Suddenly the pirate was there, wavering amidst the clutter of his cannon, gunpowder-blackened hands on his hips, white Crimean shirt soaked with blood and sea-water, blonde hair excited by the breeze, scowling defiantly at the author of his dismemberment. Fletcher Thorson Wood straightened up and faced Fokie Tom across the receding water, returning his gaze. The pirate abruptly snatched a revolver from under his belt, and before anyone aboard *Essex* could fetch and aim a musket, Tom had Fletcher in his sights.

More chagrined than surprised at being taken unawares, Fletcher could only stare back at Tom across the gun sights. The final futile gesture of a beaten man, he thought – a pistol shot from a pitching deck across fifty yards of water. Go ahead, pull the trigger. It is not my destiny to be killed by a Parthian shot.

洋神

Yang Shen

The God from the West

Book I: Landfall, 1860

James Lande

Old China Books
www.oldchinabooks.com

YANG SHEN

© James Lande, 2011
版權所有請勿翻印

The events and many of the characters depicted in this work of fiction come from documented history. The identification of many characters has been changed, and characters have been invented, to abet fictional speculation about the *un*documented aspects of these people and their times. Characters, their names, and places and events in this novel, whether from history or the author's imagination, are used fictitiously, and any resemblance to places or events or actual persons, living or dead, is coincidental.

For Weezie, who put part of herself into the author,
and Lynne 琳, who put part of herself into Yang Shen
請勿笑小巫也

These fragments I have shored against my ruins
T. S. Elliot, *The Waste Land*, "What The Thunder Said"

1st printing October 2011
1 2 3 4 5 6 7 8 9 10

ISBN: 978-0-9831454-0-0
Subject headings:
   Historical Fiction
   Historical Fiction - China
   China, 1860-1862
   Taiping Rebellion
   Opium War
   Shanghai
   Action & Adventure

On the cover

武 Wu, martial valor, warrior; first syllable of the name "Wood."
洋神 *Yang-shen* (pr. "yong shun"), the "God from the West."

Inscriptions at the temple of the Yang Shen:
同仇敵愾 *T'ung-ch'iu ti-k'ai*, "We hate the enemy for the same reason."
海外奇男萬里勛名留碧血 *Hai-wai ch'i-nan wan-li hsun-ming liu pi-hsüeh*, "a remarkable man from beyond the seas came from afar to win merit and fame [or, whose merit and fame are known to all] and left his azure blood."
雲間福地千秋廟貌表丹心 *Yun-chien fu-ti ch'ien ch'iu miao-mao piao tan-hsin*, "in this happy place among the clouds this temple will forever proclaim his faithful heart."
"Azure blood" alludes to a Chou Dynasty hero Ch'ang Hung 萇弘 killed in battle, whose blood is said to have turned to jade three years later as a sign of his loyalty.
Yun-chien 雲間, literally "among the clouds" The old name for the town of Sungkiang, site of the temple of the "god from the West." The double-meaning is rendered with less fancy as "In this happy place once known as Yun-chien…".

Contents
(Notes on adaption of historical sources appear by chapter in the Underfoot)

Book I: Landfall, 1860

In Medias Res 9
Chapter 1: Fletcher Thorson Wood 15
Chapter 2: Borrowing American Troops 29
Chapter 3: Laws are Silent 45
Chapter 4: The Englishman's War 67
Chapter 5: Fighting Fokie Tom 79
Chapter 6: Sowing Foreign Discord 95
Chapter 7: Crossing the Bar 113
Chapter 8: *Essex* at Shanghai 127
Chapter 9: Rebels and Imps 143
Chapter 10: Shanghai's U. S. Marshal 159
Chapter 11: American Consular Inquiry 177
Chapter 12: Fletcher Meets *Confucius* 197
Chapter 13: The Fitch *Soirée* 211
Chapter 14: The Lower Reaches 233
Chapter 15: The Rebel Capital 251
Chapter 16: Breaking the Siege 267
Chapter 17: The River Gauntlet 281
Chapter 18: Fletcher Meets Takee 299
Chapter 19: Tiger with Wings 315
Chapter 20: "Sumbitch Tigah Boat" 329
Chapter 21: Tanyang and Changchow 345
Chapter 22: Treachery at Soochow 365
Chapter 23: Hiring Foreign Rifles 389
Chapter 24: Fire God Temple 405
Chapter 25: Green Flag Immortals 427
Chapter 26: 1st Sungkiang 445
Chapter 27: Fourth of July 465
Yang Shen Glossary 483
Yang Shen "Underfoot" 495
Yang Shen Reading List 541

Book II: Close-hauled, 1861
(Work in progress)

Book III: Departure, 1862
(Work in progress)

Acknowledgements:
Cambridge University Press for consent to quote from C. A. Curwen's 1977 *Taiping Rebel: The Deposition of Li Hsiu-Ch'eng*, p. 229 n35.
William T. La Moy, Syracuse University Library, Syracuse, NY 13244
Christine Riggle, Baker Library, Harvard University, Boston, MA 01263
Jim Davis, First Mate, Bark *Star of India*, Maritime Museum Assoc. of San Diego
Jardine Matheson Archive, Cambridge University, Cambridge, England

Jen Yu-wen Collection, Sterling Library, Yale University, New Haven CT 06520
Maps adapted from UK Admiralty charts, 1842, UK Hydrographic Office,
  www.ukho.gov.uk
Mains'l Haul: Journal of Maritime History, Maritime Museum Assoc. of San Diego
Ch'eng Wen Reprints, Ch'eng Wen Pub. Co. 成文出版社, Taipei, Taiwan, ROC
Chris Cooper, Curator, National Army Museum, Chelsea SW3 4HT
Gary K. Y. Yang 楊克義, 杭州津诚针织纺织有限公司, Hangzhou, Zhejiang, PRC
Su Nianying 苏念英, independent historical researcher, Guilin, Guangxi, PRC
Public Records Office, London, England
British Museum, London, England
<u>Reviewers and readers:</u>
  David Franklin
  George T. Jefferson
  Kay Meggison
  R. C. Newton

Back cover photo credits:
Clipper ship – author's photo of *Cutty Sark*, Greenwich, London, 1999. See her at *www.cuttysark.org.uk/index.cfm*.
Trading junk – Davis, John F., *The Chinese: a General Description...*, Harper & Bros, New York, 1836.
Confucius – author's sketch based on Peabody Essex Museum original oil painting M1655.
6-pounder field guns – Library of Congress Prints and Photographs Division, *http://www.loc.gov/pictures/item/cwp2003001035/PP/*.
Mandarin – Bingham, John Elliot, *Narrative of the Expedition to China*, Henry Colburn, London, 1843.
Manchu bowman – http://en.wikipedia.org/wiki/File:Manchuguard.jpg. Public domain photo of "one of the Qianlong Emperor's numerous Manchu bodyguards."
Temple of Heaven – Allgood, G., *The China War*, 1860, Longmans Green and Company, London, 1901.
Nanking Chung Hua Gate 中華門 (Zhong-hua Men) – author's photo of a portion of the wall of Nanking, 2003.
Peking city wall, Anting Gate – Allgood, G., *op cit.*
Shanghai native city diagram, Shanghai gazetteer *Shang-hai hsien-chih* 上海縣志, 同治十一年 1873.

Book I: Landfall, 1860

I am publishing my own memoirs, not *theirs*, and we all know that no three witnesses of a brawl can agree on all the details. How much more likely will be the difference in a great battle covering a vast space of broken ground, when each division, brigade, regiment, and even company, naturally and honestly believes that it was the focus of the whole affair! Each of them won the battle. None ever lost. That was the fate of the old man who unhappily commanded.
  William Tecumseh Sherman, *Memoirs*

All History, so far as it is not supported by contemporary evidence, is romance.
  Samuel Johnson, in Boswell's *Tour of the Hebrides*

I cheerfully bear the reproach of having descended below the dignity of history.
  Thomas Babington Macauley, *History of England*

The columns supporting the House of History are so far apart that a novelist could drive wagonloads of fictional detail between them.
  James Lande

洋神 *Yang Shen*   James Lande 藍德

Dramatis Personae: In Medias Res

Fokie Tom   renegade English pirate of the China seas
Lay Wah-duk 李華德   Cantonese pirate, *lodaai* 老大 of Tom's fleet

China in 1860

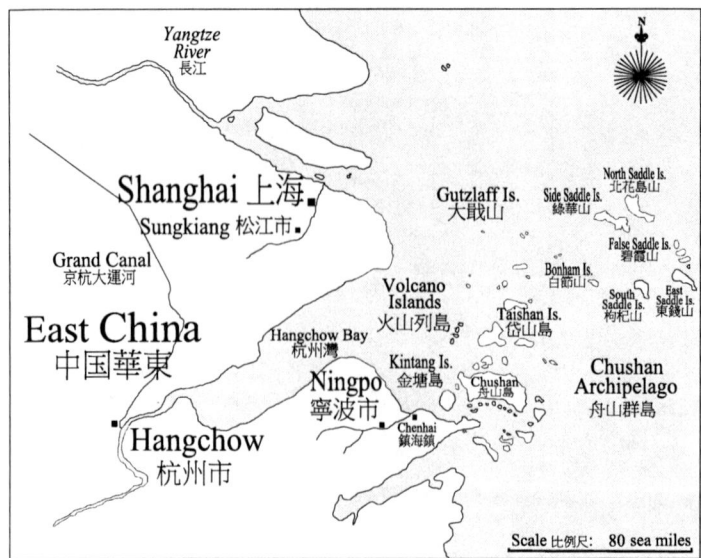

The Chushan Archipelago, the Saddles, and Bonham Island

洋神 *Yang Shen*   *James Lande* 藍德

In Medias Res ...
(In the middle of things...)

Wednesday, April 18, 1860, 6:30pm

    She was a weathered old Ningpo trader prowling in the China Sea, scudding over ocean the color of dried blood. Her grimy deck stretched aft eighty feet, from a low stem to a high, turret-like deckhouse perched above the stern. Bright blue eyes bulged under her bluff prow – one eye grafted to each side so she could find her way when her feckless pilots could not. Each huge oculus, hand-carved from camphor wood, had a stark white iris midst its lustrous blue orb. Her stern was painted blue with red facings – but without the lawful inscription for port of registry. A black-bordered red flag flew atop the tallest of her three ancient masts, and she displayed the rare extravagance of hand-carved teak railings. In the twilight, the junk's brown and yellow sails, tall and slender rectangles of woven rattan matting and bamboo battens, were silhouetted black against the orange afterglow of the sunset.

    Two days earlier, she had slaughtered the passengers and crew of a lorcha in Blackwall Pass, west of Chushan Island, and now she thirsted for the blood of an American clipper ship departing Ningpo for Shanghai.

    "晚上要小心 have a small heart tonight – be careful," said the *lodaai* 老大 – the old-great, the junk master. "I smell seaweed rotting on rocks above the tide, over here, and over there I hear the crashing of surf." He leaned out over the bow and whispered to the junk. "We are in dangerous water, and the sky will soon be black. Do you see what we search for? Look hard."

    I am your ears and nose, he thought, but you are my eyes. The *lodaai* glanced back nervously at the grisly cargo on the deck amidships. "Pay no attention to those things," he told the junk. "We soon will be far away from them."

    The junk's old eyes, wasted and worm-eaten beneath new paint, had sailed over empires of ocean. In their youth, the eyes had gazed down into the sea for quarry, like an archipelago fisher, but years of drought and famine had passed since this predator wanted fish. Now they peered straight ahead, searching for dragons disguised as mountains beneath the sea, for grasping shoals haunted by drowned ghosts waiting to clutch at passing prey, for shifting eddies that betrayed swift tidal currents and shallow depths. For imperial war junks, too – and British gunboats.

    The junk slowed, brailed up the foot of her lugsails, spilled wind, settled into her wash, and skulked silently past Show Island into the shadow of the East Volcanos. The four stark basalt crags of East Volcano Island loomed black over the old hulk as it wallowed in the quiet shallows of the narrow channel.

    The *lodaai* was short and slender, clad in cotton slippers and brown quilted cotton trousers and jacket. He had the round face of the Cantonese, with pinched features, a clean-shaven forehead, and black hair braided into a long queue down his back. His name was Lay Wah-duk 李華德, Honorable-conduct Lay, a native of Canton whose family had lived on a junk and fished in the Pearl River delta. When he was fifteen, a typhoon destroyed the family junk and drowned all aboard except Lay. A northbound trading junk picked him up, but that ill-fated vessel was attacked and burned by pirates on the approach to Ningpo. The pirates gave Lay Wah-duk the choice of becoming a pirate himself, or death, so he became a pirate. Years later, he joined a gang of pirates gathered from disbanded imperial troops and ruled by a renegade English sailor.

    Lay Wah-duk's skill at handling junks of any class won for him the rank of fleet admiral, and he became leader of the Cantonese faction of the Englishman's gang. Lay was the *lodaai* to his colleagues, and highly regarded – he talked to junks.

"Do you see it yet?" the *lodaai* murmured. The swollen eyes made only the sound of water rushing against wood. The *lodaai* was not troubled that there was no answer.

The thump of heavy boots approached from behind.

"Are you talkin' to the fokin boat again you bloody half-wit!" bellowed a voice. "You see anything yet?"

The Cantonese spun about to face a tall, heavy, florid-faced Westerner clad in black boots and trousers and a loose, long-sleeved white Crimean shirt open at the throat.

You stupid pig-shit demon, thought the *lodaai*, drown in your own piss.

The foreigner was the English freebooter Fokie Tom, notorious from Peking to Canton as a savage spoiler of the trade routes through the East China Sea. His ice-blue eyes glinted coldly from beneath bushy eyebrows and a mat of long hair as yellow, Chinese might have said, as the rooftop tiles of the Forbidden City.

"Boat see plenty, massah," Lay Wah-duk said. "Look for *bu-yi*."

Fokie Tom was born Thomas James Babbington, second Earl of Suffolkshire, but his father's hopes for Thomas at the Royal Military Academy at Sandhurst were broken when his young son struck a drill sergeant and Thomas was drummed out of school. Preferring hell's fires to hearth fires and his father's wrath, Tom went to sea and learned gunnery aboard HMS *Wellesley*, a 74-gun ship-of-the-line, at the blockade of Canton, the sack of Tinghai, and at the mouth of the Peiho during the first China war.

"Listen here, Lay, first, we tries to 'oist the buoy and carry it inshore, but if it's too 'eavy then you jump into the fokin sampan with the cold chisel and 'ammer and fetch that fokin chain up and cut it in two."

Navy discipline suited Tom no better than discipline at Sandhurst, and he deserted at Whampoa to join Chin A Po's pirate fleet as a gunner. He survived twelve years of debauchery among Chinese pirates and pursuit by British gunboats, smoking as much opium as he robbed and sold, and drinking the land dry of every kind of thrice-fired rot-gut *samshu*, Shaohsing wine and Kaoliang whiskey. He whored with every village girl that came to hand and every captive woman that fell into his clutches, as if intent on populating south China with a new race of half-breed little blond Toms. All his whelps that actually came into the light were drowned, or had their brains bashed out before the mother jumped into a well or was thrown into the Pearl River. Eventually, when age caught up and he sobered a little, he drifted north into the Chushan Archipelago and Ningpo, and began to rebuild the broken empire of his pirate mentor Chin A Po.

"Can do, mastah!"

Fokie Tom turned away and went to the waist where three wooden coffins stood side-by-side against the rail. Lay Wah-duk swallowed hard when he saw the Englishman approach the coffins – the pig-shit demon called up the dead for a terrible task. The coffins were large in the Chinese fashion, lacquered bright red, and hewn from ironwood that would sink in water. Fokie Tom loosened the rope securing the cover of the first coffin and lifted the lid.

"Mastah, mastah! What do, mastah? Mus' not open box!" The Cantonese rushed toward the coffins, but stopped several feet away.

"Go to hell you superstitious little bastard." The lid fell off and revealed a purple corpse still recognizable as a Westerner despite gaping cuts, lacerations and burns. The *lodaai* screamed, ran to the other side of the main deck, and scampered up the ladder to a small shrine before the deckhouse. A dozen Chinese were already there, on their knees before a clay figurine of the goddess of the sea, Ma Tzu Po 媽祖婆, their hands pressed together in front of their faces, muttering urgent prayers of supplication. Repeatedly, they reached beneath the altar for bills of the mock money used for ceremony – joss money – to kindle in a small red votive lamp on the altar and burn in an ash-filled bowl before the image of the goddess.

"Lay, get to the bow and watch, you goddamn little shit!"

"Mus' pay plentee *chin-chin* joss, mastah. Make god keep 'way hungly ghos'."

"Get to the bow!"

Lay Wah-duk's face turned squally with anger and fear. He fetched up wads of joss money from beneath the altar and threw them into the bowl of flaming paper. He grabbed more handfuls of joss money, scrambled down from the poop to the main deck, ran to the coffins, and threw the joss money over the rail.

"Pay *chin-chin* joss," he hissed at the pig-shit demon. Then he ran down the deck past the last coffin and threw the other handful of joss money over that rail before slinking back out to the bow.

"There now, Archie," Fokie Tom muttered to the corpse in the first coffin, "we's even providin' you with travel money, see?" Come to wish you *bon voyage* I have, he thought. You allus was my dearest friend. Moved up together in the world, from cutting purses to cutting throats, didn't we? Paid our dues loading down the bloody fokin imperial war junk captains with spoils, and freighting the bleedin' fokin mandarins with Mexican dollars. Had a high time then, chasin' down so many fokin opium schooners, them high-and-mighty British admirals and merchant princes spit blood. Cut out the middleman you allus said, or cut 'im *up*. But then you went and spoilt it all, Archie. Tried to cut me out, too. You turned out to be an old-school company man, didn't believe in newfangled notions like free-market competition, had to monopolize it all. You'd never've tried to do me in, you swine, if you had sense enough *to let the wretch who toils accuse not, hate not, him who wears the spoils*. Murderin' me would've exceeded your bloody fokin commission. Byron's probably wasted on you, too.

Fokie Tom was apologetic. Each of the corpses had been people useful to him. When the fury of his blood lust passed, he was sorry he had murdered them. Their absence was an inconvenience. Bringing them aboard for one last employment was a reprieve in Tom's view, a final opportunity for each of them to make up for their shortcomings in life and the bother they had caused him. Lay Wah-duk had pleaded to simply bring aboard another anchor to do the job Tom wanted done, and bury these bodies back on the pirate's island base. The Englishman threw a tankard of ale at the *lodaai*, shouting that an anchor was too heavy and unwieldy, and that there was no goddamn poetic justice in a fokin anchor. Rare fokin commodity justice, he said to himself, and rarer still the chance to be dishin' it up instead o' being served it out.

Tom hefted four 12-pound cannon balls into the bottom of the coffin, replaced the lid, took up hammer and nails from a box beside the rail, and nailed the coffin shut. Then he opened the second coffin and glared down at the body of a Fukienese sailor with a bullet hole in his forehead.

Yes, it's me you heathen josser, it's Fokie Tom, *whose very name appalls the fiercest of his crew*. Come to give you final orders, I have, and these orders you *will* obey. There's a big marker buoy just ahead, a nun buoy shaped like a cone and red and white like a bleedin' Yankee flag. We'll cut it from its mooring and drag it inshore under those volcanoes, where it's ever so much shallower. Then, to be sure it stay's there, we'll chain the three of you to the buoy, in your shiny red ironwood coffins, weighted with big black cannon balls. Tomorrow when you sees that big flappin' goose of an American clipper ship, *Essex* they calls 'er, come waddling up the channel, you're to pull that ship over to the buoy and run 'er aground. She'll be chock full o' gold and guns, bars of fine gold worth thousands, and fine new brass field guns, 6-pounders they are. And there's a sweet little lady, too – a white-skinned, blue-veined, pretty little bitch.

In Medeas Res

She'll be all warm 'n juicy and too young yet to know how hot a woman gets for a man, but I'll larn her. Rip off 'er rags, lay 'er over a big gun, strap her ankles to muzzle and cascabel, an' larn her good, just like I did all them others. It'll be easier'n swallerin' tiger's milk 'cause we've got our own man hired aboard as pilot. After that, you can drag down into the briny deep as many Christian souls as you can get your bony fingers into, 'cause there'll be lots that's past carin'.

Tom loaded four cannon balls into the second coffin and nailed it shut. He opened the third coffin and dropped heavy shot in beside the naked, blood-streaked body of an adolescent Hakka girl who's sunken features, except for the gash across her throat, were still gauntly attractive even in death.

Ah, Judy, he thought with a long sigh. Such a sad end for a swell tart. I never enjoyed a little laced mutton as much as I enjoyed you – at first. If you'd just stopped crying and shown a little passion. That whimpering on and on just got on me nerves – made me so angry, that's why I threw you down into the hold for the crew. All your screamin' must have made them angry too. Look what they did to you. Tsk, tsk. Well, now you're going to be in good company with Archie here. He was always partial to little southern girls.

Tom watched as dragon's blood filled the sky above the western horizon. The dark red flame kindled ablaze water yellow with windblown loess from Mongolian deserts and ochre loam from the Yangtze River watershed, transmuting the sea into a revelation of ruin. Sanguinary light sallied over battlements of turbulent clouds and suffused the salt air with forebodings of violent death.

Fokie Tom nailed shut the third coffin.

洋神 *Yang Shen*   *James Lande* 藍德

Dramatis Personae (new): Chapter 1

Fletcher Thorson Wood	*Essex* passenger, boarded at Hong Kong
Hugh Gabriel Wood	Fletcher's brother, boarded with Fletcher
Hannah Eliot Fitch	part owner of *Essex*
Elizabeth Glenna Fitch	Hannah's daughter
Cornelius Lowell Fitch	Hannah's nephew, captain of *Essex*
Ptolemy Reese	*Essex* first mate, on foremast larboard watch

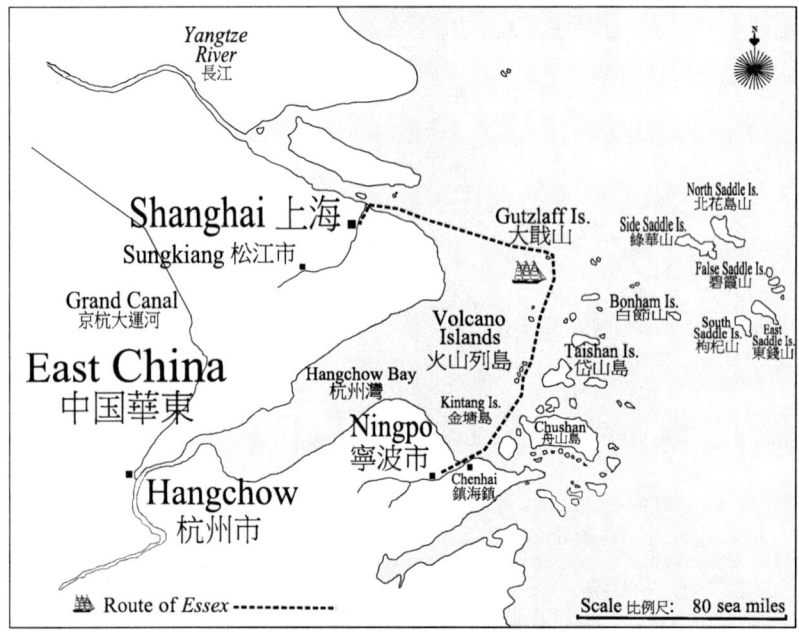

East China and the Chushan Archipelago
(based on British Hydrographic Office chart, China., Sheet IX, 1842)

Clipper ship, circa 1860
(based on Arthur H. Clark, The Clipper Ship Era, "Flying Cloud," 1912)

洋神 *Yang Shen* *James Lande* 藍德

Chapter 1: Fletcher Thorson Wood
Thursday, April 19, 1860, 7:15am

A master in hell before a minion in Heaven. I'll be a prince in China, and lord over these heathen beggars, or I'll make a great many of them wish they'd better joss – better luck – than to cross my bow. But first, we have to sail this lazy hooker through these islands without losing our precious heads to pirates, into the Yangtze without bestowing her name on some uncharted rock, and up the Whangpoo to the walls of Shanghai without sticking her into mud.

Fletcher Thorson Wood leaned against a rail of *Essex* and gazed along the channel between the cloistered islands. He stood with one booted foot upon the larboard cathead timber beam that hoisted her best bower anchor, and listened to the spasmodic snap of the canvas staysail. He savored the feel of the old hooker rolling beneath him, and inhaled deeply the salt-water aromas wafted up from where the yellowed ocean held quiet parley with the cutwater of the ship. While his eyes surveyed the water ahead, his mind raced north some seven hundred miles toward the glory and riches of Peking.

He was short and stocky, with a powerful body more suited to swinging a sledge in a mine than climbing in the rigging of a sailing ship, but he was tall enough, said many who knew, to crack a sailor's jaw with his fist. His dark-blue eyes, shoulder-length black hair, and black frock coat buttoned tightly from collar to waist acquired for him the look of a smoke-blackened iron spike driven into the wood of the deck.

Yankee clipper *Essex* was three days out of Hong Kong on 19 April 1860, bound for Shanghai, her position 30° 16' North, 121° 59' East. She was a three-masted square-rigged ship, a medium clipper 185 feet long from her figurehead of the nymph Galatea to the gleaming teakwood tafferel – the railing around her stern. Her beam measured thirty-five feet, her hold was twenty feet deep, she displaced eleven hundred tons, and atop her main mast flew an ensign with a white "AF" on a green field – the house flag of Augustus Fitch & Company. Her fore and main topsails billowed out above her main and mizzen staysails, her spanker was set over her stern, and her speed was eight knots – nautical miles per hour. She was sailing large across Hangchow Bay under a capful of southwest soldier's wind over her larboard – or port – quarter, mincing her way north from a call at the treaty port of Ningpo, through the treacherous shoals and shallows of the islands of the Chushan Archipelago.

All around *Essex,* the wild green islets of the archipelago lay scattered in profusion across the East China Sea, like jade gemstones strewn over yellow silk. Silk, he thought, of the yellow reserved by ancient sumptuary law for the emperor alone, the yellow of the great Huang Ho River, of the shifting Gobi sands, and of the opium addict's jaundiced skin. Chinese yellow.

Ahead loomed the Volcanos and Taishan Island, calm and clear in the mid-morning sun, and between them lay the northeast channel, its surface rippled by soft cat's-paws. High over the channel a pair of fishing eagles backed and filled in languid circles, their white-plumed tail feathers glistening in the sunlight, their piercing *kree* echoing across the waves. Far in the distance, a solitary nun buoy floated in the shallows under the four silent peaks of East Volcano Island. Fletcher stared into the turbid swash running under the bow of *Essex* and wondered about the water's depth.

These narrows shroud submerged rocks like rivers conceal sunken snags, and the water shallows without warning. Deep-water sailors have no more business poking about the Hangchow tidal flats than a damselfly's got inside the mouth of a snoring drunk. The captain is the owner's nephew, that's clear, because no sailor'd take 135 days

Fletcher Thorson Wood   15

洋神 *Yang Shen*   *James Lande* 藍德

around Cape Horn on a voyage needing only ninety-five in decent weather. The Oriental ran it in eighty-one days way back in 1850. And no real sailor'd risk taking a big old brawler like *Essex* through these islands. With too little ballast for the weight of her cargo, heavy yards, and tons of cannon along her rails, she's a crank ship, has a tipsy sway even becalmed – in a heavy swell she'd stagger like a drunken sailor. Loaded light, she'd have about a fathom less draft and could skip over the Hangchow Bay mud like a pebble over a pond. With a near-full load of commercial goods, and women passengers to boot, we'd do better to round the Saddles, or at least head for deeper water at Bonham Strait. Around here, fifteen-foot tides and four-knot tidal currents give the water more bump and grind than a Turkish belly dancer, even at this time of year in the lull between the monsoons, when the winds and tides are tame. Watch that damned wind, though. If it drops, the current will suck her around and spit her up on some beach.

From her home port of Salem, Massachusetts, *Essex* brought American cotton shirtings, sundries, and iron bar and nail rod for sale on consignment at the godowns – warehouses – of Augustus Fitch & Company in Shanghai. There also were contraband field guns – four brass 6-pounders with fifty chests of ammunition packed with fifty rounds each of shot and canister, covertly purchased as a favor to the Shanghai *taotai*.

Fletcher knew all about that highbinder. In times of peace, the *taotai*, or Intendant of Circuit, was the highest-ranking Chinese official in Shanghai. His rice-bowl included the precarious management of what he would doubtless consider the unpredictable, avaricious foreigners, and the imposition of tonnage dues and customs duties sanctioned by treaty on the cargoes of their ships. Every *taotai* in office since trade began under the 1842 Treaty of Nanking furtively filched from customs duties extraordinary riches never remitted to the imperial treasury at Peking. The present incumbent of this lucrative office was anxious to have a private arsenal of modern Western weapons ready for the day when the Taiping rebels would come to Shanghai to plunder from the *taotai* the wealth he had pilfered from the emperor.

Essex had dropped some of the cottons at Hong Kong and picked up a cargo of English woolens and broken putchuck root, called *mu-hsiang* 木香 by the Chinese, who used it to make joss sticks – temple incense. *Essex* carried no opium; Augustus Lowell Fitch did not allow his ships to traffic in the Poison Trade, even while they smuggled arms for Chinese mandarins. In Municipal Council meetings and letters to the editor of Shanghai's British weekly, the *North China Herald*, "Uncle" Fitch gave such violent vent to his prejudices about opium that Augustus Fitch & Company was known by the sobriquet "New Jerusalem" among traders less particular about their cargoes.

The helmsman struck seven bells of the morning watch – 7:30am – and Fletcher surfaced from his imaginary soundings. The water was too roiled with silt and sediment ever to see the bottom – too muddied by glacial tillites from the Tibetan highlands, and iron-laden red sandstone from the Szechwan Basin, and dissolved carbonate scoured from the limestone bedrock of the Yangtze Gorges. The sea was laden with alluvium swept up from twelve Chinese provinces, spewed out of the mouth of the Yangtze, and shoved south into Hangchow Bay by the East China Cold Current.

Again he gazed far ahead, sighting over the jib boom the distant nun buoy that marked shallow water in the channel, a ten-foot high, truncated cone striped red and white, like blood and bandages, gently rising and falling at anchor. The calm began to unsettle him – it was too calm. There were no fishermen casting their nets from junks and sampans. The ocean was empty – gloomy as a played out gold camp.

Alone on a wide, rough, rude sea. With no chart and only Chinese constellations and compass for navigation. Queen of heaven and dragon kings instead of Orion and Cassiopeia. Heavens crowded with all the Buddhist, Taoist and Confucian pantheons of

Fletcher Thorson Wood

China, instead of Greeks and Romans. They'll have to move over, make room for me.

Fletcher frowned at the four iron 24-pounders trussed to the clipper's main deck, underfoot of the crew working the ship. Try to bring those to bear on a moving target – half the length of the ship apart, traverse's so narrow a target'd have to be right under the muzzle. Those're the notion of some landsman who's never fired pivoted bow and stern guns at pirates in the China Sea, from a ship run aground and unable to maneuver waist guns into position. Unless they make enough noise to scare off pirates, they'll be of little more help than a mortar to a milkmaid. *Essex*'s only real hope against marauders is to trice up her skirts, bare her fantail, and run for her life.

On the main deck below, the larboard watch of many nations, predominantly British seamen, stumped up out of the forecastle – their bellies full of sourdough biscuits and spiced oatmeal skillagalee – found their duty stations, and began fumbling about the Sisyphean tasks essential to maintain a sailing vessel.

Ordinary seamen scraped at rust, chipped away corrosion, puttied cracks and painted bulwarks. Sailors were forever slapping smelly Stockholm tar onto shrouds and lines to replace worn weatherproofing. Experienced hands mended sennit, spliced new rope into chafed lines, and wormed, parceled, and served old lines – seaman's language for repairing worn, plaited rope by winding strands of twine into the grooves and wrapping rope with tarred canvas.

Able-bodied seamen – the ABs – roamed the decks between lines and lanyards, heaved taut with Norwegian steam – muscle power – on four-strand tarred Manila hemp slack with age, and resized cow-tailed rope ends where broken seizing allowed hempen strands to unravel and splay. The ABs clambered up rope ladders into the rigging, testing their weight on the hempen lines tied between the shrouds of the standing rigging that held the masts erect, and scoured the running rigging that squared the yards and trimmed the sails for signs of chafing and decay. Old hands searched among the shrouds for sun-rotted ratlines, buntlines and clew lines further up among the sails, and greased pulley block sheaves or sent blocks down for overhaul and painting,

The worn vertical grain of each length of 3¾-inch Douglas fir deck planking suffered ceaseless scrutiny for splitting and dry rot. Here caulking was ordered and there pitch was paid, wherever the packing between the hardwood deck planks chafed away and sprouted grimy blossoms of blackened oakum.

The decks and rigging came alive with the movement and activity of a full watch of eighteen men and boys swarming over their charge, smoothing, grooming and polishing her, preening and primping with all the fuss of the Queen's own couturier and coiffeuse.

The first mate crossed the main deck yelling and kicking at the crew, then stomped aft and mounted grimly to the poop deck. He nodded to the helmsman and took the officer's station at the weather rail beside the companionway, the quarterdeck on a clipper ship. At sea, he might have scrutinized the helmsman's course and ordered a correction but, while the ship was under the nominal command of the pilot, he let the Chinese give the helmsman her course and generally left them alone.

The mate was a weathered, whiskered sea-hulk in duck trousers, checked shirt, and tarpaulin cap, named Ptolemy Reese. A foot taller than Fletcher, Reese was the bull in John Bull if any man was. His proud name was the gift of his Cockney father, a corporal of engineers who served in 1801 with British troops landed in Egypt, at Abu Qir, to join the Ottoman Turks in a drive on Napoleon's Army of Egypt. The father thought it no burden for his son to bear the name of an ancient line of Egyptian kings. What the boy learned defending his name, kicking and biting in schoolyard brawls, taught him enough to fight his way out of the squalor and disease of the Liverpool slums and go to sea

Fletcher Thorson Wood

洋神 *Yang Shen*　　　　　　　　　　　　　　　　　　　　　　*James Lande* 藍德

where, accustomed to brutality and privation, he found a home.

Passengers tentatively emerged from the companionway onto the poop deck. One by one, they glanced about, discerned little welcome in the unflinching scowl of the somber mate, then turned away and clustered together at the leeward rail: Hubert Gabriel Wood, Fletcher's younger brother; Hannah Eliot Fitch, wife of China trader Augustus Fitch and part owner of *Essex*; and her daughter Elizabeth Glenna Fitch. Their elegant attire, appropriate for morning dress in any household of the Western world, contrasted vividly with the drab rigging of the sailors, decked out in work clothes of canvas drill milled – like the ship's sails – from cotton raised below the Mason-Dixon Line.

Fletcher descended the forecastle ladder and walked the length of the main deck. A couple of the seasoned hands, Chips and Old Burgoo, glanced at the grim trespasser as he crossed through their domain and noted his rolling gait. Fletcher saw them watching.

I must have the look of an escaped felon, fled from Joppa and bound for Tarshish.

In an era of disease and disaster that killed early, Fletcher was already an old man at the age of twenty-eight, and impressed his contemporaries as solemn and careworn. He had served long in both the forecastle and quarterdeck of sailing ships, and rounded the Horn many times. He had driven desperate men with fist and club, thwarted mutiny with powder keg and burning brand, and survived keelhauling, knife-blade, and musket ball. By now, his experience had aged his appearance well beyond his years.

A cabin boy, a slender, quick, blond-haired lad of maybe fifteen years, sallied forth from the saloon struggling with a wooden trunk on his shoulder and, his view obscured, collided with Fletcher.

"Ho, come about there matey!" Fletcher said, laughing. The trunk started for the deck but he caught it up, and helped balance the load on the lad's shoulder.

"Oh, beggin' your pardon, sir! Didn't see you there."

"Watch where you're goin' you clumsy halfwit!" yelled the mate from the poop deck. "Ya hafta be watchin' out fer passengers wanderin' around on the deck where they got no business to be."

"No ha'm done boy," Fletcher said, ignoring the mate. "Have you got it now?"

"Yes, sir. Thank you sir. Good morning sir."

Fletcher watched the boy weave forward on his way. He remembered thinking, when he first set eyes on this boy in Hong Kong, that the lad was no older than he was himself when first sent to sea aboard the *Hamilton*. A hard school, the sea, but with Uncle William as captain, I probably had an easier berth than this ship's boy. Second mate on my first voyage out, to Hong Kong and Canton. My watch didn't know whether to laugh at me or throw me overboard, but that changed when they saw I was a better sailor than all of them put together, showing the younger ones how to worm and parcel, scamper aloft, and go over all the standing rigging. Tone Cabot was a brutal first mate, especially to crewman who lagged, and I felt his fist or foot often enough until I hardened up, wised up, and learned instant obedience. A mate is an officer, and an officer's a *leader*, boy, Tone would growl at me, and that means you're the first one into the rigging and you see your watch safely down. How many times did Tone get that lecture about leaders from Uncle William? You're always out front, *showing* how, the first to do what's wanted. That's why we calls 'em leaders, boy, because they *lead*. Outward bound I was hated, but by the time *Hamilton* returned around the Horn, men older than my father respected me. This boy could do with a mate like Tone.

Fletcher mounted the ladder to the poop deck, nodded to the mate, and joined the three passengers beside the skylight over the saloon. The skylight was a long, barrel-shaped dome of frosted glass panes protected by thin wire rods and set between two long, polished mahogany benches. Aft of the companionway, perched upon a wooden

Fletcher Thorson Wood

pedestal of more shiny brown mahogany, was the burnished copper housing of the binnacle; through its large, round glass window the man at the helm conned the ship's compass. The helmsman stood behind a six-foot tall wheel so big it might have come off the axle of a Conestoga wagon tracking the Oregon Trail. Elegant in construction and finish, its spokes were crafted from lustrous teakwood, its felloe faced with shining brass. The wheel turned an immense steering gear inside a wood housing set before the tafferel. The ship's name was carved into one of the benches:

ESSEX

Crammed under each bench was a row of smelly wooden coops holding the last of the scrawny chickens for the passengers' meals. Further aft was a small, waist-high hatchway – the companionway – constructed of mahogany panels, with doors that opened toward the stern. Inside, a ladder descended directly into the saloon.

The cabin boy appeared at the top of the ladder, ran across the poop deck to the helm, took up an oily rag, and genuflected beside the companionway. Under the blessing of the helmsman, he rubbed devoutly on the panels with the anointed rag to beseech a brighter luster.

2

"My aunt," Elizabeth said, "writes from Charleston that her men express concern secessionists will make a mighty effort to sow discord among the delegates at the Democratic convention."

Elizabeth smiled at Fletcher and turned slightly to admit him to her audience. She was a slender, pallid brunette of nineteen bedecked in a claret velvet-and-silk visiting dress, a tight high-necked bodice with flounced pagoda sleeves and white under sleeves, and a claret capote hat held by a ribbon under her chin. Hannah Fitch insisted this style was too old for her daughter and unsuited for shipboard life as well.

"Their purpose," she continued, "is to defeat the nomination of Senator Douglas, and thereby ensure the victory of abolitionist Republicans. That, of course, would lead to the separation of the South."

Fletcher recalled mention at table that Miss Fitch recently graduated from a backwoods women's college called Mount Holyoke Female Seminary, and he felt a rising dismay at the prospect of another dreary political talk by the precocious Miss Fitch. Any girl with her looks and bearing would set him on edge. He didn't really know what to say to them, for fear of saying something rough.

"In your view, Mr. Wood," Elizabeth asked Hugh, "are they not turncoats who would not attempt every stratagem to avoid the tragedy of war?" Hugh was less intimidating, slight of build but taller than his gloomy brother, a boor in a brown frock coat over a buff checked vest, starched collar with black necktie, brown top hat, and pinstriped trousers.

"To be frank, Miss Fitch," Hugh said, "I'm too sta'tled to make an immediate response." The vision of the pert Miss Fitch so unbalanced Hugh that he had completely missed what she said. "I have always thought that ladies understood little about politics, and would not have expected most men to grasp fully the potential for disaster at the Cha'leston convention. That is one more prejudiced notion our acquaintance, Miss Fitch, may yet see me abandon." A few weeks earlier, Hugh had been a clerk dreaming of riches while scratching at ledgers with quill pen and ink in the dark, dreary offices of their father's New York shipping firm, Hugh's pallor glimmered like white sailcloth beside his brother's ruddy cheeks and rough, sun burnt hands. Composure around attractive young women was no more a strong suit for Hugh than for his brother.

Elizabeth was impatient and unappeased, and disinclined to allow the unrefined and unwanted familiarity occasioned by trifling flattery from strange men. Even after close confinement together aboard *Essex* for three days and nights, these men were still not to be permitted informalities.

The mate left the weather rail and went aft to the helm. Fletcher strained to hear the mate's order to the helmsman over the prattling of the passengers.

"Take her out more into the center of the channel. There's got to be too much mud in close to these islands. I don't like it"

"A point to starb'd, Mr. Reese, toward center channel." The mate noted the change in direction then, satisfied with the course of *Essex*, ordered the ship's boy to 'vast polishing and run forward, and went down to the main deck to see the yards trimmed.

Behind the helmsman, the Chinese pilot stood with arms folded tightly across his dark blue cotton jacket watching the mate descend the ladder to the main deck. A long black snake of a braided queue emerged from beneath his black skullcap and crept down his back to his waist. To Fletcher there was nothing at all inscrutable about the grimace of the pilot. Pirates could look like any Chinese, even pilots.

"Come moh dis side," the pilot said.

"But Mr. Reese said bring 'er into center channel," the helmsman said.

"Moh watah pote side, channah hab lock."

"You're the pilot, but Mr. Reese will not like it." The helmsman brought the wheel down just enough to change the course of *Essex* a barely perceptible half-point, and the breeze colluded with the stratagem by staying in the sails. The helmsman appeared relieved that he had cleared both the Scylla of the monstrous mate, and the Charybdis of the pox-ridden pilot. Fletcher wondered how the mate could not have felt the slight change in direction, even from the waist of the ship.

A sailor since he was eleven, a second mate at sixteen, six times around Cape Horn, and more than three years on the China coast, Fletcher told himself he knew what was wanted in a crew, and looked first for obedience. Men who refused to jump to their tasks when a moment's delay meant life or death were a danger to the ship and everyone aboard. A first mate who spent more time supervising deck maintenance than sailing the ship was a work foreman, not a ship's officer. A helmsman who changed an officer's sailing instructions was due for a keelhauling as a lesson in obedience to orders. Her sails were loosely trimmed and she wandered from her course – signs of slovenly seamanship that resulted in slow passages and late arrivals that owners would not tolerate. And *Essex* needed a lookout in the foretop, if not in the bow as well, to watch for rocks and shoals – and marauders. Bad judgment added to bad sailing galled him more than usual in these waters.

Elizabeth, her annoyance at Hugh unabated, turned on Fletcher Wood.

"What was that gibberish the Chinese man was saying? Surely, he cannot be speaking in Chinese to our sailor, can he?"

Fletcher considered the young lady for a moment. An uncongealed character, he mused, reluctant gentility working to bridle coltish intellect, blue stockings hidden under silks and crinoline. Reminds me of my sister Elizabeth, but they really have little more in common than their name – my sister is modest and quiet.

"That's pidgin, miss."

"Pigeon? Where's a pigeon? Those are gulls."

Fletcher had to laugh. "P-i-d-g-i-n is a ja'gon, Miss Fitch. Like the Portugese lorcha, a junk with a western-style hull and Chinese sail, pidgin is another basta'd born of the illicit union of native and foreign."

Elizabeth struggled to retain her poise. Why, she fumed inwardly, does he use such terrible language, without any consideration for the sensibility of others?

"I hate pidgin" Fletcher said. "With a vocabula'y of about only fifty words, nobody can understand what anybody else says. It is not much better than the sign language used by our American Indian tribes that do not speak a common tongue. Talking pidgin, you always sound like a babbling infant. It is a barely intelligible ja'gon of English words twisted into Chinese idiom and mispronounced according to Chinese syntax. It makes everyone who speaks it sound mighty stupid."

"Then why have it?"

"It is spoken between Chinese and foreigners. Chinese who do business with foreigners refuse to learn English. We speak pidgin because no one will teach us Chinese. The mandarins torture any Chinese caught teaching their language to foreigners. Sometimes Chinese who speak no mutually intelligible dialects of their own language speak pidgin English to each other." Fletcher expected to distract the obstinate young lady with this digression, but his hope was quickly dismasted.

"I still ask you, Mr. Wood, are they not traitors to their country who would see it plunged into the horrors of war before they would consider a democratic compromise?"

"Elizabeth," said her mother. "Must you inflict yourself on our passengers? Perhaps we do not want to endure more political lectures. We came on deck for *fresh* air, dear." And they did not pay passage to hear your prattle.

Hannah Eliot Fitch was the forty-year-old matriarch of the China trader Augustus Fitch & Company, descended from a proud line of Boston first families that went back to the Revolutionary War. Sea captains mostly, and Unitarians all, an uncle on her father's side was discreetly offered a cabinet position by President John Tyler in 1841, a position quietly declined. Hannah married off Chestnut Hill and out of the social register, to Augustus Lowell Fitch, without a backward glance because, she said, she knew her own mind.

"I will have my say, mother!"

"It is not ladylike, dear, for young women to flaunt pretensions to learning." Mrs. Fitch was tightly corseted in a black broadcloth carriage-dress; her gray-streaked brown hair was drawn back under a quilted black poke-bonnet, and across her shoulders lay a lace-trimmed Paisley print shawl from Scotland, popular since Queen Victoria built her castle at Balmoral. Hannah's daughter observed that her mother's style of dress was nearly twenty years out of date, as if Mrs. Fitch had abandoned fashion immediately after her marriage to Mr. Fitch.

"If not traitors to their country, then traitors to the Union," Fletcher said, thinking he need not cut and run like Hugh. "I beg your pardon, Mrs. Fitch, but the question deserves consideration rega'dless of who's askin'. In the South, they may have a different idea of country than we do, and it's entirely possible that following their idea of country, they feel themselves patriots. More's the pity, too, because their patriotic zeal may end in the destruction of everyone's notion of country."

Hannah sniffed audibly from where she sat on the bench built into the skylight over the *Essex* saloon. She knitted her brows and shot a dour glance at Fletcher. "That sounds more than a little like copperhead talk. How anyone can be so generous to a pack of rebels, who would tear their own nation apa't just so they can go on living in the past, is beyond me, Mr. Wood. It's simply very bad for business. Very bad!"

"Separatists and abolitionists have extreme intolerance in common, Mrs. Fitch," Fletcher said quietly, dismissing her resemblance to an old Puritan crone howling after Salem witches. Actually, he considered the absence of any silk garment in the dress of a female part owner of one of the largest silk trading agencies in the world to be ample testimony to her frugality and self-constraint. Her language would benefit from the same self-constraint, he thought. No man can say copperhead to me and not expect to wade knee-deep in his own blood.

"As I read," Fletcher said, "about the outrageous bickering of our country's leaders in Congress, the inflated and violent rhetoric and insults exchanged, I wonder if we could not find common ground more readily if we first locked up the extremists in some dungeon well out of earshot. One senator uses John Brown's villainy as a glove to slap the face of another senator. A representative takes up Dred Scott to use as a stick to beat another representative. Our honored legislators resort to carrying arms on the floor of the House, and fight duels to settle the differences of the nation. I wonder how well-served we are by a few dozen blockheads in Washington who won't sit down and shut up, and allow cooler and more tolerant men to work out a solution."

Mrs. Fitch's expression turned as inclement as a New England winter. Elizabeth braved that barren landscape and, with a conspiratorial smile at the men, murmured, "Careful, Mr. Fletcher Wood, you are skating on thin ice, because when you talk to my mother, you are talking to a founding member and an elected officer of the Massachusetts Anti-slavery Society."

"I have also read newspaper accounts of the arguments in Congress," Hannah said. "Politicians are what they are, Mr. Wood, and if you had seen as much of their chicanery as I have, your tolerance would be exhausted like mine. Nevertheless, I will have a law to prevent the hunting of slaves in Massachusetts. I cannot tolerate even the idea of slavery, and I will not countenance bounty hunters roaming around Massachusetts and kidnapping any black man they happen upon. I will have such a law, peaceably and with due process if I can, but I will have it."

Fletcher thought this extreme intolerance. But the ship-owner's wife took the high ground, and he'd best go around, especially seeing as she was determined to put him in his place. Anyway, he thought, I probably deserved defeat in the engagement – shouldn't have committed troops unless certain of victory. New Englanders can always mount an argument against slavery because they never have anything to lose.

"Yes, ma'am, and I believe you are the person to see that accomplished." Fletcher turned toward the larboard rail. "I do not disagree with your views, ma'am, and I hope they all can be achieved without ha'm to the Union. I do not countenance disunion."

"Nor do I, sir," she said to Fletcher's back. "Not any of us."

Your kind is no stranger to me, she thought, nettled by his arrogance. No family, no responsibility to others, no ambition to better yourself, and you contribute to no one's welfare. You waste your life in dissipation, go back to sea whenever your money's gone, sail from port to port until too old to climb rigging, take asylum in some old sailor's home, and die destitute and alone. Your fate will be to molder nameless under a marker with no epitaph until Judgment Day – then burn in hell for all eternity.

3

Essex was coming up on the southern tip of East Volcano Island, one of hundreds of tiny islands in the archipelago through which they must pass to arrive at Shanghai. From the larboard rail, Fletcher surveyed the islands ahead for inlets and crevices where a pirate lorcha might hide like a remora behind a shark's fin. He leaned out a little over the rail and sighted forward past the clipper's waist along the shallows of the island where the nun buoy shimmered in the rising heat. The buoy nagged at him, bothered him, made him vaguely disquiet. And still there were no fishermen, no drift-netters, and no draggers. Where in hell were the goddamn fishing boats?

Among many others he knew along the east China coast, he vaguely remembered a buoy like this one because he had been aboard the steamer *Antelope* when her agent ordered a buoy placed at East Volcano Island during a passage to Hong Kong. The

Shanghai branch of the American trading house Russell & Company paid for this as a favor to British authorities at Shanghai, and the imperial Chinese maritime customs.

Hannah rose from her seat, tugged at her bonnet, and smoothed her dress.

"If you gentlemen will excuse me, I must go below and see how the captain is coming with our books. Come along Elizabeth."

"I'll stay on deck a while more, Mother."

Hannah Fitch glared at her daughter for a moment while she deliberated the wisdom of leaving Elizabeth alone and unchaperoned on deck with a rugged ship's crew stumbling around her, then shrugged. "Suit yourself then. Gentlemen, I trust I may leave my daughter to your watchful charge."

Ever the gentleman, Hugh hastened to assist the stodgy Mrs. Fitch negotiate her spars down the narrow ladder to the main deck. Elizabeth Fitch strolled around the saloon skylight to where Fletcher Wood stood beside the larboard rail.

"What were you looking for so diligently from the bow, Mr. Wood?"

"Well, miss, it just pays to keep a sharp eye to the wind'ard in these parts."

"Are you on the lookout for pirates, Mr. Wood? Is that why you're keeping such a sharp eye to the *wind'ard*? At Ningpo, when mother and the captain discussed engaging that Chinese pilot, she said this course was her choice to reduce our sailing time, and save another day's wages. She said any pirates we met could just go to...well, you know where they could go."

"It's quite possible that's where they come *from*, Miss Fitch, them and the rebels."

"Rebels? You mean the Christian rebels in Nanking?"

Yes, Nanking, he thought. Foreigners who bring men, muskets and gunpowder to the Taiping become generals. Longhaired rebels will surely stumble all over each other to get an experienced gunnery officer. Both sides would. With an army of a couple hundred jack-tars and Indian fighters off the treaty port docks, I could whip anything the imperials send against me. Then this so-called Yankee filibuster will be made a general, and a mandarin, and a prince and, by thunder, maybe even sit at the right hand of the psalm-singing Taiping emperor himself, if not on the great dragon throne of China.

"Mr. Wood? Did you not hear me? Do you mean the Nanking rebels?"

"Not just Nanking, miss. The Taiping rebels attacked and burned the city of Hangchow just a month ago, and their spies and skirmishers are everywhere between Soochow and Shanghai. Unless they're imperial deserters. Sometimes it's hard to know if rebels or imps are committing the atrocities in the countryside."

"Rebels and imps," she said. "What is an imp? And I have wondered, too, how pagan Chinese rebels could become Christians."

"Imp is for imperial, miss, soldiers of the emperor. They behave that way, like imps – little goblins. I'm told the rebels call 'em that too, imp in Chinese. The Taiping rebels, far as I know, started up ten, twelve years ago near Canton. One more passel of Chinamen disgusted with mandarins, expensive rice and heavy taxes, that rose up against the emperor. Seems to be a rebellion somewhere in China most anytime."

Fletcher thought back to his readings on the Taiping over the years in the *North China Herald*, opinion of travelers in Taiping domains mostly, and of the paper's jaundiced editor. Each of them looking through a different knothole in the fence.

"The Taiping leader, named Hoong, says he's the *younger brother* of Jesus Christ and, like Joseph Smith, Hoong also *talks* with God. Hoong, however, got his religion from a foreign preacher in Hong Kong, they say, then went back and converted his village. Other villages joined up, and pretty soon there were so many that the mandarins tried to corral them. The villagers swarmed together and put to route the imperial troops sent against them. Hoong declared his Heavenly Kingdom and fought his way out of south China. Hundreds of thousands marched all the way up to the ancient capital at Nanking, a huge place surrounded by a wall I've been told is nearly twenty miles long. Hoong captured the city and made it the rebel capital. That was the early fifties."

"You think these Taiping are like the Mormons?"

"Not so much alike, miss. Just similarities. Taiping and Mormon grew from fledgling revisionist sects into violent insurrections suppressed by nation and empire – Buchanan sent federal troops against the Mormons in fifty-seven, just as now the emperor sends armies against the Taiping. Their foes hounded them from one place to another until they settled in a capital, the Mormons from Illinois to Salt Lake City, the Taiping from south China to Nanking. Charisma fires the leadership of the Anointed One, a sermonizer who says his doctrines are revelations from God, and brings order to his congregation with rules and regulations. Their religions whittle away at the orthodoxy of the Christian Bible, and recast their societies in new molds. The Taiping condemn footbinding and make men and women live separately. Mormons establish farm cooperatives that swamp local economies, and form their own militia. Both condone polygamy, for the high officers at least. Hoong is supposed to have sixty-six wives. They say Joseph Smith had twenty-seven. The comparison puts the Taiping in a more familiar context, for Americans at least."

"It cannot be a strict comparison, can it? I mean, pagan Chinese accepting Protestant Christianity, and Christian followers making a new Mormon religion?"

"Goes only so far, miss – that's right. The Taiping seem to have made a new sort of Christianity, mixed in a lot of native Chinese belief and practice."

The idea of the Christian Taiping burning joss sticks before images of Jesus and Mary and the saints did not seem peculiar to Fletcher. Catholic mass was heavy with incense. But placing bowls of rice and fruit before the cross, offering three cups of tea on the altar, and burning paper prayers to send them to heaven would offend orthodoxy somewhere. The more so if Chinese gods share the altar, the faithful ring bells to wake up Jesus, or toss little wood blocks to demand He tell their fortune.

"Westerners that have been there say the Taiping live by the Ten Commandments – but with a lot of Chinese ideas mixed in that make Taiping Christianity pretty strange. They destroyed all the pagan Chinese temples, banned Confucius, and forbade opium smoking, then appointed a lot of kings to rule over them. Imperial armies laid siege to Nanking years ago, and have been trying to oust the Taiping ever since."

"If there are so many rebellions in China, it would appear that the Manchu do not rule the country very well."

"Allowing for the rebel pretense to their misbegotten spawn of Christianity, it's hard to see much difference between Taiping and Manchu, 'cept maybe that the rebels have unbraided their queues and grown their hair long. Both have their emperor, their mandarins, their walled cities and warriors, yet the whole of the territory divided between them remains awash with famine, poverty, decay and death. And still the civil war wages on, Miss Fitch, between the heavenly kingdom of the Christian Taiping and the imperial empire of the profane Manchu."

"Why," Elizabeth said, "do they call them civil wars when they always are so extraordinarily uncivil?"

Hugh clambered back up the ladder and crossed to where Fletcher and Elizabeth stood by the rail, intent upon interdicting his brother and retaking the lost conversation.

"Your mother must be very conscientious to be working on your books while still this far away from our destination," Hugh said.

"Depend on it," she said, squeezing out as little a laugh as her chary gentility would allow. "Mother won't wait for a landfall. She is a holy terror with the account books. She will have cost and profit to the penny without delay. After the company's gain is known, she calculates the return for every one of the little adventures entrusted to her by all the retired sea-captains, pensioned widows, and foundling homes in Boston, as if each was a major shareholder in Augustus Fitch & Company." Elizabeth turned to Fletcher. Why is it, she thought, that self-absorbed men like this Fletcher Wood invite discomfiture, make you want to knock their hats off? His brother just runs in circles yapping like a lap dog. "You don't really think we are in any danger, do you?"

"Hong Kong newspaper reported two or three recent attacks in the Chushans before *Essex* sailed," Fletcher said, intent again on the surrounding islands. "Crews butchered, cargoes plundered, vessels burnt to the water. Three weeks ago the lorcha *Silvery Cross* was taken in Bullock Harbor, near Ningpo, and the master, several Europeans, and one Chinaman were murdered."

Elizabeth caught her breath. Hugh took more notice of the surrounding islands.

"The rest of the people on board were said to have escaped," Fletcher said quickly, regretting his inattention. Better leave the rest unsaid, he thought – that five days later pirates took another lorcha, the *Cleopatra*, at the mouth of the river at Wangchow, again near Ningpo, and all hands are supposed to have been murdered. "The paper warned there are many pirates cruising between Ningpo and the Yangtze River."

"But we have just left Ningpo," Elizabeth said, "and must go on the Yangtze River to get to Shanghai, is that not correct?"

"Yes, miss. We got under way from Ningpo just before first light. We will pass the Volcano Islands after three hours. We should make Gutzlaff Island tonight, and enter the Yangtze tomorrow."

"Then we are sailing through the middle of those *cruising* pirates?"

"On a beeline, Miss Fitch. Do you think it worth a day's wages?"

"Oh, come along Fletcher! You're just trying to frighten Miss Fitch."

"Not you, of course, eh Hugh?"

"Shouldn't we turn back," Elizabeth said, "or go a different way?"

"Always go straight forward, they said in old Salem, and if you meet the Devil cut him in two and go between the pieces. If anyone imposes upon you, tell him to go whistle against a northwester and bottle up moonshine."

Hugh saw Elizabeth Fitch turn pale, and silently cursed his brother the Hun.

"We're past the time," Fletcher said, "for deciding to go a different way. The arrow, as they say, has left the bow."

"Look here, Fletcher. Can't you see you're upsetting Miss Fitch?"

"*Fortuna favet fortibus*, Hugh. It's worth a risk to prove that maxim."

"For the love of God, Fletcher, talk English. What does that mean?"

"Fortune favors the brave," murmured Elizabeth.

"There, you see Hugh. The young lady has more gumption than you think. Why, I'll wager that just beneath her stylish rigging she's copper-lined and brass-riveted and will stand up in any weather. What do you say, Miss Fitch?"

"How far is it back to Salem?"

4 "Don't be alarmed Miss Fitch," Hugh said. "My brother always exaggerates."

"If you'd taken time, Hugh," Fletcher said, "to read the news while we were in Hong Kong, you might be less flippant and better informed about pirates."

"Buccaneers and privateers?" Elizabeth bravely twitted. "Jean Lafitte, Henry Morgan, and Captain Kidd? Eye-patches, peg legs, and Spanish doubloons?"

Fletcher despaired of imparting much useful information to either of them.

"Chinese pirates are a lot different, miss – different names like Shap and Apak and Fokie Tom, different loot like opium and Mexican dollars, different vessels like junks, gunboats and sampans. They swarm along the coast from the Pearl River in the south to the Peiho River in the north and prey on anything that floats."

He dredged up some of the yarns old Lynch had spun back in fifty-seven when Fletcher was mate aboard *Antelope*, about great pirate empires of the south China coast in the high days of the old Canton traders. Fleets of hundreds harbored in large pirate towns complete with dockyards and arsenals, and vulgar dens for drinking, gambling and harlotry. They preyed on the shipping routes of the opium schooners and merchant traders, just like the old Jamaican pirates plundered the sea-lanes of the Caribbean, and even rushed on shore to attack villages and ravage entire towns.

"That is incredible!" Elizabeth said. His patronizing tone annoyed her. "Surely fleets of pirates are not so bold as to attack a town on shore, not with all the gunboats and frigates in these waters? The entire English and French navies must have been off Ningpo when we set sail this morning."

"Those were war-steamers and transports of the advance squadron that we saw anchored off Kintang Island, downriver from Ningpo – part of the small expeditionary force following *Essex* up from Hong Kong to occupy Chushan Island over the next few days. Only a coincidence that we left less than a day ahead of them. In forty-one, and again now, the English strategy for advancing their fleet north is first to take and garrison intermediate stations *en route* to secure their lines of communication and supply before sailing north. And to threaten the transport of Chinese tribute grain on the Grand Canal, the Yangtze, and up the coast."

"But why do these Chinese turn to piracy?"

"There's many'll say the bloodthirsty rascals are just born to it."

"Perhaps this war of the English is a cause?" she ventured, not expecting him to take her seriously, and not at all pleased by his condescension. "I have read that these wars the English and French fight against the Chinese cause hardship among common folk, displace large numbers of people, spoil rice crops, and breed rebellion. Do you suppose that rebels and pirates, as different as they may be in their particulars, are really the same – an incarnation of misrule?"

"Maybe the wars had something to do with hard times in China," Fletcher said, "or maybe it was just coincidental, happening at about the same time. There have been pirates on the China coast – Chinese, Japanese, even Korean – a lot longer than English and French here have been peddling opium. More pirates than mosquitoes."

Fletcher leaned out over the larboard rail again and gazed aft past the clipper's stern. Her wake drifted to larboard barely five degrees, not enough leeway to matter over the short distance *Essex* was sailing. About twenty-five miles to the southeast, the Allied Expeditionary Force was probably chockablock in the harbor at Tinghai potting away at Chinese shore installations and disembarking marines to assault the town.

Better to be in action there, witness to the start of this next war against China, than here aboard sleepy ol' *Essex*, dawdling along with waspish women and emporium goods, and maybe no more than a pirate for diversion.

Essex evidently had slowed. Close by Fletcher saw the southern tip of East Volcano Island was behind them only one-half mile or so to the southwest. Forward under the jib boom was the lonely nun buoy in the distant shallows.

That's a curious buoy. On a windward flood, with the wind blowing offshore against an incoming tide, the cable should be stretched taut and the buoy standing erect, not leaning over in the direction of the current as if bowing to ancient ancestors.

A very small, shrill alarum went off in the back of his mind.

"But surely such a large number of people would not repeatedly go to the extreme of piracy without good *reason*, Mr. Wood," Elizabeth said.

"The Chinese are as exasperating a people as you may ever experience, Miss Fitch," nearly as exasperating as you, he thought. If you and my brother would stop yammering long enough, I might be able to find pirates before they find us! "They are brutal and uncivilized, and carry on such slaughter of one another as to make it quite clear that life, which we hold sacred, means nothing to them."

Elizabeth looked away. You must patronize me I suppose, but I'm not so stupid as to fail to recognize an evasion, or horse manure shoveled up to cover the fact you don't know the answer to my question. You misrepresent them, I believe, Mr. Wood – perhaps intentionally, perhaps just out of ignorance. You don't understand women any better. People don't do things without a good reason, and if the truth can be known, I will find out the reason, even if you cannot, in spite of my being just a simple-minded girl in need of guidance from pompous, strutting, vile-cigar-smoking, bloodthirsty, brutal men.

Hang it all! What's wrong with that blasted buoy? Storm make it drag anchor? Villagers divine it offends the fong-shway of the place, violates that barbarous geomancy of wind and water they invoke to measure the pulse of the sea-dragon king, and move it to where it can't offend the spirits, frighten the fish, or bring flood, famine, and foraging rebels? Or pirates? No, villagers wouldn't move it, they'd sink it or burn it; but pirates would move it, and leave it where it would ground some skylarking ship.

The clipper came about some, giving Fletcher a different view of the channel, and that jarred his memory. Without a word, he suddenly pushed past Elizabeth and Hugh toward the ladder, jumped down to the main deck, ran forward to the forecastle ladder, mounted to the upper deck, and stopped beside the larboard cathead.

Now we see their stinking trick. That marker wasn't so far inshore last time *Antelope* came through here, carrying ol' Fletch Wood as her mate. Back then, the channel had the slender waist of a Shanghai whore, and we had to cinch in our gut before we could squeeze into her. Damned pirates have moved the buoy inshore, and that Ningpo Judas, that so-called pilot, is going to use the buoy's position as an excuse to run us right over onto our beam-ends!

洋神 *Yang Shen*   James Lande 藍德

Dramatis Personae: Chapter 2

Wu Hsü 吳煦	*taotai* 道台 at Shanghai
Liu Hsun-kao 劉郇膏	county magistrate 知縣 at Shanghai
Frank Jackson	interpreter, Shanghai American consulate
Walter Lowell Grace Shanks	American Consul, Shanghai ("General" Shanks)

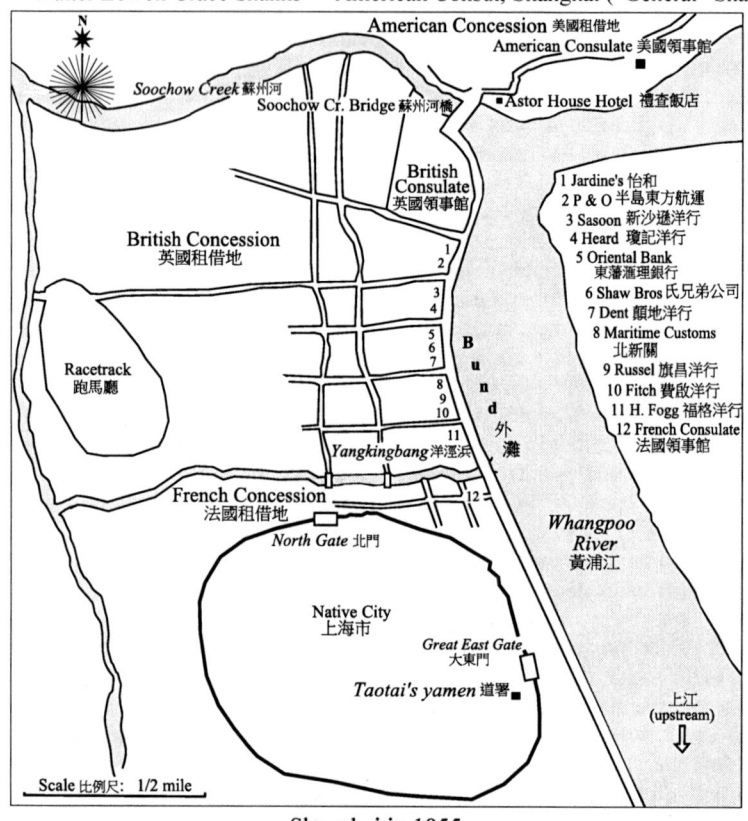

Shanghai in 1855
(based on Morse, *International Relations of the Chinese Empire*, v. 1, p. 454)

Calendars

Western	Ch'ing	Taiping
	Hsien Feng	
1851	1	1
1852	2	2
1853	3	3
1854	4	4
1855	5	5
1856	6	6
1857	7	7
1858	8	8
1859	9	9
1860	10	10
1861	11	11
	T'ung-chih	
1862	1	12

Place Names

Chinese	Western
Che-chiang 浙江	Chekiang
Hang-chou 杭州	Hangchow
Hsiang-kang 香港	Hong Kong
Kuang-chou 廣州	Canton
Nan-ching 南京	Nanking
Pei-ching 北京	Peking
Shang-hai 上海	Shanghai
Su-chou 蘇州	Soochow
Sung-chiang 松江	Sungkiang
T'ai-ts'ang 太倉	Taitsan
Kuang-tung 廣東	Kuang-tung

1860 Rates of Exchange
s = shillings   d = pence

British Pound	Shanghai Tael	Mexican Dollar	American Dollar
£1	3.0	4.16	4.80
6s 8d	**1.0**	1.388	1.60
4s 8d	0.72	**1.00**	1.15
4s 2d	0.625	0.88	**1.00**

Distance

One Chinese *li* 里 = 1894.12 feet or .278 mile

3 Chinese *li* 里 = 1.076 miles (about one mile)

28   Borrowing American Troops

洋神 *Yang Shen*   *James Lande* 藍德

Chapter 2: Borrowing American Troops
Thursday, April 19, 1860, 8:30am

小蟋蟀在歌唱 a small cricket singing. A soft, delicate high-pitched *chirrup* that repeats and repeats, swelling to fill the ears, the head, and finally the heart with sweetness, and melancholy. The song seeped out from between the tiny bamboo bars of a circular cage, framed with carved ivory, no bigger than the palm of a small boy's hand. The cricket cage hung in an open window, between shutters of yellow parchment paper pasted on carved and lacquered lattice, together with several empty cricket cages of bamboo and carved ivory turning slowly in the breeze of a warm summer afternoon. To one side on the sill there was a small dish of chopped fresh cucumber, boiled chestnuts, cabbage, seeds, and kernels of boiled rice. The other cages were empty because their occupants, raised on mosquitoes fed blood from his arm and carefully trained to kill, had all died in contests of sport, fighting with other diminutive cricket warriors owned by other small boys in battles to the death. This last small cricket he kept to hear its song. The old story of the house-cricket 促織 came to mind, and he recalled how the spirit of a small boy had entered the body of a fighting cricket and lived in a cage, vanquished other crickets, danced to music, and sung for the Emperor. Outside the window, beyond the swinging cricket cages, the man's gaze followed that of the small boy, across the rice fields and orchards of "Love and Peace County," Jen-ho Hsien 仁和縣, to the distant hills of Chekiang Province 浙江省 barely visible in the mists of faded memory.

    The sedan chair in which the man rode lurched slightly when one of its eight bearers put his foot wrong, and the *chirrup* of the crickets of his childhood blended with and disappeared into the clamor of beating gongs and the chanting and huffing of the men bearing his chair. *Taotai* Wu Hsü 吳煦 returned instantly from his memory of the rustic beauty of his birthplace to the squalid streets of Shang-hai 上海.

    Wu Hsü was a tall, slender man in his forties, with blotched skin like translucent rice paper, tight and unyielding, as if the thinnest smile would rupture his face. In his official's summer hat and ordinary robes of office 常服, he carried himself quietly and gave other Chinese an impression of solemn authority. But that impression could be contorted into obsequious servility in an instant when necessary to meet the expectations of some proud, ignorant and dense foreign diplomat. He would play that role for the American minister, when the minister came to Shang-hai from the American legation at Macao, and perhaps today for the American consul, unless the consul was too sick to care, but not for the interpreter Jackson, through whom all conversation would pass.

    Wu Hsü's actual title was Acting Su-Sung-T'ai Taotai 蘇松太道台, which meant he was responsible for the prefectures of Su-chou 蘇州 and Sung-chiang 松江, with five counties including Shang-hai, and the department of T'ai-ts'ang 太倉, with three counties, in all twenty-two walled cities. To the *taotai,* there reported three prefects, eight county magistrates, and numerous functionaries subordinate to the *taotai*'s other titles of office. For many years, the Shanghai *taotai* had also been a *de facto* foreign minister due to his proximity to the foreigners and the lack of any foreign office in the Chinese empire. When refugees from the pillaging of Taiping rebels swelled the population of the native city of Shanghai and overflowed like the Whangpoo River into the foreign concessions, the *taotai* was indirectly responsible for the welfare of probably over 1,000,000 people.

    Excluding the foreigners, of course, thought Wu Hsü. Many Chinese who have actually seen a rice-flour-faced foreigner believe they are ghosts, not people. Chinese

洋神 *Yang Shen*   *James Lande* 藍德

know that spirits, *shen* 神, and ghosts, *kuei* 鬼, live in the world together with men. The spirits do men good and ghosts do men ill according to fate. Because the foreigners, *yang-jen* 洋人, do so much evil, so it follows that they can only be ghosts materialized out of the Western oceans, and thus the people call them *yang-kuei* 洋鬼.

    Shanghai's foreign merchants grumbled and groused that the *taotai* was into everything and seemed to be friends with everyone. Doubtless, he had a legion of sly informers who prowled dark streets to listen at windows for the secrets of the Westerners, and he twisted the foreign consuls to his will with self-seeking affability and toadying deference. Rumor held that the *taotai* was one of the richest mandarins in China, possessed of a purse of Fortunatus bulging with more than a million pounds sterling. It was common knowledge that Wu Hsü acquired this fortune by pocketing public funds and joining with other Chekiang men in business ventures forbidden to mandarins by the emperor. The *taotai* and his clique were very clever at concealing their malfeasance, and his enemies had not yet uncovered sufficient evidence to support impeachment and degradation of Wu Hsü. However, many of the foreigners with whom he dealt at Shanghai looked forward to the day when the *taotai* would at last get his due.

    混蛋 damn them. Get in step!

    The *taotai*'s chair was jouncing instead of gently swaying. Carried by the usual four bearers, the ride was smoother with fewer men because it was easier to maintain the same rhythm. Eight bearers were too many to keep in step unless they carried chairs every day. Outside his sedan chair, the din of the gongs leading his procession and the criers bellowing "make way for his Excellency *Taotai* Wu" brought all traffic to a halt while the great man passed. The day was bright and through the gauze curtains Wu Hsü saw apparitions stone-still on the opaque cloth – the vague shapes of buildings and shadows of pedestrians on the Bund 外灘, the old towpath that was now a promenade along the riverfront. The chair made its way along the gauntlet of Western hongs 西洋樓 marshaled like an army of occupation. Once only, their high, square outlines were interrupted – by the upturned eaves of the old temple that housed the maritime customs.

    Behind the *taotai*'s chair followed the chair of the Shanghai county magistrate, Liu Hsun-kao 劉郇膏. Liu was born in a dragon year and Wu Hsü thought Liu's long face and protruding eyes made him look just like the astrologer's description of such people, and he was well mannered and very clever, too. Wu Hsü had to be extraordinarily careful about everything he said to Liu. The county magistrate was subordinate to the *taotai*, but Liu was intelligent, perceptive, and conscientious to a fault. Liu was much too scrupulous to applaud the *taotai*'s private enterprises and, in the years since they both had served as sub-prefects for coastal defense at Sung-chiang prefecture, Wu Hsü had contrived ways to frustrate Liu's ceaseless integrity. When broader attempts to manipulate the magistrate failed, Wu Hsü was forced to acquire subtlety. Presently, he often conferred with Liu on official business, which appealed to Liu's vanity, and also distracted the magistrate from Wu Hsü's *unofficial* business. Before starting out for the American consulate this morning, the taotai and the magistrate had attempted a mutual understanding of the task before them.

    "Sung-yen, the menace that threatens our dynasty now," Wu Hsü had said, "is the greatest in the past two hundred years of barbarian affairs." Wu Hsü called Liu by his personal name Sung-yen 松巖 – a special name called a *tzu* 字 – chosen at the age of twenty and used between friends. Liu Hsün-kao, being junior in both age and rank, always addressed the *taotai* more formally, as *Ta-jen* 大人.

    "Friendly relations would have been possible without difficulty," the *taotai* said, "when the five ports were opened under the first treaties, if there had been in place satisfactory rules 規矩, so that everyone knew their proper roles. But the Kuang-chou officials refused to allow the barbarian chiefs to enter the city, or meet with the imperial commissioner. The source of the trouble in the so-called Opium War was the barbarian merchants and their opium. Since the Treaty of Nan-ching 南京, and the opening of the five ports to trade, the barbarian merchants have had no complaint whatever. Hostilities against Chinese authority occur again today because of the conceit of the barbarian chiefs, especially the English. Thus the present difficulty derives more from the barbarian *chiefs* and less from the barbarian merchants."

"It is difficult to deal with them without great loss of face," Liu said. "Some say they should be crushed – the defeat of the British last year put an end to it all. If they saw the barbarians every day as we do, and witnessed the power of their weapons, they might understand that the barbarians cannot be repelled so easily."

The matter of face is truly an obstacle, mused the *taotai*. Many in Pei-ching are no less arrogant than the barbarians. Advanced thinking for a county magistrate – magistrates rarely deal with foreigners, and are as ignorant of Westerners as those empty rice-buckets in Pei-ching – but exposure to foreigners at Shanghai matures a man quickly. Which is another reason effort is required to confine the activity of Liu Hsün-kao to county-level matters. To have him involved with the maritime customs would be a disaster – not only would he discover my embezzlement 監守自盜, but he also would make accusations against me in memorials to the censorate 樞垣! Officials like Magistrate Liu watch constantly, looking for the slightest evidence of malfeasance. If all were to become known, banishment to military exile in a malaria-infested region would not be enough – the money is so much that even strangulation would be deemed lenient, and my immediate decapitation would be ordered.

"Now we must fight rebels and foreigners, too," Liu said, becoming incensed. "With crops failing everywhere, farmland laid fallow by war, and famine all around, how can we find tax money to buy cannons to fight both the T'ai-p'ing and the British? Rebels are everywhere in the north, and local bandits in all jurisdictions are always wriggling with desire for action. Now those Western barbarians have repudiated their treaties and attacked and occupied Kuang-chou, abducted our Governor Yeh Ming-ch'en 葉名琛, and threaten to return with war vessels to the Pei-ho River again this year."

"The blood of every Chinese is up for a fight!" Wu Hsü said. "I too gnash my teeth in bitter hatred, hungering to flay their skin and eat their flesh! But how can we expect to handle so many enemies?"

"You have said the barbarians cannot be handled successfully if we treat them as vassals or slaves, for that only makes them angry."

"Neither can we appeal to the wisdom of their sages," the *taotai* said, "because the uncultured foreigners have no sages. We cannot control them by force, as their weapons are superior. What our countrymen must realize is that the foreigners have handed to us the very things we require in order to handle them."

"What things?"

"Their treaties."

"Treaties?"

"Yes. Hold the barbarians firmly to their treaties, show good faith, humble the foreigners with reason, and mollify them with favors. Set the greed of one nation against that of another, weaken their resolve by creating dissension among them, and poison not their bread but their minds with suspicions of one another. When the foreigner becomes greedy, pretend to be indifferent."

"When he is proud, defer to him?" Liu said.

"Yes. And when he hides deceit behind false friendship, show him trust."

"Cater to his mood, and sooth his mind."

"Exactly. The Southerners were the first to meet the barbar..., the foreigners, and did not understand how to handle them, but in Shang-hai we have learned for over twenty years from the mistakes of the Kuang-chou men."

"We cannot use force until we can be sure of success," Liu said. "Evidently, we should wait for a more propitious time to act. But, how long must we wait?"

"How would I know," Wu Hsü said, sighing. "However long it may be, I am ready to sleep on faggots and sip gall 臥薪嘗膽 so that vengeance is never forgotten. One day we will avenge the insult to China, and Heaven will punish our foe."

2 Outside the curtain enclosing the *taotai*'s chair, muffled footfalls thumped on a wood surface. The din of gongs and shouts of "make way for his Excellency *Taotai* Wu" dissipated out over the water and echoed off the brick wall of the quay opposite. Pushing the curtain aside slightly, Wu Hsü saw they were crossing the foreigners' toll bridge over Su-chou Creek. Ahead were the granite gates, tall arches, and two-story buildings of the Astor House Hotel. His chair was about to enter the American Settlement, and in a few minutes they would arrive at the American consulate. He closed the curtain.

Magistrate Liu understands the questions much better than other officials. He grasped the contradiction quickly.

"How," Liu had said, "can Shang-hai manage to borrow troops from the Western nations to help fight the T'ai-p'ing rebels, when the Western nations are about to go to war against China? The situation is extraordinary – Chinese and Westerners are all very cordial in Shang-hai, even as the English and French gather their naval force in Hsiang-kang to occupy the island of Chu-shan and attack T'ien-chin. If this were Kuang-chou, Chinese and Westerners would be fighting a bitter and bloody brawl 浴血苦戰. However, it will be a profound paradox if the foreign troops fight the Ch'ing in the north at the same time they help the Ch'ing in the south 洋軍一時在北打清在南助清將是一個很大的矛盾. That we could borrow their troops is much to hope for."

"Clearly," Wu Hsü said, "if Shang-hai falls, then the rebels will have new sources of finance, munitions, and supply and the rebellion will go on without end. But if all the imperial troops are at Nan-ching, or deployed around T'ien-chin waiting for the English and French to return, who will come to our aid? The foreigners will fight only to protect their own property in the settlements."

"But we want them to protect the Shanghai walled city as well."

"Yes. The French might be persuaded to send troops to Su-chou – to protect the Christian churches – and perhaps then the English can be induced, also. Only the Americans are mainly neutral. They do not want to be involved in anybody's quarrel – Chinese, T'ai-p'ing rebel, or English and French. Americans just want to be left alone to sell muskets and powder to the longhairs."

"If the Emperor opposes the borrowing of troops to suppress the rebels, *chieh-ping chu-chiao* 借兵助剿, then there is nothing more to say. I, Liu Hsün-kao, will not oppose the will of the Emperor." When Liu got up a little fire, his eyes burned like the pop-eyes of the devil-deflecting star god Tzu Wei Ti 紫微帝 astride his lion dog – some people felt the righteous Purple Planet was staring straight at them 紫微正照.

"You need not oppose the Emperor," Wu Hsü said, with rising exasperation. "But perhaps He can be encouraged to consider another view? There certainly is ample precedent for the borrowing of troops to suppress rebels, *chieh-ping chu-chiao*. China has employed barbarians for military purposes for thousands of years."

"The arguments *against* borrowing troops are not a few," Liu said, firmly. "We say water can float a craft, but it can also sink a craft 水能載舟亦能覆舟. Borrowed troops can save the empire, but they also can destroy the empire. In the Han, barbarian mercenaries could not be controlled and revolted against the dynasty. The Ughur allies of the T'ang were querulous and disobedient, and An-lu-shan himself was a bastard barbarian in T'ang service when he rebelled. At the same time the Jesuits made cannon, they meddled in Chinese affairs. Troops borrowed from barbarian tribes were different – they learned right conduct and gave their loyalty to China. Now, if China borrows foreign assistance, what else would foreigners have to gain but the occupation of territory? Did not the French Settlement expand to the Small East Gate after French soldiers drove out the Small Swords?"

"That was only a small space, a few streets."

"And once enlisted to assist, how would the barbarian troops be controlled?"

"With honors, and rewards. With money, a great deal of money."

"If used to suppress rebels, what would prevent them from allying with rebels?"

"The same. Honors and rewards. More favors. Travel inland, trade on the Long River. Perhaps a little territory – hongs, godowns, consulates…concessions."

"If they covet only profit, then on the pretext of cooperating in bandit suppression will they not make inordinate demands?"

"Promise anything, everything. Then delay."

"Would the Westerners not just protect their own interests?"

Liu had become quite overbearing, as if he knew enough about the *taotai*'s deceptions to have no fear of his superior. It was a mistake to allow such conversations to go on too long. The *taotai* sighed deeply. He leaned back against the embroidered tapestries covering the walls of his jouncing sedan chair and wondered how they could convince the Americans to lend troops to help keep the longhaired rebels out of Shanghai, and to *not* go north to T'ien-chin together with the English and French.

"At the very least," Wu Hsü had finally offered, "we can begin inquiries with the foreign consuls, to start them thinking about lending troops."

The sedan chair stopped. Through the narrow opening between the closed curtains, Wu Hsü saw an attendant run forward to the sagging gate of the American consulate, bow stiffly to the gatekeeper and hand over the *taotai*'s gilt-edged vermilion calling card. The gates swung open and the procession entered to the report of three small cannon fired in honor of the arrival of the *taotai*. The breeze blew the white smoke from the guns into his sedan chair and the *taotai* sneezed. The chair was set upon the ground, the curtains parted, and the *taotai* stepped out into the small courtyard. Glancing to one side, he saw the blue sedan chair of the county magistrate a little to the rear of his own green chair. Liu had dismounted and was waiting to step forward behind his superior.

A retainer ran back with a large red silk umbrella and held it above the *taotai*. Arrayed before the old converted godown that served as the American consulate stood the consul, W. L. G. Shanks, the interpreter Jackson, and as many clerks, merchants and friends as the consul was able to round up in time to make some appearance of honoring the mandarin's visit. The *taotai* suppressed an ungenerous thought that he wished he were calling at the British consulate instead, lest the thought unbalance his delicate state of concentration. The two mandarins stepped forward three paces in perfect unison like birds turning on wing, clasped their own hands and shook them before their own faces, and bowed forward to the degree proper for a consul of an inferior nation.

"您好您好你們大家都好麼 hello, hello, are you all well?" each repeated in accented

洋神 *Yang Shen* *James Lande* 藍德

Mandarin. "好久沒見到你們了 it has been a long time since we have seen you."

Several foreigners responded in kind, bowing and shaking their own hands in similar fashion, and repeating "*ni hao ma*" or "hello." Some foreigners simply bowed. A rude fellow or two just smiled; the *taotai*'s runners carefully scrutinized them. The consul bowed as much as he thought dignified, and put aside a recollection that Minister Wood the year before had refused to bow at all to the Chinese emperor in Peking.

Frank Jackson bowed and shook his own hands not just once, but twice, each time with a wide grin, once to the *taotai*, and once to the magistrate, repeating their greetings in Mandarin. Frank Jackson had been from here to Piccadilly more than once, he told himself, and knew that his job was easier when he was as polite to the Chinese as they were to him. Give them much face. Anyway, being a Southerner, he calculated that he was born to etiquette and proper behavior, and Yankee insolence be damned.

Jackson believed his pride as a Southerner, and the many slights that he and his people suffered at the hands of arrogant northerners, lent him some insight into the Chinese obsession with face. A fundamental tenet of Chinese etiquette, face was not written up as such in their many books about ritual and rites, as far as he could see, but it was nonetheless the bone to which the tendons and ligaments of decorum were attached. Every encounter with a Chinese over the age of four required that one "give face," show respect and proper deference to others, and to the rules of etiquette – that is what made it possible for this nation to continue for 5000 years. Follow the rules, he thought, and things get done. Ignore the rules, and nothing gets done. Face is a constituent of Chinese blood because they start the infusion early. The toddlers are scolded *hsiu-hsiu-lien* 羞羞臉, shame-shame-face, for every infraction of the rules. Older children learn to fear loss of face 怕丟臉 over every breach of etiquette. Chinese live with this fear all their lives. In the angry face of every gnarled old Chinese man I witness snubbed, I can imagine a feint *hsiu-hsiu lien* echoing still in the back of his mind.

Mandarins walk like they're belly-deep in cold water, thought Jackson, as he studied again the appearance of the *taotai*. Wu Hsü's summer hat was round, wide and flat – a smaller model of the conical hats farmers wore in the fields. It was constructed of straw pressed onto light board, covered with long red fringe, and topped with a button of rank, a red tassel, and a double-eyed peacock's feather dangling from the crown as a mark of special honor. The button was fashioned of lapis lazuli to indicate that the *taotai* was an official of the fourth rank. A long black braid of hair descended his back from beneath the hat. His long loose gown was of pale blue silk embossed with designs of the character for long life 壽, and embroidered with a foot-high bottom hem of alternating light and dark blue diagonal bands and curled white billows representing swirling water.

Over the gown was a three-quarter length dark blue surcoat 補服, fastened with carved ivory toggles and hemmed in pale blue. On the chest and the back of the surcoat there was a large cloth square 補章, embroidered in plum and white depicting a wild goose 雲鴈 among the clouds, which was also an insignia of a 4th-rank official. An ornate clasp of pale green jade, fastening a loosely girdled thick belt of worked gold, was just visible where the surcoat parted at the waist. The sleeves of the surcoat were very long and loose, and from within them the sleeves of the gown emerged to cover the *taotai*'s hands when he lowered his arms, or withdrew his hands inside the horse-hoof shaped cuffs and held them at his waist.

The *taotai* also wore velvet-trimmed black satin boots with thick white felt soles. Attached to his belt were cases and pouches richly embroidered with silk, gold, and silver metal thread. One case held a fan, another pouch tobacco, flint and steel, or perhaps a porcelain snuff bottle and other knick-knacks. A separate embroidered pouch

洋神 *Yang Shen*   *James Lande* 藍德

held a Western pocket-watch the *taotai* had taken out on previous occasions. Descending from neck to waist there was an official's necklace 素珠, a length of 108 beads of rose quartz, coral, and tourmaline, each the size of a pigeon's egg, all perfumed slightly with musk. The *taotai* carried no weapon.

    Shanghai County Magistrate Liu was dressed in similar fashion, except that the button atop his hat was plain gold in keeping with his grade of 7th-rank official. The square embroidered on the chest of his surcoat depicted the insignia of a mandarin duck 鸂鶒 in flight above the waves. His belt was silver, his gown was pale red in color, and his peacock feather had only a single eye.

    The American consul and his interpreter, thought Jackson, were each dressed in singularly unspectacular gray broadcloth frock coats with black velvet lapels and facings. Their creased gray trousers were pinstriped, and their waistcoats were a subdued gray check garnished by a dangling gold chain and pocket watch. White shirt with stiff collar and cravat, black leather shoes, and gray silk top hats completed this sartorial array. Their hair grew in wild profusion all over their faces, instead of hanging in a tidy braid down their backs. The consul was a ruddy, wrinkled old warhorse struggling against fever to stand up straight. The interpreter was a slender, handsome gentleman of tolerant sentiment and even disposition. The interpreter had in one pocket a small briarwood pipe, pouch of Lorillard tobacco, a box of Lucifer matches, and an old Chinese chop. The chop was a small, oblong stamp made of hardwood inscribed at one end with the Chinese characters for the interpreter's name, which he used to tamp down tobacco in his pipe. In another pocket, the interpreter carried a leather wallet in which he kept various papers, and a small daguerreotype of his wife and little girl. The interpreter had no idea at all what might be in the consul's pockets. Thus, feeling somewhat unequally accoutered, the consul and his interpreter sailed boldly into the uncharted waters of the wide diplomatic sea.

    Jackson glanced furtively at the county magistrate and found Liu smiling back at him. Well Mr. Liu, he thought, travelling in bad company again I see. Take care not to let that venal old Fagin lead you astray.

    The interpreter and the magistrate first met in 1858 during the few weeks when Jackson filled in as American consul at Shanghai. Liu had presented him with Soochow pongee silk as a gift for Mrs. Jackson, under the official category of samples of home-woven from local looms. Jackson was touched by the gesture and afterwards took increased interest in excerpts of the Peking Gazette printed in the *North China Herald* when information pertaining to county magistrates appeared. Since then he had concluded that Magistrate Liu was a rare example of an upright official. Liu was the lowest level of authority in the firmament of Chinese officialdom. Provincial officers were closer to the emperor, but a county magistrate was expected to be closest to the people, to know their troubles and feel their suffering, to understand their needs, and to decide their cases with compassion. County magistrates were called the Father-Mother officials 父母官, and their role was to be parents to the people, their children, to treat the people just as they would their own family. It was an ingenuous Confucian ideal that in effect placed control of the empire in the hands of a small contingent of county magistrates of disparate character, and not a few desperate characters. But Liu was a quintessential Man of the People able to struggle up from under heaps of petitions, complaints, and other yamen paperwork and get out into the countryside to visit the folks. He worried over crops with the farmers, walked the dikes and levees, chased banditti on horseback, and took rice to childless widows. Liu was the embodiment of his title *chih-hsien* 知縣, "knows the county."

洋神 *Yang Shen*   *James Lande* 藍德

Yes, Mr. County Magistrate, I smile because I am thinking about taking my wife and child and departing from your celestial empire. Just as soon as I can somehow twist the arm of the warden of our prison, that honorable secretary of state in Washington, Mr. Lewis Cass, and make him holler "come on home" to Charleston, South Carolina. There I shall offer my services as an experienced bureaucrat of modest ambitions to the State government and settle down to wait for South Carolina to secede from the Union. If you think you have problems with rebels, Mr. County Magistrate, wait until you see the trouble this howling rebel makes for them damn Yankees.

3   The ritual exchange of greetings continued as the Chinese repeatedly took a few more steps and gestured, until they stood before the consul and his interpreter. Wu Hsü then stood up straight and shot out his right hand to the consul, and this time they shook each other's hand, while mentally Wu Hsü congratulated himself for the hundredth time on his mastery of this singular and unsanitary gesture so highly regarded by the foreigners. Magistrate Liu studied the fading emblem above the door of the consulate, so as not to be caught staring at what must be his superior's considerable discomfort at having to take the foreigner's hand. Wu Hsü knew he need not shake Frank Jackson's hand, and they just exchanged smiles.

"Please come in," the consul said in English, gesturing broadly as he preceded the mandarins into the building. Numerous bodyguards and runners, and the unwieldy red umbrella, followed the officials inside, and everyone was seated or positioned as required by protocol. High-backed armchairs with a small table between had been placed at the front of the consul's rickety desk. The *taotai* sat under his red umbrella in the position of honor on the left, and the consul sat on the right holding his topper. The magistrate sat next to the *taotai*, and the interpreter sat next to the consul. The *taotai*'s retainers stood behind the mandarins, arms folded across their chests in a stern line the length of the room. A few guests from the crowd outside stood fidgeting near the door.

During the interim, while everyone shuffled about finding their places, there came to *Taotai* Wu Hsü's mind one of the earliest images of the American barbarians. The unfortunate Imperial Commissioner Ch'i-ying had offered the impression in an old memorial to the emperor at the time of the first Western intrusions at Canton. America is in the Far West, said Ch'i-ying. It is the most uncivilized and distant country of all the border states, by itself alone and uneducated. They know nothing of proclamations and laws, and if meaning be subtle they would probably not understand. They do not follow the Chinese calendar nor accept imperial authority, and we could wear out our tongues and parch our lips and they still would only grin uncomprehendingly like a deaf person 即使舌敝唇焦乃未免褎如充耳. They would never accept status like that of the vassal states An-nan 安南 or Liu-ch'iu 琉球. Apparently, we must keep things simple for them, and use plain language they can grasp easily.

The two mandarins and the entire line of runners soon brought out their paper fans to cool themselves in the stifling little office. Acting-secretary Parrish appeared and collected the top hats then bustled off for the tea. Jackson observed that the nail of the small finger of the left hand of each mandarin was about three inches long, and that each nail was covered with a thin sheath of finely engraved silver and gold. The taotai's bodyguards intercepted Parrish, returning with a large tray of tea, just outside the doorway, the tea and sweet English biscuits were discretely tasted, and then the tea was brought in and served by Parrish and one of the *taotai*'s servants. The Americans proffered Manila cheroots, and the Chinese tucked them into their sleeves. While all this was going on, polite questions were exchanged in an uninterrupted flow.

"Has the honored gentleman been in good health?"

"Is your venerable father also enjoying good health?"
"What is the age of your honorable father now?"
"May he enjoy another 10,000 springs!"
"And your excellent brothers, are they well too?"
"And how many sons has the worthy sir now?"
"I am cursed by a miserable fate – I have only three little bugs."
"Is your honorable president in good health?"
"Is your honorable emperor enjoying health?"

The consul put his questions to the interpreter in his upstate New York accent, the interpreter spoke in South Carolina-accented Mandarin with the *taotai*, the *taotai* responded in Chekiang-accented Mandarin, and the interpreter translated into southern American. The consul replied as succinctly as he could, and relied on his interpreter to add the polite flourishes essential for ceremonial conversation in Chinese. Among other considerations, ceremony required that all references to oneself use the appropriate self-depreciating term for, in this case, officials of equal rank, rendered as "my humble self" or "this humble servant" 敝官. At one time, Jackson had learned the more complex forms of address used between superiors and inferiors, which became still more complex depending upon the distance of relationship, but he never used most of them. The British interpreters knew the terms well, as their consuls were always hobnobbing with Chinese viceroys, governors and commissioners, but the insignificant American consul only communed with district magistrates, prefects, and *taotai*s. Jackson was all too happy to allow the formal language to languish and fade from his mind.

After an appropriate number of exchanges, Frank Jackson glanced at the consul with a slight raise of an eyebrow, an expression the two Americans understood to mean that the formalities could be concluded and serious talk begun. Jackson spoke again to the *taotai*, addressing him properly as "great," *Ta-jen* 大人, the address specified for a *taotai* by the Board of Rites in Peking.

"Wu *Ta-jen*," Jackson said, "my consul asks me to thank you for your gracious visit to our lowly yamen. He understands that you are very busy with many important matters and pressed for time. The consul begs to ask if today there is any small favor he might be honored to perform for you."

"Indeed, it is this humble servant's honor," replied the *taotai*, "to be allowed the privilege of calling upon the esteemed representative of the great country of America. No relations of state are more important to the imperial court than those with Great America 大美唎駕國. It is with your honorable country alone that we now have a new treaty, negotiated and ratified last year by your distinguished Minister Jethro E. Wood. Other nations must now follow Great America in the proper management of affairs under the treaty. The English and French, having not ratified their treaties, must now petition for most-favored-nation treatment under your treaty. This humble servant recalls the sublime pleasure of discussing affairs of state with your distinguished minister when his honor was last in Shanghai. Will his honor come here again very soon?"

The *taotai*'s experience in this sort of exchange had taught him to pause after each sentence or two to allow an interpreter to do his work without having to remember an entire oration, and then nod to the interpreter when the floor was to be given to another party. Jackson appreciated his consideration, as the skill was uncommon among mandarins and helped conversations go smoothly. Jackson faced the *taotai* until it was time for the consul to reply, and then turned slightly toward the consul, who recognized the cue for his response.

The consul expected from his experience that these exchanges would always start with lighter fare, a *hors d'oeuvre* of discourse, and that if possible one or another participant would finesse an opportunity to grant the first favor, to increase the other's obligation when the subjects turned more serious. Of course, the *taotai* had the same expectation, as he himself would do the same, and each knew the other knew, so that the proceeding promptly acquired the character of an intense and, especially for the American consul, rapidly fatiguing game of chess.

While his interpreter trudged through a rendering of the *taotai*'s polite language about America, the consul's attention wandered and his brow wrinkled. Shanks had the appearance of a rough-hewn block of old Adirondack maple, with a complexion almost as florid as Northeastern autumn, dark eyes under unruly brows, and a forehead permanently furrowed by drumlins of perplexity. It seemed to him that he moved slowly through a miasma of noxious malarial vapors, for he had frequent fevers, and saw everything blurred at the edges. When the Chinese asked about another visit to Shanghai by the American minister, Shanks' pulse quickened.

Wu Hsü's opening gambit was likely to lead to something of more substance. The question quickened the tension among the two Chinese and the two Americans and established the first subtle apprehension between them. Magistrate Liu Hsun-kao sat silently with a wan smile pasted to his face while in his mind he rapidly considered each exchange from 10,000 different directions.

"The American minister," the consul said, "has told me how much he enjoyed his discussions with the honorable *taotai* of Shanghai when last here, and I am certain the minister would welcome another such opportunity. Presently, our American minister is seeing to affairs at the American legations in Hong Kong and Macau, but I believe he may have instructions to come north if the English and French go to Tientsin."

"Does the honorable consul know when the English and French go to Tientsin?"

"This humble servant has not yet heard." And the English and French would delight in hanging me for espionage if I told you.

"English and French warships soon arrive at Chushan Island. Last time, they went north immediately after occupying Tinghai, so I expect they will go to Tientsin soon."

"Your Honor is probably very correct. I am sorry to be so ignorant and unable to provide more information."

"Because the treaty between China and America has already been ratified, and the negotiations of tariff schedules and tonnage dues are now concluded, is there some other reason for the American minister to return to Tientsin?" The Emperor suspects that you Americans, and the Russians, sail north in the wake of the English and French to obtain still more gratuitous advantages. He says to keep you Americans from the sway of the Russians to limit their influence, and that you both should be separated from the English and French, in order to isolate them.

"The American Secretary of State would probably want our minister to see that American treaty rights are preserved, and that any new rights secured by other nations are secured for America as well. It is also possible that America could mediate between China and the other nations, and help to avoid an armed engagement." Lord only knows what the hell's really in the mind of Lewis Cass, but nobody here actually believes Americans can mediate in this mess, least of all the crafty old Chinese.

"Ah, I see," Wu Hsü said. "Then we need not put your minister to the inconvenience of traveling to Tientsin. We can undertake further negotiations right here at Shanghai, with imperial commissioners appointed by the Emperor. Two years ago, we negotiated tariff regulations under the new treaty – here at Shanghai."

The American consul tried not to show his feelings at the mention of the Shanghai tariff conference of late 1858, but Wu Hsü noted a change in the consul's expression and decided he had made some mistake. The American consul probably knows about the secret plan. By now everyone does. How could it remain a secret after their newspaper published the details told them by Chinese turncoats 漢奸? When they learned that the Emperor repudiated the treaty signed that summer in T'ien-chin, the barbarian chiefs were all very angry and accused every Chinese official of outrageous duplicity.

Consul Shanks was of the firm opinion that the English and the Chinese would not be in their present difficulty if, at the tariff conference, the wily old Imperial Commissioner Kuei-liang had not snake-charmed an indulgent Lord Exter into giving up the English demand for a resident minister in Peking. Now the English were back again insisting upon that right at any expense, in spite of how deeply the prospect humiliated the emperor, and regardless of the fact that a minister resident in Shanghai, with the right to go to Peking as needed, would be more effective.

Such a fuss, thought the consul, over everyone pushing north to Tientsin. Why do it? The Chinese are bending over as far as a reed can bend to make negotiation possible at Shanghai, by transferring the imperial commissioners from Canton to Shanghai – effecting the end of Canton as the locus of diplomacy, if that's what they call it. I guess the English might be more reasonable about negotiating at Shanghai if they had not captured the Canton governor's store of secret memorials and edicts. After reading the emperor's private letters, we all know now that the stubborn intransigence met at Canton did not originate with the imperial commissioners, but was because of the obstinacy of the emperor *himself*! So, the English calculate that if the emperor is going to be a pig-headed ass, he'll be just as much so in Shanghai as in Canton.

But the consul grasped another purpose in the *taotai*'s mention of the tariff discussions. Wu Hsü had served as go-between in 1858, and interposed himself in those discussions when the governor-general Ho Kuei-ch'ing could not come to Shanghai because he was up to his neck in rebels pouring out from Nanking over the countryside. Wu had brought to the consul verbal requests – for the American minister's ears alone – which Ho Kuei-ch'ing dare not put into any memorial the emperor or any officials might see. Shanks and Wu were thus present together at the inception of a small conspiracy to get the treaties working right away, despite the emperor's insistence upon delay while he attended to the English and French. Wu seemed to suggest now that the same friendly accommodations could be made again if the American minister would agree not to go to Tientsin and negotiate instead at Shanghai.

"This humble servant," replied the consul, "will relay your suggestion to the American minister, but I cannot say if the minister will consider negotiations at Shanghai when the English and French are in Tientsin, especially if America can mediate an accord at Tientsin."

"The wish of the illustrious American Secretary of State to assist in mediating to avert hostilities at Tientsin is a most friendly gesture, and most sincerely appreciated by His Imperial Majesty, the Emperor. However, there is also great danger to the American minister in the north, where he could be wounded by gunfire, or his ship could run aground, or he might be injured while being escorted overland."

"The American minister is not afraid of these risks," intoned Consul Shanks.

"Certainly the minister must be an exceedingly brave man who absolutely fears nothing," the *taotai* said, "however, I am sure that the imperial court would still be concerned for his safety. Moreover, if the minister were harmed, then Chinese would be held responsible, and be made to pay still more in reparations. Surely it cannot be just for my country to have no say about being placed at risk for payment of further reparations if American lives or property are injured."

"True, that is an important point. Your humble servant will suggest to the minister that for this trip to Tientsin he consider relinquishing the right to reparations for any accidental injury to American lives and property caused by Chinese forces, while retaining rights to compensation in case of deliberate attack."

"Deliberate? That could never happen, not to any ship flying the flowery flag of America, not now that all Chinese know America is our friend, and that we have mutual respect. That worries me also. It is most important that nothing harm the reputation of America as a friend of China. His majesty the emperor may possibly misunderstand the American reasons for coming north to Tientsin, and assume that the Americans are in collusion with the English and French, to coerce and extort further concessions. You, of course, will recall the confusion that resulted when the so-called neutral Americans attacked China together with the English and French during the fighting last year. The Emperor was very angry then, and would not accept your excuses a second time now."

"You are quite right, Wu *Ta-jen*." Excuses, thought Shanks! The American consul was immediately stung with mixed pride and aggravation at the recollection of the gallantry of old Commodore blood-thicker-than-water Tattnall's intervention to save British lives during the debacle at the Peiho River the summer before. But he quickly realized that mention of this was a stratagem of the *taotai* to unbalance the consul's concentration and disrupt his endgame. "We must not allow the emperor to have the wrong idea about the Americans. Your humble servant will be sure to remind the American minister to send letters to the court at Peking which will explain our purpose, and thus set the mind of the emperor at rest about our motives in coming to Tientsin."

It was obvious to the *taotai* that it would not be easy to deter the American minister. This involves real danger, to the minister, of course, but who cared about that turtle's egg? No, the real danger is that the Emperor will *order* his officials in Shang-hai to prevent the American minister from going to T'ien-chin, and that degradation and punishment will be served up to officials who failed. I might suffer reduction in grade and removal from office, from which disaster a quick-witted man might eventually recover. Punishment, however, could be as severe as transportation to some savage frontier like Hsin-chiang 新疆 or T'ai-wan 臺灣. That would remove me from the vicinity of my principle source of wealth, the imperial custom house – and the tens of thousands of taels skimmed each year from import and export duties levied on foreign and native cargoes under the treaties.

"Your humble servant fears that the Emperor will be very much opposed to the Americans going to Tientsin, and will order the governor to prevent that at any cost. This insignificant official will convey your responses to Hsueh *Ta-jen*, the new governor of Kiangsu Province, for his further consideration."

"Please forgive me, Wu *Ta-jen*. I can only repeat that President Buchanan will insist that Minister Wood go north to the Peiho to mediate between the English and the Chinese, and to see that American treaty rights are not infringed, and that all new rights secured by other nations are secured for America as well."

"As the honorable consul has offered all possible assistance in this matter, perhaps we should now proceed to another subject. You are aware, of course, that the rebels appear to have started a new offensive. Last month they took the city of Hangchow with the loss of 70,000 lives and terrible destruction, and in just the past few days have taken the towns of Lih-yang, Kin-tan, and Lih-shui. Perhaps it is early yet, however it cannot be unwise to prepare for the worst. Most imperial troops are engaged at the siege of Nanking and cannot help if the rebels break free of the siege and attack Shanghai. There are not enough imperial troops to subdue the rebels 官軍不敷勦辦, and for that reason we hope to borrow your bar..., your Western strength 冀因借用夷...洋力. We seek assistance from the foreign nations with concessions here at Shanghai to defend the city, and we ask your Excellency what help the Americans might offer."

"Well, sir, you know that America has no troops stationed at Shanghai, and only a very few men able to bear arms as volunteers."

"Cannot American ships of war be brought to Shanghai? Each American steam frigate has aboard several hundred marines who could support the English and French."

"Our fleet in the Far East is quite small and stationed in ports far apart."

"There is precedent for an American defense of the settlement, is there not? I was just a minor official when the Small Swords occupied the native city, but I remember the hundred or so American volunteers and sailors who came from an American warship. Together with English marines and sailors, they defended the foreign settlement against the depredations of imperial troops and drove off an army of 20,000 or more. Have you seen the tablet on the wall of Trinity Church honoring the two Americans who died?"

"Yes, Excellency, I have heard of the Battle of Muddy Flat many times, and seen the commemorative tablet at Trinity Church, but I do not believe that can be considered a precedent." Times were different then, and American consuls did not have to be galled by recitations of the history of their American countrymen from Chinese mandarins. An American sortie against imperial soldiers is hardly a precedent for engaging insurgent forces unless we are to dismiss all distinctions between rebels and imps.

"When the American minister comes from Hong Kong, he will come on a warship, will he not? If his Excellency should remain in Shanghai for negotiations, instead of going on to Tientsin, then his warship could remain here also, and help defend the city with its marines and its large guns."

"Well, sir, that is not impossible; however, Americans are under orders to maintain strict neutrality. It is against our laws to fight on either side in this insurrection."

"But you certainly would take up weapons to defend the lives and property of your citizens in the American settlement."

"But only in the American settlement."

"You would not man barriers outside the native city in order to prevent rebels from advancing into your part of the settlement?"

"Hmm. This kind of question I cannot answer without first conferring with the American minister and with the Secretary of State in Washington."

"Therefore, you would not agree to accompany English and French troops and steamers to go to the relief of the city of Soochow."

A smile struggled for possession of the consul's face when he saw where the *taotai*'s questions lead. The consul subdued the urge to smile by clenching his toes while imagining the *taotai*'s next question – if Americans will not go to Soochow, will they remain in Shanghai to provide support for nations that do send troops to aid Soochow?

"No, Your Honor," the consul said, "my country would not allow me to send troops inland to Soochow – that would unquestionably violate the Neutrality Law."

"But American troops could remain behind in Shanghai to provide support for the English and French if they sent troops to Soochow?"

"Wu *Ta-jen*, if the American minister stays in Shanghai instead of going to Tientsin, and if he comes here on a warship with marines, and if the warship's guns are trained on the approaches to Shanghai, and if the warship's marines are ordered ashore to defend the American settlement, by that time anything will be possible. Then I would not be surprised to see American marines posted on barricades outside the native city together with American volunteers. In all likelihood, I would be there myself. But that is a great many 'ifs' and I cannot promise anything now without consulting my superiors."

"This humble servant would not dare suggest that the distinguished American consul begin to make inquiries as soon as possible, but would only point out that the rebels can move fast and communications are slow. Soon the rebels will be in a position to pounce upon Shanghai like a tiger, before even the fleetest deer among the steamers can flee to Hong Kong or Japan, and it will be too late to call for help."

4   The departure of the *taotai's* retinue was somewhat like the arrival, but in reverse. Parting gifts were presented to the *taotai*, products of Western manufacture donated by the local American Chamber of Commerce. These included brandy and champagne, which Wu Hsü would pass up to his superiors. The box of Cuban cigars he would keep to give back to foreigners when they called at his yamen. The bolts of cotton cloth from English looms he would give to his wife to send to her relatives in the country. After the gifts were presented, the retinue filed back out into the courtyard, the Chinese backed away from the door grasping and shaking their own hands as before, followed by the consul and his interpreter making the same gesture and exchanging well wishes.

The mandarins backed into their sedan chairs, drew the curtains and were silent. The eight bearers of the *taotai*'s chair swung around behind the double file of runners, the red umbrella ran to the front of the left file, the four bearers of the county magistrate's chair took up a position following the first chair, and more runners brought up the rear. Signboards carried on tall poles and painted with the character *tao* 道, for the office of *taotai*, were raised front and rear above the procession. These would make known the approach of such an important official.

When everyone quit fussing and settled into line, the gates were thrown open with a sudden and unexpected clamor of gongs, struck exactly eleven stokes in accordance with rule of the Board of Rites to denote a *taotai*, and criers bellowing "make way for His Honor Wu *Ta-jen*." Passersby scrambled aside as if they were witness to the opening of the gates to the eighteen Buddhist hells.

The consul and the interpreter accompanied the procession into the street and followed it around the next corner. They stood gazing after and waving until the Chinese crossed over Wills Bridge, passed the British consulate, and disappeared into the crowd closing in behind them as the runners cleared their path to the front along the Bund.

"We should feel honored," mused Jackson, aloud to the consul. "The *taotai* normally goes about with only four chair bearers."

"Maybe it helps bolster his self-confidence, along with the rest of that ambulating shivaree," Shanks said. "He'll get a welcome colder'n Presbyterian charity anyplace he appeals for foreign troops to save Soochow from the rebels."

When the last of the procession to remain visible were the *tao* 道 characters bobbing about over the crowd on the Bund, the Americans returned to their consulate.

At Ropewalk Road, the county magistrate's chair continued toward the native city, surrounded by his own small retinue. The *taotai*'s procession turned inland from the Bund and, with some apparent uncertainty, wound through the back streets of the British concession searching for the new location of Takee Bank, T'ai-chi Hang 泰記行. Formerly, the bank was on the Street of Eternal Rest, Yung-an K'ai 永安街, in the native city. As relations between the bank and the foreign merchant community grew ever closer, the Chinese bank financed an increasing amount of the foreign merchants' trade in tea and silk. It became essential to find a location in the foreign settlement for the hong of one of the most successful and richest mandarins in the city, Yang Fang, called Takee by the foreigners. Inconvenient for me, thought Wu Hsü, but convenient for the banker Yang Fang, to foment dissension among the foreign merchants and cause them to rain down complaints upon the heads of their consuls.

Alone once again inside his chair, the *taotai* fretted over his failure. He would have to report to Governor Hsüeh Huan that the American minister was determined to go to

洋神 *Yang Shen*   *James Lande* 藍德

Tientsin, so that the governor could warn others and prepare some new strategy for keeping the Americans at Shanghai.

    My blunder may have lost the opportunity, but I'll not tell anything about that to the governor. What did I say…something that made the consul remember the Emperor's secret plan to repudiate the treaties and demand four articles entirely removed? We would have lost face completely if we took such a proposal to the English, but the Emperor was adamant there be no foreign ministers residing in Pei-ching, no inland trade, no inland travel for foreigners, and no huge indemnity. We were to tell the English that *China would abolish all customs duties forever* in return for removing these four articles from the treaty. Appalling!

    What were we to do? The Emperor demanded we carry out a stupid policy at our peril. I was ready to send out to buy my coffin. Then Ho Kuei-ch'ing and Hsüeh Huan risked all and sent memorials pointing out the drawbacks of the secret plan. They did not shout and stamp their feet, but rather took time to reveal gradually the drawbacks of the secret plan, and after several months, the secret plan finally was abandoned. The Emperor continued to oppose the four articles, and so refused ratification last year when the English and French returned, so now we have another war.

    No official who serves the Emperor can enjoy success for very long because the dogs and sheep keep coming back to bark and bleat. Barbarian expert is too dangerous a role to play – it promises large rewards but entails enormous risks if the fate of earlier experts is considered. Lin Tse-hsü, who burnt the 20,000 chests of the foreigner's opium at Kuang-chou, was banished to Ili. The huge personal fortune of Ch'i-shan was confiscated after he was accused of collaborating with the English – he was stripped of office and titles, led out of Kuang-chou in chains, and sentenced to death. Yeh Ming-ch'en, the Governor of Kuang-tung 廣東 and the Emperor's own representative, was captured by the English and imprisoned at Calcutta until he died. The negotiator of the earliest treaties, Ch'i-ying, was made to swallow poison.

    The *taotai* shivered at thoughts of degradation and loss of his fortune, or banishment to a barren military frontier, or swallowing gold leaf. He fought to keep away a vision of beheading, of kneeling in the dust wearing rags, of his queue yanked forward, of a dull, heavy blade chopping into his neck.

    Wu Hsü began to tremble uncontrollably.

洋神 *Yang Shen*   James Lande 藍德

Dramatis Personae: Chapter 3

Liu Fu-hsi 劉福喜	pilot taken on by *Essex* at Ningpo
Micah	*Essex* second mate, on mainmast starboard watch
Chips	*Essex* ship's carpenter
Doctor	*Essex* ship's cook and doctor
Bo'sun (boatswain)	*Essex* ship's officer for arms and maintenance
Steward	attends to *Essex* passengers

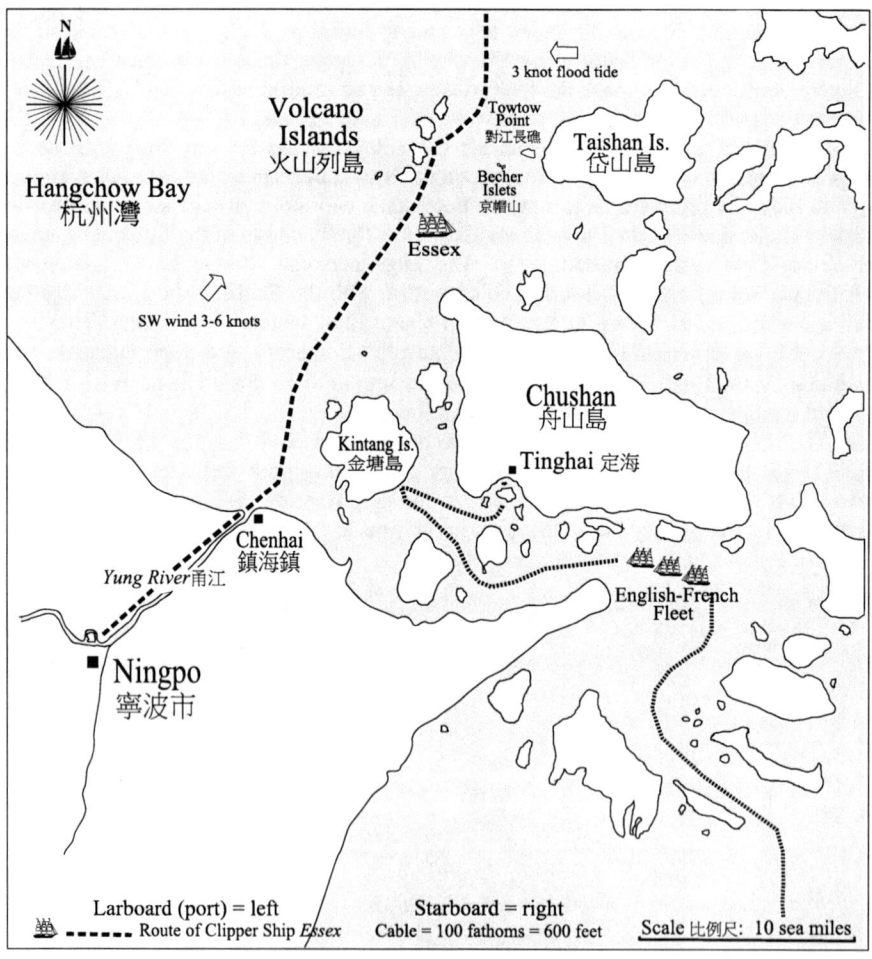

Ningpo and Chushan Island
(based on British Hydrographic Office chart, China., Sheet IX, 1842)

One mile equals 3 Chinese *li* 里. One tael equals US$1.60.

洋神 *Yang Shen*   *James Lande* 藍德

Chapter 3: Laws are Silent
Thursday, April 19, 1860, 9:00am

Fletcher Thorson Wood felt himself flying at the Chinese pilot like a well-aimed musket ball. With sudden force of will, he reigned in his emotion and quickly slowed to an amble toward the stern of *Essex* where the pilot stood with the helmsman.

Handsomely now, reef your sails, don't attract more attention than necessary, don't alert the Artful Dodger, don't wake the mate before you can question the thimblerigger.

Advancing along the larboard rail, he again searched carefully the islands about *Essex* for some sign of the enemy. The southern tip of East Volcano Island was now astern one mile to the southwest. In the distant haze about four miles to the northeast, he made out Towtow Point at the western tip of Taishan Island. Midway lay two steep rocks called the Becher Islets. If they weren't behind the peaks of East Volcano Island, they would be behind Towtow Point. Or behind the Bechers? The cliffs there were certainly high enough to hide a junk, and they were little more than a mile away.

Alert to the movements of everyone on deck, the pilot had watched the black-garbed foreigner descend the forecastle ladder, make his way along the main deck, then mount the ladder to the poop deck. Another foreigner standing at the rail, and a foreign woman, met him there. The black-garbed foreigner spoke to the woman, then yanked the other man aside and whispered in his ear. They glared at the pilot furtively, like skulking cowards, with what the pilot was certain was vicious malice in their eyes.

你白眼看我一會就紅眼看 you look at me with white eyes – with contempt – but you'll soon be seeing red. The channel will be too crowded for you, and you'll learn the sea *can* be worn away by ships. Crabs will eat your flesh, the tide will scatter your bones, your parents will freeze in winter and stifle in summer, your bastard sons will turn thieves, your daughters whores, and your miserable line will die out.

The pilot was called Liu Fu-hsi 劉福喜, Luck-and-Happiness Liu, and his native village was Tinghai, on Chushan Island. He was the last of fourteen children, the son of a fisherman, the poorest inhabitants of the island. When he was twenty, Liu passed by a pear orchard near his home village and stopped to pick and eat three pears. The owner of the orchard, who was also the village constable 地保, gave chase and Liu struck the constable in the head with an unripe pear and knocked him senseless.

Restored to consciousness, the furious constable rushed to the yamen and paid a clerk to pore through the Ch'ing penal code 大清律例 for every possible infraction. Finally, he charged Liu with the crimes of Unauthorized Eating of Fruits Taken from Fields and Orchards 擅食田園瓜果, and Assault on an Official 毆官罪. For good measure, he also charged the hapless boy with Robbery Committed with Violence 強盜, and Resisting Arrest 罪人拒捕, making him subject to bambooing and penal servitude, or banishment, or possibly even strangulation.

The pilot had watched the two foreigners when they separated. The one with the bloodless, rice-flour face, took the woman down the ladder to the main deck and, apparently, into the saloon. The other foreigner, the hard-looking one garbed in black, walked along the larboard rail toward the stern, gazing around him at the islands. *Hai yah*, this black demon has the eye of a hawk, thought the seething pilot. No matter. Look all you want foreign devil, *yang kuei-tzu* 洋鬼子, you'll never see our war junks, not until it is too late.

Liu had escaped to the mainland and drifted into Ningpo a *pai-hsiang jen* 白鄉人, a

Laws Are Silent   45

洋神 *Yang Shen*   *James Lande* 藍德

vagrant in the Shanghai idiom. On the Ningpo docks, he earned a few cash taking the place of sick coolies, loitered in teahouses where junk owners hired laborers, survived beatings by other vagrants fighting for the same work, and slept in the open under godown eaves. Finally, the boss 龍頭 of the East Gate coolie guild 東門派 noticed him.

    For half the cash he earned each day, the boss allowed him to join the guild and apprenticed him as a bearer 肩夫 who carried loads of rice and delicate Kiukiang porcelain 九江陶瓷 from the kilns of Ching-te Chen 景德鎮 on his shoulders instead of with a bamboo carrying-pole. For a long time, brigands 儸儸 and touts 跑打聽 of several gangs watched him. Finally, he was approached by the Yellow Hairs, Huang Mao 黃毛, a gang of robbers and pirates gathered from disbanded imperial troops and led by a yellow-haired Englishman.

    The pilot learned that the native leaders of the Huang Mao fancied themselves provincial heroes and, like secret society members, steeped themselves in the folk traditions of *The Water Margin*, Shui-hu Chuan 水滸傳, the perennially popular romance about a legendary band of Northern Sung dynasty brigands. They styled their hideout the Liang-shan marsh, after that of the Shui-hu bandits. They initiated new members with blood ritual and grueling question-and-answer sessions, after the fashion of secret societies like the Triads. They whispered secret words and signals, tattooed their members, and rationalized their savage bloodletting with patriotic homilies about "strike the rich, help the poor 劫富濟貧" and "oppose the Ch'ing, restore the Ming 反清復明." The pilot had not cared then if their claims sounded counterfeit. Then, he was too hungry to care. Now, he was too rich.

    You are trapped, *yang kuei-tzu*, because there are war junks behind the islands north and south. The sand bar is little more than three *li* distant, and the yellow-haired Englishman will see me throw you into it like a bag of rice, and that will signal the attack. 連你像孫悟空能打個勛斗十萬八千里還打不出我們的手掌 even if, like the monkey king, you could somersault one-hundred-and-eight-thousand *li,* you still cannot escape our grasp.

    Liu Fu-hsi had answered the questions, drunk the wine-and-blood, kowtowed and sworn eternal brotherhood upon pain of miserable death, and was marked with the sign of a panther. The Huang Mao elected to use his knowledge of local waters and made him a pilot 導航 on their war junks. He was a loyal brother and a good pilot and modest with drink, opium, and women, and he prospered. Liu Fu-hsi invested the spoils of his trade in land and houses, but not in trading junks – trading junks might be attacked by pirates – and accumulated a small fortune of several hundred taels of silver, one-ounce ingots buried in a box in the courtyard of his father's house.

    Then came his greatest opportunity. He was called to the little cabin of yellow-haired Englishman's Ningpo trading junk and given documents taken from vessels plundered by the Huang Mao, pilot's papers, and instructed to present the papers to foreign trading companies 洋行 in Ningpo. Liu did as bidden, and soon was assigned the duties of pilot on foreign ships and steamers, piloting several vessels between Shanghai and Ningpo before the yellow-haired Englishman chose a victim. When the Huang Mao learned there were field guns with ammunition aboard *Essex*, they were enthusiastic, but when they discovered among her passengers the young daughter of one of the richest trading houses in Shanghai, they were ecstatic. It was too great a temptation to pass over, even if the vessel was a large and heavily armed clipper.

    The black-garbed foreigner stopped a few feet from the pilot, leaned against the rail, and gazed for moment into the water. Then he straightened up, turned around, and leaned back and rested his elbows on the mahogany railing, staring at the pilot. The pilot

洋神 *Yang Shen*   *James Lande* 藍德

stood motionless, staring ahead, his legs firmly apart, his arms folded across his loose blue cotton jacket.

The Huang Mao had prepared for dealing with the American clipper. Liu saw to the disposal of the pilot already engaged by *Essex* and applied as his replacement. There were no other applicants after Chinese learned what happened to the original pilot, so Liu was taken on. The captain, in conference with the new pilot, decided the course *Essex* would sail. The pilot demonstrated adequate knowledge of the route through the islands, and promised to save an entire day on the run to Shanghai. The pilot then went ashore and despatched north to the yellow-haired Englishman a message confirming the prearranged location where *Essex* would be run aground and stranded. He selected as his courier a slender 35-foot "quick-plank" boat 快板船, capable of 12 *li* 里 – four knots – each hour when propelled by two spirit-sails and sculled by four *yuloh* 搖櫓 oarsmen. Thereafter, Liu Fu-hsi simply waited and watched and, when the clipper readied to get under way, he sent a second quick-plank boat north to warn the waiting pirate junks to complete their own grim preparations.

As he watched the black-garbed foreign devil through his half-closed eyes, Liu Fu-hsi savored the knowledge that this was his last trip as a pilot for the Huang Mao. After this, Ningpo will know me as the pilot on this ill-fated foreign vessel, and the yellow-haired Englishman will have to find a new pilot, one of my older brothers if I can find some way to please that inscrutable fiend from hell. Then I will retire to my property, purchase the office of constable, and wear silk robes and a fox-fur vest. I will marry some rich man's daughter and make her get sons, and I will spend the passing years watching my children, my land and money, and my influence all grow together.

"You savvee dis watah?" the black-garbed foreigner said.

"*Hai-yah*, my longtime pidgin!"

"My longtime sailee-man China-side," the black-garbed foreigner said. "My come dis watah many time. My plenti savee dis watah. My tinkee marker buoy too muchee land-side, b'longee moh watah-side."

Makah boo-i? He sees the channel marker, thinks it's been moved? Liu Fu-hsi's stomach jumped to his throat and his mind raced ahead over the water like a swooping gull. If this pig-shit black demon knows about the buoy and the sand bar, and shouts warning in time to save their damn cargo, their cannon, and the big, clumsy bottomless-hole-daughter 無底洞女兒 of the foreign trading house.... Damn him 他媽的! Kill him, quickly. With the knife strapped to your back. Then jump overboard. They won't have time to change course. But can I kill him? If I miss, if there's a struggle, I will give myself away, and he can shout out a warning. No. Delay. Keep him talking, talking until it's too late to change course. Maybe it's already too late.

"Makah boo-i no b'longee watah-side," the pilot said. "Makah boo-i all plopah. Bottom-side he changee velly muchee by'mby, alla time he changee. You look-see plenti changee now. You longtime no come dis watah, my tinkee. No moh talkee. Hab work now. You go 'way."

"Too muchee land-side," the black-garbed foreigner said. "Bottom-side he changee you bet, but he changee watah-side, no changee land-side. Makah boo-i no can go land-side. No can do."

The pilot was stunned. Stupid 傻瓜! Good-for-nothing 飯桶! Water in this place piles up mud around these islands, and marker buoys always move away from the land, never come in to the land. Damn me 該死! We're discovered! That finishes it 垮台了!

The pilot stepped toward the larboard rail and reached for the knife at the small of his back but, just as the black-garbed foreigner backed away, the white-faced foreigner

Laws Are Silent   47

emerged from the companionway. The pilot stopped, fighting to control his anger and fear, then turned his back to both of them and stared at the binnacle. He willed his outward appearance into relaxation, and all expression from his face, by concentrating on the countless strange points on the complicated face of the foreign compass.

操你媽個臭洋鬼子 fok your stinking foreign-devil mother. 我們非給你個下馬威不可 we will give you the shock of your life, 讓你看看我們的利害 show you how tough we are. 你的吃飯傢伙非先搬家不可 and your head will be the first to roll!

2

The mate suddenly burst onto the poop deck from the main deck ladder. "I told you to come about into center channel," he roared at the helmsman.

"Yes, sir, Mr. Reese," the sailor said, "but the pilot here says to lay off again because there's rocks in the channel and more water off to larboard."

The mate came to rest in front of Fletcher, jerked a thumb over his brawny shoulder toward the helm, and turned a baleful expression on his passenger.

" 'Scuse me, Mr. Wood, but I can't have you jawin' with this josser when I can't keep 'im on course."

"Just as you say, Mr. Reese," Fletcher said, retreating to the larboard rail. A bold pilot, thought Fletcher, considering as how the garlic-sodden gallows bird's probably reeling like he's all aback with his decks awash but, of course, he is dumber than a cabbage. Mud from the mouth of the Yangtze pours out into the China Sea and washes south into Hangchow Bay by the acre, and the land grows and the sea is pushed back, and the buoys move *out* with the land.

"Helmsman," Reese said with a growl, "bring her about two points to starb'd and stay in center channel, and if the josser wants to change course again, you call me first."

"Two points to starb'd," the helmsman repeated. The mate crossed to the windward rail forward of Fletcher to see how far from the shore *Essex* fell off.

Hugh Wood followed his brother to the larboard rail and, as they feigned an exchange of pleasantries, Hugh passed to Fletcher a loaded Colt Navy revolver, which Fletcher slipped into his belt under his frock coat. Hugh took up a position further aft from which he could cover the Chinese pilot, the companionway, and the ladder, should circumstances absolutely force him into an awkward attempt to fire his weapon. Fletcher went forward to where the mate stood hands on his hips glaring out over the main deck.

"Mr. Reese, a word with you?" Fletcher said. "It's urgent else I wouldn't bother you while you're at your duties."

"What's your pleasure, and be tellin' it quickly, if you please. I'm no less busy than our pilot back there."

"The buoy ahead there in the channel has been moved inshore a couple of cables from where it should be, and I believe we'll be aground soon if we stay on this course."

"Oh, 'as it now. Well, I don't know nothing about that. I got me 'eathen pilot right behind me 'ere, and that's a bloke what knows."

"Your pilot *knows* the course is wrong. Keelhaul me if he's not a pirate himself."

"Come along now, Mr. Wood, and don't tempt me," the mate said, laughing. "What's to fear. I seed this ol' josser wasn't no pirate when I took 'im on, what with his consular papers an' all. You're just startin' in to believe all those tall tales you been tellin' b'lowdecks there at the captain's table. Stand aside, Mr. Wood. You're no mate on *this* ship, but them that is 'as got better employment for their time."

"Mr. Reese, look ahead there," Fletcher said. "A long spit of sand and mud juts out from that island into the channel up there somewhere, and the water shoals."

"That's why I'm tryin' to get 'er over to center channel."

"You'll need to move a lot faster than this to stay off the bottom. Look here, Mr.

Reese, at least take a few precautions. Put a lookout in the bow, or in the foretop, to watch the water, or heave a lead."

"Mind your 'elm, there, matey. I'm not takin' orders from passengers on my own quarterdeck. I minds me own business, just as others should mind theirs, and you can bloody well bet I ain't going to have just any perisher come at me sayin' to do this and do that. For all I know, *you's* the pirate, and you's tryin' to take me off'n my course and into some rock out there in the middle of the channel. Now you get off my quarterdeck, you 'ear," roared Reese. "Get below!"

"Tarnation!" Fletcher said. "Get your saddle on the right horse, will you! I'm no more a pirate than this Chinaman here's a three-tailed pasha. Come to your bearings and send a man topside and see for yourself how the water lies."

"Get below I said!"

"The blood will be on your own head then if you don't heed my warning."

After Hugh Wood had assisted Hannah Fitch down to the main deck, she entered the saloon and crossed to the captain's cabin under the starboard rail. There she found the captain sitting alone at a small desk stacked high with books, maps and papers.

"Ah, there you are nephew. I've come down to assist with the ledgers, and to evade the dreary chatter of ship passengers. How is your bookkeeping?"

To Hannah, Cornelius Lowell Fitch scarcely looked the part of a clipper ship captain. Young and smooth-cheeked, he showed none of the weathering of old rocks and old seamen that have seen too much wind and water, and still less of their hardness. Pale as white-ash, with blue eyes and pale-blond hair, he was in command on his first voyage to China because of his family connections, and not because of any repute as a seaman. His father Elias William Fitch, older brother of Augustus Fitch, had been captain of *Essex* and part owner with his brother of Augustus Fitch & Company.

"Close the door behind you, please, aunt," he said, looking around behind her through the doorway. "I don't mind telling you that I already have enough trouble commanding this crew without having them bear witness to all the embarrassments you conjure up for me daily."

Hannah seated herself opposite the captain and pulled a ledger book across the desk. Cornelius got up from his chair and went to close the cabin door.

"Did cousin Elizabeth come down with you?"

"She is on deck in the company of the brothers Wood where, when I left her, she was occupied with displaying her blue stockings. I do not mind telling you nephew that for a while it will be a relief not to have her snagging me with those sharp little claws. How did we ever manage to survive four and one-half months of Elizabeth bored, hungry, and confined? If Unitarians had a purgatory, this passage on the *Essex* would have to be it. No wonder I stayed away in China all those years."

"Are you sure she should be left with those two?"

"Cornelius, if anyone is in danger it is those two feckless men. You do not know your cousin nearly as well as we all know you would like to."

Cornelius' ashen hue took on some color. "I am just not convinced that they are entirely trustworthy gentlemen, for all their apparent good intentions and assistance."

"Hugh Wood is closer to your notion of gentleman than his brother," she said. "However, Hugh Wood is the greater threat of the two, a possible competitor to Augustus Fitch & Company. Fletcher Wood, he is as odd as an albatross, come to the quarterdeck up through the fo'c's'le, but doesn't seem to have any definite landfall in mind. Never mind him – he is a sailor, which means he is a drunkard and a libertine, and maybe a copperhead in the bargain. What assistance?"

"At table I said that I thought Maury's *Wind and Current Charts* a little vague about the waters off the China coast, and Fletcher Wood mentioned a book with sailing directions for precisely this area – the Chushan Archipelago. S. Wells Williams' *Chinese Commercial Guide*. When I wondered why the ship's chandlers in Hong Kong failed to offer me a copy, Fletcher Wood gave me his. It's been of immense help. Has information useful about shipping, too. Have you seen it?"

"Williams is one of those annoying missionaries into everything: interpreter, *chargé d'affaires*, editor. Printed the *Chinese Repository* magazine in the fifties, until that revolting Viceroy Yeh closed him down. Yeh destroyed his inventory and press when the Cantonese burnt down the foreign hongs. Williams would accumulate such minutia of information in all the different posts he has held. I didn't realize you had no copy. We sent one back to Boston."

There came a light knock at the door and Elizabeth entered followed by Hugh Wood. She crossed the cabin and perched on the settee. Hugh disappeared.

"Land's sake," Hannah said, "man has the manners of a Tartar."

"Mother, something is wrong."

"Something is always wrong, dear."

"I mean with the ship. That Fletcher Wood started running around like a mad March Hare. Then he enlisted his brother in some conspiracy and would not tell me."

"Do you feel left out, dear?"

"I am worried."

Hannah looked up and considered her daughter over the gold rims of her glasses. Before she could inquire further, angry voices on deck above became so loud there was no mistaking an argument under way.

"That's your mate, Mr. Reese, isn't it?" Hannah said.

"Yes," Cornelius said with a sigh, "and the other sounds like Fletcher Wood. What kind of a row do you suppose they're into? I'd best go upstairs and look in on them."

"Topside," Hannah said.

The captain sighed again.

"Topside."

The mate and passenger were close to blows when Captain Fitch emerged from the companionway and approached the arguing men. "Here, here, gentlemen," said the captain, stepping between the two men. "What's the meaning of this ruckus. Mr. Reese, explain yourself."

"What!" the mate said, more astonished at what his captain said than at anything said by Fletcher. "In front of my crew?"

"Captain Fitch, this is my fault, not Mr. Reese's. I disturbed him at his work with my concern about the depth of the water we are in, and he was quite justifiably angry at being bothered by a passenger."

" 'ere you, pipe down. I can explain myself."

"That's enough, both of you. Mr. Wood, why are you interfering with my mate?"

"That buoy up ahead marks a shoal that runs out a mile from East Volcano Island almost to mid-channel, but the buoy has been moved inshore. I helped place the buoy from the steamer *Antelope* when she was working for Russell & Company back in fifty-eight. The buoy may have dragged inshore, but your so-called pilot has *Essex* drifting directly toward the shoal, and I'll be way off my course if he's not a pirate."

Cornelius Fitch swallowed hard and stared at Fletcher, then spoke to the mate. "Mr. Reese, Mr. Wood is experienced in these waters and we are not. Notwithstanding the fact he is a passenger aboard *Essex*, I welcome any advice he cares to give, if he can find some tactful way to offer his opinion. What has been asked of us, Mr. Reese?"

"Put a man topside to watch the water," the mate said, sullenly.

"Very well, that is my order then."

Reese called out to the foretopman to lay aloft and keep a bright lookout, then crossed to the leeward rail, yielding the weather rail to the captain now that he was on deck. Fletcher placed himself where he could keep an eye on the pilot. The foretopman ran the length of the main deck and scrambled up the rigging into the bunt of the foreyard. Immediately he called out.

"Mr. Reese, Mr. Reese! Shoal dead ahead! Put her helm up hard. Lift her keel. Helm up! Helm up! Lay off! Lay off!"

In that instant the minds of Ptolemy Reese and his foretopman were one thing, and Reese knew that to pass over the shoal the ship must heel over sharply to the left to lift the keel away from the muddy bottom.

"Helm a-weather!" shouted the mate.

"Helm a-weather!" cried the helmsman, snatching wildly at the spokes of the wheel.

Essex started to swing downwind and out toward the center of the channel, but the warning came too late. A sudden grating squeal echoed from the bowels of the great ship and swelled into a rasping scream as hundreds of tons of white-oak heartwood plowed into the sandy mud of the sea floor. *Essex* lurched over violently, and part of the false keel beneath the true keel sheared away. The force of the ship's forward rush, impeded by the clutching bottom, spent itself laterally, wrenching wooden ribs and planking out of line with the keel. Timber groaned and bleated and brayed. The keelson buckled and shifted the heel of the mainmast up off the keel, and the mast swayed wildly at the main truck 100 feet above the main deck. The sheer-strakes twisted away from the frame ribs and wrenched at treenails in the planking.

Cargo ricocheted through the hold. Nail-rod rolled against wooden crates, which slammed into the larboard planking. Barrels broke loose, rolled free, and smashed through the wooden staves of the animal pen and into the last pig left for the forecastle galley. The field guns lurched with the pitch of the deck, but their moorings held. The pantry door in the saloon flew open and China plates fell and broke, spewing smashed shards across the saloon floor. Elizabeth stumbled against a wall of her cabin, cracked her temple against a brass fitting, and slumped down into an iron washtub. In the captain's cabin, the straight-backed chair under Hannah collapsed and dumped her on the floor under a pile of heavy ledger books. A cooking kettle fell from the galley stove in the forward house and launched stewing chickens at the cook. In the next cabin, an open drawer spilled hand tools into the carpenter's lap. On deck, the crew scrambled for any purchase that came to hand. Masts swayed drunkenly in the air and men grabbed for rigging, but the foretopman missed his mark, flew out of the foretop, and smashed into the larboard rail before falling lifeless into the sea.

Only a moment passed before the forward momentum of the ship spent itself and *Essex* settled into the sand like a broken wave. Her wood was well aged and seasoned in salt pickle and snapped back into place like a bow after an arrow-shot. The keelson straightened, the main mast fell back into its step, and the planking settled. The cargo in her hold came to rest. For a few more moments, everything was still. The crew breathed deeply again. The shallow sea lapped against the cutwater, the masts creaked, and buntlines slapped on canvas. A solitary barrel rolled about somewhere below deck. A bittersweet aroma of aniseed oil mixed with cinnamon and camphor drifted up from broken casks in the hold and out over the deck. The frightened pig squealed from under a tumble of debris. An injured man groaned. The crew stared at each other in disbelief and uttered silent oaths, or prayers of gratitude that nothing worse had happened. *Essex* remained heeled over ten degrees to larboard with her masts lolling out over the shoal.

Slumped over on her left side, thought Fletcher, like a wagon with a broken wheel. But as long as she creaks, she holds.

Reese whirled about in red-faced fury and glared at the Chinese pilot. "Blast me if you ain't a bleedin' mooncursor! C'm'ere you 'eathen little pig-tailed monkey!"

The pilot blanched as white as weathered walrus tusk, bolted for the windward rail, and sailed over it into the water. Reese stared over the rail after him. Fletcher appeared at the mate's side.

"If ever a pale pilot was the sign of a storm," Reese said, with a wry smile at Fletcher. Rancor was gone from his voice, jolted out by the disaster facing them all. "I'll be borryin' that revolver of yours, Mr. Wood, if you don't mind."

"You don't miss much."

"Watch this."

Fletcher handed his Colt Navy to the mate. Reese stepped back from the rail and slowly and with great care thumbed back the hammer, aimed, and shot the flailing pilot in the back of the head. Then he returned the weapon to Fletcher.

"Laws are silent when drums beat, Mr. Wood. That pays for my foretopman."

Fletcher Thorson Wood watched a Union Jack flying from the mast of a Chinese junk come into view from behind the northernmost rocks off East Volcano Island. Well, Mr. Ptolemy Reese. If not exactly war, it might as well be.

The pistol shot fired by the mate alarmed nearly everyone aboard the ship. The cook and carpenter came out of the forward house, the watch below out of the forecastle, and men and boys came running to the windward rail while the cloud of white smoke from the pistol still drifted to starboard. Under the bow of the ship floated the body of the foretopman, dead because of the Chinese pilot, and beyond the stern the body of the pilot rolled out over the shoal on which he had stranded *Essex*. A crewman saw the junk and gestured toward the north point.

"What's that junk coming!"

The brown and yellow sails and towering stern of an 80-foot Ningpo trader came into view laboring hard to get into the channel against the conflicting set of wind and current. With less cargo, she rode high in the water and presented more bulk to the wind, which made her especially difficult to control.

"What kinda Frenchman is that? Is she's flyin' the Union Jack!"

Ptolemy Reese followed the gaze of the sailors amidships, then took up a glass and examined the deck of the junk. "She's crewed by a lot of pox-ridden jossers," he said, and handed the glass to the captain, who also examined the junk. Half-naked crewmen could be seen scampering her length, getting guns into service, passing out weapons and ammunition, and clearing her deck for action.

"Wait a moment," the captain said, "this one's not a Chinese. He's got blond hair. Maybe they are British."

"Pay that Union Jack no heed," Fletcher said, "the registry's easily enough bought. They'll be firing from under those false colors before a brace of shakes and Admiralty law be damned."

"There's another one!" came a cry from the waist. A smaller junk showing no colors appeared from behind the island and slowly beat up astern of the first junk. She was a deep-sea trawler – an archipelago fisher – with a large round eye, high bulwark, and high sloping horns. The horns flared up from each side of her open bow and made her look like a garishly painted manta ray. She came about and started down island toward the opposite side of the shoal to approach the clipper's larboard. That put her into the wind and, close-hauled on a starboard tack, she lost headway and the flood tide pushed her inshore. She quickly abandoned the maneuver and came back around to larboard. *Essex* could see Chinamen on her deck taking in laundry from a clothesline stretched between her masts.

"Look over here," Hugh cried. "More junks!"

The captain and the mate jumped to the tafferel. Two Chinese craft came into view, working around from behind the southern slopes of East Volcano Island. One was unmistakably a Portuguese lorcha, with the sharp prow and unrigged bowsprit of a western-style hull perhaps fifty feet in length, a white deckhouse and gaudy yellow forecastle and poop, and British colors at her main truck. The other vessel was a hundred-foot three-masted Shao-hsing trader rigged with bamboo lugsails and a large leeboard hung at the waist, and painted with a bizarre blue and red face on her large, square bow. She flew a black-bordered red flag.

Fletcher motioned to his brother and said, "One of us should go below and see that the women are not hurt."

"Hang it all!" Hugh said, "I forgot all about them! I'll go down right now. But, what should I say about our sudden callers?"

"Say only that *Essex* has run aground, the captain has signaled for help, and the crew is working to get her afloat. They'll learn the rest soon enough."

As Hugh disappeared down the companionway, a small cloud of white smoke enveloped the bow of the distant lorcha, a dim report rolled along the foothills of the Volcanos, and a tiny spout of water was raised over a mile from *Essex*. A faint clamor of gongs and tom-toms and shouting came downwind in the breeze. The crewmen at the rail amidships unriveted their attention from the strangers in the north and gaped southward at the approaching junk and lorcha.

3

"Pirates!" came a cry from the waist.

That word rattled around among the crew of *Essex* like the report of the lorcha's 12-pounder bowchaser echoed in ravines of the island, and each repetition of the word swelled the panic. A few of the older hands gazed silently toward the stern, at their officers on their quarterdeck, and waited for orders. Cornelius Fitch gripped the tafferel so hard his knuckles turned white and he dropped the telescope on the deck. Reese's eyes widened with undisguised fear.

Not the mate's cup of tea, thought Fletcher, nor the captain's cup of coffee.

The telescope slowly rolled across the deck. Fletcher picked it up.

Cornelius Fitch pushed away from the tafferel and went forward. He stopped when he saw the crew knotted together in the waist. Above the crew, in the offing, he could see the junks standing away from the north point. He watched with a falling sensation as the Union Jack disappeared from the mast of the largest junk and a black-bordered red flag took its place. The voice of the mate just behind him startled him.

"Captain," he said, "shall I give orders to man the deck guns, and break out the swivel guns, and arm the crew?"

Cornelius Fitch groaned and slumped onto the bench at the skylight. "Good Lord, man!" the captain said. "With *Essex* heeled over like this, those guns are just pointing at sky and water! They're only good for shooting birds and fish! How can we hold off four pirate junks with two-inch swivel popguns and small arms?"

The struggle in the mind of Ptolemy Reese took possession of his face. Reese hesitated, and Fletcher wondered briefly if the mate would ask again for a revolver and this time shoot the captain. Reese glanced around wildly until his gaze came to rest on the Volcanos. He grabbed the glass from Fletcher and peered through it at the island. He

Laws Are Silent

apparently saw something arresting because, as he slowly lowered the glass and placed it on the bench, the struggle ebbed from his face and in its place flowed grim resolve.

"What do you want to do, Captain?" Reese said, growling. "Just *give up* the ship to the pirates and row ashore?"

Reese bent beside the captain and pointed over the larboard quarter.

"Look at them islands in the glass, sir. Them rocks is dark where the tide 'as yet to rise, so the flow's still young. I've 'eard tell they don't hurt them that don't fight back. Maybe if we hold off shootin' at 'em, bring the boats around under the starb'd rail where they can pull out of sight of them junks, and wait for the tide to flow, we can get off before they get to us."

"That's right thinking Mr. Reese," Fletcher said, "and it's a fine thing to see a man who can keep his wits about him under fire. But I'm afraid you're over your head trying to second-guess what a Chinese pirate will do. Better to fight."

"Fight?" the mate said with a snarl. "These bricklayer's clerks that pass for a crew aboard *Essex* were mostly shanghaied out of stores 'n libraries. Say 'galley down'aul' and they'd go lookin' for it 'igh and low. I've been dry nursing this crew for months, and I can tell you they aren't up to a fight. They can 'ardly sail this ship. What's more, we didn't sail with a full complement, an' there's some what up and jumped ship in Hong Kong, so we're shorthanded as well."

"The junks with the wind will be the immediate threat, Mr. Reese," Fletcher said, quietly. Fletcher felt like the ocean looked at turn of tide: calm, quiet, flat, and reflective.

The mate checked his protest and gazed curiously into Fletcher's dark blue eyes. The captain looked up. The statement was not a revelation to either man, and neither would have objected to the truth of this simple fact, had it occurred to him. What engaged the attention of the captain was that it had not occurred to anyone but his passenger. Fletcher's calm manner and the dusky timbre of voice, like a stage whisper mid the clamor of a music-hall performance, made the bellowing mate self-conscious and drained his agitation.

"The junks to the north," Fletcher said, "cannot make good speed into the wind *and* against the current. If they come down in the lee of the island, they risk going aground just like *Essex*. So before they can close with *Essex*, they will have to cross over forward of us, where they can come about with the current. Even then, they still will be close-hauled, and junks just do not sail well into the wind. Worry less about the Englishman, and sight your guns on the lorcha and her companion."

The mate studied the approaching junks. "But our guns are out of commission," he said. Any suggestion of fear in the mate's expression and voice had subsided completely and been replaced now by the mere urgency of solving a perplexing problem.

"No matter," Fletcher said. "Pop off at 'em a few times anyway. That'll make the junks fall off and wait, while they get up more courage to attack an armed clipper. That'll give you more time, and put some spit back into your crew."

Fletcher turned to the captain. "We're not exactly high and dry, sir. Mr. Reese is quite right about the high-water mark on the rocks off the island there. We raised sail three hours ago at half-tide and, in spite of the Chinese pilot's effort to delay our departure from Ningpo and at the Yung River bar, we have arrived while the water's still low and the tide's still turning. The pirates wanted *Essex* put aground at high water, so the tide could not lift her off, but this tide is likely to flow for another two hours. There's a fourteen-foot tidal bore in some of these islands, and due west of here in Hangchow Bay there's a thirty-two foot tidal bore that flows at seven or eight knots, faster than a Nantucket sleigh ride. Surely, you can see, sir, that *Essex* is going to lift herself off faster than two shakes of a lamb's tail. All we have to do is hold them gong-beaters off for a while, and do everything we can to help the old hooker get free of the mud."

"She's not got much iron ballast under her floor heads," Reese said. "She may not right herself so easy."

"If her cargo hasn't shifted," the captain said, "she may come down to her bearings, Mr. Reese. Let's give her a chance to show us what she can do."

"Her trucks'll jump for the sky," Fletcher said, smiling. "We'll skedaddle right off."

The lorcha and the junks both north and south were now firing their guns at intervals and the dull clatter of gongs and cymbals filled the lull between reports. At a distance less than two miles, none of the pirate fire could have any effect other than, perhaps, to raise the morale of the pirates themselves. The sailors aboard *Essex* merely wondered at the great waste of powder and ball, and observed from the barely visible splash of the shot the rate at which the pirates were closing.

"Them that's south 'as the wind, but they're fightin' the current," Reese said. "If they come down at, say, three knots, that'll put 'em over the tafferel in about forty minutes. They'll have our range in twenty-five."

Cornelius Fitch stood up and looked again at the crew bunched together in the waist whispering about tales of atrocities in these waters and waiting for the captain to give orders that would save them all from imminent disaster. Fitch felt the deck swaying under his feet and wondered if he would swoon like a silly woman, then realized that he was standing perfectly steady and that *Essex*, already humiliated by being put ashore, was now being maltreated by the elements.

"Mr. Reese," the captain said, "her topsails catching the wind like that are just pushing her over deeper into the mud."

Reese jumped to the ladder and split the bedlam on deck with his bellow.

"Belay that!" he shouted. "All hands aft!" In a few moments, the entire crew still able to stand and walk was crowded around the foot of the ladder with the bully mate towering over them.

"Shut chur clam-shells and listen up! Yes, them's pirates, an' them cannon balls 're their 'ow-dee-doo. But understand this, you packet-rats! You got less to fear from those bleedin' jossers then you do from *me*, if you don't do exactly what I tell you, exactly when I tell you. We's goin' to be very busy for the next couple of hours, so there will be no slackin' off with Cape Horn fever. When you've finished some job, report back 'ere. Now, where's me darlin' second mate?"

"Here, Mr. Reese!"

"Micah, I want your watch to shake the fore and main tops'ls so's they won't keep pushing 'er into the mud. And 'eave a lead from the weather cat and sing out her depth at the bow. Jump to it. Larboard watch, lay below and check for leaks, and see that the cargo hasn't shifted. Gunner, you stand by here with me. Bos'n, jump up 'ere and turn the ensign over, then go below and break open the arms locker, get rockets and set 'em off for a distress signal, load and cap weapons and prepare to issue muskets, pistols and cutlasses. Steward, you'd better go below and attend to the passengers. Keep those women below and out of harm's way."

"On the lee side of any action, right Mr. Reese?"

"That's right, Steward, same place you're likely to be. Chips, would you and the Doctor see to overhauling the rigging and equipment and fixin' whatever's in need? Gunner, start one of those guns firing. Save your shot and just fire wads, so's we make a lot of smoke and noise."

In a few moments, *Essex* was alive again with men and boys clambering over her deck. The gunner rounded up the men who passed as his gun crew, sent two below for tools and ammunition, and then began rehearsing with the other two how to fire 24-pounder. A man at the larboard cathead called out.

"By the mark, two and a quarter!"

"Fourteen feet of water under the bow," Fletcher said to the captain. "She's probably drawing eighteen feet after unloading at Ningpo. That's a lot of mud you're stuck in. Better to warp her off than tow her, Captain."

Another crack of cannon fire from the south unnerved the captain. He glanced nervously around the stern. "Mr. Reese," he said, "what would be required to warp *Essex* off this shoal?"

"That's a tall order, Captain," the mate said, "what with them jossers bearing down on us. *Essex* only 'as the one kedge anchor. We could 'ook a pennant to it, lower it into a boat, and take it out and drop it. But without another kedge off the stern to keep the current from pushing her further into the mud, nobody can say how long we'd 'eave at the windlass to pull 'er around. There's hardly time to take out one anchor if this 'ere crew's expected to fight pirates in the bargain.

"Why not use one of the anchors on the bow?" Fletcher said. "The small bower is still fished and catted to the starb'd gunnel, so it need only be lowered to a boat. That leaves your kedge for dropping off the stern."

"We'd have to 'ook a pennant to the catted anchor and run t'other end of the pennant 'round the capstan," mused the mate, "so's you could lower an anchor to a boat. But even allowin' we could lower it like that, the small bower's more than a ton-and-half of anchor, Mr. Wood, an' likely to swamp a boat! I've heard tell of them big anchors bein' put on planks across two boats, but I must've been out pissin' when they tol' the part where a boat crew got the anchor *off* the planks and into the water. I suspect they only lifted the anchor on shore with a derrick."

"Suppose that we suspend the anchor between the boats, below the water, with just the stock across planks coated with tallow, and a long, heavy spar under the stock to lever the anchor off the planks and into the water. Who was it said that with a lever long enough he could move the world?"

"It's worth a try, I suppose," the captain said, "if only because it will remove considerable weight from the bow and help us float free. Mr. Reese!" Cornelius Fitch looked his mate in the eye and with visible effort rallied new authority into his voice. "Get your small bower anchor off the bow and ready to lower, and have the starboard watch get the boats over. And ask the carpenter and the cook to go below with the bos'n and fetch up arms and ammunition to the main deck. We will stack rifles aft here, where they will be at hand when your men need them."

"Aye, aye, sir!"

A *whoosh*! sounded in the waist, followed by the shriek of a signal rocket lifting out of a firing trough mounted by the boatswain on the starboard bulwark. The rocket climbed slowly on a swirling column of thick white smoke and yellow sparks until at a height of several hundred feet it burst into a shower of stars. The boatswain hefted another signal rocket up into the trough and lit the rocket's fuse.

Standing by the aft 24-pounder a few feet away, the gunner and his crew watched with rapt admiration as the second rocket whistled up into the sky and burst into another shower of stars. Fletcher wondered if the flares could be seen from Kintang, or over on the west side of the Volcanos. An English despatch boat between Shanghai and Kintang might spot the flares, if they're on the water this early in the morning.

"Come along then, lads, we can beat that," the gunner said. He resumed plodding through the artillery drill – devised less to achieve speed than ensure safety – as quickly as he judged the two ABs and two ordinaries could relearn the instructions they had last received months before. The duties of serving the gun had to be redistributed among the smaller crew of only five men. "Once again, me boyos, by the numbers. Stay in order, now, so's we don't have Jack with his head up the bore when I fires the gun."

The tremendous *wump*! of the 24-pounder shook *Essex* like the collapse of a brick building. Cornelius Fitch felt his stomach recoil with the gun, and he groped for a handhold, but the artillery fired Fletcher's blood with excitement almost forgotten in the years since the Crimea. Fletcher took up the glass from the skylight bench to watch for the response of the junks.

"Ha!" he shouted. "That bulldog whipped the devil 'round the stump! They're all falling off! Take a look at that, Captain Fitch, and tell me it doesn't make your heart leap and your blood run hot."

The captain took the glass and watched the south junks come about to spill wind from their sails and let the current carry them away. The junks suddenly were as quiet as the swollen cloud of white smoke rolling over the bulwark above the gun, as if the report of the ship's gun had pinched out the hullabaloo of gongs and tom-toms and shouting like a snuffed candle.

"Pour it on, gunner," the captain shouted down to the main deck. "You have them on the run! Look, Mr. Wood. You would think they are maneuvering in formation."

"Yes," Fletcher said, laughing. "That's what I'd call a perfectly executed advance to the rear. And it gives you some more time."

At the forward house Reese interrupted his orders to the second mate long enough to observe the effect of the deck gun on the junks.

"Look there, Micah. They's dropping off."

"Too bad that gun's not for'd," the second mate said. "They won't be lookin' *forever* for the splash of a ball."

"Never you mind 'bout that. Just get them boats over the starb'd rail and under the small bower. Now, do ya understand about 'anging the stock of the anchor across the planks, and 'ow to use the spar?"

"We'll getchur pretty little anchor out for ya," the second mate said, "if'n you don't drop it on our heads first, and them piraticals don' pot us."

Below deck, the passengers and steward were crowded together in Elizabeth's cabin trying to revive her when the first deafening report of the deck gun shook the vessel.

"Heavens!" Hannah said, "Can't they tell a body when they're going to make that noise? It's enough to knock your feathers off!"

Hugh had found Hannah Fitch flailing about from under a pile of ledger books in the captain's cabin and, when satisfied she was not injured, together they went in search of Elizabeth. They found her where she still lay like a rag doll unconscious in the iron washtub in her cabin. After lifting her into a bunk, they loosened the tight collar of her bodice and improvised cold compresses to apply to the bump on her forehead. The steward was sent for hot tea when he came below.

"I gather we are aground," Hannah said, "but what all is that shooting about."

"I believe the captain is signaling for help, Mrs. Fitch," Hugh said.

"Land's sake, Mr. Wood, I did not fall on my head! Signal rockets I'd expect, but one does not call for help by firing cannon. And we are not likely to get help if all our rescuers can do is beat on gongs and drums. First, it was quiet as a graveyard on deck, and now the whole crew is pounding around up there making more noise than a boatload of calves."

Elizabeth groaned, opened her eyes, and smiled.

Laws Are Silent

"I suppose we are not at Shanghai yet?"

"No, dear, we are still at sea, resting on a shoal, and judging from the particularly pale color of these gentlemen's faces, we are surrounded by hordes of screaming cutthroats. Now, just lie still. I am not yet certain because Mr. Wood thinks he is being kindly by keeping us ignorant of our true circumstances."

The steward motioned to Hugh to step outside for a moment.

"That's a helluva mouse you got coming up there," Hugh said, noticing the steward's eye.

"Yeah, well I didn't move fast enough for the Prince of Egypt. We should not be on this side, where a cannon ball can come crashing in."

Hugh returned to the women.

"Mrs. Fitch," he said, smiling, "what you have guessed is a great deal worse than our actual circumstances, so I must be candid if only to put your minds at rest. We are aground, as you so rightly concluded, and there are several native craft approaching from a nearby island, but their intentions are as yet unclear. The steward has suggested that we move Miss Fitch to the other side of the vessel, into the captain's cabin where there is more room, as soon as she has recovered sufficiently to walk."

"I can walk now, if it's to safety," Elizabeth said. She rose from the bunk and, after a few tentative steps on the sloping floor, crossed the saloon hanging on the forearms of her mother and Hugh.

"Mother," Elizabeth said, looking about the saloon, "if there is trouble, can we not set up an infirmary here in the saloon, to render assistance to the injured, and thus be of somewhat more use than anyone expects?"

"Florence Nightingale would be proud of you, my dear."

4 On the main deck, the second mate divided the part of his watch not detailed to the arms locker into two boat crews of six men each. They threw a watch-tackle over the starboard mainyard, and hooked it to a boat stowed on the roof of the forward house. Another watch-tackle was put on the same yardarm at its extreme end above the water, then brought over and hooked to the boat. Two heavy planks, a long spar and a tin of warm tallow were put aboard. The boat was lifted with the first tackle, hauled across the deck through clouds of smoke drifting forward from the firing of the aft deck gun, pulled out over the bulwark with the second tackle, then lowered to the water. Another boat was lifted over the weather side in like manner, and the crew scrambled down Jacob's ladders into their boat and sculled around to the starboard bow.

The boatswain left his helpers below loading pistols and, together with the carpenter and cook, carried armloads of rifles up to the main deck, where they stacked arms forward of the poop. Fletcher jumped down the main deck to see for himself exactly what sort of small arms *Essex* carried. He knelt beside a stack of four long guns and examined their lock plates. 1840 Tower, he thought, old smoothbore percussion musket. Here's an improvement, an 1853 Tower. That would be a .702 caliber British minié rifle. Sighted for 900 yards. Those cases of cartridges would be for these rifles.

Fletcher quickly counted twelve British minié rifles. He unstacked one rifle and examined the muzzle, barrel, and stock for wear, fished a small wrench out of a box of tools brought on deck by the boatswain, and unscrewed the percussion nipple to examine the seat at the entrance to the powder chamber. Later than 1852, he thought, rifled with four grooves instead of three – not a conversion. Shows wear, but still serviceable. With a target the size of a junk, we don't need marksmen to be effective. He took the minié rifle back up onto the poop deck and showed it to the captain.

"Captain Fitch, there're a dozen long-range rifles among that lot being fetched up on deck, effective at 1000 yards and more."

"I suppose that's better than nothing." Evidently, the previous high spirits of the nephew of Augustus Fitch & Company were precarious and liable to being doused by the lightest zephyr.

"Sir, you may not know what can be done with weapons like these. They fire a bullet the size of your thumb with tremendous smashing power. In the Kaffir War in South Africa, British marksmen used these rifles to scatter native contingents at 1200 yards, almost 3/4 of a mile! They were standard issue in the Crimea, the envy of French armed with percussion muskets, and the bane of Russians with old smooth-bores."

Fletcher paused and looked about. The pirate junks were still well away from *Essex*. He calculated there was time yet to talk these men out of their blue funk.

"There's a fine tale told of a Lieutenant Connolly," he said, "whose picket held up a sortie of 5000 Russians out of Sebastopol. One bullet from their minié rifles knocked down three or four men in a row, one behind the other. When Connelly was surrounded, he *attacked* the head of the Russian column and so confused the enemy he was able to withdraw even with his casualties! That's only one example, Captain, of the success in the face of great odds of a few bold men, armed with advanced weapons, over large numbers of less well-armed troops."

"You said 'marksmen' fired these rifles." The captain's enthusiasm had not yet been driven so far beneath his deflated appearance that a little dogged determination might not whistle it back up. "You must know as well as I that sailors can't shoot rifles."

"Captain Fitch, a feller'd hafta be cross-eyed and palsied to miss a Chinese junk at 1000 yards with even a little practice. We can form a rifle squad, and I can train them to fire the rifle. Tarnation, Captain, that's my profession! I'll even set their sights for 'em if I have to. If you would lead us, and we had a couple of sailors to help reload, we could provide covering fire against the north junks for the men on the fo'c's'le, and for the boats when they get away with the anchor."

"Well, maybe that's not such a bad notion," the captain said. "Actually, it's a capital idea, Mr. Wood! Fetch your men, arm yourselves and come forward. I'll meet you on the fo'c's'le."

Within a few minutes, the hastily assembled rifle squad gathered on the weather side of the forecastle head, to one side of the larboard watch working to lower the small bower from where it was fished below the starboard gunwale. The captain, Fletcher and Hugh, the ship's carpenter and cook, and the boatswain, made a small semicircle around an ammunition case tended by the two ABs who would reload.

"Gentlemen," the captain said, "those of you less familiar with these weapons look to Mr. Fletcher Wood for instruction, and rely on these sailors behind us here to reload for you. Mr. Wood will try a couple of shots to get the range, and you can watch his handling of the rifle and then set your sights as he does his."

"One little trick about these cartridges that we discovered in the Crimea," Fletcher said, taking from his pocket a small clasp knife scrimshawed with the image of a breaching sperm whale. "That is to shave the tip of the bullet with a knife-blade, or flatten the nose of the bullet by knocking it on a hard surface." He opened the clasp knife and cut away the blunt point of the bullet. "This causes the bullet to expand in flight and make a wound into which your fist may be inserted."

On the lee side of the forecastle, the larboard watch rigged the small bower anchor for lowering to the boats. Moving the anchor by hand required considerable care due to its extraordinary weight. Normally, the crew let the anchor down to hang beneath the cathead, anchor cable was unwound from the windlass, run out to the anchor, and secured to the anchor ring. Upon release into the sea, the anchor pulled the cable out of the hawsehole as it fell.

To lift the anchor, the crew sweated at capstan bars to the rhythm of a sea shanty, turning the capstan, which turned the windlass below in the chain locker, to wind up the cable and bring in the anchor. When the anchor reached the hawsehole, the tackle was hooked on again and the anchor fished – or hauled – up tight under the gunwale.

This time, however, instead releasing the anchor to drop to the seabed, the crew lowered the anchor with the forecastle capstan. The capstan was disengaged from the anchor windlass below, a forty-foot line was fastened to the anchor ring, and the slack taken up on the capstan. The anchor was let down a short distance, the crew whistled up a shanty and manned the oaken capstan bars, then backed off slowly on the capstan to lower the anchor to the water.

Cannon fire from the north arrested the attention of men on the forecastle.

"Lay into that!" yelled the mate. "I'll tell you when you can go skylarkin'."

The junks descending from the north opened fire. Their shot raised spouts of water some distance from *Essex*, but neither junk could close rapidly on the starboard tack, with lugsails against their masts and the wind in their teeth. Reese glanced nervously toward the stern. Shot fired from the lorcha and the south junk fell much closer than before. The rifle squad – the "Fo'c's'le Rifles" – opened with a volley toward the north, obscuring the forecastle with clouds of acrid white smoke. They continued firing at will, but the distance was still too great and most of their shots were lobbed rather than aimed at the pirates.

The small bower anchor was lowered to the water and held there. Two forty-foot longboats came below the anchor, and a half-turn of the capstan on deck allowed the anchor to swing out between the boats. This placed the long stock at the top of the anchor across the boats just above the gunwales. The anchor was then turned so the stock lay in the same direction as the boats, hovering over the empty space between. Heavy planks were placed across the two boats so that the planks lay beneath the stock, tallow was spread on the planks, and a long spar was placed under the stock to lever the anchor into the sea.

On deck, tackle was gingerly slackened, and the anchor was lowered the rest of the way onto the planks. The thick wood creaked under the heavy weight of the small bower and each boat sank down a foot into the swell, to where the ocean lapped at their gunwales, but they shipped no water and the anchor held. The tackle was unhooked and a length of anchor cable was let down to the boats before they pulled away.

Cornelius Fitch, captain of the *Essex* Fo'c's'le Rifles, hefted his Model 1853 Tower rifle, set its stock snugly into the hollow of his shoulder, and thumbed back the hammer from over the percussion cap. This frigate is going to kick like a mule – better lean forward into it more. Curious how comfortable its weight feels, heavier than my old squirrel rifle. The weight will help the rifle stay on target. Smells like black powder, not cleaned very well, have to see the boatswain remedies that after this battle. It's good we're not rocking with the swell. Wood is right about the advantages of being stuck in the mud; if we cannot run, at least our fire will be effective. Who would think of that?

The captain gently squeezed the trigger, the hammer fell, the percussion cap popped, and the rifle fired with an earsplitting report. The stock of the rifle punched him hard in the shoulder, and a suffocating cloud of white smoke swirled around him and drifted away with the breeze, but this did not distract him from imagining the path of the minié bullet's trajectory over 1000 yards of yellow ocean. He thought he saw fragments of a bamboo batten flying away from the forward lugsail of the Ningpo trader. In all the din and commotion, he almost did not recognize Fletcher's big grin and the heavy thump of his approving hand on his surviving shoulder.

"Fine shot, Captain!" Fletcher offered a small telescope. "See for yourself."

Cornelius Fitch spied the hole in the junk's lugsail, and started to reload with gusto. Impatient to get off another shot, he grabbed a rifle from the AB behind him and fired again, hitting the deck of the Ningpo trader. Again and again he fired, as fast as anyone could reload for him, and each shot swelled his confidence that *Essex* would prevail.

"Mr. Reese," shouted the captain, ramming a minié bullet down the barrel of his rifle, "silence the waist gun and send the gun crew for a swivel gun. Have the gun mounted on the stern and fired at the south junks."

"Aye, aye, sir!"

While Reese was on the main deck giving instructions to the gun crew, his watch below in the chain locker re-engaged the windlass to the forecastle capstan, locking the windlass pawl to secure the anchor cable. The boats pulled away slowly to starboard, paying out cable as they went, the crews glancing nervously to the north each time a junk fired one of its guns. The pirate trader saw boats pulling away from *Essex*, and evidently understood the ship was attempting to warp off the shoal. The trader immediately came about and put her bowchaser to work, firing at the *Essex* boats as fast as her crew could reload. The junk was still several hundred yards out of range, but a few shot skipped across the water like flat stones in a progression of small splashes until they sank harmlessly out of sight, and musket balls kicked up water close by. When the mate returned to the forecastle, the boats had reached position about half the length of *Essex* off the starboard beam.

"Let go the anchor, Mr. Reese," the captain said, quietly.

"Let go!" yelled the mate over the water to the boats. The second mate and four other sailors dropped the remaining anchor cable overboard, then took hold of the end of the spar and heaved it up to lift the stock of the anchor. They then were able to remove a plank, but the anchor still hung on the other plank. A musket ball smashed through the stern of one boat and knocked splinters into the air. Two sailors jumped forward and started rocking the boat to shake loose the anchor.

"Belay that, you fools!" the second mate shouted. "You'll capsize both boats. Take the spar forward."

The second mate followed the spar into the bow. There was just enough room between the anchor stock and the remaining plank to slip the spar under the stock. They all heaved up on the spar. The anchor slipped silently into the water.

"Boats are returning, Captain," the mate said.

"See if you can warp her, Mr. Reese."

"Man the capstan!" Sailors jumped to the capstan bars and were able to turn it several revolutions and take up slack, but when the anchor fluke dug into the mud the capstan stopped turning.

"Heave around there, mates!" Reese shouted. The men strained vigorously but could not budge *Essex*, even when Reese and several others heaved all their weight against the capstan bars.

"Belay heaving," Reese shouted. "The oak'll crack before the ship moves."

"Give me your men from the capstan for another rifle squad," the captain said, "and we will try the capstan again when the boat crews return and the tide's a little higher."

The sailors from the mate's watch ran forward to join the men firing rifles from the forecastle and, after observing a few rounds being loaded and fired, took the places of the first squad and continued covering fire for the returning boats.

5 *Essex* was now under punishing fire from the lorcha and south junk. Parts of the boom crotch, the spanker boom, and the forward house were blown away by solid shot, and the tafferel, steering gear housing and companionway were perforated with bullet holes. The gun crew tried to mount the swivel cannon at the stern, but enemy fire made the poop deck too hot for the work until the captain's rifle squad took up firing positions on the weather quarter and began volleys of rifle fire.

"That lorcha's about 900 yards out."

"Aim for the helmsman. He's exposed on that lorcha."

"Right-oh! Make 'em pay for steerage!"

The riflemen soon had the range. Most fired two rounds in a minute and some men even faster as they mastered reloading. They do not exactly rake the lorcha's deck with long-range rifle fire, thought Fletcher, but a ¾-inch thick minié ball crashing through their upper deck every few seconds, sending wood splinters flying in all directions, must have them pretty flustered. They're hugging that deck so tightly, the little toggles they have down their shirts instead of buttons are gonna get stuck to their backbones.

Suddenly, the lorcha's tiller was unmanned, and the lorcha fell off again, followed by the Shao-hsing trader. By that time, the 2-inch swivel gun had been set up at the tafferel and was making a valiant effort to launch balls junkward, but reaching little further than 300 yards.

"Save your ammunition, Gunner," the captain said.

Reese came up to the poop deck.

"How are they doing forward?" the captain said. "Any casualties?"

"One casualty, sir, an oarsman's hand ripped up by wood slivers. One boat's back aboard, and the crew's heaving at the capstan, but she's not moved an eyelash, yet. I've left the other boat down and her crew is rigging tackle to get the kedge over. They've fired off about half their cartridges."

"This case here is down by half, too," the captain said. "Mr. Reese, caution our Fo'c's'le Rifles to conserve their ammunition. These junks appear to fall off each time we can reach their decks with repeated volleys, so have your men wait until a junk is well in range before expending any more cartridges. And have a man see how it goes with the passengers below, and if there's any damage."

"Aye, aye, sir, and after that, if you're agreed, I'll put every available hand forward at the capstan to heave in relays."

The captain nodded and the mate went forward after sending a man below.

"Bos'n," called the captain. "How much more rifle ammunition have we?"

"There's one more case of cartridges for the minié rifles, Captain."

"Round up a boy and put him to work serving out cartridges, half that case forward and the rest aft."

The men looked at the half-empty case of rifle cartridges, and then at each other, and then at the lorcha and south junk coming down with the wind again. *Essex* realized that their initial success with rifles would end when the ammunition ran out.

Fletcher drew the captain to one side and asked, "Is there a chance we could get one of those deck guns up here for a sternchaser, Captain?"

"I think they are very heavy," the captain said. "Gunner!" The captain put the same question to the gunner.

"I'd guess the wrench that fits the bolts on them carriages is still back at the shipyard where *Essex* was built, sir."

Reese clambered up the ladder from the main deck.

"Beg' pard'n, Captain," the mate said. "The ladies send compliments and say they're frightened out of their wits, but otherwise tolerable and ready to tend any injured. As for damage, we was hulled a couple of times below the starboard waterline, but not hurt much – seems watertight still. I've left Micah to take care of the rate of fire of the Fo'c's'le Rifles, and to keep at the capstan."

"Well done, Mr. Reese," the captain said. "Mr. Wood, put your question to him."

"What would you say to unbolting one of the 24-pounders and heaving it up here to the poop for a sternchaser?"

Reese's expression changed from amazement to amusement. "Drop me down the hold for dunnage," he said, "if'n you ain't a ripsnorter, Yank. But one of them iron 24-pounders and its carriage weighs nearly two tons. How're we going to lift that much weight to the poop? The mainyard would hold a gun, but that skinny lil' cro'jack yard'll split like kindling. We've never even bent a sail to it before. It'd be better if we could lift a deck gun up forward to the fo'c's'le for a bowchaser. Foreyard's the same size as the mainyard, to bend the same size sail, and it'd lift a gun, no questions."

"As long as the south junks have the wind," Fletcher said, "they present the immediate threat and the greatest danger. Stuck in the mud like this, with no room to come about, a gun mounted on the fo'c's'le would have to fire across our stern to get at those junks, and we'd smash our own sticks and canvas ourselves."

Reese was staring up at the mizzenmast. "I suppose we could drop a tackle from the mizzen topyard to the cro'jack yard, to get the support of an extra yard, then rig extra braces. But then, we have to get that damn carriage up from the deck an' I don't recall as we have ever had the tools for that. Probably rusted solid. Even if we can get it loose and up to the stern, how can it be fired? The recoil'll send the gun flying."

The lorcha's bowchaser opened fire again, sending shot flying into the main top. Tackle blocks, shattered wood, and iron fittings showered down through the rigging and felled men standing below. The gunner called out the range at 800 yards and the "Stern Rifles" resumed directing volleys of rifle fire at the lorcha and the junk.

"Get me that gun," Fletcher said. "I know what to do about the recoil."

"I'll take the gunner here," the mate said, "seein' as how he and his gun crew're on holiday until them pirates comes in range of the swivel gun. We'll scour the holds for tools to get up that carriage."

The mate called to the gunner to bring his crew, and they all scampered down the ladder under a hail of shell fragments. Solid shot that whistled into the rigging smashed yards and masts and damaged the ship but, at closer range, the pirates began firing exploding shell that burst over the ship and spewed iron scrap that disabled men.

Coming under shell fire demanded a change in tactics. The Stern Rifles hastily beat for the cover of the skylight and steering gear housing, and idlers leapt off the exposed poop for the comparative safety of the main deck. The lorcha fell off once more when the Stern Rifles potted another lorcha helmsman. A short time after that Reese yelled from the waist for the starboard watch to go to one of the deck guns. Over his head, the first mate flourished a heavy iron box-wrench almost as long as one of the iron cannon.

While the mate set to work unbolting a gun carriage, the Fo'c's'le Rifles kept up intermittent rifle fire just accurate enough to interfere with the handling of the north junks. Evidently, the junks were not armed with many rifles. They did not return much fire, just charged in and fell off as wind and current permitted. A maritime illustration, thought Fletcher, of why rifles have changed artillery tactics, and rendered useless smooth bore artillery of no greater range than the new rifles.

Under the protection of the Fo'c's'le Rifles, the sailors at the capstan alternately pushed and heaved to warp the ship. They devised schemes of block and tackle that only pulled the capstan bars from their sockets. They even hammered at the capstan bars with a top maul until the oak shattered, but still could not move *Essex* out of the mud no matter how much they cursed at the capstan. More rockets went up. The crew anxiously searched the horizon for some sign of a British gunboat. The lead was heaved again.

"By the mark, two and a half. Tide's rising!"

The Stern Rifles managed to hold the lorcha and south junk at about 800 yards, through one more replacement of the lorcha helmsman, until the two vessels exchanged positions and the lorcha came in astern of the junk, where it was protected from rifle fire. The junk got off two rounds of shell that exploded over *Essex* and struck the cook, a sailor, and the cabin boy. The Stern Rifles advanced to the tafferel and set off an angry fusillade of rifle fire, raking the deck of the junk and silencing her guns. She fell off again and the lorcha, trying to stay in the lee of the larger junk, went with her. Two bodies were thrown overboard from the junk.

The wounded aboard *Essex* were more fortunate – they were taken below to the saloon and laid out on the dining table, where the passengers and the steward tended them. The cook received only a shell fragment in the thigh and, while in some deal of pain relieved only slightly by the grog served up by the steward, he was still able to engage in his other shipboard profession, that of ship's doctor. He bound up his own leg so he could go to work on the others, but was too late to help the sailor, who bled to death before the flow could be stanched. The boy remained unconscious with several wounds, which the cook cleaned with water, dressed, and bandaged. Finally, with Elizabeth attending, the cook removed the shell fragment from his own leg and wrapped the wound with a table napkin. Elizabeth stayed with the cabin boy, pressing a wet cloth to his brow, but otherwise watching helplessly as his breathing grew shallow.

After fifteen minutes of prodigious effort and jarring clang of sledge hammer on iron wrench, the gun carriage was unbolted and the 24-pounder was free. The mizzenmast was elected to work as a boom for dragging the gun astern. The upper and lower yards were lashed together for greater support. Tackle thrown over the lower yard was hooked to ropes slung from the front and rear of the gun. Six burly crewmen hauled on the tackle, while two more directed the path of the gun with guidelines.

"Handsomely now, men," the mate cooed. "Haul away. That's too fast. More handsomely still. That's right."

The tackle stretched taught. The crossjack yard groaned and squealed. All the running rigging on the mizzenmast snapped tight. Reese glanced up nervously at Fletcher where he stood at the head of the ladder. Fletcher grinned. Reese grimaced. Damn you, Yank.

"Haul away again," the mate said. The line came along, but only the mizzen yards moved – they bent over still further. The gun didn't budge. Thick white smoke from the rifle volleys at the stern swept through the mizzen rigging and swirled among the sailors hauling on the gun. Shell exploded over the stern and two riflemen sprawled on the deck. Another shell burst off the larboard quarter, throwing iron junk across the ship and into the crew hauling on the 24-pounder. The wounded dragged themselves aside and others took their place.

"Handsomely now, haul away again," the mate said. "That's right. Here she comes." The gun lifted from the deck and flew at the ladder, dragging the men holding the guideline. The mate and two more sailors leapt for the guideline to arrest the gun and steady it under the yards. They hauled the gun up another foot and secured the tackle so that the mizzenyards could swing around, but when the yards came about the gun crashed against the bulwark. The men left off turning the yards and hauled wildly hand over hand on the tackle again in order to raise the gun to a height of fifteen feet, where it would clear both the bulwark and the poop deck rail, then secured the tackle and resume turning the yards.

The gun was coming back in over the starboard poop deck rail when the standing part of the tackle securing the two yards parted with a loud snap and the crossjack yardarm carried away. The gun crashed down onto the rail, hung by a trunnion on the bulwark, then ripped out the gunwale and fell into the sea. More than one heart aboard *Essex* went overboard with the gun. Reese grimaced and stared up at the demolished gunwale. Fletcher heaved a sigh, and then called down to the waist.

"No! No, Mr. Reese, don't *throw* the guns at them. Shoot the guns!"

洋神 *Yang Shen*   *James Lande* 藍德

Dramatis Personae: Chapter 4

Francis W. A. Blaine	British Minister to China, son of the 7th Earl of Exter
Travis Trent Masters	Shanghai British Consul, wrote *Rebellions of the Chinese*
Terrance Fenton Wells	interpreter, British consulate
Chalmers Alexander	interpreter, British consulate
Seng-ko-lin-ch'in 僧格林沁	Mongol prince, imperial general defending approach to Peking, known as "Sam Collinson." to Westerners

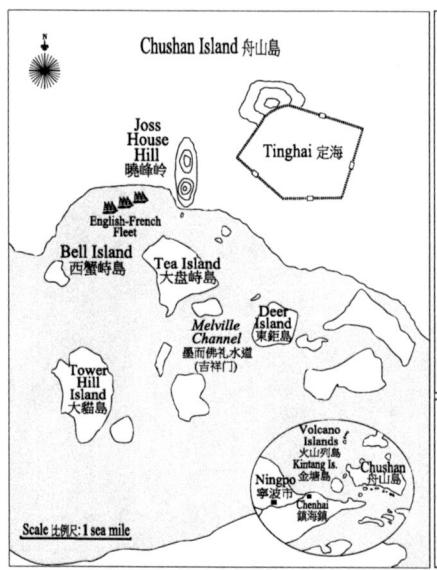

Chushan Island and Tinghai Harbor
(based on British Hydrographic Office chart)

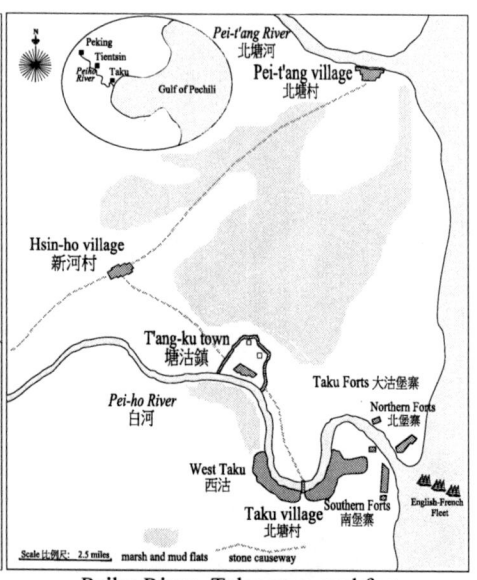

Peiho River, Taku area, and forts
(from Knollys, Incidents…China War 1860*)*

Calendars		
Western	Ch'ing	Taiping
	Hsien Feng	
1851	1	1
1852	2	2
1853	3	3
1854	4	4
1855	5	5
1856	6	6
1857	7	7
1858	8	8
1859	9	9
1860	10	10
1861	11	11
	T'ung-chih	
1862	1	12

Place Names	
Chinese	**Western**
Che-chiang 浙江	Chekiang
Hang-chou 杭州	Hangchow
Hsiang-kang 香港	Hong Kong
Kuang-chou 廣州	Canton
Nan-ching 南京	Nanking
Pei-ching 北京	Peking
Shang-hai 上海	Shanghai
Su-chou 蘇州	Soochow
Sung-chiang 松江	Sungkiang
T'ai-ts'ang 太倉	Taitsan
T'ien-chin 天津	Tientsin

1860 Rates of Exchange			
s = shillings d = pence			
British Pound	**Shanghai Tael**	**Mexican Dollar**	**American Dollar**
£1	3.0	4.16	4.80
6s 8d	**1.0**	1.388	1.60
4s 8d	0.72	**1.00**	1.15
4s 2d	0.625	0.88	**1.00**
Distance			
One Chinese *li* 里 = 1894.12 feet or .278 mile			
3 Chinese *li* 里 = 1.076 miles (about one mile)			

The Englishman's War

洋神 *Yang Shen* James Lande 藍德

Chapter 4: The Englishman's War
Thursday, April 19, 1860, 10:30am

> The
> **Boston Evening Transcript**
> Thursday, January 5, 1860
> --
> The China Question is discussed in the current number of the *North American Review* at considerable length.... The writer regards the disaster at the Peiho as the perfection of blundering on all sides, and can hardly believe that what has been so stupidly done can be justified to the extent of making it the cause of war. The review closes as follows: "Before this article sees the light, we shall know what success has actually attended [Minister] Wood's pacific diplomacy, and whether the American Treaty of Tientsin, so much scoffed at a year ago, is not the only commercial one ratified. We sincerely trust that the first fruit of such success will be [our] offer of mediation...made disinterestedly, and in perfect good faith.... We have no interests in China but those which are commercial. Great Britain ought to have no others...."

The British gunboat HMS *Roebuck*, on despatch duty for the Allied Expeditionary Force gathering at Kintang, crossed from the river into the anchorage off the Shanghai Bund and passed beneath the forest of masts and yards of closely moored square-rigged merchantmen, paddle-wheel frigates, gunboats and steam tugs. She slowed to avoid lighters and sampans and swung her beam around to the stone quay below the British Bund, sloshing water over a pontoon-landing platform opposite the British consulate. An officer in the scarlet wool jacket of Lieutenant Colonel Gascoigne's battalion of Royal Marines jumped down to the landing, hurried up the gangway, crossed the Bund through the crowd of foot traffic, sedan chairs, wheelbarrows, and equestrians and entered the consulate grounds. He double-timed up the path between the green lawns to the tall red brick façade, returned the guard's salute, and entered the building.

"Despatch for the consul," he told the reception clerk. The clerk sent for the consul's aide, Bitterman. He appeared after a few minutes, a slender and serene young subaltern in shirtsleeves, signed for the despatch, and asked the officer to wait in case there was a reply. The aide quickly glanced around the entrance, smiled and nodded to the American consul where he stood alone in the anteroom, then scurried back down the hallway and stopped outside a half-open door and peeked inside.

The British minister, Sir Francis W. A. Blaine, and Shanghai British consul, Travis Trent Masters, were engaged in one of their more sedate exchanges – not yet going at it hammer and tong. Bitterman waited at the door for a break in the conversation, flustered by the tension between the men, which was enhanced by their difference in size – the consul was well over six feet tall and towered above the smaller minister, but the minister's unusually stiff collar held his head high in an attitude of chilling hauteur.

"At times like this, Masters, one most wishes our communication wi' the Home Office was more expeditious." The minister was of medium height, portly, with a bald crown over thick flowing hair, and ruddy cheeks above a full face of cottony white whiskers. The brash plaid of a short Kilmarnock waistcoat with wide black-velvet lapels glowed between the lapels of his single-breasted black frock coat. "This departure from instructions places the entire risk for the enterprise on my shoulders alone – can na' receive the foreign secretary's approval until the time for action is well past."

Well, I'm dashed, thought the British consul. If you can't decide based on your best assessment of the situation, then who can? Certainly not the bloody parliament, half a

The Englishman's War 67

world away. You do *not* have to wait for Russell or Exter to tell you what to do.

"Well sir," the consul said, rubbing his long salt-and-pepper sideburns with thumb and forefinger, "the French minister endorses your decision not to blockade the coast and disrupt transport by sea between Chinese ports, even before he has received his own instructions from Louis Napoleon. The French minister also supports the occupation Chushan and advance on Peking...." Masters, caught unaware when the minister had barged in earlier than expected that morning, was still in an informal buff morning coat, with fitted white shirt and a loose amber cravat, skewered by an onyx-tipped gold pin, black trousers and square-toed shoes.

"French minister! Nobody gives a damn wha' the French think. They could turn on us at any time, now that they've annexed Savoy."

"...and you can expect Lord Exter will give his warm approval when he arrives at Shanghai as plenipotentiary. The foreign secretary's instructions to you did not exclude the alternative of going to war if necessary, he merely did not refer explicitly to that choice, and went on record as wishing to avoid bloodshed if possible. The way I see it, sir, Lord Russell has done as would any politician elected to high office, and has delegated the decision to the principals at the scene of the action."

Her Britannic Majesty's Minister to China was not mollified. Least of all by thought of the imminent arrival of his older brother, Lord Exter, 8th Earl of Exter and 12th Earl of Kilmarnock, to replace Blaine as Ambassador Extraordinary and Plenipotentiary. They say he has more experience, thought Blaine, and that it's na' a lack of confidence in me. But Russell's reprimand said a recourse to force was na' necessary. I'm na' censured, na' recalled, just replaced. How was I to keep that fool admiral from bolting at the forts and getting his fleet shot t' hell? Palmerston finally made it very clear that I could na' do anything from nine miles out to sea wi' no way to communicate, but I'm *still* replaced. Taku was my Waterloo.

Minister Blaine was certain that his brother, Lord Exter, would pursue war with great vengeance, because parliament and the people alike now regarded the defeat at the Taku forts as Lord Exter's fault, and he sought redemption. The houses of parliament first raised the hue and cry after Minister Blaine for starting another costly war and trampling Chinese sovereignty. Palmerston, the Minister for War, and even Russell, said Blaine was only following orders from Whitehall. Checked in that direction, Gladstone, Cochrane, Bright and others bayed after Exter for demanding there be a minister resident in Peking, and causing the Chinese to refuse ratification, and fight at Taku. By the time the howling in the chambers of parliament finally quieted, Russell had come to agree with Exter, and gave instructions that a resident minister clause would be required. The foreign secretary sanctioned the policy – and war in China again was inevitable.

Ever since the departure of the British from Tientsin 1858, the war party in Peking was on the rise and determined to set aside the treaty. Minister Blaine was certain that the defeat of this hostile party would ensure successful ratification. The minister felt it possible to contrive a defeat by patronizing the peace party through diplomacy. But his brother would choose war regardless. Exter believed the Manchu empire should be allowed to collapse of its own decay, and would hasten them to *their* Waterloo with little regard for consequences.

My brother and I still disagree about the Manchu – he would leave the Manchu to their fate. I would rather they improve and grow stronger. Perhaps, if we agreed the rebels had any capacity for government, we would disagree less about the Manchus.

The Taiping rebels could never fill any void left by the collapse of the Manchus, and Minister Blaine was determined that China never become another British colony like India. If nothing else, the cost of an administration over China could never be

洋神 *Yang Shen*   *James Lande* 藍德

justified by the pittance in trade returned. But now, the reply from the Great Court at Peking had been received, and it was known that the emperor still refused to consider ratification of the treaty. Blaine could just imagine his brother's dour face, scarlet with indignation at the arrogance of the Chinese refusal, and the eagerness with which Lord Exter would take command of the Allied Expeditionary Force and sail up the Peiho again for a final, brutal confrontation with his nemesis, the Emperor of China.

"As it happens, Masters," the minister said, "the choice forced upon me is na' the choice I would have. History has its full share of irony, and does na' need another decision for war made by a man who would be the last man to choose war. I can na' impress upon you sufficiently my belief that Grea' Britain must do all in her power to support and maintain the authority of the Chinese empire. In all the verdicts you render as British consul at Shanghai, you must support this principle. I have no compunction about saying to you 'protect Chinese sovereignty' at the same moment I order British soldiers to march against Chinese sovereignty. I can only hope you are able to appreciate the subtlety of such a policy, and possess sufficient presence of mind na' to be unhorsed by its obvious contradictions."

Unhorsed? That's a *wee* bit thick to lay on a Chinese-speaking consul, on station here in China nearly a decade, when you've just come into your diplomatic majority, so to speak. Secretary to your brother Exter on his first misadventure in Tientsin back in 1858, colonial secretariat at Hong Kong for two years in the forties and you still can't even say *chin-chin* in Chinese. I'll *na'* be your dogsbody, you cheeky beggar!

Travis Trent Masters had been a fixture in the Shanghai foreign settlement since publishing *Rebellions of the Chinese* in 1856. The inevitable controversy accompanying the book may have led the captious little foreign community to regard him as quarrelsome and cranky, and not a little strange. A Chinese linguist had to expect to be thought strange by non-linguists, but his allegedly vehement support for the Taiping, and his role as settlement policeman, further antagonized many of the moneygrubbers along the Bund. His enemies were not few, and he went out heavily armed. The consul conceded his sympathy for the goals, but not the methods, of the Taiping heavenly kingdom so, obviously, one of the contradictions the minister referred to was the consul's own equivocal views toward the Manchu emperor. Truth be told, Masters often thought, I'm more a friend of the Chinese *people* than any party of Chinese, and would prevent interference in their affairs by foreign powers. I've said often enough in meetings in this settlement that when a quarrel breaks out between your hosts, a sensible guest neither takes sides nor encourages one against the other. When the quarrel is over, the guest is more likely to remain welcome. The analogy is lost I suppose on that class who demand to have their own selfish way, and want only to humiliate the Chinese.

However, it was clear to Consul Masters that to continue to preside over British affairs in Shanghai, and in any way disregard the policy he was charged as British consul with upholding, would be the height of pecksniffery. Conveniently, he was not so devoted to the rebel cause that he confronted a crisis of conscience when directed to oppose the Taiping rebels, especially if they invested Shanghai.

"The policy you recommend, sir," Masters said, "fraught as it may be with difficulties, is not inconsistent with the responsibilities of my office, and I am in accord with your view that the principle of Chinese sovereignty should be advanced whenever it is within my power to be of influence."

There was a light knock on the door to the consul's office, followed by the entrance of the consul's chief aide, Bitterman.

"Excuse me, Consul Masters, but the American consul wishes to call on you."

"Ask the American consul to wait a few minutes, would you Bitterman," Masters

The Englishman's War

said. "Tell him I am engaged at the moment, but will be free presently."

"Bit'erman," the minister said, "be a good fellow and send in my aide."

Bitterman hesitated, the dispatch heavy in his hand, but then withdrew. A minute later, Minister Blaine's aide appeared. Blaine told him to bring the file for the American consul. On the heels of Blaine's aide, Bitterman reappeared, now wearing his frock coat.

"Excuse me again, sir, but a despatch for the minister has arrived from Kintang by the gunboat *Roebuck*. It's from General Sir Hope Grant. And I have asked the American consul to wait upon you."

"Kintang." Blaine said. "That's probably Gran' telling us he's arrived. It's less than a day from Shanghai, isn't it? He should be able to say how *many* ships have arrived at Kintang from Hong Kong. Not all of them, I'd wager, just an advance squadron to sound the channels, commissariat, hospital and the like. I would like to be present during your interview wi' the American consul, Masters, if you don't mind, as he will be wanting to know more about Her Majesty's intentions in China, but I think I should read the despatch from Kintang first. Will Consul Shanks mind waiting, do you think?"

"The American consul," Masters said, "has what the Americans like to call a 'chip' on his shoulder about the way he imagines he is treated by us and, labor as I might, there seems to be nothing I can do to remove it. Of course, he will want to know the news of the Allied Expeditionary Force."

"Well, then, let the old bugger wait!"

Minister Blaine's aide re-entered with the papers to be given to the American consul, and Bitterman handed the despatch to the minister and withdrew again. Blaine read the despatch aloud.

Aboard the Granada,
Kintang Island,
April 19, 1860
Sir:
I have the honor to inform you of the imminent arrival at Kintang of the Allied Forces of England and France under the joint command of myself, and the commanders of British and French naval forces. Our fleet of steam and sailing vessels will anchor off Kintang, opposite Chenhai, at the mouth of the Ningpo River, starting April 19th instant, and we plan to embark for Tinghai, the capital city of the island of Chushan, Saturday morning, April 21st. At such time as the full complement arrives from Hong Kong and Shanghai, our fleet will include the following vessels of war:

British	HMS Granada, flagship	HMS Imperieuse, steam frigate
	HMS Pearl, steam frigate	HMS Slaney, gunboat
	HMS Opossom, gunboat	HMS Kestrel, gunboat
	HMS Woodcock, gunboat	HMS Roebuck, dispatch boat
	HMS Creasy, troop ship	HMS Mars, troop ship
	HMS Tasmania, troop ship	HMS Walmer Castle, troop ship
	HMS Octavia, store ship	HMS Adventure, troop ship
French	HIM Saigon, steamer	HIM Du Chayla, steam frigate
	HIM Dragonne, gunboat	HIM Mitraille, gunboat
	HIM Alarme, gunboat	

In all we will number some 2000 men, including elements of the 67th and 99th regiments, Rotton's battery of artillery, and a company of engineers, as well as 600 British marines from Admiral Hope, and another 500 French marines and sailors. I anticipate no opposition to our occupation, by either Chinese civil or military authorities. After establishing a garrison to secure the island, I shall return to Hong Kong to resume preparations there for the advance to the north.

I have the Honor to be Yours,
 Respectfully,

洋神 *Yang Shen*   James Lande 藍德

J. Hope Grant, Lt. General,
   Commanding Military Forces in China

"Ay, thank you General," Blaine said. "You could na' have counted the vessels already arrived, could you?"

2   Bitterman lead the American consul to a plush leather chair deep inside the sanctuary of the consulate, offered him a cheroot, and had Chinese tea set out on the table beside him. In the corridor to the consul's front clerks and functionaries, more than he could count, tramped or trudged to and fro waving despatches and documents, intermingled with lieutenants, captains, colonels and admirals with faces full of high purpose. The bustle in just one hallway of the British consulate made his meager American establishment look like a cloister struck by cholera. And that was just the first galling indignity that reminded him that in Shanghai, America, as pa used to say, sucked Hampshire hind tit. Only now, it was Yorkshire. The English have cause, I suppose, to condemn other nations that stood to one side while British arms won pact and privilege in China, deferred upon others by no more virtue than a most-favored-nation treaty clause, but Americans have stood by Englishmen on other occasions. The first war could still make a chapter in my book about the Chinese, even if we were not much involved. Shanks let his mind wander, testing thoughts and phrases he might write in his book.

"Consul Shanks?"

The consul felt a friendly hand on his shoulder. Chalmers Alexander, interpreter for the British consulate, knelt beside his chair to speak into the American consul's face, as if sensitive to their respective rank in the diplomatic establishment, and solicitous of the consul's feelings in the humiliating role of jackal after the British lion. Consul Shanks turned in his chair and smiled.

"Alexander! Where have you been keeping yourself?" Alexander was a slight young man of twenty-eight years, in a linen sack coat with Carnelian Vest and a broad-brimmed straw hat. His short, light-red hair, sea-blue eyes and pale, freckled skin gave him a sprightly appearance – some old-country codgers expected him to sprout diaphanous wings and fly up into the nearest tree or rafter.

"Out and about, sir. They have me pressed into service aboard every transport up and down the river, in most every temple and godown where troops are barracked, *chin-chin*ing the mandarins to get decent digs for our delicate Devon inductees, and helping them break the ice. Water, food, latrines, sewage, and all the amenities have I single-handedly, or so it seems, procured for the regiments. I have even been so resourceful as to rob a few dogs of their treasures, when they weren't looking of course."

"Take care with that kind of work, Chalmers, because there is cholera on board the transports, and the threat of an epidemic on shore when the hot weather comes."

"Oh, how right you are about that, sir. Doctor Rennie has been detaching bluejackets right and left and ordering them to the temple hospitals in an attempt to nip the cholera in the bud. I've been so keen on getting transferred to consulate duty that I'm about to come apart at the seams. Come to think of it, sir, your color looks a little off, if you don't mind my being so bold as to just up and say so. Are you taking your quinine?"

"Yes, Chalmers," the consul said, "thank you." Shanks knew Alexander as a prodigious student of the Chinese language, and possessed of considerable insight into the characteristics of Chinese. No one recalled ever hearing him utter a cross word.

"Well, I'm off. Come around more often if you can. Some of us Englishmen have a very high regard for Americans."

Alexander waved and departed down the corridor, leaving the consul in the doldrums again, waiting for the British consul. Shanks endured the lull by sipping his

The Englishman's War

cold tea and relighting his cheroot. He pondered how Alexander's charm could dull the sharp edge of his impudence and make it seem like reverence. Alexander has wit and intelligence, he thought, and seems to fathom the Chinese. Chalmers was selected for the bizarre task of escorting pigheaded old Governor Yeh Ming-chen into house arrest in Calcutta, after Canton fell in 1858, where the old blackguard died the next year. The British put Yeh aboard HMS *Inflexible*, an irony surely not missed by the English. Imagine that spry young English Ariel flitting about that crabbed old Chinese Caliban, attempting to get an interview for the *Times* – better a braillist than a linguist, or maybe a phrenologist. Still, Chalmers is probably the most likely of the linguists to advance to consul, if he'd waste less time with the local drama club. On the other hand, maybe amateur theatricals are fit preparation for politics.

After what seemed the duration of a Chinese dynasty, there burst into the anteroom from the corridor the sudden apparition of a very large fellow in an ill-fitting unbuttoned double-breasted blue reefer jacket over an unfastened bright red Chinese silk waistcoat. Seeing the American consul, the fellow glanced quickly about as if for a place to retreat from rebel hordes but, finding no easy avenue of escape from the stampede of bureaucratic traffic, he surrendered to the consul's astounded gape.

"Good afternoon, Consul Shanks," he said, his flapping jacket and waistcoat coming to rest. "Nice to see you again, sir. You are well, I trust."

"Yes, yes," the consul said abruptly, recognizing Terrance Fenton Wells – broad of brow and square of jaw, with deep-set hazel eyes, a retreating hairline and wispy gray muttonchops. Wells was a pushy middle-aged sinologue – student of China – long on station with the British in China, who pestered beyond endurance all his superiors with projects for reform of the British civil service in China, from the training of interpreters to Whitehall's policy toward the Manchus. As vice-consul in 1854, he led the Shanghai Volunteer Corps in the Battle of Muddy Flat; in 1858, he was assigned as Lord Exter's interpreter for the first treaty negotiations; and now he was appointed by Minister Blaine as Chinese Secretary.

"Don't let me detain you if you must be off."

"Not at all, sir," Wells said, advancing into the anteroom. "Are you waiting to see the minister?" T. F. Wells was not immune to the community of pity felt for the American consul by British underlings delegated to alleviate his interminable stops for official attention. He felt a sleight pang of guilt for having sought to flee the encounter.

Conditioned reflex, a man of science would say. Consul looks ready for a brandy.

"Of course. That is a mighty large bundle of documents you are hauling about. You could capsize." Consul Shanks thought his diplomacy was a natural gift. His real talents were wasted in this backwater.

"Hah, translations, sir. There is never an end to them!"

"A Chinese Secretary does translations?"

"There's no one else."

"Anything interesting," the consul whispered.

"Just corrections to corrections." Wells grinned shyly. "Confidentially, I am just in a bit of hot water over an injudicious choice of language in a translation of a reply from the Chinese court to the last British ultimatum."

"I suppose I can imagine how you feel, as I have often been witness to the agony of our interpreter, Frank Jackson, over his translations, and chagrin over his mistakes. As a lay parishioner, however, I never fail to be amazed at what you interpreter priests accomplish. And, candidly, I am happy to get anything at all, mistakes or no."

"Let me confide in you further, sir. The secret is to have good native informants to keep one in the straight and narrow, linguistically speaking, and curb any immodest tendencies toward flamboyance."

"Interesting. I am not sure our Mr. Jackson relies much on native assistants."

"It has been a while since I have chatted with Frank. Perhaps I should shake loose an hour and drop by to talk shop, perhaps lend him a copy of my new Peking dialect primer based on the *Hsin Ching Lu* 尋津錄, The Book of Experiments, if he feels it might be of use. Well, now, here's Bitterman, so your relief column has arrived to take you to the minister. I'll just be off then. By the way, sir, are you taking your quinine? I have to take mine faithfully to keep the fever away."

"Yes, Wells, of course" the consul said, bridling his annoyance, "thank you."

"Then, good day to you, sir."

"Goodbye, Wells." And good riddance. Impertinent jackass, I don't need your japery, and I can take care of my own health.

3 The American consul entered the British consul's office, the three diplomats exchanged pleasantries, seated themselves on an overstuffed sofa, and Bitterman poured brandy and passed around a brass humidor of cheroots. The office was a large and well-appointed room, richly furnished like a parlor with burgundy velvet draperies, upholstered armchairs and settees, carved tables inlaid with ivory, a huge, brightly polished glass-covered mahogany desk and leather-backed chair, and a wide, thick carpet woven with the design of a crowned lion. A portrait of the Queen hung over the mantelpiece and a warm fire crackled in the fireplace below. Consul Shanks always marveled at the British consulate's allowance for furnishings.

"Have you any news yet from Chushan?" Shanks said. "I hope the occupation will go without incident."

"Yes, thank you, Consul," Masters said. "The occupation is underway. Allied troops arrived at Kintang this morning. They plan to embark for Tinghai early Saturday morning. We do not anticipate any engagement with the Chinese, as the natives at Tinghai are reported to be looking forward eagerly to the arrival of new British and French customers for their trade."

"That's very good," Shanks said. "I've only stopped by to hear if a date has been set for the departure to the north, and to check on my American prisoners in your gaol."

"I am afraid the Chinese still stubbornly refuse to parley with us," Masters said, "and that there remains no hope of avoiding a contest. Minister Blaine has recently received word from the Chinese."

"Consul Shanks," Blaine said, "the reply to Her Majesty's ultimatum to the Grea' Council at Peking has come from Commissioner Ho and still does na' offer much hope for negotiation. We gave our ultimatum demanding an apology for their outrageous attack upon us at Taku last summer, as well as passage past Taku and up to Tientsin for exchange of ratifications in Peking, and an indemnity of four million taels. As before, the Chinese still refuse to discuss specific proposals, because of what they evidently consider the impropriety of acceding to any demands at all. They would exclude all consideration of a minister resident in Peking, refuse to allow additional ports on the Yangtze River, forbid inland travel by foreigners, and eliminate any indemnity. We have replied that their answer is unsatisfactory, and that action by our naval and military authorities is imminent. Accordingly, my French colleague and I have instructed our Allied Commanders-in-chief to proceed wi' the occupation of Chushan."

Bitterman abruptly entered the office and stopped beside the British consul to whisper into his ear. Consul Masters shook his head and Bitterman hurried out. A hum of hallway traffic, bustling clerks and hasty conversations, drifted into the office through the half-open doorway. Consul Shanks glanced in that direction, reflecting on how quiet it always was in his own consulate.

"After the troops are landed at Tinghai," Blaine said, "and our administration established, the majority of the fleet will return to Hong Kong until conditions are suitable for transporting more troops to the north. Also, you may also inform your merchants that there will be no blockade of the Gulf of Peicheli, as we do na' believe such an action would be effective, nor do we wish to injure the trade of the natives along the coast and cause them unnecessary distress."

Consul Masters sauntered over to the office door and gently pushed it closed then, turning, smiled at the American consul. Shanks wondered if the British minister also put the British consul into a semi-mesmerized state, or was it his fever, or perhaps the heat from the fireplace. The American consulate was not heated.

"Moreover, I have recently received a despatch from Lord Russell saying that Lord Exter and Baron Galle have been appointed as special ministers to China, and that they have set sail for Shanghai. It is unlikely they will arrive before the third week in June. By then, we expect the monsoon to have abated and ice to have cleared completely from the Peiho up to Tientsin, and beyond to Peking. Therefore, if negotiations prove fruitless and hostilities must ensue, they cannot be precipitated by the expeditionary force until the end of June, when Lord Exter arrives at the Peiho. However, troop ships and cavalry transports will start north as soon as winds are favorable."

"I will report this to Minister Wood and Commodore Spalding at Hong Kong, and to Secretary Cass in Washington," Shanks said. The British minister handed over a portfolio of documents to the American consul.

"Here are copies of recent documents pertaining to our negotiations wi' the Grea' Council, to the occupation of Chushan, and also the copy you requested of my let'er to Lord Russell regarding the abuses in the convoy trade. Your Minister Wood felt that my let'er would add some weight to his plea to your Congress for greater authority to prosecute and incarcerate lawless citizens in the treaty ports."

"Thank you," Shanks said. "There is rumor that the insurgents have slipped out of Nanking and taken Ch'ang-chau and the district cities of Kin-tan and Lih-yang. Have you any further information?"

"I believe that at least one of the cities was retaken by imperial troops," Masters said, "but I am told that this new activity probably heralds a spring offensive along the Yangtze by the Taiping rebels. The direction of their operations suggests they are heading for Soochow. What they will do after reaching Soochow remains to be seen, considering as there are nearly 15,000 Allied soldiers on the coast at this time, and over 60 warships, but I would not be surprised to see rebels on the approaches to Shanghai come June or July. I would certainly prepare accordingly, just to be on the safe side."

"What will be the British attitude if insurgents attack Shanghai?" Shanks said.

Minister Blaine answered. "As before, Her Majesty wishes to remain neutral in the war between the Taiping rebels and the Chinese emperor, so we shall na' take any steps to actively interfere in rebel operations. However, we also must ensure the safety of the lives and property of our citizens in Shanghai, and to achieve that end we are prepared to defend the set'lement wi' support from our steam frigates, gunboats, and British marines. Thus our policy would be one of armed neutrality."

Armed neutrality, thought Shanks? Oh, this *is* high concept. Please, Lord, get me soon to Bedlam. Moreover, how can we allege neutrality, and claim that we interfere with neither side, when clearly we deny the insurgents access to the entrepot of Shanghai, deny them the opportunity to relieve the imperials of Shanghai's arms, supplies, and finances? If only the *taotai* could hear this and witness how gently doth the little lamb of logic lie down between the enormous paws of the serene British lion.

"Is it your intention to defend the Chinese city as well?"

"That is na' our stated intention," Blaine said, "but as the Chinese city is practically a part of the set'lement, I would not hesitate to incorporate its defense wi' that of ours if necessary to protect the foreign set'lement outside the walls of the Chinese city. Allied troops would take care to remain apart from any imperial troops engaged to defend the Chinese city, so as na' to give the impression of supporting imperial troops."

"I have requested American warships be brought up to Shanghai," the American consul said, "in anticipation of insurgent operations here, but have not yet received a reply to that request. American citizens in Shanghai will doubtless want to volunteer to man the barricades."

"You may rely," the British minister said, "for the protection of your American concession upon British ships of war and British marines in case hostilities wi' the rebels break out here at Shanghai."

4

Land's end of the Pei-ho River was a brown smudge of estuary, monotonous with salt marsh and mud flats that stretched away from the winding river to dull horizons north, south, and west. On the east, the river met the shifting hues of the gulf and, above the littoral, there was an irregular progression of white saltpans, soaked by spring tides and edged by brittle crusts of raw salt. Salt pools tinged with green or brown algae, or the green stems of salt weed, lay scattered about the alluvial ooze, along the edge of the saltpans, and beside the worn stone causeways.

From atop the roof of a two-story wooden temple, General Seng-ko-lin-ch'in 僧格林沁 – a squat, lumpy, round-shouldered Mongol with an undershot jaw and sunken eyes dark with weariness – gazed out 100 *li* in each of the four directions. The Temple of the God of the Sea 海神廟 stood just inside the ten-foot high crenellated mud wall of Ta-ku 大沽, a hamlet of crumbling mud huts daubed on the bank of the Pei-ho 白河, the White River. In his mind, the general followed the length of his defenses along the Pei-ho, from the Ta-ku forts northwest 318 *li* – 106 miles – to Pei-ching.

The Ta-ku forts were three *li* upstream from the mouth of the Pei-ho. Below the forts, four booms obstructed passage of large vessels up the river. Just above the booms were five forts, three on the south bank and higher up two on the north bank. Further upstream, near the first bend of the river, there were another two forts. Past them, around the second bend in the river, was the hamlet of Ta-ku.

The forts all were square enclosures surrounded by 15-foot high crenellated mud walls. Gaudy banners flapping in the breeze above the walls stood out in florid contrast to the drab umber walls and dreary mud flats. The approach to each wall was protected by a kind of *cheval-de-frise* – a barricade of sharp bamboo stakes inclined toward attackers – in front of two or three mud ditches, and sharp-pointed iron crow's feet strewn along the berm at the base of the walls. Within the enclosures there were low, broad roofed mud structures fortified by timber – casemates – that would protect the men of the garrison quartered there from gunfire, and shelter stores and munitions. The casemates were set against high walls facing the sea or river, and had many openings for firing small weapons. 9-, 12-, and 24-pounder brass and iron cannon, set in embrasures in the walls, commanded the Pei-ho with a lethal crossfire.

When the tide was low, the empty hulls of three dismantled barbarian gunboats were seen where they rested on the muddy shore below the first boom. The guns recovered from them now guarded the walls of the large south fort, where they would deal death to the next barbarians so foolish as to trespass in the river.

Seng-ko-lin-ch'in was commissioned to reinforce defenses at the mouth of the Pei-

洋神 *Yang Shen* James Lande 藍德

ho. The Emperor's edict read: defense of the Pei-t'ang district and Ta-ku both are imperative. Seng-ko-lin-ch'in has deployed defenses and cavalry as reinforcements before. His arrangements remain satisfactory. Order him to thoroughly review the circumstances and devise secret plans for defense, and prevent the barbarians from spying on us.

The general dismissed the tone of the Edict as protocol. The Emperor, he thought, the present-day Buddha 當今佛爺, was very agitated when we spoke last month of these defenses, urging repeatedly that I must emulate Kuan Yü 關羽 and protect the throne against the barbarian invaders. Last year, the invaders were careless. This time they will not be careless. The barbarian chiefs are not wild geese so startled by the twang of my bowstring they just fall out of the sky 夷酋非驚弓之雁, 聽弦音非落下天.

Defenses for the forts can be completed immediately, and chain and iron stakes for river obstructions can be wrought in the forge we have constructed below. But the ice must melt before obstructions can be placed into the river. This time when the barbarians approach, their paddle-wheel boats will meet iron stakes, weighing several tons and embedded in the muddy bottom. The stakes will destroy their paddle wheels. A boom of buoys and hawsers follows, and then another boom of chains and spars. Then more iron stakes followed by junks packed with flammables and anchored in a line across the river. Finally, there will be a large boom of junks cabled together so tightly that not even black powder charges or gunfire will blow them apart.

Seng-ko-lin-ch'in watched a messenger ride up to the temple and dismount. After a few minutes, a Mongol cavalry lieutenant mounted to the upper floor led by the general's Chinese secretary. The officer wore a broad-brimmed round black hat with two furry brown-ringed tails dangling from the back, and a short, dark yellow jacket 馬褂 over a belted long gown. He carried a long sword, a short recurved bow in a large case that hung from his belt, and arrows in a quiver strapped to his back.

"*Ta-jen*," the officer said in Mongol. "Captain Shu-t'ung-e reports that the guns you ordered shifted to the north wall of the north Ta-ku forts are now in place and adjusted to fire to a distance of two *li*."

"Yes," the general said, turning back the horseshoe cuffs of his inside gown. He straightened the front panel of the gown and smoothed the dark yellow silk. "From here I saw and heard them sighting their guns."

"The captain also says that the devil ships at the river mouth are spying through telescopes on the construction work at the forts, and taking soundings everywhere outside the bar, as well as up nearby rivers."

王八蛋 nuisances, thought the general, barbarians *and* imperial court censors. There is no need for those untried in battle to memorialize the Emperor with self-seeking language about barbarian strategy. Stupid pigs 笨豬 could guess the barbarians would have new plans this year. They saw the forts last year and sailed to T'ien-chin the year before, so of course the barbarians know the face of the land now. It doesn't need a toadying court censor to find that out. Of course, they'll come from a different direction this time, not just from the river. Maybe they will land at Pei-t'ang village, cut off the north garrison, then march down to Ta-ku, but it won't be at night! Can't cross that muck in the dark. Rumors about their plans have been all over the Shang-hai Bund 大馬路 for months, but now our spies have provided confirmation, so *now* we turn some guns toward Pei-t'ang. If we turn the guns every time we hear a new rumor, the guns will spin around so much they'll bury themselves in the marsh.

"Tell the captain I said to place more observers and messengers out on the coast to spy on the barbarian ship movements. You may return."

The Englishman's War

洋神 *Yang Shen*　　　　　　　　　　　　　　　　　　　　James Lande 藍德

The officer bowed and turned to leave.

"Wait. Have you officers been warning the men not to pillage?"

"Yes, *Ta-jen*. We tell them to treat the locals well, and pay for what they take."

"Remind them not to take anything not *willingly* offered. Tell your captain what I have said about this."

"Yes, *Ta-jen*. I most certainly will." The officer bowed again and left.

The Chinese here are angry and threaten disorder. Already they hold back taxes because of the high price of rice, and many have turned to banditry. If our troops mistreat them, the traitors 漢奸 among them will be even more likely to help the barbarians, just as they have in the past. My cavalry is well trained and well behaved, but I have less control over the rowdy troops of the other officers nearby. Even my soldiers will be a problem if I cannot pay them.

Only the best banner units should be deployed. Those from the north, from Chih-li 直隸 and Shan-tung 山東 provinces are still the most reliable, still retain their martial élan. True bannermen practice military drill, ride horseback, and shoot arrows from the back of a galloping horse. They are loyal like red-faced Lord Guan, persevere like Yue Fei 岳飛, fight with the ferocity of demons, and speak their native Mongol and Manchu tongues as well as learn Chinese. The worthless ones waste their time in idle pursuits like raising birds and insects, spinning tops, flying kites, racing horses, cooking pastries, attending operas, or singing folk songs to the beat of eight-cornered drums. Worst are the wastrels who recite poetry in teahouses with lewd women and smoke opium. If the dynasty falls, and only those worthless lumps remain, men will be able to say that the Eight Banners could not repulse the barbarians, but they carved wonderful birdcages!

It seems that the further south from Pei-ching the banner garrisons, the more effete the bannermen, the more they live among and become like Chinese, forgetting their own noble tradition and language. To believe that Mongol and Manchu could ever live together with Chinese is a fatal error. Because the Manchu have the mandate of Heaven, yes, but more because the Manchu are the conquering race. Chinese, if given opportunity, will turn on Manchu and murder us all.

For hundreds of years the Manchu were paramount in China, but now our people are impoverished and our garrisons are falling apart, and we are more and more vulnerable. Once there were walls within the walls, around the Manchu bannermen and their garrisons in the heart of Chinese cities. Now the garrison walls crumble down, and bannermen mingle with the ordinary people. But walls are still in the hearts of the Chinese, and garrisons still in their minds.

洋神 *Yang Shen*   James Lande 藍德

Dramatis Personae: Chapter 5

Gunner	*Essex* gun crew captain
Lemuel Grace	*Essex* gun crew spongeman
Ramsay John	*Essex* gun crew loader
Crusoe Weller	*Essex* gun crew runner

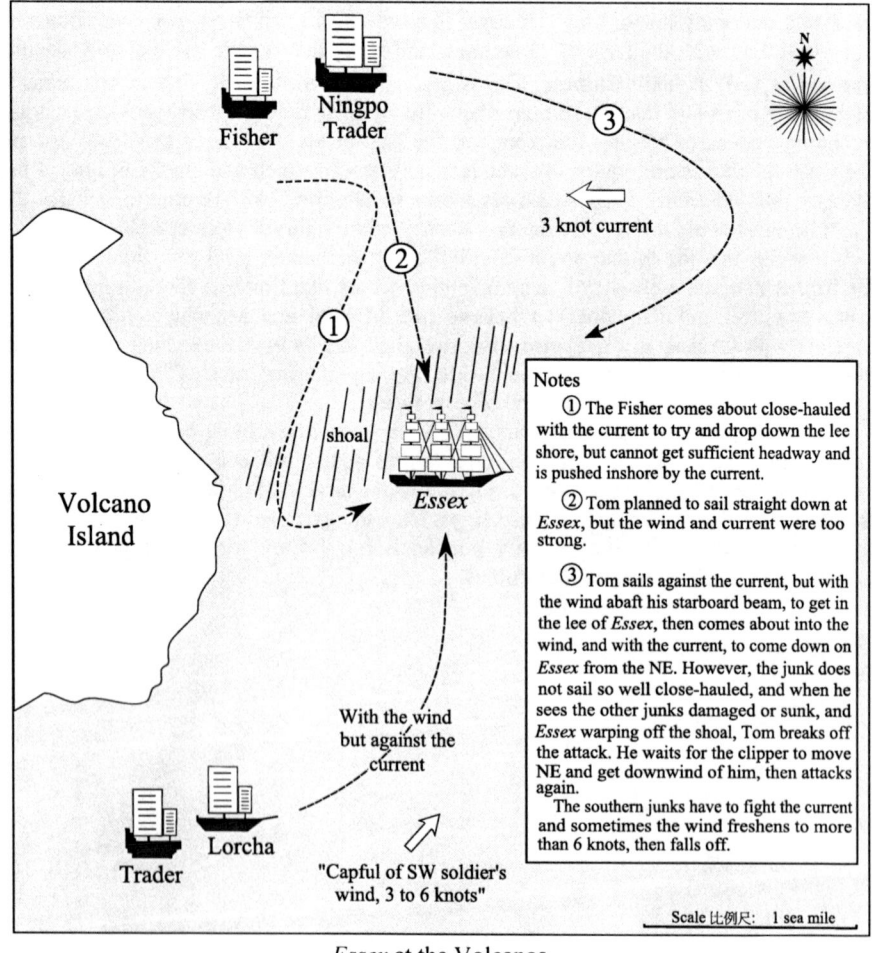

Essex at the Volcanos

Chapter 5: Fighting Fokie Tom
Thursday, April 19, 1860, 10:30am

Ptolemy Reese whirled about and glared up at Fletcher Wood, who was smiling broadly, and mighty glad the mate did not still have his Colt Navy.

"Battle the watch, Mr. Reese. There's acres of water between us yet!"

Reese shook his head. "We're chockablock now, Yank. 'Tis the bitter end."

"Not by a long chalk, Mr. Reese." Fletcher leaned forward over the rail. "We're not done 'till the last dog's hung."

Reese clenched his fists, seething. If Fletcher had been within reach, the mate would have strangled him. The captain stepped to the rail beside Fletcher.

"You've got brass 6-pounders 'tween decks," Fletcher said to Reese, "and they're light enough to lift with a burnt Lucifer match. Break one of those guns out of the hold on the mainyard, then you can use what's left of the cro'jack to hoist it clear up to the mizzen truck if need be."

"6-pounder! What'll be the good of that? We're not unhorsing cavalry."

"True, a 6-pounder is light for the work, but a well-placed shot could punch through some parts of a junk's hull, and canister will sweep pirates off decks."

"Blast me if my bleedin' gunner's ever fired a field gun."

"Leave it to me, Mr. Reese. I'll be your gunnery officer, and I'll turn your sailors into a first-rate field gun crew, too. Get me just one field gun out of your hold and up the poop deck, and I can promise you those junks won't dare come near *Essex* before you can float her free."

"With them big wheels, it'll just roll over the rail into the ocean."

"The gun will not roll, Mr. Reese."

"How'll you prevent that?"

"Hobble the gun."

"Hobble it? Like a bleedin' horse?"

"Precisely. Time's a wastin' Mr. Reese."

"Go ahead, Mr. Reese," the captain said. Reese hesitated, wondering which man he would kill first. What could be more insane than a field gun on the deck of a ship?

"Yank," the mate said, "You'd better come below and unlimber a gun for my crew else, ignorant as the blighters are of military ordnance, they'd fetch up an entire battery." In the dark of the cargo hold, he could hobble the Yank and none'd be the wiser.

The mate went forward and set crewmen to unbattening the main hatch, rolling back the tarpaulin, and removing the timber hatch cover. Fletcher followed. The mainyard was braced around and purchases thrown over the yard, one near the mast and the other on the yardarm. Fletcher vanished into the hold riding the tackle. The mate stayed on deck to handle the crew.

The crew below cut away the lashings securing the field gun last loaded, and Fletcher unhitched the carriage trail from its limber – the two-wheeled chest that carried tools for the gun. He emptied the limber of needed tools, stowed them on the gun, and sent the ammunition chest from the limber, and three other ammunition chests, up to the main deck to the lee of the poop where they would be protected from enemy fire. The 6-pounder was rolled under the open hatch, slings were passed under the muzzle of the gun, under the axle of the carriage, and through the pointing ring on the trail. The block lowered from the tackle on the mainyard was hooked to the slings on the gun.

The same six crewmen who had lifted the 24-pounder hauled on the fall of the field gun tackle and the field gun fairly flew out of the hold and up to the mainyard.

"'Vast hauling, half-wits!" the mate screamed. "Gun's no use at the main truck."

The crewmen braced the mainyard around to starboard, hauled the field gun out to the yardarm with the second purchase, lowered the gun to the main deck, removed the tackle and carried it aft to the crossjack. Just as the they started to haul the 6-pounder aft, a twelve-pound cannon ball smashed through the larboard bulwark, shattered the wrought-iron bilge pump wheels, ricocheted off the foot of the mainmast, rolled across the path of the field gun, and came to rest against the starboard bulwark.

"Well," mused the mate, as he stared at the spent shot, "they've got our range. Throw that trash overboard before someone trips over it."

The field gun was rolled aft down the deck to the poop deck, the broken crossjack yard swung around, a luff-tackle hooked to the slings on the gun, and the gun lifted over onto the poop deck. The mate ordered the gun crew from the 24-pounder up to the field gun. Fletcher called down to the mate.

"Mr. Reese, we are shorthanded on this gun crew. I'd like to take your carpenter and bos'n from the stern rifles, and we'll need one more hand."

The mate ordered four sailors aft – three to replace the vacancies in the stern rifles left by the recent promotion of the carpenter, the boatswain, and Fletcher Wood, and one more to make seven for the field gun crew. The rest of the starboard watch he sent forward to their own second mate on the forecastle, where at the capstan they were encouraged to reopen negotiations with her reluctant majesty *Essex* on subjects pertaining to getting the hell out of the mud. The old hands of the stern rifles, Captain Fitch, Hugh Wood, and the two ABs, set about training their recruits to load and fire rifles. The newly reformed gun crew gathered around the 6-pounder. Acrid white smoke from the stern rifles swirled around them. Balls and bullets struck fragments out of *Essex* and dusted them with wood chips as they parleyed about the strange 6-pounder.

"Looks kinda puny," the gunner said.

"I don't see a trigger on this thing," the boatswain said. "What I know about artillery wouldn't half-fill a thimble."

"With th'm big wheels, what's to keep it from jumpin' back across th' deck and out o'er the side?" the carpenter said.

"What ho, lads!" Fletcher said. "Why the long faces? Been eatin' oats outta butter churns? There's a fight-a-comin'. Is there any among ye *not* eager to spill blood?"

"Sure now, as long as 'taint *my* blood, Mr. Wood," the grinning gunner said. "But look here, I've nev'r fired one o' these here field guns."

"Gunner, that doesn't bother me any more'n the dark bothers hoot owls. You are an experienced artilleryman, are you not?"

The gunner stood up a little taller. "Mr. Wood, these guns is a proud tradition in me family. Me father was after bein' quarter-gunner on a Royal Navy seventy-four! And I've fired just about ev'ry kind of cannon, carronade and Columbiad aboard her majesty's ships of war." The gunner was a small, bowl-legged Irishman well past forty years of age, with deep creases in his face and black powder buried in the pores of his nose and cheeks. His sparkling green eyes relentlessly scrutinized his work, but his manner was calm and his bantering tone encouraging.

"And that, Gunner, is why you will be gun commander of the Shanghai *taotai*'s fine contraband field gun, and I will be your officer. Let us quickly assign the duties while the enemy still remains in confusion!"

"Well, sir," the gunner said, pointing to a tall, gangly sailor, "this here's Lemuel Grace, that was Number One on the deck gun, as he's got the longest reach. This other..." and the gunner pushed back the watch cap from the bangs of a redheaded sailor,

"...he's Ramsay John, the reason, if there ever was one, Englishmen's called mad dogs. He was me Number Two and nev'r put a seam under a vent."

"Very good, Gunner. Mr. Grace for Number One, our spongeman, and Mr. John for Number Two, our loader. Carpenter, I'd like you to be our Number Three, our ventsman, because you have the size and strength to hoist the gun around."

"Call me Chips, Mr. Wood," replied the dark, bushy-browed man, "and I'll spin your gun on me little finger."

"Chips for ventsman, then. Bos'n, will you be our Number Four and fire the gun? You will have a purple lanyard instead of a trigger to pull." The grizzled old boatswain blinked his sunken eyes, wriggled his white mustache, wiped his hands on his patched dungarees, and dipped his head in accord.

"This one looks able to run a mile," Fletcher said. "What's your name, sailor?"

"Crusoe Weller, sir" was the blushing response from a sleek, slender youth all peach-fuzz on apple-red cheeks.

"Crusoe Weller for Number Five, our runner. The remaining two sailors will work below on the main deck and serve cartridges up to the runner on the poop deck. Now, crewmen, let's prepare this gun. We'll work here in the lee of the helm until we're ready, then roll her out to the stern."

A distant report was followed seconds later by a splash under the stern. A crackle of musketry drifted with the wind. Lead balls thunked into the woodwork of the poop deck and kicked up splinters.

The spongeman removed the wood tompion from the muzzle of the gun. The gun crew lifted the gun from the bed of the carriage with handspikes and heaved it up to firing position on top of the carriage. Trunnions – large earlike knobs protruding from each side of the gun – slipped onto trunnion plates recessed in the body of the carriage. Metal plates – cap squares – locked them down.

The gunner screwed in the muzzle-sight and the iron support for a Pendulum-Hausse rear sight at the base of the breech – the Pendulum-Hausse, adapted from Russian service, allowed the gun to be aimed when the carriage was not level. Fletcher presented the Pendulum-Hausse rear sight, in its leather case, to the gun commander.

Near at hand, the gun crew placed a leather bucket of fresh water, handspikes, a sponger/rammer staff, sponges, a worming staff – for pulling wadding or charges out of the gun barrel – buckskin thumbstall pads for blocking the vent when loading, pouches and other miscellaneous equipment brought up from the limber ammunition chest.

Fletcher put the spongeman, loader and ventsman to work cleaning the vent and swabbing out the bore to remove packing grease. The boatswain went to prepare several lengths of heavy rope that would reach between the carriage wheels and under the barrel, and to devise rope fenders to place under the heavy trail of the gun. Then Fletcher took the gun commander, runner and two ammunition servers below to where the ammunition chests were stowed on the main deck beside the ladder to the poop deck.

"Each of these chests contains several kinds of cartridges," Fletcher explained to the servers. "We have them stowed here in the lee of the poop to keep them safe. These round-topped cartridges are solid shot, these others that have a circle of numbers on top – that's the Bormann fuse – are spherical case shot, and the cartridges with this elongated top are canister. From the gun we will call for one of these three cartridges and our runner, Mr. Crusoe Weller, will come to the ladder and repeat the order, and you fine sailors will carefully pass up to him the required cartridge. When you open another chest, also carefully pass up these friction primers, and the lanyard."

They climbed back up the ladder. Fletcher handed the lanyard to the bosun.

"There now, Bos'n," Fletcher intoned, "you're an honorable member of the Order of the Purple Lanyard."

Fletcher showed the carpenter how to use a handspike to lift the trail of the carriage – the "trail" being the wooden tongue that rested on the deck behind the carriage wheels – and explained commands for moving the gun by pushing on the wheel spokes. Each crewman took his post at the gun and together they rolled the gun aft to the larboard corner of the stern and pointed it toward the pirates coming from the south.

The stern rifles took positions to each side of the gun and continued slow independent fire that forced the lorcha and the south junk to fall off with the current after each attempt to fly down upon *Essex*. The wooden slats at the bottom of the case of rifle cartridges were now visible.

More shot splashed into the water at the stern, crashed through the sails and rigging, and sent smashed woodwork flying around the deck. Riflemen sprinted for cover. Fletcher stood to one side, out of the way of the men serving the gun, but in the open and exposed to fire from the pirates, his deep blue eyes flashing while he talked quietly to the gun crew.

Bloomin' idiot must think 'e 'as a charmed life, thought the boatswain.

"One *advantage* of being aground, gentlemen," Fletcher said, "is that the swell cannot disturb the aiming of our gun. The enemy still has the swell to contend with, which upsets both their trajectory and windage!"

A short length of heavy rope was passed under the barrel of the gun and fastened to each wheel.

"This heavy rope is sort of like a hobble on horse legs," Fletcher said. "The rope will dampen the recoil and prevent the gun from knocking the helmsman galley-west. When the recoil sends the gun flying to the rear, the carriage wheels roll backward and lift the rope, stretching it taut against the underside of the barrel. When the barrel jerks up, the trail at the rear pushes down against the deck, which arrests movement to the rear. Rope fenders under the trail protect the deck – the barrel will be elevated to allow for the fenders under the trail. Watch that rope hobble and replace it when it wears."

Fletcher stepped the sailors through the gun drill, then they tried it for themselves.

"Range 800 yards, spherical case." The gun commander repeated the order.

"Cartridge forward!" Crusoe Weller went to the ladder together with the gunner, called out the round ordered, and received the round up from the main deck in a small wicker basket. He took it to the gun commander's station where the gunner, being familiar with fuses already, pricked open the fuse at the 3-second interval and sent the round on to the loader.

"Load!" ordered the gunner, at Fletcher's direction.

Chips, the Ventsman, covered the vent with his leather thumbstall to prevent sparks from being forced into the vent.

The spongeman wet his sponge, placed it in the bore, checked the vent was properly covered, then forced the sponge to the bottom of the bore and twisted it around twice before pulling it out.

The loader inserted the cartridge, powder-bag first, into the muzzle, checking that the seam of the woolen casing would not come under the vent. Fletcher thought he could detect the odor of the pepper and camphor used as a preservative in the cartridge, even with all the black-powder smoke in the air from the rifles.

"Ram!" ordered the gunner.

The spongeman reversed his staff and started to ram the cartridge home.

"Stop vent!" shouted the gunner. "Chips, you keep that blasted vent covered."

The carpenter shot the gunner a nasty look and started to say something.

"Until the gun's completely loaded," snarled the gunner.

Fletcher intervened to avoid a brawl. "Chips, we don't want the powder set off by spark while we're loading the gun. Ventsman may seem small-beer, but our lives are in your hands."

"Under his thumb's more like it," muttered the gunner.

"Just as you say, sor," Chips said, covering the vent again. "Giver 'nother try."

The spongeman threw his weight on the rammer and forced the cartridge to the bottom of the bore, checking the mark on his rammer to be certain the round was all the way in. Rammer withdrawn, the spongeman and loader stood to one side, and the spongeman called out:

"Gun loaded, sir!"

The Pendulum-Hausse rear sight was affixed to its mount on the base of the breech. The elevation screw under the cascabel was turned to raise the gun to the $2°$ mark on the sight, for a range of 800 yards with spherical case shot. The rear sight was removed and put back into the leather pouch. The gun commander checked the direction of fire.

The ventsman moved the trail to the right when the gun commander tapped with a handspike on the right side of the carriage, and to the left when the left side was tapped. The gun commander raised both arms. The ventsman returned to his post.

"Ready!" the gunner ordered. Chips thrust the vent pick through the vent to poke an opening in the woolen cartridge inside the barrel, feeling for the resistance to be sure the cloth bag was properly pierced.

The boatswain attached his purple lanyard to the ring of a friction primer and reached over to the far side of the gun to insert the primer into the vent. He then laid the lanyard over the top of the gun, stepped back with the lanyard in hand, and called out:

"Gun ready to fire, sir!"

Fletcher reviewed with the gun commander what to check before firing: ramrod not still in the bore of the gun, cartridge not still in the wicker basket, friction primer inserted in the vent, lanyard attached to the primer, and crew well away from the gun.

"Commence firing!" Fletcher ordered.

"Fire!" the gunner said. The boatswain yanked the lanyard and set off the friction primer. The field gun roared and bucked and spit a great cloud of thick white smoke over the tafferel, but the rope hobble checked its recoil and it jumped only a foot.

The gun commander watched for the result of the discharge. Three seconds later the round exploded well behind the stern of the Shao-hsing trader, spraying her transom with musket balls. Wild cheering raked the length of *Essex* as the crew found new cause for hope. The men at the gun all stood staring upwind at the junk.

"Not bad, Mr. Wood, for such a little pop-gun," the gunner said.

"She puts a fine edge on placing shot, Gunner," replied Fletcher with a grin, "but like all her tribe she responds best to the attentive care of an excellent crew. That round took us eight minutes. Now let's work the drill and see if we can achieve a rate of one round a minute. She appears to be shooting high, so bring your elevation down a full turn of the screw. We'll try for the big junk's mains'l sheets first, lads, then try to smash her rudder."

"Lively now, me boyos," sang the gunner. "Do it man o' war fashion!"

The men rolled the gun forward and resumed with the loading sequence, varied this time by having already fired the first round. Behind them, ahead of *Essex*' bow, they heard the report of cannon fire from the north junks, and the volleys of rifle fire returned by the forecastle rifles.

The pirate junks seemed very close.

2

"Range 400 yards, spherical case shot!"

"Cartridge forward!"

"Cartridge forward, sir!"

"Load!" This time the ventsman extracted the spent primer and wiped the gun vent before closing the vent with his thumbstall. The bore was sponged and the cartridge placed in the muzzle.

"Ram!" After the new cartridge was rammed home, the ventsman helped adjust the windage of the gun to follow the lateral course of the trader. The lorcha was well behind the trader and out of sight.

"Ready!"

"Gun ready, sir!"

"Fire!"

Again, the little 6-pounder thundered and jumped and threw out more clouds of thick white smoke. One second later the round exploded amidships of the Shao-hsing trader, four feet above her main deck, clearing the deck of crewman, ripping great holes in her bamboo lugsails, and riddling her leeboard.

"Five minutes! That was a fine shot, *me boyos*," Fletcher said, winking at the gunner, "but not quite good enough yet. Junks can sail when they're flying nothing more than ladies bloomers. Once more amidships, but higher up where we can cut her sheets."

Micah called up a lusty chorus of *Rolling Home* to give the rhythm of a song to the starbolines sweating at the capstan to warp *Essex* off the shoal. The Americans in the starboard watch sang "New England" in place of "old England."

> *Pipe all hands to man the windlass,*
> *See our cable run down clear,*
> *As we heave away our anchor,*
> *For old [new] England's shores, we'll steer.*
> *Rolling home, rolling home,*
> *Rolling home across the sea,*
> *Rolling home to merry England,*
> *Rolling home, dear land, to thee!*

The song at the capstan was interrupted from chorus to chorus by shell exploding off the forward part of *Essex*, or solid shot ripping from fore topgallant to spanker through the sails behind the stern rifles and field gun crew, or crashing into the ship's superstructure. But then the song was resumed with greater passion, if that was possible.

Below, in the saloon, Hannah heard the shanty over a discordant rattle of gunfire.

"Those fools have a song for everything," she muttered.

Do sailors sing when they cast a body into the sea, thought Elizabeth? She looked away from the table in the corner of the saloon.

"Mother," she said, "it is all so useless. We do not know enough."

"Enough? We know nothing! But none of this should have happened in the first place, Elizabeth darling, so it is no wonder we are not prepared. You cannot blame yourself, dear. You cannot blame yourself, do you hear? I shall inquire further into medical conditions aboard our ships at the first opportunity but, in the meantime, I can start here. Doctor, what is in that medical chest?"

"Not much, ma'am," the cook said, "not like a regular 'ospital."

"Well, show us anyway. It might be useful. Come, Elizabeth, and see this." Hannah thought her daughter would be less frightened if she kept busy.

Elizabeth surrendered to her Mother's sway and looked into the chest.

"Ma'am, I don't know that it's proper to talk about some things with ladies."

"Don't be shy Doctor, and we shall not be either. You are pardoned in advance for mention of anything not genteel. Imagine you are talking to Florence Nightingale."

The cook opened the medical chest and lifted out the tray to look inside.

"Some dressings and bandages – the dressings're applied to the wound and the bandage is tied over to 'old 'em on. Use this lint and raw cotton for packin' the wounds. Iodine to paint the wounds and keepin' down redness and pus, and bottles of bichloride of mercury, sodium hypochlorite, and carbolic acid, all disinfectants."

"Bottles of what?" Hannah said, marveling that anyone could even say those names, much less a nearly illiterate ship's cook.

"What are you calling 'disinfectants,' Doctor?" asked Elizabeth.

"They help keep a wound from festerin', and help heal quicker. Can't say how, but I've done some readin', and others 'ave showed me. I put 'em in the wound when I lay on the dressing. Wait too long and the wound can turn more hateful than perdition. There's lots o' folks don't hold with 'em, but I seen God's truth – so I don't give a hang for what they say, unless of course they agree with me."

Cannon fire echoed through the belly of *Essex*. The women flinched with each loud explosion on deck. The cook removed some of the clutter from the chest and continued.

"Small wood splints to hold broken fingers and wrists in place. Lancets for boils and bleeding, tho' I don't 'old with bleeding, nor leeches – don't make no sense to bleed a man when we move heaven and earth to *stop* bleeding from wounds. Oil of wintergreen and *aqua vitae* for sore muscles. Quinine for inflammation and fever, if there ain't no turpentine. Opium pills and raw opium, as it's easy t' get in China, for relieving pain and bowel complaints, and bottles of laudanum and morphine for pain. Sometime I rub morphine into a wound. Castor oil as a purgative. Witch-hazel for skin conditions and itching. Rum we get from the stores. Patient drinks rum to deaden pain, but I've found splashing some on a wound sometimes keeps down redness and flare-ups around the edges durin' what they call the 'irritative period.'"

"So rum has some good use after all," Hannah said. "Hard to imagine."

"Sailors don't take sick much, but they break lots o' arms and legs fallin' from yardarms and such, so we splice and splint lots o' bones. Tweezers for picking lead out o' wounds and probin' for balls – better'n probin' with fingers. Collodion for pluggin' open wounds. Needles and horsehair thread for suturing. Small saw for amputations. Little chloroform left in this bottle. Save that for officers – rum does for sailors. Put a cloth over the mouth and nose and drip the chloroform onto the cloth until the patient's dreamin' of…er, home. Prob'ly enough 'ere to saw off an arm or leg, when the patient's dull from liquor and opiate. Only need ten minutes. Chips for the big splints. Sails for the shrouds."

"Are we doing the right thing for these wounded men?" Hannah said.

"For these gunshots and shell fragments, most important is to stop the bleeding. Then dig out the pieces and clean the wounds. Then dress, pack and bandage the wounds with one of those disinfectants. Apply the bandages wet and keep 'em wetted down. Sometimes we sew the large cuts together after cleaning and packing the wound – I draws the packin' out later when the wound's better. Keep the patient warm with blankets. Give 'em water when they wants it."

"It doesn't seem like much," Hannah said.

"After that, ma'am, it's in the hands of God."

The 6-pounder loading sequence was begun again, the aim of the gun adjusted for the change in the trader's position, and the gun fired. The shot exploded between the junk's forward and main trucks, and bamboo lugsails clattered down from both her

Fighting Fokie Tom

foremast and her mainmast into piles on the deck. Her stern swung around rapidly.

"Mains'l's parted from clew to earing, sir," the gunner reported. "Looks like she's turned tail for the old country."

The lorcha came down around the trader, all sail piled on, bowchaser manned by a dozen crewmen, firing as rapidly as they were able. Her first shell exploded off the clipper's larboard beam.

"Range 400 yards and closing, spherical case," Fletcher cried. "Clear that gun crew off her bow. Handsomely, now, *Essex*, and don't get excited. This is not a race. Follow your drill exactly no matter how long it takes. Remember your drill!"

Another shell from the lorcha's bowchaser exploded above and behind the stern, and shell fragments swept the deck and ripped into several sailors.

"Stern rifles to the fo'c's'le!" Captain Fitch shouted. "Help the wounded men down the ladder."

Fletcher saw blood trickling over the cheek and forearm of the gunner. "Gunner, you're hit!"

"Just a few scratches, Mr. Wood," murmured the gunner. He inspected his enigmatic officer where Fletcher stood against the tafferel in his tightly buttoned black frock coat. "I can stay on this deck as long as you, sir."

"I do not doubt it," Fletcher said.

"Ready!" the gunner shouted.

"Gun ready, sir!"

"Fire!"

Again the gun barked, lurched at her tether, and spewed boatloads of smoke.

"Keep at your drill, men," Fletcher yelled. "Don't stop to look. That slows you down. The gunner will tell you what happens."

Fletcher and the gunner peered through the smoke blown back in their faces by the breeze and saw the round explode over the bow of the lorcha. When the lorcha came on through the smoke, her bow was deserted – there was only the lonely gun, and a broken bowsprit. *Essex* raised a thundering cheer.

"Dead on!" the gunner cried. "Smack in her teeth!"

"Range 200 yards and closing," Fletcher said to the gunner. "Canister, now."

The gunner repeated the order. This time the crew of the *Essex*' little field gun was ready and waiting for the cartridge when it came up. The drill continued. The gunner chanted the drill to his crew, watching each man carefully, anticipating and correcting every possible deviation.

"Fire!"

The canister carried away a small corner of the lorcha's deckhouse, and the pirate swung to starboard to bring her waist guns into action. The *Essex* gun crew went right on about their business with hardly a glance at the lorcha.

"High and wide," the gunner shouted. "Range 100 yards, solid shot."

"She's coming around, Gunner," Fletcher said. "See if you can get one in under her bow and make 'er take on some water."

The next shot bounced off the hull of the lorcha and plopped into the water, but the following shot struck her hull between reinforcing beams, at the water line, and she started to ship water and gradually lost headway.

"Smoke and oakum, Gunner!" Fletcher yelled. "You knocked seven bells out of her! Now blast her gunnysack over galley stove back around to the Sandwich Islands."

The field gun at *Essex*' stern spoke again, sending a solid shot through the stern compartment below the gunwale of the lorcha and striking her rudderpost with a loud crack. When the helmsman next leaned on the tiller, the rudderpost broke apart and, rudderless, the lorcha floated away out of control.

"That thar junk's nigh 'bout fin out, Mr. Wood" the gunner said, with a wink back at Fletcher.

"And this is the damn finest gun crew," Fletcher said, "I have ever commanded. I have never seen such accurate fire." Every man swelled visibly with pride, but none more than *Essex*' own blood-spattered gunner.

A boy scampered up the ladder from the main deck and arrived at the gun breathless. "Beg pard'n, Mr. Gunner, sir," he burst out with eyes wide at the gunner's bloody appearance, "but which is Mr. Wood?"

"Standing there at the rail, boy."

"Mr. Wood, sir, I'm to say the captain sends his complements to yar gun crew, and that, and that the Fo'c's'le Rifles are plumb out of ammunition, and that if ya, if ya're done pummeling that there pirate, well sir, the captain'd be pleased for ya to carry this field gun up forward and try your luck up there."

"Said all that, did he?" Fletcher smiled at the wheezing boy.

"Yes, sir. Every word, sir." The boy grinned back.

"Well, now, you just skedaddle forward with my compliments to the captain and say the kedge anchor may now be dropped astern, and would the first mate come aft and lend a hand lifting this gun down to the main deck. Do you have all that, son?"

"Yes, sir! Every word, sir!" and the boy flew away down the ladder.

"Gunner, I am leaving the deck now to take the gun forward," Fletcher said, "and wish you would drop into the saloon long enough to have your wounds bandaged before you rejoin us on the fo'c's'le."

The gunner grinned, threw Fletcher a two-fingered salute, and went down the companionway to the saloon. The gun crew secured the field gun and its tools and moved it forward to where the crossjack yard still hung over the poop deck.

With the south junks silent, a crew could safely put out a long boat. The deck crew lifted the kedge anchor to the starboard rail, hauled it over the bulwark, and lowered it to the water, where the boat crew lashed it off the stern sheets. Once under the clipper's stern, the long boat took down one end of a hawser dropped from the deck above, bent it to the kedge, then rowed out against the current and lowered the kedge to the muddy bottom. Watch-tackle brought the hawser up taut until a fluke bit into the mud and kept the stern from pushing farther up onto the shoal.

Out of ammunition, the Fo'c's'le Rifles disbanded and the larboard watch went to move the field gun. No longer impeded by rifle fire, the north junks both swung about to bring the wind forward of their larboard beam and come up as close-hauled as their sails would allow. Their port guns opened with shot and shell, making the forecastle head of *Essex* too hazardous for work, so Micah broke off the song and sent the men at the capstan to help move the field gun forward.

The 6-pounder ascended to the crossjack, swung out over the poop deck rail, and descended to the main deck. Four sailors heaved at each wheel to roll the gun forward while the carpenter and another sailor hefted the trail with a handspike. They hoisted the gun to the forecastle head through drifts of black smoke from exploding shell, and the gun crew rolled the gun to a position just aft of the starboard cathead. From there it could fire under the ship's stays without interference from the spirit-sail yard or the jib-boom guy lines. Ammunition cases arrived in the lee of the forecastle deck. Still under fire from the north junks, the gun crew hurried to ready the gun.

"The gun'll be underfoot when we heave short to the anchor," the mate said, "but, if we put it to the weather side now, it'll blow away the jib-boom to get at them pirates.

Fighting Fokie Tom

We'll have to haul the gun over t' windward when we come outter the mud."

The mate went down on deck to get the second boat back aboard over the starboard rail. Captain Fitch called down to the mate to prepare to set sail. Reese relayed the order to the second mate.

"Micah, set your t'gallants fore and main, but point the yards into the wind and shake the canvas to keep her from pushin' her keel any further into the mud. We'll be wanting to fly outter here the moment she rights herself and pulls free, and not waste time putting on sail when them cutthroats is closest."

The gun crew laid out their tools and began the loading sequence with Fletcher as gun commander in place of the gunner.

"Range 400 yards, spherical case shot!"

"Remember your drill now. Pay no attention to all that shot and shell flying about. Steady, and by the numbers."

"Gun ready, sir!"

"Fire!"

The field gun leapt with the explosion of the charge and poured forth her white cloud of smoke and one second later, the round exploded high above the flared horns at the bow of the archipelago fisher.

"High and wide," called out the gunner as he came up on the forecastle.

"Gunner!" Fletcher cried. "Where have you been? We need you."

"Them ladies down there in the saloon is mighty...well, perlite, Mr. Wood. It was all a man could do just to tear hisself away from their company."

Examining the gunner's bandages, Fletcher said, "Well, Gunner, you look dressed for company to me. We have callers on the verandah right now, and I wonder if you would get the door?"

With a grin and a chuckle the gunner called out "range 200 yards, canister" and then he began a new loading sequence.

"Latch me gun tackles to her, me boyos," sang the gunner, "heave on the lines, and run me up into her hard and stiff. We'll prick more than a vent this time." The gunner lowered the elevation of the gun. "That's a nice tight fit in there between the rail and the stays, Mr. Wood. Comfy-like."

"Just knock a section out of the rail if it interferes with your firing, Gunner," Fletcher said, "but stay low and try not to bust the bowspr't stays."

With sidewise glance at Fletcher, the gunner dropped the muzzle a little more, shifted the trail to lead the closest junk, and fired the gun. The canister spread across the bow of the fisher, scattering the bowchaser gunners and shredding her lower foresail.

"One of you lift out that section of rail over the cathead," ordered the gunner. "It's spoiling my aim."

At two-minute intervals, and then more quickly as she recaptured her rhythm, *Essex* spread canister along the deck of each junk and sent the pirate crews scurrying for cover. On the larboard tack again, with lugsails once more against the masts and the wind in their teeth, the junks struggled in the swell to prevent the current from carrying them away from the line of attack. In consequence, their fire was imprecise, if not altogether wild at times. Shot splashed in the water all around *Essex*, or flew into the rigging, and finally the pirates ceased firing shell entirely. The mate brought the larboard watch back up on the forecastle and set them to heaving at the capstan.

Oh, Shenandoah,
We're bound to leave you.
Away, you rolling river,

Oh, Shenandoah,
We'll not deceive you.
Away, we're bound away,
'Cross the wide Missouri.

"Now let's see if we can re-design her along the water line just a little bit," said the gunner. "Range 200 yards, solid shot."

"Cartridge forward!"

"Cartridge forward, sir!"

"Load!"

"Ram!"

"Gun loaded, sir!"

3 *Essex* moved.

Her bow shifted to starboard with a groan and a bleat, loose lines slapped against her swaying masts, and the pirate junks slipped out of sight behind the bowsprit.

"Aw, now you lubbers've gone and spoilt my shot," the gunner said. "Stand to posts for moving the gun! We'll put her over to larboard where we can get a clear shot."

"Watch out for that junk bearing down on you, Gunner," Fletcher said

The wind shifted around to the south and gave the junks some headway across the current. The fisher came around close on *Essex*' larboard beam where she could bring her waist guns into action.

Evidently, the other pirate, the Ningpo trader with the blond Englishman at the helm, saw the field gun being moved to windward on *Essex*' forecastle. She came about quickly on her starboard tack and made ready to come back down across the clipper's bow. Then for no apparent reason the trader suddenly veered off toward the north and abandoned her companion junk.

The gunner aimed low and just ahead of the fisher, waiting a moment for her to come up.

"Ready!"

"Gun ready, sir!"

"Fire!"

The shot smashed into her at the waterline just behind the bow, opening a hole that began to fill with water. *Essex* broke out in wild cheering.

"Not yet, lads," Fletcher yelled. "We're not done yet. Shot that'd sink a frigate won't sink a junk. She's got probably a dozen bulkheads, and each compartment is watertight. We have to stitch her with shot at the waterline if we're to sink her."

The fisher returned fire with a shot that took away part of the forecastle deck and larboard rail, knocking men down, and a second shot that whizzed over the heads of the men heaving at the capstan. As the current pushed water into the fisher's first compartment and she fought to regain headway, *Essex* loaded canister into her field gun.

Then the clipper lurched again to starboard as she came groaning and creaking further off the shoal. Sailors that lay bleeding on the deck groaned with her.

Chips shifted the field gun trail to change the windage. The first canister cleared the crew from around the fisher's forward waist gun, and a second canister silenced the other gun. Reloading the field gun with solid shot, *Essex* sent ball after ball against the junk at her waterline amidships. Some just bounced off her, but others hammered at weaker sections of her hull and opened her up.

"Smack between wind and water!" Fletcher said.

Reese came over from the capstan and stood beside Fletcher.

"Gunner," Fletcher said, "we're going to sink this pirate. Take out her rudder then open up all her compartments."

"Yank," Reese said, "much as it galls me to say so, you do know your business."

"Easy money, Mr. Reese," replied Fletcher with a broad wink. "Nothin's better'n killin' pirates – 'cept maybe being one."

"Not today," Reese said.

The field gun got off three more solid shot before *Essex* came rolling off the shoal, taking out the fisher's rudder and hulling her twice. As the crew struggled to get *Essex* under control, Fletcher looked north into the offing where the Ningpo trader was coming about out of range of *Essex*, then watched the archipelago fisher as she shipped a sea of water and swirled away in the grip of the current. She sank fast in the shallows and came to rest with her black-bordered red flag still flying at her masthead high over the swell.

Low tide will bring her back out each night, thought Fletcher, and she'll lay there on the mud under the moonlight like a ghost until she breaks up.

"Heave short," yelled the captain from the poop deck.

The mate quickly piled on hands at the capstan and brought *Essex* around to east-north-east. The wind filled the sails and together with the current strained the kedge hawser, threatening to push her over to leeward, until the second mate was able to get the yards braced back around on the other tack and shake the sails.

Fletcher kept watch on the Ningpo trader, where she lay hove to above the island outside of the current, and wondered if she would attempt one more dash at *Essex* to return some of the punishment the pirates had received. The clipper swung on her tether and bumped along the shoal as she warped up to her anchor.

"Up and down!" the mate yelled.

Cornelius Fitch gave a succession of orders closely timed to get *Essex* under way and prevent her from being carried back onto the shoal. No longer aground now, the maneuver was much the same as getting the ship under way from any shallow anchorage, except for the kedge tethered to her stern and the three-knot current.

"Up helm!"

"Up helm, sir" repeated the helmsman, spinning the top of the wheel over to his left. The rudder swung to starboard, the current pushed the ship's stern around to larboard, and she caught some wind on her sails.

"Square tops'ls and t'gallants!"

"Squaring sail, sir!" responded the second mate. When the fore, main, and mizzen topsails and topgallants were all set and squared, the south wind began to push on the sails and force *Essex* ahead against the current. But *Essex* merely hung motionless in the flow, a prisoner suspended between the opposing forces of wind and water.

Ptolemy Reese stared aft the length of the ship at the captain. The wrong command now would put them back on the shoal – at the mercy of the pirates again. The men of his watch were already on the foreyard, and had the gaskets off and were ready to let go.

Set and square your fore course, thought Fletcher, then slip your kedge when she tugs at the hawser. Whatever else you do, Captain, don't slip your kedge without first setting more sail.

In an instant, the unfamiliar equation of wind and water and vessel was calculated and re-calculated in the mind of Cornelius Fitch, until the potential consequences of each command were clear, and he could see in his mind how the vessel should move.

"Set the fore course and jib!"

"Set fore course and jib," answered Reese. The mainsail on the lowest yard of the foremast was lowered and sheeted home, the yard was braced square, and the jib sail was hauled up on the stay above the bowsprit. *Essex* started to move against the current.

"Break her out!"

"Break her out, sir!" Reese yelled, and the watch heaved on the capstan and pulled the small bower free from the muddy bottom.

"Anchor's a-weigh!" *Essex* yanked her tether. The hawser creaked.

"Slip the kedge!"

"Slip the kedge, sir!" echoed the starbolines tending the hawser. The line was cut and slipped overboard as *Essex* gathered headway – with pirates still in the offing, there was no time to take aboard the expendable kedge anchor. The small bower anchor was brought up to the hawse-hole and left hanging, and the capstan was locked with several pawls. The small bower would have to wait while *Essex* came about in the channel.

"Hands prepare to wear ship!"

"Helmsman up your helm," the captain said.

"Up helm, sir," repeated the helmsman.

"Wear-O! Square the yards!"

Micah set his men to quickly bracing the mizzen yards around to the larboard tack, and then did the same for the mainyards. The larboard watch braced around the fore yards square to the following wind. The topsails and topgallants snapped and filled.

"Headsheets, Mr. Reese!"

"Shifting headsheets, sir!"

The first mate sent his watch to shift the headsails over to the new tack. *Essex* brought the wind across her stern to her larboard quarter and came around into the channel, once again bound north toward Gutzlaff Island and sailing large.

"Set the mains'l!"

The starbolines leapt into the rigging and loosed the main course from the lowest yard on the mainmast. Deck hands sheeted the huge sail home, and it stretched and filled and jammed the clipper forward. As the exultant cheering on board *Essex* faded away, and captain and crew began to mull over the prospect of continuing through these narrow seas without a pilot.

"Sail ho!" came a cry from the rigging.

"Where away?"

"Off the larboard beam, sir. That pirate's coming down on us!"

The Ningpo trader was moving fast to interdict *Essex*. The junk was free now of the tidal currant that flowed around East Volcano Island. The wind was on her starboard beam and nothing held her back. While *Essex* had busied herself with getting under way, the junk quietly approached to within 800 yards. She sent her greetings. A 12-pound ball from her bowchaser splashed under *Essex*' bow.

"Gunner!" screamed the first mate. "Get your bleedin' gun crew back up to the fo'c's'le now!" The gun crew came running from all quarters of the ship, released the field gun from its deck lashings, and resumed their drill like old hands. The first mate's harsh order banished from the mind of the gunner any thought of the 24-pounders in the waist of *Essex*, at least until the trader's big gun started ripping the clipper's forecastle apart, but by then there was no time to get a waist gun into action and little room to maneuver the ship.

"Range 800 yards and closing, solid shot."

The junk's bowchaser roared and poured out a cloud of smoke and another twelve-pound ball smashed through the larboard bulwark, carried away the two forecastle ladders, and tore out a section of the starboard bulwark.

"Return fire!" the captain shouted.

The gunner and carpenter wrestled the carriage around to point the gun at the junk.

洋神 *Yang Shen*   *James Lande* 藍德

The gunner studied the rise and fall of the muzzle-sight and, thinking to fire on the up swell, yelled his order at the bottom of the swell. The gun belched out fire and smoke and her shot ricocheted off the mainmast and exploded into the deckhouse of the junk.

"That one's in up to the hitches, Mr. Wood!" the gunner yelled.

The junk returned fire and carried away the forecastle rail with a crash and a burst of splintered wood two feet behind Fletcher. The gunner was felled by flying debris.

"Reese!" Fletcher snatched up the little old Irishman and carried him to the where the forecastle ladder had been. "My gunner's down. Please take him below." Fletcher gently passed the gunner down to the first mate. Blood was coursing from around a large piece of the splintered wood railing embedded in the gunner's chest. Fletcher returned to the gun crew. "Well, now we're down to the jerky and beans," he said just loud enough to be heard above the din. "Gentlemen, please silence that gun."

"Range 400 yards and closing, solid shot," Fletcher shouted. The gun crew set to their work with grim determination. When they glanced at the junk flying down at them, they imagined they could see the sweaty faces of the Chinese pirates on the junk working feverishly to load and fire their gun. At the tiller atop the deckhouse, they clearly saw the blonde-haired Englishman.

Merchant and pirate exchanged shots again. The junk's ball crashed through the forecastle rail forward of the field gun and tore out a chunk of the larboard cathead. Fletcher and the carpenter heaved the trail of the carriage to allow for the shifting positions of the duelists, and waited for the bottom of the swell, but this time Fletcher gave the order a moment earlier. The shot ripped through the crossbeam of the junk's bow, splintered the wooden carriage of the bowchaser, and ricocheted through the foremast tabernacle. When the smoke cleared, the muzzle of the bowchaser lay on the deck with the foremast lugsail in a pile on top of the disabled gun.

There Gunner, Fletcher thought, that put a line on it!

"Once more men," Fletcher said. "You bloodied her nose. Now cut her lip."

"Range 100 yards, solid shot."

"Cartridge forward!"

"Load!"

"Ram!"

"Ready!"

"Fire!"

4 *Essex* shook and filled her main course, braced up her yards, brought her head up into the wind and surged ahead. Fletcher ambled aft from the forecastle to the poop deck, following along opposite the wounded junk as *Essex* passed her, surveying the smashed wales under the trader's square bow, the water flowing slowly into her forward compartments, and the debris of the broken bowchaser littering her forward deck. He climbed the ladder to the poop deck and went aft to the tafferel. She wouldn't sink, of course, as there were perhaps ten more compartments still undamaged and watertight, but she would limp about. She certainly wouldn't cut and thrust anymore for a while.

Suddenly he was there, wavering amidst the clutter of his cannon, gunpowder-blackened hands on his hips, white Crimean shirt soaked with blood and sea-water, blonde hair excited by the breeze, scowling defiantly at the author of his dismemberment. Fletcher Thorson Wood straightened up and faced Fokie Tom across the receding water, returning his gaze. The pirate abruptly snatched a revolver from under his belt, and before anyone aboard *Essex* could fetch and aim a musket, Tom had Fletcher in his sights.

Fighting Fokie Tom

More chagrined than surprised at being taken unawares, Fletcher could only stare back at Tom across the gun sights. The final futile gesture of a beaten man, thought Fletcher, a pistol shot from a pitching deck across fifty yards of water. Go ahead, pull the trigger. It is not my destiny to be killed by a Parthian shot.

A wisp of blue smoke purled around Tom's pistol and a strangled report drifted across the water. *Essex* stared dumfounded at Fletcher – waiting for him to tumble to the deck. Then Tom screamed his favorite epithet and bent over the revolver, working furiously to reload. Wet powder! A chorus of jeers and catcalls shot up out of *Essex* and the perplexed passengers let loose their breath. When Tom looked up again, the ship was well beyond the range of both pistol shot and pirate wrath. He hurled his pistol to the deck and glared after the retreating clipper.

Essex contemplated the helpless pirate hulk as it slowly swung away with the current, and from the tafferel Fletcher touched two fingers to his forehead in an ambiguous gesture mixed of salute, farewell, and relief.

Nothing better'n killin' pirates, he thought. Unless it's bein' a pirate yourself.

洋神 *Yang Shen*　　　　　　　　　　　　　　　　　　　　　　*James Lande* 藍德

Dramatis Personae: Chapter 6

Yang Fang 楊坊, *aka* Takee	president of *T'ai Chi* (Takee) bank 泰記行, head of Ningpo Guild in Shang-hai
Hsüeh Huan 薛煥	(brevet) governor of Kiangsu Province, imperial commissioner (acting) for the five treaty ports

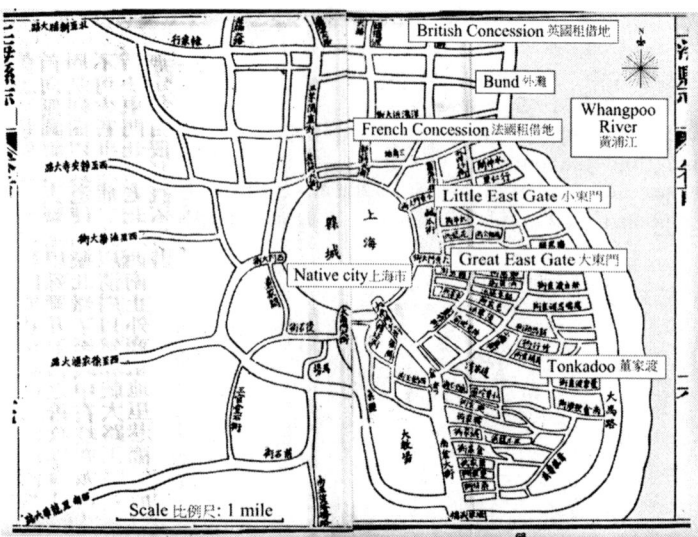

Shang-hai Native City
(based on Shang-hai County Gazetteer, 1873)

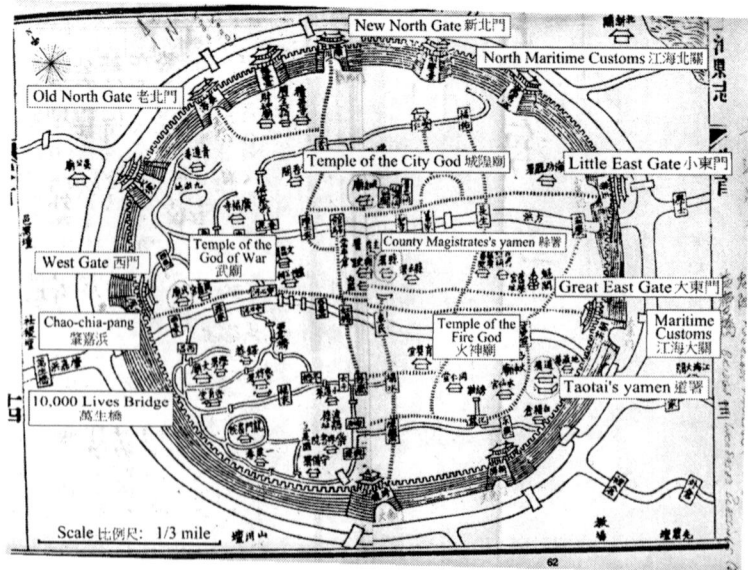

Shang-hai Native City Detail
(based on Shang-hai County Gazetteer, 1873)

94　　　　　　　　　　　　　　　　　　　　　　*Sowing Foreign Discord*

Chapter 6: Sowing Foreign Discord
Thursday, April 19, 1860, 10:30am

"大老爺大老爺 *Ta-lao-yeh, Ta-lao-yeh* Old Master, Old Master. A runner from Wu *Ta-jen*. The runner has just arrived to say that Wu *Ta-jen* is now on his way from the American consulate to call upon you, and that he will quickly arrive."

"Very well, make preparations," Yang Fang replied, dismissing his head manager with a dignified nod.

"是大老爺 yes *Ta-lao-yeh*," the head manager said. Smiling, the head manager 經手 bowed to display to his Old Master the red tassel atop his shiny silk cap, stepped back once, straightened up and turned through the door, scattering a covey of deputy managers 副手 with a hissed "hey! clear out 走開阿!"

Through the open door of his office, the Old Master watched with pursed lips holding a smile in check while his head manager swaggered down the hallway, his hands flinging themselves out toward all of the four directions like the exaggerated gesticulations of an arrogant stage actor. Upon each flick of the manager's wrist, a small troupe of clerks and apprentices hurled themselves away from stage center to fall upon some hapless task that needed doing before his Excellency the *tao-t'ai* arrived at the bank to honor their Old Master.

So, Wu *Ta-jen* comes from the Americans, thought Yang Fang. I dare say he has been kowtowing to them and asking to borrow their troops to help fight the longhaired rebels 向他們叩頭清借兵助剿. Since the rebels have attacked Hang-chou and slaughtered tens of thousands, and other cities and towns much closer are falling to rebel general Li Hsu-ch'eng's army, it cannot be too soon to make inquiries among the foreigners, even if at the same time we war with the English and French. The foreigners will protect their trade at Shang-hai regardless of whether they fight the Emperor at T'ien-chin. But how to convince them to commit their troops to defend Shanghai? Even if they understand we Chinese are too weak to defend Shang-hai. Even if they are concerned that officials who support their trade will be punished if Chiang-nan 江南 – the region south of the river – falls to the T'ai-p'ing rebels and Su-chou and Shang-hai are lost. Even if they cared that we officials will be stripped of our offices, our rank, our wealth, and banished to some far frontier, or ordered to commit suicide, the foreigners still would not lend their troops.

Yang Fang had come to Shanghai from Ningpo many years before and distinguished himself early by becoming a banker and silk merchant, then a comprador for *Ewo* 怡和, Jardine Matheson and Co., where he learned to understand and even speak some amount of English. As agent and intermediary, the comprador managed the firm's Chinese employees and transacted business with native suppliers and customers. Yang Fang prospered as comprador, accumulating in less than ten years the extraordinary amount of some several million taels, which required infinite ingenuity to conceal from rapacious officials of the empire. He also learned much about dealing with foreigners, such that he rose quickly in the estimation of a group of powerful officials and merchants relocated to Shanghai from the province of Chekiang, the Chekiang clique of Shanghai, of whose members one of the most powerful was *Tao-t'ai* Wu Hsü.

His brothers in the Chekiang clique encouraged Yang Fang to become active in civil and military affairs. When the Small Swords, also called Triads, attacked and occupied Shanghai in 1853, Yang Fang joined the struggle to dislodge them, helping to build a wall of rammed earth that shut up the Triads inside the native city and cut off

洋神 *Yang Shen* James Lande 藍德

supplies smuggled from the foreign settlement. Combined with the French naval bombardment that breached the city wall, and the attack of French regulars and imperial troops, Yang Fang's efforts were regarded by the Chinese as crucial in forcing the eventual withdrawal of the enemy from the native city, and promotion in rank and office soon followed.

Yang Fang kept his relationship with Jardine's after leaving the firm to devote his full attention to his own enterprises, which included a pawnshop in the native city, and his association with foreign merchants proved an ever more prosperous adjunct to his other banking, silk, and trade interests. Inevitably, he ascended into the Kiangsu provincial gentry, through the purchase of the opaque blue button of a 4th-rank official for 30,000 taels, and then purchased his way up through several posts to his present office of provincial salt comptroller 鹽運使司. He also was expectant 候選 *Su-Sung-T'ai tao-t'ai* – when the office became vacant, he expected to fill it next, if enough money and influence could be purveyed to secure the appointment.

The banker Yang Fang had more than enough of both. What power his wealth did not procure came from the support of his friends from Chekiang. He was influential in the Ningpo Guild 四明公所, a native-place association for immigrants to Shanghai from Ningpo. He established and supported two foundling homes in the city, and served as treasurer for the Shanghai "Houseless Refugees Fund," which collected large donations from foreigners to provide some trifling relief for the fluctuating population in Shanghai of refugees from the Taiping rebels. He helped provide funding for the local Pirate Suppression Bureau 捕盜局, which paid the American Ghent and the crew of the paddle-wheel steamer *Confucius* to protect shipping and hunt pirates. And he came to handle much of Wu Hsü's private business with foreigners, in order to help the *tao-t'ai* avoid the imperial prohibition against mandarins engaging in trade. If there was a weakness in dealing with officials that was greater than their own avarice, it was the persistent risk of impeachment and degradation to lower rank, exile, or even death should the emperor learn of their malfeasance in office. More than one mandarin had been strangled for his crimes.

Yang Fang rose stiffly and went to a rosewood wardrobe in a corner of the office. He took out his surcoat with the embroidered square depicting the 4th-rank official's wild goose among the clouds, his official's necklace of 108 beads of precious stones, and from the hat cupboard his official's summer hat with the lapis lazuli button. As he donned this finery, and thereby effected the change from banker to minister of his emperor, his mind was still occupied with the well-officered professional troops of the foreigners, armed with modern weapons, and trained in modern strategy and tactics.

If we could just borrow troops like them, he thought, from the English and French, even from the Americans. Unfortunately, the English and French are also our enemies. No matter how cleverly the governors and provincial treasurers and *tao-t'ais* all scheme to convince the foreigners to help fight the T'ai-p'ing rebels, the foreigners still regard being defended by your enemy as a paradox 矛盾.

Outside the bank, some distance up Barrier Road, the apprentice posted to watch for the *taotai* saw in the distance the character *tao* 道 dancing above the crowd, heard the clash of the gong and counted eleven strokes, and sprinted back down Barrier Road to Takee Bank to give the alert. Accountants and shroffs roused themselves with the dignity of inner office dwellers to tidy their gowns and jackets, and the tellers and canvassers of the outer office hustled to remove their work frocks and put their desks in order. Warehouseman heated water for tea and arranged the props of the reception hall, the chairs, stools, tables, screens, and small and large porcelain vases, and sent the apprentices rushing about for boxes and tins of delicacies to offer guests and small bric-a-brac to display on the tables. Official's-cap chairs 官帽倚 – square-backed armchairs of dark, satin-finished East Indian rosewood 老花梨木 – were set upon a raised dais at the end of the hall farthest from the entrance. These were chairs-of-honor, with a strut to raise the feet off the drafty dais, and a back rail projecting from each side like the wings on the mandarin's cap of earlier dynasties. Over the back and seat of these chairs were thrown folds of rich silk fabric brocaded with stylized waves and mountains, and before the chairs were set brocade-covered footstools. Around the hall, pairs of armless straight-backed rosewood chairs were arranged on each side of small tables, and thick, richly decorated carpets were unrolled and laid on the floor in front of the furniture. Gradually the flurry of re-arranging the hall for receiving officials in state subsided, the actors all came to rest at their marks beside their desks in the offices, or in the reception hall, and the head manager appeared again at Yang Fang's door.

"都準備好了大老爺 all is prepared, *Tu-lao-yeh*," the head manager said. With studied dignity, the Old Master arose from his desk, took up his official cap and placed it on his head, and left his office, pacing slowly toward the entrance of the bank. One by one, the head manager and four deputy managers fell in behind him, hands hidden in sleeves and eyes half-closed, as if these affairs were of so little importance to such eminent men that sleep was the only really appropriate response.

Yang Fang and his managers all came out into the middle of the street, where the traffic was forced to wind around them, and there they suddenly came alive with large, animated grins and grasped their hands and shook them before their bowed heads. This performance began well before the red umbrella leading the *taotai*'s procession ever turned the corner, and did not stop until the *taotai* had arrived, alighted, advanced, and presented his greeting card. The *taotai* stood serenely before them all, returning their courtesies midst the clamor of gongs, horns and firecrackers set off by bank employees, and then proceeded into the building.

The deputy managers outside the entrance continued to bow after the *taotai* passed to be sure all in the Wu Hsü's entourage were witness to their reverence and none could suspect their sincerity. The *taotai* was Shanghai's highest-ranking mandarin, who every day sentenced men to prison and exile, to strangulation and decapitation, and even flaying alive. Offending even the lowliest of his retainers risked not just death and disembowelment, but also the destruction of one's entire family, living and dead – Manchu vengeance embraced even the desecration of the graves of ancestors, and the scattering of their bones to the four winds.

2 Over the entrance to the bank hung a wide plank of wood darkened by years of accumulated grime, incense soot and firecracker smoke, in which were carved the characters for the name of Takee Bank, T'ai-chi Hang 泰記行. Between the red lacquered columns lining the entranceway, other similar old planks, carved with a variety of honorific sentiments and classical allusions, hung from the ceiling in tiers receding to the portal of the reception hall. Yang Fang led the *taotai* to the position of honor, and joined him sitting upon the dais while the *taotai*'s retinue filed in along one side of the hall, and the bank managers and higher-level employees formed a line on the opposite side of the hall. Polite conversation ensued, and greetings and felicitations were exchanged between the Old Master and his Honored Guest, and with important bank functionaries who were in the next echelon of importance in the Shanghai Banking Trade Guild 上海錢業公所, or in the Ningpo Guild. Shortly, the banker and the *taotai* withdrew from the gathering, leaving the managers to preside, and retired to the banker's office for private conversation. Here, beyond the sight and hearing of others, the two men enjoyed the familiarity of long years of association that required fewer formalities. The *taotai*, however, did not remove his cap.

"I cannot stay long," Wu Hsü said, "as I must still go to the county *ya-men* 衙門 and continue a review of open and delayed judicial cases with Magistrate Liu."

"A magistrate reviewing cases? Should that not be a prefect, or someone with higher authority?"

"The cases are mine, sent to the *tao-t'ai* for review. Magistrate Liu helps me with them. He will be a *tao-t'ai* one day."

"Then I shall not delay. Did you learn anything of interest from the American consul?" Yang Fang gestured slightly to a clerk outside the door to bring tea.

"We must give this business of borrowing troops more consideration. The American consul is not encouraging about keeping an American warship, and its marines, at Shang-hai, and absolutely does not want American soldiers to fight the rebels. We can speak again with the American merchant Elias Cage, urge him to press the American consul for an American warship at Shang-hai, but the Americans will never march to Su-chou, I'm sure of that. We must increase our effort with the English and French, especially the French. They would like the glory."

"Soon now, the time will arrive when we will be forced to act. The rebels will come before long, the foreign troops are leaving Shang-hai to go to T'ien-chin, and the Emperor is going to demand that we defend Chiang-nan."

"Even if the foreigners eventually decide to lend troops to fight the rebels, perhaps even defend Su-chou, it may not be in time to prevent a rebel victory at Shang-hai. I am in desperate straits 陷入絕境, and feeling like this is the end of my road 感到今日暮途窮. Elder brother 大哥, where do you think I can get soldiers?"

"You know better than I," Yang Fang said, "that we have no Chinese soldiers to defend Chiang-nan. The Eight Banners 八旗 are of little use. More than half are garrisoned around Pei-ching to protect the Emperor, and they all will be very busy in a month or two, when the English and French arrive at T'ien-chin and, perhaps, march on the capital."

The Eight Banners, thought Wu Hsü, of the Manchu imperial army have disintegrated over the past hundreds of years in the absence of serious warfare, and under a patrimony that has diminished their vitality. Once they were a great army of desert warriors, gathered together by the Manchu general Nurhaci to conquer China. Now Manchu generals with little interest in the plight of their Chinese counterparts command the 250,000 bannermen. If a city falls, the Chinese officials would be punished long before any Eight Banner generals.

"Troops of the Green Flag 綠營," Yang Fang said, "are few in number and they do not care to fight away from their homes. They carry out so many civilian tasks, even provide labor for public works, that they have little time for military training. Assembled in large forces from diverse provinces, Green Flag troops have no common origins, language, or customs – they even eat different foods, so they do not fight well together."

"They seem few," Wu Hsü said, "because they are dispersed to the four winds at posts of less than 1000 men. Actually, there are over 600,000 Green Flag troops commanded by provincial governors-general and governors. However, like the Eight Banners, the Green Flag army has declined. Both are hereditary armies with too many special privileges, land grants, pensions, allotments of rice and cloth, preference before the law. The soldiers are poorly trained and impoverished – even the Kuang-chou 廣州

洋神 *Yang Shen*   *James Lande* 藍德

men in the British coolie-corps are paid more – and demoralized by officers who routinely filch part of their men's allowances, officers dedicated to maintaining their own privileges and perquisites, not to improving the fighting capability of their armies. Their weapons are primitive – pikes, fowling pieces, and clumsy gingals. Their strategy is little advanced over thousand-year-old Sun Tzu 孫子, they know nothing of modern tactics, cannot use modern small arms effectively, and still less modern artillery."

"According to Tseng Kuo-fan 曾國藩," Yang Fang said, "Green Flag armies fire at their enemy with cannon and matchlocks from a great distance, but have never met a T'ai-p'ing army face-to-face in hand-to-hand fighting."

"The Eight Banners and the Green Flag armies are not choices," Wu Hsü said, with only a little exasperation, less at the wily banker than at the obstacles an unrelenting fate seemed always to be setting in the path of his ambition. "The imperial court will not allow us to raise any but a local force."

Yang Fang leaned back, steepled his fingers, and smiled warmly at his friend. The banker's prominent cheekbones and pointed chin gave his face a triangular shape, like a fox with pointed ears and a sharp little nose, thought Wu Hsü – the same gaunt shape of the faces of people who did not eat half so well. His face showed some of the damage done to his body by malarial fever during his years in Shanghai. Wu recalled how Yang's large ears poked out from beneath his official's cap like the handles on an old wine pot. They accentuated the fox-like aspect in his face, but his large ears had also always brought Yang Fang much good luck. Wu Hsü looked away. Then he too smiled his thin smile and sat back into his chair.

"As always, Elder Brother," Wu Hsü said, "you are both wise and patient. Wise to examine calmly the entire situation, and patient with my abruptness. Forgive me, as I spend too much time among uncultured foreigners. Please continue."

"吳大人我實在不敢當 Wu *Ta-jen*, I most certainly dare not presume. It is you who taught me to try to understand the strange ways of the foreigners, raised me up in the estimation of the important men of our Ning-po guildhall, and directed my steps into official office. Without your patronage, I would be a dirty coolie sweating under bales of silk carried between junk and godown. Instead, I wear silk robes – a rich merchant and high official. I dare not presume to attain the wisdom of Wu *Ta-jen*."

"那裏那裏 not so, not so." Both men smiled self-consciously at this ritual exchange. Wu Hsü felt a trifle chagrined that his impatience had provoked from his older protégé this rote, if nonetheless sincere, homage, as their friendship went so far back that such courtesies were usually unnecessary. Yang Fang was mildly amused at the younger man's discomfiture, but pleased that Wu Hsü's slip of composure allowed a rare opportunity to express gratitude.

"團練 local militia," Yang Fang said, "are useful to fight longhaired rebels foraging near villages, but a militia is only temporary, a few hundred non-professional conscripts and rowdies called together from the fields to defend their villages and drilled only during the spare time between harvests."

"Local militia," Wu Hsü said, "can barely defend themselves and their property from local banditti and pirates because they are equipped with nothing more than lanterns and long pikes. They are small and disorganized, and too unprofessional to contest with T'ai-p'ing armies for the control of walled cities and great highroads."

"勇 braves are more professional than militia," Yang Fang said. "They can be formed and disbanded by the authority of provincial and local officials, without central government approval, and the cost of their pay and rations can be met by voluntary or compulsory contributions from local gentry, the imposition of local taxes, and in Shanghai from customs revenues."

"Small units of braves gathered in armies of 1000," Wu Hsü said, "have some limited offensive capability, but only when attached to regular armies commanded by professional officers. Civil officials 文官 are not soldiers, not like military mandarins 武官. Civil officials are graduates of literature, so how can we expect them to lead braves effectively?"

"勇營 the provincial armies are better led," Yang Fang said, "better cared for, and better trained than imperial Eight Banner and Green Flag armies, or local militia and braves. The Hu-nan Army 湘軍 has engaged close to 120,000 soldiers taken from militia and braves for the siege of Nan-ching, and in fighting T'ai-p'ing armies far inland."

The large provincial armies, thought Wu Hsü, now besieging Nan-ching are unique, developed according the ideas of Ch'i Chi-kuang 戚繼光. Ch'i wrote in the Ming Dynasty about small armies of soldiers from the same region, loyal to a heroic leader who recruits his own officers, with strict discipline and careful training. General Tseng Kuo-fan's Hu-nan Army is such an army, independent of the meddling local authorities, with officers advanced on merit, and no corruption.

"The Hu-nan Army cannot come to Shang-hai," Wu Hsü said. "The Emperor will not allow it. Our imperial court, I fear, does not completely trust Tseng Kuo-fan, and suspiciously imagines so large a force could oppose even the Emperor – no matter that at this very moment the Hu-nan Army fights to defend the Emperor against the T'ai-p'ing in An-hui Province. So, we are left with braves and militia."

"And foreigners," Yang Fang said.

"But the foreigners are leaving Shanghai and going to T'ien-chin," Wu Hsü said, his aggravation rising. "Even after the hostilities in the north, and the English and French have their treaties, it remains clear from what the foreign consuls tell me that the foreign officials still will not interfere in the rebellion. No matter how much the foreign merchants want foreign troops to fight the T'ai-p'ing rebels, the foreign officials still fear sinking so deeply into the mud of China they can never pull themselves free."

"我要雇外國列兵 I want to hire a private army of foreign soldiers," Yang Fang said, quietly. "The only choice I see left is to hire Westerners as mercenaries 雇傭洋兵, like those that fight with the longhaired rebels, but where to find good men? A thousand foreigners at Shanghai will fight for silver, but all of them are screwed-up drunken rowdies 亂七八糟酒鬼. My paddle-wheel boat captain, Ghent, is the only reliable leader among them, but he will not leave the river to fight on land, and he only employs Chinese, and the men from Manila, and will not have white-men because, he says, they are all trash."

"Hmmm. Even if we wanted to spend the large amounts that would cost, how would we control foreigners?"

"As we control the foreigners of our Pirate Suppression Bureau," Yang Fang said. "I have some experience with them now. My fearless Admiral Ghent declines to fight on land, but I think that a land force similar to his water force, with trained soldiers led by officers like the Admiral, under our control just like the Admiral, is a necessary adjunct to any force of braves and militia. We have seen the foreigners fight many times in twenty years. They have excellent officers, modern weapons, and good training. Their new-style muskets – rifles – and artillery have tremendous firepower, they go anywhere in swift paddle-wheel gunboats, and their soldiers learn tactics and have astonishing bravery under fire. A handful of them can defeat regiments of rebels."

"Will mercenaries be as good as that?" mused Wu Hsü. "To equip such a force with muskets and cannon is not easy, as such are difficult to buy, and paddle-wheel boats are almost impossible. And no army, not even a foreign army, can win battles without great leaders, great generals who know how to fight and can lead men."

Yang Fang's enthusiasm faltered with this thought. "Yes. Where to find a leader?" he wondered. "Perhaps, if we cannot borrow their troops, the English or the French will at least let us borrow some of their officers."

"Here we deal with a different class of men," the *taotai* said. "English army officers will behave differently from English officials and merchants. Even if officers could be detached for Chinese service, would they be willing to lead mercenaries?"

"While their country is at war with us? I will have inquiries made among the foreign merchants to find out how they receive this idea, and if they would urge it upon their consuls."

"All I have seen," Wu Hsü said, "tells me that the English army and navy follow the instructions of the English officials. Once again, we must discover a way to compel the English officials to do as we wish."

Yang Fang swallowed a reply that he had seen instances of the opposite case, English officers ordering about English officials, but realized they may have been exceptions. Even after all his years as a comprador at *Yi-ho* 怡和, Jardine Matheson and Co., Englishmen were still a fatiguing mystery, and he still did not truly comprehend at all the complex relationships between English merchants, military officers and civil officials. He felt the need for lighter conversation.

"The English and French are eating your sheep and pigs at Ting-hai 定海."

"Mine?" Wu Hsü was incredulous.

"Yes," Yang Fang said, laughing. "阿拉同鄉者夢玉山 our hometown man Meng Yu-shan, who as you know also is a member of our Ning-po Guild here in Shang-hai, anticipated the foreigners would occupy Chu-shan again and that large sales could be made to the English and French. He sent word some time ago that he wished to make a loan with my T'ai-chi Hang to speculate in supplies for the commissariat. Some of the money I lent to him came from your private account, 5000 taels due on the 20th of next month, just some small business."

"What will be the profit?"

"1000 taels, because of the shortness of the term."

"Good, good. Anything else?"

"Trade with Japan seems to be progressing, so I am planning to start shipping merchandise to Nagasaki later this year. If you wish, I can invest from your private account in the venture."

"What sort of things can we sell to Japan?"

"Tortoise-shell is in demand by artisans. Chinese herbal medicines are also sold there, so I will also send jars of dragon's foam, and other medicines. And there is always a market for Chinese silk among the wealthy."

"Truly, the friendship of merchants makes one rich."

"豈敢豈敢 not at all, not at all."

I can only hope, thought Yang Fang, that the friendship of officials will not impoverish me.

Yang Fang picked up his cup, lifted the delicately enamled porcelain cover, and used the edge to slowly push to the back of the cup the leaves and stems floating on the surface of the tea. He took a sip, and then asked, "Where is Hsüeh *Ta-jen* staying?"

The taotai's expression did not change, but he did heave a small sigh. "In my *ya-*

洋神 *Yang Shen*   James Lande 藍德

men. It is not easy for any of the *ya-men* in Shang-hai, with so many provincial officials fleeing T'ai-p'ing rebels threatening Su-chou and crowding together into our few accommodations, but it is especially awkward to have a governor of the province just across the courtyard from your bedchamber. I suggested he might find it more comfortable to reside in one of our local temples, of the City God, or the God of War. But because he himself was the Shang-hai *tao-t'ai* three years ago, he regards my *ya-men* as his own, even showed me the renovations made when he lived there. However, he spends much time at the county *ya-men* each day, and keeps to himself at night."

"It could be worse," Yang Fang said. "You could have *both* governors of the province at your door, but Governor Hsü Yu-jen stays at Su-chou to defend his city. Hsüeh *Ta-jen*, being an expert on foreigners, can be more useful here in Shanghai. What is he doing at the county *ya-men*?"

"Today, I believe he is reviewing death sentences for retrial. He has commandeered part of that huge staff the magistrate pays for, because he has so many more responsibilities now as brevet governor 巡撫銜. Soon he will be five-ports commissioner as well, so he has little choice but to employ many private secretaries, none of whom will delay to grovel before him now that he is the new governor. My own organization is small, and he did not bring many of his own people with him, so he would be much more understaffed in my *ya-men*. I think, also, that the governor finds the magistrate's company more congenial."

"Do you think the governor will push us aside so he can build his own following?"

"No, I do not worry about that. The magistrate is too small a fish and, if anything, has to take care the governor does not swallow him up. Hsüeh *Ta-jen* is comparatively simple, and Magistrate Liu is not one to take advantage. Actually, the magistrate is remarkably capable and dedicated, and believes sincerely in his role as parent to the ordinary people 父母官. He has little time and no patience for politics. I am coming to depend upon him though, and I believe he will be a great help when it comes time to fight T'ai-p'ing rebels."

"It is too bad he is not from Ning-po," Yang Fang said. "Our Ning-po people can use strong men such as Magistrate Liu, if they show promise."

"Perhaps. But I wonder if sometimes we rely overmuch on the support of native-place relationships. In business, of course they absolutely are necessary, but in government, perhaps less so. Native-place ties do not appeal so much to an upright official like the magistrate, who purposely avoids entanglements that interfere with his official responsibilities. He does not see provinces like Ho-nan 河南, Che-chiang, or Ssü-ch'uan 四川 as readily as he sees a country he calls China 中國. This comes out of the struggle with these foreigners, when some people realize that we cannot prevail against foreigners as long as we are divided by petty regional jealousies."

"Elder brother, I have not heard you express such an idea before," Yang Fang said.

"Hsüeh *Ta-jen* likes to talk in that way. It is one reason, I suspect, that he is so popular with the British. A man who is respected by both his Emperor and his enemies is not a man to take lightly."

3   Late afternoon shadows had begun to lengthen in the foreign settlement as the *taotai*'s noisy entourage turned south on Barrier Road and set out for the native city. It was almost six *li* – two English miles – from Takee Bank to the county *ya-men*, and half a mile further to the *taotai*'s *ya-men*. Wu Hsü opened the curtains slightly and looked out on the country to the west, still broad mud flats mostly. There were more dwellings along the roadside, if that was what these filthy structures could be called, little houses of common people, with tiny, trash-filled courtyards jammed together like bricks on

洋神 *Yang Shen*   *James Lande* 藍德

edge, and the squalid shelters of ragged beggars and thieves mortared in between.

On the wide thoroughfare, his bearers were impeded less by foot traffic and could make better time, but they would slow again once in the native city. With the crowds, it would still take nearly an hour.

My chair is about the only place I have time to myself. Is it a wonder, then, that so much policy is formulated, and so many issues are decided, while I am in this chair?

As his withered body swayed slightly with the rhythm of the footfall of his chair bearers, the *taotai*'s mind considered how best to report his findings to the governor, who would still be at the county *ya-men* when the *taotai* arrived.

Hsüeh *Ta-jen* is unlike anyone else. First, he bows down and kowtows to T'ai Shan 泰山, sacred Mount Tai, then stands up and shakes his fist at T'ai Shan, and the gods still have not frazzled him with a thunderbolt. One can only shake one's head in disbelief. In the 3rd year of Hsien Feng, he was only the prefect of Sung-chiang. In the 7th year of Hsien Feng, he was here in Shang-hai as *tao-t'ai*, coming and going among the foreign officials and merchants, and leading braves in skirmishes with rebels. The next year, his fame at negotiating with the barbarians had spread so far that the Emperor called him to Pei-ching to assist in talks with the Americans, and then that autumn gave him responsibility for assisting the commissioners in the tariff conference at Shang-hai. There was no reward he could have asked for and not received.

But when the commissioners arrived at Shang-hai, Hsüeh Huan betrayed the Emperor! He dared to contradict the August One. He told the commissioners that the Emperor's secret plan to repudiate the treaties, just agreed to at Pei-ching, was wrong! That the Secret Plan would *not* work and should not be submitted to the foreign envoys! That foreigners would not accept an agreement for mere free trade at treaty ports in place of treaties! That barbarian officials are concerned less about profits in trade than about what they regard as diplomacy between equal nations!

I could not understand, and thought there could not be any race of people in the world more two-faced than Englishmen. Of course, now we know there are official barbarians, and merchant barbarians, and that they hate each other almost as much as we hate them. But how could his Excellency defy the Emperor by repudiating the Secret Plan, and still keep his head?

Barrier Road left the international settlement at the foot of the North Gate 北門 and passed over the moat and through the wall into the native city. A three-mile long sloping rampart wall of tamped earth fifteen feet thick and twenty-four feet high encircled Shanghai, built in the Ming Dynasty to protect the city from Japanese pirates. The earth of the core was faced inside and out by large gray-fired bricks laid in lime mortar on a foundation of dressed stone. Around the wall was a twenty-foot-wide moat of slowly flowing water twelve feet deep, from which the earth for the wall had been taken. Along the top of the wall were twenty arrow towers 箭塔, watch-towers and gate-towers of two and three stories, each story roofed with tile and dressed with sharply upcurved flying eaves. Beneath six of the towers were gates for roads and at four other places there were water gates 水門, for the canals that passed through the city to the river. Long before eastern Chiang-su Province ever saw carts or wheelbarrows, people in the lower Yangtze delta traveled to market on a bewildering latticework of rivers and canals that, within the city walls of Shanghai, passed near homes and shops in streets, lanes and alleys everywhere in the city.

Outside the gate, a few peddlers lingered in hopes of selling the last of the day's vegetables from their carts. Inside the gate, business was still brisk in stationary shops selling wooden chops, camelhair brushes and marble ink stones, and shops offering

洋神 *Yang Shen*   *James Lande* 藍德

sandalwood incense and paper money to burn before temple altars. The *taotai*'s procession passed through the gate, on the wall above which were cut the characters for the name of the gate, Yen Hai 晏海, Gate of the Quiet Sea, or Gate of Peace. They turned east on North Gate road toward Fragrant Flower Bridge 香花橋 and passed by deserted morning markets with empty stalls, and bustling evening markets just setting up stalls to cook supper for workers and coolies and barrow boys done with the day's drudgery. Crossing the Fragrant Flower Bridge bridge south over the canal, the *taotai*'s chair navigated through shop districts with lanes named for their wares or trades and surrounded by restaurants and pawnshops: Bamboo-dealers Alley 竹行巷, Medicine-shops Lane 藥局衖, Pastry-shops Lane 餅店衖, Southern-style Food Alley 南飯巷.

    To the foreigners, thought Wu Hsü, Hsüeh Huan praises the power and honesty of the English, tells them that he would not be too proud to learn barbarian methods. To the Emperor, he accuses the foreigners of duplicity, of conspiring against the Emperor. He tells the foreigners what the foreigners want to hear, and the foreigners praise his congenial attitudes. He tells the Emperor what the Emperor wants to hear, and the Emperor fawns on him for his adeptness at managing the barbarian. Yet we Chinese make the concessions, not the English or French. Hsüeh Huan obstructs the Emperor's Secret Plan to repudiate the treaties forced on us, gives away Chinese sovereignty to the foreigners, agreeing to honor the foreign laws over Chinese laws, and to give all nations treaty rights secured by any one nation. When the English and French return with their warships to extort more privileges, making perfectly clear the failure of Hsüeh's strategy, the Emperor promotes Hsüeh to governor of Chiang-su and promises to make him Imperial Commissioner of the Five Ports. Why has Hsüeh not lost all his possessions and been exiled for life to a far frontier?

    The *taotai*'s chair passed by the turnoff for the Temple of the City God 城隍廟 and his own *ya-men* under the Great East Gate, and continued southeast over more large bridges and canals through the wholesale district, crossing Rice-wholesalers Street, Lumber-wholesalers Street, Mat-dealers Alley, Mutton-shops Street, and Food-dealers Lane. At Three-arches Street 三牌坊街, the bearers turned south and circled around the artisans at work on Cast-iron Street, Blacksmiths Lane, Pan-factories Lane, Anchor-works Alley, and Boat-builders Boulevard. The procession skirted residential districts of houses and courtyards around temples and schools where the rich made their homes, and the slums and alleyways where common people lived closer together in the intimacy of poverty. Arriving at County-front Street 縣前街, the chair turned east and was carried up to the stone lions guarding the great main gate of the magistrate's offices. Atop the three-tiered drum-tower away in the center of the city, a watchman beat the drum signal for the hour of the rooster, 5:00pm. Realizing the lateness of the hour, Wu Hsü decided to have a runner sent on to his own *ya-men* to tell his family and staff that he would be returning late that evening.

    When the porter of the main gate 大門 of the county *ya-men* heard the gongs announcing the *taotai*'s approach and saw the dancing *tao* 道, he immediately ordered his assistants to fetch their instruments for the reception required. As the procession turned into the main gate, a blare of horns 喇叭 and beat of gongs 大鑼 from within the courtyard answered the gongs without on the street. The *taotai*'s chair squeezed through the narrow entrance into the first courtyard and approached the gaol-keeper's doorway 監門 on the left. This avoided the throng of people crowding toward the Hall of Administration through the Ceremonial Gate on the opposite side of the courtyard. His bearers, however, were forced to set down their burden and fall back around the chair to fend off a crowd of petitioners who rushed to clamor for the intervention of the *tao-t'ai*

洋神 *Yang Shen*   *James Lande* 藍德

in petty suits.

As if a *tao-t'ai* were permitted to interfere, thought Wu Hsü, in the routine administrative affairs of a magistrate. Really, these people in Shang-hai have no understanding of proper behavior 實在不懂規矩. People in this city trade gossip and rumors with hundreds of neighbors, then take on airs as if they know something, and act as if officials are here to serve them instead of the opposite. It is all I can do just to review the performance of my prefects and magistrates, and manage other subordinates, and now the foreign officials. What have I to do with these common people?

Suddenly the main gate porter appeared and gave a shout: "Clear away 走開阿! Return to the hall and dare not to pester Wu *Ta-jen* with your trivial squabbles or you'll not enter this *ya-men* again. Do not forget the penalty for *yueh-sung* 越訟, for not going through proper channels with suits, is fifty strokes of the light bamboo."

Immediately the crowd backed away and scattered in response to the rumpled, wizened little man, an apparently menial functionary of the bustling county offices who in actuality commanded great respect among gentry and ordinary people alike for his supreme power over access to *ya-men* officials. The punishment threatened also made an impression. The gate porter turned and bowed to the *taotai*, passed the runner carrying the mandarin's visiting card, and then returned to his post at the main gate.

A commotion rose again at the Ceremonial Gate. Clerks and runners poured through, herding to one side all the people milling about there, and formed two lines in a ceremonial gauntlet for the *taotai* to pass through into the second courtyard. Wu Hsü dismounted from his chair with slow dignity just as Magistrate Liu, followed by his deputies, rushed out with apologies for not being quicker to meet him, and enough elaborate salutations, gestures and bows to satisfy protocol. The gate had two small walls on either side of a narrow entrance roofed with elaborate green ceramic tiles. A third wall, also roofed with green tile, was set as a screen before the entrance, such that one had to go around the screen to enter through the gate, an entrance too small to admit sedan chairs. The characters for Ceremonial Gate 儀門 were carved into the screen facing the main entrance.

Inside the gate, Wu Hsü stopped briefly beside a small monument that stood at the center of the second courtyard under its own small roof of shiny blue-green tiles. A large stone tablet there was incised with the characters *kung sheng ming* 公生明, taken from the couplet "public life is open, private life is closed." The tablet was a warning to remember not to discuss official business outside *ya-men* walls.

If I strictly followed that injunction, thought Wu Hsü, elder brother Yang and the other high officers of the Ning-po Guild would be very disappointed.

Beyond the crowds of bystanders, the *taotai* passed between long rows of clerks offices 書使房 on each side of the courtyard and up into the Great Hall 大堂 at the rear of the courtyard, the Hall of Administration 治堂 where public business was conducted.

"Hsüeh *Ta-jen*?" he asked the magistrate.

"His Excellency went to the Temple of the City God and said we should go ahead with our judicial case review if he had not returned when you arrived."

"Very well."

Magistrate Liu conducted the *taotai* to an office that opened off the Great Hall, offered his Excellency a comfortable seat beside a large desk stacked with scrolls, called in his clerk to assist with the review, and ordered a servant to bring tea.

One by one, the magistrate opened a scroll and presented the details of a legal case for the *taotai*'s consideration. The clerk handed a copy of each scroll to the *taotai*, who slowly unrolled the scroll as he listened.

Sowing Foreign Discord

洋神 *Yang Shen*   James Lande 藍德

"The first case is about possession by ghosts," said the magistrate, watching closely for any changes in the *taotai*'s expression.

First case: The Tomb Violator

A woodcutter named Chang Hai found his wife raving as one deranged. Believing the ghost of a distant cousin Chang Wen-po had entered his wife, Chang Hai went to the house where the coffin of Chang Wen-po was awaiting a geomancer to declare a propitious day for burial. Chang Hai pried open the coffin to drive away the ghost and restore his wife's health. Chang Hai beat a gong and chanted spells but did not expose the corpse. The owner of the house complained to the local constable and Chang Hai was arrested. The judge in the case cites the statute for violation of tombs 發塚, sub-statute for opening the coffin of a dead person not permanently buried, with the intention of robbery, and sentences Chang Hai to one hundred strokes of the heavy bamboo and three years penal servitude.

"Ghosts," the *taotai* said. "Will we never suppress these superstitions?"

"We cannot easily take away their ghosts, Excellency. How else will the old-hundred-names explain strange happenings that beset the lives of common people?"

"That view is unorthodox, Sung-yen. Much human mischief is attributed to ghosts, I think. What do you suppose his wife was raving about? Did she discover his misdeeds, or was she covering her own, perhaps with the dead cousin?"

"If so, she didn't tell the judge."

"How did this Chang-hai know where the ghost came from?"

"Coincidence?" Liu said. "No one else has died in that place for months."

"Why not hire a priest to cast out the demon, why violate a coffin himself?"

"Cost?" Liu said. "A woodcutter's family would be very poor."

"Well," the *taotai* said, sighing, "no tomb was violated, so we proceed by analogy."

"There was no intent to rob," Liu said, "however a coffin was forced open."

"Again the relationship is outside of the five degrees of mourning," Wu Hsü said. "Had Chang Hai desecrated the coffin of a closer relative, the penalty would be increased. Had he exposed the corpse in this coffin, the penalty would be increased to military exile at a distant frontier."

"As it is," Liu said, "the punishment appears to fit the crime."

Second case: Criminal Excused to Care for Aged Parents

A man fired a pistol in defense of his mother and by chance, the bullet struck and killed his elder first cousin, a relationship of the third degree 大功, of the five degrees of mourning. Consequently, the man was sentenced to immediate decapitation. Upon review by the Emperor, the sentence was changed to decapitation after the assizes, because the criminal was his mother's only son. Upon further consideration, the status of the case was further reduced to that of having circumstances deserving of capital punishment 情實. Subsequently, the case was reviewed at two autumn assizes without execution of sentence, and so was transferred to the category of deferred execution 緩決. A petition was thereafter approved to allow the criminal to return home to care for his aged mother, according to the statute for wrongdoers permitted to remain at home to care for parents 犯罪存留養親.

"It was determined that the killing was accidental?" the *taotai* said.

"Yes, Excellency. It was not an intentional murder."

洋神 *Yang Shen*   James Lande 藍德

"And since then, the criminal has been in gaol at his native place?"

"For over two years now, but here at Shanghai."

"How has the mother gotten on while he has been imprisoned?"

"This we do not know. However, she signed the petition for release."

"And the death sentence has been commuted?"

"Yes, Excellency, to one hundred strokes of the heavy bamboo, and wearing the cangue for two months."

"Administer the beating here at Shanghai to be sure it is done properly."

"Then deliver him to the authorities of his native place for the rest?"

"Yes, I suppose that can be allowed. They can apply the cangue. Better his mother feed him, rather than have him starve on the streets of Shanghai because he cannot put hand to mouth."

"Mother will be caring for son, then, at least for the first two months."

"He will learn gratitude."

"If he does not already know it. Next case."

Third case: The Murdered Businessmen

Two businessmen, both named Wang, traveling together on a business trip, engaged a porter to carry their luggage. When the party stopped for the night at a tavern, the porter stole their money and ran away. The two businessmen pursued and captured the porter, returned him to the tavern, and tied him up in their room, planning to send the porter to the magistrate the following morning. The two businessmen sealed the room and slept in front of the door. The porter got loose and put poison in soup left from dinner and the next morning the two businessmen drank the soup and died. The judge in the case cites the statute for a "criminal who resists capture and kills a person attempting to make the capture," finds the porter guilty by analogy of violating this statute, and orders decapitation after the assizes.

The *taotai* quickly read the remaining particulars of the names and places of the persons involved. Then he laid the scroll in his lap and gazed out into the Great Hall. Both men were silent. Clearly, thought Wu Hsü, there is no question of the porter's guilt. He has upset the cosmic order of the universe and must be executed to restore harmony. However, it is crucial that the manner of his death be appropriate and, of course, that there be no error in assigning punishment that could be reversed by higher authority when the case is sent to Pei-ching for review. Are there mitigating factors? The porter was not related to the businessmen, so relationship is not a consideration that would increase the penalty of death. Wait – what does this say?

"The two men traveling on business were first cousins several times removed, is that right?"

"Yes," Liu said. "Both victims were surnamed Wang and related by family."

"Have your clerk look up the statute for homicide of three persons in one family 殺一家三人罪."

"Ah," sighed Liu, "the judge neglected to consider the victims were family, probably because they were outside the five degrees of mourning 五服."

"The commentary on the statute should say that all persons who live together and share food and lodging are considered as one family 一家人, even servants and persons beyond the five degrees of mourning. See if there is a sub-statute regarding the murder of two persons."

"But could the victims be said to have been living together?"

"They traveled together, stayed under the same roof, ate at the same table. The porter carried the luggage of both men, stole the money belonging to them both."

"Murdered them both, too. Even that was done to them together."

The clerk opened a book for the magistrate and pointed to a column of characters.

"For the murder of two persons in the same family, the sub-statute specifies immediate decapitation and exposure of the head."

"Yes, a heavier penalty, as I thought," Wu Hsü said.

The clerk whispered a question to the magistrate. Liu waved him away.

"What's that?" Wu Hsü said.

"My clerk is new to legal reviews. He wonders why immediate decapitation is a heavier punishment, considering the porter dies either way."

"That's all right. You can explain it to him," Wu Hsü said, interested in hearing how his magistrate would elucidate death, and if Liu might not be a little discomforted by the nuisance.

"The assizes," Liu said, "are the judicial reviews held in the autumn at the capital. Not only would the execution be delayed five months, but criminals often are treated leniently and have their sentences reduced to strangulation, exile, or penal servitude. The homicide of multiple members of a single family is far too great a disturbance to allow the disharmony caused to linger on over months."

"Immediate decapitation and exposure should be the sentence submitted to higher authority for this porter, so there is no delay of execution, and so that the old-hundred-names 老百姓 – the common folk – will see the murderer's head exposed in the streets and understand the evil of killing members of a single family."

When gongs of the governor's returning procession were heard in the early evening, answered by the din in the *ya-men* courtyard, Magistrate Liu left the *taotai* and hurried out to the front of the *ya-men* to greet Hsüeh Huan and escort him inside. He then returned to the *taotai*.

"Where did you put the governor?" Wu Hsü said.

"He is in the *wen-hsin t'ang* 問心堂," the magistrate said. "Please come this way, Excellency."

Magistrate Liu guided the *taotai* through the Great Hall, out a rear door, through a small gate in the high wall that separated the public and private worlds of the *ya-men*, and across a small courtyard to the third gate of the *ya-men*, the Residential Gate 宅門. That gate led to private and guest apartments, to the kitchen 廚房, and to a unique room, called the *wen-hsin t'ang* 問心堂, remodeled in the twentieth year of Kang Hsi 康熙 by a magistrate named Shih Ts'ai 史彩, as a place for the magistrate to meditate on the character of his work. Here, beneath a large gilt-edged tablet incised with the characters 問心 for "examine your heart," Wu Hsü found the governor sitting at a high table on which were stacked scrolls and cloth-bound books of documents, surrounded by the fuss and flurry of private secretaries and personal servants, whose principal activity appeared to be doing anything to be noticed. The governor did not seem to be examining his heart very closely.

Magistrate Liu entered, announced that Wu *Ta-jen* waited to call upon the governor, then withdrew. Immediately, the governor's round, full face engulfed the room with a jovial grin, his fat cheeks jiggling with each burst of laughter – like quivering bean curd, thought Wu – and his heavy black eyebrows arching high in great surprise with each secret confided to him. He rose up and came around the table while Wu Hsü waved his clasped hands before his face and bowed his head several times.

洋神 *Yang Shen* James Lande 藍德

"薛大人, 您好, 您好 Hsüeh *Ta-jen*, how are you?"

"好, 好, 謝謝 good, good, thanks. 你也好罷 you're also well? 吳大人, 你來的真巧 Wu *Ta-jen*, you have come at exactly the right time," the governor said in Ssü-ch'uan-accented Mandarin. "我就有事情要跟你商量商量 I have just had some matters come up that I wish to confer upon with you. Come, let's walk out to the archery corridor."

Along the east wall of the *ya-men*, at the rear, there was a long corridor open to the sky that was set aside for archery practice, the *chien-tao* 箭道. The two mandarins made their way around the private apartments to the *chien-tao* and proceeded to pace slowly together up and down its length while they talked.

"I want to raise another force of braves," the governor said, "to defend Shang-hai against the T'ai-p'ing rebels and, as I have been concerned with other matters for several years, I wish to ask the advice of experienced officials like you, and Magistrate Liu. The magistrate does not think much of the bunch we have now. They have been around too long and have lost their martial spirit and their skills at war. Where do you think I can find the best men? Are there men from your native place that would be suitable?"

Wu Hsü considered this. There was the practical, and the political. On the practical side, trash that posed as soldiers were easy to get – good men hard. So, too, were arms and ammunition hard to come by, which is why Wu Hsü had carefully accumulated such a large secret arsenal, to be used as a last resort but not to be squandered. On the political side, the Emperor would not cashier a mandarin who raised a force that successfully repelled rebels. And whoever was first to do that, he had first pick of men and arms, and would be the first to come to the attention of the Emperor. If the governor, who already had the confidence of the Emperor, did not raise a force of his own, he would certainly interfere with any force raised by another. If he were the first to raise a force, he would lessen the chance for other officials to achieve honor. If he raised a force and it failed, that would clear the way for others to conscript an army.

"I think there are not many men from Ning-po," the *taotai* said, "who would be suitable as soldiers, but there are a great many men from Kuang-chou outside the South Gate around T'ung-chia Ferry 董家渡, and in the southern suburbs around Kao-ch'ang Temple 高昌廟. They came north with the English and gained experience fighting in their ranks together with the black men from India."

I need to save our Ning-po men for later, thought Wu Hsü, and kill off the Kuang-chou men first, so that the soldiers in the last armies left when the rebels are defeated are my own Ning-po people, who will then support our Ning-po officials.

"I'm not sure I could control a force of Kuang-chou men," the governor said. "Could we use Ning-po men as officers?" There are just too few men from Ssü-ch'uan here in Shang-hai, thought Hsüeh Huan, which leaves me dependent upon the Ning-po and Kuang-chou men who swarm in this city.

"Best not to use soldiers from different native places together in one force," the *taotai* said. "Kuang-chou men and Ning-po men would not get along – would not fight together." They would probably fight each other, thought Wu Hsü. "However, we have some minor Kuang-chou officials here in Shang-hai who might help organize a force."

"That's good, too. Yes, send them to me and we'll see. Now, what did the Americans have to say? They insisted on going with the English and French to T'ien-chin, didn't they?"

"That is so, I'm afraid. Of course, this is only the first time I have mentioned it to the American consul."

"I knew it. I had no doubt. Wu *Ta-jen*, the Americans absolutely must be prevented

Sowing Foreign Discord

from going to T'ien-chin. They must not be allowed to plot together with the English and French, or the Russians, and that is exactly what they will do at T'ien-chin. The Emperor knows this, and before long we are likely to receive a memorial ordering us to keep the Americans away. Once the Emperor has ordered us, there will be very great risk. This absolutely must be avoided at all cost."

"Their decision appears not to rest with either their consul or their minister, Excellency. Evidently, the minister has already been ordered to mediate if possible by his superior officials in America."

"And we cannot talk to their president in America any more than we can talk to the rabbit in the moon. Wu *Ta-jen*, can you suggest a strategy to use against the American minister? What do you think of trying to sow discord between the several nations, so that the English and French will not want the Americans at T'ien-chin, will be suspicious of their reasons for going there and tell them to stay away?"

"好極了 that's wonderful!" Wu Hsü said. Quickly he tried to think of some way to finesse his answer to the governor. "If we Chinese cannot tell them to stay away, maybe the English can. Turning the foreigners against each other has been effective in the past and is encouraged by the Emperor. Of course, this approach was recently attempted with the French barbarians."

"The attempt to discredit the English minister with the French?"

"Yes, Excellency. Just when the barbarian merchants were most resentful of Minister Blaine, Governor-general Ho Kuei-ch'ing had me order our Chinese merchants to go to the barbarian merchants. They were to say that the affray at Ta-ku was entirely the fault of the English minister himself starting the quarrel 肇釁. Then we ordered our Chinese merchants to ask the barbarian merchants to write to their home government and accuse Minister Blaine of personally initiating these hostilities with China. When the English queen heard of the anger of the merchants, we thought Minister Blaine would certainly be punished. I then took the opportunity to send letters through the French consul and secretary to the French minister, Bourboulon, saying that we had not yet heard if there were any French casualties at Ta-ku."

"That is all that was said?"

"Yes."

"That was quite subtle. I assume that Ho *Ta-jen*'s thought was to get the French to blame the English for the loss of French troops at Ta-ku last summer. The French were said to have lost four killed, including a high-ranking officer, and twelve wounded."

"Perhaps it was too subtle, for the French anyway."

"The plan did not work?" the governor said.

"The English minister has not been recalled, and the English and French remain allies. Apparently, Minister Bourboulon did not think the small loss worth pressing claims, and merely communicated with his emperor. As for Minister Blaine, there was a tempest in the English parliament, however his official superiors supported the minister, and now he is quite puffed up about his success and often orders the barbarian merchants to his *ya-men* for lectures. If anything, he is stronger now than before."

"That will not be good for the Governor-general. Since I have been assisting Ho *Ta-jen* manage the affairs of the five ports, his outspokenness has often caused the Emperor to be impatient with him. If Ho *Ta-jen*'s enemies at court report this incident as another failure with the English and French ministers, his influence will suffer still more. That would be a shame because everything Ho *Ta-jen* has said over recent years has been very sound 實在有道理."

"Yes, I agree completely," Wu Hsü said in a slightly dejected tone. It occurred to him that if Ho Kuei-ch'ing fell from favor because of his common sense, where would that leave Hsüeh Huan and himself? For one thing, they would no longer have the Governor-general between themselves and the Emperor, writing memorials in his own name but with their recommendations.

"Well, those were the French and the English," Hsüeh Huan said. "The Americans might be very different. The English and the Americans were bitter enemies once, you know, and have fought two wars, one when the Americans rebelled against the oppression of English rule in America, and again forty years later when the British kidnapped some American sailors from a ship at sea. They are always a little suspicious of each other anyway. 於深悉控馭咪夷之方利益匪淺 learning well to control the Americans would bring no small *advantage*."

"It has been my belief," Wu Hsü said, "that, for a long time now, implicit in the American motives has been their growing anger over the way the British proudly flaunt their opening of the five treaty ports, and the collusion of the other nations with this deception. This is a weak point in their coalition, and one reason why the Americans distance themselves from the other barbarians."

It is also the American barbarian's strength, thought the *taotai*. They stand apart from the influence of others in politics and business. So, they are the first to have the advantages of a new treaty and, as Yang Fang has shown me, the first to find new ways to accumulate wealth and riches. The Americans are abandoning old methods of doing business, changing from agencies and commissions to direct investments that create capital and earn interest. And theirs will be the first steamship companies to transport merchandise on rivers and coasts all over China. 於深悉控馭咪夷之方贏利匪淺 truly, learning well to control the Americans would bring no small *profit*.

"Perhaps we can use the bitterness of the Americans against themselves," Hsüeh Huan said, "and turn the foreigners against each other more effectively."

"We can send the expectant *tao-t'ai* Yang Fang among the foreign merchants with false rumors of harmful actions planned by each nation against the other nations, and get them all excited and anxious. For example, the English have decided not to blockade the north coast and stop trade when they go north, but we could say they have had a change of heart and now plan to blockade the north coast. That would stir the resentment of the Americans against the English, and anger all the foreign merchants as well."

"Yes, yes, a good idea," the governor said, rubbing his hands together as he warmed to the thought. "What else?" he asked in the hoarse whisper of a co-conspirator.

"We could say that the Americans plan to ask the Emperor to grant exclusive trading rights on the Long River 長江, and inland. That would frighten the English merchants into thinking they will be shut out of their trade on the Long River, and they will yell at their officials not to let it happen."

"太好了 very good. Very good."

"And we could let it slip that the Americans plan to get to Nan-ching ahead of others, negotiate with the T'ai-p'ing rebels, and secure exclusive trading rights from the bandit Hung. That will cause the English merchants to fear Americans will close off trade on the Long River, and they will angrily write letters to their rulers in England."

"頂好 top notch! Wu *Ta-jen*, you are truly too smart 你實在太聰明! Your ideas would cause much trouble. Even 1000-year-old foxes 千年狐狸 could not stir up so much trouble!"

Sowing Foreign Discord

洋神 *Yang Shen*　　　　　　　　　　　　　　　　　　　　　　James Lande 藍德

Dramatis Personae: Chapter 7

Delevan Slaughter　　　Yangtze River pilot

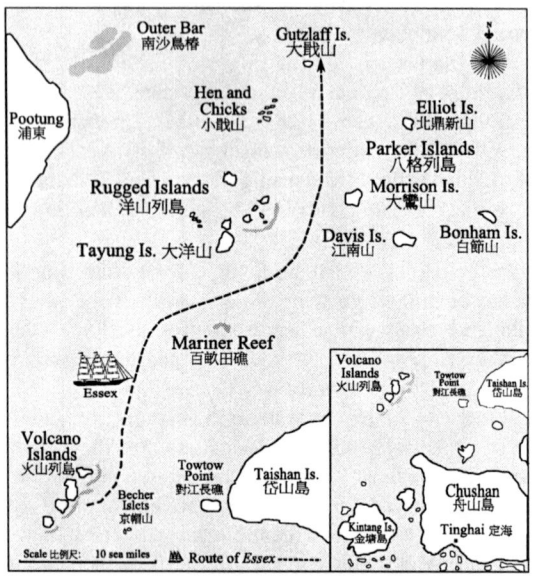

Volcano Group to Gutzlaff Island
(based on British Hydrographic Office chart, Yang-tse-kyang, Sheet IX, 1842)

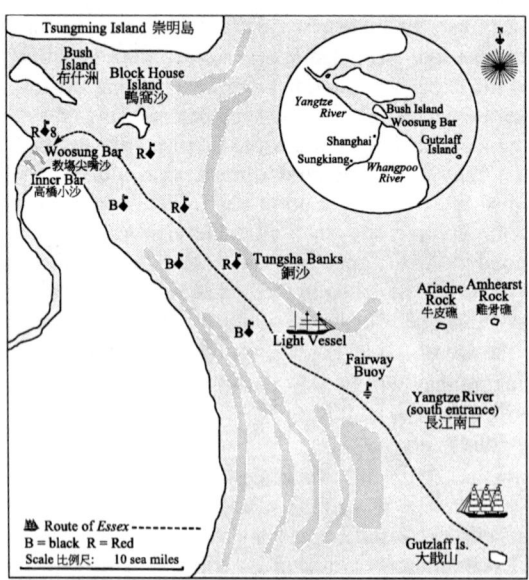

Gutzlaff Island to Woosung Bar
(based on British Hydrographic Office chart, China, Sheet VIII, 1843)

knot (nautical mile): 6076 feet (Br. knot = 6080 feet), 798 feet, or 15%, longer than a land mile.
cable: one hundred fathoms　　**fathom**: six feet.
larboard (port): left　　**starboard**: right.

112　　　　　　　　　　　　　　　　　　　　　　　　　　*Crossing the Bar*

Chapter 7: Crossing the Bar
Thursday, April 19, 1860, 12:30pm

Ptolemy Reese stood beside the helmsman on the poop deck of the Yankee clipper *Essex* watching carefully the sea ahead. For all his bravado about sailing by the book, the book unnerved the mate because he was not certain he could understand everything he read. Were there other rocks yet unstruck waiting to be named "*Essex*"? Reese sent a man to the foretop to watch the water ahead for reefs and shoals, reminding him that one hand was for the ship, but the other hand was for himself. And he damn well better hang on tight, because losing one foretopman on this voyage was one too many.

"'ow the 'ell do we find that bloody island without a bloody pilot?"

"Land o' Goshen!" Hannah Fitch whispered aloud as she surveyed the battered deck of *Essex*. She had just come up on the poop deck from the saloon for the first time since the beginning of the attack, having left Elizabeth in the saloon to continue ministering to the remaining wounded. Her eyes widened in astonishment as she tallied the ship's gaping wounds and piles of splintered debris. Slowly, she passed her fingers over the holes and tears in the polished mahogany panels and rails.

"Careful, Ma'am," Ptolemy Reese said quietly as he looked up from the compass. "There's still jag'd edges of sharp metal embedded in the wood." Captain Fitch stood in conference at the binnacle together with the mate and the helmsman.

"It's a wonder," she returned absently, "there's so little of this metal embedded in you men. Surely we have not seen all the casualties down below in the saloon."

"Only the worst of them, I expect, ma'am," Reese said. "Most'd want to tend each other's wounds, as they always 'ave. Ain't none ever been tended by ladies 'board ship. Say nothin' 'bout the ship owner's wife and daughter. They'd feel pretty strange."

Hannah dismissed with a grimace all men too foolish to be cared for properly.

"Look at this ship, Cornelius! It is a terrible mess! What will it cost to repair all this damage? Oh, if only I could get my hands on those pirates now; they would be made to suffer all the torments of Hades for this!" Hannah glared out over the main deck of *Essex* with growing dismay and rising anger.

"A storm at sea would have done as much, Aunt," the captain answered. "We're always replacing or repairing yards and rigging."

"I want a reckoning of all this damage," she said with a sniff.

"Not now, Aunt. I find myself pressed into the office of pilot, since we have shot the first one, and must determine how we can safely make our way to Gutzlaff Island."

"Beg'n your pardon, ma'am," Reese ventured, "but if I might be allowed to mention it, each of them pirates killed'll bring £20 sterling from the Admiralty when it's reported, and that much money will make a lot of repairs aboard *Essex* after compensations are paid out to the crew."

"Well, for that matter, I suppose there will be insurance." Hannah was somewhat appeased by the realization that the Netherlands Indian Marine and Fire Insurance Company, and not Augustus Fitch & Company, would pay the cost of repairing *Essex*. Then it occurred to her that the company would get back such a large return on the staggering premiums paid for insurance that she could afford to be more generous.

"Actually, Mr. Reese, whatever prize money is received will be used to compensate the crew of *Essex*. Augustus Fitch & Company will see to the ship's repairs."

Hannah turned to go below again, muttering "well, I never in all my born days..." as she descended the companionway, and no one left topside could be quite certain whether she was rattling on about wounded men, damaged ships, or insubordinate nephews.

"The crew'll surely be glad to hear that, ma'am," said Reese after her.

"Do you understand these sailing directions, Mr. Reese?" The captain picked up a book from the bench, a copy of *The Chinese Commercial Guide*.

"Pretty much, Captain. Chart makes more sense with sailing directions."

"Compliments to Mr. Wood. This is his own copy he's given us."

"Says Mariner Reef has five feet under her stern at low water – glad we're passin' at 'igh water."

"Almost like having a pilot."

"Better'n that last poxy blighter."

"Before I forget, Mr. Reese," the captain said, "see that a double-round of grog is served out to the crew as soon as possible. I know rum would calm my jangled nerves."

Reese smiled. "I'll do that, sir. When it's known around Shanghai that Mr. Fitch serves up double rations of grog and pays out prize money to his men, there'll never be any shortage of sailors for crew aboard Fitch vessels."

Reese glanced to the northeast, considered the wind direction and velocity, and noted the compass setting. "Keepin' 'er due north for at least six miles should put 'er well past Mariner Reef," he said, "then we can bear north-northeast for the first of the Rugged Islands, and the channel between them and the Morrison Islands. Like to shorten sail, Captain, the better to gingerly feel our way north. If the wind and weather hold, and it stays clear so we can see these islands, we should raise Gutzlaff Island well before the sun sets. I don't know what we'll do if we raise a fog."

"Very well, Mr. Reese. Inform me of each change in course, and call me if there are questions or doubts. Set both watches to repairing damage. I do not wish to be any more of a spectacle than necessary at Shanghai."

Below in the saloon, Fletcher found Elizabeth and the cook tending six men wrapped in blankets, sitting on tables or benches. The gunner lay on a table in a corner of the room, beside the cabin boy, and the sailor. They all three were still, ashen, lifeless. Fletcher walked across to where they lay. Elizabeth came and stood beside him.

"They're all dead," she said. Her voice quavered.

"I'd hoped for better."

"We did everything we could for them."

Fletcher saw the blood splattered on her dress. He looked into her face and saw her eyes were brimming with tears. Another casualty. He looked back down at the bodies.

"Did you know them?" she said.

"Actually, miss, I did. This one was the cabin boy. Someone had him passing out cartridges to the riflemen when a shell exploded above the deck. Same shell that got the cook, and that sailor."

"Why was a boy on deck at all?"

"This other one's my gunner. Plucky little Irishman you couldn't keep down. I sent him down here once and you bandaged him. Then up he comes again, gargling about the perlite ladies below, and takes back command of his gun. Stood there with lead flying every which way and never flinched. Said his father was a quarter-gunner on a Royal Navy seventy-four. Did his father proud, if you ask me."

"It's just too much."

"No use to cry over what's lost, miss. They wouldn't want it. They're no better off for it, either. When it's your time to stop by, you stop, and the rest of us move on. No regrets for a life lived."

"Life lived, you say. What life lived? That boy wasn't even fifteen years old."

Elizabeth turned abruptly and went back to the living.

The cook limped over to Fletcher.

"The boy dying in her arms unsettled her. Do you know the time, Mr. Wood?"

"Near one, I'd guess."

"Only one? We grounded about what, nine?"

"Sounds right. Three, four hours ago."

"Only a few hours. Seems longer."

"A lot's happened," Fletcher said. "In just a few hours, we put out two anchors, warped a clipper out of the mud, trained a field gun crew, and fought off pirates. Training a gun crew normally takes weeks. What happened with this boy?"

"He was cut up fiercely by shell fragments. Shrapnel of all kinds of junk, not smooth lead balls. I just could not find all the places where he was bleedin'. Thought we had it all, but must've been more inside. He suddenly woke up screaming in pain, and there was pools of blood beneath him. We gave him more rum, give 'im something to bite down on, and told 'im to think of queen and country while I dug about tryin' to find the leaks. No use. Damn pirates."

"You did the best you could, Doctor."

"Fortunes of war."

"Fortunes of war. Does he have kin?"

"Orphan I think."

"D'you bury them at sea?"

"Most times. Only a day away from port, they'll probably take 'em on in."

"They're British?"

"All three of 'em."

"Burial in the sailor's cemetery."

"Yes, sir. With a consul to say some words over them."

"What would a consul know about them?"

Elizabeth Fitch entered her cabin and closed and locked the door. She shut her eyes and stood collapsed against the door for a half minute until she felt composed. Opening her eyes, she unbuttoned the tight collar of her bodice, breathed deeply for the first time in hours, and inspected her clothing. The claret-colored velvet trim was utterly ruined where sprays of blood had beaded upon it, and the silk skirt was stained by water and smelled of spilled rum, the cook's remedy for pain. Beyond hope, she thought, completely beyond repair. It just breaks a person's heart to have to put such a beautiful thing in with the trash, with the bloody bandages.

Slowly, she unbuttoned, untied, and removed her bloodstained outer garments and threw them in a corner. She opened each of her four travel trunks, removed the upper trays and set them aside, then removed each article of her wardrobe and arrayed them on the bunk, her walking dresses, visiting dresses, evening dresses. These were only her best dresses, for there was not room in the trunks for her ball gowns, her dresses of second choice, or all the bonnets, belts, shoes, and other accoutrements; those rested in seven more trunks below in the hold of *Essex*. She passed her hand lovingly over walking dresses trimmed with wide passementerie, velvet bows and ornaments, plaits, guipures and *point de Genes* lace. She lifted the folds of visiting dresses of brocaded silk with silk and velvet bouquets, of French taffeta *a l'Imperatrice*, Pekin velvet, and tarletane with gimp florets. She smoothed her evening dresses of white tulle over blue taffeta trimmed in bouillonnes and felt blossoms, of light green tulle over white organdy bordered with seaweed-colored taffeta, and of white satin covered with tulle illusion and speckled with gold stars. The bodices of the evening dresses all had extreme décolleté edged with pleated ruches and delicate Brussels lace.

She held an evening dress to her shoulders and turned to see herself in the crude mirror on the cabin wall. Lowering the dress to just beneath the swell of her breasts under the sheer muslin of her chemise, she considered how easily this sight excited men.

There is nothing quite so stupid, she thought, as a drooling man crowding up against a woman wearing such a dress and trying to peek down into her bodice without being noticed. You look away, they stare down, you look back up at them, and they snap the eyes back so fast you'd think they were going to pop right out of their heads. You look away again, twist this way, turn that, perhaps bend forward a little, and watch them suffer for knowing they're staring at something they can never have. You taunt them with sweetness and charm, and tease them with the unspoken suggestion of delights promised but never delivered, and punish the bumbling idiots for never being what you want them to be, for taking from you what you can never have back again. And then discarding the damaged goods without another thought. Oh, Richard!

Elizabeth laid the dress over the back of a chair and turned again to the mirror, shivering slightly in the cold cabin. She pressed her palms up underneath her breasts, felt with her fingertips the firmness straining at the thin material, and closed her eyes. After a moment, she clenched her eyes and thought: No! Stop it. Proper young women do not have sexual feelings.

But she could not shut out the memory of his lips on hers, his thin mustache where it tickled under her nose, the warmth of his hand under her breast. No, she thought again! Stop it. You've already caused me to be driven a Magdalene from Boston, ruined my life. What more do you want? Leave me alone!

Aloud she whimpered, "Leave me alone," and continued crying quietly. After a few minutes, she looked up again at the mirror, then hesitantly raised both her hands, closed her eyes, and began slowly to caress her breasts. Her nipples hardened and stood out under her roving fingertips. After another minute she stopped. No, she mused, it is just not the same. Frigidity may be easier to cultivate than I thought, now that I can no longer feel anything. That will make me the apotheosis of modern woman. A demure little handmaid to the Gospel, an efficient auxiliary to the great task of renovating the world that Mary Lyon and Mount Holyoke would have had me, a pious, pure, submissive, frigid little house slave.

2

Fletcher Thorson Wood stood with his back to the larboard forecastle rail of *Essex* and watched the crew repairing the damage to her superstructure. Ptolemy Reese walked the length of the deck, stopped at the foremast and ordered a relief into the foreyard, then crossed to the new forecastle ladder, a solid contrivance of beams and one-by-eight planking jury-rigged to replace the ladder blown away by Fokie Tom.

"So, Yank, today we truly sail 'by the book,' " Reese said as he mounted the ladder. "My leadsman is marking every sounding on a chart we're working up."

"You will be the envy of the admiralty, Mr. Reese," Fletcher said. "And you can add cartographer to your impressive list of accomplishments. After this voyage, your reputation will spread up and down the China coast as the pirate hunter who dismasted Fokie Tom, and you will be in great demand aboard every ship in the China Sea."

"Yank, I have never heard anyone so *full* of shyte!"

"Well, mate, you could just come right out and say so."

"You son-of-a-bitch – I could ring your neck as easy as fartin'."

"Sure you could, Mr. Reese. You're a big man, and strong. But before you strangled me, you would think of what you owe me."

"Why would I think of that?"

"Because you're a righteous man, Mr. Reese, not an outlaw like the bloody, death-dealing pirates we left floating in our wake at the Volcanos."

"Wha'do I owe ya?"

"Your life."

Reese glared into Fletcher's face. Fletcher returned his look with unblinking, unintimidated serenity. After a few tense moments, the mate yielded.

"Supposin' that were true, what would I owe you for my worthless life?"

"We're even, Mr. Reese. I saved my life, too. You helped. The slate is clean."

Reese chuckled and leaned against the rail beside Fletcher.

"You can joke all you like, Yank…er, *Mister* Wood, but every man aboard knows we are here this afternoon because of you this morning. It's not like it's something a man can say right out, but if ever you're in a tight place, just yell 'Essex' and twenty or thirty able hands will come runnin' to spill blood for you."

"From you, Reese, 'Yank's' better. I know you. It galls you to knuckle under, just as it does me. You owe me nothing."

Reese turned around and leaned out over the rail. "Look here…*Yank*. We're all mighty curious about what you're going to be doin' when you gets to Shanghai. I mean, it ain't nobody's business but yours, an' nobody wants to pry, but there's rumors flyin' about all kinds of opportunities for men who can take their punches. They say that a feller can hire himself out as a soldier for a hundred dollars a month.

"I guess I've heard those rumors."

"They say there's plunder to be had ransakin' the cities an army occupies."

"I've heard that, too."

"Well, Mr. Wood, might you be knowin' of anyone getting up such an army?"

"Well, Mr. Reese, I am not acquainted with anyone like that, but I'm sure I'll know where to find you if such a person comes to my attention."

Fletcher noticed that the ship was silent. The arguments and oaths and sawing and hammering that a moment before had whirled over the deck were suddenly gone.

"Either that's more pirates," Reese said, "or a woman on deck."

They walked to the forecastle ladder. Elizabeth approached across the main deck, dressed now with less formality in a long broadcloth skirt with narrow blue-and-white stripes, a high-necked, close-fitting blue bodice with tight sleeves, and a simple narrow-brimmed white bonnet. The crew fidgeted, trying to get a closer look without looking directly at her. Reese groaned and started down the ladder.

"I'll leave this to you, Mr. Wood."

At the bottom of the jury-rigged ladder, Reese spun about and almost bumped into the girl, growled "miss," then stomped off shouting at the malingering crew. Elizabeth snatched up a little of her long skirt and nimbly climbed the ladder, taking the hand stretched down by Fletcher to help her up.

"What is wrong with that mate?" she said. "He just about bit my head off."

Fletcher quickly appraised the young woman's appearance. Her manner of dress was now much closer to the spirit of a sailing ship, simple and practical, without the frippery of crinolines and lace. With some luck, thought Fletcher, one more change of costume and we'll have her in white duck and flannel.

Squads of abundant dark-brown hair pushed out in ringlets from under the narrow brim of her bonnet, emerged from encampment about her small ears, and formed into a line of skirmishers across her forehead. Her brown eyes looked almost directly into his. The sexual impulse excited in him by her bold presence was muted by manners acquired in what little New England society he mixed when ashore, and was only a distant cousin to the barely restrained response pulsing through the body of the *Essex* sailors. For

Fletcher, the urge was no more than a brief, unvoiced fancy, a whisper carried off on the breeze with the scent of her French perfume, prevented by rule of law and custom from being echoed in any hall of social congress.

"Probably doesn't hold with having female passengers forward, miss – distracts men from their work. Every crewman with a hammer will be pounding on his thumb."

"Well, it's my father's ship and I'll go where I want on it, and the crew will just have to mind their manners."

Fletcher returned to the larboard rail. Elizabeth followed.

"I suppose I should ask your pardon, Mr. Wood, for snapping like that. Of course I'll try to stay out of the way of the crew, but I just have to get out of the cramped little cabin and away from...that part of the ship."

"You are upset. About the boy who died?"

"Oh, yes, I guess so. Wait – that's a stupid thing to say. There's no *guessing* about it. That and, well, it just seems like nobody really cares! Men have died today, an innocent young boy died in my arms, and I could do nothing to prevent it, and nobody...nobody cares." She heaved a deep breath and made a visible effort to fight back tears. "Why do you all seem so unconcerned about that boy?"

"Listen to me," he said softly. "There is a fatalism that informs a sailor's view of life. He has the same subdued response to a crewman fallen overboard or a kitten washed away. No use to raise a wild hue and cry like the landsman, and weep and wail over what's lost. A sailor's not indifferent, really, but rather too often he's seen a friend snatched away overboard and never been able to go back. And he knows, too, that he's always one slip away from the same unrelenting fate. Put him on land, and he's the first into the burning barn or swollen stream to save a life, all the more quickly because at sea he could not, because the cold sea is not so conveniently contained, and swallows her victims in a single swift gulp with no remorse."

"It...it just seems so inhumane, And cruel."

"It is cruel. Every man here knows that, and would agree with you if pressed to speak out. But it is not a man's way to speak overmuch of things that can't be helped. A woman can learn to distinguish between a man's pained silence and his indifference."

"How do you tell?"

"It is in his eyes. And sometimes in his tone of voice, or in what he chooses to say, or chooses not to say. But it is always in his eyes. That's why a man sometimes looks away, so his eyes cannot be seen."

"I don't think I see any pain in your eyes, Mr. Wood."

"The dead pass on, the living rejoice, Miss Fitch. I have said a prayer for the boy who died, and now I rejoice that I am still alive. And all the rest of you, too. But now I am elated that once more I have cheated death. A person cannot understand that, if they have not faced death, but I have many times, and still my luck has not run out. The ocean has tried to drown me, but I kicked free. A Bolivian firing squad was ready to shoot me, but I escaped at the last moment. My crew mutinied, and I knocked in the top of a powder keg and threatened to shove in a burning brand if they did not come to order. I was ready to take me, them, the whole ship with me – and I was this close to doing it, too, when they saw my threat was real and they backed down. Death does not yet have dominion over me, Miss Fitch, or the grave any victory. Lord willing, I will go on to cheat the devil of his due, many more times."

Elizabeth frowned, tired of so much talk about death. She recalled conversation at table about Wood's earlier time in Shanghai.

"Shanghai could be an unsettling place," she said, "with so many different nationalities and languages and habits that I don't understand."

"Yes, miss, the world's a babble of voices all right, and some knack with languages would make life easier for us all. You'd do well to study on the pidgin that passes here between foreigners and Chinese, even if you have to do it on the sly. I've tried a little of the Chinaman's own talk that I could pick up, but teachers are hard to come by because the mandarins froth at the mouth and start whacking off heads when a Chinaman's caught teaching his language to foreigners. As for them runes they write, well, my head aches just to think about all that scratching."

Elizabeth was silent for a minute. It occurred to Fletcher that she did not seem very well prepared for what he believed lay before her.

"What made you leave Salem? Have you any idea of what to expect in China?"

"What I have heard," she said, "makes me concerned about what lies ahead. I believe that like Mr. Hawthorne, and Mr. Melville, and Mr. Emerson, each of us has formed his own different impression of our own country, each according to his different experience of it. So, I *can* understand how there might be many different impressions among Westerners of a country as big as China. But which is the impression upon which I can *rely*? After that, I hesitate to even think about the several impressions we Westerners may have made upon the Chinese."

"Viewing China, is a tough job. So I've heard tell from at least one great captain of academia that sailed into the deep waters of studyin' up on the Celestial Kingdom. Kinda like estimating distances with one eye closed, or navigating some great, uncharted ocean by dead reckoning. Simple sailor like ol' Fletch Wood can't even fetch wood when it comes to havin' the gumption to stay with book learnin', and have it stick like it does to some. But even if it's knock wood for me when it comes to big bore studyin', there's still a lot to be learned out here at the front, right close up to action, so to speak."

Fletcher walked forward to the larboard cathead, straddled it, and sat with his back against the rail. Elizabeth followed and leaned against the rail beside him. Evidently, if the conversation were to continue, she would have to follow him around the ship.

"Did your parents describe nothing to you of life in Shanghai?"

"Not much. They were too busy building their business to write often, and never at home long enough to talk at length. Mother joined father in Shanghai when I was young, and I stayed with family in Boston until I went off to finishing school." In any case, she thought, one could hardly expect them to thrust upon the tender sensibilities of a young girl an account either comprehensive or candid about the more sordid aspects of treaty port life. Nor can you expect me to be candid about the reasons for my being rudely thrust out of Boston social life and dispatched upon a sea voyage.

"Well, Miss Fitch, I do not have an everyday acquaintance with your class of people in the American community at Shanghai. I can only imagine you will live in a large house with many Chinese *amahs*, servants, cooks and gardeners, a house with fine view of the shipping in the distant harbor, in some exclusive part of the American settlement. You will rise late, attire yourself in morning dress, and nibble at your toast and tea. You will call for your carriage and be driven out along the Bund for your airing, return home and re-attire in afternoon visiting dress, then go out again to call upon one or another of the other young ladies in the American, English, or French settlements. Daughters of merchants like your father they will be, or of naval officers on station, or consular staff. You will return home, change to evening attire and greet mater or pater upon their return from the hong and the godowns, and supervise intractable Chinese servants in the preparation of dinner."

"Goodness, how dreary," she said, stepping over to the rail. Many small green islets studded the yellow ocean. High on the slope of one island a small red brick temple stood surrounded by groves of tall bamboo and camphor trees. Farther down the slope, a thin

Crossing the Bar

column of white smoke rose from the dun-colored towers. The islands were quite rugged, as named, with many bare stone outcroppings accessible only to the sea birds.

"You have sailed to many countries, Mr. Wood, and lived among many different people. Has it been your practice to learn the languages of those places?"

"Well, miss, after a fashion, I suppose. I had to learn some Spanish in the Americas and Mexico, and some French in the Crimea, and some still rattles around in my head, but I wouldn't bet my life on any of it."

"What made you want to travel so far from home?"

"Perhaps it's because I am tormented with an everlasting itch for things remote, that I love to sail forbidden seas and land on barbarous coasts."

"Well, then, better to be named Ishmael than Fletcher!"

"So now you, too, sail to barbarous coasts, and land in pagan China."

"It is curious. I would not have expected to trade literary allusions with a sailor."

Fletcher pushed away from the rail and offered her his arm. They started back toward the passenger's cabins.

"When I went to sea, I sailed with a sea-chest full of books, as many as I could carry. I read them during those long, quiet watches when the ship sailed itself for great distances and there was little else to do. I swapped with other sailors for books not yet read. And in dusty little out-of-the-way bookshops at foreign ports-of-call, I turned over my entire library for another chest full of books. Often, I returned to Salem with a new collection containing not one of the books I took to sea. This stubborn habit was also the cause of my advancement, 'though not for any knowledge I got by reading."

At the ladder, he offered a hand to stabilize her descent in her long skirt.

"When I was a wild boy in Salem and went aboard my family's ships at anchor, it became clear I could not stay before the mast – the light was too poor to read by. Many ships had no oil lamps in the fo'c's'le, and sailors had to make light from strips of cloth cut from rags and set afloat in a metal cup half-full of fat rendered down from food. But in a mate's cabin, now there was luxury – oil lamps to read by! Why, if I was a mate, I could read twice as many books, because I could read by night as well as by day! So my course was set, and my first appointment was as a ship's officer. Still, I am nothing more than what you'd call self-educated, just an ordinary fellow, salt of the earth, or sea rather, as just at home in your parlor as in a ship's fo'c's'le."

"In my limited experience, Mr. Wood," she said, smiling again, "men are usually one or the other, but not both."

"But I do have wanderlust, Miss Fitch, and unbounded ambition to always be somewhere else. Any woman who sets her heart on having the comfortable home and large family, like a substantial man of business would provide, would do better to consider a more stable man. Consider, by way of contrast, my brother Hugh, who is one inclined to stay at home, one more likely to be content with the joys of home and hearth. A woman could do worse than Hugh. He will live a long and happy life while I, well, my life is more likely to end like that of Alexander the Great."

Elizabeth suddenly felt chill.

3 Late the same day *Essex* grounded, she sighted the small, round 210-foot high lump that was Gutzlaff Island – in spite of the disquiet of Ptolemy Reese over piloting the archipelago alone. Captain Fitch scanned the horizon for any Western vessel flying the pilot's flag, but found none, as pilots were more likely to cruise on the north side of the island, where traffic from the Saddles into Shanghai passed. *Essex* dropped off toward the east, against the tide turning toward the mouth of the Yangtze, then picked up a westerly breeze and pushed around the island. It was dusk when she arrived within sight

洋神 *Yang Shen*   *James Lande* 藍德

of the small rock off the north shore of Gutzlaff Island. Northwest in the gloaming, a dim masthead light flashed at intervals and, in the glass, *Essex* could just make out the hazy lines and fading red blur of the two-masted lightship twenty-three miles distant. More importantly, close in under the light there was on approach a small schooner, painted black, and flying the horizontal red and white flag of a pilot vessel. *Essex* set off a signal flare and backed her mainsail to heave-to and bring aboard yet another pilot.

    The little fore-and-after swung out to the northeast and came around skillfully, setting her sails to catch sufficient wind to move her slowly against the current, then spilling the wind enough to come gently alongside under the clipper's leeward rail.

    "Shanghae Foreign Pilot Schooner" was painted in white letters across her stern. She was the *Molly Mog*, a 76-foot American model schooner of 101 tons burden, lightly built of American oak and elm. The outlines of old gun ports were still visible in her bulwarks – in earlier days when she was the Dent, Beale & Co. opium clipper *Lightfoot*, she had mounted brass 18-pounders to protect her opium cargoes from Chinese pirates. *Molly Mog* tossed up lines and put over fenders and *Essex* unrolled a Jacob's ladder over the side. When the vessels were steady, the schooner disgorged a huge man at least six and one-half feet tall, whose great weight, when he lurched forward and jumped onto the rope boarding ladder, seemed to roll the clipper to starboard like a small swell. Hands jumped to the rail ready to save the ship, then stared jaws agape at the spectacle of 300 pounds swinging from side to side on the creaking ropes of the tiny ladder. The pilot climbed up to the clipper's deck and over the rail with amazing dexterity, much like the mountain ascending the ropes to the climber.

    "*Que milagro!*" moaned the new foretopman.

    "*Que magnifico!*" exclaimed the steward.

    "Mother of all the Maccabees," muttered Ptolemy Reese.

    The pilot, for so he turned out to be, heaved his bulk sternward along the bulwark. The sleeves of his white silk shirt billowed out like studding sails, and his red suspenders hauled his trousers up so high that his cuffs were the companion of his thick calves. With all sail flung wide, and surging against the buntlines above his broad deck, the pilot might have been mistaken for a Yankee clipper under full sail. He backed his mainsail, hove to at the foot of the poop deck ladder, and glared up at the captain.

    "Delevan Slaughter, atcher service Cap'n, if you be the Cap'n."

    "Captain Cornelius Fitch."

    "All right, Cap'n. Here's my license, and the company's book of rules." He set the articles on a step of the ladder. "Whatcher draft, Cap'n? Looks to be eighteen feet fully laden. Ten Mexican dollars a foot for pilotage from Gutzlaff to Shanghai, Cap'n. What's left of you 'pears to be about 200 foot, so you'll be wantin' to scare up $2000.00 Mex. Judging from your sorry looks, you left all your hard cash with them fellers back there in those islands. How about it, Cap'n? You got the scratch?"

    The captain sighed, and aside to Reese said, "why does every revival-tent charlatan and side-show freak from New York to Shanghai pick me for their mark? The rate is in our book of sailing directions." Reese grinned.

    Cornelius Fitch leaned over the railing and hissed down at the pilot. "The published rate is five taels a foot, from Gutzlaff Island to the Shanghai Bund, set by the board of the Shanghai Pilot's Association. You will be most promptly reported to them for this infraction of the rules if you do not start immediately to act like someone born in a house instead of a bordello."

    "Well," the pilot hesitated, "the rates have changed since you was here last. You'll just have to take it or leave it, because no other pilot's going to take you in if you don't go with me. You can be swinging at anchor off the Bund by noon tomorrow, or you can

Crossing the Bar

spend the rest of the week picking your way between Tungsha Banks and Amhearst and Ariadne Rocks. It's all the same to me."

"This is tantamount to highway robbery!" snapped Captain Fitch. "I won't pay it! Are there no honest pilots in China? Must *Essex* suffer all the crooks?"

"Call it what it really is," said a voice behind the captain. Fletcher stepped to the railing. "If it's Delevan Slaughter you're dealing with, it has to be called piracy."

Slaughter started visibly, and then sneered at Fletcher. "You all done with your filibustering, now, Fletcher? What makes you think Shanghai will have you, when we set dogs on beggars and whores? Cap'n, you should know that man's a wanted criminal, and that the American authorities will hang him right along with William Walker if he ever tries to go back to America. Better put him in irons and hold him for the marshal."

"Piracy is the old Delevan Slaughter specialty," Fletcher said, "and I haven't forgotten, I once swore I'd see him swing for it. I'd just bet Slaughter hasn't either. I'd swim into Shanghai towing *Essex* from a rope in my teeth if it meant I could watch him dangle. Matter of fact, somebody get me a rope, and we'll finish this right now – let me lynch this blood-gorged cutthroat!"

Fletcher started for the ladder. The captain clutched his arm and held him. "Empty wagons rattle the loudest," the captain said, "but *Essex* still needs this noisy pilot to get to berth. I'd be obliged if you hanged him another time. For that matter, if you'll just wait 'till we get to safe harbor, I'll hold his legs while you tie the knot."

"He's not to be trusted," Fletcher said, "and he'll put you aground fast as a powder flash if he smells money in it."

The captain looked back down at the pilot. "Listen here, Mr. Delevan Slaughter. A pilot has already been killed on this voyage." The captain paused to let that sink in. "One more dead pilot won't make the difference of a pig's whisker to me or anyone else aboard this ship. No one aboard will hear an ill word said against Mr. Wood, and I'd not put him in irons for any reason, and most certainly not for the murder of a bloated rascal calling himself a pilot. Now I am going to pay you the standard rate for pilotage, and you are going to wave that schooner away and come up here, send up your pilot's pennant, and go to work with my mate standing beside you. He will be ready to gut and skin you for a circus tent if *Essex* comes anywhere near shoal water or rocks. You will do your job or, as God is my witness, I'll have your hide on a hayrack!"

"In a pigs eye!" bawled the pilot. He turned and started for the rail, then stopped short. The schooner *Molly Mog* was already a cable's length away into the gloom.

Essex passed the night anchored in a calm sea off Gutzlaff Island. Early the morning after the fight with Folkie Tom, at three bells of the Middle Watch – 1:30am – the larboard watch began to make ready to get the ship underway. Her jibs and fore staysails were set, as were her fore and main courses, topsails and topgallants, and her spanker. By four bells, *Essex* was sailing north by west at five knots for the lightship at the entrance to the Yangtze River, and Shanghai beyond.

By the time passengers started coming on deck around 7:00am, *Essex* was passing the bare masts of the dull-red lightship. The clipper changed her course to N 63° W and made for the Kiu-t'oan beacon tower on the south bank of the Yangtze, upriver from the entrance about sixteen miles. On the opposite tack, not more than a cable distant – 600 feet – another clipper ship approached, a ship larger than *Essex* that was just setting the last stitch of sail possible, evidently intent on bursting out of the Yangtze River into the East China Sea in all her glory. Fletcher put a glass on her.

"Hello," he said. "That's *Game Cock*. Hugh, look at this. She's a grand clipper ship, 200 feet long, about 1400 tons, and she's putting on *full* sail, at least 8000 square yards

洋神 *Yang Shen*   *James Lande* 藍德

of canvas. *Game Cock* spreads nearly as much sail as *Flying Cloud* and, with all sail set, she must have the same magnificent appearance. You'll never see this again in your life. Quick, jump down and tell the other passengers to come up on deck right away." Word also passed quickly among the *Essex* sailors that *Game Cock* was about to pass by them under full sail and, as passengers gathered at the poop rail, sailors crowded together above the larboard forecastle.

With studdingsails reaching well out beyond her fore and main yardarms, and skysails set below her trucks, *Game Cock* looked like an enormous white cumulus cloud bearing down from the horizon upon the passengers and crew of her smaller sister *Essex*. She loomed larger and larger until she filled the sky before them, humming along toward them with a bone in her teeth. She had the sharp bow of the kind of extreme clipper no longer constructed, built more for speed than capacity, and her slender stem sliced through the waves with barely a ripple. Her figurehead was a fighting gamecock, carved with its head thrust forward beneath her jib, ready to leap out and bury a spur into the spars of all that contested her ferocity.

"Ahoy, *Game Cock*," shouted Captain Fitch through his brass trumpet, "good morning from Captain Cornelius Lowell Fitch of the good ship *Essex* out of Salem. Where are you bound?"

"Ahoy, *Essex*," came the answer. "Morning to you from Captain Clement P. Jayne out of East Boston, bound in ballast for Nagasaki, Japan, to fetch back horses for the Queen's Royal Cavalry. What's your cargo?"

"Sundries for the emporiums of Shanghai."

"You look a little shot up, Captain Fitch."

"Fell afoul of pirates at the Volcanos."

What fool'd come that way, thought *Game Cock*?

"You should see yourself from here," Fletcher shouted.

Captain Jayne grinned and waved up at the firmament of canvas sail above him.

From the *Essex* forecastle came a parting shot: "'Ear, now, I 'ave a game cock, and you won't hafta wait long to see it put on a fine show in Bamboo Town!" Jeers, catcalls, and obscene gestures returned in a fusillade from men on the yardarms of *Game Cock*.

"Couldn't have come down from Shanghai," Reese said, "and be here at this hour, could she Pilot?"

"She came down yesterday noon, and moored inside the bar to bide the night for a boatload of limey quartermasters what's come up from the Chushans to go to the Japans and buy horses for the generals to ride at the Peiho River."

"Where's the Peiho?"

"Up north – runs to Peking from the ocean. The limeys is goin' up north there to kick the emperor's royal arse, they is. You'll find out lots more when you get ashore – always lots of amateur theatricals to keep a feller entertained."

Game Cock came about behind *Essex* and took possession of the channel out to the open sea. Her canvas snapped and her crew sang out as they hauled on her braces and sheets to trim her square sails and heaved at her windlass to secure her anchors.

Captain Fitch kept a weather eye on the lightship, straining anxiously to hear her signal gun. If *Essex* steered the wrong course, and threatened to run aground in shallow water, the lightship would fire a cannon and run up pennants giving the course correction in Marryat's code. Gradually, the masts of the lightship faded into morning mist as the red and white striped brick of the Kiu-t'oan beacon tower emerged from the murk, and the only sound heard was the scream of gulls. Captain Fitch began to feel a

Crossing the Bar

shade more confidence in the pilot, as if the lightship crew had confirmed the course given *Essex* and upheld the pilot's judgement. That is, if anyone is aboard that lightship, thought the captain, and not asleep or murdered by pirates.

Fifteen miles or more north, a low contour emerged from the mists on the horizon, the shoreline of Tsung-ming Island – an accretion of silt deposited in the embouchement of the Yangtze and called the "tongue of the river" by the natives. As *Essex* approached from center channel, the brown haze to the south a mile or two grew into broad, flat, reedy marshland only a little higher than sea level, unrelieved by the swell of any hills. The common impression was of a tedious and uninviting landscape. The river itself, however, invited a variety of bustling activity – all manner of junks under sail, and sampans sculled by *yuloh* sweeps at their sterns, moved along the shoreline and in and out of creeks and inlets.

Where the channel took *Essex* closer to the south bank, mostly only the tops of trees and farmhouses were visible above the dikes. With a telescope, there sometimes could be seen low farmhouses clustered in hamlets on a rise enclosed by stands of bamboo, mulberry, and fruit trees. Cotton and wheat fields surrounded them, and rice paddies divided by creeks and ditches, tree-shaded fishponds, and shallow pans for evaporating salt. Water buffalo tugged at wooden ploughs to furrow the paddies, or turned the large wooden cogwheels of irrigation machinery that employed an endless chain of square hardwood pallets in a wooden trough to raise water from creek to field.

At the Kiu-t'oan beacon tower, *Essex* changed course to N 15° W and proceeded up the river between a sparse line of black iron nun buoys on the larboard, and red buoys on the starboard hand, looking for the trees on Block House Island, eight miles further on. Finding the trees, she set out to search for the beacon off Bush Island. She could be grateful the trees on Block House Island were not torn out by typhoons, or chopped down for firewood.

Essex descried her proximity to the mouth of the Whangpoo as she passed the Bush Island beacon. In the distance, she saw several large Western ships anchored in the Yangtze, just outside the bar, where they waited on wind and tide to cross. While she was still well away from that anchorage, the mate sent the ship's boy to call Captain Fitch on deck for the maneuvers required to bring the ship around to a starboard tack and take her over the bar. The boy also alerted the passengers that the ship was at the Whangpoo River, should they wish to come on deck to observe the crossing of the bar.

Stone fortifications defended each bank at the mouth of the Whangpoo. Ancient cannon on the walls of each fort pointed out over a busy junk anchorage inside the bar, where all manner of brightly painted Chinese boats, from numerous ports along the coast and up and down the Yangtze, together created a gaudy and raucous scene. The pilot ordered the spanker let off to slow the ship's approach to the river mouth, and then explained the aids to navigation placed on the riverbanks to show where to cross the bar of mud across the mouth of the Whangpoo.

"That #8 red buoy, that marks the north spit. Steam tug *Meteor* pulled a vessel off there not two days ago, bark *Templeman* it was, stranded out on that spit for a whole week. Farther up the Whangpoo, on the west bank, you can see three sixty-foot high poles on that stone fort. The two red poles in the rear have crow's nests. The white pole in front has the bull's eye target. Over on the west side of the entrance, that's the Paushan Tower, and there's a beacon just in front of it. We stay on a line for that beacon until the white pole lines up between the red poles, and then we steer for the target on the white pole. That'll take us along the narrow trough through the outer bar. Pass close to the red buoy, taking care not to slam into the ship that's sunk near there. Stay on that side of the river, past the poles, past more sunken junks, up to the town of Woosung."

洋神 *Yang Shen*   *James Lande* 藍德

The first mate called all hands to stations, and then went forward to command his watch at the foremast. The second mate rehearsed with his watch at the mainmast what each man was to do, and threatened to take a belaying pin and make soup out of the head of any man who failed to do exactly as told. The third mate posted his watch around the mizzenmast. The captain ordered the fore and main courses set, and braced square sail around sharp to catch the wind coming broadly over her larboard bow. Close-hauled on the larboard tack, she threatened to shake her sails and lose control in the current. So she eased off her spanker, and put her helm over to starboard five points to get up speed and find the balance between on and off the wind that would make a successful turn. By the time the square sails were set again, *Essex* had enough momentum to risk bringing her back around full-and-by, and she was turned five points back to larboard.

"Ready about."

Preparations by all watches were complete. Sails were properly trimmed, weather leeches tight, halyards and sheets laid out, lines on the lee side loosened from their pins.

"Masts manned and ready sir!"

The helmsman turned the wheel downwind just enough to start the turn, but not so much that the rudder might slow the ship. Crewmen stood tense at their lines and sheets, intent on the trim of their yards and sails and waited for the next commands. The mates glared out over the deck, their gaze jumping quickly from man to man, and shouted oaths in anticipation of every possible mistake.

"Helm's alee!"

Essex started around toward the mouth of the Whangpoo River. The crew hauled the spanker boom to larboard, where the wind could fall upon it again and force the stern around and the bow across the wind. The square sails commenced to shake.

"Raise tacks and sheets!"

Frantically, *Essex* hauled up her main course and doused her main and mizzen staysails. A moment later, the upper square sails slapped against their masts.

"Mains'l haul!"

The crew began hauling on the mainyards to brace them around for the starboard tack. As *Essex* continued her turn, and her bow cut through the wind, the mainyards started around and the sails began to draw. Wind in her sails helped brace the mainyards around the rest of the way needed.

"Let go and haul!"

Now she braced her foreyards around on the new tack, reset the main and mizzen staysails, lowered the main course, and trimmed all sails. She eased her spanker off to reduce lee helm and keep the ship close to the wind.

"This is not the best wind for this," muttered the pilot, "but we do it all the time during the summer monsoon."

Essex started into the river mouth, pulling for the wind, pushing against the ebb, eager to vanquish the bar. Then she faltered, her sails began to shake, and the wind threatened to clap her in irons.

"Pilot!" cried the helmsman, "she's drifting! She won't answer the helm!"

Essex lost headway and began to shudder in the swirling current. She was about to miss the channel, and ride her beam-ends into the muck of the shoal.

Crossing the Bar

洋神 *Yang Shen*   *James Lande* 藍德

Dramatis Personae: Chapter 8

Ezra   *Essex* third mate, on mizzenmast watch
Jamie   *Essex* helmsman
Stockton Hull   U. S. marshal at Shanghai

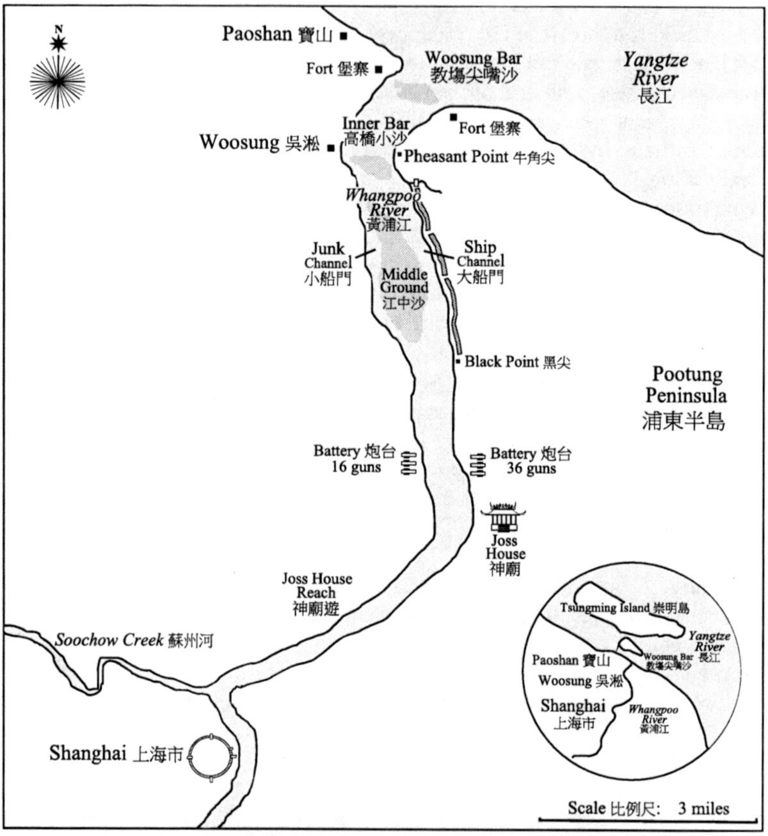

Whangpoo River, Woosung Bar to Shanghai Harbor
(based on British Hydrographic Office chart, Yang-tse-kyang, Sheet IX, 1842)

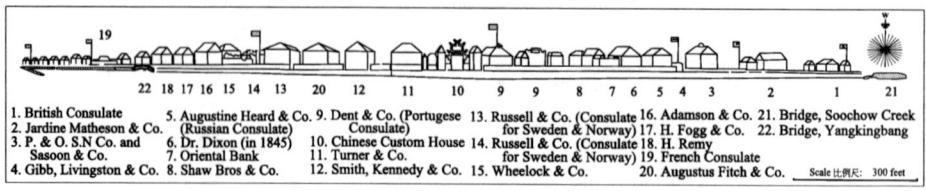

Shanghai Bund in 1857
(from H. B. Morse, The International Relations of the Chinese Empire, 1918, Vol. 1, p. 464)

knot (nautical mile): 6076 feet (Br. knot = 6080 feet), 798 feet, or 15%, longer than a land mile.
         cable: one hundred fathoms   **fathom**: six feet.
         larboard (port): left   **starboard**: right.

126   *Essex at Shanghai*

Chapter 8: *Essex* at Shanghai
Friday, April 20, 1860, 12:00pm

"Easy, now, helmsman," Delevan Slaughter said, "don't getchur wind up. I'm sticking to you like bark to a tree. When I say the word, you give me a point to larboard, just when we need more wind in her sails for an extra push. Captain Fitch, I must have the spanker braced more to starb'd to get more weather helm."

Damn your hide, thought the captain – the spanker should've been braced before we started across. The captain yelled his commands to Ezra, the third mate, where he stood ready aft of the mizzenmast, and six crewman loosed the spanker sheets and pulled with all their might on the outhaul to swing the heavy spanker boom out three feet to starboard against the wind. The captain could feel the 185-foot long ship come around slightly and inch forward over the bar.

"Now, helmsman," the pilot said quietly, "a point to larboard."

"Point to larboard," repeated the helmsman.

Essex swung to larboard in response to her helm, and the wind fell more fully on her close-hauled courses, and the spanker, and increased her momentum.

"Now bring her back a point."

"Point to starboard."

The helmsman smiled as he turned the wheel, realizing the maneuver had overcome the force of the crosscurrents and nudged *Essex* forward across the bar.

The first mate was careful to record in the ship's log the details of the run into Shanghai from the open ocean. There were far too many hazards for sailing ships here – too many narrow passages, sunken ships, and too much uncharted bottom. He needed some record, copied out of the log of *Essex*, in preparation for the next time he came around the world to land at Shanghai. The *Essex* log recorded a figure for leeway as well as location, wind, current, course and speed. Leeway was the drift away from a course caused by the force of wind and current, which in a single day could result in navigation errors of miles on broad oceans, less in narrow seas and rivers.

Log of Ship ESSEX, Augustus Fitch & Co.

Date & Time	Lat & Long	Wind (est.)	Current (est.)	Course	Speed	Leeway
Ap 20, 1860, 2:00am	N 30° 47' 0" E 122° 10' 0"	SW 6 knots	SE by E, 1¼ knots	N by W ¾ West	5 knots	½ point

(Reese) Departed Gutzlaff Island with pilot Delevan Slaughter from Molly Mog at 4 bells of the Middle Watch, tide out of the Yangtze River at quarter ebb. Under fore and main courses, topsails and topgallants, jibs and staysails. Daybreak at 5:21am. Shallow water, narrow trench, heaved much lead to stay in line. Expect more difficulty during neap tides. Lem Grace arm sliced in fight started by Ram John. Weller drunk on watch. (Fitch) Ship's punishment: Ramsay John – 20 lashes and forfeiture of month's pay. Crusoe Weller – forfeiture of week's pay.

Date & Time	Lat & Long	Wind (est.)	Current (est.)	Course	Speed	Leeway
Ap 20, 1860, 7:10am	N 31° 7' 30" E 122° 0' 30"	SW 7 knots	NW by W, 1 knot	North 63° West	6 knots	¼ point

(Reese) Raised lightship 24 miles from Gutzlaff. Steered north 63° west for the beacon tower at 6 knots, too fast in this shoal water but pilot refused to reduce speed. Spoke clipper <u>Game Cock</u> bound for Nagasaki. Entered Yangtze River channel on last of flood tide, red buoys on starboard, black buoys to port. River narrows, channel southerly. Lee helm with wind forward made her drift off much – doused fore and main

洋神 *Yang Shen* James Lande 藍德

courses, sheeted spanker to board for better headway. Carried by flood. Sighted red and white beacon tower and south shore. Passed Block House Island, North 15 ° West, 8 miles beyond beacon tower. Raised beacon at Bush Island. Levi left his station. Ord talking at work. (Fitch) Ship's punishment: Levi Haskett and Ord Strikeleather, extra hard duty for one week.

Date & Time	Lat & Long	Wind (est.)	Current (est.)	Course	Speed	Leeway
Ap 20, 1860, 12:05pm	N 31° 23' 30" E 121° 28' 10"	SW 10 knots gusting	WNW, 1 knot downriver	ESE against current	5 knots	¼ point

(Reese) High slack-water at 11:10am – will lose the flood before getting to Shanghai. Raised Woosung Bar, distance from Gutzlaff 58 miles, 12 miles to Shanghai up Whangpoo River. Starboard tack to enter river. Scraped some barnacles crossing outer Woosung Bar, have to sight on poles on west shore to cross at deepest water.

Essex passed the junk anchorage at Woosung, the swollen terminus of the straggle of anchorages that accompanied the left bank of the river all the way up from inside the outer bar. Large sea-going trading junks from the north lined up stem to stern with iceboats, pigboats, ungainly Foochow junks loaded with thousands of poles, cotton freighters built at the tongue-of-the-river – Tsung-ming Island – and numerous other brightly painted junks, lighters and sampans packed into the narrow spaces of the anchorage. The town of Woosung rose up from the shore behind the anchorage as an assembly of gray mud walls and dark tile roofs interrupted by the sudden contrast of vividly colored, sharply upcurved temple eaves reaching up from the roofs of the town into the heavens. Beyond the boundaries of the town, farmhouses clustered together in villages at the intersections of creeks, where boughs of willow drooped and camphor trees and small fruit orchards scented the air.

"This is not Shanghai is it? It is very small," Hugh said.

"This is Woosung," Fletcher said, "downriver maybe twelve miles from Shanghai. If a person couldn't tell any other way, those receiving ships moored there mark the place as Woosung."

"Which are the receiving ships?" Elizabeth said.

"That little fleet over there at permanent anchor without sails or rigging," Fletcher said, examining them closely through the telescope. "The topmasts have all been taken down. Appears to be six of them left now, *Ann Walsh* – that would be Augustine Heard's ship – *Ariel*, *Emily Jane* is Dent's if I recall, *Lady Hayes* is Jardine's, *Swallow* and *Wellington*. Used to be eight when I was last here. Little bark called *Nimrod* is gone; that was Sassoon's, and there was a *Sea Horse*, too – belonged to one of the other Parsee trading houses. These opium hulks come and go."

"Opium?" said Elizabeth.

"Sure," said Fletcher. He paused, for no more reason than to aggravate her.

"Sure? Sure what!" He succeeded.

"What?"

"What about the opium hulks, Mr. Wood?" Mentally, he could see her stamping her little foot.

"Oh, right. Well, the opium clippers that used to carry the drug up the coast from Hong Kong, on consignment to British, Jewish, and Parsee merchant houses, always transferred their cargoes to these old opium hulks instead of taking the opium up to Shanghai, where customs would make them pay duties. That was after the drug was treated as legal in practice, but before it became legal by treaty in fifty-eight. At any one time, an opium hulk might have 4000 to 5000 chests aboard. The Chinese buyers would just come alongside the receiving ship for their opium. The drug would find its way from here up the Yangtze, or up the coast. Even the Americans had receiving ships here once. All the treaty ports had them."

"Why did they let these ships stay here?" Hugh said. "Surely the Shanghai authorities knew about opium smuggling going on here under their nose at Woosung."

"The British actually put the receiving ships at Woosung themselves, to separate the illegal trade from the legal trade that lands in Shanghai – nothing if not organized, the Brits. If the British consul can't see an opium hulk from out his window, he doesn't have to go aboard and examine its manifest and charge duties, and he can ignore the opium."

"The British," Hannah said, "insist it is the responsibility of the Chinese authorities to collect Chinese duties. The consuls go along some distance to observe the treaty regulations, but if the opium is outside the consul's treaty port jurisdiction, it is not in the British consul's interest to press British merchants for duties, and the consuls of the other nations follow along with the British."

"One would have expected," Hugh said, "the Chinese authorities to object to all this, the viper in their bosom, so to speak. I mean, opium is against their law, is it not, so why did they not stop it? Why did they not drive away the receiving ships?"

"I'm not certain I understand all that, Hugh. Of course, if Chinese tried to board one of these hulks and seize the opium, and the crews *didn't* blow 'em to pieces, then there'd just be another big row with the British merchants. And the British consuls, who are here to back up the merchants when you come right down to it. The merchants'd drag the mandarins into consular court and yammer at 'em about property rights, and treaty rights, and extrality, and everything else in our laws that the Chinese hardly understand."

"What is extrality?" Elizabeth said.

"Extraterritoriality, they call it – you can see why we shorten the word. It means foreigners are not subject to Chinese laws, only to the laws of their own nations. Anyway, the opium hulks would just turn up somewhere else. If you asked me to guess, I'd say the trading houses that trafficked in opium probably paid off the mandarins to leave them alone."

"You have some doubt?" Hannah said. Fletcher smiled.

2 At the wheel, the captain, mate, and helmsman conferred again with the pilot.

"Now we're coming up on the second complication," the pilot said, "the inner bar. A little farther upriver, we'll come to a long shoal called the Middle Ground. East of the Middle Ground is the channel that takes us up to Shanghai. On the other side, that's the junk channel – too shallow for anything but them flat-bottomed junks. To get over into the ship channel to Shanghai, your vessel starts across the current toward the east shore, crosses over the inner bar, then comes about into the ship channel before running up onto the east shore. Inner bar is marked by them two little boats just coming into view beyond Pheasant Point, moored over there toward the east bank – the white boat, and the red boat farther upstream. The little white house on the far shore, that's in Mr. Henderson's garden. We cross the river going between them two little boats, keeping a bearing on the little white house."

Sampans sculled across the path of the clipper, laggards tugging frantically at their *yuloh* sweeps to clear her cutwater. Fletcher observed carefully the sinister-looking junks that stood off at a distance with no respectable business to be about. Watching the advance of the huge ship, he thought, ready to pounce on her the moment she goes aground in this narrow space where there's hardly room to swing a saber, strip her bare, and be gone before help can even be summoned.

"Betcha never thought it'd be this easy," the pilot said.

"I've seen worse," the captain lied. "Let's get to it."

"Helmsman, two points to larboard!" barked the pilot.

"Two points to larboard," repeated the helmsman. The rudder swung to one side, but the ship did not respond. The wind had dropped off suddenly, and the ebb was still not very strong. Without the pressure of water against the rudder, the ship would not turn. *Essex* just drifted to larboard. She was slowly starting back downriver, working up sternway in the slight current.

"Pilot," the captain said, "the ship is not responding again."

The pilot peered ahead around the main course. "Not responding, hmm? You must have her cargo loaded wrong. Her center of balance must be too far aft."

"The devil you say!" Reese said with a growl. He shouldered the huge pilot aside, pushed in front of the helmsman, and violently spun the wheel to bring the rudder over full, as far as it would turn.

A large junk nearby hauled up her lugsails and started drifting toward the clipper.

"Cap'n Fitch," the pilot said, "I'll not be responsible for your vessel if…."

"Be quiet, Pilot!" the captain said. "Mr. Reese, what are you doing?"

"Giving her all the rudder she can take, sir, so's the current has the full face of the rudder to push against, and can swing her around enough to put more wind in her sails."

"Cap'n…," said the pilot.

"Pilot!" snarled the captain. "You stand right there and answer every question I put to you as if your life depends upon it." Captain Fitch turned to the pilot and stared up into his face. "Because it does."

What captains and owners feared, what experienced sailors knew would happen when a ship lost the wind in a narrow roadstead with a slack current, was happening now. The wind could not catch her close-hauled sails and take *Essex* across the river. She would slowly drift onshore with the indifferent current unless turned to get her head off the wind and fill her sails.

The first mate was thinking as fast as anchor chain rattled out of a hawsehole. Too little sail forward – but choirboys could set a headsail, in minutes. Too much sail aft. And the spanker's still braced to starboard and pushing the bow around into the wind.

"Micah!" Reese yelled. "Set the foretop staysail. Ezra! Ease off the spanker, and douse the main and mizzen staysails. Smartly, now, any man who wants to stay afloat."

With the change in sail, the stern slowly inched to starboard and the bow swung over toward the east shore. The current pushing against the flat of the rudder nudged *Essex* around a little. The headsails began to draw. Further into her turn, the rising wind filled the rest of her sails. She came about and sluggishly set out across the current. The little bit of wind she sliced through blew now on a great deal more sail and carried her away from the Middle Ground. The current rushed full against her rudder, her speed surged, and Reese finally was able to steer again.

Reese put the helmsman back at the wheel and stood to one side, quietly whispering instructions. *Essex* headed over to the east shore and, when within three cable lengths, came about to starboard, where she found the narrow channel upriver to Shanghai. The following junk fell off toward Woosung, presumably to await another victim.

The SW wind falling behind her starboard bow pushed her along slowly beside a 20-foot-high crumbling earthen dike, built to protect the east bank, and notched at intervals with vents to release overflowing water. She passed the junk anchorage above the Middle Ground, and Black Point. By then, the pilot's attention to the handling of the ship struck Reese as no better than distracted, like a for-hire horse returning to its stable, so the first mate stayed beside his helmsman.

"Captain," the pilot said, "up ahead there's an old temple, dirty red brick, collapsed walls. That's where the river turns right for five miles southwest from the Joss House up to Shanghai. This wind'll be coming smack down the middle of the river, close to ten knots, and maybe the ebb is two knots by now. You're making about six knots with the wind near 'cross your beam. If the wind and current hold for that stretch up to the creek, you could make your way – if your crew can beat to windard that far. You wouldn't be the first that's done it under sail, 'gainst the summer monsoon. If the wind falls off, 'tho, you'll be looking for a steamer. Too bad we didn't get here sooner."

"Good Lord, I think they're getting ready to *sail* up to Shanghai," Fletcher said. He was standing at the tafferel with Hugh. The ladies Fitch were below.
"Why wouldn't they?" Hugh said.
"The wind and current will be squarely in her face."
"And square-rigged ships don't sail well into the wind?"
"Not like *Vivid*. She will have to make many boards to get to Shanghai.
"Boards? Is that like tacking a fore-and-after?"
"Yes. Many tacks back and forth across the narrow river, all the way."
"Sounds like a lot of work."
"For even the best of crews. This bunch will be very busy."
"Not much room in this river, is there? A mile wide?"
"Less than a mile, maybe four or five cables for turns – a half mile."
Opposite the Joss House, *Essex* followed the bend of the river and came about several points upriver into the wind – as far as she dare without shaking her sails. She struck out diagonally across the river, ready to sound near the opposite bank for shallows where she would have to change direction. She crossed the current on a starboard tack, with the spanker sheeted a little to windward to keep her from falling off. The captain and the helmsman watched the weather leeches of the sails, constantly adjusting the helm to keep the sails filling.
Mid-channel of the first board the depth was six fathoms – thirty-six feet.
600 yards from the flat, grassy shoreline, the depth was five fathoms – thirty feet.
At 400 yards, the depth was three and one-half fathoms – twenty-one feet.
"Ready about."
"All masts manned and ready, sir!"
On the captain's order, the helmsman started the turn, and *Essex* came about into the southwest wind.
"Helm's alee!" the helmsman shouted.

Essex struggled back and forth across the river many times, each time more quickly than the last, and with fewer mishaps. Finally, the pennants of foreign ships beyond Pootung Point came into view, waving in the afternoon sun, and a row of Western-style buildings loomed up over the Shanghai Bund. The pilot pointed to the closest one.
"That's the British consulate," he said. "Steer for that red brick building, at the mouth of Soochow Creek, where the *chow-chow* water is. To get past there without any grief, you want to come about up into the anchorage before you get out to mid-stream. Have your fore and main topsails and topgallants set again before starting your turn."
Essex approached the harbor like a timid yet restless green sailor, slipping gingerly into his first noisy grogshop, bowled over by the rush of girls to get at his towrope. The anxious ship would not turn, and her momentum advanced her past the channel into the flux where the current shoved at her hull, the wind blew on her bow, and she menaced the lighters and sampans sculling headlong around her. She bellied up to the *chow-chow*

Essex *at Shanghai*

rip, slammed against it, and offered drinks for all. But the flow out of Soochow Creek surged up and bounced her back out into the channel before she could swallow. She picked herself up, blinked at the light, shook her sails a few times, gazed about for a new bearing, and then staggered away, chastened but cheered by her narrow escape.

Abruptly, a bold panorama that occupied the entire western horizon arose ahead of *Essex*. The narrow confines of river, town, and clipper ship fell away upon all sides and a broad sweep of the chaotic municipality embraced the ship, before which a wide anchorage of hundreds of vessels ranged along the shoreline. Passengers gathered at the starboard rail, above the poop deck ladder, from where they could have the best view of the harbor, and the newcomers beset the Old China Hands with inquiry about historical and cultural landmarks. The watch off duty mustered on the starboard forecastle head for their view of the harbor, and listened to older hands hold forth on the landfall of consulates, trading houses, sailors' homes, grogshops, opium dens and brothels.

A towering framework of crisscrossed masts, yards, booms and spars in the foreign anchorage off the Bund advanced south up the river for over a mile, and beyond them the native junk anchorage continued on another three miles. Nearly three hundred merchantmen and ships of war, anchored stem to stern in the river, rolling with the incoming tide. Tier after tier of closely moored brigs, barks and ships lolled in haphazard ranks, with their jib booms rigged in and cockbilled yards lifted like saber salutes to the Union Jack, Tricolor, Old Glory, and the flags of lesser nations. Dozens of side-paddle steam frigates and smaller gunboats seeped black smoke from their tall stacks and tugged at their moorings. So much shipping was crammed into the anchorage that barely 600 yards remained for the channel on the east side of the river.

"My goodness, mother!" Elizabeth said, "will you look at the warships! Are they going off to fight the Taiping rebels?"

"No, dear," Hannah said, "this is part of the expeditionary force. The warships at Hong Kong are the larger part of this fleet. More were arriving as we sailed."

"Some of these warships'll go north to Peking to fight the emperor," Fletcher said. "Others are on permanent station in Shanghai or downriver at Woosung. A few will go north to reconnoiter, the rest south to Chushan for the occupation. They'll leave a garrison at Tinghai and return to Hong Kong – join the fleet there, waiting for the ice to melt in the north. Rumors in Ningpo said that Tinghai'll be much too busy getting ready to do business with the troops to consider defending the place. The mandarins'll climb all over each other to be the first aboard the frigates and rent their yamens – their official residences – to the officers for headquarters."

"The English will never commit troops to fight the rebels," Hannah said, "not while they continue to pout about what they consider the bad behavior of the Chinese emperor, and his stubborn demand to have negotiations here."

"Why must the English go north and fight a war if the Chinese want to negotiate at Shanghai," Elizabeth said.

"The high mandarins in Peking refused to ratify the new treaty," Fletcher said, "in rather certain terms. But that probably upset the English less than the monumental affront to their precious dignity of seeing their general unhorsed and their admiral dismasted by second-raters. Tired of nursing their wounded pride, the English now come forth to chastise the Chinese for beating them so soundly at the Taku forts last year. The mighty English navy stymied by a few squadrons of Sam Collinson's Mongol cavalry – that really sticks in their craw. They say it was enough just to have the Union Jack torn down from the truck of the *Arrow*, and Taku adds injury to insult."

"You do not have to read the *Times*," Hannah said, "to know that opium smugglers

– Jardine, Dent, and the others – have been prodding parliament to declare this war. The French, they have no business to speak of in China, not like the English. I do not understand why they want to get involved in a stupid little war like this one about to be perpetrated on the Chinese."

"The French have gotten uppity about the murder of some Catholic priests," Fletcher said, "but all they really want is glory. The French haven't seen glory on the battlefield since Sebastopol, back in fifty-six, and Louis Napoleon is looking for a few spectacular victories to impress the rabble that keeps him on his throne. A fine pair of allies the French and English will make. Their armies'll probably catch Hong Kong fever, go into shivering fits, and turn on each other long before they see any Chinese."

Elizabeth considered the fleet of warships for a moment, and then replied, "Do you mean to say that at the same time the English are defending the Chinese government against the Taiping rebels surrounding Shanghai, they are attacking the Chinese government in Peking?"

Fletcher chuckled. "Well, not defending Shanghai, not officially. The meticulous English insist they're neutral in the squabble between longhairs and Manchus. But ask me, and I'd say the English figure Shanghai is theirs, just like Hong Kong and, if they fire on Taiping rebels, it's more to defend an English settlement than a Chinese city."

"But Hong Kong was ceded to Britain by a treaty, wasn't it? Surely the Chinese didn't give away Shanghai as well."

"Now, dear," Hannah said, clucking, "you shouldn't bother yourself with rebels and wars and treaties. Such things are not the concern of a proper young woman. All one needs to know is that governments make wars and treaties, and that governments are run by men, not women, so it is no wonder that everything in the world is topsy-turvey."

"Mrs. Fitch," Hugh said, "the English march on Peking for Queen Victoria."

"Hugh Wood," Hannah said, "you know very well Queen Victoria is no more than a prim little figurehead, and that Palmerston is the power in parliament, where the decisions to go to war are made. The English march on Peking in the name of Palmerston and empire. And free markets for woolen goods, and opium in Chinese treaty ports. I'll thank you to remember you are an American, and not party to the hypocrisy of governments that take refuge behind cries of 'queen and country' while they send innocent young men off to die in foreign lands for English mercantile policy."

Essex slowly passed the churning froth of the *chow-chow* water at the confluence of Soochow Creek and the Whangpoo River. Approaching closer to the west bank, the growing din of activity along river and creek subdued the noise of the contending waters: shrill steamer whistles, songs of boatmen and cries of sampan men. Strident gongs and piercing high-pitched horns and strings, temple drums and violent bursts of firecrackers. Hammering on anvils, sawing on wood, the wailing of street hawkers. Swarms of fetid odors that would plague the newcomers until they left Shanghai drifted out over the river from the creek and joined the assault upon the senses: paddle-wheeler smoke, garbage and night soil junks, stagnant water in ponds and ditches. Sesame oil from cooking pots, burnt peanut oil in frying pans, temple incense and firecracker fumes. Bitter vapors from silver refineries, human excrement in open drains, rotting fish and refuse under jetties. And decaying cadavers floating with the tides. All contributed to the swirl of sound and scent swept down the creek into the harbor.

"Brings to mind," Fletcher said, "the remark of the Scotsman about to arrive home. Sweet Edinbro, ah smells thee noo."

Junks and sampans thronged off Soochow Creek, many more than at the Woosung anchorage. Shanghai lighters hugged the stone quays together with Ningpo ice-boats stinking of the catch from the fishing grounds, Tsung-ming cotton junks, white-hulled Fukien traders, black-hulled Soochow junks, and disheveled lorchas, all with bulwarks painted in the bright colors of their ports of origin. Brick-boats, wine-boats, firewood-boats, and fishing-boats jammed tightly together left little room for the dense traffic in and out of the creek. Boats tangled with each other while boatmen laughed and waved and longshoremen shouted gratuitous warnings.

Immediately behind *Essex* was the American Settlement at Hongkew, north of Soochow Creek, a motley collection of docks and wharves and shabby buildings scattered behind the dapper Astor House Hotel. The American Episcopal Church Mission stood on the bank of the Whangpoo, its tower long a welcome sight to the captains of ships coming up the river from Woosung to Shanghai. Just before the mouth of Soochow Creek, on an alley in a swamp at the edge of Hongkew, stuffed in between coal sheds, a sailor's boarding house, and the dockyard, was the ramshackle building that passed as the American consulate.

"Russell and Company built it out of charity," Hannah said, "as a refuge for the American consul."

Across the mouth of Soochow creek, within sight of the miserable accommodations of the American consul, were the broad and spacious grounds of the British consulate, with consular residence amidst manicured lawns and shrubbery, and a court house, post office, and jail enclosed by a substantial brick wall.

"Here in China," Hannah said, "where the people know nothing of political relations between foreign countries, wealth and power are judged by public display of pomp and ostentation – and we have the American consul living in a shack across from the Buckingham Palace of the English magistrate. Even the French are embarrassed, and Lord knows how pompous they are. Can anyone blame the Chinese for considering us Americans as nothing more than second-chop Englishmen?"

3 Western concessions followed the river along the old towpath foreigners had come to call the Bund, a half-mile long quay of river mud exposed at low tide. From the American settlement, the Bund extended south beside the British concession from Soochow Creek to the *Yang-king-bang* creek. The *Quai du Whangpoo* – the French Bund – continued south from the *Yang-king-bang* and ended at the Shanghai city wall. The riverbank from there to the East Gate was the Chinese Bund.

The foreign settlements little resembled the Chinese city. The British Bund was a wide, tree-lined path paved with coal cinders and granite chips, and lined by closely crowded buildings. The Western-style wooden facades rose to a uniform height of one or two stories, with large, orderly rows of windows looking out over the jetties and harbor – a small incarnation of High Street in London. The *Quai du Whangpoo* was a muddy track edged with an aggregation of a few smaller European buildings enveloped by Chinese hongs, godowns, emporiums, temples, hovels, and empty ground. The incongruous profile created by the colonial architecture of the foreign hongs, godowns, shipping offices, and hotels facing the Bund, stretched off toward the southern horizon until interdicted by the high, stone-faced ramparts of the Chinese wall.

The largest merchantmen moored off the British Bund were the American clipper ships *Fanny McHenry*, *Forest Eagle* and *Indiaman*, each as large as *Essex*. Next in size was Dent's ship *Hurricane*, and Russell and Co.'s ship *Matilda*. The rest of the merchants were brigs and barks, English and Dutch mostly, of 500 tons or less, each consigned to one of the larger trading houses:. Hannah thought that, as before, one or two were probably under charter to the queen to carry troops and supplies. The warships included the paddle-wheel steam frigate *Furious*, the gunboats *Nimrod* and *Woodcock*,

洋神 *Yang Shen*　　　　　　　　　　　　　　　　　　　　　　　　*James Lande* 藍德

and several other steamers and troop transports.

Upriver from Hongkew and Soochow Creek, the throng of Shanghai harbor life off the British Bund was still more animated. Yangtze River trading junks set out into the stream with crew singing in lusty chorus as they hauled up sail. Bawling peddlers in sampans sculled about hawking their wares or vegetables, and barber boats bumped alongside merchantmen to offer haircuts. Dentists drew up to anchor chains and waved crude paintings of bright teeth, and lighters of all sizes unloaded cargo for the godowns and loaded cargo to stow aboard ships. Sampans of all types ferried passengers to and from the jetties. Barges laden with farm produce lumbered into the harbor, and barges passed upriver back to the farms loaded with human fertilizer. Several thousand junks and smaller vessels lay at rest in the narrow water between the anchorage and the Nantao suburbs around the city wall. Moored under the wall there was a floating municipality of permanent boat-dwellers.

The major Western trading houses lined the Bund south from the British consulate to the perimeter of the French Settlement. A row of large Western-style buildings facing the river, interrupted by one Chinese temple compound, extended nearly to the Chinese walled city. Fletcher pointed up the Bund to the American trading house of Augustus Fitch and Company, lodged in an imposing, three-story building with long verandahs and a huge portico above the entrance. Steps ascended from each side to a landing midway up, and thence from the landing up to the front, where large pillars stood on each side of the entrance. The grounds were scrupulously landscaped with bushes, flowers, and trees around a closely trimmed lawn of yellowing grass.

Elizabeth studied the facade of her father's trading house, relieved that it was a substantial structure able to hold its own with any other trading house on the Bund. Her gaze then passed along the scattered foreign buildings queued up along the *Quai du Whangpoo* to where it ended abruptly at the somber wall that enclosed the native city in a circle of gray stone. Fletcher called that wall the *omphalos* of Shanghai, the middle of all things, the navel of the settlements he might have said. The prospect, she thought, was not at all like that of the America from which she had taken leave three months earlier. Here in Shanghai, no tidy progression of shipping passed into the anchorage, none like that below the somber gray of the State House dome that dominated the rose-red brick face of Boston. Salem, too, had the civilized and confident aspect of a center of commerce and culture, a grand port of the American east coast, where an industrious and orderly people launched vital enterprises and built great industries.

Nonetheless, she was already prepared to admit to herself her excitement at the romantic spectacle of this exotic land, captivated like so many traders and merchants of her own family's stock, seafarers and adventurers before her. Its strange and mysterious aspect suggested the peril of imminent cataclysm in the events at hand, and vague possibilities she could not yet begin to comprehend. She felt within her that something was coming to life in the chill and colorless winter countryside of her New England soul, and she tingled in a vague anticipation of a change in her life, conscious of the proximity of its promise while still ignorant of its form. It felt like the moment before the first dawn she had ever seen at sea – if the aura alone could cause such excitement, how could she survive the event itself?

"China seems a kind of Longfellow land," she said to Fletcher, "full of people and places with curious names. By the shores of the gitchee-goomee, and all that. I am almost regretting I shall be here for only one year before we all return home to Salem."

Fletcher laughed.

"Oh, go ahead and laugh your smug laugh at my sentiment, Mr. Fletcher Wood," Elizabeth said, "but just bear in mind that it is laughable only because it is exaggerated, not because it is unsound."

"Unsound! But Elizabeth, it *is* unsound. So unsound that sound should never be given utterance to such sentiment. What ever is life's meaning can be seen sooner from atop the masthead of a foundering ship than from the pianoforte of a genteel Beacon Street drawing room. People like your precious Ralph Waldo Emerson, or Julia Ward Howe, they might just as well live in bottles for all they know about life!"

"Emerson is a great philosopher!" she said. "A teacher, and a lecturer."

"Emerson is a poet and a preacher, with little practical experience."

"He toured Europe, and wrote about the English."

"Taking the Grand Tour hardly qualifies as experience – Thoreau is more practical. I reckon that even you, miss, will know more about life by your next birthday than all the Boston Brahmins put together will ever begin to con. More's the pity of it, too."

"Oh, why pity, Mr. Wood?"

"You're a nicely bred lady, Elizabeth Fitch, but for everything got something's lost in the getting. Gentility does not thrive in China."

"Come now, surely matters are not as bad as all that. Innocence must be lost in some time, and at some place, and it may just as well be in Shanghai as in Salem."

Fletcher stared at her for a moment as he quelled some exasperation. "Matters are much worse, Miss Fitch. While delicate young girls struggle to avoid the loss of their innocence, the innocence of nations is blasted. If there is to be a civil war at home, some people expect that perhaps as many as 200,000 or more soldiers will die on American battlefields. I have read that more than one hundred times that number, over 20,000,000, may die before this Chinese civil war is over, a civil war that Americans know little and care less about. It is too far beyond our borders, across too much water, for us to concern ourselves with what happens in China. We treat the Chinese like the primitive Africans, as just another barbaric race of coloreds, good for nothing but coolie slaves because they have no steamships, no telegraph, no railroads, no civilization as *we* know it."

Elizabeth smirked perceptibly as she said, "But is it not that very same disdain for an inferior race, Mr. Wood, which makes it possible for adventurers and cutthroats to make their illicit fortunes in China? To spill the blood of innocent people, without so much as a 'pshaw' in condemnation from the authorities?"

Fletcher's jaw tightened visibly and the enthusiasm drained from his voice. "Yes, it is, Miss Fitch. Perhaps that American ignorance of conditions in China is best after all; otherwise, the land would be overrun by soldiers of fortune who would regard China as only the next American frontier. A frontier only a little ways beyond the Rocky Mountains and Columbia River valley, another wilderness of wild natives and abundant land, and resources from which more empires might be carved. God knows the Chinese are plagued enough now by bible-thumping, psalm-singing foreign missionaries, larcenous foreign traders, and addle-brained foreign consuls."

If this dynasty is in its death throes as I have been told, she thought, but would not say aloud, then no wonder that it is overrun by vultures and carrion feeders *sacking the town* as Lord Byron has it. Elizabeth gazed out over the harbor wistfully, wanting to feel charity for the teeming millions of poor Chinese, but able to feel only pique for Fletcher Wood. She began to recite aloud.

> *Then there were foreigners of much renown,*
> *Of various nations, and all volunteers;*
> *Not fighting for their country or its crown,*
> *But wishing one day to be brigadiers;*
> *Alas to have the sacking of the town,*
> *A pleasant thing to young men of their years.*

"Is that what you are, Mr. Wood, a soldier of fortune, a mercenary, wishing one day to be a brigadier?"

She thought she saw him flinch and wondered if it was her imagination.

"Something more, I hope, miss."

"Elizabeth," called Hannah, "it's time we changed out of our traveling clothes and finished packing our trunks. Gentlemen, good day to you. I trust you will call upon Augustus Fitch and Company at your first opportunity. Elizabeth."

Hannah turned toward the companionway. Elizabeth smiled sweetly at Fletcher and Hugh, then fell in behind her mother and went below. She found her mother waiting at the door to her cabin.

"Elizabeth, did I overhear you say to Fletcher Wood that we have come to stay in Shanghai for only a year, after which we will all return home to Salem."

"Yes, I believe I said something like that."

"Elizabeth Glenna Fitch! You have no more discretion than a servant girl. What is in your head? What kind of a fool would prattle about private family matters to complete strangers or, worse yet, voracious birds of prey like those two Wood brothers?"

"Mother, Fletcher and Hugh aren't strangers. Fletcher is sincere, if uncivil sometimes, and I'm certain that Hugh Wood takes a special interest in me."

Hannah took her daughter by the arm and pulled her into Elizabeth's cabin, shutting the door behind them.

"You know nothing about those men, Elizabeth. Nothing! Except that they are potential competitors to your father's company. Of course they are friendly – how else could they solicit your trust and obtain private information about our business. If that information were known, our business could be damaged, even destroyed. That your father plans to leave Shanghai in a year is information that could be used to his disadvantage. Your father depends on his personal contacts with suppliers. Suppose an important supplier of tea or silk heard that Augustus was leaving Shanghai for good. Suppose that supplier, upon hearing this, decided to sell to someone else, with the result that our company could not find tea to purchase this season because all but the poorest teas were already committed to other houses. Suppose that meant the loss of $100,000 in profit, and that without that money your father could not afford to leave Shanghai."

"I, I guess I just did not think."

"That is how a twelve-year-old behaves. Children never think a thing all the way through to its consequences. And you are too much occupied with playing the coquette. Well, this is the last time you will ever be forgiven for not thinking. From now on you *will* think, do you hear? This is fair warning. I have already retrieved you once from disgrace by taking you from Salem and bringing you out to China. I thought it was only at some inconvenience, but now I see it is with no small risk to our very business. If you are ever, ever the cause of trouble to your father's business because of careless prattling like that I just heard, as God is my witness I will disown all responsibility for you, and put you out on the street where you can fend for yourself."

4 *Essex* began preparations to come to anchor as she approached the extreme boundary of the foreign anchorage off the Teenhow Temple, near the mouth of the *Yang-king-bang* creek, closer to the Augustus Fitch and Company godowns. That end of the anchorage was less crowded with square-riggers and steamers. Captain Fitch had wanted to go directly into the docks at Hongkew, where he could unload and start to work on repairs, but the pilot advised against it.

洋神 *Yang Shen*   *James Lande* 藍德

"With the spring tide up this high," the pilot had said, "ten feet or more, the Shanghai Dock Company wharf over at Hongkew is nearly awash, like the jetties along the Bund. They've docked vessels with as much as seventeen foot draft at high water down at Hongkew, but until you're unladen you're still going to draw close to eighteen feet, and I wouldn't want her to have to sit in the mud at low tide. Unloaded, she draws, what, twelve or thirteen feet? Best drop anchor upriver, closer to your godowns. When her cargo's ashore, you can have the steam tug *Ta Yung* or *Meteor* tow her back downriver for repairs."

The pilot also proposed engaging a steam tug to tow *Essex* into a mooring, rather than risk collision, but the captain declined the suggestion. Picking up a mooring in this swarming anchorage was the kind of difficult challenge by which others judged a captain's skill and mettle. Successful captains were highly regarded by owners and masters, toasted by insurance agents, and warmly welcomed in the maritime society of ports and harbors. Anyone as clumsy or unlucky as to tangle with another ship when coming to anchor might just as well have the mark of Cain upon him, for all the hospitality he would receive ashore.

In any case, the tide had turned and the ebb was not yet strong. That greatly simplified the stratagem for occupying a berth. Moreover, it would be a final pennant in the breeze of her brave pirate-fighting crew if they could bring their ship to rest without fouling another ship's moorings, smashing a bowsprit, or snarling rigging. *Essex* unfished her anchors and hung them from the catheads, and cable was bent and several lengths overhauled forward of the windlass. She shortened her fore-and-aft sails and clewed up her topgallants. As she approached her ground and slowed, she braced around her main topsail to spill its wind, and put her foretopsail aback to deaden her way.

"Let go the larboard anchor!" the captain shouted.

"Let go the larboard anchor."

The carpenter struck with his maul at the pin securing the chain and the anchor rattled out of the hawse and splashed into the water. The first mate signaled from the forecastle the amount of cable paid out, and the direction the cable lay. Ezra's watch hauled the spanker to windward to counter the ship's tendency to drift out of line. When the breeze had nudged *Essex* forward twice the length of chain she would ride by when moored, she dropped her starboard anchor. The main topsail was braced around and put aback so that, with both fore and main topsails aback, the ship came to a stop in the rising current and began to gather sternway. Thirty-two men leaned into the bars of the windlass to take up the slack of the first anchor dropped and warp the ship aft, sweating to the chant of *The California Song*.

> *I come from Alabama with my wash-bowl on my knee;*
> *I'm going to California, the gold dust for to see.*
> *It rained all night the day I left, the weather it was dry;*
> *The sun so hot I froze to death, oh, brother, don't you cry.*
> *Oh, California, that's the land for me,*
> *I'm going to California with my wash-bowl on my knee.*

At length, *Essex* came to rest with the same scope of cable payed out to each anchor. She hoisted her anchor ball pennant to announce to the harbor that she was at rest, and the crew set to work squaring up the yards and furling sails. Lighters and chopboats with watermelon-shaped roofs flocked about below her waist, clamoring for cargo to carry to the jetty. By the time the customs lighter came alongside, *Essex* was at repose in the falling tide. The customs inspectors, one Westerner and one Chinese, looked over the passenger list and the cargo manifest, taking special notice of the contraband artillery listed openly with the rest of the cargo, then went below to inspect the cargo itself. In the bustle of getting the gangway over the side and bringing the tidewaiters aboard, no one paid attention when the pilot clambered over the side and went ashore in a lighter.

The inspectors seized and impounded the four contraband 6-pounders and set them aside to go ashore in a special customs lighter, but instead of threatening to levy fines for this breach of the treaty, they conferred briefly, and then struck the guns from the cargo manifest. That discreetly concluded the transaction. Fletcher assumed the guns would go to the custom house, which was under the authority of the *taotai*, where they would stay until transferred to the *taotai*'s personal armory, and whatever financial consideration was involved would be handled quietly between Augustus Fitch and the *taotai*. Within two hours of the crew's going ashore, everyone in Shanghai would know that Augustus Fitch had brought the *taotai* four contraband 6-pounder field guns aboard *Essex*, and the news probably would reach Taiping rebel camps that evening.

The contraband items disposed of, the customs inspectors accepted the ship's *Application to Land Cargo*, authorized unloading, instructed Captain Fitch to deposit his ship's papers and manifest with his country's consul within 48 hours, and disembarked. The passengers clambered down to sampans lined up beside the gangway. The Wood brothers took one sampan after assisting Mrs. and Miss Fitch into another, and together they were sculled over to the private jetty of Augustus Fitch and Company, passing under one towering bow after another in the swaying line of progressively smaller merchant ships: *Invincible, Howqua, Heroes of Alma, Celestial, Fenimore Cooper*.

The moorage ended some distance from the riverbank. Plank walkways connected narrow stone landings, sunk at intervals into the embankment, with floating platforms that rose and fell with the tide. An odor of rotting garbage and trash arose from the debris and river mud piled high against the upstream wall of stones. To her relief, Mrs. Fitch smelled none of the reek from rotting corpses that often lodged against the jetty instead of floating downriver with the tides.

Elizabeth's still could not contain her excitement over the strange new sights and sounds, and her gaze fluttered about like a songbird in a bamboo cage. She chattered brightly to her mother until their sampan came downwind of the Fitch jetty and the noxious fumes rising from the refuse there overcame them both and they lunged into their baggage for handkerchiefs and smelling salts.

Beside Fletcher in their sampan, Hugh rambled on about starting a trading house of his own in Shanghai until he, too, was overcome by the stench and placed a hand over his nose and mouth. Fletcher was barely able to contain his own excitement at returning to China and landing at Shanghai, and could pay his brother but scant heed for the ditty echoing in his own head.

> Oh, I come from Salem City, with my rifle on my knee;
> I'm a going to Shanghai, China, to rule in that countree.
> It rained all night the day I left, the weather it was dry;
> The sun so hot I froze to death, now, Chinee, don't you cry.
> Oh, Shanghai, China, that's the place for me,
> I've come to Shanghai, China, with my rifle on my knee.

The gentlemen landed first and helped the ladies out of the ungainly craft. After stopping a moment to gain their balance on the pitching jetty, they mounted a wooden gangplank and crossed over bare mud flats to the quay. When Fletcher stepped down to the walkway, a large man in a black beaver stovepipe and black frock coat stepped out from between bales of cotton piled on the Bund and blocked his way. His face was gaunt and leathery, with bristly black eyebrows, and a thick, tobacco-stained mustache that swept down over his mouth like water over a rock. He looked like an undertaker.

"You Fletcher Thorson Wood?" the man asked brusquely. Some distance down the Bund, Fletcher saw Delevan Slaughter leaning against the wall of a building and grinning like a mangy Missouri mule munching briars.

"Yes, I am."

"Fletcher Thorson Wood, I am placing you under arrest on my authority as United States Marshal at Shanghai." The man tugged a lapel to one side and hooked a thumb in his belt. A large, shiny badge was pinned to his vest, and the pearl handle of a huge Colt Walker .44 revolver gleamed under his coat.

"May I know the charge?" Fletcher said.

"Violation of the Neutrality Law. You armed?"

"There is a Colt Navy revolver under my coat at the small of my back. If you intend to disarm me, perhaps you should remove it yourself, so that no misunderstanding leads to an accident." Here I've just slaughtered God knows how many wily Celestials down the coast, and now I'm arrested on a trumped up charge for that old business in Sonora, Mexico, cleared up long ago. Tomorrow, pigs sprout wings.

"Unbutton your coat." The marshal reached under Fletcher's coat to remove the revolver, placing it under his own belt. Hugh appeared under his brother's lee.

"Here, now," Hugh said. "What's the difficulty, ah, Marshal. My brother and I have only just arrived in port. Surely he cannot be in trouble already."

Hannah hove to on Fletcher's windward, with Elizabeth in tow.

"What is the meaning of this!" Hannah spat a tiny squall into the face of the marshal. "You cannot detain this man. He has done nothing wrong. He helped to save our ship. We are indebted to him for our lives. What are you doing? Put those manacles back in your pocket. Listen here, I don't care a fig about who you are – that badge means nothing to me. I am Mrs. Augustus Fitch, of Augustus Fitch and Company, and if you have even a glimmer of what's good for you, sir, you will desist this moment from detaining our Mr. Wood."

The marshal pocketed his manacles and held up his hands as if to fend off the sudden interlopers. He glanced wryly at the broad smile on Fletcher's face.

"Mrs. Fitch," the marshal said, "just settle down and I'll explain."

"Settle down!" she barked. "I'll settle you down! Just who on God's good green earth do you think you are!"

Fletcher stepped in front of the advancing Hannah Fitch to block her way.

"Mrs. Fitch," he said quietly. "This officer is just doing an errand he was sent upon, and I can guess what has happened. That pilot, the one called Delevan Slaughter, who brought us upriver, I expect he's involved in this, and up to no good as usual."

"Man name o' Slaughter made the complaint to the consul not more 'n half-hour ago. How'd you know?"

"It was easy enough to guess, Marshal. Delevan Slaughter made the same false accusation to Captain Fitch when Slaughter came aboard as pilot. Of course, the captain of *Essex* set no store by his word. Mrs. Fitch, let us not interfere with the marshal. To be of help, you might take this matter up with the American consul instead. The consul issued the order for arrest on the strength, I expect, of nothing more than the word of that lily-livered pilot."

"To be of help!" Hannah flared. "Hah! Wait until I get a word with that feckless consul. I'll have this straightened out mighty fast, you can wager. Marshal! What do you intend to do with Mr. Wood?"

"I shall take him to the jail at the English consulate, where he'll be held until examined by the American consul."

"So, our consul *still* does not have his own jail. Very well. But you take good care of Mr. Wood, Marshal, or you shall have me to deal with. And believe you me, mister, you do not want to deal with me. No, siree!" Hannah turned and stomped across to the anxious menials from Augustus Fitch and Company who huddled together at a prudent distance from the ruckus. Elizabeth gave Fletcher a quick smile and hurried after her mother, who was already venting another outburst of indignation on the hapless griffins.

"Hugh," Fletcher said, "go on ahead to the Astor House and reserve our rooms. Join the Fitches when they meet with the consul. Some of these people feel indebted to me, Marshal, but no such notion need hamper you. Mrs. Fitch is just naturally excitable."

The marshal cocked his head slightly and smirked. "I took this job because it was *not* some frontier settlement with Injuns to raise my hair. I'm not sure what's happened here, but I'm inclined to feel beholden. Name's Stockton Hull."

The marshal gestured for Fletcher to accompany him, without producing manacles. Fletcher shouldered his canvas seabag, and they crossed the Bund to a waiting carriage.

Out at sea, the wind shifted around to the northeast as the last of the winter monsoons prepared for a final assault on the model settlement of Shanghai. From Kagoshima to Taiwan-fu, barometers fell in submission to a line of cold squalls advancing out of the east, the vanguard of gale winds and cold rain welling up from under thunderheads over the Saddles and Rugged Islands. Thunder erupted over the Yangtze delta like volleys of cannon fire that rolled up the river and out over the flat plain. Lightning inside clouds set them glowing a deep red like the core of a hot kiln, and tinged the terrified faces of native junkmen flying before the storm.

洋神 *Yang Shen* James Lande 藍德

Dramatis Personae: Chapter 9

Chang Kuo-liang 張國梁 — Imperial General 江南提督 at Nanking
Li Hsiu-Ch'eng 李秀成 — Taiping Loyal King 忠王, *Chung Wang*

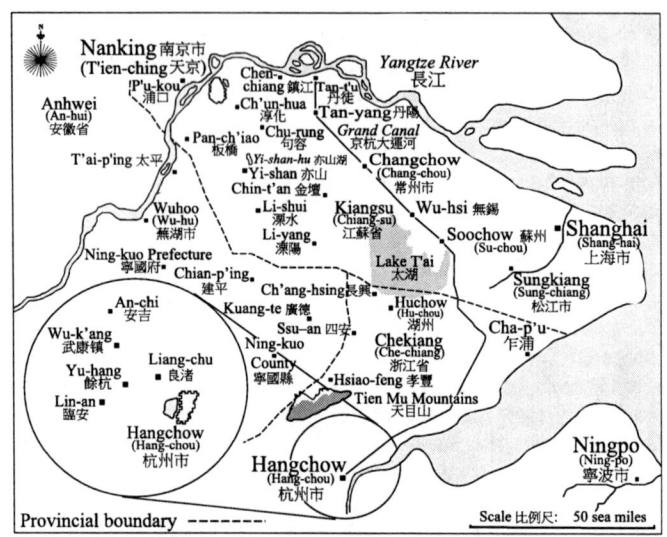

Nanking (Nan-ching) Southern Approaches
(adapted from Kuo T'ing-yi 郭廷以, *The Taiping Kingdom Day by Day* 太平天國史事日誌)

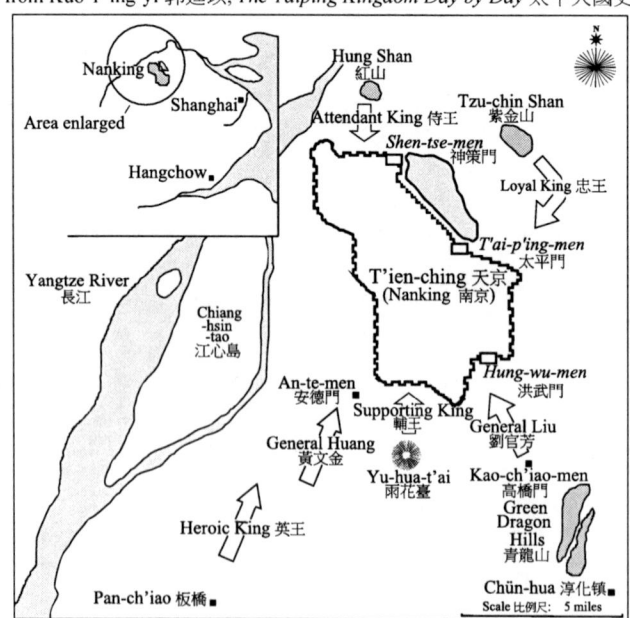

Assault on the *Chiang-nan Ta-ying*
(based on Curwen, *Taiping Rebel*, Map 3, Nanking…, and Kuo, *Taiping Kingdom Day by Day*)

One mile equals 3 Chinese *li* 里. One **tael** equals US$1.60.

142 *Rebels and Imps*

洋神 *Yang Shen*   *James Lande* 藍德

Chapter 9: Rebels and Imps
Friday, April 20, 1860, 12:00pm

There were no rebels 賊 in Hang-chou! They all disappeared overnight! They stayed only long enough to slaughter 60,000 soldiers and townspeople, and then were gone. And since then, they have captured Kuang-te 广德 and Chian-p'ing 建平 in An-hui 安徽 province, and Li-yang 溧陽 and Chin-t'an 金壇, in just over three weeks. Three weeks!

These thoughts plagued the mind of imperial General Chang Kuo-liang as he gazed northwest from atop the highest summit of the Green Dragon hills at the encampments besieging the walled city of Nan-ching. A rebel vanguard of only a thousand or so briefly engaged imperial troops at Hang-chou, but the next morning there were no more rebels in the city. Rebel general Li Hsiu-ch'eng's flying column truly can fly – straight for our throats. Again he has the initiative and we are controlled by him rather than controlling him. We all knew this was a ruse to draw troops away from Nan-ching, just as before when we were lured to Ning-po, but what else could we do – we had to go to Hang-chou. We did not need to send so many, but that fool Ho Chün dared not send fewer lest they be defeated and the Emperor's wrath fall upon him. Three thousand would have been enough. So now, we are understrength and tens of thousands of rebels approach. My spies in the rebel camp have already sent word of the rebel order of battle:

> The Supporting King Yang Fu-ch'ing attacks the south encampments from Yu-hua-t'ai 雨花臺.
> The Heroic King Ch'en Yü-ch'eng attacks the south encampments from Pan-ch'iao 板橋.
> The Loyal King Li Hsiu-ch'eng attacks the east encampments from Tzu-chin Shan 紫金山.
> The Attendant King Li Shih-hsien attacks the north encampments from Hung Shan 紅山.
> General Liu Kuan-fang attacks the south encampments from Kao-ch'iao-men 高橋門.
> General Huang Wen-chin attacks the south encampments from Yu-hua-t'ai 雨花臺.

As a signal for the attack to begin, Taiping units will ride out through An-te-men 安德門 and attack imperial encampments from several directions at once. When the encampments in the southeast are destroyed, the columns in the south led by the Heroic King and the Supporting King, and Generals Liu and Huang, will sweep around to the west and attack encampments under the west wall.

太奇妙 wonderful! Perhaps Ho Chün can tell me how to prevent 120,000 rebels approaching east, south, west and north 東南西北 from annihilating the 20,000 soldiers left in the *Chiang-nan Ta-ying* 江南大營, our Great Southern Imperial Encampment.

The general turned his pony and went back down to the trail to rejoin his detachment. He was going to the town of Chün-hua 淳化镇, twenty *li* southeast of the Nan-ching city wall, to protect the long canal, reinforce the garrison, and encourage them to fight, or try to prevent them all from running away at the first sign of rebel banners. The commander there would be indifferent to resisting the rebels, and reports said Chün-hua was not prepared for defense. The commander would complain he did not have enough men to dig trenches and erect ramparts. The men were sullen, and would not work when there were so few. If he pressed them, they would mutiny – and he would probably lead them! Moreover, like all the imperial soldiers of the *Chiang-nan Ta-ying*, their pay was in arrears and issued so infrequently that in effect pay had been reduced to two-thirds for many. They had not enough to send to their families, or even pay for their own incidentals. The soldiers at Chün-hua would not be the first to refuse to fight.

If I had command of this army, there would be no such problems. Commanders

洋神 *Yang Shen*   *James Lande* 藍德

would pay their men, and on time, or their heads would hang from the city gates in bamboo cages. Musters would be accurate and not bulge with dead men whose pay and rations are filched by officers. Provisions would not be diverted from the men. Ogres like that filth Wang Chün, who appoints favorites to high rank, forces officers to pay him bribes, and steals the pay of his troops, he would not be protected by a certain imperial commissioner named Ho Chün! The entire army would be like my troops – braver, smarter, better-trained and more disciplined soldiers than any trash that old fool can put into the field, troops that always make his levies look craven.

My authority would not be impaired by incompetent old Manchu dogs 滿狗子, whose bungling causes so many dead imperial soldiers. Tseng Kuo-fan's force, the Hsiang Army, has clear lines of command and is loyal to one man – Tseng himself. Even my bandits were more loyal than the dogs of the *Chiang-nan Ta-ying*, loyal to me! But would the councilors and secretaries in Pei-ching appoint me over this army, make me commander of the *Chiang-nan Ta-ying*, give command to Chang Kuo-liang?

No! Chang Kuo-liang was a bandit. Chang Kuo-liang is not a Manchu. For eight years, I have coddled the Manchu incompetents the court sends here, conscripted their armies, trained their soldiers, fought their battles, defeated their enemies, lied about their success, and buried the bodies behind them. I have done all this. I crushed the rebel bandits 賊 time and again – not those effete old Manchu dogs Hsiang Jung and Ho Chün! Does the Emperor 皇上 see this? Does the Emperor see Chang Kuo-liang?

2   General Li Hsiu-Ch'eng 李秀成, the Taiping Loyal King *Chung Wang* 忠王, swayed in the padded wooden saddle on his Mongolian pony as his mount trudged along behind a regiment of rebel foot. Flashing banners and flapping pennants led a procession of pike men, archers, sappers and musketeers, all uniformed in bright reds and yellows. Behind the Loyal King rode his adjutant, officers, mounted messengers, and two Corsican mercenaries in Western dress.

Seven thousand rebel soldiers in three light columns converged upon the ancient walled city of Nanking 南京, renamed T'ien-ching 天京 in 1853, when the Christian rebels captured the city and made it their capital. The rebel army advancing on T'ien-ching was grimly intent upon raising the long imperial siege, and massacring every imp in the strangling horde of the camps and siege works of the *Chiang-nan Ta-ying*.

Each rebel column had two wings. The Loyal King's wing moved in three sections of men and women – vanguard, center, and rear guard – according to the instructions on military strategy personally received by the Eastern King 東王 from the Heavenly Father and the Heavenly Elder Brother Jesus. Each section was a light regiment without baggage, coolies or commissariat. A captain 旅帥 and his officers, scouts and conscripted local guides led each section. Tough women warriors – 105 strong – led by a fearless woman called the Iron Lieutenant 鐵卒長 augmented the center regiment. The rear guard pickets and vedettes – mounted sentinels – lagged far behind the column to watch for pursuing imperial detachments. The demon troops 妖兵 of General Chang Yü-liang 張玉良 might catch up at any time.

We went to Hang-chou, thought the Loyal King, because we wanted to decoy demon soldiers away from T'ien-ching, not to cause the death of who knows how many thousands of innocent people. Too, too pitiable 慘極慘極. Father in Heaven, please forgive me. Shame, shame 慚愧慚愧. Elder Brother Jesus, please forgive me.

The Loyal King was in his early forties, of medium height, light and wiry, with a high forehead, large flashing black eyes under heavy black brows, a straight nose and small mouth with sharply chiseled lips, and a dark complexion. He was dressed simply in black trousers, white sash, a scarlet quilted jacket, and a scarlet hood, with an undress coronet mounting a ruby flanked on each side by four gold medallions. A jade-handled long sword hung from his leather belt, and lashed to his saddle there was a recurved Tartar bow in a burnished leather scabbard, and a quiver of arrows with bright red fletching. A devout follower of Jesus since the beginning of the Taiping insurrection years before, the Loyal King felt genuine sorrow over the carnage at Hang-chou.

The slaughter was inconceivable. There were only a few thousand imp soldiers 妖兵 there, and my holy soldiers 聖兵 killed some of them. Mobs of townspeople attacked and killed more of the imps caught pillaging in the city. But when people saw our banners on the hillsides, and heard the explosion of our mine under the Ch'ing-po Gate 清波門, they lost their reason 喪心病狂 and committed suicide by thousands! Men hung themselves after cutting the throats of their wives and children. Women drank gold leaf or jumped down wells. There was no way to stop them.

Li Hsiu-ch'eng was lively in conversation and on the battlefield self-possessed but, on horseback, the plodding gait of his pony lulled his senses, deflecting him from his anguish. Vagrant chatter from the ranks of sappers directly ahead drifted back to him.

Happy: Aren't we there yet? How much farther?
Eight Epochs: We'll be there when we get there 到就到.
Happy: Don't you ever get tired of walking?
Eight Epochs: Can't be helped. Had to join the army, else I'd've had to work for a living. Can't swim, so I couldn't be a sailor 水師.
Happy: All the places they make us march to. March to Hang-chou, then march back to T'ien-ching.
Eight Epochs: Used to think that all you do in an army is wait. But then they put me in this flying column, and now they make me march day and night and never wait.

"Happy" was Ch'ing Ko-hsi 青可喜, an 18-year-old flag caretaker and ensign bearer with a quick smile, tall and thin like a bean sprout 豆芽菜. He slouched along in brown drill leggings, baggy green trousers, and a loose red jacket. Hemp rope over his shoulders held a cloth backpack with rations, a water gourd, and army flags.

"Eight Epochs," Chu Pa-chieh 諸八節, was a grizzled old grumbler at the age of 38, a senior sapper engineer with a huge belly, stout limbs, fat jowls and bushy black brows that shot up at the ends. His olive drill trousers and jacket stretched tightly around his ample 大腹便便的 proportions, and he wore straw sandals and a small, square cap like that of a Taoist priest 道士冠.

Happy: I didn't want to go to Hang-chou.
Eight Epochs: I didn't want to stay in T'ien-ching, bedeviled by the demons all around the walls. Everybody in T'ien-ching feels like turtles in a pot 壺中之龜 pestered by cruel children. There are only 20,000 holy soldiers left in the garrison there, communications are broken, and the people are near starvation.
Happy: I didn't want to stay in T'ien-ching either. Somebody said the imps have 40,000 soldiers in 130 camps surrounding the city, and over 100 li of ramparts 壁壘 and trenches 渠溝 around the walls. How could anyone get food into the city past them?
Eight Epochs: Ay-yah, these years, the heavenly capital has suffered as many reverses

洋神 *Yang Shen*   James Lande 藍德

	as copper cash on a long string. When the generals all massacred each other and their families and followers four years ago, we were bled dry of our military genius. For such a long time now, it has been near impossible to fend off the imp stranglehold. Many sold out and joined the demons. That is why we lost all the countryside north of the Long River. Now the imps and demons surround T'ien-ching on all sides.
Happy:	Hang-chou was a disappointment. I'd heard the city walls were a hundred feet high, the moat was a hundred feet deep and full of crocodiles, and there were fifty-thousand bannermen there all armed with new-style foreign breach-loading rifles.
Eight Epochs:	And you believed it, of course. Before that, you believed Hang-chou was populated with demons 妖怪 lusting to rip off your flesh with their great fangs, boil pieces of you in huge cauldrons, and eat you up with soy sauce and ginger – *hung-shao* 紅燒 Happy!
Happy:	My stomach's hungry again. Think we'll stop by that lake?
Eight Epochs:	Midday cold rice. Every day. Why no fires at noon? That's always been their most stupid rule.
Happy:	I had a warm *tsung-tzu* 粽子. That peddler back before Chin-t'an had a basket-full.
Eight Epochs:	Who has money for *tsung-tzu*?
Happy:	Just a couple of cash.
Eight Epochs:	All my cash is gone every payday.
Happy:	Well, save a little and you'd have cash for *tsung-tzu* along the road.
Eight Epochs:	他媽的 damn you, stick your warm *tsung-tzu* up your—.
Happy:	罵人幹麼 why cuss me? When I'm a general, you'll be more polite.

3   That sapper is not far wrong, thought Li Hsiu-ch'eng. We lost a generation of military genius when the generals massacred each other at T'ien-ching, in the 6th year of T'ai-p'ing. Jealousy, greed, and wild ambition dealt us a staggering blow far more disastrous than the war against the Manchu. Slowly, however, a new generation of generals is taking up the burden of leadership: Heroic King Ch'en Yü-ch'eng 英王陳玉成, Attendant King Li Shih-hsien 侍王李世賢, Supporting King Yang Fu-ch'ing 輔王陽輔清, and myself – all of us fierce in battle. Prospects seemed brighter, at least back then, when the Heavenly King's cousin, Hung Jen-k'an 洪仁玕, arrived from the south and was appointed the Shield King 干王, as well as T'ai-p'ing prime minister. Still, how many times did I have to plead for support of my plan to break the imperial siege, even with our depleted strength?

"Draw the enemy away to reduce their numbers," I told them, "and then destroy those remaining with overwhelming force. That is how this siege of T'ien-ching will be broken. Encircling Wei to save Zhao 圍魏救趙之計 is an old, old strategy that almost always is successful even though it is known to all generals, and even to literary graduates." Finally, the prime minister agreed to support my plan.

"Now, it would be difficult for the besieged capital to counterattack," he said. "We must forcefully attack their rear from the direction of Hu-Hang 湖杭, Hu-chou and Hang-chou, compel them to the rescue of Hu-Hang, wait for them to disperse troops far and wide, then quickly return and break the siege. Disguised in imperial hats and uniforms 纓帽號衣, the Loyal King and the Attendant King can together attack both Hu-chou and Hang-chou."

洋神 *Yang Shen*   *James Lande* 藍德

    This time we encircled Hang-chou instead of Wei, to save T'ien-ching instead of Zhao. At least 15,000 demon soldiers under the command of imp General Chang Yü-liang rushed from T'ien-ching to save Hang-chou, leaving the heavenly capital surrounded by no more than the 20,000 or so that now remain. When all ten of our columns come from the four directions and take up their positions for the attack, more than 120,000 holy soldiers will be ready to sweep through all the camps of the enemy demons and drive them terror-stricken into the Long River.

Jupiter: Ha! Bean sprout 豆芽菜 thinks they're going to make him a general 軍帥. Ha! Who lives *that* long?

Rock of Ages: Ask again when you have lived as many years as I have lived.

    "Jupiter" was T'un Ching-yi 涒京乂, a 30-year-old sapper mole assigned to dig tunnels. His officers thought him typical of the recent ilk of rebel recruits, who joined for pay and pillage, and professed Christianity only if a full bowl of rice was set before them. Jupiter dressed to impress girls, in garish green pongee trousers, blue pongee shirt, a fancy red vest, red turban, and black cloth boots with felt soles.

    "Rock of Ages," Shih Lao-shih 世老石, was a worn and wizened 44-year-old in scruffy black cloth slippers, brown drill leggings, blue cotton trousers, black padded cotton jacket, and a conical straw hat, who usually looked half-asleep and spoke with a thick southern accent. A Hakka 客家人 with the God-worshipers from the first uprising at Chin-t'ien 金田, Rock of Ages started as a sapper, became a spear-carrier protecting sappers, and now was corporal in charge of four privates.

Happy: Just one more battle's all I need – I'll take so many heads they'll be crazy to promote me.

Jupiter: Give me *hsiao wanyir* 小玩藝兒, the little plaything of some sweet girl with tiny feet, in the next town.

Eight Epochs: 哈，又吹你的牛屄通紅 ha, blowing your ox-crack bright red again!

Rock of Ages: Haven't you had enough of little playthings yet? You had many very interested at Hang-chou.

Jupiter: Don't remind me. Those little playthings could kill a man. Them I've had enough of.

Happy: He knows nothing. All these country village girls have ugly big feet.

Jupiter: Country villages have no money either. When do we get to a town?

Rock of Ages: Mistreat the common folk, the old-hundred-names 老百姓, and you'll go to hell!

Jupiter: I'm not there now? Why don't you go find a church to pray in?

Rock of Ages: Loyal King will whack off your stupid head if you molest common folk.

Eight Epochs: And hang it from a city gate. Wouldn't that be a pretty sight.

Jupiter: Well, if I die, I'll still go to heaven – I'm a Christian.

Rock of Ages: 呸呸呸 *pei, pei, pei*! Don't talk about dying – it's bad luck.

Jupiter: Nothing wrong with thinking about *hsiao wanyir* – nobody'll catch me.

Rock of Ages: Think about this – seems like a good idea to leave the villagers alone, since they have no money and the girls all have big feet.

Eight Epochs: Anyway, if the imps get there first nothing's ever left but blood, bones, and burnt houses.

Jupiter: No wonder the T'ai-p'ing are generous with the old-hundred-names.

Rock of Ages: It's good policy, too – if the foreigners think we T'ai-p'ing love the people, they won't oppose us.

洋神 *Yang Shen*　　　　　　　　　　　　　　　　　　*James Lande* 藍德

Jupiter:　　　　狗屁洋鬼 dog-fart foreign devils. 管他們 to hell with 'em.
Eight Epochs:　那麼勃起太硬 if you've still got such a hard-on, why don't you go over there and march with the Iron Lieutenant and her women? Show them what you've got. Tell 'em about the Manchu girls in Hang-chou.
Jupiter:　　　　哎唷, 嚇死人 *ai-yo*, scare me to death! 佣抱她們一個鐵娘子前還好幹牛鬼蛇神 I'd sooner do ox-headed devils and snake demons before I'd even hug one of them iron viragos. And will you all shut-up about Hang-chou?
Eight Epochs:　How do we get rid of this blockhead 阿斗?

　　The Loyal King's scouts rode ahead looking for high, dry ground where his wing could camp protected by natural features. Following the heavenly regulations of the Eastern King, soldiers who knew the towns and terrain reported the distance to each objective. If none knew the area, then locals were conscripted as guides, or spies probed the route and estimated the distances. Soldiers found ferries and secured ferryboats on both sides of rivers. Scouts reported enemy troop movements, rugged terrain, road junctions, sources of water, forage for animals, and sites for camps. At road junctions, officers posted aides, having proper credentials with the general's seal, to wave flags and show the way to approaching troops. The route of march and order of battle were distributed to the units, memorized by the officers, and reviewed at the start of each day.

　　A rebel flying column traveled light, with no large cannon, wagons, or baggage, and foraged off the enemy's captured equipment and supplies. The army was a colorful procession of uniforms, and mufti worn in spite of regulations – generally black trousers, a red sash and sleeveless red jacket 背心號衣 trimmed in yellow, and a red hood or turban. Cloth squares on the front of a private's uniform read "Taiping" 太平, and on the back "Holy Soldier" 聖兵. A wooden block 腰牌 attached to a soldier's belt and stamped with a seal identified his unit and commander.

　　Each soldier carried his or her own weapons and equipment, a thin quilt, collapsible lanterns and candles, a gourd of water, a cooking pot and five days of provisions. Rations included tea, rice, rice meal for gruel, dried shredded pork, preserved duck eggs and pickles, red peppers, garlic cloves, sesame oil, salt, dried fish, bamboo shoots, fruit and vegetables.

　　Swords and spears predominated, either long two-handed swords or short swords, and iron spikes set on bamboo poles eight to eighteen feet long. Some carried matchlocks, and an occasional musket or pistol, and recruits from the north Tartar bows. Squads of four carried a long, heavy gingal musket and tripod. Young ensigns brandished the showy banners particular to each of four lieutenants in a company, and lead the way into battle. In defensive combat, they loaded weapons for their musketeers.

　　When camping at night, each unit settled within a few arrow flights of the commanding general's tent, posted their banners and flags, and established a unique signal with gong and rattle to help stragglers locate their bivouac in the dark. Other signals by gongs called officers and men to quarters for assemblies or emergencies. The company of women pitched their tents only a little to one side of the men.

　　Rice was cooked and meals prepared in the twilight after a day's march, and in the dark of early morning before striking camp, when the midday meal was also prepared in advance. Officers mustered their men for daily roll call and inspection, assigned gingal and cannon to individual squads, remedied discrepancies with equipment, and recorded the sick and wounded and sent them for care.

　　The Heavenly King demanded strict adherence to the Sixty-two Heavenly

洋神 *Yang Shen*   *James Lande* 藍德

Commands, on pain of decapitation, burning, quartering, wearing the cangue, beating with a bamboo, or reduction of rank. A holy soldier had to be obedient, loyal, brave, upright and honest. Murder (of anyone but imps), rape, robbery, smoking opium or tobacco, selling gunpowder, damaging property, drinking spirits, gambling, theft, sleeping on duty, wasting supplies, or cooking food outside of camp along the route of march all merited harsh punishment for both the soldier and his sergeant. A soldier who left camp without permission or loitered in towns had his head cut off and displayed.

Peddlers of tea and rice gruel by the roadsides were not to be impressed to carry arms or baggage, otherwise where would other holy soldiers buy tea and rice gruel? Mounted officers were to give up their mounts to carry the wounded and infirm. Officers of the mess ensured the wounded ate properly so they could recover. Even the Loyal King visited sick wards. Nearby relatives could care for the sick or wounded, else their brother warriors would care for them, because all were brothers in Christ. Officers supplied the guard with food, clothing and bedding, even if an officer had to lend his own robe to a guard for the night. Soldiers worked in turns when pitching camp, one half their number digging trenches and latrines and raising tents, while the other half stood guard or patrolled perimeters. Following these regulations, wrote the Eastern King, soldiers are grateful and secure in camp, and submit to discipline.

Several riders approached from the front of the column. The leader was all blue silk with yellow trim, and had the insignia of a black bear on the brow of his hood. The adjutant rode forward to meet him, wide-brimmed straw hat flapping in the breeze, and then returned with a report.

"*Chung Wang*," the adjutant said, "the captain of the vanguard reports that the right wing of our eastern column, led by the Attendant King General Li Shih-hsien, is ahead of us on the road to Chü-jung 句容. He clears the route forward of imps."

Li Shih-hsien will do that well, thought the Loyal King, carefully scouring the hillsides, the ponds enclosed by rushes, the thickly-weeded hollows and woods with heavy undergrowth, searching for demons hidden in ambush, and imperial spies.

"Where are the other columns?" the Loyal King said, distracted for a moment by the peonies and white clouds embroidered on the adjutant's straw hat. Each time the gaudy hat caught his attention, he wondered if he was right to relax the Heavenly King's strict regulations for uniforms.

"The center column led by the Supporting King General Yang Fu-ch'ing, left Li-shui yesterday and is approaching Chiang-ning. The west column under the Heroic King Ch'en Yü-ch'eng is still on the other side of the river. He will send word when he arrives opposite Tung-liang-shan."

"Send word to General Li that we march north behind him, and have passed through Li-yang 溧陽 and Chin-t'an 金壇. Tonight my troops camp with their backs protected by Yi-shan Mountain 亦山, and their right flank guarded by Yi-shan Lake."

The adjutant rode forward.

Twelve days now, thought the Loyal King, since we all decided on the final strategy for smashing the siege and left Chien-p'ing 建平, following three routes of approach: west, central, and east. Three hundred *li* lie between Chien-p'ing and the heavenly capital. General Chang Yü-liang's demon army will pursue us all the way, and demon garrisons will harry us along the routes.

Another rider cantered up from the rear and called to the Loyal King.

"*Chung Wang*. Report from the rear guard." The rider wore a rattan helmet 號帽 inscribed on the brow with Taiping 太平 on one side of a rampant black bear, and

洋神 *Yang Shen* James Lande 藍德

Kingdom 天國 on the other.

"Captain?"

"Up to now, all progresses well. My vedettes continuously rotate to the extreme rear to observe the imperial advance."

"Still no sign of pursuit from Hang-chou?"

"Strangely, we have heard nothing of General Chang Yü-liang. Only rumors that the Manchu garrison commander has kept him at Hang-chou, and that Su-chou demands he go there to defend that city, and that Ch'ang-chou also wants his troops for defense."

"Of course," said the Loyal King, "these could be false rumors spread to confuse us as to his whereabouts."

"If so," said the captain, "they are very successful, because I have absolutely no idea where he is."

"I should have sent someone all the way back to Hang-chou. Even so, Captain, we have a good plan, as good as when I broke the siege of imp General Hsiang Jung 向榮."

"*Chung Wang*, I have heard of this Hsiang Jung, but that was before I enlisted."

"His was the first siege of the heavenly capital. We destroyed that blocade in the same way we will destroy the present one. In the 6th year of T'ai-p'ing, the Eastern King sent our T'ai-p'ing holy soldiers in a feint at Ning-po 寧波, same as Hang-chou now."

"So, Hsiang Jung fell into the same kind of trap?"

"Yes, he detached part of his siege force around T'ien-ching to relieve Ning-po and Chen-chiang 鎮江. We fought against the remaining 20,000 or more of Hsiang Jung and Chang Kuo-liang's troops until, finally, we drove them out of their stockades among the tombs of the Ming emperors. They retreated south to protect Tan-yang, where Hsiang Jung hanged himself in shame at his failure."

"He killed himself? A brave officer would die in battle."

"He deserved to be flayed alive. Hsiang Jung was an opinionated bastard. He listened to no one. His character became clear to me as early as the 1st year of T'ai-p'ing, when his soldiers surrounded us at Yung-an 永安. We slipped away from the town one rainy night while he stood around arguing tactics with his generals. He was demoted for that blunder. He could not cooperate with anyone then, or later when he laid siege to T'ien-ching. I think his successes in the field really were because of Chang Kuo-liang – everywhere Hsiang Jung went, there were Chang Kuo-liang's banners."

"And we still fight General Chang Kuo-liang," the captain said. "Always that bandit Chang is there to make us stumble, fighting our armies to a stalemate."

"He is the greatest of their generals, but this time we will defeat him."

"I would like to see his expression when he realizes our feint at Hang-chou was successful, and that he was tricked the same way *again*."

"The most humble army," the Loyal King said, "even of charcoal-burners fighting with nothing more than sticks and stones can, if they have virtue, crush armies of soldiers armed with swords and shields and cannon and bring down city walls. Time and again we have shown this is so, that the T'ai-p'ing were chosen by the Heavenly Father and given the Mandate of Heaven to bring down the demon dynasty. We absolutely cannot fail, because we are a Righteous Army 義兵."

4 Two months earlier, the Loyal King had set out from Wu-hu for Ning-kuo prefecture 寧國府 – their first major objective on the raid southeast to Hang-chou. Ning-kuo was under the command of an imperial provincial officer, and the town bristled with imps on the defense who would not come out from behind their wall to fight.

The Loyal King knew siege warfare was completely wrong for his flying column –

attacking a city always was a tactic of final recourse in the cannon of Chinese military lore, after disrupting an enemy's plans, breaking his communications, and attacking his army. Building siege machinery and complete excavations took months. A besieging army would grow old and slow, and innocent people would die.

In late February, the Loyal King passed by Ning-kuo prefecture rather than delay – if the demons would not even step outside their gate, they were unlikely to rush to the relief of other towns along the way. General Li Shih-hsien's right wing did take the Ning-kuo county seat 寧國縣, and then caught up with the Loyal King after leaving behind a small rebel garrison.

Kuang-te, however, could not be passed over – it was a junction on the retreat and had to be controlled. Two days later, the entire column surrounded Kuang-te with banners waving. The imp garrison fired a few matchlocks and gingals from the south gate tower, then threw open the gate and lunged through the rebel lines, leaving the townspeople to the mercy of the Taiping. The Loyal King entered Kuang-te with a small detachment, collected some of the local gentry and calmed their fears with assurances the Taiping would not harm their people or property.

> *I, the Loyal King, have swept Kuang-te clear of demons and restored your town. Be content now and go about your affairs with no fear and glad hearts. The T'ai-p'ing will not disturb or harm you nor plunder your goods. Some of us will stay here to give guidance in the ways of Heaven and protect you from the demon imps. Do not gather together in large groups or carelessly resist our soldiers. Reform and accept the reward of peace – resist and be punished."*

A small garrison remained to hold Kuang-te, commanded by two rebel officers in place of the local magistrate, who had fled together with the imperial soldiers.

The Loyal King and his general Li Shih-hsien continued their march toward Hang-chou, and over the following nine days captured An-chi 安吉 in Che-chiang 浙江, and the towns of Ch'ang-hsing 長興 and Ssu-an 四安. The men rested for a day while the Loyal King considered reports from Hu-chou and Hang-chou, then decided to divide the force and attack each place separately to further confuse the enemy.

General Li Shih-hsien led his wing off toward Hu-chou in the northeast, near the south shore of Lake T'ai. Two days later, he attacked and captured the poorly defended city, posted his pickets, and settled down in Hu-chou to await the arrival of the enemy imperial relief force rushing south from the *Chiang-nan Ta-ying*.

The Loyal King's troops unpacked imperial uniforms and unit banners captured along their route, disguised themselves as imperial soldiers, and set out on a forced march for Hang-chou, taking first the town of Wu-k'ang 武康.

By this time, however, the breathless local magistrate from Kuang-te had finally reached Hang-chou and cried his warning. The city scraped together a detachment of 400 braves 勇, commanded by a literary graduate appointed provincial judge, and send them flying west to intercept and delay the rebels. Braves and rebels collided at Yu-hang 餘杭, but a larger part of the rebel wing slipped around the imps and continued on toward Hang-chou with all speed, along less-traveled byways.

Surprise was no longer possible, but the rebels were very close and knew from their spy inside the city, an old man disguised as a fortuneteller, that it was imperative to arrive before a defense could be prepared and the gates closed against them. The following day, the Loyal King's vanguard of 1,250 holy soldiers reached the northwest Hang-chou suburb of Liang-chu 良渚 without being detected.

Roughly 200 miles northwest at the *Chiang-nan Ta-ying* surrounding T'ien-ching,

洋神 *Yang Shen*   *James Lande* 藍德

imperial general Chang Kuo-liang 張國梁 called together the highest ranking officers commanding the siege and informed them that Taiping rebels had captured Kuang-te and An-chi in Che-chiang. Confessions under torture of captured rebels revealed a rebel campaign to cut off supplies and provisions for the *Chiang-nan Ta-ying* by taking Hang-chou. Chang Kuo-liang knew he must protect the supply lines for his siege force. If he could not lead troops south himself, he would propose General Chang Yü-liang 張玉良 be detached to rush to the defense of Hang-chou.

Chang Kuo-liang listened quietly to the fulmination of his officers about an obvious trick to deplete the strength of the siege force, and then asked them what other choices there were – under any circumstances, Hang-chou must be protected. After much squabbling with Ho Ch'un 和春, the Manchu imperial commissioner 欽差大臣 commanding the siege, Chang Kuo-liang issued orders for 13,000 imperial troops to march south with the greatest haste to Hang-chou. Then he wrote an urgent memorial to the Emperor explaining the sudden decision, and apologizing for his precipitous action.

The celebration of Bhuddha's birthday was underway at temples everywhere in China. Candles and incense were alight at night, and solemn drums sounded while water scented with sandalwood, musk, or ambergris was poured over the statues of the Buddhas to wash away dust and grime of the year. Monks scrambled to catch the residue to sell to the faithful for potions and physics. Followers lined up to splash teacups of water over the statues and toss copper cash, while holy choirs chanted "blessings of the Buddha be upon you."

The holiday was a chance for some of the Loyal King's holy soldiers to exchange their imperial disguises for those of Buddhist monks – not entirely disagreeable, as the saffron yellow monk robes appealed to the Taiping taste for garish colors. Once inside the city walls of Hang-chou, they passed intelligence to rebels outside the walls, spread false rumors, and feigned utter terror and frenzy to rouse alarm of impending calamity among townspeople, and fear of a Taiping massacre among imperial soldiers.

Rebels dressed as monks and imperial officers mingled with the throng of pilgrims and refugees and passed through the Hang-chou city gates. Once inside the wall, some disguised rebels were exposed when caught stealing horses – the gates slammed shut, and travelers and militia were left milling about outside the walls until rebel shell started exploding against the Wu-lin 武林 and Ch'ien-t'ang 錢塘 gates, and everyone leapt for cover under the bridges over the moat. Militiamen driven away from guard posts in the suburbs ran to the city wall and pounded on the gates but, even if the city wanted to let them in, they could not be distinguished from rebels and died in the first barrages.

Expecting a rebel onslaught, the city turned upon itself – turmoil reigned, and the suicides among the townspeople began.

A general 提督 of the Manchu Bordered Yellow Banner commanding the Manchu garrison at Hang-chou sent his few hundred bannermen out of the garrison to the walls at the Wu-lin and Ch'ien-t'ang gates, to safeguard both the garrison and the populace at the north of the city, where the rebels were expected to attack. If the rebels could not he held back and came over the wall, the bannermen would withdraw into their garrison. They would bar the gates of their own little walled Manchu and Mongol bastion, shut out Taiping and Chinese alike, and defend themselves from atop their garrison walls.

The Manchu general also sent urgent orders up the coast to the banner garrison at Cha-p'u 乍浦 for more muskets – several days later a brigade-general 副都統 of the Mongol Plain White Banner arrived from Cha-p'u leading four hundred musketeers to reinforce the Hang-chou garrison.

洋神 *Yang Shen*   *James Lande* 藍德

Hundreds of braves and militia abandoned outside the city wall gathered into gangs and fanned out into the suburbs to sack and burn. The literary-graduate-appointed-provincial-judge and his braves found an opening in the rebel lines, dashed wildly through to the city wall, and implored the guard to let them back inside. Some unruly militiamen tried to follow the braves of the provincial judge back into the city, but were singled out again, and the gate once more was slammed shut in their face.

Then suddenly all was quiet, as if the rebels had withdrawn.

The Loyal King had no desire to lay siege to Hang-chou, but it was too soon to withdraw. A siege would have been an unnecessary waste of men and material. All he need do was prance about making threatening gestures and loud noises to frighten the city, and then be sure that all the panic-stricken imperial messengers escaped unimpeded through the rebel lines carrying urgent pleas for help to Su-chou, and the *Chiang-nan Ta-ying* besieging T'ien-ching. His spies would bring him word daily of the progress of the imp relief force and, when confirmed to be close, he would withdraw, first for Kuang-te, and then T'ien-ching.

In the meantime, the Loyal King's vanguard set to work dressing the stage around Hang-chou for the great rebel puppet play 太平天國大傀儡戲. Flags and banners were planted everywhere along the Wan-sung foothills 萬松嶺 and other hillsides within sight of the city walls. Extra banners were unrolled and set out to look like three or four times the actual number of rebels – they made the fluttering slopes seem like market day at a county seat. Rebels ran about just out of musket range yelling and jeering, slapping their fannies, and dashing toward the wall on horseback to irk the defenders into wasting ammunition firing at them.

The *chunk* of axes on wood echoed over the hillsides as small pines and camphor trees were felled and quickly thrown together in facades of wooden stockades under waving Taiping banners. Holy soldiers ransacked Taoist and Buddhist temples in the hills and suburbs for wooden statues of the pagan gods, carried them back to the outworks, dressed them in Taiping uniforms, and sat them in rows atop the stockades. From sufficient distance, the gleeful gods of wealth and health, the solemn gods of longevity and literature, and the grimacing god of war, together with Kuan Yin 觀音 and the lesser bodhisattvas looked quite like a large army of besieging longhaired rebels. More quiet than their rebel brethren, the new recruits glared out over the Hang-chou audience from their hilly proscenium and never flinched, even when struck occasionally by a musket ball. The people of Hang-chou were convinced tens of thousands of Taiping swarmed around them.

As the Loyal King waited in the wings of his stage play for word of the imperial relief force, the rest of his column arrived from Yu-hang. While imps from the north were still days away, there was time for more elaborate construction to reinforce the impression of siege. Again, the sound of axe against tree carried on the wind. Engineers went to work over the next few days erecting ten more large stockades along the shore of West Lake, outfitting them with numerous fluttering unit ensigns, and posting more wooden conscripts along the parapets.

Eight Epochs devised a plan for several tunnels from the stockades down to the city gates, and Jupiter and other sappers began digging. Men and women dug into the sandy loam day and night with hand tools – shovels, spades, picks, mattocks and pikes – opening entrances seven and one-half feet high and eight feet wide, hauling out the dirt in wheeled carts. In the galleries, Eight Epochs ensured proper reinforcement foot by foot with posts and beams. Outside, rebels raised a din of music with flutes, horns, drums and gongs to cover the sound of the digging operation. To the defenders, of course, that meant longhairs tunneling. Sappers dampened the smoke from their lanterns, and repeatedly sealed cracks in tunnel walls, to reduce the risk that smoke would seep out. At night, they dimmed their lanterns to prevent light escaping the tunnels, and muffled the rattle of cartwheels.

Once more, the literary-graduate-appointed-provincial-judge sallied forth to attack the Loyal King's troops, but was driven off. Another force that arrived shortly after from Cha-p'u took one look at the countless rebel banners flying and ran for their lives. The next day the Loyal King defeated another detachment of imps at Kuan-yin-t'ang 觀音塘. Then came word that imperial general Chang Yü-liang had arrived at Su-chou and was getting very close. Nine days had passed since the rebels first arrived at Hang-chou – it was the time for the next tactics in the strategy, to place a few more stones on the *wei-ch'i* 圍棋 board.

5   The explosion at the Hang-chou Ch'ing-po Gate lifted tons of rock, stone, and packed earth out of the city wall and sent smashed blocks high into the sky atop a huge yellow fireball, scattering broken brick over rooftops and into fields. Rebel sappers had packed cartloads of new Western gunpowder, smuggled to the rebels by foreign mercenaries, into their tunnel under the wall, not knowing how much more powerful it was than ordinary black powder. The earsplitting blast was heard as far away as Ning-po, where early risers peered into the cloudless dawn and wondered how there could be thunder. The explosion generated a wave of shock and heat that crushed soldiers, flattened houses, bowled over sappers, and knocked over wooden effigies of rebel soldiers bestride stockade parapets far away in the Wan-sung foothills. It was more terrible for coming unexpectedly so early in the morning.

Taiping holy soldiers clambered over the wreckage in the breach and stormed into the southwest quarter of Hang-chou, quickly overwhelming and opening to more rebels the sparsely manned P'u-chin Gate 浦金門 on the west, Feng-shan Gate 鳳山門 on the south, and Wang-chiang 望江, Ch'ing-t'ai 清泰 and Ch'ing Ch'un 慶春 gates on the west. The Loyal King's vanguard of 1,250 men and women streamed into the city through the unguarded portals and charged the main body of defenders on the north wall from the rear. Rebel spies within the walls wound their heads with red cloth to identify themselves to other Taiping, and guided holy soldiers through the enemy stronghold.

Before the tremors had dissipated, and the city's defenders could recover their senses, the rebels took possession of the south end of Hang-chou, and threatened the north. But while the wall may have yielded to the rebels, the fierce spirit of the Manchu defenders did not, and the bannermen rallied to the barricades and halted the onslaught.

The Taiping pressed hard to break the deadlock. Shells from small rebel cannon exploded and set fire to houses in the northern quarter and Manchu garrison, and started conflagrations fanned by wind that raged through the city day and night. Sorties of rebel foot rushed the barricades and were repulsed by flights of arrows and mortar fire.

Even the Iron Lieutenant and her women warriors flung themselves into the melee, and now and again they found themselves wielding sword and spear against other women – Manchu mothers and daughters defending home and hearth.

Hang-chou local militia defending the gates abandoned their posts, ran into the streets, and preceded the rebels in plundering private shops and homes. Furious at this betrayal, the townspeople took up arms against the marauding militia, opening a second front of battle within Hang-chou. They struck down the first militiamen with tools and sticks of furniture, and then chased after the rest with swords and spears taken from the militia they had killed. Howling mobs of angry citizens pursued militiamen through the streets and into cul-de-sacs where they cornered their prey, dragged them out to the thoroughfares, and hanged them from building rafters and gateposts as a grisly warning to the rest of the mutinous militia.

The gates of the Manchu garrison – the small walled fortress within the city where Manchu lived separately from Han Chinese – were suddenly thrown open, then as quickly closed again. Mounted Manchu and Mongol officers led a sortie of banner foot out through the rampaging rebel army into the streets in order to subdue the militia and try to pacify the citizenry, lest the garrison be forced to fight against rebels, militia and townspeople, all three together.

Gradually the battle lines consolidated, with the Taiping and impressed civilians in control of the southern part of the city. Behind barricades across the streets, a force combined of Tartar bannermen, local militia, and civilian volunteers held the northern part of Hang-chou. The Loyal King could not press the assault without bringing in the rest of his wing, and he did not anticipate the barricaded defenders being supplied with food and arms over the Grand Canal from Cha-p'u, so the battle raged to a standstill.

Terrified the rebel army would cut them to pieces, bannermen and militia were desperate to halt the surge of rebels being led through Manchu lines by red-turbaned spies. Somehow, the defenders of Hang-chou had to hold out long enough for a relief force to arrive from Su-chou – if one was coming at all.

Eight Epochs received orders to open new tunnels in an attempt to get past the barricades and under the walls of the Manchu garrison. He started from within buildings opposite the garrison wall, to cross the shortest distance and hide the excavated dirt. Once more, hundreds of sappers plunged down into the loose earth and shoveled their way under the streets, with wood and rafters torn out of the buildings providing easily accessible supports for the tunnels. Jupiter strayed from the rebel lines toward the inner city, wanting to go look for *hsiao wanyir* with tiny feet, but his sergeant chased him down, boxed his ears, and dragged him back. Rock of Ages stood by the entrance leaning on his spear and grimaced as Jupiter marched into a tunnel.

Rock of Ages: Ayah, Jupiter, someone caught you! Maybe there's some down below.
Jupiter: Sure, ox-headed devils and snake demons underground. Go find a church to pray in.
Eight Epochs: Says he's a Christian, right? Can sappers find God in a tunnel?

Jupiter spaded and scooped for hours, relieved at intervals for brief rests by other sappers, until they struck the foundation of the garrison wall and stone rubble fell into the gallery. They dug under the baked brick of the outside face of the wall, which became their gallery ceiling, and under the tamped earth that filled the center, solid under thousands of pounds of pressure, then continued on under the inside face of the wall and the floor of the compound.

Inside the garrison, the tunnels that made it under the wall were detected when the defenders noticed depressions in the sandy soil along the base of the wall. Bannermen dug down several feet into the depressions, dropped in bags of black powder, and lit the fuses, setting off explosions that collapsed the tunnels below.

Jupiter heard a frightening blast and, as the ceiling collapsed all around him, he covered his face with one hand, took a deep breath, and with the other hand thrust his short spade straight up above his head.

Suddenly all was black, but he was still conscious and, inhaling slightly, he smelled the odor of old sod. Quickly he began twisting the spade and thrusting up, knowing that there was no mountain above. Only a few feet of earth separated him from blue sky. The spade moved slightly.

Rebels and Imps

洋神 *Yang Shen*   *James Lande* 藍德

As the sandy loam loosened, he could twist the spade full turns. Like an earthworm, Jupiter worked open a space above him, gasping desperately behind his hand for each thin breath, until he could thrust his other hand into the opening and slowly pull himself up out of the rubble. When finally he managed to claw his way up out of the breach, he found his *hsiao wanyir* waiting for him.

They were not exactly what he had imagined – Manchu girls were spearing the surviving sappers that clambered up out of the ground. With a shout one girl in black trousers and a short tunic, her hair in long black braids tied with blue ribbons, thrust an iron-tipped length of tasseled bamboo spear at his throat. Jupiter deflected the spear with a clumsy parry of his short-handled spade. Iron clanked on iron and threw dull orange sparks as slowly he backed into the open trench.

Jupiter stumbled and fell on his back into the tunnel opening, certain he was about to be killed by spear thrusts from a screaming semicircle of the little playthings. Twelve inches of cold iron hovering at his throat squelched his last cry, and he watched helpless as the girl flexed her shoulders and prepared to shove it into him.

Suddenly there was a clank of iron. Her spear point disappeared, knocked aside by a spear from behind him, wielded by Rock of Ages. Tasseled spears thrust and parried and flailed about over his prostrate body like a theater performance.

Rock of Ages: Get moving, stupid! I can't hold them off forever.

Jupiter twisted over and crawled on his belly between the legs of Rock of Ages and back into the dark.

Iron kettles filled with burning artemisia wood 遊火箱 were swung on chains into the tunnel behind the retreating rebel sappers – the artemisia smoke carried oil that, in confined subterranean spaces, caused fatal convulsions, if the sappers were not simply asphyxiated. Stinkpots were thrown into other open tunnels not blocked by debris, followed by buckets-full of rusty iron caltrops. A kind of heavy *cheval-de-frise* of thick bamboo with sharp stakes pointing into the tunnel was wedged into each opening and made fast with long iron spikes, and Manchu girls were posted to guard the entrances.

Rebel soldiers broke through into the garrison and hand-to-hand fighting with enraged bannermen ensued. Despair enfolded the hearts of brave defenders as fire and smoke enveloped them – many gathered their families and one-by-one cut the throats of their terror-stricken wives and children or dropped them into wells before rushing headlong back into the battle wild for vengeance.

Exasperated by the slow pace of the imperial relief force, which was delaying his withdrawal and causing unnecessary casualties on both sides, the Loyal King reduced the number of sorties, and placed captured muskets on rooftops with orders to maintain desultory musket fire into the barricades.

Just less than two weeks after the first Taiping arrived at Hang-chou, the first of General Chang Yü-liang's relief force finally arrived at the Wu-lin Gate from Su-chou, and the Loyal King knew his plan had succeeded – time for more stones on the *wei-ch'i* board. Word of Chang Yü-liang's arrival was sent to the Attendant King, so that he would know to withdraw from Hu-chou and start back to Kuang-te. Skirmishers engaged Chang Yü-liang's soldiers outside the north wall, forcing them to entrench there instead of approaching any closer to the southwest wall.

Government troops at several other towns in the area threatened to cut off the Loyal King's return – haste was crucial if the rebel wing was to avoid capture. The Loyal King decided to employ the stratagem of withdrawing with insufficient troops 缺兵撤退計 to gain additional time. He ordered unit ensigns and banners raised all over the portions of

洋神 *Yang Shen*   *James Lande* 藍德

the city wall held by his men to give the appearance of greater numbers, and mislead Chang Yü-liang into thinking more rebels had entered the city.

At the same time, to the Loyal King's delight, the Tartar officers defending Hang-chou refused to allow Chang Yü-liang to enter the city because of the rebel spies in his ranks – those picked up along the way, who reported to the Loyal King on the progress of the relief force. Sheltering fire was stepped up from the rooftops above the northern quarter inside the city and, under the concealment of darkness, the Taiping quietly withdrew through the Ch'ing-po and Feng-shan gates, and quickly set out around the south end of West Lake for Kuang-te.

Whatever the reason – delay by suspicious Tartars, or apprehension about a larger rebel force – Chang Yü-liang did not enter the city for another day and night, and then had to wait while his soldiers pillaged everything not yet molested by Taiping rebels and local militia. The general mustered a detachment of cavalry and pursued the Loyal King through the Wan-sung foothills as far as Yu-hang, but there he turned back to await the arrival of the rest of his force at Hang-chou.

The Loyal King marched through Yu-hang to Lin-an 臨安 and then crossed west over the Tien Mu Mountains 天目山 to Hsiao-feng 孝豐 and on to Kuang-te, arriving ten days after leaving Hang-chou burnt and broken. He rested his troops and conferred with the first of his generals to arrive, and waited for the others.

On his way to Kuang-te, the Supporting King General Yang Fu-ch'ing captured Red Forest Bridge 紅林橋 near Ning-kuo prefecture, and dispersed the threat of imperial pursuit from the southwest.

The Attendant King General Li Shih-hsien delayed his withdrawal from Hu-chou until confident the larger part of Chang Yü-liang's laggard relief force had finally arrived at Hu-chou, then quietly withdrew unseen through early morning mists and retired to Kuang-te.

The report the Loyal King received at Kuang-te told of the staggering 匪夷所思 number of suicides caused by his ruse at Hang-chou – over 60,000 people perished. Cadavers thrown without ceremony into trenches below the eastern wall numbered in the thousands. At the gates, the bodies of the dead crowded out the living and blocked entry to the city. Among the dead were the governor of Che-chiang province, the provincial grain intendant, several *taotai*s, department directors, and county magistrates, military officers and civil officials. Other officials fled to nearby jurisdictions. Much of the civil administration of the city was wiped out. Taiping casualties were equally incredible – less than a few hundred.

Several days later, nearly the entire general command of the Taiping army left Kuang-te and converged on the town of Chien-p'ing, west of Kuang-te, drove out the imp garrison, and settled in for their final conference on the strategy for smashing the siege of T'ien-ching, unaware of the imperial spies of general Chang Guo-liang eavesdropping in their midst.

洋神 *Yang Shen*   *James Lande* 藍德

Dramatis Personae: Chapter 10

Williard Harris Parrish	half-time acting-secretary of the American consulate
Mr. Wong	doorman and gaoler (jailer) for Stockton Hull

Shanghai Custom House on Bund in 1857
(From Morse, *The Trade and Administration of China*, 1908)

Chapter 10: Shanghai's U. S. Marshal
Friday, April 20, 1860, 3:30pm

Marshal Stockton Hull ordered Fletcher into a black double-brougham carriage and sat opposite his prisoner. On an order to the Chinese driver, the carriage swung about and set off down the Bund in the direction of the British consulate.

Fletcher looked past the Fitch jetty at *Essex* moored in the anchorage. Floating jetties jutted out over mud flats exposed by the falling tide all the way down the Bund to Soochow Creek.

"More jetties since I was here last," Fletcher said. "Like rungs on a ladder."

"Riverbank'd probably be all built up by now," the marshal said, " 'cepting the Chinese won't allow that old tow path to be removed. Not so many boats towed there now – before long won't be none at all."

"Seems to have grown a lot. Larger houses, more godowns."

"Still not much bigger'n a tiny postage stamp on a big Chinese parcel. But the old timers say that until a few years ago this place wasn't more'n a few cow paths out to a Chinese anchorage, so I guess it just sort of growed like Topsy."

"Not enough to get the roads paved."

"That ship looked pretty well shot up. What happened?"

"Pirates jumped us in the Volcanos. Three junks and a lorcha. We potted away at 'em for nearly two hours after running aground. Pirates moved the buoy marking the shoal. The pilot we took on at Ningpo was in cahoots, and deliberately put us onto muddy bottom. They were led by a blonde-headed foreigner I'd guess was Fokie Tom."

"Tom's been heard of recently down around Ningpo," the marshal said. "You may be right. Sure like to loop my lasso over the horns of that maverick."

"Read about the American marshal when I was on the coast in fifty-eight, and I'm wondering if you are not the same man."

"What'd you read?"

"As I recall, there was a scuffle between some Manilamen and Chinese, over gambling debts, and a Chinese was stabbed dead. Well, it happened in Bamboo Town, the American concession, the marshal's jurisdiction. So, when the murder was reported, the marshal went out in the dead of night to track down the killers, no matter the victim was only a Chinese, and caught up with 'em aboard the steamer *Confucius*."

"Yeah," the marshal said, "that *Confucius* was run by a self-styled Admiral named Ghent, hired out by the mandarins to suppress piracy. Crewed the steamer with a pack of wild Manilamen."

Near Mission Road Fletcher glimpsed the wide verandahs and tall columns of the two-story British colonial-style buildings housing the offices and living quarters of the American trader Russell and Company, surrounded by godowns.

"The marshal," Fletcher said, "went aboard and confronted this Ghent, probably expecting to be gutted and stuffed for long pig. But Ghent searched *Confucius* and turned up bloody knives, poniards they called the Manilamen's bolos, among the belongings of two of the crew, and gave them over to the marshal without opposition."

"That Ghent feller, he's still commands *Confucius*, still chases pirates in the Yangtze and on the coast, and I am still that marshal."

"Well, Marshal, I am glad now I never kicked up too much dust in Bamboo Town. I'd rather be brained with a belaying pin that by that horse pistol under your coat."

"Gun that serves as a cudgel saves ammunition. $50 a month marshal's pay and court fees don't hardly buy cartridges when the marshal pays all his own expenses."

洋神 *Yang Shen*   *James Lande* 藍德

The marshal lowered one of the brougham's retractable windows. A whiff of temple incense drifted through the carriage. Fletcher imagined the streets west of the Bund where the Chinese swarmed, the scent of sandalwood joss sticks smoldering before pagan altars in gaudy temples, the deep vibrato of shivering brass gongs, the *tock-tock-tock* of teakwood on red-lacquered wooden temple blocks, a monotonous hum of prayers to entreat the fickle gods of China. He was awakening again to old sensations.

"When exactly were you out here?"

"Sailed to Hong Kong in forty-seven," Fletcher said. "On the China coast in fifty-one, came out before the mast and lay over in Shanghai, worked on an old opium hulk for a few months down at Woosung, when they still had trouble with pirates. Called at Hong Kong as mate on *Black Warrior* in fifty-four, on my way out to the Crimea. Back out again in fifty-seven, stayed almost two years, mostly aboard *Antelope*."

The carriage came to a high Chinese gate, with stacks of green-tiled roofs and upturned eaves, a temple converted for use by Chinese Maritime Customs, then crossed Custom House Road – another street leading away from the Bund past the homes of the rich and hovels of the poor. Behind the mansions and godowns of the foreigners, the mud walls and thatched roofs of native houses crowded together beside the slate-colored brick walls and green tile roofs of their rulers. Secluded inside high walls of plastered brick, wealthy natives – traders, compradors and mandarins – built their homes of stone and marble under glazed ceramic roofs supported by lacquered columns and massive carved beams.

"Don't set much store by steamers," Fletcher said, "being a deep-water sailor, but as far as they go, *Antelope* wasn't half bad. Samuel Hall built her in East Boston, my part of the country, in 1855 or so. She was a 415-ton screw auxiliary rigged as a bark, and a smart little opium clipper for the run up to Shanghai, until she was chartered by Uncle Sam to go to the Peiho."

"Sure, I remember *Antelope*. The Russell steamer, right? Haven't seen her around Shanghai for a while. Russell and Company sold her a year or two ago. Portagee now, down in Macao, call her *Fernando* or something like that."

"At the Peiho, her decks were awash with Navy brass and braid saluting every which way, and State Department starched-collars and creased-pants stumbling along her rails. Got to be more'n I could take, them spit-n-polish boys, and I disembarked for more lively surroundings."

"Anything to this flap about Nicaragua?"

Clerks in short sleeveless jackets, and compradors in rich silks brocaded with the characters for happiness, longevity, and luck deftly sidestepped farmers leading wagons drawn by oxen, peddlers pushing carts or wheelbarrows, and long-robed officials lounging in lacquered sedan chairs borne by toiling coolies. Westerners threaded through the crowd on horseback and in carriages and, rarely, a Western official appeared aboard his own sedan chair, lording it like a Chinese nabob.

"Will you look at that – a white man in a mandarin's chair," Fletcher said.

"Not many. That's the Prussian consul. The mandarins're exact about the privileges granted Westerners under the treaties. Sedan chairs for consuls have to be built the same, have the same color, and same number of bearers as a Chinese official of equal rank. What about Nicaragua?"

"Sure, I was with Walker all right, but earlier than Nicaragua – in Sonora, Mexico. Spent a few months training recruits mostly, but we had some differences of opinion because your gray-eyed Man of Destiny was more than just a little loco, and I left Mexico late in fifty-three."

A cacophony of string, drum, horn, flute and firecracker tumbled down the riverbank from an elaborate procession of junk sailors attended by a wildly cavorting golden lion with red tassels, papier-mâché ears, and a torso of shining silk.

"The next year, after Walker himself was arrested, I was in San Francisco and about to ship on *Westward Ho*, when a marshal *there* detained me after the authorities found out I'd been with Walker. Judge didn't think there was enough evidence for charges, mostly because I left Walker's service voluntarily. Wasn't prosecuted, so now I'm just persecuted. Since then, I keep running into people who want to tar me with that same brush as Walker, but you'll find upon inquiring with the Federal Courthouse in San Francisco that President Buchanan has considered the matter and declined to prosecute."

"That's not an inquiry for me to make. The American consul here in Shanghai decides such matters; I just catch the crooks."

"This time the crook got away. You've got his victim."

"Could be."

One after another, the carriage passed in review of the foreign hongs until it reached Consulate Road. The British opium runner Dent was neighbor to the colonnade portals of Shaw Brothers and the Oriental Bank. The brown brick face of American trader Augustine Heard overshadowed tiny Gibb, Livingston and Company back off the Bund. The P. & O. steamship offices crowded together with Sassoon and Company, and Jardine Matheson snuggled up to the British consulate.

"That one used to be Blenkin and Rawson. Sassoon's now. Parsee."

The carriage approached the gate of the British consulate grounds and was waved through by the Queen's guard. They proceeded along the path through broad close-cropped lawns and between tall red brick buildings toward the rear of the compound.

"Jail must still be around back of the consulate building," Fletcher said. "Last time I was brought here, before your time I expect, Marshal Hull, that little jail was so full of wicked offenders they had to release me back to *Antelope* with orders I was to be confined for a week. I was confined only long enough for the authorities to go ashore."

The British jailers greeted the marshal with long faces.

"Awfully sorry about things over 'ere today, Marshal 'ull. You see, there was a terrible brawl aboard one 'er Majesty's frigates. A number of our ratings being impatient to get on with the fighting at Peking, they took it upon themselves to rehearse 'ere in Shanghai. The upshot of it all, I'm afraid, is that a great many are now the guests of 'er Britannic Majesty's consul, them what isn't in irons aboard ship. You're welcome to look for yourself."

The marshal took Fletcher with him inside to examine the state of affairs and found at least one-hundred men crammed into the close atmosphere of the eight tiny cells with hardly room to stand.

"*Déjà vu*," Wood said.

The marshal shook his head and motioned Fletcher out.

"You'll have to stay in my rooms."

2 "Parrish? Have we any more cases to hear today?" American consul Walter L. G. Shanks shouted through the door of his tiny office to his half-time acting-secretary.

In the anteroom, a wisp of a young man with thin blond hair and silver-rimmed spectacles stared blankly at a pale shaft of sunlight that entered from a low angle and fell across the blotter on his desk. Another day of servitude to his overseer would soon end, and then a week, a month, a year. Surely, he'll have to go back before then, and leave me to my own inventions. Otherwise, he will certainly die of fever here in Shanghai. Which would be the same to me. Just let's not dawdle.

Williard Harris Parrish left his desk and came into the consul's office. "No sir, nothing more today. The deputy saw fit to return the remaining defendants to the British jail when Marshal Hull was called away to apprehend this sailor Fletcher Wood."

"Did you locate the lodgings of the plaintiff, that mountainous fellow calling himself Delevan Slaughter?"

"Yes sir, he is to be reached through the Pilot's Association. I left instructions for Mr. Slaughter to appear here at the consulate tomorrow morning at 10:00am to give his testimony in consular court."

"Very well. See that he brings his pilot's papers. What else have we to consider?"

The acting-secretary considered for a moment. In his gray suit, Parrish gave the impression of a pillar of drifting gray cloud preceding the Israelites in the desert. He dressed better than a half-time clerk could afford, especially since the State Department had cancelled allocations for consular pupils in 1857. The other half of his time was spent as a griffin at Russell and Company, where he kept company officers apprised of affairs at the American consulate, and the state of the consul's health.

The consul was aware of the Russell and Company spy in his midst, and actually found it mildly comforting that anyone cared even as little as the China trader Russell for how he conducted his office. Parrish might even send for help if the consul fell out of his chair. But Shanks still handled the most sensitive correspondence himself, which was just one more thing that made the position of consul so debilitating.

"This morning," the acting-secretary said, "I sent over to Russell and Company the $100.00 draft for quarterly rent on the consulate building, so that's done. The ledger book for reporting *Return of Fees* has only enough room for another three or four months of entries, so a new ledger book should be ordered from Washington, along with despatch paper. Another grommet fell out of the flag this morning, and I had to tie what remains of our poor old flag to the rope on the flagpole."

"It's too expensive to have a flag made," the consul said, "and Washington will not send a flag, so I have no choice but to call upon one of our warships and humbly beg a flag of them, perhaps from Commodore Spalding when, or rather if, he comes to Shanghai. As for the ledger, go ahead and write the usual letter requesting what we need, and I will sign. If that's all the urgent business taken care of, let us finish the draft of my letter on the suspension of trade."

The acting-secretary fetched the draft from his desk in the anteroom and made ready to take the consul's dictation.

"Read to me what we have so far," the consul said.

"To the Honorable Lewis Cass," began the acting-secretary, "Secretary of State, Washington. Sir, I have the honor to inform you that the trade at this port with the Chinese has materially diminished during the last few weeks, and the usual trade at this season of the year is virtually suspended. The insurgents, we are told, are withdrawing to a certain extent from Nankin and dispersing in parties over the adjacent country. The result of these movements is that they take possession of a wider tract of country. Hovering along the borders of this Province, they make it hazardous for the Chinese Merchants to keep up with their trade in the interior. Connected with these movements of the insurgents to create more or less alarm and ill feeling, may be mentioned the impending hostilities between Great Britain and France and the Government of China."

Parrish indicated that was all, and the consul continued while the acting-secretary took down his words.

"The British and French forces are now arriving in this vicinity preparatory, the British minister tells me, to proceeding north in the course of a few weeks. What will be the effect of their actions upon the Chinese mind, it is out of the question to foretell."

Out of the question, thought Parrish. Ha! *All Chinee man, him tinkee dat plenti big* stinkee bobbely. That's your effect on the Chinese mind – a big, stinking hullabaloo.

"I have no doubt that the Chinese Authorities, and the well-informed Chinese, regard the Government of the United States and its citizens as friends. However, in case of an outbreak I presume the mass of the Chinese would regard all foreigners in the same category. And in such case, in my judgment, the Chinese Authorities would be utterly powerless to maintain order and afford the necessary protection to the lives and property of citizens of the United States at this port. There is a large amount of property at this port, afloat and ashore, belonging to citizens of the United States—"

Especially my property, thought Parrish, all my shares in the tea, silk, and opium in Russell godowns. My taipan masters want to hear that you are requesting warships, Mr. Consul, to come to Shanghai and protect our property.

"—and the same is accumulating because of suspension of the trade. This port, being nearer to the movements of the insurgents, and to the anticipated theater of hostilities, than the other open ports, will be likely to feel the effects the soonest."

A commotion started up in the hallway beyond the anteroom. Hearing the Chinese doorman greeting several people, the counsel grimaced at his acting-secretary and concluded his dictation.

"I have, therefore, thought it proper to request Commodore Spalding to send a man-of-war here immediately. He has not yet visited this port. I have the honor to be, Sir, Your Obedient Servant, Walter L. G. Shanks, U. S. Consul. Parrish, see who that is bursting in upon us, will you?"

A minute later the acting-secretary returned to announce that Augustus Fitch, and several others, wished to report an act of piracy. Five people entered consul's office. Parrish introduced them as Augustus Fitch, Mrs. and Miss Fitch, Captain Cornelius Fitch, and Hugh Wood, and together the bunch of them made the little room seem a great deal smaller.

"Good afternoon, Mr. Consul," Augustus Fitch said. "This must be the most miserable building in all of Shanghai. How you receive callers here is beyond me."

The consul recognized Fitch's greeting for what it was, an opening salvo intended to intimidate the enemy and put the consul at a disadvantage from the start of the interview. Augustus Fitch was a tall and portly man in his fifties, with a ruddy complexion, slate-gray eyes behind gold-rimmed spectacles, and thinning gray hair and salt-and-pepper muttonchops. Fitch was dressed simply in an inexpensive charcoal woolen suit with a plain black cravat knotted under a stiff white collar. The collar and elbows of his coat were visibly worn, and buttons were missing from the cuffs, because he would never waste his money more than once on frivolous fashion. He was reported to have refused to read Dickens after 1844 because he could not forgive the author for his attacks on America in *American Notes* and *Martin Chuzzlewit*.

Usually the consul ignored the merchant's boorish lack of manners, if only because it required too much effort of body and mind to fence with the man, but today Consul Shanks felt disinclined to be ridden over roughshod and replied in kind.

"Your government's representative, Mr. Fitch, is lodged in this manner as a result of the charity of the American merchant Russell and Company. The largess of any other public-spirited American company in Shanghai not forthcoming, your consul can expect to remain so lodged until the American constituency in this metropolis sees fit to make our needs clear to the American Congress. Now, what is this about a piracy?"

"My ship *Essex* was set upon by pirates at the Volcanos, my wife and daughter's lives put at risk, four crewmen were killed, and at least $15,000 of damage done to the ship. What is more, your bumbling marshal has gone and locked up the one man I am told did more that any to save the ship and the lives of its passengers and crew, a Mr.

Fletcher Thorson Wood, an American citizen. I am here to see justice done to Mr. Wood, and to report this outrage on my ship and learn what you intend to do about it."

"Have your ship's captain give the details of the attack, and of the men who died, to my secretary and a report will be duly made of the incident – for your insurance records. What were the nationalities of the seamen who died."

"All British."

"Buried at sea?"

"They are aboard *Essex*."

"Very well. I'll see the British consul is notified and the bodies remanded to his custody for services and burial. As for this Fletcher Wood, he has been arrested on a charge of violation of the Neutrality Act and his case will be heard in consular court."

"That charge is just so much nonsense," Hannah said, "trumped up by the worthless pilot that came aboard our ship at Gutzlaff Island. During our voyage, Mr. Wood told us about his experience with William Walker, but all that happened a long time ago. Yesterday morning he saved us from miserable death at the hands of blood-thirsty pirates, led by a blond-headed Englishman they called Tom, and that certainly has to outweigh any silliness from way back when."

"What exactly did Mr. Wood do yesterday morning?" the consul said.

"We were about finished," Cornelius Fitch said, "then Mr. Wood says to lift one of the *taotai*'s 6-pounders out of the hold. He put my sailors together with the gun and in minutes, he had them working it like they were old hands. Sailors my mate could hardly get to stand up straight! It was amazing. Even the mate could not help admitting that he – that is, Mr. Wood – was a sailor's sailor. What did Mr. Reese say, Aunt Hannah?"

"Rope yarn for hair and Stockolm tar for blood."

"Yes, that's it. Wood kept his head, stood there as calm as vespers, with solid shot and musket balls chipping away wood from the rails and masts all around him, and the rest of us just ran amok like...." Cornelius hesitated.

"Like chickens with a fox in the coop," Elizabeth said. "And he really talks just like that too, your Honor, all the time."

"Well, Miss Fitch," the consul said, charmed and smiling. "I guess I'll just have to have a chat with your large talking hero before I decide what to do with him. May I presume, then, Mr. Fitch, that Augustus Fitch and Company will stand guarantee for Mr. Wood, if there turns out to be no cause to hold him or return him to the United States?"

"He helped to save many lives, the ship, and its cargo. There is no amount too large to set for his bond. And he certainly should not be repatriated. A man of his experience can be of great moment in the events about to come to hand here in Shanghai."

"What is this about the *taotai*'s 6-pounders?" the consul said. "You know that traffic in armaments is illegal under the treaties."

"Ah, I have just learned," Augustus said, with a hard look at his nephew Cornelius, "that some light artillery pieces were transshipped from Hong Kong on the authority of the *taotai* of Shanghai, and were seized by the imperial Chinese customs and removed from on board my ship. My company did not engage in any illegal arms traffic, but merely carried arms in an official capacity for the Chinese government. You had best speak with the *taotai* himself for clarification."

The consul guessed that the circumstances were quite different. Hardly smuggling when Chinese officials are on the receiving end. Anyway, if the guns are already in the *taotai*'s hands, there'll be no evidence. And Fitch's argument relies on the ambiguity of transporting arms for official purposes. How could I be held remiss in my duty, especially as Shanghai will need that artillery quite soon, when screaming rebels come over the walls of the Chinese city, and surround the foreign settlement?

"I will look into this matter of the guns. Mr. Wood's case will be heard at 10:00am tomorrow morning, at which time I will consider the facts and decide if he is still a risk to the community of Shanghai, or can be released to you under bond from your company. As you are standing bond, I invite you to be present at the hearing. And anyone else that cares to testify as to the man's character."

"Does he have to spend the night in jail?" Elizabeth said.

"I will see that your Mr. Wood is taken care of, Miss Fitch. If conditions in the British jail are inadequate, then I shall have him removed to the marshal's quarters, where he can be more comfortable."

"I want to know why there are no American ships of war cruising the sea lanes to protect our vessels," Hannah said. "Americans have a great deal invested in China, and we ship many expensive cargoes, yet there are no American gunboats or steam frigates in these waters to protect our shipping. Why did no gunboat to come to our rescue?"

"I'm surprised you saw none," the consul said, with apathy swelling in his voice, "because there are dozens between here and Chushan supporting the occupation of that island by the combined British and French expeditionary force. If you were attacked at the Volcanos, perhaps you were outside of the usual sea-lanes? But in any case, Mrs. Fitch, our situation here has not improved since your last stay, and we are still dependent upon other nations for protection of our ships at sea and citizens ashore. We have no navy of our own patrolling the coasts, no American gunboats to rely on. We depend on English gunboats to suppress piracy, and on the English municipal council to arrange civil matters, the English postal service to deliver the mail, and the English fire brigade to fight our fires. English ships survey coastal waters, not American. English jails hold American criminals, not American jails. English initiative, not American, takes the lead in dealings with the native government, and the insurgents' government for that matter."

"But English interests come first to Englishmen," Hannah said. "The English extend help to us only when their own affairs are in order."

"Repeatedly," the consul said, "American consuls have written to our State Department pleading for greater American presence in these waters, greater American influence in affairs in China, but to no avail. Even the threat of insurgent attack against American holdings in China does not seem to be enough to bestir Congress to allocate a force for these waters. Even now, I am begging Washington to send the *Hartford* or the *Saginaw* up here from Hong Kong, so there will be a steam frigate on station to shell the advancing insurgents when they come, and to take away American citizens if need be. I wish I had a better answer for your question, Mrs. Fitch, but there is no other."

"Well all I can say is that it is a mighty sorry state of affairs when Americans cannot scratch up even one little gunboat to protect our merchantmen. I suppose we will have to hide behind British skirts from the rebels, too. No wonder we're regarded as no better than second-chop Englishmen."

3

The Fitches returned through deepening twilight to their home in the British settlement. Hugh Wood returned to the Astor House to eat his supper alone and wonder if the consul would release his brother. Hugh was not at all prepared to admit to himself, especially as he was the older, that he wanted to stay in China without Fletcher. In his heart, he knew Fletcher's experience and bravado were his own shield and buckler and, without their comforting proximity, Hugh might just as well wander naked into the wilderness and be eaten alive by the Laestrygonians.

To Frenchmen on the Bund, the Fitches' landau driving past presented a familiar and heartwarming sight. It was one of few landaus in Shanghai and, with the top down and Elizabeth's bright parasol hovering above the crowded thoroughfare, the Americans looked recently transported from the Champs-Elysées. Stylishly dressed young women promenading along the Bund on the arms of young gentlemen, none of whom themselves possessed a landau or any other carriage, gazed with undisguised envy at the fashionable, if slightly vulgar, impression made by the unknown American newcomer. Every one of the seventy-five or so foreign women living in the settlement knew each other, and thus immediately recognized the young girl as a stranger.

Arriving at Augustus Fitch and Company, the party alighted like royalty under the imposing white portico and ascended the steps to the landing, turned for a final presentation to the ordinary mortals below Valhalla, then disappeared into the building.

Elizabeth found all this studied parade down the Bund to her new home much more satisfying than their first hurried dash to collect her father for the raid on the American consulate. This time she savored every moment of her arrival, every self-conscious gesture, as though it was her debutante's promenade.

Once past the drab offices at the front of the establishment, she discovered in the Fitch house a blend of Victorian and Chinese decor collected over years by Hannah. In her free moments, Elizabeth wandered about rooms, pushing aside the draperies at each entrance, always expecting to make new little discoveries. Thick Chinese carpets covered the dark varnished wooden floors with brilliantly colored and intricate designs of flowers and phoenixes. Among the more utilitarian wicker chairs in the parlor and other front rooms, she found overstuffed chairs, divans, sofas and ottomans. Exquisitely designed painted porcelain vases perched on small tables constructed to special order by Chinese craftsmen in a common Western style, but carved elaborately and inlaid in Chinese fashion. Western paintings of landscapes hung one above another on wires suspended from the ceiling molding, or from picture rails, and reminded the occupants of the fields and farms, the mountains and streams, of home.

Her rooms upstairs included an unused and dusty bedroom with attached sitting room, where the Chinese grooms and gardeners had left her trunks. There were more Chinese servants than she could keep in mind: grooms, gardeners, cooks, maids downstairs and upstairs, and messengers. A young Chinese girl, dressed like the other female Chinese servants in a three-quarter length high-collared black silk jacket over black silk trousers, was introduced to Elizabeth as her personal maid, or *amah*; she said that her name was Ah-mei, and that she spoke English "plitty good, you bet."

Elizabeth had discreetly watched her father's face ever since his first great surprise, followed by barely concealed fury, at seeing her with her mother when together the two women had burst into the firm's offices and demanded he drop everything and accompany them to rescue Fletcher Wood. Elizabeth anticipated the storm she and her mother would have to "weather under bare poles." It was about to break.

The afternoon, she decided, she would spend upstairs, supervising the cleaning of her rooms, and the unpacking and arranging of her wardrobe. She ordered Ah-mei to collect two more maids and begin the project, and was pleased to discover the Chinese women knew exactly what was needed without being told, and bent to the tasks with energy. Among themselves, the maids giggled and chattered in their country dialects, expressing with soft "ah"s and "ai-yo"s surprise mounting to amazement that any one young woman could have so many dresses, enough to clothe entire villages back home.

Alone with her finally in his private rooms, Augustus swept Hannah into his arms, ignoring her flinch, and whispered into her ear.

"I've waited so long to see you again, to have you by my side, in my arms. Are you ready, my darling? Are you ready to give me what I want, what I need so desperately?"

Hannah threw her head back and smiled at him. He went on.

"Will you give me everything that I want, all that I ask for?"

"Yes, my darling," she said. "Oh, yes! Here it is!"

Hannah swept her dress aside and dropped to one knee, gazing lovingly up into his face. Then she threw open the lid of the travel trunk beside them, lifted out the top compartment, and grasped and pulled up on a garter-stay affixed at each side of the bottom. The bottom of the trunk lifted up out of the box, spilling the pile of clothes onto Augustus' shoes. He leaned over Hannah and peered down, not at the swell of her bosom, but at the swell of her bullion, at thirty one-pound bars of shining gold.

"Hannah, darling! After all these years, no one can thrill me as much as you."

"Some people are thrilled with less than $50,000."

"In this little travel trunk?"

"There are four more trunks like this across the hallway in Elizabeth's room, packed with Elizabeth's ball gowns."

"From Edward?"

"Yes."

"Good. That confirms my expectations of the advantages of branching into London. When the civil war starts in America, our shipping can be declared neutral by using British bottoms."

"This bullion is only a loan, Gus, at ten percent per annum; it's not an investment at risk with Augustus Fitch and Company – not even a rise in our commission rate to two percent could persuade Edward to invest. Use the gold as you will for one year, then I must pack it up and take it home. Edward feels very strongly about preventing British gold and silver from making its way into China, and for that reason he will be doubly apoplectic if this is lost."

"What else have you brought me?"

"Elizabeth?"

Augustus grimaced. "Besides Elizabeth?"

"Cotton shirtings and drills."

"We can't sell what we have now. As my alter ego at Abraham Hart and Company has been heard to say, I know everyone expects the Chinese will all jump straightaway into cotton shifts when this paper treaty is made, but the reality is they will not. What the Chinese make on their home-looms is always of a lesser quality, but it's so much cheaper, they can't help but be satisfied with it. It's just as warm."

"I've been ashore in Shanghai only half a day," Hannah said. "and already whispered rumors say that our firm is insolvent. Have you heard any of this?"

"That is because I'm holding back every payment I can until our tea comes down to Shanghai. With godowns full of tea, we will have credit once more, and I will be able to issue drafts for our expenses. Of course, with this gold bullion we are already back in business – this gold can be leveraged to complete the purchase of our tea."

"But rumors of insolvency will damage our trade, will they not?"

"Perhaps, but not for long if my gamble pays off. It is a risk – but a risk worth running. I'm privy to clandestine information that the rebels are starting a spring offensive against Soochow, perhaps even Shanghai. With this gold, I can rent armed steamers and fighting men to bring out the tea. If I can get the earliest crops of summer tea out of the countryside ahead of the rebels, I will be one of only a few traders with any tea, and I will have a corner on the market. Come July or so, Augustus Fitch and Company will be firing and scenting our own tea in our Shanghai godowns, and selling it for three times, maybe ten times, what we sold it for last year. Then your silly rumors won't be worth any more than the fuzz on a puckered little Yankee gnat's ass."

"Have your plans changed since I was away?"

"No, Hannah, they have not. I remain appalled by the threat of financial ruin likely under the new customs regulations of the Treaty of Tientsin, and I still plan to leave the China trade. That is why I have brought Cornelius out to China, to take over the business after we leave, in spite of his inexperience. He is the only man left in our family who is young enough and ambitious enough to keep the concern growing. But it will have to take a different direction, and I am not certain what that will be. No doubt, our firm will have to start investing more of our own money into enterprises in China instead of just other people's money. But not me. I am getting too old, and so I have played my last hand. Now, tell me what possessed you to bring our daughter to this godforsaken pesthole, and what on earth makes you think that our precious, genteel daughter, with her tender sentiments, could possibly survive the callous brutality of life in China."

"You underestimate Elizabeth's strength," Hannah said. "What makes you think the girl could grow up so different from the mother? Or from her aunts? My sisters raise more hell than I ever could, and they have made as much of a rebel out of Elizabeth as they could out of any girl attending a female seminary. Of course, she still has many of the silly notions of a young girl, but she will not long mourn the loss of any gentility, she struggles against it so. She is intelligent, resourceful and industrious, and together we decided that if she is to ever have an opportunity to do something important with her life, spending some time learning how a business is built and run couldn't harm her. So, I have brought her out to China for a year as my protégé, to learn the business from me, and from you to the extent you can give her time."

"And you expect me to believe that she prefers that to rounds of *soirées*, tea parties, theater, lectures and the whirl of social life in Boston?"

"Elizabeth is a very level-headed girl, and she realizes she can do all that next year when she returns to America. The experience she will take back may give her much more to offer a young man just starting out in business."

"She could do as much in Boston or New York."

"I would not entrust her to anyone outside our family. Her uncles would be sincere yet deficient teachers for a woman, always patronizing her and never allowing her any real responsibility. Men never assume a woman can do anything that men can do. A woman always knows she can do better."

"You think you can do better with a precocious girl that elicits from your heart as much jealousy as tenderness? And you expect me to stand by and watch as you make a harsh Hannah of my sweet Elizabeth, play Dr. Frankenstein and make a virago of an innocent girl. What could be done with such a *menage a trois* as the three of us?"

"Listen, Gus, there is more to this than you know. You want to take a risk for gain, put all your money into upcountry tea. All right, I want to take a risk for gain also, with Elizabeth. She has growing within her a conceit about her bluestocking intellect, and a contempt for her less substantial contemporaries, which must be arrested before it ruins her life by making her unfit for any society. Time to put seminary learning behind her, and learn the lessons of the real world. After a year in China, seeing how harsh the world can really be, and how hard one must work to be successful, she may learn some modesty about her own growing prowess. And some empathy for the rest of the world that suffers along without her talents. And maybe just a little fear of God."

"Playing with a life is not the same as playing with commodities."

"Gus, if this were your son, you would be eager to send him out into the world to test his strength. Why must you deny the same opportunity to a daughter who is every bit as fearless as any son?"

Augustus still suspected that the situation concealed some much more serious issue. Something has happened to Elizabeth. Women's rights is being trotted out, as usual, to masquerade a truth. Hannah is counting on my reluctance to confront that truth, whatever it might be, because I can't bear to see my little girl change into a woman, and because she knows as well as I that exposure of the masquerade may do us damage. So, she is right, and I will not confront the truth and possibly humiliate my only daughter. She evidently cannot go back to America, or she wouldn't be here in China, so I will not send her back, at least not until I see signs of her distress.

"All right, Hannah. Elizabeth can stay and I will take her into the firm, as a 'lady griffin' of all things, if she's up to the work. You survived the experience, even thrived, so perhaps she can too. Especially if you are there to relate to her all the many mistakes you made, so she can avoid them."

"Augustus, you are a tolerant and forgiving man, and God will reward you for your generosity of spirit."

"Sure, are you? Perhaps you might also tell me when – in this world, or the next."

In any case, he thought, Elizabeth here will quell any rumors of my leaving the trade, and give the firm some protection against any failure of confidence.

"But the moment she falters, the moment she starts to show any sign of breaking, back she goes to America."

4

The marshal's carriage crunched to a halt before a large two-story Western-style house faced with red brick and surrounded by a high brick wall topped by broken crockery set in mortar. The house was located on Minghong Road in the American concession, about one-half mile from the American consulate on Soochow Creek. A small stable occupied one side of the front courtyard, and iron bars enclosed the first-floor windows of the house. Bars were common enough to keep intruders out but, in the case of the marshal, they were also intended to keep prisoners inside the rooms in which they were housed when the British jail was full.

The marshal and Fletcher Wood departed the carriage at the front door of the building, leaving the driver to tend to the horse. A Chinese servant in black jacket and cap, carrying a large ring of jangling keys, unlocked and opened the front door.

At the doorstep, Fletcher again caught the smell of familiar odors hanging on the damp air outside – sandalwood incense laced with smoke from oil lamps glowing against the gloom, and charcoal in braziers kindled for evening meals. In the tiny vestibule, the Chinese took their coats, and the marshal's hat, and put them away, then locked the front door behind them and took a seat beside the door.

Four rooms opened off the downstairs hallway, which led through another locked door to a rear courtyard enclosed by another high wall. The house had attached a small room for a servant, and there was an outhouse. The marshal's deputy met them in the downstairs parlor, where a fire was already burning in the fireplace. The deputy, called Simmons by the marshal, reported that the two prisoners then in custody in rooms at the rear of the house were well enough. Seeing he was not needed, Simmons withdrew to his quarters in one of the upstairs rooms, saying he would look in on the prisoners later at supper. The marshal did not introduce Fletcher Wood, nor did the marshal say that Wood was a prisoner. The deputy did not ask.

"You'll sleep in one of the rooms we keep for prisoners but, if you don't give me any trouble, you can have the run of the house until we put the lights out. A feller couldn't get out of here without raising a ruckus anyway. Considerin' as how you've got the Fitches to vouch for you, I figure I can put you on your honor, and we can have a bite to eat and set a spell in the parlor with brandy and cigars."

"You have my word, Marshal Hull. I shall do as you wish, and make my appearance before the consul as directed. I do not want to become a fugitive over something as trivial as the matter that has brought me here."

"I'll keep your revolver here with me. You can fetch it anytime after you are released by the consul. Setchur self down there by the fire. Mister Wong!"

They seated themselves in deep leather armchairs. A jangling of keys in the hallway was followed by the appearance of the Chinese doorman at the entrance to the parlor.

"Yes, ma-shah?"

"Two brandies, and more wood on the fire, if you please."

"Lite alay, ma-shah."

"Still can't tell if he's saying 'marshal' or 'master.' But he's a good man, brave as a bulldog. Had a prisoner try to escape once. You probably think those keys are to lock and unlock doors around here. So did I, until I saw my doorman wallop that prisoner with those massive keys. Reason enough to be respectful around the man. But I would be polite anyway. I have found that the best way to be with the Chinese. Make a show of respect for them, and they will do the same for you. I'm marshal for everyone living in my jurisdiction. Chinese, too. They know it, know I'll stand up for them just as soon as for a white man, so they help keep the peace."

"And you go in the dead of night to track down the murderers of a Chinese."

Mister Wong appeared with brandy, soda, and glasses on a lacquered wood tray.

"Him belly good ma-shah, you betcha."

"Thanks, Mister Wong. That's all for now. Supper at 7:00pm."

"Yes, ma-shah. You likee sma' tiffin now, can do."

"All right, slice up some of that sweet ham with crackers."

"Yes, ma-shah, lite alay."

The marshal took down a large scrapbook from a bookshelf, and opened it on a table to one side of where Fletcher sat.

"Here's a clipping of what you probably read."

The clipping was of a letter to the editor of the *North China Herald*, dated March 13, 1858, and signed AMIGOS. Fletcher read quickly through the letter, and then stopped where it read:

> ...surely if the American government can afford to pay seven hundred dollars for a flagstaff, they can manage to have a decent prison and not continue, when they have desperate characters to confine, to be solely and entirely dependent upon the British jail.

Fletcher looked up and considered the austere Stockton Hull for a few moments while the marshal poured two glasses of brandy.

"I would not be surprised if you had written this letter yourself."

The marshal chuckled. "Soda?" he said.

"Neat."

"Every so often a man just gets fed up," the marshal said. "With the stupidity that expects him to risk his life, and the lives of people that come to depend upon him, without the equipment to do the job. With the parsimony that will not provide adequate facilities to do the job. The American consuls, they don't like living in penury either, but they don't risk their lives. When I went aboard that steamer for my little parley with your Admiral Ghent, I was never more than the breadth of a very fine hair away from having my hair, or in this case head, lifted by Manilamen bolos, and becoming just one more mysterious disappearance. Well, when my hand stopped shaking enough, yes I wrote that letter. S'pose it was just self-aggrandizement, but writing 'disgrace to the American government' felt as good as letting off a .44 round. Still got no jail, 'tho."

"I heard quite a bit about *Confucius* when I was last on the coast. She was out chasing pirates while *Antelope* was ferrying attachés and interpreters to the north."

"Yeah, you can bet I've paid closer attention to *Confucius* since I had to take off those Manilamen. She was a pirate-killer from the start, way back when Captain Dearborn skippered her for Russell and Company and hunted pirates in the Chushans. Then Dearborn went and built his own steamer, right down in Woosung, would you believe it, called her *Yang-tsze*, monstrous thing 200 feet long and a thousand tons burden, but with only a 9-foot draft so it could just about walk on water. That's when he sold *Confucius* to the Chinese, to a guild of merchants, for $90,000, which must have paid for some small part of *Yang-tsze*.

"I remember *Yang-tsze*," Fletcher said. "She ran mail up from Hong Kong. Beat the official P. & O. mail steamers so often, folks called *Yang-tsze* the official mail boat."

"Yeah, Dearborn the bounty hunter turned Dearborn the postman. Last I heard, *Yang-tsze*'s in trade and running up to the Japans now. *Confucius*, however, did not stop hunting pirates just because Dearborn changed colors. Dent, Beale and Company took over management of her for the Chinese. When she was not hunting pirates, her owners worked her on the river towing deep-draft vessels between Woosung and Shanghai. When Dent put your Mr. Simon Rhys Ghent in charge of her, though, I guess they knew they had another American fire-eater at her helm, just like the previous administration. Right off the new captain went in *Confucius*, together with the gunboat *Hornet*, to escort a fleet of Chinese merchant junks carrying imperial grain tribute up to Tientsin."

Mr. Wong returned with a large tray he set on side table.

"Sugar-cured and slow smoked," the marshal said, "in a little house out back. Made 'em myself until Mr. Wong got the knack. Now he makes smoked hams and sells 'em in the Chinese market."

Mr. Wong served the sliced ham and English crackers on Chinese porcelain plates.

"Those two gunboats," the marshal said, "went about their work in a very professional manner and left nothing to chance. They chased away all the pirates out of the Saddles, swept south around Raffles and through the Ruggeds down to the Volcanos and beyond, then came back up and cleared the way north around Shantung to the mouth of the Peiho and upriver to Tientsin. *Confucius* has continued with the work since. Every so often you'd read in the *Herald* about how the 'Chinese war-steamer' *Confucius*, now in the service of the Chinese government and commanded by 'Admiral' Ghent, now promoted to Chinese rank, sank some pirate lorchas at Shantung or burned a fleet of Cantonese pirate junks off Ningpo."

Stockton Hull had a slow way of talking, a drawl like a bowie knife drawn slowly over a dry whetstone. Sometimes he seemed half-asleep on his feet, until he did something sudden. He caught a falling fireplace poker with the quickness of a gunslinger slapping leather. A glint of humor was always at the ready in his blue eyes, and his shy grin shook at the mustache to get out from behind. Together with Fletcher's eyes, Stockton Hull's eyes made for an ocean of blue between them.

"Was in *Confucius* myself for some action," the marshal said, "just couple of months before I had to arrest those Manilamen. The American consul and the *taotai* had me take *Confucius* to intercept the ship *Wandering Jew* out on the Yangtze just beyond Woosung. We removed a couple hundred coolies that'd been enticed on board for a few dollars each and told they were to be soldiers at Shanghai, or work on board ship, but never told nary a word about being shipped off to some foreign country. Ship's captain and crew were somewhat disinclined to give up their cargo – bunched up around me, the consul, and his interpreter, and fingered their knives and flashed their eyeteeth."

The marshal offered Fletcher a Manila cheroot from a ceramic humidor. They each took one and lit up while Mister Wong piled wood on the fire.

"Looked like they were going to throw us in among the coolies, until Ghent saw the trouble and put aboard a squad of his meanest-lookin' Manilamen, all armed with Sharps carbines, Colt revolvers and big bolo knives. When they came across the deck in a skirmishing line, the muzzles of those rifles looked 'bout as big as hawseholes and you'd like to hear our voices echoing down their barrels. That was all it took to scatter the ship's crew. So Ghent was not a stranger to me when I came to arrest his two crewmen and, come to think of it, I suppose that helped me some 'bout the time the rest of his crew were wondering which end of me to start whittling on first."

Outside the barred windows of the marshal's house, the afternoon light faded, distant lightning flashed dimly, and several miles to the east thunder rumbled like empty wagons rolling over a corduroy road.

"You appear to know a lot about the good 'Admiral' Ghent," Fletcher said.

"All part of a policeman's job, know everything about everybody, always have on hand a satchel full of facts and juicy gossip which – when properly employed – can make the job a little easier. That's a rule you learn in politics, too."

"There was some more hubbub over the *Wandering Jew*, was there not," Fletcher said, "over and above the ceaseless argument about the coolie trade? *Antelope* ran more silk down to Hong Kong about then, and everything'd blown over when we got back."

"Well, sure, the merchants squawked like they always do at any interference with their precious trade, and English merchants consider the pig trade legitimate. Accused the consul of exceeding his authority, and got four of the two-hundred coolies we landed to say they were prevented from lawfully emigrating to a foreign country, 'tho they couldn't say which foreign country, not Cuba nor anywhere else."

Stockton Hull poured himself another glass of brandy. "See any action at the Peiho back then, in fifty-eight?" he said.

"Watched the Allied Expeditionary Force blow apart the Taku forts."

Fletcher told the marshal about the long delay while the belligerents straggled into the shallow anchorage off the mouth of the Peiho, unloading and reloading cannon and heavy equipment in order to get across the bar, and the frantic efforts of the Chinese to erect batteries, build embankments, sandbag breastworks, and entrench stockades.

At about 10:00am on May 20th, there were at least two dozen warships and gunboats assembled. *Cormorant* led the attack by steaming through a hawser stretched across the river and running a gauntlet of cannon fire from the forts on each side of the river. *Nimrod* followed, opening fire on the south forts, then the other ships joined in the bombardment. Fort by fort, the men-of-war were towed into position, followed by the gunboats, where they all poured shot, shell, grape and rockets into a fort until its guns were silenced, then moved methodically up the line to the next fort.

"Guns fired and guns answered, until the noise sounded as if all hell was poundin' bark. Most of the Chinese cannon fire went high, striking yards and masts instead of hulls because, as it later came to light, the guns were elevated for high water and the tide had already fallen. After two hours of shelling, all the forts were silenced, and a landing party of close to 2000 marines, English and French, went ashore to finish demolishing the abandoned forts."

"Strange, isn't it," Stockton Hull said. "Two years ago, you were part of the expeditionary force sent to the Peiho – fought their way upriver to Tientsin, forced the Chinese to sign a new treaty. Now, you return two years later, and what looks like the same Allied Expeditionary Force is gathering in Hong Kong. It has many of the same men-of-war, preparing to sail north to the same Peiho, fight their way upriver to Tientsin, and force the Chinese to sign the same treaty they wouldn't sign the first time."

"With all those men, ships, and huge treasure expended, and all the trouble the British have in Canton, India, and Persia, you'd think they would get their treaty the first time and not have to come back and do it all over again. Cobden and the peace party in the British parliament must be feelin' just about as crabbed as a wounded bear."

"And hungry for Palmerston stew," the marshal said, chuckling. "What brings you back to China, Fletcher Wood?"

"My thought is to come upon the dry land to seek my fortune. I understand there are legitimate opportunities in China for officers with experience at war."

"Why leave the sea? Many's the time as a boy I wanted to ship out."

"I think my heart was divided ever before I went to sea, between becoming an officer of infantry, or the master of a ship. Actually, I started off for the Mexican War first, when I was fifteen years old. They caught me before I reached the county line, returned me to Salem, and sent me to sea as second mate on a China bound clipper called the *Hamilton*. Keep that under your hat, 'tho, because I'm fond of saying I came to ships through the fo'c's'le. So, the sea became my first enterprise, and I've never regretted it, but I have always wondered if a man mayn't have more than one calling. Came back from that voyage determined to learn soldiering. Even tried for West Point."

"Any man worth a pinch of salt," Hull said, "has worked several lines, to my way of thinking, unless he's got himself an education. I was railroad detective and a family man, 'till the cholera took my wife and children, a trolley conductor, gold prospector, and senator's assistant, and a policeman in Sacramento, until I was knocked unconscious and put on a ship bound for Shanghai. Once here, I decided it wasn't so bad and took the marshal's job. Never looked back. But if you were at West Point, then you have an education that makes knocking about unnecessary."

"My only schooling in military subjects was a few months of study at a military academy in Vermont. They taught the basics of tactics, strategy, and military engineering. Some in my class found it a desperately lonely place, being away from home for the first time, but I'd just sailed to China and back as second mate on a clipper ship and, in some respects, was already much older than the other boys my age. The family fortunes were at low tide in forty-eight and my father couldn't afford to give me more. He wanted to but, as he has said repeatedly, many successful men started with much less, and I could do just as well with what I had. Since then, of course, I've acquired practical experience in South America, Mexico, and the Crimea, which built upon that foundation from the Vermont academy, so time and money were well spent."

A carriage drew up to the entrance. Keys rattled, the front door was unlocked, and the doorman's could be heard bowing and scraping. Over the sound of thunder from outside, a deep, weary voice asked to see the marshal, and Stockton Hull went into the hallway and returned with the American consul.

"I can't stay but a moment, Stockton," the consul said. "They told me at the British consulate that you had brought your prisoner away because their accommodations were full up. Do you have him here?"

By the light of the fire reflected in the consul's normally florid face, Stockton Hull recognized another flush, the reddish hue that accompanied the return of the breakbone fever. Has he started taking his quinine again, the marshal wondered? If he does not take better care of himself, or leave Shanghai as he wants, he will take his place in the cemetery among all the derelict sailors he himself has committed to rest there.

"Yes, sir, right here. Mr. Wood?"

Fletcher Wood stood up and approached them.

"Mr. Consul," the marshal said, "this is Mr. Fletcher Wood."

"How do you do, Mr. Consul," Fletcher said, offering his hand. The consul started to take his hand, then stopped.

"Marshal, isn't this man your prisoner? Why is he not under lock and key? Why is he sitting in your parlor drinking brandy and smoking cigars?"

"Er, in my estimation, sir, it is sufficient that Mr. Wood is being detained in my custody until brought before you."

"Step into the hall for a moment, Marshal," the consul said. Together the consul and the marshal left the room, closing the door behind them. Fletcher glanced at his pariah hand, which had begun to feel chill, then stuffed it into a pants pocket for warmth. Through the closed door, Fletcher heard clearly enough the jangle of Mister Wong's keys as he hurried up the hallway stairs, followed by the sound of the men's voices.

"What do you mean in your estimation? It is not your place to render judgment on prisoners. That is the prerogative, the duty of the consul."

"I rendered no judgment, sir, except perhaps as to how I choose to incarcerate the man. Surely I am allowed some latitude in how I treat my prisoners."

"A man is no prisoner if he is being treated like royalty, with the courtesy shown a crowned-head of Europe. Lord, man, I'm not regarded half that well when I call on the goddamned British consul. There I'm treated like a tradesman, and have to stand on line at the desk of his secretary, knowing all the while they just have not the brass to order me around to the servant's entrance. Not only have I no secretary, but just an acting-secretary, whom I cannot pay enough to promote, but I also might just as well have no desk, if all I can have is that rickety old hand-me-down crate from Russell and Company. I even have to borrow a carriage from Russell to go out in the rain."

"The man is only detained for hearing, Mr. Consul. He is not convicted of a crime like those others back there. Mr. Wood is innocent until proven guilty, and I am merely treating him as such."

"Oh, so now you're going to tell me the law. I cannot bear any more of this, simply cannot bear it. You...you have your prisoner at the consulate by 10:00am tomorrow morning. Good night!"

Marshal Stockton Hull returned to the parlor, looking a good deal more world-weary than before. Fletcher rose from his chair and gave the marshal a look that said "should I return to my cell?" but the marshal just waved him back into his chair beside the crackling fire and poured himself three fingers of brandy. He swallowed the brandy in a single gulp, then poured two more glasses.

"Consul Shanks," the marshal said, without noticeable rancor, "has a lot on his mind. But, seein' as how I work for him, and you will appear before him tomorrow morning, I can't in good conscience say more. Let's see about supper."

But deep in the sanctuary of his own heart, Stanford Hull believed the old consul was about to crack.

5

The American consul's carriage rolled through the dark, rain-puddled streets of the American concession. Inside, the consul's mood was as black as the weather outside.

Insubordinate marshal. How dare he preach "innocent until proven guilty to" me? If I thought I could replace him in less than a year, I would discharge that iniquitous villain instantly, but who would take his job at his pay? Who could face up to ministers, merchant princes, missionaries, and drunks and wharf rats like my marshal, sail into a sailors' brawl and end it with the barrel of his dragoon pistol? Actually, except for the cumshaw and squeeze, Stockton Hull is not all that unfit. But that Fletcher Wood, he must be very smooth to win over my granite-hearted marshal that way, and also that old skinflint Augustus Fitch. Well, Mr. Wood, you will not get around me so easily.

We already have witnessed overmuch the "depredations of renegade foreigners" in China, fighting in the rebel ranks, selling arms and ammunition to the rebels, and we certainly have no need for any man so experienced as to have served with that filibuster Walker in Nicaragua. I will have Mr. Wood back on a ship bound for the United States so fast his head will swim.

A jarring burst of thunder was followed immediately by a brilliant flash that illuminated the interior of the carriage with white light. The consul winced violently and shrank into his seat. A few minutes passed before he was again composed.

I wonder what is in the Neutrality Law? If the State Department would provide consulates with an adequate library of reference books, we would not have to *guess* at how the law should be administered here. Statutes at Large, Opinions of Attorneys General, Wheaton's International Law, Blackstone – by themselves they are simply insufficient. Where are my sources for the laws of shipping, partnerships, principal and agents, commercial law? How am I to equitably resolve disputes, to know what punishment to mete out to the defendants I convict? And this Neutrality Law. I cannot very well apply the law as it stands now, even if I knew the law, because any offense would have been committed some time ago. When did they say Wood was with Walker, in 1853? I would have to apply the law in force then, and how on earth am I to find out what the law was in 1853, when I cannot even ascertain what the law is now!

They must give me a leave of absence, at least a year. No man can perform this job without some relief. No one can keep his health in this debilitating environment. No one can cope with the infinite trials a consul must endure. No home leave, inadequate pay, staff, and facilities, Congress, the State Department, the Treasury Department, war, insurrection, treaties, regulations, articles, codes, currency questions, duties and tariffs, coolie trade, opium trade, shipwrecks, navigational aids, ships' flags and registers, smuggling, bills of exchange, British pounds, Mexican dollars, Chinese taels, American, British, French, Russian, Spanish, Dutch ministers extraordinary, plenipotentiaries, consuls, mandarins, *taotai*s, naval officers, customs officers, interpreters, translators, merchants, compradors, missionaries, ship captains, sailors, pirates, rebels, deserters...and filibusterers. Lord, please do not let anyone hear me *scream*! And where shall I find more time to complete my book on the Chinese, to complete the research necessary – on Canton and the early treaties, the Chinese courts, the other treaty ports – for a work worthy of being dedicated to General Cass. Just one year, Lord, anywhere else in the world.

What shall I say, how can I put it in a letter to the Secretary of State? "I have the honor...." No, too feeble. "I regret to inform you" is more direct. "I regret to inform you...that I cannot remain here another summer at this port without a change of climate. Since I arrived here in 1858, this unhealthy climate has impaired my health, and I am fearful my constitution has been affected from the amount of quinine I must take for the fever." That will not be enough, however. I must have corroboration. I must include a physician's statement. Yes, a note from my doctor.

洋神 *Yang Shen*   James Lande 藍德

Dramatis Personae: Chapter 11

Hannibal Arlen Benedict   a gentleman from North Carolina

Shanghai in 1855
(based on Morse, *International Relations of the Chinese Empire*, v. 1, p. 454)

Early Astor House Hotel 禮查飯店 (about 1900)
from Virtual Shanghai *http://virtualshanghai.net*
photo courtesy of Getty Research Institute *www.getty.edu/research*

176   *American Consular Inquiry*

洋神 *Yang Shen*   *James Lande* 藍德

Chapter 11: American Consular Inquiry

Saturday, April 21, 1860, 8:00am

The following morning Fletcher was already dressed when the marshal unlocked the door to his room and called him for breakfast. Deputy Simmons had escorted his two prisoners out into the damp, foggy rear courtyard for morning exercise. The marshal ate breakfast at the same place he and Fletcher had eaten supper the evening before, at a small table in the kitchen, near the warmth of the wood-stove.

"There's a copy of today's paper on the table. Thought you'd want to look it over. You've already got your name in the papers."

Fletcher sat to table and opened the *North China Herald* with apprehension, expecting to see a headline jump out at him: **NOTORIOUS FILIBUSTER WOOD ARRESTED AT SHANGHAI.** Marshal Hull chuckled at Fletcher's expression.

"It's not that bad," he said. "You're in the passenger arrivals."

Relieved that his reputation was not already compromised before he had even one foot out onto the flemish horses of Shanghai, Fletcher devoured the rest of the news along with stacks of fried ham and eggs.

The
North-China Herald
Shanghai, Saturday, April 21, 1860

Latest Dates
England Feb 28   Singapore Apr 3
Bombay Mar 16   Hongkong Apr 14
Calcutta   New York Feb 12
Galle   Mar 26

Passengers
ARRIVED: Per *Azof*, from Kanagawa, Messrs Aspinall, Marshall, Burgy, Wetmore, Cheney, Shearer & Lelez. From Nagasaki, Mrs Walsh, and Mr Nunjeebhoy. Per *Chevy Chase*, from Hongkong, Dr & Mrs Bridges and child, Mr. & Mrs Pollard, Messrs Delano, Gregson, and McNair. Per *Aden*, Mrs Rickomartz & child, Admiral Charner, Captain L. Ladebat. Per *Essex*, from Hongkong, Mrs & Miss Fitch, Messrs H. Wood and F. T. Wood.

There were the Shipping notices, Notices of Firms, Insurance notices, sundries For Sale, copies of the U. S. Treaty with China on sale at the *Herald* office, notices of Public Auction, Houses & Land, and miscellaneous situations wanted, periodicals for sale, and rates at the Shanghae Hospital. Old Kupferschmid was unloading his most recent cargo of commodities "at very reasonable prices." Also: H. Fogg & Co. Ship Chandlers, Saekee & Co. silk, and the ever-present announcement for Lea & Perrins Celebrated Worcestershire Sauce for perfectly digested food. Heaven knows, he thought, the way we eat in Shanghai, one man at supper ingesting enough comestibles to feed a company of corsairs, we need all the assistance modern science and the culinary arts can invent. Now I know I have arrived home again, welcomed as I am by my old friends Mr. Lea and Mr. Perrins.

The P. & O. steamer *Aden* will leave for Hong Kong on the 29th with room for 2200 bales of silk. Another Sassoon, this one named after Father Abraham, was admitted as a partner in the Parsee tribe of Sassoon traders. There's a notice of *Cleopatra* being taken by pirates near Ningpo. Yokohama is in a very unsettled state...the prince of Meto attacked and severely wounded the Japanese regent...no one is to go out after dark.

Her Majesty the Queen of England's

THE SHANGHAI HOSPITAL AND DISPENSARY

H AS been enlarged, and can accommodate Private Patients with comfort.
The terms are,
    For Private Rooms....Tls 2.0.0 a day
    " Officers   Do. .... " 1.5.0 "
    " General Wards .... " 1.0.0 "
    Washing one tael per month extra
    The Lowest charge is Seven Taels
    F. C. SIBBALD, M.D., *Surgeon*
    Mr. NEWMAN, *Apothecary*

☞ The DISPENSARY is well stocked with Medicine, which may be had upon application to the Apothecary.
tf   Shanghai, July 17th, 1857

American Consular Inquiry

洋神 *Yang Shen*   *James Lande* 藍德

ultimatums to the Chinese Government are unalterable. Here're a hat full of letters whining about late arrivals of mail on the P. & O. mail steamers. Rebels are operating near Ch'ang-chau, and the district cities of Kin-tan and Lih-yang have fallen.

"Rebels are active around Ch'ang-chau," Fletcher said. "Where exactly is that?"

"That'd be Changchow. No two people spell anything the same way in this country. 'bout halfway to Nanking, on the Grand Canal."

"I need maps. Shanghai, Soochow, Hangchow, Nanking, and the Yangtze."

"Only Admiralty maps are any good. Hard to come by. Chinese maps are useless."

"I wonder if those fallen cities mean the Taipings are coming our way? If they take Soochow next, then Shanghai would have to follow."

"They may return to Hangchow. There're no foreign men-of-war off Hangchow."

Island of Chushan is probably now surrounded by British and French men of war and "the people will be only too delighted at the prospect of the revival of the old state of things...and dollars are plentiful...." Pity the poor islanders, Fletcher thought. What will they do next year when the treaty's been signed and the Emperor and the Queen are closer than two peas in a pod, and the English do *not* occupy Chushan?

Consul Shanks was at his desk in the American consulate early that Saturday morning and, while waiting for the hour of the Consular Court, he considered the vexing problem of handling American lawbreakers in Shanghai. Before him on his desk was a copy of a letter from his superior in China, Minister Jethro Wood, to Shanks' superior in Washington, Secretary of State Lewis Cass.

Official No. 3
Legation of the United States, Macao
February 22, 1860

To the Honorable Lewis Cass
Secretary of State

Sir,
I have already referred to the humiliating position in which I find our consuls in China.... My predecessor forwarded you a strong petition, which had been presented to him by the shipmasters at Shanghai requesting adequate facilities and support for judicial punishment of wrongdoers.... Knowledge that our consuls have no adequate power to punish crime in treaty ports emboldens our lawless citizens to act out their wickedness.... Chinese authorities persist in their dislike of an expansion of intercourse with foreign nations because of the repetition of such acts, scores of which the majority of foreigners never hear of, and grievances like those described in Minister Blaine's letter to Lord Russell, a copy of which I enclose and recommend to your attention.... A tax of $10 levied on every American ship coming into a port would aid the funds needed for this purpose and relieve the Government of the entire expense of prisons and marshals....
I have the honor to be,
  Your obedient servant,
  Jethro E. Wood

They would have just received this letter in Washington, as it was sent in February. Perhaps they already are over their pique at receiving yet another such plea from distant China. Shipmasters would petition, of course, because of the frequency they must receive back on board malefactors they are trying to get off their ships. And the Chinese chafe under the restrictions of extraterritoriality that too often result in a slap on the hand for foreigners who commit crimes against Chinese as serious as murder. In a good year, a $10 tax on each American ship would yield several thousand dollars, sufficient to build and operate a jail, and to pay marshals enough to make graft unnecessary, at least at Shanghai. At the smaller ports, the income might be inadequate, but pooling of resources might be possible. Melancholy? Outrageous would be closer to the facts.

The consul next examined an attachment to Minister Wood's letter.

Summary of replies from U. S. Consular officers in China treaty ports...:
- Consuls have used the jails belonging to the British consulate, placed prisoners on board U.S. men of war, put in irons on board their own ships, or in consulate rooms.... At Shanghai, 191 persons had been brought before the consul during the year ending in July, 1859.
- Prisoners could not be confined in the yamun of Chinese officials or in Chinese prisons because it would be impossible to ensure adequate measures for their health and safety.... A prison building at Shanghai might cost $2000 to $3000 to build; at Ningpo, perhaps $1200 to $1500; at Fuchau a building could be rented for $800 annually, with $600 for initial outlay; at Amoy a building would rent for about $200 annually. All of the consuls disfavor a floating prison.
- All consuls report instances where convicted prisoners, released because of the want of facilities for their incarceration, have resorted to assault, kidnapping, ransom, black mail of native fishermen and tradesmen, and piracy. American vagabonds have a large license everywhere in China... Extraterritoriality now operates as a shield between the felon and the laws of China, and the consequence is abounding and unrebuked crime.

So, the extraterritoriality – or ex-territoriality, or extrality – intended to shield foreigners from the iniquities of Chinese justice – arbitrary laws, torture in the courts, death by being flayed alive or beheaded – now shields the crimes of foreigners from just prosecution – heinous crimes like brutal extortion, rape and murder.

Such, then, are the crimes of renegade foreigners. Many are the depredations a notorious filibusterer like this Fletcher Thorson Wood might choose. He comes here with no visible means of support, no position already secured, and his only calling soldier of fortune – ready to offer his sword to the highest bidder. What do you think he will do? Mend ladies' parasols? Sell shaved ice on the Bund? Preach the gospel?

He appears to be a leader as well, as he demonstrated aboard ship, which makes him all the more dangerous. He could easily round up a contingent of motley sailors and terrorize the surrounding countryside. I wish I could be certain I had the authority to put him on a ship back to America on suspicion alone. It would not be difficult to execute. The marshal escorts the man aboard a ship at time of sailing and gives the master a voucher for his expenses, and the man is confined to quarters until the ship is at sea.

2 Before he could finish reading the letter, the consul heard footsteps at his office door and a knock. Parrish entered with Marshal Hull and the defendant Wood.

"Take a seat, gentlemen," the consul said, "while we wait for the plaintiff and the other persons interested in this case." Parrish busied himself arranging the office for a court hearing. Fletcher examined the consul's office, but his impression of the establishment did not improve. He had already noted the tiny emblem representing the United States poorly painted over the entrance to the building, and the ancient American flag that looked as if it had been in the thick of Revolutionary War battles. On a table under a window, there were open ledger books entitled *Arrivals and Departures of Vessels*, and *Return of Fees*, and in a dark corner of the office, there was a large iron safe standing half-open. A slightly moldy odor seemed to emanate from the safe, as though old books and ledgers stored inside had fallen to pieces with age. The odor reminded him of the trunk of books, musty from long exposure to damp salt air, which he had traded at the old Simon Bolivar Bookshop in Valparaiso. The windows of the consul's office were dark with grime and a thin layer of dust lay in the sills. There was a large map on the wall.

"Look at this map," he whispered to the marshal. Stepping over to the wall, Fletcher pointed to Shanghai, Soochow and Nanking on the map. Between them Changchow and the two cities reported in the newspaper as taken by the rebels were arrayed in a line of attack like pieces on a chess board, about one-third of the distance from Nanking toward Soochow.

"Look at how the rebels chose the three cities, Changchow, Kin-tan and Lih-yang, in a line advancing on Soochow."

After a short while, the Fitches arrived with Hugh Wood and took their seats. When the pilot Delevan Slaughter had not arrived by 10:15am, the consul instructed Parrish to send a runner to find him.

"Let us, while we are waiting for the plaintiff," the consul said, "conduct an informal inquiry into the charges. Mr. Wood, you are charged with violation of the Neutrality Act, specifically for having served with William Walker in Nicaragua. There seems to be no question about this, as you are reported to have told the story of your service with Walker on board ship."

"That's pretty close to the truth, your Honor," Fletcher said. "Actually, I was with Walker in the summer of 1853, when he was campaigning in Lower California and Sonora, but everybody just assumes it was Nicaragua, because Walker's most closely associated with Nicaragua."

"State your full name."

"Fletcher Thorson Wood."

"Where were you born?"

"Salem, Massachusetts, your Honor."

"What is your age?"

"Twenty-eight."

"How did you come to be with Walker?"

"I sailed from China on *Gold Hunter* in April of fifty-three, carrying coolies to Mexico. Left the ship at Tehauntepec, transshipped some of the coolies from Oaxaca up to Sonora, and heard about an army of foreigners there. I'd had some military schooling, and been first officer aboard clipper ships, so I was signed on to train recruits in close-order drill and later to train artillerymen. Well, after a while, three or four months maybe, I was not getting on all that well with Colonel Walker, because of the ways he insisted on doing some things. So, after an argument, I up and quit and went off to be a Texas Ranger, then a drillmaster in the Mexican army, then joined up with a partner to collect scrap-iron in Mexico. When that scheme busted, I jumped aboard a mule and rode through Mexico to California, thinking to ship out for again for China."

"When was that?"

"Late in fifty-four, your Honor. I'd left Walker for almost a year when he was arrested himself for violation of neutrality, the first time. When I was about to ship out from San Francisco on *Westward Ho*, the authorities detained me because of my service with Walker in that so-called Republic of Sonora. The Federal Court in San Francisco dismissed the case for lack of evidence when I told the judge I'd left Walker long before the collapse of his republic. When Walker went to Nicaragua, I was already in the Crimea, commissioned as a lieutenant in the French artillery. When Walker was president of Nicaragua, I was on the China coast as a mate in the Russell and Company steamer *Antelope*. This Walker business is old news, and you wouldn't be bothered with it if not for crooked old Delevan Slaughter."

"Can you tell me," the consul said, "the names of the officers who arrested you?"

"No, sir. Just U. S. Marshals."

"The court where your hearing took place?"

"The courts were just numbers, some district in San Francisco, I'd guess."

"The judge who reviewed your case?"

"Harvard Lansing, Junior. Him, I remember."

"About this pilot, who has not seen fit to appear and give testimony, is there anything more to be said about him?"

"Much more," Fletcher said. "There was a time Slaughter passed himself off as a river pilot, and he was hired to take this little Yangtze steamer carrying specie through rebel territory for a Shanghai guild of rich Chinese merchants. Well, come nightfall Delevan Slaughter deliberately ran the steamer aground in rebel territory, where I guess he'd arranged to be picked up by some junk. He packed up a couple of satchels full of gold at gunpoint, abandoned the crewmen, who had gone into the water to free our vessel, and left me and a dozen others under rebel fire."

"Are there other witnesses to this?"

"No sir. In the dark, I jumped into the river and swam out to a passing junk, but it turned out to be swarming with rebels and they hauled me aboard. From what I could hear – gunfire, screams and then silence – I had to guess the rest of the crew were past salvation. Tried to convince the rebels that Slaughter and the fleeing junk were much more valuable prizes then me. The rebels finally gave chase, almost had her when finally the steamer came off of the mud shoal, uncovered a 12-pounder sternchaser, and opened fire. Disabled the rebels, and I was able to slip over the side and eventually make my way back to Shanghai. The pilot had disappeared by that time, of course, down the coast somewhere, but I swore then that I would kill Delevan Slaughter on sight."

"When was this?"

"Back in early fifty-seven. I went aboard *Antelope* not long after."

"I believe I was consul then. Why was this incident not reported to me?"

"Chinese vessel? Must've been reported to the *taotai*, unless the merchants that made the charter weren't on the up and up."

"Why did you not report the incident?"

"Me? Reporting to consuls is the business of captains and mates, not ordinary seamen like I was back then. What's more, I doubt anybody could've reckoned what authority had jurisdiction. I don't think there were any two men of the same nationality on board." Why would I want to get tangled up with consuls and their courts? They say Chinese dread their courts – where mandarins torture even the plaintiffs – and stay far away from them, and that's always seemed a wise policy to me.

"What business brings you to China?" the consul said, hoping that Wood would stumble on this question and reveal some mercenary purpose that would form the basis of an excuse to deport him.

"I seek my fortune, sir, just as might any man. Like my brother Hugh, for example, who has removed himself from his position as a shipping clerk in our father's New York firm, where both he and I gained experience in commerce, and come out to China to go into trade. I have already established myself in Shanghai in earlier years, on the coast, as some gentlemen at Russell and Company, the owners of *Antelope*, can testify. Many choices are open to me, in trade with my brother, at my old profession in the coasting trade, or elsewhere that I have not yet discovered."

"Mr. Wood, you openly avow your calling as a soldier, a mercenary serving in foreign armies, and claim to have served as an officer. I think you may have come to Shanghai to continue in that calling. No, no, don't bother to deny it. Your record speaks for itself and renders ludicrous the thought of a man of action like yourself in trade."

"Mr. Consul!" Augustus Fitch said. He stood and stepped forward to the consul's desk. "You have no call to make such an allegation against Mr. Wood, no evidence at all. Mr. Wood can take a place in my firm at any time, and that should be all the guarantee the man needs."

The consul jumped up and leaned forward.

"Fitch, this is my consulate, and while in any other venue I am constrained by public sentiment to defer to you, I'll be damned before I will allow you to swagger about here. Sit down, sir, and speak only when you are spoken to, or by God I'll have my marshal put you into the street!"

Fitch fumed for a moment, and then took his seat. "The man is not even represented by legal counsel," he said, spitting the words.

"There is no court in session here," the consul said, spitting the words back. "This is merely an informal inquiry." Hannah Fitch took her husband's arm in hers and Fitch withdrew into sullen silence.

"Mr. Wood," the consul said, taking his seat, "indigestion attacks my stomach each time I contemplate the mischief you are likely to cause if I allow you to remain in Shanghai, and my stomach is always right in these matters. If you weren't so well liked in influential circles, I would jail you on the testimony of my stomach and have you put on the first ship outward bound to any destination as far as possible from China."

"Stomach?" Augustus Fitch said, snorting in disgust.

"I hasten to beg your Honor's pardon," Fletcher said quickly, "for any discomfort I may inadvertently cause the court, but in all sincerity I fail to see what 'mischief' I might cause when so many legitimate pursuits beckon."

"You are aware of your government's policy in this civil war between the Taiping rebels and the lawful Chinese government, are you not?"

"Neutrality, of course."

"That means that it is against the law, Mr. Wood, for American citizens to render assistance to the Taiping rebels – to join their army, to supply them with weapons, or sell to them any contraband material. The British observe the same scrupulous policy, and all other Western nations follow that policy. Any American apprehended rendering aid to the rebels is subject to arrest and punishment, at my discretion."

The consul's office was silent while all present considered the present impasse. Fletcher wondered just how serious an obstacle to his plans this consul really was. At that moment, the consul had called his hand, and Fletcher was vulnerable because he might be taken directly aboard an outbound ship if the consul could not be convinced to continue the play. Somehow, he had to get out of Shanghai, beyond the reach of the consul and his marshal, onto the river, and up the Yangtze to rebel territory, before he could discover what to do next. He had not yet been at Shanghai long enough to find out the true conditions among the rebels. He was not prepared to go over to them until he was certain of a number of things, of how they would receive him, and treat him, and their actual strength and prospects for victory.

The consul's acting-secretary went to answer a knock at the door. He returned to say that the pilot Delevan Slaughter was reported to have left Shanghai that morning on a steamer bound for Ningpo.

"Well, that squares it, does it not?" Augustus Fitch said.

The consul stared at Fitch for a few moments before asking slowly, "what is your meaning, Mr. Fitch?"

With a barely concealed effort to control himself, Fitch answered, "it means, your Honor, that without a plaintiff, without a warrant for Mr. Wood's arrest, without witnesses, and there is no case against Mr. Wood."

"And suppose I have a complaint made against Mr. Wood by the United States, and swear out a warrant here and now on the strength of Mr. Wood's own admissions."

"You said this was an informal inquiry!"

Marshal Hull stepped forward. "Your Honor, might I address the court with a suggestion?" The marshal's intercession cleaved the angry atmosphere and arrested the struggle between the consul and the China trader. Consul Shanks sat back and allowed his fury at Augustus Fitch to subside somewhat, then smiled at his marshal.

"Yes, Marshal. What is *your* suggestion?"

"Mr. Wood might make his start aboard one of the Chinese steamers on the Yangtze, helping to ensure the safety of river commerce by suppressing piracy, which is not against any law that I know of. It's no violation of neutrality, and it is more in line with his calling as a soldier and sailor."

The consul considered this mutely. True, neutrality does not apply to pirates, only to rebels. The work is appropriate enough for his background, and finding such a berth is not difficult. The American Ghent could find a place for him. Wood would be in the employ of the Chinese, raising questions about whether American law still would protect him, and whether he should be indemnified by the United States. We have not yet clarified the status of Americans in the employ of the Chinese government. Even our recent appointment of an American agent to the Chinese custom house has not required any decision. Of course, once upriver, he could go over to the rebels. But even if he stays in Shanghai, I can't see how to prevent that. At least, we would know if he defected from some Chinese steamer. Then he would be *persona non grata* in Shanghai, and arrested on sight. If Fitch was not involved, I could just chuck the ruffian on board some ship but, if I did so now, my cause would be questioned immediately. I cannot deport the man without sufficient cause, not with only the scant authority granted a U. S. consul, so the next best solution is to give him some rope to hang himself.

"Mr. Wood," the consul said, "do you understand the suggestion?"

"Yes, your Honor. I am acquainted with Admiral Ghent, and the work done by *Confucius* for the Pirate Suppression Bureau of the Chinese."

"Can you say that you are qualified for a berth on a steamer like *Confucius*, and willing to do the work. It would be a place for you to start your career in Shanghai, whatever that may ultimately be."

"Yes, your Honor, I would accept the berth of mate on such a vessel."

"I shall consider, then, what you have told me about the character of your service with Walker in Sonora, Mexico, your gallant actions aboard the merchant vessel *Essex*, and the willingness of a prominent business firm like Augustus Fitch and Company to guarantee your conduct."

"Thank you, sir." Fletcher stood up to leave.

"Just a moment – sit down. I am prepared to release you in the charge of Augustus Fitch and Company, under the recognizance that you shall seek employment aboard a steamer responsible for the suppression of piracy upon the Yangtze River. Should you fail to serve in such a position for at least six months, Augustus Fitch and Company shall be liable for any damages arising out of your breach of this trust, and you yourself shall be liable to immediate deportation out of China. Do you agree to this, Mr. Wood?"

"Yes, sir, I do."

"And you, Mr. Fitch, for your firm?"

洋神 *Yang Shen*   *James Lande* 藍德

"Yes, I do. Am I expected to post a bond?"

"Not at this time. Mr. Wood, you are released to the custody of Mr. Fitch and are to hold yourself ready while I make inquiries on your behalf with responsible persons. Leave your address with the clerk and be available on immediate notice. That is all, ladies and gentlemen. You may all leave now."

The erstwhile litigants all filed out of the consulate building and crowded into the Fitch's landau. The marshal and the consul watched through an office window as the Fitch carriage crossed over Soochow Creek.

"Think he'll go over to the rebels?"

"If he does," the consul said, "we shall never see him nor hear from him again. He will die fighting in the rebel army. And good riddance."

The marshal left the office. Alone, the consul went to his ledger books where they lay open on a table and made the following entry in his *Report of Judicial Cases*.

Return of Suits from 1st day of January 1860 to 30th day of June 1860

CASE	PLAINTIFF	DEFENDANT	NATURE OF SUIT	JUDGMENT	FINES	FEES	DISPOSITION OF FEES	APPEAL
44	United States	Fletcher Thorson Wood, USA	Violation of Neutrality Laws	No Cause of Action	None	$8.00	Marshal: $4.00 Clerk: $4.00 $8.00	None

As the Fitch carriage drove out of the American concession, over Soochow Creek, and along the British Bund, Fletcher secretly exulted in the ride as a victory parade, and silently celebrated turning to his advantage the vitriol of Delevan Slaughter, and the weathering of yet one more squall besetting the course of his ambition.

"Excuse me, Consul Masters," Bitterman said, "but another despatch from General Sir Hope Grant has just arrived for the minister. The courier awaits your convenience."

Sir Francis W. A. Blaine, Her Britannic Majesty's Minister to China, raised his eyebrows and turned to the British consul Travis Trent Masters. "So now comes General Hope Grant to tell me what my policy hath wrought in the Chushans."

"Bitterman," the consul said, "bring in the courier from General Grant."

Bitterman withdrew and Minister Blaine's aide entered with a document for Blaine's approval, the memorandum of the meeting the previous week with British and French ministers and generals, and their decision about blockading the Gulf of Peicheli. Blaine studied the final version while waiting for the courier from the Chushans:

Les Soussignés ont résolu à l'unanimité qu'un blocus immédiat, comme opération isolée, serait probablement plus préjudiciable aux intérêts de l'expédition que nuisible au Gouvernement Chinois, et qu'en conséquence il n'était pas désirable de l'établir jusqu'à ce que les préparatifs de l'expédition fussent plus avances.	Resolved unanimously, that immediate blockade, as an isolated operation, would likely prove more prejudicial to the interests of the expedition than hurtful to the Chinese Government, and that it was not therefore desirable to institute it, until the preparations for the expedition were further advanced.

It occurred to the minister that other participants were at that meeting whose signatures were not on the memorandum – the British merchants of Shanghai. Of course, they were not invited, but they were there in spirit, impinging on the conscience of the minister after having called upon him in a body the day before, in an attempt to sway his sentiment, if not his opinion. Well, they got what they wanted, and there will be no stoppage of trade along the coast north to Tientsin, not yet anyway, but we shall not waste time waiting to see how Shanghai's British merchants express their gratitude.

Bitterman returned with a young lieutenant, uniformed in the scarlet wool jacket of

洋神 *Yang Shen* James Lande 藍德

the 99th Regiment of Royal Marines, who stood ramrod stiff at attention waiting to be acknowledged. Blaine initialed the memorandum and handed it to Bitterman.

"Give that to my aid, please, Bitterman, and tell him to make it ready for signatures. Now, Lieutenant, stand at ease. I am Minister Blaine. You have a despatch for me from General Grant?"

"Yes sir," the officer said as he handed the despatch envelope to the minister. "General Grant sends his respects and his best wishes for your good health, sir."

"Where did you leave the General?"

"Aboard the *Grenada*, sir, off Joss House Hill, in the harbor at Tinghai."

The despatch described the cordial reception of the allied force by the Chinese on the island, and the convention agreed upon among the allied commanders for the occupation. Chinese arms were to be surrendered, soldiers disbanded, foreign magistrates appointed, the authority of the civil mandarins retained under the surveillance of the foreign magistrates, military posts occupied, and the city policed by combined English and French troops. There were no casualties other than those attributed to accidents. The natives were busily furnishing supplies of every description, some financed in advance by speculators from Ningpo. Proclamations posted in Tinghai, exhorting the population to behave properly, were to have read "British Occupation," but the Allies objected and suggested "European Occupation," which subsequently was changed to "Foreign Occupation" because the Chinese had no word for "European."

Blaine dismissed the courier with instructions to return the next morning for a reply. Alone with the British consul, he related the content of the despatch from Chushan.

"It is difficult to comprehend," the minister said, "the complete indifference of the population on this coast toward their emperor's quarrel with our Queen. I presume it shows just how isolated and ignorant of true conditions in China the Manchu dynasty really is, which makes me wonder if protecting the sovereignty of China is not a task so large as to require Promethean efforts."

"Pray," Masters said, sighing, "that we are not all chained to a rock for our trouble and eagles sent to gnaw our livers."

3 The Astor House stood alone on the north bank of Soochow Creek, inside a walled compound entered through a gate of granite pillars. Across the frontage road, a picket fence ran along the berm of the levee where the creek met the Whangpoo. Within the wall stood two wooden buildings each of two stories, connected by a recessed one-story arcade with seven tall East Indian arches in the front wall. "Astor House" was inscribed over the entranceway through the middle arch. Tall windows glazed with multiple panes lined the lower floor dining room in the west wing. On the verandah above, outside the second-floor ballroom, or on the open promenade over the arcade, guests could take in the morning air, or sit afternoons with cold drinks and survey activity in the harbor and along the entire length of the Bund south all the way up to the walled city.

A long flight of wide steps ascended toward the entranceway to a level above the reach of spring tides that flooded the Hongkew shoreline with vile-smelling river water and left foul flotsam at the door of the hotel until washed away by Chinese doormen.

The establishment catered mostly to a bachelor brotherhood of American taipans, ship captains and naval officers, who satisfied obligations for its posh accommodations out of either the profits of trade, or the public purse. Consequently, the fortune of the Astor House was secured by the shipping in harbor, and the present disagreement over treaties between Great Britain and China. The business outlook for 1860 was quite as encouraging as it had been for each of the previous two years.

Hugh Wood bubbled like champagne with enthusiasm during dinner at the Astor

House that evening, delighted that Fletcher would not be sent back to America, and that he himself would not be abandoned in Shanghai.

Man seems just as happy as if he had good sense, thought Fletcher.

"As God is my witness," Hugh said, "I did not know how I would cope by myself here alone. I was committed to returning with you, if it came down to that."

"Your rifling's just a little crooked, brother, that's all. You know damn well you're a very capable fellow, able to chart your own course and avoid the dangerous waters I'm always being blown into. That's the best of the differences between us, isn't it? Your approach to life is careful and considered while mine is wild and carefree."

"Wildly exaggerated is closer to it. You do take many risks, but so do I, now. A few years ago, I would have only dreamed of coming to China. However, there is conservatism in your risk-taking, Fletcher, which I have seen. You delight in pushing circumstances to their limit, in testing everyone's patience, but you go only so far, sometimes right to the edge, and then you pull back. As though you want to see how close you can get to danger without actually being *in* danger."

"The odds are generally in my favor when I do something like that."

"Were the odds in your favor when, if you said the wrong thing, the consul was ready to clap you in irons and toss you aboard a ship bound for San Francisco?"

"Yes. I knew I had the advantage of the man."

"Confound it, I don't see how!"

"You had to look more closely at the consul. Beneath his moldy old beaver hat and black velvet lapel is a tired, timid public servant tormented by his circumstances. He's underpaid, overworked, sick with the breakbone fever, and humiliated by having to knuckle under to rich, arrogant American merchants. He might oppose Fitch, or even Heard or Russell, but the issue would have to be very, very important. Fletcher Thorson Wood was just too insignificant for the consul to cross blades with Augustus Fitch. As long as the taipan was prepared to be my guarantor, the consul could do me no harm."

Fletcher and Hugh sat together at a small table under the red velvet-flocked back wall of the Astor House dining room. Spermaceti candles in English cut-glass chandeliers imported from Thomas Webb and Sons brightened the center of the room; whale-oil lamps set in mirrored niches in the walls cast a weak, flickering glow into dim corners. Regency-style furniture, constructed to order from catalog drawings by local Chinese craftsman, rested upon thick Chinese carpets. The claret draperies, Sheffield flatware, and lead crystal goblets were as foreign to Fletcher as to the Chinese. He felt slightly uncomfortable in these sumptuous surroundings, especially as the room was full of British and French colonels and captains. But Fletcher felt his brother's near giddy relief at the outcome of the day's events, and allowed Hugh to cajole him into an expensive dinner to celebrate.

"Expect a fellow for dinner," Fletcher said, "called Hannibal Arlen Benedict. Stumbled on him in the hotel bar as I was coming in earlier, says he stays here sometimes. A gentleman from North Carolina, a gallant and experienced soldier who, likely as not, is itching for a good scrap."

"Gentleman? A slaveholder then? How do you know him?"

"A slaveholder, perhaps. The less mentioned on that subject the better. Hannibal has pronounced southern sentiments, but he and I go back to the Crimea, fought together on the side of the French. He was a plucky lad – won a battlefield promotion for bravery by single-handedly fighting off Russian cavalry overrunning his artillery battery at Inkerman in fifty-four. It's typical of the man that I never learned about that until much later, when I stopped over in London after leaving Sebastopol in late fifty-five. French officers we knew in common told rousing stories of Hannibal crouched on the ramparts giving cover to gunners scrambling to reload and fire. Dismounted horsemen right and left, shot Russians out of the saddle with a pistol, parried saber thrusts and unhorsed riders with a ramrod like a jousting knight from the days of Arthur and Merlin. I hope to make use of the man, whatever schemes we hit upon here."

"Good Lord! I'd have to be completely drunk to dare that."

"Maybe he was – he has a reputation for hard drinking. You can stand on a wall and wave flags at cavalry without ever being shot by a mounted carabineer, but I would descend from the ramparts when infantry muskets came within range."

"And you would consider him in spite of his disunionist temper?"

"In spite of that, yes."

"But you boast how you'd like to throw all secessionist rabble into some deep, dark dungeon and lose the keys."

"That rabble has not yet applied to officer my army in China. Hannibal Benedict must be an exception, I suppose, if we can keep talk of slavery out of the officers mess."

"Perhaps I understand how you leaven theory with reality, Fletcher – patriotism with practicality – but I believe it would be indiscreet to put it in banner headlines in the *Herald*. What is our bold Hannibal doing here in Shanghai?"

"Waiting for his opportunity, like you and me. There'll be others like him, I'll wager, who will come forward to join a cadre of fighting men, a little band of brothers if you will, when the word gets out. Tell me now, brother, have you any more thoughts on what you will do here?"

"Well, I think I shall not join your service, Fletcher, not if I have to jump on parapets and swing at the enemy with a wet sponge. But maybe I will provision your army. From what I've seen of Augustus Fitch, and what I've heard in conversation at table last night and this morning, I'm beginning to think that I was silly to contemplate griffin when I can go straight to taipan. There are many more opportunities in Shanghai, at least over the short run of a few years, than are being taken. How does 'Wood and Company' sound to you?"

"Good, of course. Where will you get the money?"

"Yes. Well, the few times I've been able to steer a conversation to the subject of partnerships, I was left shivering in the cold and dark. There seem to be too many difficulties with partners in Shanghai. They depart prematurely, with either their pile or yours, or they up and die of Asiatic fever, cholera, typhoid, or dissipation. Establishing one's own firm seems to have come to be the method of choice. I shall write to father with my estimate of prospects here, and ask if he would care to help me get started. It would be like opening a branch of his company here in China, or that's how *he* will think of it, anyway."

"Be sure to tell him I have other plans."

"Yes," Hugh said, chuckling, "in his view, it would change the character of the risk if you were coming and going all the time. I hate to say so, because I have tremendous respect for your brass, Fletcher, and I am with you whatever you choose to do. By the way, what *will* you do."

"As long as the American government insists I hunt pirates for the Chinese government, it seems I'm destined for that branch of international diplomacy."

"Lord help the pirates."

"Lord help the Chinese government."

"The Lord need not bother. The English and French will do that."

"Your Wood and Company may turn out to be a godsend, Hugh. Whatever I do, I shall need arms and ammunition – difficult to come by hereabouts. All we ever see are hand-me-downs from the Crimea, and the ancient matchlocks the Chinese use."

American Consular Inquiry

"Arms are going to be difficult to come by anywhere for a while, if there's a war back home. All production in the north will be dedicated to equipping Union troops, and the South will be out shopping for the rest of the world's production of weaponry."

"That's my thought, as well, which is why Wood and Company can be useful. Arranging to buy arms from here in China takes much time, but an agent in the United States can go directly to Sharps or Spencer or Colt and plunk down cash for a special production run. Cash on the barrel-head, and a little discretion, will see arms shipped to China when nothing else will do."

"That is an interesting idea. How do you get money to buy something that costly?"

"Someone else pays for it, of course. Both sides in this war here are fat with cash."

"Well, I guess the emperor and his mandarins are rich, but why would the British give you money for arms?"

"Not *that* war, blockhead. The civil war. The *Chinese* civil war."

"You're not thinking of joining the rebels, are you? That's insane!"

"Shhhh! Pipe your voice down and prick your ears up." Fletcher listened for lapses in conversations rippling about them, but perceived that little could interrupt the incredulity of chauvinist French officers confounded by the kowtowing submission of the entire population of Chushan Island to yet another invasion by European masters.

"Look here, I don't know where I'm going to land until I can chart *my* course, and I won't decide until I've been out and about and can judge from what I see. The rebels have untold riches from all of their plundering, but the mandarins milk that custom house for tens of thousands to fatten their public coffers, and we all know they skim a lot of cream and butter for their private larders, too. They've got more scratch than they know what to do with, and they've got hordes of rebels coming to take it all away from them. That makes them mighty motivated, to my way of thinking. It is not a question of where to get the money, just which side."

"Surely you don't think the rebels can conquer China?"

"I don't know. All I know is there're a lot of other people – Westerners – who believe in the Taiping dynasty. Even the British consul in Shanghai thinks the rebels will win, or so folks say."

"Fletcher, you can't go over to the rebels. Fitch and his friends say the rebels are just a ragtag lot of cutthroats, no better than Fokie Tom and his kind. Everyone here in Shanghai is against them. Going over to the Taiping would be like betraying your own kind. And how would it look for me, my brother with the rebels?"

"Calm down, Hugh. I'm not going to jump until the pan's good 'n hot. And that's why taking a berth on a Chinese gunboat is the best thing that could happen right now."

"Well, on the Yangtze I guess you can find out a great deal about rebel strength and movements. Hopefully that will show you how stupid it would be to join the Taiping."

"More than that can be learned. Gunboat captains on the river parley with the rebels all the time, meet up with their officers, sometimes their generals and maybe even a *wang*, a king, and listen to their offers to make them altar boys for the cause of the Heavenly Kingdom. Amidst all those promises of glory, the gist of their plans has to come out. What's more, this Ghent fellow, he's the 'Admiral' of the Chinese gunboats, sounds like he knows more than just about anybody around here about the true state of affairs. If I kind of sidle into the subject, and he's a talkative sort, I shall gather intelligence of great value to my enterprise. Like who pays his salary, and who finances the gunboat fleet and weaponry. If I keep my nose in the wind, I should be able to track down someone to finance me a private army. Like Ghent's gunboat, 'cept on land."

"Well, that would keep you on the right side, anyway."

洋神 *Yang Shen*   *James Lande* 藍德

Over his brother's shoulder, Fletcher saw Hannibal Arlen Benedict heave to at the entrance of the dining room and scrutinize the clientele with a slow, sweeping gaze. Fletcher waved and watched him as he crossed the room. By the light of the dining room chandeliers Hannibal – in gray frock coat and black cravat – looked older and darker than Fletcher remembered. His walk was a determined amble enhanced by a slight crook at the knee that made him rise and fall slightly like a moored ship in an uncalm sea, apace with a geniality that seemed forced and unnatural. In Hannibal's large, rheumy eyes, Fletcher imagined he saw apparitions, or maybe the mists of *ignis fatuus* – eerie marsh lights – or maybe just broken hopes.

"Ah, mon cher ami! *Beaucoup de sang, beaucoup de gloire, une troupe d'aventuriers, une famille toujours heureux.* Ah my dear friend! Much blood, much glory, a troop of adventurers, a family always happy! How the hell are you, Fletcher my friend? *J'ai soif*! I'm thirsty!"

"*Je ne suis sur le bord de ma tombe, grace a la faveur divine*, not yet close to my grave, by the grace of divine favor. Waiter! Another bottle of Perrier and Jonet!"

"And oysters, by God," Hannibal said, "a stew full of them!"

Fletcher introduced his brother and Hannibal's dark eyes flashed with feeling as he fervently shook hands. Hugh observed the pall in Hannibal's face – surrounded as it was by long, black, curly hair and a full black beard – routed instantly by an expression of warm and sympathetic concern, and was taken by his easy amiability. But Hugh flinched in his hard and bony grip.

"Fletcher," Hannibal said, "you look about as nervous as a frog in a French Quarter restaurant. Are we both out of place among all these splendid officers and gentlemen and fine linen and silver? Too many brass hats and satin sashes for me, all eavesdropping on each other's conversations, like at a Washington reception. I'd prefer to squat with Manilamen on a fo'c's'le deck and dine on a bowl of fried rice, but I'll suffer through oysters and champagne if I must be induced to entertain your proposition. Pour me some of that bilge water, *mon ami* – I'm as dry as a powder house."

"Hannibal used to hit the bottle pretty hard," Fletcher said "but I've heard he has mellowed at the ripe old age of twenty-four."

"Oh, I still have my dram, and I am especially partial to a brandy sour some mornings to fend off gastritis. That's brandy mixed with sugar, lemon, and lime, then strained through chopped ice when clean ice can be found. It's verruh popular in North Carolina. But old demon rum has not had me by the throat for many a year – I find the thrill of battle much more intoxicating. You may now consider me a lush for battle"

"You'd be up to a little freelancing, then, if the opportunity arose?"

"Most assuredly. A man cannot make his pile as a ship's mate."

"So, then, you're back aboard board ship?"

"Steamers. Came over on *Edwin Forrest* last October. Ferried silks and sundries to Hong Kong on *Formosa* for a few months, until I fell out with that Cap'n Brown – man's worsen even old William Bligh. On *Shanghai* now, running supplies and despatches to the Chushans." Hannibal cupped his hand over his mouth, leaned forward and rolled his eyes and in a stage whisper said: "For the Frogs and Limeys."

"Your performance is wasted on this bunch," Fletcher said, chuckling. "They're all too puffed up with their own importance to regard wharf rats like us."

"*Shanghai* has been chartered by Louis Napoleon for service with the expeditionary force," Hannibal said. "Going back down to Chushan again, leave tomorrow, but back pretty soon. Before *Formosa*, there was *Pluto* – Chinese run her now – and *Confucius*. Captain named Ghent crews her with bloodthirsty Manilamen and hunts pirates for some so-called pirate-suppressing bureau, really just a pack of native Napoleons of finance,

American Consular Inquiry   189

scared shitless of losing their precious tea and silk trade to rebels and bandits. Pay Ghent a fortune to ride shotgun for tea junks on the river and coast. Keep the waters free for Mercantilism, in a manner of speaking. Watch out for that Ghent, 'though – he's a mean old bastard, and it requires a strong decoction of Seneca and the Stoics to tolerate him. I'll be damned if the oysters in this stew are not a day's run apart! Waiter, bring me a plate of oysters. Two plates!"

"Why should I expect to have business with this Ghent?"

"Oh, come along now, Fletcher. Shanghai may look like a city, but it really is just a very small town. All the white folks learned you were seconded as mate to *Confucius* twenty minutes after you left the office of the American consul, and the *taotai* after only ten minutes. You can't sneeze at one end of the Settlement without someone at the t'other end muttering 'bless you.' And you know that sailors in port – after all those long nights of lonely watches at sea – are the world's busiest gossips. Every freebooter in Bamboo Town is chuckling in his Bass Pale Ale about your sentence, as if being sent upriver was exactly what you'd want if you had a mind to parley with rebels."

Hugh looked up startled. Fletcher leaned closer to Hannibal.

"Heave to there, sailor. No one said anything about rebels. You'll be wanting to mind your helm more closely and shorten sail if we are to ship together on any voyage that brings a profit. For a while, I shall only cast about in these troubled waters, and learn all I can about the contestants. Weather's changed since I was here last. There's a lot *more* weather, for one thing, and I do not wish to end up sailing against the wind."

"All right, all right, have it your way. There's time yet. But as I see it, really makes no matter on which side you fight – there's no more difference between imperials and rebels than between abolitionists and Conscience Whigs, and ain't none of 'em worth a sack full of goober-peas."

"I'll have to satisfy myself about that, Hannibal. The story changes with each storyteller. First, I'm told the rebels are Christian saints destined to overthrow the terrible Tartars who renege on treaties and have to be chastised by Queen Victoria and Louis Napoleon. Then I'm told the Manchus are the salvation of China, and that rapacious rebels perpetrate the atrocities committed in the countryside. Too many conflicting accounts to sort out here in Shanghai – I'll go upriver and into the countryside to see for myself. And, if it's any consolation, while I do not countenance disunion, I am not an abolitionist."

"Well, being from New England is almost the same. The rest of the country is content to live as they choose, and to let others do the same, but not the God-almighty Yankees. I tell you there certainly *should* be a parting of the ways, but it is New England that should secede, and leave the Union to the rest of us. They are not Americans in the north, for they neither believe in nor uphold American values. Let Massachusetts become a part of Nova Scotia, or Iceland. No one from the South would fight to prevent New England from leaving the Union. And so there'd be no war."

Hannibal began this invective harshly, spitting out the words, then quieted, as if to allow the venom to take effect. Finally, he sat back limp, his face like cold cinders after the fire burnt out of his eyes. Hugh was shaken by the unexpected vehemence, and began to doubt Fletcher's trust in the volatile Southerner. Can you work your spell on this one, thought Hugh, like you did on that Ptolemy Reese?

Hugh had long since ceased to be mystified by what seemed a physical intensity that sometimes emanated from his brother. Often it was as palpable as the repelling energy of a magnet – something that could actually be felt. He ceased as well being envious of Fletcher's success at wielding that curious intensity to influence others – nowadays he simply waited to see whether it would emerge, as it had aboard *Essex*. The power seemed to crouch somewhere deep within Fletcher and creep forth when some obstinate quarry came close enough to thwart his brother's will. Not everyone succumbed, as far as Hugh could see, but any capable of sensing it were always taken aback, if not slightly mesmerized. Whenever Hugh was close enough to sense that predator rising up in Fletcher, the hair on the back of Hugh's neck stood up as it did now, and he knew better than even to speak, lest he chance becoming a victim himself.

"Hannibal." Fletcher said only the one word, then reached over and grasped the man's shoulder lightly. Hannibal winced and stiffened at the touch. He stared at Fletcher with a harsh expression, homicide in his eyes, then both men slowly smiled.

"Hannibal, if we are to co-operate," Fletcher said, "we must disagree cordially. I know your sentiments well enough, and you know mine, but if those feelings are allowed to interfere with the work at hand, then we shall fail miserably."

"No, no, Fletcher. I must be allowed to blow off some steam from time to time, lessen the pressure. However, I shall not allow our differences to hinder our association. It would be madness not to keep faith with your venture, else how shall I become a rich man. Let us agree upon an *entente cordiale*, an informal coalition, a cordial alliance. You decide on your course of action, and I shall cleave to your plan of campaign – let's have more champagne! Here's a toast to us all – to victory in civil war, but first in China. America's civil war will have to wait a while longer."

"Victory in war," echoed Fletcher.

4 Benedict left them after they finished dinner. Fletcher and Hugh stopped inside the verandah at the hotel entrance for a smoke.

"You can trust him?" Hugh said.

"When the pot's full, yes," Fletcher said. "He'll want money. You do not?"

"Want money? Surely. Trust him? No. His temper is too freakish. Gives me the whim-whams. I don't know enough to question his or anyone else's military experience, more's the pity, but I have to wonder how much loyalty money will buy."

"They won't serve without plunder, I'll grant you, but they will come for *me*, Hugh. I won't have men I cannot hold in my sway. Even if I have to sacrifice experience, I *must* have dominion over my men, dominate them. For experience I can substitute training – inexperience can even be an asset, when experience would object to rigorous training and harsh discipline. But there is no substitute for loyalty and without it men will not follow. The dodge is to enlist men capable of loyalty, simple men who don't question things too closely, who just do what they are told. The clever ones always quibble, always want what you have for themselves."

From the Astor House, a dirt road ran north into the American settlement and Bamboo Town, a slum of dozens of the haunts frequented by sailors and riff-raff who could ill afford a night at the Astor. Fletcher heard the noises of drunken revelry that drifted down Bamboo Town Road.

"They must be having a good time," Hugh said, dryly.

"Yes, I suppose. It's only by chance that I'm here tonight instead of down they're carousing with drunken sailors."

Hugh glared at Fletcher. "Maybe that's where you belong."

Fletcher gazed out over the confluence of the rivers. His brother seemed to have no end of grievances against him. The old bitterness welled up again, as he recalled how often Hugh had taken their father's part against him. He could not content his brother any more than his father, and maybe he would never understand why.

"It's only a short walk from the Astor House into Bamboo Town, if I wanted that."

"I've always imagined that as a ship's officer you were above it, mostly."

"Mostly. Getting drunk and flopping with some doxie is an easy way to catch some loathsome disease – frightens me more than a regiment of screaming hussars. For one night of Venus, you suffer six weeks of silvery suggestions of Mercury from one of those exquisite little ebony and ivory urethral syringes waved about by ships' doctors. That or my Yankee doodle'd rot off. Oh, you can imagine me in those surroundings, though. Just a collection of ramshackle buildings, Chinese saloons, grog shops they call 'em, boarding houses, brothels and opium dens."

"No churches, I suppose."

"The Mission church isn't far away. Some of those carousers'd be fined by their captains if they didn't make it church come Sunday morning in port."

"Feel a little like your own crew, do they?"

"Perhaps. The sailors from *Essex*, and other ships. In some of those grog shops, I have old friends from years past who'll dance a lively hornpipe to see me again."

"I don't remember you as much of a church-going man, Fletcher."

"Measure me by your holy rood, Hugh, and I'll come up short. I can be if need be."

"Another guise you take up in order to achieve your ends?"

Fletcher laughed. "Guise? *Moi*, me? Brother, you surprise me – is it possible you think me less than completely honest, someone other than a simple sailor, or a ship's officer aboard square-rigged clippers?"

"Only God knows, Fletcher. I've watched you match the expectations of Hannah Fitch, Ptolemy Reese, and Hannibal Benedict – they're the ones I've been witness to on this voyage. Only the Good Lord knows how you got around the marshal and the consul – they'd be hard put to say who you really are. You seem to me like water – you find your way around every obstacle. You lose yourself in this role of mercenary soldier-of-fortune, Fletcher, and maybe your soul to boot."

"My soul has nothing to with it," he said, quietly. "I'm just practical."

"Sometimes, even I am unsettled by your changeability."

"If I'm not what I appear to be, it's probably because I'm still becoming myself."

"So, you encourage Mrs. Fitch to believe you're shiftless, the mate to suppose you're invincible, Hannibal to suspect you're venal, the marshal to imagine you're trustworthy, and the consul to hold you harmless."

"These *guises*, as you call them, are a practical necessity. Comes from running into so many ornery cayuses."

Fletcher's face glowed in the flare of a lucifer match he struck and put to his cheroot. "If it needs a name," he said, "let us call it practicality, or maybe self-reliance. There's little philosophy to filibustering – it needs practical action, not abstract theory."

"Some are motivated by higher ideals, Fletcher. By love of country, or public service. You have ideals – like your devotion to the Union. I cannot fathom how you set your ideals aside so easily when it suits you."

"Ideals I keep in one pocket, practical concerns in another."

"Some would say your ideals fit in your watch pocket with room to spare."

"Nope, I need my watch."

"Still, it rattles me to witness their disesteem for you. You have none of the wanton disregard for principle associated with mercenaries. I've been there when you placed concern for others ahead of yourself."

"Well, if it's any consolation, perhaps my practicality will become a philosophy one day. In my wide reading under the Southern Cross, I have come across advocates for the idea that practicality should prevail over principles, and that the purpose of thought should be to pilot action." Fletcher's mind wandered. Practicality...*tacitly carpi*?

"Some would say that principles should pilot action."

"Faith plots a compass course, not principles," Fletcher said. "Before all else most men need faith, to believe in God or principles, or anything they can't understand or explain. The rest don't need faith because they believe in nothing more than what they know, like a .36 caliber revolver."

"Maybe your practicality is just a substitute for a dearth of principle – maybe you substitute practical *for* principle. Would you call good whatever serves the *individual* instead of the community? Even the pack would disappear, and we would all become solitary predators and turn upon one another."

"And the strongest prevail? I'm content to leave the theorizing to others, like Mr. Emerson. To me, self-reliance is just another word for 'taking action,' like *carpe diem*. Maybe that would be the proper result of self-reliance, to calmly consider what can be done today, and leave tomorrow alone. Having much thought for the future, that's for fools that think they can plot the course of the present, kings and presidents and tycoons of trade and industry. Can't be done, if only because God has placed men like me here in the present, to frustrate the conceits of powerful old praetorians who would keep their hoarded riches from the greatest number of us."

"You're not what you make yourself out to be, Fletcher, not at all. You've never led an army, a brigade, or a regiment. By your own account, you only commanded a battery in the Crimea, and taught Mexicans the manual of arms at Juarez. Reading books about war does not make a field commander. I fear for your safety. I fear you'll convince some ignoramus to let you command an army and lead it into the field, and then your little bit of military school and book learning will fail you. I fear my only brother will die on some lonely battlefield because he thought he understood more than he really knew."

Fletcher turned and stepped under one of the arches, leaned against a fluted column, and stared up into the dark night at the constellations overhead. "A twinge comes to the pit of my stomach," he said, "when I realize that these stars in the Chinese sky are the same stars under which I once sailed along the Aqua Vitae Ledge, with *Vivid* heeled over so far that her scuppers were awash with sea foam. Then I was alone and free and responsible for no more than the sloop and myself. These days I'm not always so confident of the course I plot. While the stars might be the same stars by which the youth navigated, the man must now steer a different course, into dangerous waters. You mention church-going, Hugh? I can tell you this much – when a man starts getting closer to death, it's some comfort to get closer to God at the same time. And the Lord knows we are surrounded by death in this place."

5

Several days later, the sedan chair of the banker Yang Fang entered the Bund from Custom House Road and wound its way among coolies and carriages to the Chinese Maritime Customs office, where Yang was summoned to meet with the *taotai* shortly after noon. The message from Wu Hsü had said only 申江古廟申正 – Huang-p'u River, old temple, second hour of the monkey. No purpose for their meeting was given, so Yang assumed the matter was confidential, if not clandestine, and went alone.

Once the old temple had stood alone on the foreshore of the river, but now it had become a custom house surrounded by the square, red brick hongs and godowns of the foreigners. It appeared as strangely out of place as a junk moored among merchantmen. Four small green-tiled roofs, stacked high above one another over the entrance gate in the wall facing the Bund, sheltered a plaque of white marble incised with the black characters for North Maritime Customs 江海北關. Further back in the courtyard, the green tile roofs over the Great Hall gleamed so brightly in the sun that they were visible to sailing ships as far downriver as Pootung Point.

Yang Fang's sedan chair was admitted through the bustle of clerks, compradors, examiners, inspectors, tidewaiters, ship's officers, shippers and consignees and passed beneath the gate. The chair was set down at one side of the courtyard under the flying eaves of the rough white stone and red brick building that secured seized contraband and impounded cargoes. Yang left his bearers in the shade of the eaves and entered the Great Hall. Newly converted to offices, the hall was a noisy warren of English-speaking Chinese clerks, Chinese-speaking foreign linguists, accountants who spoke the still more obscure language of ledgers, and copyists, who spoke only Chinese. He advanced through the clamor of clerks, exited into the courtyard behind the Great Hall, and crossed to the old dormitory, now converted to a godown.

Within the wooden walls, stained black with age, the godown was dark and cool, and it took a few moments for the old man's eyes to adjust to the dim. Wu Hsü was there; he bowed quickly and saluted with clasped hands before his face, whispering, "老兄弟你沒事罷 elder brother, you are well?"

"沒事沒事 fine, fine."

"那好 that's good. 請你隨我來 please come with me. 我後房有東西給你看看 I have something in the back room to show you."

Yang Fang caught his breath when he turned a corner and nearly walked into four gleaming brass cannon arrayed against a back wall. Large chests were stacked beside the guns, and beyond them were two-wheeled carts mounted with chests.

"Elder brother!" Yang Fang whispered. He went from one gun to the next, examining them, caressing the satiny brass finish of each gun. "6-pounders I think, small dragons, judging from the size of the mouth."

"Yes. These cannon were purchased secretly in America and brought here by the merchant Fitch, as a favor to me. You should have your people remove them to our private arsenal. There are fifty chests of ammunition back there. Well, a few chests less, not as many as I purchased, because the luckless ship *Essex* fired many rounds at the pirates that attacked them near Ch'u-shan Island. Those two-wheeled chests carry ammunition and tools – they are pulled by horses, I believe, judging from the harness attached to the shafts – and the cannon are attached to the two-wheeled chests. So we must look into acquiring horses and grooms, as well, and prepare a place to keep them."

"We will need to train reliable men to fire these guns, as soon as we can, so they can be used if the rebels approach the city. My paddle-wheel boat captain can train them, as he trains his men to fire the cannon on *Confucius*."

"Elder Brother Yang, you have just reminded me of a thing. The American consul and his assistants paid a formal return visit at my yamen this morning. His first surly complaint was about pirates that attacked an American vessel *Essex*, belonging to the merchant Augustus Fitch, near Ch'u-shan. On board the Fitch vessel, there was a man who, they said, fought bravely and fired the cannon. The American consul examined this man three days ago, evidently because the man is some sort of fugitive 亡命之徒, and the consul wants to send him back to America. The consul is a timid man whose main concern is avoiding difficulties. But the American marshal, whom you will recall is absolutely not timid, suggested this man, named Wood, might make a good officer aboard a vessel of the Pirate Suppression Bureau. I told the consul I would mention this to you, and that you would contact the consul when you had information."

"Hmmm, named Wood 木頭?"

"More like warrior *wu* 武."

"Oh, yes!" Yang Fang's face glowed with delight. "That is perfect. That is a good omen, a man named *Wu* 武, just when we need a warrior. Wood. *Woo-duh* 武德, a man of martial honor? The war-god Kuan Lao-yeh 關老爺, must have sent this man to us. If he is useful, I will make a sacrifice at the temple of the God of War. And I will talk right away with Admiral Ghent. He will know how best to use the man. Then I will tell the timid American consul."

"Good. Good," the taotai said. "You are right, Elder Brother, it is a good omen, a soldier named *Wu* 武. I like him already. Is there other news?"

"The merchant Fitch deposited 20,000 taels in gold bullion yesterday morning."

"No doubt it came on his ship. He probably has received much more. It is lucky the pirates did not capture the ship."

"His comprador told me that Fitch has put all his cash into upcountry tea, and was so short of funds that he has been holding payment of ordinary bills. If he has purchased a great deal of tea, then he must try to get the tea down to Shang-hai before the rebels stop all shipments."

"Yes. If he can do that, then he will be one of only a few foreigners with tea to ship abroad from Shang-hai. But he is taking such a great risk – some of these foreigners truly fear nothing at all 奋不顾身."

"He will want paddle-wheel boats, crews, and arms to bring out his tea."

"Yes," Wu Hsü said, laughing, "you are right! Paddle-wheel boats and arms are a much more secure investment than tea right now. You ought to have a word with his comprador about suggesting that Fitch rent *Confucius*. That way, he can get the men and arms together with the paddle-wheel boat, and know the crew will give no trouble."

"Actually, they are not together," the banker said. "It is a small matter, but the paddle-wheel boat rents for 500 taels per month, or 200 taels per week. Other costs are separate and paid by those who rent the paddle-wheel boat. The pay for the crew is negotiated with Admiral Ghent, arms not already on board are extra, cost of ammunition depends on shots fired and powder expended, and rations have to be provided."

"Ai-yah, you have it all precisely calculated – as I would expect."

"That Fitch comprador is a greedy rascal. He'll probably demand five percent."

"Give him two percent and remind him that 'he who does not soar too high will suffer less by a fall'."

They both laughed.

"The American consul wanted me to send *Confucius* to Ch'u-shan Island to hunt the pirates that attacked the Fitch vessel."

"Oh, that would not do, as Fitch may ask for *Confucius* right away."

"That is not a problem. I suggested to the consul that he ask the English to look for the pirates, as the English are already there at Ch'u-shan Island."

"Will he do so?"

"I'll learn of it soon enough."

"And if he does not?"

"The pirates live another day."

"You will not send *Confucius*, will you?"

"胡說 silly talk."

洋神 *Yang Shen*   *James Lande* 藍德

Dramatis Personae: Chapter 12

Confucius (*k'ung-fu-tze* 孔夫子)	Chinese side-wheel paddle steamer (gunboat)
Rhys Simon Ghent	American captain of *Confucius*
Vincente Macanaya	Manilaman second mate, *Confucius*

The Chinese war-steamer *Confucius* (showing walking-beam steam engine amidships)
(sketch © 2011 James Lande. Based on an untitled original oil painting by an unknown Hong Kong artist, oil, 18x13 inches. A gift of Mrs. J. T. Coolidge in 1947 to the Peabody Essex Museum, Salem, MA; M1655)

One mile equals 3 Chinese *li* 里. One tael equals US$1.60.

196   *Fletcher Meets Confucius*

Chapter 12: Fletcher Meets *Confucius*
Wednesday, April 25, 1860, 2:00pm

Fletcher Thorson Wood
Astor House, Shanghai
Wednesday, 25 April, 1860, 10:00am
Sir:
The Chinese war-steamer <u>Confucius</u> is now in port for repairs at the Shanghai Dock Company in Hongkew. You are to go to that location without delay and present your mate's papers to Captain R. S. Ghent, who will examine your suitability for employment with the fleet under his command.
Willard Harris Parrish for
  W. L. G Shanks
    U. S. Consul, Shanghai

Early in the afternoon after receiving word from the American consul to go aboard *Confucius*, Fletcher Thorson Wood sat upon an upturned wooden barrel at one end of the dock where the steamer was tied up behind the clipper ship *Essex*. He lit a cheroot and considered the steamer, as had countless mates before him considered their new berths. Here were the two vessels in his life on that day, the ship he was leaving behind, so to speak, and the steamer to which he was going. *Essex* was the proud nymph Galatea, her chariot drawn by dolphins across the shining sea – for whose present abused and battered state he was at least partly responsible. The steamer astern was a dark, brooding and unquiet Polyphemus. Its name was in large smoky-white letters over the wood filigree grille of the wheel housing.

CONFUCIUS

Repairs to *Essex* had progressed briskly. Chips was busy with saw, adze and mallet replacing smashed planking shot away from the forecastle. The sailor's bunks inside were exposed to view like a rib cage of bison bones bleaching on the prairie. New forecastle railing and ladders gleamed with fresh varnish, most of the forward house was restored, and everywhere along the dock swirled the sharp odors of pine shavings, shellac and turpentine. Gazing up at the graceful form of *Essex*, and sensing her majesty, Fletcher felt a pang of regret when he saw how terribly she was hurt. He was a little heartsick at the thought of parting from her beauty, the music of the wind whistling through her shrouds and stays, the slap of her buntlines on canvas, her perfume of tar and hemp, her quiet meditations. The other he was going to was short and stout, noisy and dirty, but tempted him with offers of wealth and fame his first love could not match. He would leave the one to the solace of her solitary tears, and go to the other who could advance his career, in an ages-old marriage of convenience.

  The carpenter waved and beckoned. Fletcher left his seabag on the dock and went aboard *Essex*.

"How do you like her, Mr. Wood? Comin' along right nice, wouldn't you say."

"Looks fine, Chips. You do good work."

"Thankee, sir. Proud to hear you say so. Take a look around if you like."

Fletcher slowly walked the length of her deck, observing that her broken bulwarks were replaced and painted, and another kedge anchor was stashed behind the larboard forecastle ladder. The musket balls and shell fragments dug out of her woodwork filled a small cracker barrel left sitting at the poop rail, and the wounds had been closed with white wood putty and awaited only paint and lacquer to remove the last of the blemishes from her mahogany complexion. Fletcher went to the stern and leaned on the tafferel, lit another cheroot, and returned to his study of the sulking Polyphemus that was to be his next berth.

This hulk was a wooden American-model side-paddle river steamer, with a low black hull, one deck, a long house amidships, and spindly masts fore and aft. Her burden might be around 460 tons, but he could not recall directly because, being Chinese now, the *North China Herald* no longer reported her in shipping lists. She looked to be 150 or 160 feet long, maybe forty feet shorter than *Essex*. Her beam width was about twenty-five feet, and Fletcher guessed she drew eight or nine feet of water unladen. Atop the house, forward of the smokestack, was a white-trimmed wheelhouse with large glass windows and armor of wrought-iron plate that dropped down over the glass. Her huge side-paddle housings were so far astern that she looked as if, with good head of steam, she could lift her bow up out of the water and howl at the moon.

A forty-foot tall black bullet-riddled smokestack thrust high into the air above her house. The stack was secured by five forestays running to bulwarks and eight backstays made fast aft, and still looked like it was about to fall over. Partly obscured behind the stack stood a twenty-foot high ironbound wooden A-frame on which balanced the steam engine's eighteen-foot walking beam, an open frame of wrought iron shaped like a squat diamond that reminded Fletcher of a gallows. Her bow stem was a serious piece of work. Thick plates of iron on each side of the stem, riveted together in a sharp edge, covered the stem from below the waterline up to the blunt bowsprit.

That pretty Polly's for ramming junks.

Her bowchaser was a 32-pounder howitzer mounted on a pivot carriage behind a bulwark of foot-thick teakwood planking standing three feet above her iron bulwark. The foremast was square-rigged, with yards for a mainsail and a topsail, but without the rigging needed to support the highest part of the mast, the foretopmast. The mizzenmast aft of the wheel housings was fore-and-aft rigged, with an unusually long spanker gaff rigged more as a hoist to extend out over the paddle-wheel housings and cargo hold. A flapping canvas awning partly sheltered the aft portion of the poop deck.

Awning can be struck after tea and crumpets are served and more working room is needed. The silly masts're just a damn nuisance – they'd have to be housed then stepped every time she wants to pass through a water gate. And she'll never set a topsail. Spanker gaff and boom probably never saw sail set either. Not at all a pretty prospect – more like a skinny old maid schoolmarm.

But Fletcher had warmed to her enough to regard the steamer as a "she," a very distant in-law, a poor cousin, of clipper ships. Her boilers were still being blown out with steam, and the rhythm of some steam pump deep in her hold made her sound like she was quietly breathing *sss-chunk…sss-chunk…sss-chunk*. To the superstitious Chinese on the dock, the fire-wheel-boat 火輪船 was a thing alive and of awesome power and grandeur, a water dragon to be propitiated by offerings.

Suddenly the water dragon spoke: *whoosh*! A cloud of white steam billowed up out of her stack and Chinese on the dock jumped back. Even a Chinese oiler who helped dismantle and reassemble her cylinder and piston eyed her circumspectly.

Fletcher only grinned and thought *whoosh*! to you too, you old smudge pot.

The likeness of a man emerged from the wheelhouse, descended the ladder, and clumped forward to the rail. He was of medium height, with a dark complexion, and as fat as an alderman, but he moved with assurance, even authority, in spite of favoring his right leg. He was rigged in dark trousers under a dark-blue double-breasted jacket cut like a naval uniform with dingy gold epaulets and tarnished gold buttons. His pockmarked face was sun-bronzed and streaked with soot, and a meerschaum pipe formerly of white clay, now nearly black, dangled from beneath his heavy gray mustache. He stopped at the rail and glowered down into the space between the two vessels, then glanced up to the stern of *Essex* and saw the stranger staring down at him.

"Top 'o the day to ye, Admiral," Fletcher said.

The man shot Fletcher a purser's grin – a sneer. "So, now they put the figureheads of jackasses at the stern of sailing ships?"

Fletcher grinned like a jackass eating briars. Now here's a squally master, he thought, as hard as a twice-baked biscuit.

"We can't all boast 'owitzers for figure'eads, can we Admiral?"

For a long moment, the apparition stared hard at Fletcher, wrinkling his moustache as though he had found something unpalatable in his soup. Fletcher stood up straight and folded his arms across his chest so that his measure might be better taken.

Can't tell from the way a cat looks, he thought, how far he can jump. If this biting old grumbler doesn't help Vulcan forge thunderbolts in the furnace of his boiler room like the Cyclops, he could be a tolerable old splicer.

"Why don't you stop posturing like you was a simple-minded sailor, Mr. Whats-your-name, and come aboard like you was told to by your consul?"

Fletcher settled on a high stool in the wheelhouse, recalling the parting shot of the *Essex* carpenter.

"Are ye goin' aboard that steamer, Mr. Wood?" he had asked and, when Fletcher said he was considering the prospect, the carpenter replied, "Steam boat's no place for a deep-water sailor, Mr. Wood. Muckin' about in all that noise and black soot. I've knowed it to ruin many fine sailors and good men, sir, and I shorely hope it does not do the same thing to you. Evening, sir."

After that Fletcher could not shake the vision of Elijah on the dock at Nantucket waving a bony finger at the *Pequod* and intimating premonitions of a terrible fate for any who sailed with that suffering old Captain Ahab.

In a chair opposite sat the master of *Confucius*, Captain R. S. Ghent. He had two sound legs, *two* sharp eyes, hazel in color, and dark wavy hair. He appeared to be in his mid-forties. Fletcher reproached himself for allowing harpies of outlandish allusion to drag his own good common sense overboard, and for giving the good captain less than the benefit of some reasonable doubt.

Comes of reading too damn many books. Overboard with your tattered Bullfinch!

"The American consul recommends I take you aboard as a mate," Ghent said. His voice was low and rough, like a saw cutting wood, and he often coughed to clear his throat. "You're not the first rum-soaked derelict foisted off on me by Uncle Sam, and if Bill Shanks' judgement isn't any better than before, you might just find yourself rolling out with the next tide. Now who the hell are you?"

"Mate on Captain Lynch's *Antelope* back in fifty-eight."

Ghent looked up at him with tamped-down surprise, then slowly packed tobacco into his pipe and put a flaming lucifer match to the bowl. He looked at Wood again. "Where was you 'bout June and July of that year?"

"On the Peiho, ferrying diplomats and interpreters to Tientsin."

"Why did you leave that berth, and when?"

"Went back to New York about January of fifty-nine, took a position in my father's trading firm, to learn a little more about the workings of the home office. No, I was not forced to flee for killing anyone, least of all any steamer captains."

The yellow flare of another lucifer match was reflected in Ghent's eyes. Fletcher watched him struggle to keep his pipe lit.

"*Antelope?*" Ghent said. "Maybe I remember something about a mate. Can't be on this coast long and not be known. It's a small community, mostly of inbred English and French retards. Lynch maybe mentioned a mate some time back then, impressed how nothing ever seemed to rile the man."

"Not musket balls nor sudden shoals, not mutinous crews nor rebel gongs and firecrackers. Captain Lynch was not a man to flinch when there was a fight."

Ghent looked up angrily, opened his mouth to respond, then held his counsel. He stood up, crossed to the wheel, and stared out the window at the stern of the clipper. "What was you doing aboard that goddamn sailboat?" he muttered into the glass.

"Came up in her from Hong Kong. She was damaged in the Volcanos, and I wanted to see her repairs." Fletcher began to wonder if Ghent had not just flinched. That was a harmless enough remark about old Lynch, he thought, to have touched a raw nerve.

"You're one of those deep-water sailors, aren't you, from those big old square-riggers. The kind of sailor that hates steamships and treats sailing ships like living, breathing goddesses of the ocean, worships all the arcana of winds and weather and canvas and ropes, who can't pass a steamship at sea without sneering like some posh passing an outhouse."

Ghent whirled about and rested his back against the wheel, as if leaning on his steamer for support.

"I've carried your kind of mate before and put up with their arrogance until I could taste gall and then kicked 'em back on shore. Steamer duty's not so glamorous as sailing ships. You get your hands dirty. Hell, you get dirty all over and you stay that way, because you work hard with the machinery. Over there on that ship, you're a carpenter and a sailmaker, trades nice 'n clean and sweet-smelling, but over here you're just a grimy machinist."

"And a painter, pipefitter, rifleman and artilleryman. Sure, Captain, I've been on quarterdecks, but I've spent time in wheelhouses too, and you might make a mistake by dismissing me too easily" *or by measuring your pecker by my bushel, old man.*

Fletcher jumped down from the stool and planted himself before the captain. Ghent startled and leaned forward slightly into a fighting stance.

"It's just an accident of fate," Fletcher said, suppressing his anger, "that consul intervened. Just as likely, I'd've been blown down here to the docks looking about for a river steamer on my own account. Because it suits me, and not some worn-out wreck of a civil servant. I only agreed to the consul's proposal because it *did* suit me. If I knew the consul's name would be no recommendation here, I'd've looked elsewhere."

"I suppose," Ghent said, "that clinking noise I heard when you came up the gangway was your brass balls?"

Wood and Ghent bristled with rage, each wishing the other would just so much as raise a hand. For a moment, anything could have happened, but Fletcher remembered his precarious situation, willed himself to relax, and shifted his gaze out into the harbor. Ghent glared at his profile and wanted to crush Fletcher's jaw. Had anyone else been present, the outcome would have been different, but Ghent recognized he'd been yielded right-of-way, however grudgingly, and could give way without noticeable loss of face.

"Sit down, and tell me why the hell you are back in China."

The captain seemed to relent when confronted with commensurate mulishness, or maybe he got an inkling of Fletcher about to refuse the commission. Fletcher wondered if Ghent was desperate for a mate. *Should've asked around more at the sailor's home about this crank, depended less on the marshal's testimony. If he wants to match wills in the wheelhouse, I learned long ago how to play that game. The real test comes later.*

"I am looking for a berth suited to my talents and experience, maybe one where brass balls are indispensable. Events in China are poised for change, the country's being forced open to trade, great opportunities are just ahead, and I want to be there at the brink when they come. I don't promise to be a mate on your vessels very long, but while I am you can expect a good job done without shirking. I'm just as hard a man to shave at steaming as I am at sailing."

"My last mate was shot dead."

"Bad luck. Respect to the dead. Maybe he was looking the wrong way."

Ghent tamped the tobacco in his pipe with the head of a large nail, then struck another match and put it to the stuff. Swirls of sweet-smelling blue smoke enveloped Fletcher. Ghent picked up Fletcher's packet of sailing papers, looked them over again, and handed them back.

"This's not an easy crew to handle. Half's Chinese, the other half's Manilamen. Tough as this nail. You have to be tougher or they'll flay you alive. That's the only kind of man can survive in this line of work. It's a very thin line between the hunters and the hunted. Lynch's boat is a pampered mail packet compared to *Confucius*. You show any weakness, and you'll find your guts strung out for fish bait in our wake."

"I'm not exactly a cloister-educated celibate. I've seen tough crews."

"That mate, he was killed by the crew. I can't prove it, or who, but there was black powder all around the hole in his face. He wasn't shot from very far away."

"Mate must not have been worth a Bungtown copper."

"Oh, he was a bully mate, all right, right out of a dime-novel. Then right away, he lost his ballast, fell out with the Manilamen, ran about kicking and screaming, never gave the crew a moment's peace. I was going to trade him in for a rabid bulldog when we got back, but he drew the hanged man before we made port."

"How long was he aboard?"

"Two weeks."

"You're still kicking."

"That's because I respect Manilamen and their ways. Oh, I'm a tough sonofabitch all right – they find that out first, but I give them leeway and don't come down on 'em hard 'cepting as I have a damn good reason. Like a good horse or dog, ill treatment can wear on them, until their spirit dies and they become cringing, worthless curs. Treated properly, they're good fighters, without fear, fierce and hardened mountain men. Loyal to the death, if you can win their loyalty. If you can't, you're finished."

Fletcher began to feel like he had the man's measure. Ghent did not want to fight, maybe not again, maybe never before. He relied on the ferocity of his crew, and a good mate, to keep up the appearances that baffled his Chinese backers. It was just a guess, of course. The real test always came under fire.

"Then I shall follow your example, Captain, and give them respect but, at the same time, I shall be ha'd enough to give them reason to respect me."

Ghent's face relaxed. A moment later he said: "All right, you can have the berth as mate. Here, on *Confucius*. I'd inquire about you with Captain Lynch, but he went to Macao with *Antelope* when Russell auctioned her off to Fernandes. He ever turns up again in Shanghai, we can pay him a curtsy call – if you're still aboard. You appear ready to start, so let's look her over. Black gang's below, with a Chinese assistant engineer. Crew's not, won't be for another day or two, but you can get the layout now."

"What's the pay?"

"Berth pays 75 taels a month, $120.00 US."

Fletcher said nothing. Ghent's eyes narrowed.

"That's the same as my engineer, and a third more than the 2nd mate. Engineer and

洋神 *Yang Shen*   *James Lande* 藍德

first mate're paid top dollar aboard *Confucius*. Hell, everybody is. Even a Chinese AB gets more than a Chinese army officer."

"I'd guess a Chinese sailor takes more risk aboard your boat."

"Look here, Wood. $120.00 US isn't just pocket change. That's $1440.00 a year, if you're here that long. Maybe less than a worn-out wreck of an American consul, but more than his clerk or interpreter. Beats $30.00 a month for mate's berth on a sailing ship. You won't get rich drawing pay, but it more than enough for anything you want in Shanghai. Wine, women, song – what's yer poison?"

"Pay's first chop, Cap'n." About the same as *Antelope*, for the same work. Won't draw pay all that long anyway.

At the door to the wheelhouse, Ghent stopped and turned a baleful eye on Fletcher. "One more thing. You are to address me as captain, or sir, but never again as admiral."

2   Ghent led Fletcher from one end of the steamer to the other, beginning with simple particulars, then warming to the task and expounding a story for her every bolt and blemish. He sparked first to Fletcher's obvious acquaintance with the 32-pounder and description of the Crimea, rankled at Fletcher's contempt for his steamer's standing rigging, then flared at a remark about the greater merit of screw-steamers.

"Listen here! *Confucius* was *custom* built for this duty on the China coast, in the United States in 1853 by Thomas Collyer, for Tom Dearborn and Russell & Company. Collyer was no journeyman boat builder – he made everything from towboats to racing steam sloops in his day, and knew how to design a river steamer for the lower reaches of the Ol' Miss around New Orleans. Him and Tom set to on a plan that would suit work in China, with shallow draft but plenty of cargo capacity below deck, and hardy construction that could stand up. So she's shorter and narrower, more like an ocean-going packet, and she's *twice* as deep as any goddamn screw-steamer, which is why she's rated for twice the burden as river steamers with the same length and beam."

The foredeck was open and had plenty of working room around the hatch over the forward hold. The house was paneled with what looked like white oak trimmed with varnished larch or chestnut. On deck at the front of the house, there was a small wooden tabernacle streaked with gray incense ash where the Chinese sailors aboard *Confucius* held pagan ceremonies for their guardian deity. A porcelain figurine perched inside – some Chinese god of war Fletcher judged from its dark expression.

"Old Tom was her first captain and brought her out to China through Singapore and Hong Kong under her own steam when she was still just a maiden. Tom wanted no flimflam – just a solid, sturdy, working boat that he could steam across the Pacific and put to work in rough Chinese coastal waters, and on a big river like the Yangtze."

A narrow passageway led back through the house to the saloon. Under the wheelhouse, up forward, there was a spacious machine shop that smelled of oil and grease, and a smithy with a small kiln of red brick and soot-covered tools. Further aft there was a boatswain's locker full of coiled rope, hardware and tackle, and an arms locker with a door that opened to larboard as well as a companionway that led directly to the powder locker below.

"Hulks they put on the Mississippi and the Ohio back then was just rafts loaded down with too many boilers and a pounding high-pressure engine roofed over by a towering jigsaw superstructure of deck piled upon deck. Like a goddamn floating wedding cake they were, 'specially at night with all the candles lit up."

The passageway continued aft between six cabins, past the galley and pantry, around the base of the smokestack, and into the saloon. The six cabins all smelled of fresh paint. The captain's cabin was not large – sleeping quarters and a sitting room that doubled as an office. The other smaller cabins – each a spartan cubbyhole with bunk bed, mosquito netting, chair, desk and cabinet – were for the pilot, mate, engineer, and a Chinese officer assigned to the crew. The last cabin was for passengers, but when dignitaries came aboard, the pilot gave up his cabin and moved forward to bunk with the mate, or the hands in the forecastle. The first mate followed, after the pilot. The black gang had part of the forecastle to themselves, separate from the deck crew.

"Weren't no more than canvas and papier-mâché held together by old string and sealing wax, all glint and glitter like a New Orleans bordello. If one of those whores of Babylon ever put to sea, why the ocean'd rebel – rise right up and smash it down into so many pieces that beachcombers could collect enough spittoons and shreds of red velvet from the surf to furnish a town full of gaudy saloons!"

Fletcher and Ghent stepped into the galley and Ghent poured two mugs of black coffee from a pot steaming slowly on a wide black iron stove.

"Her burden is 468 tons, she's 161 feet long, with a beam just under 27 feet, 11½-foot depth of hold, and an 8-foot draft in ballast. Her engine's a simple low-pressure model, not nearly so dangerous or expensive to operate. She has two boilers 26 feet long by 3 feet in diameter that get up 20 pounds of pressure each. Chinese bought her in fifty-five and converted her into a gunboat to ride shotgun for their merchant junks. She convoys for the silk and tea guilds, hunts pirates when the occasion arises, and even works as a tug sometimes to keep busy. Occasionally, she charters for 200 taels a week."

They entered the saloon from the galley, crossed through the saloon and back out of the house to the larboard rail, then walked aft to where the walking-beam loomed over the house and paddle-wheel housings. Ghent turned around and pointed to the forward end of the walking beam, where the wall of the saloon and extensions of the house walls and roof enclosed a cramped platform with a bank of valves, rods, levers and dials.

"Engineers work the vessel from there when *Confucius* is underway. She's a vertical beam design, used mostly in American steamers. Over there, that's her cylinder. Stroke of the piston inside the cylinder lifts one end of the beam nine feet high, pushes t'other end with the crankshaft down nine feet. Turns the paddle wheels. Boat moves."

Aft of the control platform there was an iron cylinder ten feet high and five feet wide. At the center of the engine was the walking beam atop the A-frame, with piston arm at the forward end of the beam, and crankshaft arm at the aft end, connected to the shaft on which the paddle wheels were mounted.

"Her stroke is a lot longer than what you see in most British steamers. She'd be better with two engines, so the side wheels could be turned independently when a really tight turn is needed. But, one engine's a lot cheaper to build and operate, so she's equipped with a clutch that can disengage one or t'other of the paddle wheels when the engine is stopped. She runs at about twenty rpm. With two paddle wheels thirty-two feet in diameter, that gives us up to 430 horsepower. Simple!"

"Don't see engines on the decks of steamers much any more, do you?"

"Used to be a passel of these engines on western rivers in America. Now they make the cylinders horizontal so they can fit below deck with the boilers. But these machines are unique, make no mistake, and suited for work here in China. They're simple and reliable, even if more's exposed than's good on a gunboat. The way they go up and down at each end looks like they're walking up the river, so we call 'em walking beam engines. Same as vertical beam."

"You say she's a river steamer, but I've heard of her putting out to sea."

"We take her up and down the coast, and that's sort of ocean going, but she's not constructed for regular crossings of the Atlantic or Pacific. She's an American model M river steamer, Class 5, Rate A1. I'll give you a book to read up on the technicalities, but for now, the M means she's classed as towboat with an open-standing pipe. Class 5 steamers are built for sounds, lakes and rivers only – smaller than the Class 1 through 4 ocean-going steamers with two or more decks, one or two engines, enough spread of sail to be of some use, and watertight bulkheads forward and aft of the engines and boilers. Her A1 rating refers to improvements on the standard construction, like reinforced propeller bearings and rudder post, a coppered hull, heavier boilers, and bilge injection and independent steam pumps. All that mumbo-jumbo will mean more to you later."

Where the tafferel would have been at the stern of *Essex*, the steamer had a 12-pounder sternchaser mounted like the bowchaser on a pivot carriage and protected behind a bulwark of heavy teakwood planking. A long flagstaff jutting out over the rail flew a small flag emblazoned with a rampant golden dragon.

"Stars 'n stripes'd look a damn sight better there," Ghent said with a snort, "but that's what ol' Takee give me to fly an' Takee foots the bills, so we fly a silly dragon. Supposed to be a Tartar national flag, but don't mean much if'n you've got no nation."

They returned to the house and, at the rear of the saloon, descended a narrow metal companionway down into the hold. The scent of hemp and camphor wood dunnage mixed with the odor of oily metal shavings, mildew and stagnant bilge water. Far forward long iron spars bolted to the wood ribbing, larboard and starboard, buttressed heavy iron plates laid against the bow stem, clearly for reinforcement when ramming some hapless junk. Under the reinforced bow were the chain locker, and the forecastle with twenty-four bunks, and a row of chairs and tables bolted to the floor. The forecastle was also accessible from a forward hatchway.

Aft of the forecastle was the forward hold. Empty it appeared spacious, but when underway with a cargo of opium, tea or silk, it was walled off and made accessible only through the forward hatch, so the hold could be sealed and bonded.

Amidships there was the powder locker – located as far away from the boiler fireboxes, galley, and smithy as practical – and lockers for sail, paint, spare parts and pipefittings, water and dry goods, rope and chain, and bunkers for coal.

Immediately forward of the companionway from the saloon there were two long grimy cylindrical boilers of riveted wrought-iron plates, placed lengthwise to the hull, with fireboxes under the aft ends of the boilers, enclosed with firebrick and latched shut with iron doors. The boilers rested on cast-iron brackets just under chimneys that led up into the smokestack through a tangle of copper and iron pipes, valves, and gauges.

"Coal is loaded into those bunkers from dockside, or in baskets passed up from sampans if we're in backcountry. There's room for fifty tons below, and we can make room for more. That's enough coal for about 125 hours of steaming, or fifteen days at eight hours a day under the best circumstances. Water for the boilers comes from the river or ocean, first by gravity through feed valves because the boilers are below water level, then from steam-driven feed pumps through a hot box to warm the cold water before injecting it into hot boilers. Cold water in hot boilers causes boilers to explode. Among other things."

Aft of the companionway, the four heavy iron struts of the A-frame supporting the walking beam above deck passed down through the center of the ship to where they were bolted to heavy beams secured to the keel. Looking up between the A-frame struts, Fletcher could see the underside of the engine. Iron and copper steam pipes led up from the boilers past the condensers to the cylinder containing the huge piston that lifted the walking beam. Aft of the cylinder, there was the hotwell and air pump, and past that the iron framework supporting the paddle-wheel shaft. Back of the paddle wheels was the aft cargo hold.

"She'll carry up to 750 tons if we strike the main-deck cabins, but really she's a floating arsenal, not a cargo boat. You've seen the artillery. That airtight powder locker holds fifty drums of black powder and 500 rounds of shot, shell, and canister. We'll load that ammunition tomorrow and the next day, and learning how we safely stow it will be one of your first duties. Our armory also boasts fifty Beecher's Bibles – Sharps 1859 model .52 caliber rifled percussion carbines – and half that number of Colt, Kerr and Le Mat revolvers. No other armory on the coast, not even aboard British frigates, has as many breach-loading rifles. The next best have only rifled muskets. Our crewmen all train as riflemen. They fashion their own paper cartridges."

Fletcher and the captain climbed back up the companionway into the saloon and stepped out on the main deck. A cool breeze off the Whangpoo River was a relief after even a few minutes standing beside the hot boilers and fireboxes. They walked aft and sat on the cargo hatch. The men on watch at the engine controls were all Chinese. One stepped forward and spoke as Ghent and Fletcher passed. The others fell back against the bulkheads as if to get out of sight of the captain.

"All plopah, Cap'n," the Chinese said.

"My engineer is a Dutchman, but he's ashore right now for parts, so the fires are banked. He's trained these Chinamen pretty good, though, especially that one who spoke up – he's good enough to spell my engineer when we're at rest, but none of them are rated for operating the engine. I really need a second engineer, but they're hard to come by, so we run *Confucius* like a banker's office, shut her down every evening."

Ghent pointed up to the mizzen-top and the smokestack.

"With an eleven-and-a-half-foot hold, and eight feet under water, the main deck is three-and-a-half feet above water, bulwarks five feet. Main cabin's seven feet above the deck, and wheelhouse's another six feet above that. That's sixteen-and-a-half feet from the water line to the top of the wheelhouse. The smokestack rises forty feet over the water and the foremast's another thirty feet above the stack. The masts can always be sent down to get under obstacles. The stack can come down, too, at least long enough to clear a low bridge, if you don't mind a hot deck and a little soot in your face, and hearing the engineer scream bloody murder about how the engine will be damaged without a proper funnel. If she can't get under them any other way, we blow the bridges away with the bowchaser."

From the aft cargo hatch, they walked forward toward the wheelhouse.

"That walking beam's a different matter – could bring down the beam with some effort, but the A-frame's bolted to the heart of her and can't be moved. A-frame needs another eight feet of clearance above the wheelhouse. The paddle-wheel housings are two feet higher than the wheelhouse, and the housings come off easily enough, but they're lower than the engine frame, so not much point in dismantling the wheel housings. Many's the time I wished I could. Housings are something of a blind spot when you're looking back over your shoulder to see what's bearing down on you from behind – have to turn her a little to port or starb'd to see behind the housings. That's another problem they don't have on the Ohio – lorchas and war junks beating down on your stern."

Ghent stopped again in the galley for more coffee, and then led Fletcher back up the narrow stairway into the wheelhouse. Standing at the wheel, he twisted around to each side and pointed back at the tall wheel housings, which clearly obscured Fletcher's view of the harbor traffic surging around downriver behind the steamer.

"*Confucius* is a little big for some of the work she's asked to do," the captain said. "Can't negotiate the water gates at most inland cities. But since she draws only eight feet, she can go anywhere on the river, been all the way up to Hankow, and inland to more than a few towns. She's respected wherever she goes by imps and rebels alike.

None of them dare challenge her, else she'd smash 'em to kindling. She's unique in the world, a Chinese steamer, crewed by natives, officered by foreigners, financed out of a Chinese purse, and she comes and goes wherever she likes. I'm doing what the Shanghai taipans have been chompin' at their bits to do for years now, navigate inland waterways, steam upriver to ports on the Yangtze. Maybe this new treaty the British want will open the river to all the powers and, if it does, then we'll see a great many steamers in the Yangtze, but until then *Confucius* is queen of the river."

Of the river, thought Fletcher, and *only* the river. *Confucius* can't go inland because of her draft, or clear water gates because of her size. Too bad she can't get over to the Grand Canal and all the little streams and creeks that saturate this delta and consolidate the towns and villages between Nanking and Shanghai.

"Bring up your seabag. Stow your gear in your cabin, then come back up to the house. I'll set you to work on the pidgin not yet completed. We're still loading coal, but most important is getting more ammunition on board, because this trip we're chartered to steam up river and fetch down tea to market, and I want to be certain we have plenty of powder and shot for any cocky imps or rebels. We'll take on part of the tea as our cargo, and the rest will be aboard barges and junks we'll escort back to Shanghai."

Fletcher felt he now had a little more of the man's measure. Ghent knew *Confucius* well, every bolt and blemish, her pedigree and performance. But Fletcher understood her potential better than the captain, whose perspective was confined to the river. Ghent was so close to *Confucius* that her beams were his bones, but that was not all there was to be said about the man. Fletcher guessed there would be more.

3 Fletcher stayed on board *Confucius* and spent the days following supervising the loading of coal, cargo, and ammunition, and overseeing refitting on deck. Inspection and cleaning of the engine, and repairs below deck, were carried out by the black gang – the wheezing old Dutch engineer called Schnapps, and a handful of Chinese oilers and coolies. The days in port were awash with overhaul of the paddle-wheel outer bearings, scalding the lubricators to remove dirt, lightly scaling one boiler, clearing mud from the injection seacock, and pumping out the bilge.

Ghent fetched out copies of river charts drawn by Commander J. Wood of HMS *Actaeon* during Lord Exter's expedition up the river in 1858. Fletcher pored over them, struggling to memorize the piloting of 200 miles of the lower reaches from Woosung to Nanking, then scrambled all over the steamer learning the pipes, as he called it, the same as he'd learnt the ropes on sailing ships.

After knocking off work, Fletcher walked up to the Astor House to join Hugh for dinner and listen to his scuttlebutt about Shanghai, the occupation of Chushan, American and British traders, and the prim Miss Elizabeth Fitch.

"Here's your invitation to the Fitch *soirée*," Hugh said one evening, handing Fletcher an embossed envelope. "Combination debutante's ball and hero's welcome."

"Who's the hero?"

"You, of course."

"That's silly. I'm no hero. Make some excuse for me."

"I think not, Fletcher. All the Fitches are dead set on honoring you. Everyone in Shanghai, who is anyone, will attend. Fitch will send a runner for you."

"When is this – maybe I'll be on the river?"

"Saturday night. Consider, brother – you'll probably meet the people who will either help you, or hinder you. What was that about 'know your enemy'?"

"Know your enemy, know yourself, one hundred battles fought and won. The *Art of War* – Captain Partridge made us read that at Norwich. Ancient rules of war still followed now. I suppose you have a point."

"Do you think any of the Chinese in Shanghai have read that book?"

"Who knows? I'll probably find out on some Chinese battlefield."

"Maybe you should read it again."

Later each evening, Fletcher returned to his cabin aboard *Confucius* and, after he had carefully arranged his small library on jury-rigged shelves, and on the floor against the hardwood wainscoting, he spent several hours reading in Prescott's *History of the Conquest of Mexico*.

Early Friday morning, Fletcher was in the wheelhouse going over charts of the river at Nanking, when the captain entered with a Manilaman under tow. "Mr. Wood, this here's Vincente Macanaya, our second mate."

Macanaya was a slender, lithe Manilaman in his middle twenties, with oil-black wavy hair and deep black eyes who, thought Fletcher, no doubt broke the hearts of swarms of señoritas when he left Manila. Around his left wrist, there was a bracelet of what looked like large white shark teeth, which clicked when his hand moved.

"*Magandang umaga* Vincente. Good morning," Fletcher said in Tagalog only vaguely remembered. "*Ang pangalan* Fletcher *ko* my name is Fletcher. *Kumusta ka, pare* how are you, friend?"

The Manilaman looked at Fletcher as if he was some kind of talking parrot. "*Humihinga pa. Ikaw? Po?*" he answered suspiciously, "Still breathing. You? Sir?"

"*Nakakaraos naman, sa awa ng Diyos* barely surviving, by the grace of God. The captain tells me that you are the leader of the Manilamen in this crew, and that you translate into Spanish and Tagalog for them."

"*Sige, iyon lang pala* sure, why not? You speak much Tagalog?"

"*Hindi pa* not yet, Vincente. *Pero, puedo hablar un poco espanol* but I am able to speak a little Spanish."

"*El señor, el señor donde aprender a hablar el espanol* sir, sir, where did you catch on to speak the Spanish?"

"In Mexico, and in South America. I was a *soldado*, a soldier in those countries. Ships in which I sailed have landed at Manila, and I departed with some words of your language. *Taga-Manila ka* you are from Manila?"

"My home in mountains south of Lingayan, in Pangasinan, on island of Luzon. Many year before, my grandfather leave Tondo, go north to Pangasinan, make home in mountains, grow rice, sugar cane. My grandfather speak some Spanish, so make him headman at Salasa, *un cabeza de barangay*, a don. Some people not like Tagolog *cabeza* in Pangasinan *barangay*, say bad things, make lies. Then Spanish military officers, *peninsulares*, take away grandfather and father to execute. I escape with mother, brothers and sisters back to home in mountains, then I go back down to Salasa. I find those officers, I cut off heads with bolo and throw heads in barracks, set barracks on fire and burn Spanish *soldados* to death. In Heaven, my grandfather and father listened *con mucho gusto* to screams of Spanish pigs. Then I run away to Manila, float under guns of Fort Santiago on Pasig River, go to sea in Chinese trade junk. Just fifteen years old."

Fletcher smiled into the dark eyes of the Manilaman – he and Vincente were the same height. "Where I am from, we burned the witches, *las brujas*. In Salem, Massachusetts, in America. I was a mate on sailing ships, a captain of artillery in the Crimea, and mate on the China coast steamer *Antelope*. Do you know her?"

"Of course. Before, meet sometimes, anchor at lightship and play cards all night. But I not think you, yourself, burn many witches, Mr. Wood, any *mangkukulam*."

"There's time yet," Fletcher said. "Captain says you are a good artilleryman."

"The best, *señor*. My gun can burst coconut at three hundred yards."

"I looked at your guns. They are well cared for. When we reach a quiet stretch of water, you can show me how you burst coconuts at three hundred yards?"

"*Con much gusto, señor* with much pleasure, sir."

"Macanaya," the captain said, "ask Mr. Wood about the box."

"Yes, Captain. There is equipments in box with 32-pounder, I think some kind of gunsight, but not understand mechanism. Perhaps you know how it work?"

"You mean you burst coconuts at three hundred yards with bare iron sights?"

"Sure. One does what one must, no?"

"Let's go look at your gunsight."

An hour later Macanaya went ashore to begin rounding up his crew, and Fletcher returned to the wheelhouse to study his charts. Fletcher liked the Manilaman.

And perhaps he can be of value, maybe even a *compadre*. Yes, you'll do, Señor Macanaya. You may be my Queequeg or, better, my Chingachgook.

"So?" Ghent said. "Is it a gunsight?"

"Russian *hausse*. Not for the howitzer, but it can be used with your sternchaser. I showed him how to mount it on the 12-pounder."

"You never said you speak Manilaman, or Mexican. That will make you a lot more acceptable to my Manilamen. Any other languages?"

"Some French, from the Crimea. Not spoken at all like Frenchman insist it be, but adequate for an artillery battery of French, English, Italians, Bavarians, and what have you. Don't know how much I can remember, now."

"No matter. It still can be useful. Chinese?"

"Chinese makes my head ache."

"Mine, too," Ghent said, chuckling.

Relieved of the extra work, Ghent began to relax more around Fletcher and, as he observed his new first mate's even temper, knowledge of steamers, and attention to every detail, actually turned a smidgen amiable. Fletcher interrogated the captain about this warning marked on the river charts and that landfall, working his way on the charts slowly up the river from town to town toward rebel territory, and into the captain's confidence, but mentioned nothing about rebels. Before long he knew the lonely old man was itching to tell his tales of rebel encounters, and he could bide his time.

Fletcher might have warmed to the captain despite his gruff manner, which was of little account between hard men, but his own father had taught Fletcher all he needed to know about men who hide away weaknesses like pilfered cargo down in the dark, damp bilge of their soul. Ghent neither said nor did anything to ease Fletcher's misgivings about his mettle. Fletcher sensed something with a coppery taste about the captain.

That evening, Fletcher wrote to his sister.

Dear Elizabeth,

How are you, darling sister? I hope all goes well, and that you and mater and pater are all in bouncing good health, and that my little brother has also written to you, so that you may compare our letters and discover our exaggerations. Since Hong Kong, Hugh and I have meandered up to Shanghai. The voyage up was uneventful, with the exception of being attacked by pirates at some islands called the Volcanos. Four men died in a terrific battle, and the ship was heavily damaged.

Our more seriously wounded are at the Shanghai Hospital and Dispensary, in an open ward, which I believe to be unhealthy with so much disease in the city. But when I took up the matter with the ship's owner, he refused to consider moving them to private rooms because of the cost (and perhaps because all five of them are English). The open ward is one tael per day, a little more than $1.50 American, and a private room only twice that, but the old

洋神 *Yang Shen*   *James Lande* 藍德

skinflint raved about being cash-poor and facing bankruptcy, which is absolute drivel. Hugh and I scratched up $90.00 we can spare, which will keep the five men in a private room for a week. I passed a hat among the rest of the "Essex" crew when I saw them in Bamboo Town a few days ago, and collected enough for another week in a private room. I also inquired after the remains of their dead comrades, and the funeral arrangements (they were not buried at sea because we were only a day from port). No one besides the sailors themselves really cared, because there was no political hay to be made from the incident. As none of them had next of kin here, the British consul did nothing more than chuck them into graves among the derelicts in the Sailors Cemetery across the river. They deserved more than to be abandoned in Shanghai.

Hugh considers the prospect for business encouraging, and insists I remain on hand while he gets himself established. I have been invited to resume my former calling as first mate, on a Yangtze River steamer called the "Confucius," which should provide an opportunity to discover better prospects. We move already among the elite - when I last dined with Hugh at the Astor House, he handed me an engraved invitation to a big "do" the skinflint is being forced, feet to the fire, to throw for his daughter's arrival in town. The old man has to invite us – his darlin' dotty dotter wouldn't be here but for our intercession with the China corsairs.

There are so many men with the name Wood running about Shanghai that it is quite easy to be taken for a person of consequence. There is the U. S. Minister Jethro Wood who, so anxious was he to meet the Chinese emperor, rode to Peking in an oxcart flying a pennant that declared in Chinese he was a "tribute bearer from America." He thoroughly redeemed himself later, especially if that story is true, by refusing to kowtow to the august personage of his imperial majesty of all the wily celestials, Mr. Heen Foong. Then there's John Wood, the captain of the Brit frigate "Actaeon." To date he has done nothing remarkable, but quite likely is gazetted for heroism beyond the call of queen and country when he arrives at the Peiho and tries to pass upriver to the Forbidden City. Then there's yours truly. Confucius say, "come aboard, mate" – that's my call to glory.

The minister named Wood trails his titles in a travois, there are so many. He's an Envoy Extraordinary, an extraordinary title, and a Minister Plenipotentiary, which I suppose they have to call him because that's what the other ministers are called; following the most-flavorful nation principle, if your minister is a plenipo, then my minister gets to be a plenipo, too. We call them "plenipo" for short. I've looked up plenipotentiary in all the dictionaries I could lay a hand on without finding the word - until I do, I'll have to assume that it means the fellow has "pleni" of "potential" for...making a mess of everything.

Best wishes,
  Your loving brother,
    Fletcher
      Shanghai, China, April 27, 1860.

Fletcher Meets Confucius   209

洋神 *Yang Shen*   *James Lande* 藍德

Dramatis Personae: Chapter 13

Alphonse de Bourboulon	French minister to China
Claude de Montpellier	French commanding general
Jeremy Whitfall	head of Jardine's Shanghai office
Elias Cage	American trader, Russell and Co.
Chase Steven Cummings	editor of the *North China Herald*
Charles Balfour, RN	commander, HMS *Assistance*
Frederick E. Budd, RM	captain, Royal Marines

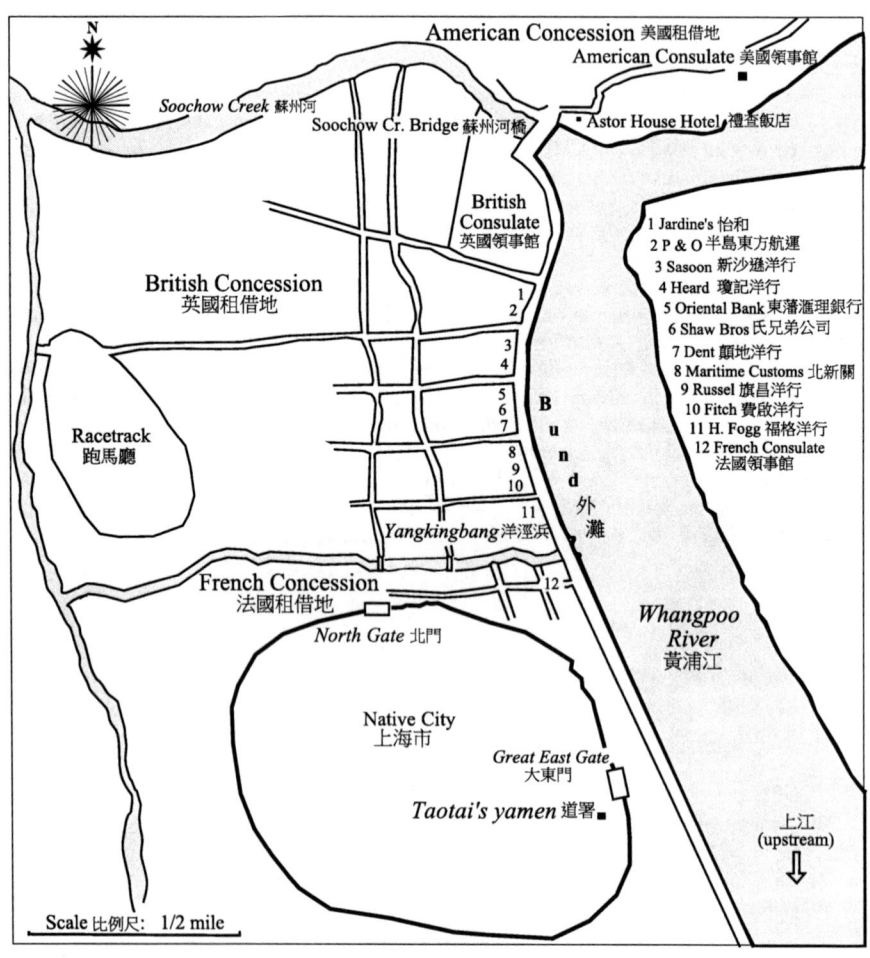

Shanghai in 1855
(based on H. B. Morse, *The International Relations of the Chinese Empire*, Vol. 1, facing p. 454)

The Fitch Soirée

Chapter 13: The Fitch *Soirée*
Saturday, April 28, 1860, 11:00pm

Late in the evening of the soirée, when the gentlemen had repaired to an Astor House drawing room for brandy and cigars, Fletcher joined Augustus Fitch where the taipan was pouring himself a brandy at a sideboard. Fitch looked up at him without expression, then back down at his snifter.

"You have made quite an impression here tonight," Fitch said quietly.

"Actually, I was quite subdued. The laurel of hero rests uncomfortably."

"You might have called less attention to yourself. Instead, you just about caused a skirmish with British officers, earned a rebuke from the British minister, and then tangled with Jardine Matheson. That is not the kind of reserve for which we New Englanders are noted."

Fletcher could not have been more startled if a plateful of clams had suddenly jumped up and started barking and yowling at him. "Some of your treaty port luminaries need to come down a button-hole or two," he said softly.

"Confound all, your manners are worse than Penelope's suitors! Don't you understand how dangerous it is to provoke the British lion?"

Fletcher began to wonder if, as Elias Cage had implied, American traders in Shanghai were so hornswoggled by the almighty British, and so addicted to the opiate of British men-of-war and gunboats, that they dropped to their knees and knocked their heads nine times whenever an Englishman belched.

"No, Mr. Fitch, it had not occurred to me that I need kowtow to the British."

"Have some Hennessy's, Mr. Wood," Fitch said, and then abruptly he turned away.

The night of the Augustus Fitch & Company *soirée* at the Astor house, Shanghai was soaked by a sudden squall of the southwest monsoon that swelled the streams and creeks and staggered the Whangpoo like an overburdened coolie. The river shouldered up onto the land and within hours flooded the Bund and other low-lying ground near the waterfront. Foul river water crept stealthily up dark paths from the Hongkew wharves toward Broadway. The water seeped under the floorboards of shabby grog shops and dilapidated squatters' shacks, and charged the air of the American settlement with a stench of offal the rain could not keep down.

The settlement roads metalled with coal cinders reclaimed from steamship furnaces developed a thin layer of slippery black film, but otherwise held their contour. Unsurfaced roads in the Chinese city and suburbs of the settlement turned to a deep brown muck that clutched at the wheels of heavy carriages and hobbled horses' hooves. Unfortunates out in a coach in such weather were wise to strap a pair of wooden planks atop the axles so as to have a little bit of temporary roadbed to place under carriage wheels mired in the mud.

Frigates and gunboats swung at anchor in the rising water of the roadstead and stretched taut their chains as if to brace their decks for officers in fancy dress descending into gigs to be rowed ashore for the evening's entertainment. From the British paddle-wheel steam frigate HMS *Furious*, 16 guns, 1287 tons, recently returned from the Chushans, came Captain O. J. Jones. The British troopship HMS *Assistance*, screw steamer, 6 guns, 1793 tons, discharged Commander C. Balfour, Royal Marine Lieutenant Colonel March, Royal Marine Captain Budd, and several more infantry and artillery officers. British gunboat HMS *Firm*, 4 guns, 232 tons, just back from Kintang, gave up Lieutenant W. R. Boulton. From the French steam frigate HIM *Entreprenante*,

洋神 *Yang Shen* James Lande 藍德

60 guns, 2550 tons, emerged General Claude de Montpellier and his staff, Captain Devaux, and Lieutenant Vergue. More lieutenants came ashore from the French screw gunboat HIM *Avalanche*, 10 guns, 536 tons, arrived that morning from Tinghai, and from the 4-gun, 1200 ton French steam transport HIM *Gironde*.

Carriages and traps of prominent taipans issued from between the wrought-iron gates of grand merchant mansions and turned down the muddy Bund toward the Astor House. From Jardine Matheson came Jeremy Whitfall, preceded by Arthur Dent and wife of archrival Dent & Company. Allan Howe and Randolf Isaac Frazer, with their wives, represented Abraham Howe & Company, followed by Elias Cage and Tobias Wright and wife of Russell & Co., Augustus Allan Hayes and wife of Olyphant & Co., and Darius Sassoon and wife of Sassoon & Co.. Augustus Fitch escorted Hannah and Elizabeth Fitch.

Rented sedan chairs loosely sealed to keep out the wet called at the doors of the consulates to fetch the emissaries of great nations – America, Spain, Portugal, Germany, Prussia, Hamburg, Bremen, Schleswig, and Piedmont. Their governments maintained these gentlemen in such penury that, if not personally wealthy, they could not afford the fine carriages and horses of the British and French ministers. They could only take consolation in the conspicuous honor accorded them by the Chinese empire of riding in a green chair with *four* bearers.

Beneath the brightly lit windows of the second-floor reception rooms of the Astor House, calash, brougham and phaeton coaches closed tight against the weather drew up before a jury-rigged platform of wooden planks, run out from the broad steps at the entrance and laid across cracker barrels set in the road. This allowed the ladies in their voluminous hoop skirts and crinolines to debark without stepping into the muddy street. The hotel already bulged at its seams, like an overheated steam boiler, with British and French officers billeted there until the departure for the north of the Allied Expeditionary Force. Now the Astor House gracefully spread wide the East Indian arches supporting its portico in order to receive the cream of foreign society at Shanghai then converging upon its entrance.

Fletcher Thorson Wood stood at a distance, with rain pouring off his black southwester, surveying the throng invited by Augustus Fitch to receive his daughter into their society, and coincidentally do Fletcher honor. He seriously considered a tactical retreat back to his bunk aboard *Confucius*, where she was berthed alongside the Hongkew wharf. Instead, he waited under a protecting eave until the traffic dwindled, then went into the hotel bar and found Hugh in all his frippery: tan sack coat edged in black cord, matching buff and black check vest and black trousers, and flowing black cravat. Sitting in the company of the corps of neglected officers billeted in the hotel, the brothers sipped brandy and casually scrutinized the distinguished guests of the *soirée* checking their cloaks and top hats and ascending to the second-floor reception rooms.

"Fletcher," Hugh said, grinning, "Mr. Fitch is having a conniption fit because you are not up there in his reception line greeting these luminaries. But then you are not exactly dressed for the occasion, are you. Can you not wear something beside that dreary old black frock coat?"

"Our Mr. Fitch strikes me as a bit choleric and prone to apoplexy regardless, Hugh, so a simple conniption fit is probably an advance over his usual temperament. And you know simple garb suits me. There is far too much sartorial splendor mincing about upstairs to be agreeable. I'd rather wait until they settle and I can sidle in unnoticed. They'll be dancing another hour before dinner is served."

"Hardly the way for a guest of honor to conduct himself. By the way, here is a newspaper clipping I saved for you while you were mucking about in that steamer. All

Shanghai knows now what happened aboard *Essex*."

Fletcher quickly glanced over the clipping. "Well, I suppose they must have their hero, seeing how little can be done about pirates along the China coast. But I do not feel cut out for the role based on so little merit as that fracas aboard *Essex*, and it will be all I can do to keep from being the skeleton at this feast."

Hugh chuckled. "There is some irony in all this fancy display, when you consider the troubles outside the door – allies occupying Chushan, gathering to storm Peking, and rebels threatening the countryside round about."

"Appears to be a great many officers here already, even with most of the Allied fleet still in Hong Kong, or at Chushan."

"I certainly wish they would depart from Shanghai, or at least the Astor House. Aboard your steamer you do not have this hoard of gregarious fellows underfoot, overburdening the hotel service, drinking up all the wine, and filling all the comfortable chairs."

"Some of them will be departing for Nagasaki, I hear, aboard the British steamer *Chusan*, with three hundred of their Chinese 'Bamboo Rifles,' whatever those are. They'll be fetching Japanese horses for the cavalry to use in the north."

"Yes, I have heard from officers here that quite a few of the horses they tried to transport by sea from India got sick and didn't make it past Hong Kong."

"The British general, Sir Hope Grant, is going back to Hong Kong, too, now that he has conquered Chushan, and he'll be taking some of the fellows with him. The rest of these officers will likely stay on as garrison, until the Allied Expeditionary Force finally leaves Hong Kong for the Peiho. The French general, de Montpellier, has just returned victorious from Chushan only to be ordered to take off his spurs and set a spell here in Shanghai, so you can expect more officers to be coming and going between here and Chushan."

"Probably won't have the hotel to myself again until the war's over."

"That could be a while, if the Chinese and British go on squabbling over treaty terms. Front stoop could collect hundreds of British and French officers, if the Chinese ambassadors stall negotiations much longer to keep the allies from going north, and give Sam Collinson additional time to prepare his defenses. Then the anchorage will fill up with troop transports, and the ships in harbor, and temples and godowns all over Shanghai, will be crowded with angry soldiers howling for the fray."

North China Herald
Shanghai, 28 April, 1860

Piratical Attack in Chushans

Recently we learned of an attack on the Fitch & Co. clipper *Essex* by pirates in the vicinity of the Volcanos on the 19th ultimo. *Essex* was bound for Shanghai from Hong Kong under the command of Captain Cornelius Fitch; Mrs. Hannah Fitch, and Miss Elizabeth Fitch, wife and daughter of the ship's owner Augustus Fitch, were also aboard. Four pirate junks surrounded the ship after it stranded on a shoal, apparently due to the perfidy of a Chinese pilot with consular papers engaged at Ningpo. The crew put up a valiant defense with rifle and cannon, inspired we are told by the bold leadership of a passenger, F. T. Wood. A former officer of artillery in the Crimea, Mr Wood directed the crew in the firing of a 6-pounder field gun found in the hold and pressed into service on deck. While under fire, the crew warped the ship out of the mud using a small bower and kedge, got free of the ambush and sailed to Gutzlaff Island to meet the pilot schooner, and a pilot was engaged to take her to Shanghai. Four lives were lost aboard Essex: the ship's gunner, an able-bodied seaman, a cabin boy, and a foretopman, all British citizens. One pirate junk sank, two were severely damaged, and at least 20 pirates were killed. A blond-headed white man thought to be the notorious apostate Englishman Fokie Tom led the pirates who, it is said, may still be skulking about the islands near Chushan. We are of the opinion that as long as they are there in Chushan with little else to do, British and French gunboats can render great service by hunting down the nefarious Tom and putting an end to his piratical enterprise.

"I overheard a naval lieutenant a few minutes before you came in, Fletcher. He said that a ship called the *Forbin* has just come back from reconnoitering at the Peiho, and that some of her officers disguised themselves as Chinamen and got close to the forts in sampans to get a good idea of fortifications on the river front."

"By thunder! That's showing some mighty fine initiative. What a pickle they'd be in if they just nonchalantly sailed up to the forts and found a Sebastopol there!"

"Are they going to have to take the Taku forts again?"

"Well, if so, they best beat to quarters pretty soon, or this delay will have them in their red wool tunics smack in the middle of the hottest weather."

"Speaking of delay, Fletcher, it is time we scaled Parnassus."

The reception room on the second floor of the Astor House was festooned with colored streamers and bunting, and a few early spring garden flowers that struggled to bloom in the recent cold. Together these gave the adjoining reception, dining and ball rooms a festive atmosphere. Displayed behind the reception line were the flags of the nations attending the ball, with the Stars and Stripes and the Union Jack at the center, and flags of other nations in alphabetical order on the right and left. Under the showy decoration, the rooms were furnished in the same Regency style as the first-floor dining rooms, with thick carpeting and heavy draperies in rich claret, and gaily lit by large imported English chandeliers of cut glass that cast reflected candle light into every corner. At the back of the ballroom, a pianoforte and a trio of piccolo, cornet, and clarinet were quietly improvising *Barbara Allen*. On loan from the Royal Marine band aboard HMS *Assistance* on short notice, they would provide music for the gathering until the full orchestra arrived to play for the ball.

Fitch's guests transformed the rooms into a dominion of high fashion amply populated with diplomats in striped trousers and tailcoats garnished with ribbon sashes, decorations of honor, and ceremonial swords. Army and navy officers were in full dress uniform awash with gold buttons, braid, and bright ribbons and medals. Men of the settlement were bedecked in frock coats, elaborate vests and silk cravats, and their ladies arrayed in rainbows of swirling silk gowns and taffeta skirts abounding with lace and ribbon. Even the Chinese menials were fitted out in double-breasted gray livery trimmed in maroon especially for the occasion.

Fletcher and Hugh arrived as the reception line was breaking up to begin the dancing, but not so soon as to be overlooked by the officious little Austrian manager of the Fitch hong. He took them in tow and ferried them over to where Augustus Fitch stood in black tailcoat and trousers, double-breasted white waistcoat, and black bow tie, chatting with Hannah and Elizabeth.

"Ah, Mr. Wood," said Fitch, "I should be upset with you. I wished you to join us in the reception line and be introduced to our friends here in the settlement. That is so much easier than dragging you about the room to make introductions. Did my runners not find you?"

"Good evening, Mrs. Fitch, Miss Fitch," said Fletcher, smiling to the ladies. Hannah seemed begrudgingly chic in a purple striped organdy dress with matching striped cape and broad sleeves with white under sleeves. Elizabeth was dressed to the nines for the role of perfect debutante in a lime-green flounced taffeta gown trimmed in point lace with under dress of white *glacé* silk and flaring pagoda sleeves.

"Kind of you to invite my brother Hugh and me to your little shindig. As for your runners, Mr. Fitch, they did find me, but I was unavoidably detained. Perhaps, however, we can dispense temporarily with formalities and settle for a toast at dinner? In the meantime, I can just drift about on the tide of conversation."

洋神 *Yang Shen*   *James Lande* 藍德

"Now you are exasperating me, Mr. Wood." Fitch leaned closer, as if in conspiracy. "I would not loose you in this room if my fortune depended upon it. We have here tonight ministers, consuls, taipans, and high-ranking military officers – just about everyone of consequence in Shanghai, including three VCs. Unless you know to whom you are speaking, there is great risk of compromising your excellent credentials, which I remind you are of my procuring, and doing injury to your already superlative reputation. Dancing will begin shortly, and dinner will be at 8:00pm, so humor me by staying close until then and I shall make your acquaintance known to at least some of the guests."

Mr. Fitch anchored Elizabeth to himself on one arm and Hannah on the other and embarked on a modest promenade about the room, stopping to hail each assembly of guests, with Fletcher and Hugh directly behind buoyed in the hollow formed by the ladies enormous skirts. A swirling Babel of conversations paused and parted to regard the passing entourage, gurgled pleasantries, then swam together in their wake. Fletcher could understand a little of the French and Spanish, and some of the diplomats even had their interpreters with them.

Therefore, he thought, anything that is not said in English probably isn't worth listening to anyway.

Conversations Encountered During Promenade at Augustus Fitch *Soirée*, Shanghai, April 28, 1860

Royal Marine Captain Budd, recently returned from Hong Kong aboard HMS *Assistance*, in scarlet single-breasted tunic with eight gold buttons, blue piping, blue collar with gold crown and star, three gold stripes above blue cuffs, blue serge trousers with crimson stripe, black bell-top shako, half-basket guard dress sword with gold acorn knot in steel scabbard suspended from white morocco leather shoulder strap with gilt buckle embossed with lion and crown, globe and laurels, fouled anchor and motto *Per Mare Per Terram*, Baltic Medal, Crimean War medal with Sebastopol clasp, Indian Mutiny medal with Relief of Lucknow clasp, sipping from a crystal flute of ruby dinner claret, to…	Lieutenant W. R. Boulton, commanding gunboat HMS *Firm*, in blue double-breasted tunic with two rows of ten crown and laurel buttons, gold lace collar and gold epaulets with fouled anchor emblem, black silk cravat, one gold stripe on each sleeve, blue trousers with gold stripe, blue cocked hat with black and gold bullions, dress sword with half-basket guard in steel scabbard hung from black morocco belt, Second Burmese War medal with Pegu clasp, Baltic medal, Crimean War medal with Sea of Azof clasp, Sardinian medal:

"You must have read that the Whitworth gun is far superior to the Armstrong – it uses tin instead of flannel cartridges. Tin cartridges transport easily and safely, stay dry, and load easily. And the Whitworth has less recoil – forty grooves in the Armstrong rifling cause much heat and resistance. The older Armstrongs wanted a river of water at hand to swab out the barrel and keep the gun cool, but now Armstrong has perfected a lubricated cartridge – don't need to sponge out the barrel so often. We test fired the Armstrong earlier this year while still at Hong Kong, and it performed with the accuracy of a rifle – hit a man-sized target at a mile! It's the rifling – machined on a lathe to tolerances of 1/3000 of an inch. Shell explodes into as many as fifty jagged fragments and is extraordinarily lethal to advancing foot and horse alike. So, we have brought several batteries of Armstrongs to introduce to Old Sam Collinson and his Tartar cavalry."

The Fitch Soirée

洋神 *Yang Shen*   *James Lande* 藍德

Elias Cage of Russell & Co. with thick cheek whiskers and mustache, tailcoat, velvet collar and waistcoat, black bow tie, and eyeglasses suspended from waistcoat button to…

Captain Smith of the Howe & Company clipper *Fanny McHenry*, loading for Hakodate, in shiny black broadcloth frock coat, starched collar, gray cravat with emerald pin, and gray spats:

"I hear that the *Progressive Age* will probably be condemned. She is rotted through and would cost at least 3000 taels to repair, and is not worth 2000 taels as she floats. I fear her repairs will hardly come under insurance either, so it will be hard upon her owners unless the agent can foist the brig off on some gullible buyer. I am glad she is not mine – I would never allow a vessel of mine to fall into such a state of disrepair. Even her timbers and fittings would not bring enough to recover her costs. She has so little she cannot be given away. Not even Chinese would want to rebuild her. No one wants her!"

Captain of Royal Engineers in scarlet single-breasted tunic edged with blue velvet facings, gold collar embroidered with crown and star, full-dress gold braid shoulder strap, dark blue trousers with gold lace stripe, busby with white plume affixed by gold flaming grenade, Russia leather belt, gilt buckle with crown and laurel insignia, dress saber with engraved gilt-scroll hilt in silver scabbard, Victoria Cross, Punjab Campaign medal with Mooltan clasp, Crimean War medal with Balaclava clasp, Indian Mutiny Medal with Dehli clasp, twirling a sweating glass of iced Perrier & Jonet champagne, to…

Captain of Royal Marine Artillery in blue single-breasted tunic with eight gold buttons and scarlet piping, scarlet collar with gold crown and star, three gold stripes on tunic sleeves, blue trousers with scarlet stripe, half-basket guard dress sword with gold acorn knot in steel scabbard suspended from white morocco leather shoulder strap. cocked hat of black beaver with gold and crimson bullions and white plume, Baltic medal, Crimean War medal with Alma and Inkerman clasps, Turkish Crimea Medal with ring suspender, Indian Mutiny Medal with Relief of Lucknow clasp:

"Shanghai must be one of the most dreary places on the face of the earth! Certainly there could be no more terrible a station for any man without regular business to occupy his time, and no one but a fool set on getting rich overnight could tolerate living here. Only one racket court, no club, a stiflingly hot little room of book shelves called a library by the residents, and a forlorn old mud puddle encircled by fetid ditches local wags have dubbed a race-course are the entire domain of public amusements. And have you noticed how much in evidence the native population is in the concessions? There's no escaping bloody Chinese wherever you go. The one saving grace is the liberality of the city's merchant princes in spending their wealth on the hospitality of an open house like this one here tonight. For storekeepers they certainly do lay a good cloth."

Olyphant & Co. taipan with trencher beard, wearing gray double-breasted frock coat with black velvet collar and lapels, black shawl-collared double-breasted vest, baggy plaid trousers, to…

Sassoon & Co. trader with mutton chop sideburns, wearing black coat, turned-down collar with small black bow tie, dotted pearl-gray satin vest, gold watch chain:

"First they say they will stop the trade, then they say they will not. How is one to prepare successfully for profitable business? If there is no interruption of the native coastal junk trade by this campaign in the north, we can expect increasing demand for foreign trade goods before long, and can hope to empty some of our godown shelves of long accumulated inventory. A great many junks will come up the coast from Canton and Foochow, and many more down the creek from Soochow and Huchow, just as soon as they can be sure of impunity and security. But it cannot happen if the British and

洋神 *Yang Shen*   *James Lande* 藍德

French ministers stop the coastal junk trade."

| French Consul with imperial beard, monocle, light blue frock coat edged in gold braid, medals, ribbons on blue sash across white satin vest, ceremonial sword, black trousers with gold stripe, to… | Captain Lee of the Russell & Company ship *Matilda*, in somber suit of gray: |

"*Que nul ne pourra désormais s'etablir à Ting-hai sans avoir au préalable sollicité et obtenu l'autorisation de la Commission Mixte Instituée par les Officers Generaux Commandant.* I am very sorry, Monsieur, but no one shall henceforth be permitted to establish himself at Tinghai without having first solicited and obtained the sanction of the Mixed Commission of the General Officers Commanding."

| Young lady in ball gown of canary-yellow silk, under mantlet of black taffeta to… | young lady in evening dress of white corded silk trimmed in black velvet with under dress of blue silk, reading a dance card with Chinese characters: |

"Shang-hai 上海 – what does it mean? It says here that it translates as 'the higher sea, or to go upon the sea.' Does that mean that when the Yangtze River reaches the coast it goes out to the sea? Or that a boat upon the Yangtze River goes out to sea? Shall we say Go-to-sea? Go-to-sea, China? Like Battersea, England?"

2   At 8:00pm, a chime rang the call to dinner. The guests flowed out of the ballroom and reception area and into the adjoining dining hall, glowing in the light of imported cut-glass chandeliers. Elaborate centerpieces and place settings of glazed dishware, bright silver Sheffield flatware, and crystal wine glasses crowded three long tables covered in white damask. Gilt-edged place cards embossed with a national flag or unit crest rested next to each gold-rimmed porcelain plate. Fitch factotums consulted seating charts and deftly directed guests toward their assigned seats. The dinner party of sixty-six was comprised of small islands of taipan families surrounded by a sea of single diplomats, officers, and traders. An American taipan hosted each table, with Augustus Fitch at the head of the first table, and the British and French ministers and General de Montpellier in seats of honor. Hannah Fitch sat at the opposite end of the table, with the guest of honor Fletcher Thorson Wood, Hugh Wood, and Elizabeth Fitch.

There were only eleven ladies, owing to the dearth of any women at all in the foreign population of Shanghai, and each was flattered by several men vying to escort them to table and draw chairs to clear passage for their voluminous hoop skirts. A rig or two did threaten to fly up, but were wrestled onto seats with sufficient fullness at the stern to reduce upsweep at the bow, and gentlemen sitting to each side pushed their way in past the aggressive hoops. Ladies wearing long evening gloves removed them. Within ten minutes, the assembly was settled and plates of *pâté de foie gras* were being served.

Iced buckets of Giesler's Creaming Champagne, and Perrier & Jonet, were arrayed strategically beside the tables and served by the liveried Chinese Ganymedes. Ruby dinner claret was set out in rows of cut-glass decanters down the center of each table. The wine lists included Hennessy's Pale Brandy, Bass's Pale Ale, Misa Pale Sherry, hock, Madeira, port, and porter. A seemingly endless procession of Chinese waiters brought plates of roast beef, legs of mutton, roast pheasant and partridge, and chicken and rice curries. There were joints of cold salt pork, California smoked salmon, baked and sautéed vegetables, and baked and stuffed potatoes. Desserts included plum puddings, custards, pastries, and cheeses, oranges, figs, raisins, walnuts, and blancmange

The Fitch Soirée

– a sweet pudding flavored with almond extract and rum.

Fletcher found himself seated between Chalmers Alexander, interpreter at the British consulate, on his left and Jeremy Whitfall, head of Jardine's Shanghai office, on his right. Opposite Fletcher was Captain Budd of the Royal Marines, and to Budd's left Rudolph Isaac Frazer of Abraham Howe and Co., the Russell & Co. trader Elias Cage, and Cummings of the *Herald*. Fletcher noted the absence of missionaries and their wives from the dinner party, and wondered if that said anything about the relations between the religious and trading communities of Shanghai – between God and mammon. The male civilians at table tended toward a portly, flushed appearance and dull expression characteristic of overindulgence in the food, drink and tobacco that served as some of the few consolations of treaty port life. Chalmers Alexander's slight build, light-red hair and pale freckled skin were a lively contrast, and his sea-blue eyes suggested intelligence and wit.

"Keep you busy," Fletcher said, "all these soldiers and sailors in port?"

"Very," Alexander said, "I'm pressed into their service day and night to find accommodations and resolve disputes with the local Chinese – and the troops here now are just the advance party. Only a few of us here that speak the language. Frank Jackson does the deed for your side. That's him, with his wife, there at the end of the last table."

"I envy your mastery of the language, all the more so as I lack any ability."

"May seem singular to non-linguists but, believe me, I know next to nothing at all."

"Not speaking the language of a place is like going to sea as a passenger."

"How very apt, Mr. Wood," Alexander said with a chuckle.

Augustus Fitch rapped with a silver fork on his gilt-rimmed wine goblet.

"Ladies and gentlemen, thank you all for coming this evening. I am especially pleased to welcome the British minister, his Excellency Mr. Francis W. A. Blaine, and the French Minister, his Excellency Monsieur Alphonse de Bourboulon. Also with us is commander of the French expedition General Claude de Montpellier. British commander Sir Hope Grant has returned to Hong Kong and sent his regrets he could not attend this evening. My purpose in bringing you together is twofold. First, I wish to introduce to the settlement my daughter Elizabeth Fitch, just arrived from America on her first trip to the Orient. To Elizabeth."

The men at the tables rose to offer their glasses to Elizabeth Fitch, those that could find where she was sitting. The more confused, tipsy, or less practiced in English followed the gaze of others, or the direction in which champagne glasses pointed, to offer their toast. Then all set down their glasses and extended a round of polite applause.

"I wish also to honor the brave fellow who was singularly responsible for saving the lives of my wife and daughter, and the crew of the Fitch vessel *Essex*, when she was attacked by a fleet of pirates in the Volcanos a week ago. Fletcher, please stand up. Gentlemen, I give you Fletcher Thorson Wood."

Fletcher reluctantly rose to his feet, with a grin Hugh later called sheepish, and accepted the toast. A louder round of applause ensued, punctuated by "hear, hear!" Fletcher turned to Augustus, bowed slightly, raised his glass to his host and patron.

"Thank you, Mr. Fitch," he said.

"Please enjoy your dinner," Augustus said. "I've spared no effort, nor expense, to gratify every taste. After dinner there will be refreshments in sitting rooms and in the ballroom more dancing to waltzes played by Her Majesty's Royal Marine band."

Augustus and Fletcher resumed their seats, and the procession of Chinese servants delivering the many courses continued. Rudolph Frazer caught Fletcher's attention. He was an amiable-looking youth with wavy blond hair, blue eyes, and a bemused expression, wearing a swallowtail frock coat of glossy black broadcloth, and a narrow standing collar with black bow tie skewered by a diamond stickpin. He had only recently arrived from New York and was working as a griffin for Abraham Howe.

"Mr. Wood," Frazer said, "please satisfy my curiosity. I read in the *Herald* that you fought off those pirates with nothing more than a little 6-pounder."

Fletcher sighed inwardly at the call for yet another performance and launched a small recital that summarized the events as quickly as possible, describing the junks, their locations, and the distances. "When they came down to 1000 yards, the captain organized rifle squads that kept up a hot fire and potted quite a few pirate helmsman as they closed in. It was only after the ca'tridges for the rifles were gone that we thought of the *taotai*'s field guns down in the ship's hold."

Elias Cage interrupted.

"I am certain we are all grateful to have such a brave fellow among our number. We are all mighty amazed at your resourcefulness, Mr. Wood. How did you get experience with field artillery?"

Cage was large man with a broad forehead, gray hair parted on his left and brushed over to the right, and thick cheek whiskers conjoined by a heavy mustache. His sunken eyes suggested long residence in inhospitable climes. Fletcher noticed that his left eye lacked the luster of the right and wondered if it was glass.

"Most of my experience with light artillery, I received in service with the French in the Crimea," he said with a nod to the French at the opposite end of the table. "I arrived there late in fifty-four, served as an officer of artillery for about a year, and saw my last action of the war at the fall of Sebastopol. Since then I've had occasion to train artillery in Mexico and South America."

"And aboard Mr. Fitch's clipper ship *Essex*!" volunteered the captain of *Furious*, O. J. Jones, who offered his glass in a toast. "Here's my glass to you, Mr. Wood, to your courage under fire."

"Here, here!" echoed the dinner guests.

"Mr. Wood," Captain Budd said, poking at the tablecloth with a fork. "What regiment did you fight with, in the Crimea?"

"Joined the 2nd Corps D'Armée at Inkerman. That's a Sebastopol clasp on your ribbon, isn't it?"

"Yes. How's a Yankee come to fight with Frenchmen?"

"They needed artillery officers – I took the first offer."

"How'd you know enough about artillery to be an officer?"

"A mate aboard ship learns about the guns."

"So, you served in the navy?"

"I sailed on merchant ships."

"Merchants don't have guns."

"Some do. Especially in China."

Budd stared at Fletcher silently. His fork had opened a hole in the damask.

"You stayed only one year? War wasn't quite over. Why did you leave?"

"A difference of opinion with a superior. I resigned."

"You mean you quit."

"No, I resigned."

3 Jeremy Whitfall of Jardine Matheson & Co. rapped lightly on his wine glass with an *hors d'oeuvre* fork.

"Mr. Fitch," he said, "I wonder if I may not put a question to Consul Shanks? Considering that the American treaty with the emperor was ratified last year, and is now in force, why do the Americans consider it necessary to once more accompany the British and French forces returning to the Peiho?"

The Fitch Soirée

Ha, thought Elias Cage, there's the long arm of *Taotai* Wu and Governor Hsueh at work again. The *taotai* dispenses his favors and Jardine helps work his will. The local corollary of the Most Favored Nation clause – known as the Most Favored Taipan.

"President Buchanan," said the American consul, standing to orate, "has asked that Minister Jethro Wood remain at this post until peace has been restored, and afford the belligerents every opportunity of using the good offices of Americans as intermediaries. And there remain the details of regulations for tariff and trade."

"Many of these things can be resolved here at Shanghai," Whitfall said, "or in the other treaty ports. As for mediation, do you not think it is quite late for that? I do not see the need for American presence in the north. It would only complicate matters further, and distract the Chinese from negotiations with the British and French." And it would give you Americans a lucrative opportunity for business directly with the Chinese government in arms, shipping, and grain transport. We know your Russian friends are whispering in the emperor's ear to let Americans ship rice to Peking.

"You may be right, sir," Shanks said, "that it could be too late to mediate. Sadly, hopes for this prospect seem rather to ebb than flow. However, Minister Wood firmly believes there would be no prospect at all were Americans to shirk their destiny and not be present. The minister feels that the role played by Americans in the diplomatic relations with the Chinese Empire has been regarded for some time as subordinate to that of other treaty participants. He wishes that America now take responsibility commensurate with her stature under the first of these new treaties."

The American consul took his seat. Fletcher stared at Whitfall beside him for a few moments, and then said, "He's right you know."

Whitfall glanced condescendingly at Fletcher.

"I am sure I do not know what you mean, sir."

Hugh was seated too far away to kick his brother's shin, and was reluctant to ask Captain Budd to kick Fletcher for him. Fletcher noted that his status as hero was no coin-of-the-realm with Jardine Matheson.

"That Americans have not been given due credit for their diplomacy here."

"With respect, sir, I submit there has not been much to American diplomacy in China, following as it does British policy."

"More, perhaps, than you British allow. An example I read about happened a few years back, when Triad insurrectionists took the Shanghai and drove the Imperial Customs out of the native city. The American commissioner Marshall collected duties in specie from American traders and turned them over to the Chinese. British consul took promissory notes from British merchants and never gave anything to the Chinese. Instead, British merchants clamored for a free port."

Whitfall turned round to confront Fletcher.

"How you Americans manage to think you fool anyone is quite beyond my comprehension! At the very same moment Caleb Cushing addressed your Congress to boast of American respect for the laws and sovereignty of the Chinese empire, your American taipans at Canton gleefully violated old Commissioner Lin's trade embargo by smuggling English cargoes all over South China. Down to the present day, you have kept up your hypocrisy and presented yourselves as creatures of the light superior to us benighted English devils. But no one believes such poppycock except maybe the ignorant, gullible American public. Certainly no Englishman in England or China believes it, nor dare I say does any Chinese. I would not wager a farthing on a bet that the Americans here in Shanghai believe it. You know which are the Americans – they're the pale, gaunt ones slavering from their jowls where they sit off to one side waiting for the lions to finish the important work at hand."

"Inevitably," Fletcher said, smiling, "we return to that tiresome cliché about the jackal following after the British lion. I would have thought it laid to rest by now, after the fracas at the Taku forts last year. The 'pale, gaunt ones slavering from their jowls' were not the ones who retired from the field with a black eye and a bloody nose."

Chairs groaned and several officers made as if to rise, but the Commander Balfour, of HMS *Assistance*, was on his feet ahead of them.

"Gentlemen. Keep your seats."

Commander Balfour shot a stern look down the table at Fletcher, and then resumed his seat. The officers remained taut, poised for action. Minister Blaine stood up.

"While I can na' agree wi' his tone," Minister Blaine said, "I do share some of Fletcher Wood's sentiment. Gentlemen, let us give credit where it is due, and recall that the gallant American Commodore Tattnall defied his own orders last year wi' the cry that 'blood is thicker than water' and leapt into the fray to save British lives. He rescued the wounded Admiral Hope, and joined wi' British sailors in the loading of their guns. A shot that barely missed the commodore killed his coxswain, and the commodore's barge sank along wi' the four British gunboats. But that did na' prevent him from bringing up a flotilla carrying 500 men to storm the enemy positions. Who among you will say that is how a jackal behaves?"

Blaine paused. There was no response.

"Moreover, when British and French forces withdrew, Americans did na' follow after them, but went on up the river to the Forbidden City and entered into the negotiations for the treaty. They could find no justification for retiring from the field together wi' the British and French, and thereby disobey the explicit instructions of their President. They saw an opportunity, afforded to them alone, to achieve a grea' triumph that would benefit all the nations involved, and especially those gripped so tightly in struggle that they could na' parley. I submit to you, gentlemen, that this is na' the behavior of a self-seeking country, some solitary predator, some jackal, or some second there merely to hold the British coat. These were the acts of a responsible member of the community of nations, na' totally unprepared to answer the call of fraternity when it can be done without stain upon her own escutcheon."

The room was silent for a few moments while the men measured the consequences of any response. Some agreed that the Americans had perhaps come of age and taken some responsibility. Some, who valued commitment to the longer course, wondered if Americans would withdraw when America plunged into civil war. Some believed that with this brash harangue the English, on behalf of the Americans, had actually flung a gauntlet at the feet of everyone gathered there.

"Hear, hear, Minister!" burst forth from the opposite end of the table, followed by rising applause round the room mingled with the chinking of wineglasses.

"Most eloquent rhetoric, Minister," Whitfall said, with seeming approval. Then his tone hardened.

"But it would have been better not to have gone to Peking at all, rather than be humiliated by being bounced about in an unsprung oxcart, flying a little yellow pennant declaring them to be 'tribute bearers from the United States.' That little cavalcade in their 'carriage of honor' caused all foreign nations great loss of face in the eyes of the Chinese. It invites still more contempt from a race we must repeatedly force, at no small sacrifice in blood and treasure, to respect us."

"That, sir," Consul Shanks said, "never happened except in the minds of reckless British and French journalists, no offense to Mr. Cummings here. European journalists. Their malice for the United States diplomatic initiative, from Minister Reed in 1858 forward, has so distorted their judgment as to cause them to fabricate tales to discredit the American mission, and even mislead the English parliament and people. Witness the incredulity, upon hearing these false reports, of not only of Minister Wood, the man who refused to kneel to the Chinese emperor, but also of the two very competent interpreters who accompanied him, Dr. Williams and Mr. Martin. Those men were quite capable of reading any Chinese, had such appeared, and of fiercely contesting such a sham. Minister Wood said it was true that for a short part of the trip, he rode in a cart, as is much more common in the north, but it was so uncomfortable that he soon got out and walked. I grant you that short part of the passage was somewhat less than entirely noble, but it was of short duration and there was no little yellow pennant."

The British Minister picked up his wineglass. He was thinking that, Minister Wood's sadly amateur statesmanship to the contrary, even Americans given enough time might learn diplomacy. But the American Minister had been raked over coals quite enough. Godfrey, he's even had to endure low blows from the French, from his eminence the Holy Roman Minister de Bourboulon, as if those blithering idiots had any ground to stand on! In any event, judging from the way London treated me after the Taku debacle last year, it would seem the inevitable fate of ministers to China to be pilloried in public and in the press. If we had been successful, England would have cheered – instead, even Philadelphia wanted me tried for high treason.

"Wha'ever the case, gentlemen," Minister Blaine said, smiling conspicuously at Whitfall, "Minister Wood's refusal to kowtow to the Chinese emperor was an act that certainly reclaimed more than enough American pride to outweigh any other inconvenience or slight. He was quoted widely as having said 'I bow only to God and woman!' Isn't that right, Consul Shanks?"

"Yes," the American consul said, with a disconcerted smile. "Minister Wood told me that it occurred to him only later that the idea of bowing to women probably only confused the Chinese with unfamiliar notions of Western chivalry. They did mention that their emperor *is* God but, recalling nothing to that effect in *our* catechism, he disregarded the remark."

"Every so often," Fletcher said *sotto voce* to Chalmers Alexander, "the *Herald* prints a letter from an American consul in Japan. Have you seen same, Chalmers?"

"Townsend Harris?"

"That's him. In Japan it would appear that the British follow the Americans, sharing the treaty rights won by the great patience of Townsend Harris, and reaping the benefits of American diplomacy, without any effort of their own."

"You Americans should have credit for that."

"Well, I probably should not say so – my tone is not agreeable. He exiled himself in some obscure seaside village for years slowly wearing away Japanese resistance like water dripping on stone, until they agreed to a commercial treaty. The Japanese have been secluding foreigners at Nagasaki, just like the Chinese have confined foreigners at Canton. Harris secured trade privileges, toleration of missionaries and teaching, and rights of diplomatic residence in several places, all without a war like the one the English wage now against the Chinese."

"Nagasaki, Kanagawa, and Hakodate. The village of his exile is Shimoda."

"Ah, then you have followed this."

"Closely. Your Harris was consul general in fifty-five, and minister in fifty-nine. To be fair, however, I would point out that, while Harris did not war on Japan, he quite effectively used the threat of war – pointing suggestively to British warships then in Japanese harbors – to win his treaty."

"Coercion, Mr. Wood." Jeremy Whitfall pinioned Fletcher with a flanking glare. "Call it by any name you wish, but it is all coercion. Americans have reaped no less a whirlwind in Japan than has Great Britain in China. The murder of the *tairō* can be laid at your doorstep, along with all the chaos following your treaty."

"Gen'lemen, perhaps we can put to rest our disagreements," Minister Blaine said, "at least for this evening. When we quarrel wi' each other, the Chinese witness a weakness among us they see can be put to their own advantage. In spite of our setback at the Peiho last year, the more cunning among them know quite well they can na' defeat us by force of arms, so they devise strategies to set us at odds with one another, to create suspicions between our several nations, to divide and conquer. Whenever our cooperation falters, and one of our nations gets out of step, we can expect the mandarins to be right there to take advantage of the slip. They whisper in our ears 'look there, your brother's flocks are larger, his orchards yield more fruit, he is more handsome and more favored by God, so why do you na' go and kill your brother and take for yourself the things that are his'."

Injured feelings were assuaged somewhat if not cured completely by the denouement of exchanges and conversation that dissipated into smaller circles. Around the compass rose, Fletcher fended off several hard stares from the part of the establishment with a growing notion of Fletcher Wood as a potential troublemaker.

"Who is this tie-row?" Fletcher whispered his question to Alexander, careful this time not to attract more attention from Jardine Matheson & Company. Alexander glanced toward Whitfall and rolled his eyes – the taipan's attention was elsewhere.

"Elder statesman," Alexander said in a furtive whisper. "His name was Ii Kamon no Kami, second after the Japanese *shōgun*, very powerful. The treaty angered many Japanese because the *tairō* took it upon himself, and did not seek approval from the Japanese emperor, the court nobles, or the clan leaders, and they all opposed him. It was like stepping on a hornet's nest. Rumors over two years have been that the *tairō* has been cutting the hair of all who opposed the treaty, removing some from office, sending some abroad. Even assassination."

"So now they have assassinated him?"

"Yes. It was only a few weeks ago and too soon to say, but it was probably a band of fanatical supporters of the Japanese emperor who take umbrage at any insult to him, real or fancied. Their war-cry is *sonnō jōi*, expel the barbarians."

"Is there a gang of fanatical Chinese also wanting to expel *us* barbarians?"

"In Peking, and in the provinces, there is a war party, and there is a peace party. They both hold office together, like Republicans and Democrats in your Congress, flailing away at each other to gain the support and approval of the emperor. Chinese are not homogenous silk. They are alive with the variety of color and texture of your old tweed smoking jacket, which anyone can see clearly when they look closely at the fibers of the cloth. We English make the mistake of assuming that because the letter of an agreement with the Chinese has been ratified, that the rules of a treaty will be observed. In point of fact, ratification seems to mean nothing to them, and so we regard them as perfidious rascals, and China as the most corrupt nation on the face of the earth. But it is hardly that simple. Our own House of Commons debates the discretion and judgement of Lord Exter and Minister Blaine, and Palmerston and Derby skirmish over the prime minister's chair so each can guide England's course in China according to his own view. So why would you not expect disagreement among Chinese about how to treat with us."

Alexander noticed Jeremy Whitfall listening again. He stopped whispering.

"If we English," Alexander said, "were able to learn enough about the politics of the Chinese empire, we might influence the opinion of its ministers, advance a caliber of men able to treat rationally with foreign powers, and avert a show of force."

"Utter nonsense!" Whitfall hissed. "Balderdash from griffins not long enough in China to discover first hand that Chinese have no principles or scruples. British politicians measure war with China using the same rod they measure war with France, and conclude they need only deal with 'political motives.' But the Chinese emperor and his mandarins have no concept of 'political motives,' or of truthful dealings, or of the cruelty caused by the lack of ethical principles. Their dumb god Buddha from time immemorial has taught only duplicity, and the whole of what passes for their social fabric is based on falsehood. Only force will 'motivate' them to behave in a civilized fashion. Repeatedly, the greatest nation on earth has humbled itself before the Chinese emperor, and still the British cabinet hopes to avert war. This offering of milk and water will not suffice – now is the time to chastise the Chinese emperor so severely he will not again dare confront the family of nations."

Dashed if tha' does na' sound jus' like my brother Lord Exter, thought Minister Blaine. And t' think this Whitfall has the ear of the prime minister.

Inflict upon her the chastisement of her perfidy, thought the French consul.

Sounds like a war party now, thought Fletcher.

4 Shortly before 10:00pm, Augustus Fitch lightly tapped again on his wineglass with a dessert spoon.

"Ladies and gentlemen, sitting rooms just down the corridor have been prepared, one with brandy and cigars for the gentlemen, and the other with light refreshment for the ladies. More refreshments are in the ballroom, where the Royal Marine band will play another hour for dancing."

Once more gallants came to the assistance of ladies navigating their ungainly hoops from between table and chair, offered their arms, and escorted them out of the dining room and into the ballroom, or down the hallway to the door of their sitting room. Some others of the dinner party cordially begged off and, claiming the lateness of the hour and the demands of the following day, returned to their ships, hongs, and hotels, or repaired to more nefarious haunts. A few remained chatting at table; those not a part of the brandy-and-cigar crowd went down to the bar; the rest sauntered into the room appointed for their after-dinner ritual. As the last of the brandy-and-cigar men left the dining room, Fletcher and Hugh rose and followed them.

Beyond the windows, the sky was stygian black, as if the river below was not the Whangpoo, but the Styx. Occasionally a bright arc of white lightning split the black night. Inside the room, a bright fire burnt in a fireplace at one end of the room and together with moderator oil lamps on console tables reflected warm light throughout. Plush leather-covered overstuffed chairs were drawn into circles for conversation and bottles of Hennessy's Pale Brandy and decanters of port and Madeira were set out on a sideboard with gleaming snifters and boxes of cigars and cheroots. A Chinese boy stood beside the sideboard ready to fetch drinks.

A fleet of Augustus Fitch & Company ship captains sailed right into the room, took on cargoes of brandy and cigars, navigated to a corner table, pulled up chairs, then brought out cards and got up a game of whist.

"Cavendish rules?"

"Of course."

Standing at a window, Fletcher watched the light flashing over the dark river, briefly illuminating the silhouettes of square-rigged ships. Elias Cage joined him.

"Mr. Wood, we Americans here in Shanghai are men of business, and guests, as it were, of a powerful nation that takes responsibility for representing the Western powers to the Chinese authorities, and for securing and preserving order in our Settlement. The representatives of the Queen graciously consult with our consuls and, as landholders and ratepayers, we have a voice in the management of the Settlement, but it is always *sotto voce* in deference to the very real fact of British leadership in Shanghai. We do not feel it our place to delve deeply into military and political topics that are rightly the affair of the Queen's officers. Our custom is to confine our conversation to matters of business and related subjects."

"And you believe I should do the same?"

"This is a small community, and the behavior of any one of us reflects on all Americans here. Life is easier when we all are more cordial."

"A word to the wise?"

"I can only hope so."

Conversation ebbed with departures and flowed as empty chairs filled. Imbibed liquor, and the late hour, began to have a liberating effect on discourse, and a few guests even began to slip the common constraints of ceremony. The representatives of the Court of Saint James took up positions on one flank of the Americans, and representatives of the Court of the Tuileries occupied the chairs opposite the English. The French General Claude de Montpellier and Minister Alphonse de Bourboulon engaged in a hushed but spirited argument.

"*Enrichissez-vous, voila ma devise!* Become rich, that is my motto!" de Montpellier said, clenching his fists. The fringe of the yellow epaulets of his uniform flew about with his flamboyant gestures. "But before riches, glory. France demands glory. The emperor demands glory, and great conquests. So, what will Paris think of Chushan? Nothing." The general waved his empty palms. Few who did not know de Montpellier well ever noticed the sneer beneath his thick dark mustache.

"Nothing? At all?" de Bourboulon said with a sigh. He was long accustomed to the general's acerbity. The French minister was easily the smallest man in the room, even smaller than the Chinese boy, but de Bourboulon was agile and precise. His sharp perception missed little and, had his tongue been a rapier, the halls of the French court would long since have been littered with the victims of his riposte.

"*Rien est rien*! Nothing is nothing!" de Montpellier said. "They rowed out to our ships and said 'here, please take the key to the city.' There was no fighting. It was just a waste of time, and men, and supplies and money. And the place is of no use – it is too isolated. We would be better provisioned out of Shanghai. Closer as well to Soochow."

"Shanghai is too small, too crowded. And what is your idea about Soochow?"

"We must defend the city. We cannot allow the Catholics there to be butchered by the Taiping."

"We shall see," de Bourboulon said with another sigh.

"You give me no battles to win, and no authority to win them. Why must I share authority with Baron Galle? He knows nothing of military affairs, and will simply be in the way."

"The baron has much experience, and the army must have a political conscience," de Bourboulon said.

"Political conscience," the general hissed. "*Vous me ferez raison de ce mystere,* you will have to explain to me this mystery."

"*N'en parlons plus,*" the French minister said, "let us speak no more of this. Others are listening."

"Minister Blaine," Consul Shanks said, "I read in the Herald that your Mr. Herbert believes that the Treaty of Tientsin is a *fait accompli*. That seems inconsistent with the situation here in China."

"Yes, well, I believe tha' Mr. Herbert was referring to the House of Commons, where both sides of the House have accepted the treaty. It is a *fait accompli* in England. We just have not yet convinced the Chinese emperor."

"Prime Minister Palmerston," said Shanks, "appears quite optimistic that the emperor is in a state of mind to make an apology to Great Britain, and that perhaps hostilities will not be necessary."

"No, no, no," General de Montpellier said. "There certainly will be the war. Even if the English resolve weakens, the Emperor of the French demands satisfaction. London is far behind events. They live in the ether."

"It is true," Minister Blaine said, "tha' news travels slowly to and from London. We have only jus' received word of the China debate in parliament in early March. Palmerston has na' yet heard tha' the Chinese emperor has refused my most recent terms. If the prime minister knew of this, he might be less optimistic."

"Palmerston evidently has been told that the Chinese emperor regards the fighting at the Peiho last summer as merely an incident, caused by an impetuous British commander. But the prime minister vindicates your action last year, Minister Blaine. That must be some gratification."

"Yes, it confers greater confidence in following one's instructions, doesn't it," Blaine said. "However, it seems tha' all the hubbub has been stirred up by – of all people – the Chinese themselves. They read the *Herald* in translation, learn about our quarrels in parliament, and then attempt to play one party off against another, and sway the opinion of the English people, just as in China they attempt to set one country against another. They recognize our factionalism because, of course, it is the same as theirs. It is as if the mandarins were sitting in the gallery of the House of Commons."

"It was Viceroy Ho's doing, I'm told," Consul Masters said. "He sent his lackeys to our merchants to say that the altercation was the fault of Minister Blaine – never the peace-loving Chinese – and that the minister should be sacked! The Chinese goaded certain of our traders," he said, glancing casually around the room, "who are always predisposed to favor the interests of their trading partners, to write letters home accusing the minister of starting a quarrel, thinking this would stir up sentiment for the minister's punishment. Then our precious *taotai* sends letters to the French consulate suggesting that the death of French troops in the fighting was the fault of Minister Blaine!"

"And so the Chinese try and drive the wedge between us," Minister de Bourboulon said. "Naturally, I recognize this as a tactic to pit the foreigners against each other. I have never thought Minister Blaine, or England, to blame for what happened at the Peiho. Only the fool would be taken in by this gambit."

"Thank you very much, your Excellency," the British minister said. "I am glad to have your confidence."

"The Chinese, they wriggle like the worm on the hook," de Bourboulon said. "Having experience only with barbarian tribes from the north, they mistake Frenchmen and English for the same. Curiously, the Chinese learn about our politics at home, that the English have the parliament and House of Lords and House of Commons, as if mandarins sit in the gallery, as you say. Yet they employ against us the same simple-minded tactics they use against nomad tribes, instead of sitting down at table and frankly discussing issues. They have no concept of the diplomacy. Perhaps they never will, not until they learn there are many countries, and not just one emperor of the whole world."

The circle of diplomats quieted. The drone of conversations from other quarters drifted around the room. The laughter of the ladies swirled in from the next room.

"Augustus has a very good idea here," Allan Howe said to his griffin Rudolph Frazer, the amiable-looking youth with wavy blond hair. Howe was tall and portly, with hazel eyes, graying hair and muttonchops. He wore a black double-breasted frock coat, brocaded waistcoat of dark blue satin, with a gold watch chain. They sat together in a small circle with their guest for the evening Aleksandr Rastopof, captain of the Russian bark *Potemkin.*, and several other Howe & Company ship captains: Wiley of *Union*, Holmes of *Progressive Age*, Smith of *Fanny McHenry*, and Hardy of *Mountain Wave*.

"A *soirée* for his daughter?" Frazer said.

"No, I mean gathering all these high nawobs and heap big chiefs to the feeding trough, stuffing them with wine and rare victuals, and getting in with them thick as thieves. Having those politicos in our waistcoat pocket would be better than any gold watch – think of the advantage we'd have over other taipans, access to information, influence on policy. Obviously, that is a next step, if I can become Russian *chargé d'affaires*, and can sway affairs for American benefit in the Shanghai consular meetings. Throwing shindys like this one for ministers and admirals at big hotels in the city would just get Howe & Company in all the more tighter with the powers that be around here."

"*Spasibo*," the Russian said, "thanks." He was swilling brandy as fast as the Chinese boy could fill his glass. The other captains looked on with mild amusement, nodding in response to his oafish grin, and wondering if perhaps the Russian empire had forfeited all its brandy in reparations after the Crimean War.

"I am lots drinking!" Rastopof gurgled in a deep, gruff voice. The Russian was thickset and solid, with short arms and legs, and appeared even larger in a woolen coat. His face was browned by the sun, thickly grained by wrinkles, and gnarled by wind and rain. Slav and Mongol struggled for precedence in his narrow eyes.

"Vhen sheep go on reever, make plenty mawney?"

Both Howe and Frazer were instantly alert and glanced about to be sure no one was in earshot. Fletcher noticed their agitation.

"Shhh, captain," Howe whispered. "No talk about that outside the office."

"*Da*, yes, beeg seecret."

Frazer recalled the conversation that morning with the Russian captain. They had told him that next year they would have their own steamer on the Yangtze.

"We call her the *Draco*, for the dragon in the sky, the constellation."

"Vhat kind sheep?" Rastopof said.

"*Draco* is a side-wheel paddle steamer, built of wood, 678 tons capacity. We secured subscriptions for $100,000 and put in the order last November."

"Gawns?"

"No, no guns – she a trader, not a gunboat. Howe & Company will be able to carry trade goods up the river and sell them at all the inland ports."

"Mehny steemers on reever?"

"After the treaty is ratified and the rebels are put down, there will be more steamers, but we will be among the very first and will be established before the others. The cream of the trade will be ours."

Tobias Wright, Russell & Company taipan, stopped by Allan Howe's chair.

"A word, Allan?" Howe nodded, smiled charitably at the Russian, and followed Wright to one end of the fireplace, out of earshot. Fletcher sat down in front of the fire.

"Allan, about that letter from General Ignatiev. I hope there is no misunderstanding about why I opened it. The letter was handed us by some native Christians, and was addressed to 'Our Consular Agent at Shanghai,' but there was no one on hand who read Russian. I surmised from 'Gowe' in the salutation that it was for you, knowing that H becomes G in Russian. Are you Russian consular agent, Allan?" Something was going on with the Russians in Peking. Old rival Abraham Howe & Company appeared to be bedding down with them.

"No matter, Tobias," Howe said. "Actually, I'm glad that you sent it along to me – in spite of our occasional disagreements. Rastopof said it was quite important – I assumed he is the consular agent it was meant for."

"The letter was to be forwarded to Rastopof, aboard *Potemkin*?" Howe would be a hard clam to pry open.

"Yes," Howe said, after a moment. "I took it to him." You're pushing the margin, Tobias – being Americans doesn't make us colleagues. Actually, Howe thought, the letter was a desperate call for help. Ignatiev wrote that ratification of the Russian treaty was stalemated in the face of China's imminent war with England and France, that he had told the Chinese he was being recalled to St Petersburg, and that he urgently requested a ship be sent north for him from Shanghai.

"And Rastopof will be leaving soon for the Peiho?"

"Well, I suppose he has to go somewhere, doesn't he?"

"Well, Allan, do I need a team of wild horses? Ignatiev is in Peking, isn't he?"

"That's no secret. The Russians have had a hostel there for a long time now."

Ostensibly a religious mission, Howe thought. From whence Ignatiev issues forth daily to conduct diplomatic relations with the Chinese empire. Not very successfully, though. The letter also said that the Chinese forbade Russian warships to come to the Peiho, and that Russians were not allowed to travel between the coast and Peking. The Chinese want Ignatiev to return overland. They are probably anxious the Russians will reconnoiter their fortifications at Taku and sell the information to the British.

"What is Ignatiev doing in Peking?"

"What do Russians do anywhere?"

If it got out, Howe thought, that the Russians had come overland to Peking with a shipment of fifty cannon and ten thousand rifles for the Taku forts, and were negotiating territorial concessions along the Amur River, all hell would break loose in the Settlement. And now General Ignatiev was as close to being held hostage in Peking as he could get without actually being shackled and imprisoned.

"Why would Rastopof go north to the Peiho?"

"He's loading a cargo of our tea is all I know." If Ignatiev has been recalled, he'll want *Potempkin* to come fetch him home, but you don't need to know that. Rostopov said there was some confusion over sending letters, and travel, and warships at the Peiho, there being no provisos in the treaty for such things. This is probably why the letter came the way it did, hand-carried by native Christians. I suppose the Chinese are nervous over their preparations for the coming war.

Well, Wright thought, maybe that confirms where *Potempkin* will go. "You're sure there's going to be a war, Allan?"

"I'm only sure that you know as much as I."

"D'you think they are talking about us?" Jeremy Whitfall said with a smile.

The Howe ship captains had helped Captain Rastopof stagger out of the hotel and had returned to their ships. Howe, Frazer and Wright looked about for a welcome, sensed a pulsing animus at the center of the diplomatist's circle, then joined Whitfall, Cage and Cummings in a cabal of taipans.

"Let them speak of whomever they please," Cage said. "They will soon be gone, while we remain."

"That Wood fellow does not look like he plans to leave soon," the *Herald* editor said. "Does anyone know what are his intentions?"

"He's a nobody," Whitfall said. "Having a moment of glory. He's no concern."

"Under most circumstances I would agree. His kind washes up in Shanghai, drifts through Bamboo Town, and disappears. However, our Mr. Wood's reputation precedes him. I cannot help but wonder about the motives of a notorious filibuster in a chaotic place like China, and about the kind of trouble he could stir up."

"All I have heard," Howe said, "is that Shanks released him to Augustus."

"He has been taken aboard that Chinese steamer *Confucius*," Wright said.

"Rumor says *Confucius* is about to run opium up to Nanking," Frazer said.

"Rumor says Takee has opened a large account at Fogg's," Whitfall said. "For the quiet purchase of firearms. What does a banker want with arms?"

"Firearms!" Cummings said. "If they are for Takee, then they are for the *taotai*. The one does not pour tea that the other does not drink. The *taotai* might be preparing to arm more braves, or the governor."

Fletcher appeared behind Frazer's chair.

"Gentlemen. Why not put to my face the questions you ask behind my back, and we can clear up any confusion as fast as alum clears muddy water? Of course, I am the guest of honor but, as Mr. Fitch is out of earshot, we can dispense with formalities."

After a moment's hesitation, in which several of the taipans quietly seethed over the effrontery of this common sailor who, before this fortuitous night, could not beg their slops, the *Herald* editor finally dared rise to the provocation.

"Very well, since you insist, I was wondering what intentions you might have here in China, Mr. Wood, considering your reputation as a filibuster with the notorious William Walker. Quite frankly, we here are opposed to filibustering, and our community will not abide it. We do not wish to have here the kind of wicked depredations that are committed by lawless soldiers of fortune."

Fletcher wearily sensed again the diaspora of prejudice that emanated from the office of the American consul and had spread through the Settlement like a cholera – bloated remarks that had to be kept at arm's length to avoid pollution.

"Gentlemen, believe me, I have never entertained thoughts of a career as a filibuster. That business with William Walker was an indiscretion of long ago, a misunderstanding that still dogs my steps wherever I go."

"Understandably so," Whitfall said. "People believe the leopard cannot change its spots, and that a fox may grow gray, but never good."

You are one to talk, thought Fletcher. Depredations! As if your lying, swindling and smuggling does not sap the life of Chinamen, steal their land, and rob their wealth. You damned hypocrites! You're all in it together, one hand washing the other, journalist and trader, Pilate and Sanhedrin.

"We do not require mercenaries, Mr. Wood," Cummings said. "If the rebel army comes here, we will be ready for them, and they will find out that our volunteers can dispatch a rebel as easily as a bird on the wing. But before that happens, we here in Shanghai have no need for troublemakers gallivanting about the countryside stirring up the rage of the Taiping and causing them to take revenge upon our settlement."

"Is that what you expect of me?"

"That, or that you might join the rebels."

"Quite a few ex-seamen are in their employ now," Cage said.

"Yes, and tomorrow all you taipans will join the clergy."

"You're spending your little bit of credit rapidly."

"Getting up a vigilance committee?"

"No need for that – we are the law."

"What law is that? Lynch law?"

"You are pushing your luck."

"Lady luck is too capricious."

"You have missed my meaning."

"Perhaps you were too vague."

"Men disappear every day," Whitfall said.

"In the hold of Jardine ships?"

"Who knows?"

The Fitch Soirée

洋神 *Yang Shen*   *James Lande* 藍德

"We'll see."

5   A large crystal chandelier brightened the ladies' salon. Brass candelabra and moderator oil lamps glowed on console tables around the perimeter of the room. Large windows looked out over the confluence of creek and river and up the Whangpoo. Elizabeth could see dim lights in the windows of banks and hongs along the waterfront, and yellow lanterns flickering in wisps of river fog drifting through the anchorage.

"Imagine," Elizabeth said to her mother. "There were no casualties at Chushan."

"Sounds like they just walked into the Chinese parlor and sat themselves down."

"If the Chinese are going to be so gracious, perhaps there will be no war after all."

"Chinese are always gracious, dear, but Chushan is a long way from Peking."

The walls of the room were paneled below with dark mahogany and, above, the dado was covered in French flowered damask. Overstuffed chairs – their lions-paw feet discretely draped by print covers – and rosewood end and tea tables were arranged in a wide circle around a plush deep-purple pile-knotted carpet with gold-crowned rampant lions woven into the borders. A blazing fireplace at one end of the room faced a gilt-trimmed white pianoforte against the wall opposite, at which Mrs. Wright was softly playing a Chopin étude while Mrs. Hayes turned pages of sheet music. Ladies still up for the dancing came and went between the ballroom and the sitting room.

"Where is Yeddo?" Elizabeth said.

"In the Japans," Hannah said.

"One of those traders told me that each night they must carefully inspect the residences of the foreign ministers to look for strangers hiding in the shadows, and combustibles secreted on the grounds during the day, to be used for burning down the buildings after dark. The regent of the country was attacked and beheaded by some prince, and even the British minister's Japanese servant was murdered. Is it going to be like that here in Shanghai?"

"That would be Mr. Wetmore," Hannah said. "He's just returned from the Japans. The political state of affairs there is confused and very dangerous, and living conditions are not so advanced as in our Model Settlement here at Shanghai. Foreigners in Japan are at much greater personal risk."

Hot tea, chilled lemonade, ginger beer, and sarsaparilla were set out on a sideboard with desserts from the dinner: puddings, custards, pastries, and a variety of cheese with crackers, more blancmange, oranges, figs, raisins and walnuts. Several young Chinese girls in livery passed the refreshments *a la Russe* among the ladies.

"They are so slender and graceful, the Chinese women," Elizabeth said.

"Oh, Miss Fitch!" Mrs. Fogg said. "You have arrived at just the right time! Why, our season's just starting up here in Shanghai. The gardens are about to bloom, the races are ready to start, and new amateur theatricals are being performed."

Mrs. Fogg, a mercantile wife, was perhaps ten years older than Elizabeth. The only guests not in trade, the Foggs were slightly outside the pale of the established taipan circle, and gravitated to the new arrivals. Elizabeth Fitch was, of course, the youngest of the ladies. Most were of her mother's generation.

"And for who knows how long, we'll have all these grand men-o-war back and forth between Hong Kong and the north. They are all of them simply packed with dashing young British in their scarlet tunics, and French naval officers and marines, who will come ashore and compete for the privilege of escorting young ladies of Shanghai to our many cultural events."

"Thank you, Mrs. Fogg," Elizabeth said. "I am so glad to hear this. I truly had no idea of what to expect when I set sail from America."

"Did you have a pleasant trip out, Miss Fitch?" Mrs. Sassoon said.

Hannah smiled blandly as she watched her daughter with rising concern. Elizabeth might not realize that her character was being appraised by these innocent questions, that her gold was being assayed to determine her quality.

"The novelty fled after a few days," Elizabeth said, "and left only increasing monotony until we reached Cape Horn. There we had a month of abject terror as we were passed about from one storm to the next. At times, the waves were so high I might have fallen out of bed over my feet. In the Pacific Ocean, we sailed back into monotony – the ship may have been moving, but mother and I were in the doldrums."

"The crew of course," Hannah said, "had work to keep them busy. The male passengers observed the operation of the ship, and even pitched in with the work." Don't be carried away, Elizabeth – if you cannot manufacture some semblance of modesty and reserve, and deference, you risk losing the regard of the small community of Western women here whose consideration could make life more convenient and enjoyable, even if aggravating. If you are rash or patronizing, these ladies will set you aside. And Heaven help you if you blurt out again the name of that English pirate.

"However," Elizabeth said, "to women accustomed to the daily enterprise of running a household or, as in my case, the stimulation of attending lectures, and calling on friends and receiving guests, newspapers, gossip, letters and what-have-you, the confined life of a woman at sea is an awful bore. Reading and sewing change from pastime to refuge. Had I neglected to bring along Mr. Darwin and Mr. Dickens I'm sure I would have gone stark-staring mad."

Hannah wondered what she had been thinking – how could Elizabeth not say anything that came into her pea-brained head? She tried to give her daughter a sign she was overboard already.

"How do you like Shanghai so far?" Mrs. Dent said.

"When we arrived, China seemed a kind of Longfellow-land of strange people and places with curious names – by the shores of the gitchee-goomee, and such. But a fellow passenger thought the notion unsound, and that gentility might not thrive here."

"Well, it can be a struggle," Mrs. Dent said, anticipating her opinion would be shared by all present, and confident that her audience would tolerate without demurrer another aspersion on the character of Chinese. "These Chinese are filthy, heathen beggars, to whom the idea of gentility would be bizarre, and I often wonder how I am expected to live among them!"

"Ah, what passenger told you this, Miss Fitch?" Mrs. Whitfall said.

"Our guest of honor tonight, Fletcher Thorson Wood."

"Oh, my goodness!" Mrs. Whitfall said. "The American filibuster!"

"You would do better to avoid such as him, my dear," Mrs. Dent said.

"Oh, yes, like the plague," Mrs. Sassoon said.

"He should be deported from Shanghai."

"He should be expelled from China."

"The Bastille is too good for his kind."

The Fitch Soirée

洋神 *Yang Shen*   James Lande 藍德

Dramatis Personae: Chapter 14

Old Huang 老黃 (Lao Huang)	Yangtze river pilot, *Confucius*
Yang Hsi-hai 陽喜海	pirate-suppressing mandarin, *Confucius*
Chester Hicks	passenger, Shanghai businessman

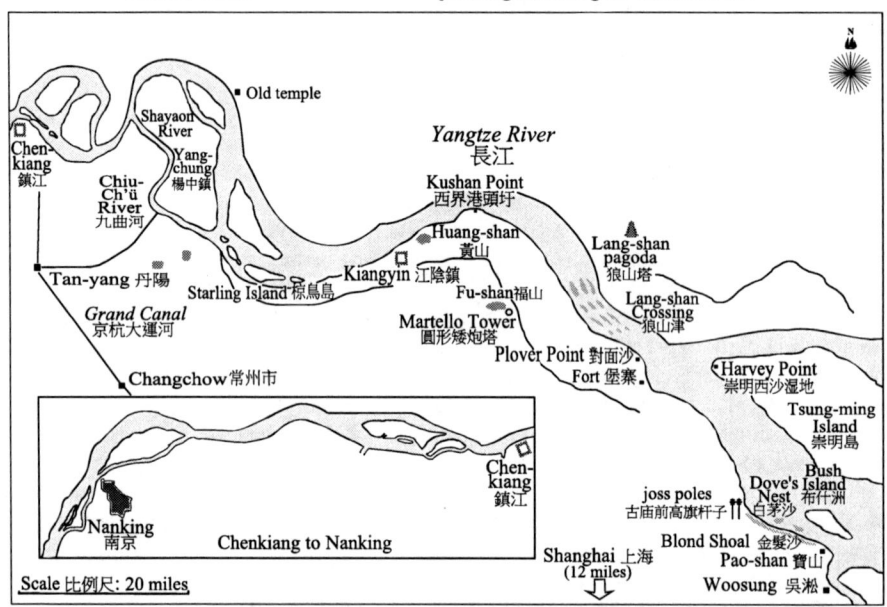

Yangtze River, Woosung to Chen-chiang (Chenkiang)
(based on British Hydrographic Office chart, China., Sheet IX, 1842)

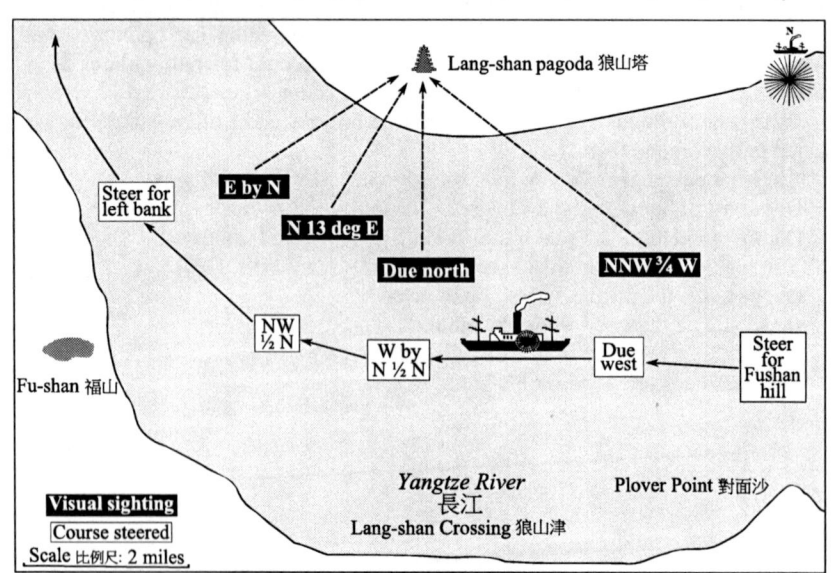

Directions for the Langshan crossing
(based on S. Wells Williams, *The Chinese Commercial Guide*, 1863. Sailing Directions, p. 146-8)

The Lower Reaches

洋神 *Yang Shen*   *James Lande* 藍德

Chapter 14: The Lower Reaches
Sunday, April 29, 1860, 12:00pm

Confucius came to life with people moving on her decks, wheezing smoke and steam, and seeping the odor of burning coal into the air. The first mate came up out of the hold, made a turn around the foredeck, then climbed the ladder to the wheelhouse.

"Last of the ammunition and powder's secure, Captain," Fetcher said.

"Good. I told Macanaya to have his crew aboard after *tiffin*."

"Schnapps says all the black gang is aboard. Any passengers yet?"

"We are still shy our Chinese pilot, our official pirate-suppressing mandarin – the bureau's agent and a source of great entertainment aboard *Confucius* – and two passengers, Fitch's comprador and a Mr. Chester Hicks. If the full company is not aboard by 1:00pm, start sending crewmen out to round them up. Macanaya's men know where to find them. I want to be underway by 2:00pm."

Deep in the belly of *Confucius*, the black gang set about getting up steam. Old Schnapps opened the feed valves to start water into the boilers, and opened the gauge cocks to let air out through them. While the boilers filled, the stokers cleared the furnace firebox and ash pit of ash and began to lay the fires. Coal was spread evenly over the firebox grating from front to back in a layer of about four inches. More coals were piled at the front, and kindling was set over them and waste oakum placed beneath the wood. The oakum was set afire and the furnace doors closed. When the coals were completely ignited, the furnace doors were opened for the greatest draft and the burning coals pushed back over the other coal. The smokestack created a strong draw that quickly ignited all the coal. Old Schnapps opened the throttle a little to keep it from jamming when heat expanded the metal. He checked all the moving parts of the engine for sufficient clearance, and removed some wood shims left from repairs. He blew the glass to be sure the glass water gauge reading would be correct, then as he limped about he kept the gauge in view to be sure the water level stayed right.

The official pirate-suppressing mandarin came aboard without summons. He arrived quietly at dockside in a sedan chair carried by two bearers, and dismounted with all the dignity his rotund configuration would allow. The arrival of their mandarin, always in the full regalia the officials stubbornly insisted upon wearing at sea and upon the river, was ever a novelty aboard *Confucius* and all eyes were upon him immediately. Atop his shaved forehead a black-lacquered straw hat, covered in long red fringe and topped by a gold button, balanced like an upside-down salad bowl. Over a long light-blue gown, he wore a dark-blue jacket with large, square embroidered emblems of rank front and back. A string of large precious stones hung down his chest, and several embroidered pouches dangled from a silver belt – the possible contents of the pouches always excited the curiosity of onlookers. A pair of white-soled blue velvet boots served as the substantial foundation of his rig. Alone and without ceremony, he bravely clambered up the gangway under his own wheezing steam, grasping the rope hand-over-hand. At the top of the gangway, he stood swaying for a moment before stepping down. Once on deck, his pudgy hands disappeared inside his long sleeves and reappeared only when the ship lurched and he grabbed for furniture to help him stay upright. The captain met the mandarin with a courteous bow and escorted him into the saloon.

Runners took word to the Fitch passengers and, before long, they came together in sedan chairs surrounded by a heavily armed guard of twenty men winding down the Bund from the Augustus Fitch & Company offices. Chester Hicks was a stout, middle-aged man in a brown coat trimmed with black velvet, and a gray top hat. The coat he

洋神 *Yang Shen* *James Lande* 藍德

exchanged for a more practical buff canvas jacket once in the saloon. The other passenger was a young, slim Chinese in a black skullcap and modest black jacket over a long dark-blue gown. His name, Fletcher was told, was Tang Sung-kee, called Ah-sang or Sankey by the captain, and he was the son of Fitch's Chinese comprador. Sankey came aboard accompanied by four burley servants dressed in like manner, but armed with broad Chinese cutlasses in scabbards strapped to their backs, and short muskets slung over their shoulders. Between them, they carried two small wooden chests that presumably contained the treasure to pay for cargo upriver. The captain greeted Sankey with a courteous bow, they shook hands foreigner-style, and the party was escorted into the saloon. The chests were taken into the captain's cabin, secured in a heavy safe there, and guards posted at the door with swords drawn to discourage the curious.

The Chinese pilot, a slender round-faced Cantonese in black Western-style trousers and a smelly old black pea coat, was the last to come aboard, having been delayed by his previous charge. As the pilot entered the wheelhouse, the captain greeted him with a sarcastic flourish.

"Welcome aboard, Mr. Huang. Nice of you to come along with us. Make yourself comfortable over there by the fire. Have some tea."

Huang just grinned at Fletcher and shook his head. "Catchee one dum' sumbitch cap'n. Too dum' savee pote not stahb'd, catchee *chow-chow* watah at ol' livah, kissum big gunboat, takee 32-poundah down mouth likee lovee-dovee sing-song gel, sing plenti high note now goddamn."

"Oh, that's a great one," Ghent said. "Who helped you think up that whopper? Meet Fletcher Wood, my new mate. This here's Old Huang, pilot, such as he is."

Huang tugged vigorously at Fletcher's yardarm. "Yoo 'melican, Fechawood?"

"'Bout as 'melican as they come," Fletcher said.

"Good! Need 'melican mate keep company fo' cap'n. Talkee lingo allo samee plenti much homeside scutt'butt," which Fletcher interpreted to mean, "speak the same language so they could talk over the news from home." While he said this, Old Huang fished a greasy porcelain teacup out of his coat pocket, stood on a chair and filled the cup half-full of tea leaves from a dented tin painted with black dragons he fetched down from a shelf above the small coal stove. He soaked the tea leaves in boiling water poured from a battered pot heating atop the stove, then plopped into a chair beside the stove and savored the aroma of the steeping tea. "Need cap'n savee pote-side not stahb'd-side, too," he said, grinning from behind his teacup.

The captain just smirked and shook his head. "Peckerwood."

"What yoo las' ship, Fechawood?"

Fletcher just pointed to *Essex*.

"Ahhh. Bad time on dat ship. Lots bad pilot. All bad pilot China coas' come good ship Ah-sacks. Bad Chinee pilot, got killum dead. Bad 'melican pilot stinkee dlunk allo time, lie, steal. Cheat ca'ds, too. Yoo takee close lookee heah, Fechawood," he said, tapping his finger on his chin, "at Ol' Huang. Cap'n Get, Ol' Huang longtime flen' many yeah. My save Cap'n Get ass, Cap'n Get save Ol' Huang ass. Ol' Huang save *K'ung-fu-tze* ass plenti time. You no shootum Ol' Huang, hokay? Mebbe sumday Ol' Huang save Fechawood ass, too, whatchatinkee?"

Fletcher laughed. "Hokay, Ol' Huang. No shootum pilot this time out. We'll just shoot pirates."

For a moment, Old Huang was serious. "Fechawood, sumtime pi-*lot* an' pi-*rate* belly close, hard to tell apot. Yoo savee diffahlence?"

"Sure. Pi-*rates* 'r always tryin' to sink me, get my feet wet. Pi-*lots* 'r always tryin' to keep me afloat, keep my feet dry."

洋神 *Yang Shen*   *James Lande* 藍德

Old Huang raised his teacup in a toast. "Dly fleet," he said, with a twinkle in his eyes that made Fletcher wonder if the pun wasn't intentional.

Below deck, the fires in the heart of the old Dutchman rose like the fires under his boilers, and he hobbled about more spryly to see that his gang had the boilers filled, and the fires properly laid and lit. He checked the gauge cocks and safety valves were closed, and the water level in the boilers was correct. The firebox doors, compartment doors, and hatches were flung open to send fresh air into the fires, the lubricator wicks were trimmed, and the engines cranked a few revolutions by hand. As the smokestack expanded with heat, coolies ran up on deck to loosen the funnel stays. Steam pressure slowly built toward twenty pounds, and the steam gauge rose past 3, 4, then 5 inches.

In the wheelhouse, the captain sounded his telegraph bell and set the pointer to **AHEAD SLOW** on the annunciator dial, and Old Schnapps yanked on his telegraph lever to sound the answering bell and set his pointer to **AHEAD SLOW**. Schnapps dropped the hooks to engage the long rods connected to the shaft that opened and closed the valves automatically with each turn of the shaft. The paddle wheels turned a few slow revolutions. Every three seconds the huge piston rose and fell and, above the piston, the enormous iron frame of the diamond-shaped walking beam rocked on its axis. Black smoke poured out of the stack and clouds of steam began to rise from the engine.

"You're burning up all my goddamn coal," the captain shouted into the wheelhouse voice pipe.

"Good head of steam to start up in this narrow river is worth a bushel of your *godverdomme* coal, *oetlul* captain," muttered the engineer. "Where will you be if you lose steam in the middle of a crowded roadstead, eh?"

At 3:00pm, *Confucius* started up her shrill whistle at intervals as she slowly maneuvered herself away from the dock, through the crowd of lighters and sampans, past the northernmost tier of merchantmen moored off the British Bund, and over to the Whangpoo ship channel below Soochow Creek.

With the wind on her stern and the tidal current beginning to ebb, *Confucius* set out north down the Whangpoo, skipped across the inner bar at the place where she knew there was always at least twelve feet of water, and just over an hour later came up on the opium hulks at the Woosung anchorage. Ghent slowed *Confucius* in center channel, brought her about, pointed her back upstream, and then drifted her across the slow current to a position just above *Ann Walsh*. Fletcher let go the anchor, and the steamer slowly came alongside the receiving ship. The captain ordered the starboard paddle wheel disengaged, and kept the larboard paddle wheel revolving slightly at dead slow to counter the drift of the stern with only one anchor in the mud.

Gangplanks were run out, and Sankey and two of his men lurched across and boarded *Ann Walsh* carrying one of Sankey's small wooden chests of treasure. Shortly afterward, crewmen from the two vessels began carrying over to *Confucius* fifty chests of Malwa opium. The captain closely supervised topside, to be certain no part of the cargo disappeared over the rail. Below deck, Fletcher carefully directed the stowage of the opium in the forward hold, and discouraged any pilferage.

A half-hour later Fletcher started up the steam winch and weighed anchor. *Confucius* re-engaged her starboard paddle wheel, swung about into the stream, and rambled carelessly downriver out over the shallowest channel through the outer bar. Fletcher watched his crew secure the foredeck, then went to the wheelhouse where he found Chester Hicks with the captain and the pilot. Hicks popped the cork off an iced bottle of Perrier & Jonet champagne, poured into chilled glasses for all, and toasted the journey.

"Large profits," Hicks said.

The Lower Reaches

洋神 *Yang Shen*   *James Lande* 藍德

"Deep water," Ghent said.
"Confusion to the enemy," Fletcher said.
"一路平安 peaceful journey," Old Huang said.

Confucius came about to NW¼W from the red buoy off Woosung, opposite Bush Island, twelve miles north of Shanghai, and began churning up the broad Yangtze. Old Huang told Fletcher the Yangtze was called the *ch'ang-chiang* 長江 by Chinese, the Long River, or by the older name *ta-chiang* 大江, the Great River.

"You come long livah befo', Fetchawood?"
"Never past Woosung."
"Plenti long livah, many name, many big town. Livah go allo way big snowy high mountain, ten-t'ousand *li*. Staht belly littee, call *chin-sha chiang* 金沙江, Gold Sand Livah. Changem by-an'-by to *ch'uan-chiang* 川江, Ssü-ch'uan Livah. Dat part middah livah. Den come Long Livah, same name Big Livah. Hab got *ch'ung-ch'ing* 重慶, yi-chang 宜昌, han-k'ou 漢口, nan-ching 南京, shang-hai 上海, allo big town."

Old Schnapps stood at the controls aft of the house fussing over his engine, keeping vigil over the glass water gauge, and feeling the bearings with his hands for overheating. He also watched the Chinese oilers closely to be sure they tended the lubricators, oiled the bearings and connecting rods, and lubricated all the different pumps.

After an hour of steaming against a two-knot current abetted by the ebbing tide, the vast reach of water began finally to narrow from six miles wide and the suggestions of shoreline emerged north and south. The steamer kept toward the south shore until the pilot pointed to a clump of trees on the mainland.

"Blon' Sho', Cap'n," the pilot said.
"This is the approach to Blond Shoal, Mr. Wood," the captain said. "Go forward and heave the lead. Watch for the joss poles I told you about."

Fletcher found the water along the bank shallowed gently from six fathoms, to five, then to four fathoms. *Confucius* followed this channel northwest, guided carefully by Fletcher's soundings. The high embankment that held back flood waters from village and field concealed all useful landmarks except two slender joss poles that sometimes could be seen above the embankment when a vessel had cleared the end of Blond Shoal. But there was not enough light so late in the day to see the poles. *Confucius* had to continue sounding for the end of the shoal, then steer NNE on an approach for Tsungming Island. She could only hope to come up short of the Dove's Nest, another menacing swarm of shoals where two vessels of Lord Exter's expedition up the Yangtze, *Cruizer* and *Furious*, went aground in 1858.

Like an old blind woman tapping her cane on cobblestones, *Confucius* bumped her lead along the bottom of the Yangtze, gingerly feeling her way across the river toward the Dove's Nest. For all the experience guiding her, she could not know if she would find her depth in time to veer away from the ravenous grasp of the river.

Fletcher sounded six fathoms and sang out, and Ghent violently threw the wheel over and came about to NNW½W, sounded the bell and shouted "full speed, pour it on Schnapps!" into the wheelhouse voice pipe. The captain peered intently into the heart of his brass compass, gripping the wheel and steering desperately to match his steamer's course to those fine black lines waving about on the compass face. *Confucius* surged against the ebbing current, her huge paddle wheels churning enormous froth, edging her way along the treacherous banks, and this time did not go aground. Gradually, she pushed her way over into the deeper channel that would take her up to Plover Point another hour away. Blond Shoal and the Dove's Nest fell behind her, but they would be there waiting when she returned.

Fletcher left Macanaya in charge on the fore deck during the next stretch of quiet water and went to the saloon. The bureau's mandarin sat stiffly on one side of the spartan room, wedged uncomfortably between a narrow table bolted to the floor and the padded bench along the wall, and sipped at tea served by the Chinese steward. Sankey sat opposite, silently between his bristling guards, his eyes closed as if asleep. Chester Hicks waved a greeting and, after pouring himself a cup of water, Fletcher joined Hicks at a table near the door.

"Nice little bit of river you got us over there, Mr. Wood," Hicks said. "Seems the old admiral has got himself a good mate again."

American, Fletcher quickly surmised – northerner, sounds like New York, and in trade. "You've sailed with him before, then."

"Only way to get upriver without losing your hair, this steamer. The admiral's brought out many a cargo of tea and silk for me."

"I thought foreigners are not allowed to go inland. Have you been to Nanking?"

"Certainly. And beyond all the way to Hankow, too. That's the advantage of knowing the right Chinese, those with their own armed steamers and foreign captains. Mandarins along the river may object that foreigners are out of bounds beyond Shanghai, but they can do nothing unless they have imperial war junks to send out after us. In which case, we send a little silver on a short journey across some imperial junk commander's palm and consequently I would guess *Confucius* is always reported to be too swift to be apprehended."

"What exactly is your business, if you don't mind my asking?"

"No one here will ever tell you exactly about their business, Mr. Wood. Business here is all done with the deepest, darkest secrecy and you can trust only that someone will always be listening to discover your secrets and steal away your trade with a better offer. But this much I will tell you, I came to China years back eager to introduce a brand of machines for dredging the rivers and, finding only occasional success, I have since branched out into a number of other enterprises. Yesterday, I may have introduced a buyer to a seller for a fee, tomorrow I may receive a consignment of ladies undergarments for the fashionable salons of Shanghai, but today I am assisting with brokering the purchase of a cargo of tea. A man of many trades, Mr. Wood, that is me, with income from so many sources, I can hardly keep track of the thousands, or perhaps millions, I am owed. Can't stop to count it all while the play is still on, but I seem to never lack for a soft brandy and a sweet cigar." Hicks withdrew a cheroot from an embossed leather case he took from inside his jacket and offered it to Fletcher.

"Isn't brokering tea a comprador's business? And I thought Fitch did not tolerate traffic in opium, so why do we have fifty chests of the weed on board *Confucius*?"

"Well, sir, you are now a principal in this enterprise, so you are entitled to know more, especially since this transaction is already underway and unlikely to become common knowledge throughout the settlement after a night of carousing on the Bund. As for the comprador, the sleepy gentleman on your left, flanked by his menacing minions, is merely the son of the Fitch house comprador. Still a little wet behind the ears, as we would say, quite young yet to be carrying $150,000 Mex in treasure inland and dealing on his own with opium smugglers, imperial officers, and rebel generals. The arrangements for this trip were made in haste and, as the father is still upcountry himself on other business, the son was accepted in his father's place, with the proviso that I accompany the son, and provide him with the benefit of my experience, both on the river and in these dealings."

Hicks twisted out from behind the small table and motioned for Fletcher to follow him out on deck. In the fading twilight, the shoreline was barely visible, and only the occasional torch of a small craft and the lanterns of the cormorant fishers flecked the dark river with points of light. The two men stood at the rail, while they talked and smoked, and watched the black birds come and go under the sallow lantern-light glowing about the fishing sampans. The racket from the incessant rocking of the clangorous walking beam muffled their voices.

"Do you know much about the trade in tea, Mr. Wood?"

"No more than necessary to carry tea to Hong Kong on occasion."

"It is a fascinating subject, full of romance and adventure, if one is inclined to view the world in such terms. Each year there are several crops of tea from the Bohea district in Fukien province. The first crop, on the market in April, is the most important, and the Fitch comprador was upcountry in March with advances on this crop we are to bring down. With tea, as with silk, the sellers often require partial payment in opium, which can be difficult to purchase upcountry, and with so many competitors chasing after the crop, one has little choice but to carry the drug."

"In spite of the sentiments over at New Jerusalem."

"Exactly. In consideration of his feelings, Augustus Fitch is simply not told the details of exchange. By the time he has read in his ledgers of the opium traded, it is too late for anything but the remonstrations of hypocrites. Before this season is over, Augustus Fitch & Company will send nearly a half million dollars upcountry, paying five to six dollars for each half-chest of pekoe, oolong and souchong tea. I will show you more about the tea when we take our cargo on board. This crop we are buying is brought overland from the more northerly parts of the tea district around Taiping, in Anhwei province, and sent down to the Yangtze to Wuhoo."

"Is that is our destination, then – Wuhoo?"

"Yes. Coming back, we will pay duties to the rebels at Nanking, and again at Shanghai when the tea is landed at the Fitch godowns. If it cannot be avoided we may also have to pay something I will not grace with the name 'duty' to imperialist scavengers and pirates on the way downriver."

"Isn't Wuhoo in the hands of the rebels?"

"Yes. The town of Wuhoo is the last reach of the ocean tides, and the last reach as well of the rebel stranglehold on the river above Nanking. But imp or rebel, all the Chinese along that part of the Yangtze are anxious to trade in arms and opium."

Another hour of steaming carried *Confucius* past the small village and solitary tree that on the chart marked Harvey Point, then upriver ten more miles to Plover Point, forty-six miles west of Shanghai. The last light of day was already gone from the sky, and only a few dim yellow lanterns stippled the darkness surrounding another small village and the breastworks of an old abandoned fort low on the right bank. The pilot's landmarks at best were shadowy in the dim light of the half-moon, and often shrouded in darkness by cover of clouds. So, even though Captain Ghent had run this part of the river in the dark more than once, no urgency pressed them to take the risk on this night. *Confucius* was turned out of the stream and brought to anchor in seven fathoms of quiet water, not far from the colored lanterns and domestic clatter of Chinese fishermen and traders living aboard their boats in the junk anchorage at Plover Point.

Old Schnapps released hot water from the boilers then started up the donkey engine to gradually pump cold water back in to cool the boilers without precipitating salts. When all the water was out, the boiler was blown through with steam, burning coal in the fireboxes was doused and ashes were hauled, and the engine wiped down. Melted tallow was poured into the grease-cups round the piston rods to keep dirt out of the

洋神 *Yang Shen*   James Lande 藍德

glands that prevented fluids from leaking past joints in the machinery. The old Dutchman examined the lubricators, slide-rod end bearings, paddle-shaft outer bearings, piston glands, and supervised the tightening of the holding-down bolts. When the smokestack cooled, coolies went up on deck to tighten down the funnel stays.

A watch was posted – Sharps rifles and Colt revolvers fore and aft and in the waist. The rest of the deck crew and black gang were served supper and began a boisterous game of monte that lasted well into the night. The passengers were served supper too and, immediately afterward, Sankey and the pirate-suppressing mandarin retired to their cabins. Sankey's guards stretched out on the saloon benches until called for their next watch over the treasure. The captain, pilot, Old Schnapps, Chester Hicks, and Fletcher Wood conversed until a late hour over brandy and cigars in the wheelhouse, relating many stories of foreigners on the river, of the rebellion that raged along its banks, and of the often strange fate that brought the two together.

Log of Steamer CONFUCIUS, chartered by Augustus Fitch & Company

Date & Time	Location	Wind (est.)	Current	Speed	Cargo
Sunday April 29 1860 9:00pm	Plover Point, Yangtze R, Kiangsu	NW 3 knots	3 knots	8 knots	Tea

2 *Confucius* awoke the next morning to sheets of cold rain falling out of gray clouds rolling south over the river. The weather put her in a cranky mood, and she rolled about reluctantly in the muddy water, gobbled down shovels-full of black coal for breakfast, and finally worked up enough steam to come *sss-chunk…sss-chunk…sss-chunking* away from the shore. The pilot brought her to where the old fort at Plover Point was just about south of SW, then pointed into the west where in a glass Fletcher could see a low hill crested by white houses surrounded by trees.

"Fushan Hill 富山, Cap'n," the pilot said. "Closs ovah livah to Langshan 狼山 now. Mus' hab plenty small heart dis place, Fetchawood. Mus' be plenty kayfoo."

"Must be careful?" Fletcher said.

"Olo woof mountain plenty mean one piecee rivah, alla time wantche takee big bite outta *K'ung-fu-tze* bottomside!"

"Now we begin the Langshan Crossing, Mr. Wood," the captain said, "the most difficult of all the obstacles on the lower reaches. There should be a pilotage here, and there will be one day when there's more steamer traffic on the river. But until then, we thread our own needle. This mutton-headed pilot will tell you Langshan means wolf mountain, and that the crack-brained locals swear by Buddha's blood that the shallows 're haunted by the ghosts of hapless Chinese eaten by wolves that live in the river."

"Plenty woof *on* livah too, Fetchawood," Old Huang said with a grin.

"We steer for Fushan hill there in the west," Ghent said, "where that martello tower stands on the slope below, and at the same time watch the north shore for the Langshan pagoda to come into view atop the highest of three hills. She'll change course several times, according to our bearing on the pagoda, in order to make the crossing. We make a broad right turn with the direction of the river, steaming just enough to keep headway where the current meets the rising flood tide. All the while, we'll sound our depth as a safeguard. Go forward, now, and put men to heaving the lead port and starb'd, and singing out our depth, and singing especially loud if we come up on six fathoms or less."

What, no barking dog? Fletcher snatched up an oilskin coat and clambered down to the deck. The captain pushed open the front windows of the wheelhouse to better see and hear the men at the bow.

"Vincente," he called out, "heave a lead off the starb'd bow." Macanaya took a position well forward of where the anchor was suspended under the starboard bow, and

The Lower Reaches   239

Fletcher took a similar position on the port side. Captain Ghent brought the Langshan pagoda to bear NNW ¾ W where it was just visible in the heavy rain, then immediately swung *Confucius* about to the west. The two mates called out the depth several times each minute as the steamer crept forward against the wind, and Ghent constantly changed speed and touched up her steering to allow for the drift of the current.

"Six fathoms!" Fletcher shouted suddenly.

The captain spun the wheel, rang the telegraph bell, and shouted "ahead full, Schnapps!" down to the engineer, and the steamer came about to the starboard and sluggishly increased her speed.

"Nine fathoms," Fletcher shouted.

"Half speed," ordered Ghent as he brought her back around to the west. When the pagoda bore directly north, the captain changed course to W by N ½ N.

"Five fathom!" Macanaya shouted.

The captain spun the wheel again and once more rang the bell and shouted "full speed, Schnapps!" down to the engineer, and the steamer veered away from the shoal on her starboard.

"Eight fathom," Macanaya shouted.

And so, *Confucius* caromed up the channel across the river, bumping onto one shoal, then rebounding and brushing along a shoal on the opposite side of the passage. Twice the pagoda was completely obscured by rain clouds hanging low on the hills, and Ghent slowed *Confucius* to where she hung motionless against the current until the pagoda reappeared. When the pagoda came down to N 13 deg. E, the captain changed his course to NW½N. When the pagoda was finally E by N and the steamer was seven miles upriver from the beginning of the crossing, *Confucius* crossed over to the left bank of the river and came up to full speed for the run to Kushan Point and beyond.

The deluge of rain turned to showers, then to drizzles, and finally the rain clouds broke apart and scattered northward over the prostrate delta. But rain-swollen streams and creeks continued to pour yellow-mud runoff into the river. The captain observed with satisfaction that would put more water over the rocks and shoals that crowded together where this part of the river narrowed.

Through the mist lifting over the north shore, the pilot sighted a wedge-shaped hill ninety feet high glowing in the sunlight.

"Kushan Point 頭圲, Cap'n," the pilot said. *Confucius* steamed out to mid-channel and was set free to charge upriver without fear of further obstructions.

A few more miles west, Huangshan 黃山 stood up like a yellow island in the middle of the river until, upon closer approach, it fell back among the few other low hills that broke the tedium of flat horizon.

"Toward the end of the year, when the river's lowest, the flood tide is much stronger, and catching it in the early morning will make for a lot cheaper run. In December, the flood is felt as far upriver as Wuhoo. When the river's low and flood's strong, there can be slack water even on stretches of the Yangtze."

Past Huangshan bay, the river narrowed quickly from five or six miles to a quiet flow one mile wide and, for a while, both banks were visible at once. The north shore remained low and level, with a thick foliage of bushes and bamboo atop the levees and an occasional osier or weeping willow. Along the south shore, the levees parted at intervals for the outflow of creeks, or at gates that controlled the inflow of irrigation water. Through the foliage one might catch a glimpse of a small lake of wind-rippled water bordered by mulberry trees and vegetable gardens, cultivated fields surrounded by low wooded hills that sloped down to the riverbank, or snug little thatch farmhouses shaded by willows and bamboo. Further on, the steamer came up on a neat little bund on the south bank that led up to a walled city beneath high hills covered by evergreens.

"That's Kiangyin," Ghent said. "British occupied the town briefly, during the first war back in forty-two, before going on up to attack Chenkiang and Nanking. There's a stream back there, behind all the pretty flags on them imperial war junks and mandarin boats in the anchorage, that leads from the river southwest over to the Grand Canal, just a shortcut really. The canal itself comes out further upriver near Chenkiang, but for vessels coming up the canal from Hangchow or Soochow that don't draw a lot of water, cutting east over to Kiangyin from the Grand Canal saves near sixty miles on a trip down to Shanghai."

"Can *Confucius* go that way?" Fletcher imagined her steaming up the Grand Canal to intercept the rebel army, maybe all the way to Nanking.

"Not likely. Never see many large vessels, just little country boats and the like, especially since the rebels took up squatter's rights in the territory south of the river. An honest peddler can't work his sampan between creek and canal these days without some gang of rebel thieves holding him up at every flash-lock and slipway. Canal's not much use now anyway. Channels filled in, dikes collapsed, locks broken, and nobody cares to keep it in repair. Beats that Great Wall all to pieces, if you ask me; build a stone wall and it just sits there, not much maintenance, but the effort needed to keep up a thousand miles of man-made waterway is beyond imagination. And it's all we can do just to dredge the bars at Woosung and keep the channel open to Shanghai."

Upriver from Kiangyin, the river widened and *Confucius* moved to mid-channel, then over to the left bank to approach the lee of Starling Island. After a second day's run of fifty-four miles from Plover Point, about 100 miles west of Shanghai, she came to anchor within sight of the pagoda atop Chowshan. The storm that morning had brushed onto the mountain's three peaks a few white strokes of late-season snow.

A long, slender war junk rowed by twenty men shot out from among a small clutch of imperial junks anchored off the left bank. An officer hailed *Confucius*. The pilot shouted back and went to fetch the pirate-suppressing mandarin, who shuffled out on deck hands-in-sleeves and went to the rail to identify the steamer and her business. When after some discussion, the imperial officer made as if to come aboard the steamer, the mandarin's voice rose half an octave and his fat palms fluttered to wave the man off. Almost as if he knew better, thought Fletcher, than to let those thieving river dogs on board, where they'll bow and smile and sniff around for anything of value to tell 'em if she's worth pissing on when she comes back downriver.

Manilamen sauntered into the half-light and stood on each side of the mandarin with their carbines cradled closely to their chests. They grinned and joked with each other in Tagalog, as if the war junk were just another piece of spinning driftwood. The mandarin placed his hands back into his sleeves, stood up straight with a broad smile left and right at his convoy, and leaned his belly into the rail.

"再見 good-bye," he said, so quietly to the officer that he was heard all over the river. The imperial officer glared up at *Confucius* for a few moments, then sniffed and disappeared into the bowels of his boat, which fell off into the current and swung back around for the left bank.

"Dat sojah say plentee big pidgin on livah," the pilot told Fletcher. "Tell mandalin hab got many piecee lebel go Nanking, many piecee empalah sojah go Nanking now, mebbe catchee big fight soon, mebbe *K'ung-fu-tze* go Nanking see big battah. Whatchatinkee, Fetchawood?"

"Old Huang, I think a big battle is no place for a little steamer."

Fletcher set small store on rumor, and less on being caught between imps and rebels. However, he did begin to appreciate the virtue of having on board an official gold-button mandarin all their very own, who remained in costume in order to hold court with all the other imperial mandarins along the river. The pirate-suppressing mandarin looked a good deal less ridiculous than when he had come aboard, and Fletcher began to take closer notice of the man.

As on the previous night, the steamer bedded down and an armed watch was posted. Supper was served to passengers and crew, the Chinese passengers retired, and the deck crew and black gang played mahjong late into the night. Fletcher joined Ghent, Schnapps, Hicks and the pilot in the wheelhouse where they sipped brandy, smoked cheroots or cigars, and competed at yarning tall tales and true about their adventures at sea and on shore. When the conversation began to ebb, Fetcher and Hicks got up a game of stud poker, which they had to teach to the pilot, before they finally retired to their cabins. Once that night the crew and passengers were abruptly awakened by the echoing crack of a Sharps, fired by the watch to warn off a junk that approached too closely.

Log of Steamer CONFUCIUS, chartered by Augustus Fitch & Company

Date & Time	Location	Wind (est.)	Current	Speed	Cargo
Monday April 30 1860 9:00pm	Chowshan, Yangtze R, Kiangsu	NW 2 knots	3½ knots	7 knots	Tea

Confucius arose with the next dawn. While the black gang got up steam, Fletcher went to the galley for two mugs of steaming coffee to take to the wheelhouse, where he and Ghent went over the chart of the river from Starling Island to Chenkiang.

The river was in a subdued and contemplative mood that flattened its surface into an unfretted calm. Without the clamor of war, death and destruction, the world above the river warmed quietly in the deepening glow of sunrise. Ancient stone steps wound down into the depths through thick green foliage parted by tall osier, mulberry and willow that reached out across the river. Small boys scampered past a lone fisherman dangling line from a thin pole of bamboo. Above the evergreen hills, the tiny cinnamon daub of a pagoda stood atop a peak white with a dusting of snow from the recent storm. As the sun rose gradually above the horizon, the tableau turned slowly to burnished gold. Gangs of silent black cormorants swooped low over the water. Ragged formations of long-necked swans trumpeting in chorus passed overhead high in the air. For a few minutes, the world stopped still, captured as a protean thought in the mind of a river, then disappeared in the ripples of a rising breeze.

In the galley, the Manilaman cook danced a bright jig around his stove where by himself he prepared all at once breakfast for three nations. Thick-sliced ham, scrambled eggs, and toasted bread for the Americans. Hot rice congee flavored with pickled vegetables and preserved eggs, pork noodles, and steamed buns for the Chinese. Fried garlic rice mixed with sun-dried anchovies and shrimp for the Manilamen. All staple fare nonetheless filling for being simple.

The crew not yet on watch filed past the galley to fill their bowls then dispersed along the rail where they busily worked their chopsticks to shovel breakfast from bowl to mouth while *Confucius* got under way. The steward carried breakfast into the saloon for the officers and passengers, but not for the pudgy mandarin. When the commotion in the galley came to rest and the cook sat down to eat, a Chinese servant went into the galley and, over heat from the embers banked in the stove, prepared a much less simple repast for the delicate palate of the pirate-suppressing mandarin.

Much time was lost the third morning working the steamer over shoals and sand banks that had shifted with the rising volume of water since the pilot's last passage upriver. With no other steamer along to give a tow, and the river too wide to throw a line to shore, *Confucius* was left with few stratagems. At the moment of an unexpected impact under the bow, the man at the wheel shouted "reverse engines!" down to the engineer. While the hull still grated and whined its way into the river bottom, the helmsman threw the wheel over to where the current pushed downstream against the rudder. When this was not sufficient to lift her off a shoal, the steamer paddled full astern while the crew shifted equipment and cargo from one end of the vessel to the other. Occasionally, no act of man could budge her and she could only wait on the tide coming upstream from the ocean. In this part of the lower reaches, the river might rise by as much as six feet during spring tides.

"Not so easy," the captain said, as they floated free of another bank of mud. "In some of them little rivers, a feller can get hold to something and haul hisself around tight bends and over shallow bottoms. Met up with a pilot in Shanghai that came off the Colorado not so long ago. Said they'd sometimes have to turn one o' them little flatbed boats they mount with locomotive engines right plumb around and back her up sternwise so's the wheel could just *dig* its way through the mud to cross a shoal."

Silence in the wheelhouse.

"It's true! It's true!"

Muffled guffaws.

"I swear it's getting' so around here a man *has* to lie because nobody'll believe the truth when it's told."

Ten and a half hours steaming brought *Confucius* to the reach approaching Chenkiang, 155 miles west of Shanghai, where the Yangtze curled around low hills and out onto the broad and flat alluvium of the delta. Abundant thickets enveloped and softened the outline of the black crags of Silver Island silhouetted against the sanguine glow of sunset. Oil lamps in brick compounds and thatch huts on the south shore at Chenkiang began to flicker in the falling light. Lanterns aboard imperial sea-going war junks moored off Kwachow glimmered in the gloaming. *Confucius* deftly shifted her helm to and fro through the eddies that surged around large rocks submerged just below the surface between Silver Island and the Chenkiang anchorage, on the lookout especially for the Furious Rock, where in 1858 Lord Exter's gunboat *Furious* went aground. Gingerly through the dark, *Confucius* neared the lee of Silver Island, found a quiet place to settle, and anchored for the night.

The officers of *Confucius* met again in the wheelhouse after supper to swap stories about Chenkiang which, like Kiangyin downriver, was occupied by the British in 1842.

"British massacred a couple thousand Tartar bannermen here," Ghent said.

"Why would the British bother with Chenkiang?" Fletcher said.

"Put the Grand Canal out of business, cut off the supply of rice shipped to Peking. When the British squadron showed up, Tartars just about went berserk searching for Chinese traitors who might sell food or information to the British. Chenkiang was terrified – Chinamen fled the town in droves."

"Sounds like Tartars and Chinamen don't cotton much to each other."

"Bannermen are as arrogant as any occupying force, Chinamen don't care to have little mobs of very disagreeable Tartars in the heart of their cities."

"The Manchus keep pretty much to themselves," Hicks said, "in garrisons in important cities around the country. Every senior Chinese mandarin outside the capital holds office together with a Tartar official of the same rank, to keep an eye on the Chinese – that's how the Manchu govern China. Of course, Peking's thick with Tartars."

"That's one almighty big chowdah," Fletcher said. "Sta't with a solid stock of native Chinese, and there's all different variety and dialects of them. Pour in a conquering race of Manchus, or Tahtars or whichever-you-call-'em. Simmer for 200 years, then add British coming at you with opium and gunboats, and top it all off with Christian rebels itching to smash the Tahtar dynasty. Middle Kingdom ought to be called

洋神 *Yang Shen* James Lande 藍德

the muddle Kingdom."

A gunshot echoed through the wheelhouse. Ghent quenched the oil lamp, and the little assembly edged up to the windows. A solitary sampan was barely visible in the dim moonlight, sculling quickly away toward the Chenkiang quay, Manilamen following along the larboard rail. Fletcher stepped out onto the wheelhouse ladder.

"*Que pasa?*" he whispered. "What's happening?"

"*Nada señor*, nothing sir," came a hoarse voice from the rail. "*Solamente una barka pequeña – ahora bien* it was just a little boat – okay now." Fletcher went back inside, the lamp was relit, the spilled brandy wiped up.

"Chenkiang," Hicks said, "was one more terrible flare-up between Manchu and Chinese. The Manchu arrested and imprisoned hundreds of Chenkiang townspeople. The Manchu commander even accused the Chinese district magistrate of being a traitor, and threw him out of town when the magistrate objected to the wholesale arrest and execution of the Chinese population."

"No wonder there's a rebellion against the Manchu," Fletcher said.

"The Royal Navy went on to Nanking," Ghent said, "where they extorted $21,000,000 silver dollars in indemnities at gunpoint. After the smoke cleared and the treaty was signed, they come to find out the Chinese had long since gotten wind that the English wanted to cut the Grand Canal. All the Chinese tribute grain had been shipped up the canal to Peking months before the English even arrived at the Yangtze."

"So, the massacre at Chenkiang," Fletcher said, "was needless slaughter."

"Put a quick end to the war," Ghent said.

"At extraordinary cost," Hicks said.

Log of Steamer CONFUCIUS, *chartered by Augustus Fitch & Company*

Date & Time	Location	Wind (est.)	Current	Speed	Cargo
Tuesday May 1st 1860 9:00pm	Silver Island, Chenkiang, Kiangsu	NW 3 knots	3 knots	6 knots	Tea

Early the following morning, the sudden gruff cawing of thousands of rooks and jackdaws rent the calm as the birds rose up through the river mists around Silver Island in a swirling black mob. They circled above *Confucius*, and then swarmed across the river to settle upon the desolation of Chenkiang. Fletcher's gaze followed the birds and, in the rising light, he was stunned to see the magnitude of destruction wrought by the rebels, amply evident even at a distance through a glass, upon what by all reports formerly had been a bustling entrepôt of river commerce. The remains of Chenkiang were just a burnt-out cinder, and little more than an enclave for carrion-feeders. In places the town wall lay in heaps of dirt and broken masonry, towers were shattered and gates smashed, and buildings and arches collapsed, warehouses flattened and wharves awash. For a mile around the town, the suburbs were a fire-blackened ruin overgrown by weed and thistle that gave shelter only to wild pheasant and waterfowl. From the breaches in the town wall to the broad plains beyond, not a single tree stood standing. Shadows of men moved slowly like wraiths among the collapsed hovels.

"There is your Kingdom of Heavenly Peace," Chester Hicks muttered. "Once Chenkiang was a thriving marketplace of 100,000 people. Here at the junction of the Grand Canal, it was perhaps the busiest crossroads in the empire. And the rebels who destroyed this town would rule all China."

There was no missing the bitterness in the trader's voice. After the previous night's lengthy exchange of river tales, during which many salient facts about the rebels came forth from Chester Hicks, whose volubility advanced apace with his intake of brandy, Fletcher was rather less than surprised at the man's sentiment. Similar indictments were heard with increasing frequency in the gilt and velvet lobbies of expensive Shanghai hotels, and in the fashionable parlors of Shanghai homes, many more than in 1859 when Fletcher was last on the coast.

"But the rebels *do not* rule here, do they? Have I not been told that Chenkiang is now under imperial control," he said, wondering why Hicks would still blame the long-absent rebels for the condition of the town. "Chenkiang must have rebuilt after the British assault in forty-two, as did Shanghai after the Triads were driven out in fifty-five. Chinese are nothing if not industrious – if rebels have been gone from Chenkiang for over three years, why are the walls and buildings not rebuilt? Why have the people not returned to their homes? Why is the town not restored to life, instead of left to molder?"

"The rebellion casts a long shadow, Mr. Wood. A pall remains over this town, over every town along the Yangtze threatened by the Taiping. They don't have to possess a place to cause it to wither and die – the population believes that rebels understand only how to kill and destroy, and the people are terrified by nothing more than fear of what the rebels might do. Just their presence in Nanking threatens the sun, and Chinese must live from day to day with the likelihood that rebels will return at anytime to rape and pillage and destroy, and that threat is enough to destroy all enterprise."

Fletcher considered how nothing more than the nearby presence of the Taiping caused an entire countryside to wilt away and millions of acres of rice land to lie fallow for years. What kind of imperial siege allowed the rebels to come and go?

"How do they get in and out, with Nanking surrounded by imperial troops?"

"Silver can be more effective than artillery at breaching imperial lines."

Fletcher squinted through a telescope, beyond the riverfront, at the remains of the twenty-foot high town wall. Few soldiers were on the walls or at the town gates. Evidently, the imperials were not wasting many men on the garrison at Chenkiang.

"One would think that regardless of the threat from Nanking, a walled town in imperialist hands and protected by the emperor would fare better."

"There is nothing to be done. The populace has fled and there is no one left to till the fields, no rice in the imperial granaries, and no relief from Peking or elsewhere. If the emperor restored Chenkiang, the rebels would just return and raze the place again. This desolation cannot be restored until that infamy at Nanking is utterly destroyed."

Fletcher looked about him and noted that in spite of its proximity to the ruined town of Chenkiang, Silver Island had not suffered any similar calamity. The island was still thick with trees and vegetation, fields lay undisturbed below bright temples perched four hundred feet up on the higher slopes, and a soft down of damp mists as white as gull-feather clung in the rocky clefts between green moss-covered cliffs. The deep peal of a bronze bell rolled out across the river from high on Silver Island, followed by a dim echo of the droning chant of Buddhist priests at prayer.

"Perhaps this destruction is necessary," Fletcher said, "to topple an alien dynasty no longer wanted by the people, a reign of terror needed to exterminate completely any lingering affection for a decadent aristocracy."

"The Reign of Terror accomplished nothing, only lead the French into another autocracy under Napoleon Bonaparte, and that because common Frenchmen were no more prepared to rule in France than these rebels are in China. Revolutions collapse into anarchy when they discover the futility of ruling a nation without good men dedicated to the purpose of good government. The Great Ch'ing dynasty has a few hundred years of experience administering China that, even at the very worst, still make the Manchu the lesser of the two evils."

"If Chenkiang is an example of rebel policy, it's a wonder there are still any Westerners left who would support their cause."

"Yes, well, among us there are Westerners who would see a Christian dynasty installed in China regardless of the cost. That is, if they cannot make China a protectorate under British authority. Can you imagine a British China, like a British India? Lord save us! So far, the British authorities in China seem able to hold on to some horse sense, and content themselves with interfering only in matters of trade. They usually manage to turn a deaf ear to the incessant caterwauling of the British mercantile community for the takeover of China by British troops."

"Just what is your attitude toward the Chinese, Mr. Hicks?"

"Same as my attitude toward anyone. Ambivalent."

Expecting delay at Nanking, Captain Ghent was anxious to depart Chenkiang at the earliest opportunity, so that *Confucius* would not have to pass the coming night anchored within range of the rebel cannon in the forts at Nanking. If the truth be told, thought Fletcher, everyone aboard is unnerved by the gloom of this ghostly town of Chenkiang, and would flee its noxious threat without delay.

3 *Confucius* weighed anchor at 8:00am and slipped cautiously past Furious Rock out into the middle channel, steaming west under a five-story pagoda and several temples on Golden Island, and crossing over to the north channel. Ten miles further upriver, she passed another imperial war fleet at the salt mart of Iching, the last major imperial station before entering the rebel-controlled river. Between Chenkiang and Iching, Fletcher had counted close to 100 large imperial sea-going war junks mounting from ten to sixteen old cannon each, with hundreds of smaller oar-driven war junks and other fighting craft among them.

Beyond Iching, the river began to narrow to a little over one-half mile, low hills rose up behind the banks, and ranges of higher mountains were seen well inland. Shortly before noon, the outline of the Pingshan pagoda rose in the distance, followed by Theodolite Point, and then the Nanking forts. Macanaya's crew "unlimbered" the guns fore and aft, Sharps carbines and cartridges were issued to a part of the crew, and the passengers were confined to the house so that sight of them on deck would not invite unnecessary curiosity on the part of rebel authorities. Fletcher began to wonder what the captain really expected.

The city slowly grew in size as *Confucius* closed in, until it was evident that the walled city of Nanking was at least six or seven times larger than Shanghai. Outside the hewn stone wall, the suburbs lay in ruins. The wall itself appeared to be in excellent condition, as much as eighty feet high in places, winding along the south shore for miles. It followed the contour of a low range of hills that sometimes seemed to be a part of the wall. Artillery batteries on both north and south shores gave the rebels complete mastery of the river passage. Several batteries were positioned outside the city wall in front of a high, fortified mound above the riverbank.

The captain motioned to Fletcher. "Take the wheel, Mr. Wood. I want a mate who knows enough about the thin places to take her through if I'm down and the pilot's out. Bring her 'round this way to star'bd to keep her in the channel."

East and west of the city stood high, sharp-peaked hills on which perched several tall, slender pagodas. Between the hills and the city, long lines of banners and pennants fluttered above the encampments of the imperial army besieging Nanking. The imperial siege line only partially surrounded the city walls – the sweep of imperial flags met the Yangtze a mile or two above and below the city, leaving control of the river immediately opposite the city in rebel hands. Beyond the farthest western boundaries of the city and imperial camps, the Yangtze dwindled around a bend toward the south.

"Keep her over toward the right bank, Mr. Wood. We have no choice but to look down the muzzles of their guns. The deepest part of the channel passes within a pistol-shot of the batteries that fired on Lord Exter's little armada two years ago. *Confucius* was here then, with *Pluto*, witnessed the rebels welcome the British. All hell broke loose – half-dozen frigates, brigs and barks steamed up and down in front of the city pouring rockets, shot, and shell into the forts for a half-hour before it got too dark to fight. The rebels gave as good as they got, hulling every one of the ships. Next morning, the British poured it on again and, before long, all the forts were quiet. The devil-ship bombardment was too much for the rebels. Then the imperial war junks opened fire on the silent rebel batteries – from two miles away!"

Confucius was still east of Theodolite Hill when Fletcher looked more closely at the north bank fortifications and the junks anchored below them.

"Captain? Aren't those imperial banners flying from those junks?"

Ghent took up a glass and surveyed the shoreline. "I'll be damned," he whispered. "You're right as rain, Mr. Wood. The imperial fleet's taken those batteries again and plunked a nickel's worth of war junks right down on the counter across from Nanking. That'll mean rebel communication with the north bank is broken and they're cut off from their supplies and their army north of the river. It also means that for the time being, *Confucius* is not threatened by rebel fire from the north bank."

"Unless we stumble into their crossfire."

Fletcher noticed a rebel junk flying a riot of bright flags and pennants coming out from the anchorage before the city, hastily putting out her oars and raising sail to catch enough breeze to put her on a course to interdict *Confucius*. On the junk's deck, her crew was frantically loading her guns.

Ghent followed Fletcher's gaze and saw the interloper getting under way.

A second rebel junk put out her oars and prepared to stand away from the anchorage to follow the first junk, which was now closing in on the steamer. The first junk was less than half the length of the huge side-wheel steamer, but she was at least as well armed, with a 32-pounder in her bow and more guns in her waist.

"Mr. Wood, go forward and have Macanaya swing the bowchaser around on that junk." Ghent rang the telegraph, and into the speaking tube, he barked: "Schnapps! Slow to half-ahead." Then he swung *Confucius* around to larboard just enough to point her bow right into the face of the rebel junk.

"Now, you coolie-kings will please to shit or get off the goddamn pot."

Fletcher stood with the Manilaman gun-crew at the bow of *Confucius* and watched the rebel junk waver below the mountainous steamer bearing down on her on a collision course. At a distance of fifty yards, the junk came about, raised oars, and ordered her crew to stand away from their guns. Satisfied of a less belligerent welcome, *Confucius* gave a short snort on her steam whistle, came about to starboard, and slowed until she hung in the current. The junk struggled over close enough to throw a line, pulled herself up against fenders lowered together with a boarding net from the steamer's rail, and two Chinese jumped for the net and swung themselves up over the rail into the waist.

Fletcher left Macanaya in the bow and went to the larboard rail to examine the meddlers more closely. They were a motley-looking collection, rebel officers and crew alike. Instead of the somber blue effect characteristic in other Chinese cities, rebel sailors apparently delighted in wearing a gaudy mix of wild colors. Below, red or green trousers held by a white or yellow sash. Above, a red tunic edged in blue or orange. Yellow or black cloth squares front and back were embroidered with large characters for what Fletcher guessed were rank or unit. Their heads were unshaven, and they wound strips of colored silk into their long hair and queues. Several each had a length of red silk cord woven into the plait of the queue, which was then wound round their head like a turban with the tassel of the cord hanging down over the left shoulder.

They don't cut off their queues, Fletcher thought. Of course not, else how would their spies pass into imperial cities, or maybe they all're just hedging their bets.

On the cheeks of a few of the sailors, he could make out a black tattoo 太平天國, the brand the Taiping burnt into the faces of their slaves. On others, there was a white scar where the tattoo had been removed with quicklime. Old Huang said the tattoo meant "Taiping heavenly kingdom."

A reward, no doubt, for exemplary slaves, for conduct above and beyond, the insurgents' Victoria Cross.

The rebel officers wore red or yellow robes embroidered with square insignia, and tall, square black caps unlike those worn by the mandarins outside of rebel territory. From a distance where their colors first struck the eye, the rebel crew presented a cheerful picture, but closer inspection found them generally dirty and disorderly, unwashed and unkempt.

As though being under siege was an excuse for never putting soap to body or clothes. They say there are only two classes of people in Nanking: soldiers and slaves. An empire of soldiers and slaves ruled over by coolie-kings. The old man is letting them cool their heels.

The two rebel officers stood alone on the deck looking about them and apparently wondering what to do next. After five minutes, the two rebels were quietly fuming and began to argue with each other. Then Captain Ghent slammed open the wheelhouse door and slowly descended to the deck behind his pilot. Old Huang looked a little queasy at the prospect of facing rebel officers. He attempted what sounded like polite conversation, but was interrupted immediately.

"你們這艘船下江為甚麼沒有在天京停留?" the Chinese yelled in Mandarin heavy with the accent of the Anhwei countryside.

"He say *K'ung-fu-tze* come down livah why no stop dis place."

"Tell 'em I ain't got time to stop for every pirate that waves a gun in my direction on this river." The pilot winced.

"船主說沒時間隨便停留 the captain says he had no time to stop at random."

The rebel officer's black eyes flashed under his long black eyebrows, and he stared for a moment at the pilot, then for a longer moment at the foreign captain. Slowly resignation stole into his expression and mingled with the anger there, and he seemed to make an effort to speak more calmly.

"船上有甚麼人?"

"He want know got what people on boat?"

"Tell 'em it's none of his goddamn business."

"沒甚麼人 - 只有我們的船員 no one in particular – just our crew."

"你們上到那裡去?"

"He say where boat go?"

"Tell 'em we're going to hell, and he's welcome to come along."

"我們到蕪湖買茶去 we go to Wuhoo to buy tea."

Ghent heard "Wuhoo" and glared at the pilot. The rebel officer paused again while he scrutinized the pilot and the captain, as if something visible about their expressions or posture, or Heavenly intervention, would reveal the truth of what they said. Fletcher guessed that Ghent's tone kept an already hostile Chinese brusque and resentful.

"你們船主要隨我來見見我們團長芳大人 - 不能不去! 你懂不懂?"

"He say cap'n go with him, see big boss-man, callum Fang, He say mus' go."

"You blithering idiot! What've you gotten me into now?" Ghent spun on his heel and called to Fletcher as he climbed to the wheelhouse. The rebel officer knitted his brows at the retreating captain, then turned to the rail and shouted down to his officers on the deck of the junk.

"預備放槍 ready to fire muskets!"

Rebel sailors ran to the junk's starboard side, cocking flintlocks and blowing on matchlock fuses. Manilamen lined up at the steamer's larboard rail with rifles at the ready. In the wheelhouse, Ghent grabbed coat and cap, took a revolver from a drawer, checked its load, and tucked it under his coat.

"Last time coming down from Hankow, we didn't bother stopping here, no point in paying duties twice if it can be avoided, but after we passed the forts they sent a junk out after us." Ghent took another revolver from the drawer and handed it to Fletcher.

"Junk was against the wind, but I guess somebody remembers us and wants his due. I'd tell 'em all to go suck eggs, but it's not going to be worth being shot at from those batteries coming back down from Wuhoo. We'd best go ashore and parley. Find Chester Hicks and tell him – and tell him to keep those passengers out of sight inside the saloon until I get back. When that's done, go forward and prepare to drop the hook while I put her over toward the anchorage, then get ready to go ashore with me. Throw a coat over that pistol and stay a couple of feet behind me all the time to cover my back."

"What if they try to board *Confucius* while we're gone?"

"Macanaya won't let that happen."

Fletcher climbed down from the wheelhouse wondering who would cover him while he was covering the captain. Over his head, the captain yelled down to the pilot.

"Tell that horse's ass to get back in his goddamn boat and get it the hell out of the way so I can drop anchor out of the stream!"

Log of Steamer CONFUCIUS, chartered by Augustus Fitch & Company

Date & Time	Location	Wind (est.)	Current	Speed	Cargo
Wednesday May 2 1860 12:00pm	Nanking, Kiangsu	NW 3 knots	3 knots	7 knots	Tea

洋神 *Yang Shen*   James Lande 藍德

Dramatis Personae: Chapter 15

Reverend Walter J. Russell	American Protestant missionary
Hung Jen-k'an 洪仁玕	Taiping *Kan Wang* 干王, Shield King

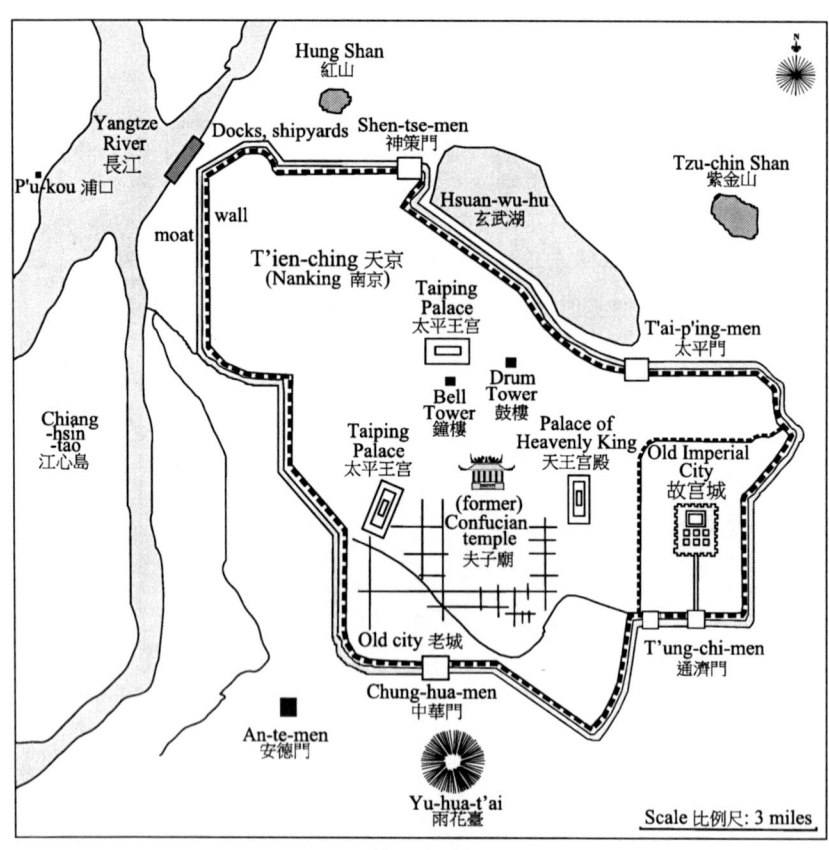

Nanking in 1860
(from several sources, noted in Underfoot*)*

Three Chinese *li* 里 = one mile.

250   *The Rebel Capital*

Chapter 15: The Rebel Capital
Wednesday, May 2, 1860, 1:30pm

Rebel officers took Captain Ghent, Fletcher Wood, and the Chinese pilot Old Huang off *Confucius* and put them aboard a long sampan, trimmed with fluttering flags and flashing banners, which landed on a stone wharf inside the junk anchorage. Squads of menacing foot soldiers armed with swords and pikes crowded in around the three men, forming a sinister gauntlet of derisive laughter and sneers through which the foreigners were hustled. They stumbled past the bloody, dirt-caked remains of a half-dozen dead bodies sprawled in a cabbage patch of severed heads, presided over by a swollen, rotting head impaled on a pike driven into the rusty earth.

"Old Huang," Fletcher said, "you walk between me and the captain."

Opposite the wharf there was a hill surmounted by the wooden stockade of a fort. Above the fort flew a swarm of black flags that snapped in the breeze over the hoods of musketeers pointing their matchlocks down at the foreigners. Fletcher imagined he could see wisps of black smoke rising from smoldering fuses, and smell the odor of burning hemp and, for a twinkling, he felt as if transported out of the 19th century and back in time to medieval Europe. He expected at any moment to see the flash and hear the report of a musket on the wall, or to be yanked roughly aside and made to kneel and suffer some terrible torture at the hands of the rebel soldiers. However, the foreigners were merely herded into an open two-wheeled cart drawn by two sleepy Mongolian ponies driven by a single carter. The soldiery dispersed, but neither the cessation of the soldiers' curiosity, nor the ridiculous conveyance in which they were placed, eased at all any of Fletcher's swelling apprehension for the serious risk they undertook placing themselves at the mercy of these rebels.

The brusque officer from the rebel junk dispatched a messenger off toward the east wall. The officer mounted a horse and preceded the jouncing cart over a near-deserted path under the eastern wall for a distance of two or three miles. Imperial regimental banners and flags flapped in a breeze over rudely constructed ramparts in a line off to their left. They came to a two-story wooden tower atop the wall, below which was a huge iron-studded gate over which were carved in the stone the three characters 神策門.

"Gate fo' god big plan," the pilot said, which enlightened no one.

Before they could enter the gate, a sudden blast of horns and beat of drums reverberated out of the tunnel, causing their little Mongolian cart-ponies to snort and shy, and back the cart away from ranks of rebel cavalry that cantered forth from under the wall. The tramp of hundreds of foot soldiers and the clank of their equipment followed behind the rumbling din of horses' hooves. Troop after troop shouldering muskets and matchlocks, gingals and iron-tipped bamboo spears, marched out and turned south along the city wall in the direction of the Tartar barracks.

"Lebel makee big bobbely. Mebbe big fightee."

"Rebels do look like they're up to something mighty big," Fletcher said.

"Maybe we should've taken those rumors downriver more seriously," Ghent said.

"What do you think is happening? Ever seen anything like this before?"

"No, never. Don't s'pose they come out and fight every day."

"Have we blundered into the middle of Armageddon?"

The guards passed them through the gate, a cavernous echoing vault faced with flagstone, then through a second gate into a city suddenly as vacant and quiet as the deserted road they had just traveled from the river. In the next two miles through the Nanking streets, no crowd of curious bystanders gathered to gawk at the outlandish foreigners. There were no shops or peddlers or beggars, no yamen runners rushing about on official business, no one living in the relatively undamaged but nonetheless empty houses along the streets. The few stragglers they encountered no more than glanced their way with the gaunt and pale expressions of the half-starved.

"This place is a ghost town," Ghent said.

Walls and gates were posted with notices and circulars the pilot said were put up by mandarins and generals telling the people to "pay tax, burnee temple, fightee Tatah imp, play to God." On each side of doors and gates were pasted strips of red paper painted with black characters saying, "Worship heavenly fathah, sing song to God, no dlinkee, no sweah, behave plopah." Fletcher saw columns of smoke at the southern end of the city and, at intersections, he wondered if he heard the dull hubbub of commerce drifting in the breeze; perhaps just the northern half of Nanking was abandoned.

Further toward the west, the city opened out into gardens and fish ponds surrounded by willows and bamboo, an occasional temple burned to charred ruin, or the collapsed walls of some rich man's villa, knocked down and stripped of its wood. Eventually they came to an old wooden building of three stories, with upturned eaves painted red and gold, surrounded by a high wall and flanked by open ground. On the closer ground, near the wall of the building, three Chinese soldiers, stripped to the waist, knelt in the dust with their shaved heads bowed, and their queues pulled forward by the hand of a rebel officer. To one side stood a burly, bare-chested Chinese examining the edge of a stubby broad sword. The cart halted in the street opposite the execution ground and waited while the two foreigners and their pilot watched with sinking stomachs as the executioner stepped to the first victim and, with a single roundhouse swing, lopped off the man's head. He then stepped over the fallen body and proceeded quickly to behead each of the next two men. One of the officers swung his victim's head by the queue a few times then dropped it in the dirt. A few minutes later, the ground was deserted of all but the bleeding corpses. The foreigner's cart rolled forward to the door of the building.

The three foreigners were ordered off the cart and led through the first gate, a courtyard, a second gate, a second courtyard, and up a flight of steps into an open hall. Straight-backed chairs lined each side of the hall and, at the far end, there was a large table on a raised dais covered with tiger skins. Menacing rebel guards stood in ranks on each side of the hall. Fletcher didn't notice much of this right away — he was working to get out of his own head the twisted grimace that dangled at the end of the dead Chinaman's queue. Old Huang was wide-eyed and pale and stumbled up the steps. Only Ghent retained his bitter composure.

"Chop off all their goddamn heads!"

Years before, on the execution ground at Canton, Fletcher had seen men beheaded, but from a distance – never from just a few feet away. He had been out on a lark with shipmates from *Antelope* after delivering a cargo of tea. They had wandered half-drunk out of the part of town set aside for foreign sailors and come upon a crowd of Chinese packed in around something they assumed was street theater or a puppet show. He balanced precariously on the thighs of two of his companions to get a view over the crowd, and saw a dozen Chinese led out into an open space before a crowd held back by armed guards. Each had a wooden signboard strapped to his back in such a way that what must have been the name of his crime waved about over the victim's head.

A man's signboard was jerked away, his queue pulled to stretch his neck, and a sword fell. With each stroke, the crowd gasped, some cheered, and when all twelve bodies lay separated from their heads, the crowd surged forward to poke at the bleeding torsos, and gape at the disembodied faces. Some women dipped cloth in the pools of blood, then screamed and waved the grisly tokens for all to see. Fletcher fell down and retched in the dirt. When they saw the foreign sailors in the street behind them, the crowd set to howling and gave chase. Fletcher had to run for his life with the others, and they didn't stop until they were back on board, where the captain flogged the sailors for going out of bounds and fined his mate. But for Fletcher even flogging would have been superfluous. Before that day, he had thought a little smugly that he had seen all the brutality of which men were capable. Afterwards he wondered if he ever could see it all.

A commotion on the dais announced the arrival of some high rebel mandarin, who marched onto the dais accompanied by four attendants and took a seat behind the table. The mandarin was a tall, slender young man with a square face, a high narrow nose, and large black eyes. He was dressed in yellow robes embroidered with dragons in gold and silver thread and fancy borders of stripes and waves, and wore a tall, square black cap in which was set a red stone. He looked up at the foreigners and smiled, then gestured them forward into chairs at the front of the room. His voice boomed across the hall.

"歡迎歡迎洋老兄! 請坐請坐!"

Old Huang was so surprised at this that he broke into a large grin and whispered to the captain and the mate, "Mandalin say welcome, welcome, foreign brothers. Please sittee down. Foreign *older* brothers. Belly polite." The rebel officer who had been their escort into the city took a place on the other side of the hall opposite the foreigners and listened without expression. The rebel mandarin then addressed the Chinese pilot, who stood quickly and bowed.

"老兄你能做翻譯麼 elder brother, can you interpret?"

"不敢大人實在不敢 I wouldn't dare your Excellency, I truly dare not."

"好的好的. 你們請等一等 all right. You please wait a little."

Sometime during the delay, when Fletcher finally regained his wits completely and began to pay closer attention to his surroundings, there was another commotion at the rear of the hall and a foreigner bustled in from a dark side entrance. He was a short, dowdy man, dressed in gray trousers and a black frock coat, with thinning white hair that waved about above his ears and brilliant blue eyes behind silver-rimmed spectacles. Behind him, a large man dressed in what seemed to be Western clothes stopped in the entrance, partly obscured by the crowd of rebel attendants and barely visible in the dim light. There was a quick exchange in Chinese between the white-haired man and the mandarin, the man nodded briskly to the Chinese, then turned to the foreigners.

"Gentlemen, how are you? Please forgive my delay in arriving. I am the Reverend Walter J. Russell, here in Nanking at the invitation of his Excellency the Heavenly King Hoong to translate scripture and preach the gospel of Jesus. You sit before his Honor, Regimental Commander Fang, second-in-command of northern defenses, supporter of the celestial institutes, and who has too many other distinctions to narrate here. He wishes me to welcome you to Nanking. I have been asked to translate."

The missionary turned to Commander Fang and nodded. The mandarin began speaking and Russell followed along in English.

"Jesus was the first begotten Son of God. The Heavenly King Hung Hsiu-ch'üan is the second Son of God. Jesus ascended into Heaven and the gospel was proclaimed on earth for eighteen centuries while China was yet in darkness. The Heavenly King Hung Hsiu-ch'üan was commissioned by God to commence anew the work of evangelization, which would be carried on until all mankind acknowledge the true God. Moreover, as the American people are worshippers of Jesus, they are in consequence of one family with Hung Hsiu-ch'üan and his junior brethren. Hence, it is entirely correct that there should exist no strife between such closely allied kindred. Welcome, foreign brothers, to the Heavenly Kingdom of the T'ai-p'ing. Please tell me your names."

Fletcher was dumfounded, and dug his fingers into his arm to keep a straight face. The Lord knows I am not a fastidious Christian, but I respect Him in my way. I just never expected to come 10,000 miles to China to be preached a Sunday sermon from a Taiping pulpit. Can this pompous Holy Roller be serious? They actually do think Hoong is the younger brother of Jesus Christ! Will they still cut off our heads?

Captain Ghent stood and spoke.

"Thank you your Honor. We're proud to be here. My name is Rhys Simon Ghent, and I'm captain of the merchant-steamer *Confucius*. This here's my first mate Fletcher Wood, and the other's my pilot Old Huang."

Russell's translation into Chinese made the rebel mandarin chuckle.

"The commander asks," Russell said, "if the steamer truly is called 'Confucius'."

Ghent actually smiled. Finally, he thought, someone gets the joke. "Yessir, that's her name. Finest merchant-steamer on the Yangtze River."

"You say merchant-steamer. Is that vessel not owned by the foreign usurpers of the Chinese empire, the Tartar imps and demons?"

"No, sir. She is chartered to Shanghai merchants, but I am her owner."

"What kind of trade do you pursue?"

"Tea and silk, mostly. Sometimes I charter to other merchants."

"Do you ever transport weapons or opium?"

"No, sir. Never. We just carry enough weapons for her defense."

"Where are you bound now, and for what purpose?"

"To Wuhoo. To pick up a cargo of tea for Shanghai."

"Do you understand that when you return downriver, you must stop here at our capital and pay duties on your cargo?"

"What I understand is that since the treaty of 1858 Westerners are exempt from paying taxes."

"You do not understand. That treaty is with the Manchu demons, not with the Heavenly Kingdom of T'ai-p'ing. You are *not* exempt from paying taxes here."

"Oh, well, yes sir. If you say so. By the way, do you happen to know how much the duties might be?"

"Oh, some trifling amount. Nothing important. You carry no opium?"

"No opium."

"No weapons? We wish to buy guns and ammunition, and will pay a good price. We treat especially well anyone who can bring us arms."

"Sorry, your Honor. No weapons."

"Spy-glasses, lucifer matches, umbrellas, pocket watches?"

"We carry none of those things."

"Liar!"

The man out of sight at the back of the hall now suddenly heaved his huge bulk forward through the crowd of attendants and spoke up.

"Black liar!"

2

"Damn your eyes, Slaughter," the captain said, spitting the words. "Where on earth have you turned up from? I'd've bet a year's wages your bones'd been picked over by the crabs long ago."

"Ghent, you old pirate," Delevan Slaughter said, "crabs'll get you sooner 'n me."

"Should've expected you'd turn coat," Fletcher said acidly, staring marlinespikes into Slaughter's gargoyle face, "and go to soldier for the rebels."

"Too bad they didn't ship you back to America, Fletcher. You might not be getting' out of this scrape so easy tho' – I'm in good with the Loyal King, an' one word to him'll see your head out there with all those others. Better to be perlite."

"Now you keep the hell out of this," Ghent said, "or by God you'll regret it!"

"Blow steam all you like, Captain," Slaughter said, sneering. "But if I tell this 'ere chief that you're carryin' the Fitch's comprador on board, with $150,000 of specie to boot, and that you took on fifty chests of opium at Woosung, I figger you'll be the one doin' the regrettin'."

"Figger all you want, renegade. Do you no good."

"Be nice to have a tidy little war-steamer of my own."

"You'll never lay a hook on my steamer, you rum-soaked shit-faced whore-poxed turncoat black cutthroat. If I'm not back aboard in another hour, Macanay'll open fire on everything in sight and lay your anchorage, your wharf, and your wall to waste. And that'll bring the imp armada charging in from across the river to finish the job with even bigger guns. Somehow I just can't see as how your precious Heavenly King'll appreciate you much after you call down upon them the wrath of God."

"Ha!" Slaughter snorted, "God would have nothing to do with you. God excommunicated you from the human race years ago."

The rebel mandarin was becoming openly impatient with the exchange and said something sharply to Russell. "Gentlemen, his Honor wants to know what you are arguing about."

Slaughter turned to the mandarin, but said nothing and turned back to Ghent with a big grin on his grotesque face. "Russell, just tell his Excellency Commander Fang these men are to be released to continue upriver."

"What kind of treachery are you up to now?" Ghent growled.

"Ghent, you guessed closer that you'll ever know, but no one here has time to prove your noisy bluffing. We had to find out if we'd caught *Confucius* supporting the enemy, but it's clear you're just lying and cheating your way up and down the river as always. Get the hell back on your steamer and away from Nanking before night falls, 'cause if you're still here tomorrow you'll never get away."

"What the hell're you talking about? Who the hell d'ya think you are anyway, tellin' me when to come and go?"

"Fool! You haven't got the sense God gave chiggers. Tomorrow we launch an offensive to end the siege and break out of Nanking. I'd just as soon gut 'n pluck you all and turn your guns on the imp war junks, but the chiefs here don't want no trouble with foreigners, even think they can make a treaty with the British, which only goes to show you're not the only fool inside these walls. So, today I have to spare your miserable lives, but this'll be one more item on my side of the ledger that someday you're going to square with me. I just want you to know that, and also that you can't do anything I don't know about. Reverend, see these *gentlemen* are issued a pass." Slaughter laughed, then heaved around, barged back through the rebel attendants, and disappeared into the dark.

"That explains the troops marching from the gate we entered," Fletcher whispered to Captain Ghent. And explains, too, why the northern part of the city is deserted. The south of Nanking faces the besieging enemy, and the remaining garrison is marshaled there ready to storm out against the imperialist camps.

The rebel mandarin shouted so loudly that the missionary winced. Fletcher hastily decided on a diversionary tactic to restore some of the face stolen by Slaughter from the commander, whose sway alone might keep their heads on duty at their present stations.

"I have a very fine pocket watch right here, Your Excellency," he blurted, stepping forward. He took his own watch and chain from his pocket, and handed it to the missionary, who gave it to the mandarin. "A gift from my grandfather on my eighteenth birthday. Gold-plated and inlaid with an ivory square-rigger. It may be a little worn, but it has been dear to me, and helped me go around the world several times in clipper ships. Please accept it as a gift from your American brother."

Commander Fang inhaled sharply at the sight of so precious an item, then grinned broadly and nodded as if saying, "Yes, yes." He turned the watch over several times, and opened and closed the cover while the missionary spoke to him again in Chinese. At the mandarin's order, an attendant produced a large document and spread it flat on the desk, then handed to the mandarin a writing brush dipped in ink from a marble stand on a side-table. The mandarin regarded the brush reverently and, holding his writing sleeve out of the way, quickly dashed several characters onto the paper. The attendant stamped the document with a large chop, folded the paper and laid it on the desk. The mandarin handed the document to Russell and issued his instructions.

"Commander Fang says to thank the American brother very much. He says that this is a splendid gift, and that he is not at all worthy to receive such a marvelous watch, especially because he has nothing comparable to give in return. He says he will not forget your generosity. This trivial document he gives to you is a river pass from the *Kan Wang* that will convey you safely through T'ai-p'ing territory. You need simply show it to any T'ai-p'ing officials, and they will comply with any reasonable request, or they will lose their heads. The commander asks me to accompany you back to your steamer."

The mandarin rose and left the hall, followed by his attendants and the rebel officer who had escorted the foreigners from their ship. The diminishing echo of the pocket watch cover clicking open and shut echoed back into the hall. The missionary led the three men out of the hall to the front of the building, where they found four sedan chairs waiting. After returning to the wharf, Fletcher was able to make several inquiries of the Reverend Russell. He had been in Nanking for several months. He was treated well. He spent many hours daily interpreting the bible in classes for the children of the Taiping *wang*s, or kings. The most important kings after the Heavenly King were the *Kan Wang*, or 'Shield King,' the *Ying Wang*, or 'Heroic King,' and the *Chung Wang*, the 'Loyal King'. The missionary had attempted to preach the gospel, but found himself frequently in conflict with the doctrines of the Heavenly King.

"They have their own curious kind of belief. In our religion, we tell of the Chosen People, and of the temptation of Christ, and the Sermon on the Mount, and so much more. These Taiping know nothing of these things. Their 'Christianity' is a barely recognizable jumble of misunderstood bible stories and native idolatry."

"It would seem that the interpretation of what is a religion is quite narrow."

"For heaven's sake, man, to accommodate the Taiping version of Christianity our definition would have to be so broad that you might just as well include the Hindus and Mussulmen. It is not always easy to reconcile the Taiping religion with Christianity as I know it, but I do my best."

"What do you know about that fellow called Slaughter?"

"Well, he's highly regarded, comes and goes pretty much as he pleases and no one interferes with him. I know he's not a missionary, and it seems the only other kind of foreigners employed here are mercenaries. I believe he has come since my arrival, for I do not recall seeing him until recently. Your captain seems to know him quite well. Perhaps he can tell you more than I can." Fletcher was not sure he knew the captain well enough to ask about Slaughter. There might not be anyone who knew Ghent that well.

"Mr. Russell, what do you know about this offensive to break the siege?"

"Only that they have been boasting about their plans ever since I came here. They had me translate their strategy to Slaughter. I didn't understand all of it, of course, but it involved an attack on Hangchow, to draw imperial troops away from Nanking."

洋神 *Yang Shen*   *James Lande* 藍德

Then the rebels were not marching on Soochow at all, thought Fletcher. When they captured those cities reported in the *Herald*, the ones I saw on the consul's wall map, they must have been on the march west *back* to Nanking, not east toward Shanghai. That would lure more imps away from the walls of Nanking. At the same time, they blocked the return of imps chasing them north from Hangchow. That was no simple strategy, if it was not an accident – it would be wisest to assume not. Does the presence of such large fleets of imperial war junks, at Kwachow and Iching, mean that the imperials know what the rebels are up to?

"Mr. Wood," the missionary said, "you really have no opium aboard?"

"Of course not, Mr. Russell. We just took on ballast and rummage at Woosung. You know, you need special packing in the hold when you carry tea, to keep from spoiling the leaves. Mr. Slaughter does not know as much as he thinks." Fletcher wondered if there was a special punishment in hell for sailors who lied to men of God.

Delevan Slaughter entered alone into a compound in the south of Nanking, near the palace of the Heavenly King, and stood quietly before guards flanking the entrance to a room in the spacious residence of the *Chung Wang*, the Loyal King Li Hsiu-ch'eng. The *Chung Wang* was the rebel chief to whom the mercenary rendered his loyalty. The general's patronage gave Slaughter the freedom to roam about the city. He came and went as he chose between the Loyal King's residence and the barracks that housed the riff-raff recruited from Shanghai, but he still was not at ease with his circumstances.

Too many kings: Attendant King, Shield King, Heroic King, Loyal King, Eastern King, Western King. Lord only knows how many more, all under orders from that crazy old coot the Heavenly King. Never shows his face, never minds military affairs. Just sits in his palace diddling with his wives, and writing poems to his big brother Jesus. There's too much confusion – better one boss, and a single, straight chain-of-command.

Slaughter had discovered more rebel commanders who coveted his service and sent lackeys to ply him with tempting offers of gold and glory, or lure away his men with secret promises of opium and women. There was growing in him an unsettling premonition of officers wavering in their defense of a starving city, and squabbling between rebel *wang*s and rival commanders over territory, weapons, men and stores just when imperial regiments storm the walls. He wanted to be gone when that happened. Only the Loyal King impressed him as having the vision and vigor to keep the rest of the mob in line, but the sand in the glass of the Loyal King was running low too.

When Slaughter was called into the room, he found the Loyal King still in conference with the *Kan Wang* Hung Jen-k'an, Prime Minister of the Heavenly Dynasty, the Heavenly King's chief civil administrator and secretary for foreign affairs. While the mercenary waited once more to be acknowledged, he wondered again how the Loyal King managed to slip in and out of Nanking so often without being caught by the impish horde surrounding most of the city.

Shouldn't be hard to sneak in from the river no matter how many imp patrols prowl the shores, but I swear more 'n once he's come through their lines from the south slicker 'n goose-grease. Not even a ghost could drift through all that many Tartars – they're so close together they can't reach t' itch without scratchin' some other feller's balls.

Comparing the two Hakka officers, Slaughter laughed to himself at the thought of the feeble *Kan Wang* – in his forties, tall and portly and dressed in long yellow robes – attempting to make his stumbling way through enemy lines. Yet if Slaughter understood it correctly, the *Kan Wang* was plotting to take command of all the rebel armies. The man was as pale as a bank clerk, obviously never lifted anything heavier than a writing brush or a chopstick, and always had this mealy-mouthed grin on his simpering face. It was the kind of grin full of the nauseating benevolence contracted from overexposure to psalm-singing missionaries.

The general made ten of the minister. His black eyes, heavy brows, straight nose and dark complexion sometimes made him appear as much Mediterranean as Chinese. He wore an unassuming scarlet quilted jacket instead of long robes, with a scarlet hood under an undress coronet that reminded Slaughter of a Gypsy fortune-teller. General Li was animated and fidgety, always shifting his legs, tapping with his foot, working his hands, and moving suddenly, which Slaughter thought a curious contrast to the general's quiet discipline on the battlefield.

Under fire, Li was perfectly cool, and often calmed those about him with a musical flow of language in a low, soft voice. Sometimes you might even catch him wearing a pair of foreign spectacles for reading. Doubtless, thought Slaughter, a very un-Chinese thing to do, but it beats holding a book against your nose to read like the *Kan Wang*. General Li came from solid peasant stock of *Hakka* charcoal-burners and worked his way up through the ranks to the command of as many as 150,000 men. It was one of the largest armies in the world and bigger than anything Slaughter expected West Point generals would ever command in the war about to start at home. To his mind, the general was the epitome of a Chinese military commander in appearance and bearing, even if on occasion Li appeared a little careworn. The brilliant strategy Li had worked out with the prime minister to break the siege of Nanking demonstrated he had the intelligence needed to lead rebel armies to victory.

The missionary Russell came in and both foreigners were motioned to take chairs beside the large table at which sat the minister and the general. Russell again struggled along as interpreter.

"Mr. Russell," the prime minister said, "did our guests return safely to their ship?"

"Yes, sir. I watched them get up steam and take up their anchor before I returned in response to your summons."

"That is good. Ask our friend here to tell me what he thought of them."

Russell put the question to Slaughter.

"Your Excellency, Mr. Slaughter says that the captain lied about who was on board the ship, and about the cargo, but that he is acquainted with the captain and is certain the steamer is not here to aid the Tartar demons. The captain has been hired by an American firm at Shanghai to bring down tea from Wuhoo."

"It is to be expected," the prime minister said, "that the captain would not wish to reveal that he is carrying a great deal of money and opium."

"Your Excellency, the mate, Mr. Wood, assured me the steamer does not carry any opium." The minister gave the missionary a compassionate smile.

"However," the prime minister said, "he may find that he has picked an inopportune time to go to Wu-hu."

"Yes," the general said, smiling, "the last of our northern armies may still be crossing the river at the Hsi-liang Shan, the West Pillar. The great number of junks encountered there may surprise the steamer. Mr. Russell, say to this fat foreigner 胖子 that the minister and I have decided that when we have broken the enemy siege, I shall go on to capture Su-chou and approach Shang-hai in order to meet with foreigners at that place. Therefore, I shall want his force of foreigners ready to go into the field very soon. I believe I may want to station some of our foreign troops in garrison at towns close to Shang-hai, in case we encounter foreigners. Will his men be ready?"

"Your Excellency, Mr. Slaughter says that his men are ready now, but that they need to be better armed to be truly effective. He says that it would have been good to take some of the arms from the *Confucius*, and that it is not yet too late to do that. She

洋神 *Yang Shen*   *James Lande* 藍德

could be boarded at Wuhoo."

"As long as the steamer does not act against us in any way," the general said, "we shall not interfere with her. It is our policy to respect the neutrality of the foreigners and to seek to convince them of the superiority of our cause. That will be all for now."

3   As soon as the two foreigners left the room, the prime minister arose from his chair and began to pace the room. "Brother Li," the prime minister said, "you were rash to tell the foreigner we plan to capture Su-chou and Shang-hai. That has not yet been decided. Must I remind you that we cannot win ten thousand victories in ten thousand battles with separate armies going wherever they wish. We must have a plan of conquest, agreed to by all our generals, approved by the Heavenly King and controlled from the center."

"And you wish to be at the center where you can be in command?"

"No, Brother Li, I do not wish to be at the center. That will always be the role of our Heavenly King. Our difficulty is that today the power of life and death is in the hands of our several individual armies instead of in one single hand. Control must be in one hand and all our armies must act together or we cannot prevail."

"Of all our generals, my hand is the strongest," Li Hsiu-ch'eng said. "Surely you can see that I must lead our armies for that reason. The Heavenly King will understand this and give me supreme command."

The prime minister stopped pacing, smiled at the general, and took his seat again. "Yes, yes," he said nodding. "Perhaps that would be the best decision. You are strong enough to command all the others. In any case, we must have agreement. After we have broken the siege, all the generals will be called together to discuss future strategy. Each must be heard and given due consideration or they will not cooperate. The Heavenly King then will decide. Until that time, no one can say what our plan will be."

The minister waited for a moment, hoping that the general would express agreement. The general was silent, but his fingers made small rapid circles on the gilt cover of an ink stone on the desk. "I know I can trust your judgement," the prime minister continued, "but I still find it very hard to believe these foreigners, and many other brother *wang*s agree. If this man Slaughter were to desert us now, he could warn the British that we are considering the capture of Su-chou, and the British might tell the Tartar imps, who would send an army to protect Su-chou."

"你放心好了," the general said, "put your mind at ease. First, the British know we will attack Su-chou sometime, and then come to Shang-hai – this is not a mystery to them. Only the date is not known, no more to them than to us at this time. Second, after we have scattered the Tartar demons from the *Chiang-nan Ta-ying*, the usurpers will not have enough troops south of the river to come to the defense of Su-chou. Third, I never confide very much information to foreign mercenaries. Each knows only a little, and what each knows is different from what the others know. They do not know enough to be harmful. Fourth, has not our country over the centuries employed the principle of borrowing talent from foreign lands, *chieh-ts'ai yi-ti* 借才異地, and used barbarians to fight barbarians. The best among these foreigners know much about waging war and fighting battles, and can get cannon, rifles, pistols and ammunition when we cannot. I will not deny there is some risk, as in all things, but the rewards are sufficient to be worth the risk if foreign mercenaries are only a small part of our forces and tactics."

"Employing the foreign refuse of Shang-hai docks is hardly an example of *chieh-ts'ai yi-ti*," the prime minister said, dryly. "In the past when foreigners were employed, they became a part of Chinese forces, and combined their skills with our own. When even this dynasty of usurping Tartars has used Russian soldiers, they were made a part of the Eight Banners. Adventurers who merely follow along, drawing a few gold coins

The Rebel Capital

in pay, ransacking towns for wine, women, and opium, who do not believe in our cause and are not even decent Christians, how can you say they ever would do more than simply protect their own interests? We are accepting too many who are not Christians, who do not share our thinking, and they weaken our army, our kingdom, from within."

"That is all I expect them to do, follow along for a few gold coins. Their deaths are of no concern."

"Perhaps your contempt for these men blinds you to their danger. There will be much to concern us if the demons can make the foreigners fight *against* us."

The general rose and paced to a window. After a moment, he returned to his chair but did not sit down. He stood behind the chair gripping the chair-back with alternate hands as he worked to banish from his voice any hint of acrimony. "When we approach the walled city," he said, "if we are careful to clearly inform the foreigners of our peaceful intentions toward them, and careful not to cross boundaries or fire into their concessions, they will limit their aid and not conduct an offensive. Besides, how can they defend the Tartar dynasty at Shang-hai while they attack the same dynasty in the north? It makes no sense."

"General Li, brother, do you not think that once they have settled their treaty differences, the foreign devils may join with the demons? How long will their neutrality last when traders like Jardine and Dent pressure their government at home to intervene? Even if the treaty port consuls were able to maintain the most precariously balanced neutrality in spite of demands by merchants, the merchants both Chinese and foreign at Shang-hai can still form their own private armies of foreigners under Ch'ing authority to protect their trade. We must at all cost try to impress the foreign community at Shang-hai that the T'ai-p'ing are the next rulers of China and cause them to give their support to us, if only to prevent them from fighting *against* us."

"Brother Hung, your spies obviously keep you very well informed." The general's tone was too ungracious for the minister to be flattered by this remark. Too well informed, thought the general, and too knowledgeable about Tartar mandarins and foreign traders to be trusted. How could we in T'ien-ching know so much about affairs in Shang-hai unless we were in close contact with the enemy – and prepared to go over to the Tartars whenever our kingdom appears about fall?

"What you say has merit," the general said, "but I cannot entirely agree. Yes, it is important to win the support of the foreigners and keep British ships of war from shelling the Heavenly Capital of T'ien-ching and sacking our city, like they did Chen-chiang many years ago. However, private armies of foreigners are not possible and can never have any influence on the outcome of this war. Believe me, I have seen the kind of insignificant foreigners available to make private armies and, while some individuals may be of value, as a group they are impossible to lead. Moreover, such units would be too small to be effective, and only foreigners could lead them. There are no such foreigners in China, and the demons would not allow foreigners to lead private armies."

The Prime Minister paused. He recognized the familiar old border in the terrain of his conversations with the *Chung Wang* and, with a reserve of patience learned in the past, the wily old catechist and evangelist refused to cross over from conversation to conflict. Other kings might be more willing to listen, but the Loyal King was the most dogmatic of the ignorant Taiping generals. Great patience and gentle counsel was required to manage the Loyal King. After the Heavenly King, the Loyal King was the main reason the prime minister needed much more time to set his plans and reforms in motion. Hung Jen-k'an rose and walked slowly to the entrance of the room and through the door asked a guard to bring more tea. Then he returned to his seat.

"What happened at Hang-chou?" he asked.

"I cannot delay returning to where my army is encamped at Tzu-chin Shan 紫金山, but I will hurriedly tell you a little about Hang-chou. I started with only a small force, but by the time the first imps attacked, our reinforcements had arrived and we could count 6000 men in ten stockades. After that, the enemy dared not attack – they fled when they saw us. At the Ch'ing-po gate, we placed a charge and blew down part of the wall, rushed in and chased out all the enemy *yung* soldiers and militia. Taking the city was not difficult, as we had learned from one of our spies, disguised as a fortune-teller, that there were fewer than 3000 soldiers inside the city. But the Tartar garrison held out so, when we received word that Chang Yü-liang's troops were arriving from Yang-chou, I ordered my men to employ the old trick for withdrawing without sufficient troops. On the walls, we set up all those filthy wood statues of Taoist gods wearing our uniforms, and straw soldiers made by stuffing empty uniforms with grass, and flew all our new banners and flags, then left behind a few men to beat gongs and drums while the rest of our army withdrew. Later I was told that the mighty general Chang Yü-liang waited outside Hang-chou one day and one night before he was allowed in, and then his troops plundered the city."

"Our plan has worked very well," the prime minister said.

"And now we are ready to strike!" the Loyal King said. With a flourish, he unrolled a large map across the table and pointed to locations forming a triangle surrounding the imperial camp. "The enemy's supplies are cut off and their men are hungry and they have not been paid for weeks and many refuse to fight. Their reinforcements are cut off and their strength is weakened by our diversions, and our spies tell us their leadership is troubled by jealousy and bickering."

General Li pointed on the map to four separate locations across the territories surrounding T'ien-ching.

"Our four kings and their generals have today been notified to begin the attack tomorrow. Each of five commanders has two columns, a total of 100,000 holy soldiers in ten columns, positioned to split the gourd and separate the armies of generals Ho Ch'un and Chang Kuo-liang."

On the map, General Li traced his path north from Hang-chou to T'ien-ching.

"Our holy soldiers," the general said, "outnumber the imps by over ten to one. The enemy is starving and dispirited. There can be only one outcome. We will be victorious and chase the imps away from the capital and back to hell where they came from!"

If the Loyal King is victorious, thought Taiping Prime Minister Hung Jen-k'an, it cannot be too soon. Our own garrison is very small now, and supplies are dangerously low. General Ho Ch'un has strangled our capital with his demon soldiers, stockades, and trenches encircling our wall. The imps blockade our communications on the Long River and cut us off from the north bank. Starve us or storm us, the demons will destroy us soon if we do not strike them first.

He stood at an open window of his library and gazed out into the garden. When there is no need of it, time pours slowly like thick syrup. When there is much to accomplish, time flows quickly like thin gruel, like water that evaporates into air or sinks into sand. All my plans would bear golden peaches of immortality if only given enough time, but the Tartar oppressors close in upon us from without, and argument and opposition within slow the progress of reform. Had I come to the Heavenly Capital many years ago instead of only last year, I would have more time now. But how could I leave my aged mother and still be considered a filial son? Surely, our clan lost its good fortune when the evil Tartar demons dug up the graves of our ancestors and scattered our forefathers' bones to the four winds.

洋神 *Yang Shen*   *James Lande* 藍德

In all the years I was a catechist and preacher, I was never faced with anything like the obstinate ignorance of these unlettered T'ai-p'ing generals, the petty-mindedness of the *T'ien Wang*'s palace relatives, or madness of the *T'ien Wang* himself. But perhaps my ambition is also a liability. My first important memorial, *A New Treatise on Political Counsel* 資政新篇, was probably too broad in its scope, too sweeping a program of political, economic and social changes, to be accepted all at once. But liberal reform is absolutely necessary to lessen the harsh character of T'ai-p'ing government and improve foreign relations. Our commerce must be revived. We must provide relief for the distressed. We must prevent girl-babies from being drowned at birth, care for the aged, disabled and destitute, do away with foot-binding, extravagant ceremony, raising birds, cricket fights, and excessive personal adornment. We should foster scientific progress through the study of Western technology.

The prime minister's library was an outward semblance of his inner mind, furnished with the bibelots and curios of his many interests and pursuits. There were several timepieces: an hourglass, a small sundial, a model of a water clock, a pendulum-driven ormolu mantle-clock, a brass chronometer salvaged from a wrecked clipper ship, and a small collection of ornate pocket watches. There were also two brass telescopes and a sextant, a world globe map, several crucifixes and a large King James Bible presented to the minister by friends from the London Missionary Society in Hsiang-kang – Hong Kong. There were wheel lock, flintlock, and percussion derringer and pepperbox pistols, a mercury barometer, thermometer and a telegraph key, a model steam locomotive, and a model side-wheel steamship. Scrolls of Chinese Christian prayers authored by the minister hung on the walls, and western books about the physical sciences and religion were crowded onto shelves and cabinets.

Strange elements of Chinese practices creep into our Christian ritual. They require only simple changes. Worshipers may be allowed to drink the three cups of tea placed on the altar, and it is not necessary to burn written prayers in order to send them up to heaven. However, there are more sensitive subjects of doctrine that the Heavenly King will oppose – the T'ien Wang, the man who went up to heaven to visit God and his elder brother Jesus. No one denies that the Heavenly King has his head up in the skies, while my feet are planted firmly upon the ground. He understands nothing of such concepts as the Holy Trinity, or original sin. Our liturgy makes not one single reference to the holy name of Jehovah. And the *T'ien Wang*'s notions of the Heavenly Mother, and the Heavenly Sister-in-law, are adapted from Chinese thought and have no place in Protestant belief. We have changed the calendar, established laws of marriage, and reordered the examination system, but these accomplishments are nothing compared to what will be necessary to remove mistakes from our religion.

If we can break this siege of T'ien-ching, that will prove the necessity of centralized military planning for conquering all of China, and perhaps our generals will see the wisdom of giving up some of their precious autonomy, instead of increasing their autonomy and becoming independent kingdoms. Then our military effort will cease to be compromised by political undercurrents fed by the rivalry of generals like Li Hsiu-ch'eng, and I will begin to command some respect from all these little *wang*s.

Finally, we must establish relations with foreign nations according to the principle of the equality of nations, and not insist that other nations be our vassals and pay tribute. The enmity between the Westerners and Pei-ching can be put to our advantage. If we can impress the foreigners with our good intentions and accomplishments, they will favor us over the Ch'ing government. But how long can we keep foreign envoys from learning the truth about our Heavenly King, that he still believes he has been sent by God to carry out a holy mission, and that he is the divine ruler of the whole world?"

洋神 *Yang Shen*   *James Lande* 藍德

The prime minister felt a light tug on his gown just below his belt. The one brave little holy soldier who dared go anywhere in the kingdom of the prime minister's household, where neither the minister's wife nor servants dare go, stood at his side. The boy held a picture book written in Chinese and English, from which he was learning to speak English, after a fashion. The son placed his hand into his father's hand and lisped in English "good evening, Father, how do you do?" The minister swept the boy up into his arms and exclaimed joyfully in English "very well, thank you!" He seated himself at his desk and plopped his son down in his lap so they could begin the evening's lesson.

Too fast, thought the prime minister. If it all happens too fast, they will never agree. Such changes must be accepted gradually. But do I have enough time?

4   At dusk, two short columns of rebel cavalry in battle dress 號衣 emerged from the palatial T'ien-ching residence of the Loyal King. Behind them rode the Loyal King himself, arrayed in scarlet jacket and undress coronet, mounted astride a spirited Mongol pony. Two more short columns of personal guard brought up the rear. They made the impressive spectacle intended, ribbons and banners streaming and weapons bristling, a brief piece of high-theater to lift the morale of the besieged and starving city. Their horses pranced down the largest thoroughfares of the city toward the Taiping Men 太平門, the Gate of Heavenly Peace, in the east wall. The rattle of hooves echoed off walls and down narrow alleyways. The scarlet jackets and hoods of the Loyal King's army glowed in the last light of day.

Empty water jars make the loudest noise when rapped, thought the Loyal King, and that empty old jug – the so-called prime minister – certainly makes the hollowest of all sounds when he puts on airs and tries to impress everyone with his fancy brush strokes. T'ang poetry and Sung prose are no mystery to me. I have read all the romantic novels. Astrology I learned in the hills of Hang-chou at Hsi-hu 西湖, West Lake, from a ninety-year-old sage who instructed me for seven days and nights, then disappeared without a word of farewell. He was like the mysterious old wizard in novels who waves his horsehair scepter, bestows supernatural powers upon a heroic swordsman, then dissolves in wisp of smoke. What kind of military experience does that empty old jug have? What battles has he fought, what cities captured, what imp generals opposed? What strategies has he thought of? None – he has not written a single thing worth reading. He knows nothing about waging war, but he knows a great deal about how to take credit for the ideas of others. In military council at Wu-hu, empty old jug told the other generals that we should employ the strategy of encircling Wei to save Zhao 圍魏救趙之計. As if I had not already thought of the plan to attack Hang-chou, and draw the imps away from T'ien-ching. As if I had not already discussed it with him over and over.

When the general's escort arrived below the wall, the guards saluted smartly and passed them through the gate and over the drawbridge beyond, then raised the drawbridge and closed the gate against the night. The general and his guard continued in the direction of the reddish-purple glow from the peak of Tzu-chin Shan, a hill of purple shale that rose abruptly just a mile or so beyond the Taiping gate in the eastern suburbs. As his pony plodded over the scorched and torn earth, the general surveyed his defenses.

Before my army took back this place a few days ago, I would have had to steal out of the city under the cover of dark, uniformed as an imperial foot soldier foraging for firewood. I had to enter that wet narrow tunnel hidden behind all the earthenware jars of black powder in the magazine enclosure next to the T'ai-p'ing gate, and cross under the city wall to where the tunnel comes out inside the abandoned well down in that hollow. Today I can ride high over the folds in the land – where before I had to conceal myself within them, and crawl through dirt and dust to cross the demon lines. The imps have changed the landscape while they camped here, built walls and excavated trenches, steeped up mounds and piled debris for cover, busy as stupid little ants, but we will change the landscape back to the way it was long ago when first we cleared the terrain.

Read Master Hsü Hsüeh-fan 許學範, I told them – look at the tactics in his *Essentials of Military Preparedness* 武備集要. Master Hsü tells us to clear away all of the villages, towers, and pagodas within one li from the outer moat, does he not? A simple man like myself – unable to read the many ancient manuals of war except, perhaps, the Art of War 孫子兵法, which every good general has committed to heart – even I can read Master Hsü's book. It has much good theory and many practical examples from actual warfare. Even a romantic novel like *The Romance of the Three Kingdoms* 三國演義 has good strategy. Master Hsü tells us that the defenders of a walled city must have an unobstructed approach, raze the countryside before the wall, and deny all useful materials and cover to the enemy. So we burnt the suburbs, brought into the city thousands of villagers who could warrant they were not spies, and drove away the rest. We leveled the hills, carted away dirt that could be used to fill the moat, cut down groves of trees that might be used for boats, ferries, ladders, firewood, or shelter. Grasses and weeds were burnt lest any become fodder for horses, and the wells were filled. We have kept it that way for seven years, except when the imp soldiers camped on our land, and put back much of what we so diligently took away. Again, we take it away – my soldiers have already bridged General Ho Ch'un's trenches here, knocked down parts of Chang Kuo-liang's 10,000 *li* wall across the foot of Tzu-chin Shan, and demolished and flattened the nearby imp stockades.

Ahead of his men the reddish-purple shale summit of the mountain still gleamed faintly in the final glow of sunset, but the parched and rugged cracks and fissures of the bleached-white limestone cliffs below the ancient summit were already lost in the darkness. Only General Chang's wall stood out in the twilight, where it slashed across the thigh and foot of the mountain like a white scar.

Chung Shan 鍾山, Goblet Mountain, once was its name, he thought, but the local folk call it Tzu-chin Shan 紫金山, Purple-gold Mountain – the unusual color of its shale peak. So did the name of the city change with time. Literary men fond of old allusions called it Chin-ling 金陵, Golden Tomb. The Ming called it Nan-ching 南京, Southern Capital. Now, we call it T'ien-ching 天京, Heavenly Capital.

An eerie silence settled in about the Loyal King's personal guard as they passed near the tomb of Emperor Chu Hung-wu. Soft earth dulled the sound of horses' hooves, and the creak of wooden saddles and clank of iron weapons was muffled by air dank and heavy with the odor of decay. The soldiers fell silent in response to the oppressive feeling of the place, and some began to glance furtively into the dark about them.

Deep within the shadows of the monument, at the rear of Chin-chu Shan 金珠山, Golden Pearl Mountain, behind which the remains of the dead emperor were buried, they clearly heard a high-pitched, hollow cry that echoed up the mountain and died slowly away. Horses pricked up their ears and snorted, and riders shortened their grip on reins. The lonely cry of wild peacocks among the Ming graves sounded like the moans of the lingering ghosts of the Ming lords. The sepulchral cry came again, then again. Some riders heard only the cry of peacocks. Others feared the lament of Ming ghosts, of emperor Hung-wu crying out from his tomb under the mountain, and of his dead ministers, answering from their secluded graves scattered in the wild places outside the city. The desolate cries made spines shiver and skin turn cold with bumps like chicken-skin. Without any word of command, the horsemen quickened the pace of their mounts.

My men are frightened of hungry ghosts, but that is not right. This is the tomb of

洋神 *Yang Shen* *James Lande* 藍德

Chu Hung-wu! Was Chu not a native Chinese rebel leader like me? Was he not from a poor peasant family like me? The founder of the Ming Dynasty was just another simple man who joined a monastery and became a monk when his family died of plague and left him without a single coin. He wandered about the countryside with only a begging bowl to live by for years, until he returned to his home village and organized a band of peasants to fight injustice. They donned the red turban and waved the red banner, and Chu began to build an army of 100,000 armored soldiers, and a fleet of 1000 fighting warships to defeat his rivals and consolidate his power up and down the Long River and across the delta. That was almost five centuries ago, when Chu Hung-wu pulled down the foreign Mongol dynasty and raised up the native Ming dynasty.

Five hundred years later, I now battle for possession of the Long River, from An-ching 3000 *li* downriver to Su-chou and Shang-hai, and one day I will again march on Pei-ching to drive out the foreign dynasty of Manchus. These noisy ghosts of the Ming, if that is what we hear in those black shadows, most likely are casting their powerful spells to aid and support the T'ai-p'ing cause, and lifting their weird voices, not in lament, but in encouragement. The ghosts of the Ming join with the T'ai-p'ing against the Tartar imps, to help the T'ai-p'ing drive all foreigners out of China.

洋神 *Yang Shen*   *James Lande* 藍德

Dramatis Personae: Chapter 16

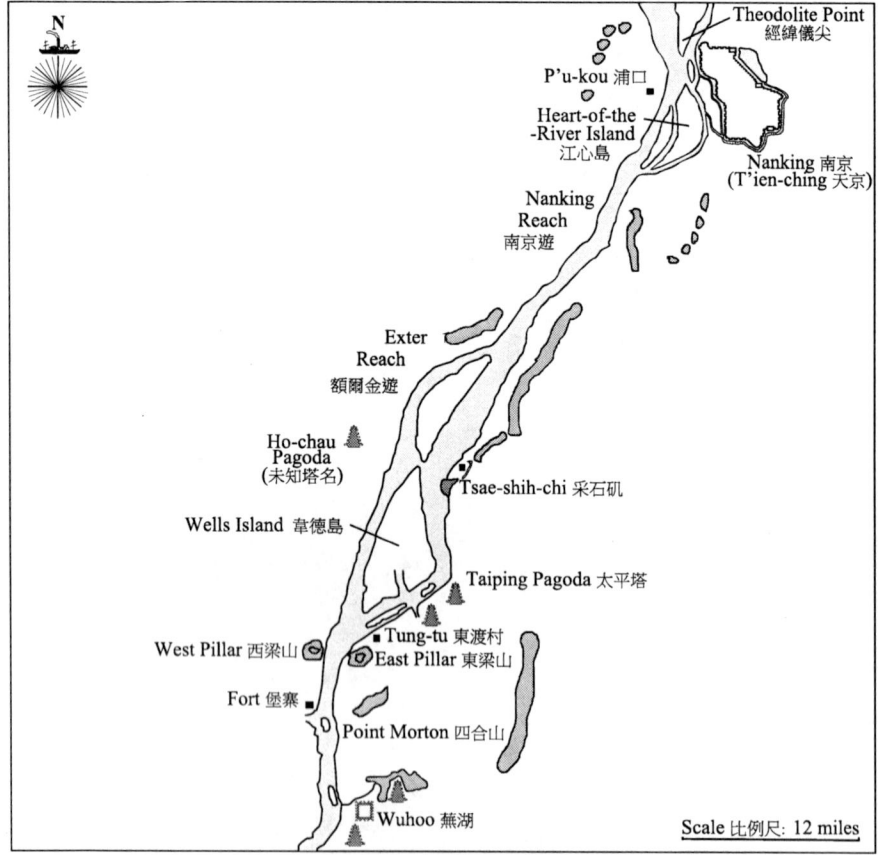

Yangtze River, Nanking to Wuhoo
(from British Hydrographic Office chart, Yang-tse Kyang, Nanking to Tu-ngliu, 1858)

One cable = 100 fathoms, or 600 feet.

Breaking the Siege

洋神 *Yang Shen*   *James Lande* 藍德

Chapter 16: Breaking the Siege
Wednesday, May 2, 1860, 3:30pm

Confucius weighed anchor and bolted from Nanking in mid-afternoon.

"Pour it on!" the captain shouted repeatedly down the voice pipe to Old Schnapps.

Ghent was determined to be well away from the battle imminent at Nanking. His late departure meant he would have to steam well into the night before raising the Pillars, fifty miles upriver. The captain did not relish piloting his steamer in the dark, but neither did he want to be caught between warring imps and rebels.

"The sooner we're away from Nanking, the better," was his muttered reprise until *Confucius* found her southerly course from P'u-k'ou 浦口 up the middle channel, and Nanking disappeared from view behind Heart-of-the-River Island 江心洲. The run south through Exter Reach was clear of obstructions and quickly traversed, and Ghent was just beginning to rue his intemperate manner, even contrive a half-apologetic grimace, when the rebels fired so close over *Confucius* that the captain spilled his coffee.

The sheer face of an extraordinary limestone rock, a half-mile long and two to three hundred feet high, protruded into the river from the right bank at Tsae-shih-chi 采石矶, the first of many uncommon sights in the highlands above Chenkiang and Nanking. Beyond the rock, Tsae-shih village 采石村 was protected by two small mud forts at the water's edge, and a camp on a rise behind the forts. An imposing display of flags flew from the battlements. The mutilated remains of several recently decapitated imperialist soldiers lay on the open ground between the forts.

As *Confucius* quietly steamed past the second fort intent upon her commerce, some loud rebels in gay colors mounted the wall of the battery and shouted and flailed the air with their arms and waved battle flags, then fired their gingals and matchlocks. The balls from the larger weapons fell short with a pitifully small splash and *Confucius* waved back and continued on her way. Then the battery brought a gun to bear on her, and got off one shot that whistled over her deck.

There was never much look-see pidgin in what passed for beat-to-quarters aboard Ghent's steamer – no bosun's pipe or drum and bugle to quicken the hot blood of sailors and marines scurrying to their stations, eager for glory and bounty. Only the first mate, new to his berth, noticeably broke the studied rhythm of the crew. He jumped down from the wheelhouse, instead of stepping calmly down the ladder, and shooed passengers from the deck into the saloon. Macanaya's gun crew walked – sauntered really – to the bow and "unlimbered" the 32-pounder about as casually as bellying up to some grog shop bar to demand *samshoo*. The Chinese deck hands appeared at their action-stations, calmly alert. The captain abruptly became very self-possessed and quietly spoke his instructions down to the engineer.

"Ahead full, Schnapps."

Confucius came about with a growl and bared her fangs at the batteries. Clearly, she did not appreciate being shot at – the more so because she assumed that she was minding her own business – for once – as well as traveling under the protection of no less than a Taiping Heavenly Kingdom river pass. Just upstream from the redoubt she slowed, settled in with the flow, and drifted sideways to a position opposite the battery. Her 32-pounder bellowed and belched enough thick, white smoke to hide a barn, and the shell from her gun *whoosh*ed across the water and exploded with a reverberating *whump* at the foot of the battery. When the smoke and dust cleared, the wall of the battery lay in rubble, and through the breach rebel gunners were seen scampering to the rear with their loose yellow and red robes flapping in the wind. *Confucius* quickly came about just in

Breaking the Siege

洋神 *Yang Shen*   *James Lande* 藍德

time to avoid the shallows and resumed churning her way upriver.

That was the only incident to mar the otherwise quiet passage away from Nanking. On the approach to Wells Island, there was much evidence of rebel troop movement at places along the right bank, and on inland roads leading east to Nanking. However, the rebel army appeared resolved to reach its holy city, and no more reckless rebels offered to challenge the steamer. The captain put Fletcher at the wheel and directed him to take *Confucius* west around Wells Island. In that channel, there was no bottom at eight fathoms, and they could avoid shallow ground on the right bank 3½ miles WSW of the Taiping Pagoda. They could avoid as well a dangerous shoal that stretched out into the eastern channel abreast of the village of Tung-tu 東渡村.

When they came out from behind Wells Island, opposite Tung-tu, where the river narrowed to less than a mile, it was already 9:00pm, dusk had fallen, and the forests above the shoreline were a black outline beneath the last light. Increasingly loud noises drifted down the river to within earshot – the thumping of wood and clatter of metal, and an occasional drum roll or crash of gongs. Lights on the river and shore came into view and *Confucius* slowed. In the black night, they could see the dim glimmer of dozens of flickering lamps in the fortifications and gun emplacements that clung to the nearly sheer face of the West Pillar 西梁山. Much fainter lights glowed across the river on the wall of the East Pillar 東梁山.

Ahead of the steamer, hundreds of lanterns strung out across the river swayed in the dark. A weir of soft light illuminated the passage of countless shadowy junks and sampans drifting across the current from the west shore to the east and back, apparently ferrying soldiers of the rebel armies from north of the Yangtze toward their rendezvous at Nanking. Captain Ghent allowed *Confucius* to drift to within fifty yards of the nearest junks before calling for just enough steam to suspend her mid-stream, and ordered a crewman forward to hang two kerosene anchor lanterns from the jackstaff. Together with Fletcher and the pilot, the captain peered out through the wheelhouse window at the incandescent spectacle blocking passage upstream of his vessel.

Some rebel boats were the small green and yellow imperial war junks Old Huang called "quick-ferry" boats 快渡船, about seventy feet long with twenty oars to a side, a rattan war-shield painted with a tiger's head above each oar, and small cannon fore and aft and gingals in the waist. These generally were burdened with twice their complement of forty men. The rest were mostly sampans and cargo-ferries, either the smaller forty-foot Wuhoo cargo-ferry 擺江子, commandeered to transport twenty closely-packed soldiers, or the larger Nanking or broad-beamed Hankow-style lighters and cargo-boats 駁船, overloaded with as many as six-hundred soldiers or more. As each boat touched the east bank, the soldiers jumped down, splashed ashore, formed quickly into ranks according to the insignia on their square and triangular flags, and to the clamor of drums and gongs marched off company by company in the direction of Nanking.

A war junk detached itself from the line of cargo boats and dropped down to hail the steamer. From her, *Confucius* learned that thousands of soldiers had passed over the river, and thousands more waited to cross.

"Jehoshaphat!" Ghent said, fuming. "I steamed upriver forty miles to get away from that plague of rebel locusts."

"They'll take hours more to ferry the rest," Fletcher said.

"Might as well pass the night here," Ghent said, "under the West Pillar."

Confucius dropped anchor out of the stream. She was just settling down when rebels hailed her from the shore battery at the foot of the West Pillar, pushed out in a sampan with a lantern shining in its bow, and approached the steamer. Fletcher was still

洋神 *Yang Shen*   *James Lande* 藍德

on deck and chose to lower the boarding ladder instead of merely drop a boarding net over the side, to which gesture he attributed the relaxed and courteous manner of the rebel officer who came aboard. The pilot came on deck to translate the officer's perfunctory questions as to the steamer's business on the river. Then the officer's expression changed, and he asked if *Confucius* had fired at a rebel battery downriver. For a moment, Fletcher considered whether to acknowledge the infraction, or even admit they knew it had been a rebel battery, but he remembered the Taiping river pass issued to *Confucius* at Nanking and showed it to the officer, who read in Chinese the following:

> *Founder of the Dynasty and Truly Loyal Chief of Staff of the T'ai-p'ing T'ien-kuo, Commander of the Right Army, the Kan Wang, Hung Jen-kan:*
> **By the order of the Kan Wang:**
> *All personnel at checkpoints and gates are informed:*
> *Now, the captain Mr. Ke-na-t'e of a foreign country ascends the Long River in the foreign steamship Confucius to trade at Wu-hu. He is to be allowed to proceed to Wu-hu and to return to T'ien-ching. Upon being shown this pass, you are ordered to permit passage and not block the way. This is urgently commanded.*
> *Issued at the Heavenly Capital of T'ien-ching on the 22nd day, 3rd month, 10th year Keng-shen of the T'ai-p'ing T'ien-kuo of the Heavenly Father, Heavenly Elder Brother, and the T'ien Wang.*
> *Countersigned by Fang Lo-wen, Regimental Commander, second-in-command of northern defenses, supporter of the Celestial Institutes.*

    The officer caught his breath, reverently folded the document, and touched it to his forehead before returning it to Fletcher. Without further questions, but with many smiles and good wishes, he hastily retreated down the ladder, jumped into his sampan, and disappeared into the night.

    "Old Huang! What is in that document?" Fletcher said. "The poor fellow flew out of here as if pursued by all the devils from Chinese hell."

    The pilot laughed. "Pletty good tlade, huh? Lebel livah pass fo' ol' pockee watch you catchee off dum' sumbitch pilot in goddamn stud pokah game at Sta'ling Island. Yoo say let ol' Huang win back watch! Now whatcha do, Fechawood?"

Log of Steamer CONFUCIUS, chartered by Augustus Fitch & Company

Date & Time	Location	Wind (est.)	Current	Speed	Cargo
Wednesday May 2 1860 9:00pm	West Pillar, Yangtze R. Anhui	NW 3 knots	3 knots	7 knots	Tea

2   When Fletcher Wood came on deck the next morning, the sky was dark with threatening clouds surging upriver, and the air had chilled considerably from the previous day. The two rocks called East and West Pillar, or The Gate, were large in the morning light, and seemed like an immense stone gateway to the lower reaches. The passengers argued about just how high the Pillars were – some said over 600 feet high, while others snickered that they weren't more than 250 to 300 feet high. Fortifications and batteries pocked the nearly vertical face of each rock, base to summit. At the foot of each, there was a small village surrounded by ramparts quickened in appearance by the fluttering of rebel colors. Fletcher found the captain and Chester Hicks at the rail, listening intently to dull pounding coming out of the northeast. The river was deserted.

    "Sound like thunder to you, Mr. Wood?" the captain said. Fletcher listened for a moment to the irregular and often simultaneous reports of varying intensity.

    "Too much to be thunder," he said. "It's gunfire, some 32-pounders."

    "I was afraid you'd say that – but I'd've said it too. We've just missed being smashed between hammer and anvil. Trick now is to get back downriver past Nanking with a cargo of tea, and towing a barge."

    "We could wait it out at Wuhoo," Fletcher said.

Breaking the Siege

"No, sir," Hicks said. "I am sorry Mr. Wood, but this kind of engagement can go on for weeks or months, and I cannot delay the transport of tea I have contracted to deliver to Augustus Fitch in Shanghai before May 10th. Even setting my promise aside, time is of the essence in processing the tea quickly and getting it to market – the cargo will spoil if left on board here near the damp of the river."

"Suits me," Fletcher said. "I'd just as soon take a look at what's happening over yonder at Nanking. Even from the deck of a passing steamer."

"You want to see the sights, Mr. Wood," the captain said, with a snort, "you buy yourself passage on some gilded stern-wheeler. S'pose I have to heed the wishes of my passenger, tho', at least if there's a reasonable or better chance of squeaking past that hullabaloo in one piece. Get under way for Wuhoo, Mr. Wood, and we'll see how things stand after the cargo is aboard."

Half an hour later, *Confucius* had her steam up, raised her mud hook, and worked her way out to mid-channel between the tall pillars of The Gate. Fletcher stayed at the wheel with the captain, Chester Hicks, and the pilot. The captain pressed Hicks into duty as assistant pilot for the stretch of river that Hicks had passed over four months earlier.

"Every man must be his own pilot, Mr. Wood," Chester Hicks said.

"From the Pillars, the course up the river is southerly," the captain said. "Keep Morton Point close aboard, and pass to the eastward of the small, flat island you'll see there. Three miles further south, there's a rock or shoal about a cable's length off the right bank. That right, Mr. Hicks?"

"Yes, Captain," Hicks said. "The rock just shows in November, and six feet of it was dry in December. The mud shoal around it was exposed, but in May who knows how much water lies over it."

Fletcher began to get a feel for handling the large side-wheeler. He noticed that in this narrow stretch of the river, *Confucius* wallowed some while she forced her way upstream in the swifter current due to the weight of her guns. With all the propulsion at her waist, she tended to fantail easily in fast water – like a waggely-tailed little tart in a tight skirt, he thought – and required constant attention at the wheel to keep her in line. So far inland, almost 240 miles from Woosung, the ocean tide no longer had much effect. The ebb no longer hastened the downstream flow, but neither did the flood hurry the steamer forward, and she relied increasingly to her own none too stable propensities.

"How did you like your visit to Nanking, Mr. Wood?" Chester Hicks said.

"Hospitality was a little rough," Fletcher said. "Their mandarins could not desist from lopping off the heads of unbelievers long enough to set out a service of tea. Even concocted an amateur theatrical for our salvation – sent three poor fools to meet their Maker. Other than their tiresome Christian homilies, however, they seem not to differ much from their quarrelsome imperialist brothers."

"Did you see many rebel soldiers?"

"The rebel garrison was out paying court to the imps at the time, so I could not get a reliable idea of their actual strength. They seem poorly equipped, with medieval matchlocks and halberds mostly, and in great want of simple necessities right in the very heart of their kingdom. Don't impress you much as a going concern. More foreigners in the city than I expected – mix of missionaries and mercenaries. Turncoat named Slaughter appears to have wormed his way into their trust."

"Ho, Captain!" Hicks said, chuckling. "Your nemesis materializes again."

"Some little devil left the barn door of hell open," Ghent said, snorting "and that abomination sneaked out."

"Well, bad pennies will turn up," Hicks said, laughing. "It's no surprise Delevan Slaughter's among the rebels. The captain may have his private reasons for hating the man, but the rest of us waste no affection upon him either, and he dare not show his face in Shanghai. He's said to be the reason they invented the quip 'mean enough to steal the coppers off a dead man's eyes'."

"Man's as savage as a meat axe." Ghent spat.

"Slaughter fell prey to a common failing among China coast pilots," Hicks said. "He sacrificed his career to demon rum, and in a state of intoxication caused a terrible collision in which many lives were lost, then jumped overboard when he could have stayed and helped to save passengers and crew. That's what most folks know, anyway."

"Don't say – man's making a career of treachery," Fletcher said. "He was a river pilot when he grounded a steamer I was on, stole thousands in gold specie, and caused more than a few deaths. Wonder what he'll do for the rebels?"

"Run guns, recruit mercenaries, maybe even fight. Who knows what goes on inland? Won't preach the gospel, I'll wager. Seems these days every worthless pilot on the China Coast turns up in Nanking for a spate of duty with the rebels. The Taiping are not very fastidious about the company they keep, if Delevan Slaughter is at Nanking. Any other foreigner there would suffer the onus of being in bad company."

Confucius kept her mid-channel course for several miles of the Wuhoo reach, until she came up on an anchorage protected by several mud forts on the right bank. Inshore under a range of low hills mounted by a pagoda there was the wall of a town. Fletcher kept the steamer away from the right bank below the anchorage, then steered into the anchorage to avoid a small islet about 1½ cables from shore. Hicks told him that in December there were dry mud shallows for about two miles approaching the anchorage.

"They tell me," Hicks said, "Wuhoo means 'weedy lake,' which explains why we anchor here and load cargo from lighters. They come down that stream from the town. Past Wuhoo, the stream goes into to the rice-growing country beyond, and eventually to the Grand Canal. I'd guess you don't have to go inland far to find rebels in possession of the villages. Rebel control of the river ends here – there are imperial posts ten miles upstream, and flotillas of gunboats to harass your passage."

Chinese clad in rich, shining silks hailed the steamer from where they balanced precariously, waving and grinning, on the bows of two sampans that set out together from a junk in the anchorage. Chester Hicks and Sankey waved back and shouted a greeting, and were informed by the sampans where best to moor the steamer. While Ghent and his crew slowly maneuvered *Confucius* to anchor, the Chinese from shore quickly came aboard and went up to the wheelhouse to be introduced to the captain. Before Ghent had an opportunity to grouse that he was busy at the wheel, the guests were hustled back down to the deck and into the saloon.

Bottles of Giesler's Creaming Champagne and some expensive *samshoo* were broken out to celebrate the arrival of the steamer, and the prospect of a large and profitable business transaction. On shore, a crowd of brightly dressed onlookers, rebel soldiers and civilians, gathered waterside to marvel at the appearance of the remarkable foreign steamer. As he waited at the bow for the command to drop the anchor, Fletcher noticed what a lively contrast the colors of high fashion in the rebel community made next to the somber indigo blue prevailing elsewhere in China. This blithe impression reversed a turn, however, when at a far corner of the anchorage, on the bank just above the waterline, he saw a pack of snarling dogs tearing at the remains of a human body.

Welcome to Wuhoo, he thought.

After the steamer was secured, and rebel officers had sculled out to conduct the formalities of arrival, the captain ordered Fletcher to accompany the shore party.

"Arm yourself discreetly, Mr. Wood, and don't let Chester Hicks out of your sight for very long at one time. He is in his element here, of course, certainly more than I am, but if I must err, let it be on the side of caution. I will see to arranging for the coal, ballast and stowage in our hold, and will expect you within two hours or so, with our passengers in tow, and with the first loads of tea to bring aboard."

The morning air was crisp and smelled of incense and smoke from charcoal braziers cooking morning meals. Fletcher, Hicks, and Sankey and two of his bodyguards boarded the sampans and were sculled over to a small junk, a dull and grimy Kiangsu trader that was making ready to ascend the stream to the town. Sankey's other two men stayed aboard *Confucius* to guard the treasure. The junk caught the rising northerly breeze and made the old stone quay under the city wall in half an hour, better time than Fletcher expected from such a clumsy old hulk.

A sailor couldn't spend two years coasting in China, he occasionally thought, and come away with no understanding at all of the infinite variety of fascinating contrivances the Chinese put on water. Fletcher recognized, even appreciated, more than a handful of Chinese ocean going and river junks, boats, sampans, lighters, gigs and punts, even some rare idiot paddling about a harbor in a wooden washtub. Such were called "kettle-boats" by what he was sure had to be the most mendacious Chinese under Orion. He found none of the Chinese vessels more engaging, however, than what he called the "five-card stud" junks, the Kiangsu traders, "sah-choon" he'd heard them called, "sand-boats."

Where the graceful sail contour of the classic junk opened up like a paper fan, the five tall rectangular lugsails of the Kiangsu trader were raked forward at the bow and backward at the stern like five cards fanned out in the hand of a precise and fastidious poker player. At sea, he once saw a 170-foot ocean-going model scudding north for Peking, but mostly they were 80-foot little brothers of maybe 100 tons burden, like this one. They rarely went to sea, and were largely confined to the Yangtze estuary.

While Chester Hicks and Sankey observed the proprieties with the tea agents in the laodah's cabin, Fletcher was free to wander the length of the vessel. He called her "Poker Hand" for want of knowing her real name, having discarded "Two Pair," "Three-of-a-kind," "Full House," and "Straight Flush" as less germane. The unexpected delight he took in examining all her corners and crevices, was a welcome distraction. He wandered through the house, where his quick smile and hesitant air gained for him the same courtesy in return from the Chinese crew, who could see his keen interest and appreciation of the rare vessel of which they were justly proud. He sauntered past a smoky cooking stove in the starboard alcove, past cabins with upper and lower berths for the crew, past the rice bin and workroom, and the inevitable shrine to the Chinese Stella Maris, the goddess Gone Yeen. On other junks, she was depicted as the savior of sailors, Ma-zoo-po, but always she was present in some incarnation in every Chinese junk he'd ever boarded.

Suspended on a pole lashed haphazardly over the starboard quarter, a candle enclosed in a crude isinglass-like box that served as a sort of sallow navigation light, one carried by no other junks Fletcher had thus far seen in China except Kiangsu traders. At her mainmast head spun one of the most curious devices anywhere – a revolving wooden egg supporting a six-foot slender red pennant, with smaller pennants above, topped by a palm frond. The people are easy to read and understand, he thought – it's the palm fronds on the main trucks of Kiangsu traders that are inscrutable.

He guessed that below deck, a couple of her dozen or more bulkheads would be storing fresh water or housing crew or storing ropes and sail and sea anchors. The boat-builder had rabbeted the curved deck beams into the curved frames of the hull, and extended the transom into a 10-foot gallery over the stern. That served as a balcony over the world sweeping past, and made it easier to work on the rudder. He wondered how a

70-foot spar of Oregon pine had made its way down the Columbia River through Astoria to China to become the main mast of a Chinese junk.

The little company of tea-buyers disembarked on the quay, where they were greeted by still more silk-clad agents and their servants, and were conveyed into large godowns roofed by green tile supported on red brick columns erected close by the river. Hicks and Sankey were escorted into the richly appointed offices of the tea-sellers' agents to make their arrangements and taste samples of the teas. Fletcher and Sankey's guards waited outside under the eaves. Coolies under close supervision of the tea agents began carrying tea chests out of the godown to small lighters at the quay. Wuhoo cargo-ferries and more lighters queued up nearby to come alongside.

Fletcher stood on the smooth, hard-packed floor and peered into the dark, narrow openings that led into the godown, from where a melange of rousing odors roiled forth. His nostrils flared as he sniffed at the rich mix of flowered tea scents, and he traced with his fingertip the elaborate Chinese characters of the chop marks painted on the stacked wooden tea chests, evidently the brand names that identified the origin of the teas.

Servants of the tea-sellers' agents bustled out with rattan stools and a small table on which they arrayed teacups and pots of steaming water. They invited Sankey's men to sit, and gestured to Fletcher. Tea leaves were sprinkled into the cups from a newly opened packet of tea, covered with hot water, and closed to steep. After a few minutes of awkward silence, the guards gestured to Fletcher. He removed the cover to find the water swimming with tea leaves – Chinese fashion. In the past, when he had not yet learned to push the leaves to the back of the cup with the lid, he had wondered how to drink the stuff without choking on the leaves. He took a sip.

Several rebel officers accompanied by armed soldiers came in turn to the godowns, and each time Fletcher and Sankey's guards went and stood at the entrance to the offices, not quite sure of the protocol, but not about to allow armed men to enter. Each time, a tea sellers' agent came out to escort the officer inside, while the soldiers fell into conversation with Sankey's guards. About an hour after they first arrived at Wuhoo, Chester Hicks emerged from the godown offices and joined Fletcher.

"Good. They've already got the loading started," Hicks said. "What are all these soldiers here for?"

"They came with the rebel officers."

"Oh, of course. Always a nuisance, these fellows. Clamoring to buy cannon, muskets or pistols. Offer a king's ransom in silver for anything they can get their hands on – fowling pieces, clocks, watches, even metal files. They can't very well walk off with chests of tea, but I'd watch them anyway. How'd you like your tea?"

"It was bitter."

Hicks chuckled. "Must've served you the stuff we rejected. We'll be off shortly now that all the dickering's done, go back down on that junk so the opium can be unloaded into her. Then we'll start loading the tea from these lighters into your steamer. She'll take most of 5000 chests, the more expensive Bohea pekoe and Keeling pekoe, and some of the Saokee pekoe. The barge and the junk will be loaded here at Wuhoo and brought down tomorrow morning."

"Who watches the tea loaded here, to prevent the chop-boat coolies from passing up a chest with two tallies stuck to it, or slipping a package overboard?"

"You have done this before, haven't you? That will have to be left to Sankey, and the sellers' agents can pretty well be trusted to see our contract honored. Those old boys will still be here after the nameless coolies have disappeared. When Sankey brings the treasure back up here and turns it over, we can have his men watch some of the loading, and ride shotgun on the lighters going downstream to discourage pilferage."

"You could say that I've been in a steamer that carried tea, but I never learned more than how to stow it properly."

"Look here at this chest. The characters, or chop, written on it tell where it came from, but not its quality. You must learn which kind of tea is represented by what chop. Take this chest here, for example. I don't read Chinese, but I know those characters 武彝 stand for Bohea, the name of some place in Fookien, which produces a high-quality black pekoe for which we pay $29.00 Mexican per chest. The earliest leaf buds in the season still have their soft down. They are quite delicate and careless firing will destroy their flavor. The next best pekoe, with these characters 旗嶺 on the chests, is called Keeling. The Keeling pekoe has open black leaves mixed with blossoms, and we pay $16.00 per chest for it. The cheapest kinds of tea we're buying are Saokee and plain orange pekoe. Over here, in this chest with the characters 小池, we have Saokee pekoe, called 'small pool,' which has green leaves mixed in and we buy for $10.00 a chest. Those over there with the characters 上香, which I'm told means 'superior fragrance,' hold plain orange pekoe, also are $10.00 a chest. The leaf is small and curled with a yellowish hue and whitish tips like pekoe. Most of it is exported to the United States. These teas are all from the earliest crops in the hinterlands, so they have the best taste when flavored and fired. Even more important, because the rebels are likely to cause a major disruption of this year's tea trade, not as much tea will get out and demand for the limited supply is sure to drive up prices. We purchase for Augustus Fitch a total of 8780 chests of tea at a cost of $128,300. If we can get it all downriver past the Taiping, Fitch stands to come by as much as ten times that in profits."

Fletcher spent that afternoon in the hold of *Confucius* overseeing the unloading of the opium onto the tea-agents' junk he had dubbed *Poker Hand*. After the hold was clear of opium, he directed the stowage of 4800 chests of Bohea and Keeling pekoe tea from dozens of Wuhoo lighters that crowded the little stream down from the city. The captain had done a creditable job of preparing the fore and aft holds for the tea. The bilge was pumped clear of water, and thousands of small round stones had been dumped in over the keelson. Clean boards of pine and camphor wood covered the stones, so that the tea would not touch the ballast. A great quantity of split bamboo was set against the sides of the hold to cushion the chests and prevent damage to them. Atop this, the flooring chop of tea chests was to be laid in, followed by tier after tier of chests rising up to the underside of the deck above. The teas described by Chester Hicks all came in lead-lined wooden chests of different sizes wrapped in oilpaper. Canvas spread on top warded off water during the voyage and prevented spoilage by damp.

Fletcher decided himself how to pack the tea chests. Stout a vessel as she was, Confucius still could not carry more tea than even a very sharp clipper ship. The holds fore and aft each stored 2400 chests more or less in tiers 10 feet high with room for access and ventilation. Had there been no barge or junk to carry the additional load, the steamer's forecastle could have been appropriated and filled some 660 chests, and the crew and black gang made to sleep on the saloon floor and on deck. Another 250 or so chests might have been stuffed into four cabins, and the officers formerly resident there sent looking for other accommodations. Any chests remaining would have been chucked down to the barge when it arrived, as Confucius was a war ship and would not clutter her decks with baggage that might get underfoot in a fight.

When each lighter unloaded, the chests were carried up over the side by a line of coolies, tallied and stamped by the captain, Sankey, and one of the agents, and lowered into the holds where they were carefully stacked and secured by the Chinese hands.

When the last chest came aboard, the count was short by twenty cases. The Chinese tea agent rattled off what Fletcher assumed was invective about worthless coolie thieves, too many boats to watch, and too little time to load, then jumped down into the last lighter and beat back up toward Wuhoo to fetch back chests to make up the discrepancy. After the captain, and Sankey under Chester Hicks direction, examined the stowage of the tea, and counted and recounted the cargo, the holds, forecastle and cabins were sealed and the crew came on deck to find twilight had already fallen.

"Glad to be rid of the opium," Hicks said. The officers and passengers had finished supper and Hicks joined Fletcher at the rail for a smoke. "Whatever else a person might think of the poison trade, it's too great a temptation to skullduggery when on board. Now word will go out that we've unloaded the stuff and robbers will lose interest."

"As long as they aren't interested in tea," Fletcher said. "I am in agreement with you and glad to be free of the risk, but happy too just to be rid of the drug. I don't take it, and I don't like anyone who does, have no use for them at all. Opium has already caused more than its share of mischief here in China."

"Maybe the Chinese would be better off if the British did not import opium, or maybe they'd just grow it themselves. The point is moot as long as opium is the only alternative to silver for buying Chinese tea and silk. The West has nothing else the Chinese want in trade."

"They want steamships, don't they? And artillery and other arms. I've wondered sometimes why we don't trade steamers for tea and silk."

Hicks chuckled. "Nobody has that many steamers."

"You mean foreigners buy a lot of tea and silk?"

"Heaps. But there is something to your idea."

"About steamships?"

"Yes. Of course, most Chinese still dislike the idea of railroads, telegraphs, steamships and modern artillery, but some progressive fellows among them look to the future and see such things are unavoidable. Gradually, reaction against our Western toys will lessen. The understanding of what's needed to develop modern technology, and the supporting structure of economy and education, will become less an anathema to conservative Confucians. Most of that's a ways off. But maybe not steamships."

"Like *Confucius*, steam-powered gunboats, or war-steamers as they are called in the newspapers? Captain Ghent seems to think that there will be a lot of steamers on the Yangtze, after the river is opened to trade under the new treaty."

"The merchant houses in Shanghai think that once they've got steamers up the Yangtze, they can unload all those cotton and woolen goods stuffed into their godowns behind the Bund. But Chinese upriver don't want cottons or woolens any more than Chinese elsewhere. Furs are preferred to wool, and homespun cotton is a thriving cottage industry. However, suppose enterprising persons were to establish a steamship company to transport Chinese goods up and down the river, and out to the coast. Fast, reliable, and hard for pirates or rebels to attack. Now there's something I'd bet the Chinese would want very much."

"That would take a pot o' gold, wouldn't it, to finance a steamship business? Who would do it? Certainly not the merchant princes of Shanghai – they never put any of their own money at risk. Overseas investors are too far away from China, and the conservative Chinese you mentioned would not take the risk, would they?"

"I would not sell your merchant princes short just yet," Hicks said. "After all, this is the 19th century, and the times are changing rapidly, as I see it. If you listen to traders like Augustus Fitch, the commission business has already seen its zenith, and other enterprises are supplanting trade. You must have seen in our own country how much

洋神 *Yang Shen*   *James Lande* 藍德

money is going into factories, railroads, and such, like those textile mills down in your neck of the woods, at Lowell. More investment is going into manufacturing that builds up the wealth of a country, so that when the business is finished, you have your profits but you also have something more to point to, something lasting that will continue to be of value, something you can pass on."

Later that evening, the tea-agent's junk *Poker Hand* returned downriver laden with 1280 chests of Saokee pekoe tea. The junk towed a barge laden with 2700 chests of Saokee and orange pekoe tea. They stopped for the night beside the steamer. Several of the silken-gowned Chinese agents, each with a somber, worried expression, clambered aboard under oiled-paper umbrellas and gathered in a corner of the saloon in hushed conference with Sankey and Hicks. After the agents disembarked, Hicks met with the captain and Fletcher alone in the wheelhouse.

"All hell has broken loose at Nanking," Hicks said. "At least ten rebel columns, over 100,000 men, are attacking imperial stockades surrounding the city. Some of imperialist camps have already been smashed, and the soldiers scattered across the countryside toward Soochow. Most of the armies are still engaged, but vastly greater numbers of rebels are overwhelming the camps. Every sign points to the imminent probability of a crushing defeat of the imperial armies. If we start downriver now, we are likely to pass dead center through a storm of fire, and come out on the other side among hordes of defeated soldiers ravaging the countryside and plundering the river."

Log of Steamer CONFUCIUS, chartered by Augustus Fitch & Company

Date & Time	Location	Wind (est.)	Current	Speed	Cargo
Thursday May 3 1860 9:00pm	Wuhoo, Anhui	SE 20 knots	3½ knots	NA	Tea

3 All that long dark night, marauding southeasters one after another assailed the shivering river. Storms shouldered their way between the Pillars, and pummeled the foreign steamer hunkered down like a wet dog in the anchorage. Purple clouds loosed packs of howling winds that dashed over her decks, bayed at closed portals and locked windows, nosed under loose vent covers, slunk between ill-fitted jambs into cold cabins, and rubbed roughly against skittish men, chafing the skin and abrading the patience.

No one aboard *Confucius* slept soundly that night, and there was no tranquil sunrise to wake to, so the crew quickly came to stations when called early the next morning. *Confucius* was under way steaming for Nanking by 6:00am, through showers of hail the size and hardness of musket-balls, followed by *Poker Hand* towing the barge. Droves of ugly black thunderstorms stampeded down the river and eastward toward the delta, sending down hail that clattered on the steamer's roofs and decks like dancing stallions. Some swollen black clouds spread out over the water and mingled with white mists of damp fog. Visibility was so reduced that the steamer had to reverse engines to slow, or steer completely out of the current, and wait until she could see the river again, almost causing the trailing junk to pile up under her stern until more distance was put between them. At other times, there was no delay between light and sound. Thunderclaps louder than a park of 64-pounders rattled every loose thing in the wheelhouse – coffee cups, window latches, and teeth – and made brave men flinch, then laugh at one another to quell their fright and salve their injured bluster. Fletcher wondered half-seriously if the angry heavens had not opened up in furious response to the violence likely being raised by the holy soldiers of the Heavenly Kingdom at Nanking.

Winds of tremendous velocity thrust at the slab-sided steamer from all directions, heeling her over out of the channel and toward the shallows. Winds fell suddenly on her bow, reduced her speed by a quarter, then punched into her stern and kicked her forward so fast that the captain hollered for reverse engines. After six hours of such pummeling,

洋神 *Yang Shen*   *James Lande* 藍德

grounding twice, and watching thick columns of black ash downriver grow larger and swirl up into the storm, a very tired and testy *Confucius* came finally within sight of the city of Nanking.

    Battle smoke rising into storm clouds obscured the spectacle she witnessed there, and thunder mingled with the roar of heavy guns impaired her hearing. Often enough, however, the shrouding curtains of smoke and cloud blew aside to reveal the bloody proscenium of the battlefield, and the broad approaches to the walled city smoldering in the flames of war. *Confucius* slowed to just a knot faster than the current, barely enough speed to steer a course. For the hour it took to steam from the southern-most spit of Heart-of-the-river Island to the north wall of Nanking, her officers and passengers, and even some of her hardened crew, looked on in fascinated horror much as awed Zoar must have gazed upon Gamorah. And the smoke of the country went up as the smoke of a furnace, thought Fletcher.

    Fletcher peered through a telescope out over encampments of rebel tents along the shore opposite Heart-of-the-river Island. The fluttering banners and flags and bright uniforms of a rebel column could be seen three miles distant trudging north through the thick mud of towns and villages west of Nanking. In the wake of the rebel army lay the ruins of smashed wooden stockades that for months had protected imperial regiments camped near the southwest corner of the city. More stockades nearby roared and crackled with white heat like huge crematoriums, encircled now only by armies of decapitated imperial dead.

    "Rebels are marching on the imperial stockades outside the walls of the city," Fletcher said. "They have joined with rebels coming out of Nanking, and are attacking one stockade after another, and driving out the imperial soldiers."

    Confucius came closer and watched as rebel skirmishers fanned out from the body of the rebel army. They approached another wooden stockade held by imperial troops, outside the west wall of the city, north of the rebel army's position. Atop the stockade, puffs of white smoke appeared between the whipping banners and pennants of the defenders. The rebel skirmishers fell back into the column, which divided and took up separate positions about two-hundred yards apart, just beyond the range of the muskets atop the stockade. Rebel artillery moved to the right flank, from where it could enfilade the log parapet and cover the rebel infantry rushing the moat at foot of the stockade. A reserve of rebel marksmen armed with matchlocks, muskets and gingals moved out to form ranks before each half of the column.

    Outside the gate of the imperial stockade, where the wooden drawbridge lay in the moat, four 6-pounders, two at each side, opened slow fire on the rebels. The shells fell short, but were in range of the approach to the stockade wall. The rebel column waited. Suddenly a troop of rebel horse wheeled around the far side of the stockade, galloping between the moat and the stockade, and charged the guns. At the same moment, the rebel infantry stormed forward under the cover of the crossfire set up by their reserves.

    Canister fired from the gate thinned the first ranks forward, until cavalry cut down the imperial gunners and withdrew out of musket range, after dragging the guns into the moat. The next ranks picked up discarded scaling ladders and continued running for the stockade. If the onset of the rebel attack was the lightening, the sound of their signal gongs and drums and war cries was the thunder that arrived seconds afterward, far away on the river, as only a thin, disjointed echo from some hollow part of the battlefield.

    The rebels raised their ladders high and dropped them across the moat, then ran over the ladders to the opposite side, quickly but precariously, some soldiers holding their arms out for balance, or over their heads like a monkey walking a rail. Soldiers disappeared into the ditch and reappeared scrambling up the far side. Some fired from

Breaking the Siege

the cover of the ditch. A few used their long bamboo spears to vault across the moat.

Fusillades from the reserves raked the top of the parapet and kept the defenders from approaching too closely to the edge, causing their gingal fire to fly high over the heads of the attackers. Falls of arrows and arrow-headed rockets loosed from within the stockade flew over the parapets and into the attackers, shredding the rebel ranks. The rebel battery responded from the flank with a loud volley of canister and rockets that chipped up bark and splinters along the length of the palisade.

The attackers yanked up the ladders, ran them up against the palisade, and began climbing toward the parapet. Avalanches of heavy stones, boiling water, and slurries of urine and feces crushed the first soldiers up the ladders. Stinkpots dropped over the wall exploded into clouds of choking, corrosive gas and suffocating fumes that drove back the first echelon of attackers coughing and vomiting, which prompted the reserves and artillery to step up their sweeping fire.

Troops of Tartar cavalry charged from south of the stockade, and rebel gunners on the right turned their guns completely around and began firing on the Tartar horsemen. Companies of rebel foot on the right flank wheeled away from the main formation and ran to protect the rebel guns. When the rebel foot came abreast of their own guns, the inside files halted while the outermost files continued past, until they had extended in a long gauntlet on each side of the southern approach to the guns. Musketeers detached from the reserves and joined the line. Gingals took up positions along the lines, and halberdiers advanced to the front of them.

The scarlet plumes and waving banners of the imperial cavalry advanced in waves up the rise and charged. The rebel guns opened fire with grape and canister. When a regiment of Tartar cavalry was almost upon the rebel artillery, there burst forth a sheet of flame along the entire length of both sides of the flanking lines of infantry, followed by the rolling report of musketry mixed with rasping cough of the heavy gingals. Tartar horsemen fell like scythed wheat. While the first echelon of imperial cavalry struggled to retreat through the rebel lines, the next echelon advanced and met the same kind of decimating volley. Those who attacked the lines and tried to trample the enemy ran full on lances set firmly in the ground by kneeling spearmen. The rest fell beneath a continuous fire sustained by musketeers running in a circle from the front to the rear of their files, loading as they ran behind and firing when they came to the front. Hundreds of the enemy fell to these singular infantry tactics before the rebel cavalry reappeared from behind their batteries and flew to the attack, sometimes leaping completely over the guns to get at the Manchu and Mongol horsemen. Imperial officers cantered back and forth before the troop of horse, apparently rallying the cavalry for another charge, but the troop hesitated and then slowly dissipated, leaving its furious officers standing alone, shaking their swords over the dead and dying cavalry and fallen horses writhing and screaming before them.

A strange calm crept over the ground after the Manchu cavalry retired, and the field of battle fell silent and motionless in a *tableau vivant* of mud-caked battle-weary soldiers leaning on their pikes or sitting in the mud with their muskets across their knees. A momentary break in the clouds allowed a swath of sunshine to sweep over the river and warm the shore before passing through the armies on the plain like a theater light. The light brought briefly to life the incongruous whistle and chatter of songbirds, setting to music a poignant irony no one could have explained, but which most of the onlookers understood in some way.

The tide of battle did not change so much as merely reach slack high water, and the battlefield simply halted to rest amidst its carnage while it caught its breath from killing.

Abruptly a bright flash of yellow lit up the entire field, and even the underside of the oppressing storm clouds. Black smoke billowed out from the stockade and, when it lifted, there was a gaping breach in the palisade. With a loud cheer, the rebel army, almost 10,000 men, lurched forward *en masse* over the shattered logs. What took place inside the stockade could not be seen from the river, mercifully so thought many aboard *Confucius*, and it did not last very long.

Fields on the plains surrounding Nanking, once ripe with abundant harvests, disappeared beneath shouting armies surging across the blood-soaked, smothered land. Troops of cavalry charged about the armies and crashed down upon one another, sending men and horses sprawling across the earth. Cannon, gingal, and musket drenched the land in a shower of lead almost as fast as the storm poured down rain. When the wind shifted in the direction of the river, there came the distant clamor of gongs, beat of drums, boom of cannon, pop of musketry, clang of swords, and the wild cries of screaming men and horses. The wind carried with it as well the pungent smell of damp wood smoke, and the acrid brimstone odor of exploded black powder, mixed with the unmistakable savor of burning flesh. The pale horse of death, thought Fletcher, flies behind the red horse of war outside the walls of Nanking. Has any living man ever come closer to a vision of the Apocalypse?

"Lord, have mercy," whispered Chester Hicks.

洋神 *Yang Shen*   *James Lande* 藍德

Dramatis Personae: Chapter 17

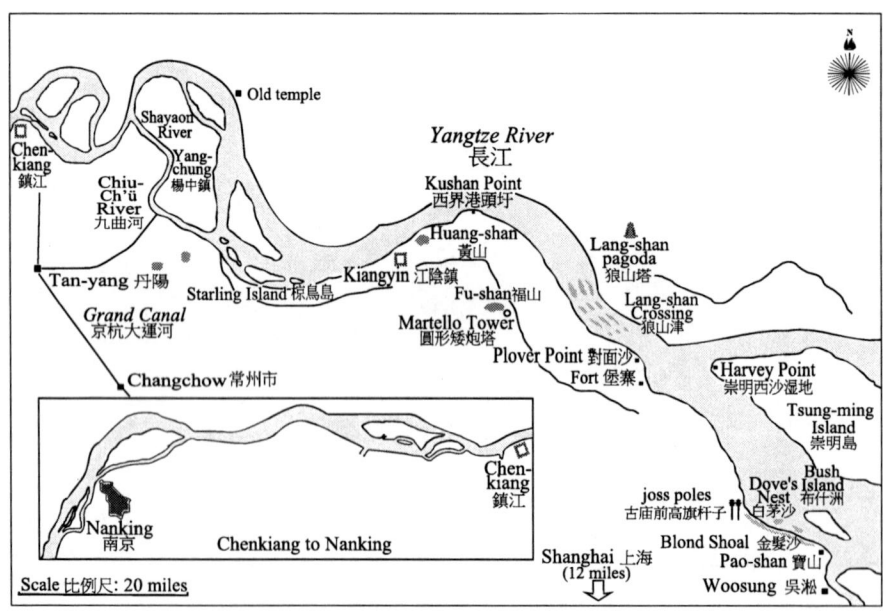

Yangtze River, Nanking to Woosung
(based on British Hydrographic Office chart, China., Sheet IX, 1842)

Mex = Mexican dollar

Chapter 17: The River Gauntlet

Friday, May 4, 1860, 11:00am

Grimly, Captain Ghent left the wheelhouse in the care of the pilot long enough to go below, issue arms to his crew, and send them to their battle stations. Crews fore and aft readied their guns. Fletcher gathered the passengers into the saloon and gave instructions for protecting themselves from injury when under fire. *Confucius* rounded the north wall of the city and slowed to determine the condition of the rebel batteries. Across the river below P'u-k'ou, the imperial camps on the north shore were a smoking ruin, and rebel soldiers worked feverishly to revamp the damaged batteries. At the water's edge, flames leapt from imperial war junks aground in the mud and under punishing shell and canister fire from nearby rebel war junks. Somewhat less surprising was the disheartening discovery that rebels manned the guns of the forts in front of the city as well, and rebel war junks already were putting out their oars and getting under way toward the steamer.

"You'd think they'd have too much on their minds to bother with us," the captain said, "but now they've got their north shore guns back again, and they're giving the imps such a pounding, I guess they feel pretty well puffed up with themselves. I suppose we'd better stop and parley."

Ghent sounded the telegraph bell and barked into the speaking tube "ahead half," then told Fletcher to go aft and wave off "that goddamned stupid barge and junk before they smash into us again." Inwardly, Fletcher sighed in relief that Ghent chose not to test the rebel guns, but was not at all certain any rebels should be allowed aboard to parley.

The larger rebel junk swung downriver a short distance then came back around on a line for the foreign steamer, rowing against the current and tacking slowly back and forth across the stream, her bowchaser pointed down at the steamer's waterline. Macanaya's gun crew readied their 32-pounder and pointed their gun down, too, at the heart of the threatening war junk. The other rebel junk came along side and called out for the steamer to stop and drop anchor. Ghent steered *Confucius* out of the stream, slowed speed still more, and then reversed engines to hold her in the slower current. The tea-agents' junk and the barge came about into an eddy below Heart-of-the-river Island and drifted into the calmer water of the anchorage, but misjudged the wind and smacked up against a line of junks moored there, all of which erupted in a volley of oaths.

"Better them than me," Ghent muttered. Fletcher let go the steamer's larboard anchor, Ghent eased off until he could be certain the anchor would hold, then allowed the current to swing her stern slowly out to larboard around her chain until her bow pointed upstream and she held her ground. The bulwark was opened and a boarding ladder lowered against the side. The nearer junk swung about with her oars kicking up water as she rowed wildly to get out of the steamer's way before falling alongside. An officer jumped onto the ladder and climbed up to the deck, accompanied by a bodyguard of one soldier armed with an oiled-paper umbrella to keep off the drizzle.

"As I live and breathe," the captain said. "It's that same trigger-happy old crust of a bastard that stopped us the last time."

"你們船上帶來甚麼東西," the officer said with a growl. "要算運輸稅金." His heavily accented Mandarin, severe expression, brusque manner, and flashing black eyes under long black eyebrows were familiar to *Confucius*.

"Dis man, he wantchee know what cahgo on boahd, talkee mus' pay taxee."

"Taxes!" Ghent whooped. "Armageddon is upon us and all Nanking is aflame with the hot fires of hell, and this jackass wants to collect taxes! Never in all my born days.

Well, that'll be between him and Sankey. Mr. Huang, tell him he has to see the comprador. Mr. Wood, you wait here with this longhair while my pilot talks to him, then bring the rebel inside the saloon." Ghent left them standing at the rail and went to find Sankey and Hicks.

When Fletcher escorted the rebel officer into the saloon, leaving the officer's umbrella-armed escort at the door, he found Sankey seated behind a table at the far end of the saloon flanked by his armed guard. Chester Hicks stood behind him whispering into his ear. The smiling comprador offered the officer a chair and tea was served with decorum, as if the whole world a few hundred yards away was not blowing apart. Sankey sipped from his cup, but the officer only glanced at the tea leaves floating in his own cup. The discussion got under way in Chinese between Sankey and the officer, with many pauses while Sankey and Hicks conferred quietly in pidgin. For ten minutes the prattle rose and fell, together with echoes of the storm and war without, before they asked Fletcher to accompany them into the hold to examine the cargo.

At the rail, the officer shouted an order down to the deck of his junk and, in a moment, another officer commandeered a sampan that sculled across the anchorage from the rebel junk to the tea-agent's junk. In the hold of *Confucius*, Fletcher showed the rebel officer a tally of the different teas and a count of the chests. Back in the saloon, more tea was poured and ignored, and the negotiations resumed with a higher pitch and more emphatic gesticulation by both parties, until the other officer came on board, reported, and was dismissed. Finally, Chester Hicks left the two Chinese alone and joined the captain and Fletcher at the other end of the saloon.

"This fool is going to break us," Hicks said. "He is demanding $4.00 Mexican per chest, which is exorbitant and beyond our capacity to pay. The tea has already cost us more than $128,000 of our $150,000, and we cannot afford to pay another $35,000. That is more than we have, and there are still other expenses. We offer him $2.00 per chest, but he will not take it. He says that if we do not pay $4.00 per chest, the tea will be confiscated and held here at Nanking until the duty is paid."

The three men considered the problem silently while the report of distant cannon fire drifted through the room. Finally, Ghent said, "I think I know a way to bust this stalemate. I got something he likely wants more than money." Ghent went into his cabin and emerged with a shiny new Sharps 1859 model .52 caliber rifled percussion carbine. He dropped the rifle on the table in front of the officer, whose startled expression changed to keen interest in the Sharps. He looked up at Ghent.

"Sankey," the captain said, "you talkee he, no mountain-high money can buy one-piecee this first-chop rifle. No hundred dollah, no thousand dollah. You talkee he, can catchee one-piecee rifle. Me, lowdah, give him, he catchee two dollah Mex one-piecee tea chest. You talkee he, what can dollah catchee in Nanking?"

Sankey translated. The officer folded his arms across his chest and stared at the Sharps, said something to Sankey, then grimaced at Ghent.

"He talkee tlee dollah Mex, Cap'n," Sankey said.

"Two dollah Mex," Ghent said.

Fletcher appeared at the other side of the officer, leaned against the edge of the table, lifted the rifle up and levered open the action. The rifle made a slick metallic sound that filled the small room. Fletcher grinned with the satisfaction of men who know and appreciate fine weapons and showed the open action to the rebel officer, chatting as he did so in English.

"This is a very good rifle. Never been fired. Look at how smooth the action is. It even smells good." Fletcher inhaled the odor of the well-oiled action, sighted down the barrel at the floor, swung the rifle around and peered down the barrel. He grinned again at the officer and repeated a small circular motion with an index finger to indicate the rifling. The officer glanced at the black cavity of the muzzle. Fletcher offered the rifle to the officer, who stood and accepted the weapon, worked the action, sighted at a porthole, then handed it back to Fletcher. But Fletcher smiled and held up his hands and would not take the rifle back, gesturing that the officer should keep it. The officer looked down at the rifle for a few interminable moments, then cradled it in the crook of one arm and turned and said something to Sankey.

"Him talkee catchee ammo?" Sankey said.

Ghent disappeared into his cabin and returned lugging a wooden case half-full of paper cartridges, and the deal was done. Sankey paid out $14,000 Mexican, because of course *Confucius* had cheated on the count, and received a receipt stating that all duties were paid. The cargo was free and clear, and not to be molested anywhere in the Heavenly Kingdom. Within half an hour, *Confucius* had her steam up, swung back around into the current, and the little convoy got underway again.

"Hicks, you pirate," the captain said. "You owe me one first-chop rifle."

With the plodding little *Poker Hand* and her barge dogging the steamer's heels like a pair of lazy Pekinese lap dogs, *Confucius* steamed downriver away from Nanking toward Chenkiang and Silver Island. They expected to cover the thirty-nine miles in three to four hours and anchor for the night in the lee of Silver Island, if rowdy imperial soldiers did not already overrun the place. As the river descended into the delta plain, the weather thinned and eventually began to clear in places. Occasional sunlight was a welcome relief after the constant storms and chafing winds of the previous several days, and helped to dispel some of the gloomy clouds that had settled over the hearts of the witnesses to the butchery at Nanking. The engagement had spread along the river too, and *Confucius* could see signs of skirmishing between rebel and imperial fleets as she descended the river past Iching, and across the river from Chenkiang at Kwachow.

The steamer was not long past the tall, slender pagodas on Golden Island, and Silver Island was off her starboard quarter when behind her Old Huang spied the long bowsprit, sharp bow and the rusty-red lugsails of a large lorcha sneaking out from behind the upriver end of Silver Island. The lorcha was on a bearing to interdict *Poker Hand* and her barge.

"王八蛋 bastards!" he muttered.

"What?" Ghent said, without turning from the wheel. He'd heard that nicety from his pilot so often he barely took notice.

"Hab real tea party now, Cap'n," the pilot said.

"Make sense you blockhead!"

Fletcher looked over at the pilot sitting in a corner, then followed the pilot's gaze out the rear window and over the stern.

"One mo' piecee chinaman come *chin-chin K'ung-fu-tze*, Cap'n." Old Huang turned and saw Fletcher peering through the haze astern.

"Whatchatinkee, Fetchawood?"

"Captain," Fletcher said. "Rebel lorcha astern." Fletcher was out of the wheelhouse and down the ladder in a moment. He called out to Vincente as he passed the house and raced for the stern.

"Hands on deck! Man the sternchaser."

Ghent twisted around to look, but the smokestack and the engine A-frame obstructed his view. He steered slightly to port. The rebel lorcha was directly astern and coming about. The tea junk and barge were off the steamer's larboard quarter.

"Damn! Where'd that thing come from?"

洋神 *Yang Shen* James Lande 藍德

The lorcha was almost as long as the steamer, over 130 feet and maybe 300 tons burden, with the usual drab yellow forecastle, poop, and dirty white deckhouse. She was trimmed in countless whipping flags and pennants that clearly identified her as a rebel war-fleet river auxiliary, probably commandeered from some hapless foreign firm caught trading illegally on the river. Whatever her seedy origins, she was apparently detached from naval duty upriver and, with the imperial war-fleet preoccupied at Kwachow, free to forage on her own unmolested. Any of the small boats that skimmed swiftly past *Confucius* downriver could have carried orders from that touchy rebel tax collector to plunder the steamer's cargo. That the lorcha was a rogue rebel turned temporary river pirate was manifestly clear — her gun crews were stationed about her forward and waist guns with smoking matches in hand. The steamer's Taiping river pass and her official Heavenly Kingdom receipt for cargo duties paid meant nothing now.

Confucius did not wait for the interloper to open fire. She would have to turn toward the Silver Island shoreline and risk the shallows rather than turn into the deeper water and chance a collision with her charges. Ghent lunged at the telegraph lever, set the annunciator dial to **STANDBY** and shouted into the voice pipe.

"Full turn to starboard 180 degrees! Unhitch the starboard wheel and turn at full ahead. Same drill as always."

"Full turn to starboard," the Dutchman shouted from the engine control panel. The wheelhouse telegraph bell sang out and the engine responder dial swung to **STANDBY**.

Old Schnapps briefly took charge of the steamer to complete the maneuver ordered. Steam was throttled back to slow the paddles, then fully closed, and the piston given steam in reverse to stop the wheels completely. The starboard paddle shaft clutch was disengaged to remove power from the starboard paddle wheel, then the engine was throttled back up and full power applied the larboard paddle wheel. Schnapps rang his telegraph, set the speed to **AHEAD FULL**, and Ghent rang confirmation. While the starboard wheel slowly revolved in the wash of river water, the larboard wheel churned furiously and pushed the steamer around while she drifted 600 feet on the river current. When she had swung around to about 10 degrees short of the full turn, the captain rang for **STANDBY**, his signal for the engineer to slow and engage the starboard paddle wheel. When the starboard wheel began to turn under power, the captain rang for **AHEAD FULL**.

The crew had quickly manned and loaded her sternchaser and was able to get off one shot across the rebel's bow before the steamer started about out of the river proper and back up along the shore of Silver Island. She left the main channel open wide for the junk and barge to forge past.

Thick white smoke suddenly enveloped the lorcha's waist and, a moment later, a cannon ball *whished* along the steamer's starboard bulwark so close to the rail that crewmen flattened themselves on the deck. The ball sent up a column of water fifty yards beyond her stern.

"Man forward gun," Vincente shouted.

The lorcha had already started downriver after the junk and barge when a sudden gust of southerly wind over her starboard beam slammed her main lugsail, which was hung to starboard, against her mainmast. The wind gust filled her foresail and pushed her bow around to port and out into center stream. Her helmsman struggled to straighten her out, but she lost headway and had to beat back around toward *Poker Hand* and the barge. She crossed their wake little more than the lorcha's length behind. When she came about to port and started downriver once more to give chase the wind slapped her main lugsail tight against her mainmast again and caused her to lose more headway.

Confucius suddenly careened out across the river from the shore of Silver Island with side-wheels pounding water white, her walking beam thrusting skyward, and her steam whistle screaming. She let go with her 32-pounder right into the face of the lorcha. That juggernaut descending upon them like a fire-breathing river-dragon 龍馬 apparently was too much for the nerves of the rebels struggling to handle their vessel against the wind. The lorcha immediately fell off and crossed the river toward the left bank. *Poker Hand* and her barge came about close in to the right bank below Silver Island and wallowed in the shallows. *Confucius* was about to congratulate herself for driving off the rebels and start downstream again when she ran up onto a sucking shoal that took hold of her more tightly than the clammy embrace of an octopus and held her dead in the water.

Not again, thought Fletcher! Not here, not now.

"Full astern," the captain shouted down the voice pipe as he rang the bell. Gradually the towering walking beam slackened pace, and the huge paddle wheels slowed to a stop, reversed direction, and began to throw up a froth of white water under her bow. The reverse rotation made her predicament unmistakably clear to the lorcha.

Swiftly the lorcha came about from the left bank with the wind over her port bow, her main lugsail now close-hauled, sailing with much greater speed and maneuverability than any clumsy flat-bottomed junk. She crossed back over the river almost straight at *Confucius*.

"*Bangkâ, bangkâ*! Boat come!"

2

Macanaya saw the lorcha approaching and shouted a warning from the bow. His gun was already loaded and he had only to swing it around and bring it to bear on the rebels, but the lorcha got off the first shot anyway. Her forward gun was also a 32-pounder. When it fired from 500 yards, the bow of the lorcha disappeared behind white smoke and the roar of the gun arrived just before a ball that raised a spout under the steamer's bow and sprayed water over the Manilaman gun crew.

Fletcher appeared in the wheelhouse. "Six feet of water, Captain," he said. "She's buried herself in black ooze."

"Damn!" Ghent shouted. "More steam, Schnapps!" he yelled into the voice pipe. "It's that cargo of tea's got us weighted down," he said to Fletcher, "or we wouldn't be in so deep." The pitch of the captain's voice changed, and he began glancing nervously out at the advancing lorcha. "Couldn't of been a junk, damn the luck. Look at it comin' straight across the river like it was walkin' on water. Got our range, too."

Macanaya's gun roared back. The round shredded a lower corner of the foresail and exploded 30 yards beyond the stern of the lorcha. The rebel crew jumped for their muskets and lined up on either side of their bowchaser firing haphazardly. Musket balls began chipping at the teakwood around the steamer's gun, bouncing off the walking beam and rails, and clanking into the black smokestack. Ghent lowered the wrought-iron plate armor over the glass of the wheelhouse windows. Musket balls thunked against the metal.

"Hafta do better'n that, Macanaya," he shouted out a side-window.

The lorcha fired again. Fletcher later swore he could see and hear it coming. The ball crashed into the larboard corner of the wheelhouse, just below the roof, and tore away several square feet of planking in a loud explosion that threw debris all over the room and knocked the captain, the pilot and Fletcher to the floor. Fletcher was unhurt, but the pilot was bleeding from a scalp wound where the roof fell on him, and the captain lay in a corner, pale and shaken. Fletcher yanked the towel from under a tray of smashed coffee cups and bound the pilot's head to stop his bleeding. The pilot stood and took the wheel, pressing the towel against his head, and waved Fletcher toward the captain. Fletcher saw no injuries on Ghent and gently helped him to his feet.

"Mr. Huang," Fletcher said, "if you will stay at the wheel and keep trying to back her off this shoal, I will help the captain down to his cabin."

Fletcher waved through a side-window at Macanaya on the bow, to let him know they were all right in the wheelhouse, then got a secure hold on the woozy captain and helped him down the ladder through the gun-smoke swirling over the deck. Chinese crewmen and stokers were struggling to swing a pair of stern davits out over the larboard quarter rail and lower a dinghy to the water. While the captain watched, several of the Chinese crew who could swim leapt over the rail and made for Silver Island.

"Maybe they've got more sense than we give 'em credit for," Ghent said. "We'd all have a better chance ashore."

Inside the saloon, the passengers were in a panic, but a handful of Manilamen and Chinese riflemen in the crew waited anxiously for weapons. Chester Hicks came up to Fletcher, with Sankey and his guards bunched at his heels like ducklings behind a mother duck.

"Is the crew abandoning ship?" Hicks asked in something closer to a whine than Fletcher had heard before. "Are we really in so much danger? Is the captain all right? What happened to the junk and barge?"

Fletcher glanced about. The mandarin was collapsed in a heap on a corner bench, pale and wide-eyed, but breathing rhythmically, if quickly. The rest of them seemed in tolerable working order.

"Mr. Hicks," Fletcher said as he continued on to the captain's cabin. "The captain is just a bit dazed from being struck by flying debris. Our other vessels are waiting in the lee of Silver Island. You could be of considerable help by *calming* yourself, and Sankey and his men, putting all of them somewhere out of ha'm's way, and then seeing to our pirate-suppressing mandarin. He does not seem to be in a condition for suppressing pirates, although now is a damn fine opportunity."

Fletcher did not wait to see the effect of his request, but took the captain directly into his cabin, laid the man on his bunk, then secured the armory keys and tossed them out to the crew.

"Break out rifles and ammunition," he ordered, then he went to the rifle rack on the wall of the captain's cabin, took down a Sharps, and filled his pockets with paper cartridges and percussion caps from a wooden box on the floor.

"Mr. Wood, what are you doing?" the captain said. "We should abandon ship. That lorcha's got the better of us. It's almost our size, equally well armed, and a damn sight handier than any junk. Once those rebels get aboard *Confucius* we won't have room to turn around, and the passengers will be at risk. On the island, we would have room to defend ourselves. If we are not aboard, the rebels will just take whatever comes to hand and can be carried away, but they won't know how to run a steamer, and after they've gone we can come back aboard."

"Captain, we don't have to go ashore. We can trounce that lorcha, believe me. Just give us a chance. Your second mate is already giving them a helluva beating."

"Are you refusing to obey my order?"

"No sir, Captain. I will see the passengers and crew ashore if you insist upon it. But all it takes is a bit of gumption to see this through."

"If you're calling me a coward...."

"No, captain, but maybe you're just a little shaken by being damn near blown up in your wheelhouse."

Fletcher levered open the action of the rifle and inserted a paper cartridge, jerked up on the lever and closed the action with finality, set a cap on the nipple, then clicked the hammer down and stared at Ghent.

"Rest a few minutes, Captain, while I go save your ship. If things still look bad when you're up and around again, lower another lifeboat and start the passengers ashore. I'll follow."

Fletcher didn't wait for an answer. He ran into Hicks listening just outside the entrance to the captain's cabin.

"Are we going to make a stand?" Hicks said.

Fletcher led him into the saloon. The mandarin was stretched out on the floor next to an inside wall, and Sankey and his guards sat on either side of him with their backs to the wall. Blankets were piled around them to catch flying glass.

"Sure," Fletcher said. "Bring a rifle. The blankets were a good idea, Hicks."

"What about the captain?"

"The captain wants to abandon ship and row ashore. Pay him no heed."

Hicks went to the captain's cabin, nodded to Ghent, took a Sharps from the rack on the wall and picked up a handful each of cartridges and caps. He left without further word to the captain, crossed the saloon, and stopped just inside the door when he saw Fletcher standing outside.

"Mr. Wood," Hicks said, peering gingerly around the door, "there are an awful lot of musket balls flying about you out there. Are you not concerned that one of them may hit you?"

"No, Mr. Hicks," Fletcher said. "None of those balls have my name on them, nor yours neither. Come on out and take a few potshots. We'll give the fellows manning the gun on the bow some cover."

Fletcher ran forward along the larboard rail to the bow and took a position beside the bowchaser Macanaya and his men were loading. Hicks followed and joined Fletcher behind the jury-rigged bulwark protecting the gun. The other armed crewmen stood along the rails on either side and kept up a rapid fire at the approaching lorcha. One of the gun crew sat inside the bulwark with his back against the teakwood pressing his shirt over a head wound to staunch the flow of blood down his chest.

"I am not at all certain I should be out here, Mr. Wood," Hicks said.

"Why not? You'd just be underfoot anywhere else. Can't imagine a man like you would want to cower in the cabin like that worthless mandarin detailed to *Confucius* by the Pirate Suppression Bureau. Man wants to save his life, sometimes the safest place is in the thick of the fighting."

Vincente Macanaya looked up from his work at the gun and pondered Fletcher's face. Tough talk, *dayo*, but little banty roosters always crow the loudest – let's see if you can shoot as good as you talk.

The Manilaman's stare caught Fletcher's attention. "Don't mind me, Vincente. I won't get in your way. Fire whenever you're ready." Macanaya's gun crew went about their business quickly and efficiently and put Fletcher in mind of the artillery duel between *Essex* and Fokie Tom only two weeks before. He thought of the jaunty old Irish gunner from *Essex*, and the few words of praise the crew of *Essex* had insisted he say at the gunner's burial in the Sailors Cemetery at Shanghai. It occurred to him that he did not want to see Vincente Macanaya or any more of his men get hurt in this encounter.

The gun roared again and Macanaya's shot smashed into the bow of the lorcha just above the waterline to one side of the stem.

"Water-tight bulkheads, Vincente," Fletcher said. "At least six of them stem to stern. We could pound her forever in the teeth and she still would not go down. Rake her decks with canister, and I will see if I can undress her a little."

Fletcher studied the slight roll of the foremast as the oncoming lorcha bounced over the swell. He judged the distance to be about 100 yards, put the rifle to his shoulder, aimed slowly, and fired. It was too far away to say for certain, but it seemed that the .50 caliber rifled bullet nicked the wood of the fore masthead, and he conned the immeasurably small delay between the moment he pressed on the trigger and the strike of the bullet.

The rapid fire from the other Sharps carbines together with canister shot from the 32-pounder was taking a toll among the musket-bearing rebels on the lorcha's bow and slowing the work of her gun crew, but it would not take her long to close 100 yards. Fletcher chambered another round, waited for the foremast head to reach the end of its arc and start back, gave it a little lead, and then fired. The loud report and white smoke were swept across the river by the wind, and a moment later the fore masthead burst apart with a loud clap. The foresail halyard parted from the foremast and the halyard and block fell to the deck on top of the crashing lugsail, burying the lorcha gun crew in bamboo matting. Macanaya stood up and peered with a growing smile at the lorcha. Hicks' mouth opened wide in surprise.

Fletcher reloaded. If a British rifleman can hit eight out of ten targets from 800 yards, I certainly can hit a bouncing halyard block at 100 yards, even with a short barrel.

The lorcha's mainmast was easily eighty feet high and five inches thick at the masthead. The lugsail on the mainmast was suspended from the halyard without parrels to hold it to the mast and, close-hauled before the wind, it bellied out as much as its stiff bamboo battens and taught running rigging would allow.

Fletcher's rifle barked again, surrounding him in swirling billows of white smoke, and an instant later the crack of the bullet smashing into the thick hardwood of the lorcha's main masthead echoed over the river. More musket fire from the bow of the lorcha answered Fletcher's shot, and balls whizzed wildly over the heads of the men standing on the bow of *Confucius* and ricocheted off the raised iron walking beam with a *clang* like a broken church bell.

"They're coming very close," Hicks said.

"Makes the shot easier," Fletcher said.

Fletcher fired again and again, each rifled bullet smashing into the main masthead with explosions of splintered hardwood. The third shot blew the pendant off the mast. The pulley and halyard flew away from the main masthead, running rigging slipped through blocks or parted entirely, and the mainmast lugsail was carried out over the leeward bulkhead. The wind stretched it taught and settled it gently upon the water like a great shroud of bamboo matting, then the current pushed it into a bundle at the lorcha's waterline and dragged the lugsail down under the hull. The lorcha swapped headway for leeway as the current clutched the vessel and dragged it helpless down the river.

"Gracious me!" whispered Hicks. "How on earth did you think of that? I would not have thought it could be done."

"Isn't desperation the mother of invention, Mr. Hicks?" Fletcher said, with a grin. "That, and the threat of miserable death at the hands of bloodthirsty rebels and pirates."

"You missed your calling, sir. You could make your fortune in a music hall performing magic tricks."

"I plan to make my fortune right here, Mr. Hicks, in China. I'm just waiting for the right opportunity to come along. As it happens, there goes one opportunity right now, floating downriver."

"You would join the rebels, Mr. Wood?"

Together they watched the lorcha drifting away.

"Well," Fletcher said, "not those rebels."

On board the lorcha, the remaining crew labored furiously at any tactic to regain command of their craft. Without fore and main sails, the wind could not hold her across the current, and the vessel drifted out of control in a slow spin toward center stream and came up to speed with the 3-knot current.

"There're many that have joined the rebels," Fletcher said, "and done well in the bargain. I'm a soldier, Mr. Hicks, and I have sold my services all over the world, in the Crimea, Central America, South America. It's just a trick of fate that now I am here in China instead of in Italy fighting with Garibaldi to create a new Italian state."

"I think you would do better fighting *against* the rebels rather than *for* them, Mr. Wood," Hicks said. "The tide of battle is beginning to turn against Nanking, in spite of what we have recently witnessed. If the rebels have broken the siege at Nanking, it is because the imperials have held them in a loose grip. The time will come soon when they tighten their grasp."

The lorcha by now was completely clear of *Confucius*. Fletcher saw that the crew of *Poker Hand* must have realized that the lorcha was going to drift helplessly past their position because the junk's crew was suddenly active fetching muskets and loading their own small cannon. The lorcha would have to undergo more hazing before it would be free of them entirely.

"The balance of power is shifting as well, Mr. Wood. The British are going to be trading on the river. They will expand the sphere of Western interests up the river all the way to Hankow, and seal the bargain in Peking. Today you have Western gunboats under Chinese registry escorting Shanghai merchants upriver, but tomorrow British and American steamers carrying on their own trade in silk and tea will pass under the walls of the rebel stronghold in Nanking every week. The rebels may fume over the intrusion of our gunboats, maybe even attempt to extort tariffs, but they will be powerless to treat with us as equals. The foreign mercantile community in China has lost whatever illusions, or hopes, it might have had about the heavenly kingdom of the Taipings, and settled on the present Manchu dynasty as the only hope China has for any future as a sovereign nation. I guess you know that British gunboats and soldiers go wherever Jardine and Matheson want them. The rebellion is not over yet, may not be for some time, so there will be many opportunities for employment of your services by the side in this war that is most likely to prevail in the end. Your best chances are in Shanghai, Mr. Wood, not in Nanking."

"You mean with Chinese merchants, the ones behind the so-called Pirate Suppression Bureau, who foot the bill for this steamer and pay our gallant captain to protect their junks trading on the Yangtze? Who is this Tacky fellow, anyway?"

Hicks was silent for a second as he calculated how much information he should divulge to this brazen, quick-witted freebooter who a moment before had admitted he would as soon sell his sword to one side as to the other. It is always the same difficulty, he thought, with this avaricious class of legionnaires – how to make an appeal superior to their greed, ambition, or their vanity…how to get hooks so deep down their throats they can never tear free. But then, when one takes into account the class of Chinese employing these desperados, the only conclusion is that they deserve each other. It makes me wonder how I ever got involved with any of them, and makes me wish I were just starting out again to sell dredging machines…anywhere *but* China.

"I'm sure," Hicks said, "that there will be many people in Shanghai eager to express their gratitude for your help here today when Captain Ghent makes his report. Not the least of which will be myself. You have not lost an opportunity, sir; you have merely exchanged one opportunity for another."

"Good," Fletcher said, "because I have a plan that I want to discuss with anyone that can finance an army. Now, tell me about this Tacky."

Inwardly Hicks sighed in resignation. This Fletcher Thorson Wood is far too persistent a man to be put off for long, and if I do not introduce him to Takee, Wood somehow will find his own way to the man, especially after this incident today. I cannot prevent the man's reputation from reaching that wily old Chinese banker, with his hand in the pockets of the *taotai*, and thence the imperial customs revenues, and ears everywhere in Shanghai, nor would I wish to as long as I can get a piece of the transaction. But in any case, I can still demonstrate the usefulness of Chester Hicks by bringing Wood to Takee, and bag a large fee in the bargain. And if necessary, I can squash any unflattering rumors about Captain Ghent that might arise from today's work. Ghent and his steamer are still very much needed, for my own plans, and for those of others, no matter how little others might understand that.

"It's pronounced Tah-kèe. He is the mandarin responsible for this steamer, and the other steamers of the Pirate Suppression Bureau. He arranges for the pay of the crews, and sometimes commissions the steamers with specific missions. He is an important official, and a very successful banker and merchant of some note in Shanghai. While at Jardine Matheson, Takee worked out a method of silk purchase we now call the 'Soochow system.' A comprador takes opium from Shanghai to the silk region of Soochow – one junk takes delivery of perhaps five chests of opium at Woosung, to divide the risk – and in Soochow exchanges the opium for silk. Within a fortnight, the proceeds are paid at Shanghai in cash, or transferred between accounts. Takee is one of a handful of Chinese who understand something about foreigners, and who is not completely hostile to them. He is a go-between by very high authorities, and has the ear of at least the governor, which makes him very powerful and influential. He has control over a great many of the expenditures from the provincial and imperial treasuries. He is worth at least a million in sterling himself, and can recommend taxes levied as well. If anyone can finance a private army, Takee is that man."

Fletcher decided it was time to hunt up the "admiral" and his lusty crew and shake *Confucius* clear of the shoal. He would mull over what Hicks had just told him.

When Fletcher left Chester Hicks in the saloon and returned to the wheelhouse, he saw through the window that the debris had been cleared and that the captain was alone at the wheel. Fletcher loitered outside for a minute while he subdued his excitement and calmed his unsettled mind.

Have I stumbled right into the berth I've been looking for? If this Takee is even half of what Chester Hicks says, then my course can be plotted from here. I can only take Hicks at his word, which will be reliable only when his interests are furthered. He has purposes he's not divulging. But why misrepresent Takee when the truth so quickly will out? Had I not seen the chaos in Taipingdom for myself, I could not trust all the many things he has been whispering in my ear. Was that an offer to go partners in a steamship enterprise on the river? Why suggest such a grandiose scheme to an obviously threadbare drifter like Fletcher Thorson Wood, unless to incite what he would arrogantly assume was a poor man's lust for riches, to appeal to greed? Of course, I would have to side with the imperials. It's hard to get up any more enthusiasm for the rebels after seeing that debacle at Nanking, but neither do imperial troops behave like crusaders for a valorous cause. Not as easy as the choice between Union and Confederate.

Fletcher entered the wheelhouse.

"Doing some redecoration here, Captain?" Fletcher said. "New skylight, I see."

"Yeah," Ghent said, with a snort. "Steamboat gothic."

Fletcher suppressed a chuckle, and thought that a high pulpit and rope ladder like

Father Mapple's might do as a replacement. Better for sermons to calm raging rivers, and to evangelize the gospel of western mercantilism to multitudes of Chinese on shore.

"You're feeling better, Captain?"

"Yes, Mr. Wood, thank you. I've sent the pilot to his cabin. You're to be congratulated for your presence of mind in this action. That was a clever trick, shooting out the halyard pulleys. Chinese rigs are vulnerable that way, aren't they?"

"Didn't hit block or pulley, Captain, just blew away part of the masthead where the pendant secured the halyard pulley. Standing rigging on junks is usually pretty flimsy. Didn't think to have Vincente fire canister at the mast, but it's a good idea. It was just a little piece of luck, even at fifty yards. If that lorcha'd been on another bearing, she'd have carried into us with or without sail, and we'd still be in a pickle of a fix."

"Your modesty is as becoming as your garb is somber, Mr. Wood, but I hear those brass balls we spoke of clinking again like chunk-ice in a glass of Irish whiskey. And, by the way, about that conversation we had in my cabin – it never took place. Nuff said?"

"Forgotten completely, Captain."

"What about getting my steamer unstuck?"

"Tide'll turn in another hour or two, and the moon is near full. Rise from behind those clouds downstream in maybe an hour or two, I'd guess. On a spring tide, just two feet would be enough for her to paddle herself off the rest of the way. If the weather stays clear, we'll have bright moonlight to pilot by, if you want to continue on down the river tonight."

"By moonlight? We haven't seen the moon for nearly a week."

"On the ocean for so many years, living and working according to the phases of the moon, knowing her appearance and path through the sky gets to be second nature. Could say I know the changing face of the ageless moon better than I knew the face of the pilot's old pocket watch."

"I guess we can go on down the river tonight. For quite a distance, there should be little risk except from floating debris, if we stay in the center channels, over deep water. There's too many angry imps and rebels between Chenkiang and Nanking out lookin' for trouble and, if we stay here, we'll be certain to light into more. You take your crew below at 9:00pm, and I'll stay on deck and try to get underway for the first half of the run back down to Starling Island. At 2:00am, I'll call your watch to make the last half of the run. Remember to roust out that old Chinaman when you come on deck, too, because you'll need his knowin' of the ways of the river if you're to pilot by moonlight."

Log of Steamer CONFUCIUS, chartered by Augustus Fitch & Company

Date & Time	Location	Wind (est.)	Current	Speed	Cargo
Friday May 4 1860 9:00pm	Silver Island, Chenkiang, Kiangsu	SW 3 knots	3½ knots	8 knots	Tea

Fletcher slept little. He lay in his bunk, and listened through the thin walls to the activity outside the tiny cocoon of his cabin. The junkmen shouted as they brought *Poker Hand* and her barge to anchor behind the steamer. Bare feet tramped across the deck as chests of tea were unloaded onto the barge. On two occasions, distant musket shots were answered by rifle fire from the deck of *Confucius*.

The clang of metal on metal echoed up from the engine room, swathed in Dutch oaths from Old Schnapps and his Chinese black gang, who had learned from their boss to swear in Dutch. Inert machinery sluggishly squeaked into motion, boilers began to hiss and spit, walking beam to rock, and paddle wheels to turn. The steamer strained mightily to yank loose her tethered bow, wooden wheels biting into the river, and a slightly annoyed first mate rolled gently in his bunk as *Confucius* swayed side-to-side in the weakening grip of the muddy river bottom.

The River Gauntlet

洋神 *Yang Shen* James Lande 藍德

When the steamer finally lurched backward, the current brought her stern around downstream. The wheelhouse bell clanged loudly, the captain shouted for **AHEAD FULL**, then dropped anchor. She came to rest in the stream twisting slightly on her chain. Soon there were more bare feet trudging about on deck, bringing cargo back aboard from the barge. Later, when the steamer was underway, Fletcher finally was lulled into sleep by the rhythmic hiss of the steam valves, the chatter of the walking beam bearings, and the slap of the flat wooden paddles against the surface of the river.

When called to his watch, Fletcher came on deck together with the pilot to find the steamer dead center in the river, drifting along under a bright moon on the ebbing tide, with the engine at half power. Several crewmen at the forward gun held long boat hooks and ropes over the bow, dangling oil lamps just above the waterline. The lamps cast a nimbus of ambient pale yellow on the river ahead of *Confucius*.

When Fletcher relieved the captain and took the wheel, Ghent stayed in the wheelhouse and chatted quietly with Old Huang in their outlandish pidgin while the Chinese peered out through the windows at the river. Old Huang shook his bandaged head, pursed his lips, and crossed the wheelhouse to peer out at the other side of the river. He stared up through the gaping hole blown out of the wheelhouse roof at the bright full moon, which in turn shined down to illuminate all the many gnawing doubts crowding into his thin, worried expression. But in spite of the pilot's silent misgivings, the run continued pretty much without mishap until an hour after dawn.

Fletcher was still at the wheel and the captain below when *Confucius* missed her bearings within sight of the Chowshan pagoda and grounded on a sandy shoal that stretched partway across the river. The high water, river current, and ebbing tide combined to pull her off after a few minutes, but then she hung up again on more sandbanks in the boat channel between Starling Island and the left bank. From these she also broke free after only a small delay, drifting into the anchorage in the lee of Starling Island and coming to rest for the morning, much to the relief of the first mate.

Poker Hand and the barge passed over the same shoals with draft to spare and anchored beside the steamer. Another small imperial war junk of twenty oars approached from the left bank as before when *Confucius* had passed upriver. This time Old Huang hurried the steamer's official mandarin out on deck before the war junk could come alongside and, after some gesticulation and shouted explanations, the imperial junk withdrew and the steamer's crew settled in to sleep out the morning under the guard of watchful sentries.

Old Huang gestured to Fletcher from below the wheelhouse window. Fletcher slammed the window open.

"Mandalin, he say plenty tlouble at Lang-shan. Woof wait fo' boat."

"What kind of wolves?"

"Not sure. Mebbe lebel, mebbe wah-junk – tigah-boat."

Fletcher turned and glared intently out over the bow toward Langshan, as if from Starling Island he could just see an ambush of tiger boats waiting to light into *Confucius*.

3 The watch below was called on deck at 10:00am and joined the rest of the crew preparing to make Plover Point by dusk that evening. *Confucius* got underway without incident, steaming against the flood rising into the narrows, away from the wide river and featureless shoreline west of Starling Island. Soon the landscape gave way to the low foothills, cultivated fields and tree-shaded farmhouses surrounding the walled city of Kiangyin. South of the Kiangyin bund, the levees closed in upon the river, and the steamer passed between lines of weeping willow toward the high yellow hills at Huangshan. When the hills astern had become a distant yellow island in the middle of the river, Kushan Point opened up, warning of the approach to the Langshan Crossing.

Fletcher was himself to steer the cramped passage across the river at Langshan. When he took the wheel, with Ghent at one elbow and Old Huang at the other, a three-knot SE wind over the steamer's bow raised a swell across the river and rolled her a little from side to side. Fletcher gently nudged *Confucius* away from the left bank toward the middle of the river while carefully observing over his left shoulder her bearing to the Langshan pagoda on the north shore. The seven-mile run to Plover Point began when the pagoda came to bear E by N. Fletcher listened through the open wheelhouse windows for the leadsmen on the bow to call out the depth, then made the first of his several course changes. Gradually, he pointed the steamer's bow from south to east over the southeastern quadrant of the compass, in a wide left turn that kept her within the narrow confines of the channel cut by the river across the soft rock of its bed.

Poker Hand and her barge slowed about a quarter of a mile upriver of the crossing and waited for *Confucius* to get well along before starting down. They steered their own course close to the wind, and easily cleared shoals that might ground the deeper-draft steamer, but held back to avoid overrunning *Confucius*. They had just begun to make headway and enter the crossing when they sighted two small green and yellow imperial war junks rowing swiftly for them out of the shallows along the right bank.

Pandemonium broke out aboard *Poker Hand*. Wild arguments about what to do that were carried back upriver on the wind toward Kiangyin and never heard by *Confucius*, intent as she was on making the crossing. By the time it occurred to someone aboard *Poker Hand* to fire their guns to get the steamer's attention, the war junks were less than a half-mile off and closing fast.

Fletcher leaned out of the wheelhouse larboard window and looked back over the heads of crewmen running for the stern. He saw the line of twenty orange-and-black striped tiger-faces on the rattan shields above the oars propelling each of the war junks bearing down on his charges, then jumped to the voice pipe and yelled, "Stop engines!" Then he remembered to ring the telegraph bell.

"If those goddamn pirates think we can't do anything to save our tea just because we're halfway over the crossing," the captain said, "they've got another guess coming. They're counting on us having no room to come about."

Fletcher rang for **FULL ASTERN**.

A 4-pounder fired from the bow of the leading war junk spouted water just ahead of *Poker Hand*. Immediately, *Poker Hand* fell off toward the left bank.

"Those fools!" the captain screamed. "Look at them run for shore. We'll lose the cargo if they go to ground and the pirates follow. They have to come down here to us where we can protect them. I'll take the wheel and hold her position so Vincente can bring the 12-pounder to bear. You go tell him I said to put a shot across our junk's bow to keep her from going ashore. Then put him to work whittling down those damn imperial pirates."

Fletcher started for the wheelhouse door.

"Mr. Wood," the captain said.

"Sir?"

"Be ready to go to the forward gun if I bring her about."

Fletcher jumped down out of the wheelhouse and ran to the stern. Macanaya's crew had their gun loaded and he was sighting on the imperial war junks. Riflemen stood at the rail with loaded carbines ready to provide covering fire for the gunners. Macanaya lined up the iron sights and waited for the roll of the swell. The gun fired, filling the poop deck with white smoke that carried upriver toward the tea junk, and the round exploded twenty feet above the bow of the leading war junk.

"*Bóbo!* Stupid!" the Manilaman said under his breath.

"Vincente," Fletcher said, "the captain says to put shot across the tea junk's bow, don't let them go in to shore, keep them coming downriver to us here."

"*Si, entiendo* yes, I understand," Macanaya said, and he set his gun crew to work shifting the position of the 12-pounder while he set the fuse of the next round. It occurred then to Fletcher that with *Confucius* treading water in a rolling swell, Macanaya would have difficulty hitting a barn, not to mention a coconut, with the 12-pounder. While the gun was being loaded, Fletcher went to the armory and fetched back the leather case containing the rear sight Macanaya had asked about that first Saturday morning Fletcher had been aboard. He returned just in time to see a round explode fifty yards inshore from the bow of *Poker Hand*.

A burst of a round fired from the steamer got *Poker Hand*'s attention. At the larboard quarter rail, Chester Hicks, Sankey, and his bodyguards all waved wildly to signal the junk to come downriver. *Poker Hand* came about into the wind tugging at her barge, heeled over to larboard, and lumbered for the safety of her escort with as much speed as any junk towing a clumsy barge could make.

"Vincente, you asked me once to show you how this gun-sight works. I think this is a very good time to demonstrate, when the ship is rolling in a swell."

"Now, *señor*?"

Confucius' stern began to swing a little to starboard. The 12-pounder's iron sights swept slowly up to one of the imperial war junks, and then past. Macanaya spoke quiet orders to his crew and they leapt to bring the gun back around enough to bear on the war junk. *Confucius* stopped her turn, and Macanaya sighted the gun.

"Adjust for the swell, Vincente," Fletcher said.

"What else?" Vincente said.

Macanaya called out adjustments, sighted again and fired. The round splashed into the water twenty feet shy of the leading war junk, skipped under her bow, and exploded on the other side. She was unhurt, but her oars all stopped moving as if she were wounded. Across the water, the crew on the deck of the steamer imagined that even upwind they could hear the frantically screamed orders of the war junk's officers before her oars began pushing at the river again.

Fletcher smiled. "Now, *señor*."

"Quickly, then – dog be on rabbit in only few minutes."

The iron seat for suspending the sight on the 12-pounder had been screwed into the base of the breech and left there on that first Saturday morning. Fletcher needed only to affix the sight to the iron seat. The sight was a length of sheet-brass weighted at the bottom by a bulb of lead and incised with a quarter-degree scale over which traveled a brass slider. He explained the working of the sight while Macanaya set the fuse on the next round and the crew began to load the gun.

"This is a Pendulum-Hausse sight, Vincente. I attach the center of the sight to the breech of the gun with this screw so that, as you can see, the lead weight at the bottom of the upright bass plate of the sight makes it swing freely and always remain vertical in the swell. You shift the gun on its traverse to adjust for windage as before, and set the slider on the scale for elevation as with any breech sight, then line up the iron sight on the muzzle here in this opening atop the brass slider on the rear-sight. Wait until *Confucius* reaches the bottom of the swell, then fire as your sights pass up and the junk comes in line with the sights. We can't sink her, so try to kill the helmsman or destroy the rudder."

Macanaya sighted the gun. "Through here?" he said.

"Yes, like this," Fletcher said, and he drew the sight picture in the palm of his hand with an index finger.

"*Si, si, bueno*, yes, yes, good," Macanaya said. With one eye, he followed the white bead atop the muzzle sight down across the house of the leading war junk. In a quiet rattle of Tagalog, he ordered the gun shifted slightly, twisted the elevating screw a quarter-turn. He sighted again as the muzzle of his gun drifted down across the stern of the junk, waited for the swell, and yanked on the friction-primer lanyard. The gun roared and spit orange fire and clouds of white smoke that the wind whipped out over the river. A moment later, a bright explosion over the aft quarter of the war junk shredded the mizzen lugsail in a burst of bamboo splinters and cleared the stern of officers and helmsman. Before another hand could go aft to take her tiller, the war junk's rudder swung hard over and she came about slowly to starboard like a drifting leaf while a few oarsmen forward continued stroking her down toward *Confucius*.

"I like your gun-sight, *señor*," Macanaya said. "It has a nice swing to it, like a tick-tock clock on a wall, or the stern of some of those big Portuguese women at Macao." Macanaya's gun crew suddenly was all big grins and chattered quickly among themselves while they sweated to load the gun. They stole quick glances at the sight standing erect above the breech of the gun, and at their revered boss Vincente and his *compañero*, the short, dark and slightly Spanish-looking Fletcher Wood, who spoke a little *gringo* Mexican.

The 12-pounder fired again and blew away part of the house of the second war junk. The first war junk finally came under control, with what looked in a glass like an ordinary sailor in command on the poop and an oarsman at the helm. They straightened out on a line for the steamer while crew on her bow loaded the 4-pounder and lugged gingals forward and arrayed them on either side of the gun. But before the junk could approach close enough for effective fire, Macanaya lobbed a couple of shot into her stem and exploded spherical case shot above her bow. After that, she came about for the left bank, reassembled some of her bruised firepower, and began another attack on an easier target.

Poker Hand had come down to within several hundred yards of the steamer, but the other war junk was closing from above the barge, putting *Poker Hand* in a light but, for her crew of tradesman, unnerving crossfire of cannon balls, gingal pellets and musket balls. Even with only one gun and some rifles, *Confucius* had the advantage of greater range and heavier caliber. She would have damaged the war junks severely and forced an end to the engagement, if only she could have held her position and not drifted larboard onto a shoal.

When *Confucius* heeled over and her stern started to come around downriver, no traverse of her 12-pounder could bring the gun to bear on the imperials. Immediately, as her paddle wheels cranked full astern to back her out into the current, Fletcher and Vincente led the riflemen and gun-crew forward to the bow, readied the 32-pounder for action, and put some riflemen to work potting at the imperial junks. *Poker Hand* and her barge beat down under the steamer's bow just as *Confucius* began making sternway. The captain reversed her engines and brought her up to full-speed forward, slowing her descent and steadying her drift so the gunners could get their best shots. The wheelhouse window slammed open and Captain Ghent yelled out.

"Mr. Wood, get those lollygagging leadsmen back to her stern! Can't anybody see we have changed direction?"

Poker Hand tacked frantically to keep from being run down by *Confucius*, and the war junks sprinted a zigzag course, one junk crossing in the other's wake, to keep from being blown out of the water. Their tactic soon became a cat-and-mouse game when the junks discovered they could hold just to one side of the 32-pounder's field of fire and not be hit no matter how close they approached, and then change positions when the steamer's gun-crew shifted their gun to bear on them. When the captain discovered that this tactic was slowing Vincente's rate of fire, he leaned his ruddy, pockmarked face out of the wheelhouse window, snatched his soot-blackened meerschaum pipe from beneath his thick gray moustache, and yelled down to his crew on the forecastle.

"Quit moving the gun! I'll move the boat!"

Their breezy cat-and-mouse game turned into a deadly duck-shoot, with the war junks as the ducks. Vincente secured the traverse of the gun dead center over the bow. Ghent steered *Confucius* to larboard enough to bring the gun to bear. Vincente cut loose with repeatedly telling fire. While the pilot leaned out of a wheelhouse side-window to watch the river behind her stern, and listened for the depths called up by the leadsmen, the captain stood at his wheel and imagined *Confucius* to be something like a huge floating gun carriage. He aimed at the war junks over the jackstaff as if it were an iron rifle sight, shifting the steamer's position from port to starboard to follow the evasions of the renegade imperials. Within minutes, the drama was done, and the imperial war junks were limping away raw and bleeding toward the anchorage at Plover Point. Aboard *Poker Hand*, several crewmen were nursing injuries. *Confucius* was not hulled even once. Fletcher secured the crew from battle stations, saw the weapons returned to the armory, then returned to the wheelhouse to report to the captain. Ghent nodded and smiled, obviously distracted by the challenge of piloting backwards.

"Aren't you going to turn her around, Captain?" Fletcher said.

"Never done this backwards before. Think I might just as well finish the crossing this way. Like to be able to say I done it."

Fletcher smiled, imagining how for months the shipping reports would be full of steamers going aground while trying to descend the Langshan crossing backwards.

Confucius reversed her direction when she came opposite Plover Point. Together with *Poker Hand* and the barge, she came in close to shore below the point and dropped anchor for the night. The remains of the imperials higher up in the anchorage above the point seemed a safe distance away.

Log of Steamer CONFUCIUS, chartered by Augustus Fitch & Company

Date & Time	Location	Wind (est.)	Current	Speed	Cargo
Saturday May 5 1860 9:00pm	Plover Point, Yangtze R. Kiangsu	SW 3 knots	3½ knots	6 knots	Tea

The night's watch passed quietly and the steamer and her charges were underway again the next morning by 8:00am. Carefully, they negotiated a passage through the Dove's Nest, passed the joss poles at Blonde Shoal, raised Bush Island, and crossed the bar at Woosung on a rising tide. From there *Confucius* whistled her way shrilly through the swarm of lighters and sampans off the British Bund at Shanghai while Chester Hicks opened another chilled bottle of champagne in the wheelhouse. He congratulated the officers on the successful completion of one of the most harrowing voyages he ever had the pleasure of taking.

"Big bonuses," the captain said.

"Future endeavors," Hicks said, winking at Fletcher.

"New allies," Fletcher said.

"Dly fleet," Old Huang said.

4 *Dear Darling Sister Elizabeth,*

The Yangtze River at midnight under a full moon is a romantic experience if walking hand-in-hand with your gentleman-friend along its quiet shore teeming with soft night sounds. But it is a dreadful and often eerie adventure in a paddle-wheel steamer rushing

洋神 *Yang Shen*   *James Lande* 藍德

downstream at a death-defying six knots per hour. Engaged for the past week as mate on "Confucius," I was obliged to journey from Shanghai up the treacherous river to Nanking in rebel territory. Actually, the Yangtze is no more forbidding than our own Mississippi, where shoals and shallows change position after every storm and drifting debris always threatens to stave in hulls and smash paddle wheels. The Yangtze is at least as long – Meriwether Lewis and William Clark measured the Mississippi to the headwaters of the Missouri. At the river mouth, the Yangtze is miles wider and much deeper. Shanghai would be like New Orleans, inland a ways from the ocean as is New Orleans from the Gulf, and Nanking would be somewhat like Baton Rouge, (west) upriver about 230 miles through a broad floodplain similar to the Mississippi delta.

    Returning downriver, we went aground while engaging river pirates and were not able to get afloat until well into the evening, whereupon we decided to continue on downstream by the light of a full moon. Many of the Chinese will not go on the river after dark because, they say, that is when river ghosts come out, and the spirits of men drowned in the river attempt to pull down vessels to the bottom and exchange their ghostly existence for the lives of the living. The shadows in the water and along the shore do create fantastic impressions.

    There was an American on board, Chester Hicks, representing a tea buyer, and from him I learned things about the situation here that incline me toward the imperials. A decision to fight with the imperial side cannot but be influenced by the absolute brutality of the rebels. They run rampant over the country, leaving utter destruction and hopelessness in their wake. They make no effort to rehabilitate or govern the territory they conquer, but instead ravage the land for plunder to carry back to Nanking. Ironically, it also is difficult to muster any feeling for the imperials, who are no less depraved. The imperial practice, if not a de facto policy, is to commit terrible atrocities in the countryside and cause the blame to fall upon the rebels, to undermine any support among the populace for the Taiping.

    A man of principle would regard the choice as one between the lesser of two evils – even then, only Solomon could decide which evil is the lesser. Still, there is no question but that I am a Union man and would not be a rebel. In America, of course, the choice does not involve such ambiguity and clearly is one between good and evil. When and where in China is anything ever that clear?

    Best wishes,
        Your loving brother,
            Fletcher
                Shanghai, China, May 6, 1860

洋神 *Yang Shen*   *James Lande* 藍德

Dramatis Personae: Chapter 18

Yang Ch'ang Mei 楊常梅	daughter of the banker Yang Fang (Takee)
Hsüeh Ch'un 雪春	Ch'ang-mei's slave girl 丫鬟, her maid
Hung Hsiu-chuan 洪秀全	Taiping Heavenly King, the *T'ien Wang* 天王

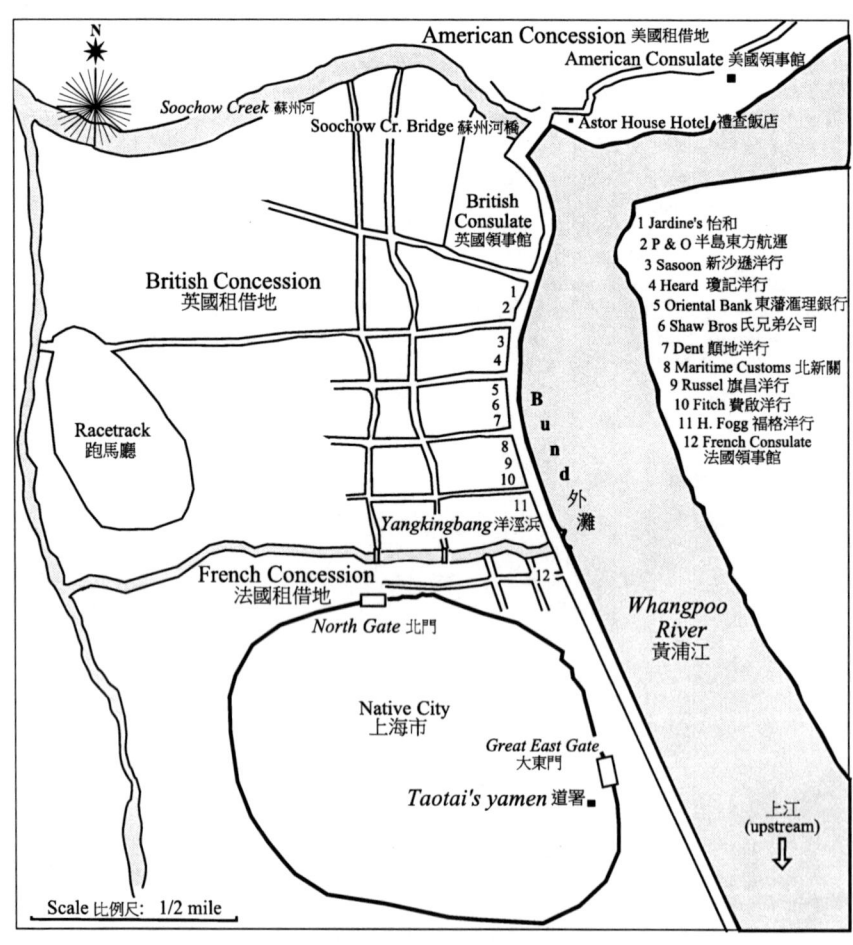

Shanghai in 1855
(based on Morse, *International Relations of the Chinese Empire*, v. 1, p. 454)

Fletcher Meets Takee

洋神 *Yang Shen*   *James Lande* 藍德

Chapter 18: Fletcher Meets Takee
Monday, May 7, 1860, 7:30pm

The
North China Herald
Shanghai, Saturday, May 5, 1860

England...... Mar 10   Singapore.....Apr 15
Bombay......Apr   1   Hongkong....Apr 25
Calcutta   ----   New York....Feb 12
Galle...........Apr   6

REBELS: ...The Nanking rebels are expected soon to surrender their city. Circumvented on all sides and incessantly harassed by Imperialist attacks, destitute of sufficient supplies and without the prospect of relief from without, it is affirmed that they cannot hold out much longer. Their object now is to cut their way through the Imperialist lines and thus save themselves from merited destruction.

    Monday morning, Chester Hicks sent a runner to the Astor House with a message for Fletcher Wood. Hicks had spoken with Takee the evening before, not long after *Confucius* returned to Shanghai, and would Fletcher to be available to call upon the mandarin this evening. Fletcher spent the day roving the Bund and quays and streets and alleys of the foreign settlement and the Chinese city, taking time to oil the surging waters of his rising excitement and give calm thought to the plan he would present to the Chinese. When he returned to the Astor House at the appointed time, he found Hicks waiting with a pair of sedan chairs.

    "No barnacles stick to your hull, Mr. Chester Hicks. I expected to be beached high and dry for a long spell before parleying with mandarins."

    "It has never been my policy to wait for my ship to come in, Mr. Fletcher Wood, when I can row out to get it. After Admiral Ghent regaled Takee with the rousing tale of our ascent past Nanking in *Confucius*, and your bold command of the steamer and those exasperating Manilamen, I mentioned something of what we discussed. The old mandarin really got his boilers up to hear your offer. Insisted I bring you around right away *chop-chop*. And you may have heard something on the wind today that makes this the best possible time to approach the Chinese."

    "What's to hear? I've been in the native city and suburbs all day and just returned."

    "The rumors on the Bund say that the rebels have chased away all the imperial troops from Nanking. Instead of surrendering the city as we all were expecting, the siege of Nanking has been broken and the Taiping have soundly defeated the imperials."

    "Good Lord! Was that what we watched from *Confucius*! If it's true, then what's left between Nanking and Shanghai to stand up against that rabble? They could be here in a week or two. And that confirms what we learned at Nanking about the rebel advances against those towns they took the day I arrived – the rebels were luring imperial troops away from Nanking with a feint instead of advancing on Soochow, and that's why they evaporated out of Hangchow after only a week. Another feint. The coolie-king that thought up that busy little stratagem is someone to be reckoned with."

    "Exactly," Hicks said. "And you can bet Takee has received the same news and worked up a high fever trying to prevent all his banker friends from packing their steamer trunks full of treasure and taking passage back to Ningpo, or Hong Kong if Ningpo is too close for comfort. So, we are off to the French concession."

Fletcher Meets Takee

The chair-coolies started up the creek from the Astor House to the Wills bridge, stopped for Hicks to pay the bridge toll, then huffed their way over Soochow Creek, singing out at other foot traffic to give way. They loped past the British consulate and south along the British Bund, past the verandahs and brightly lit windows of the great trading houses. The last office on the British Bund was the ship's chandler H. Fogg & Company, the principal hardware and mercantile trader for the settlement and, Fletcher noted again as they passed, the most likely source of general supply for a small force of mercenaries. From H. Fogg's, they swung across the footbridge over the *Yang-king-bang* creek onto the *quai du Whampoo* – the French "bund" – then turned up *du Consulat* street toward the western suburbs. A few streets short of their destination they stopped and dismissed the sedan chairs.

"Chair-coolies know too much of everybody's business," Hicks muttered. "Shanghai is an emporium of infiltrators and informers, Mr. Wood. Between rebel spies and the *taotai*'s lackeys alone, more information passes than would fill your morning *Herald*. Scoff if you wish, sir, but you will find, if you do not already know it, that it is not possible to be too careful with one's business in this place."

Shortly, they came to a high wall of plastered masonry stained dull red and bristling with jagged shards of broken pottery and rusty iron set in mortar along the top. "Here begins the old gentleman's *cittadella*, Mr. Wood, Takee's private seraglio of mansions, gardens and pools, complete with hareem of wives and concubines forbidden to strangers, and down this street we shall eventually arrive at his Sublime Gate."

Fletcher could see a large, tile-roofed gate another 200 feet further along the wall. If one side is 400 feet long, he thought, then there are four acres of ground behind that wall. In the foreign settlement that is something to boast about.

"Judging by his lodgings, your Takee might actually be able to pay for an army."

"Oh, he has the scratch all right, Mr. Wood, make no mistake about that. If the *taotai* is rumored to have the purse of Fortunatus, then Old Takee has got the ill-gotten gold of Tolosa, pilfered from the *taotai*'s custom house squeeze, widows and orphans, homeless refugees, pawnshop profits, and who knows where else. He makes a better Yankee than us Yankees: water's the rum, sands the sugar, wets the codfish and tobacco, then goes to prayers. But also mind you this: he is an agent of the Tartars, and has the ear of none other than the emperor himself. Be guarded with Takee until you know him well, and never divulge any more than you must. Be light of foot, Mr. Wood, if you want to dance with the devil and pay no due."

They found the gate closed but, between the planks of the two large doors, flickering lantern light was visible within. Hicks rapped on the wood. A panel in one of the side doors snapped open. A yellow paper lantern on a long stick appeared above them at the top of the gate and swathed the two foreigners in sallow light broken by the shadows of flitting moths. Sullen eyes set in a face yellowed like parched earth peered through the open panel.

"干嘛 what d'ya want?"

"My wantchee Takee," Hicks said. The malevolent eyes slowly looked them up and down, the panel snapped shut, and the lantern was withdrawn and extinguished. Hicks and Wood stood in the moonlight for five minutes.

"Armed guards walk the perimeter of the wall inside," Hicks whispered, "regular soldiers, 'braves' we call them, for the Chinese character for bravery sewn on the back of their uniforms. Takee says the district magistrate lends them, because Takee himself is a kind of *taotai* in waiting, after the sitting *taotai*, Wu. So stay close to me and do not stray into any of the gardens, or any further than the first courtyard and the big hall. Beyond the big hall, that's the hareem, so to speak, where no strangers are allowed. Just never go anywhere in the house that you are not invited."

I wasn't raised in a barnyard, Mr. Hicks, Fletcher thought. You still have me confused with waterfront riffraff.

A rusty bolt rasped a harsh demurral, the side-door on the left creaked open, and a stark light stabbed through the crack.

"Remember," Hicks said, "the byway into hell runs right next to the gateway into heaven. No missteps now, no wrong turns!"

A thin hand thrust through the opening and a long bony finger beckoned in the thin glare, then disappeared. After a moment, the parched-earth face of the old caretaker appeared suddenly, impatiently raking at them with his bony finger, gesturing them in through the main gate 大門 and left around a large wooden barricade that loomed out of the shadow immediately behind the gate.

Spirit screen, Fletcher thought. Maybe they keep out Chinese ghosts and devils and other straight-line navigators, but they obviously do not keep out foreign ghosts and devils, *yang-kuei-tzu* like us. Damyankees chart a course any which way.

Off to his right, Fletcher could see gardens in the moonlight, sparkling pools spanned by fragile little arch bridges, stone-lined white paths that led among the shadows of tall, wispy trees and disappeared in the dark. Somewhere at the back of the gardens, he imagined he heard whispered voices and the clink of metal. The gatekeeper called out and another servant appeared and led the foreigners across a small arched bridge over a pond lush with floating white lotus blooms, through a smaller tile-roofed gate 小門 set into another wall, then around another spirit screen of weathered green marble into a broad, rectangular courtyard paved with flagstone.

On each side of the yard, a row of squat buildings perched upon rough granite pedestals that raised the structures four feet above the stone pavement. Ornate staircases of ebon wood and white marble ascended to open verandahs of polished teak and mahogany hardwood that passed along the facade of each building under broad eaves of heavy timber. Into the facades were set windows of thin parchment or oyster shell laid upon a fragile bamboo lattice. Below the verandahs, intricate lattice panels concealed the open space under the buildings. The foreigners followed their shuffling guide across the courtyard, entered the reception hall 大堂, and were invited to sit in one of the two guest halls 客堂 at each side of the reception hall.

"Must have caught the old man unawares," Hicks said. "Usually he makes a great show of rushing out to greet his guests."

The two foreigners sat in straight-back chairs of glossy rosewood at one side of the guest hall where the astonishing wealth of the household was displayed. Rotund vases of sea-green crackled porcelain enamel on copper, inlaid with ivory cranes and cinnabar peonies, loomed in recesses like garish menials attending guests. Everywhere on rosewood and ebony tables were arrayed rich bronzes inlaid with silver, white jade and green jade jars, cups and bowls, and carved lacquer-wood trays and boxes. Delicate gilt screens embellished with garnet and lapis lazuli stood beneath elegant hanging tapestries depicting grimacing lions and soaring cranes embroidered in gold and silver thread, and long white scrolls of jet-black calligraphy. High among the carved and painted rafters of side-chamber balconies hung slender bamboo cages in which thrushes and other quietly chattering songbirds flashed bright tints under the smoke-dark ceiling.

Carpets thick with elaborate designs of dragon and phoenix lay atop burnished floor tiles that roused the room to a riot of color and detail. They seemed to Fletcher almost a reproach of the foreigners' somber rigging, Hicks in his black-velvet trimmed gray coat and gray top hat, Fletcher in black French field cap and black frock coat. Servants bustled in with wide toothy grins and steaming cups of tea in elegant porcelain cups on lacquered trays piled with strange-looking confectionery. The faint aroma of sandalwood incense drifted in from the burners on the altar visible at the back of the reception hall.

Hicks motioned toward the altar. "Behind that wall," he said in low voice, "is the inner courtyard, the family's private sanctum, the realm of Takee's wife, son, and daughter. Actually only one concubine, I've heard. Shanghai tells a remarkable story about the concubine. Seems she and her sister were part of some kind of traveling carnival run by a Chinese edition of P. T. Barnum. She was skilled in repartee, telling jokes and making riddles, and reciting poems in the fashion appreciated by patrician Chinese. Her sister displayed martial talents that excited the rubes, was an agile swordswoman and a superb archer, and an acrobat as well. Together they traveled the cities and towns of China attracting large audiences until they arrived in Shanghai, by which time the women had learned a thing or two and threatened to take over the carnival for themselves. That was too much for the Chinese Barnum, and he auctioned the women off. The district magistrate bought the lady of martial temperament for 3000 taels, and now she dons a soldier's uniform and joins the magistrate's forces when he goes out to do battle with the rebels! The lady of literary temperament became the second Mrs. Takee. Rumor has it – and rumor is the only way one hears about these cloistered Chinese women – that she is quite resourceful, and in part responsible for her husband's remarkable success here in Shanghai and at court in the Forbidden City."

While Hicks rattled on, Fletcher heard an echo that drew his attention to the balcony of a side chamber at the end of the guest hall. A flitting shadow disappeared behind a cinnabar column carved in relief with entwined dragons. Something was up there, in the dark under the rafters.

2

"Cha-ssu-tah, Cha-ssu-tah, olo flen!" A thin voice sounded up a corridor and Yang Fang swept into the guest hall flanked by servants. The two foreigners stood. "Solly too muchee you wait so long. Please sit, *ch'ing tso* 請坐, *ch'ing tso* 請坐. Hab tea? Good?"

"*Chin-chin*, Takee," Hicks said, "*maskee, maskee*, it's all right. Here, I have brought you Fletcher Wood."

Fletcher put forth his hand, but the Chinese clasped his two hands together and waved them before his own face, smiling broadly. Fletcher remembered the Chinese gesture of greeting. Foolish of me to offer him a handshake, he thought, but it didn't seem to fluster him as it does others. Fletcher joined his hands before his chest in a similar manner, and then took his seat.

"Wu-te? Fetcha Wu-te? Please to know you, Fetcha Wu-te. Please to know you. My name b'long Yang Fang, but Cha-ssu-tah talkee my name Takee. You talkee my name Takee, *maskee*? Please sit now, *ch'ing-tso, ch'ing-tso*. Drink tea?"

Yang Fang motioned for a chair to be put on the right facing the foreigners and flopped down into it, spreading his gilt-embroidered gown around his feet. He leaned back and steepled his fingers, and through a warm smile peered into the foreigner's face, endeavoring to read in Fletcher's deep blue eyes whatever was there to be seen.

Wu-te is small in stature, thought Yang Fang, but strong, and dark in complexion, like a Chinese. His size will not impress men, not like Chang Fei 張飛 or Kuan Yu 關羽, heroes over eight feet tall, and he looks like neither a warrior nor a scholar. His appearance is more like ordinary Chinese than other foreigners, and so Chinese will feel he is more like themselves. So much hair on his face, over his mouth and on his chin, but his mouth is full-lipped, not thin-lipped or mean. How do these foreigners grow so much hair on their bodies? They always smell, too, of either horses, unwashed bodies, or strong soap. He is alert and intent, his eyes are penetrating and his smile reserved, and he looks directly into my face. I see...curiosity, determination...but feel no threat.

"Chin-chin, Takee, pleased to know you too. I hear you are a very big man in Shanghai. Good of you to invite me to your house."

Takee has a gaunt, hungry air about him, thought Fletcher, and an expression evidently wasted by the recurrent fever they say he endures. All bony cheek and sharp chin, and ears that poke out from under his little hat like handles on a sugar bowl – maybe the better to eavesdrop on foreign secrets. The angular face by itself is enough to inspire his reputation as a fox. Confident, and not intimidated by the foreigner's strangeness. Takee gazes directly into your eyes with never any question about whether he is your equal. Seems to understand some English, too, at least simple phrases.

"Wu-te! You come my house allo time allo samee!" Yang Fang hesitated imperceptivity as he realized his mistake, then added: "Cha-ssu-tah, olo flen, why you no come see me mo'? You come allo time, too!"

"Takee, I do not speak your language," Fletcher said, "and my pidgin is not very good. So, I want to ask if you think we should have an interpreter when we meet."

"*Maskee*. Wu-te talkee 'Melican, no talkee pidgin."

"But Takee, can you understand me if I speak American?"

"My sabee belly good," the Chinese said, laughing. He pointed to an ear, then to his mouth. "Takee eah plitty good, Takee mouth plitty bad. Can sabee belly muchee, *maskee* mus' talkee pidgin. Takee long time *mai-ban* 賣瓣, complado' at *I-ho* 怡和, you call Chahdeen, big English tlading hong, learn belly muchee English word."

"Takee was a Jardine comprador for years in the fifties," Hicks said. "He was very important in helping Jardine's Shanghai office develop their business in upcountry silk, and now he's become a very rich man. Richer, they say, than Howqua was in Canton back in the 40s. What do you think, Takee, are you richer now than Howqua?"

Yang Fang waved his hands. "Oh, no, my not so lich now. Howqua belly lich man, mo' lich den Takee. Takee money in bankee now, money allo b'long Takee bankee."

The Chinese paused to sip tea and secure a moment's respite from the clumsy foreigner's rude remarks about his personal wealth, sighting Fletcher over the edge of his steaming cup. Suddenly, he called to a servant to bring brush, ink and paper.

"Wu-te, you hab belly good name. 'Wu' mean sojah...woyah. 'Te' mean honah. 'Woyah honah,' belly, belly good name Wu-te. Belly lucky. All Chinee mus' call you dis name, hokay? You say 'my name Wu-te, *wo chiao wu-te* 我叫武德.' " It was common language, he thought, but easy for a foreigner.

After a moment, Fletcher grasped Takee's meaning: warrior-honor.

"My teachee you talkee Chinee, Wu-te," Yang Fang said. "Litee bit."

Fletcher smiled at the twinkle in the old man's eye – Takee had a sense of humor. That quality could go a long way to surmount the language barrier.

"Sure, Takee," Fletcher said, laughing, "but *only* a little bit."

"Write dis way, Wu-te."

Takee dipped the brush in ink and quickly stroked out 武德

"You're not going to make me *write* that, are you?"

"No, Wu-te," Yang Fang said, laughing again. "Jus' talkee."

"My name is Wood," Fletcher said, "Woo-duh. *whoa jeeao woo-duh*." When the paper with his name dried, Fletcher folded it, touched it to his forehead following the Chinese gesture of thanks, and placed it in his pocket.

His composure regained, Yang Fang fired off a rapid volley of questions about where Fletcher came from, his parents, and his family. When Takee asked about a wife, Fletcher became self-conscious and maneuvered for high ground in the conversation.

"Are you from Shanghai, Takee? Do you have a large family?"

"Takee no b'longee Shanghai, Wu-te. Takee b'longee Ningpo. Ningpo south flom Shanghai, close by ocean like Salem. Takee family b'long Shanghai now, hab got *t'ai-t'ai*, one piecee stupid boy, one piecee ugly gel." After this quick parry came the repost. "Wu-te, what you' pidgin?"

"My pidgin." Fletcher mulled while he formulated a succinct response.

"Pidgin," Hicks said, "can mean business or employment, apart from the polyglot pidgin tongue we are all forced to speak in this place."

"For many years I was a ship's officer, a first mate on clipper ships sailing to China and trading in tea and silk."

"Oh, Wu-te, come China befo'?"

"Several times," Fletcher said. He slowly related his resume, like a scroll unrolled leisurely. Takee peered into his face with an unchanging expression and nodded with the name of each vessel. *Hamilton, Russell Glover, Black Warrior, Gold Hunter, Westward Ho, Antelope*. Takee said he knew *An-ti-lou-pu*.

"Fetcha Wu-te, you long-time sailo'-man, go many placee, see all under sky." Takee seemed almost envious. He had never been further from Ningpo than Shanghai. While he was not sure he actually wanted to go anywhere else, he could still appreciate someone who had traveled the world.

"Yes, but I am a soldier, too." Now Fletcher unrolled the military pages of his scroll. Schooling at Norwich Academy in the basics of military drill, tactics, strategy and military engineering. Training Walker's recruits in Lower California, soldiering with Garibaldi in Peru and Bolivia, officer of artillery in the Crimea, and fighting for Juarez in Mexico. Even Hicks was impressed. He had not yet heard all of this.

Unlikely as it was that Takee knew the places Fletcher mentioned, at least he appeared to be listening carefully. Fletcher spoke slowly, watching the Chinaman's face for signs that he understood, but not a flicker of pursed lip or raised brow ever disturbed Takee's placid expression. Fletcher swallowed the impulse to simplify his language, so that he could learn just how well Takee understood this English.

"Wu-te, you first b'long sailah, how fashion now b'long sojah?"

"That came of meeting the Italian named Giuseppe Garabaldi. He is in Italy now, fighting for independence. He became my genius – my hero. We met in San Francisco, about ten years ago, when he took command there of a ship bound for Canton. I was a ship keeper rotting away with inactivity in a dusty office, and he came to me on some kind of business. We discovered we both were sons of shipmasters, both left home early and went to sea, and both were experienced deep-water sailors in command on ships 'round the Horn."

Fletcher guessed Takee was not following much of this, but the wind was in his sails. Anyway, Hicks was listening closely, and Takee was also watching Hicks.

"Garibaldi was raising funds for a new revolutionary movement in Italy, and I accompanied him to several dinner parties of rich San Francisco families sympathetic to the cause of liberation in Italy. He was twice my age, a fierce orator, fearless yet gentle, and he told tales of adventure in foreign lands that lit a fire in my blood. I wasn't sure how to go about becoming the liberator of some God-forsaken fly-blown backwater, but I knew enough to get off my stool and put to sea."

Fletcher expected the old man's eyes to glaze over about the time Garabaldi and Italy came aboard the conversation, but there was no change in the wan smile pasted on the Chinaman's face, even though Hicks was looking restless. Fletcher decided to press on quickly to a close, but he would remember that Takee had never even flinched when hearing English he could not possibly have fathomed.

洋神 *Yang Shen* *James Lande* 藍德

Yang Fang recalled other foreigners he had known and compared them to this Wu-te. They were businessmen, mostly – Yang Fang did not see foreign consuls and military officers as did the *tao-t'ai*. Foreign traders were smart, and calculating, with minds like an abacus, clicking constantly to evaluate profit and loss. They lived garishly in pretentious dwellings, overindulged their senses, and displayed their tawdry wives like half-naked streetwalkers. Mostly, they were disrespectful, even contemptuous, and often arrogant. Wu-te was strong, even overwhelming, but not disrespectful or arrogant.

"Wu-te, you sabee lebel? Lebel belly bad man, kill muchee piecee Chinee man, do muchee bad thing. You sabee lebel come Shanghai?" Yang Fang was showing signs of wear from too many strange names and places, too much incomprehensible English.

"I have a plan to keep the rebels away from Shanghai."

Yang Fang sat up straight as bamboo. "What plan, Wu-te?"

"I want to muster a force of men to fight the rebels. If I can enlist an army of several hundred men, soldiers and sailors from Shanghai, give them guns, train them to march and fight, I can defend Shanghai and keep rebels out of the city."

"How fashion can do, Wu-te?"

"I would establish a training camp, somewhere to the west, and enlist infantry and artillery officers, and sergeants and corporals here in Shanghai. I would find good men who know how to train other men as soldiers. At the same time, I will buy rifles, muskets and pistols in Shanghai, and artillery. Field guns, 6-pounders and 12-pounders. When the training camp is ready, we will find men to be our soldiers, give them arms, and train them to shoot and to fight together. When they are ready, I will march them against rebel strongholds."

Fletcher undid two buttons of his frock coat and withdrew a paper that he unfolded and handed to the Chinese. "Look there, Takee, that is a map of Shanghai and the country all around. You can see Soochow, and the Yangtze River, and Nanking. All the country in a circle around Shanghai, and across the Whangpoo in Pootung, must be secured. All the rebels anywhere around there now must be driven out, then we must protect the important towns around the area to keep the rebels out."

"Ho, Wu-te, dat soun' like belly good plan!"

"Some things are needed, Takee. The army will be small, to move fast and hit hard, and cannot garrison the towns we capture, so we must have Chinese troops come to garrison the towns, to live there and hold the places so the rebels cannot return."

"Yes, yes, my sabee. Can do, Wu-te. My talkee Wu *Tao-t'ai*. Wu *Tao-t'ai* catchee Chinee Gleen Flag tloop."

"We will need money to buy arms, Takee, much money. We must have breach-loading rifles if we can get them, but certainly rifled muskets, and older smoothbore muskets only if unavoidable, but all in good condition, and pistols. We'll need maybe two or three hundred rifles or muskets all together."

Yang Fang hesitated, calculating the cost. "Yes, can do. Catchee muchee piecee lifle, Wu-te. My godown have muchee piecee lifle, can use fo' sojah."

Wood hesitated. He could guess what kind of weapons were in Takee's godown. Old smoothbore muskets, or worse yet flintlocks and matchlocks, museum pieces and other useless trash bought cheap for resale at outrageous prices to the imperials, or even the rebels. They would buy that trash because they knew nothing about guns, preferred swords and spears, bows and arrows.

"Well, I'll look at what is in your godown, but it may not be of much use. First chop weapons are needed, Sharps rifles and carbines in good condition, and Tower rifled muskets of recent vintage. Nothing old and broken."

Yang Fang seemed a little crestfallen for a moment. "No *maskee* godown lifle, Wu-te. My catchee new lifle."

"No, Takee, I must buy the guns."

The Chinese looked up quickly. "My catchee lifle allo samee."

"No, it is not all the same." Fletcher looked directly into Yang Fang's black eyes and spoke softly. "You're a banker, not a soldier. I'll wager in your whole your life you've never even fired a rifle."

Hicks, whose unctuous deference to the banker rarely failed, fidgeted in his chair at this amiable provocation. Yang Fang slowly shook his head.

"No, I didn't think so. You must trust me in this, Takee, because the weapons we buy are very important, and I know what we must have. You will have to arrange for credit in my name at Fogg's, and at Jardine's, and I will charge my purchases to your account. This is the only way it can be done."

Yang Fang struggled to look away from the compelling blue eyes of the foreigner. For a few moments, the only sound heard was the song of a thrush echoing among the rafters. Then Yang Fang looked up and nodded.

"I can help out there, Mr. Wood," Hicks said. "I have contacts that can put their hands on some rifles that Sharps sold to the British back in fifty-five. There are some of those still around in private arsenals that I can track down for you."

"Same terms, Mr. Hicks. Good condition, reasonably priced. I reserve right of refusal for anything bought on my behalf, and whatever I refuse you and Takee are stuck with at no cost to me."

"The Manilamen aboard *Confucius* were using Sharps that I procured for the Admiral, so do not be too concerned – what I find for you will be the same quality."

"I also require artillery. We will need more money to buy artillery."

"Yes," Yang Fang said with a grin, "big cannon, belly big cannon. My takee you catchee cannon, Wu-te."

"To move the army, we will need steamers, Takee. Gunboats with shallow drafts that can pass through water gates, armed with heavy guns to shell towns and smash city walls. Can you get steamers?"

"Hab got *k'ung-fu-tze*. Tell Gan-tuh no chase pilate, chase lebel."

"*Confucius* is too big, Takee. She is a good boat on the Yangtze, but she can't go inland too far because her draft is too deep. We need smaller steamers."

"Mebbe can catchee, Wu-te," Yang Fang said cheerlessly. "Takee look-see catchee littee steamah."

"Soldiers must be paid. They must have uniforms and equipment. They must be fed and doctored. Soldiers should get $100.00 Mexican dollars each month. Sergeants $150.00 Mex. Officers pay should be from $300.00 to $400.00 Mex, with extra for artillery officers. I receive $500.00 Mex each month. At least $25,000.00 for soldiers' pay, and another $18,000 for commissary and medical, food and medicine. That's over $40,000.00 Mexican dollars a month to start. And the sum will grow as the army grows. No hanging back about pay – every soldier receives his pay every month without delay."

五萬五千兩銀子多 more than 55,000 taels, thought Yang Fang! He pursed his lips and squirmed in his chair. Each month!

"And that's not all," Fletcher said. Yang Fang's eyebrows flew up and furrowed the thin, mottled skin of his translucent brow.

"Mo'?"

"For every small town we capture, I receive $45,000.00 Mex. For every big town we take from the rebels, I receive $133,000.00 Mex."

Yang Fang's jaw dropped and his eyes opened wide. 十八萬四千兩銀子 184,000 taels! Even Chester Hicks exhaled audibly. Hicks turned in his chair. Yang Fang left his chair entirely and slowly paced the length of the hall.

"You have sand, Fletcher Wood," Hicks said in a low voice. "Yesterday, you were a simple mate on a river steamer, yet tonight you demand a king's ransom for sacking rebel towns. And here I thought I was audacious. Obviously, I should go for a soldier in your army if I do not wish to remain a pauper in my own calling. Old Takee is too polite to ask if you hab got watah topside, if you're crazy, but he must be wondering."

Fletcher ignored Hicks and watched Takee, waiting for him to come to anchor. Setting aside the pirate-suppressing mandarin aboard *Confucius*, this was the first mandarin Fletcher had actually met, the first Chinese man of wealth, class, and power. He remembered calling on the Peabody family, and the Crowninshields, in their sitting rooms – the riches of the patrician aristocracy made a lasting impression on a small boy. Takee was a banker so, of course, Fletcher imagined the old man's mind clicking away like a Chinese abacus calculating cost but, personally, he seemed to alternate between gushing, courteous deference, and calm, pensive reflection. Takee's riches could not be seen from outside – the gold and jade were modestly secluded inside dusty brick walls. His family was nowhere evident, no portly wife nagged for introductions, and he probably never drank anything stronger than tea. If foreigners only meet beggars, singsong girls and servants, he thought, no wonder they have a low opinion of Chinese.

這個小子的膽子相當大 this rascal has a lot of nerve. 我把他幹掉怎麼樣 what if I throw him out ? Yang Fang glanced quickly at Fletcher Wood, only to find Fletcher looking directly into his face, his dark-blue glowing like sapphires.

Yang Fang returned to pacing. A house servant started to ask what the *Ta-lao-yeh*, might be wanting. Yang Fang hissed at him, "滾蛋 get out!" The servant vanished.

That is a lot of money! We know nothing about this rascal except that he fought a few river pirates. So much money! And if we have such an army, how can it be controlled, how can this impudent rogue be managed? Such money! This is simple extortion! Wu-te knows there is a lot at risk, large money, large property, and he is gambling that we will pay much to protect our wealth and holdings from the longhaired bandits. I cannot be responsible for such a decision – this must be discussed with Wu *Ta-jen*, maybe even the governor. But if we financed such an army, it would have to be kept secret from the Emperor until successful in battle, lest blame for failure fall on our heads. Where would we get money like that? No Chinese army is paid so much, and I certainly don't want to pay it myself, nor from T'ai-chi Hang! How many towns can this upstart capture? I must consult with Wu *Ta-jen*.

Fletcher watched the old mandarin's face closely and tried to guess his thoughts from his impassive expression and stooped posture. Might just as well try to read bibles in a dark bilge, but he does not like the money, that's clear. What can I do here to make tongue 'n buckle meet? Hicks said Takee helped defend the Chinese city against the Triads back in the early fifties. Built a wall northeast of the native city and cut the Small Knife rebels off from supplies smuggled from the foreign settlement. He was a hero then, and maybe became rich as a consequence.

Fletcher rose from his chair, which brought Yang Fang to a halt.

"Where go, Wu-te? Please to sit. Hab mo' tea. 來人來茶 someone bring tea!" he called out. "*Ch'ing-tso, ch'ing-tso,* please be seated, 請請 *ch'ing, ch'ing*."

Fletcher and Yang Fang both sat again and, while servants fled in and out with hot tea, Fletcher went to work on the old mandarin, staring hard into Yang Fang's eyes and speaking slowly with many pauses to allow the old man's comprehension to keep pace.

"Look here, Takee, we know the rebels are going to come to Shanghai, and we know there are not enough Chinese soldiers to fight them. We also know that British and

Americans are going to enforce neutrality in this civil war, so they are not going to put a force into the field against the rebels. The French may talk about sending soldiers to Soochow, but in the end the French will do as the British."

Well, he must know something if he knows that, thought Yang Fang.

Fletcher raised an eyebrow as if to say "do you understand me, old man?" Takee understood and nodded quickly as if to answer "yes, of course I understand, so please get on with it." They were learning an unspoken language of expression and gesture to assist their ungainly speech. Fletcher began to gesticulate more to buttress their mutual comprehension and circumvent the Chinaman's reluctance to admit ignorance of a word.

"Yes, Wu-te. Flench allo time do same as Blitish. Folla 'roun like littee dogee."

"The foreign nations will defend the settlement, of course, with volunteers and marines and frigates firing from the Whangpoo on rebel positions and approaches to the settlement, and maybe they will defend the Chinese city as well. The French can hardly avoid that, being right under the wall as they are. But you know yourself what can happen if rebels get into the Chinese city. You were here when the Triads took the city years ago, you helped to fight those rebels and defeat them, but you know what it cost, too. Thousands died, and the city and suburbs were destroyed."

Fletcher paused again to let his last remark sink in deeply, as well as to rest from the unaccustomed calisthenics of the conversation. Westerners all laughed at the way hands flew when Chinese talked, but he was beginning to see why that happened when two people did not speak the same language.

Yang Fang realized the foreigner expected him to say something to show that he understood the English. "Oh, yes, Wu-te. Many piecee Chinee man allo dead, an' allo Shanghai burn up."

"Now," Fletcher said, "six or seven years later, nothing's changed. If the Taiping come near Shanghai, the British will set fire to outlying districts, and your suburbs will go up in flames again. Of course, that will never bother the British, because after the war they'll just go into business of selling the materials to rebuild the suburbs, and you Chinese will have to pay for it all. Does it cost more to finance an army than to rebuild a city destroyed by fire? One army for one year costs, what – half a million dollars Mexican? Close to 700,000 in your little silver shoes. Even if the army costs a million or more, it is still going to cost, how much – ten million to rebuild the suburbs? And how much more if you add the cost of all the lives lost and towns burnt in outlying areas?"

Fletcher leaned back to sip his tea and let a moment of silence punctuate the argument. He deliberately clicked the porcelain lid against the cup several times to heighten the tension. He could see the old mandarin dangling on his direct stare like a carp caught on a bamboo pole. "No one else in Shanghai is willing to go into the field against the rebels except me! Only I can defeat the rebels and save Shanghai."

Fletcher set his teacup down with a loud clink that rattled the lid and paused again for effect. He let Yang Fang off the hook and gazed around the hall. His glance caught a movement on the balcony of a side chamber at the end of the guest hall, opposite the great hall. Behind a large red-lacquered column supporting the balcony, he made out two shadowy figures with the flowing gowns and high headdress of women. He continued looking about so that his gaze would not betray to Takee what he had seen.

There is something fragile, he thought, and insubstantial about this kind of dwelling that is different from the solid old manse of brick and mortar, built to keep out the elements. Here sun warms courtyards open to the weather, wind whips through long, wide corridors, snow piles up on exposed verandahs, rain tears the delicate rice-paper coverings of bamboo lattice windows. All the sounds of nature from the crack of thunder to the gentle drip of rainwater must echo through the whole house. As changeably warm, wind-swept and wet as the place can be, it must feel like living in the fo'c's'le of a clipper ship. Slowly, Fletcher turned back to his host. The two figures were still there, eavesdropping from the balcony.

"It cannot be all that hard to find the money, can it?" Fletcher said. Taxes can always be raised from somewhere, and I guess you don't need me to say where, because I could not begin to imagine all the different kinds of logrolling and pork-barrels that come to hand in China.

Not from T'ai-chi Hang, thought Yang Fang, not with my money. From our brothers in the Ningpo Guild 四明公所. And Wu *Ta-jen* has official sources, the customs revenues 關稅, *li-chin* taxes 釐金, and special levies 關徵.

"Of course, you must have your own people with the army, to see that the accounting is done correctly and that the money is being spent properly, and so you'll have your own people to explain why expenses rise, and why Wu-te has to ask for more money every month. Imagine how Shanghai will praise you if you finance the army that saves the city. You'll be a hero again just as before, when the Triads captured Shanghai. Everyone will want to do business with Takee Bank. You will be honored by the *taotai*, by the governor of the province, even by the emperor! Maybe then the emperor will make Takee the next *taotai*!"

Maybe the Emperor will have my head, thought Yang Fang, smiling thinly at the thought of becoming *tao-t'ai*. Wu Hsü already ably fills that office, and our partnership is successful. If I were *tao-t'ai*, who would be the *tao-t'ai*'s banker? But this Wu-te has much enthusiasm and confidence, and he anticipates much of what will also occur to Brother Wu. Perhaps he could lead an army of foreigners, as they must have a leader. Besides his bravery aboard our paddle-wheel boat – reported breathlessly 熱情洋溢地 by nephew Yang Hsi-hai – he also helped defend the Fitch trading ship, the owner of Fitch & Company guarantees him, and the American consul sent him to us. That does not mean he is a leader, or even reliable. He is a different kind of person from the foreign traders, or the foreign consuls, or the Christian missionaries. He is too unsettled for trade, too brash for diplomacy, and too arrogant to submit to any god. But there is his name, *wu-te*. He is a good omen when we most need a warrior, this man named *wu* 武, warrior, *wu-te* 武德 a man of martial honor. I will go to the *tao-t'ai*'s yamen and discuss this with Brother Wu but, on the way, I will visit the temple of Kuan Lao-yeh, make another sacrifice to the God of War, and consult his oracle about this Wu-te.

"Wu-te, you hab belly good plan. My tinkee you one belly good man, Wu-te, mebbe can do fight lebel. *Maskee*, no belongee Takee pidgin. Mus' talkee muchee piecee man, mus' tinkee where catchee big dollah. Allo belongee *tao-t'ai* pidgin, Wu-te. My talkee Wu *Tao-t'ai*, mebbe Wu *Tao-t'ai* wantche talkee you, Wu-te. Hokay?"

"As you wish, Takee. I'll wait." But not too long, Takee. Might not be enough time.

3 From where they stood concealed behind large red-lacquered columns in the gloom of a balcony at the end of the guest hall, two women watched the foreigners depart from Yang Fang's house. One was Yang Fang's daughter Ch'ang Mei 常梅, and the other was Ch'ang Mei's slave girl 丫鬟, called Hsüeh-ch'un 雪春.

"They are just too ugly, those foreigners!" the slave girl said. "They should not be allowed inside the house. Finally they're gone." Hsüeh-ch'un was indignant. Her mistress was about to go out into their private garden to view the moon when the awful foreigners came pounding on the gate. Of course, the two women could not allow themselves to be seen outside their secluded rooms, so the little slave girl had missed a coveted opportunity to dawdle in the cool evening air along ornate little bridges over ponds reflecting the moonlight. At least she had induced her mistress to steal out to a dark corner and eavesdrop on the interlopers.

"The smaller one looks somewhat like a Chinese," Ch'ang-mei said, her curiosity aroused by the apparitions in strange Western clothing, and the odd, piggish grunts and squeals that passed for language between them and her father. In her memory, foreigners had seldom come to their home – a privilege rarely granted even her father's close Chinese friends, who were always met in tea houses or restaurants. It was unnerving to have two very large and boisterous foreign men appear suddenly in their guest hall. She sensed, too, tension between them and her father, and took a dislike to them. She was certain she could smell their strange odor over the scent of sandalwood incense.

Ch'ang-mei was twenty-one years old and unexceptional in appearance. Her black eyes were close-set in an oval face, her nose wide and flat, and her mouth full. Her forehead and eyebrows were cleanly shaven, and her long hair was gathered tightly at the nape of her neck with a beaten gold sleeve. She wore a light blue skirt and embroidered belt, white silk blouse with large open sleeves and, over her shoulders, a blue mantlet edged with white lace trim. She carried a round fan of translucent bird's-egg blue silk painted with yellow and black swallow-tailed butterflies and mounted on a slender handle of ivory carved in the shape of a willowy woman.

"Mistress, let's return now, and wait for the stink of their sweat to disperse."

"All right." Ch'ang-mei's embroidered silk skirts swirled as she turned away, and Hsüeh Ch'un dutifully followed beside her, lightly supporting her arm. The small, mincing steps Ch'ang-mei took on her golden lilies – her bound feet – were firm and unwavering and made her skirts swish. In the long years the two girls had lived together as mistress and maid, Hsüeh Ch'un had endured with her mistress the ordeal Ch'ang-mei suffered learning to walk with skill on her heels in beautifully made but extraordinarily clumsy platform shoes of blue brocade only four inches long. The slave girl fluttered constantly at the side of her mistress, but really was needed only when they came to stairs, and sometimes to help her mistress stand.

The room that was Ch'ang-mei's world, her "all under heaven 天下," faced east with double doors opening onto a wide balcony that looked out over the private garden, with its scaly green porcelain dragon undulating along the top of the wall. Beyond were the outer gardens and outer wall topped with shards of broken pottery and rusty iron scrap. Each window in the balcony doors let in light through opaque gauze under a wooden lattice. Inside, wide bamboo blinds could be rolled down to hold back the dawn until Hsüeh Ch'un's mistress was ready to view the new day.

Ch'ang-mei was slow and poised, and had more education than other girls of her age and station. Her Little Mother gave her reading lessons beginning when she was eleven years old, and taught her poetry and some history as well as the more usual sewing, weaving, embroidery, and other domestic arts. She had two mothers really, her own mother, Yang Fang's first wife, called Ta Niang 大娘, and her Little Mother, Hsiao Ma 小媽, who was in fact the lady of literary temperament Yang Fang had purchased. Constant in Ch'ang-mei's thought was the tension between her two mothers: the first wife, and the little concubine.

Hsüeh Ch'un was eighteen years old. She had straight eyebrows, a thin nose, and a rosebud mouth. A large *faux* pearl on a gilded chain dangled from each earlobe. She dressed in a long, loose white silk skirt, white blouse with flowing sleeves, a small black vest with lapels embroidered in gold and silver, and a matching embroidered belt. Hsüeh Ch'un could not read, and often scolded herself for being so stupid. She made up for her lack with ready perception, a nimble mind, and a sweet disposition. She was given to broad gestures with her hands that made her sleeves swirl about like birds on wing.

洋神 *Yang Shen* James Lande 藍德

Ch'ang-mei was demure in her movements – her sleeves hardly ever fluttered. The mistress was a serene white egret, and the maid a clever lark, if not a mischievous jay.

"We precious daughters 千金小姐 choose smart, quick-witted slaves who can sing and tell jokes. You entertain me, and are my eyes and ears outside of the boudoir and beyond our walls. So you have to be at least as smart as me, which, as you know, is not difficult. If you do well, then when I marry I will be certain that you also are married well as part of the bargain."

Young as she was, Ch'ang-mei already bore a profound sorrow. She was bad luck. Engaged to marry at a much younger and more appropriate age, her intended had died. Regardless of how rich and important her father might be, no one would consider her for marriage now that she had "spilled her tea," frightened they too would die because of the inscrutable working of her sinister fate. She could only believe her betrothed had cursed her with his dying breath. He certainly had doomed her to long lonely years as an old maid, never to have a home of her own, never to have children, never to have happiness. But for Hsüeh Ch'un her slave, Yang Fang's daughter was imprisoned alone in her own boudoir, where the only part of life she could taste was her own tears. She often cried herself to sleep to the lament of Ts'ui Ying-ying 催鶯鶯, the cloistered heroine of *The Romance of the West Chamber* 西廂記.

> The maiden's room has long been lonely 蘭閨久寂寞
> She has no will to enjoy the fragrant spring 無事度芳春
> That fellow who is walking by, humming 料得行吟者
> Ought to have pity for the grieving girl 應憐長歎人

When Ch'ang-mei's engagement ended, it was clear that she would never marry. Hsüeh Ch'un became frightened that she, too, would never marry and, together with her mistress, would grow into an old maid. Ch'ang-mei's own mother lost all consideration for her after the engagement failed, abused her as a worthless thing the family must feed and clothe forever, and threatened to sell her to the rebels if she misbehaved or, worse yet, to the *yang-kuei-tzu*, the foreign devils!

4 The heavenly capital celebrated. Two-hundred miles upriver from Takee's reception hall, the city of T'ien-ching was in the midst of ten days of roisterous celebration of the end of the siege and the collapse of the *Chiang-nan Ta-ying*. The incessant *rat-tat-tat* explosion of strings of firecrackers and the din of music on drum, flute, horn and gong was everywhere. Towering commemorative wooden gateways 木牌坊 proclaimed 10,000 years of the great Taiping kingdom and the Heavenly King Hung. Swinging lanterns and gaily-fluttering banners hung from poles raised above walks and from balconies. Gaudy lions and dragons danced in the streets.

The populace bathed and put on new clothes and went out into streets to enjoy the festivities with loud cries of "Congratulations 恭喜恭喜!" and "Taiping Kingdom Forever 太平天國萬歲!" Everywhere they ran into friends and relations they had not seen for months and thought dead, but who were only hiding in dark corners of ruined houses for fear of violence in the streets and outside the city wall. Acquaintances together again pulled and pushed each other into newly reopened teahouses and celebrated old friendships in freshly restored restaurants all over the city.

Rice, vegetables, pigs and chickens carted into the city from outlying captured cities or landed from boats on the Long River were distributed to new markets opened for the occasion – despite injunctions against peddlers within the city limits. Tables were set out along the streets for sale of all variety of goods and provisions. Red paper strips with gilt characters were pasted up on walls, doorposts, and lintels along with red paper squares

洋神 *Yang Shen*   *James Lande* 藍德

inscribed in black with the character *fu* 福 for happiness turned upside down to show happiness had arrived.

Water was splashed on doors, shutters, and woodwork, chairs and utensils were cleaned, and clothes washed. Smoldering incense, fruit and bowls of food were set out on family altars before the wood tablets inscribed with the names of ancestors and the crucifixes that long since had replaced the idols of the old gods. Christian devotees went to church, and mothers brought their new babies for baptism. People bustled about on ceremonial visits to superiors or bundled gifts of food and clothing to aged parents. Acrobats performed in the marketplaces, historical plays were enacted, and puppet shows put on all around the city center.

On the evening of the sixth day, the greatest Taiping generals were called together for a military conference in the palace of the Heavenly King. The palace grounds covered an immense area in the southeast of the walled city, just west of the old Manchu citadel. A high yellow wall surrounded the grounds and enclosed drum towers, lakes, pavilions, and acres of green, gold, and scarlet roofs over public and private buildings and attendants' quarters. The procession of the Taiping generals first entered beneath a high carved stone memorial arch, the Taiping Dynasty Archway 太朝牌坊. Three narrow bridges crossed a broad moat and approached the wide, tile-roofed Taiping Dynasty Gate 太朝門, which opened into a wide courtyard with signal drum pavilions on the east and west of the entrance. Workmen still came and went within the compound, as construction of the palace was not nearly complete.

The generals continued alone through the entrance, past broad chambers between small offices for secretaries, scribes, and other menials. In the audience chamber an orchestra of musicians played at each side of the doorway. Beyond the audience chamber were the apartments of the palace functionaries, another court, the Heavenly Hall where the *T'ien Wang* worshiped, and then the private rooms of the *T'ien Wang*'s wives and concubines, the forbidden harem where only women served. The generals took their places on each side of the chamber, at the foot of the heavenly throne.

The *T'ien Wang*, Heavenly King Hung Hsiu-ch'üan 天王洪秀全, wore a robe of yellow silk, with scaly five-clawed dragons embroidered in blue and gray silk, and an embroidered yellow silk cap with the characters *T'ien Wang* 天王, Heavenly King, between a pair of embroidered green dragons. He sat upon a raised throne draped in yellow silk and flanked on each side by a four-foot tall white porcelain ibis with wings outstretched. The Heavenly King was close to fifty years old, about five and one-half feet tall, muscular in build, with the even features that commonly made Hakka men handsome and Hakka women beautiful. He was light skinned, with a round face, small round ears, and a long and thin black mustache that furled around the corners of his mouth. He spoke in a rich and mellow voice that charmed, even enchanted, his listeners.

"Thanks to the Heavenly Father for allowing us to crush our enemies and scatter them across the land. Now our Father in Heaven demands to know how we will use this great opportunity He has given us. Each of you is commanded to express your thoughts about our next strategy. We will consider all that you say and decide on a plan."

The *Ying Wang*, Heroic King Ch'en Yü-ch'eng wanted to send an army to An-ching to prevent an attack by the Hsiang Army of Tseng Kuo-fan. Ch'en Yü-ch'eng was bent on protecting his own territory north and west of the Long River.

The *Shih Wang*, Attendant King Li Shih-hsien, said they should continue to press into Fu-chien and Che-chiang, rich provinces where the Taiping could gather wealth to pay for more expeditions to conquer the entire country – all present understood that Li

洋神 *Yang Shen*   *James Lande* 藍德

Shih-hsien was intent on securing for himself territory south and east of the Long River.

The *Chung Wang*, Loyal King Li Hsiu-ch'eng, argued for a strike to the east at Su-chou, Hang-chou and Shang-hai because they were closer, only 1000 *li*. There he would spend a million taels to buy twenty steamers and send them up the Yangtze to take hold of the river and cut off movement of imperial troops and provisions by water.

The *Kan Wang*, Shield King Hung Jen-kan, agreed with Li Hsiu-ch'eng that they should capture the cities of Chiang-nan, and then send armies to conquer Hu-pei and regain control of the entire Yangtze river valley.

The *T'ien Wang* agreed with Hung Jen-kan and appointed Li Hsiu-ch'eng commander of the Eastern Expeditionary Force. "General Li, you are to capture Ch'ang-chou and Su-chou within one month. You will be the Lord's White Rider, as is written in the Holy Bible, revealed when the First Seal was broken.

> *When the Lamb opened the first seal,*
> *A great noise of thunder resounded,*
> *And behold there was a white horse,*
> *Upon the horse sat a fierce bowman,*
> *He was a great king wearing a crown,*
> *And the bowman went forth to conquer.*

The first horseman of the Apocalypse went forth to conquer, and so shall the *Chung Wang* go forth as the White Rider to conquer the cities of the east."

One month, thought General Li Hsiu-ch'eng. The eastern expedition 東征 must move quickly. The armies must cooperate closely to support my advance. We will fly out of T'ien-ching like an arrow shot straight down the Grand Canal at the heart of Shang-hai. No power under heaven will stop my holy soldiers. Thirty days. We'll sweep into Tan-yang, crush Ch'ang-chou, and attack Chen-chiang 鎮江 to hold the imp garrison there. Next, Wu-hsi 無錫 and Su-chou 蘇州. Finally, Sung-chiang 松江 and Shang-hai. A string of priceless pearls – town after town strung out along the Chiang-nan Canal. Thirty days. We'll have the imps by the throat before they know what has happened, and Shang-hai will be ours. We will see what the foreigners say when my army burns the Chinese city and surrounds their settlement. Then they will not be so arrogant – then they will beg the T'ai-p'ing Heavenly King for his beneficent mercy.

Fletcher Meets Takee

洋神 Yang Shen　　　　　　　　　　　　　　　　　　　　　　James Lande 藍德

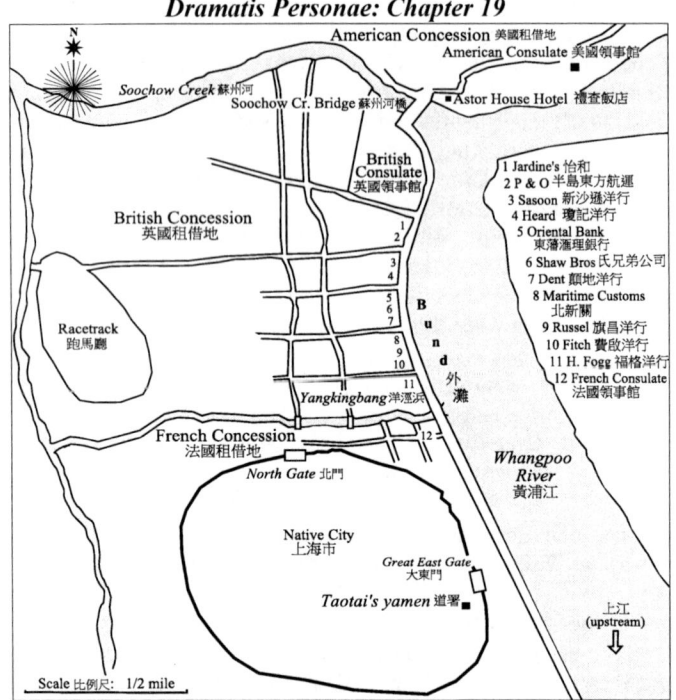

Dramatis Personae: Chapter 19

Shanghai in 1855
(based on Morse, *International Relations of the Chinese Empire*, v. 1, p. 454)

Grade	Button		補章, 補子(Pusa)		Belt	Honorific
Civilian 1	Plain red coral	仙鶴	$hsien^1\text{-}hao^4$	White Crane	Agate	Ta-jen
Military 1		麒麟	$chi^3\text{-}lin^3$	Unicorn		
Civilian 2	Embossed red coral	錦雞	$chin^3\text{-}chi^1$	Golden Pheasant	Worked Gold	Ta-jen
Military 2		獅子	$shih^1\text{-}tzu^3$	Lion		
Civilian 3	Sapphire	孔雀	$k'ung^3\text{-}ch'ieh^4$	Peacock	Worked Gold	Ta-jen
Military 3		豹	bao^4	Panther		
Civilian 4	Lapis Lazuli	雲鴈	$yun^2\text{-}yen^4$	Wild Goose	Worked Gold	Talaoyeh
Military 4		虎	hu^3	Tiger		
Civilian 5	Crystal	白鷳	$pai^3\text{-}hsien^2$	Silver Pheasant	Plain Gold	Talaoyeh
Military 5		熊	$hsiung^2$	Black Bear		
Civilian 6	Opaque white adularia	鷺鷥	$lu^4\text{-}ssu^1$	Eastern Egret	Tortoise Shell	Talaoyeh
Military 6	Translucent feldspar	羆	$p'i^2$	Mottled Bear		
Civilian 7	Plain Gold	鸂鶒	$ch'i^1\text{-}chih^4$	Mandarin Duck	Silver	Laoyeh
Military 7		彪	$biao^1$	Tiger Cat		
Civilian 8	Embossed gold	鵪鶉	$an^1\text{-}ch'un^2$	Quail	Ram's Horn	Laoyeh
Military 8		海馬	$hai^2\text{-}ma^3$	Seal		
Civilian 9	Embossed gold 壽壽	練鵲	$lien^4\text{-}ch'iao$	Paradise Flycatcher	Black Horn	Laoyeh
Military 9		犀牛	$hsi^1\text{-}niu^2$	Rhinoceros		

Civilian and Military Insignia of Rank in the Ch'ing Dynasty
(from Giles, *Chinese-English Dictionary* (1892, 1912), Table I: Insignia of Official Rank)

洋神 *Yang Shen*   *James Lande* 藍德

Chapter 19: Tiger with Wings
Friday, May 11, 1860, 10:00am

"184,000 taels!"

Wu Hsü struggled to retain composure. "I thought rebels and disbanded imperial soldiers were brutal robbers, but this Wu-te is the biggest robber of all!"

Like a Yangtze gorges boatman hauling a heavy junk upriver against the stream, Yang Fang had slowly tracked his way for half an hour to this point of the conversation. He understood that the *taotai* would be frightened about the money. It was necessary first to extol the foreigner's qualities, and recite the testimonials of others about him, before discussing Fletcher Wood's plan to save Shanghai. Wu-te's plan must be presented item by item, beginning with small chits and working up to the large vouchers. The *taotai* had to have a good grip and a firm footing before the earth started to shake – after all, this business might mean wealth or poverty, even life or death.

Yang was not above subtly manipulating his friend, if it were in Wu's best interest, or that of the Ningpo guild. He would not manipulate Wu for his own purposes, even if so inclined – the *taotai* was too sharp for that. Yang avoided any conflict of interest by keeping Wu's purposes in harmony with his own. In this manner, Yang Fang had carefully guided his friend into risky investments that initially had alarmed the *taotai*, each a little larger than the one before, and helped Wu Hsü gradually feel more confidence in matters of trade. But an army of foreigners, thought Yang, is an enterprise larger by several times than our business investments – because of the rapacious ambition of the foreigner. Still, it is not as large as administering a district or province.

Wu and Yang sat close together in glossy teakwood armchairs, steaming tea and cold sliced melon between them, in the guest hall 上房, of the *taotai*'s yamen 道署 in the native city. The guest hall was well appointed with richly finished furniture, embroidered silk wall hangings, and colorful carpets of elaborate design. There were enough intricate jade carvings and glazed porcelain ceramics to ensure that guests were properly impressed with the wealth of their host. On the rear wall, there was a large painting of a scene from the widely cherished tale *The Romance of the Three Kingdoms* 三國演義, in which three heroes of ancient times meet in a peach garden to swear brotherhood and eternal fealty.

The hall was at the very back of the building, next to the family quarters, away from inquisitive secretaries and runners. Trusted guards stood at each entrance. When more refreshments were required, Wu called to a guard, and their conversation turned to lighter matters as servants traipsed in and out; when alone again, they leaned close together and spoke in a conspiratorial whisper to frustrate the ears in the walls.

"Yes, Elder Brother," Yang Fang said, "it is much money, more than any one of us has now. I must defer to your opinion in this matter, as I am unable to bear the burden of such expense. In government, one always can make opportunities. In trade, one must wait upon opportunity, which cannot be predicted. Perhaps this plan of the foreigner is just such an opportunity, and should be treated as another business enterprise, in which case we must weigh the profit and loss. If there can be a profit in such an army, then we should find the capital to invest."

"If we can convince the British and French to lend troops to defend Soochow against the rebels, perhaps we will not need an army of *yang-ch'iang* 洋槍, foreign rifles, certainly not one so expensive. If the foreigners will defend Soochow, then surely they will defend Shanghai as well if the rebels come here."

"Elder Brother, do you really believe the British and French will lend soldiers to defend Soochow?

Tiger with Wings

"I must appear to believe," Wu Hsü said. "The Governor wants me to go to the foreign consuls, to humble myself before them and ask for their help, for the loan of foreign troops to defend Soochow."

"If they do not lend troops, and we are not prepared for the rebels, there could be a great calamity. Even Wu-te understands this – he knows what happened when the Small Swords captured the city, of the cost in lives lost and property. The cost to rebuild was more than ten millions, and it might be the same if the British fire the suburbs again. Wu-te says that for one year an army of foreigners may cost a million. I would rather pay one million for an army than ten million for a city."

Wu Hsü sighed deeply. "有道理 makes sense."

"Let us consider Wu-te's plan?"

"Very well."

"He would employ Western officers and soldiers."

"That sounds fine," Wu Hsü said, "but where does he get such men? If he tries to get soldiers and sailors, the British will certainly object and cause trouble, and ship's captains will complain if he takes their crews. All that is left in Shanghai is trash, sailors waiting for ships, deserters, drunken rowdies, worthless things."

"He would train the men in Western tactics."

"Can the men he finds be trained in time to fight the rebels advancing from Nanking? We may have only several weeks. And where would he train them?"

"He would use rifles for greater accuracy at longer range, breach-loading rifles for greater rate of fire, and artillery to breach walls and knock down gates."

"Yes, I can see he must have superior weapons, but need they cost so much?"

"Shallow-draft paddle-wheel boats. These boats travel by water to any place in Chiang-nan 江南 – south of the river – quickly and cheaply. They carry many soldiers, and have large guns for breaching walls and gates. He says that two or three shallow-draft paddle-wheel boats can go anywhere in the rebel territory, attack Ch'ing-p'u 青浦 in morning and Chia-ting 嘉定 in the afternoon, carrying several hundred soldiers with artillery – the rebels won't know where to expect them because they move so fast."

"Western soldiers. Western weapons. That I might expect. But paddle-wheel boats that need no wind, with flat-bottoms that can go up any small creek, and carry men and guns as fast as the wind – that is a tactic that I have never read in our books on war. Giving his army paddle-wheel boats would be like adding wings to a tiger 給虎添翼. This I like, very much. I think that would really frighten the rebels."

"Wu-te says we should limit operations to the area surrounding Shanghai, making small the land we defend and garrison. The towns west to Feng Huang Shan, east to P'u-tung, north to Wu-sung, and south to Sung-chiang could be defended by his force. Chinese Green Flag troops, *yung* 勇, could be stationed in captured towns to hold them, so that the foreign rifles, *yang-ch'iang*, would be free to strike again anywhere."

"Can Green Flag soldiers hold a captured city? That is a weakness in his plan. *Yung* are not *yang-ch'iang*, and Wu-te will not have time to train Green Flag troops to be any better than they are now. Besides, Green Flag troops add to the cost."

"Wu *Ta-ge* 大哥, Elder Brother Wu, your questions are all very excellent, but I have no way to answer. I wish to neither support nor oppose Wu-te's plan, but merely to discuss his ideas. Many of these questions cannot be answered without giving him a try. If he is successful, if he makes a profit in captured towns and dead rebels, we can dare to invest more; if not, we can withdraw. In the end, it all rests with this man, Wu-te."

"Well, can he do it? What have you found out about him?"

"He says he attended a military academy in America, and fought wars in many countries. He has come to China many times, and was on a coastal paddle-wheel boat here for two years. My nephew Yang Hsi-hai reported that on board *Confucius*, Wu-te gained the confidence of the men and they followed his commands. He even disabled an attacking junk by shooting down its sail with a rifle! A moving junk! He brought the paddle-wheel boat downriver by the light of the moon, his first time out on the Long River 長江. He trained the Manilaman 呂宋人 gun crew to use a special aiming device at the same time they fought off imperial war junks. Captain Ghent, Chester Hicks, the Manilamen – they all believe he is a hero come down from heaven. I myself would not have thought there could be such a man 自己也沒想到會有這麼一個人."

"That is similar to what the merchant Fitch told the American consul. The merchant Fitch guarantees him, and he is under the control of the American consul. Perhaps he is of a better quality, but it is not very much information."

"Lu Pei 劉備 and Chang-fei 張飛 did not know much about Kuan-yu 關羽 when they all first met, yet they quickly understood one another and became fast friends 談的很投機. The next day in the peach garden 桃園, they burnt incense and swore allegiance as blood brothers of different surnames 異姓兄弟, and comrades in war."

Wu Hsü smiled and glanced at the painting on the rear wall. "Yes, perhaps if I meet with Wu-te, I shall find out what I wish to know about him. I suppose you have already made long ledgers of what things this army will need."

"Rifles, ammunition, uniforms, Western equipment – the things they carry. When I tried to list such things, I realized that I have not paid very close attention to them. There's that bag they wear on their back, a small container of water on their belt, a long knife that attaches to the mouth of their rifles. If we are going to be buying much of this stuff, we'd better find out what it is."

"What about the men?"

"Wu-te says he has one officer selected already, name of Bai-nah-dee-ke-te. First Wu-te will hire sergeants – men who know how to train other men – and take them to a remote place for training. I think Kuang-fu-lin 廣富林 would be good for that. When the sergeants have been trained, then they will train the soldiers."

"Kuang-fu-lin? It's out of the way, a barren, unhealthy, mosquito-infested place."

"With few people to hear the report of guns. Chiang-nan will hear a sound like distant thunder, and villagers will assume cannon are being fired somewhere south of the river. For a while, too, rebel spies will not understand why there are foreigners firing guns at Kuang-fu-lin, and that may give the first soldiers of the *yang-ch'iang* time to train unmolested. What's more, the Green Flag braves of Colonel Li Heng-sung are headquartered near there. Colonel Li can keep the foreigners under close surveillance."

"And it is far from the bars and brothels of the Shanghai waterfront."

"Yet close to rebel approaches to the towns of Chiang-nan," Yang Fang said. "From Kuang-fu-lin, Wu-te's *yang-ch'iang* could move quickly to Ch'ing-p'u, Sung-chiang, Chia-ting or Shanghai."

"Indeed, very small paddle-wheel boats will be needed to get around on the creeks and streams in that backwater."

"We can give him the paddle-wheel boats *Confucius* and *Pluto* to start, along with small junks, while we seek out smaller paddle-wheel boats to purchase or rent. We will have to arrange with the Western merchants H. Fogg, and Jardine Matheson, for credit to purchase equipment, but I will watch closely what is bought to be sure it is never more than the money we have collected for the *yang-ch'iang*. Wu-te wants a place within the Shanghai city walls, away from the prying eyes of foreigners and the patrols of the British and French, where he can keep men to be examined as recruits before sending them out to the training camp."

"The place for that would be the Temple of the Fire God 火神廟, opposite my yamen. My people can watch carefully the trash he takes into his army. You watch the money at Fogg, and Jardine, and I'll watch the men at the temple. Now I feel a little better. Let's get on to how we are going to find money to pay for all this."

"The merchants who subscribe to the Pirate Suppression Bureau will certainly shriek they already pay too much for the paddle-wheel boat *Confucius* and crew."

"Yes," Wu Hsü said, "they will bawl that they are not money trees to be shaken at every convenience, at least not until the longhaired rebels are at the Shanghai gates."

"Our Ningpo guild brothers will be just as loath to subscribe to such an expense, until some calamity befalls us. When Hangchow fell and 60,000 died, and the city was looted and burned, even that was not enough to get guild subscriptions for the defense fund – because the rebels left Hangchow after a week."

"And because the calamity was in Che-chiang 浙江 province and not in Chiang-su 江蘇 province. It was too far away to be of concern."

"Yes, too far," Yang Fang said. "Now the scandalous defeat of the *Chiang-nan Ta-ying* and the scattering of the imperial armies have sent our brothers scurrying into the guild hall to shake and moan and wet their sleeves with tears. But even such a catastrophe is not going to be enough to pry loose their strings of cash."

"However, now that the *Chiang-nan Ta-ying* has fallen, there is nothing to prevent the rebels from advancing on Soochow and Shanghai."

"Exactly. At the first rumors of skirmishing rebels, our fellow Ningpo guild members will shoulder aside Pirate Suppression Bureau subscribers to get into Takee Bank, knock their heads on the floor and beg me to take their bags of silver."

"If your foreign warrior Wu-te can make good his proud boasts and recapture towns from the rebels, then we can tax the prosperous merchants and landowners in the places that are retaken, and they can bear some of the cost of saving their property. Perhaps, too, I can squeeze more from the custom house revenues. Yes, that's perfect! Then the foreigners themselves would fund the army, indirectly out of customs taxes. How many towns can this upstart capture, I wonder?"

"Another thing troubles me, Elder Brother," Yang Fang said. "If we have such an army, how can it be controlled, how can this impudent rogue be managed?"

"You must have your own people with the army, of course, to see that the accounting is done correctly and that the money is being spent properly. As for control of the foreigner, you say he wants only to be paid, but he seems too intelligent to be content with only money. Other things must tempt him, and if we discover what those things are, then we can better control him. These Americans are so inscrutable, I wonder if they can be understood at all. You have spoken with the man, and with others who know him, so naturally you are in a position to judge him, and to say if he is capable."

"True, however, as we say, it is easy to paint a tiger's skin, but difficult to paint a tiger's bones 畫虎畫皮難畫骨 – I have seen his face, but how can I know what is in his heart? Perhaps it is time for you to speak with him, as well?"

"Very well, very well. I will arrange a time at the custom house, late in the evening. Bring him to me there. For now, we must carefully keep all this secret. I know you understand there is great risk if it should reach the ears of the Emperor that we are financing an army of foreign rifles led by this strange American."

"Kept secret at least until successful in battle. Otherwise, we will be blamed for failure and heads will roll." The image of his head under the executioner's dull blade unnerved Yang Fang. Foreigners were ignorant of Chinese ways, and unpredictable in their own. Wu-te might so provoke the court that the Emperor would strangle them all.

洋神 *Yang Shen*　　　　　　　　　　　　　　　　　　　　　　James Lande 藍德

2　　Fletcher did not have long to wait. A few days after he met with Yang Fang, a Chinese concierge knocked at his door late in the evening with a note on which was written 武德, brought by a messenger who was waiting downstairs at the Astor House entrance. The concierge tugged at his sleeve saying "*k'uai-ti k'uai-ti*, hurry hurry. English sojah beat up Chinee boy."

Fletcher arrived at the hotel verandah to find a drunken Royal Marine officer pulling a whimpering Chinese about by his queue, while several more hulking Royal Marine officers loomed over the frightened boy. Fletcher stepped into the half-light midst the scarlet ring and grasped the boy's arm.

"Excuse me, will you Lieutenant, this boy was sent to find me."

"The hell he was – I say he's a bleedin' rebel spy. Look at his long hair, down to his bum it is. That's what they calls 'em, right – longhairs?"

"The rebels grow the hair on *top* of their head long," Fletcher said calmly. He tugged off the boy's skullcap. "This boy's pate is shaved clean as a billiard ball. He's as loyal a subject of his Manchu emperor as are you of your English queen."

The marine officer looked up from the Chinese boy to inspect Fletcher Wood. "Here, now, just who the 'ell 're you," the lieutenant said, sputtering, "and I'll thank you not t' be mentioning the Queen in the same breath as that Tartar pug we're going to blow to smithereens."

"Apologies to your Queen, gentlemen – if I have given offense, it was not intentional. But I must beg you to release this messenger boy, or I shall not be able to find out what he wants to tell me."

"You're a bleedin' Yank, aren't ya. Tell by the way you mangle the Queen's English. You Americans 'd be well advised to stay out of British affairs, and not be kowtowin' to no more Tartars."

"Come now, Lieutenant," Fletcher said, "forgotten Commodore Tattnall so soon?"

One of the other scarlet tunics chuckled.

"He's got you there, Rodney."

"The 'ell 'e 'as!"

"Hold on there, old man," the scarlet tunic said, "I was aboard *Cormorant* last year when we was aground at Taku, with the Admiral wounded and me mates dead and dying all about me. Chinese gunners was potting at us from shore batteries when a boatload of Yankee bluejackets comes swarming up over the side and sets to loading and firing our guns for us. Sent the Chinamen scampering out of range and helped us hold 'em off. So, if this gentleman's a Yankee, then I'm all for him." The officer extended his hand to Fletcher and, in order to shake with him, Fletcher let go of the boy's arm.

"Here, Rodney, let go of the Chinaman and shake hands with…begging you pardon, sir, what is your name?"

The scarlet tunics cordoned off Fletcher and the lieutenant from the Chinese boy, and together Fletcher and the soldiers all marched into the hotel bar to toast Admiral Hope and Commodore Tattnall.

"Here's to your doughty Fighting Jimmie!"

"Here's to the ol' blood's-thicker'n-water Commodore!"

"Here's to Bass's Pale Ale, what's thicker 'n blood *or* water!"

The messenger was still waiting in the shadows of the verandah when Fletcher managed a tactical withdrawal from the Royal Marines. The boy whispered into his ear, "Takee wantchee come now. You follow."

Fletcher needed nothing more than his Navy Six, already under his belt at the small of his back, and an extra cylinder in each of his two frock coat pockets. He followed the

Tiger with Wings　　　　　　　　　　　　　　　　　　　　　　　　　　　　　319

light of the boy's paper lantern out to the quay, across Wills Bridge, and up the Bund. He was wondering if he was going to have to dog this kid all the way to the native city when the boy disappeared under the green-tiled roofs above the entrance gate of the gaudy temple that served as the Chinese Maritime Customs office. When a few moments later Fletcher arrived at the temple entrance, he found Takee standing in a small doorway beside the closed gate, bowing to him in the sallow lantern light.

"Wu-te, you come wit' Takee?" Yang Fang said with a grin. "Come take tea."

"This is a long way to go for tea, Takee." The courtyard inside the entrance was dark except for the boy's lantern, which threw long, eerie shadows against the brick walls of the foreign hongs surrounding the courtyard.

"*Tao-t'ai* here, Wu-te."

So, thought Fletcher, not at the yamen in the native city. Cause too much stir among the Chinese, I suppose. Must be that Yang and Wu want to keep this business a secret. Wonder how the *taotai* managed to come here without his sedan chair and retinue of bearers? It's like Chester Hicks said aboard *Confucius*. Business here is done with the deepest, darkest secrecy.

"*Ya-men* wall hab ear," Yang Fang said, as if reading Fletcher's thoughts.

They mounted the steps to the great hall and entered the customs office, passing along a cordon of waist-high counters in front of tiny offices partitioned off by thin wooden panels, until at the back of the hall they came to a large office dimly lit by lanterns. The small nameplate on the office door read "Horatio Nelson Lay, Inspector-General," but through the glass panes of the door a Chinese was visible inside. He was dressed in a simple gray gown, a padded blue jacket, and a black skullcap. He sat behind a western desk piled high with green ledger books.

Lay might be a Cantonese name, thought Fletcher, but the *taotai* cannot be named Horatio Nelson. We must be borrowing a manager's office. They've cleared the place of staff and it all looks harmless enough, but the shadows're probably bristling with armed guards. That boy's disappeared again, too.

Wu Hsü remained seated when they entered the room. Yang Fang quickly bowed then made a simple introduction.

"Dis man *tao-t'ai*, name Wu."

The office was paneled in dark wood and lined with bookcases. Behind the *taotai*, there were shelves stacked with a mix of both western and Chinese books. Fat books with large characters on the spine. An equally fat Bible. Tall, dark-blue tomes titled with various Western legal subjects regarding trade and commerce. And boxes containing bound and single issues of the *Chinese Repository* and the *North China Herald*. On the desk, there was a daguerreotype of a severe-looking Western woman surrounded by four well-scrubbed children, and another of four young Western men in formal dress standing around an older couple, probably their parents. A small gallery of oil portraits and landscape paintings – sun-drenched English countrysides and manor houses mostly – hung in spaces between bookshelves stuffed with sets of Thackeray, Trollope and Dickens. Straight-back chairs conferred together quietly in corners with Chinese porcelain vases on small rosewood tables. Documents in Chinese and English lay amongst the piles of ledgers atop the desk, which together slightly dwarfed the slender, middle-aged Chinese who peered sharply at Fletcher from behind the ledgers.

Fletcher clasped his hands before his face and bowed slightly, saying "Pleased to make your acquaintance, Wu *Taotai*. It is a privilege to meet such a high official."

"Belly good, Wu-te," Wu Hsü said, with a thin smile that worked very hard to find a purchase on his face. "No wantchee shakee han'."

"No, sir. Not plopah Chinee fashion."

"My no talkee belly good 'Melican, Wu-te. Belly solly. Mus' talkee pidgin."

"My savee, Wu *Taotai*. Maskee, my no talkee belly good pidgin."

"Takee help, Wu-te. Please to sit, *ch'ing-ch'ing*."

Fletcher set aside Elizabeth Gaskell and Wilkie Collins from the seat of a corner chair and placed it, and another chair, in front of the desk for himself and Takee. The old banker was so surprised by this courtesy that he broke into a big grin and spontaneously began gesturing for Fletcher to sit first.

"Oh, come now, Takee," Fletcher said. "We're all friends here. Let's everybody sit down as he pleases." Fletcher lowered himself little by little, following Takee as he lowered himself, until they both finally hit bottom. Fletcher grinned and mopped broadly at his brow. Takee smiled.

The exchange proceeded forward against the current of mutually unintelligible language, backing and filling in a generally forward direction, while Wu Hsü and Fletcher Wood became accustomed to one another's parlance and pronunciation. The image of *Confucius* bumping her lead along the bottom of the Yangtze like an old blind woman tapping her cane on cobblestones came again to Fletcher's mind, and he wished for a better pilot than Takee. There was little of the litany of polite phrases that encumbered the beginning and end of the *taotai*'s discussions with consuls – it was simply too difficult, if not ludicrous, in pidgin English.

A knock on a glass pane of the door interrupted them, and the messenger boy entered with a pot of tea and teacups on a tray.

"Belly solly, Wu-te," Wu Hsü said. "Only hab tea. One day you come *taotai* yamen for belly big tiffin."

"That's all right, sir. Tea's fine."

When the boy cleared out, and Yang Fang had watched him retreat to the front of the great hall, they resumed their talk. Fletcher repeated the essence of what he had explained to Takee, knowing that Takee had doubtless already given the *taotai* every detail. Even so, it required almost an hour of plodding explanation to lay everything out and show Wu Hsü the map of the towns surrounding Shanghai.

"Wu-te can take dis town?" Wu Hsü said, pointing to each town that he knew from experience the rebels would try to take and occupy. T'ai-ts'ang, Chia-ting, Kao-ch'iao, Hsiao-t'ang, and Nan-ch'iao. Fletcher knew some of the towns, but made a pencil-mark beside the others and said he would go see what they look like.

"Dis place call Kuang-fu-lin," Wu Hsü said. "Good place fo' camp."

"Camp?" Fletcher said. The place was near the western periphery of the cordon he proposed to protect, not quite as far as the hills they called Feng Huang. Sungkiang was to the southeast, Tsingpoo to the northwest. It appeared quite far from Shanghai. "This Gong Foo Lin, how would I go there. How long would it take?"

"My takee you, Wu-te, see allo towns," Yang Fang said.

"Good," Wu Hsü said. "Mus' do chop-chop, Wu-te. Lebel come belly soon mebbe. Empalah tloop all gone now, no one stop lebel. Lebel mebbe go Soochow firs'. Aftah Soochow – take many town, heah, heah, heah." Wu Hsü pointed to each of the towns, all in a line west toward Shanghai along the Grand Canal. "Den Shanghai. Litee time, Wu-te. Litee time."

"Little time. Yes, sir. But I'll be ready." Fletcher was not sure he could be ready, but he knew he had to say so, or risk their confidence in him. He could reconnoiter around Shanghai while the Shanghai hongs were gathering his arms and provisions. That would save time. The men he could gather quickly, if he were not too fastidious, at least at the start, if he could begin now. One more thing he needed – a hedge.

"Takee. Wu *Taotai*. There is a promise I want you to make to me."

"What plomise?" Yang Fang said.

"Please promise that if I am not successful at first, you will give me another chance." It was a risk to suggest any possibility of failure, but Fletcher needed to keep them from throwing him overboard too soon. "Victory may need more than one try."

The *taotai* frowned, but Yang Fang spoke to him. "A second chance is a good idea – there will be a great deal of money invested in this, and it will all be wasted if we are too hasty. It may take more than once for him to understand how to fight the rebels."

"Hokay, Wu-te," Yang Fang said. "Hokay."

Wu Hsü sat back and looked again into the foreigner's face, searching for the answer to the nagging anxiety that Wood would not do as he was told, that they would not be able to control him. His foreign independence and unpredictability was a double-edged blade – it allowed him to do things that would not even occur to a Chinese, but it placed the Chinese associated with him at the great risk of displeasing the Emperor. Wu Hsü grew cold again at the memory of the fate of earlier barbarian experts: loss of office, exile to the frontier, maybe even execution by strangling. This stupid barbarian understood nothing of the risk the Chinese would undertake, or the calamity Wood could bring upon them all by doing as he wished and not as they demanded.

"Wu-te, all sojah got boss sojah!" The *taotai* barked this out at Fletcher with a sudden and unexpected vehemence. "Got sahghent say what do, where go, when go. Sahghent got captun. Captun got genlah. My got guvnah, guvnah got Empalah. So, Takee say you wan contlol all sojah, belly good. But my wan know who boss you, Wu-te. Who say what you do, where you go, when you go? No can hab no boss, Wu-te. Mus' hab boss fo' you. Who dat?"

"Takee would be my boss."

Reflexively Yang Fang started to repeat, "不敢當 I dare not," but caught himself and stifled the impulse. The self-deprecating phrase was a customary Chinese deflection of homage or flattery that seasoned every polite conversation but, in this case, if Yang Fang didn't dare, then who would? Anyway, Wu-te wouldn't have understood the Chinese phrase, still less its significance.

"Hokay, Wu-te, Takee you boss. He say what do, where go, when go. Now, who Takee boss?

"I guess that would be you, sir."

"So, my say where you go, you go?"

"Yes, sir. It would be best if you tell Takee, and then can Takee tell me."

"What say when Takee not heah? Takee some oth' place."

"Then I would do as you say."

"Wu-te, guvnah my boss. Guvnah say Wu, you do this, my do it."

"Wu *Taotai*. I can see where you are going with this. You want to know who I report to, and we agree I should report to Takee, then to you, and to the governor. But if the governor wants me to go somewhere, he should send orders to you, and you should send orders to Takee, and Takee should send orders to me, and I will order my men. I cannot have Takee giving orders to my men. I cannot have the *taotai* giving orders to my men. I cannot have the governor giving orders to my men. Western armies all have what's called a chain of command. One officer gives an order to a lower officer, who gives the order to a still-lower officer, who orders the soldiers. Generals do not give orders to privates. It is very important you understand this – my men fight for me, and if someone else tries to command them, my men will not fight."

Wu Hsü was silent while he digested all this English. When he was confident he grasped at least the essence of the argument, that an officer commands those immediately below him, he nodded to Fletcher, and then addressed Yang Fang.

"There's something to that. Any official has authority over Green Flag troops – I can order our Green Flag commander Li Heng-sung to attack Ch'ing-p'u, and Governor Hsüeh Huan can order Li Heng-sung to attack Chia-ting. But the provincial army of Tseng Kuo-fan fights rebels in Hunan only upon the orders of Tseng Kuo-fan. Tseng's Hsiang Army is made up of Hunan men, all from his own region, who owe allegiance to him alone. He appoints his highest officers, then they appoint their subordinate officers, and those officers appoint their subordinates. Each level of command owes allegiance to the level above. The Emperor did not originally approve of this, but Tseng insisted that only personal loyalty can build an army that will serve successfully and defeat the rebels. The men only take orders from their own commanders."

"But Elder Brother," Yang Fang said, "the more I think about this, the more complicated it becomes. First, I have many other responsibilities and cannot always be with Wu-te's soldiers. You are the same – you cannot always go to battle for the same reason. Second, I am not in office and so I have no authority. I cannot tell Li Heng-sung to garrison a town, and I expect that Wu-te will need someone in authority, a Chinese officer, to assist his army. You, of course, are in office and have authority in military affairs. You can tell Li Heng-sung to garrison a town. You also talk directly with Governor Hsüeh Huan – you are a 'link' in what Wu-te is calling a 'chain of command.' I am afraid that if I command Wu-te, I may fail him when he needs us most."

Wu was silent again for a moment while he considered this.

"Wu *Taotai*?" Fletcher said gently. "Is there some difficulty?"

Wu Hsü looked into the foreigner's face and saw in his flashing dark-blue eyes an earnestness and concern that buoyed his confidence in Wu-te. Wu Hsü could not have explained why, but he felt he could trust Fletcher to do whatever was needed. Perhaps the impression was induced by the manifest admiration of Yang Fang for the foreigner, a remarkable sentiment for the usually reticent Elder Brother Yang. Whatever way Wu Hsü came by it, this novice conviction induced him to see the solution for the problem of command. He smiled at Fletcher and spoke briefly again with Yang Fang.

"Here's what we'll do. We shall *both* command the *yang-ch'iang*. That is to say, you and I together will give Wu-te his orders, but he will command his own troops. When I am available, I shall be in authority and accompany his troops, but he will command his troops. When I cannot be there, then you will be in authority and go with him. When we can both accompany the *yang-ch'iang*, you will be in authority after me."

Now it was Yang Fang's turn to mull over the idea. The three of them sat in silence. Fletcher willed himself to be still. He wished very much then that he spoke their language, so that he could understand whatever it was that concerned them so deeply, and be able to coax them toward his way of thinking. Then he chided himself for the thought. No, Fletcher, you will never speak very much Chinese, and you will always have to rely on other ways of imposing your will upon these wily celestials. You'll have to do without the language.

"But will he accept this arrangement?" Yang Fang said.

"He'll have to," Wu Hsü said, smiling at Fletcher. "Yes, I'm sure he will."

The *taotai* explained to Fletcher that he – Wu Hsü – and Yang Fang would exercise a joint command of the "foreign rifles," following the arrangement he and Yang Fang had just discussed, but that only Fletcher would give orders to his troops.

Fletcher had his misgivings about this arrangement, but more with the idea of the mandarins accompanying him into the field at all, rather than with who would command. Obviously, the *taotai*'s authority had to prevail, and likely would be useful to get things done with the Chinese. Wu could accomplish things Yang could not. Yang for the finances, Wu for the power. But the notion of these two mollycoddles scrambling

洋神 *Yang Shen*   *James Lande* 藍德

around the backwoods in their robes of office, getting underfoot and delaying the movement of his "foreign rifles," had no appeal at all.

"I understand, Wu *Taotai*. Takee is my direct superior, then Wu *Taotai*, then Governor Hsieh." With a grin, Fletcher added, "Then the emperor."

The mandarins both looked startled, and then realized that the foreigner was only making a joke. But Fletcher saw their fear, and he began to sense something of the threat the emperor meant to these men.

3

If only, thought Governor Hsüeh Huan, there were more educated men from Ssŭ-ch'uan in Chiang-nan, people with the same dialect and the same heart, instead of so many officials from Kuang-chou and Ning-po. Always it has been so difficult for us to get good teachers in the remote districts. Learning was so much more arduous that even the best of us became discouraged and ceased to study. When first I was prefect at Sung-chiang, and inspected the level of education there by giving a standard test of classical learning 經學, they laughed into their sleeves. They japed that nobody from a backwater like Ssŭ-ch'uan would have any classical learning, and that I was fit only for giving tests of children's books like the *The Trimetrical Classic* 三字經. No one elsewhere knows the humiliation suffered to become a graduate scholar 舉人 in Ssŭ-ch'uan, or the torments endured after leaving that place. Certainly not anyone like this Wu Hsü, who purchased his degree and official's cap.

Wu Hsü sat next to the governor in the "examining one's heart" hall 問心堂 of district magistrate Liu Hsun-kao's county yamen. The large silk scroll on which the characters "examine your heart," 問心 *wen-hsin* 問心, were written black on white still hung in an alcove, where the taotai could not help but see them, gently chiding him to contemplate his own motives. No matter where Wu Hsü looked, he could not escape the view of those huge characters. They were always in the corner of his eye, glaring over his shoulder.

"Wu *Ta-ge* 大哥, do the Americans still plan to go to T'ien-chin with the British and French?" The two mandarins had not yet gotten beyond the preliminaries of rehashing old business, and Wu Hsü had settled comfortably into this conversation rather than advance to the onerous topic he had on his mind. The meeting with Fletcher Wood ended on a minor key, but that did not lessen Wu Hsü's growing certainty that he had found a way keep rebels away from Shang-hai. But how to convince the governor?

"Yes, *Ta-jen*, that has not changed. There is still time, however, as the American minister will not arrive for perhaps two weeks."

"The Americans must be prevented from going to T'ien-chin. They must not be allowed to plot together with the English and French or the Russians. Has the banker Yang Fang been successful at spreading discord among the foreigners?"

"Expectant *Tao-t'ai* Yang Fang has started rumors that the Americans plan to get to Nan-ching ahead of others and secure *exclusive* trading rights from the rebels. Also that the Americans have asked the Emperor for *exclusive* trading rights on the Long River and inland. Also that the English have changed their heart and decided to blockade trade along the north coast when they go to T'ien-chin. Soon the foreign merchants will not know what to believe about the Americans and the English. But it is difficult to know how the foreigners will behave, and they may not respond as we hope."

"Do not worry, Elder Brother!" Hsüeh Huan said, with a big moon-faced grin. The governor's heavy black brows arched high over his dark eyes as he confided his secret. "馭夷之法全在順其性而馴之 managing barbarians is simply a matter of conforming to *their* nature in order to subdue them. The Emperor tells us that if we can create discord between the several nations, then the English and French will be suspicious of the Americans, and of why the Americans want to go to T'ien-chin. If they think the Americans want to add *exclusive* trading rights on the Long River to their treaty, the British and French will tell the Americans to stay away from T'ien-chin. It is the nature of barbarians to be suspicious and jealous, so we give them a pretext for conforming to their own nature 順他們自己的性. Do you not agree?"

"Of course, *Ta-jen*, of course. That is simply too clever!" Wu Hsü shifted in his chair to get the big black characters 問心 out of the corner of his vision. He paused to take up a small porcelain pot from the table between their chairs and, lifting the long sleeve of his robe of office, carefully pour more hot tea into the governor's cup.

The governor registered the *taotai*'s obsequious tone, but another issue had come to mind, and he absently picked up the teacup and slowly sipped from it before continuing.

"When you last came to see me, I said I wanted to raise a force of Green Flag soldiers, *yung* 勇, to fight the rebels. You suggested the Cantonese around T'ung-chia ferry 董家渡, and Kao ch'ang temple 高昌廟, the ones who came here with the English. You've probably heard the governor-general commissioned an officer to raise 600 *yung* and take them to Soochow. Each man was paid two taels to enlist, but when the boats stopped midway, half of the recruits jumped ashore and scattered in all directions. Now the officer has returned to raise another 300 men. Such a small loss of face will not prevent enlistment, but how easily mistakes are made. I wish to make no mistakes.

"That is how it is, with that sort of men," Wu Hsü said, seeing his opportunity. "The *yung* soldiers we have now have been here too long, and have lost their martial spirit, and their skills at war. I have come to speak with you regarding a better alternative, a way to have an army that will fight rebels and defeat them."

"Ah, Wu *Ta-ge*, what alternative?"

"Expectant *Tao-t'ai* Yang Fang has found a foreign officer I believe can form an army of foreign fighting men, armed with Western weapons, experienced in Western methods, that can defeat rebels and keep them away from Shanghai!"

"Ahhh, Wu *Ta-ge*, we have been talking about borrowing troops to help extinguish rebels for a long while now, but cannot convince the British or French to lend troops to China, certainly not while they are at war with China."

"Not French or British regular troops. Mercenaries, Americans we hire and pay."

The governor turned to the *taotai* with bushy black eyebrows raised so high they threatened to push his official's cap backwards off his head. Wu Hsü held his breath, watching the governor's eyebrows descend slowly to their former station.

"Tell me," Hsüeh Huan said.

Fletcher's plan for the defense of Shanghai went on parade yet again, this time led by the *taotai*, with the governor in review. Wu Hsü remembered Yang Fang's manner of presenting the plan, leaving the more controversial aspects for last to avoid causing resistance before all detail was assembled. Employ Western officers and soldiers trained in Western weapons and tactics, armed with rifles for greater accuracy at longer range, breach-loading rifles for greater rate of fire, and artillery to breach walls and knock down gates. Transport the *yang-ch'iang* by shallow-draft paddle-wheel boats – attack Ch'ing-p'u in morning and Chia-ting in the afternoon. Garrison captured towns with Green Flag *yung*, leaving the *yang-ch'iang* free to strike again anywhere.

"Giving the *yang-ch'iang* paddle-wheel boats is the best idea," Wu Hsü said. "I like that very much, and I think that never knowing where the *yang-ch'iang* will strike next would really frighten the rebels. That will be like adding wings to a tiger."

The governor asked many of the same questions that had occurred to Wu Hsü, but

洋神 *Yang Shen*   *James Lande* 藍德

in a more perfunctory manner because his mind was preoccupied from the start with three questions: pay, control, and imperial mandate.

"Elder Brother, how will these *yang-ch'iang* be paid? Already I pay thirty thousand worthless *yung* several hundred thousand taels each month, and still they are disloyal and cannot be controlled. The province has no money to pay for an army of foreigners."

"Your Excellency need not pay the cost of the foreign soldiers. They would be supported by funds from the Pirate Suppression Bureau, by subscriptions from merchants and guild members, and from customs fees. If necessary, additional taxes can be levied in recaptured areas for pay the cost of garrison troops."

"A great deal of money comes from that custom house, isn't that right? Perhaps we should be using customs revenues to fight rebels all over the province."

"*Ta-jen*, there could be difficulties with using customs revenue elsewhere, because the money comes largely from Western trade, and the Westerners insist upon having a say on how the revenues are spent. However, all agree on use of customs revenues for the defense of Shanghai because both Chinese and Westerners live here."

"Yes, well, these foreigners have a say in a great many things that are properly the right of the Emperor to determine. I shall look further into how customs revenues are handled another time. So, perhaps the *yang-ch'iang* can be financed, but how will they be controlled? Who will give them orders, and will not the Western consuls want to be in charge of the *yang-ch'iang* if the soldiers are all foreigners?"

"They foreign troops will be commanded by Wu-te, but Wu-te will take orders from the *tao-t'ai*, and the governor."

"How do we know he will listen to us, this Wu-te?"

"He has given his word. Expectant *Tao-t'ai* Yang Fang trusts him, and so do I." Again, the *taotai* noticed the scroll hanging in the alcove.

"Ahhh, Elder Brother, what a man says can be different from what is in his heart. 口欲受而心欲辭 the mouth accepts but the heart rejects."

"Considering that expectant *tao-t'ai* Yang Fang recommends and guarantees Wu-te 報薦武德, and that they seem well-suited to each other 彼此極為相得, we probably can believe the foreigner. Yang Fang has been with foreigners for many years and, if anyone can understand what is in their hearts, it is our Yang *Ta-ge*. I have never seen him this enthusiastic. If in the end we still have trouble with Wu-te, if he will not follow orders, then we will simply get someone else who will."

"Would these *yang-ch'iang* go to Soochow?"

"*Ta-jen*, the British and French are still needed to defend Soochow against a rebel advance – the Foreign Rifles would not be ready in time for Soochow, and probably would not be a large army anyway. If the British and French could prevent the longhairs from taking Soochow, that would break up the rebel advance, and the *yang-ch'iang* could be used to retake other towns in Chiang-nan."

"We cannot expect the British to lend troops to go to Soochow," Hsüeh Huan said. "The British minister is concerned that if Western troops go inland, they may stay and carve out little empires from Chinese territory. Once there, they might never leave."

"And that would interfere with British influence."

"But even if the British and French are willing to defend Soochow, the Emperor would not have it. Repeatedly, memorials return with the Emperor's vermilion rescript saying that borrowing troops to extinguish rebels is unacceptable. The Emperor rebukes us saying foreigners must not go upriver, and we must never beseech the foreigners for help against the rebels. The Emperor says that if China accepts aid from barbarians, our country will lose face, and when the barbarians have no respect for China, there will be no end to the calamity that follows."

洋神 *Yang Shen*   *James Lande* 藍德

"There are many local gentry who feel as you about borrowing foreign troops. Can we not enlist their support to convince the Emperor?"

"Perhaps," Hsüeh Huan said with a sigh, "but that will take time. No one is eager to risk rebuke over a signature on a petition. As for this foreign force 夷勇, we can expect that the Emperor would not approve, especially when relations with foreigners are collapsing. There are too many possible problems. Would the force answer to foreign demands, would other foreigners interfere, or complicate treaty negotiations? Would the force side with the barbarians and turn on us, or go over to the rebels. What would become of me if I established the *yang-ch'iang*, and then I was ordered by the Emperor to disband the force? I would not stay governor very long."

"Suppose we made it clear that the *yang-ch'iang* are employed by merchants, not by the Chinese government, so as to avoid the impression of official sanction?"

"It may come to that, if the *yang-ch'iang* ever get started. But for the time being, under the present circumstances, we cannot risk forming a foreign force without angering the Emperor. As circumstances change, perhaps so too will the amount of risk. Perhaps being overrun by rebels will soon become the greater risk. So, my counsel is to continue making inquiries and preparations, so that at any time in the near future you will be ready, but do not form your *yang-ch'iang* yet. Wait, Elder Brother, wait."

After the *taotai* left, the governor sat alone and truly did examine his heart. The way to defeat barbarians is not by pitting them one against another, hoping they will destroy themselves, but by acquiring the weapons of the barbarians to use against them. When China can make rifles and ammunition, cast cannon, build ships, and train our armies to use the weapons with the same tactics, then we can defeat the barbarians and drive them from our country. The French will sell us materials, and provide craftsmen to show us how to manufacture, but it needs time. We must delay the foreigners, tempt them with petty rewards, and distract them while we build factories. We must find ways to collect the money needed to finance it all. Then one day, foreigners will discover a new China has emerged to confront them and – as they say themselves – they will stare down the barrel of the same kind of gun that today they point at the heart of China.

我國家多事之秋,人人皆知以和為貴,而和若稍不審慎,則後患無窮.惟欲盡如我願,審時度勢,亦有力不能到者. Now is the autumn of affliction for my country. Everyone knows that peace is to be treasured, but if peace is even slightly imprudent, endless calamity will follow. To get all we want, as conditions are now, we still have not yet attained the strength.

洋神 *Yang Shen*   *James Lande* 藍德

Dramatis Personae: Chapter 20

Iluminada	gunner aboard *Confucius*
Lao Chang 老張	Kiangyin waterman
Ah-shan 阿姍	Lao Chang's wife

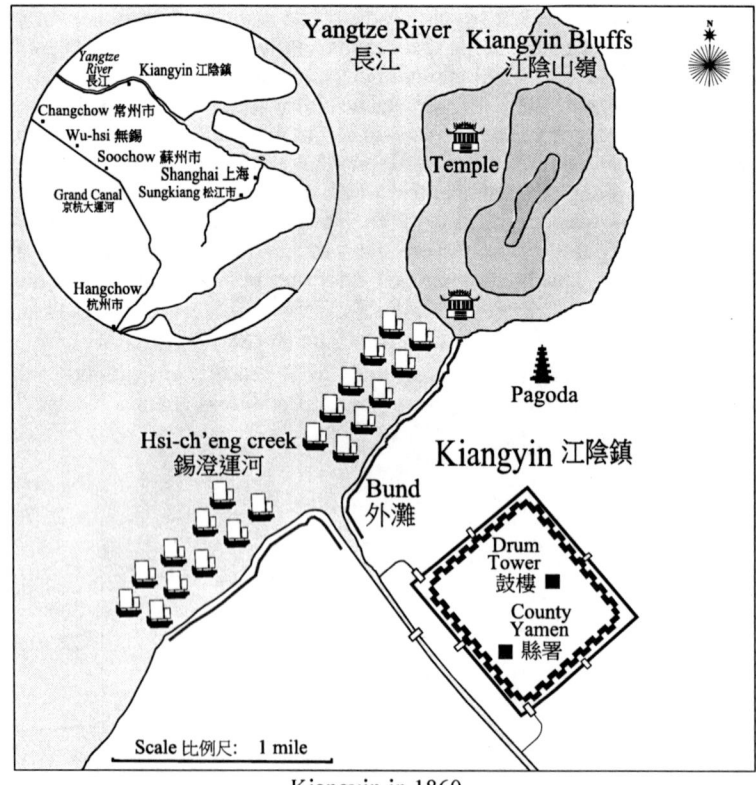

Kiangyin in 1860
(from Kiangyin city map 江陰市區圖, and Oliphant, …*Earl of Elgin's Mission to China*…p. 293)

Sumbitch Tigah Boat

洋神 *Yang Shen*   James Lande 藍德

Chapter 20: "Sumbitch Tigah Boat"
Tuesday, May 14, 1860, 7:00pm

> The
> ***North China Herald***
> Shanghai, Saturday, May 12, 1860
> --
> **Latest Dates**
> England.....Mar 10   Singapore......Apr 15
> Bombay....Apr 1   Hong Kong...Apr 25
> Calcutta   ----   New York.....Feb 12
> Galle.........Apr 6
> --
>
> REBELS: Our correspondent is unusually brief this week in his report upon rebel movements. The Great Southern Imperial Encampment, the imperialist force at Nan-king, according to his statement amounts to some 70,000 men....
>
> From another source we learned, on the 8th and 9th instant, that the besieging Imperialist army under Chang Kwoh-liang had sustained a very serious defeat, and that he himself was badly wounded. Whether the rebel garrison had received any reinforcements or not was not stated, but they had made a sortie on the position nearest the walls, where the besiegers had considered themselves so secure as to have established a sort of market. Over-powering the troops there stationed, they followed up their attack with great success, and it is said have possessed themselves of an immense amount of Imperialist artillery and stores, besides destroying the works of circumvallation on which their enemy had spent enormous sums.

    On a muggy Monday evening in mid-May, *Confucius* dropped downriver from the Shanghai anchorage, crossed the Woosung bar, and moored in the lee of several square-rigged merchantmen waiting for the spring tide to put enough water over the bar so they could proceed up to Shanghai. A full complement of officers and crew were on board *Confucius*, with Fletcher Wood as first mate. Her published objective was pirate suppression but, actually, she was looking for rebels.

    In the dark of that moonless evening, Ghent left Macanaya in charge of the steamer and, together with the pilot Old Huang, took Fletcher and put out in a skiff with a sallow lantern swinging over the bow to call on the clipper ship captains moored at the Woosung bar. At each ship, they introduced Ghent's new mate Fletcher Wood and passed out a few small luxuries the vessels were likely short of after months at sea. Newspapers to *Gibraltar*, a Jardine ship of 1237 tons arrived from Liverpool, port wine to Rimi's *Kate Hooper*, a ship of 1488 tons returning from Nagasaki, and apples to *Red Rover*, an 1150-ton bark up from Hong Kong for Abraham Hart. Aboard *Sarah Galley*, a Wetmore ship of 1366 tons arriving from New York, the pilot set to chatting with the green crews about what to expect going up to Shanghai. Ships' captains were about the only breed of man with whom Ghent was sociable, and these negligible courtesies won him regard among sailor-folk somewhat larger than his dismal reputation among the community ashore as a gruff old reprobate. And, thought Fletcher, these captains will all think of Ghent first when they need a steam tug to pull their ships out of the mud.

    Earlier that evening, Yang Fang had gone aboard *Confucius* with the governor's message to wait before executing Fletcher's plan to recruit an army of foreigners.

    "Wu-te is aboard our paddle-wheel boat," Wu Hsü had said. "Let him go back into rebel territory and watch the longhaired rebels 長毛賊. We will pass on to him all the information about rebel movements that we receive from our spies. When the time is

Sumbitch Tigah Boat

right, we will tell him to gather his army."

Captain Ghent was enlisted in the collaboration and, after hearing the particulars of Fletcher's plan, grumbled that it was probably wise to bide their time anyway. Time would give them an opportunity to reconnoiter the towns around Shanghai, as well as go back up into rebel territory and find out what the rebels were really up to. With so many rumors coming into the city from the western marches, the only reliable way to get accurate intelligence was to go there.

"When they start for Shanghai," Ghent said, "they'll come down the Grand Canal. Always do. They'll come straight down the line of the canal to Soochow, then Sungkiang, then Shanghai."

Fletcher laid out a chart and traced the path of the canal with tip of an unlit cheroot. "See here, Takee?" Fletcher said. "This straight line from Chenkiang to Soochow, that's the Grand Canal, and it runs in generally the same direction as the Yangtze. *Confucius* can steam down the Yangtze River, starting from Chenkiang, and follow along on the river as the rebels advance along the canal."

"*K'ung-fu-tze* no can go far flom livah, Wu-te?"

"Well, I don't know yet. What do you say, Captain, can she get into the canal, or go very far up any of these creeks that run south from the Yangtze to the canal?"

"It may yet be too early in the year for the entrance to the canal at Chenkiang. I doubt we could get eight feet of water in most places along there."

"A junk could cross over to the canal, right?"

"Sure, and maybe even pass under all those little bridges, if she could strike her mast, but I'd not want to waltz into rebel territory without artillery. If you're fool enough to take a junk from the river, then you can meet the rebel route of march pretty near anywhere. Just takes more time to cover the distance from river to canal and back."

"Wu-te, you takee livah junk go canal?"

"Hire one, or buy one if the junkmen won't go among the rebels. Might be the only way to get close enough, Takee. That's why we'll want shallow-draft steamers."

"Takee know many piecee man at Chiang-yin, at Chen-chiang, can takee Wu-te to canal. Many livah man hab pidgin wit' Takee Bank. My catchee name fo' you, Wu-te."

Anticipating a need for smaller vessels, Yang Fang brought a list of junkmen on the river that did business with customers of Takee Bank. He also brought bills of exchange 憑票 for 5,000 taels, which the pirate-suppressing mandarin could take to little clearinghouses 錢莊 in river towns and exchange for silver to pay expenses. The clearinghouses were small native banks, developed predominantly by Ningpo men during the preceding century, which issued notes, offered accounts for cash transactions, and extended simple credit to customers.

"Yeah, and I know a few junks in river towns that'll go over to the canal," Ghent said, "if there's enough scratch offered." Ghent had observed with bitterness how chummy the Chinese banker was with Fletcher Wood. Another time it might have irked him – Takee had never been so affable with Ghent. But the captain's meager gratitude still suckled the memory of Fletcher Wood's silence. As long as Wood was quiet about Ghent's failure of nerve at Silver Island the week before, the captain would overlook just about anything, and Wood and Takee could go bugger each other for all he cared.

Confucius slept quietly at the Woosung bar and woke early to a waning half moon in the southeast and a rising neap tide. By 6:00am, she was steaming up the foggy Yangtze for Kiangyin, an 85-mile run from Woosung that could be made in anywhere between ten and twenty-one hours depending on tidal flows, river currents, and luck at the Langshan crossing. The smaller neap tide this morning might push the steamer

洋神 *Yang Shen*   *James Lande* 藍德

upriver at perhaps only four or six knots, instead of the eight to ten knots of a flooding spring tide, and *Confucius* might make Kiangyin in the early evening.

    The sky over the lower reaches was clear, but upriver beyond the western horizon she sometimes heard distant thunder and saw the faint, brief glow of lightning on the underside of leaden clouds. A torrent of storm-driven water rushing down the Yangtze could raise the high-water mark and swell the ebbing tide. Then *Confucius* might do less than four knots against the current, and not make Kiangyin until well past midnight.

    After nearly two hours in the crossing that morning, the Langshan pagoda finally was brought E by N, seven miles upriver from Fushan Hill, and *Confucius* was taken over toward the left bank for the run full-speed to Kunshan Point. Fletcher began to truly appreciate the skill of the captain and his old Chinese pilot after this crossing at Langshan. Only twice had the steamer nudged into shoal sand, and each time it was enough to reverse her engine and paddle backwards into the center of the channel, then start forward again. Most vessels got stuck deeper and more often at Langshan, and not a few had to wait on the tide to get free.

    For the rest of the day, *Confucius* plodded upstream against an increasing ebb and greater volume of water in the narrowing river. Kunshan Point and Huangshan came and went, and then the river narrowed to a mile wide and white egrets could be seen gliding over both banks. Fletcher began to take more interest in the clumps of osier and weeping willow along the south shore, for they often marked where the levees parted for the outflow of creeks. He was looking for openings large enough to pass a junk, if not a steamer, into creeks that might go inland to the Grand Canal.

    During the long stretches of deep water, Fletcher took time to learn more about the others on board. Vincente he passed time with when moored, as one or the other of them was always required on deck when the steamer was under way. When relieved by Vincente, Fletcher rounded up Old Huang – if he was not needed on deck – and together they went in search of their pirate-suppressing mandarin. Fletcher remembered how this unassuming-looking, pudgy little gold-button mandarin had so deftly handled the imperial officer at Chowshan the week before, preventing him from coming aboard when *Confucius* anchored there for a night and was challenged by an imperial war junk. That was when Fletcher began to take serious notice of the man, and now he wanted to learn something more about him, if only a name other than pirate-suppressing mandarin.

    Old Huang at first was reluctant to approach the mandarin. When at Fletcher's urging Old Huang finally knocked at the mandarin's cabin door, all the pilot's flamboyance with foreigners was exchanged for an uncertain deference. He stood at the end of the corridor, hands clasped before him, almost whispering and, when a round moon-face appeared in the cabin doorway, Old Huang started bowing and chattering in Chinese. Whatever he said, it worked just fine, because the pirate-suppressing mandarin broke into a big grin, clasped his fat little hands together, and emerged bowing to Old Huang. He paused and peered around the pilot at Fletcher.

    "Hallo," the pirate-suppressing mandarin said.

    After everything the three of them had been through together aboard *Confucius*, it was surprising that this was the first time they actually had spoken to one another. The mandarin gestured toward the saloon, and they all settled onto the padded benches behind the narrow tables bolted to the floor. Then Old Huang suddenly jumped up.

    "Get tea," he blurted as he hurried out of the saloon, leaving Fletcher and the mandarin grinning foolishly at each other. A moment later Old Huang returned with the Chinese steward, who set the tables for a tea party – Chinese war-steamer style.

    "What should I call him?" Fletcher said. "What is his name?"

    "Mandalin name Yang Hsi-hai 陽喜海," Old Huang said, "allo samee 'Love

Sumbitch Tigah Boat   331

Ocean' Yang. He belong same family Yang Fang – man you callum Takee. Maybe you call mandalin 'Mistah Yang,' 'cause he only littee mandalin."

"Tell Mr. Yang that I think he handled things very well on the river last week."

"Mistah Yang say dat littee pidgin, not impo'tant. Mistah Yang say you belly blave man, Fetchawood. Save *K'ung-fu-tze* ass plenti time alleady. Mandalin belly happy meetcha, Fetchawood. Me too. Littee mandalin not such bad chap aftah all."

Fletcher *chin-chin*ed the mandarin. "It was nothing, Mr. Yang," Fletcher said, in his best imitation of Chinese courtesy. "Just a little target practice. I don't know many mandarins – how did he become a mandarin, and get this job suppressing pirates?"

Before long, the three-way conversation settled into something manageable, and Fletcher gradually came to understand that Mr. Yang was actually Takee's nephew. His father had been a magistrate in some remote district, but died while his son was still young, so the boy was sent to family in Ningpo, and then to Shanghai to stay with his uncle. Over time, the boy tried hard to learn his letters, but the classics eluded his feeble memory, and he failed the local examinations three times. Rather than prolong that embarrassment, he asked his uncle if there were not some other way he could be useful. At the time, Takee wanted someone aboard *Confucius* to furnish the paddle-wheel boat with official representation on coast and river, so Takee purchased entry-level official rank – the gold button – for his young relation and assigned him to *Confucius*. At first, Mr. Yang was seasick very often, but in time that went away and he actually came to like the duty. Now, with rebels everywhere as well as pirates, it had become important work, and essential to protecting the business of T'ai-chi Hang in tea and silk.

Afterwards when their paths crossed, they still observed a certain formality in deference to Mr. Yang's rank, but at least they were cordial and able to work together more easily. Fletcher wondered if the new acquaintance wasn't something of a burden for Old Huang, however, as in the past he could pretend the Little Mandarin didn't really exist. Now he had to balance two roles aboard *Confucius* – raffish pilot for foreigners, and deferential subject for mandarins – and sometimes the sudden change from one to the other unhinged everybody.

2 When *Confucius* came churning up to the neat little bund on the south bank that led to the walled town of Kiangyin, the sun was setting and Jupiter emerging as a tiny point of bright light above the western horizon. Instead of the usual crowd of curious onlookers gathered at the distant quay to gape at the outlandish fire-wheel boat of the foreigners, there was a disorderly row of dirty tents along the bund.

"Full stop, Dutchman! Then reverse," the captain shouted into the voice pipe as he rang for **STOP ENGINE**, then for **ASTERN FULL**. "With all that rabble on the bund, I don't want to get too close for our guns. Tell me again what range you settled on with the 32-pounder's fuses modified, like you did in the Crimea?"

"Three, four hundred yards at the closest, Captain," Fletcher said. During their run up to Wuhoo, Fletcher had shown Vincente how to modify their Bormann fuses to delay ¾ second, and ½ second, and reduce powder charges for slower velocity. There was much less range of fire on rivers than over open ground or at sea, so *Confucius* needed rounds that would explode at shorter distances. With sufficient care, the additional risk to gunners was small, and Vincente and Fletcher had tested the modified fuses and powder charges on the river.

There were more dirty tents in clearings under the city wall, with clutches of imperial soldiers armed with muskets or gingals loafing about. Fletcher handed a glass to the captain. "Look over this side, Captain, beyond the town where that large creek opens into the anchorage. They look like imps, but they're acting like pirates."

洋神 *Yang Shen*   *James Lande* 藍德

Scattered along the banks of the creek were numerous small junks and sampans huddled mutely like deer before prowling tigers – seventy-foot imperial war galleys mounting cannon and gingals fore and aft and brandishing orange-and-black tiger's heads painted on rattan war-shields hung above each oar. Imperial soldiers aboard a snarl of war junks and lighters instantly set upon unwieldy merchant junks under sail that descended the creek through this gauntlet into the Kiangyin anchorage. The soldiers closed around the hapless merchants firing matchlocks and arrows, leapt aboard with drawn swords, slaughtered the crews, then lugged bundles and bags of freight up from the holds and tossed them all over onto the decks of the lighters.

"Tell Macanaya to man his guns," the captain said.

Confucius slowed her engines and sidled out into the anchorage to get room to come about. If she had sleeves, thought Fletcher as he stood watching Vincente and his gunners ready the 32-pounder, she'd be rolling them up. Instead, look at how she sends her crew scurrying about to prepare for a scuffle long before they ever receive any order.

The pilot stayed with the captain in the wheelhouse. The only other non-combatant aboard was Mr. Yang, now known as the Little Mandarin. On his way back from the bowchaser, Fletcher heard Old Huang shout down from the wheelhouse window.

"Littee Mandalin!"

Fletcher waved to the pilot and ran into the saloon, where he found Mr. Yang calmly sipping tea behind one of the tight little tables bolted to the floor. Fletcher couldn't even guess if the Little Mandarin was going to understand pidgin English.

"Mister Yang, big fight now, many guns, many rifle shoot. You stay cabin, okay?"

"Hokay, Fetchawood. Now we killum sumbitch tigah, sinkum sumbitch tigah boat. Whatchatinkee, Fetchawood?"

"My tinkee you talkee too muchee Old Huang pidgin," Fletcher said with a laugh as the Little Mandarin scuttled out from behind the table. The round moon-face peeked back over a shoulder at him with a sly grin as it disappeared into the cabin.

"Plitty good pidgin, too?" his voice echoed – then the door clicked shut.

"Schnapps, secure for action, lower your pressure!" Captain Ghent yelled down the wheelhouse voice pipe as he rang for **STANDBY**. This he felt more seemly than shouting "battle stations!" as if *Confucius* was a frigate or corvette. Schnapps would value the warning no less. Too often, the steamer had not enough notice when going into action.

Below the Kiangyin bund, two 70-foot imperial war junks put out from the docks toward the center of the anchorage 400 yards away – directly for *Confucius*. Each war junk carried forty or more soldiers bearing muskets or matchlocks with smoking matches at the ready. Sweating oarsmen pulled behind rattan shields as large as three feet across, each emblazoned with a rampant orange-and-black tiger and woven so tightly each could stop a musket ball. Crewmen loaded 4-pounders fore and aft and gingals in the waist. A din of gong and drum rose from within the bowels of the junks and echoed out over the water.

The old Dutchman ordered tools set out within reach: spanners, sledges, hacksaws, chisels, canvas, thin sheet-iron and copper plates, shoring. Stokers packed bags of coal around the steam chest like sandbags, filled the boilers with water to their crowns, and spilled water into the bilge to increase her draft – if *Confucius* went aground, pumping the water out would quickly float her again. They stoked the fires and opened the safety valve to reduce steam pressure to atmospheric to more easily control damage to boilers. The boiler hand-pump was readied in case of fire, and a pipe from the feed-pump was taken up to the main deck and fitted with a hose to shoot steaming-hot water at the enemy in close quarters, a tactic especially useful against pirates. Oilers went up on deck to stand by the walking beam.

"Action stations," the captain yelled as he yanked at the cord of his steam whistle. On deck, ordinary seamen ran to the armory to draw pistols and carbines. Below deck, gun crews wrestled with cases of shot and canister and requisitioned primers. Fletcher armed himself with a Sharps carbine and a pocketful of paper cartridges and caps and climbed back up to the wheelhouse.

"Captain," Fletcher said, "aren't those imperials? Maybe we should parley first?"

"In a pig's eye! Get your head out into the daylight, Mr. Wood, and gaze about you. See any banners, any bright and colorful flags identifying the force? Tell me where're their insignia, and why are they not sending out a deputation instead of a war-party?"

"Desahtah, Fetchawood. Bad sojah, desaht ahmee, lun alay."

"That's a great many deserters," Fletcher murmured.

"That's what's left of their Great Southern Imperial Encampment, which you and I witnessed get their asses whupped last week, Mr. Wood. For a while, until the Tartar generals get 'em all rounded up, deserters'll be thicker 'n ticks on a Mississippi coon-dog everywhere south of the river."

Ghent stuck his head out a wheelhouse side-window.

"Open fire, godammit!"

Macanaya's gun roared. White smoke spewed back over the wheelhouse and a round of spherical case shot burst ten yards short of the closest junk.

"Macanaya!" Ghent shouted out the side-window. "Don't be so damn bashful!"

With the second shot, Vincente got the range and case shot burst over the stern of the closest junk, clearing the deck of helmsman and officers.

"Macanaya!" the captain yelled out a wheelhouse window. "Slow down, dammit! I wanna ram one o' them bastards!"

Make up your crazy *dayo* mind, *señor*.

Ghent spun the wheel and brought *Confucius* around with engines growling and whistle shrieking. He slapped the cap off the voice pipe.

"Ramming speed, Dutchman! Pour it on! This elephant's gonna kill some goddamn tigers!" The bell sounded **AHEAD FULL**.

The quick turn swung the steamer's stern high and wide. When the side-wheels reached back into the water, the sudden forward thrust settled her stern and raised her bow high up onto a frothy wave. She leapt out of the crimson sunset toward her prey, paddle wheels pounding the river, walking beam flailing the air, steam whistle screaming. *Confucius* abruptly became the incarnation of a writhing river-dragon 蟠龍, mounting onto a white cloud, enveloped in thunder and fire. The dragon rose up and crashed down on startled imperial sailors. Her iron stem smashed into the slight bulwarks of the junk, down through the hold to the keel, and cracked the vessel's backbone, throwing crew in all directions. The junk shivered and lifted at stem and stern. Crewmen grabbed for any purchase and clung for their lives to the broken hulk. On shore, hundreds of deserters rushed to the shoreline and gaped in consternation as the foreign steamer shattered their war junk.

As the first junk fell away, the other opened fire from her bow and waist, sending a two-inch ball bouncing off the planking protecting the steamer's bowchaser, and raking the foredeck with a flock of half-inch balls and broken iron. One of Vincente's gunners fell wounded. The angry Manilamen swore unholy oaths in Tagalog and sweated to double their rate of fire. A round burst over the helm of the second war junk, followed at twenty-second intervals by bursts over the forward deck. Soldiers and oarsmen scrambled for cover or jumped overboard to escape the explosions passing slowly from aft to fore of the junk. In a few moments, the junk was vacant and adrift, pushed by a

洋神 *Yang Shen*   James Lande 藍德

breeze out toward the river, followed in the sights of a dozen carbines.

The orphaned halves of the first war junk, sheltering a few stray soldiers and seamen in the darkening water, quietly purled away from her drifting companion back toward the Kiangyin docks, where her remains were abandoned when they touched land.

Confucius slowed her paddle wheels, backed off, and settled down into a frill of coffee-colored river froth.

"Damn," Ghent muttered. He stepped over to the riverside window and struck a lucifer match to light his pipe. "Cut her right in two. Can you believe it?"

"We are told," Fletcher said, "that we are commissioned to fight rebels and pirates, but everywhere we go we have to get through gangs of imps first."

"Beats sellin' ladies shoes."

Kiangyin harbor became remarkably quiet. The war junks and lighters at the mouth of the creek ceased their predation and warily eyed the foreign fire-wheel boat, waiting to see what it would do next.

"How about that gang of pirates over at the creek?"

"Nah, be darker'n a room full o' black cats real soon now. If the dumb sumbitches are still at it tomorrow morning, we'll make cauldrons of tiger stew then. Let's back out of here and move up to where we've got the river at our backs. Yeah, just like cavalry troopers in Arizona or Texas. Don't want to be outflanked by any of them Apaches."

The loud rattle of chain paying out of her lockers echoed across the anchorage as *Confucius* dropped anchor in the dark shallows out of the stream. After tending her wounded, she settled into a nervous night under the watchful eye of the walled city – with her guard tripled. A couple of late arrivals from upriver were surprised when rifles volleyed across their bow as they made for the Kiangyin anchorage. Boats already at Kiangyin gave the steamer a wide berth after they heard her snap at their neighbors.

Log of Steamer CONFUCIUS, *Shanghai Pirate Suppression Bureau.*

Date & Time	Location	Wind (est.)	Current	Speed	Cargo
Tuesday May 15 1860 8:00pm	Kiangyin, Kiangsu	SSW 2 knots	-	-	-

Fletcher went down to the forecastle looking for casualties from the day's action and found Macanaya sitting on a lower bunk beside his wounded gunner, talking quietly. The place was dank and dark, and smelled of mildew, unwashed clothes, and unwashed men. Fletcher squatted beside the injured Manilaman.

"*Que tal hombre* how are you fellow?" he asked in Spanish.

"*No muerto, señor* not dead, sir."

"How badly is he hurt, Vincente?"

"Iron piece many place, leg, foot. No dance good now, *ahora no puede bailar bueno, eh, Iluminada*?"

"*Aun tengo mi cohones, otros no importante* still got my balls, rest not important."

"Shouldn't he have a doctor?"

"We take care each other, *señor*. I take out iron piece. See?" Vincente opened the top of a canvas pouch behind him on the floor. Inside, slender metal instruments glinted in the low light. "Wash with whiskey, bandage. Tomorrow, next day, send to Shanghai hospital on junk."

"Will he have the money for the hospital? I can give some." Rates at the Shanghai Hospital and Dispensary are damn high.

"Yes, *señor*, captain always pay money. Hospital know *Confucius*."

"*Nagúgutom* hungry?" Fletcher asked Iluminada in Tagalog.

"*Uhaw na* thirsty."

"*Sandalí lang* wait a minute." Fletcher went to his cabin and fetched back a pint of

Sumbitch Tigah Boat   335

rum. It passed slowly between the three of them.

"Where are you from, Iluminada?"

"Luzon. Mountain very nice, *señor*, you should visit. Life good, eh Vincente?"

"Without Spanish, maybe."

"Life in pueblo good," Iluminada said. "Simple. Live in bamboo hut, thatch with nipa palm, sleep in hammock, drink nipa wine, chew betel nut, hunt boar in forest, swim and fish in stream and ocean, trade for rice, corn, *cigarillos* at *tianggi* – weekly market."

"Simple," Vincente said. "Little clay oven for cook. Wood mortar for rice, grindstone for corn, baskets for carry. Men make tables, chairs of wood and rattan, use only *bolo* knife. Women weave clothes from *abaca* hemp and *piña*. Forest very pretty, remember, Iluminada? Always rain, everything always wet with rain like good woman, light come down through trees, shine on wet leaf. Sunlight shine between trees, make mist glow. Not dirty like China."

"Yes," Fletcher said, "must be like the sun when it rises through river mists and makes the air glow with iridescence, shine with many colors."

"Yes, like that...I think," Iluminada said.

"Grandfather tell me," Vincente said, "when Spanish come soldiers go in villages and take everything, take man to slave in field, take woman, leave Christian friar to make all Christian. The Spanish, *señor*, they say missionary bring catechism good thing for Philippine people. So now, *Indios* – native Filipinos – we must speak Spanish, say *Dios* not *Bathala*, forget old gods, recite Angelus morning, noon, and night, wear *sapatos* – shoes. *Indios* slave at work, pound rice for priest in church, wash church floor and wall, dig in field and harvest crop, for no pay, for nothing, Slave like ant is holy, play like grasshopper is sin."

"They did not pay for the work?"

"In my country, *señor*," Vincente said, "Spanish have *polistas* – slave labor – called *polo*. Spanish mayor, he collect all tribute and say who must labor every year forty days in *polo* for government, or for Christian friars. Also control rum, and cockfight. When Spanish come, take all land. Spanish soldier say how live, Christian friar say how think. Chinee mestizo make all money. *Indios* sweat and starve, and listen for chapel bells."

Fletcher and Vincente toasted their last tot of rum and turned in, Fletcher to his tiny cabin, Vincente to his bunk in the forecastle. On deck, alert Manilamen cradled their carbines as closely to their chests as they would a warm woman, and carefully watched over every movement in the anchorage. Bright Jupiter set in late evening, and Saturn followed later. By midnight, the moonless sky was dark except for the white glow of millions of stars. *Confucius* slept.

3 "Captain, how far up that creek can *Confucius* go?" Fletcher said.

"Hell, you don't know enough to be assistant janitor in a corn crib if you think I'm risking my steamer up there – I can piss more water than's in them piddly little creeks."

"Some say new occasions teach new duties."

"Hang it all, don't try my patience with trite preaching! Even with spring tides or rains upriver, there's not eight feet of water most places. Embankments fall in, bottom shoals up, and maybe the widest is 120 feet, so there's never room to turn around. You'd have to back down all the way. There're bridges too – much too low for this boat to get under, so you'd have to endear yourself to the locals by shelling their damn bridges to get past. If you did find your depth, after going ashore God knows how many times, the river'd drop and you'd be stuck out there for God knows how long surrounded by hostiles and no wagons to circle. You could be there months until the next rainstorm."

"We could survey the creek in a junk and not take the steamer unless..."

"You're barkin' up the wrong tree, Mr. Wood. I'll hear no more about it."
"Well, I still want to take a junk up that creek."
"That's your business, as long as I stay here in Kiangyin."
"How long?"
"Rebels won't wait for us."
"Another day?"
"One day."

Fletcher set out to find the Takee bank clearinghouse, taking Old Huang, the pirate-suppressing mandarin, and four heavily armed Manilamen in a sampan to the Kiangyin bund. Another sampan ferried ashore a dozen more heavily armed Manilamen. Two crewmen stayed to guard the sampans. At the north gate, deserters challenged the shore party, confirming Fletcher's expectation that no civil authority ruled in Kiangyin. Sharps carbines leveled at the deserters' heads were enough to convince them to put down their weapons and lock themselves in the gatehouse. Four crewmen remained to hold the gate.

Bystanders directed the shore party to Banker's Alley through progressively smaller streets and lanes littered with broken baskets and other refuse, past shabby storefronts from which they were eyed warily by shopkeepers and old women. The nervous crewmen hoisted their rifles to the ready. Fletcher began to doubt a bank branch could be located in a slum Bill Sikes or Fagin would fear to enter. He struggled to remember the way in case they had to retreat through the dark little passageways. Getting in is easy, but getting out through this warren of alleys and lanes might be a *tour de force*.

They stopped under a dusty arcade in front of a rundown shop with iron bars over the windows and door. Fletcher could not believe this was a bank, a correspondent of the great Takee Bank of Shanghai, but Mr. Yang sailed right in. Fletcher left four crewmen outside and he and the rest crowded in behind – there was not room for more. Inside, the tiny room was dark and smelled strongly of sandalwood from the incense burning on a small altar high over a door at the rear. A wall of dark wood closed off half the small room leaving only a narrow passageway. In the wall there was a single window enclosed by an iron grille. The sudden apparition of so many rifles must have frightened the banker, because the shutter behind the grille jerked shut with a loud snap. Mr. Yang spoke softly to a gruff voice behind the wall for several minutes before the shutter opened a crack in response to his entreaties and a lone, bespectacled eye appeared in the crack to examine Mr. Yang's bill of exchange.

"我是泰記行來的," Mr. Yang said. "I'm from Takee Bank."

Then the window opened wide and greetings flew as if between long-lost relatives. The door at the rear opened and Mr. Yang disappeared into the dark interior. Fifteen minutes later, he emerged and explained that they had credit for several thousand taels, showing them a bag full of silver ingots and copper coin secreted under his jacket. He also said that a man from the clearinghouse would come to *Confucius* and take them to talk with trustworthy junkmen in the Kiangyin harbor. Then a boy from the clearinghouse led Fletcher's party back to the North Gate.

That afternoon a man from the clearinghouse brought Fletcher, Old Huang and four armed Manilamen ashore in a large sampan. As the sampan approached the Kiangyin bund, Fletcher could see a small crowd of townspeople gathered at the wharf and along the bund, which made him a little nervous – foreign experience held that a crowd in China had the potential of quickly turning ugly and dangerous.

"Lao Huang, what are all those people there for?" Fletcher had noticed that the Little Mandarin called the pilot Lao Huang, using the honorific "Lao" where an

American would have said "Old" out of respect, and started calling the pilot Lao Huang.

"Come see you, Fetchawood! Nevah see too many steamboat, too many white man in littee livah town."

As the sampan came alongside the wharf, Fletcher realized that it was *Confucius* that had people all gawking out into the harbor, and at the spectacle of foreigners coming ashore in a sampan. As he passed time in towns along the river, Fletcher eventually grew more accustomed to the inevitable crowds, and alert to the different appearance of ordinary folk and possible troublemakers, but his awareness of the potential of a crowd to turn suddenly ugly never completely settled.

Behind the sampan, the *whump* of the 32-pounder aboard *Confucius* and the crackle of Sharps carbines began echoing off the pine-covered hills north of the anchorage.

"*K'ung-fu-tze* got tlouble, Fetchawood?"

"Judging from the direction, the captain is putting *Confucius* to work on the tiger boats at the mouth of that creek." He added, "*Confucius* killum sumbitch tigah boat."

"Oh, Littee Mandalin, he like dat belly much. Bet he got big smile."

The clearinghouse man walked the bund with Fletcher and Old Huang, stopping at an occasional junk to examine the vessel and speak with the junkmen. Fletcher's tutelage in small Chinese craft advanced quickly as they examined all the sampans and junks at Kiangyin. Some junks looked just too far-gone, unkempt and falling apart from old age. Others had too much draft for the creek, or masts too large or difficult to unstep for passing under bridges, or no house where a foreigner could stay out of sight. At Kiangyin mostly were vessels of the middle river. They looked at salt junks, rice junks, inland traders, brick boats, lime boats, peddler boats, post boats, even rafts and "kettle" boats, those old barrels cut in two and paddled by hand.

The clearinghouse man stopped before a slender, rough-looking fifty-foot long junk. Old Huang said it was a north-of-the-river junk 江北船, a cargo lighter with a capacity of forty tons, twelve-foot beam, and five-foot draft – shallow enough for the creek. It had a squat house with galley and living quarters inside, a rudder as well as a *yuloh* sweep at the stern, and two sweeps at the bow.

"No," Fletcher said, "look at the mast. It must be fifty feet high."

"Hey, Fetchawood," Old Huang said, "mas' come down chop-chop, boat go undah fifteen-foot blidge."

"Oh?" Fletcher was looking more closely when a short, pudgy woman on the junk came to the rail and looked him up and down. She wore a grimy gray padded jacket, ankle-length gray trousers, her short black hair spilled over a red cloth band, she was barefoot, and her front teeth were black with decay.

"你是誰?" she said, laughing.

"She wantchee know who you, Fetchawood," the pilot said.

"*Wo jeeeyao Woo-duh.*" Fletcher thought he'd try his new Chinese again.

"*Ai-yo!*" she cackled. "洋鬼子說中國話 the foreign devil spoke Chinese!"

"She say…"

"Yeah, yeah. I can guess. What do we call her?"

"She say name callum Ah-shan 阿姍."

Old Huang said something more to her and, shouting at the low house, she jumped to the mainmast, grabbed a dangling line, and went aft. Two scruffy-looking fellows crawled out from the house. She shouted again and they ran forward and attached one of the long *yuloh* sweeps to the base of the mast, rigged a line from the top of the mast to the forward end of the sweep, and ran purchases from the forward end of the sweep to iron rings on each side of the bow. The woman began hauling on her line, which ran up to the masthead, while the two men paid out line through each purchase. In a matter of seconds, the fifty-foot mast canted backward to only eight feet above the deck. The woman took a stance with both hands on her hips and black-toothed grin at Fletcher.

"怎麼樣洋鬼子?" she shouted. "How's that, foreign devil?"

Fletcher was surprised at how quickly the mast came down, having spent little time around junks that worked on inland streams and creeks. The *yuloh* sweep became a kind of sheerleg that, joined to the foot of the upright mast, formed a right angle that the quick operation simply lay down on the deck: ╲╱. He stepped back, placed his hands on his hips, then held up a thumb and barked, "*Ting hao* 丁好, great!"

The entire crew of the junk laughed and repeated several times, "*ting hao*." Neighboring junkmen took up the chorus "*ting hao, ting hao*." Old Huang told the woman they wanted to hire the junk for a day.

"She say mus' talkee *lao-ta* 老大, old-great," Old Huang said. "*Lao-ta* go makee pidgin at teahouse."

"Ask her what teahouse, and what is the *laodah*'s name?"

"She say boy takee. *Lao-ta* name Old Chang, *Lao* Chang 老張."

A small barefoot boy in shorts burst out of the house and jumped down from the junk, reached out and took Fletcher's hand, and started off up the bund toward the city gate with Fletcher's outfit in tow

"Go me," the boy said.

A moment later, they turned off to a street behind the bund and climbed stone steps to a higher street.

"哎呀小張釣了一條外國魚," came a shout from the crowd following in their wake. "Hey, Little Chang has caught a foreigner-fish."

"Worth more than a fish!"

"Look at his nose. It's so big!"

"His money-purse must be even bigger."

"Probably that's not all that's big."

"Lao Huang," Fletcher said. "What are they saying?"

"Oh, jus' say welcome foreign man come Chiang-yin."

They arrived at the ornate door of a large, low building with open shutters the entire length of the side facing the harbor. Blue skullcaps, wispy white beards, wafting teacups and waving chopsticks filled the proscenium of windows above the sill. Faces in the windows became alarmed when Fletcher approached the door and entered. Several attendants raised their hands and stepped in front of him to block his way, but the boy just pushed between them dragging his foreigner into the large tearoom.

"爸爸 *pa-pa*." The boy's shout was lost in the welter of conversation, storytelling, haggling, shouting waiters, winning gamblers, and performing musicians.

"爸爸 *pa-pa*!"

"小張, 在這裡 Little Chang, over here."

The boy pulled Fletcher across the crowded room to a table close to the wall where three men were seated

"爸爸這位外國先生要談生意 pa-pa, this foreign gentleman wants to talk business."

"很好 very good," said a tall, angular man with a thin, wispy gray beard. He wore a glossy black gown of embroidered silk and a black skullcap brocaded with gold thread.

The clearinghouse man made the introductions to Lao Chang, explaining they were from Takee Bank – at which point the other two men rose and politely withdrew. On the man's invitation, the clearinghouse man, Fletcher, and Old Huang seated themselves at the table and hot tea was brought. The boy disappeared into the cloud of tobacco smoke

Sumbitch Tigah Boat 339

that filled the room. Noticing, however, that the attention of the entire room was riveted on their conversation, Lao Chang suggested they adjourn to the street and return to the bund. He told his story as they walked back down to the anchorage.

The junkman Lao Chang had been associated years before with Takee Bank in Shanghai and later returned home to Yang-chou on the north side of the river. When shipping fell off under rebel control, Lao Chang relocated with his lighter downriver to Kiangyin, and carried cargo between there and Shanghai. He had brought the junk up Soochow Creek, along the Grand Canal, and down to Kiangyin on the Hsi-ch'eng Canal 錫澄運河, so not only was he guaranteed reliable, but he also knew the water. The clearinghouse man bargained a price of three taels for a day's use of the junk as far as the Grand Canal, and transport for the wounded crewman to the Shanghai Hospital on the following day. The fee set the faces of the Lao Chang and his wife to beaming. Fletcher assumed the amount was much more than fair, and that the clearinghouse man would have his part of it. It was Takee's money, and the Chinese had their own ways.

"Sumbitch junk man now belly lich," Old Huang said. "My catchee junk, work fo' you, pay me too muchee Takee silver, whatchatinkee Fetchawood?"

"My tinkee Lao Huang belly good pilot, numbah one *ting-hao* pilot."

"*Ting-hao* 丁好? Talkee too muchee Chinee, Fetchawood."

When they returned to Confucius they saw that above the town, where the creek entered the anchorage, small junks and sampans came and went without hindrance, no longer pestered by prowling tigers. The imperial war galleys were gone, except for the masts of one sunk, and the burning remains of another driven ashore.

Log of Steamer CONFUCIUS, *Shanghai Pirate Suppression Bureau.*

Date & Time	Location	Wind (est.)	Current	Speed	Cargo
Wednesday May 16 1860 9:00pm	Kiangyin, Kiangsu	SW 2 knots	-	-	-

4

"*Soldados*!" Vincente called out. "Soldiers!"

The junk was rounding the foot of a temple at the waterside in one old town, and Fletcher and Vincente were forward of the mast where they could see ahead. As he shouted, Vincente pointed forward to where the creek passed between the vertical pillars of a low, gray stone bridge. Atop the bridge stood six men armed with muskets. Several more with pikes stood on steps leading up to the bridge.

"Ah-shan, drop the sail! Imperial soldiers." Fletcher shouted.

Old Huang relayed the command in Chinese. Ah-shan shouted her order and the crewmen jumped to the mast and brought the lugsail down with a crash. The junk slowed to a stop, held in the current by the stern sweep. The crack of a musket fired from the bridge echoed over the creek and a ball whizzed past the junk's house and splashed into the water aft.

"混蛋 bastards!" Ah-shan's sudden howl echoed back up the creek as loudly as the musket shot, surprising the junk's passengers as much as the soldiers. "打我們幹麼 what are you firing at us for?" She shouted at Little Chang and he jumped into a hold.

"停船 stop boat."

"狗屁 dog fart!" Ah-shan screamed.

"小畜生還敢罵人 little bitch, you dare cuss people!"

Fletcher was waiting to see if Ah-shan actually could shout her way out of this, but when the muskets started rising to firing position, he and Vincente took over the conversation with a loud volley of rifle fire. Two soldiers staggered backward off the far side of the bridge and into the water below, followed by the splash of their muskets. The remaining three muskets fired wildly and bolted off the bridge on the heels of the rest of the fleeing braves. Vincente's crewman got off a rifle shot and felled the last soldier retreating down the path beside the creek.

"好棒!" whooped Ah-shan. "Really great!"

The door of the junk's house opened and Lao Chang looked out. "甚麼事那麼嘈嘈鬧鬧 what's all the ruckus?"

"沒你的事 - 回去" Ah-shan said. "No business of yours – go back to the game."

"啊, 好了 oh, okay." Lao Chang disappeared back into the house.

When Fletcher had arrived at the mist-shrouded anchorage early that morning with Old Huang, Vincente, and a Manilaman – all but the pilot were armed with Sharps carbines and Colt revolvers – the junkman's wife was on deck with the two crewmen and Little Chang. Fletcher could hear voices and laughter and the unmistakable clacking of mahjong tiles coming from the house. Inside, he found Lao Chang in his embroidered black gown and brocaded black skullcap seated at a low table with three cronies in the center of the room. All four were too intent on their game for more than a quick wave, whether in greeting or dismissal Fletcher could not tell. When Fletcher glanced back at the junkman's wife and raised an eyebrow, she shook her head and waved a hand – clearly a gesture of dismissal.

"不要管他們," she said.

"She say maskee dat junk man, Fetchawood," Old Huang said. "She *lao-ta* now, she junk cap'n."

"比他好," she added.

"She say she bettah junk boss."

Ah-shan shouted orders to Little Chang and her crewmen to raise the lugsail while she hurried to the stern and manned the *yuloh* sweep. A few quick twists of the sweep took the junk away from the bund. The wind caught the lugsail and the junk made for the creek that went south to the Grand Canal.

"Not cleek, Fetchawood. Ah-shan, she call canal 運河, likee Gland Canal." Ah-shan had said that the Hsi-ch'eng was part of the southern Grand Canal system and was over two thousand years old.

When Fletcher left *Confucius* that morning, Ghent was still in a funk over the delay, but it had occurred to Fletcher that making friends with these officials up and down the river could be beneficial in several respects. He would be less dependent on the intelligence passed to him from the Shanghai *taotai* and Takee if junkmen and even mandarins enrolled as his eyes-and-ears on the river. His own intelligence would provide independent corroboration of whatever he was told by his sponsors and, perhaps, deliver espionage outside their capability. He wondered how to enlist the loyalty of his own sources – money, of course. Was something more needed to prevent information for him alone, and about him, from going astray?

The canal was eighty to one hundred feet wide and flowed between mud dikes four to eight feet high at low neap tide. They pushed against a slow current running toward Kiangyin, with a fitful southwest breeze that gave her headway of three or four knots. Whenever the breeze fell off, the sweeps nudged her forward. They met mostly sampans and country boats, and smaller junks like their own. Imperial war-junks were probably too big for the canal, Fletcher thought. He and Vincente traded off sounding the canal depth, which varied from five to fifteen feet in the morning and rose another two feet with the incoming tide.

For much of the distance the banks were black mud walls under windrows of tall brown reeds; they could not see the fields behind the dikes. Now and again, the junk

洋神 *Yang Shen* *James Lande* 藍德

passed large sluice gates built of short, square beams set in stone piers in the dikes. In some places, beams were removed from the top of a gate until water could flow from the canal into the fields. Barefoot farmers with mud-caked legs and broad straw hats trudged along the berms beside yellow oxen pulling two-wheeled carts loaded with produce or refuse. Stray imperial soldiers halted to stare down indignantly at the passing junk.

"Lao Huang," Fletcher said, "tell Ah-shan to have her crewmen watch for imperial soldiers with muskets. Vincente and I will do the same."

Each village they passed through had several bridges where the junk's crew had to lower the lugsail then help Ah-shan bring the mast down to the deck. Ah-shan lay into the stern sweep and, together with the crewmen on the bow sweeps, they drove the craft underneath each bridge. The underside of more than one bridge ground away a little of the canted masthead. One little arched bridge was so small that the bow sweeps had to be taken in and the mast tugged down even closer to the deck to clear the opening, and the junk's gunwales still left splinters hanging on the stone walls under the bridge.

After the encounter with the deserters on the bridge, the junk meandered south about twenty miles before the canal ended at a high slipway that crossed over to the Grand Canal. A shallow channel that passed alongside the Grand Canal from the east fed water from Lake T'ai into the Hsi-ch'eng Canal. To get over to the Grand Canal, a junk would have to be pulled up the slipway on one side by ropes taken up on buffalo-powered capstans, and then released to slide down the slipway on the other side. At low tide, the haul up the slipway could be a long distance for a fully laden cargo boat of forty tons like Lao Chang's junk, and it was probably necessary sometimes to unload cargo to avoid damage to a vessel.

Clearly, thought Fletcher, large craft cannot take this route into the Grand Canal.

The junk dropped anchor beside the slipway. Fletcher and Vincente stepped ashore and hiked up to the huge capstans perched on top of the slipway. The Grand Canal was wide here, perhaps forty yards across, and alive with vessels of perhaps six or eight feet of draft moving under sail. There was a great deal of traffic, all in one direction – east away from Changchow and the approaching rebels, but there were no rebel troops within sight. It had taken six hours to reach the canal from Kiangyin, including several delays to get off shoals and return the fire of foraging deserters. Returning, the wind would be abaft their beam and they'd be with the current. If the junk could get up to six or seven knots along clear stretches, they might make Kiangyin in as little as four hours.

Fletcher could think of no steamer on the China coast that could have made this trip. They all were too long and drew too much water, a drawback to the concept of using steamer firepower inland he had advanced to Takee. He knew there were river steamers small enough – screw steamers without bulky side-wheels, with the same beam as the junk, only ten or fifteen feet longer, and having even less draft, which could mount 12-pounders, maybe even 32-pounders. But searching out such steamers would take time. Building new ones would take much more time, maybe a year or more.

When Fletcher and Vincente returned to the junk, a hot meal of steaming beef noodles was waiting. Long after the junk arrived back in Kiangyin late that afternoon, and Fletcher and his men had returned to *Confucius*, the mahjong game was still in play.

Log of Steamer CONFUCIUS, *Shanghai Pirate Suppression Bureau.*

Date & Time	Location	Wind (est.)	Current	Speed	Cargo
Thursday May 17 1860 9:00pm	Kiangyin, Kiangsu	SW 3 knots	-	-	-

Mate and crew put aboard junk bound upstream from Kiangyin for Grand Canal

The next morning was unusually cold. A slender crescent moon hung above the

Sumbitch Tigah Boat

洋神 *Yang Shen* James Lande 藍德

creek at Kiangyin harbor when Ah-shan sculled her junk over from the bund through white wisps of frost smoke and tied up alongside the steamer. While *Confucius* got up steam, Iluminada was carried aboard the junk and settled in the house. Old Huang sat for a few minutes with him, and Ah-shan and Little Chang, to be certain they knew how to find the hospital at Shanghai, would hire a chair to carry Iluminada from the Bund, and would accompany the Manilaman all the way. Fletcher had asked the Little Mandarin to write letters for Takee, one telling of the steamer's exploits to date, the other – as pointedly explained to Ah-shan – commending Lao Chang for his service on the river and recommending he be given more work. Fletcher looked to ensure the steamer's crewman would be treated properly as well as to buttress the junkman's allegiance.

Fletcher and Ghent quickly went over their charts for the sixty-five miles from Kiangyin to Chenkiang, noting places likely to have changed. "With spring tides a few days away," the captain said, "the depths shown on the chart should be pretty close."

The tide would run for another four hours. With a breeze out of the southeast, as on the day before, *Confucius* could make good time, carried on the rising flood and pushed by a quartering wind. For the twenty-five miles to Starling Island, the run was mid-channel, as the right bank quickly shoaled to a fathom – six feet. They would pass the island to leeward, where the shelf scoured by the river plunged to sixteen fathoms – 96 feet. The narrow passage on the following fifteen-mile reach north to the Old Joss House often was only twelve feet deep. Past the joss house, the river curved west around the flat expanse of Great Sand Island and meandered beside several more sandy islands over bottom six to nine fathoms deep – thirty-six to fifty-four feet – to Chenkiang.

With Fletcher at the helm, *Confucius* left Kiangyin at 7:00am together with Lao Chang's junk. The steamer turned upriver for Chenkiang. The junk slipped downstream for Shanghai. Ah-shan looked up from her sculling to wave at the steamer as it vanished into haze. From beside the 12-pounder, Vincente watched Iluminada carried out of sight.

"*Diyan na kayo, páre* goodbye, my friend."

Sumbitch Tigah Boat

洋神 *Yang Shen*   *James Lande* 藍德

Dramatis Personae: Chapter 21

Lin Ch'uan 林全 (Lao Lin), and his wife   Chenkiang boat people

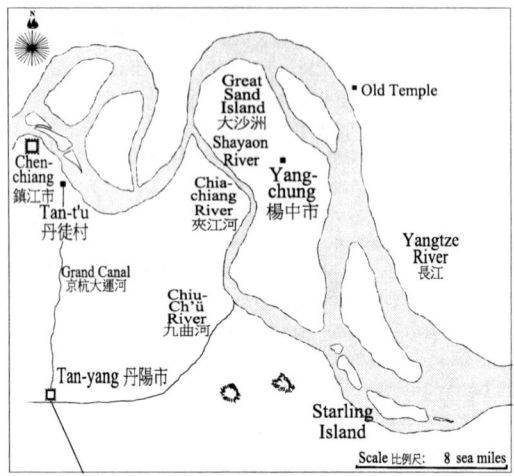

Chia-chiang and Chiu-ch'ü Rivers at Yang-chung
(based on British Hydrographic Office chart, China., Sheet IX, 1842, and contemporary maps)

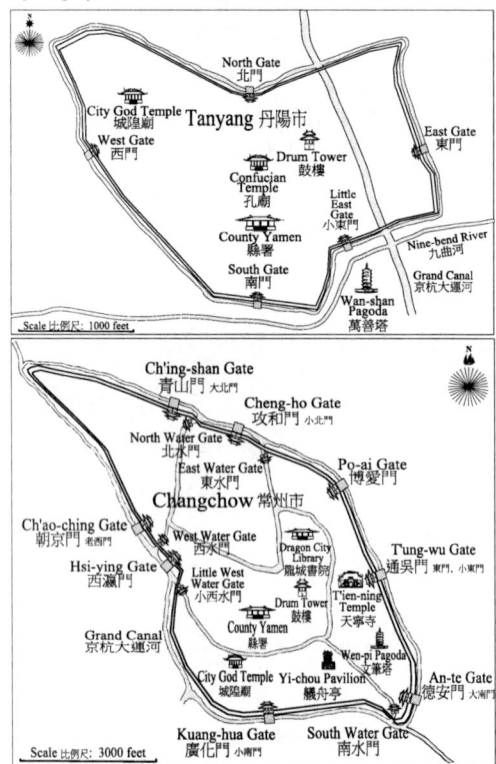

Tanyang and Changchow in 1860
(adapted from present-day maps)

Chapter 21: Tanyang and Changchow
Friday, May 18, 1860, 7:00am

Wisps of gossamer mist whorled around the hull of *Confucius* as she worked her way up the river toward Chenkiang through legions of murky white ghosts drifting on the current, eerie apparitions of frost smoke that sent superstitious Chinese boatmen splashing frantically to shore – frightened the river ghosts were rising. As the Yangtze widened again and the tedious banks receded into mist, the river felt more like an ocean and the steamer seemed afloat on a formless sea. Distant sounds echoing out of the fog along the shoreline were the only token of beings living beyond her penumbra – a bell struck in a temple atop a hill, the belligerent crow of a cock, the lowing of an ox.

"When'll we raise Silver Island?" the captain said.

"Well," Fletcher said, "barring delays, take maybe seven hours, about 2:00pm?"

"Barring delays? Hedging, aren't you, mister? Where's your nerve?"

"Not a fortune-teller."

"Where's your crust, mister?"

Crust, thought Fletcher! I guess you'd know about crust.

"Gold eagle says you can't raise Silver Island by 2:00pm."

"Whoa, ten dollars is a lot of scratch. Give or take a half hour?"

"More temporizing. Half-hour margin, then. But no dawdling."

"All right, Captain, I'll take your gold eagle."

"Show some color, mister. Put 'em next to the wheel here."

"Like Ahab's Spanish gold ounce."

The sun rose higher and the wind started up out of the southeast and the ghostly legions dissipated, leaving a better view ahead of lurking hazards. Fletcher rang for **AHEAD FULL**. The left bank emerged from the haze to reveal ragged bands of imperial soldiers striking their tents and resuming a disorderly march east. Tiger boats came down the river, the seventy-foot imperial war galleys pulled by forty oars, plunging into the wave crests, pushing against the leeward flood, reluctantly yielding wide berth to the huge steamer. The tiger boat officers glared across the water at *Confucius*, scowling like the orange-and-black tiger heads on their war-shields.

Chowshan appeared, now a gray nubbin from which all the snow had finally melted. Fletcher crossed over to the lee of Starling Island. That swirling black mob of raucous rooks and jackdaws resident along the approach to Silver Island swarmed squawking and yawping over the steamer and followed along high above her. Fletcher slowed past the Old Joss House, and managed to stay out of the sand along Great Sand Island and as far as Little Sand Island. Even before she started to scrape, the crew leaned on the shoal with their long poles. Fletcher called quickly for **FULL ASTERN** and nudged her off. Minutes later, the black crags of Silver Island loomed around a bend. Old Huang and the captain stood one on each side of the first mate as he steered *Confucius* safely past Furious rock. Fletcher checked the time and glanced over at Ghent.

"Two of the clock and twenty-one minutes, Captain."

"You think I can't tell the time! Take your money."

Ghent pushed gruffly past him and stomped noisily down the wheelhouse ladder but, by now, Fletcher had come to recognize the occasional wrinkle of a smile underneath all that hair on the captain's face. Ghent was pleased with Fletcher's handling of *Confucius*. It meant Fletcher could spell him on long runs, and take over if he were disabled. Fletcher listened to the satisfying jingle of the two coins in his pocket.

"Cost of crust, Cap'n."

洋神 *Yang Shen* James Lande 藍德

Immense rafts of noisy ducks floated downriver between Silver Island and Chenkiang, and long lines of black cormorants flew around the island on their way upriver, rising high to pass over the steamer then descending back to the water. The island was as before, green with trees and vegetation, temples on the higher slopes, moss-covered cliffs. From high in the hills, the same deep peal of a bronze bell echoed out over the river, accompanied the chants of Buddhists at prayer. *Confucius* continued carefully around to the lee side of Silver Island, from where the bund at Chenkiang harbor was visible, and dropped her hook without incident.

Log of Steamer CONFUCIUS, Shanghai Pirate Suppression Bureau

Date & Time	Location	Wind (est.)	Current	Speed	Cargo
Friday May 18 1860 3:00pm	Silver Island, Chenkiang, Kiangsu	SE 3 knots	3 knots	5 knots	-

Confucius hailed sampans from the Chenkiang anchorage and disembarked two details. One, lead by Vincente, was to sound the depths of the entrance to the Grand Canal, where it left the river at the west end of the anchorage. The other was a shore party, lead by Fletcher, to transact the business of Takee Bank. Under the warm May sun, Fletcher, Old Huang, and six armed crewmen escorted the Little Mandarin a mile through the bleak suburbs to the east gate. Not a single tree remained standing and everywhere they flushed wildfowl and small musk deer out of the abundant overgrowth. At the east gate, they found the town was under the command of imperial Brigade General Feng Tze-ts'un, 總兵馮子村. The general had regrouped his dispirited troops and was hastily repairing his defenses. The gate commander assigned an officer to guide the steamer's mandarin and his companions through the bustle of imperial soldiery.

Inside the town along Hua Shan Road 花山路, there appeared little to defend – only burnt buildings, and refugees huddled in reed huts. Soldiers removed debris to clear open ground for defense, filled breaches in the walls, repaired gates and smeared them with mud to suppress flame, and raised fluttering flags and banners along the parapets. Serviceable guns recovered from the rubble were placed back into action atop the town walls and new guns installed beside them. Bundles of arrows and crossbow shafts were stashed next to embrasures, together with long bamboo staffs to push away storming ladders, and large stones and cauldrons of oil to set afire and drop over the parapets. Listening devices to detect enemy tunneling – geophones made of hollow crockery sealed with a thin hide membrane – were placed in wells sunk every few yards along the inside of the southwestern wall.

"The ch'i 氣 of this town," the officer said, "flows to the south and southwest, toward the yang 陽, so this is a male town, supplied from the swift river that protects the town on the north, and guarded on the south by the mountain Nan Shan 南山. The walls may be broken down, but this location above the river and at the foot of the mountain is fortuitous, our stores of rice and water are plentiful, our leaders are brave, and our rewards liberal. Defended resolutely, the enemy cannot take Chen-chiang."

At the street of clearinghouses, Mr. Yang found the Takee Bank correspondent and, as in Kiangyin, established credit for silver taels, less than in Kiangyin because of the impending rebel threat, He also received the names of a few junkmen who had returned to the harbor. The clearinghouse manager arranged with the yamen officer for a clerk to accompany Fletcher's party to the bund to search for a junk. Mr. Yang remained at the clearinghouse with four of the armed crewmen.

At the anchorage, thousands of imperial soldiers sent to reinforce Chenkiang crowded the decks of junks and sampans, where they were quartered when there was no

Tanyang and Changchow

room left in the town. As the armed foreigners passed, the soldiers quieted suddenly and eyed them warily, some hungrily, thought Fletcher. Soldiers today, deserters tomorrow. Without this officer, we'd be in a heap of trouble.

A cacophony of Chinese music drifted up the bund, and shortly they came upon a junkman's wedding underway aboard a large harbor lighter. The newlywed's junk was decorated bow to stern with colored streamers dangling from the masts, paper lanterns twisting in the breeze, and lighted red lanterns on the poop deck. Shiny strips of gold paper inscribed with black characters for good luck 福 and marital bliss 囍 were pasted around the doors, and fresh scrolls of sentiments appropriate for the occasion decorated the cabin walls. Ancestors' tablets stood on an altar outside the port cabin, and offerings of smoldering incense and food lay before the altar. All over the main deck, tables were piled high with food for the banquet: platters with baked pigs, tureens of braised beef and roast chicken, plates of seafood casseroles, and boxes of sweet cakes and fresh fruit. Crates on deck held honking geese and quacking ducks, and their racket mingled with the noise of a small group of musicians playing on horns, flutes, drums and a two-stringed *er-hu* 二胡. Strings of firecrackers rattled off explosions that sent red paper scrap flying over the railings.

The clearinghouse clerk stopped at a wharf-boat 小碼頭船 and called out. The junk was perhaps fifty-five or sixty feet long, twelve feet wide, looked to be about five feet deep, and was propelled by a *yuloh* sweep at her stern, with provision for two more *yuloh*s that mounted on bumpkins on her bow. There was one mast stepped forward, set with a spritsail and easily removed and, instead of the usual awning aft, there was a small makeshift house where the family lived. She was a cousin to the larger cargo boats downriver, used for transporting cargoes of at least twenty tons, and as a harbor lighter. Around the doorways, there remained only the worn and faded remnants of characters for good luck and marital bliss not yet peeled away.

A disheveled woman with graying hair looked out and muttered a few words to the clerk. He told Old Huang to wait and ran back to the wedding party. Small bells jangled from the house and a little girl toddled out on deck and over to the rail, followed by a fat black chow-chow. The girl had large, shiny black eyes, long pigtails tied with red ribbon, and wore a short blue quilted jacket, black trousers, and an anklet of small silver bells. She, and the dog, stared under the rail at the foreigners.

"Well," Fletcher said, only half to the little girl, "always know where you are."

"大鼻子," she said, pointing at Fletcher and laughing. "Big nose."

"What is she saying, Lao Huang?"

"She say likee big foreign man."

The clerk returned from the wedding celebration leading a tall, barefoot junkman wearing a black headband, a short black jacket with a white cloth belt, and knee-length black trousers. The junkman leapt aboard his junk without a glance at the foreigners and yelled at the house. The woman came out with bamboo stools, then fetched tea things and set to preparing tea over a small brazier at the mainmast. The little girl crossed to her mother, bells jangling, dog following. The junkman gestured to the clerk.

Fletcher, Old Huang, and the clerk went onboard and sat with the junkman. The junkman, too, had large, shiny black eyes – and a penetrating stare. His head was big for his body, with a broad, square forehead, large mouth, round nose, and weathered skin pockmarked as from smallpox. He said he had been associated with Takee Bank in Shanghai and recently returned to Chenkiang to be closer to his aging parents. He was called Lin Ch'uan 林全, or Lao Lin 老林.

The clearinghouse clerk explained what was wanted. While Lao Lin's wife served tea from a tray, he boasted that he knew all the streams between the lower reaches and the Grand Canal. In his eight years on the river, they had been all over the delta, from Hangchow to Yangchow, Woosung to Wuhan, even tracked upriver through the high gorges from I-ch'ang to Ch'ung-ch'ing. They had also carried foreign arms to the rebels, but Lao Lin kept that to himself. The creeks and streams of Kiangnan were too shallow in winter, but his junk could go over to the canal on the current spring floods.

The junkman's wife collected the teacups, which she stacked on the tray. Lao Lin looked up at her and, without a word, just stood up and followed her to the mainmast. To Fletcher it seemed that Lao Lin was not entirely in charge aboard this junk.

"Lao Huang, can you hear what they're saying?" he said.

"No can heah," the pilot said. But Old Huang also wondered about the junkman, and his wife. The teacups got him started – she had put them in two stacks, two cups in each stack. Triad killers, and brothers in other secret societies, placed teacups in different arrangements as signals to one another.

"妳派茶碗陣幹麼?" Lao Lin said to his wife. "Why play with teacup formations? One of these outsiders might understand."

"這個水很緊 this is rough water. 木楊城裡是乾坤 the City of Willows is our whole world. If we are not careful and we make mistakes, we could lose everything and become again like rolling dragons, if we're not feathered."

They spoke in a secret language of the Society of Elder Brothers, the *Ko-lao Hui* 哥老會, another of many secret societies, like the Triads, dedicated to the overthrow of the Manchu. The language varied from place to place, used local dialect to confuse the uninitiated, and had elaborate arrangements of tea or wine cups, and tobacco pipes or opium pipes, to convey secret messages, as well as a vocabulary of posture and gestures.

Lao Lin's wife had told him "this is a dangerous situation. The *Ko-lao Hui* is our world now, and if not careful we could lose our rank in the lodge, become outsiders and have to live miserable lives again, if we are not thrown into the river."

"You are assistant lodge master 輔山主," Lao Lin said, "and my superior in these matters. I would only give counsel. We *Ko-lao* are sworn to drive foreigners from China, so why would we help foreigners opposed to our T'ai-p'ing brothers?"

"We can get many fat hens – silver ingots – for our *Ko-lao* brothers from this foreigner," she said. "We can also find ways through him to get arms for both the *Ko-lao* and the T'ai-p'ing, new advanced weapons to replace the trash we have now, weapons to slaughter tens of thousands of demon soldiers 斬盡殺絕妖兵千千萬. Afterwards we could feather him 把他毛了, toss him into the river."

"唉呀, 把他做了不簡單 ai-yah, doing him in would not be easy. He comes and goes on that big fire-wheel boat. But you are the stove-keeper, and you make the decisions. Tell me what we should do, and I'll do it."

Lao Lin did not protest the price of one tael per day for two days' use of the junk offered by the clearinghouse clerk, but he had another objection.

"Junk man," Old Huang said, "he say mus' go temple, ask god if now good time."

Lao Lin said that when he returned from the temple later that night he would hang three white lanterns from his mast if the signs were bad, or three red lanterns from his mast if the signs were good and he accepted the offer of the foreigner. Then he would bring his junk out to the steamer.

2

Confucius settled in to pass the night in the flow above Silver Island. Fletcher's shore party came back from Chenkiang without incident, after returning to the clearinghouse and fetching the Little Mandarin and his guards. Aboard the steamer, Mr. Yang's freight of silver ingots and copper coin was unloaded and locked into the heavy safe in the captain's cabin. Later on that moonless evening, the captain and his officers convened again in the wheelhouse, where conversation turned once more to the rebellion, while a watch of Manilamen paced the decks below. Just above the northern horizon, bright Jupiter took sleepy Venus to couch beneath the pale rings of Saturn.

"Ever met any of these rebel kings," Fletcher said, "*wang*s, I guess they're called?"

"The coolie kings?" Ghent said. "No, and I can't say as I want to, neither. Vicious lot o' cutthroats. What you read about 'em comes mostly from the *Herald*. Was one book a few years back – *History of the Insurrection in China*, as I recall. There's a tattered old copy in my cabin, if you want to look it over. Doesn't have much after the rebels took Nanking. Hasn't been a lot to write about until now, I guess, they've been so quiet up there, if you don't count them massacring each other. The book's a mish-mash, but some facts stated there are worth knowin'."

"You know more about them, don't you, more than they know in the treaty ports?"

"Sure, this worthless pilot and me, we keep our noses to the wind when we're upriver. There's a passel o' them kings, hundreds."

Ghent held forth for the next hour on the rebel kings and their command of the countryside on both sides of the river, until Old Huang tapped Fletcher on the shoulder and pointed out the wheelhouse window. Across the harbor, three red lanterns dangling from the mast of a wharf-boat. The red lights started to sway as Lao Lin sculled his junk out from the bund and started across toward *Confucius*.

"Vincente, the junk from Chenkiang has started over to us. Best alert your sentries not to shoot at her."

Vincente went on deck to make ready for the junk's arrival, and the rest of the wheelhouse rabble dispersed shortly after. Rope fenders were let down and the boarding ladder dropped. A beam of lantern light from *Confucius* cut through the dark night and picked out the junkman at the stern-sweep. He hailed the steamer, sheered over to her side forward of the huge paddlewheel, bumped against her fenders, and threw lines up to her deck. Secure beside the looming black hulk of the steamer, the little wharf-boat snuggled up against *Confucius* like a piglet against a warm porker. Fletcher and Old Huang climbed down to the junk, where they were greeted noisily by Lao Lin, his wife, child and barking dog, and put on stools around the charcoal brazier under sallow light from paper lanterns hung on the mainmast. The wife stoked the flames, then went to the house and brought back a bottle of Chinese liquor and poured it out into tiny cups.

"乾杯 *kan-pei*, dry cup!" the junkman blurted, downing the drink with a flourish and holding the empty cup out upside down. Mrs. Lin shook her head and retreated into the house with the child and the dog. Crewmen leaned over the steamer rail and grinned with anticipation. Fletcher looked down into the depths of the thimbleful of clear liquid wondering if there truly was a bottom to it.

"*Kan-pei, kan-pei*," the junkman said, coaxing him.

"Lao Huang, what is this stuff?"

Old Huang sniffed his cup and smiled, but only touched his cup to his lips.

"Callum *mao-t'ai chiu* 茅臺酒, Fetchawood. Dis belly good glog!"

"Grog? Where did you learn to say grog? And I see you're not drinking it."

"My no dlinkee likker, Fetchawood. You longtime savvy my no dlinkee."

"*Kan-pei, kan-pei*," the junkman urged, waving his upside down cup.

Fletcher sniffed the brew and fumes raced into his head and made his eyes water, but could not place the musty scent.

"You plentee blave man, Fetchawood. Blave sailah-man can dlinkee, my tinkee."

"Hero, you think? Well, can it be worse than keelhauling? Here goes." Fletcher downed the drink is one swallow and instantly decided it *was* worse than keelhauling. Liquid fire seared his mouth and throat. A fireball descended past his lung and heart to his stomach, setting aflame every organ it surged past.

"Whew!" he finally managed to say, and would have sworn blue flame leapt from his mouth. Guffaws drifted down from the crewman above. When he could see again through his tears, Fletcher gallantly held out his cup upside down and muttered "*gonebay*. No wha... wha... wonder the cups are so tiny."

The junkman promptly refilled his own and Fletcher's cups.

"Is the second one any easier?"

Old Huang just laughed, which made the junkman laugh, which made the crewmen laugh. Fletcher decided the second cup *was* easier, if only because his mouth and throat were already numb from the first cup. This ritual was repeated several times and shortly the junkman became more voluble.

"This foreigner is not so bad," he said, Old Huang interpreting.

"Tell him I'd rather drink paint thinner," Fletcher said.

"Yes, I know," the junkman said. "Paint thinner's good, too."

"Ask him where he's from," Fletcher said, "and do they all drink this stuff?"

"Call me Lao Lin. I was born in Wu-hsi, just down the canal, by Lake T'ai."

Lao Lin kept Fletcher's little cup full and made Fletcher keep pace with him. The junkman wore a jacket with sleeves cut off at the shoulder – Fletcher noticed dim tattoos on each upper arm.

"What do his tattoos mean?"

Old Huang hesitated to ask. They were criminal brands, not tattoos.

"What did he say?" Lao Lin asked.

"Ah, please do not take offense," Old Huang said, "but he asks about your...tattoos."

"Oh, yes," Lao Lin said, setting down his cup and self-consciously placing his hands over the burns. "I forgot about them."

"It's no matter," the pilot said quickly.

"No, no. If I don't tell him now, you'll have to tell him later. Best let me tell it." He pointed to his right shoulder. "This one says rapacious criminal 蠹犯. And the other one says wicked clerk 奸胥."

"They brand criminals like that?" Fletcher said.

"Not usually." Lao Lin said.

The junkman moved his stool to where he could lean back against the mainmast and poured more *mao-t'ai*. Gesturing for them to come closer, he poured another for Fletcher, who guessed that the opaque white bottle was now half-empty and wondered if they would soon be telling time by bottles of firewater consumed. The crewmen aboard *Confucius* drifted away, leaving only the watch on deck. By fits and starts the three-way conversation lumbered along, like the earlier conversation with the pirate-suppressing mandarin aboard *Confucius*, and Fletcher grasped what he thought was a tolerable rendering of the junkman's story.

Lao Lin remembered his family's land was difficult to both cultivate and harvest, but his father could gather a little cotton by each Autumn Festival. With spinning and weaving cloth, they had enough to exchange for rice and get back the family's winter clothes from pawnshops. But when Ch'ing-ming – the tomb sweeping festival – arrived in the spring, they had to pawn the family's clothes again to plant a new crop of cotton.

"People think that farming near a large lake, such as Lake T'ai, must be very good," Lao Lin said, "but if the streams are not kept flowing and the dikes are not repaired, the water cannot come to the land. That kind of land keeps people poor."

After many years of neglect, the water officials 水官, finally dredged the Huang-p'u River, and Su-chou Creek, and the streams and channels near his family's land.

"Now the same land made people rich. We grew black-seed cotton 黑核花, which had a high yield of fine, soft fiber and was very good for spinning yarn and weaving cloth. From that time, the junkman's family followed the path to riches. As poor farmers, they acquired adjoining plots with access to water and became rich farmers. They became farmer-merchants when they hired help and sent Lao Lin on rounds to collect raw cotton from other farmers, and cotton cloth to sell in the local markets. Finally, they acquired more land, rented the land to tenants, and became farmer-landlords.

"Father's sons now had time to be educated in the classics. Oldest brother passed the exams and became an official. But I repeatedly failed the exams, and finally gave up and became a yamen clerk at Wu-hsi. During my five years there, I became rich taking bribes for transacting business, exorbitant fees for handling lawsuits, and payments to release innocent people I myself accused and arrested. Most of my money I hid away or invested – I bought a pawnshop in a nearby town, and I loaned my wife's brother money to buy cargo junks. Then disaster struck."

Rebels swarming over Chiang-nan forced Lao Lin's parents to give up their land and flee for safety, stopping in Chen-chiang. His oldest brother was impeached for malfeasance in office, reduced in rank, and dismissed from his appointment. Then the magistrate of Lao Lin's yamen was impeached for consorting with prostitutes and was demoted, sentenced to sixty blows of the heavy bamboo, a month wearing the cangue, and deportation. A new magistrate audited the yamen finances and discovered some of Lao Lin's embezzlement – a greedy collaborator in the yamen sold him out. So now, the harsh Manchu legal code 大清律例 finally caught up with Lao Lin himself. He was dismissed from the yamen, prosecuted as a "wicked clerk," sentenced to sixty strokes of the heavy bamboo, and penal servitude for one year.

To alleviate the beating with a heavy bamboo, he paid a fewer-stroke fee 少打錢, of four hundred taels – ten taels for each stroke – to secretly reduce the strokes to twenty. He paid a light-beating fee 輕打錢, to reduce the force of the remaining strokes. But when he refused to pay more fees, the runners burnt the characters for "wicked clerk" into one shoulder with a red-hot iron. Then he was charged paper-and-ink fees by the clerks, food-and-water fees and cell-sweeping fees by the jailers, and shoe-and-sock fees by the runners. When at last he had no more ill-gotten gains to hold back, he was forced to sign over ownership of the pawnshop and, out of pure malice, his other shoulder was branded with "rapacious criminal."

Fletcher had long since called for **AHEAD SLOW** on the bottle of *mao-t'ai* and, taking his cue from Old Huang, stopped emptying his cup. By that time, Lao Lin hardly noticed, being three sheets to the wind himself, and simply kept pouring his own. The story ended when he slumped senseless against the mast. His wife appeared, and together they all lifted the junkman into the little house, then Old Huang helped the none-too-steady Fletcher negotiate the boarding ladder back up to the steamer's deck. The junkman's wife came out, called to the steamer watch to cast off her lines, sculled the junk off a short distance toward the current, heaved to, and by herself set her anchors for the night.

3 When Fletcher struggled out of his berth and made his way through the bright, piercing light to the pitching deck of *Confucius*, he found the wharf-boat riding quietly at anchor a little way off the steamer's rail under a casual watch of Sharps carbines. Aboard their junk, Lao Lin, his wife, child and dog huddled around a charcoal brazier heating rice gruel and frying dough sticks, their happy prattling punctuated by an occasional yip from the chow-chow at long-nosed river dolphins 白鱀豚, blowing under the junk's bow. Further off, mists swirled about each end of the anchorage like a down of white feathers.

Fletcher shuffled into the saloon and made for the coffeepot, then took a seat opposite the captain, who was finishing his breakfast.

"Welcome back aboard, Mr. Wood," Ghent said. "Nice of you to join us this morning, or do you plan to return to your bunk? You look ready for your coffin."

"Oh, captain. Quietly, please. This morning sounds are like the blasts of steam whistles in my ears."

"I'd've thought you too smart to get drunk with a Chinaman."

"That firewater creeps up slowly and ambushes a man."

"Well, coffee up. You have duties to perform."

"Are we going over to the canal?"

"Not from here. Like I thought, entrance here's still too silted up. Every winter, when the water falls, that stretch beneath the town wall opposite the British concession silts up. Vincente couldn't find five feet most places. Sampans get in, not many junks. We'll drop back downriver the five miles to Tantu and see how much water the noontime flood brings. From there it's less than a half mile to the canal, then mebbe eight or ten miles to Tanyang. However, like I said before, we'll not find eight feet of water in most places along there, so I'm keeping my money in my pocket."

"But won't there be at least six hours of high water? Higher than usual on a flood tide with spring flows. Water and time enough to get to Tanyang and back."

"You've not had enough coffee yet, mister. Higher water lowers the bridges."

Confucius got underway just after 7:00am, coming about around Silver Island with Lao Lin's junk in her wake. A brisk east wind cleared the fog and shoved the rising tide up against the downstream flow hard enough to raise whitecaps and quash the current. The steamer had to burn nearly twice the coal to maintain eight knots, and had the junk not found refuge from the force of the wind just aft of *Confucius* she would have quickly fallen off. When she could no longer keep up, a line was thrown to her and she was towed the rest of the way. They still made Tantu in less than an hour, anchoring out of the stream near the Tantu canal. The junk came around into the lee of the steamer.

Fletcher and Old Huang went aboard Lao Lin's junk and arranged for him to enter the channel at Tantu and sound the depths out to the canal proper. When the junk reappeared an hour later, Fletcher and Old Huang went back aboard but, before they could ask about depths and bridges, the junkman flatly refused to go back into the Tantu canal. Rebel troops, he said, were swarming all along the canal between Nanking and Tanyang – anyone taking the Tantu canal toward Tanyang would be caught in front of the advancing rebel army and surely be taken for spies and slaughtered.

Fletcher and Old Huang reported the junkman's story to Captain Ghent.

"Captain," Fletcher said, "since the junkman won't go, there seems little choice but to take *Confucius* in as far as possible."

"Can't do it," Ghent said. "Even if the way was clear and the water deep, it would be insane to just waltz right into the path of the rampaging rebel army."

"But did you not say that *Confucius* could go amongst the rebels and send them scurrying with one shot from her 32-pounder? That has not changed, Captain – you most surely are the one adversary on the river who could hold them off."

"Now don't you try to soft-soap me with *that* blarney! No 100,000 rebels are going to tremble before a single gun. Think of Gulliver tied down by Lilliputians!"

"Well, I still must go there. Hell, that is what Takee is paying us for."

He's not paying you yet, son, thought Ghent. Not me, neither. You want to kick up a big shindy to impress Takee Bank, that's your affair. Why should I take the risk so you can be a hero?

"Offer more money," Ghent said. "Promise an exclusive, lifetime contract from Takee Bank to carry wool mungo and marmalade upriver from now to kingdom come."

Fletcher and Old Huang offered the junkman two taels, three taels, then five taels a day plus a twenty-tael bonus, to go to Tanyang. Lao Lin just shook his head. Then his wife said something Old Huang could not understand, and Lao Lin brightened a little.

"There's a better way," Lao Lin said. "We avoid the fighting if we go up on the other side of Tanyang."

"We know all the streams over to the canal," the junkman's wife said. "And we'll take your last offer of five taels a day and a twenty-tael bonus, *if* you will go our way."

"Of course," Lao Lin said. "We can get to Tan-yang from the north on the Chia-chiang River 夾江河, along the west side of the Great Sand Island 大沙洲, and the Chiu-ch'ü River 九曲河 from below the town of Yang-chung 楊中市 on Great Sand Island."

"Chia-chiang River," Old Huang said, "mebbe you callum Littee Yangtze?"

"East of Tanyang, would we not meet imperial deserters?" Fletcher said.

"Some. Bring your fire-wheel boat as far as possible for protection, and we will continue on my boat, carrying your men with those fast-firing foreign guns to scare the imps away. Imperial troops will be as afraid of your fire-wheel boat as they are of rebels." And with luck, thought Lao Lin, maybe the rebels can find a way to trap your fire-wheel boat in a shallow channel and massacre all of you.

Back aboard the steamer, Fletcher and Old Huang searched their charts the passage described by Lao Lin. Along the western and southern shore of Great Sand Island, there was a narrow channel with depths of two to eight fathoms – fifteen to forty-eight feet. Called the Chia-chiang River by the junkman, and the Shayaon River on the chart, the passage separated Great Sand Island from the mainland and skirted the island town of Yang-chung, but there was no stream running southwest to Tanyang.

"Not on the chart!" the captain said, fuming. "You got a screw loose to take the word of just any flimflammer about some pissy little creek you've never seen before and isn't on your chart. Who the hell is this suck-egg houn' dog anyway? You spend a few hours drinking yourselves blind on Chinee tanglefoot and now you're friends for life?"

"Well, he's Takee's man, that's all I know about him." Fletcher was less rattled by the captain's abuse than embarrassed for Old Huang. Ghent would say anything in front of anyone. No wonder he was a pariah in the concessions, banished to wander on this river. Imagine the pilot staying with him for so long – Lao Huang seems impervious to the old man, waterproofed, Ghent-proofed. So I suppose the pilot's regard for the mate remains unruffled. Yet the old bugger's authority must dominate, exist alone and supreme, with none other acknowledged. A Lilliputian Ahab. A small-beer Bligh.

"The junkman's offhand description of the locale matches the chart – that's evidence that his claim to know this place is not just arrogant swash."

A chill like frost smoke filled the wheelhouse. Ghent stiffened, balled a fist, and glared at Fletcher. Fletcher glared back. Old Huang turned to look out the window.

"You wantchee me go on deck, Cap'n?"

洋神 *Yang Shen*　　　　　　　　　　　　　　　　　　　　　*James Lande* 藍德

A spate of acid retorts sped through Ghent's mind before he remembered with a spasm of remorse, if not repentance, the incident of the lorcha on the river, and his rush to abandon the ship, and the conversation that never took place in his cabin. Ambivalence crowded the anger from his mind. He hated the mate for his hold over him, but he begrudgingly prized the mate for his presence of mind and panache. With patent reluctance, the captain stood down.

"No, peckerwood. Here's your place: the wheelhouse. *Mate* goes on deck."

"That's right Captain. I am the mate," Fletcher said quietly. Ghent has to be knocked up the side of his thick head with a shovel to get his attention. Fletcher went to the door.

"And I still need your pilot for my interpreter when I go aboard this junk," he said over his shoulder. "To Great Sand Island."

"Take him then. Vincente will do me as well."

"And I'd like six of his Manilamen as an armed escort."

"Take 'em, damn it. Just bring 'em back alive!"

Lao Lin's junk started downriver with Fletcher aboard, and Old Huang and six steamer crewmen armed with pistols and carbines. As the junk swept past *Confucius*, Fletcher stared up at the glum face of the captain frowning down on him through a reflection of scudding white clouds in the glass of a wheelhouse window. Mate on *Confucius* was a temporary hindrance, and soon Fletcher would throw this bunch over and strike out on his own. No need to antagonize Ghent any more than necessary.

Lao Lin mounted two *yuloh* oars at the bow and Fletcher ordered the crewmen to man them, so they were able to make almost five knots by his reckoning, raised Great Sand Island in less than two hours, and came about into the Chia-chiang. Fletcher and Old Huang stayed with the junkman and his wife at the stern, where Lao Lin pushed and pulled at the aft *yuloh*. The child sat in the shade of the house, tethered to an iron ring in the deck, and tended by her chow-chow *amah*.

A northwest breeze cooled the warming day, fanned the spritsail, and assisted the *yuloh* oar sweep the junk over slack water. The south bank was fallow and featureless; a flatland repeatedly built up and leveled by millennia of inundation, by the advance and retreat of the river onto the shore. Further inland from the south bank, a range of low hills lay in the shadow of massive white cumulus drifting above and, in the distance behind the hills, two squat mountains emerged from haze. The river was about a thousand yards wide and ran southeast toward the two mountains. The earth above the bank on each side of the river was pale green with new growth.

"Cotton," Lao Lin told Old Huang. "Like my family used to grow." Lao Lin gazed out over the farmland, shading his eyes against the glare. Where the bank dipped low, broad fields of newly planted cotton lay over the land like a soft coverlet. "Closer to the river here, you can see the furrows ploughed in the earth and deep channels between, where we chopped the weeds day after day. We spread as many as sixty squares of bean-cake over each acre for fertilizer, so the plants would grow to just the right size. Our fields did not stink of night soil – they smelled of fragrant *tofu* instead."

Old Huang struggled with his mangled English to convey Lao Lin's jargon, and Fletcher filled in the lapses with the little he knew about cotton farming in the American south. It seemed to him that, as a place for growing cotton, the Yangtze delta was not unlike the Mississippi delta, and he was about to ask if Chinese had spinning wheels when, suddenly, he heard the scream of a distant steam whistle – *Confucius* was approaching from astern.

"You lost, Captain Ghent?"

"Not as lost as you'll be if you go in there alone."

"Your concern is touching, Captain."

"Takee'd want to know why I let you get your throat cut."

"Well, *Confucius* is a comfort."

"Vincente looked the charts again. This stretch is all right. Wide and deep."

"I won't ask you to take her into the tight places."

"Well, I won't holler till she's squeezed pretty hard."

Bluffed you old man. You just can't allow yourself to be shown up to Takee, can you? If you had better sense, you'd just forget what happened on the river, because you'd know I would never mention the incident. You're the victim of your own cantankerous temper, hoisted by your own petard.

Confucius took her crew back aboard and continued on south behind the junk. The two mountains grew larger as the steamer approached the southern horizon. After another hour, *Confucius* saw the junk veer right into a narrow opening.

"How's my steamer supposed to turn around in there, mister?"

"It was supposed to be a river. Maybe we should sound the passage from the junk?"

"Day's half over, mister. Sound the channel now, and you'll be amongst the Philistines in the dark when you come back from Tanyang."

"You'll have to reverse engines and back out of there," Fletcher said. "A narrow stern-wheeler would do better."

"Sternwheeler! Sternwheeler be damned. It would not be the first time this old girl has backed her way out of a jam, if you'll recall the Langshan crossing."

"Wide river, strong current. This piddly little creek could get quite crowded."

"So it might. Well, as you reminded me earlier, you're the mate."

"Yes?"

"So, shag a lead and start heaving!"

4 Mulberry trees crowded the entrance to the stream, willows brushed slender stems over the water's surface, and the steep banks were thick with wild clematis and berry brambles. *Confucius* trod lightly onto this new threshold. The stream was perhaps 125 feet wide and raised at least ten feet over its bed by spring rains and the flood tide. Captain Ghent took to following in the wake of Lao Lin's junk, passing between sampans heaving lustily at their sweeps to avoid the huge steamer, expecting that the junkman would lead the way along the deepest channels and around threatening obstacles. Refugees with possessions piled on their backs or in barrows crowded along the levees, hurrying away from Tanyang. Occasional detachments of imperial cavalry rode past toward Tanyang.

The battle still rages, thought Fletcher, if the soldiers haven't yet fled.

The steamer churned up brown froth as it scraped over the muddy bottom between eroded banks and fallen tree trunks, twisting around shoaled sand and submerged debris, even the skeleton of a stranded junk. She went into mud several times, but was able to back out and go around. Some turns were so narrow and sharp that *Confucius* dug her stern into embankments and collapsed walls of earth into the water.

"This is insanity," the captain muttered. "If the river drops now, we'd be stuck here for who knows how long, just like that wreck we passed. Months maybe, until there's another rainstorm upriver."

They passed several tributary streams where the steamer might reverse direction. After another two miles, they came to a stone bridge across the stream that joined a village spread out along both banks. The junk quickly unstepped her mast to pass under, but the bridge was too low for the steamer, and she came to a quick halt atop a brown collar of frothy water. Villagers dropped whatever they were doing and hurried over to gawk at the foreign fire-wheel boat. Some grasped the threat and called to their friends to climb quickly onto the bridge, where they set to waving and shouting at *Confucius*.

Abruptly, Ghent was no longer faced with the choice of destroying the bridge to get the steamer past, not unless he was prepared to massacre a village. *Confucius* put Fletcher, Old Huang and the six crewmen aboard the junk, then started up her engine **AHEAD SLOW** and let the current gently drift her stern back down toward the last tributary she had passed. Abreast of the tributary channel, Ghent rang for **AHEAD HALF** to suspend *Confucius* in the current while he read the water. The channel was full and fast, and about eighty feet wide where it entered the stream.

"Vincente," he shouted out a wheelhouse window, "heave the lead."

Ghent threw the rudder over to starboard and let the current carry her stern closer to the channel opening, but he could see nothing that told him the depth there or what obstructions might lie beneath the surface. Vincente heaved the lead as far as he could and signaled the captain when he felt it touch bottom. The channel appeared to have some depth, and the line did not catch on a sunken tree. Effluent from the fast-flowing channel scoured the bottom, and undermined and collapsed the opposite embankment, widening the stream. Ghent drifted the steamer across to the opposite bank.

"Vincente, what are the depths on this side?"

Vincente called out fifteen feet, twelve feet, and then ten feet when *Confucius* was only two yards from the embankment. Ghent took her back to center stream and gazed up the channel. It appeared comparatively free of debris. If *Confucius* could shove her stern up into the channel about forty feet without digging her paddlewheels into mud, he could let the current bring her about and swing her bow downstream.

Lao Lin's junk continued on southwest, then west, toward Tanyang. The steamer crewmen were put to work again sweating at the forward *yuloh*s to sustain headway against the current, which was growing hourly with the ebb of the tide. The two squat mountains were still visible off to larboard through the trees. In some places, the mulberries and willows thinned and the stream opened up. The countryside flattened out into broad stretches of ripening cotton.

As the junk approached Tanyang, the villages they passed beside or through became noisier with surging crowds of frantic people, and the bridges more choked with refugees. Closer still to Tanyang, the stream filled with small river craft fleeing toward Yang-chung and larger, more unruly crowds swarmed along the levees. Fletcher and Old Huang witnessed many melancholy scenes of refugees struck down in the road by imperial cavalry, the weak and elderly robbed by brigands of their few trinkets, people thrown over embankments senseless or dead, and barrows and carts of possessions thrown down after them. Where the brush cleared, the exposed embankments appeared streaked with alabaster clay, and cluttered with white sticks, stones and broken pottery tumbling down the slopes. Through his telescope, Fletcher saw that the white rubble was a mix of human skulls and bones, and the alabaster clay was bone powder and ash.

Further upstream, the sky began to fill with black smoke. The reports of cannon and shouts of armies eddied in the wind. Bugle calls and drumbeats echoed across the water. The gray stone of the Tanyang town wall rose slowly above a horizon obscured by swirling dust and smoke. The riverbank fell away and the ground before the wall soared up bristling with the garish banners of the rebel army. Columns of rebel infantry advanced and wheeled into position. Rebel cavalry charged across the field of battle.

Cannons fired, rockets flared, musketry rattled, and men shouted and screamed. The air filled with the acrid smells of scorched wood, burnt powder, and seared flesh.

Lao Lin and his wife were first stunned and then terrified by the abrupt appearance of war at their very feet. Fletcher gave a shout and waved toward the south bank, across the stream from Tanyang, to stop the junk before going too far into the melee. The junkman's wife recovered her senses, picked up her child, and ran for the safety of the house. Lao Lin seemed about to follow her, then mastered his terror and bent over his oar. He wildly sculled the junk to larboard into a slow eddy in shallow water, just avoiding the chaos of rafts and sampans splashing frantically to escape from the armies before the town wall.

"*Venga aqui*, come here!" Fletcher shouted to the crewman at the bow. He gathered them together, with Lao Lin and Old Huang, out of sight behind the junk's house. They warily peered over the house and watched the battle like groundlings at an Elizabethan stage play. Fletcher walked back to the stern from where he could more clearly observe the Taiping troop disposition and engineering work.

They faced a section of town wall about four hundred yards long and thirty feet high, and outside the wall at one end, there was a stockade. The rebel effort was concentrated on a large iron-studded wooden gate in the town wall, before which they were excavating a low breastwork and several trenches. Light iron cannon atop the breastwork fired at the gate, with little effect, and rockets flew in the direction of the wall and stockade. Rafts lying across the moat did temporary duty as pontoon bridges.

Units of several thousand rebels waited behind the breastwork, beyond range of archers atop the wall. Each side appeared to have a few men armed with matchlocks or muskets who merely fired at random. Lines of rebel foot kicked up white bone dust along the opposite levee as they were marched into position. Mongol ponies harnessed to gun carriages emerged from behind the rebel ranks and took up a position facing the gate. The battery consisted of three 6-pounder field guns, attended by rebel gunners, but commanded by an officer in Western dress. The artillery went to work on the gate and adjacent wall with effective fire, but the guns were too light to do much damage quickly.

Flags waved. A unit of several hundred rebel infantry armed with swords and spears suddenly rose up from behind the breastwork and stormed toward the gate, with guidons flashing, for a *coup de main* – a direct frontal assault – while a reserve of musketeers opened fire at the walls to cover the assault. The infantry was led by a large black flag, and at the rear there followed a rank with drawn swords. When several soldiers backed away from the attack and sought to flee, they were caught and instantly beheaded by the assassins of the rear rank.

The rebels advanced to the moat against a barrage of arrows and arrow-headed rockets, and either crossed over the rafts or leapt into the moat. Their reserve failed to follow on, the infantry advanced beyond their covering fire, and the men who crossed the moat were cut down. Those in the moat were protected because the wall had no flanking embrasures. Unable to reach the rebel infantry with arrows or musket fire, the defenders threw stinkpots over the wall down onto the scarp and into the moat, where they exploded in bursts of flame and asphyxiating fumes.

Chinese walls, thought Fletcher, round and square, have no flanking defenses built into them like star or polygon-shaped forts with protruding bastions. Towers give cover for bows and muskets, but are too flimsy to mount guns. The only outworks are wooden stockades. When Chinese want to protect themselves, they think first of a wall, around a city, or across the steppes. Their notions of constructing and besieging fortifications seemed to have changed not a whit since the middle ages. There must be a wall in their minds, as well, one they cannot see over, fortifying their veneration of the obsolete.

洋神 *Yang Shen* *James Lande* 藍德

    Unexpectedly, the reserve of rebel musketeers finally leapt up, driven by new officers and their command flags, and sprinted along the approaches to closer positions, from where they directed enfilade fire against the battlements. Fletcher thought the rebel muskets would clear the wall of imps, but suddenly the imperial soldiers just disappeared from the battlements. One moment they were there, the next moment they were not, as if en masse they had deserted the wall. With no more arrows or stinkpots raining down upon them, the remaining 100 or so infantry were able to clamber out of the moat and retreat to safety behind their lines.

    For the first time, Fletcher considered Chinese walled cities from the point-of-view of siege craft. In all his layovers at Shanghai, he had never thought much about the city's wall and moat as a fortification. In the context of Vauban's old book on siege craft, a Chinese walled town was of little consequence compared to European fortifications. There was no glacis – no wide slope beyond the moat, engineered to protect the foot of a wall from enemy fire and expose advancing attackers on the open approach – and so no 3rd parallel was needed. In Vauban's scheme, an attack against a wall moved closer through three parallels: the 1st parallel was the farthest out, the 2nd parallel advanced halfway under cover by the digging of trenches, and the 3rd parallel arrived at the foot of the glacis. Against bows and muskets, Fletcher needed only guns of sufficient power – a Chinese wall could be quickly breached from the 1st parallel. The rebel 6-pounders would need many hours and much ammunition to blast through the Tanyang wall, 30 feet thick and of rammed earth faced with a foot or two of square stone blocks. A 32-pounder, or rifled artillery, would break through much more quickly.

    Imperial cavalry galloped out from inside the stockade, followed by a thousand or more shouting foot soldiers, and drew up with a clamor of blaring horns and rattling drums in ranks along the front of the stockade. Detachments of more imperial horse came up from several directions to reinforce their line. From the center of the field, a counter-cacophony of horns and drums started up when companies of rebel pike and musket wheeled out from behind the breastwork and dashed into positions directly in front of the imps.

    The rebel 6-pounders turned toward the stockade. The opposing forces stood there grappled by anger, pennants and ensigns flashing, horns strident and drums pounding, ponies prancing and men shouting and waving their weapons. A high-pitched command came from the artillery battery and the field guns fired, followed by a volley of rebel musketry. The artillery shot exploded against the stockade wall and musket balls fell man and horse but, to Fletcher's amazement, not one arrow flew and not one shot was fired in return by the imps – the entire imperial force simply flew apart and scattered in all directions away from the field. They ran away! They all spun on their heels like a flock of frightened birds turning together on wing and, in an astounding display of cowardice before the enemy, completely deserted the field. Fletcher had never seen anything like it – not in the Crimea, not in Mexico, nor in Bolivia or Peru. If this was the empire's only defense, he thought, then the Manchu were doomed like Sodom and would be annihilated by the Taiping. Have I chosen the losing side, he wondered?

    Fletcher slowly moved the telescope from right to left noting what kind of soldiers served under the different rebel banners. Unexpectedly, the circle of his lens was filled by the glaring face of a wraith with intense black eyes and heavy black brows under a curious sort of coronet with a ruby flanked by gold medallions. Fletcher flinched at the sudden apparition and lowered the telescope. The wraith was a rebel officer. His detachment of horse kicked up clouds of white dust around him as it reigned in atop the narrow levee opposite Lao Lin's junk. The officer wore a simple scarlet quilted jacket, scarlet hood, and the undress coronet. A Tartar bow and a quiver of arrows were lashed to his saddle, and a long sword set with bright green jade pommel hung from his belt. The hooves of his skittish Mongol pony kicked up swirls of dust from the sun-bleached human bones and broken skulls that covered the slope of earth down to the water, the neglected remains of victims of the warring emperors of China.

Li Hsiu-ch'eng saw the small, dark foreigner peering at him through a polished brass telescope. He was puzzled that anyone would want to see him that closely, and wondered why a foreigner would be at Tanyang on a Chinese junk. He looked straight at the man, with a brazen glare that he intended should melt the foreigner's brass devil-glass. The man lowered the glass and stared back. Now the Loyal King saw a dark glow of blue in the foreigner's eyes, and the form of an individual took shape, a man of strong character and penetrating vision. There rose in him the urge to kill this man, whose devil-glass may have seen within him, and discovered the secrets of his heart.

Fletcher heard an order given. A horseman descended to the water's edge.

"你們是甚麼人, 這有甚麼事?" he called across the water.

"Lao Huang," Fletcher said, "what'd he say?" Fletcher wondered if the coronet meant he was a rebel king, a *wang*. The man had a straight nose and an olive complexion that to Fletcher made him look as much Greek or Italian as Chinese.

"Who you, what do here?" the flustered pilot said. The crewmen of *Confucius* jabbered excitedly about the sudden manifestation – a rebel king, or the devil incarnate?

The junkman almost called out a reply. He wanted to say "I am your brother, your *Ko-lao* elder brother, please do not harm my family and I will kill this foreigner!" But the noise and smoke and rebel cavalry so frightened him that he could not make any sounds come out of his mouth. He moved to the edge of the house and put his hand on the throwing knife inside his jacket. One throw, kill the foreigner. The longhaired brothers and the *Ko-lao* elders all will congratulate me.

"太平天國大忠王李秀成要知道," the officer screamed above the growing din. "The great Loyal King of the kingdom of T'ai-p'ing demands to know!"

"Fetchawood," the pilot hissed. "Dat Loyal King!"

Fletcher stepped to the rail of the junk, his attention captured entirely by the general Li Hsiu-ch'eng, the Loyal King. He seemed very young for a general. Don't we all, thought Fletcher. But, damn – right out of the Knights of the Round Table!

The junkman came from behind the house, up behind Fletcher. The pilot followed.

Li Hsiu-ch'eng's eyes narrowed in anger. He was about to reach for his bow and send an arrow into the impudent foreigner's heart, when a great shout of voices arose from the direction of Tanyang.

Fletcher started to say "Tell him...," but the Loyal King snapped a curt order, and the horseman turned away from the water's edge. In a few moments, the Loyal King and his riders all had disappeared off the levee toward the town in a cloud of white bone-dust thrown up by the hooves of their ponies.

他媽的 damn, thought the junkman! Don't ride away. Now they are all gone. They can no longer see me kill him.

Damn, thought Fletcher, I could have ended the threat to Shanghai right here and now by putting a pistol-ball into the head of that rebel general. Gone before I thought of it. Our first exchange, and no shots fired! Only curious glances, like dandies at a debutante's ball. If staring across a piece of water at an enemy like Fokie Tom or the Loyal King won battles, I'd sure be a general and a hero by now.

"You wantchee see lebal king, Fetchawood," Old Huang whished. "Close 'nuff?"

"Much too close, my tinkee," Fletcher said. "Let's get the hell away from here before they come back." He turned around to find the junkman standing at his back, his hand inside his jacket. "Lao Lin," he said. "Go back now."

洋神 *Yang Shen*   *James Lande* 藍德

"回去," the pilot said. "Go back."

Lao Lin hesitated, his black brows knitted by both fear and frustration, but at last he went to step his mainmast and set his spritsail, then returned to his oar at the stern and began sculling. Fletcher called to the crewmen to man the forward *yuloh*s, and together they brought the junk around into the clamor of refugee sampans and started downriver.

Fletcher heard pounding hooves and whirled about to see a dozen armor-clad horsemen above the embankment galloping for the retreating junk, charging down the path through the crowd of refugees, shouting wildly at them to clear a path, trampling any too slow to sidestep the wheezing ponies. As their mounts leapt across prostrate bodies, the riders yanked bows out of their sheaths.

"*Compañeros* fellows!" Fletcher cried out. "*Enemigos atrás* enemies behind!"

The Manilamen unshipped their oars, unslung their carbines, and leapt for cover behind the mainmast and the house, chambering rounds on the run. Fletcher saw the horsemen nock their arrows. He jumped to the stern *yuloh*, tugging his Colt Navy revolver out from under his coat.

"Lao Huang," he shouted, "take Lao Lin behind the house. Quickly."

On a clear stretch of road, the riders loosed a flight of arrows at the junk. The arrows thunked into the deck, and into the thin wall of the house. The junkman's wife screamed.

"Stay inside!" the junkman shouted. "Lie with the child under the big mat!"

The crewmen responded to the arrows with a volley of rifle fire that cloaked the junk in a cloud of white smoke, snapped tree branches and smashed into houses behind the horsemen, and pitched one rider into the dusty road. The downed rider disappeared beneath a knot of menacing bystanders that quickly tightened around him after the rebel cavalry passed. Spiders, Fletcher thought, to suck out the juices.

Now only Fletcher was exposed on deck, desperately hanging on to the stern *yuloh*, sweating profusely in the hot sun. One moment he was looking forward over the house, trying to keep the junk centered in the stream and moving with the current. The next moment, he was glancing across the stream and getting off another shot at the horsemen dashing pell-mell off the larboard quarter. Manilamen came to the rear of the house to give their first mate better cover. Fletcher squatted down behind the sweep. More arrows flew at the stern. One notched the sleeve of his frock coat.

"Stay down, *señor*!"

"I *am* staying down! Keep shooting!" The ponies can't keep up that pace forever, and the rifles must take their toll. What the Sam Hill's got 'em chasing after me? So much for the liturgy that the rebels want to be friends with Westerners.

Swiftly, Fletcher replaced the expended cylinder in his revolver.

The rebel horsemen raced along the embankment, scattering refugees and jumping obstacles to keep up with the fleeing junk. In the first village they came to – spread along both sides of the stream and joined by a bridge – Lao Lin bolted out from behind the house to strike his spritsail and pull down the mast. The clamor of pursuit echoed off the walls of the houses – the clatter of the ponies, the crash of flattened roadside stalls. One pony collided with a snack peddler's cart and tumbled to the ground in a tangle of flailing hooves, grilled sausage, fried dumplings, and dim sum. The next pony stumbled over the first and sent its rider flying over the embankment and into the stream.

Hard pressed just to stay in their saddles for much of the distance, the riders could not nock an arrow, and the *Confucius* riflemen hesitated to fire for fear of hitting people on the road. When the rebels' sweaty, foam-flecked ponies began to flag, the remaining horsemen dropped out of the chase, until the last rider clattered out to the middle of a stone bridge and loosed an arrow that fell short of the stern.

洋神 *Yang Shen*   James Lande 藍德

Fletcher thumbed back the hammer and took aim at him, raising his sights a smidgen for the distance. He was same horseman who had shouted the Loyal King's demand to know who Fletcher was. Fletcher thought he could see the rider's defiant expression, and judged he would face him and refuse to stand down, even if it meant death. Fletcher fired, but only after shifting the revolver away slightly. The ball struck up a bright flash of orange sparks beside to the rebel horseman where it glanced off the stone balustrade. Hell, Fletcher thought, you fellows gave a mighty chase, but none of us was hurt, not much anyway. That shot's just so you know your life's been spared.

As Fletcher watched the tableau of the rebel on the bridge recede, his anger surged. Getting soft, old man, he wondered? No, that one no longer posed any threat, no longer stood in my way. Many more will come athwart my hawse – cross my moorings. Those who do not stand aside, them I *will* cut down, with no regret.

5

"Looks like you ran into a war party," Captain Ghent said.

"Yeah. We have some arrows," Fletcher said, glancing along the length of Lao Lin's junk as it skirred on downstream. "Now, I just need a bow."

Ghent smiled. "Got to see some rebels?"

"Nobody'd believe what we saw. Tanyang's fallen."

"Figured as much, what with all the refugees."

"I see you got her turned around."

"Nothing to it. But the minute we faced downstream, we sorely wanted the 32-pounder pointing upstream. Got so more Tartar soldiers were comin' away from Tanyang than refugees, outnumbered 'em two or three to one. Running lickety-split for their lives, all over hell and half of Georgia, like they was chased by a corpse."

"That's how it was in town – imps just broke and ran when rebels charged."

"Them damn imp *braves* ain't worth shucks; not a goober peanut neither."

Lao Lin's junk continued downstream after putting Fletcher's party back aboard the steamer. At Great Sand Island, there was not enough light to go on safely, so they anchored mid-stream in the Little Yangtze, south of Yang-chung. Captain Ghent got Fletcher to tell him all that happened at Tanyang and, after mulling their choices over several fingers of brandy, agreed to stay on the river and follow the rebel advance.

"In light of the dismal imperial defense of Tanyang," Fletcher said, "I'm guessing the rebels will move much more quickly now. Changchow is next. Lao Lin says there's a Tsao River from Kiangyin, but it goes to Wuhsi, and we'd have to go back along the Grand Canal to get to Changchow. Other streams below Starling Island might go more directly. If Lao Lin can find a way in from the river to Changchow, I could wait and see if Changchow was the Loyal King's next objective and, if so, how long before it falls."

Log of Steamer CONFUCIUS, Shanghai Pirate Suppression Bureau

Date & Time	Location	Wind (est.)	Current	Speed	Cargo
Saturday May 19 1860 6:00pm	Great Sand Island, Kiangsu	SW 3 knots	2 knots	-	-

Mate and crew took junk over to Tanyang from river

Sunday morning *Confucius* dropped down past Starling Island behind the junk and stood by in deep water while Lao Lin searched along the shallows of the south bank for likely streams. Early in the hot afternoon, they sighted a trickle of sampans and junks standing out from one stream in particular and, by late afternoon, the trickle had turned to a flood. Lao Lin sculled over to *Confucius* to report that these craft were fleeing from the rebels advancing on Changchow. Fletcher decided he would go in to Changchow on the junk the next morning and, with the junk in her lee, *Confucius* settled out of the flow to sleep on the river another night.

洋神 *Yang Shen* *James Lande* 藍德

Log of Steamer CONFUCIUS, Shanghai Pirate Suppression Bureau

Date & Time	Location	Wind (est.)	Current	Speed	Cargo
Sunday May 20 1860 6:00pm	below Starling Island, Kiangsu	SW 3 knots	3 knots	-	-

The following day Fletcher delayed until close to noon, waiting on the tide, then took Old Huang and six crewmen dressed in Chinese clothes aboard Lin-ch'uan's junk and set off up the stream to Changchow. Many small craft came downstream, with all variety of passengers – refugees, officials, bandits, imperial soldiers. Fletcher stayed in the house much of the time to avoid attracting unnecessary attention. In Chinese clothes, the Manilamen did not look so different from Chinese and, after putting their rifles out of sight, they stayed on deck and sweated at the oars.

Miles before the Grand Canal, the western sky already was black with churning clouds of smoke. Smoke in the air joined with sounds of roaring cannon, shrill horns, banging drums, shouting men and all the other insane clamor of war. The roadway beside the stream swelled with fugitives, every manner of common folk, patricians and plebeians alike – as well as imperial soldiers stampeding away from the town, lions heedless of the lambs in step along the roadway beside them.

The stream finally came upon a slipway that crossed over to the Grand Canal. A small junk balanced on the top of the slipway, stern gallery swaying high in the air, about to slide down into the stream. Fletcher waved Lao Lin over to the west bank, they tied up, and Fletcher and Old Huang jumped ashore and walked to the top of the levee. War junks and sampans packed the canal. Not far off, the thirty-foot high gray stone face of the Changchow wall was surrounded on all sides by armies, rebel and imperial. On the plain before the town, countless rebels in brilliant colors massed together, several armies Fletcher estimated, with thousands of flags snapping in the breeze.

"The flags tell what armies are on the field. If I knew the flags better, I could tell you what *wang*s lead these armies before Changchow."

The imperial army was encamped outside the town gates, along the foot of the wall in rows and rows of tents behind numerous stockades large and small. Some of the stockades were on fire; a pall of black smoke smothered the town. Near a tall pagoda outside the east gate, a Buddhist monastery was in flames.

Imperial cavalry carrying burning brands dashed in among the houses below the wall, followed by imperial infantry, and set house after house on fire. The infantry prowled through the houses rounding up people that did not manage to escape and drove them shrieking into the town, past more soldiers coming out of the town toting pokes, pouches, and bags. It took Fletcher a few minutes to realize what was happening.

"What in blue blazes?"

Through his glass, Fletcher saw imperial soldiers coming and going through the east gate loaded down with loot of every description.

"What see, Fetchawood?" Fletcher handed the telescope to Old Huang.

"I'll be jiggered if the imperials are not looting and burning their *own* town! The town they are supposed to be protecting. Who on earth is in charge here? Isn't this where the viceroy has his yamen?"

Old Huang stood silently beside Fletcher for some time. The pungent stench of smoldering wood seemed different, as if ancient wood burned with an ancient smell.

"Dat why people hate sojah, Fetchawood. Any sojah. All sojah." They all are vermin, thought Old Huang, all are savage frogs, poisonous centipedes, and hungry vipers 都是蠹蟲都是猖狂蛤蟆惡毒蜈蚣饑餓毒蛇. You are no different, *yang-kuei-tzu*. Your army will pillage, rape and murder just the same as these vermin.

Tanyang and Changchow

洋神 *Yang Shen*   *James Lande* 藍德

"Look," Old Huang said, pointing with the telescope at a small bridge halfway between the canal and the town wall. Fletcher took the glass. A lone figure of a man in a long blue gown stood on the bridge watching the conflagration, now several miles wide and spreading across the outlying houses before him. People crying in terror fled in every direction, some carrying bundles on bamboo poles, others pushing wheelbarrows and carts, some not even fully dressed. Soldiers with swords drawn ran among the refugees, snatching away their bundles and cutting down the men, ripping the clothes off screaming women and dragging their bare bodies out of sight into empty houses, putting torches to doors and rafters and hurling firebrands through windows. A temple burst into flame. A rich man's villa kindled, and then ignited. The lone figure on the bridge turned away with his face in his sleeve. Obviously, he could not bear to watch.

"Dat you ahmee, Fetchawood?" the pilot hissed.

Fletcher turned on Old Huang. The pilot's eyes were brimming with tears.

"No." Fletcher looked straight into Old Huang's face. "No – no army of mine will ever do this." Fletcher slowly turned back to the gruesome field of battle before the wall of Changchow, loath to watch more.

"I will never allow this, never allow my soldiers to harm innocent people. As God is my judge, I will shoot dead without any hesitation any man of mine who does what you see being done here today."

Fletcher and Old Huang returned to Lao Lin's junk. The junk found its way back through the crisscrossing streams and arrived on the river at twilight, and Fletcher's party boarded *Confucius*. He reported to Captain Ghent that the rebels were attacking Changchow, and that they need wait only a short while for the emperor's own army to slaughter everyone in the town and burn it to the ground. Captain Ghent received the report without remark and ordered Fletcher to turn in. For all his animosity toward Fletcher, Ghent was still able to read pain in the somber eyes of his normally resilient first mate, and despair in the dejected expression of his usually jocular Chinese pilot.

Log of Steamer CONFUCIUS, Shanghai Pirate Suppression Bureau

Date & Time	Location	Wind (est.)	Current	Speed	Cargo
Monday May 21 1860 9:00pm	Kiangyin, Kiangsu	SW 3 knots	3 knots	-	-

Mate and crew took junk over to Grand Canal and Changchow from river

Confucius had only a few miles to make Kiangyin, so she spent the night in the deep water of a friendly anchorage. Ah-shan sculled out to the steamer with baskets of fruit and fried dumplings, waving and grinning at the Manilamen on watch. She sniffed at Lao Lin's upriver junk, then with a shout hauled on her sweep, came about, and returned to the Kiangyin bund singing the songs of mountain girls all the way.

"再見, 洋鬼子 see you again, foreign devil!"

The next morning *Confucius* paid off Lao Lin and returned to Shanghai.

Tanyang and Changchow   363

洋神 *Yang Shen*   *James Lande* 藍德

Dramatis Personae: Chapter 22

Li Wen-ping 李文炳	Soochow expectant *taotai*
Artemis L. Fuller	H. Fogg & Company purchasing agent

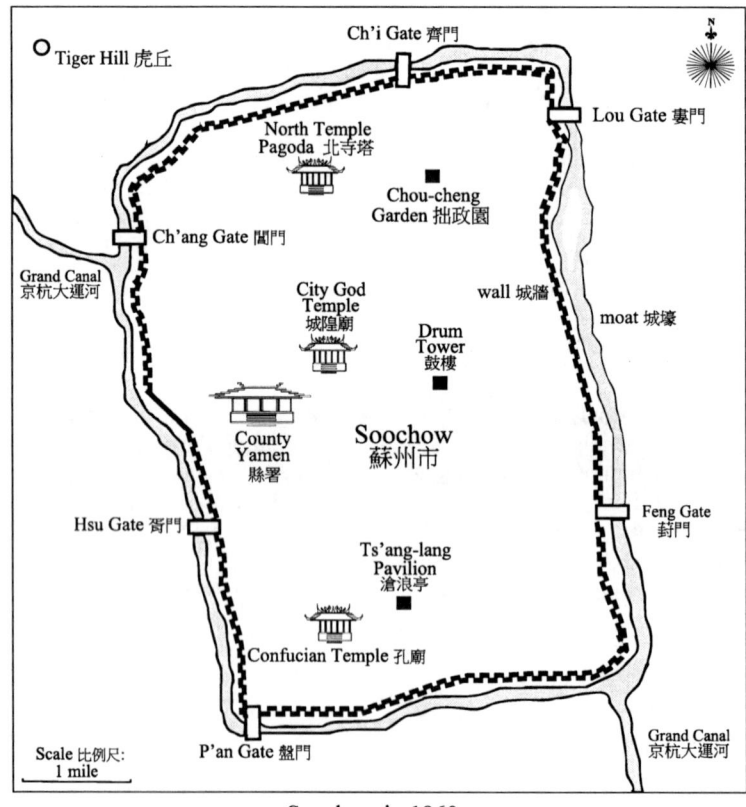

Soochow in 1860
(from Su-chou gazetteer, and present-day maps)

Treachery at Soochow

Chapter 22: Treachery at Soochow
Friday, June 1, 1860, 10:00am

> **Shanghai, 26ᵗʰ May, 1860**
> The Undersigned issue this Proclamation to tranquillize the minds of the people.
> Shanghai is a port open to foreign trade, and the native dealers residing therein have large transactions with the foreigners who resort to the place to carry on their business. Were it to become the scene of attack and of civil war, commerce would receive a severe blow, and the interests of those, whether foreign or native, who wish to pursue their peaceful avocations in quiet, would suffer great loss.
> The undersigned will therefore call upon the Commanders of Her Majesty's Naval and Military authorities to take proper measures to prevent…Shanghai from being exposed to massacre and pillage, and to lend…assistance to put down any insurrectionary movements among the ill-disposed, and to protect the city against any attack.
> Signed:
> **F. W. A. Blaine**, C.B., H.B.M. Minister Extraordinary and Minister
>   Plenipotentiary in China
> **Bourboulon**, *Envoy Extraordinairé et Ministre Plénipotentiaire de Sa*
>   *Majesté l'Empereur des Francais en Chine*

From the battlements of the Su-chou city wall, expectant *taotai* Li Wen-ping 李文炳 gazed northwest over a shimmering sea of rebel flags and banners – yellow, green, and red silk tossing and furling in the breeze like windblown waves. One comber after another, he thought, cresting up under the city wall and rolling back out into the swell of armies. Ling-yen Hill 靈岩山 and T'ien-p'ing Hill 天平山 in the west were green islands adrift in a sea of iridescent soldiers. Rebels came by foot and horseback along the road from Wu-hsi, and in thousands of boats southeast over the *Ching-hang Ta-yun-ho* 京杭大運河 – the name in Su-chou for the Grand Canal. He watched for the pennants of Li Hsiu-ch'eng – the Loyal King would decide the fate of Su-chou.

"李大老爺 Li *Ta-lao-yeh*, these T'ai-p'ing bandits will kill us all," Chou Wu said. "There are no other soldiers left to defend the city. How can we remain here ourselves?"

The expectant *taotai*, a 5th-rank official with a silver pheasant 白鵰 *pusa* and crystal button, was attended by Kuang-chou 廣州 hometown associates expectant prefect Ho Hsin-yi 何信義, and Chou Wu 周五, each in their robes of office with mandarin duck 鸂鶒 *pusa* and summer hats with plain gold button of 7th-rank officials. Waiting below for orders was the 500-strong regiment of Kuang-chou braves they commanded, all terrified of certain death in an attack on the rebel horde outside the wall.

"General Chang Yu-liang's troops," Chou Wu said, "have all withdrawn through the Pan Men 盤門 gate and fled southwest for Hang-chou."

Ho Hsin-yi sneered. "The cowards that General Ma Te-chao's left behind have already laid down their arms and taken off their uniforms."

"And our Su-chou garrison has not even 4000 soldiers," Li said. He turned to the other side of the battlements and surveyed with indignation the devastation imperial soldiers wrought in the name of defending Su-chou against the T'ai-p'ing. The city was an inferno, the suburbs a holocaust.

Only yesterday, he thought, the army of imperial General Ma, retreating from defeat by rebels at Wu-hsi, ran wild through the streets of Su-chou looting shops and burning houses, completely beyond the control of their officers. The general struggled to curb his soldiers, offering immediate pay and large bonuses to any who would return to their ranks, but nothing would turn them from pillage.

After the locusts of Ma Te-chao swarmed away, imperial General Chang Yü-liang and his army came to pick over the leavings. General Chang wanted to enter the city, but Su-chou knew rebels in imperial uniforms swelled his ranks on the retreat from Wu-hsi, and we would not pass him through the Ch'ang Men 閶門 gate. Then he promised that only his personal guard would enter, but longhairs crowded together with them through the gate, and now the Loyal King's spies fill the city.

Wu-hsi fell and the imperial defenders flee across Chiang-nan. Before that Ch'ang-chou, and Tan-yang. Now Su-chou. Three days we gave the suburbs to pack their possessions and flee, before soldiers set shops and houses on fire to deprive the rebels of cover. Thousands of refugees crowd into the thoroughfares. Homeless persons driven outside the city camp by the wall together with the refugees from the suburbs – people throw food down to them. Dead bodies lie about by the hundreds, unsanctified, strewn over open ground. Ripening crops left uncut wither in the heat of the sun. Even the squalling of abandoned infants rises from the pandemonium 烏煙瘴氣 of evacuation.

A fleck of gray ash settled on a sleeve of Li Wen-ping's fine blue silk surcoat. He snapped open a fan carved of bamboo and tortoiseshell and gently whiffed away the ash. No residue remained on the silk, and he was pleased, too, that no ash had besmirched him in the years since the Small Sword uprising at Shanghai, in the 3rd year of Hsien Feng. Then he was known as Li Shao-hsi 李紹熙, the rebel leader whose Kuang-chou brethren slew local officials, including the county magistrate, and looted the yamens and temples of the native city, sparing only *tao-t'ai* Wu Chien-chang 吳健彰 – Wu they expected would be more useful alive, and he too was Kuang-chou hometown brethren.

The old Li Shao-hsi smuggled guns from Americans at Russell & Company into the native city, until Yang Fang built his wall and cut the rebels off from the foreign settlements. Together with his American friends, Li arranged for the *tao-t'ai* to escape from the native city so that, when Li quit the Small Swords and went over to the imperials, Wu Chien-chang accepted his surrender – and 30,000 taels he had plundered from the county yamen to purchase rank – and saw to his appointment as Su-chou expectant *tao-t'ai*. Since coming to Su-chou, he had made many new friends, influential hometown men who helped him advance, and gave him his own regiment of Kuang-chou braves. Truly, he thought, 竊國者侯 steal a country and you're made a prince.

Su-chou once was vain and arrogant, especially toward Kuang-chou men – proud of their riches, their pretty women, and their silly gardens. Now they flee in terror at the approach of the holy soldiers of the T'ai-p'ing, or lie moldering in fields, or stopping up wells and cisterns with their drowned bodies. Now they know sorrow, now their vanity and arrogance floats away with the ash on a breeze. Their riches are despoiled, their women defiled, their gardens destroyed. The rich men and wise officials have abandoned the place, and now their literati recite only poems of lament.

Li Wen-ping looked again for the pennants of the Loyal King. The only question remaining is should I lead my Kuang-chou braves into battle against the Loyal King, or should I open the gates of the city and welcome the Loyal King inside?

2

Ten days earlier, when they had come off the river, the report Fletcher and Ghent took to Takee about Tanyang and Changchow just about gave the old Chinese a fit – his eyes widened, his hands trembled, and his breathing nearly stopped. Takee recovered only enough to hear them out. When they left, fear that the Loyal King was about to knock down his gate and walk into his house was still in his face.

They agreed that while they could not start recruiting without the sanction of the governor, preparations should begin without delay. Takee would arrange for credit at H. Fogg and Jardine Matheson, set up accounts for transferring funds between clearinghouses, and notify his backers in the Ningpo Guild and other associations that he needed their donations. Fletcher would make ready to conjure up an army, beginning with the purchase of arms and equipment at H. Fogg. As soon as the preparations were underway, Takee would arrange to help Fletcher reconnoiter towns around Shanghai.

Takee's comprador had come to the Astor House early the next morning with letters introducing Fletcher to purchasing agents at Fogg's and Jardine's, and a black satin purse containing ten gold eagles. The Chinese cautioned him to be very quiet about making purchases, especially guns and ammunition. Gossiping clerks would let everyone know Takee had opened new accounts at Western hongs, but the fewer details to get around the better. This advice caused Fletcher to decide against sending a letter to Chester Hicks about purchasing arms – better to meet and discuss the business out of earshot. He sent a runner with a message asking Hicks to come to the Astor House.

Later that morning, Chester Hicks found Fletcher at the hotel. They filled plates at a buffet and secreted themselves away in a corner of the second floor verandah looking out over Soochow Creek. A waiter brought hot coffee and tea.

"Have you heard," Hicks said, "that our plenipos are about to declare British and French marines will defend Shanghai against rebel attack?"

"That should be worth a few pounds sterling on the local exchange."

"And it is now rumored that the fleet left Hong Kong on the 15th and sailed directly north, and the force at Chushan is sailing out to join them, leaving a garrison of Indian troops. Chutney will do well at Tinghai. Where are the rebels?"

"Approaching Soochow. That's why I wish to speak with you."

"Of course. If the notorious filibuster Fletcher Wood has just returned from a week on the Yangtze river, been to Tanyang, been to Changchow, and then to Takee Bank, it only follows that he'd be out shopping soon. What are you looking for?"

"Same as we discussed with Takee. You mentioned rifles."

"Yes, that lot, from fifty-five. Actually, I have since located better sources. The Allied Expeditionary Force – AEF – is nothing if not well-equipped and, with so many British gunnery chiefs in Shanghai having little to do but drink and whore themselves into debt, I have turned up unexpected opportunities."

"Are these English not rather attached to their rifles?"

"Bless my soul, Mr. Wood. I would never separate a soldier from his rifle. No sir, I deal in bulk with non-commissioned quartermasters. The old guzzlers have a surplus of arms they store aboard ship because they can no longer be issued, percussion minié rifles replaced by Enfield rifles and such."

"It must give you a pain to reveal that."

"Of course, however to conclude a sale I feel I must assure you of abundance."

"Minié rifles are what our bo'sun found aboard *Essex*, Tower 1853 models. He said *Essex* looked to be armed out of some English ship-of-the-line."

"Sounds right. I'll see what I can scout up and let you know very soon. Approached anyone else?"

"You ask with whom you will compete? I think you have taught me better."

"For rifles, perhaps. But an army needs much than rifles, which I cannot supply. I merely would increase my value with advice to your advantage. For example, you doubtless will go to Fogg's. There you will be given over to one Artemis L. Fuller, purchasing agent, and I can tell you about that pirate, and several more dealers in arms who will become dizzyfied with visions of Takee silver."

"All right, Chester," Fletcher said, chuckling, "*add* your *valorem*."

"Fuller has, as we say, been to Piccadilly and back and is a clever critter. He's been in China since the early fifties, even served as American Vice-consul for a while in fifty-eight. That must have been quite tedious for him, and likely without profit, so he shucked the position after a couple of months and went back into commerce, I suppose after he had learned all that could be to his advantage. I have not seen them, but rumor says he has hundreds of surplus arms brought from the Crimea hidden away in a Shanghai godown. He may argue states' rights to put you off, but under those muttonchops, he's really just a whitewashed Yankee. And he's the kind of Yankee that makes other people swear a Yankee soul'd fit inside a turnip seed."

"Sounds like a hard man to shave."

"You'll have to stay awake if you expect to get your money's worth. Here's another pointer – when he won't bend enough for you, mention Clark, that's another ship chandler close by, and McKenzie, just up the *Yang-king-bang* creek."

That same afternoon, Fletcher crossed Wills Bridge over Soochow Creek and walked south up the Bund to ship chandler H. Fogg & Company, located near the Stone Bridge to the French Concession. Fletcher was shown into the long mercantile showroom – on its high walls were hung a wealth of wood and iron implements, and on its shelves were arranged all variety of jars, bottles and trays of wares "useful for home and workplace."

"Military ammunition?"

"Ball and powder for rifles, and waterproof cartridges and caps for Colt, Adams, and other revolvers. On the wall there we have some older military models, muzzle loaders mostly, some percussion."

"Breech-loaders?"

"There is not much, sir. Under the treaties, can't import firearms. At the end of the row, there is a Martini-Henry .45/90 caliber falling block model, and two Sharps .50 caliber carbines on consignment from military officers. These Sharps models are still in early production and, with the chance of war in America, they are getting hard to find."

"Set aside the two Sharps rifles."

Fletcher asked for the purchasing agent and was shown into a small office and introduced to Mr. Artemis L. Fuller. The agent was a stringy little man with pale blue eyes, thin gray hair to his shoulders and gray muttonchops.

"Yes?" he said through his large nose in a high-pitched New England twang that would have certainly given away his origins even if his politics did not. He wore a dapper tan and white check waistcoat under a tan Chesterfield double-breasted with black velvet collar that he likely kept on against the chill of the drafty building.

"Mr. Fuller, sir, this gentleman is asking about military arms."

Fletcher handed over his letter of introduction. Instantly, the agent leapt to his feet and showed Fletcher to a plush leather chair by a window looking out over the busy foot traffic beside the *Yang-king-bang* creek, rather more a ditch here. He called for tea.

"Mighty glad to meet you, Mr. Wood. Your name precedes you."

"Oh, really? I would not have thought so."

"Come now, Mr. Wood, why so modest? Your adventure has displaced even the longhaired rebels and the English war with China in conversation at the club bar. Not so often do victims of piracy turn the tables and give the pirates such a mighty hiding."

"That notoriety won't last long."

"No sir, it won't. Nothing ever does. But you can believe me it's a welcome respite from other tiresome news that never lets up."

Tea was served, followed by cheroots. Fuller waved his about like a band conductor's baton, with little regard for where the ashes flew.

"We looked for someone to come over here from Takee Bank, when he opened this account, but perhaps not so soon. How can I be of help?"

"Here is my list," Fletcher said. The purchasing agent sucked in a deep breath.

"You're clearly not just supplying *Confucius* to hunt pirates. This is for an army!"

Fletcher had seen this coming and realized there would be no keeping his purpose secret from weapons suppliers. He had hoped to divide immediate orders between several local suppliers to conceal the total ordnance purchased, and order additional ordnance from abroad over time, but in Shanghai only large, well-connected hongs were both able and willing to trade locally in arms. He could swear them to secrecy but, as Takee was fond of saying, "wall hab ear," and in the end, he had to trust that the promise of profit from large transactions would assure their silence.

"Pirates we could handle with a few field guns and rifles. To defend Shanghai against Taiping rebels, give them a mighty hiding as you have put it, we need an army."

"Not everyone will agree, least of all the English. That is the Englishman's rice-bowl, and he will not welcome having it broken by interlopers. However, as it happens, I do agree. The Chinese themselves are hopeless, the English and French have other fish to fry at Peking, and even if our American commodore would lend us marines, they would not be enough. A vigilante committee is needed, like they had in California during the gold rush. A vigilance *army*, really. It appears Chinese merchants will fund your army. Quite a novelty."

Fuller examined the list again.

"Rifles, muskets, bayonets, pistols, uniforms, pouches, mess kits, canteens, tents, packing crates, camp tables and chairs, picks and shovels, canvas cloth, rubberized muslin, field guns.... Rifles and muskets are contraband under the American treaty, of course, since the end of fifty-eight."

"The *taotai*," Fletcher said, "is rumored to have an arsenal of weapons, and I wonder if there are not other collections of arms right here in Shanghai. At this time I have one other source for rifles."

"Oh, who is that?"

"Jardine Matheson."

"No bargains there, and the treaty puts Jardine under the same legal restrictions."

"What prices can you offer for the other equipage?"

"Field guns, I don't know for certain – nothing on hand of course. Field guns must be purchased through non-treaty importers, or locally, in which case a buyer would not want to inquire too closely into the sources. Let me see…" Fuller took down a heavy book from a shelf and fanned through the pages. "Here we are. An ordinary 12-pounder – accurate to 1400 yards, weight with limber about 2500 pounds, requiring six horses, with a life of about 800 rounds – should cost you about 300 pounds."

"Really? At four pounds four shillings to the U.S. dollar, that's about…$72.00. I have heard of older field guns, Napoleons, for only 150 pounds, $36.00."

"You would have muzzle loaders, Mr. Wood?"

"Yes, if necessary. What about Armstrongs?"

"Breechloaders are more difficult to come by out here – the expeditionary force has cornered the market on that item. An Armstrong 12-pounder – with a range of 5000 yards, weighing only 800 pounds, pulled by only four horses, and still new after 3500 rounds – costs 350 pounds. They say it can hit a man at a mile, and uses only one-half the powder of a muzzleloader. I'll have to inquire further about artillery, the contraband restrictions and such, to be sure imports can be gotten through customs."

"Purchases are by the authority of the *taotai* and not subject to restrictions."

Treachery at Soochow

"Even so, arrangements must be made – until now there's been little call to determine if the treaty rules prohibit import by the Chinese government, or by its subjects. The custom house, you may know, is chaperoned by foreigners, who're sometimes quite fussy. With adequate preparation and proper documents, it should be possible to acquire arms on the up-and-up."

"The *taotai* is the custom house."

"Yes, so I am told. Still, English manage the place, don't they? Anyway, why tolerate representatives from leviathans like Schleswig or Piedmont if they can't make themselves useful by importing arms without restriction by treaty? The beggars couldn't survive here unless we toss them a few crumbs."

"In Hong Kong, an Armstrong 12-pounder was quoted at 250 pounds, $60.00, Mr. Fuller. Your estimates seem consistently high."

"Hong Kong is 865 sea miles from Shanghai, Mr. Wood. Shipping is not yet without expense. In any case, the rest of this can be done. Muskets, muskets might be found for perhaps ten to fifteen taels…"

"Best quality, Mr. Fuller. No trash. Percussion, smoothbore only if rifled is not available, all in good condition."

"Yes, yes."

"Fifteen taels is about $24.00 American – much too expensive."

"Well, this is Takee's equipment. He can afford it."

"No – this is my equipment. My arms. My army. Every weapon at $24.00 is one less weapon I can buy at $12.00 American. You are quite mistaken if you think I do not know the price of a percussion minié rifle."

"It will cost more than 8 taels to buy a musket, Mr. Wood."

"What are your other prices?"

"500 muskets at fifteen taels each is 7500 taels, or US$12,000.00."

"At $12.00 each, they cost only US$6000.00. Haversacks?"

"500 haversacks at, say, two taels each is 1000 taels, or US$1600.00."

"At $2.00 each, they cost US$1000.00. At $1.00 each, US$500.00. Serge shirts?"

"100 serge shirts I might have made for two taels each, so 200 taels, US$320.00."

Fletcher chuckled aloud. "Mr. Fuller, you are not allowed to fund your retirement at the expense of Takee Bank. Please provide estimates in accord with my wishes and current market prices, not marked up to almighty high heaven."

"Mr. Wood. I can appreciate your attempting to drive a hard bargain, but it is clear that you are new at this."

"All the more reason to be reasonable, Mr. Fuller. Fogg's should not take advantage of a buyer simply because he is a griffin and not a taipan."

"'H' Fogg, please. And H. Fogg will not sell at cost to Takee Bank. Neither are we a public charity."

"Mr. Fuller. Look at me. Look in my face. This is not Takee. You are dealing with me, Fletcher Wood. And if you want me to save your city from a rebel onslaught, you will want to cooperate."

Try as he might, the agent could not escape the intensity of Fletcher's expression and, for a moment, he just stared back into Fletcher's face with a quizzical expression. Finally, he twisted away and stared wearily out the window at the *Yang-king-bang* ditch.

"Your terms are not satisfactory," the agent said. "I decline the privilege."

"Others may accept my terms, and make up the difference on volume. I believe I shall just step around to Clark & Company, or maybe up the street here to McKenzie."

Fletcher stood up and started for the door.

"Takee opened an account here," Fletcher said. "Takee can open accounts with them, too. Theirs will have transactions. H. Fogg's will not."

"A moment, Mr. Wood."

"Yes?"

"Neither Clark nor McKenzie are reliable. Best use H. Fogg. You can be sure to get what you want on the date you ask for delivery. If you can document a lower price from anyone for anything we sell to you, H. Fogg will accept that price in payment."

Fletcher returned to the window and sat down, smiling broadly at Mr. Fuller.

"Percussion minié rifles, $12.00 each?"

"All right, but darned if I don't feel I've been pummeled by a paddle wheel!"

"Bite down on your Latin grammar, Mr. Fuller. I shall require prior signed approval and receipts for all purchases cash or credit. And my own copies."

"That can be done. Duplicate copies for quartermaster and comprador."

"I have no quartermaster yet, but give me little time. How do you get paid?"

"We submit a monthly accounting to Takee's comprador."

"Terms?"

"No terms, Mr. Wood. Chinese pay immediately and in full – cash on the barrelhead." This seemed rather more a declaration than a simple explanation, an anthem to the Chinese business precepts that Fuller thought everyone should practice. "You were bluffing, weren't you Mr. Wood."

"No, I was going to walk out. You do not know how lucky you are, Mr. Fuller – I am the most extraordinary fellow it is your good fortune to know."

"Don't say?" Fuller said, laughing. "Well, make it my *great* fortune and I'll be bound to share that high opinion." Fuller considered what more was needed to persuade Fletcher Wood to do business with H. Fogg. How much risk, he wondered, is there in showing this young Bellerophon the arsenal he clearly suspects is mine? It must be an open secret by now, like the *taotai*'s purse of Fortunatus. I'll wager my rifled muskets are much more comely than the *taotai*'s old smoothbores. Once gazed upon, how could any lothario resist their charms?

"We have some of what you are looking for on hand," Fuller said quietly, thinking he'd best set his hook quickly before the fish spit it out – no point in giving the competition any advantage.

Fletcher followed the purchasing agent out of his office, down several dark hallways, to a large padlocked door deep in the building. Clicking open the lock, Fuller pushed on the door, squeezed through the opening and beckoned Fletcher into the dark. A lucifer match was struck and put to the wick of an oil lamp, and Fletcher followed in the dim glow of yellow light that flashed among shelves of stores along the walls, until Fuller stopped at a row of tall cabinets, also padlocked. He turned and smiled at Fletcher for a moment to prolong the anticipation, then one by one unlocked each cabinet and opened the doors. The yellow light shined on dozens of muskets with well-oiled stocks and glinting barrels, each with a long, slender bayonet mounted on its muzzle.

"A treasure trove, Mr. Wood, the riches of Ali Baba at your feet, if you like rifles."

"Lordy!" Fletcher said, visibly impressed by the display. "What are they?"

"British minié rifles, mostly," Fuller said, recalling that older goods were always presented best in dim light. "An Enfield or three, and a few museum pieces, Brunswicks, Brown Bess flintlocks. There are eighty here, and another four hundred in my godown up the *Yang-king-bang* creek."

"I have to admire the way you close a sale," Fletcher said, laughing. "I could not have been more surprised if P. T. Barnum had arranged for Jenny Lind to jump out and began singing the Star-Spangled Banner. How did you get them all?"

"British military surplus, of course, from the Crimea, and from the Allied

Expeditionary Force sent here in fifty-eight and fifty-nine. The Enfield has gradually been replacing minié rifles in more far-flung regiments, reached India in fifty-seven, much to the exasperation of the British Empire. Some miniés were shipped from England after the Crimea, the rest came from ship's stores, courtesy of chief gunners who hoarded replaced models for private sale, most recently from the *Octavia* at anchor now out there in the Whangpoo."

"I guess I shouldn't be surprised that far-sighted traders would stock up on guns in a country like China."

"Doesn't take a blind Tiresias to see they will be in demand when the rebels come to Shanghai. We cannot import guns, but nothing prevents older rifles from being sold."

Fletcher removed a rifle from the rack for inspection. It was a Tower.

"May I assume you have ample powder, bullets and caps?"

"Ample."

"And this rifle will cost me $12.00?"

"$12.00."

"It's good you have them so well stored. I can take delivery as I need them."

"Take as many as you wish. I'll hold whatever's paid for until needed."

"Would you mind completing your estimate for the other equipage on that list?"

"Right away. Where are you staying? I'll send it along directly."

"Astor House."

"Fiddlesticks, man. That's too dear. I have rooms for you, spacious, convenient, with a comely Chinese hired girl to cook and clean, and warm your bed if you like. A large bungalow with a deep verandah on North Gate Street in the French Concession. You may lodge there at no expense – that will definitely stretch the old banker's dollar."

"And keep you privy to my business?"

"What matter, if all your business is with H. Fogg?"

"I would not want to limit my options."

"You will fare worse anywhere else."

"Oh, by the way," Fletcher said, "add a dozen American flags to that list."

Fletcher had just spent a fortune amounting to over $12,000.00. There was a brief elation, a shout in his soul, that accompanied the transaction, but his bleak New England frugality quickly silenced any siren's song of extravagance. How much time is there, he pondered? Changchow, Wuhsi, Soochow – what, seventy-five miles overland, the distance from Salem to New Bedford? Judging from what I saw at Tanyang and Changchow, the rebels could be in Soochow in little more than a week. Once in Soochow, they might take time to consolidate their administration of the city, and ready their army to start out for nearby towns. That would allow me more time to pick up shipments from suppliers. And recruit an army. A week, two weeks, three weeks at the most before the rebels begin probing into the countryside around Shanghai? Three weeks to train an army? How can I possibly equip and train an army in three weeks? Cadmus had dragon's teeth.

Behind him on the British Bund Fletcher heard a familiar blaring of horns, beating of gongs, and calls of Chinese lictors announcing the approach of some great oriental potentate. He recognized the thirteen gong beats and the character *tao* 道 dancing above the procession and realized that his new friend Wu Hsü must be inside that sedan chair. The mandarin's retinue backed and filled on down beside the Whangpoo River and came about into the grounds of the British consulate. Fletcher wondered what mischief his new sponsor *Taotai* Wu would be up to there.

3 The racket of the *taotai*'s procession ceased at the consulate gate. Between the curtains of his sedan chair, Wu Hsü could see the imposing red brick building of the British consulate surrounded by wide lawns of short green grass. So much grander than that disgusting hovel the Americans should be ashamed to call a consulate, converted from an old godown, with its sagging gate and tattered old American flag.

Pacing deliberately to and fro on the building steps, waiting to welcome the mandarins, were two British officials in top hats, formal black frock coats and gray trousers, quiet waistcoats with narrow lapels, and stiff standing collars with black cravats. One was the British consul Masters, and the other the interpreter Wells, evidently on loan from the British minister's staff, where Wells was Chinese Secretary. The *taotai*'s informant had said that the consulate interpreter was ill, but Wu Hsü believed the British minister just wanted his own man there to listen in at meetings with the *taotai*. Masters speaks Chinese well enough, thought Wu Hsü, better than Wells, so why would the consul need an interpreter present?

Both Englishmen were extraordinarily large, giants like Guan Yu and Chang Fei, dwarfing the Chinese around them, appearing less like foreign diplomats than immense mountains obstructing the flow of discourse. Wu Hsü recalled without generosity that Masters was a supporter of the Taiping rebels who, at his best, was an ill-tempered and cantankerous bully roaming the streets armed like a ruffian with guns and knives. Stars fell and rivers flooded the morning he was born. Wells was no better – his bellicose arrogance at the Tientsin treaty negotiations two years before was in some part the cause of many present difficulties. Hens turned to roosters the night he was whelped.

The *taotai*'s green chair was lowered, the curtains parted, and Wu Hsü emerged decorously onto the consulate grounds. The umbrella-bearer ran forward and raised the large red silk umbrella over him. The blue sedan chair of county magistrate Liu Hsun-kao stopped a little to the rear and the magistrate stepped out. Another attendant ran forward through a small crowd of foreigners and presented the *taotai*'s gilt-edged vermilion calling card. When Wu Hsü and Liu Hsun-kao stepped forward three paces, Wells signaled a marine corporal to set off three small cannon beside the entrance. Only two cannon went off. Wells leapt down the steps at the corporal.

"You bloody idiot!" he hissed. "Get it right!"

"Y-yes, sir," the corporal stammered. "Wet primer, sir. Sorry, I'm sure."

"Well get another!" Wells barked. "And be quick about it."

The corporal fumbled in his blouse pocket for another friction primer, replaced the primer in the vent and attached a lanyard, then stood back.

"Will you step away, sir?"

"Damn!" Wells said.

The third gun fired. Wells spun about and tromped back up the consulate steps. The crisis apparently over, each of the placid and completely self-possessed Chinese gently clasped his own hands and in unison shook them before his face while bowing forward to the proper degree.

"您好您好你們大家這機天都好麼 hello, hello, have you been well these past few days?" Wu Hsü said in his Chekiang-accented Mandarin. The *taotai* was dressed today in an embossed red silk gown under a three-quarter length red surcoat. He wore his long necklace of precious stones, red-fringed summer hat with 4th-rank lapis lazuli button, and double-eyed peacock's feather. County Magistrate Liu was dressed in similar manner in a blue gown and purple surcoat with a silver belt and a single-eyed peacock feather that dangled from the 7th-rank gold button of his summer hat.

The crowd of foreigners moved aside and the two Englishmen stepped forward and bowed, shook their own hands in similar fashion, and repeated "*nin hao*" or "hello." Wu Hsü gestured for the consul to precede him, repeating "please, please, *ch'ing, ch'ing* 請請," and Masters gestured for the *taotai* to precede him, repeating "*ch'ing, ch'ing*."

"Please come in," Masters said finally in English and went along before them. Wu Hsü's factotums followed the officials inside and took places in the office or hallway. Tea and sweet English biscuits were served while the initial formalities were observed.

The opulence of the British consul's large office, richly appointed with furniture, draperies, carpets and a huge mahogany desk, contrasted with the musty, stifling little office of the American consul, and his stiff high-backed armchairs and rickety old desk. A portrait of the English queen hung over the British consul's mantelpiece and a warm fire crackled in the fireplace. The Americans had no fireplace, and a dusty portrait of their first president *Hua-shun-dun*, only half completed, sat on the floor against a wall.

With power comes prestige, then arrogance. The Americans have no power, and so they cannot begin to match the British for arrogance. The British love to shout and pound on tables. In that way, they are very much like their gunboats – which scream and fire cannon. Opposite me are two towering, hairy-faced British gunboats, dressed in frock coats, waistcoats and stiff collars. They sit in chairs in very un-gunboat-like manner, about to lecture to me on neutrality and the rule of laws, while their gang of gunboats 炮船幫派 sails north to fire their guns at my Emperor.

"So, Wu *Ta-jen*," Wells said, "what news have you?"

"What?" the *taotai* said. Wells spoke Mandarin with a heavy Cantonese accent that Wu Hsü often could not understand. Moreover, Wells was abrupt and ill mannered and talked about issues immediately without polite overtures.

"What news have you brought us?" Wells said, laboring to crush his unruly nine Cantonese tones into four.

"What?" Wu Hsü said, intent upon controlling this insolent barbarian clerk.

"*Ta-ren*," Liu Hsun-kao said, "I think he asks if we have news for the minister."

"Ah, yes," the taotai said, irked that Magistrate Liu could sometimes be so dense. "Today I hasten here to inform his Excellency, your minister, that rebels have reached Chang-chou, the city is under siege, and thousands flee for the safety of Su-chou. Our generals have fallen back, and Chang-chou is defended now only by militia and must soon fall. Then nothing will stand between the rebels and Su-chou. The city is in a great state of alarm and preparing to close the gates. In seven years, the rebels have never come this close to Su-chou, or to Shang-hai. The defense of Shang-hai is of paramount importance. Please inform the minister that we desperately need the help of the British to defend Shang-hai, and ask him what are his intentions?"

"The minister is in conference now with the French minister Bourboulon," Consul Masters said, "to discuss possible alternatives for defense, I believe. They will decide very soon, and I will communicate that decision to you immediately when it is reached."

"The situation is desperate and of the greatest urgency. Tens of thousands of rebels are reported between Ch'ang-chou and Su-chou."

"We appreciate your concern, Wu *Ta-jen*, and please understand that his Excellency is equally concerned." But I'd have to clap my own eyes on those rebels before I believed your fancy tales, Mr. *Taotai* Wu. How often have you reported as fact information that proved the very next day to be cotton wool?"

"The Emperor may be persuaded to accept treaty terms if the British demonstrate they have helped to protect the people in Su-chou and Shang-hai."

"Shanghai and Suchou are separate cases. Probably best not to treat them as one."

"Many officials at court who believe the British always seek quarrels will think differently if they see the British are allies against the rebellion and support the people."

"I have yet to see how anyone could reconcile warring with the emperor in the north and defending the emperor in the south. I believe the minister would prefer to ratify the Treaty of Tientsin before reconsidering policy toward the Taiping. Of course, I cannot speak for Minister Blaine."

"There are many Catholics at Su-chou that the rebels will put to the sword unless the city can be protected. The French are anxious to protect Su-chou."

"The French have a particular interest in protecting native Roman Catholics."

"I have spoken with the French General de Montpellier about raising a relief force of 1500 French troops to be sent to Su-chou. Could not the minister send British marines along with the French soldiers?"

Wells interrupted. "1500 is not very many if the rebel army is large, and there are hundreds of thousands of people in Su-chou. In my opinion, sending a force that is too small would be worse than sending no force at all."

The consul gave Wells a look that said, "let me handle this."

"British policy regarding the rebellion all along has been neutrality. If anyone is to change that policy, it would be the minister acting under instructions from the Foreign Secretary Lord Russell at Whitehall."

"The holy fathers at your Shang-hai churches, and the taipans of your Shang-hai businesses, all would support sending troops to Su-chou to save the city."

"The priests and taipans do not decide British policy, your Excellency." Is the *taotai*'s mainspring wound so tightly, Masters wondered, that he will never unwind?

Eventually, the *taotai* went away empty handed. Wells retreated to his own office to transcribe the minutes of the meeting. Consul Masters was notified when Minister Blaine's meeting with the French minister ended and, a few moments after, Blaine came into the consul's office and sank into a chair before the fireplace.

"Does it seem too early in the day for a brandy, sir?" Bitterman said to the minister.

"Achh, na' too early young man, na' at all. Masters, why are we always in meetings? All day long, day after day, interminable meetings. If I knew at the start wha' I know now about the diplomatic service, I might have chosen some other kind of work. At least a smithy sees his finished work on the hoof and can watch the dumb beast trot away satisfied. Even a highwayman has his immediate satisfaction, although I suppose that work has its ups and downs. Wha' new demands did the *taotai* make of us?"

While the consul summarized the discussion with Wu Hsü, Bitterman placed a tray with brandy and glasses on a table between the two men and poured two small brandies. Blaine held up three fingers and waved away the seltzer.

"He also asks for help to defend Shanghai, and wishes to know your intentions."

"My intentions? Plucky lit'le beggar, our *taotai*. He would embroil Grea' Britain in a fight with the Taiping so he can get out of ho' water with his emperor and report tha' he has saved his district from the rebels, wi' a lit'le help from his *vassals* the British and French. The *taotai* thereby avoids degradation and punishment, and can go on pilfering from the custom house. He is sacrificed if he tells the truth to his emperor, and sacrificed when the truth will out and inevitable calamity befalls him. It would na' be impossible to feel some compassion for the man if he were na' such a complete bounder. I am certainly na' about to be hoodwinked into getting involved in his infernal schemes."

"Will the French accede to the *taotai*'s request to send troops to Soochow?"

"Bourboulon and I are discussing the merits of tha' request, if there are any. In the meantime, we agree to issue a joint statement committing our military forces to the defense of Shanghai."

"Wu also spoke to Montpellier, about a relief force of 1500 French for Soochow."

"Colonel Foley thought he had 400 marines he could detach, but will do nothing without my sanction."

"Are you seriously considering that, sir?"

"I think not. Too many things weigh against such an adventure. To begin, the marines are assigned for duty at Shanghai, na' anywhere else. Fugitive imperial soldiers swarm into Shanghai and daily pose an increasing threat to the security of foreign concessions. To reduce our defense force here would na' be responsible."

Shadows lengthened over the consulate lawns and fog began to creep up paths from the river. A gloom settled into the consul's office and the room grew chill. Bitterman stoked the fire and added coal, and then refilled the brandy glasses.

"For that matter," the consul said, "I believe we need to take control of two of the gates to ensure we can get into the native city in case of a rising. Insurgents would first seize the gates and, if we are to defend the place, having to breach the wall would be a costly waste of time and treasure, and also appear not just a little silly to our constituency back home."

"Yes, tha' is right. Make the suggestion to the *taotai* but, regardless of the response, have detachments ready to secure the gates in short order on your command."

"Yes, sir." Masters went to his desk to jot down some notes. Bitterman took a light red and yellow afghan from a side cabinet and placed it over the minister's shoulders.

"Returning to the subject of Soochow," Masters said from his desk, "we really do not know what the rebels intend, what is their number, or what is their objective. We are given a great deal of information that cannot be confirmed, and usually proves to be erroneous or exaggerated within a day."

"And wi' no adequate intelligence, sendin' a small force so far inland, wi' no reliable communications or supply, is extraordinarily hazardous. It's na' just the risk to the men – the failure of such a mission would damage the repute of our military forces and compromise future operations, and tha' would put our laddies at still more risk."

"I also emphasized our policy of neutrality again."

"Neutrality. To protect British trade with the natives, we have to protect the natives, too. Wha' kind of neutrality is that? Anyway, if our policy of neutrality is to be revised in favor of the imperialists, I would prefer the change take place after the present treaty crisis is resolved and there are no other mitigating factors to interfere wi' a clear evaluation of the alternatives."

"Even after the treaty is ratified," the consul said, "and the force returns from the north, Her Majesty's government would still find it difficult to determine just who to support against whom. The reports I receive have rebels attacking government troops, militia and deserters attacking ordinary people, and the people rising up in self-defense against militia, perhaps even against the so obviously negligent government itself. If our marines are sent to Soochow, whom would the mandarins order them to attack – rebels, runaway troops, or the people?"

Blaine sighed. "Damned if we do, and damned if we do na'."

A signal gun fired in the anchorage, followed by the call of a bugle. A gun answered from within the consulate compound and another bugle started up. The commands of the marine guard lowering the flag echoed in the building entrance.

"I have no confidence." the minister said, "tha' any intervention on our part would be fairly represented to the Chinese court, regardless of the promises of our feckless *taotai*. To my knowledge none of our services to the dynasty have ever been reported to the emperor, na' even our many successes in suppressing piracy. Frankly, I can na' see any reason at all for considering a relief force. Native Catholics have ample opportunity to flee the city. Churches can be rebuilt."

洋神 Yang Shen					James Lande 藍德

4   It was said that 60,000 imperial troops submitted to the Loyal King when the turncoat Li Wen-ping threw open the gates of Soochow. Actually, there were a great many less, and they surrendered from imperial camps outside the walls. The Taiping army entered the city unopposed, on June 2 1860, six days after they took Changchow, and two days after the fall of Wu-hsi.

The savory aroma of frying sausages drifted above a campfire beside the Chinghang Canal where a squad of rebel sappers sat cooking up a mid-day meal. Their unit, the 5th company, Front Regiment, the Loyal King's division, had halted while their officers went ahead into Su-chou with the Loyal King.

"Su-chou is a good place," said Shih Lao-shih, Rock of Ages, the worn and wizened old spear-carrier who usually looked half-asleep and spoke with a thick southern accent.

"What's good about it?" said flag caretaker Ching Ko-hsi, Happy, the young and ever-smiling bean sprout.

"No fighting at Su-chou," Rock of Ages said. "I will always remember this place with thanks to God because we did not have to fight our way into the city."

"No wall to blow up," said sapper mole Ching T'un-yi, Jupiter. "Cities like Su-chou will break our rice bowls. They'll come and say they don't need sappers any more. Then where will we be? Back in the infantry." Jupiter was the farmer's son who longed for *hsiao wanyir* 小玩藝兒 – the little playthings of sweet girls with tiny feet.

"Careful there or you stupid eggs will burn the sausages," said sapper engineer Chu Pa-chieh, Eight Epochs, the grizzled old grumbler nicknamed Pigsy because of his huge belly, stout limbs, fat jowls and bushy black brows.

"Why was there no fighting?" Happy said.

"Some city officials sold out," Eight Epochs said. He had been to the Ch'ang Men gate in order to study the engineering needed to sap the wall. "Betrayed the imps and opened the city gates to our army."

"They'll be made Taiping officials now, what do you think?" Jupiter said. "Chief Attendant of Umbrellas?"

"Chief Attendant of Sedan Chairs," Eight Epochs said, laughing.

"Attendant of Firewood," Rock of Ages said.

"Did the governor of Chiang-su sell out?" Happy said.

"No," Eight Epochs said. "I heard that he tried to escape with his seal of office by jumping into the canal. That seal of office was probably too heavy, because he drowned. Anyway, they say the Loyal King ordered the governor's body be prepared for the proper burial of a high official, the corpse dressed and placed in a coffin and prayers said over him, because he was a loyal official who died honorably."

"If you think about it," Rock of Ages said, "the graves of loyal officials we have buried on this eastern expedition form a long line along our route of advance."

"Are the imp soldiers still there in Su-chou?" Happy said.

"Sure, tens of thousands of them," Eight Epochs said, laughing.

"And we don't have to fight them?"

"*Lao-pai-hsing* 老百姓 the old-hundred-names – the ordinary folks – are fighting them for us," Eight Epochs said. "Demon soldiers pillaged and torched temples and yamens and shops and houses everywhere in the Ch'ang Men and Hsü Men suburbs and made ordinary people really angry. They snatched up rakes and hoes and attacked the soldiers, then went at them with dead soldiers' swords and pikes. Dead imps are strewn everywhere in the city and suburbs and along the roads from Tan-yang to Su-chou."

"了不起 that's really something," Rock of Ages said. "The *lao-pai-hsing* are killing government troops so we holy soldiers don't have to. That's really something."

Horns and drums sounded a call to formation. The sappers hurriedly put out their campfire, gathered up their weapons and equipment, and fell into ranks still chewing on the last of their sausages. 5th Company was marched east along the canal toward the distant Su-chou city wall, past low hills on the south, together with many other companies of rebel infantry and horse. In time, they came up to the Ch'ang Men gate and marched through behind a detachment of horsemen on prancing ponies, with banners streaming from their lances.

"Ai-yah, I hate walking behind horses," Happy said.

Large signs over the doors of shops and houses inside the gate read, "welcome Taiping Heavenly Kingdom holy soldiers" and "join together and slay all the government soldiers of Chang and Ho!" Heedless of the signs, rebel soldiers were escorting imperial officers over to the canal and assisting them and their families aboard junks and sampans.

"Look at that," Jupiter said. "They're even giving them food."

"Money, too, I heard," Eight Epochs said.

"I'm hungry, and they get the food," Happy said.

"Only our Taiping army would do that," Rock of Ages said with evident pride.

"Well, didn't we steal the money from their provincial treasury?" Jupiter said.

"Some people don't deserve to be holy soldiers," Rock of Ages snapped at Jupiter. "你不要臉 you should be ashamed."

"Go find a church to pray in, old man."

They marched past a yamen where imperial soldiers stood in lines inside the open gates. The sappers assumed the imps were prisoners but, when the company halted there briefly, they saw the imps still had weapons, and they were being issued rebel uniforms. More imps came out of the yamen wearing red, yellow and green rebel colors and discarding their imperial uniforms.

"Now how are we going to tell the difference," Eight Epochs growled.

"Why would we care?" Jupiter said. "Aren't they our new brethren now?"

The company was broken up and dispatched to different places in the city for work details. The sapper squad joined another rebel squad in front of a common well, a little one about three feet wide that served a small neighborhood of houses.

"Corporal, get rope," a sergeant said to Rock of Ages, "and lift the bodies out of this well. Let's see if you are as good in wells as you are in tunnels."

The sappers suddenly felt some alarm and stepped back from the well.

"You two go look in those houses for long ropes," Rock of Ages said to Jupiter and Happy. "Be quick about it." Then Rock of Ages exchanged a swift grimace with Eight Epochs. Together they stepped forward and peeked over into the well. There were too many bodies piled one on top of another to count them.

"Pigsy, why do we do this?" Rock of Ages whispered.

"You mean ruin perfectly good wells by jumping into them?"

"No, of course not. My meaning is why do we kill ourselves when rebels come? Holy soldiers don't torture people or rape their wives and daughters. There's no reason for mass suicide." Rock of Ages dare not look up right away because of his tears.

"They do not yet understand Christian love, old friend," Eight Epochs said.

Jupiter and Happy returned with great coils of hemp rope. Rock of Ages ordered the skinny bean sprout Happy down into the well to put rope around the bodies. They looped a rope under his arms and put him over into the opening – he grabbed the edge and looked up pleadingly at his corporal.

"Are their ghosts still down there?" he whimpered.

"Their souls are with Jesus," Rock of Ages said. "You're all right. Let go."

Slowly, they lowered Happy down. He managed to get a second rope around the stomach of an adolescent girl. Hand over hand they hauled her up, drew her limp body out streaming with water, and laid her to one side on the ground. Immediately, three soldiers from another squad – in clean uniforms that meant they were new brethren – bent over her and ransacked her body for valuables. The sappers were too stunned at such sacrilege to do anything but gape at the soldiers while they yanked at her jade bracelets, tugged roughly at her gold finger rings, and ripped silver earrings from her earlobes. Then they set to quarreling over the spoils, pushing at each other and shouting. Rock of Ages and Eight Epochs stepped between them.

"What are you doing?" Rock of Ages cried. "This is not Christian behavior."

"Stop fighting," Eight Epochs said.

"幹你娘," one of the new brethren shouted, "fok your mother."

"Stand still," Eight Epochs said angrily, hefting a shovel.

"滾蛋," the second hissed. "Scram! This is our stuff."

"You guys are God Worshipers, aren't you," the third said. "Go away."

"No, pull up another one." The second soldier laughed.

"C'mon," the first said, "roll dice for this stuff 打骰子. Has to be divided evenly."

The three new brethren scuttled over to the wall of a building and squatted down to throw dice. The sappers just stared after them. Even Jupiter shook his head. Once they had divided the jewelry between them, the three new brethren lit up pipes of tobacco and just watched the sappers without making any effort to help.

Happy shouted up from the well.

"Hey, it's cold down here, and really, really strange. Next one is tied. Hurry up."

They hauled up the body of another girl and lifted her out. While they pulled Happy up out of the well, the three new brethren scrambled up off their haunches, tapped their pipes on their palms, and crossed over to the second body. Rock of Ages snatched up his long iron-spiked bamboo spear and leveled it at them.

"氣死我了你們死傢伙真氣死我了," Rock of Ages shouted, "piss me off, you guys really piss me off! Just come a little closer so I can slice open your stomachs and spill your innards out onto the ground. Then you can roll dice for your guts."

"Ai-yah, take it easy old man."

"You will not desecrate the body of this girl."

"Okay, but what happens to her valuables? Somebody has to have them."

"They are collected by our officers and placed in the central treasury."

"Ah, of course. The officers never keep them for themselves."

Eight Epochs knelt over the body, clasped his hands and gave a quick bow of his head, then began gently removing the girl's jade bracelets. He touched each piece of jewelry to his forehead, and then placed it on the hem of her skirt. Almost reverently, he removed the gold rings from her fingers and the gold hoops from her earlobes. He took a silk kerchief from one of her pockets and wrapped the jewelry in the kerchief, then walked across the street to a rebel officer and gave him the bundle.

"You're joking." The new brethren spat. "Who'd believe these stupid pigs?"

The officer came over to the well and faced the three new brethren.

"You men help out here with the bodies in this well," he told them. They just laughed, turned and walked away. One of them called back over his shoulder.

"We are assigned down the road and were just resting here."

The officer started after them, but stopped when he saw a detachment of horsemen approaching. He recognized the Loyal King riding with his officers, messengers, and foreign mercenaries.

"Please let them go, sir," Rock of Ages said. "We don't want them, these so-called new rebels. They're not Christians. Just now they broke too many heavenly commandments – desecrated the dead, stole jewelry, fought over stolen goods, gambled for the jewelry, smoked tobacco and swore…and disobeyed an officer."

"Is that what the new brethren are going to be like?" Eight Epochs said.

"They do not understand," the officer said. "They will change, or lose their heads."

"We are not the same," Eight Epochs said. "We should *not* give them our colors."

"No matter," Rock of Ages said. "It will not be hard for us to recognize them."

"Us – of course," Eight Epochs said, "but wearing our colors, the *lao-pai-hsing* will think *they* are us."

"So what?" Jupiter said.

"When they murder, rape and pillage," Eight Epochs said, "ordinary people will not know old soldiers from new. To them, they will *all* be Taiping soldiers."

What has the Loyal King done, wondered Rock of Ages?

The Loyal King's detachment came up to the well and slowed. Li Hsiu-ch'uan took in the scene, the men at the well with ropes, the bodies beside the well, and slowly shook his head. He noticed Rock of Ages holding upright his long spear and smiled at him. Rock of Ages smiled back, wondering again about the new brethren.

What has the Loyal King done?

The Loyal King rode on through the streets of Su-chou, oblivious to any personal danger. He wanted to see that his army followed his orders and harmed no one, damaged no property, suppressed fires and aided the injured. And he wanted to encourage righteousness by his presence. It was not difficult to see that the armies of Ma and Chang had already done terrible damage and that, if his army was to avoid blame for the tragedy of death and destruction at Su-chou, he must show the people that the Taiping army was not their enemy. He would take money and valuables from government yamens and wealthy families for the treasury at T'ien-ching, but he would also hold back as much as he needed to begin the restoration of this city and its people.

The future is before us, thought the Loyal King. We are here, actually here, within thirty days, and Su-chou is ours. This is a fine place, a large city on the Ching-hang Canal, close to the foreign emporium of the port of Shanghai and the western ocean, surrounded by rich farmland, and at no small distance from the heavenly capital. Su-chou would be a good base for me. Just as the other *wang*s have their all-under-heaven 天下, their own sphere of influence, I could have the same for myself here in the east.

I will convince the citizens that I will govern fairly and peacefully, even go out into the rural districts myself to pacify the people and show them they will prosper under my rule. The gentry will participate in governing the countryside. Academics and literary men will gather together where they can flourish. I will suppress crime and punish criminals so that commerce can succeed. Rice, silk and cotton farming will be reestablished and encouraged. Silk production around Su-chou is nearly ruined, but I will bring it back – I can imagine increasing production under good administration to tens of thousands of bales each year.

We will relocate displaced persons to where they can live happily, establish them with rations of rice, and help them build new homes. Towns and villages will have special streets for trading and people will flock to local markets from everywhere. Our government will lower taxes and offer fair prices for goods. We will loan money to businessmen, charge no interest, and allow them to retain generous portions of their profit for reinvestment. Shops and factories will spring up like mushrooms after spring rain, and even foreigners will want to invest in our commerce. I will show the foreigners a Su-chou richer and more successful than anyone ever saw under the decadent Manchu demons. Su-chou will be a heaven within a heaven. And we will strike out from Su-chou into the surrounding country, capture all the towns and cities, and bring them into the sanctuary of the heavenly kingdom of the T'ai-p'ing.

5 Kiangsu Governor Hsüeh Huan sat behind a polished table carved of heavy red mahogany and draped with embroidered red silk runners at the center of a wide dais in the rear of the great hall of the Shang-hai county yamen. A stately audience of men in long silk gowns sat upon rows of polished teak and rosewood chairs that lined each side of the hall beneath embroidered silk tapestries and scrolls of T'ang dynasty poetry. When a messenger from Su-chou arrived at the gate, Hsüeh Huan was hearing petitions for relief from the many Wu-hsi and Su-chou gentry displaced by the Taiping rebels.

The messenger, a gold-button secretary from the office of the Chiang-su provincial judge, recognized many of the refugees in Hsüeh Huan's audience hall, so he whispered that his report was secret lest his news cause a furor. Many from Su-chou in the audience recognized this petty official from the provincial yamen and were immediately alarmed, and alert to hear what he would say. The messenger was taken up to the dais and waited there until the governor motioned to him.

"*Ta-jen*," the messenger whispered, "rebels have entered through the Ch'ang Men gate of Su-chou and taken the city. The governor has killed himself."

The governor's heavy black eyebrows arched so high that they raised his black cap of office, and his usually jovial expression disappeared. Some in the audience saw the sudden change in the governor's face and fear knotted their stomachs.

Hsüeh Huan quickly recovered his composure, so as not to alarm others. As brevet governor for months, he had been next to succeed to the office, and thought he was prepared for this message, but momentarily he could not think of what to do. He would have to take over as governor. He should hear the report in private. But only he could hear the petitions before him, and if he withdrew now the room would erupt in hysteria. He motioned to an assistant.

"Take this officer to the next hall, close the doors, and wait there with him."

The supplicant presenting his petition continued, and the tension in the hall gradually dissipated. After a suitable interval, Hsüeh Huan surprised the supplicant by cutting short his complaints and granting his petition straightaway. The governor clapped a wooden block on the table, announced a recess until early evening, and then chatted for a minute with his law secretary, to allay any anxiety in the crowd before rising and leaving the hall.

"Make arrangements to house the officials coming from Su-chou," Hsüeh Huan told *Taotai* Wu Hsü. "The office of Chiang-su provincial governor will temporarily be transferred here to Shang-hai."

"How many families? How many have escaped?"

Wu Hsü had been in the great hall of his own yamen when the governor's urgent summons came. He broke off from hearing intelligence about the Russians and went immediately in his sedan chair to the county yamen. The month-old report from the English-speaking Chinese boy he had placed at the Fitch soirée as a waiter – about the prattle of the Russian ship captain, and the conversation between Russell and Howe taipans about the Russian Ignatiev – would have to wait. Wu Hsü had much evidence that the Russians were inciting the Americans to go north to the Peiho, as well as

洋神 *Yang Shen*   *James Lande* 藍德

meddling in British and French policy for Russian advantage.

"More families than Ch'ang-chou or Wu-hsi," Hsüeh Huan said. "The rebels *released* many of them. Put them on boats, gave them food and money."

"What? Put them on boats? Didn't slaughter them?"

"Yes, it's very strange, don't you think?"

"They will be arriving over the next few days, then?"

"Tomorrow. I'll wait to see what government appointments to make. The temples of the City God, and the God of War, can they be readied to receive provincial officers?"

"Of course, *Ta-jen*. I'll see to that. Is money being brought from Su-chou? We'll have many mouths to feed."

"Probably not." the governor said. "The rebels certainly will not let any money get away. Revenue will have to be redirected here from elsewhere. The custom house, additional local taxes and surtaxes."

"Will the rebels stay in Su-chou, or are they going to attack Shang-hai?"

"No one can say yet. If they do come on to Shang-hai, there are no forces to oppose them. Chang Yü-liang's army fled from Su-chou as the rebels arrived, and I have not yet learned where he has gone."

"Not to Shang-hai, or I would have heard," Wu Hsü said. "Hang-chou probably, if they open the gates to him. His army treated Hang-chou quite roughly."

"Where is Yang Fang's foreigner, that Wu-te? Our last resort now is the army of foreigners, our so-called Foreign Rifles."

"Wu-te is here in Shang-hai, waiting for my orders."

"Well, get him started. How will he be paid? Where will you get the money?"

"The source of the money is not yet definite." He could not reveal Yang Fang's preparations for payment of the force, or Hsüeh Huan would want the money for the provincial government at Shang-hai. Anyway, Wu Hsü really did not know all the intricate, if not labyrinthine, arrangements made by Yang Fang. "Yang Fang is starting with the subscribers to the Pirate Suppression Bureau, and he may be discussing matters with the Ning-po Guild. For now, it will be done on credit, arms and equipment from the Western hongs. Soldiers' payroll later, after the army has been established."

Hsüeh Huan measured the hesitation in the *tao-t'ai*'s response and decided Wu Hsü was lying. What else could be expected from this Wu Hsü? However, both must have money – the provincial government in exile at Shang-hai, and the Foreign Rifles – so there is little point in pressing the question now. Time enough later, after the financing is in place, to open a small artery of the banker Yang Fang.

"Keep a close eye on this foreigner," Hsüeh Huan said. "Remember that no one must know we have sanctioned these Foreign Rifles, not until they win battles. If they lose, then let them die quietly."

"Su-chou has fallen," Wu Hsü said, "and Hsü Yu-jen has drowned himself. Hsüeh *Ta-jen* is permanent governor now. He tells us to have Wu-te enlist his Foreign Rifles."

"Su-chou!" Yang Fang said, shaking his head. "Did Wu-hsi fall as well?"

"Yes. Two days ago."

"There could not have been much fighting at Su-chou in two days."

"There was no fighting at all," Wu Hsü said with a sigh.

"What? Su-chou did not fight?"

"This morning traitors called out their welcome to the Loyal King from atop the city wall, and then they opened the Ch'ang Men gate to the rebels."

"漢奸 traitors?"

"That clique of Kuang-chou trash sold out and joined the rebels. You remember Li

Treachery at Soochow

Wen-ping and his ilk."

"We should have killed him when we drove the Triads from Shanghai, but he was protected by the *tao-t'ai* then, Wu Chien-chang."

"After the loss of so many cities," Wu Hsü said, "Chang Yü-liang's army probably became too dispirited to oppose any rebels. At Su-chou, even the *lao-pai-hsing* rose up against his army, in revenge for soldiers plundering the countryside, so it all must have seemed very bleak to General Chang. He sneaked out the Pan Gate and fled."

"Where has he gone?"

"Hang-chou, it would seem. Haven't heard yet."

"He won't be welcome in Hang-chou, not after what his army did to them last month. His is an army without a country."

"And ours is a country without an army."

"We have the Foreign Rifles," Yang Fang said.

"All right," Wu Hsü said. "Foreign Rifles. Wu-te wants a place within the walls where he can gather recruits. The best place still is the Temple of the Fire God, across from my yamen. Tell him to take his recruits there. Hsüeh *Ta-jen* says we are to keep a close watch on them, and this time I agree. With the temple close by, it will be easy for my people to watch what he does there."

The same Chinese boy that had guided Fletcher to the custom house three weeks before, to meet the *taotai*, came to fetch him to Yang Fang's home – any other place, such as Takee Bank, Fletcher guessed would attract too much attention. He was more aware now of how many rebel spies were in Shanghai, disguised as fortune tellers or chair bearers, lurking in the shadows, listening for information useful to the Heavenly King. Takee was waiting in his guest hall.

"Wu-te, belly bad news. Lebel takee Su-chou today."

"Already? Sooner than we expected. Was there much fighting?" Takee must be very upset. He didn't even call for tea.

"No fight, Wu-te." Yang Fang sighed heavily. "Jus' give up citee."

"You're joking. They surrendered without a fight?"

"No fight."

The despair in Takee's voice, and his downcast expression, moved Fletcher in a curious way, as if the banker were a friend as well as a financier. He tried to imagine what this news meant to Takee, his family, his business, his city. After all the fuss over protecting Soochow, it was hard to believe they just *surrendered* the damn city.

"I'm sorry."

Yang Fang looked up at the foreigner, into his strange blue eyes. Wu-te's eyes often made him think of the riveting stare of the star gods, the dwarf *k'uei hsing* 魁星 or the purple planet Tzu Wei 紫微, malevolent in appearance, but benevolent of purpose. Apparently, Wu-te also seemed moved by the tragedy. Yang Fang had known many foreigners over the long years, and had seen abundant anger and lust and greed in their faces, but rarely…what? Compassion 同情?

"Su-chou belly close. Today lebel takee Su-chou, tomollah takee Shang-hai. All lost, Wu-te."

A servant brought tea on a lacquered tray and set it on a table between them. Fletcher watched the servant withdraw, and thought he saw a woman's figure in the dimly lit hallway. Someone else knew Takee's anguish, and watched over him. Fletcher poured tea, holding the lid of the pot in place with two fingers.

"Have some tea," he said, offering the mandarin a cup. Yang Fang stared at the cup, then at the Fletcher, then accepted the tea as if waking from a dream. Fletcher held his own cup with one hand and lifted it with the fingers of the other in a gesture often witnessed but never performed. It seemed a sort of condolence.

"Not all is lost, Takee. Not before I have something to say about it."

6

Fletcher found the steam tug *Ta Yung* slowly fading into rising river mist where it was moored in the river off the Teenhow Temple, near the mouth of the *Yang-king-bang* creek. He paid a waterman to scull him out to her, climbed aboard, and gave a shout when he saw the deck and wheelhouse were deserted.

"Yayuss," came a deep, rasping drawl from the house. Hannibal Arlen Benedict was holed up in the cramped, grimy little saloon sipping coffee doctored with brandy.

"Well, as I live and breathe, *mon cher ami* my dear friend Fletcher Wood, the notorious adventurer. Come to witness my degradation have you?"

"*Ah, mon pauvre ami* my poor friend Hannibal,*"* Fletcher said, laughing. Benedict appeared somewhat worse than he did at the Astor House the month before. He was thinner, and his eyes were even more dark and rheumy. Even in half-light, his face contrasted noticeably with his long, black, curly hair and full black beard, and he appeared more pale than before. "Keeping track of you is a chore. I have spent half a day just trying to find your whereabouts. Someone said you'd finally gone from *Shanghai* to *Ta Yung*."

"Olympus to Hades. Gunboat to bumboat. First-class to steerage. Mate on a tugboat. Never thought it possible, *déclassé*."

"*Qu'avez vous donc ami* what troubles you friend? What happened aboard *Shanghai*? You said you thought you'd see something of the Chushans."

"Been easier to carry a struggling, snarling, snapping Cerberus to Tinghai and back. Didn't get on with Cap'n Townsend this time out – he'd've had me wear a dress and spin wool on Omphale's wheel while he wore the lion skin."

Fletcher was dismayed. No man's a mate who can't mind his captain.

"Hannibal, there's no denying your eloquent manner of expression, but it does not tell me a whole helluva lot. I've come here for an officer, not a mutineer, or a poet. What would Townsend say of it? Insubordination?"

"Insub..., hell no! It was all right until we got to Tinghai. Time before we stayed out in the anchorage, discharged and loaded from lighters. This time, a longboat full of cocked hats, brass buttons and gold braid came aboard, and the ol' cap'n, his eyes glaze over and he starts breathing heavy. Stood up taller than a Georgia pine, puffed up bigger than a bull under a cow chip, and started ordering us all about like we were cabin boys. Wouldn't let me do my job – just pushed me aside and gave all the orders himself. It was just about the most addle-headed display you could ever expect to see. I thought it impolitic to oppose the captain while the Frogs were aboard, but once they were out of earshot, I ripped into that ol' cuss, told him I was first mate on *Shanghai* and...well, enough of that. Suffice it to say, we did not agree, and I was invited ashore when we returned to port – but no faster than I got ashore myself."

"Not much of a recommendation." Hannibal has no more patience for brass hats and satin sashes then I do. If the story is not just mendacity, the gold braid would have rubbed him the wrong way as much as anything else. If Townsend lurched into the wake of the French, Hannibal would have fallen off and found his own wind. But this sort of thing appears to have happened a lot recently.

"Fletcher, if I did not stand up to that captain, then I'd be about as sorry as a worn out old shoe. But you and I, we go back a lot farther than *Shanghai*, way back to the Crimea. We have experience together, and we respect each other. You know I will take any bastion and hold any barricade, and I know I can place my life under your orders confident that I will not be shot apart for any stupid reason. Wet-nursing a supply boat is nothing at all like the freelancing venture you have in mind. Marching at the head of a regiment of infantry is a great deal farther than a stone's throw from being reduced to a larn-pidgin on a coal bucket."

Fletcher remained silent, partly waiting to see if silence would unhinge Hannibal any further, partly waiting for divine guidance. If Hannibal could keep close to the straight and narrow, he would be a brave officer men would follow, but it is never easy to tell which way he will jump. In Shanghai, one could grow wrinkled bark and green moss waiting for any better choice.

"I have sworn that when you decide your course of action," Hannibal said, "I shall cleave to your plan of campaign." And why not. I could have my own army if I wished it, but command is a heavy burden best taken up by another if there be one competent. The money's the thing – I do not relish going hat in hand to these smug and supercilious mandarins and abasing myself at their feet, knocking my head on the floor nine times, to get their money – rather be kicked to death by grasshoppers. Groveling for Chinese cash – that, too, is best left to another, to some bloodsucking leech like Urea Heep that craves licking Chinese…boots. They won't be regulars either, Fletcher's little army. More likely wharf rats and derelicts, hard to train, harder to discipline, whose backs will bleed with all the bamboo chow-chow they'll need to keep them in line.

"There will be just the two of us for a while, another like yourself, one Elias Fell, an officer I met in South America nearly ten years ago, wrote to say that presently he is bond slave for several *zaibatsu*, those large trading companies in Japan, where he interprets English, and does not expect to cut free soon. He says he speaks Chinese, too, but as I recall his brush always had a lot of paint."

"We can hope his Chinese is better than my Hindustani. By the way, I assume you made your investigation upriver, aboard *Confucius* with the indomitable Captain Ghent. So, what is the plan of campaign? Of even greater interest, on which side do we fight?"

"We defend the emperor against the rebels."

"Ever the unionist, eh? Pity the poor rebels. When do we start?"

"As soon as you can leave this watch."

"An engineer's below. He can take over. I'll pack my seabag, scribble a note of heartfelt resignation, and leave it with the engineer. Where are we off to?"

"The native city. One of their temples, for a king of fire, Takee said."

"What does the work pay?"

"As my second-in-command your monthly pay is $400.00 Mex, with bonuses for towns captured."

"Four hundred! Whew. There's another excellent reason you can most assuredly depend on me, Fletcher, *mon ami*. Or should that be 'sir'? Or captain, or colonel? What are our ranks, anyway?"

"Haven't given that any thought yet."

"Well, I recommend you for a colonel to start, and I'll be your major."

"'Fletcher' and 'Hannibal' will be all right in private – but formal military courtesy will always be necessary in front of our men."

"Yes, of course. That would be needed to maintain discipline."

Fletcher rented two sedan chairs on the Bund. They crossed the footbridge over the *Yang-king-bang* creek into the French Concession, passing the French consulate and the Ningpo Guild joss house on the way. The chair coolies turned onto the Great East Gate road and loped toward the city wall, passed through the huge gate at a wave from the French guard and imperial sentries, and halted just inside the wall. Fletcher paid and dismissed the chairs, remembering that Chester Hicks never took a strange chair all the way to any destination, since any coolie could be a rebel. He took out a document written in Chinese with a map drawn on the back.

"Is ever the sailor without his chart?" Hannibal said. "What have we here?"

"I sketched this from Takee's directions. This's the east gate, that's the *taotai*'s yamen, and this building opposite is supposed to be our bivouac, the temple of a fire king. At least that's gist I got from Takee."

"Right under the eye of the *taotai*. No mistake there – he'll keep a close watch on how his cash is spent. Our men will have to be on good behavior, considering they'll be on the *taotai*'s very doorstep."

Fletcher led Hannibal past the *taotai*'s yamen to a walled compound across the street. On the north side of the compound they found a crowd of people coming and going through the entrance of a large temple festooned with scores of yellow lanterns under the eaves of the gate. Above the entrance were the characters 火神廟, which matched those Takee had written on the map. The temple walls were ochre with cinnabar trim, and over the entrance there was a high roof of three tiers of black tiles. Around the ochre spirit screen, there was a large courtyard in front of an open main hall, with corridors along each side leading to the rear. Along the sides of the courtyard, there were many small stands, one offering roast corn and red pastries, another serving bowls of noodles, and others selling whatnots including paper effigies, candles, holy icons and incense. Dozens of people stood in front of a small stage watching marionettes dressed in elaborate military uniforms, each with sword and lance and a clutch of pennants at their backs, waging war across the boards.

"Ah," Hannibal said, "our first recruits. Look at them fight!"

The crowd parted and watched warily as the two foreigners crossed the open space, mounting stone steps to where a four-foot tall iron urn entwined by a black dragon stood before three altars draped in red cloth. Wisps of sandalwood incense smoke drifted out of the urn and down the steps. The long, low tremor of muffled brass gongs and the tock-tock-tock of tapping on wooden fish – hollowed-out camphor wood blocks lacquered red or gold – echoed through the smoke-blackened rafters. Life-size effigies of Taoist gods crouched on tables behind each altar, with a large red-bearded fellow in their center. His face and hair were bright red, he had three eyes, a headdress like a fishtail, and a red robe embellished all over with symbols of broken and unbroken lines in groups of three. But all the god's red-faced ferocity could not evoke nearly the curiosity and fear from the worshipers edging around them as did the two foreigners.

"Do you suppose we're welcome here?" Hannibal said.

"You not accustomed by now to Chinese staring at you?"

"Well, certainly – they just don't know any better. But these aren't smiling."

Their foreboding vanished with the appearance of a short, bald priest in an amber robe, dangling a rope of walnut-sized brown beads over one wrist, who greeted the foreigners in Chinese. Fletcher showed him the document from Takee, the priest softly chanted the characters, then broke into a wide grin and bowed several times.

"How's that for a smile? Feel better?"

"Colonel, you are amazing. Where can I get such a letter?"

The priest led them down one of the side corridors to the rear of the main hall where there was another courtyard with a smaller hall at the rear. There were many small rooms around the sides of this courtyard, most occupied by what appeared to be pilgrims and travelers, spilling out into the corridors. Blind mendicants sat against the walls with begging bowls in their laps murmuring chants and fingering their beads. Fletcher and Hannibal were taken to one of the rooms and left to themselves. The room was warmly lit by several dusty lanterns, and furnished with a wood-frame wicker bed along each side, mosquito netting, chairs and small tables, and a wardrobe. At the back, there was a crockery water pitcher, and wash basin on a table, and on each bed there were two large folded quilts of heavy cotton covered in embroidered satin.

"I do believe we're expected," Hannibal said. "They've laid out their best linen."

"Looks like this will be our headquarters for the time being, a staging area where we can hold recruits in transit to a training ground. Can you manage that priest, see how many rooms we can have?"

"I suppose so," Hannibal said, sighing, "with ample sign language, point to a room then point to me. However, we must enlist an interpreter soon."

"For the past month, I've had the pilot aboard *Confucius* as my interpreter, and I sorely miss him now. Takee can provide someone temporarily, but we'll have to get a proper interpreter for the army, the 'foreign rifles' as Takee calls them."

"Foreign rifles, huh? All right, we're the Foreign Rifles."

Late into the night, Fletcher reviewed for Hannibal what had passed in the discussions with Takee and, later, the *taotai*. After they turned in, Fletcher could not sleep on the hard wicker bed and his restless mind went from one bugbear to another until he settled on the enigma of Hannibal.

He will be one of my lesser risks, thought Fletcher, and perhaps one of my greater assets. In the field, he will excel, understanding the purpose and details of tactics, and leading his men from the front and not the rear. In garrison, he will be as harsh as necessary to keep the drunken rowdies in line, so that my capacity to lead will not be so compromised by punishments. Men who cannot be ruled by their own rudder will be ruled by the rock of his hard fist.

His attitude toward the coloreds, his contempt for Hindustanis and Chinese, that could be a liability. Yang and Wu will quickly sense his cold temperature, and that will impair his effectiveness with them, and leave them to me alone. I will have to try early to coax him into congeniality toward our sponsors, else he may do violence to their regard for us. That is – more violence than is inevitable already.

洋神 *Yang Shen*   *James Lande* 藍德

Dramatis Personae: Chapter 23

Nigel Falconer   Drill sergeant, 2nd Queen's
Darby Garden   Sergeant 2nd Queen's, former drill sergeant

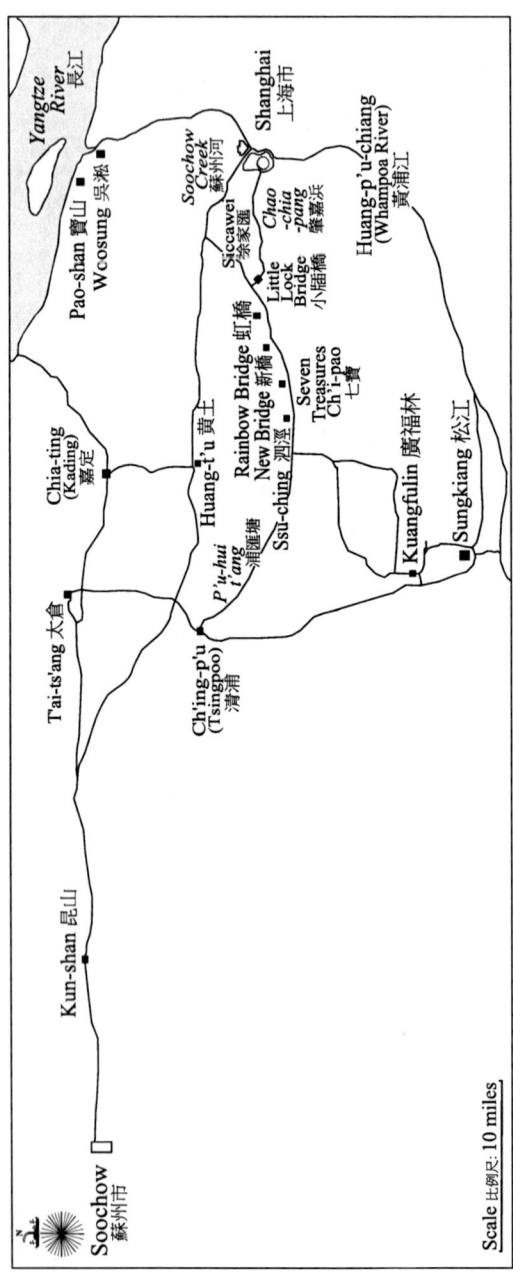

Country west of Shanghai
[from several sources, noted in Underfoot*]*

Hiring Foreign Rifles

Chapter 23: Hiring Foreign Rifles
Monday, June 3, 1860, 8:00pm

The
North China Herald
Shanghai, Saturday, June 2, 1860

England......Apr 10   Singapore......May 14
Bombay......May 1   Hongkong......May 25
Calcutta   ----   New York......May 27
Galle..........May 6

Shipping Reports. By the *Bustard* from Chushan we have received the following, dated 27th ult. – On the morning of the 22nd ult., a combined expedition on a small scale took place against a horde of pirates whose den was situated between the island of Latee and Chushan. The force employed consisted of H. M. Gun-boats *Bustard* and *Woodcock*, the marines and two cutter crews of the *Imperieuse*, and one Company of the 99th Regiment, the French Gun-boat *Alarme* and a few French troops. ...Most of the pirates got into the main land of Chushan and escaped. The land force should have been there to receive them, but it came up two hours late. As it was however, twelve or fifteen were killed and about forty made prisoners. Amongst the latter is the wife of "Fokie Tom," the pirate leader, who is said to be an Englishman. She is a rather pretty Malay girl. The *Bustard* got ashore in her channel and remained there until next day, when she returned to Tinghae with 17 junks, the *Woodcock* 7, and the *Alarme* 2, and 6 were burnt.

Fletcher's black frock coat contrasted sharply with the redcoats at the Crown and Anchor as he and Hannibal Benedict pushed their way inside early the next evening, just after the report of the evening gun at the British consulate. The room was packed like a crate full of boiled lobsters, with men clad in the scarlet or red undress uniforms of their regiments, topees, shakos or forage caps in hand, or the blue jackets of their ships. Some men wore mufti, but most evidently never expected to be in Shanghai long enough to forage for shore togs. The gamut of Chinese girls working the crowd ran from brassy hustlers at the bar in high-collared slit skirts of glistening ruby or sapphire silk, to demure empresses in quiet silk jackets over short gray or black satin gowns holding court at tables. Between the music of a concertina, an accompanying round of *All Jolly Fellows*, and the din of shouts and oaths it was hard to hear much.

The Crown and Anchor was in the British concession, a few blocks west from the Bund on Park Lane, called by the Chinese the Great Horse Road 大馬路, the *maloo*. The Crown had been a two-story wooden teahouse that a fortuneteller divined would earn riches as a grogshop when foreign ships first arrived at Shanghai. The large, windowless room downstairs was lit by oil lamps and smelled of stale rum. Along one wall, there was a long mahogany bar with a wooden foot-rail and brass spittoons at convenient intervals. Enclosed booths lined the wall opposite, with simple wooden tables and chairs crowded into the space between. Play was underway at a billiard table in the back. The furnishings were kept bare and utilitarian, as they were smashed to splinters every week. The Crown made fortunes for woodshops on the *maloo* that turned out expendable furniture and billiard cue sticks for Western drinking establishments.

Upstairs there was a more elegantly appointed tearoom, with stiff benches at the entranceway for the pretty young girls who welcomed guests to the Crown, and private rooms and alcoves in the rear. The 2nd floor was encircled by a narrow verandah for dallying over cool drinks on lazy summer days, and the roof was covered in brightly glazed green tile with sharply upturned eaves.

The Crown was habituated by British non-commissioned officers mostly – sergeants, quartermasters, boatswains and other petty officers – the ordinary ranks of soldiers and seamen being disinclined to sit and drink with the brutal NCOs that daily lashed bloody the backs of enlisted men. Warrant officers – mongrels damned to wander in a perpetual limbo between enlisted hell and commissioned heaven – came and went unchallenged, but commissioned officers were even less welcome at the Crown than a master-at-arms. The two Americans probed along the bar until they found a breach in the wall of revelers.

"H'lo, Yank! What're ya drinkin'?"

No one ever mistook Fletcher for anything but an American.

It was still early enough for the British crowd to be convivial. Earlier in the day, Fletcher and Hannibal had started off for Bob Allen's, the American boarding house across the river on the Pootung side, to begin recruiting ship's officers and seamen. As they considered how to fill their muster, it occurred to them that they first needed military men rather than seamen – reliable men that could set up an encampment, lay out field fortifications, and train riflemen. Drill sergeants.

"We want three stripes or more," Fletcher said, "older men with service as far back as the Crimea. The 44th was there, and in India."

The Allied Expeditionary Force temporarily garrisoned at Shanghai was, of course, a fountainhead of British noncommissioned and petty officers champing at their bits for action after long delay. The troop transport *Octavia* had been moored out in the river for almost two months since she left Chushan, and had aboard scores of sergeants seasoned by service with the 67th and 99th Regiments. Most of them weathered their doldrums at the Crown and Anchor.

"Be no ha'm if we bought the drinks, would there?" Fletcher shouted. "Ahoy there, barman. Open a case of champagne and pour drinks for the boys here at the bar." Immediately the crowd on the main deck began to drift over toward the bar, and the girls started circling like little requiem sharks.

"Geezah?" asked the Chinese behind the bar.

"Old man? Oh, yes, Giesler's champagne." Fletcher tossed down a golden eagle. "That can pay for the glasses, too."

"Coo, there's some bloody rhino."

"Uncle Jonathan, yor heart's in the right place!"

"God bless ya mate!"

"Now there's a proper bloke!"

"There's no bloody emperor in Pekin. He's right here!"

"Yank, you's a bloomin' toff."

"Who's payin' for this?"

"The Yank down there, one t' looks like a clergyman."

"The one that can't say 'r' any better than a Chinaman?"

"Is he touched then?"

"Cheers, pukka sahib!"

"What's the occasion, Yank?"

"A toast to soldiers of the Queen! Hear, hear!"

"You can soldier in my army anytime, Yank."

"Truth be told, I am looking for men to soldier in *my* army."

"What army's that?"

"An army to fight the rebels around Shanghai," Fletcher said loudly. "I want brave men and true, a band of brothers. Pays $100 Mex on time every month."

Word of his offer flew about the Crown like an electric telegraph message. Fletcher walked along beside the bar, toasting the men, examining chevrons and faces, and came to a sergeant of the 2nd Queen's with three gold chevrons and a crown on his single-breasted red tunic. The tunic had gold piping, brass buttons down the center, and a yellow collar and cuffs. He also wore a white crossbelt, white waist belt with cartridge pouch, and his trousers were dark Oxford gray with a red seam. On the bar in front of him lay a white topee – cork helmet – wrapped in a white linen pugaree.

"With the gallowglass you'd call mercenaries," said the sergeant in a deep bass voice, "discipline is difficult, especially when there's loot to plunder."

The sergeant was a large man, mid-thirties, over six feet tall, solid as plug of pig iron. His grizzled black hair and muttonchops coiled around a ruddy face with a broken nose. His eyes were obsidian-black.

Hannibal joined them as Fletcher stretched out his hand to the sergeant.

"This is Colonel Wood," said Hannibal, "and I am Major Benedict." Fletcher shot Hannibal a quick glance of disapproval. A small imposture, perhaps, but the Crown was no place to boast of filched rank.

"Sergeant Nigel Falconer." The sergeant inspected the Americans as if they were recently paroled.

"Know something about mercenaries, do you sergeant?" Fletcher said.

"Yes, sir, usually to my regret."

"Nigel, here, he knows all the laddies." This testimonial came from another three-striper standing at the bar behind Sergeant Falconer.

"Sergeant Darby Garden," Falconer said, jerking a thumb over his shoulder.

Garden turned to spit out a quid of tobacco, wiped his mouth, and then stepped around to shake hands with Fletcher and Hannibal. He looked a mix of Gael and Norse, in his mid-thirties, tall and lean, with reddish hair, a thick reddish waxed mustache, and light blue eyes. He wore the same uniform and insignia of the 2nd Queen's as Falconer.

"The rum barrel's empty, Yank" Garden said, burring his 'r's, "an' th' treasury's depleted, so your champagne's not unwelcome. Been here too long – marooned you could say."

"Came up from 'ong Kong on *Assistance*," Falconer said, "and was detached for a little garrison duty at Shanghai. Now our ship's sailed to Chushan and we're waitin' to go north with the 99th aboard *Octavia*."

"Marooned," Garden said, and he drained his glass. "We've been sitting on our bums in this bloody harbor for so long now it seems like home service. And na' a bean left. *An droch staid*," he added in Scottish Gaelic, "were in a bad condition."

It occurred to Fletcher that many of the Queen's soldiers had probably run through all their shillings while marooned at Shanghai, and now they were desperate for ready cash. One more burr under their saddles that the money he offered would brush away.

"Sergeant Falconer," Fletcher said, "you look as if you've seen a war or two."

"Or three, now," Garden said. "A bonny ol' rat-catcher, our Nigel."

"Right, sir," Falconer said. "I first took the Queen's shillin' with the 44th Regiment. At Alma we were with the 3rd Division, in the reserve at Inkerman, and after stormin' back and forth for months at Sebastopol finally saw action at Dockyard Creek and the cemetery. Long wait for little glory, that 'n. The fightin' kept on for months before the city fell, an' what we saw there when we marched through – the piles of rotting corpses – well, it was 'orrible."

"But not so horrible as Lucknow," Garden said.
"Or Cawnpore. That was the worst," Falconer said.
"Have you ever been wounded?" Fletcher said.
"More 'n I can count, bayonet, shrapnel…".
"Na' countin' cuts from broken rum bot'les," Garden said. "How many wounds have *you*?"
"At least as many as Alexander the Great," Fletcher said stiffly.
"Never mind Darby's chaff," Falconer said. "You seen some action too, sir."
"Crimea," Fletcher said. "Crossed over by steam packet and took a coaster to Gallipoli. Joined a battery of 12-pounders attached to the French 2nd Corps D'Armée at Inkerman. The British Light Division under Pennefather was taking a terrible beating on the eastern heights against charge after Russian charge until French infantry and artillery finally advanced."
"There now, I knew of that General Pennefather," Garden said. "The Good Lord himself would blush at the man's profanity, but he held ground like a bulldog in the Alma heights, and the foggy valley at Inkerman."
"We were ordered," Fletcher said, "to set up our guns close to the Russian line and, when the fog cleared, we cut loose at the Russian right flank, drove them back down the slopes. French artillery cleared the entire length of the line, and French infantry and Zouaves poured down the ridges and drove the Russians back. Ivan tried one riposte but was cut down by French artillery and British minié rifles."
"Colonel Wood commanded that battery," Hannibal said.
"Would either of you happen to be a drill sergeant?" Fletcher said.
"That I am," Falconer said. "Darby here was a drill sergeant with the 93rd some years back."
"Ay," Garden said, "I ken the firing drill as well as any blighter, and I can train marksmen wi' any weapon, be it Brown Bess, Brunswick, minié rifle, or Enfield."
"Let's get to closer quarters," Fletcher said. "Too loud here for talk."
Falconer liberated a bottle of champagne with glasses and led the way upstairs. Hannibal remained behind to continue working the 1st floor. A gauntlet of pretty Chinese girls delayed Falconer's advance at the entrance to the tearoom. The girls jumped up and surrounded the redcoats, fragrant perfume drifting up from sachets buried in their elaborate coiffures, embroidered silk dresses gleaming in the half-light. The huge men hesitated to step forward for fear of crushing them. A fat old Mother Goose rushed up honking and flashing her wings to shoo her goslings back to their perches and extricate the men. She waggled over to a table by the verandah and the men followed her. They waved away three girls the Mama Goose brought to their table.
"An army of any kind needs disciplined leadership," Fletcher said. "That's why I want you." He went on to quickly describe his purpose, what he expected from them, and the rewards he offered. They discussed the authority for Fletcher's force, the disposition of the rebel army, the terrain to be defended, overall defensive strategy, tactics of assaulting walled cities, and the specifics of recruiting, supplying, and training soldiers of varying experience. Throughout the exchange, the sergeants remained skeptical in expression and tone. Fletcher became anxious that he might not be able to win them over after all. Falconer finally summarized their view of the proposal.
"Well, Colonel Wood, here's…."
"Please, just Mr. Wood. If anything, 'colonel' would be an honorific title."
"As you wish, Mr. Wood. I believe I can speak for Darby here when I point out, no offense intended, that you're an unproven commodity, and we risk losing a great deal. Penalty for desertion is severe, and it means twelve or fourteen years for naught."

"Assuming we are na' shot by the Taiping rebels," Garden said.

"So, you believe you cannot do it?"

"Ach, to be sure we can do it," Garden said.

"What you set out seems quite practical," Falconer said. "You've given it all some thought, and my experience says it's workable, given enough time. Ah, but the time, that's the rub now isn't it? You have said the rebels are near us now in Soochow, maybe southwest seventy miles. That is very close."

"They'll be on us quicker tha' dogs on a fox," Garden said, "and tha's na' much time to find, equip, and train an army large enough."

"It's an unusual situation, Mr. Wood," Falconer said. "I mean, armies have long since come out from inside their medieval castles. We fight now across broad expanse of lands, with long-range rifles and artillery. We'd have to go back maybe five hundred years to find a 'istorical parallel. You say the rebels will be determined to capture walled cities, and not descend upon us like 'owling 'oards of barbarian 'orsemen, taking little advantage of their superior numbers. In that case, a small and nimble army could successfully wage an irregular campaign, a guerilla campaign, so to speak."

"My idea, exactly," Fletcher said.

"I like his notion of armed steamers, Nigel," Garden said. "It's like cavalry on water, a flying column that can almost be in two places at once. Still it's a lot to expect in so little time."

"My advice to you, Mr. Wood," Falconer said, "is to make haste slowly, and do not allow your army to be put in the field before it is ready, or where it cannot be effective. Your strategy and tactics will always be that of the small force against the large, so you must never be where you are expected."

"Yes," Garden said, "leave garrison duty for Chinese soldiers so your army can fly away in an instant."

"Yes, good advice, which I will not disregard. So, what do you think?"

Falconer and Garden begged off a hasty decision and said they'd consider it. Fletcher left them to their deliberation, and went downstairs somewhat disappointed at their reserve, and disconcerted about their reservations. Punishment for desertion was a serious threat to the lifers, and Fletcher's lack of credibility discouraged the veterans.

Hannibal was at a table with two more sergeants, one in the 99th Regiment, the other in the 2nd Queen's. Their names were Colin Allbright and Byron Boxer. Hannibal's badinage elicited that Sergeant Allbright was formerly a London costermonger who took the Queen's shilling in 1854 and served with the 57th in the Crimea and the 64th in India and was now a drill sergeant in the 99th. Sergeant Boxer had been apprenticed as a chimneysweep in his youth, but in 1855 bolted for glory to the 2nd Queen's and saw service in India before coming to China. He was thoroughly stewed and prostrate in a brothel when his transport left Shanghai several weeks before, and now was reassigned for temporary duty and waited with the 99th to go north. He had been a drill sergeant with the 2nd Queen's, but knew he had come a cropper, and would gladly take $100 Mex a month over what he expected now would be the Queen's farthing. Fletcher had not even thought to ask where Falconer was from. Clearly, Falconer was English, and Garden a Scot, but he had to wonder at the difference between the information he and Hannibal elicited from a recruit. He later learned that Falconer came from Liverpool where he started as a waterman on the Mersey, and Garden was born in Aberdeen and was a laborer on London's West India docks when he enlisted.

"These boys are ready to sign up," Hannibal said.

"Well done," Fletcher said. "An army needs disciplined leadership, and that's why I want you drill sergeants."

"We know that, sir," Allbright said. "Drill and discipline make British foot soldiers the world's best."

"We know 'ow to discipline men all right, sir," Boxer said. "Never you worry."

Fletcher was not certain he liked Boxer's tone, and almost replied "if discipline is correct, punishment is not necessary," when Falconer and Garden joined them.

"We are with you, Colonel Wood," Falconer said. "How shall we start?"

"You'll all need to go get your kits, and change to shore togs. The British Marine patrols will be less likely to question you if you're not in your red tunics. Be at the East Gate of the native city in two hours, and we'll be sure you pass through the French on duty there." Fletcher handed them each a small red envelope. "The characters on these envelopes say 'Temple of the Fire God,' which is our rendezvous point in the city, and you need only show the characters to a chair bearer if you get lost. There's also five dollars Mex inside, and some Chinese cash."

"Weapons, sir?" Falconer said.

"Rifles we'll have for you by the time we arrive at our training camp. Bring along handguns and utility knives if you have them, telescope, compass, or whistle – any useful small equipment."

The four British drill sergeants left the Crown and Anchor. In the street, they separated, two for the Bund to get a sampan to take them to *Octavia*, and two for their godown barracks.

"Look 'ere, Falconer," Boxer said, "d' ya' think this 'ere Colonel Wood is the genuine article?"

"His plan is sound, and his bearing commands respect, which is more than I can say about some officers I've served under. Not much risk to go and see what he's up to."

"The money's genuine," Garden said, clinking the Mexican dollars in his pocket.

"That's right," Allbright said. "We've time enough t' go off on a lark. We can collect 'is pay, fight some rebels, and be back to muster on board *Octavia* before she sails north."

"We'll be missed at roll call," Boxer said.

"Ask to go to 'ospital, and have a chum report ya on sick leave."

"Ask your officer for shore leave," Garden said.

"Yes," Falconer said. "If you're back late you'll still not be a deserter."

2

"The British consul is on to you."

Artemis L. Fuller poured two glasses of brandy and handed them round. Fletcher and Hannibal had gone from the Crown and Anchor to Fuller's rooms on North Gate Street in the French settlement for the equipment and provisions Fuller had sent word were ready there. They found small crates packed with canvas shelter tents, canvas trousers, shirts of cotton, worsted, and serge, leather boots and wool socks, canvas leggings, blankets, two cast iron pots, and two bugles. There were also cartons of dry foodstuffs: coffee, sugar, crackers, jerky, beans, dried fruit, and tapers and lucifer matches. Fuller told them the rest of the order was in larger crates in the H. Fogg godown beside the *Yang-king-bang* creek. Carts would be needed to transport those.

"We can take these crates back with us tonight to the temple," Fletcher said. "What about the consul?"

"Masters sent a marine corporal to fetch me to his consulate this morning," Fuller said. "Told me he had word that I was selling arms to one Fletcher Wood, and that I was to cease forthwith."

"How does that concern the goddamn British consulate?" Hannibal said, fuming. "They have no jurisdiction over Americans."

"I thought better of denying the transaction," Fuller said, "as Masters obviously had reliable intelligence – there's no keeping secrets from staff in hong or godown. So I told him Takee Bank had placed an order for supplies, including some of our older issue muskets, which are quite legal to sell, and that I had no idea who was to receive the order until Takee's comprador told me where to send it all."

"Who would tell the consul?" Fletcher said.

"You have enemies here in Shanghai, Mr. Wood, or don't you know that?"

"Enemies!" Hannibal said. "Already? We are not yet past the starting post."

"I guess I can imagine," Fletcher said. "Augustus Fitch introduced some of them to me – Cummings, the *Herald* editor, chief among them, and now Consul Masters."

"Consarn Minnows," Hannibal said.

"Who else did you approach?" Fuller said.

"Takee opened an account at Jardine Matheson, but I have not been there yet."

"Ah, Whitfall," Fuller said.

"We had words at the soirée," Fletcher said, "but why would he want to ha'm me – he wants to do business with Takee Bank."

"He would not be above interfering with H. Fogg in order to force our business together in his direction."

"That I would not have expected," Fletcher said.

"Have you taipan's no conscience?" Hannibal said.

"Pity I'm just a clerk and cannot answer your question," Fuller said.

"I'll have to have another talk with Mr. Whitfall," Fletcher said.

"I told Masters it was none of his business and stormed out. Made a grand show of it, so all the consulate knows. But I'm not certain that's the end of it. Keep an eye out for British Marines."

Fletcher and Hannibal beat a course further up Broadway Road to the Hawse Hole. The place was nearly empty, and the only answer they got was from a drunken sailor.

"You're what? An army! Think a little louse like you can fight? I've got tougher lice under my collar. Go knock at the foundling home."

Hannibal wanted to knock the man down, but Fletcher would not allow it.

The Gunner's Daughter was crowded with better prospects, sailors from the USS *Hartford* and USS *Saginaw* in whites or mufti, a couple of weeks up from Hong Kong, *en route* to Tientsin with the American minister – together the ships mounted nineteen guns. The "Gunner" was a one-story shack near the Hongkew docks that looked a lot like the downstairs of the Crown and Anchor, with a long bar, tables and chairs, and a billiard table. The place was a drinking establishment and didn't employ girls, but the entrance was crammed with gabbling girls of diverse allure beseeching any jack to take them ashore, and inside there were a few at the tables.

"Barkeep," Fletcher shouted, "a case of your best champagne for the boys at the bar to splice the mainbrace." That was certainly the easiest way to clear a path to a place at the bar. The eagle Fletcher ostentatiously dropped on the bar spun a noisy pirouette and had the attention of the crowd before it was still.

"Hey, cock your weather eye on that!"

"Now, don't that beat all!"

"That's for me! I'm as thirsty as a shipwrecked rumpot."

"Tumble up, barkeep, a bottle over here!"

"Don't get in such a pucker – your turn'll come."

"Are ye celebratin' sumpin, Cap'n?"

"A new army," Fletcher said.

"What army be that, Cap'n?"

"An army to fight the rebels here at Shanghai," Fletcher shouted above the din. "A stalwart band of brothers to flog the longhairs. Pays $100 Mex every month."

A cordon of sailors ringed him round.

"You're joking, aren't you mate?"

"A hundred dollars is a half year's pay for some of these boys."

"This yokel has got too much paint in his brush."

"Here now, I'm a gunner's mate. How do I join?"

"When it comes down to the short sixes, we can beat ten times our number."

While the clamor around Fletcher grew, an old petty officer slipped out through the gauntlet of girls at the front door and hurried off down Broadway Road.

Fletcher and Hannibal went to a table and began to talk about the adventure to a dozen excited sailors sitting and standing around them. As he rattled through his oration on discipline, leadership, the rebels, and the terrain, Fletcher examined the eager young faces and realized that sailors aboard a small American sloop of war would not have seen much action, nothing like a British tar over the past ten years. This was all green wood and, with the exception of the gunners, would be a liability to the Foreign Rifles. With a knowing glance at Hannibal, he veered off into grim detail about hardships, dangers, and punishments he conjured on the fly. Some of the sailors began to drift away.

An American naval officer in navy-blue frock coat with three gold stripes on the sleeves, white shirt and black satin cravat, and cap with patent-leather visor appeared inside the entrance of The Gunner's Daughter, followed by two burly chief petty officers in summer whites. The sailors at the bar made way for their officer, and the jabbering at the table fell away as the room became aware of his quiet presence.

"What's that officer doin' in here?" a sailor muttered.

"Who is he?" Fletcher said.

"Barnet," the sailor whispered, "lord o' the larbolines."

"On *Hartford*?"

"Yeah. This's our hole!"

"Reef your canvas, sailor," growled one chief. "You're three sheets to the wind."

"Thinks look squally, mate. Douse your skys'l, haul down and clew up."

Fletcher's stomach sank. The lieutenant commanding USS *Hartford*'s larboard watch, he thought, with what are probably two masters-at-arms in tow.

Barnet waited a minute for the hubbub to subside before he salvo'd. Legalities aside, he felt off limits, a trespasser on the crew's sordid retreat from shipboard life, and thought he owed respect, at least to start.

"Please don't stop on my account, Mr. Wood," Barnet said. "I'd like to hear the promises you are making to my crew."

"The riches of Montezuma, a kingdom at your feet, life everlasting?" Barnet had him dead to rights. When confronted by a superior enemy, beat a tactical retreat? Let us make this graceful. Barnet's probably a good officer, or he would not be here now.

"Yes, that has tremendous appeal, Mr. Wood," Barnet said with a smile. "Certainly to gullible young men in search of adventure far from home. Why would I not want to join you myself?"

"I could use an officer like you, Lieutenant Barnet." Fletcher was serious.

"I'll bet you could. Would you take my gunner as well? What say you Hanford, will you go with this adventurer, for his Aztec gold?"

"Well, sir," stammered Hanford, the USS *Hartford* chief quarterdeck gunner. "No sir. We were, we…."

"I know. Just listening, to an old shellback spinning his fantastic yarn. No harm in that. What's the reality, though – the part he hasn't told you? That you'll be marched off to some fever hole with defective equipment and spoiled provisions, if any, and run through a few days of inadequate drill passed off training? Then together with a few hundred other chowderheads, you'll be shuffled in front of ten thousand screaming rebels and ordered to charge full on? Did he say that when you're wounded, you'll be left on the field for the enemy to cut to pieces, that your flesh will rot and your bones bleach in the sun, and your father, your mother, your family will never know what ever happened to you? Bones of rebel victims lie beside the waterways of this hardscrabble in some places a foot thick. Did he mention that if you survive it all, you'll live out your days on the run as a deserter and that, if apprehended, you might be hanged? This *is* a time of war."

"It will be nothing like that at all," Fletcher said.

"For your sake, Mr. Wood, I sincerely hope not. But I have encountered mercenaries and witnessed their handiwork. I would not wish their fate on a cur."

"There is more to this, Lieutenant Barnet. Rebels threaten this city."

"You will *not* take any of my men, Mr. Wood. Understand me clearly. You will not encourage any man of my crew to desert. As God is my witness, if one of my men goes to you, I personally will hunt you down and blow your brains out."

"You can't threaten us," Hannibal grumbled, rising. Fletcher also stood, mostly to keep Hannibal from leaping across the table to avenge a slight to honor.

"You *mis*understand, sir," Barnet said, almost in a whisper. The room was stone silent. "Mine is not a threat. Mine is a solemn oath."

Fletcher edged into Hannibal to start him toward the door.

"Lieutenant," Fletcher said, "I understand your concern, and respect your wish. In your place, I would feel the same, and do no less. I have no desire to interfere with your command, so I will not enlist any man from the *Hartford*, nor the *Saginaw* for that matter." At least not tonight, but I can pick off a few just before you set sail, when you have no time to come chasing after me. Likely as not, your ships won't be back, either.

Fletcher remained between Benedict and Barnet all the way out the door.

Falconer and the other three sergeants were standing outside the East Gate when Fletcher and Hannibal arrived. Fletcher needed only to say "good evening" in his American-accented French and they were passed through the gate. Food vendors were still serving in the courtyard when the six foreigners crossed through to the rear of the temple and found their rooms. Ten of the other men enlisted had found their way to the temple, and Fuller's coolies had come and gone carrying all the Foreign Rifles supplies on shoulder poles. After settling in and examining the crates and cartons, Fletcher sent the men back out into the temple courtyard for their first adventure – sampling Chinese street vendor food.

"Don't attempt anything that isn't cooked," he warned them.

3

"Heya, Fetchawood, you wake up!"

Old Huang tugged at Fletcher's shoulder. The pilot said he came from *Confucius* and that she was tied up at a wharf at the Bund opposite the East Gate. A great many

洋神 *Yang Shen*   *James Lande* 藍德

large boxes from Chester Hicks were aboard. And Ah-shan was tied up in the *Chao-chia-pang* 肇嘉浜, the creek that ran through the native city a short distance north of the Temple of the Fire God.

"Takee say Ah-shan takee you Kuang-fu-lin. Why go dere, Fetchawood? Only got big musky-toes 大蚊子."

Why indeed, thought Fletcher. Because Kuangfulin is where Takee and the *taotai*, my generous and trusting sponsors, have told me I must go. Four hours away, exposed to the enemy, impossible to maneuver in without boats, and under surveillance by the *taotai*'s men. Just a moment – I can think of *some*thing good about Kuangfulin.... Ah, yes, the men cannot get in trouble in Shanghai, the British are not likely to look there for deserters, and maybe Li Heng-sung's irregulars close by will be of some advantage, and not just under foot.

Ten days before, Takee had come away from his bank to Ah-shan's junk and together they had reconnoitered the waterways west of Shanghai all the way to Sungkiang. The old man was as good as his word – he displayed spirit as a campaigner, came aboard in simple dress, dark trousers and a quilted blue jacket and skullcap, and stood long hours beside the sweeps. Surprisingly, most of the waterways he knew well, and for the rest they simply asked directions. At Kuangfulin, they met imperial soldiers encamped nearby, and their brigade commander Li Heng-sung. This officer went aboard the junk and guided them to ground east of Kuangfulin where the Foreign Rifles would drill, old cotton fields overgrown with green clover and barley after the harvest the previous autumn. Li Heng-sung told Takee that the cotton farmers who left the land fallow fled the rebels and were not there to plant this spring. Takee also said that Li Heng-sung would be what sounded to Fletcher like the Chinese alter ego of the Foreign Rifles. From Kuangfulin, they went on down a maze of creeks and canals to the north wall of Sungkiang, entering through the north water gate on a canal that took them through the south water gate, intersecting a smaller creek that Takee said crossed the town from east to west. This "cross town" creek also passed under the town walls, through water gates at the east and west gates. From Sungkiang it was four miles south to the Whangpoo, then twenty-seven miles downriver to Shanghai.

Fletcher roused his men and told Hannibal to find someone outside the temple gate with a large wagon or cart. Hannibal returned with a Chinaman and a wagon drawn by a yellow ox, brought it into the temple courtyard, and ordered the men to load it up with their crates of equipment and cartons of provisions. Then they gathered up their things, put their shoulders to the back of the wagon, and helped push it through the foggy streets behind Old Huang to Lao Chang's junk. Both sides of the murky creek were chockablock with junks and sampans along the stone quays and muddy banks.

"Eh, *yang-kuei-tzu*!" Ah-shan shouted. "How ah yoo?" As ever, she was barefoot in her grimy-gray padded jacket, loose gray trousers, and red cloth headband. Fletcher tried to imagine coming home to her every night. Lao Chang was at her side in a long blue gown and a big grin, hands together before his face *chin-chin*ing their fairy godfather, and Little Chang was beside him with an equally big grin waving at Fletcher.

"Chinese family reunion, Colonel?" Hannibal said, laughing. The exuberant welcome surprised the sergeants as well. To Falconer, the Chinese seemed quite sincere.

While they removed the load from the wagon and carried the cargo aboard the junk, Ah-shan called Old Huang to the stern sweep and, after a brief exchange, the pilot went forward to where Fletcher stood at the larboard rail.

"Ah-shan, she say how yoo get cah'go off boat? No mo' wagon. Load many mo' box from *K'ung-fu-tze*."

"Confound it!" Fletcher said. "I did not think of that." He glanced back to the stern and threw Ah-shan a salute. "Can't carry it all into the camp – too far. We'll need some sort of dray at Kuangfulin, a cart or a wagon." What else have I forgotten, he wondered?

"Ah-shan, she say Kuang-fu-lin mebbe no can get wagon. Some wagon takee in pieces, wheel come off, can buy in Shanghai."

After unloading and stowing their cargo, Fletcher paid the Chinaman and went aboard the junk. Lao Chang and his wife both pitched into the *yuloh* oars this time. They managed to come about in the narrow, crowded creek and pushed out through the East Gate water gate and down to the Whangpoo, where *Confucius* loomed out of the fog over the Bund. The Manilamen on watch hailed Fletcher and, in a few moments, Fletcher was surrounded on deck by Vincente and dozens of Manilamen, all smiling and jabbering and pounding him on the back.

"Iluminada much better now," Vincente said. "Ah-shan and Lao Chang take good care at hospital. *Maráming salámat páre*, thank you very much friend."

"*De nada, púre*, nothing to it, friend," Fletcher said.

Captain Ghent stepped out to the landing of the wheelhouse stairs and shouted down "'bout time you turned up, *Mister* Wood. I have ten crates of rifled muskets for you, with ball and powder, from a mutual friend who supports your enterprise."

"Glad to hear it, Captain. Good to see you, too"

The pirate-suppressing mandarin, Yang Hsi-hai, poked his head out from the saloon and gave Fletcher a big grin and a wave. Vincente ordered his crew to unload the heavy crates onto Lao Chang's junk and, following Little Chang's gesticulations, Hannibal led his men in the stowing of the crates in the hold. The British sergeants looked at "Colonel" Wood quite differently now, as he obviously was efficient, commanding the respect of priests in Chinese temples and calling up junks and steamers like Aeolus called up the winds. He had the confidence, even the admiration, of the crews of the steamer and the junk, especially that grizzled old captain of *Confucius*.

Fletcher went up to the wheelhouse to palaver with Ghent. "Captain, can you do without your pilot for a few days, maybe a week? I have no interpreter as yet, and we are going inland to Kuangfulin today where there's no one but Chinese."

"Alone among the heathen, eh?" Ghent said. "My plan is to work *Confucius* as towboat for a while here in the harbor, be close at hand when you want her, so I will not have much use for that peckerwood pilot for a while. Sure, take him."

Ghent yelled out the door: "Huang, get your seabag, go with Mr. Wood."

"Aye, aye, Cap'n."

"I'll light the boilers under our banker friend about getting you an interpreter," Ghent said. "I'm also casting about for another steamer. Have a line on *Pluto* – she's too big for inland creeks, but she'll have to do for the time being, until we can dredge up smaller steamers."

"Would you mind if I took some of your Manilamen with me as well?

"Man, why not take 'em all, and swamp that junk as well. How many do you propose to leave me?"

"Only take four, Captain, of Vincente's choice."

"Oh. Well, that's not so many. Go ahead. Sorry the old girl can't come inland with you – we have to miss all the damned action, just steam up and down the ol' 'Poo craning our necks to see your smoke."

"We may be awfully glad one day to see *your* smoke, Captain."

Old Huang met Fletcher at the foot of the wheelhouse stairs.

"Hey Fetchawood, numbah one Shanghai pilot no good on litee stleam like dat," he said, pointing to the *Chao-chia-pang*. "Yoo got Ah-shan – what want me fo'?"

"You are promoted from peckerwood to interpreter."

"Me? Intapatah? My no talkee goddamn 'melican. You clazy?"

Fletcher placed a gold eagle in the pilot's hand, gave Old Huang a moment to register the eagle, then closed his fingers over the coin. "My tinkee," Fletcher said, mimicking Old Huang's pidgin with a wide grin, "you talkee plentee good 'melican, Lao Huang. Can you say 'eagle'?"

Old Huang looked up and smiled with great sincerity at Fletcher Wood. "Eeee-gull," the pilot said.

"Belly good. Buy another watch."

Vincente recommended four of his stalwarts as Fletcher's Manilaman bodyguard. He called them into formation along the rail and named each man selected: Ongoy, Inabayan, Tigas, and Salangsang. In Tagalog, he told them "go with this friend of Iluminada, this *kaibigan*, and keep our older brother, *kúya*, from harm."

"Four good men, *púre*," Vincente said. "Now nothing hurt you – live forever!"

Lao Chang, his wife, and their son leaned on their sweeps and pushed out across the native city. The Chinese on the junk took the place for granted, and Fletcher had come this way before – repetition slowly abraded the novelty. Some of the foreigners aboard saw only filthy water floating dilapidated boats, trash-ridden narrow streets, and poverty-stricken rabble, but Falconer found the passage diverting – a singular excursion into a peculiar place. The Chinese built water gates for streams and creeks to pass through 30-foot high walls and allow highways of water to convey boat traffic through the city. They passed the Temple of the Fire God, the crowded fish market, and under endless arched bridges carrying bustling foot traffic on north-south streets across the creek. The junk sculled between hedgerows of tile-roofed houses, shops, warehouses and temples surrounded by the early morning clamor of industrious people. The foreigners were barely noticed, as if no one ever expected to see outlandish barbarians on a junk in the dirty *Chao-chia-pang*. Approaching the west gate, Falconer gazed at another extraordinary temple, not knowing what it was, but noting with appreciation its tall timbered gates, blue-green glazed tile roofs, and sharply pointed eaves.

The junk slowed at several places quayside where Lao Chang asked about a collapsible dray, and finally stopped at the stone embankment near the Temple of the God of War. Lao Chang led Fletcher, Old Huang and two Manilamen ashore through a maze of streets and shops to a yard that built wagons and carts. Shortly after, they returned to the creek pulling two large two-wheeled carts. They removed the axle pins, dismounted the wood-spoke wheels, and carried the flat cart beds and wheels aboard.

"Does anybody know where we're going?" Sergeant Boxer yelled.

Lao Chang's junk had just crossed through the West Gate water gate, passed under the Ten-thousand Lives Bridge 萬生橋, and sculled away from the city wall in a southwesterly direction past Hsu-chia-hui 徐家匯, a Roman Catholic enclave known to the foreign community as Siccawei, where the creek was called the Siccawei River.

"Yes," Fletcher shouted. "To a camp near the town called Kuangfulin. If you want to know where you are, just ask Lao Huang here. Time you conned your course, gentlemen. Use your compass and timepiece and draw your own maps."

"Hey Fetchawood, my no sabee dis litee watah."

"Ask Ah-shan. She and I have been over these streams and creeks."

When an east wind came up, Ah-shan yelled and together with her Lao Chang and Little Chang raised the tall, slender lugsail into the lemon glow of morning. Fletcher expected that with another easterly breeze the junk might average six knots against the current, when not obstructed by other traffic – going any faster risked collision. Ah-shan went to the stern *yuloh* and Fletcher crooked a finger at Old Huang to join them.

"Listen, and watch, pilot, that the Good Lord may bless you with rare knowledge of these litee waters."

Ah-shan called out the milestones of their route, with Old Huang right behind her, trying his best to render the obscure Chinese of place names into meaningful English. The way to Kuangfulin was a snarl of streams and creeks, rights and lefts, north and south turnings that passed through three counties – Shang-hai 上海, Lou 婁, and Ch'ing-p'u 清浦 – and was barely large enough in some places for a wide junk. They sailed west by southwest from the native city along the narrow *Chao-chia-pang* creek in the midst of a cavalcade of boisterous junks and sampans transporting raw cotton and farm produce to eastern market towns and finished goods and foreign imports westward into the countryside. The junk made better time when they had put some distance behind her.

After the first hour Lao Chang's junk reached Little Lock Bridge, *Hsiao-cha Ch'iao* 小牐橋, just beyond where *Chao-chia-pang* creek flowed into a larger canal called the *P'u-hui-t'ang* 浦滙塘, which appeared to be a major thoroughfare inland from Shanghai judging from the volume of traffic it carried.

After two hours *P'u-hui-t'ang* canal had taken them past Rainbow Bridge, *Hung-ch'iao* 虹橋, and New Bridge, *Hsin-ch'iao* 新橋, and they reached Seven Treasures, *Ch'i-pao* 七寶.

During the third hour they skirted *Ssu-ching* 泗涇, which Old Huang could not or would not translate, and turned south by southwest from where the *P'u-hui-t'ang* canal went on to Ch'ing-p'u.

After four hours they sighted Kuangfulin 廣福林, "Big Luck Forest" according to Old Huang. Bamboo stakes encircled fish pens and duck ponds in lagoons along the approach to town. In town, open galleries of shops under tall willows lined each side of the creek, and behind the shops the green tile roofs of private homes peeked over white plaster walls. Long walls without doors or windows sometimes ended in a large, circular entrance with a round door instead of a square gate. The round door caught Fletcher's attention and, as they floated quietly through Kuangfulin, he enjoyed the opportunity to consider this architecture at leisure, without the threat of rebels close at hand. Towns in the Yangtze River delta grew up around the waterways – alongside the streams and creeks, as might a town elsewhere embrace roads and footpaths. Like Venice in Italy, everyone got about by boat, and water came to just about every front door.

"They construct these buildings," he said to Hannibal, "with all the anatomy spread out to see, supporting columns and roof timbers exposed to plain view, carved and painted. All the bones and sinews of a Chinese house are naked to the eye, not hidden inside walls."

"Houses all made of wood and covered by roofs of tile," Hannibal said, "but city walls, towers and fortifications all built of stone. Citadels of stone, like a medieval romance – *Waverly* or *Ivanhoe*."

"Stone stairs and flagstone walkways, too."

"Yes, and bridges – public edifices. I suppose they do not have enough stone for private dwellings, certainly not in a river delta, so wood, tile, bamboo, and plaster must suffice. The temples are elaborate, but there seems little variety in everyday structures."

Falconer joined them. "And do you see that the walls bear no weight?" he said. "Weight's all supported by columns. And the columns don't go into the ground, either – they rest on blocks, like that one there, with the wooden posts set atop stone plinths."

"You would think they'd all blow over in a stiff wind," Hannibal said.

洋神 *Yang Shen*   *James Lande* 藍德

"And they all 'ave those spines curving upward. I've wondered why."

"Keep evil spirits away is what I have been told," Hannibal said. "If I were an evil spirit, I would not come near one of those sharp rooftops."

"You *are* an evil spirit, Hannibal," Fletcher said. "We are all *yang-kuei-tzu* here."

"So, then, I should not go up on any Chinese roofs."

Fletcher glanced at the rooftop ridges that curled gracefully upward at the ends into sharp points. "Edges of roofs curved upward." he said, "let in more light when the December sun is low in the sky, so as to lift everyone's spirits on dreary winter days."

The junk lowered its mast for a steeply arched footbridge of stone with carved stone balustrades swept by the hanging branches of weeping willows. Women squatting on stone stairs beside the bridge, holystoning defenseless clothes in the creek, stopped giggling and looked up with alarm at the vile foreigners on the passing junk. Farmers in broad conical hats and straw sandals came and went over the bridge, their wives and daughters with long cotton sleevelets and brightly painted scarves draped over their hats to keep away the sun. Down the road from the bridge, there was a small temple with a tall roof and flying eaves, the Temple of the City God, Old Huang said. Every town is protected by its own city god, thought Fletcher, and every field by its earth god, *toody-goon*g Lao Huang calls him, all of them powerless against the rampaging rebels.

From the center of town, smaller creeks branched off in a weave of waterways. Lao Chang's junk came about into a wide, shallow creek that led east out into an expanse of fields surrounded by fetid swamp and salt marsh crisscrossed by sloughs and ditches that gave off brackish odors of decay. Looking astern, Fletcher could see that the receding hamlet of Kuangfulin was adrift upon a wide wetland, evidently invaded by saltwater tides, probably highest during summer and autumn, like those the junkman Lin Ch'uan had mentioned flooded his family's cotton fields. Sun and moon reached down and hauled the sea up onto the shallow land, and the weight of a great ocean pushed saltwater through channels and out into creeks and sloughs, like blood seeping from arteries into arterioles and capillaries, and briefly swelled the wetland ponds and ditches with brine. Long marshes and fens grew up in depressions where freshwater from the higher ground mixed with saline and gave rise to scattered white mulberry and osier, impenetrable stands of tufted rushes and other sedges, rose mallow and hollyhock, and stray cotton plants. Herons and egrets stalked the shallow pools for tadpoles, shrimp and salamander, wild geese and ducks flocked to the ponds, cormorants skimmed over the creeks, and long winding lines of swans glided high over the marshes. Marsh music of countless croaking frogs and chirping crickets filled both the day and night.

The creek was wide and shallow. Even midstream, the junk's hull rattled and scraped over the gravelly places. At intervals, the crew on the junk could see down along one or another marshy channel on the south to where a footbridge crossed between fields. From the creek, the southern horizon undulated with hummocks and rises surrounded by brushy, low-lying marsh that hemmed the higher ground into dry little islands where the farmers could grow their cotton. After perhaps twenty minutes, they came upon an undercut in the south side where the junk could drop anchors fore and aft next to the steep embankment and be stable enough to let down a gangplank. The creek was still 100 feet wide there and gave the junk room to come about for the return to Kuangfulin. Fletcher and the men went ashore and walked up a slight rise to where they could see the land, a forty or fifty acre tract of fallow cropland covered in green clover. As with the other land they had seen, this piece was wreathed by foul-smelling marsh and, as they immediately discovered, held by a host of ravenous mosquitoes. In the center of the high ground, there was one small white tent.

Now I remember, thought Fletcher. Mosquito netting! And those mosquito coils that burn like incense.

Together they unloaded and reassembled the two drays, unloaded the crates of rifles, and tied down the rest of their cargo on top of the rifles. Under a sweltering sun, they hauled and pushed the wagons up the slope and through patches of muck to their new stomping ground. A Chinese brave occupied the tent, a soldier under the Green Flag commander Li Heng-sung. When he saw the first of the foreigners approaching, he turned and trotted off toward the southwest.

"He's on his way to notify the commandant that we have arrived," Fletcher said. "His own Green Flag garrison is off there somewhere to the southwest."

"I will bet a month's rum ration this place was selected by *Taotai* Wu," Hannibal said, "so he can have one more flunky to oversee his investment."

"He not flunkee," Old Huang said, with a polite smile. "Li Heng-sung 李恆嵩 belly big sojah, him *ying-tsung* 營總, you say *ka-man-tan-t'e*, hab many blaves, *chuang-yung* 壯勇, mebbe ten-thousand sojah."

"It *is* a friendly watch he has over us, Hannibal," Fletcher said. "What I gather from Old Huang here is that this Lee-hung-soong is commander of a brigade of irregular Green Flag braves, so I have hopes his troops will come off better than the usual braves. I expect to see his brigade in the field as our support, and our garrison detachments will come from his ten thousand. He is the fellow who arranged for this site – we cannot just squat on some poor old sod's land. This Lee has been our go-between with the elders at Kuangfulin, and his pickets will keep the local natives at a distance from us. So, when you meet him, be cordial."

"Cordial!" Hannibal said. "Well, you may think your precious brigade commander walks on water, but I've seen this Green Flag rabble gallop into a village, trample all the men, rape and kill all the women, and burn every house to the ground. They're more vicious than the hounds of hell, and they'll slaughter everything that moves."

Ah-shan was sent back to Kuangfulin while the Foreign Rifles laid out the camp and unpacked and stowed the equipment and provisions. An hour later, she returned with some of the things the men could remember they had forgotten: bamboo poles for the tents, mosquito netting and mosquito coils, and a few luxuries like fresh vegetables, fresh pork, and four squawking chickens in a large split-bamboo cage.

Shortly after, a detachment of Chinese cavalry was sighted on approach from the southwest. They filed over a heavy footbridge onto the open ground and reined to a halt – a dozen horsemen armed with sword and bow, some bearing long pikes with flashing pennants, and at their center a solitary rider in armor.

"Don't like the look of that," Hannibal muttered. He nudged open the lid of a crate of minié rifles. "Looks to me like they're on the warpath." The sight of Russian cavalry charging his Inkerman battery flashed through Hannibal's mind. He unbuttoned his frock coat, reached in and yanked his holster forward, and unsnapped the keeper.

Sergeant Falconer reached into his knapsack and took out an Adams revolver.

"Don't anybody get spooked now," Fletcher said. "That has to be our imperial officer." He waved to the horsemen.

The armored rider started forward. On command, the ponies lunged after him, coming on at a hard gallop, kicking up sod in green clumps. With a great shout, the riders charged straight at the foreigners' camp.

洋神 *Yang Shen*   James Lande 藍德

Dramatis Personae: Chapter 24

Li Heng-sung 李恆嵩	Green Flag brigade commander 綠營鎮標營總
Wen Chia-pao 文甲胞	major 遊擊, Li Heng-sung's brigade
Bob Allen	inkeeper, Pootung American boarding house
John Colter	1st mate, American merchant ship *Fenimore Cooper*
Mr. Fan	Takee Bank clerk drafted as interpreter
Paco *Cockfighter* Dalogdog	Cebuano crewman, Chinese steamer *Confucius*

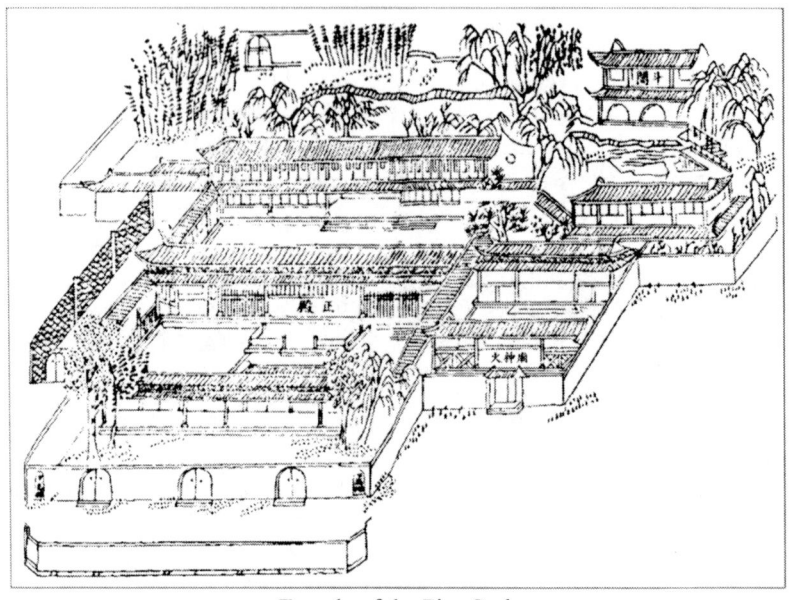

Temple of the Fire God
(based on Kuan-ti Miao, Shang-hai County Gazetteer, 1873)

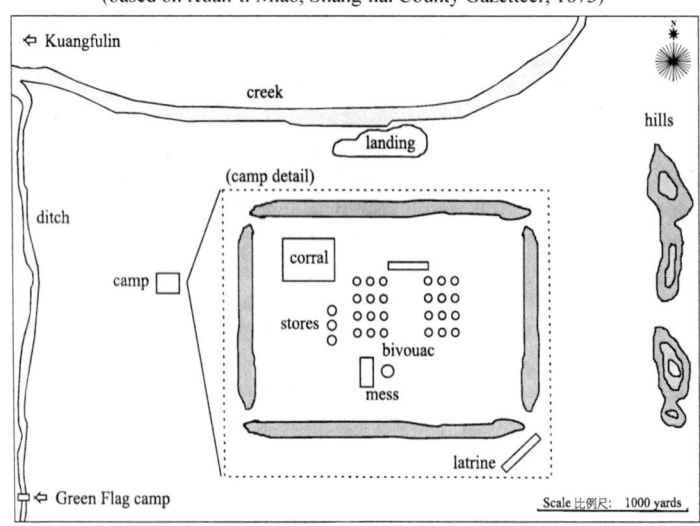

Foreign Rifle Camp near Kuangfulin

Chapter 24: Fire God Temple
June 6 to June 23, 1860

> The
> ***North China Herald***
> Shanghai, Saturday, June 9, 1860
> --
> **Latest Dates**
> England......Apr 10   Singapore...May 15
> Bombay......May 1   Hongkong...May 25
> Calcutta   ----   New York...May 27
> Galle......... May   6
> --
> **(*Communicated.*)** On Tuesday, the 5th inst., at the earnest request of the Taoutai of Shanghai and with the sanction of the Hon'ble Mr Blaine, a force of 400 men and officers of the Batallion of Royal Marines under Lieut. Colonel Gascoigne, with three howitzers, [after reconnoitering defensive positions seven miles up Soochow Creek, returned] with the tide to the Joss House Post near the Stone Bridge (Soochow Bridge). ...The next day, orders were given for 100 men to remain for the defense of the Joss House Post (which is a good position just above the Stone Bridge), and the remainder rejoined their quarters at the Godown Barracks and the *Octavia* transport. ...This post [near Stone Bridge] is now occupied by Captain Little's Company of 100 men, and communicates by patrols with the Company under Capt. Budd at the Ningpo Joss House. ...There is a small party of Blue Jackets also posted at the above Yamun. A portion of the Royal Marines have been withdrawn from the Ningpo Guild Hall and quartered within the outer and inner North Gates of the city. A party of French are similarly placed at the South Gate.

Fletcher slipped his Colt Navy from beneath his frock coat.

Sergeant Falconer stepped forward and stood beside Fletcher, cocking the hammer of the revolver he held at his side. Hannibal moved to Falconer's side.

The other men moved behind the drays and stacked crates.

Fletcher was no longer certain this armored apparition was Li Heng-sung. He did not clearly remember the man, and hardly expected an attack by imperial cavalry. They did not appear to be rebel cavalry. He thought of Inkerman and, for a moment, wished he had canister instead of a six-gun.

The horsemen came on line at a gallop just behind their officer, riders high in their stirrups, leaning forward, their pennants fluttering. They closed the distance in ten seconds. When only a few yards away from the three men facing them, the warrior in armor shouted a command, the line of horsemen shouted in unison and abruptly reined up in a flurry of dirt clods. Blowing hard, the little Mongolian ponies drooped under the weight of high-backed wooden saddles, massive stirrups, and heavy riders. One rider kicked his pony forward several more steps.

"這位是綠營鎮標營總李恆嵩 this is Green Flag brigade commander Li Heng-sung! 你們是誰 who are you?"

"Lao Huang," Fletcher said, "say I am the foreigner that came here with Takee."

The officer stiffened in his saddle, and then leaned forward. His iron helmet, with embroidered neck and ear flaps, and a spike on the crown dangling a tassel of red horsehair, obscured his face. He walked his pony forward to where Fletcher stood. The other horsemen followed.

洋神 *Yang Shen* James Lande 藍德

It was Li Heng-sung. A 4th-rank official's stone of lapis lazuli was mounted on the brow of the helmet. Fletcher put away his revolver. Li dismounted, moving quickly despite the encumbrance of armor. He was tall and sturdy – too large for his small mount. Standing close, Fletcher saw his square face and sharply angular features – nose, cheeks and chin that looked chiseled from stone. His quilted armor had three-quarter length sleeves and a knee-length skirt vented for riding – all covered with thin copper plates and copper studs – and iron shoulder guards covered in embroidered green satin, worn over an embroidered sea-green silk gown with long sleeves, horsehoof cuffs beneath carved ivory disks, and a vented skirt.

The horsemen dismounted. One had a black bear embroidered on the chest of his jacket, three others had tiger cats, and the rest of the bowmen had the characters 壯勇 – Fletcher recognized the 勇 for brave. They all wore blue surcoats with black cuffs and collars over embroidered blue silk gowns with long sleeves, horsehoof cuffs 馬蹄袖, and vented skirts over black trousers and knee-high riding boots 馬靴. Their porkpie hats had red crowns and black turned-up brims.

Li Heng-sung *chin-chin*ed Fletcher with a barely civil expression. Fletcher returned the gesture. There was no other pretence of the customary Chinese etiquette. Through Old Huang, the commander welcomed the Foreign Rifles, and said they should come to him with any problems. He gestured brusquely to Fletcher and walked out into the field. The black bear and tiger cats followed.

Commander Li pointed to the four corners of the acreage – the land within was for their encampment. Trenches were to be excavated on the other three sides and the dirt used for ramparts. As there were not yet many Foreign Rifles in camp, he would send detachments to dig the trenches and men to guard them as they worked. A stockade could be erected for them if they were to be there very long.

Fletcher turned away and looked for the Feng Huang hills. He did not know if they were close enough to see from Kuangfulin, or just obscured by mist. His anger at being set upon without apology and told what to do by this arrogant Chinese slowly subsided.

"Thank the commander for sending men to help. Each day we will have more men." And when I am at full strength, you will not be so arrogant, and I will give the orders.

Returning to the horses, Li Heng-sung noticed the open crate of minié rifles, and his perfunctory attention turned instantly to keen interest. He asked if his officer could look at one. The officer was one of the three tiger cats, a major named Wen Chia-pao 文甲胞. He carefully examined a weapon and worked the mechanism. Fletcher recalled seeing the same quiet eagerness in the face of the Taiping officer that had received a Sharps rifle from *Confucius* the month before – evidently not all Chinese so loved their swords they could resist a dalliance with rifles.

Falconer stepped forward, offered the man a percussion cap, and pointed to the nipple. Major Wen cocked the hammer and pushed the cap on to the nipple, then stood to one side and fired at the ground with a satisfying pop and flash, and swirl of pungent white smoke. Falconer gave the major large face before his superior, thought Fletcher, and wondered if this bearish martinet Li Heng-sung, who towered over the Chinese, might be the man to work together with them. Falconer handed one of the curiously shaped minié bullets to the major to examine.

"Mr. Huang," Falconer said, "please tell him that whenever he returns here, I will gladly show him how to load, aim, fire, then field-strip this weapon, if that's the right thing, Colonel Wood."

"Yes, Sergeant, that'll do," Fletcher said. What's another Chinese rifleman more or less. He won't be much use to me.

Fire God Temple

洋神 *Yang Shen*   *James Lande* 藍德

The same Chinese private remained behind as a messenger when Li Heng-sung departed. The private would join the Foreign Rifles in setting up their camp and help get any supplies they might need from Kuangfulin, only half an hour away on foot.

Old Huang was not all together delighted at staying behind as interpreter and, while fumbling at pitching his tent, grumbled and groaned that he did not want to stay in this wild and desolate country very long, not for a pot full of eeee-*gull*.

"Ever the sailor longs for the sea, eh Lao Huang," Fletcher said, laughing, "and the pilot for his rivers."

Fletcher and Hannibal took the sergeants aside and talked them through what was wanted for the camp: tent sites, commissary, sanitation, drill field, and a practice range that would effectively stop bullets and prevent strays or ricochets from flying off at Kuangfulin or into some farmer's field.

A night watch of two was to be posted from the very start. Rebels, imperial soldiers, villagers – they all had reasons to come skulking around camp in the dark and were to be regarded as a threat. Sentries were to be posted during the day as well, to watch for rebels and to report the approach of imperial troops.

Fletcher had Old Huang give Lao Chang and Ah-shan their instructions before leaving, telling them to find another two or three reliable junks to carry more men, and to be ready at *Chao-chia-pang* creek near the Temple of the Fire God the next morning. Before leaving for the junk, Fletcher gave each of the sergeants two gold eagles as an installment on their first month's pay.

"You can rely on us, Colonel Wood. We'll pull this camp together."

"Su-chou is ours," the Loyal King said, "but the people still oppose us."

The Taiping Loyal King Li Hsiu-ch'eng, arrayed in a bright yellow robe and a crown of beaten gold mounted by an orange tiger with fiery eyes and fangs of pearl, sat upon a dais behind a carved dark-red rosewood table listening to the reports of his officers. His wire-rimmed spectacles rested atop stacks of written reports sent by rebel officers from yamens in counties of Su-chou prefecture immediately surrounding the city. Behind him were displayed the gaudy banners and flags of the divisions and regiments of the rebel army occupying Soochow. A multitude of rebel officers, adjutants and couriers, impatient to conduct the business of the new administration, crowded in between the dragon-entwined carved pillars and yellow tapestries of the great hall of the Kiangsu provincial yamen at Soochow.

"*Tien-hsia* 殿下, your Highness," said General Ch'en K'un-shu 求天義陳坤書, "these people – militia, ruffians, vagabonds from outlying areas – wildly looted shops and homes under the city wall again last night. They willfully disregard the Loyal King's proclamations and will not be pacified. You need only give the order, and I will send a company to cut them all down and put an end to this chaos."

"No, we cannot win their hearts by killing them," the Loyal King said. "Continue as before, ride amongst them, fire weapons and frighten them away. And today I will take a large number of boats and go myself to Yuan-ho 元和, Wu-hsien 吳縣, and Ch'ang-chou 長洲, the counties where these reports are coming from, and state our policy and persuade the people to lay down their arms."

An adjutant approached the Loyal King with a soldier in the uniform of an imperial brave and said, "a spy from the ranks of Li Heng-sung at Kuang-fu-lin reports foreign soldiers are there."

"What would foreigners want at mosquito-plagued Kuang-fu-lin?" the Loyal King mused aloud. "Are they British, do they have cannon?"

"No, *Chung Wang*, they are several kinds – Americans, English, and others – all

Fire God Temple   407

paid by the *taotai* at Shanghai. They have no cannon, only one hundred modern rifles."

"How many are they?"

"Eight, and two officers, the first day. They make a large camp – more will come."

"Very well," the Loyal King said. "Watch them closely and send word about the number of men, their movements, and their arms. I want to know if they get cannon." The Loyal King wondered if these foreigners at Kuang-fu-lin had any relation to the American *yang-kuei-tzu* in Shanghai who bought rifles and other military equipment from H. Fogg & Company. That *yang-kuei-tzu* was said to be shopping for cannon.

2 Late that afternoon, Fletcher and Hannibal were back in Shanghai. At Takee's house, Fletcher announced that the Foreign Rifles had landed – at Kuangfulin – and introduced Hannibal Arlen Benedict. Hannibal was cordial and effusive and set to rest Fletcher's immediate concern about how his second-in-command would get on with the Chinese sponsors. Fletcher reported four sergeants, four men, and 100 British minié rifles at Kuangfulin, and mentioned again his need for an interpreter, and for more money. Takee was clearly satisfied with their news about Kuangfulin, and wrote out a draft in Chinese. He sent them on their way with his profuse thanks. At Takee Bank, they received $100 Mexican in exchange for the draft. Flush with cash, Fletcher and Hannibal stopped by the National Hotel for oysters and porterhouse steaks. The distant report of the evening gun could just be heard above street noise as they left the hotel. Hannibal had made a list all of the grogshops in the Shanghai settlements and divided them by seven nights.

"Some of those places are more brothel than bar," Fletcher said.

"Some Lotharios set up shop in brothels, and several poker games are bound to be floating about the concessions. The Hongkew grogshops are bung-full with sergeants and petty officers most any time of the day now. The Astor House bar and the Imperial are awash with officers every evening. And if that's not enough, then we have troop deployments from last week's *North China Herald*." Hannibal took a clipping from a coat pocket. "Here it is: 'troops have been landed from British and French men-of-war to protect the city.' And it gives their *locations*! 100 British marines and light infantry at the Ningpo Guild House west of the North Gate. A guard of 200 French men and officers of artillery near the Cathedral at Tonkadoo. 200 more French artillerymen quartered in buildings on the French side of the *Yang-king-bang* creek. 200 more British marines quartered at the Sin-tuck-kee hong. Evidently, the newspaper thinks rebels do not read English. We can bag marines and artillerymen as they leave their quarters for dinner. My plan is nothing if not comprehensive."

They also had settled on the way to get the men out of the city.

"Sending them to the French at the East Gate," Fletcher said, "seems to work. That avoids the wooden fences erected by the district magistrate, at who knows how many places around Shanghai. British man some of those barriers together with the Chinese militia. The French guards posted at the East Gate care only about French deserters. They will pass Americans with little thought. Any Frenchmen we enlist can be sent through the British at the North Gate."

Over bottles of Perrier & Jonet champagne at Charlie Noble's, they listened sympathetically to the crew of *Fannie McHenry* grumble about how awful it was to be in port for nine weeks, and how they were about crazy with prolonged confinement at Shanghai. Two ABs from *Fannie McHenry*, Charles Abby and Silas Cabot, vowed they were ready to go and fight anywhere. Fletcher gave them directions to the temple.

At The Mizzentop they accepted two Irishmen, the 2nd mate from *Dakotah*, and the 2nd mate from *Jubilee*, and gave them the same directions.

洋神 *Yang Shen*   *James Lande* 藍德

Around 10:00pm, Fletcher and Hannibal arrived at The Jolly Tar. It was overflowing with soldiers from the 99th, in residence aboard the troop transport *Octavia* out in the harbor, and none too ready to go back on board. The ship had been in harbor six weeks, and the bored inmates were ready to sink the asylum. Some of the 67th were also on board. That was all the excuse the 99th needed for some monumental melees.

When the champagne had flowed, and a tide of soldiers risen to the lure and ebbed away, four serious candidates were left high and dry. All were from the 99th, uniformed in black forage cap with chinstrap, scarlet tunic with a long row of brass buttons down the middle, white crossbelt and waist belt with black patent-leather pouch, and black trousers. Two were corporals, Duncan Dinwiddie and Alister Lithgow, and two were privates, Dean Dobbin and Gordon Coppersmith. None looked a day over twenty-one.

"Do ya know how long they've had us cooped up on tha' ship, Mr. Wood?" said Dinwiddie, a slender Scot of medium height with black hair, blue eyes and fuzzy sideburns down to his jaw. "I'm glad to go off wi' ye if I can get free of Shanghai. We run out of things t' do."

"Asked for patrol duty ashore," Lithgow said, burring his 'r's, "but the marines have the lock on tha'." Lithgow was a ruddy Scot, with the red hair and whiskers of Viking raiders, sorrel eyes, and a square, freckled face. "Then we fished some in the river, caught perch, bream, flounder, even eel – nothin' very appetizin'. Threw the pi'iful lot back."

"For want of else t' do, Mr. Wood," Coppersmith said, a blonde, clean-shaven English lad, "Dobbin and me, we sit at th' bow of *Octavia* and count ships in 'arbor. Today th' British ship *Ranee* arrived fro' Liverpool, and th' American *Competitor* fro' New York, and th' barks *Sappho* and *Tilton* sailed, along with a schooner, *Luisa*. Yest'day, th' *'eroes of Alma* came fro' th' Japans."

Fletcher did not mention the sergeants of the 99th already at Kuangfulin, lest the prospect of serving under the same brutal drill sergeants deter them from enlisting. He gave them directions, passed on Falconer's suggestion they ask for shore leave or go on sick call, and said to change clothes, get their kits, and meet that night at the temple.

At the Flower Boat, the reception line of giggling girls was downstairs at the front door, and only nimble navigators cleared the entrance without the grapnels of one or two boarders firmly hooked into their yardarms. The Wandering Rocks came to mind as Fletcher jibed to port then starboard and hove to on the other side.

"Masts and spars intact" Hannibal said.

"All hands accounted for," Fletcher said.

At the tables the girls badgered the men for full-priced drinks that were only tea, smiled and fondled them beneath the tables, cooed "oooh" and "ahhh" at what they discovered there, and urged them to come upstairs right away to their rooms. Every few minutes a sailor yielded to the overt temptations and allowed himself to be led by the hand up the stairs behind swishing silk, usually meeting another sailor being led down the stairs, and closely examining his sheepish grin for signs of contentment, even exhaustion.

"Hey, cock your weather eye on that!" Hannibal said.

"She wants to show him her crochet collection," Fletcher said.

Two girls led another sailor upstairs – one girl on each arm.

"That one will be shown how to double crochet."

Fletcher and Hannibal found a large Swede and two Swiss temporarily adrift at the bar, ordered champagne, and set forth their proposition. The Swede was an AB, one Lars Johansson, who had deserted from the Dutch brig *Christian Louis* the third week in April, run through all his cash, and now was desperate for a ship – he accepted immediately. His Swiss companions from *Henry Ellis* and had been at Shanghai for six weeks. One was the

Fire God Temple   409

2nd mate, Helmut Schmidt, and the other, Otto Shapiro, was an AB. Schmidt turned to an American further down the bar.

"Robert, come hear this. Robert also is AB on my watch."

The American, Robert Harrison, loosed himself from his nightingale and joined them and, after a few minutes of cajolery by the 2nd mate, he also agreed to come along. Fletcher gave them directions.

At midnight, Fletcher and Hannibal arrived at The Joss House, a grog house near the American Episcopal Mission church in Hongkew. All the men there were crew discharged from *Progressive Age* seven weeks before, when word got around she might be condemned and broken up. Charles Jackson, the 2nd mate, was a thirty-year-old of medium build from Savannah, Georgia, with dark blond hair and berry-blue eyes. The sailmaker, Farley Masters, was the oldest of the *Progressive Age* sailors, from Charleston, South Carolina. He looked like he belonged to the sea, with sandy hair, eyes the shade of green kelp above and heavy swells of side-whiskers. The foretopman and the maintopman were brothers with the unlikely name of Bean – the homespun wisdom of the Ozark hills around Springfield, Missouri, conferred upon them the folksy appellations of Ham, and Tater. As Hannibal thought Fletcher and he should make one more stop, they gave *Progressive Age* directions and sent them off to the temple.

Hannibal led Fletcher into the British concession, past Mission Road to an old building off the main road that once had belonged to Russell & Company, and was now an infamous "sink of iniquity" deplored by the Settlement. The uproar from the place tumbled down the road, across the Bund, and out into the Whangpoo: blaring music, singing, firecrackers, shouts and screams. Fletcher shifted the position of his revolver.

"What do you expect to find here?" he asked Hannibal.

"Just being thorough, Colonel."

A sign Lao Kee Cheong 老旗昌 hung over the door. Drunken men and tawdry women lolled beside the entrance and on the second-story verandah, peering out over starving beggars and scavenging dogs. Crippled Chinese, cadaverous Parsees, emaciated Manilamen, and gaunt English sailors cringed near the door, begging for cash and yowling at the taunts from the mob. A pack of a half dozen scrofulous dogs snarled and snapped at each other in the street. A drunken sailor stumbled outside and lurched down the road, and a moment later a gang of beggars and dogs followed. Shouts, a cry, and the beggars and dogs slunk back and took up their moorings at Lao Kee Cheong.

The room inside was large and crowded with raucous soldiers, sailors and Chinese girls at tables and standing along a bar that ran along three walls. Above the bar, a narrow second-story balcony festooned with red paper lanterns, and packed with more tables of rowdy customers and chintzy women, was suspended over three sides of the room. Small apartments glowing with pale red lights inside opened onto the balcony. Women appeared and disappeared in the dim light of the little rooms. The harsh smoke of cigars and cheroots mingled with the sweet odor of opium and incense and hung on the stale air.

A fight broke out between two sailors over a girl and was joined by a half dozen more sailors and escalated into a brawl between rival regiments. The donnybrook ended when all the combatants knocked each other senseless and the girls began squabbling over the money they took from the pockets of unconscious soldiers.

"Most of these boys're too far over the bay to be any use to us," Fletcher said.

"Place has changed. Lot worse than I remember."

"We have collected sixteen men tonight. Let's go back."

The temple courtyard was a calamity when Fletcher and Hannibal returned some time after midnight. They walked into a violent fight between four of the men, the Bean brothers and Jackson and Masters. They were beating each other bloody, and the smaller Beans were getting the worst of it, while all the rest except the Swede sat around guzzling rum and brandy and laughing and cheering them on. Lars Johansson was sitting on a stone drum by the entrance to the rear courtyard nursing a cut lip – he was the only Foreign Rifle recruit who was sober. Respectable-looking Chinese were huddled together with mendicant priests against the far wall and in corners, looking on in terror.

"I try stop fight, Mr. Wood," Johansson said, "but I vas no good. Dey make lots of trouble. All dos 2nd mates are too drunk to help." The *Christian Louis* AB tried to stop the fight, thought Fletcher, because the 2nd mates – from *Progressive Age*, *Dakotah*, *Jubilee*, and *Henry Ellis* – were acting like flyblown sots instead of ship's officers.

Hannibal crossed the courtyard and entered the affray, casually stepping between the warring parties, North and South, and ordering the two larger men to stand down. Jackson lurched at Hannibal with a roundhouse punch. Hannibal leaned away and sapped him down hard. Masters yelled and jumped for Hannibal. He was sapped down on top of Jackson. Hannibal turned toward Ham and Tater Bean.

"We're done, we're done," they said, laughing and showing their empty hands.

"Clean yourselves up. Get to your bunks," Hannibal growled. "All of you, cork those bottles and turn in." Even in their stupor, the loud pop of Hannibal's sap on thick skulls of the two American southerners startled the rest of the men. They struggled to their feet and into the rooms, some beginning to wonder what they had gotten themselves into.

"Those rooms all empty now 'cause dey kick out all d' Chinese," the Swede said. Lars Johansson was a slender man, close to fifty, draped in ill-fitting clothes from some slop chest, with white hair, blue eyes behind wire-rimmed spectacles, and a thick mustache stained brown by tobacco juice. "Dat monk, he vas so mad like I don' know vat! Make big ruckus."

"Hannibal," Fletcher said, "have you noticed we seem to be shy six men?"

"Really? Which ones, I wonder." Hannibal looked in each room. "The two from *Fanny McHenry*, Abby and Cabot," he said, "and the whole lot from the 99th Regiment. Do you suppose they just got lost?"

"We can hope so," Fletcher said. "We'll look for them tomorrow night. Are my directions wrong?"

"Maybe for soldiers."

Jackson and Masters groaned and, after a minute, got up rubbing their heads.

"You sapped me!" Jackson said.

"Next time stop when I say," Hannibal said, "or kiss the gunner's daughter."

"Goddamn, my head's splitting," Masters said. "And I thought you're with us."

"Good discipline is required in all camps."

"Hang it all! Come to offer our services, and you serve up belaying-pin soup. What kinda army is this?"

"Yeah, and when do we get paid."

Fletcher went to them and handed each a golden eagle. "Take this on account. Now get to your bunks and lay off the firewater."

3 The first tidings of the next day were that Jackson and Masters had skedaddled.

"And with my money," Fletcher said with a sigh.

"It's desertion, plain and simple," Hannibal said. "Ought to be shot."

"From camp, it would be desertion. From here, well this is not camp yet. But if I see them in Shanghai, I'll take what they've spent of my eagles out of their damned hides."

Hannibal got the men up, sent them to wash, then took them out to the front courtyard to the Chinese food stalls for a meal, warning them to eat only what was boiled or grilled over fire. As they finished, he sent them back to the rear court where Fletcher sat down with each one, got his particulars, and confirmed their experience. Ham and Tater Bean once barked squirrels in the Ozark forests and would make good riflemen, corporals to train the others. Robert Harrison, the American AB from *Henry Ellis* had handled blasting powder in Colorado gold mines, during a furlough from sailing two years before, and could set charges under city walls. The families of both Muldoon and Rafferty left Limerick and went to Boston to escape the potato famine, and then they went west together to fight under General Zachary Taylor against the Mexicans and saw action at Monterrey and at Buena Vista against Santa Ana. They had been at sea ever since, but their military experience was valued nonetheless.

At mid-morning Fletcher, Hannibal and the remaining eight men left for Kuangfulin.

"*Ta-jen*, I should not trouble you with these small matters," said the bald priest from the Temple of the Fire God. "Please forgive me."

"It is no trouble," Wu Hsü said. "Speak up."

"Thank you. *Ta-jen*, those awful foreigners in your temple, they are truly too frightening! They drink too much liquor, and then they yell and shout and hit people, and have terrible fights with each other. They got drunk and drove the pilgrims and other traveling guests out of their rooms, and threw all their things out into the courtyard! I tried to talk sense to the foreigners, but they were very impolite, they shouted in that foreigner talk. Of course, I do not know what they said. They took the rooms for themselves and drank some more and then started fighting again. They didn't stop until that other foreigner – I think you call him Wu-te – until he returned long past midnight and told them to stop fighting. *Ta-jen*, now everyone is afraid to enter the rear courtyard because of the *yang-kuei-tzu*."

"These men were there alone, without Wu-te?"

"Yes, *Ta-jen*. They started arriving in mid-evening, after the Hour of the Dog."

"Are they still there?"

"No, *Ta-jen*. They all have left. Two of the men sneaked away this morning after the Hour of the Tiger, before any of the other foreigners were awake. The rest all left before noon, at the Hour of the Horse."

"Very well," Wu Hsü said, "someone will look into this. Return now, and report back to me tomorrow."

"Yes, *Ta-jen*."

Wu Hsü was glad to be rid of the rowdy foreigners, but uneasy with their being the responsibility of Li Heng-sung.

"We 'ad a row with the Chinese," Sergeant Falconer said.

"Major Benedict," Fletcher said, "get these new men settled in. And keep clear of that tent with the sick men. Now, sergeant, what kind of a row?"

"When they came to dig trenches this morning, they refused to place 'em properly. Words were exchanged, tempers flared, and they went off in a 'uff. I've just come back from their camp after mending the fences. Garden went to reconnoiter the area."

Lao Chang's junk had landed the Foreign Rifles at the Kuangfulin camp in mid-afternoon. Only a few tents were standing at the site and, but for two Manilamen, Tigas and Inabayan, the camp appeared deserted. A dray had been drafted as a cook table and placed next to a pit campfire. The Manilamen were roasting chickens on spit, next to a pot of baking beans. Inside one of the tents, someone began retching.

Falconer returned and, a short while after, Garden. Falconer told Fletcher that the previous afternoon he and Garden had erected the six shelter tents and scooped out a pit campfire then, together with the Manilamen, they fetched water from the creek. Dinner was roast pork and baked beans flavored with jerky. Allbright and Boxer drank most of the evening. Falconer and Garden split watches, each with two Manilamen, and during the night fired several rounds at moving shadows, so no one slept much, except Allbright and Boxer. This morning, while the guards slept in, they got up and drank some of the water – by afternoon, both were sick with cramps and diarrhea. The Chinese private had given them each a dozen pellets that looked like rabbit turds and smelled of creosote and, an hour after being coaxed into choking them down, both men were feeling better.

Green Flag troops had arrived in the morning to dig trenches, but argued with Falconer about where the trenches were to be placed. Seeing only six tents, the Chinese started digging close by, and would not dig further out where Falconer told them. After the Chinese left, the two sergeants and the Manilamen dug a long trench latrine, unpacked and conditioned some of the muskets, and stacked them in a tent. Falconer then took the Chinese private and Old Huang and went to the Green Flag camp to find Major Wen, the Chinese officer he had shown how to fire the musket. Wen agreed to send another detachment the next morning and dig where asked. Garden took Tigas and Inabayan and reconnoitered west to the Chinese camp, south through cotton fields to low hills, and east over shallow creeks to a marsh, then mapped the terrain.

"All in all," Hannibal said, "a marvelously successful first day at the Foreign Rifles camp. What more do you suppose can happen? Did you smell those pills?"

"Actually, Falconer showed resourcefulness," Fletcher said. "going like that, into the lair of the Green Flag army. I think we can rely on him, and Garden."

Before returning to Shanghai, Fletcher met again with Falconer and Garden, commended their initiative and effort, and worked out with them an ambitious training regimen. They were to start with basic close-order drill – facing movements, marching to cadence and in column formation, flanking turns and turns to the rear. Then continue with guard mounts, signs and countersigns, field communications, bugle calls, hand signals, packing gear, pitching and striking camps, bivouac in the open, and field sanitation.

Weapons training was to begin with the manual of arms, weapons familiarization, loading and firing a minié rifle on the short range, and the school of the bayonet. Advanced training would drill loading under fire and on the run, and long-range target practice to 800 yards.

The officers and NCOs would practice field tactics for offensive and defensive maneuvers, flanking maneuvers, skirmishing, and picketing, and then siege tactics for walled cities, enfilade fire, crossing moats, escalade with ladders, trenching and ramparts, and sapping to undermine walls. The infantry square could wait for a full roster. When there was time and manpower they would dig more deeply into field fortifications.

"Drill them hard, sergeant. Keep them too tired for mischief."

Lao Chang's junk took Fletcher, Hannibal, and Old Huang back to the Temple of the Fire God, and Fletcher and Hannibal went again to Takee's house to report their strength of sixteen men. Takee said an interpreter would join them the next morning and they could send the pilot back to *Confucius*.

"That will please Old Huang," Fletcher said. "He was so unhappy on dry land, frightened of Chinese braves and sick foreigners, that we brought him back today."

"Wu-te, *tao-t'ai* belly unhappy, too," Yang Fang said. "He say sojah belly bad, makee tlouble at temple."

"Well, perhaps they got a little out of hand," Fletcher said. "They were drinking is all – no one was hurt."

Yang Fang hesitated for a moment trying to think of some gentle way to make the foreigner understand.

"Wu-te go church, yes?"

"Sure, sometimes," Fletcher said. "At sea, captains conducted services."

"What fashion in church, Wu-te? Dlink whiskey, shout at pliest, hit people?"

"What?" It took a moment to realize that Takee thought the pagan temple was the same as a Christian church. Hannibal stared at the old banker as if he were deranged.

These arrogant foreigners, thought Yang Fang, have no respect for Chinese temples as places to worship Heaven. They believe only theirs is the true religion. But when the trappings of religion are stripped away, the Heaven our Emperor prays to, and the God foreigners pray to, they are the same unknowable being. The manifestations of Heaven are worshipped in many ways, and wise Chinese observe all those ways, not just one, and pray in all the temples: Taoist temples 廟, Bhuddist temples 寺, and Confucian temples 宮. We would pray in the Christian church, Jewish synagogue, and Mohammedan mosque, if there were more of them. Not knowing which is right – or if any of them are right – it is best to respect them all.

"Why do in temple what not do in church, Wu-te?"

At Charlie Noble's they found waiting the two ABs from *Fannie McHenry*, Charles Abby and Silas Cabot, seabags at their feet, only a little worse for drink.

"We thought we lost you boys," Hannibal said.

"Didn't help that we was drunk as bees on a berry bush," Cabot said. "We set out like Columbus looking for the New World, and got lost in the West Indies."

"Yeah," Abby said, "and we lost your little red paper with the Chinee squiggles."

"Well, you're not the only ones lost," Fletcher said. "Come on with us while we try to collect them."

The soldiers of the 99th were kicking up a shindy at the Jolly Tar, the two corporals, Dinwiddie and Lithgow, and the two privates, Dobbin and Coppersmith, all in mufti and with their personals stashed out of sight. They, too, had lost the red envelope with the Chinese characters, and spent half the night walking around the walled city and evading British marines.

"Hello, Yank," said a familiar voice behind Fletcher. "Getting' up an army, are ya?"

"Ha, don't' you beat all," Fletcher said. "Still hot for plunder, Mr. Reese?"

"Sure as sharks bite, matey. Been waitin' on you for a while."

"Where's your ship?"

"Off to the Japans, or somewheres. I collected my papers."

"I figured you'd be up for captain of their next ship, or replace Cornelius."

"Man can't get too far working for New Jerusalem, Mr. Wood. That Fitch family's got a stranglehold on the company an' outsiders isn't welcome."

"Well, you're mighty welcome here, Mr. Reese."

Fletcher quickly gave Reese the particulars as they stood then, and explained that he was about to take the others up river to the temple.

"My things are stashed close by. I'll be back in ten minutes."

While they waited for Ptolemy Reese, Fletcher worked up tactical maneuvers for skirmishing with the redcoat patrols he knew were certain to be laying for them, and tried to get the 99th to stop singing *The Girl I Left Behind Me* long enough to pay attention.

> *I'm lonesome since I crossed the hill,*
> *And o'er the moorland sedgy.*
> *Such heavy thoughts my heart do fill,*
> *Since parting with my Jenny...*

They all said they knew the National Hotel, on Barrier Road up from the Barrier Road Bridge – or at least they thought they did. Finally, Fletcher asked Abby to stay with two of the soldiers, and Cabot to go with the other two. When Reese returned, they trooped out the rear door into the wet backstreets. The 99th was still in fine fettle, however, and would not stop singing. As they made their way down a narrow street of godowns parallel to Broadway Road, their song echoed up and down each cross street, their dreams of freedom and plunder overwhelming common sense. As was inevitable, they saw the patrol of redcoats cross between the buildings of an intersection ahead.

"Quiet you fools," Dinwiddie whished, and they slipped into the shadows.

"If them marine buckos get wind of me," Coppersmith said, "it'll be the cat again, and then gaol."

"Damn, here they come," Lithgow hissed.

"Scatter!" Fletcher whispered, and they bolted in all directions. Fletcher, Hannibal and Reese walked back out into the road as the diversion.

"Stand fast there!"

"Well, Captain Budd, isn't it?" Fletcher said.

"Ahh, Mr. Wood, the American. What sort of trouble are you stirring up tonight?"

"Nothing at all, Captain. Just making the rounds, like you, sort of."

"These gentlemen are Americans, too?"

"My associate, Mr. Benedict, and Mr. Reese is an English merchant sailor."

"Who were those others that skipped into the shadows while you stopped to chat?"

"Bless my soul, Captain. No idea. The streets are full of revelers."

"Well, I have no business with you. Not tonight, anyway. On your way."

Late that evening, Fletcher knocked at the door of Bob Allen's American boarding house across the river on the Pootung side. The verandah was empty and the bowling alleys deserted because of the cold from the rain. The boarders, fifteen or so, were all in the front sitting room drinking, playing cards, or reading old copies of newspapers from home. One table stopped their game and beckoned him over.

"You're Wood, aren't you?" asked a grizzled fellow in red flannel shirtsleeves.

"Yes, that I am. How did you know?"

"Couple fellas that came in here."

"That'd be Jackson, and Masters. I thought they'd be here."

"That's them. My name's John Colter. You come about soldiering?"

"Yes, I have a good proposition for sturdy men."

"You crimping 'ere for some ship, eh Wood?" boomed a voice Fletcher recognized. He turned around.

"Bob Allen," Fletcher said. "Not gone to Fiddler's Green yet."

"You know they won't let me in there." Allen was short, dark, heavy man, close to three hundred pounds. His black hair was slicked back with some glossy gunk. He didn't walk so much as heave his bulk forward, and he wheezed and the wood floor creaked with every step. "If you're going to crimp my sailors, you'll owe me a percentage."

"I'm not a crimp, Bob, and not hiring a ship's crew."

"Well, I guess I know that. Jackson and Masters are out back."

"Paid with a gold eagle."

"Yours, I suppose. They say you hired 'em to fight rebels."

"They ran off, with my money. I'll get it back before I leave."

"Back off, Wood. Round here I'm the one throws his weight around."

Fletcher unbuttoned his coat, took the Colt Navy from the small of his back, and shoved it into his belt over one hip. Allen was startled and concealed it poorly.

"I know your dogs, Bob, You keep 'em leashed and we all can have a quiet *chin-chin*." I should not have to display arms to have my way, thought Fletcher. But neither can I allow anyone to take advantage, or I'm finished. I must improve my opening gambit with these people.

"You have me wrong, Fletcher. I don't employ crimps anymore." This remark caused some stifled guffaws and throat clearing around the sitting room.

"And I'll thank you to step aside and not be interfering."

"What's your offer?"

"$100 a month, canvas tent and rations, extra for gunners, bonuses for all."

"Doggone! I'll go with you myself!"

"Soldiers, Bob, not innkeepers. Look at your belly and those bandy legs. Yours is a comfortable life, Bob – you'd not survive a day's march."

"Maybe so. But I can crimp a soldier as easily as a sailor."

"No crimping, Bob. This is all on the up and up, open and aboveboard. Hardened men, Bob, none of your bully boys or shanghaied shoe-clerks."

"Get too particular and you'll not find many takers."

"What I want," Fletcher said, in a voice everyone in the room could hear, "are tough, experienced daredevils, eager for high pay and plunder, who'll fight to keep the Taiping rebels away from Shanghai."

"This is not your recruitment center, Wood."

"As a courtesy, Bob, a quid on each man you send me, after today, that I can enlist, and who will stay. Hell, Bob, an establish proprietor like you – a man of business – you ought to be paying *me* for protecting your establishment from the Chinese rabble."

"A quid? That's a deal," Allen said, and he wheezed and creaked his way back to his little office.

Colter approached. "Mr. Wood, I'll take your shillin', as the English say. I was first mate on *Fenimore Cooper* until first week of May. I have four more good sailors."

"Very well, men. Fetch your things and we'll leave straightaway. Mr. Colter, where are Jackson and Masters."

"Little room at the back of the second floor."

While the five men were gathering their belongings, Fletcher went upstairs to the room where Jackson and Master were staying. He knocked and pushed his way in when they opened the door.

"You men have my money."

Shouts and sounds of scuffling came down the hallway and into the front sitting room, followed by the two men themselves pulled and pushed by Fletcher. They stumbled down the stairs, across the room, and out the front entrance into the street. The sailors in the sitting room jumped to the windows, but heard only thuds and groans and saw only the flicker of shadows in the dark, rain-swept night. A few minutes later Fletcher came back inside with clothes wet and mud-slicked and knuckles bloody.

"Those two each took a gold eagle from me and ran off," Fletcher said. "They had only one left between them, which they have returned, and I have taken the rest out of their hides. Mr. Colter, are you and your men still coming with me?"

"I'd've given'm more than a thrashing," Colter growled. "Sure, we're coming."

Early the next morning the men were rousted, sent to wash, and shown the Chinese food stalls in the front courtyard. There were seven more stalls, with new offerings like fried onion pancakes, and grilled octopus. Fletcher interviewed the new men after the meal and recorded their particulars. John Colter had been a wagon-master on the Oregon Trail. He was thirty-three, over six feet, with black eyes, grizzled hair and beard.

Originally from Fort Leavenworth, Kansas, he was the son of an army colonel and had managed to stay in school through the 8th grade. Colter grew up roaming the prairies and became wagon train scout on Oregon trail in 1845. Two years later, he took over his first wagon train and guided it to Oregon. The next year he left the Willamette Valley for Sutter's Mill to pan for gold, went bust, and drifted to San Francisco in 1850, from where he shipped out to sea. The scar at his hairline was from an arrowhead.

That morning Fletcher and Hannibal set out for Kuangfulin with twelve new men, and a new interpreter, a fussy little Cantonese called Mr. Fan, a clerk from Takee Bank. When Mr. Fan reassured Fletcher that he could "talkee-talkee belly good 'melican," Fletcher almost threw him overboard and, before they left, he sent an angry note to Takee: we want to translate into English, not into *pidgin*! Get me a decent interpreter. Old Huang returned to *Confucius* without any regrets.

Upon arrival, Sergeant Falconer reported on conditions in camp.

"Two men 'ave deserted, sir."

"Deserters already? Damn it all! Which two?"

"The Irishmen from *Dakotah* and *Jubilee*, Muldoon and Rafferty."

"They've only been here one day! Did they have some problem, sergeant?"

"We took away their liquor, sir. And they 'ad your eagles in their pockets."

"We cannot tolerate desertion – otherwise it will *all* come unraveled."

"Their ships're probably still in the 'arbor at Shanghai, Colonel."

"They'll have to be brought back, and a harsh example made of them."

"With the twelve you've brought, we have twenty-six now – four sergeants, and two corporals. Enough for a small platoon to begin close-order drill."

"Two of the new men are corporals. The man Reese was a first mate and will do as a sergeant. The new interpreter is Mr. Fan, but he translates into pidgin not English. Let me know if he's no good."

"Green Flaggers came back and excavated the trenches and ramparts."

"Yes, they're positioned for a much larger camp. You're more optimistic than me."

"There'll always be setbacks, Colonel. Allbright and Boxer are up and about again, if a little wobbly."

"The little rabbit turds weren't so bad, then. Get more in Kuangfulin."

"Chinese started a large rampart on the eastside to back a rifle range. It'll be ten feet high and as thick so that bullets will lodge in soft earth. Could use a cook, sir."

"I'll look in at the regimental mess."

Fletcher turned Reese over to Falconer for indoctrination. Falconer had gotten out just a few words when Reese looked up with a big grin and interrupted.

"Wayo! Are me ears foolin' or is tha' Merseyside I hear janglin'," Reese said.

"No woollyback here – bona fide Scouser. Ows it goin?" Falconer said.

"Donnelly docked when I last heard a Scouser."

"What language is that?" said Fletcher, laughing.

"Liverpoool, Mr. Wood," Falconer said. "Me an' Mr. Reese here, we're both grew up beside the Mersey River in Liverpool."

"Janglin', that's talkin'," Reese said. "Wayo's just a minute, when Donnelly docked is a long time ago, and a Scouser's anyone born in Liverpool."

"And woollybacks is all the poor sods what ain't," Falconer said with a chuckle.

Fletcher had a new assignment for Hannibal as well.

"You'll have to hold things down here at camp. We cannot prevent desertions at Kuangfulin when we are both at Shanghai."

"That's just as well. I'd rather be in the field anyway. And an officer is needed – the sergeants are regarded too closely, like one of their own. They require a stronger hand."

"Then I'll not stay over. The review of progress with drill, and conditions in camp, I'll leave that to you, and go back now. The earlier I'm in Shanghai the easier it will be to track down those deserters and bring them back."

"Yes, and upon their return I shall most certainly make an example of their company punishment."

Li Heng-sung respectfully reports to Taotai Wu Hsü on the barbarians at Kuang-fu-lin

Respectfully, Li Heng-sung 李恆嵩 submits this report to my superior. I have received your instructions and hasten to obey completely. My men watch carefully all the activity of the Luzon barbarian soldiers 呂宋國夷兵. Captain Yang Fu-han knows a little of the foreign speech, wears the garb of a private, and sleeps in a tent at the camp.

Last week his Excellency Yang Fang brought the Luzon barbarian chief Wu-te to Kuang-fu-lin. I took them to the place of the encampment. I carried out all of your Excellency's instructions about assisting the barbarian soldiers.

The first day eight barbarian soldiers were brought to the camp on a cargo junk, with the barbarian chief Wu-te, a second chief, and a translator, Huang. Four of the foreign braves are Luzon men. Four are barbarian sergeants 把總.

At their camp, I instructed the barbarian chief where to place entrenchments, explaining that his soldiers are to protect my right flank. This barbarian chief Wu-te does not know proper decorum and was arrogant. The translator Huang is incompetent and disrespectful, but I remembered Excellency's instructions and did not immediately cut off the translator's head. Major Wen Chia-pao inspected their rifles and gained the confidence of a barbarian sergeant, who will show Major Wen the firing of these rifles.

The barbarian sergeants put up tents and dug a small trench. Two of them drank liquor until after the Hour of the Boar, nearly midnight. The other two barbarian sergeants and the Luzon soldiers unpacked and cleaned rifles and cooked a meal. They put water from the creek in barrels for washing, posted a guard, and fired muskets and pistols at my men in the dark without hitting anyone. I remembered your instructions and did not attack and slaughter them all.

The second morning I sent a detachment of soldiers to dig the trenches. A barbarian sergeant told them to dig in the wrong place, and the translator Huang could not make the barbarian sergeant understand, so the men left. These barbarians do not communicate very clearly and cause misunderstandings. Their interpreter is a low person who does not know English well and talks to the barbarian chief without respect and in unclear pidgin. This is the principal cause of mistakes.

Two barbarian sergeants drank creek water and became ill. Captain Yang Fu-han gave them 橙露球 orange dew balls and they quickly became better. One barbarian sergeant came to my camp and begged Major Wen to allow our soldiers to return and dig entrenchments, and I approved. Another barbarian sergeant and two Luzon soldiers walked many miles all around their campsite and used a compass 指南針 to draw maps.

After the Hour of the Horse, about noon, on the second day eight more barbarian soldiers came to the camp with the two barbarian chiefs. These soldiers were given tents and made to march until very tired. The barbarian chief went back to Shanghai and took the translator Huang, who was ashamed and apologized to Major Wen.

During the 3rd watch, after midnight, two barbarian soldiers left camp and walked to Kuang-fu-lin. They stole a small boat and floated north on the creek. My men followed and have just returned saying the two foreigners lost their way, capsized, and nearly drowned. My men pretended to be common people and saved their lives. They wanted to go to Shanghai. My men took them through the city, identifying themselves to the gate

洋神 *Yang Shen* James Lande 藍德

guards, and down the Huang-p'u Chiang to Hung-k'ou, the American settlement.

This morning my soldiers went to the barbarian camp and dug the entrenchments where the barbarian sergeant wanted. He also told them to make a high rampart 高壘 at the extreme east of the camp for a target range, which I also approved.

The barbarian chief is expected to return soon with more soldiers.

Respectfully wishing your Excellency well-deserved happiness.

    Heng-sung 恆嵩 prudently submits this report.

Written after the Hour of the Dragon on the morning of the 7th

4   By means of broken English, abundant gesticulation, and rough drawings Fletcher directed Lao Chang's junk around Shanghai to the Whangpoo and down to Hongkew rather than through the city.

"He wants you to go to Hung-k'ou 虹口," Little Chang said.

"Ahh, that's simple enough," Ah-shan said. "Why didn't he just say so?"

Off the mouth of Soochow Creek, the junk entered a small creek that ran north in the same direction as Broadway. Ah-shan found a place to moor and Fletcher went ashore. That late in the evening, the Mizzentop was a hubbub of drunken sailors, so Fletcher did not notice one sailor scurry out the back way. Fletcher made a circuit of the room, asking about Muldoon and Rafferty, and then went on to other grogshops. The Irishman had boasted of quitting Kuangfulin, and men in the bar who recognized Fletcher could easily imagine the deserters' fate if the bully mate caught them.

At the Joss House, a palsied old Caliban in black peacoat and watch cap careened over to him, followed by a mangy black chow-chow. His dark lascar face was corrugated with welts and wheals and his clothes stank of spilled rum. He called himself Jared and, with a larcenous grin, whispered that for $5 Mex he would take Fletcher to where the Irishmen were holed up. Jared was the apotheosis of decrepit old shellbacks cast up penniless on foreign shores who survived on swill and swag. The Irishmen must have a high sense of humor, thought Fletcher, to send along this timeworn old villain.

    They left through the back way and went down a street, up a narrow lane, and into a dark alley. Jared knocked on a door four times, an obvious signal. The door swung open, Jared disappeared inside, and Fletcher followed, shouldering the door hard. He felt it splinter against someone and send him sprawling. They came at him with a canvas tarp, but he sidestepped, reached out to find something to hit, and let fly. He hit what felt like a nose and teeth. Then they were on him.

Jared went down first. The Irishmen were the solid, experienced scrappers Fletcher expected 2nd mates to be and they hit hard. Fletcher dragged them flailing into the dim light of the doorway. Once he could see them and land a few heavy blows, it ended quickly, with Muldoon and Rafferty unconscious on the floor. He yanked the ropes out of the belt loops of their trousers and tied their hands, and unlaced their boots and tied them together. He took back his $5 Mex from Jared and found some water to throw on him and, when he came round, poked the barrel of his revolver into Jared's face.

"You're going to carry one of these micks where I say, or you'll suffer worse than a beating." Jared nodded. They each shouldered an Irishman, made their way down to the creek, carried them aboard Lao Chang's junk, and laid them against the mainmast. Fletcher waved Jared ashore.

"What th' hell?" Rafferty said with a groan. Fletcher yanked on his collar.

"You swore an oath of service, you and this bucko, remember? You said 'I do solemnly swear to serve loyally and obediently the Foreign Rifles under Colonel Fletcher Thorson Wood, and to obey the orders of Colonel Wood and his officers, and to defend the Chinese empire against all rebels and insurrectionists, so help me God.'

Fire God Temple

You'll be held to that until your hitch is up or you're dead."

Ah-shan started back to camp on the flood tide into Soochow Creek. When they arrived at Kuangfulin just before dawn, Fletcher marched the deserters into camp, woke up a bugler and had assembly sounded. The men formed ranks, roll was called, and Muldoon and Rafferty were marched before them.

"These two are guilty of desertion. All hands to witness company punishment."

Hannibal wanted to give them 100 lashes each, but Fletcher said that would incapacitate the men far too long, if they survived the whipping, and settled on forty strokes each, two weeks imprisonment on half rations, and loss of a month's pay.

Hannibal shook loose the thongs of two cat-o'-nine-tails, upturned a dray, and ordered the deserters' wrists strapped to the top and their backs stripped bare.

"You can't do this to us!" Muldoon screamed. "We're free men! This is no better than a damned ship."

"Who the hell d'ya think y'are!" Rafferty shouted.

Sergeants Boxer and Allbright laid on the lash. Major Benedict counted the strokes. Both prisoners passed out and were revived and whipped some more. The punishment complete, the company was dismissed, and the prisoners manacled and chained to a post at the far end of the encampment. John Colter dressed their wounds. The sentries were made responsible for seeing the deserters were fed and watered, and placed in a tent at night. Muldoon and Rafferty shouted and cursed at everyone in camp until punched several times into silence. The routine of tending the prisoners aged quickly and, after two weeks, the Irishmen were much older. No one was much wiser about how to end double-desertion, to prevent deserting from the Foreign Rifles men who had already deserted their regiments and ships.

Later that day, two sergeants and a corporal – Allbright of the 99th, Boxer of 2nd Queens, and Corporal Lithgow of the 99th – came to Fletcher and requested his permission to be dismissed from the Foreign Rifles and allowed to return to Shanghai.

"Service is not what I expected," Allbright said.

"Food's bad," Boxer said, "and it's too far from Shanghai."

"Conditions are too severe," Lithgow said. "Discipline's too strict. I can get my beatings from sergeants in the regiment."

The irony of brutal sergeants objecting to harsh discipline – after they obviously relished whipping the Irishmen – was amusing, but rather than have more desertions, Fletcher paid them off and returned them to their drinking and whoring that afternoon.

At H. Fogg & Company Artemis Fuller reported another shipment ready at the *Yang-king-bang* godown. "There are ten Sibley tents, camp tables, chairs, and picks and shovels. Provisions include eight 100-pound tierces of Hamburg salt beef, eight 150-pound casks of salt pork, four 100-pound sacks of bacon, flour in four 100-pound canvas bags, ten tins of butter, and sugar in six *gutta percha* sacks. I have also donated four small kegs of mustard, my compliments to the officer's mess."

"Mustard? Where's my artillery?"

"I have word of Napoleons in Egypt, and my agents are inquiring after Crimean surplus, however nothing is conclusive. Will you want more muskets from the godown?"

"At the moment, we have more rifles than men. Arms are more at risk of loss in Kuangfulin than in your godown, so I'd rather leave them for now, and have them for later. What I want is artillery."

"Yes, yes, I understand. We are expediting the inquiries."

"Have you been paid yet?"

Fuller shot him a sidelong glance. "Yes, yes. Payment is not the problem, not yet anyway. When I presented our invoice to Takee Bank, the comprador appeared quite astounded by the amounts, pulled a long face, and clicked away on his abacus, but it was paid in full the next morning."

"Sounds like an entertaining performance. I'd like to be there when they get the bill for a steamer. Boats will come for the cargo tomorrow morning."

"Watch out for the patrol. They've been snooping around my godown."

"So – you weren't able to allay the good consul's concerns?"

"He would have stationed British marines on my doorstep unless I agreed not to transfer arms. Now we are paid daily visits by the conscientious Captain Budd."

"Well, look on the bright side. You'll have fewer break-ins."

"And at the queen's expense."

"By the way, how can I have a horse? I need a better way to get around Shanghai."

"A horse? Do you ride, Mr. Wood?"

"Western. I'm no wrangler, but I've crossed mountains and deserts on horseback."

"Then take one of mine. The stable is behind our rooms. Here, I'll have a note sent now to my groom Mafoo saying that you should have use of the gelding Arion. He's a distinguished old gentleman, not given to flights of fancy – a gray Arab."

"Arion – what kind of name is Arion?"

"The horse of Hercules, a gift of Neptune. Neptune struck the earth with his trident and created Arion, a horse that ran like the wind and spoke in Greek. All my horses have old names, Mr. Wood: Bucephalus, Balios, Cerus, and Actæon."

"*Actæon* is a British gunboat."

"Actæon was one of the snow-white horses of the Greek sun god Helios."

The horse was waiting when Fletcher went to the stable behind Fuller's rooms, saddled in modest English manner, with nubbins for pommel and cantle. Arion was impressive, gray with black mane, forelock and tail, tall and broad-chested, alert and listening, not at all a common jade. He obviously was cared for well. Fletcher stroked Arion's satin-soft nose. The horse nickered softly, blinked languidly, and seemed to be looking straight into his eyes.

"Oh, he likee you," Mafoo said, handing a pair of spurs to Fletcher. They had no rowel, just blunt nubs. Fletcher waved them away.

"No spurs, thank you." If the horse did not respond to unadorned heels, Fletcher thought, he could learn. Better than stabbing the poor beast. Everyone in this town wears spurs, like an artifact of Western horse-culture and, if they all do it, then I certainly will not. Besides, I have to *win* my spurs.

Mafoo exchanged the spurs for a crop. Fletcher was about to refuse that as well – the light touch of a rein on the horse's neck should be all that was needed – but the crop had the appeal of a swagger stick, the scepter of a soldier, and would add to the dramatic effect. He accepted the crop.

"No hittee ho'sey, massah."

"No, Mafoo. I'll not hit the horse." He shook the crop. "This is just for look-see pidgin – I'll tuck it out of the way."

Arion watched him shove the crop into his boot and nickered again.

From H. Fogg & Company, Fletcher rode Arion to Takee's house and knocked on the gate while still mounted. This time when the gatekeeper threw open the panel, the malevolent old eyes set in that face yellowed like parched earth snapped wide open with surprise and drew back. When the gates finally parted, the horse clattered around the spirit screen prancing as if he knew he should make an impression. Arion might have been snorting flame, such was the effect on the banker's household. Takee came out through the little gate and stood clapping his hands, like a man who could appreciate a theatrical effect, and two comely young women could be seen briefly just inside the gate, peering out at the horse on their doorstep. When Fletcher's weight shifted to dismount, Arion quieted immediately, and he wondered if the horse could read his thoughts as well as speak Greek.

"Where get ho'se, Wu-te?" Yang Fang said. He was still excited by the appearance of this apparition, this dramatic sign of the advancement of his protégé. A servant took Arion, and Fletcher explained the loan of the horse as he and Takee entered the little gate, crossed the courtyard, and entered the reception hall.

"We have twenty-three men this morning, Takee."

"Include desa'tah?"

Whoa there, Takee! I only took them back this morning. How on earth could you know about them already? "What about deserters, Takee?"

Yang Fang anticipated this question would surprise Wood, and Wood's expression did not disappoint him. The banker wanted to give the impression that he knew all that was happening, as a way to control Wood, to dull the sharp edge of his ambition. There was risk – knowing Takee had the intelligence, Wood might learn where the intelligence came from. At Kuang-fu-lin, he thought, Wu-te is like a frog in a well and cannot escape being watched by Li Heng-sung. But one day Wu-te will climb out of the well and hop about, as he is today on his big fancy horse, and Li Heng-sung will not be able to get so close. The solution is to have my own men with Wood's army to watch him, like nephew Yang Hsi-hai aboard *Confucius* watches Captain Ghent. But how can I get a Chinese into his army? For payroll, perhaps, and supply.

"Two men takee boat, lun away Shanghai," Yang Fang said.

"Anything else?" Yesterday's news, Fletcher thought, glumly. Li Heng-sung would have known that, and reported to the *taotai*. In one day? That is fast. Oh well, stop kicking. There'll always be spies. They may know some of what you already have done, as long as they never know what you plan to do.

"Why hab desa'tah, Wu-te?"

"These men, they...." Fletcher realized his mistake. "Wait, Takee. We agreed I would command my men and you would not interfere."

"Yes, yes, hokay Wu-te." Takee almost whined. "No my pidgin."

"I will handle them. Now, I want to say this – Artemis Fuller was paid for our supplies. Thank you, for being so prompt. It was a large amount of money."

"Oh, yes, Wu-te. Belly big money, many dollah. Makee ol' Takee jump!"

"You know this is just a start. We must spend much more for cannon, for steamers."

"My unnahstan', Wu-te. Steamah not so bad – steamah makee money. Gun jus' sit."

That same afternoon and evening, Fletcher rode Arion to several more haunts of redcoats and bluejackets. From Fat Jack's he collected six Frenchmen. At the Chain Locker, he found seven sailors from *Progressive Age*. When the Maidenhead opened to him, she yielded up six sailors from *Heroes of Alma*. The Albatross contributed three sailors from *Mandarin*, three from *McLeod*, one from *Emma*. Among the *Progressive Age* sailors, there was a cook, one Augusto de la Torre, or "Gus," who was assured of a heartfelt welcome at camp. And an experienced quarter gunner, John Seamount, came from the crew of HMS *Octavia*.

Around midnight, Fletcher returned Arion to the care of Mafoo and hired one of the sedan chairs that frequented the boarding houses on North Gate Street. At the Temple of the Fire God, he found the crews of *Progressive Age* and *Heroes of Alma* completely pixilated and dancing around a bonfire of furniture from the temple's guest rooms. Their host at the temple, the long-suffering bald priest, just stood off to one side rigid, arms folded, looking very severe. His expression did not change even when Fletcher handed him a fistful of Mexican dollars.

Twenty-seven men boarded Lao Chang's junk bound for Kuangfulin next morning, but they came very close to never reaching the camp.

Instead of leaving the native city west on the *Chao-chia-pang*, Ah-shan sculled east to the Whangpoo, downriver to the Yang-king-bang, and up the creek to the H. Fogg godown to load supplies for the camp. The godown was open and Fuller was waiting.

"Morning, Mr. Wood," Fuller said, counting the men on board the junk. "You appear to have many hands to put to the task."

"The better to load up quickly and be out of here," Fletcher said. He signaled to his men and they started hauling crates and barrels out of the godown. The gunner from *Octavia* broke out of line.

"Colonel Wood, sir?" John Seamount said. "Beggin' yor pardon sir, but the British patrol 'creabouts, don't they?"

"They'll be at mess this time of day, but we post a watch at each end of the street."

"They won't care about these sailors, but me 'n the Frenchies 'r takin' a big risk."

"Take the French marines into the hold of the junk until we're underway."

Seamount hesitated. "They might inspect th' boat, sir. Do they 'ave authority?"

"So they would. All right, hide in the godown." Seamount called out the French marines and together they disappeared into the building. Fletcher went to the junk.

"Don't leave these crates on deck, men. Take them below out of sight."

Five minutes later a Chinese boy came running down the street and breathlessly yammered something at the door of the godown. Fuller rushed out.

"The British are coming!"

"Damn!" Fletcher muttered. "You men, push those barrels back inside. On the junk, bring your loads back. No, no – there's no time to stow anything more below. Hurry up! Into the building. Quiet in there!"

Once they were all inside, Fuller locked the godown doors behind them. He strolled over to the junk, checked no cargo was visible, then strolled back to the building just as the scarlet mob rounded a corner and marched down to the godown doors.

"Mr. Fuller," Captain Budd said, "you're out early this morning sir."

"Can't be too careful these days, Captain. Pays to check on these native watchmen."

"Right you are, sir." Captain Budd glanced at the padlock on the godown doors, then at the crowd of junks tied up in the creek. "Not open yet, this late in the morning?"

"Late? Captain, this is early for Americans. Haven't had my bacon and eggs yet."

"Anyone inside, Mr. Fuller?"

"The night watchman, I hope."

"Well, sir, we come 'round every hour or so, so don't you worry."

"Ah, you make me feel much better, Captain. With British marines on patrol, who needs watchmen?"

"Well, good day to you sir."

The captain marched his marines down the street and around a corner. A Chinese boy sitting by the creek watched the marines pass, and then got up to follow them. Five minutes later, the boy returned to the creek and resumed his seat on an old piling. The boy smiled, gave a sign, and Fuller unlocked the godown doors so the loading of cargo could continue. When the last barrel was aboard, Fletcher made a head count, and Lao Chang's junk nudged its way around in the narrow creek – just about as wide as the junk was long – and made its way down to the river and back to Kuangfulin.

5 Sundays were good pickings for recruits because jack came ashore to get drunk, and many scudded over to the new Sailor's Home near the Old Dock in Hongkew, to compete ship-against-ship in the two ten-pin alleys. Fletcher's haul there included an armorer from USS *Hartford*, Zeke Campbell, handy to have for assembling, testing, and repairing firearms. The "colonel" piloted his new recruits up to the temple that sunny Sunday afternoon without interference from patrols or sentries, these sailors being from merchantmen, and upon arrival discovered four more Manilamen, who came from *Confucius* with Vincente's blessing and wanted to sign up. They all deferred to one called Paco Dalogdog and, when Fetcher asked if he knew of others, Paco said a Spanish brig *Tiempo* had left some Manilamen in February and that he would go talk to them.

Fletcher pledged the men to sobriety and quiet, then took Lao Chang's junk from quayside on the *Chao-chia-pang* out to the Whangpoo and down to *Yang-king-bang* creek. He jumped ashore, sent the junk further on down to Hongkew, and fetched his horse from the French Settlement. At the Crown and Anchor, he struck a short vein of military experience and mined with vigor. Hand Webley was an English quartermaster of the 99th Regiment, Elisha Cook a yeoman, and Harry Drinkwater a sergeant. They all were quartered aboard the transport HM *Octavia* and moored in the river for six weeks.

"Moored and bored," Webley said, sighing.

"Here's two more fine fellows," Drinkwater said. "Corporals Mark Merryweather and Joe Smythe, of the 2nd Queens."

"We're all goin' balmy on that bucket," Smythe said, "rarin' for any action."

Paco Dalogdog brought four more Manilamen to the temple that night. All came from Manila aboard *Tiempo* and jumped ship at Shanghai.

Sometime after midnight, what Takee had said woke Fletcher from fitful sleep. *Taotai* very unhappy – soldiers very bad – make trouble at temple. Now the *taotai* was witness to the congenital stupidity of these men. Fletcher's mind flooded with foreboding, with apprehension about a growing menace to his management of the force and control over the recruits – men I am compelled to take because of the *taotai*'s own reckless haste. Wu's impression of me is just as likely come from these waterfront wharf rats as it from a disciplined army. That will make Wu even more difficult.

After eight days of dredging Shanghai's bars and brothels, and tossing out many trash fish, Fletcher was able to report to Takee a roster of seventy-two Foreign Rifles, four sergeants, and two officers. And they had an armorer and a quartermaster.

"When can fight, Wu-te?" Yang Fang said.

"Soon, Takee. They train now." Ask me, Fletcher thought, how many can hit a rifle target, how many rounds can they fire in a minute, how far can they march and how fast. Not just "when can fight, Wood-ah?"

"Spy say lebel come flom Su-chou belly soon."

"The men must train, Takee. If a soldier is not trained, he loses his life, and you lose your army. Money wasted." Fletcher almost said "training men means saving money," but that was just too facile.

"*Tao-t'ai* ask when can fight, Wu-te."

"It's only been eight days!" Fletcher's grip eased a little and his annoyance slipped out. Yang Fang was taken aback and fell silent. Again, Fletcher realized his anger was misdirected – Takee was afflicted by that scoundrel *taotai*.

"Look here Takee," Fletcher said, smiling. "Finding the right men takes time. Training takes time. We turn away more now, so recruiting takes even longer." The British major came to mind – but he probably should not regale Takee with his failures.

The old Chinese had only so much understanding, or patience.

The British major, of the 2nd Queens, had accosted him just days before at the Astor House, wanting to know about service with the *taotai*. "Can't talk here," the major whispered, and Fletcher debated the risk of giving a British officer the location of the Temple of the Fire God. Finally, Fletcher gave him one of the red envelopes with the characters for the temple and told him to go there at 9:00pm, and bring all the NCOs he could round up, but the major never appeared, and Fletcher had not seen him since. Hard to get the experienced officers, he thought – too much for them to lose.

At Kuangfulin, Falconer and Garden began training seventy-two men in close-order drill and target practice. A few days later, another batch of recruits was organized into three platoons, with the new men in the 3rd platoon. Now, they counted ninety-two men, five sergeants, and two officers. Fletcher decided this would do as full strength for the time being. The mixed lot needed a regimen of hard training to get into condition.

"With men for three platoons, we have our first echelon," Fletcher told Hannibal. "I've had enough of Shanghai for a while, and of grogshops and brothels for a lifetime."

"Those joints could wear down all the angels and saints in a week."

"In Shanghai all I ever hear is 'too muchee dallah' and 'when go fight lebel?' My time can be better employed here with the training."

"With both of us here," Hannibal said, "training will progress faster."

"That's most important. It's not as though I am hiding from the mandarins, even if that is a consequence. The rebels are not going to sing psalms in Soochow forever. Our men must be trained quickly."

"Perhaps we should make loading and firing the rifles a first priority. If time runs out, better they can shoot than march. Which is not saying a lot for an army."

"How much longer do you think they will require?" Fletcher said.

"Another month for the basics. Three months practice to make it all second nature."

Ten days later, gray clouds crept up from the east and massed above Kuangfulin. A dull red glow came up behind the gray over the southeastern horizon, like ruby satin under wispy cotton gauze, and slowly spread into the west. Overhead, the clouds turned to lustrous orange of an intensity that brightened and dimmed in the shifting gloom.

A blue and white striped lugsail emerged out of the incandescent western sky, on approach for the Foreign Rifles camp, bearing the order to go to war.

洋神 *Yang Shen*   *James Lande* 藍德

Dramatis Personae: Chapter 25

Ying Shou-yi 英收怡   interpreter for Governor Hsüeh Huan
Hao Yi-hsin 豪宜新   captain 都司, Li Heng-sung's "immortals"

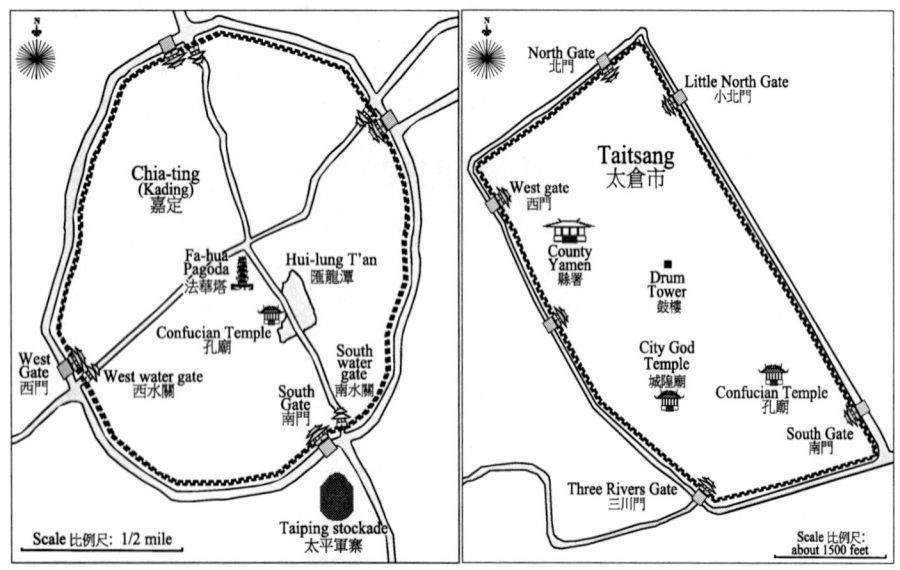

Walled Town of Chia-ting (Kading)   Walled Town of T'ai-ts'ang (Taitsan)

洋神 *Yang Shen*   *James Lande* 藍德

Chapter 25: Green Flag Immortals
Monday, June 23, 1860, 7:00am

> **The**
> ***North China Herald***
> Shanghai, Saturday, June 9, 1860
>
> ---
>
> **Latest Dates**
>
> England......Apr 1   Singapore.......May 14
> Bombay......May 1   Hongkong......May 25
> Calcutta   ----   New York........May 27
> Galle............May 6
>
> ---
>
> **Rebels.** We are without any authentic reports of the proceedings of the rebels since the date of our last. ...At Soochow it is alleged that the disbanded troops committed great atrocities. ...The terror...seems to have infected the mandarins in this and other neighboring cities, the inhabitants of which...have fled to the country districts in great numbers. This has especially been the case at Sung-kiang Fu, about 30 miles distant from Shanghai. At the instance of the Taoutai of Shanghai, HMS *Nimrod* and HIM gun-boat *Mitraille* have been sent up the river to lie off the country leading to the city, but their arrival does not appear to have interfered with the exodus of the inhabitants, who were continuing to remove families and furniture... Within Sung-kiang Fu itself the greater part of shops were closed, and even the presence of foreigners was insufficient to bring together a crowd.

    Two Americans were on sentry duty at Kuangfulin, standing atop the north rampart. One watched through a telescope the striped sail of an approaching junk as it drifted in the red glow along the creek. When the junk stopped at the camp landing, he called to the other sentry.

    "Amos," Tobias said, "what junk has a sail striped blue and white?"

    "How in the name of all that's holy am I supposed to know?" Amos said. "I'll go fetch the sergeant."

    The Chinese brave resident in the foreign camp noticed the sentries stir and climbed up onto the rampart himself. He could just see the sail and recognized the junk as a constable boat 飛蟹, doubtless with a dispatch for the barbarians from *Taotai* Wu. Commander Li Heng-sung would want know about this. He climbed down from the rampart and sauntered over to a trash pile within earshot of the barbarian chief's tent, squatted on his haunches, and sifted through the discards for something of value.

    A lowly gold button mandarin in a long robe came from the junk, in a mountain chair with two bearers and a gong beater, all brought along to spare the notable any inconvenience. As the mandarin approached, the gong was beaten seven times, at intervals, as for the arrival of a magistrate. When the sentry sergeant could finally believe his eyes and ears, he sent for Mr. Fan to receive the delegation, and notified Colonel Wood and Major Benedict. Mr. Fan hurried out in simple black surcoat and skullcap, bowing repeatedly, and led the officer back to Fletcher's tent.

    "He flom *Tao-t'ai* Wu, hab big papah fo' you," Mr. Fan said.

    The mandarin slipped a small scroll out of his sleeve and, without expression, handed it with both hands to Fletcher. Fletcher received it with two hands and the suggestion of a bow. There were two parts, one in Chinese and one in English. The name of the town T'ai-ts'ang 太倉 was written as Taitsan, Chia-ting 嘉定 was written as

Green Flag Immortals   427

Kading, and Ch'i-pao 七寶 was written as Kipao.

> *Wu-te,*
> *Rebel come Taitsan now, come Kading. You take foreign brave, go with Li Heng-sung on boat, meet Governor in Kipao tomorrow noon, go Kading fight rebel, go Taitsan fight rebel, take town back.*
> *Wu*

"Tell me I am mistaken," he said as he handed the document to Hannibal. "This says we are to move on the rebels."

"This soon?" Hannibal said. "We are not ready." Hannibal glanced at the execrable English, wincing inside at the whopping ignorance of the Chinese whose orders he was bade to follow. "This is insanity," he said angrily.

"Where does this mandarin go now?" Fletcher said.

"He go Li Heng-sung."

After the sounds of the mandarin's clashing gongs receded, Fletcher called a staff meeting in his tent with Hannibal, Falconer, and Garden. He gave them a moment to settle after reading the order to them, then asked for comment.

"Colonel, sir, there's not been time enough t' train with the full strength," Sergeant Falconer said. "They're not ready for the field."

"Mr. Wood, Colonel," Sergeant Garden said. "They have just learned to march in step and maybe half of them can hit a foot-wide target at a hundred yards. A peck o' Limehouse pimps could wipe a privy with the lot o' them."

"Sergeant Garden," Fletcher said, "can you be a little more, or less, specific?"

"Volley fire by rank," Garden said, "gives you firepower, Colonel, but their timing is off because they have na' yet got the hang of squashing minié bullets down a tight barrel. Takes some practice to get a big bullet into a lit'le billet without hurtin' her, and we get a lot of barrels jammed full of lead that would blow up in a bloke's face if a kindly and considerate drill sergeant didn't yank the rifle away."

"Colonel," Falconer said, "they're only what you'd expect after ten days. Their close-order drill is only tolerable…"

"When they're in step," Garden said.

"…when they're in step," Falconer said, "their flanking movements are ragged, hand signals botched, bugle calls buggered. Pardon my French, sir, but that language is necessary to keep 'em from being sent lambs to the slaughter. Today they 'ave potential to be an army, but not if they're all dead tomorrow."

"They'll take us to some walled city I'd wager," Hannibal said. "We do not yet have guns to breach city walls. Are we expected to *storm* over the walls?"

Fletcher waited for the exchange to subside.

"Not going is out of the question, gentlemen," Fletcher said. "So, given the unpreparedness of our force, what do you recommend?" Fletcher already knew what the force would do, but he wanted the NCOs to conclude that for themselves.

"Don't mix in," Garden said, with hesitation. Falconer exchanged a look of resignation with him.

"Yes, sir, I agree," Falconer said. "If we offer support, say with musket fire, and do not place our own in harm's way, we will have done our duty, both by the Chinese, and by the men."

"I will rely on you, then," Fletcher said, "not to accept any order you know puts your men at risk."

"We'll have to keep them well in hand," Hannibal said. "Especially the looting."

"Ach, you're right about that, sir," Garden said. "They'll be after the loot."

"Then we must keep them out of the town," Fletcher said.

"This thing gives me the hypos," Hannibal said, after the sergeants withdrew.

"Probably shouldn't," Fletcher said. "This may be a Chinese show."

"Why would you think that?"

"The governor. If we are to meet him on the way, he will be leading the excursion."

"Ah, yes. He will want the limelight to be on him, so he can report to his emperor about how he conquered the enemy legions."

"Without any foreigners."

At 7:00am the next morning, the Foreign Rifles marched west to a creek near Kuangfulin where the water was deep enough for the draft of the two 70-foot green and yellow imperial war junks – during the neap tides the creek was too low for the war junks to come all the way down to the camp. The foreigners were a motley collection got up in all variety of slops – regimental trousers, flannel shirts, hats and caps, British and French belts, haversacks, pouches, and bayonets. Only their Tower rifled muskets were the same.

On carts they brought bamboo ladders with wood planks strapped to them for crossing creeks and ditches and scaling walls, long coils of Manila rope, and extra weapons, ammunition and rations. The beds of the carts were reinforced with sufficient planking to stop a musket ball fired from a distance – the carts would be dismantled and taken along to serve as mantlets for protection against rebel musketry.

"I've half a mind to leave the ladders behind," Fletcher said to Hannibal. "I think we should not be climbing any walls, and leave that to the Chinese."

"We still need to cross ditches and moats. Best take them along just in case."

Half the men were put aboard one junk with Hannibal and sergeants Garden and Drinkwater, and the other half boarded the second war junk with Fletcher and sergeants Falconer and Reese, and sat in long files down the center of the fifteen-foot wide vessel. When the last of the twenty war junks carrying Green Flag troops passed, the two Foreign Rifle war junks fell in behind. The war junk commander shouted and twelve oarsmen on each side shipped oars and began to pull with the current. The formation of war junks snaked its way back along the same waterways on which Lao Chang's junk had conveyed Fletcher's recruits from Shanghai. Fletcher had never been on a galley under way, and its quiet progress was much more straight and steady than smaller junks with yuloh and sail.

Morning sun low in the east inundated the river and drenched the rushes and reeds along the west bank in an amber glow. A crescendo of light rose like flame in a concerto for dawn and filled the periphery of the river with reflections of gold, then gradually diminished through graduations of saffron, citrine, and lemon to the haze of another day. They passed through dappled sunlight between silent mist-covered marshes and wide lagoons as scenes of village life drifted by – women washing clothes in the creeks, young boys astride gray water buffalo, startled pheasant bursting out of the reeds, duck and cormorant flashing over the sparkling water. The siren of landscape seduced some from qualms about battle, briefly.

Fletcher took Mr. Fan to the stern and asked the war junk commander if these streams and creeks had names they could put on a rough map. The commander pointed out a local man who knew the waterways and could tell them about their route. Mr. Fan did not find it any easier to render the Chinese names into pidgin than had Old Huang but, with strident haggling over each name and conflicting recommendations from other crew, the three Chinese together eventually came to agree on most of the names they wrote down. At their first destination, about two hours later, Fletcher had recorded:

> Fu-lin Ho 福林河 river north to Kao-liang Ching 高梁涇 creek
> From there east on unnamed cut to Pai-hua Pang 百花浜 stream
> Pai-hua Pang 百花浜 stream east to T'ung-po T'ang 通波塘 canal
> T'ung-po T'ang 通波塘 canal north to Chuan-hsin Ho 磚新河 river
> Chuan-hsin Ho 磚新河 river east to another unnamed waterway
> Unnamed waterway north to the Ching T'ang 涇塘 canal
> Ching T'ang 涇塘 canal east to Ssu-ching 泗涇 town
> Ssu-ching 泗涇 town east to the Pei-mao Ching 北泖涇 creek
> Pei-mao Ching 北泖涇 creek to P'u-hui T'ang 浦匯塘 canal
> P'u-hui T'ang 浦匯塘 canal east to Ch'i-pao 七寶 town

The Chinese added the characters. Not until Fletcher saw all these canals and streams and creeks in a list did he begin to grasp the enormity of the spiderweb of waterways throughout the lower Yangtze estuary. Everywhere the people traveled on water the same as people rode horses and drove carriages on the roads of Salem and Boston. They went by boat to visit parents and uncles and aunts, they channeled the water for irrigation, boiled the water for tea, raised fish in the water and ducks on the water, and washed their clothes in the water – some even swam in the water, children mostly. If there was no water, you could not get there, maybe. And maybe that meant that only the towns accessible by water were liable to be taken by the rebels – inaccessible, out of the way villages possibly had less to fear from warring factions if they could not be reached by boat.

At Ch'i-pao, the formation of war junks stopped for ten minutes and news shouted back from stern to bow finally reached the Foreign Rifles bringing up the rear.

"He say govanah boat go flont now, you wait."

While the boats were underway, the Foreign Rifles were distracted by the novelty of the war junk and activity along the river, but the halt began to wear on their sobriety. A brandy bottle appeared and passed among devotees before being intercepted by Falconer. Restiveness overcame foreboding and scuffles broke out over trifles. The sergeants cuffed some belligerents into grudging silence.

"Now you men settle down," Falconer shouted the length of the vessel. "Else I will crack some skulls!" Like a skittish horse, the fear felt by the raw recruits had to be reigned in while it could still be controlled. The sergeants prowled the deck.

2

Finally, the flotilla came to life, the oarsmen shipped their oars and leaned into them, and the war junks started north along a creek called the Heng-li 橫瀝. In less than an hour, they came to a large river which Mr. Fan called the Wu-sung livah 吳松河.

"Allo samee Su-chou cleek at Shang-hai. Wu-sung livah go Shang-hai."

That meant this river they were turning west into would, if traveled east, take him all the way to the Astor House hotel and the Whangpoo River. Elizabeth Fitch came to mind, brilliant in her debutante's ball gown at the soirée, caught up in the fuss over her, and rapt with the admiration of hot young officers. He had not thought of her, or any woman, until now, but this was no time to be distracted. He put her from his mind.

They went up the Woosung River another hour, to a town Mr. Fan called Huang-t'u 黃土, Yellow Earth, and there turned north on another small, unnamed waterway. One more hour took them to the stream that went to the southwest gate of the town of Chiating. Farmers in their fields turned to stare dumbly at the war junks crowding into their creek, and rebel outriders spun their horses about and spurred them toward the town.

Any chance for surprise was lost by approaching too closely without reconnoitering.

The procession came to rest and the leading junks began landing soldiers. A runner came from the front of the formation with a message for officers to assemble with the governor. Fletcher told Hannibal to disembark and form the men while he took Mr. Fan and went forward. Aboard the first war junk, Hsüeh Huan stood in a circle with Li Heng-sung, Major Wen Chia-pao, and several other officers. The governor was unarmed and wore no uniform or armor, but instead wore the embroidered blue silk gown of a civil official, with a golden pheasant *pusa*, a long necklace of rose quartz and coral beads, an embossed red coral button atop his summer hat, and a one-eyed peacock feather. He grinned widely when he saw Fletcher approach.

"這是我們的武德協台罷," Hsüeh Huan said, gesturing Fletcher forward with a wave of his hand. "This must be our Colonel Wood."

"Govanah say you *ka-na-le* Wu-te," Mr. Fan said with evident surprise, and Fletcher surmised that the governor had addressed him as "colonel." Another courtesy. The governor seemed a particularly jovial fellow, with a round, fat face, an easy, perhaps nervous, laugh, and immense bushy black eyebrows that would not stay still. Fletcher bowed and *chin-chin*ed the governor.

"Govanah say how ah you?"

"Please tell the governor I am fine, and I hope he is as well," Fletcher said, amused at such elegant pleasantries in a council of war.

Mr. Fan looked perplexed, hesitated, then rattled off some Chinese. Fletcher despaired that anything comprehensible could get through the miasma of his translation.

"Govanah say what *ping* 兵 come you?"

Now Fletcher's anger surged and he glared at the Cantonese.

"What?" *The governor is impatient to get on with planning, and here this mealy-mouthed imbecile is jeopardizing my participation.*

"The governor asks how many soldiers came with you," said a soft voice behind him. Fletcher turned and found himself facing a Chinese boy of perhaps eighteen, in a brown quilted jacket and black skullcap. Mr. Fan spun around in disgust, stalked away, and clambered off the junk.

"One hundred riflemen," Fletcher said, puzzled.

"The governor says that very good. They will be useful. We talk plan of attack."

"I'm Fletcher Wood," Fletcher whispered. "Who are you?"

"My name Ying Shou-yi 英收怡, Colonel Wood. Call me Shou-yi – I am governor's English interpreter, and he wants me to tell you what they say."

"Thank the Lord," Fletcher said. The governor had the presence of mind to bring his own interpreter. Fletcher repeated the boy's name. "Showy."

"Yes, exactly," Shou-yi said with a smile. "I was taught by God's missionaries, so I also thank your Lord." Shou-yi repeated the governor's deliberation with his officers. Like a creek unimpeded by submerged rocks and fallen trees, his rendering often flowed more smoothly without the obstacles of plurals, articles and infinitives. Even so, Shou-yi was giving Fletcher English instead of pidgin, and that was a great relief, and close enough so that, as he listened, Fletcher simply tossed in the missing particles wherever intuition suggested they belonged. He relaxed knowing that, at least for the moment, his participation was no longer jeopardized by poor translation, that he could get a clear understanding of what these Chinese were thinking, and maybe even influence the outcome for the better.

"I have six hundred men," Hsüeh Huan said. "Colonel Wood has one hundred."

"I have brought one thousand men," Li Heng-sung said.

"Chia-ting is not a big place," Hsüeh Huan said. "That should be enough men to retake it. What do you think? What is the best plan? Remember – I want to attack T'ai-ts'ang as well. We must take both today, before rebel reinforcements come."

Li Heng-sung stared expressionless at the governor for a moment. He has no plan, thought Fletcher!

"Excuse me, Governor Sieh," Fletcher said, "but how can you take a walled town without artillery?"

"That is not difficult," Hsüeh Huan said, hoping that the vast ignorance of the barbarian chief was not going to be an encumbrance. "We have done this quite often. Artillery is good, but not always needed. When we capture a town – imperial troops or rebels – we take local people for the army, shopkeepers and farmers, to guard the town, and the real soldiers leave to attack the next town. Ordinary people have to be trained to be good soldiers, which takes time, and until then they are easily frightened and will run away at the first shout, no matter how much they want to protect their town. The rebels have been here at Chia-ting only two days."

"You believe they can be scared off," Fletcher said.

"That doesn't work so well," Li Heng-sung grumbled, forgetting his customary deference, "after they have held a place for a while."

"So, that's just why we must take both places at once," Hsüeh Huan said. His busy black eyebrows snapped together over the bridge of his nose in a frown at Li Heng-sung. "Surely you can see that?"

"Of course, sir," Li Heng-sung answered quickly.

"Have you reconnoitered the town yet?" Fletcher said.

"Rec..?" Shou-yi stumbled.

"Gone to look at the town, see its defenses, how to approach it, count the enemy – that's rec-ah-noi-ter."

"We have only just arrived," the governor said with a chuckle, "but you are right. Let's go look at Chia-ting."

"Dressed like that?" Fletcher said. "The rebels will see you a mile away, governor."

"Ha, and not recognize you?" Hsüeh Huan said, laughing. "Tell me your idea."

"Let me take one of those small junks down there, fishing poles, and a couple of men dressed like Showy here, and see how close we can get on this creek."

The governor grinned. "Hurry back!"

Major Wen removed his sword, turned his cotton jacket inside out, took off his pork-pie hat, then went down and commandeered a junk and found fishing poles. Fletcher exchanged his black frock coat for a soldiers's tunic turned inside out and he and Shou-yi followed. Aboard the junk, Shou-yi mentioned that the governor's name was Hsüeh Huan, and that instead of "Sieh" Fletcher should say "Hsüeh."

"Shoe-ay," Fletcher repeated.

"No," Shou-yi said, giggling. "That's 'water'. Say Hsüeh."

"Shoe-eh? And Major Wen, that's 'one,' right?"

"Close enough."

Putting to work what he'd learned watching Lin Chuan and Ah-shan, Fletcher manned the stern *yuloh* and put the junk within sight of Chia-ting's west water gate in ten minutes. The town wall was about twenty-five feet high and enclosed what seemed only a small area – Chia-ting, as the governor said, wasn't very big. There were three cannon in the tower above the gate, but the moat could not be seen from the creek. They dropped their fishing lines over the side and watched.

There was little activity in the creek, which was blocked by empty war junks near the gate, but rebel soldiers were rushing along the parapets, and out to a stockade that stood near the south gate, about 100 yards from the wall. In the ten minutes they watched, as many as six hundred rebels went into the stockade. Then horsemen came out of the west gate, halted and examined the creek, then cantered over to the bank above the junk. One dismounted, lit his matchlock fuse, and glowered down at the backs turned toward them.

"What are you doing there?" the horseman shouted.

The men on the junk silently shifted their fishing poles. Shou-yi was shivering with fright, but stayed where he squatted at the rail. Fletcher calculated how quickly he could draw his six-shooter and plug the horsemen before the matchlock could get off a shot. Major Wen just smiled and hummed a little tune.

"Hey you, *on the boat*! What are you doing there?"

"Fishing, you dope!" Major Wen sang out. "Are you blind" Suddenly his pole began to shake up and down and he jumped back and forth at the rail.

"Caught one! Caught one!" he yelled.

"Come up here."

"No, no," yelled the major, waving the horsemen away, "I've caught a big fish!"

Gongs beat and horns blew at the west gate. One of the horsemen barked an order and they all turned their horses for the gate. The dismounted rebel spit at the junk, remounted his horse, and rode off after the others.

"Let me see that big fish," Fletcher said, pointing to the fishing rod.

"魚 fish?" The major lifted his rod and caught the bare hook. "甚麼魚 what fish?"

"Ask the major about this," Fletcher said. "Suppose that Commander Li's imperial braves march southeast, then turn back and attack the south gate. At the same time, my men will fire on the stockade from this side. If we can make them think we are attacking the stockade from both sides, they might become afraid of being cut off and withdraw to the south gate. My men will then fire at the wall here to keep the rebel muskets pinned down while the governor's soldiers attack this gate."

"And the rebels will all escape from Chia-ting through the north gate," Major Wen said, laughing. "Good idea."

"Will Commander Li follow this plan?".

"If I suggest this, he will agree, because I command one of his two regiments, as an acting lieutenant colonel 參將. Anyway, if you tell him, then he must obey your order."

"My order. How can that be?"

"The governor made you a colonel 副將 at our meeting, when he called you *hsieh-t'ai* 協台, the informal title for a full colonel. Li Heng-sung is a *ying-tsung* 營總, a commander of special irregulars 壯勇. You outrank Li Heng-sung. Me too, Colonel," Major Wen added with a grin.

So that is why I am a colonel, thought Fletcher. The governor has put Li Heng-sung under my command. What other explanation is there?

"The *taotai* never said anything."

"The *taotai* does not have the authority to appoint a full colonel. That requires a governor or someone higher in rank."

One moment I'm a bum, thought Fletcher, and the next moment a Chinese colonel. No pomp and circumstance, just a few words – I dub thee colonel. Please piss on the arrogant commander whenever you wish. Well, it is easy enough to prove by just telling the commander what to do…or, maybe I should not chafe him. He'll be more tractable if I give him face, Chinese style, rather than cause him to lose face.

"Major, perhaps it would be best if you suggest this plan."

"Of course, *hsieh-t'ai*, if you wish." Interesting, thought the major, this man is not just a little smart. Barbarians are always insolent and high-handed. This one does not bark and bleat like the others. Li Heng-sung will listen to me and follow the barbarian's plan, and then we will see if this so-called colonel has any ability 有沒有把握.

"And when we take Kading," Fletcher said, "I will say that you caught the big fish."

Li-Heng-sung's two Green Flag regiments set out across the fields toward the southeast banners flying, drums beating, and horns blaring. No one in the town would have any doubt about their location. The Foreign Rifles started off a little later along the creek, behind the governor's braves, a motley crew of volunteers and conscripts arrayed in the uniforms of a dozen regiments and armed with some matchlocks and gingals, but mostly bows and arrows, spears, and swords.

Braves, thought Fletcher? With a sense of humor these Punchinellos might seem like soldiers. Takee said something about the governor trying to hire several hundred Cantonese or Ningpo men to fight rebels and half of them running away after being paid. How reliable could the governor's rag-tag harlequins be?

The imperial flotilla continued up the creek to just outside the range of the rebel guns. The governor's soldiers kept marching until the guns in the tower opened up together with several hundred muskets on the parapets above each side of the west gate. Shot and iron junk tore into the ranks, and musket and gingal balls whizzed among them. They turned to run for their lives, but found themselves looking down the barrels of the barbarian rifles. At the rear, the Foreign Rifles were beyond range of the rebel matchlocks and gingals on the wall, but the longer range of the British minié rifles allowed Sergeant Garden's 1st platoon to put random rifle fire along the parapets and into the tower to quiet the guns. The 2nd platoon with Sergeant Falconer took a position on the right and opened volley fire on the stockade while the 3rd platoon under Ptolemy Reese held back as a reserve.

The rifle fire signaled the Green Flag troops to start for the south gate, and they came up over a rise with banners waving, muskets firing, men shouting, gongs beating and horns blaring. To the Foreign Rifles, it all looked like a Fourth of July parade down Main Street, and was an effective diversion if nothing else. But the hullabaloo must have shaken rebel nerves, because all six hundred rebels in the stockade bolted together for the south gate through a hail of musket balls and shower of arrows from Li Heng-sung, who closed in behind them and almost reached the gate before it slammed shut. Li's men threw powder bags against the gate, lit fuses, then dashed back over the bridge across the moat. Hsüeh Huan ordered his men against the west gate.

"2nd platoon," Sergeant Falconer yelled, "direct fire at the gate to your left." Musket balls kicked up dirt a few yards in front of them, and gingal balls, some of pitted stone, rolled up to their feet, but Falconer paced unperturbed behind the ranks intoning psalms of musketry like a monk at matins.

"Fire high at the enemy on the parapet."

"Take care not to shoot our Chinese allies below."

"Mind your target, fire with care."

"Don't be in a hurry now."

The bridge over the moat had been removed but, under cover from the Foreign Rifles, the governor's troops were able to bring two rebel war junks into the moat to make a bridge and send a detachment over to the gate. The screaming defenders poured hot oil, rocks, even night soil down from the tower, but a handful of the governor's soldiers were able to plough through the rubbish and plop down powder bags against the wooden gate. They set short fuses and scurried back into the war junks just before a tremendous explosion blew away one door of the gate, followed by a more distant explosion from the south gate. Rebels leapt into the opening and threatened the governor's soldiers with hundreds of spears and they hesitated before the gate.

"Governor," Fletcher said, "please call your men back."

Hsüeh Huan gave the command and, when the storming party had retreated, Fletcher ordered fire directed against the gate. The 1st platoon volleyed from the front, the 2nd platoon fired from the flank, and several small cannon on the war junks opened up from the moat. Ten seconds later, when Fletcher called out for cease-fire, heaps of dead and wounded lay before the gate. Scaling ladders strapped with planks were put across the moat and Hsüeh Huan's troops charged the open gateway into Chia-ting.

The Foreign Rifles were recalled to formation and stood at ease outside the gate, listening to the fighting inside the walls, eager for plunder. Fletcher left Hannibal in charge of the Foreign Rifles, trusting he would keep them in check where they stood, and with Shou-yi accompanied the governor and his bodyguard into the town. By then, the battle was all over except for the looting. The rebels had fled out the other two gates and were stampeding toward T'ai-ts'ang. Li Heng-sung's regiments were called into formation at the south gate, but the governor's braves were too hell-bent on plunder to heed any recall. They rushed through billowing smoke from gate to gate, smashed into shops and homes, ransacked cabinets and closets for gold and silver, ravished wives and daughters and servant girls. The screams of the women finally provoked Fletcher.

"Governor, we don't have time for this."

Hsüeh Huan frowned. "You are right."

The governor sent a soldier to Li Heng-sung with orders to bring a detachment, then started forward into the streets with his own bodyguard. The soldiers commanded the looters to desist, calmly shooting dead those who refused. Shots rang out from the direction of the southeast gate. Officers swept through the town ordering soldiers to return to formation and fired volleys over their heads. When the rampage subsided and the governor's troops finally regrouped, the remainder were marched out the west gate. Eighty-four of Hsüeh Huan's men were dead – thirty-five killed looting – and one hundred twenty were wounded too seriously to continue on to T'ai-ts'ang. Li Heng-sung lost fourteen dead and twenty-six wounded left behind.

A garrison was assigned to Chia-ting and local men conscripted – this time by the imperial troops instead of the rebels – for defense of the smoldering town. Before the garrison took control, a mob of local people looted the stockade of military supplies and dragged several rebels out of hiding and cut them to pieces.

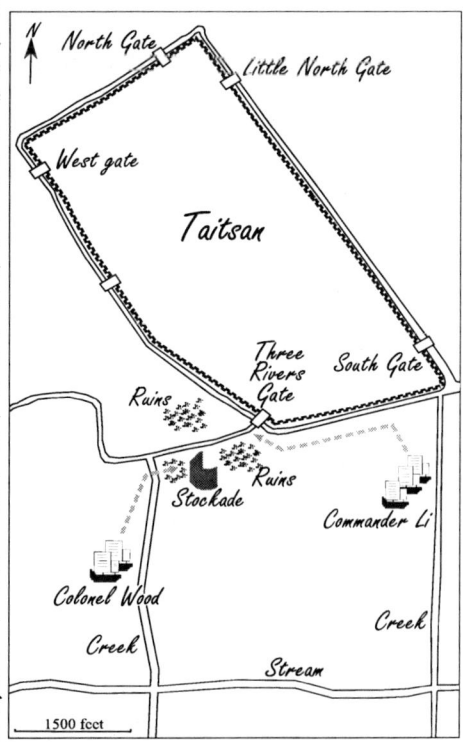

Imperial Recovery of T'ai-ts'ang, June 1860

By mid-afternoon, Hsüeh Huan's expedition was back on the water, making for T'ai-ts'ang an hour away northwest. Forewarned by rebels from Chia-ting, the T'ai-ts'ang rebel garrison prepared, and sent cavalry to meet the imperial flotilla. Harassing fire met the boats well before the town wall came into view, and accompanied them all the way.

Heavy iron stakes in the creek blocked the imperial war junks a half-mile from the T'ai-ts'ang south gate. Squads of muskets disembarked to suppress fire from the rebel cavalry that still pestered the imperial advance. Reconnoitering revealed outworks erected beyond some brick ruins outside a gate at the southwest corner of the city wall, including a half-completed stockade concealing several hundred rebels, and large bastions projecting over the gates that exposed an attack on the gates to flanking fire. A creek led past the incomplete stockade and up to the gate on the west. Another creek from the south ended at the stockade. The bridge over the moat was intact.

The imperial officers conferred again to devise a plan of attack. The iron stakes in the creek could only be removed with hoisting apparatus that would take too much time to jury-rig. An advance on the south gate would, therefore, have to be by foot over open ground and without defense against rifle and cannon fire from the walls. There had to be another way.

3 The sun was not very high above the western horizon when Major Wen Chia-pao led his regiment of *chuang-yung* – Li Heng-sung's "immortals" – out across the open rolling ground before T'ai-ts'ang toward the western gate. In the lead was the crack detachment of sixty daredevils led by Captain Hao Yi-hsin 豪宜新, men who lived for battle and laughed at fear. The major had placed his best archers at the front and rear of his formation to greet the charge of any rebel cavalry.

The walls were suspiciously quiet as his men marched past. Why no muskets, thought the major? They can't all be at the gates. Maybe they're too under strength to man the walls between the gates, or haven't the arms. Muskets are hard to get. Take them from the dead, or buy them from foreigners. Those damn foreigners better be at the stockade on time. Stupid to rely in them. We don't need barbarians. That Wu-te, he's not so bad, but his men are trash. Unreliable. They better be there.

Somewhere a loose roof tile rattled in a gust of wind. A musket ball whistled past the major's head. Damn, that's not roof tiles, that's a volley of musketry. We've gone too close to the wall!

"向左轉 to-the-left turn!"

The regiment moved away from the wall to get beyond musket range, but left four men behind dead. Stupid egg, thought the major! Misjudged the distance in the failing light. Careless! 計遠近上將之道也 a great general calculates distances correctly. There, move them into that low-lying swale. 善守者藏于九地之下 the general good at defense hides below in the nine secret recesses. Keep them behind that crest. 夫地形者兵之助也 using natural formations in the land greatly assists the soldier. Send skirmishers under the wall, and out on the flanks as diversions.

"馬兵 cavalry! From the rear!"

The rear guard is fanning out. Not too thin, good. Now let fly! Yes, again, another flight. Yes, this snake has a stinger in its tail. They won't be back soon.

Shadows of the old ruins rose on the horizon black against the sky. The major placed his regiment where the land fell away below the ruins. Captain Hao's detachment silently filed out and vanished between the shadows. Major Wen waited.

"Keep low, follow me," Captain Hao Yi-hsin whispered.

Sixty men crept away from their regiment and into the ruins outside the southwest gate of T'ai-ts'ang. Quietly, they settled in among the chipped old brick and crumbling

洋神 *Yang Shen*   James Lande 藍德

mortar. What was this place, wondered Captain Hao? Looks like old foundations, but of houses? Only rich men have brick houses, but inside the town wall, not outside. A kiln maybe. Is sixty enough. More would be too many – more would stumble into each other, more would give us away to the enemy.

"Put on the rebel clothes," the captain whispered.

He pulled his disguise from under his tunic and put on a rebel's green jacket, green head-scarf, and a yellow cape. Stupid clothes, he thought, like a puppet play. Eh, there go the foreign soldiers 洋兵. Their rifles sound like thunder echoing off the town wall. What will they do now, open the stockade, or open the gate? Listen to those rifles, as fast as drumbeats, how do they reload so fast? Wouldn't like to be in the stockade right now. Oh, cannon, too. Must be the war junks, firing their little playthings. Just bored, I'd guess. Can't hurt stockade logs much. I'd be bored too, just sitting on a damn boat. Better here. Wait, was that a light there, did the gate crack open? Wait, is that a lantern in the stockade. Better run fast if you're going to show a lantern. It's the stockade!

"Hold your fire," the captain whispered.

He couldn't hear, but he expected the major was giving the same order. Here they come, running fast, falling down and struggling up, what stupids! There's the last one out of the stockade.

"Get ready to follow me. Stay close together!"

The captain watched the last shadow in the line of rebels as it came abreast of his men. He also caught the movement of men coming out from behind the stockade. The foreign soldiers are following 洋兵追上了!

"追 follow!" the captain shouted.

His men rose up out of the ruins like ghosts out of a graveyard and flitted after the rebels, holding back to avoid attracting the attention of the hindmost runners. Captain Hao heard the volley of the foreign rifles from behind them, and saw rebels fall from the top of the wall. Good, he thought, but keep firing high or you'll hit me! The foreign rifles sound different, louder. There, a door in the gate is opening, opened halfway.

The captain and his men crowded in to pass through together with the rebels.

"Wait!" a guard shouted, a rebel private 伍卒. "Who are you?"

"嘉定來的 - 逃走的 from Chia-ting – we escaped," the captain said. The private looked at the second rifle slung over the captain's shoulder.

"Why the extra rifle?" the private said. "That's one I've never seen. Wait here." The private turned and called inside the gate.

"伍長 sergeant, please come ov–"

The sentence was cut short by a knife in his throat. Twenty of Captain Hao's daredevils shouldered their way inside and dropped the closest guards with their first volley, allowing twenty more daredevils to tumble in through the opening. The first twenty turned and heaved against the huge wooden door to push it open while the rest of the men knelt on each side of the entrance and fired at the rebels inside. Exactly as planned, thought the captain.

However, he had not planned on the rebels from the stockade turning together and charging back toward the gate. The first rank of ten rebels were dropped by volley from Hao's extra rifles, but another fifty rebels crushed into the open space, pushing the imperials to each side, trying to carry them into the moat. Suddenly ten rebels at the center of the gate clutched at their chests and fell. Behind them another twelve dropped. That time the captain heard the report – foreign rifles! The foreign soldiers are shooting into the center of the rebels and killing them. How can they keep from hitting us?

"壯勇躺下 *chuang-yung* lie down!"

One more volley from the Foreign Rifles caught a few rebels who had not taken cover, who had not seen their comrades fall for no apparent reason in front of the gate. For a few moments, the echoes of the last volley drifted down the wall. The gate was silent but for the moans of the wounded and dying. Then a screaming horde of imperial soldiers led by Major Wen boiled up out of the twilight, pounded across the bridge, and surged through the open gate into the town. Captain Hao and his men opened the doors wide and stood guard for the rest of the evening until relieved to return to Kuangfulin.

As Major Wen Chia-pao led his regiment toward the T'ai-ts'ang southwest gate, imperial war junks carrying the Foreign Rifles made their way down and around and up the creek leading to the half-built stockade, Fletcher told Ptolemy Reese to take the 3rd platoon ashore first; the other two platoons would follow. The best riflemen aboard were assigned to the three ranks of Reese's platoon. The remaining twenty riflemen were sent to the forecastle where, from a few hundred yards out, they could enfilade the ground from the landing back to the stockade, to clear it of rebels and divert attention from Li Heng-sung's advance. Reese ordered rifles loaded. Oarsmen jumped ashore with lines from the war junks and hauled enough for the slow current to push the junks to the bank.

"3rd platoon, over the side," Reese growled. "Follow me." He led his men to within twenty yards of the stockade, where there were ruins for cover, while the riflemen on the forecastle of the war junk chipped away at the stockade loopholes.

Dozey of dem rebels, he thought, not to rip out these old brick walls from in front of their little stick house. "Now do this right, one rank at a time, you know who you are. 1st rank, ready, fire!"

"2nd rank, ready, fire!"

"3rd rank, ready, fire!"

When they settled into it, their rate of fire reached between ten and twelve volleys each minute. In the first minute, over one hundred .702 caliber minié bullets tore away fist-sized chunks of pinewood from the stockade wall and let in dim rays of light through a blur of dust. Reese sent to the junk for more ammunition. The 2-pounder and 3-pounder guns aboard the closest war junk opened up on the stockade as well, not to Sergeant Reese's liking. The balls whished overhead so closely they raised his hair, and he felt hot metal fragments and burnt wadding.

"Sergeant Garden," yelled a voice behind him, "go make those idiots stop firing – they'll hit our men."

After three minutes the fusillade had raised a pox on the rough complexion of the gnarled bark. Large holes were chewed in the stockade logs and bullets whizzed inside. That was when the rebels broke out of the stockade and ran for the southwest gate. Reese was able to count them in the half-light, and no more came out after 151. Reese jumped up and chased after the last of them.

"C'mon men, after 'em!"

Most of his platoon followed after him. Only a few heard Colonel Wood shouting for him to come back, and they remained behind. As he came up on the next ruins, Reese saw the imperials dressed as rebels burst out of nowhere and dash after the running rebels. He halted his platoon.

"First rank only, independent fire, at the top of the wall." His men lined up across the path and began firing randomly along the parapet, into the tower, and at the bastion loopholes to provide cover. The first rebel hit fell from the parapet to the ground in front of the gate and the 3rd platoon let out a whoop.

"Quiet there. Pay attention. Aim high, mind your targets, fire at will."

The rebels from the stockade reached the gate and one tall door swung halfway open. The imperials crowded into the gate behind them but were stopped.

"Cease fire. Reload. Hold your fire."

There was a scuffle at the gate, the imperials pushed the door further open and fired a volley inside. When the smoke lifted, Reese could see the rebels from the stockade turn and rush back to the gate. He couldn't see what to do until dozens of rebels crowded through the open door and tried to push the imperials off to the side and into the moat.

"Ready. Drop those rebels coming out the gate, in the center. One volley. Aim. Fire!" Maybe ten rebels dropped. An easy shot. A second volley, and another dozen rebels fell. He saw the imperials at the gate fall flat on the ground, and at the same time on his right the earth rose up and launched toward the gate. The other imperials, he thought. Look at 'em all – where did they come from? Time for one more volley before they block the field of fire. He ordered the volley, then cease-fire, but by then there was hardly anyone standing below the gate. The empty path over the bridge suddenly was full of fluttering imperial banners.

Never saw 'em, he thought. How could that many men hide in so small a place? Never saw 'em at all. Them jossers is somethin' else. To see 'em rushing through that gate you'd never think it was the same blokes parading around the battlefield banging drums and blowin' 'orns an' shoutin' an' waving flags like it were Guy Fawkes Day.

4 Six days after T'ai-ts'ang was retaken by Hsüeh Huan, the Loyal King captured the prefecture seat of Ch'ing-p'u, called Singpoo or Tsingpoo by foreigners. Two days after Ch'ing-p'u fell the Loyal King dispossessed the Manchu emperor of the prefecture seat of Sung-chiang, which foreigners knew as Sungkiang. At Sungkiang, the Taiping rebels were only twenty-seven miles upriver from the Model Settlement.

Corporal Ptolemy Reese was despondent, and nothing anyone said cheered him. Yeah, he would tell you, they gave me a $100 Mex bonus for action at Taitsan. Well, maybe I saved the lives of some o' them imp jossers at the gate. And, sure, if I was in the British army they probably would've given me a bleedin' VC, and the whole platoon a unit citation, maybe a medal with a ribbon that said Taitsan . But then Colonel Wood busts me to corporal for failure to obey a command I didn't even hear, and tells me I'm lucky not to see a floggin' and gaol. Money with one hand, slap with the other. An' now I'm s'posed to bite on a bullet?

For a few days, Corporal Reese was a campfire pariah because of his gloomy mood. Of course, he was a still an NCO in the minds of his men, and kept at the middling distance allotted for non-commissioned officers. In proportion as time healed the corporal's slight, and the men were distracted by other grievances, he was rehabilitated in his mind and their estimation, and it helped that "Colonel" Wood, the author of his disgruntlement, was frequently away from camp kowtowing to the Chinese sponsors. He had been gone two days since they heard Tsingpoo was taken by the Loyal King. The southerner, Major Benedict, was left in charge.

In the absence of marching orders, Hannibal ensured the camp followed a semblance of routine practical for men generally hung over the first half of each day. For most of them, *reveille* was more difficult than a charge up Balaclava Heights, or so remarked the old soldiers of the Crimea, hardened veterans of thousands of hung-over reveilles, disciplined by the cat and lash to instant obedience. The recruits emerged blinking at the light from the hot, stuffy tents that, by now, were ordered in small enclaves by community of prejudice. At the north end of the tent rows, with signs over each tent that read *White House*, *Imperial Hotel Bar*, and *Boston Common*, dwelt the Yankees, as far away as possible from the Dixie tents at the south end, signed *Possum*

洋神 *Yang Shen* *James Lande* 藍德

Trot, *Old Holler*, and *Blue Ridge*. The French quarter, signed *Bas-de-Montmartre*, and *La Rive Gauche*, was in the west, across the continent of tents from the Germanic tribes, the Prussians and Swiss, in *The Matterhorn*. The Scot and Irish bailiwicks, *Solway Firth* and *Blarney Castle*, were removed to a safe distance from the English, in *Whitehall*, and *Crystal Palace*, the Manilamen huddled in their *El Barrio Bajo* and sang old songs about powerful heroes. The NCOs and officers were segregated into their own nameless little cantonment. Select nonaligned vagabonds were admitted to an established dominion – the Swede joined the Yankees, and the Peruvian was a guest of Dixie – or scattered about, the Greeks, Italians, and Portuguese being found anywhere. From such dissimilar congregations of dissension, Hannibal remarked, were great nations built, and the Foreign Rifle tent camp at Kuangfulin was quite possibly a hopeful young democracy. Out of their tents they stumbled dizzily for the latrines or for the water barrels. No canteen washes, no baptismal sprinkling would do – they violently splashed water, dumped water from pots, or just bent over headfirst into a barrel – a full emersion, a ritual purification, absolution by ablution.

When a bugle sounded *assembly* for roll call and guard mount, they could see their way bleary-eyed into ranks, stand almost straight, and usually answer to their name. Sentry duty was divided into two guards of twelve hours, each with three reliefs of four men each. Another guard mount at *retreat* assigned sentries for the night. At full strength, a man usually had sentry duty once every four days, but only for half a day, which was thought less tedious for men tetchy in garrison. Banging on a pot always signaled mess. The bugle for *fatigue call* invariably inspired the genius of both novice and practiced shirkers alike in the mimicry of ordinary and exotic illness. As there still was no medical officer at camp KFL, Sergeant Garden and John Colter stood in for a doctor – each having had some experience, Garden in military service, and Colter on the prairie. Both men were skilled at detecting fraudulent disability, which tended to occur in cycles congruous with disagreeable fatigue duty, and were much less charitable than any MD. Serious cases were sent to Shanghai; the walking wounded were treated in camp. Otherwise, any man who breathed and wasn't bleeding was reported fit for kitchen police, camp cleanup, digging new latrines, and hauling water. Then there was a *drill call* that signaled long distance marching, tactical field maneuvers, the manual of arms, target practice, and building field fortifications.

The training regimen set out only weeks earlier had not yet progressed to advanced levels. As the sergeants had pointed out just before the Foreign Rifles went off to Kading and Taitsan, basic skills were only just tolerable. Since then, Fletcher's emphasis had narrowed to the basics of moving in open formation under fire. The Foreign Rifles were training to move rapidly over open ground in coordinated skirmishing order both to disrupt the enemy's aim and to reduce exposure to enemy fire, halting often to rest in prone position and recover. No one who had served in the Crimea wanted to repeat the carnage accrued by marching rank after rank directly into the face of enemy fire. Infantry squares and siege tactics waited on progress with simpler maneuvers.

The last two bugle calls heard in camp were *retreat* for afternoon roll call and guard mount, and *taps*. Calls conspicuous by their absence were *stable call*, *boots and saddles*, and *watering call*, obviously not needed in a camp with no horses. Artillerymen drilled with the infantry, as there were not yet any cannon.

Sergeant Falconer made a round of the camp each evening. The same men were always drinking and fighting. American alliances were generally by origin of maritime species, and thus *Mandarin* usually clashed with *McLeod*, *Challenger* with *Progressive Age*, and *Heroes of Alma* with everyone. With Charlie Jackson and Farley Masters gone, Ham and Tater Bean had no southerners to scuffle with, and were despondent until the

Cassidy brothers vowed to accommodate them almost any time for next to no reason at all. When Lars Johansson felt left out, his mates commiserated and *Challenger* invited him to fight *Progressive Age* with them. The Swiss from *Henry Ellis*, Helmut Schmidt and Otto Shapiro, were savage at checkers and backgammon – their shouting and swearing, together with *Lorena*, *Barbara Allan*, and *Sweet Betsy from Pike* sung to banjo and harmonica by Corporal Dinwiddie and Private Dobbin, filled the night.

When live chickens were first brought back from Kuangfulin for the mess, the Manilamen Paco Dalogdog and Balla Gumarang absconded with a couple of the roosters, armed them with home-made bamboo spurs that would do until steel spurs could be gotten from Shanghai, and trained them to fight.

"My cock *Lam-ang* very best fighter," Balla would crow after his bird won a match. The camp believed the eight-pound Langshan rooster won because of its larger size and greater weight, but Balla knew it was because the cock was called *Lam-ang*, after the hero of Ilocano legend. The magical rooster of *Lam-ang* could topple houses with a flap of his wings, and Balla's *Lam-ang* terrified other birds with merely a shake of his bright red comb and wattle.

The camp decided that, inasmuch as the camp cook could take the combatants for *arroz con pollo* or cock-a-leekie at any time, training the cocks did not break the rules about keeping pet animals. The cockfights that ensued caught the attention of many who might otherwise have been fighting each other, so camp management encouraged the Manilamen in their old pastime. A special excursion to Kuangfulin was arranged so that Baboy Abinsay, Espada Inabayan, and Naguapo Tapay could shop in the market for promising cocks of their own to augment the pool, and increase the stakes. The Chinese caught on, and began to offer a better quality of rooster for this new business. Cartels formed to control monopolies for fighting cocks, and the sport spread to the villages – if there was gambling, the Chinese wanted a piece of the action.

The rest of the Foreign Rifles were more prosaic in their pastimes. They played endless games of poker, reread old newpapers and magazines, darned socks, and washed clothes. Clothes and blankets examined by lantern-light for lice and chiggers were solemnly committed to deep cauldrons of boiling water. A few quiet seaman carved wood and bone scrimshaw, recalling the flavor of life at sea.

On his rounds of camp Falconer heard a lot of griping adrift around campfires and in lantern-lit tents. The talk had an edge that the usual portion of soldier's complaints did not, a tone of men with hair-trigger tempers close to the limits of toleration. The men had been paid, but had no place to spend their money, so drinking started early. Falconer and Garden knew better than to tolerate the practice, and when Colonel Wood was in camp it was not allowed. Major Benedict, however, did not much care if the men drank after drill. He did himself. The sergeants knew that with this lot of blighters, discipline could not be enforced successfully without support from their officer. Barracks-room barristers would say they have to drink rum or brandy because they can't drink the water, and point to what happened to Allbright and Boxer. That would lead to a chorus of caterwauls about other conditions in camp besides "why can't we have clean water?"

"Why can't we get decent food?" always led to gripes about how no rations were coming from Shanghai, and how nobody would go to Kuangfulin for rations, because it was no one's job, and how there was no money for rations because there was no commissariat. Sometimes they were reduced to hardtack and coffee. Even aboard ship the food was better.

"Why isn't there a decent doctor here?" also was a old lament heard again that morning. Fergus Cassidy, gunner from *Fenimore Cooper*, was too drunk a few nights before to close his tent flap and drape his mosquito net around his cot, and the mosquitoes swarmed in and nearly picked him up and carried him out. The next morning his face, neck, wrists and ankles were swollen with huge red welts.

"I'm not after bein' excused fatigue duty, your honor," Fergus said with a groan, "I just want proper care."

Falconer thought it best to address some of the complaints himself. The previous afternoon, he had decided to go to Kuangfulin for supplies, but Mr. Fan said "mahket close now, no food, mus' go belly elly en day." So this morning at 7:00am, Falconer walked into Kuangfulin, taking Colter, who also knew something about provisioning, Webley the quartermaster, Cork the yeoman, Mr. Fan, and the Chinese private. Not so many, he thought, as to frighten the inhabitants. The tall, grizzled, normally taciturn Colter seemed to have been keeping something on his mind.

"Sergeant, do you find the camp a mite edgy these days?" Colter thought it best to test the depth before wading in.

"So, you 'ave noticed something as well, 'ave you?" Falconer had wondered if this quiet man of the American West would ever open up. He'd surely be a sergeant himself, if the Foreign Rifles did not already have too many. Falconer wondered best how to draw him out without compromise to Colonel Wood's authority.

"It's hardly any wonder they drink and fight. The inadequate conditions at this camp would crab any grizzly, goad any force of men into rowdiness." If the sergeant is willing to consider the problem, thought Colter, that should be sufficient for an opening.

"They are a rum lot. What 'ave you seen? You can speak freely. Colonel Wood is my officer, but I 'ave found him open to suggestions."

"Some things I need not detail – this trip itself tells me you are aware that having no commissariat is a nuisance. A medical officer is needed, and engineers to put this camp in shape. The living conditions – food, health – betray poor preparation from the very beginning. Someone who served in the Crimea would recognize such a situation, according to what I have been told."

"God's truth. Crimea did start off just like that. Why, the 44th barely put boot to the brown dirt of Scutari before men started catchin' the cholera. It were wrote later that in the first three months over two 'undred English and seven 'undred French died of it, and then it spread to the fleet. No way to know really 'ow many bluejackets died of cholera – buried 'em at sea, polluted the ocean. French thought it was in the air and kept changing camps. It got so's a man'd get a belly ache, minutes later he'd double over with terrible cramps, and a few hours later he be dead. After Mrs. Nightingale brought her nurses and cleaned up the hospitals it was better, but cholera plagued the regiment until we left."

"On the Overland Trail, anyone who didn't drink river water, and drank only tea and coffee made in boiled water, and some who swore by whiskey only, never got the diarrhea on the trail when others did."

"That's been my experience. We had two sergeants 'ere the first week, Allbright and Boxer, that drank water from the creek and took real sick. Since then, no one drinks creek water. Chinese themselves don't drink water, just boil water for tea. If there's no tea in the water, then it's called 'white tea' – poor people that can't afford a shillin' for tea drink that. You wonder about the water foreigners drink in Shanghai 'otels and restaurants. And the ice."

Colter offered more about the Overland Trail. A scout told him that cholera was caught once by a wagon train that drank rainwater out of pits left by other wagon trains – possibly pit latrines. The only unboiled water that was safe on the trail came from mountain springs. Cholera and fever got into water somehow but boiling killed the disease and made water safe.

"After that," Colter said, "I made strict rules about boiling river water and standing water of any kind and never again did I see any cholera in my wagon trains or have much trouble with the diarrhea or dysentery."

"You think we should do that 'ere, then. Boil all the water?"

"Water for drinking. Boil creek water in cauldrons, remove scum from the surface, mix in powdered charcoal, cool it down, and store it in barrels marked drinking water. Use the purified water for cooking, and have a *water call* for men, instead of horses, to fill their canteens."

"The fatigue duty men that 'auls the water could do that. It'd take a while to convince the men the water's safe."

"Prepare the water like that, under supervision, and I'll drink it – and I won't get sick. But sergeant, what's really needed is a well. Chinese drink well water, or at least boil well water, if your story is true. Well water would be free of all the impurities in creeks and rivers, filtered through sand – I'd still boil it, but it would be a great improvement over that dirty creek."

"Need engineers for a well, and for better field fortifications around the camp."

"I'm a little surprised, sergeant, that we don't already have commissary, medical, and engineering. Surely there are swashbucklers in those lines as well as infantry and artillery. Is the colonel not recruiting them?"

Falconer hesitated. It went against the grain to speak ill of his officers. "Well, the colonel and the major are a little new at all this. Mind you, that's not criticism – I'd not offer an opinion of my own officer to anyone else, nor should you. However, from what I've been told, they 'ave experience as line officers in action against the enemy, but 'ave never served on staff. So they 'ave these things to learn by trial and error."

"Do you think I should speak to the colonel," Colter asked softly.

"Yes, I think he's open minded. He'll listen."

Colter, however, did not bring it up until after the disaster of 1st Sungkiang.

洋神 *Yang Shen*   James Lande 藍德

Dramatis Personae: Chapter 26

Beau Moreau	Marine sergeant, French steamer HIM *Forbin*
Paul Bernard	sailor, French merchant ship *Ville de Dieppe*
Alexandre Petit	Marine corporal, French steam frigate HIM *Entreprenante*
Luc Delacroix	gunner, French steam transport HIM *Gironde*
Kirat *One-eyed* Banta	Tagalo crewman, Chinese steamer *Confucius*
Naguapo *Handsome* Tapay	Cebuano crewman, Spanish brig *Tiempo*
Vito Ferrara	Italian AB, American brig *Progressive Age*
Nuncio Ricci	Italian ordinary seaman, American brig *Progressive Age*
Angus Blackwood	Scottish AB, American merchant ship *Competitor*
Callum Blackwood	Scottish AB, American merchant ship *Competitor*
Fergus Cassidy	Irish sailor, American merchant ship *Fenimore Cooper*
Fester Cassidy	Irish sailor, American merchant ship *Fenimore Cooper*
Other Foreign Rifles	foreigners in action at 1st Sungkiang

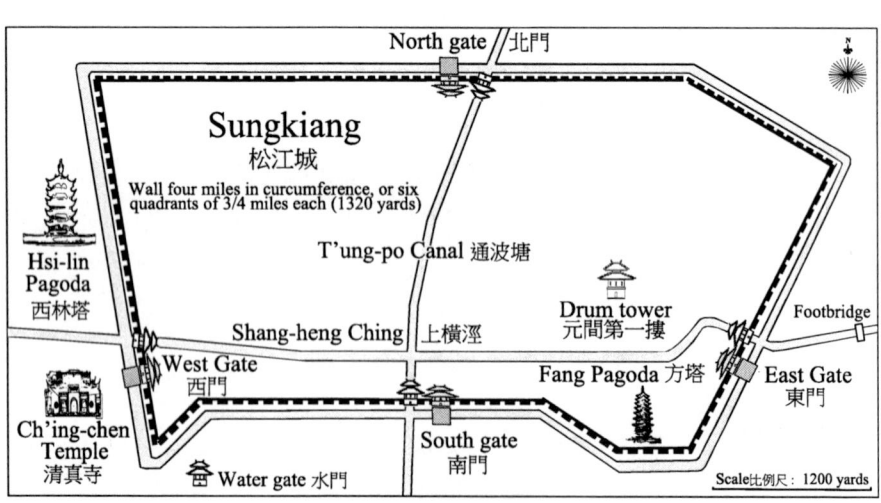

Walled City of Sungkiang
[based on Sungkiang Gazetteer, *Sung-chiang fu hsü-chih* 松江府續志, 光緒九年 1883]

444   *1st Sungkiang*

Chapter 26: 1ˢᵗ Sungkiang

Monday, July 2, 1860, 7:00 am

> **BRITISH CONSULAR NOTIFICATION.** HBM Consul has received instructions... that it is a legally punishable crime...to take any part in the internal struggles now going on in this country. ...it is made unlawful for any British subject within any part of China to assist either the existing Chinese Government or any party engaged in opposition to that Government, whether by personal enlistment or by procuring other persons to enlist, or by furnishing or procuring warlike stores of any description, or by fitting out vessels, or by knowingly doing any other act for either party for which neutrality may be violated. ...British subjects have...neither a dynasty or established government to defend nor a country to free, and cannot hire themselves to either party, or take life or aid and abet in the taking of life, without being guilty of the lowest mercenary ruffianism.... The undersigned warns...that he is empowered to punish the offences...by imprisonment for two years and a fine of five thousand dollars.
> TRAVIS TRENT MASTERS,
> *H. M.'s Consul*
> British Consulate, Shanghai

Kuangfulin had been bustling for hours with people and carts converging on the town's small market. It was not difficult to find – Falconer just followed the crowd to the town center where hundreds of stalls were crammed together under cloth awnings. In a town this small, the separate markets started at different hours. The meat market opened earliest, slaughtered the morning's animals, and hung cuts of pork, beef, and chicken in stalls together with roast ducks, sausage strings, jars of snakes, and the occasional dog. The fish market opened next, laying out fresh perch, croaker, catfish, bass, mackerel, and eel in orderly rows between holding tanks brimming with fish raised in pens along the canals and creeks. Seafood fresh from Shanghai arrived later: shrimp, octopus, squid, oysters, mussels, clams, limpets, periwinkles, and seaweed.

The vegetable and fruit stalls opened after the farmers brought in their loads. Empty oxcarts filled the streets outside teahouses around the market entrance, where the drivers idled the day away after hauling produce. Mr. Fan engaged an oxcart for the morning from among them, and then helped select the freshest of the meat and fish for the camp. Falconer wandered between narrow aisles of rhubarb, turnips, Chinese peas, knurly bitter melon, beets, *bak choy*, cauliflower, sweet potatoes, yams, garlic bulbs, bean cake, bean sprouts, chestnuts, and preserved duck eggs, and he bought great quantities of inexpensive cabbage, onions, green beans, corn, squash, mushrooms, and chicken eggs. The fruit stands displayed carambola, bananas, guava, kiwi, mango, papaya, muskmelon, watermelon, and he bought pears, apples, and oranges.

The last to open were the china and bamboo ware shop and the dry goods store, where townsfolk bought their soy sauce, sesame and peanut oil, vinegar, pepper sauce, rice wine, *samshoo*, sugar, salt, rice, and tea. In front of the dry goods shop, there were half a dozen large bins of different grades of rice, and inside on the shelves dozens of grades of black and green tea. Camp condiments came from the dry goods store.

By mid-morning, small stands at the market entrance were heating up water for noodles and firing grills for savory sausage. Falconer stared at the large Chinese sign 五金行 above the entrance to a nondescript little storefront festooned with multicolored scrub brushes and lanterns. Farmers in conical straw hats and short pants, shopkeepers in silk jackets and skullcaps, and pudgy housewives attended by servants and slaves all stepped around the tall, ungainly foreigner as he stood gawking into the store. Mr. Fan brought him here to buy tools and utensils – he called the place a "five-metal-store." From the open front of the shop, the sergeant could see down long aisles with neatly ordered shelves and trays. To Falconer it looked like an ironmonger's, a hardware store, and he marveled briefly that Chinese should have such a thing, like those just up from the Liverpool wet docks.

The shop owner hustled out to welcome the foreign guest with appropriate fanfare. While Mr. Fan read the order and haggled over his percentage of kickback on each item, the sergeant slowly browsed the aisles and allowed the curiosities there to evoke musty childhood memories. Closer examination showed some familiar objects, and others less so. Chisels, adzes, planes, and wire saws pulled instead of pushed; scythes, mattocks, split bamboo; ceramic tile and water conduit; Chinese calendars, calculators for *feng-shui*, abacuses, loom shuttles, spindles, treadles, heddles, paddles, reeds, and combs; artifacts of Chinese workaday life for farmers, carpenters, stonecutters, weavers, and geomancers. Falconer settled on picks, shovels, cakes of pungent soap, mosquito netting and mosquito incense coils, paper lanterns, iron pots, woks, cleavers, ladles, pans, pails, wheelbarrows, mallets, hammers, rope, wire, cord and string. He paid for everything out of his own pocket.

The "foraging" party returned from Kuangfulin at about 11:00am. Falconer rounded up Gus de la Torre and the best of the Manilaman cooks and put them to work preparing a grand lobscouse of stewed pork, onions, cabbage, and turnips for the camp's dinner. While the supplies were being doled out, horsemen rode in from the direction of the Green Flag camp and called out to the Chinese private. The private hurried to locate Mr. Fan, and the interpreter scurried through camp to find Hannibal. Their intelligence was that the Loyal King had that morning vaulted the walls of Sungkiang and captured the town – some of Li Heng-sung's braves were witness to the assault. Hannibal called his sergeants together to pass on the report.

"In the absence of orders from the colonel, gentlemen, we can only hold our ground. I'm told that the Green Flag commander himself is away at Tsingpoo, so we should assume no help from that flank. Put the men on alert, weapons ready, double the sentries, and send out pickets in the direction of Sungkiang."

In mid-afternoon, another blue and white striped lugsail approached from Kuangfulin and stopped next to two war junks anchored at the landing. Li Heng-sung's spy, the Chinese private, again saw the bright sail of the dispatch boat from Shanghai and meandered over to within earshot of the barbarian major's tent. The same gold button mandarin came from the creek in his swaying mountain chair, preceded by the noisy gong beater, and was met by the obsequious Mr. Fan and taken to Major Benedict.

"Hab message from *k'a-na-le* Wu-te," Mr. Fan said.

> Major Benedict,
> The rebels captured Sungkiang this morning and are only a few miles south of you. Keep the men on alert, rifles loaded and ready, and post extra sentries. With Li Heng-sung at Tsingpoo, it is not impossible the rebels will attack. Expect skirmishers. Pitch every tent we have. I'll return tonight after meeting with the Governor.
> Wood

"What will we do if attacked, sir?" Garden said.

"Defend ourselves as best as we can. Retreat only in the face of overwhelming force. The Chinese have brought down the two war junks I asked for – with the spring tides now, the creek is up, and they were able to come all the way to our landing. Assign

洋神 *Yang Shen*   *James Lande* 藍德

one platoon to cover a withdrawal to the creek *if necessary*. And send pickets up the creek toward Kuangfulin, so we can get word if rebels come that way."

2   Two days earlier Fletcher had been recalled to Shanghai. The rebels had captured Tsingpoo, and Takee sent Ah-shan to fetch Fletcher back for a war council with the mandarin godfathers of Fletcher's misbegotten army of miscreants, their honors Takee, Wu Hsü, and Hsüeh Huan. Fletcher's first stop, however, had been at H. Fogg for a quiet word with Artemis L. Fuller.

"Where in hell is my goddamn artillery!"

"Colonel, please, calm yourself," Fuller cooed, offering a cheroot.

"You know where you can put that!"

"Colonel, we have had agents in Hong Kong and India, the Middle East, even the Japans, all toiling to find cannon to fill your order. But, Mr. Wood, it takes more than 'open sesame' or abracadabra or a mere snap of the fingers to locate, purchase, and ship large guns. We completed purchase – by telegraph only yesterday – on two Napoleons, part of an entire battery of Crimean war surplus from some Turkish pasha armed by the British to fight the Russians, but they are still weeks away by ship."

Not Napoleons, thought Fletcher, if they're from the Crimea. More likely 12-pounder howitzers, but to the uninitiated I guess all guns of that sort are Napoleons.

"I need those guns now. Walled towns all around us are falling to the rebels and I must have guns to breach those walls. Where are there guns on this coast?"

"Only the British and French have them."

No, not only the British and French, recalled Fletcher. Our *taotai* has guns too. What has he done, I wonder, with those 6-pounders that came on *Essex*? And would he give them to me if he still has them?

"Send word to Takee the moment the ship carrying those Napoleons reaches Gutzlaff Island. They will belong to the Chinese government, but I want no monkeyshines with the Chinese custom house."

"Certainly. I'll see they get instructions when they arrive at Hong Kong, and have them put a letter aboard the pilot launch at Gutzlaff Island. Several other orders are completed, or nearly so. When will you want to come for them?"

"I'll be back tomorrow," Fletcher said, "to examine the invoices, and I will arrange for transport of this lot out to Kuangfulin on the next day. Same place as before, your *Yang-king-bang* godown?"

"Yes, it's most convenient. The British patrols can't sneak up on us there."

Takee and Fletcher took sedan chairs the two miles from Takee Bank to the county yamen in the north of the native city, leaving the international settlement at Barrier Road and passing through the Old North Gate. After his experience storming the walls of Kading and Taitsan, Fletcher was paying closer attention to this fortification, to the twenty-foot-wide moat said to be twelve feet deep, the arrow towers, watch-towers, gates and gate-towers of two and three stories.

Seeing Takee's chairs approach, the main gate porter of the county yamen immediately shooed people out of the way to clear a path into the courtyard without the usual fanfare for a high official. Their chairs squeezed though the narrow entrance and set down in the first courtyard and the gate porter showed Takee and the foreigner up to the ceremonial gate with elaborate gesticulation. They entered into the second courtyard, passed a small stone monument and rows of small offices, and entered the great hall.

When they arrived, Governor Hsüeh Huan was in official session, sitting behind a huge table draped with red silk atop a dais in the great hall of the yamen of the county

1ˢᵗ Sungkiang   447

magistrate. Anxious Chinese in long silk gowns stood along the walls beneath elegant tapestries and scrolls hung on the walls, evidently waiting for the governor. Fletcher and Takee were taken to a room off the next hall. Ten minutes later, there was a sharp clap of a wooden block from the great hall and a loud voice, and a few moments later a servant came to take them to a room in the rear. As they entered, Takee pointed to characters on the wall and said they meant "lookee in heart." Tables were stacked with scrolls and cloth-bound books of documents, and there were several pair of square-backed rosewood chairs around the periphery of a thick carpet embroidered with strange, fabulous animals. Wu *taotai* was already there with the governor and his English interpreter, Ying Shou-yi.

"啊我們地武德協台到了," Hsüeh Huan said with a bright grin that puffed out his bean curd cheeks and hoisted his bushy black eyebrows as if his face had set sail.

"Our Colonel Wu-te has arrived," interpreted Ying Shou-yi. The governor's words checked even the normally sedate *taotai*, who shot a look at Takee, and Fletcher could only guess this was the first they heard of his new rank.

"Our new colonel is a hero already!" Hsüeh Huan said. "He was victorious at T'ai-ts'ang. Captain Hao is most grateful to him for saving their lives at the gate."

"Saving their lives?" Takee said.

"The Foreign Rifles," the *taotai* said, "stopped a rebel counterattack at the west gate by firing all their rifles together several times." Li Heng-sung had reported the action.

"Captain Hao's daredevils are very fond of Colonel Wood now," Hsüeh Huan said, "and they all want to have foreign rifles 洋槍. Hao was particularly impressed by their accuracy and fast rate of fire, like drumbeats, he said. In an instant, the Foreign Rifles killed twenty-two rebels in the great gate. I agree with him, and am considering training special braves with rifles at Kuang-fu-lin."

"Did you say he's a *hsieh-t'ai*, a full colonel?" Wu Hsü said.

"He is to me. Of course, his appointment depends on the will of the Emperor."

"*Ta-jen*, have you memorialized this?"

"Not yet, not yet – too soon. But of course, if I call him colonel, then everyone will call him colonel." The first click of a tumbler fell into place in Fletcher's mind – it was like a brevet rank, and he would be a real colonel only at the whim of the emperor. Even Hsüeh Huan did not have the final say. These mandarins do not have independent authority like generals in other countries – the emperor has a hold on *everything* they do. No wonder their initiative is so fragile. However, I suppose that's not unlike, say, ministers dependent upon Washington or London for *ex post facto* approval of their practical decisions abroad. Except that Secretary of State Seward is not going to remove Minister Wood's head for a *faux pas* at Peking, and whatever Hsüeh Huan's mistakes, they will not be splashed across the yellow pages of every sensationalist newspaper in America and England. How blissful to be ignorant of journalism.

"Now let's speak of Ch'ing-p'u and not of confidential matters," the governor said.

"Li Heng-sung was ordered to Ch'ing-p'u, Excellency," Wu Hsü said. Actually, Li Heng-sung implored the *taotai* to send his army to Ch'ing-p'u.

"Will he be able to retake the place?" Hsüeh Huan said, recalling how Li Heng-sung remained silent while his officers, even the barbarian, all put forth great ideas on how to attack the walled towns. "My own braves suffered heavy losses at Chia-ting and T'ai-ts'ang, but the Foreign Rifles could go to Ch'ing-p'u."

"Li Heng-sung believes he can do it," Wu Hsü said, knowing that Li did not want the Foreign Rifles overshadowing Li's own accomplishments.

"Just the same, can Colonel Wu-te march on Ch'ing-p'u if needed?" The *taotai* glanced at Fletcher.

"My men are not ready, Excellency."

"What's that? Your men went to T'ai-ts'ang and fought well."

"We marched around and fired a few volleys. Li Heng-sung took the towns."

"Lebel already go Ch'ing-p'u, Wu-te," Takee said, arresting the tension rising between Wood and Hsüeh Huan. "Mus' not wait."

"Takee, send them before they are ready and they will be slaughtered. You won't have any Foreign Rifles."

"They seemed quite ready at T'ai-ts'ang," said the governor with some acid, and his black brows colliding over the bridge of his wide nose.

"Please, Excellency," Fletcher said. "They need more time to train."

"I am told they are quite well trained at Kuang-fu-lin," Wu Hsü said. Fletcher sighed inwardly – by your spy, no doubt, as if he would know.

"Not yet," Fletcher said quietly. "And there is another matter."

"And that is…," the governor said.

"I have no artillery yet. Artillery is needed against walled cities."

"We did well enough without artillery," the governor said, his mind turning from the argument to the arguer and beginning to suspect the problem was this barbarian. Untamed, tyrannical pride 桀驁不馴, he thought. We only know of barbarians as rash and restive 惟思夷急躁, yet here's one I can't get to move!

"We were lucky, sir," Fletcher said, "because the rebels hastily garrisoned the towns with untrained militia. The rebels are not going to open their gates like that very often. But they can do nothing against a breach in their walls."

"For that," Wu Hsü said, "we tunnel under the walls and lay explosives." He recognized storm clouds of bushy back brows gathering over the governor, and picked up the thread of argument as much to distract the Hsüeh Huan as to frustrate the barbarian. Wu-te is less subtle and more direct, thought the *taotai*, than his countrymen the minister and the consul. Of course he is – he is a soldier. What would you expect? Consuls don't lead armies to war. Consuls just talk.

"Artillery shortens the war," Fletcher said, speaking slowly so that Showy had time to find adequate words in Chinese. "But tunneling is time-consuming and requires many hands. Often it requires many tunnels over a long siege as the enemy discovers tunnels and collapses them. Sieges take too long and are costly, whereas artillery can knock a hole in a wall and let through thousands of attackers in hours, not days or months."

"Well, I suppose that makes sense," the *taotai* said, himself a little frustrated.

"A wall hates a gun, Excellency, because a wall has no defense against a gun."

He could see that whatever Showy had intrepreted got their attention. Fletcher wanted to go ahead and ask about the *Essex* 6-pounders, but decided that such an interrogation of the *taotai* in front of the governor would be neither politic nor productive. Try to let what little brains you have prevail over your abundant bluster.

"What's more," Takee offered, "the rebels would fear big western guns, perhaps run from them."

"We need artillery, Excellency."

3 The Temple of the Fire God was left to peaceful ministrations, and Fletcher went to room with Artemis Fuller when in Shanghai, or stayed with Hugh at the Astor House. During the time Fletcher spent with the mandarins, Hannibal and the sergeants oversaw management of the camp and training, and Fletcher communicated twice each day with the camp at Kuangfulin, sending Ah-shan or one of her trusted cousins as couriers.

The second night after the bootless conference with the governor, Fletcher rode Arion to Hongkew under a full moon bright and round like a paper lantern perched on a rooftop. Together, he and his brother Hugh again retired to the red-velvet opulence, the imported cut-glass chandeliers, Regency furnishings, and crystal goblets of the Astor House dining room. Fletcher recalled his brother's bewilderment the first night they had dined there nearly three months before and wondered if Hugh had come back to his bearings. As before, the hotel was congested with English and French officers, and bachelor taipans as well. Fletcher noticed conversations pause as he entered the dining room and he did not like the attention. Where before this assemblage had received him cordially, now there was little welcome in their expressions, and he sensed an underlying animosity. Hugh felt the coldness as well. Guilt by association.

"How soon they forget," muttered Fletcher as they sat down at a corner table. "Hero of *Essex* one day, blackguard the next."

"More bitter because some think it a betrayal."

"A hero falls from a greater height."

"They thought they had you corralled by the consul."

"And bonded by Augustus Fitch. How are you getting on with Elizabeth Fitch?"

"Elizabeth is awfully busy at her father's company. She seems more distant."

"Well, I hope no tar from me has rubbed off on you."

"So what if it has? Anyway, I for one am glad to hear rumors you are buying arms on the Bund and hiring Hessians. After Soochow fell, alarm rose to fever pitch in this backwater, and now the rebels have taken those other towns. Everyone fears that the rebels are just waiting for the Allied soldiers and gunboats to go north before they launch themselves at Shanghai. Will you have an army to defend us?"

"Raw stock. About a hundred still training and largely untried, but our strategy is to beard the lions in their den, retake the walled cities and keep rebels from approaching Shanghai. To do that, my men require more time to train and better arms, but impetuous rebels and impatient mandarins press me on all sides – no one will wait for us to train."

"Rumor has it you are persuading British soldiers to desert their regiments."

"Persuasion is not needed – some practically beg to be taken. After only a few days, men began showing up at the temple gate on their own and uninvited, mumbling in foreign tongues at the Chinese, scaring the worshipers and pilgrims. Apparently, word was getting out and our location at the Temple of the Fire God was passed among the destitute community of sailors at Shanghai. Droves of foreigners down on their luck found their way to the temple to sign up. British soldiers in field uniform leave their guard posts at the gates of the native city and come in their scarlet tunics with brass buttons down the middle looking for the Foreign Rifles. Sailors abandoned in port and down to the last of their second-hand Petticoat Lane rags – re-seated trousers, surcoats re-cuffed and re-collared, tattered cloth caps – gave me such hard luck stories as you would not believe. I've had to turn away dozens of men with wives and children, decommissioned old duffers, fugitives and cripples that are holed up in this town. Even a one-legged fellow on a crutch – he said he was stranded here by the ship that broke his leg and let it fester so it had to be cut off at the hospital. Of course I turned him away too, though with a silver crown in his pocket. Men are not hard to get."

"Arms should not be hard to get either," Hugh said. "I've inquired myself on your behalf, just out of curiosity."

"We have enough old British minié rifles, and I'm waiting on Chester Hicks for Sharps breechloaders. Artillery is deadlocked and I need some urgently."

"There's none in Shanghai?"

"None's turned up."

"What about the guns from the *Essex*?"

"When it was clear the *taotai* was not going to volunteer them, I confronted him about those guns and asked for them. He said he no longer had them, said they had been sent to the Green Flag troops attacking Tsingpoo. Later I asked Takee why the *taotai* would not give me the guns. He said 'mebbe *taotai* flaid lose gun,' which I thought unusually candid for Takee. Anyway, 6-pounders put on a good show, but they're too light to get through these city walls before an enemy sends cavalry against them, in which case the *taotai* would have good reason to fear losing his precious guns. No, we need 12-pounders at least. Better with 32-pounders."

"I could order cannon from the United States," Hugh said, "but of course it would not arrive in time for this crisis. And demand is rising now as the north and south prepare for civil war."

"Later perhaps, if this enterprise pans out. You must be in business by now." Hugh took a name card from his wallet. Fletcher smiled broadly as he read it.

"Wood & Company. Congratulations, Hugh. Here's a toast to your success!"

"It's father's money, and his company is my agent for most lines. Still, it is a start. Offices are on the Bund, between the Oriental Bank and Augustine Heard."

"It's a man of substance you are, laddie. Probably does you no good to be seen in my company."

"They can all go to hell! My brother's solid gold, and will be the Wellington that saves their Model Settlement from the Taiping. And here we quarreled because I thought you might join the rebels."

"We quarreled for the same reason we always do."

"What reason is that?"

"Old man's meager attention."

"Are we not over that."

"Undercurrents remain."

Early the next afternoon Takee Bank sent runners all over Shanghai looking for Fletcher. They found him at H. Fogg and gave him a message asking him to go right away to Takee's house. It was a ten-minute walk from the Bund, but Fletcher rode Arion anyway – it was convenient, and he was flattered by the impression he imagined riding horseback made on others. Takee's gate was opened to allow Arion to come clattering into the courtyard and a servant took hold of the reins. Takee was pacing in his doorway, his hands knotted together as if in supplication.

"Oh, Wu-te! Lebel takee Sung-chiang!"

The *taotai* had received word from the Green Flag camp near Kuangfulin, conferred with the governor, and sent a message to Takee. Sungkiang was captured by the Loyal King that morning, Li Heng-sung was at Ch'ing-p'u, so the Foreign Rifles were ordered to retake Sungkiang at once. Alone.

"Without artillery?" Fletcher said.

"Mus' do, Wu-te. *Tao-t'ai* say mus' do."

"I need more time, Takee. The men are not ready, and we have no cannon." The rebels didn't attack Sungkiang, thought Fletcher, until Li Heng-sung was drawn away from Kuangfulin to relieve Tsingpoo – knight to king's bishop three. The Loyal King thought up that move, I'd expect.

"My unnahstan', Wu-te, but mus' do. *Tao-t'ai* say hab give muchee dollah, many lifle. Cost belly muchee. You say can takee town. So – go takee Sung-chiang."

Fletcher quelled his rising anger, knowing that Takee was simply repeating what came from the governor and the *taotai*. Takee probably does understand, he thought, and would allow time if he wasn't frightened terribly by the thought of approaching rebels. How could 100 men take a walled town without artillery, a town surrounded by a four-mile wall and a wide moat? When we drifted through Sungkiang aboard Ah-shan's junk, the moat we crossed was thirty feet wide and, how many, nine feet deep? The north and south gates are as large as those I saw at Nanking, iron-reinforced teakwood, maybe some double-gates. Drum towers over the gates, arrow towers, narrow streets, suburbs probably razed by now, new stockades. How close can we approach the walls under cover – is there any cover? What's the size of the garrison, how are they armed? We can reconnoiter on the approach but, regardless of what we find there, we'll have to attack.

"Takee, you must do something for me. Remember that creek from Sungkiang to the Whangpoo?"

"Yes, my know."

"Tomorrow night after dark you must send *Confucius* and two war junks up that creek that goes to Sungkiang, as close as possible to the town wall."

"Yes, Wu-te, can do. Why fo'?"

"My men will go to Sungkiang from Kuangfulin, but from Sungkiang we will want to send the wounded to Shanghai and, if it does not go well, the war junks can bring us downriver too."

"Tomollah nite, *K'ung-fu-tze*, two junk, Sung-chiang cleek, can do, Wu-te."

"That's good, Takee. I'm depending on you."

Fletcher wrote a message for Hannibal reporting the fall of Sungkiang and presence of rebels close by Kuangfulin, and left Takee's house for the native city, riding Arion down Barrier Road through the Old North Gate. When he left Takee, he was intent on protesting to the high mandarins, but his resolve receded the closer he came to them. Takee had given him an order and, as they agreed, he was honor bound to carry out the order. Wu and Hsüeh doubtless would ignore his protests as before, and by challenging Takee's authority and going over his head, Fletcher risked injuring the mandarin's fragile trust in him, and damaging his relationship with the old banker. Takee would always be the easiest to deal with – if Fletcher rashly undermined their confidence that Takee could deal effectively with the Foreign Rifles, they might replace him.

Fletcher went first to the magistrate's yamen, found the *taotai* there with the governor, arranged for his message to be taken to Kuangfulin by dispatch boat, then returned Arion to Fuller's stable and went up the *Yang-king-bang* to where Ah-shan's junk was being loaded with supplies from Fuller's godown. All the while, he pondered on how to take the walled town and, later that evening, pondered all the way to Kuangfulin aboard Ah-shan's junk. There was no alternative – the town had to be taken by storm, under cover of darkness, if the clouds would oblige him by covering the moon.

The approach to the Kuangfulin camp landing looked somehow ominous as the junk slowed. Just past the landing, two imperial war junks were moored end-to-end in the channel, and Fletcher could see the silhouette of men on watch at the stern of the nearest war junk. Dim moon shadows moved above the landing, and there was a glint of metal, then dark shapes loomed up out of the gloom and challenged the colonel. Yes, he said into the night, it is me, it is the colonel. The camp was tense with expectation and he was challenged several times as he neared the tents, slightly luminous in the moonlight. There must have been 100 glowing tents – a rebel spy would conclude there were between four and six hundred men in camp. Fletcher detailed men to unload the junk and went looking for Hannibal.

"All quiet here at camp," Hannibal said. "Reconnaissance reports the rebels at Sungkiang have been tearing down houses on the east side of town to clear ground before the east gate, and there are stockades outside the wall on the northwest and southwest. Rebel cavalry left the town late this afternoon in the direction of Soochow.

That's from two corporals I sent with the Green Flags this morning to watch and see what the rebels are up to, reconnoiter the town just in case we have to go there."

"Well, we do. Our sponsors again send us afield without adequate preparation."

"Them mandarins! Hell is so full of high mandarins you can see their feet stickin' out the windows. Did you bring back any artillery?"

"None."

"Well damned if that does not put us in the cleft of a forked stick." Fletcher saw a shallow riffle in Hannibal's face, a flinch suggesting a submerged snag.

"You up for this?"

"Sure," Hannibal said, after a brief hesitation. "If it's easy as those first two towns, the rebels'll come down fast as a rubber balloon tied to a lead weight. What's the plan?"

"Drop down amongst them tomorrow night. Under cover of darkness, take war junks on the creeks down to Sungkiang, within sight of the town, disembark and march in platoon formation to the east gate suburbs where there's more concealment. Cross the moat on ladders and set off charges against the gate."

"That ought to wake 'em, about as fast as earthquakes wake weasels."

"Rush the breach and drive the rebels out."

"Like Kading. Do we know how many they are?"

"No. Not yet. I'll see if any of Li Heng-sung's men know or can find out. If the garrison's large, we can only wait for Li Heng-sung to return from Tsingpoo."

"*If* he returns."

"I'll take the 1st platoon, with sergeants Falconer and Reese – ah, Corporal Reese – and corporals Merryweather and Smythe. You take the 2nd platoon, with sergeants Garden and Moreau, and corporals Dinwiddie and Durand. We'll divide the 3rd platoon between us, and leave a small watch in camp."

"I'll give the men the word."

"Not the men. Tell the sergeants, but wait until late tomorrow to tell the men. I don't want them to have the whole day to work up hypos about going into action – this bunch is still quite raw. Carry on with the usual training."

The next morning Fletcher asked the Chinese private to inquire at the Green Flag camp about the size of the rebel garrison at Sungkiang and, if not known, try to have someone go in disguise to the town and find out. Then he took Mr. Fan to meet with Ah-shan and the imperial war junk captains at the landing. Both captains had taken boats to Sungkiang before and knew the waterways. Together with Ah-shan, he drew a map so there would be no mistakes about the route they would take, where they would land, and how long the boats would wait. The junks would go south from Kuangfulin on what Ah-shan called the Fu-lin Ho river 福林河, take an unnamed cut southeast to Chang-chia Ching creek 張家涇, continue east to the T'ung-po T'ang 通波塘 canal, then south several miles to the landing site. Ah-shan told Fletcher that the stream on the south side of Sungkiang leading to the Huang-p'u Chiang 黃浦江 river

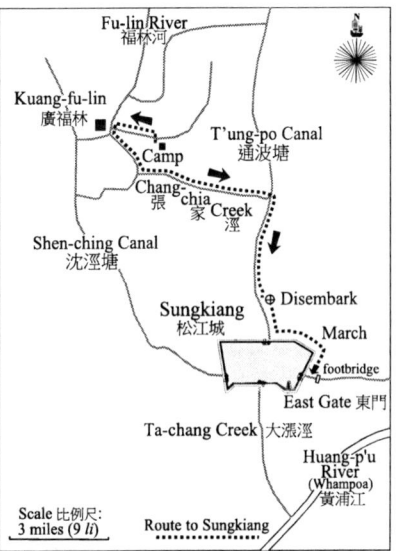

Water Route, Kuangfulin to Sungkiang 1860

was called the Ta-chang Ching 大漲涇 creek. He told the junk captains to wait two hours after the shooting started and, if the Foreign Rifles had not returned by then, to return to Kuangfulin.

4 Late that afternoon, the Foreign Rifles received marching orders and supplies were loaded. A dozen kegs of Curtis and Harvey's gunpowder for petards to blow gates, four bamboo ladders strapped with wood planks, long coils of Manila rope, and extra weapons and ammunition were stowed aboard each junk. The reinforced drays were dismantled and one put on each junk to carry equipment and serve as mantlets to fend off rebel musketry. The 3rd platoon was divided and reassigned.

As the hour neared, revelry in camp increased, and by late-evening drunken song could be heard by the crews of the Chinese war junks down at the landing. The full moon low over the southern horizon inspired rounds of toasts to the Old Man in the Moon, lonesome sweethearts back home gazing at the same moon, and then to Chinese moon-dwellers.

"They say there's a rabbit in the moon," Desmond Cafferty gurgled, maintopman from *Dakotah*. "So, here's to that li'l ol' moon bunny."

"I don' see no moon bunny!" said Paddy Rafferty, 2nd mate from *Jubilee*, squinting.

"Look again, me boyo," Cafferty said. "The great god Buddha put 'em there, so he's sure enough there."

"Hey," said Gavin Muldoon, 2nd mate from *Dakotah*, "see a princess? A cute li'l judy in Shanghai tol' me about a Chinese princess that lives inna palace onna moon."

Most of the men settled down after evening mess to write letters home, or chat quietly with chums about anything except Sungkiang. They had been to battle just days before, but not bloodied, and night action unnerved some. They occupied themselves with small pursuits that might quiet their unspoken apprehensions, and tried to ignore the uproar of the others who drank to quell their fears. Evenings were more restrained when the colonel was in camp, and Fletcher had confiscated more than one contraband bottle of liquor and punished the offender. It troubled him that he was still ambivalent about dealing with the heavy drinking. He would not have been concerned if he commanded disciplined soldiers, but he had to take the manpower available and was burdened with an extraordinary number of degenerate alcoholics. Some of the NCOs were all right, and the Manilamen. As for the rest – take away their rum and he might have no army, but overlooking their drunkenness invited disaster. He did not really know how to handle them. When finally the Irish commotion provoked him to distraction, Fletcher left off writing to his sister Elizabeth and came out of his tent.

Falconer was standing outside his own tent listening to the camp.

"Colonel," he said, "that Blarney Castle is becoming a real nuisance. I suppose they think they will be excused if they are too drunk to march."

"This has to stop," Fletcher said, "before they all are too drunk."

"I'll see to it, sir."

A bugle sounded and the camp assembled for roll call. Four Irishmen too drunk to march – Rafferty, Muldoon, Cafferty, and Quinn O'Sullivan, private from the 99th aboard *Octavia* – were arrested, manacled, and put under guard by the six men that were to remain in camp in the charge of Sergeant Drinkwater. Four men from the camp guard replaced them. The two platoons formed ranks, each with forty-two men, two sergeants, and an officer, head-counts were taken, equipment checked, and ammunition issued. The Foreign Rifles were the same chowchow legion as before, armed with Tower muskets and rigged in a mix of regimental trousers, slop chest shirts, hats and caps, and British and French equipage. They marched to the landing and boarded the same green and

洋神 *Yang Shen* 　　　　　　　　　　　　　　　　　　　　　　　*James Lande* 藍德

yellow shallow-draft imperial galleys, *k'uai-tu ch'uan*, that had taken them to Kading and Taitsan. The soldiers sat in long files down the center of the vessel between twelve oarsmen on each side – some of them even remembered each other from the earlier expedition and smiled or grimaced in acknowledgement. On command, the oarsmen shipped oars and started pulling up the creek for Kuangfulin. There was no word on the size of the rebel garrison.

The first imperial war junk grounded in mud as it turned away from the camp landing. The second imperial war junk came about and set off ahead of the first. Watching the second war junk pull away, Fletcher never imagined that this small deviation could doom the operation.

The second junk carried the 2nd platoon – commanded by Major Benedict and sergeants Garden and Moreau, with corporals Dinwiddie and Durand. They took the lead and pulled ahead, pursued by a chorus of catcalls from their stranded mates.

Aboard the stranded junk, the 1st platoon was commanded by Colonel Wood and sergeants Falconer and Reese, with corporals Merryweather and Smythe, all of whom excepting Reese had fought in the Crimea five years before. As the 2nd Platoon stood off toward Kuangfulin, Fletcher assumed his own junk would catch up and pass Hannibal's junk, placing the 1st Platoon back in the lead. After all, there was plenty of time, nearly two hours, before they came within sight of Sungkiang.

For the first hour, the army was hushed, bridled by the disquieting prospect before them, from which there was no turning. The only sounds were the oars dipping, the slapping of the lugsail, and the Chinese coxswain calling time for the galley crew rowing by moonlight. The junks turned south from Kuangfulin, southeast into a narrow cut, and east into a larger creek. Before they reached the T'ung-po canal, their rising jimjams stirred the 2nd platoon to song again and they started a run through the common repertoire, the songs the American half of the platoon knew best: *Old Dan Tucker*, *The Girl I left Behind Me*, and *Sweet Betsy from Pike*. Fletcher ordered his galley to quicken pace and catch up, and he shouted over the bow at them.

"You men be quiet! We depend on surprise at Sungkiang. You're not going to a choir rehearsal!"

Many in the 2nd platoon thought they were too far away to care about that yet.

"What did the colonel say?" Paul Bernard asked in French. He sat midships with the Frenchmen and was a little deaf anyway. There were thirteen Frenchmen in the 1st platoon, mostly deserters from French frigates *en route* to the Peiho. Bernard was the only merchant sailor, left in Shanghai by *Ville de Dieppe* when he was still weak from typhus. The Shanghai Hospital would not accept a destitute French sailor, but the innkeeper at Fat Jack's put him in a room apart and nursed him back to health.

"The colonel ordered quiet," Dominique Leroy said, a marine private from HIM *Entreprenante* who had been in hiding at Fat Jack's. "That's the boat to be on. They're having all the fun."

"They're idiots," Luc Delacroix said. "They can probably be heard on the Bund in Shanghai." Delacroix was the gunner from HIM *Gironde*.

"Why do we have to attack at night?" Corporal Alexandre Petit said, another French marine deserted from HIM *Entreprenante* and hidden at Fat Jack's. "In Saigon those little monkey-men attacked at night and we lost many good Frenchmen in the dark. We should fight in the daylight."

"Would you rather be in Saigon, Alex?" Delacroix asked, laughing.

"*Merde* no! It's too damn hot in Saigon."

"I heard you bagged 500,000 franks when you took Saigon," Delacroix said.

1st Sungkiang

"If they did, they did not give any to me."

"Is Saigon where you were before here?" Paul Bernard said.

"Of course," Petit said. "We went to make the monkey-men's little king, Tu Duc he is called, stop killing Catholic missionaries, then came this war with China and they took a thousand of us for the Anglo-French expeditionary force. A lot of us from Annam were aboard *Du Chayla*, *Renomee*, *Entreprenante*, and *Gironde*."

"They kill Catholic missionaries?" Bernard said, astonished.

"A dozen in ten years," Petit said. "Missionaries are good at dying for the faith."

"*Les héroes extrêmes* illustrious heroes," Bernard said, sighing, "*du devoir et du sacrifice* of duty and sacrifice."

"Listen to those idiots up ahead," Petit said.

"It's the Americans," Delecroix said. "Those Americans have no honor, *n'est-ce pas* is it not so?"

"*Ils sont inouïs* they are outrageous!" Petit said. "The whole bunch is a stinking herd of swine. Loud, boorish English, drunken Irish, and all these little monkey-men."

He glanced forward at the Manilamen running patches down the already immaculate bores of their minié rifles and whetting their gleaming bolos.

"Look at this walleyed specimen," Petit said, nodding at Kirat Banta, called "one-eye" because of the bluish-white iris of one of his eyes.

"*Savez-vous le français* do you know French?" Petit said. Kirat Banta smiled and shook his head.

"*Savez-vous le français* do you know French?" Petit said, harshly.

All the Manilamen looked up at the Frenchman, glared at him.

"What's wrong with that donkey's ass," Baboy Abinsay said in Ilocano.

Kirat Banta hefted his bolo and stared at Petit.

"He'd better be polite," Kirat said, "because maybe my bolo wants French blood."

The Manilamen laughed and returned to their work.

"These white men all smell of fear," Naguapo Tapay said, one of the Manilamen who deserted from the Spanish brig *Tiempo* when it called at Shanghai in February. Naguapo was a 20-year-old Cebuano born in Balamban on Cebu Island to an indentured silversmith who, in a Chinese shop on *Calle Colon* in the Parian slum of Cebu City, hammered out delicate little silver chains for the bored wives of high-caste Spanish *peninsulares*. Naguapo had light brown skin, jet-black eyes, a small gold ring in one nostril, and waves of glossy black hair. He wore a loose, collarless white shirt outside his trousers, a *camisa* hand-loomed from delicate *piña* cloth, received at his confirmation and now tattered and begrimed from long use.

"We do not have such a smell," Kirat said.

"We are not afraid." Paco Dalogdog said. He was larger than the others – Fletcher's size – with light brown skin, hazel eyes, dark brown curly hair, and teeth lightly stained reddish-black by *buyo*, betel nut. He wore black cotton trousers and a black *camisa* belted with a red sash, from which hung a long, sinuously serpentine *kris* in a hardwood sheath. He too was Cebuano, born in Consolacion on Cebu Island. He had recruited the Manilamen from *Tiempo*, and he knew Naguapo from younger days in Cebu City.

"No need to be afraid while our guardian angels watch over us," Naguapo said. His good looks and easy smile, and many pure silver finger rings, attracted loose women and to afford their charms he resorted to games of chance. Naguapo was a devout Christian, but an unfailing loser at cards, skulking into a confessional after every cockfight and game of monte. He visited confessionals frequently. Paco said that if Naguapo won a peso for every contrite Our Father and Hail Mary he ever recited he would be rich. Instead, Naguapo accumulated much more debt than he could ever repay and, when a

洋神 *Yang Shen* James Lande 藍德

Sangley gang threatened to lop off his little silver fingers, Paco helped him ship out from Cebu on a China trader. Fate brought them together again in Shanghai.

"Vincente should be here," Paco said. "He has no fear, and is bullet-proof as well."

"Who is Vincente?" Naguapo asked.

"He is a Tagalo from Manila, mate on the steamer *Confucius*, where most of us come from. A very cool fellow, tough, brave, very *guapo* – handsome like you – and a gentleman, generous to his friends, and always watches out for his comrades in arms."

The Foreign Rifles reached the T'ung-po T'ang canal and turned south again. The helmsman on Fletcher's junk was late into the turn and they lost headway and fell off some. Ahead of them the singing started up again, raucous and slurred now, like a barroom chorus braced by rum and brandy.

After a couple of miles, the 2nd platoon was well ahead and growing belligerent. They decided they should be first into the breach at Sungkiang, and Major Benedict declared a $50 bonus for the first man over the wall. So they cheered the oarsmen on, and then in an exuberant flourish the two Blackwells, the Cassidy brothers, MacDonald and McKenzie all jumped down beside the oarsmen and helped to pull. The junk captain objected but Hannibal waved him away.

"Let 'em have their fun," he said. "For some it will be the last. Lean into it you Cape Horn dawdlers!"

A dozen more men scampered about the galley and joined Chinese oarsmen. Near twice the crew pulling made the ponderous junk fly over the water and leave the other junk too far behind for the colonel to be heard shouting for them to slow. His shouts were thought to be birds or wind.

From their benches, Warwick Derby, Boyd Brenner and Joshua Lowe, three of the *Heroes of Alma* manning the oars – American ABs all – called for *Comin' 'Roun the Horn* to pace their rowing.

> *Oh, I remember well, the lies they used to tell,*
> *Of gold so bright, it hurt the sight, and made the miners yell*

The other three *Heroes of Alma* – Heath Ashton, Otis Coolidge and Robert Hewlett – passed a bottle of brandy between them at a pace with the song. They offered the brandy to the coolies rowing beside them, but the Chinese just wrinkled their noses at the stuff and pulled at their oars.

> *We stopped at Valparaiso, where the women are so loose,*
> *And all got drunk as usual, got shoved in the calaboose;*
> *Our ragged, rotten sails were patched, the ship made ready for sea,*
> *But every man, except the cook, was uptown on a spree.*

They would have rowed clear up to the walls of Sungkiang if the junk captain had not yelled at his own men to stand away from the oars as they approached the landing site. The helmsman brought the junk around toward shore then swung her back out just as she touched bottom and threw over an anchor. Gangways were run out fore and aft and Sergeant Darby Garden marshaled his detachment to carry the dray down the forward ramp and unload the gunpowder and ladders. Sergeant Beau Moreau directed the rest of the men to shore from the stern quarter, formed them in ranks, loaded weapons and fixed bayonets. In less than ten minutes, Major Benedict's platoon was marching for the objective. In many places, the men slogged through water over paths covered ankle-deep by the high spring tide that pushed the creeks up over their banks.

Colonel Wood's junk came to rest behind the first junk just when the 2nd platoon broke out in song again and disappeared from sight toward Sungkiang. As Falconer and

1st Sungkiang

Reese disembarked men and equipment and loaded weapons, the 2nd platoon's *a cappella* receded into the distance, their lusty chorus led by Dinwiddie and Dobbin – Fletcher remembered their voices from the temple a few weeks before.

> *Out on the prairie a bright starry night*
> *They broke open whiskey and Betsy got tight*
> *She sang and she shouted and danced o'er the plain,*
> *And showed her bare arse to the whole wagon train.*
> *The injuns came down in a wild yelling horde,*
> *And Betsy was scared they would scalp her adored;*
> *Behind the front wagon wheel Betsy did crawl,*
> *And there she fought injuns with musket and ball.*

The colonel was furious, but there was little to do except chase after them. All hope of surprise would be soon lost, Major Benedict's 2nd platoon would be cut down if they did not withdraw, and 1st platoon could only hope to reach them in time to provide covering fire. Fletcher ordered his platoon forward at double-time. They lumbered along for half a mile on the waterlogged banks of the canal until they caught sight of the 2nd platoon and then slowed to a march. Corporal Reese dropped back to where Sergeant Falconer brought up the rear to prevent anyone from dropping out of line.

"Ows it goin' Scouser?" Reese said.

"The 2nd's on a proper bender now, raisin' a high wind," Falconer said.

"It's sure doin' the gaffer's 'head in – 'e 'as a real cob on," Reese said, "colonel's really angry."

"Tha' cackhanded corksucker Benedict'll put paid to us all," Falconer said, "that incompetent American Benedict will get us all killed."

"It's turned out dodgy, ain't it, a sort of a blind scouse," Reese said. "We don' know nothing about what's there at Sungkiang."

"Well, we berra leg it on up there before they're all derby ducks."

We should be stormin' the north wall in moonshadow, thought Falconer. On the east side where the moonlight shines down bright on us we'll *all* be derby ducks, ducks in a barrel as they say. There's sure no surprising the rebels now.

Benedict's men came under the shadow of the north gate tower and followed the wall around to the left into the moonlight and disappeared into the ruins of some demolished houses. Wood's men saw shadows flitting on the battlements as they approached but the rebels did not fire. Streets led off between houses and vegetable plots alongside smaller canals that passed under high arched bridges. The suburbs close by the north gate had been burnt and walls and houses collapsed so that the ground within 100 yards of the town wall was flattened rubble. The bridges and distant ruins offered protection but the ground adjacent to the moat had been razed to deny cover. There was one stockade outside the northwest wall. Inside the town, a tall pagoda towered over the wall, alone and aloof.

5

Atop the north wall of Sungkiang the rebel sentries called their corporals. No one could understand why a troop of foreigners would be coming to Sungkiang and singing out loud as they marched around the walls. Did the foreigners come to fight the rebels or to join them? There were already many foreigners on the side of the Taiping, and no one wanted to be responsible for shooting at friends, if that is what they were. A corporal thought of shouting down to them, but decided he could not speak enough English to understand any answer they gave, and didn't even know what language they spoke, so instead he called out his sergeant. One of the rebel privates was taken by *Sweet Betsy from Pike* and started humming along with the singing. A corporal told him to shut up.

"Don't let the foreign devils hear us up here!"

When the sergeant arrived on the wall, the other troop of foreigners had come into view. There were too many, he thought, to risk assuming they might be friendly. The rebel sergeant passed the word for two companies to come and man the east wall, and to be quiet about it. He wondered if these were the foreigners from Kuang-fu-lin that the Loyal King has told them about. Were they *all* drunk? The full moon shined down on them as they approached and the sentries imagined they could see into the foreign faces. They looked like every kind of ugly flesh-eating demon, ghost and monster 妖魔鬼怪. Then the sergeant saw the ladders.

"Stupid egg!" he hissed at the corporal. "Look at that! Your friends bring their own ladders instead of just walk in through the gates? There is no egg in the entire world more stupid than a corporal! Load your muskets!"

Oddly, there was still no sound of rebels mounting the wall to defend the town.

Major Benedict's 2nd platoon came to a halt within sight of the east gate. The gate was deserted. Before the gate, a tall, square structure stood against two large wooden posts – a raised drawbridge no one had expected. A creek ran under the wall on the far side of the gate. Shadows of broken houses stood about seventy yards behind them. Six hundred yards further on past the east gate there was a stockade. Sergeant Garden ordered the dray unloaded while Sergeant Moreau positioned rifle squads. The two Italians, Ferrara and Ricci, and the two Portugese, Braga and De la Fuente, all sailors from *Progressive Age*, hauled the four ladders off the dray, grabbed four coils of rope, and started toward the moat. The six American *Heroes of Alma* came behind them carrying kegs of gunpowder. The dray was upended and became a mantlet.

Braga and De la Fuente set down a ladder three feet from the edge of the moat.

"Will she no be long enough?" Ricci hissed.

"Why you ask me now?" Ferrara said. He tied a line to a middle rung and together they pushed the ladder up and over across the moat, slowly lowering it until it rested on the other side with feet to spare.

"Son-of-a-gun. She fit okay!" Ricci said, pleased. He glanced up anxiously at the battlement of the nearest part of the wall. Nothing. How can an entire town be struck deaf, he wondered?

Ladders rose up and were lowered by attached ropes. Americans crowded forward.

"Hey now, no cutting in front! I'm first here," Warwick Derby muttered to Heath Ashton. "You was always under foot 'board *Alma*, but you'll not get my fifty bucks."

"Quit cher shovin' Derby," Ashton said. "Push again and you'll be lookin' for yer money in the moat."

"Shut yer clamshells you two," Sergeant Garden spat. "Get a move on."

Drunken soldiers did not gracefully negotiate narrow planks strapped on ladders – they wobbled and flailed and then ran across – two fell into the moat and were pulled out with ropes. Sergeant Garden peered at the gate tower. The sound of the splash sent a chill up Garden's spine – how could sentries not hear that? Twenty-two men crossed with Sergeant Garden and Corporal Dinwiddie and crouched at the foot of the wall while the Americans carried the powder kegs to the gate and vanished into the recessed portal. The last men over the moat pulled up two ladders and carried them to the wall. Not enough ladders, thought Garden. Need four against the wall. Need to leave some over the moat, tho' – or we won't have a way to get back. Other platoon has ladders. Where *is* the other platoon?

Still no sign of rebels. The Foreign Rifles wondered how they could not be heard.

The 1st platoon approached in skirmishing order along the periphery of the ruins.

洋神 *Yang Shen*　　　　　　　　　　　　　　　　　　　　　　*James Lande* 藍德

Seeing them, Major Benedict ordered the remainder of his platoon across the moat. Looks like we're going to surprise them after all, he thought. He saw the Americans come back around from the gate and dash toward the others under the wall. Benedict reached the wall just as a huge explosion engulfed the gateway in smoke and stone shards. When the rain of debris ceased he ran to the gate – it was undamaged! The charge had only blackened the teakwood doors.

"Not enough damn powder." He turned to the men at the wall. "Go!" he shouted. "Before the entire garrison is called out!"

Moreau pulled himself up hand over hand, rifle barrel banging his head, sweaty palms slipping on bamboo rungs. He and Garden glanced at each other as they clambered up and each pushed harder to stay ahead as if they were running a footrace. Moreau saw a large shape rising from behind the gate tower and recognized it as another tower, at a right angle from the gate tower – there was another gate inside the first gate! I should tell Colonel Wood, he thought. Suddenly the battlement was alive with contorted, screaming faces where an instant before there was only blackness. He reached to unsling his rifle. The gaping black maw of a musket in his face exploded with an ear-splitting roar and bright yellow flash, and Sergeant Beau Moreau tumbled backward through a yellow haze into eternity, and with him fell Sergeant Garden.

Moreau and Garden had reached the top of their ladders when the fusillade of musketry exploded in their faces and they fell back among the men at foot of the wall. A barrage of musket balls and arrows flew at the platoon from the battlement and the tower over the gate. Dozens of rebel muskets fired and fired again, sending musket balls smashing into men on ladders, cutting down men under ladders, and kicking up plaster dust around the men of the 1st platoon concealed in the ruins. Men tumbled through the air and crumpled on the ground. The ladders were pushed over on top of them.

Colonel Wood ordered return fire against the wall and the tower. Two ranks of twenty men each fired in volleys that raked the wall and riddled the tower with nearly two hundred minié bullets and pistol balls in the first minute. Rebel fire dwindled and then swelled, and then tapered off again. Colonel Wood led half the 1st platoon forward seventy yards to the 2nd platoon's dray and continued volley fire from there. To fire at the attackers, the rebels on the wall had to lean over the parapet and were easy targets for the 1st platoon. The rebels hidden in the gate tower were more difficult to see, but the Foreign Rifles fusillade quickly chewed into the wooden walls of the tower.

Benedict and the men still alive huddled for protection at the foot of the wall returning fire as best they could. The first rebel volley slaughtered the *Heroes of Alma* to a man – the major could see where they lay in a heap as if tackled in a football scrimmage. De la Fuente was hit by three musket balls and Ricci was hit twice in the back as he dragged his wounded friend to the foot of the wall. Dinwiddie and Dobbin lay dead where they fell together when Sergeant Garden's ladder was pushed over. Ham and Tater Bean were covered in blood but leaning back-to-back quickly reloading and firing as if barking squirrels. The rebels stopped shooting over the battlement and began throwing rocks over and pouring down boiling cooking oil. Corporal Durand crawled from body to body taking loaded rifles from the dead who had no chance to fire them. As he bellied toward the major, Durand passed the rifles out to the living.

"Nineteen dead, sir," he said to Major Benedict. "Twelve wounded." The wounded were so anesthetized by alcohol that few of them felt much pain. In the next minute, Corporal Durand watched four sailors, Church, Harvey and Wright from *Mandarin*, and Miller from *McLeod*, die in a shower of musketry and arrows from the tower. They were being ripped up from the flank.

"Fire into that damned gate tower," Major Benedict yelled.

"Get under th' gate," Angus Blackwood shouted, and he and Callum Blackwood made a break from the wall. Both were shot down.

"Sure now," Fergus Cassidy to his brother Fester, "Angus has a pretty good idea."

"More like he *had* one," Fester said, staring after the fallen Scots. "What idea?"

"That tower cannot be hittin' us if we're under the gate."

"Right-oh. Fetch yourself up a Blackwood on the way." The Cassidy brothers leapt up from the wall and bolted toward the gate, halting to pick up the two Scots.

"This one's still breathin'," Fergus wheezed.

"Mine too," Festus said.

"Ow!" Fergus cried. "Now I'm hit too. Laid one across me back like a lash."

"Well, c'mon then. You're used to the lash. Grab your Blackwood." The brothers hoisted their bundles and hobbled to the gate. Festus caught a ball in his calf on the way. From the cleft of the wall where the first volley knocked them down, MacDonald and McKenzie heard Angus shout, grasped his meaning, and pulled and pushed each other across the bloody ground to shelter under the gate.

The rebel fire diminished. Colonel Wood signaled for recall. The trill of a bugle echoed along the wall of Sungkiang. The Manilaman Paco Dalogdog stepped back from the mantlet and saluted.

"*Koronel! Necesito ayudar los heridos*! Colonel, we must help the wounded!"

"*Si, vaya! Rapido*! Yes, go. Quickly!" the colonel said, waving toward the wall.

"*Mga kapatid, táyo na*! Brothers, let's go!" Paco shouted to the other Manilamen. As a body twelve of them lay down their rifles and rose up from behind the mantlet and sprinted to the moat, musket balls flying all around them. Rifle volley followed volley from the 1st platoon, and Colonel Wood repeatedly emptied his revolver and replaced the cylinder. Rebel fire fell off under the withering salvo of rifle fire and the Manilamen were able to get across the moat on the remaining two ladders and to the wall without serious damage. Musket balls hit them each, but most ripped through their jackets and haversacks. Paco and Naguapo went from body to body and loaded those still alive onto the shoulders of a *compadre* to carry back across the moat.

"Keep going all the way to the ruins!" Paco shouted.

The respite from rebel fire allowed Major Benedict to rouse his men, pick up the wounded sheltering under the gate, and cross back over the moat.

The rebel fire ceased. Evidently, the rebels were letting them take away their wounded. Colonel Wood called for cease-fire. In the ensuing silence, Paco could see rebel faces peering out from the splintered tower, but they held their fire. Paco and Naguapo found one last man alive. Paco picked him up, shouldered him, and crossed back over the moat with Naguapo immediately behind. As they approached the upturned dray, a single shot rang out and Naguapo cried out and fell.

Paco lay the man he carried down behind the dray and went back for Naguapo. He was lying face down where he fell, blood oozing from a small hole in the middle of his back. Paco turned him over and rested Naguapo's head on his thigh. Blood surged from a gaping tear in the boy's chest.

"*Tugnaw dinhi sa Tsína*, it is cold here in China," Naguapo said, choking.

"Yes, cold," Paco said. "Not warm like back home."

"*Unsay among buhaton*, what should we do?"

"Lie still," Paco said. He knew there was nothing anyone could do.

"*Pila*, How many did we kill?" asked Naguapo, weakly.

"*Syento*, one hundred."

Paco heard a shot come from somewhere behind the wall, too far away to be intended for them. A thought came to his mind: perhaps a rebel officer had executed the

1st Sungkiang

lamias – the slave of the devil – that killed Naguapo after the cease-fire.

"*Amigo ta ka, y*ou are my friend," said the boy.
"*Oo*, yes," said Paco.
"*Mahimo bang mangutana*, may I ask a question?"
"*Oo*, yes."
"*Aduna bay Diyos sa langit*, is there a God in heaven?"
"*Oo*, yes."
"*Diay ba*, really?"
"*Oo*, yes."
"*Tabangi ko*! Help me!"
Naguapo choked up blood.
"*Amay sa langit palihug tabangi ako*! Father in heaven please help me!"

From within the dark recesses of the east gate tower a rebel sergeant silently finished counting the foreign corpses strewn across the bloody ground along the foot of the wall. Twenty-three. At least seventy of their own men were killed or wounded. The sergeant watched the last Manilaman carry a body off the field.

"那些黑鬼子好棒, 很勇敢," the sergeant said, "those black devils were truly great, very courageous."

"是很勇敢的 yes, very brave," a rebel officer behind him said.

"他們罷了 they're finished now," the sergeant said.

"Let them go," the officer said. "Call our men away from the edge. We've lost too many already."

"Who fired that last shot?" the sergeant said.

"Some fool who's been sent to hell."

6 The Foreign Rifles gathered up their wounded on their backs and on carts and limped away from the east gate of Sungkiang. The creek that ran from the south wall to the Whangpoo was about a half-mile or more away. As they skirted the stockade just out of musket range, the Union Jack and the Tricolor came into view in the moonlight, snapping at the mastheads of junks and lorchas where they waited at anchor in the creek. High tide had brought the junks to within a quarter mile of the south gate, so the men did not have to carry their wounded as far. Manilamen dropped back to cover the retreat and the boarding of the junks, and to bring away the bodies of their fellows when daylight came. Fletcher detailed a sergeant to stay with the Manilamen, and two junks to wait for them. He stared hard at Hannibal when finally they met, but said nothing while they were within earshot of the men, busying himself with getting the wounded aboard and accounting for the dead. An accounting with Hannibal would come later.

The war junks carried the wounded down to where the mouth of the creek emptied into the Whangpoo and put them aboard *Confucius* and *Pluto*. Takee was better than his word – he had sent nearly thirty imperial war junks and two steamers, both flying the Stars and Stripes. Sometime after dawn, *Confucius* got up steam and took the wounded down to the hospital at Shanghai. At mid-morning, war junks carried the rest of the men back to the Temple of the Fire God. After the men had collapsed into their bunks, Fletcher called Hannibal out into the front courtyard of the temple.

"What's the butcher's bill, Major?" Fletcher asked morosely.

"Over twenty, at least." Hannibal was hesitant.

"I counted twenty-six dead in three minutes." Hannibal just nodded.

"Twenty-four wounded. Forty intact." Hannibal nodded again.

"A forty-five percent casualty rate. It's almost unheard of, and you are responsible."

Hannibal looked up, face full of anger, and almost spoke. Fletcher cut him off.

"Your men made more noise than a panther and a pack of hounds. You *permitted* that drunken shivaree to wake all Sungkiang and lost all hope of surprise."

"Yes, yes. I know we made some noise. But their blood was up. They believed they would prevail. They were convinced. So was I."

"Without artillery. Without surprise. In moonlight."

"The rebels would have opened fire if they heard us. So we thought, anyway."

"So you underestimated the enemy."

"I surely did. I played a pair of deuces against a full house."

"That's not much consolation for Darby Garden and Beau Moreau."

"They, they were good men, first up the ladders. I'm sorry to lose them."

"Them, and corporals Dinwiddie and Durand, and privates Frazer and Campbell, and Sears and Appleton, and fifteen more in the 2nd platoon who entrusted their lives to you, their besotted major."

"All right, I was wrong!" Hannibal flared up. "But men die in war, you know as well as I. You cannot command when you're feeling sorry for yourself because you lost some men. What shall I do to atone? Blow my brains out because other men die?"

"A pistol ball would not be enough to atone for so many good lives."

"A moment ago they were drunken sots, and now they're good lives, the honored dead. That's very convenient. Well, the regular army'd probably court-martial me, but the regular army has many more officers. You have but one."

"When you're drinking, I do not have even one."

Hannibal breathed deeply and stared into the dark courtyard. Finally, he spoke.

"Never again on duty. As God is my witness, never again a drink on duty."

"How you square yourself with God is your business. I also am witness to your oath, and if you ever break it, as God is *my* witness, I will shoot you myself."

洋神 *Yang Shen*   *James Lande* 藍德

Dramatis Personae: Chapter 27

Morton Harris	marine major, 2nd Queens
Celestial	small British clipper ship
William Black	captain, China trader *Celestial*
Mrs. Black	wife of Captain Black
Mr. Roarke	first mate, China trader *Celestial*
Archibald Evans	assistant chief superintendent of customs
Vulcan	American stern-wheel paddle steamer
Jabez Reach	captain, river steamer *Vulcan*

Sternwheeler *Vulcan*
(sketch © 2011 James Lande. Author's imaginary rendering based on textual sources.)

洋神 *Yang Shen* James Lande 藍德

Chapter 27: Fourth of July
Wednesday, July 4, 1860, 7:00 am

The
North China Herald
Shanghai, Saturday, June 23, 1860

Latest Dates

England......May 3	Singapore......June	3
Bombay......May 1	Hongkong......June	14
Calcutta ----	New York......May	27
Galle......... May 6		

Rebels. The most important news of the last week...if it be true, is the degradation of Viceroy Ho Kuei-ts'ing...[who] was to be sent in chains to Peking and Tsang Kwoh-fan the Pacificator of Kiang Si to be acting governor general of the Two Kiang. Independently of the aggravation of Ho's cowardice which we alluded to last week, in firing upon the people of Chang-chau when forcing his way out of that city, the whole of the blame of the rout before Nanking was cast on him by the Governor Sü [Yu-jin], when the deserters in thousands first came flocking around Soochow. ...It is reported that Ho has since urged strongly on the Emperor the necessity of peace at any price with foreigners.

American Independence Day was celebrated up and down the Shanghai Bund with great noise and spectacle. American flags flew everywhere, and red, white, and blue bunting was hung out windows and over entrances of American hongs and boarding houses and draped from the yards of American ships. Guns were fired at intervals by ships in the river all day long starting at 4:00am and, of course, Chinese firecrackers were set off in front of every American hong, and all the boarding houses, grog shops, gambling dens and brothels in Hongkew from dawn to dusk. Church bells rang and military bands came ashore to parade about, playing *Yankee Doodle*, *Star-Spangled Banner*, *America the Beautiful*, and other patriotic American songs, and to accompany tea dances and balls at the larger hotels. The ladies of the Hongkew Church of Our Savior and the American Episcopal Mission put up baskets of fried chicken and potato salad, and fried rice and dumplings, and invited the staff of the Presbyterian mission press to ride out in decorated carriages to a picnic with native Christians at Siccawei.

Impromptu parades started up from time to time throughout the day, usually beginning as a line of rented sedan chairs wrapped in bunting and carrying inebriated sailors from the Albatross, Maidenhead, or Charlie Noble's up and down Broadway. Chinese grog shops pooled their cash and paid long, sinuous red and yellow lions to dance through the streets of the American concession shivering and shimmering, leaping and twirling to the rhythm of beating drums, wailing horns, and clashing gongs. Wild wheelbarrows with loads of drunken jack-tars burst out of side streets and charged through Hongkew, spilling over Soochow Creek and racing up the Bund. The band from USS *Hartford* alighted at the Astor House and performed intermittently into the late evening, accompanying a large fireworks show on the Wills toll bridge over Soochow Creek. The Americans celebrated this Fourth of July with dogged mirth, as if they suspected they might not celebrate another for some time.

Gunfire and fireworks in Shanghai echoed the earlier rattle of musketry at Sungkiang as Fletcher Wood walked through the north gate into the French Concession.

He went to his room at Fuller's boarding house, slept for a few hours, awoke in the early afternoon, ate sparingly, then got Arion and rode down to the Shanghai Hospital and Dispensary to see after his wounded. The hospital building was a converted rooming house with private rooms and officer's rooms on the first floor, open wards on the second floor, and in the rear coal-fired woks for cooking, a water closet, and accommodations for staff and servants. Fletcher's men occupied almost all the beds on the second floor – eight from the 1st platoon with mostly superficial wounds of the extremities, sixteen from the 2nd platoon with serious wounds. They were packed into four small rooms with ten beds in each. The surgeon, a Dr. Sibbald, had operated on De la Fuente that morning, as he was the most serious with three gunshot wounds, but the Portuguese was awake and, if not chipper, at least alert and talking with Ricci.

"Ricci save my life, Colonel."

"Aw, he pretty tough guy, Colonel – three little ball no kill De la Fuente."

A nurse said that Dr. Sibbald had been working all morning on the Foreign Rifles and that MacDonald and McKenzie, and the Blackwoods, all were in stable condition. The Beans, and the Cassidy brothers, also were doing well – Fergus on his belly yammering into his pillow, and Festus with his bandaged leg crooked under a sheet.

"I guess we made more noise that a tin pan packed with parched peas," Festus said.

The other men were in various states of repair, but would get on well enough. Fletcher expected he would never see them again once they were released, just like he would never again see the twenty-six dead men, except that these in the hospital were…*humihinga pa*, still breathing, as Vincente would say. He put the dead from his mind again. Downstairs, he found a clerk and made sure the hospital knew who was paying the bills and that the men were to have the best of care. He also paid the clerk to arrange for the two wounded Frenchmen, Paul Girard and Dominique Leroy, to be kept out of sight. Their ships had sailed north already, but in a private room they were less likely to be found by French officers.

On his way out a voice called to him from one of the officer's rooms. It was the British major, Morton Harris, from the Astor House, who never arrived at the Temple of the Fire God. His head was in a bandage.

"From what I've been hearing," the major said, "you went out for wool and came back shorn. Perhaps I am lucky to have been injured in Shanghai instead of joining up."

"What happened to you?" Fletcher said.

"Struck by a swinging block while moving cargo. Marines are clumsy on ships. What happened to you?"

"We had a little setback – it didn't go quite as we expected this time."

"Little setback? You don't look much worse for it. They say you were drunk."

"Only a few." The exaggeration nettled him, and would distort the truth if it persisted.

"I asked around about you, Mr. Wood. You were a ship's officer."

"Yes. A first mate." Fletcher began to think this was none of the major's business. But then – who else could he talk with? Hannibal should have been his confidant, but Hannibal was a cause rather than a compensation. This morning Fletcher keenly felt his own lack of experience with more than just an artillery battery or a watch aboard ship.

"Then you understand the need for strict discipline, so that orders are executed without hesitation. Why did you not enforce their discipline?"

"They were not on a ship at sea. They all were experienced. I expected them to do as they were told."

"And yet you allowed them liquor? Why did you not curtail their drinking?"

"There're a lot of hard cases among them. Half would have been in the brig."

"And when they came out of the brig, either they would have stopped drinking or quit your service."

"Had there been time I might have whittled the number down that way."

"Do you think your army somehow is different?" Harris spoke harshly. "That your irregulars face death willingly simply because you pay them a king's ransom in gold? Men do not walk willingly into withering fire, not for any reason – they must be *forced*. Or be too drunk to know better."

"They knew what had to be done. They signed the articles and took the eagles."

"All those men died at Sungkiang because you *allowed* them to liquor up. Undisciplined men waver, stop to think, to question, to fear, and get drunk. Because they were allowed to hesitate, by your own indecision, by your own blatant failure to discipline them. *You* killed them Mr. Wood, not the rebels, just as surely as if you had put your pistol to their heads and pulled the trigger."

"These were the wrong sort of men for discipline."

"Now there's a thought – blame the men for not following, never the officers for not leading." Major Harris lay back and heaved a sigh like a death rattle. "You discipline them to follow orders. Go forward, go back, don't drink – it doesn't matter what. One day, you may see the difference, if you do this very long."

Fletcher got up to leave. The major was obviously tired, and Fletcher resented the unsolicited lecture.

"At the Lahore Gate," Harris said in just above a whisper, "I watched a platoon of the 60th Rifles shrink away from their lieutenant when he called them forward. Our company was slogging through the narrow streets of Delhi, under fire from hidden snipers dropping our comrades all around. The men were close to panic and about to bolt, when all they needed was a determined rush and a few bags of gunpowder stacked against the gate to blow it open. Only one platoon followed their officer – the men of the other platoon refused orders and fell back. The officer and men that made the assault were caught against the gate and cut to ribbons. Thousands died in the six days it took to relieve Delhi. That was September of 1857. We hanged hundreds of sepoy mutineers. Tens of thousands of Indians wandered into the countryside homeless. And I was shown, with unprecedented clarity, the only real difference between a good and a bad officer. You can't really tell by looking at them – only by who follows them."

"And discipline made them follow." That was the easiest thing to say, but the major's story did not make much sense to Fletcher. The problem was not getting the men to follow him – they went in ahead of him. But the major was right about the failure to discipline, to bend them to his will.

"Of course. It certainly was not brotherly love."

Fletcher was too distracted to worry much about where Arion wanted to go – he relaxed the reins and allowed the horse to follow its own inclinations. He tended to amble toward stands selling fragrant crispy buns and dough-sticks. The major's upbraiding had upset Fletcher enough to provoke him to ponder all that had taken place since the fall of Soochow a month before. He could not deny that the confused haste of it all – convincing the mandarins, purchasing arms, equipment and supplies, recruiting the men, training, fighting – had not left much time to reflect.

Arion's plodding gait lulled his senses enough to set his mind free to wander. The ultimate responsibility for the debacle lay with Fletcher Wood – the major was not mistaken on that account. Fletcher blamed himself for the deaths of his men, and knew he should – that was the burden of all that led men into battle. The burden was borne either like a crucifix, or like the cross of Calvary, depending on the leader. If the men were drunk and loud, Hannibal may have abetted their negligence, but Fletcher should have prevented their failing in the first place. He began to doubt himself, doubt that he had chosen the right enterprise, doubt that returning to China with the expectation of great gain and glory was even reasonable. For a moment, he even considered going back aboard a ship and sailing off into oblivion. But those heresies passed quickly from his mind. Hannibal was close to the truth of one thing – you cannot command when you're feeling sorry for yourself over men lost. Assign that duty to others. Delegate death.

My mistake was taking on such men. Their class is too independent to be subject to command. If a British cat could not flog discipline into them, why would I expect them to follow my orders? Had I understood this better at the start I would have been successful, and not risked the confidence of my backers, and not lost the lives of many men who, because of my mistake, will never again set foot upon a quarterdeck or see the inside of another grogshop. Commanding an army with hundreds of men is quite different from commanding an artillery battery or a watch of seamen. Among so many men, many differences lead to confusion unless the men are selected from a single consistent stock and made to understand clearly what is expected of them.

When he looked up again, Arion was on the British Bund. Fletcher dismounted and led the horse through the bustling crowd over to the quay side of the road and along the anchorage. Old Glory flew everywhere and reports of cannon swept round the harbor. The music of a marching band – playing *Yankee Doodle* yet again – drifted on the air mixed with the squeal of gulls. Fletcher chewed on the irony of all this celebration in the wake of his defeat at Sungkiang, then spit it out.

He found himself standing beside *Confucius*.

The steamer was tied up along the quay, her wheelhouse draped with flags and bunting. She seemed deserted until Macanaya appeared at the top of the wheelhouse ladder and waved.

"*Hoy, páre, saan ka galling* hey, friend, where have you come from?"

"*Diyan lang, kumusta ka* here and there, how are you?"

"*Humihinga pa* still breathing. *Malakí ang kabáyo* big horse."

"Yeah. *Siya puwede magsalitá ng…*, he can speak…. How do you say Greek?"

"Greek? Like Greek sailor?"

"Yup."

"*Griyego.*" Sounded more like gringo.

"*Siya puwede magsalitá ng Griyego* he is able to speak Greek."

"*Gusto mo bang magpasyal sa itaas* would you like to stroll up here?"

Fletcher hitched Arion to the bollard forward of the steamer, crossed the gangplank onto *Confucius*, and mounted the wheelhouse ladder.

"I'm very sorry about Naguapo, Vincente. *Lo siento mucho.*"

"*Si, que será*, yes, whatever will be. Paco tell me about Naguapo. I not know him, but Paco bring him back, and we will bury him in sailor cemetery. All your wounded, we take to hospital."

"Thank you. I have just been to see them. They will be all right, with care." Paco brought back his one man, thought Fletcher, and I left so many behind. One friend you can grieve for but twenty-six strangers just leave you numb. One friend you can bury in a cemetery plot with a headstone, but what can you do for corpses left on the field with the enemy. What will the Taiping do with them? Leave them to rot, throw them into a pit with quicklime, burn them with fire and let their nameless ashes blow in the wind?

"Where's Captain Ghent?"

"Captain ashore, buy supply for *Confucius*. What about horse – speak Greek?"

"A joke, Vincente, *un broma*. He is called Arion – after a magic horse in the legends of ancient Greece."

"Five dollah say Arion Greek better than you Tagalog."

"Ha, no bet *señor*! Vincente, your Manilamen were very brave at Sungkiang. They lay down their rifles and ran unarmed in under the wall and brought out a dozen wounded men."

"Always brave, *señor*, work hard, never drunk on boat. Only in grogshop."

"I am very glad you sent them to me, Vincente. They are good soldiers."

"You call us Manilamen, *taga-Maynila kamí*. Truly, we not from Manila, come from many places. Luzon, Visayan, Cebu, others. We are Tagalogs, Ilocanos, Cebuanos, more. High mountain, lowlands, islands, farmers, fishermen. Many kind, yet much is same for us. We all learn be brave, have courage, have respect, love family, love God. Work hard, live simple, spend little. Like adventure, too."

"Then I guess Manilamen is not the name to call you, when you come from so many different places. What should we call you then? You *are* all from the one place, the Philippine Islands."

"Once, maybe. Many people in Philippines, so we go other places, look for better life. Go to sea from same place, mostly Manila and Vigan, in Ilocos Sur. At sea we stay together, learn sailor talk – swab deck, brace yard, lay aloft – help each other. Later come Shanghai, go sailor home – full of Manilamen, all old friends."

"Maybe we should call you Filipinos, meaning all men from the Philippines."

"No, *señor*, not so good. Call me and Paco Filipino, how anybody know I am Tagalo and he Cebuano?"

"Countries have many kinds of people, but they're still one country. In America, we have New England, Appalachia, the Ozarks, but we're all Americans. Like a family, I suppose, father-mother-son-daughter are all different, but all are called Smith or Jones. One family. One people. Maybe something is lost, but something is gained."

"We are like that, a family. Whatever place we go, we stay together, like one family, strong family. Many old story about my people – we tell story many time in fo'c's'le of *Confucius* and at campfire. Ilocanos story tell about brave and clever boy called *Lam-ang*. Every Manila boy know this story. *Lam-ang* travel many place, win many battle, have many adventure. His enemy, the tattooed Igorots, spear him many times, but he never hurt. He dive into river and kill big crocodile, then tell women pull out crocodile teeth, keep for charm, protect on journey."

Vincente shook his wrist and rattled his bracelet of large white shark teeth. At least they looked like shark teeth, but Fletcher assumed shark would do as well as crocodile for one who knew the old legends of his people and believed in the magic of supernatural heroes. Bullfinch overlooked *Lam-ang*.

"*Lam-ang* fight enemy Samarang, catch enemy spear in hand, spear enemy, call wind carry Samarang away over nine hills. *Lam-ang* get swallowed by big shark, wife Kannoyan find *Lam-ang* bones in sea, bring home, magic rooster flap powerful wings, bones rise up and *Lam-ang* come back to life. We much same like *Lam-ang*, *señor*. Very brave, travel far, stay together, even have rooster fight. Life very hard, *señor*, but Manilamen face life like one family, very strong."

"With an army of Manilamen, I could conquer China. A few magic roosters would help, too." Fletcher was not above a little extravagance, not so much to flatter, but rather to commend Vincente's race. He did not expect Vincente's answer.

"You can have that, *señor*. I can get for you. Manilamen, not rooster."

That took the sailor aback – Fletcher looked into Vincente's face to see if they were still making jokes. The Manilaman was perfectly serious.

"Are there many of your people here? How many can you get?"

"One hundred, easy. Maybe two hundred."

"How are there so many in Shanghai?"

"We are many everywhere."

The distant *ssu-chunk, ssu-chunk, ssu-chunk* of a loud steamer engine in serious need of adjustment reached their ears. Fletcher turned and stared out the wheelhouse window. A small stern-wheel paddle steamer was making her way into the anchorage, puffing up great clouds of black smoke. He fished his brass telescope out of a coat pocket and examined her more closely.

She could not have been more than sixty-five, seventy feet long, much smaller than other vessels in port, and had no long, stacked decks of passenger accommodations that made Mississippi river boats look like floating shoeboxes. She looked to be a working boat. Her hull was too shallow for holds – cargo would be carried on her main deck. Where the boiler deck would have been on a larger boat, there was a short cabin supported on columns, with space beneath for more cargo, and a pilot house atop the cabin. She had a jackstaff on her bow, vertical spars instead of masts, and a telescoping smokestack that could be lowered by a wire cable to pass easily under most inland bridges. High above the deck, a hog chain suspended on spars fore to aft kept her hull from sagging under heavy loads. Her beam did not look more than twenty feet wide – a steamer of that size would have a draft of three feet or less and could make the Kuangfulin camp landing even during neap tides. And she could mount heavy guns, and carry maybe a hundred men, closely packed.

"What is that steamer over there, Vincente?"

"She called *Vulcan, señor. Pequeño barka, no*, a little boat? Very noisy, need overhaul." Fletcher recognized the name – the British had an HMS *Vulcan* on station with the expeditionary force, a six-gun steam frigate of 1700 tons, much larger than this lurching little river steamer called *Vulcan*. HMS *Vulcan* was the troopship that delivered the 2nd Queen's Royal Regiment of Foot to malaria-plagued Hong Kong and brought them north in early May, just ahead of the fever. He recalled seeing the same HMS *Vulcan* in Balaclava harbor unloading marines for the assault on Sebastopol in 1855, dwarfed by Napier's flagship *Duke of Wellington* with her 131 guns on three decks.

"Do you know who owns this little *Vulcan*?"

"Captain know – he know all steamers."

"Will your Manilamen go to Kuangfulin and train?"

"They go any place you say."

"They'll all be sailors? They won't have fired rifles before, or cannon."

"If they never fire gun on ship, they learn."

"There won't be much time, Vincente." Fletcher wondered how he would turn beached sailors, dunnage mostly, into proficient riflemen in only a few weeks. The drill would be hard for undisciplined recruits – they'd have to be kept too tired to misbehave in camp, or they'd bolt for their Shanghai bars and brothels.

Fletcher turned around to Vincente.

"Will you come with me?"

"Of course, *señor*. I will be your *tagatanore*, your…guardian angel."

"Well, you can be my personal guard, my aide-de-camp." My Chingachgook.

"*O, sige*, okay! That's done then. I go find men."

2 *Confucius* was tied only a few doors up from the Oriental Bank. Through a window of his new offices next door, Hugh Wood saw his brother riding on the Bund and went out to meet him.

"The story of your defeat at Sungkiang is all over the Bund.

"Let's eat. I'm famished. You may buy your elder dinner."

"My blessings never cease, Fletcher. But I am glad to see you've no fantods after your…experience."

"I just don't show them, brother. I suppose it's the Astor House again?"

"Yes, to see how Shanghai treats us, now that you've met their expectations."

"No better than last time, I'd wager. They'll want to see my tail between my legs."

The Fourth of July celebration was in full swing at the Astor House – flags waving, bands playing, and fireworks on the quay. Late in the summer afternoon most of the crowd was still nursing their iced drinks up on the verandah, so a dinner table was available immediately.

Together with Minister Blaine, Consul Masters watched the Wood brothers enter and was inspired to a snide remark about the American Independence Day.

"Can't say they've done all that well since 1776."

"What about British flags flown at Sungkiang?" Blaine ignored the incivility.

"Yes, one of our chaps went up to Sungkiang this morning with some friends and found two steamers, *Confucius* and *Pluto*, flying American flags, and over thirty junks, a mix of imperial war junks and lorchas, some of the latter flying the Union Jack and the Tricolor. He was told there had been a battle with the rebels and it would be dangerous to approach the town. But he went on anyway, trusting his party would be safe, and about a mile from the east gate found a group of blacks camped out before the wall."

"What, Sepoys?" Blaine said, incredulous.

"No, Manilamen. Our chap became convinced his party risked being fired upon if they approached more closely. He said that Wood's vagabonds stood outside the wall within sight of rebels staring daggers across the open ground, and that the national flags there could only cause the rebels to think they were attacked by the western powers. The two steamers at the mouth of the creek flying American flags certainly provided encouragement, even if they did not join in the engagement."

"Surely the American flags were flying for their holiday today."

"And the spineless American consul will likely have nothing to say about a Chinese steamer flying the Stars and Stripes. I would – it's too obvious to let alone."

"The junks flying our flags, were they of British registry?"

"Can't say, sir. But this beggar has a lot of cheek to come here after his illegal depredations incite the rebels against us. At the very least, the rebels may disrupt trade in silk and tea if they conclude foreigners are taking the field against them. Or pay us back in our own coin, as it were, and attack Shanghai. Fletcher Wood should be in gaol instead of dining at the Astor."

"I dinna see what can done as long as he hides behind the robes of the *taotai* and is na' in violation of any country's neutrality. However, can we na' go after his hirelings, the British drill sergeants he is reported to have incited to desertion? And canna the Spanish consul be induced to control these bounders from Manila, round them up and gaol them or ship them away from Shanghai?"

"Yes, sir, we will pursue the British in Wood's ranks. In addition, I have put the community on official notice that violation of neutrality by British subjects will be prosecuted and punished by imprisonment of up to two years and fine of up to $5000. Circulars have been distributed, and the notice will appear in the next issue of the *Herald* and other China coast newspapers. I have also sent word to the Spanish consul, but he writes back to say only that he will look into the matter, so we will not see much action on that front. However, should we not also discourage the *taotai* from employing a mercenary force like this? Our failure to suppress the reckless actions of the *taotai's* Foreign Rifles compromises our claims to neutrality between the empire and the rebels. In the eyes of the rebels, our doing nothing is the same as supporting the empire, just as our support for trade supports the empire. How can we insist we are neutral?"

"Ah, Masters, it is a conundrum. To support trade we canna be strictly neutral. To be strictly neutral we canna support trade. Damned by the belligerents if we do, damned by the traders if we do na'. As for the *taotai*, I believe I would rather have the central authority deal directly with him instead of us."

"But, sir, Peking has given authority to the governor for raising militia against the rebels and, through him, to the *taotai* – the governor and the *taotai* are responsible for putting these irregulars into the field."

"Yes, I am aware of that, Masters. However, her majesty's government canna continue forever dealing wi' one Chinese authority in Peking and another in each province. This pernicious system of independent provincial Government must cease, and I shall press for redress shortly when we march into Peking. Dealing with this *taotai* simply strengthens his hand against the central government when I am coming to believe our policy should do nothing to weaken the central government in this time of crisis. I say again – we must protect Chinese sovereignty. Good Lord, man, we canna get mired down in China like we are in India."

Masters fumed inwardly. Damn your Hyde Park palter! Why not simply own up to your preference for the Manchu over the Taiping and have done with this inane pretence of neutrality? In the meantime, the *taotai* you decline to deal with gathers an army of desperados to send against the rebels.

Hugh and Fletcher ignored the British and sat at a small corner table.

"The news," Hugh said, "is all over Shanghai. Just how bad was it really?"

"A rout. Paid off the uninjured men this morning. The wounded are being cared for. Some men elected to stay on. I sent them back out to Kuangfulin to relieve the guard and secure the camp. The camp guard was paid off and shipped back here."

"Artillery would have made a difference."

"Yes, and the right men, too. Most importantly, I should *not* have let the Chinese prod me. They said 'must do this' and I thought I had to go do it. That was wrong. From now on, I shall do as they do – say 'yes' to everything, but do nothing until ready. When they object, well, 'something came up,' or 'I forgot.' When I'm successful, they won't care if I was insubordinate. And next time, I will be successful. I've just found another wellspring of warriors – Vincente Macanaya's Manilamen. He thinks he can round up a couple hundred. They will be easier to handle, and they are truly fierce fighters. With Manilamen, artillery, and perhaps a small steamer, I *can* take Sungkiang."

"The rebels will attack Shanghai, won't they? All the defenses are going up here."

"Often a place is best protected from a nearby location rather than inside the place itself, as in chess when a knight might best defend a king from a short distance away, and obstruct other approaches. Sometimes it's best to be the knight."

Chester Hicks appeared beside their table.

"So, the vagabond king has returned. The British consul's eyes are going to pop out of his head if he continues to stare so hard at you, Mr. Wood."

"Ah, join us Chester, as long as you are still talking to me. Few are. Never mind the consul. He can't touch me, regardless of how much he might wish to."

"I'll stay a moment, if only to parade my loyalties. You may be the butt of many jokes now, but that fracas at Sungkiang was only a temporary setback, if I know you."

"They'll all holler for help loud enough when the rebels come," Hugh said.

"Where will you get your army now, Mr. Wood? You cannot very well bury dragon's teeth in the old mandarin's garden."

"Vincente and his fierce crew are the very sons of the dragon's teeth."

"Yes, the Manilamen. That makes sense – and there are a great many of them skulking about, to give credence to the complaints about their wild ways ashore."

"In the field I believe they will be sober and disciplined."

"I would agree, having seen them in action. But you must not expect they will stay garrisoned out in the backcountry very long at one time, away from the grog houses and brothels of Shanghai. And pay close attention to what Manilamen say – they will want to avoid telling you anything they think you will not like to hear, a common Oriental failing. Together with a Spanish fondness for exaggeration and highfalutin oratory, it is easy to mistake their meaning. By the way, I finally have received those Sharps rifles we spoke of once. One hundred 1855 Sharps breech-loading rifled carbines, .52 caliber, 21 inch barrel, Maynard primers, stamped with Crown and V.R., issued to British cavalry in 1857, which you may have for the bargain price of US$20.00 each. Complete with powder and ball for 100 rounds, primers and implements. An additional 1000 rounds of ammunition can be had at 100 rounds for US$15.00. Arm your Manilamen with these and you will have a force of immortals."

"Cavalry would want Maynard primers – next batch, try for Sharps primers."

"Is there a problem with the Maynard primers?"

"Nothing I can't deal with. Under field conditions the primers malfunction – damp paper tape won't advance properly, and the primer magazine fouls with dirt, but training can remedy those drawbacks. Hold the rifles for delivery."

"Have you found any guns yet?"

"I expect to hear presently. Do you have any?"

"No, sir. Guns are hard to come by, there being so much demand for carnage around the world. What will you do for artillerymen?"

"A handful have volunteered, enough for one battery. Looks like I'll be training Manilamen for the rest."

"Manilamen? The rebels will not wait several months for you, Mr. Wood."

"I have trained troops before, Mr. Hicks. A few weeks will do."

"A few weeks? That I would like to see."

After dinner, Fletcher fetched his horse from the Astor House *mafoo* and rode back to the French concession. Fortified now with new ideas and old French wine, he was ready to meet with Takee. He could expect that the banker had already heard rumors about Sungkiang, because none of the *taotai*'s spies were around after the two junks that carried the Foreign Rifles to Sungkiang had returned to the Kuangfulin camp. Unless the *taotai* had spies among the rebels, which was entirely possible.

As he turned up *du Consulat* Street toward the western suburbs, he wondered what he could say about the defeat that would deflect the dismay of the mandarins. He dismounted and walked the last stretch beside the dull-red masonry of Takee's wall trying to anticipate the different reactions the banker might have to the news. Lantern light flickered between the planks of the tile-roofed gate. Fletcher rapped on the gate with his crop and was admitted. Perhaps Takee would threaten to withdraw support of the foreign legion and close the accounts at Jardine and H. Fogg.

The moon was just rising above the garden wall and illuminating the sparkling pools, fragile little arch bridges, and white stone-lined paths under tall trees he had seen the first night he went there, full of bluster and great aplomb. A servant took charge of his horse, and another servant led him through the gates, along the corridors, and up the marble steps into the reception hall. Once more, he sat amidst ostentatious wealth of polished wood, gleaming enamel, glowing bronze, and green jade. The thin smoke of sandalwood incense came from burners on the altar at the back of the great hall. A servant brought steaming tea. Fletcher heard once again the quietly chattering thrushes in their slender bamboo cages under the smoke-dark ceiling and remembered the bargain he had wrested from Takee. He had not heard the birds in the rafters when he visited on the several occasions since that first night, not until tonight.

"Wu-te, Wu-te, solly too muchee you wait." Yang Fang's thin voice preceded him out of a corridor, followed by the rustle of his stiff satin gown, and finally the man himself appeared. Fletcher rose to his feet. They each clasped their own two hands together and waved them before their faces.

"請坐. Please to sit. What news?"

It felt as if they were starting all over again from the beginning.

"Not good. We did not take Sungkiang." He was careful not to say "failed."

"No? What happen?"

Fletcher described the action, shamelessly beveling the corners and sanding sharp edges to soften the lines of the story and avert blame from himself. He mentioned several times having no artillery, that the rebels heard them coming and called up reinforcements, and the moonlight. He did not mention that the 2nd platoon was drunk.

"Twenty-six men died, twenty-four were wounded and taken to the hospital."

"So many! Oh, Wu-te, dis belly bad, belly bad. *Tao-t'ai* be belly anglee."

"We'll go back. We'll take Sungkiang next time."

"Lebel still in Sung-chiang, Wu-te. Come soon Shang-hai."

"They won't be there long. Next time I'll beat them."

"Mebbe no nex' time, Wu-te. Mebbe *tao-t'ai* say catchee no moh dollah."

"We can't quit now. This is just a setback, a false start."

"So muchee dollah, so many pieces dead man. Mebbe *yang-ch'iang*, foreign lifle, not good idea."

"You have to give me another chance."

"Not know, Wu-te. Allo belongee *tao-t'ai* pidgin."

"No Takee! No belongee *taotai* pidgin. Belongee Takee pidgin. You promised."

"My plomise?" Yang Fang knew the word "promise" from the early days at Jardine's, where traders *promised* to deliver but rarely said when, or at what quantity and price. The English was no less vague than the Chinese *hsü no* 許諾 that he associated with "promise." *Hsü* 許 inferred "agree" and "assent" and was wedded to many variants of "betrothal," none of which suggested the compelling and absolute character of a promise in English. Certainly, no agreement between Yang Fang and a foreigner would ever be as conclusive as a "betrothal."

"You promised."

"What plomise?"

"At the custom house that night. The first time I met the *taotai*."

"*Tao-t'ai* too?" Yang Fang struggled to remember that night at the custom house.

"You agreed that no matter what happened, you would give me another chance."

"No, Wu-te, no makee plomise. Plomise no good – hab too muchee dollah, too many pieces dead man. No plomise."

"Yes, promise. You agreed to give me another chance, and I will hold you to that. Anyway, you have spent much money – it's too soon to stop, else your money will be wasted. Don't waste your money. I can do this."

"Mus' talkee *tao-t'ai*."

"I know. But tell him that next time I will have better soldiers, I will have artillery to blow down the gates, there will be no moonlight, and the rebels will not hear us coming. Tell him that. Don't waste the money you already have invested."

"When go fight Sung-chiang, Wu-te?"

"Now don't start!" Fletcher flared up. "Don't push me. We attacked too soon this time, and many men died because of it, and we did not win. No! *I will tell you* when I am ready. Until then *you wait.* Understand?"

Yang Fang looked like he'd swallowed bile. "My wait," he whimpered.

He was not certain about the *tao-t'ai*, but Yang Fang was confident this report of defeat should be delivered in the presence of the governor. When Wu-te's determination to attack Sung-chiang again was mentioned, the governor would say "Of course, let him try again!" However, Takee knew he would not say to the governor anything about Wu-te telling them to wait – the governor already was discontent with Wu-te's arrogance. "夷人嗜利好勝 barbarians crave profit and power," the governor would intone. "武德心尤難測 Wu-te's heart is especially difficult to understand."

The governor told them they must "默為截制化武德桀驁不馴 quietly constrain Wu-te to change his untamed, tyrannical pride, 不然有尾大不掉之患 otherwise he may become a tail too big to be wagged."

Fletcher returned Arion to his stable late in the evening. Mafoo was waiting anxiously to feed and water the animal and scolded Fletcher for keeping Arion out too long and making him miss his dinner. Artemis Fuller was still up and almost as anxious as Mafoo on another subject.

"Your Napoleons are on their way and will be here in two or three days! The cargo of two brass 12-pounder howitzers and eight brass 6-pounders – two light batteries – left Macao this morning on the British ship *Celestial*, complete with limbers, caissons, battery wagon and forge, ammunition, and fifteen horses – two teams of six horses for the heavy guns, and three spare horses."

"Finally – there's good news from you. You're even bringing me the horses. I wonder, will we need horses for the light guns? The French in the Crimea had a great many horses for their artillery batteries."

"How many men are needed to heft a 6-pounder?"

"Four men can move a field gun if they must, six more easily. But horses will be needed, I think, to take guns any distance over land."

"You may be moving our guns on junks, mostly. Might not need horses."

"Maybe so, with all the canals and creeks. I have not moved guns on boats – I'll have to ask my regimental gunners how that is best done."

"Need heavy planks, and ropes and pulleys to secure the guns while crossing on planks to and from shore, so they aren't lost in a river or creek."

"On clippers we'd hoist them on a lower yard. On steamers, we might have to jury-rig a derrick if there's no cargo hoist. Don't know about junks. They must have a way of lifting heavy cargo. Or do they take only cargo a thousand coolies can carry aboard?"

"How many horses would be needed, if men can't pull the guns?"

"Eight more guns will need, what? Forty-eight horses. And you say there are two caissons, a battery wagon, and a forge? Another eighteen. And there will be forage wagons, and ammunition wagons for the light guns that have no caissons."

"We don't have so many horses here in China, not even at the Shanghai racetrack. Unless you pilfer an Allied transport, the only other horses are Chinese."

"The Mongolian ponies? They're not exactly draft horses."

"They're sturdy enough, the ones I've seen. Can't gallop, but they'll pull."

"Can you get some of them?"

"Have the *taotai* requisition horses from the imperial camp at Kuangfulin."

"Perhaps. I think a flying column is best not saddled with a lot of horses."

"You'll be wanting a farrier."

"Yes, and a smith, for the forge, to repair broken wagons and the like. Not as easy to recruit as riflemen."

"Our people take their horses out to Evans, the English smith with a workshop out at the racetrack. A few pounds might convince him to stop by Kuangfulin from time to time to catch up on any ironwork needed. Until you get your own."

"He could show us how to work the forge, maybe start an apprentice."

"So you see, Mr. Wood, the deeper you get in all this, the more your camp becomes a community, with you as the mayor and your officers as city fathers."

"I'm more interested in mogul than mayor, Mr. Fuller, but if you turn up a book on civil administration, send it along. My officers are ill-prepared."

"After the guns clear customs inspection, they can be offloaded directly to lighters and taken out to Kuangfulin. You can avoid Captain Budd."

"Yes, no marines, thank you. But there again – the horses. How to get them off a ship and into a junk? British transports either walk them down a gangplank or barge them ashore. We might have to use cargo lifts, or put them ashore first and then walk them on board a junk – which could be ticklish. Something else to look into." A horse, thought Fletcher, looks so silly suspended in a sling and being hoisted ashore by a crane. *Equinus ex machina* – flying horse.

"If you are still in Shanghai, you could attend to the customs procedures yourself and ensure there are no difficulties. Authorization from the *taotai* to receive the guns on behalf of the Chinese government might clear many obstacles."

"If the British consul doesn't get wind first and interfere with customs. But documentation from the *taotai* is a good idea – you're a great help, Mr. Fuller. Also – I saw a small steamer come into the anchorage this afternoon, the *Vulcan* I was told was her name. Not the British steam frigate HMS *Vulcan*, but a small river steamer, maybe seventy feet long, maybe a three-foot draft. To see her, just walk down to the Bund."

"Yes, a Russell & Company utility boat. Noisy old girl. Engine'd wake the dead."

"I'd like to charter that little boat. Use her to take the guns and horses to camp."

"Sure. She'll receive cargo more easily, and go on inland streams and creeks."

Fletcher made a mental note to arrange with Hicks for delivery of the Sharps carbines aboard *Vulcan* if she was chartered for the Foreign Rifles.

"Have you cannoneers to fire the guns?"

"A few. The rest I'll train."

"Train? Won't that take time? The rebels are only few days' march away."

"My men will be ready."

Fuller stared at Wood for a moment while he considered the man's audacity.

3 Three days later *Celestial* was in Shanghai harbor off the British Bund, sails tightly furled on their yards, tugging quietly at her moorings on the river side of the anchorage. Early that morning Fletcher, Vincente, and six Manilamen boarded a sampan and were sculled from *Confucius* out to *Celestial* where they expected to meet the H. Fogg agent and oversee the transshipment of Fletcher's cargo.

Celestial was half the size of the largest clippers in harbor, a small square-rigged ship of under five hundred tons, fifty feet shorter than *Essex* and probably narrower by a third. Fletcher knew her – she was one of the earliest British tea clippers and a China trader in Asian waters throughout the 1850s. She had a narrow Aberdeen bow, designed by thrifty Scots to have less tonnage by the measurements of that day, so she would pay less in tonnage dues. Two white lifeboats were overturned on a wood rack over her main cargo hatch, four swivel guns perched on her poop deck rail, and two larger brass guns,

9-pounders Fletcher guessed, peeked out through open ports on her starboard side, and there would be two more on the larboard side. She was armed quite well enough to hold her own against Chinese pirates. Fletcher's artillery would be mixed in with rattans and other cargo aboard *Celestial* consigned to the trader Gilman & Company.

The high-pitched New England twang of Artemis Fuller suddenly cut through the morning quiet of Shanghai harbor. He stood on the deck of *Celestial* toe-to-toe with another little man just as spare as himself, flailing his arms in argument. The captain stood to one side like a burly bare-knuckle referee ready to step between them. Fletcher figured his years at sea were wasted if he did not know a ship's captain at a glance.

"Five to one Fogg-man throw custom-man in harbor," Vincente said with a smile.

"You men from Manila gamble too much," Fletcher said, laughing. "Fogg-man and custom-man are not your damn chickens."

The sampan bumped up between the ship and a customs boat and Fletcher jumped onto the rail and scrambled up to the deck, followed by his Praetorians. The whinny of a horse came from the hold.

"So," said the flustered Fuller, "here's Mr. Wood, finally. He'll have the documents." Fuller's adversary was a short wicket-stump of an Englishman rigged in a gray single-breasted suit with high collar and black cravat. His square face was bracketed by thick black sideburns and a shiny monocle was scrunched into his left eye. "Mr. Wood, this is Mr. Evans, from the custom house." The customs officer turned an anxious monocle on the armed boarders. His eye was doubled in size behind the glass and unnerved the Manilamen.

"Archibald Evans, assistant chief superintendent," he said, failing to muster much bluster. As the fierce-looking Manilamen arrayed themselves across the waist, Evans edged closer to the leeward side of the captain.

"This other gentleman is Captain Black of *Celestial*."

Fletcher nodded to the customs officer and extended a hand to the captain. "Fletcher Wood," he said, then handed his papers to the Fogg-man. The confrontation resumed.

"I don't care if the emperor of China signed a release," Evans said, "these guns stay on board until the British consul approves of unloading them. They are contraband." Evans had been called to the British consulate late the previous afternoon after *Celestial* arrived to meet with Consul Masters. The consul was adamant that any guns aboard that ship were not to be landed regardless of circumstance. The consul reminded the customs officer of personal incidents Evans would not want made public, and promised that he would be watching from a consulate window and would send British marines if needed to enforce his will.

"They're not contraband!" Fuller bristled.

"They are contraband under British treaty regulation," Evans repeated sternly.

"The treaty regulation does not apply to Chinese property. It's perfectly clear from the purchase orders and bill of lading they're Chinese property."

"And just why are you receiving Chinese property, anyway?"

"Here is the release authorizing Mr. Wood to take delivery of the cargo on behalf of the Chinese government and transship the cargo to *Vulcan*. Note the big red chop of the *taotai*. By the way, where is *Vulcan*, Mr. Wood? Should be here."

"Listen for her. Sounds like empty water barrels rolling over cobblestone."

"This is…extraordinary. And highly irregular," Evans said, sputtering. "I will not be responsible. This must be taken up with my superiors at the customs office. Captain, Mr. Fuller, please gather up your paperwork and come with me."

"Blast!" the captain said. "You'll have me here all day before I can start to unload."

"Can't help that," Evans said with a sniff. "Come along whenever you are ready."

In a moment, he was over the side and into the customs boat.

"Stand by, mister," the captain shouted after him. "We'll come in your boat."

The captain hissed and fumed like an old steamboat, pitched below and rolled back up with an armload of papers, then made for the ladder. Fuller followed him.

"Captain," Fletcher said. "We want to begin unloading our shipment."

"Go ahead," grumbled the captain over his shoulder. "Your agent paid *Celestial* when he came aboard, so you're welcome to anything on your bill of lading. The mate will supervise for you. You can answer to the damn customs yourself."

As the customs boat sculled down the line of merchant sail with Artemis Fuller and Captain Black in the stern sheets, a loud rumbling and clanking started up from the direction of the Hongkew docks and the little sternwheeler *Vulcan* stood out into the river on approach for *Celestial*. Ten minutes later the steamer came up alongside, a window in the pilothouse jerked open, and a thin voice shouted out.

"Tide be risin', slack water pretty quick, so I can ride the current on your hooks."

"Giver a try, Cap'n," the mate yelled. "We'll haul up short and holler if she drags."

Crewmen aboard the steamer put out fenders, threw lines over *Celestial*'s rail, and tied up along her larboard bow opposite the ship's forward hatch. The steamer was less than half the length of the ship and looked like a whale calf nuzzling up against a humpback cow. Fletcher asked *Celestial*'s mate, Mr. Roarke, for the bill of lading and, after glancing it over, took the mate and three Manilamen aboard the steamer. The steamer captain hailed them from his tiny pilothouse and came down the forward ladder to the deck. He was in his early thirties, with auburn eyes, long hair and short beard the color of honey, and he wore a gray frock coat and cloth cap with black visor.

"Captain Jabez Reach at your service, gentlemen," he said, taking in the escort bristling with guns and bolos. "You're packin' a lot of haadware – expecting trouble, are you?" Reach was thin, hard and pale like an aspen, and his "a" was long and flat, as if squashed by a passing High Street omnibus.

"Nothing we can't handle, captain," Fletcher said, grinning. "I am the fellow who chartered your steamer, and this is Mr. Roarke, mate aboard *Celestial*." Fletcher quickly explained the immediate task at hand of transshipping the cargo, handing the bill of lading to Reach, and that the steamer would be going to Kuangfulin for at least a week.

"Suits me," Reach said, "if you have comestibles for my crew of twelve where you are taking us. Didn't bring much, not knowin' your plan. Anyway, Russell & Company have received payment in advance for the first week, so *Vulcan* in all her majesty practically belongs to you. This is a pretty big list. Look at that – fifteen horses! Wondered how I could hear horses whinny in the middle of the ol' 'Poo. And artillery! Gonna be crowded here. Say, I guess I have heard of you, Mr. Wood."

"Don't set store by what you hear. Shanghai needs to be skinning its own skunks."

"Well, your accent tells me it's likely we both're hewn from the same close-grained and durable New England maple. That being so, we share a somber and severe Puritan heritage that says he who searches for sin in others had best look first into his own heart. I prefer to *reach* my own conclusions."

"To business, then," Fletcher said. "What's your tonnage and draft?"

"Fo'ty-five tons, three foot fully laden. Empty now and riding high. Mr. Roarke, where's the cargo stowed and what do you think's the weight of this here cargo?"

"Reckon at about twenty tons, sir, stowed in holds forward and aft."

"That'll only take her down a little over a foot. I'll keep steam up in one boiler and fires banked in t'other so she'll have power to keep her deck opposite which ever hold you're unloading. Now, what about these horses?"

"We built stalls for them in the hold. First thing to do is to strike the stalls a few at a time and set them up on your deck. Put a canvas sling under a horse's belly, hook up to tackle, lift 'im up out of the hold, swing 'im across under the mainyard, and lower 'im onto your deck. It all goes very quickly once started."

"How'd you care for them?"

"Two grooms came with them from Constantinople," Roarke said. "Horses're fed and watered twice a day with hay, oats, bran mash, and six gallons of water – they can drink your condensed steam. The grooms care for them, walk them in the hold for exercise, clean up after them, disinfect the stalls, wash the feeding troughs and horses' nostrils with vinegar, and be sure they get good ventilation. You'll want to have large scuppers kept open to carry away the urine."

"Let me come over with my mate and see your horses and how the cargo's stowed," the captain said. "That'll give us some idea of how to stow it all on *Vulcan*, so that the shipment can be properly inventoried before we get underway."

After inspecting Fletcher's cargo in *Celestial*'s hold, Captain Reach and his mate returned to *Vulcan* and disappeared into her pilothouse. Shortly afterwards, the first dismantled stalls were swung across under the mainyard and the transfer of cargo was underway. The cargo space under *Vulcan*'s cabin had capacity for the stalls and horses, ammunition boxes, powder barrels, smaller equipage and gun implements, and the first of the artillery "furniture" – the dismantled forge, limbers, caissons, and their wheels. The forward deck would take the rest of the dismantled wagons, and four 6-pounder field guns. The other guns, all mounted on their carriages, would be lashed down on the after deck. When Captain Reach was satisfied his mate and crew knew what to do, he returned to the pilothouse and left them to their work. Fletcher crossed back and forth between the two vessels until he was sure the other crew had the task in hand, then went to the pilothouse. From there he could observe most items on the bill of lading as they were taken over to *Vulcan*.

"Captain, I do not recall *Vulcan* from when I was here before, nor recently."

"We don't take her out all that much," Reach said, " 'cause her capacity's so small and she's not ah'med. Sternwheeler won't do for a tugboat in a harbor with such large ships, nor a gunboat neithah, and not all ca'go's economical for her to carry upriver or inland. When she's idle, or another captain takes her out, that's when you'll find me helpin' out ovah at the harbor master's office."

As Fletcher gazed out the window, a chestnut mare slowly drifted past behind the captain's head.

"Aren't many steamers like her 'tho, that can squeeze into the little creeks inland. Ironical how many folks confuse her with the British steam frigate *Vulcan*, because of the name, you know. They're more like David and Goliath. Those Manilamen are from *Confucius* aren't they."

"Yes. Some of them have joined up with me now."

"I thought I recognized that mate from *Confucius*. She's a grand old boat, a mighty scrapper. She'd be a step up from *Vulcan* for a riverboat captain. Don't mistake my meanin', now – old Ghent's salt of the earth – but I sure hope to be around if she ever needs a new master."

Jabez Reach was from Falmouth, Massachusetts, and left home at age twenty-two for the far west: Cleveland, or Louisville. Coming to the Ohio, Mississippi and Missouri rivers, he broke his journey a while to work on steamboats as an engineer's striker, an apprentice assigned the drudgery of oiling, cleaning and tending boilers, and overhauling machinery. Of necessity, he learned blacksmithing, as would any steamboat engineer, and could make just about anything out of wrought iron with a hot fire, hammer and anvil. After three years on rivers, Jabez hankered to sail on water not strangled between two narrow banks, and made his way down to New Orleans where he enlisted for a hitch in the Navy.

"These Manilamen," said Captain Reach, "that follow you about like goslings, how did you ever tame them? More to the point, why have you bothered?"

"Good men are hard to come by," Fletcher said, "and bad men abound, as I guess you know, Captain. I enlisted some white men to go soldiering and took them into the field, but they would not follow orders, and drank to excess, and came to a bad end. These Manilamen are cut from different cloth. I've seen them in action. They are courageous yet respectful, sober and disciplined, yet fierce. They look out for each other like family, and most are devout Christians. I have better expectations of them." Fletcher declined to mention they were a holy terror when they came on shore to carouse, tetchy over imagined slights to race or honor, and prone to tantrums over trivialities.

"You may not be far off course, to judge by my experience," Reach said. "I encountered something like that in the Louisville-New Orleans trade, same sort of differences, except between Irish and German deck hands and Negro slaves. The Irish deck hands usually were insubordinate and downright lazy, even drunk on duty, while the black river men were always genial, docile, and obliging. Of course, they were slaves and had no choice, but as a class the work was much easier with the affable Negroes, and a trial with the cantankerous white men."

In the Navy, Reach had served as a shipfitter, bending and twisting sheet metal into plumbing fixtures, and was promoted to warrant officer and duty as boatswain and became an expert on the hulls of ships. His last berth was aboard USS *Powhatan*, the steam frigate that took the American minister north to the Peiho together with the British and French in late 1859. Reach's hitch was up then and he was honorably discharged at Shanghai in June, before the name of USS *Powhatten* was written indelibly into the history books. Reach settled down in Shanghai, where his experience on steamers was a rare assist to the harbormaster.

Lao Chang's junk appeared off the mouth of Soochow Creek and worked her way up alongside *Vulcan*. At Fletcher's request, Captain Reach ordered crewmen to make her fast and drop over a rope ladder, and Fletcher went down to her. Barefoot Ah-shan greeted him with her black-toothed grin and another "how ah yoo?" and motioned to long wooden crates at the mast, ten of them. He pried up the lid of one crate and found ten Sharps rifles packed inside, cavalry carbines with saddle rings. So while caissons were being lifted onto the steamer deck from *Celestial*, the crates from Chester Hicks were put into cargo nets, hauled aboard from the junk, and taken below. Fletcher climbed back aboard the ship as the first of the 6-pounder guns came up out of its hold. Unexpectedly, a small blue-eyed brunette woman in green gingham came out of the saloon and stood on deck watching. Her unsettling appearance shanghaied his attention.

"You 'ave a very big gun there, if it be yours," she said pertly.

"It's certainly quite large for so small a ship," he said, looking her up and down. There's a salty wench, he thought. What tavern does she call home?

"Small? I'll say. None 'as ever mistaken us for that 'ulking American *Celestial*." The American clipper *Celestial* was twice the size of this ship and a famous competitor in the tea races of the fifties.

"Your *Celestial* has the better pedigree, ma'am. Among the earliest of the tea clippers, isn't she, the Aberdeen model, long frame and slender bow, and a great many winsome curves?"

"Ah," she said with a broad smile, "clearly you know a good ship when you meet one. Not just pedigree, tho' – performance, too. Shanghai to London in 100 days."

"You don't say? That'd make for a fresh cuppa tea in Camden Town. Considering your last port 'o call and that cargo of rattans, I guess you're in the coasting trade now"

"For a while, until the next teas. See 'ere now, you can't just stand around and chat all morning. I require that you get your 'eavy guns and filthy 'orses off my pretty ship. It will take a 'ercules to clean her up enough to carry another cargo of tea."

"Your ship? You talk like you're the captain."

"The captain's wife, if you please. *Mrs.* William Black."

"Fletcher Wood, ma'am. In another life, I was a ship's mate and heard sometimes how a bold woman went to sea with her captain. Sailed the seven seas, so to speak, fought tooth and nail through terrible storms, quelled dreadful mutiny. However, I've never clapped eyes on such a marvelous woman. Not until now."

"Lady, Mr. Fletcher Wood. Marvelous lady."

They burst out laughing together. While more of the 6-pounders in Fletcher's artillery battery were carefully hoisted out of the *Celestial*'s hold, swung over to *Vulcan*, and gingerly lowered to the steamer's deck, Mrs. Captain Black remarked on the course of their voyage. The ship's usual outward cargo was coal, but this year after delivering her tea and silk to London in late April, and refitting during May, she was chartered in early June to pick up artillery in Constantinople. After this delivery, she would dawdle along the China coast for a few months until the next teas were ready at Foochow, then load up with silk and less expensive late season tea and return to England. Mrs. Black was convinced that Foochow had eclipsed Shanghai as a port for tea, due in part to the threat of the Taiping rebellion.

"We'll not see the old business until this bloody rebellion is over." She sighed.

The last 12-pounder from the clipper was being lowered away when *Vulcan*'s engine started up and she belched billows of black smoke. Captain Reach crossed over to *Celestial* and hailed Fletcher Wood at the entrance to the saloon where he was talking to Captain Black's wife.

"Beg your pardon, folks, don't want to interrupt, but here's the bill of lading – everything on the list is on board *Vulcan* and accounted for."

"Very good," Fletcher said. "Cranking her up already, I see."

"Anxious to be under way, captain?" Mrs. Black said.

"I would not be in such a haste, ma'am, as to discharge my ramrod, but there's a gander-party of the Queen's own yonder rowing thisaway from the Bund, and looking mighty riled. You appear to have waked a few snakes, Mr. Wood."

Tiffin was approaching when Consul Masters had a moment free from business and went upstairs to a room with windows that looked out over the harbor. Through a telescope he took from a bookshelf, he saw the steam tug *Tayung* chugging out into the channel down river towing the French steam frigate HIMS *Du Chayla*. Finally, he thought, there goes Baron Galle off to the Gulf of Pecheli. Now that both of the plenipotentiaries have left for the north, we need only be rid of the American minister to have some peace and quiet in the consulate.

In the week between their arrival from Hong Kong and their departure for the Peiho, Exter and Galle had caused endless clamor and confusion and accomplished little to reduce English and French suspicions of one another's motives.

With Exter away from Shanghai, Blaine will be a minister again and less unpleasant than when he was a sibling as well, reminded daily how his older brother displaced him from the fortunes of the Exter and Kilmarnock earldom, and knighthood. Harbor seems smaller now that most of the ships of the expedition have left, and taken with them the troops. All we have left are the six hundred of the Loodianah Regiment, four hundred Royal Marines, and the French say they left behind two hundred, mostly invalids.

There's *Celestial*. And that looks Fletcher Wood on board her – dressed like an undertaker as usual. Evans did well to bring her captain and Artemis Fuller in to the customs office. Excellent. Wait…is that a steamer tied up beside her? Yes, that's the old rattletrap *Vulcan*. Blast!

"Bitterman. Bitterman! Where is that slowcoach?"

Blast! That's a gun being hauled up from *Celestial*'s hold.

"Yes sir?" Bitterman said from the doorway.

"Those blighters Russell & Company have gone and chartered Wood a steamer. The bounder is taking his guns! Get me the marine officer on duty. I want a detail to go aboard that ship *Celestial* and take that damned Fletcher Wood in charge."

"The American, sir?"

"Yes, confound it, the American."

洋神 *Yang Shen*   *James Lande* 藍德

Yang Shen Glossary

Dialects of pronunciations are (M) Mandarin, and (C) Cantonese. (WG) indicates a Wade-Giles romanization. Phonetic pronunciations (*pr.*) offered for Chinese words are spelled in a manner that will result in a fairly close rendering of Mandarin by most American speakers of English, at least where the same sound exists in both languages.

The English glossary is followed by a brief Chinese-to-English glossary.

(Dana) indicates a word or phrase from Dana, 1863 *Sailor's Manual*. (Smythe) indicates Smythe, 1867 *The Sailor's Word Book*.

English Glossary

a la Russe – in the Russian manner, as Susan Lasdun tells us on p. 116 of 1981 *Victorians at Home*, which was to set the food out on a side-board from which servants handed the dishes around to guests to help themselves, and was an obviously more frugal way of serving less food at a large gathering.

AB – able-bodied seaman.

aback – sails pressed against a mast instead of filled out by the wind.

abaft – toward the stern; behind.

aft – toward the rear, or toward the stern of a ship.

a-lee – in the same direction the wind is blowing; with the wind, not into the wind; sheltered from the wind. Helm a-lee: the wheel turns downwind, causing the rudder to turn toward the wind, which brings the bow of a vessel around into the wind, against the direction from which the wind is blowing.

amidships – in the center of a vessel.

An-nan 安南 – (M) Annam, old name for Vietnam.

arm – the extreme outward tip of a yard, as in yardarm.

assizes – sessions of a high court held periodically to hear cases, of a legislature or assembly to make laws. In 1967 *Law in Imperial China*, Bodde and Morris explain there were two assizes in imperial China (p. 134-43), the Autumn Assizes 秋審 for hearing capital cases from the provinces, and Court Assizes 朝審 for cases originating in Peking. Cases not meriting immediate execution often were put off until after the assizes to allow time for review.

astern – in the rear, behind the stern of a ship.

athwart – across a ship rather than in line with the ship (fore to aft; Dana).

athwart our hawse – across the bow; to cross in front. Cross my path (Dana).

avast heaving – arrest the capstan, stop it from turning (Smythe).

a-weather – toward the direction from which the wind blows; into the wind, not with the wind. Helm a-weather: the wheel turns upwind, causing the rudder to turn in a direction away from the wind, which brings the bow of a vessel around with the wind, in the same direction as the wind is blowing.

bankâ – a small boat in the Philippines, or a boat of any variety.

bannermen – see Eight Banners.

barangay – the smallest unit of Philippine government administration in the 19th century. Rizal wrote that a *cabeza de barangay* was a headman and tax-collector for a group of about fifty families, for whose "tribute" he was personally responsible. Rizal, 1912 *The Reign of Greed*.

barrio bajo – slum (Spanish).

Bashi-Bazouk – Turkish ruffians, noted by fastidious Englishmen for their unkempt dress and filthy habits. They joined the British and French in irregular units fighting the Russians during the Crimean war. See Brewer, 1970 *Dictionary of Phrase and Fable*, p. 82, and photo in Lawrence, *Crimea: 1854-1856*, 1981.

battlement – in a castle or on a Chinese town wall, the elevation of a wall at the very top that provides protection for soldiers and frequently has notches for shooting arrows or firing weapons.

beat – sailing into the wind by tacking a vessel; moving forward slowly, with great difficulty.

beating the booby – beating the hands against one's sides to warm up (Smythe).

Beecher's bibles – contemporary slang name for Sharps rifled carbines.

belaying-pin soup – beat with a belaying pin until the consistency of soup, strike in the head with a belaying pin, ill-treatment of enlisted men by officers. On a sailing ship, a belaying pin is an iron or hardwood rod two or three feet long to which lines are tied.
Bellerophon – young hero of Greek myth who mastered Pegasus, the flying horse, and slew the Chimera.
bend [a rope] – tie or fasten a rope, generally to something, such as a belaying pin.
betel nut – see *buyo*.
blancmange – a sweet pudding made using almond extract, milk and gelatin, and flavored with rum.
blind scouse – lobscouse with no meat. By analogy, a risky enterprise with an unpredictable outcome.
board – starboard, larboard; aboard. The distance between changes of direction when tacking. Board originally was used for the side of a ship, but the etymology of later use is vague.
board her in the smoke – to take by surprise by firing a broadside and boarding in the smoke (Smythe).
bow – the front-end of a vessel.
bower – a large anchor carried at the bow of a vessel.
brace – as in "brace the yards, trim the sails." On a square-rigged sailing vessel, with yards hung on a mast, to turn a yard and change the angle of a sail to the wind, using a rope (brace) run through a block at the end of the yard (yardarm) and down to the deck. See trim.
brace the yards – pull hard on the tackle holding yards in place (Dana).
braces – lines that turn yards (Dana).
brail, brailing – to take in sail; shorten sail.
brave – see *yung* 勇; also *chuang-yung* 壯勇.
breakbone fever – disease transmitted by *aedes* the mosquito, with symptoms of headache, joint pain, and rash; aka dengue fever. *Aedes* also transmits yellow fever. Use of the term breakbone fever dates from 1860, and may then have been thought to also mean malaria.
breeching – heavy rope secured to the cascabel (*q.v.*) of a gun to dampen recoil.
brevet – temporary appointment or commission in a higher position or rank.
Brown Bess – smooth-bore flintlock musket of .71 caliber in British service into the early 1840s.
Brunswick rifle – percussion rifle of .704 caliber in British service from the mid to late 1840s.
bung-full – (etymology vague) completely full, as with a barrel so full that the bunghole (where a wood faucet can be inserted) must be stopped to prevent leakage; filled up to the bunghole.
bunt – center area of a sail. The bunt of the foreyard is the center part of the lowest yard on a foremast.
buntlines – lines that fall across the front of a sail and are used to haul up the sail.
burgoo, loblolly and skillagalee – names for seasoned oatmeal (Smythe).
butcher's bill – count of dead and wounded (Smythe).
buyo – Betel nut, prepared for chewing by wrapping a piece of areca-nut with a little shell-lime in a betel-leaf. Rizal, 1912 *The Reign of Greed*.
by the mark, two and a quarter – a manner of calling out a depth of water, or the depth as "marked" in a sounding line dropped into water. Two and a quarter fathoms (fathom = 6 feet) is 13½ feet.
cable – a measure, either 600 feet (U.S.) or 720 feet (U.K.) long, equal to the length of an anchor cable. 100 fathoms.
Cadmus – in Greek myth, the founder of Thebes. See dragon's teeth.
Cape Horn fever – a sailor who feigns illness to avoid duty has caught Cape Horn fever.
capstan – on a sailing vessel in the 1860s, generally a vertical post or cylinder with horizontal bars extending out like spokes on a wheel, each bar manned by a sailor who pushes on the caps'n bar and turns capstan around to take up slack in a chain or rope.
carpe diem – sieze the day; enjoy today and forget about tomorrow.
cascabel – metal ball on the back end of cannon where breeching (*q.v.*) was secured.
casemate – reinforced shelter in a fortification, or protected enclosure on a ship, from which artillery is fired through openings (embrasures) generally large on the inside to allow access to a gun and small on the outside of the casemate to protect the men inside.
cathead – a heavy timber that extends out over each side of the fore end of a vessel, from which an anchor is suspended.
cat's-paw – a gentle breeze that ripples water surface as if touched softly by the paw of a cat.
catted anchor – from the verb cat, to suspend a ship's anchor from the cathead. A catted anchor is one that has been raised to the cathead and suspended there, usually waiting for the bottom of the anchor to be drawn further up to the railing and secured for a voyage.

cayuses – *pl.* wild horses, from an Indian word for ponies on open range. Cayuse.
censorate 樞垣 – (WG) *shu-yuan* (M). Office in the Chinese bureaucracy charged with oversight of the performance and behavior of officials. Some censors travelled circuits, checking on local authorities.
century – a unit of 100 men in a Roman legion.
Cerberus – a terrible three-headed hound that stood guard at the gates of Hades.
cheval-de-frise – usually a log with many wooden spikes, used to obstruct advancing cavalry or infantry,
ch'ien-chuang 錢莊 – (M) clearinghouse, bank. *Ch'ien-chuang* were small native banks, developed predominantly by Ningpo men during the 18th century, that issued notes, offered accounts for cash transactions, and extended simple credit to customers.
Charlie Noble – sailor's nickname for the galley stovepipe.
Chenkiang 鎮江 (WG) Chen-chiang, *pr.* chen as "jun" in junk: "Jun-jee-ong" (M). Town on lower reaches of the Yangtze river, 155 miles west of Shanghai, 39 miles east of Nanking. Aka "Chin-kiang." S. Wells Williams translated it as "Guard of the River."
Chiang-nan – see Kiangnan.
Chiang-nan Ta-ying 江南大營, (M) the Great Southern Imperial Encampment that laid siege to the Taiping in Nanking during the 1850s.
Chiang-su – see Kiangsu.
Chiang-yin – see Kiangyin.
chin-chin – (1) "please, please, *ch'ing-ch'ing* 請請, an essential of polite address;" (2) a gesture of greeting or respect; (3) any worship of a god: "chin-chin joss"; (3) a chat, a chin-wag (Merriam-Webster). Giles, in his *Glossary of the Far East*, says that ch'in-ch'in is "a corruption of the Chinese salutation 'Ch'ing, Ch'ing,' which answers to our goodbye, etc. To 'ch'in-ch'in joss' is to perform religious worship of any kind.
chuang-yung 壯勇 – (M) "irregular braves," a category of Green Standard soldiers assigned special duties. In 1860, *chuang-yung* were trained in western weapons and tactics and operated together with the Foreign Rifles in action against the Taiping army around Shanghai.
cittadella – citadel (Hungarian). Specifically, a fortress in Budapest.
clew to earing – literally, the diagonal of a square sail; figuratively, from top to bottom (*A Naval Encyclopedia*, L. R. Hammersly & Co., 1881)
close-hauled – relating to how the wind blows against a sail to gain propulsion. A vessel is close-hauled when the vessel moves into the wind at the sharpest possible angle, nearly head-on. By contrast, the vessel is not close-hauled when the wind blows directly on the face of the sail, at an angle perpendicular to the sail. Aka "full-and-by."
comanch – slang for Comanche Indian.
comprador – Chinese agent of a foreign firmn who deals with Chinese customers and suppliers.
con – perceive, understand; swindle or manipulate; study or memorize.
conjee – rice gruel (Smythe).
Conscience Whig – early manifestation of New England Republican, prominent in the late 1840s, opposed to slavery, which is why a southerner like Hannibal Benedict would have thought them the same as abolitionists.
contemn – to view with contempt or scorn; British usage, 1860.
copperhead – northerners who sympathized with the South in the American Civil War.
costermonger – British name for one who sells fruit and vegetables.
course – the lowest and largest sail on a square-rigged mast. Fore course is on the foremast; main course is on the main mast.
crank ship – a ship that is top-heavy, unwieldy, or easily tipped over.
cro'jack – see crossjack.
crossjack – *pr.* "cro'jack"; a name for the lowest yard on the mizzenmast, the aft mast of a ship.
cutwater – the part of the bow at the waterline. The sides of a ship's hull where they come together under the bow and "cut" through the water.
cyclops – giants in Greek myth with one eye in the middle of their foreheads.
dayo – Tagalog meaning foreigner, immigrant, or visitor. Also, "white man."
descry, descried – to discover something, or catch sight of something in the distance.
doxie – girlfriend; floozy, woman of loose morals.
dragon's blood – a dark-red color, as in the palm resin used for varnish; Emerson, *First Essays*:

洋神 *Yang Shen*　　　　　　　　　　　　　　　　　　　　　　*James Lande* 藍德

"Siegfried, in the *Nibelungen*, is not quite immortal, for a [linden] leaf fell on his back whilst he was bathing in the dragon's blood." See Brewer, 1970 *Dictionary of Phrase and Fable*.

dragon's teeth – In Greek myth, teeth from a sacred water-dragon that guarded the spring of Ares, the god of war. When planted in the ground, they sprang up as fierce warriors, fully armed and keen for battle. With five such warriors, Cadmus founded the city of Thebes and, with Medea's help, Jason defeated such warriors in Colchis and went on to win the Golden Fleece.

dunnage – loose wood stowed amongst cargo to prevent its motion; worthless scrap (Smythe).

Eight Banners – Manchu soldiers, as opposed to native Chinese soldiers. Manchu families all were organized under eight banners, of various colors, at the time the Manchu conquered China in the 17th century, and the organization persisted throughout the Ch'ing dynasty (Mongols also were under eight banners, as were Chinese who joined the invaders). Banners were distributed between Peking and small provincial garrisons, where their officers held joint authority with Chinese civil officials. Native Chinese were organized separately – see Green Flag.

Enfield rifle – percussion muzzle-loader firing a .577 caliber lubricated bullet (the grease was blamed for the 1857 Sepoy Mutiny) in British service from the mid-1850s into the 1860s.

extrality – shorter form of extraterritoriality, the convention holding that, while abroad, a foreign national has the right to be tried under the laws of his own country, and is exempt from prosecution under the local laws of the host nation..

fantods – the fidgets of officers (Smythe).

fathom – a depth of six feet.

felloe – the circular rim of a spoked wheel into which the outer ends of the spokes are fitted; the "tire" fits around this rim.

fender – on a vessel, this is a cylinder of soft material that hangs over the side to protect the hull.

filbustier – French for filibuster (*q.v.*; Smythe).

filibuster – a congressional delaying tactic, or a fomenter of foreign insurrection. Also, a native of the Philippines accused of advocating separation from Spain – Rizal, 1912 *The Reign of Greed*.

Flemish horse – an additional footrope at the end of topsail yards (Dana).

fo'c's'le – (*Pr. foke-sull*) a sailor's pronunciation of the word "forecastle."

fore-and-after – a ship or boat rigged with fore-and-aft sails in line with the direction of the vessel, as opposed to square sails rigged at right angles to the direction of the vessel; a schooner, for example, is rigged with fore-and-aft sails on two masts.

forecastle – *pr.* "fo'c's'le" (*folk-sull*); the part of the vessel forward of the foremast (the mast closest to the bow of a ship). The deck above the forecastle was the forecastle head, where the capstan and catheads were located, from which the anchor could be suspended. Inside the forecastle were the bunks and living area for ordinary sailors.

foretopman – sailor whose duty station was at the top of the lowest section of the foremast on a sailing vessel, and who was responsible for the lines and sails adjacent to the foretop. Masts on larger square-rigged vessels were stepped in several sections to achieve height, one atop the other; the foretop was the top of the lowest and largest section of the foremast. The foretop usually had a small platform around the top where, on war vessels, marine marksmen were placed during battle.

foreyard – the lowest yard on the foremast of a sailing vessel.

Fortunatus – a medieval German hero who owned a purse that was never empty of wealth. See Brewer, 1970 *Dictionary of Phrase and Fable*, p. 430. Reference to Wu Hsü's purse of Fortunatus appeared in the *North China Herald* of July 21, 1860.

Frenchman – sailor's term for any strange vessel (Smythe).

friction primer – a short, slender tube filled with a mixture of gunpowder inserted into the vent of a cannon and used to fire the cannon. A short friction wire grooved with teeth and affixed to a ring was pulled through the explosive compound to cause a spark, which detonated the gunpowder compound.

full and change – the days when the moon is (1) fullest, and (2) when it is new.

full-and-by – see close-hauled.

gabion – a bottomless cylindrical basket used in building entrenchments.

Galatea – an ocean nymph. See Brewer, 1970 *Dictionary of Phrase and Fable*, and Bullfinch.

Galle – fortified city at the southwest end of the British crown colony of Ceylon (now Sri Lanka). Galle was colonized by the Dutch in the 17th century, and later taken over by the British East India Company. Some say that Galle was the Tarshish that traded with the kingdom of Solomon.

gallowglass – a soldier, from the mercenaries hired by Irish chieftans called *gallóglach*.

gally dawnhaul – a thing that does not exist (literally, a line to haul down a ship's galley which, generally, is affixed to the deck and moves neither up nor down, except with the ship).

Ganymede – cupbearer, after the Greek myth of a youth made cupbearer to the gods on Olympus.

gingal – (gingall, jingal, jingall) a Chinese blunderbuss. From the Hindustani "jangal," a swivel. A large musket, in China generally fired from a swivel fixed on a wall or wooden post, but sometimes with the barrel resting on a second man's shoulder. Giles wrote that "there is very little recoil in these weapons as they weigh about 20 pounds and the charge is not rammed home, but just dropped down the muzzle" (1878 *Glossary of Reference on... Far East*). In 1975 *The Chinese Opium Wars*, p. 248, Jack Beeching adds that a gingal was about seven and one-half feet long and had a range of only 100 yards.

glacis – (*pr.* glacee) a gentle slope or incline that runs downward from a fortification and functions as a buffer, impeding approach to walls and denying a foothold at the base of a wall (Smythe).

godown – warehouse. From the Malay "godon," in Colcord, 1945 *Sea Language Comes Ashore*, p. 87.

godverdomme– "goddamn" (Dutch).

Green Flag – aka Green Standard, Army of the Green Standard. Native Chinese soldiers, as opposed to Manchu soldiers. Green Flag troops, land and water, were under provincial authority, and supplemented by local *yung* (*q.v.*) irregulars, and militia. Speaking very broadly, bannermen were "national" soldiery, and Green Flag regulars were "local" soldiery distantly similar to American "state" guardsmen. See Eight Banners.

griffin – clerk in a trading house; typically a young man still in his teens come out to China to make his fortune. Griffins worked as assistants to the taipans, the older China traders.

grogshop – British slang for a low-class bar; a dive.

grumbler – discontented but hard–working jack (sailor; Smythe).

gunwale – the upper rail of a vessel.

gutta percha – a kind of rubber from Southeast Asia that came into Western use in the mid 19th century.

Hakka 客家人 – a proud southern hill people of China, distinct in appearance, manner and customs from other southern Chinese. Many of the first Taiping leaders were Hakka.

halliards – lines that hoist yards (Dana).

hawsehole – opening in the side of a ship at the bow through which passes chain or cable.

heave the anchor – raise the anchor up (Dana).

heave-to – to stop the headway of a square-rigged ship by turning into the wind, or by backing sail.

helm a-lee – see "a-lee."

helm a-weather – see "a-weather."

helm up – turn the wheel (helm) steering a ship upwind, into the wind, into the direction from which the wind blows. In vessels rigged so that the rudder swung opposite to the turn of the helm, "helm up" would cause a vessel to turn downwind, with the wind, in the same direction as the wind.

hen frigate – vessel with the wife and/or family of a captain, master, or owner on board, especially so if they interfere with the running of the ship.

highbinder – a crooked politician.

hong 行 – *pr.* "hawng" (M). Business. From the generic Chinese term for a company.

horse – shove, push, or move something by means of great force. Also, provide horses.

hotwell – the hotwell collects water condensed from a steam engine for reuse in the boiler.

howitzer – artillery piece originally designed with a medium-length barrel that allow it to serve as both a cannon and as a mortar, shooting at a low angle for long range, and at a high angle for lobbing shells over walls and into encampments.

Howqua – (Houqua) Cantonese hong merchant highly regarded by the English of Opium War days and thought to be worth at least £26,000,000. In the 1917 *Encyclopedia Sinica*, Couling says on p. 240 that Howqua donated £1,100,000 of the £6 million ransom for Canton.

humihinga pa – still breathing (Tagalog)

idlers – sailors who don't go aloft, such as the carpenter and cook (Dana).

imps – short for imperials. "Imperials" is used throughout in place of "imperialists" to indicate "imperial government" and avoid the connotation of "nation building."

in medeas res – in the middle of things, at a time when the action is already underway, rather than at the chronological beginning of the story or epic poem being related.

instant – in the present month; as in "Tuesday, the 5th inst." for the 5th of this month.

洋神 *Yang Shen*   *James Lande* 藍德

irons, in irons – the bow of a vessel cannot be made to come about one way or another when attempting to turn (tack) through the wind to a new direction (Dana). A ship caught between the equal forces of wind and current can also be said to be "in irons."

jack – a sailor.

Jacob's ladder – in marine usage, a rope ladder with wooden rungs lowered over the side of a vessel.

jibber the kibber – to decoy a vessel onto the shore for plunder. See mooncurser.

jonathan – an American (Smythe).

joskins – yankee slang for hayseeds and townsmen aboard ship, in Cole, 1934 *The Irrepressible Conflict*.

joss – a corruption of the Portuguese word for God, *Deos*, originating in Macau and spreading along coastal China in the 19th century as a pidgin word for things related to religion; e. g. joss idols, joss sticks, joss money. Joss also came to mean "luck."

joss-house – Chinese temple. The Victorian name for a Chinese temple, the place where a joss was kept (Kieth Stevens, "The Taking of Chapu," JHKBRAS, Vol. 34 (1994), p. 119, n. 7).

Kaffir Wars – aka Xhosa Wars, nine wars fought by native Africans against European settlers in South Africa over the years 1811 through 1879. Fletcher refers to the war fought in 1856-58.

kedge anchor – a small anchor used to kedge a vessel – to shift the position of a vessel.

keelhaul – to secure a man by the wrists with rope and drag him from one side to the other *under* a vessel. Used for hazing or punishment in the old days of sailing, the victim had to be able to hold his breath for the duration he was submerged in water in order to survive the experience.

keelson – a small keel over the main keel of the hull of a vessel, the keel being the central beam that runs the length of the bottom of a vessel.

Kiangnan 江南 – (WG) Chiang-nan, *pr*. "Jee-ong-non" (M). Literally "South of the River," meaning in the broadest sense all China south of the Yangtze River, a sort of Chinese Mason-Dixon line, but more often thought of as the broad expanse of the Yangtze delta, south from Nanking to Hangchow, and east to the Pacific Ocean.

Kiangsu 江蘇 – (WG) Chiang-su, *pr*. "Jee-ong-soo" (M). East China province in which are located the city of Shanghai, and the towns of Sungkiang (Sung-chiang) and Tsingpoo (Ch'ing-pu).

Kiangyin 江陰 (WG) Chiang-yin, *pr*. "Jee-ong-yeen" (M). Town on lower reaches of the Yangtze river, 90 miles west of Shanghai.

kiss the gunner's daughter – to be thrown over the breech of a cannon and whipped.

knot – "nautical" mile, about 1.15 land miles.

krummholz – sparse and stunted forest at high elevations and along timberlines.

K'ung-fu-tze 孔夫子 – (M) Mandarin pronunciation of "Confucius."

lanyard – a small cord or rope used for securing or suspending small objects.

laodah 老大 – "old-great"; *pr*. "lao-dah" (M); *lodaai* "low-dai" (C). Honorific for a man in charge, or the captain of a vessel; the "oldest and most accomplished, or wisest." Also romanized as *lao-ta* (WG).

larboard – old term for port, or left. Board originally meant the side of a ship.

larbowlines – the larboard, or port, watch (Dana).

Laestrygonians – in the Odyssey, a tribe of cruel cannibals that murder many of Ulysses' men.

lee – see leeward.

leech – vertical edge of a square sail; weather leech is the edge closest to the wind.

leeward – in the same direction toward which the wind blows; downwind; with the wind. Opposite of windward, which is toward the direction from which the wind blows. *Pr*. "lew-ard."

leeward rail – when the wind blows across a vessel, one rail, or side, is closest to the direction from which the wind blows, and the other rail is farthest. The closer rail is the windward rail (wind'rd rail), and the farther rail is the leeward rail (lee'rd rail).

left bank – the bank on the left when facing down a river.

li 里 – Chinese measure of distance, about ⅓ of an American mile, or ½ of a kilometer; "Chinese mile."

lifts – lines that tilt yards (Dana).

limbered – equipped with a limber; a limber is the part of a field gun carriage to which the trail is raised and attached for pulling the gun with a horse. By itself, the limber is essentially an ammunition box mounted atop an axle and two wheels. When attached to the gun carriage, the limber in effect changes the gun carriage into a four-wheel wagon.

Liu-ch'iu 琉球 – (M) Okinawa.

lobscouse – a sailor's stew of meat, vegetables, and bread. See blind scouse.

洋神 *Yang Shen*   *James Lande* 藍德

lodaai 老大 – (C) Cantonese for *laodah*.
Long River – the Yangtze River, *ch'ang-chiang* (WG) 長江.
loose the sails – loosen sails and let them fall open to catch wind (Dana).
lorcha – junk with a Western-style hull and Chinese sails. Portuguese first built lorchas in Macao.
lubricator – device for lubricating moving metal parts through copper tubes fed oil from cloth wicks.
luff – a sail that ripples and shakes when the wind shifts (because the wind is blowing across the face of the sail) is said to be luffing. Also, to steer the bow of a ship into the wind.
luff-tackle – a block-and-tackle with two blocks, a double-block (a line passes through the block twice) and a single-block (a line passes through the block once) used for lifting very heavy weights and for hauling tight the running rigging that controls a ship's sails and yards (sheets, braces, halyards).
mainbrace – the line that turns the main yard.
main-truck – truck at the top of the mainmast. See truck.
manila rope – rope that did not have to be tarred (Smythe).
mantlet – a portable shelter for protecting soldiers when attacking a fortification.
Manilaman – contemporary name for people from Manila, i.e. Filipinos. The term "Filipino" had not yet come into common use in 1860.
mares tails – a change in the clouds which indicates a wind rising (Smythe).
maskee – pidgin English of ambiguous pedigree. "All right," "never mind," and "however" are all valid readings depending on context. See "Maskee" in the Underfoot, Chapter 18.
Minié rifle – percussion muzzle-loader of .702 caliber, firing an expanding bullet instead of a ball, that was in British service in the early 1850s.
miss our stays – to fail to complete a tack (when a ship cannot turn her bow across the wind).
moderator oil lamp – Susan Lasdun, on p. 56 of 1981 *Victorians at Home*, describes this oil-lamp as having a small tube through which oil was forced up to the wick in a controlled amount by a spring-operated piston. It was displaced by the kerosene lamp in the late 1860s.
monsoon – seasonal wind that blows from the southwest between about April and October (summer monsoon), and from the northeast between October and April. In east China, in particular, the monsoons greatly influence seasonal rainfall, typhoons, and ocean currents.
mooncursor – a person who deliberately causes shipwrecks. A mooncursor might tie a lantern to a hobbled horse on a dark and stormy night lure an unsuspecting ship into bad water. In the south of old England, such an evildoer would curse the moon when it was so bright as to reveal the shipwrecker's stratagem. From Colcord, 1945 *Sea Language Comes Ashore*, p. 131. See "jibber the kibber."
Mount Tai – mountain holy to Chinese for over 3000 years, located in Shan-tung Province. The emperor worshiped heaven there, and pilgrims still visit its many temples.
mouse, to raise a mouse – to strike a blow that raises a lump (Smythe).
Mrs. Grundy – a prudish arbiter of social behavior; from a character in an 18th century novel *Speed the Plough* by Thomas Morton.
mungo – see wool mungo.
Ningpo Guild 四明公所 – (WG) Ssu-ming Kung-so, *pr*. "Soo-ming Goong-suo" (M). A native-place association of Chinese from Ningpo formed for mutual-assistance between men who shared a common origin and dialect, and whose families usually still resided in the native-place. Also known generally as *T'ung-hsiang-hui* 同鄉會, "same-place association."
nun buoy – a buoy that tapers from a wide base to a narrow top.
oakum – strands of jute or hemp soaked in tar and stuffed into cracks and seams as caulking.
oculi – *(pl.)* a circular opening, a window; eyes.
oetlul – "bloody idiot" (Dutch)
Omphale's wheel – Hercules was a slave for a year to Omphale, who made him wear women's clothes and hold wool for her spinning wheel. An allusion implying servitude and humiliation.
pansit – a soup made of Chinese vermicelli. A Philippine noodle dish. Rizal, 1912 *The Reign of Greed*.
parapet – an elevation of earth, stone or wall for the protection of soldiers.
parcel – see worm, parcel and serve.
Parsee – Generally, natives of Bombay, descended from Persians originally resettled in India in the 10th century, who are Zoroastrians.
Parthian shot – a shot delivered while retreating; from the mounted archers of ancient Parthia know for the stratagem of twisting around on their galloping horses to release arrows at an enemy in pursuit.

洋神 *Yang Shen* James Lande 藍德

pawl – on a geared wheel, a wood or metal spur that rests on the gear teeth, clicking on the teeth as the wheel turns in one direction, then falling in between the gear teeth to lock the geared wheel in place when the direction is reversed.
pay off – when a vessel's head falls off from the wind (Dana).
pecksniffery – sanctimonious hypocrisy; from a character in Dickens, *Martin Chuzzlewit*.
pendant – a short rope or strap, fixed to a mast or yard, that has an metal eye spliced into the lower end to receive the hooks of the main and fore tackles (Smythe).
pennet – sailor's word for a rope or line.
Per Mare Per Terram – by sea and by land (motto of British Royal Marines).
petard – a container of explosives used to blow apart barricades, gates and walls. "Hoisted by his own petard" is someone who has fallen victim to his own, usually nefarious, schemes.
pidgin – "business" in pidgin English.
polo – forced labor in the 19th century Philippines; from *polista* (Spanish). See Arcilla, *An Introduction to Philippine History*, p. 24.
Polyphemus – a cyclops; son of Poseidon. In the Odyssey, Polyphemus is made drunk and blinded with a burning brand so that Ulysses and his men may escape being eaten alive by the cyclops. In Ovid, Polyphemus is the jealous suitor of Galatea (*qv*).
poop deck – the part of the main deck aft (behind) of the mizzenmast (the mast closest to the stern of a ship); called the quarterdeck on naval vessels. Many clipper poop decks had a skylight over a saloon below, a companionway leading down to the saloon, and a binnacle (which held the compass) and helm located along the center of the poop deck, but the appointments varied.
pugaree – a cloth wrapped around a helmet to protect the back of the neck from the sun.
pukka sahib – Hindi for excellent fellow
purser's grin – a sneer (Smythe).
pusa 補子 – (M) a badge of rank. A large cloth square, *pu-chang* 補章, embroidered on the chest and the back of the surcoat of a mandarin or his wife, which used a symbolic bird or beast to represent one of the official grades 1 through 9, civil and military.
quarterdeck – the part of the main deck aft of the mizzenmast on a naval vessel (the mast closest to the stern of a ship); called the poop deck on clipper ships.
quarter gunner – a petty officer subordinate to a gunner in a ship of war. The quarter gunner generally was assigned to care for four guns, keeping them in good condition and ready for service.
que magnifico! – "How magnificent!" (Spanish)
que milagro! – "Such a miracle!" (Spanish)
ratline – ropes tied as steps up the shrouds of a square-rigged ship.
right bank – the bank on the right when facing down a river in the same direction as the flow.
runner – in the context of Chinese officialdom, low-level yamen functionary who performed a variety of menial tasks for the magistrate – policeman, guard, messenger, jailor, doorman and so on. Chü T'ung-tsu has a chapter on government runners in 1969 *Local Government in China under the Ch'ing*. Runners often abused their authority and apparently were not greatly loved by the Chinese populace.
running rigging – lines and cables that control the movement of sails of a vessel.
samshu – pidgin for a Chinese liquor, clear in color, distilled from rice, sorghum, or maize. The name *samshu* probably comes from the Cantonese for *shao-chiu* 燒酒, but "*samshu*" was likely used for any variety of Chinese liquors that are clear in color, including rice wine 白酒 or 米酒, *mao-t'ai* 茅臺酒, *kao-liang* 高粱酒, *wu-liang-yeh* 五糧液 (firewater made from five ingredients: sorghum, wheat, corn, and two kinds of rice), and so on.
sangley – old Tagalog word for Chinese (of unmixed blood).
screw steamer – steamer with a propeller instead of paddle wheels.
sennit – interwoven strands of rope yarn.
seraglio – Italian (from Turkish) for the palace of a sultan, containing a harem in which wives are secluded, and other private quarters. A seraglio is entered through a Sublime Gate.
serve – see worm, parcel and serve.
sheer – the curvature of a vessel's hull. Sheer strakes are the longitudinal planking with the greatest curvature fore and aft.
sheerleg – spar used for raising or lowering a mast. Worcester, 1971 *Junks and Sampans of the Yangtze*, p. 75, differs from definitions of a sheerleg as a kind of floating crane. The idea for using the yuloh

洋神 *Yang Shen*　　　　　　　　　　　　　　　　　　　　　　　　　　*James Lande* 藍德

sweep as the spar came from http://corribee.org/technical/mast/. Sheerlegs are used today to form a tall tripod with a pulley at the apex for stepping and unstepping masts.

sheer-strakes – the line of plank on a vessel's side, running fore and aft under the gunwale. They were attached to the ribs of the ship's body with large wooden dowels called treenails.

sheet – rope attached to the lower corner of a square sail that spreads the sail and keep it taught (Dana).

shivaree – a loud reception, a burlesque for newlyweds.

short sixes – a fight (Taylor and Whiting, 1958 *Dictionary of American Proverbs…*).

shot and shell – shot was solid iron and did not explode. Canister shot was a projectile filled with small iron balls that spread in flight – canister did not explode either. Shell was a hollow iron ball packed with powder – set off by a fuse ignited by the discharge of the cannon – that exploded in seconds and spewed iron fragments. Shot was for damaging things – ship's rigging and stone walls. *Shell was for killing men and horses.* Spherical case was sometimes called "shot," but strictly speaking any hollowed-out exploding projectile was a shell (as in "hollow shell").

shroff – one who measures the weight and quality of gold and silver.

shrouds – lines supporting masts from the sides (Dana).

skillagalee – a watery gruel or porridge; also, a worthless fellow.

skirr – move along at a rapid pace; hasty departure.

soldier's wind – a wind so easy to sail in even a soldier could sail a vessel in it.

spanker – a large fore-and-aft sail hung off the mizzenmast of a square-rigged vessel.

speak a ship – to hail her, as *Game Cock* hailed *Essex* near Woosung (Dana).

splice the mainbrace – jargon for issuing drink to a crew; serve grog after severe exertion (Smythe).

splicer – (*archaic*) sailor; a marlin-spike seaman; rope expert. One who splices rope.

standing rigging – shrouds and stays (lines and cables) that hold the masts of a sailing vessel in place.

starboard – the right side of a ship. "Star" came from steer, and "board" for the side of a ship, and "starboard" originally was used for vessels propelled or steered by a paddle or oar on the right side of a vessel. *Online Etymology Dictionary*, www.etymonline.com.

starbowlines – the starboard watch (Dana).

stays – lines supporting masts fore and aft, forestays and backstays (Dana).

stern – the rear of a boat or ship.

stinkpot – a Chinese clay or ceramic weapon filled with noxious chemicals and thrown by hand; a sort of hand grenade.

stokehold – opening at front of a boiler through which fuel is passed into the boiler.

strake – longitudinal planking of a wooden vessel.

supercargo – officer concerned with the commercial activities of a ship.

sycee – Chinese silver made in the shape of ingots, from two to about six inches in length, that were often called "shoes" because of their resemblance to footwear.

Ta-jen 大人 – (M) polite term of address for an official; "great man." Excellency.

tabernacle – on a junk, "a housing, or case, extending from a foot or so above deck level to the bottom of the junk," into which the mast is placed, like a rose stem in a slender vase, and braced with chocks between the mast and the bulkhead. Junk masts have no stays and shrouds for support of a mast in the manner of square-rigged clipper ships. Worcester, *Junks and Sampans of the Yangtze*, p. 75.

tack – (1) to turn the bow of a ship through the wind. (2) The side of a vessel on which she has the wind ("starboard tack" – wind is on the starboard side). (3) Rope or tackle leading forward from the weather clew of a course (large sail at the bottom of a mast; Dana). See tack.

tael – *liang* 兩 (M). Chinese silver currency which, in 1860, was common in the form a small "shoes."

tafferel – also "taffrail"; the part of a vessel's rail above the stern (Dana).

taotai 道台 – (WG) *tao-t'ai, pr.* "dow-tai" (M). "Intendant of circuit"; Chinese official. "The chief local magistrate is the *taotai*, who is the governor of two *fu* and one *chou*, having altogether 22 *ching*, or walled cities, under his jurisdiction; from Smith, 1847 *Consular Cities of China*, probably referring to a particular *taotai*. In 1938 *Clippers and Consuls*, p. 46, Griffin notes that the Treaty of Wanghsia placed consuls on a level of equality with a *taotai*, or a prefect.

tap the admiral – said of one who'd drink anything. "He'd tap the admiral to get a drink." from the sailor who stole spirits from the cask in which a dead admiral was being conveyed to England (Smythe).

taper – a long, thin candle used to light other candles or lamps; the wick or cord in an oil lamp that feeds fuel to the flame.

tarred with the same brush – blamed for something for the same reason as another (Smythe).
tayo na! – let's go! (Tagalog)
thimblerigger – a swindler; one who employs an old shell game to swindle the rubes (place a pea under one of three inverted cups, shuffle the cups, and invite a sucker to guess under which cup lies the pea).
three-tailed pasha – pasha or bashaw, a Turkish officer of high rank, the lesser pashas being preceded by only two or one horse-tail on march or in camp. Brewer, 1970 *Dictionary of Phrase and Fable*, p. 808.
thumbstall – a sheath that protects the thumb when blocking a vent (*q.v.*), when loading an artillery piece.
tidewaiter – A customs official who boarded ships as they arrived in port on the tide. Colcord, 1945 *Sea Language Comes Ashore*.
tiffin – noonday meal, a word brought from India by the British and grafted into treaty port jargon.
tillite – a mix of dirt, sand, and rock detritus pushed along around the foot and margin of drifting glaciers.
ti-pao 地保 – (M) village constable. The *ti-pao* was part of the Qing *bao-chia* 保甲 system for local security based on units of ten households, the later rendition of the *li-chia* 里甲 system established to manage tax collection and labor service by the first Ming emperor Ming T'ai-tzu 明太祖. On p. 190 of *The District Magistrate*, Watt uses "village constable" for *ti-pao*. Giles calls the *ti-pao* a beadle in "The Fighting Cricket" story from *Strange Stories from a Chinese Studio* 聊齋誌異.
Tiresias – Soothsayer of Thebes, a seer blinded by the gods, either for telling their secrets, or for coming upon Athena naked in her bath. As if that was not enough, Tiresias was changed by Hera to a woman for seven years when he offended her; he had to live as a prostitute. The shade of Tiresias in hell, called up by Odysseus, warned the hero of dangers ahead. Tiresias appears often in art and as a walk-on character or allusion in literature from the Odyssey to the Alexandria Quartet.
toff – British slang for gentleman.
Tolosa – city of ancient Gaul (roughly the location of modern France) plundered by the Romans in 106 BC. A large store of gold and silver was taken from the Druid temple of Apollo. See Brewer, 1970 *Dictionary of Phrase and Fable*, p. 472.
tompion – a plug or cover for the muzzle of a gun (a cannon).
trail – the part of a field gun carriage that "trails" along on the ground behind the gun. The trail is lifted and moved right or left to point the gun. The trail is also hooked up to a limber, a "wagon harness," so that the gun may be pulled by a horse.
treenail – wooden dowling used to hold together parts of the hull of a vessel, as the planking to the ribs or other beams.
trim the yards – adjust sail to catch the wind by moving the yards (Dana).
trim, trimmed – as in "brace the yards, trim the sails." On a sailing vessel, (1) to adjust the angle of a sail so as to most effectively catch the wind; (2) to arrange cargo, ballast or passengers so that a vessel floats evenly in the water without any undue list, tilting to one side or the other, or fore or aft.
truck – small platform or wood cap at the top of a mast, from which pennants and flags may be flown. Also, the wheel of a gun carriage.
trunnions – projections on each side of a cannon that rest in recesses on the top of a gun carriage.
ultimo – in the month preceding this month; as in "Tuesday, the 5th ult." for the 5th of last month.
VC – Victoria Cross, England's highest medal for courage above and beyond the call of military duty.
vedette – a mounted sentry that ranged forward of pickets.
vent – a small passage from the outside of a cannon into the gun's powder chamber; a friction primer was inserted into the vent.
Vulcan – Roman god of fire; smithy to the gods on Mount Olympus. The Chinese equivalent, Huo Wang 火王, is described in the Underfoot, Chapter 24.
waist – the "waist" of a vessel, its middle portion; the part of the main deck that lies between the forecastle and the quarterdeck.
Wandering Rocks – rocks at sea said to smash ships and scatter the remains. In Homer's Odyssey, Circe, the sorceress, tells Odysseus about the route past Wandering Rocks and on toward the monsters Scylla and Charybdis.
warp – to move a ship by attaching a line to a fixed object and taking up the line on the ship's capstan.
watch-tackle – a small block-and-tackle, a luff-tackle, with a short fall (the rope pulled on), easily moved about, and used for various purposes about the deck of a ship.
water gate – *shui-men* 水門, an opening to allow passage of a stream through the wall of an old Chinese city, just as a city gate allowed passage of a road through the city wall. All manner of boat traffic

洋神 *Yang Shen*   *James Lande* 藍德

entered the city through the water gate, just like foot traffic, but the dimensions of the water gate, perhaps only ten feet high, limited the size of vessels that could pass.

wear – to turn the stern of a ship through the wind.

weather – toward the wind, on the side exposed to the wind. "Weather braces" are braces – ropes that turn yards – on the weather side of a yard. A ship with a "weather helm" tends to steer into the wind.

wei-ch'i 圍棋 – Chinese game of military strategy employing black and white stones on a board (called *Go* in Japan).

whistling psalms to the tafferail – giving advice that is not being heeded by the listener (Smythe).

windlass – a device for winding chain or rope.

windward – toward the direction from which the wind blows; upwind; into the wind. Opposite of leeward, which is in the same direction as the wind.

wool mungo – reclaimed wool of poor quality and short staple, used as a textile fiber for making yarn.

worm, parcel, and serve – a practice on old square-riggers for preserving rope. To worm is to wind twine into the spiral grove of a plaited Manila rope, to fill the groove to keep water out, protect from chafing, and create a smooth surface. Parcel is to wrap the rope tightly with canvas. After parceling, a rope is served by winding cord closely and tightly around the rope to further prevent chafe and wear. A rope wormed, parceled, and served can then be coated with tar or varnish.

worming staff – think "corkscrew for a cannon" – intertwined metal coils that catch hold of trash (wadding, cartridge bags) in the barrel of a cannon so it can be drawn out. Manucy, 1949 *Artillery Through the Ages*....

yang-kuei-tzu 洋鬼子 – (M) foreign devil (many Chinese today are embarrassed by the term 洋鬼子).

yamen (WG: ya-men) – administrative office and residence for mandarins at several levels of Chinese government, aka yamun.

yard – the "crosspiece" hung on a ship's mast. The clipper ships of the 1860s generally had three vertical masts (*fore*mast, *main*mast, and *mizzen*mast), and each mast had five yards, hung at intervals up the mast, from which sail was suspended. The lowest yard was named according to its mast: foreyard and mainyard; the lowest yard on the mizzenmast was the exception, called the crossjack yard (*pr.* cro'jack). The next higher yard on each mast was the lower topsail yard, then the upper topsail yard, the topgallant yard, and the royal yard.

yardarm – the extreme outward tip of a yard.

yuloh 搖櫓 – *Yao-lu* (M); a long sculling oar, a sweep, for propelling and steering small to medium sized water craft in China, mounted usually at the stern, and sometimes also at the bow. The boatman stands and pushed the *yuloh* from side-to-side.

yung 勇 – (M) "braves," irregular soldiery generally called up by provincial authorities in times of crisis.

Chinese Glossary (^{G12345} refers to the Giles dictionary number for a character)

Places along the lower Yangtze

蕪湖 – *Wu-hu*, Wuhoo   太平 – *T'ai-ping*, Taiping
和州 – *Ho-chou*   浦口 – *P'u-kou*
天京 – *T'ien-ching*   鎮江 – *Chen-chiang*, Chenkiang
焦山 – *Chiao-shan*, Silver Island   丹徒 – *Tan-t'u*
江陰 – *Chiang-yin*, Kiangyin

江陰運河 – Kiangyin Canal. When the old canal from Chenkiang to Wu-chin could no longer be used, traffic moved to the shorter route that flows from Lake T'ai through Wu-yang and Kiangyin to Huang-t'ien-kang 黃田港.

句容 – Chü-jung

鹿茆口 – *Lu-mao-k'ou*. "Deer-park." *Mao* 茆 is a "water-mallow"^{G7696} sometimes used for *mao* 茅. Pai-*mao-gen* 白茅根 is the root of rushes, used as a "febrifuge," an agent that reduces fever.

狼山 – *Lang-shan* (Wolf Mountain). Opposite Fushan, on the left bank, bearing roughly 7 miles NNE (see 江蘇全省與圖, p. 249, and Williams *Commercial Guide*, p. 147). In 1860, this location was the most difficult patch along the lower reaches of the Yangtze.

福山 – *Fu-shan*, Fushan
福山口 – *Fu-shan-k'ou*

洋神 *Yang Shen*   *James Lande* 藍德

福山塘 – *Fu-shan-t'ang*. Flows from Fushan to Chang Shu, and thence to Soochow
白茆口 – *Pai-mao-k'ou*
白茆塘 – *Pai-mao-t'ang*. Flows from Pai-mao-k'ou to Chang Shu, and thence to Soochow
寶山 – *Pao-shan*, Paoshan
吳松 – *Wu-sung*, Woosung
崇明島 – *Ch'ung-ming-tao*, Tsungming Island
崇寶沙 – *Ch'ung-bao-sha*, Bush Island. In the old maps of Che-chiang, the island just northwest of Woosung, between the Huangpu and Tsungming Island has this name. It should be northeast of Wu-sung now. If you look at the name, it seems obvious that it means "the sand bank 沙 between Tsungming Island 崇明島 and Paoshan 寶山. Of course, that was 140 years ago – now it should be called 崇吳沙, for the sand bank between Tsungming Island 崇明島 and Woosung 吳松!

Detail locations cited above along the river were found in Maps of All Kiangsu 江蘇全省輿圖, *based on the edition of the 21ˢᵗ year of Kuang-hsü* 清光緒二十一年刊本, *reprinted by* Cheng-wen Publishers 成文出版社.

Towns on the Grand Canal 京杭大運河
丹陽 – *Tan-yang*, Tanyang   常州 – *Ch'ang-chou*, Changchow
武進 – *Wu-chin*   無錫 – *Wu-hsi*
蘇州 – *Su-chou*, Soochow   杭州 – *Hang-chou*, Hangchow

Other locations in Kiangnan
江南 – *Chiang-nan* (Kiangnan)   南京 – *Nan-ching*, Nanking (T'ien-ching)
安徽 – *An-hui* province   寧波 – *Ning-po*
金壇 – *Chin-t'an*, Kintan (south of Changchow)   崑山 – *K'un-shan*
太倉 – *T'ai-ts'ang*   嘉定 – *Chia-ting*, Kading
清浦 – *Ch'ing-p'u*, Tsingpoo   廣福林 – *Kuang-fu-lin*, Kuangfulin
松江 – *Sung-chiang*, Sungkiang   高橋 – *Kao-ch'iao*, Kaojiao
黃浦江 – *Huang-p'u-chiang*, Whampoa River   金山衛 – *Kin-shan-wei*
广德 – *Kuang-te*   建平 – *Chian-p'ing*
溧陽 – *Li-yang*   金壇 – *Chin-t'an*
南橋 – *Nan-ch'iao*, Nanjiao   楊中 – *Yang-chung*
鎮江 – *Chen-chiang*   丹徒 – *Tan-t'u*

Shanghai Localities
黃浦江 – *Huang-p'u chiang*, Huang-pu River; Whampoa River
吳淞江 – *Wu-sung chiang*, Wu-sung River; Soochow Creek
虹口 – *Hung-kou*, Hongkew
外灘 – *Wai-t'an*, the Bund
洋涇浜 – *Yang-king-bang*, Yangkingbang Creek
大北門 – *Ta bei-men*, Great North Gate
關帝廟 – *Kuan-ti miao*, Temple of the God of War (Kuanti Temple)
城隍廟 – *Ch'eng-huang miao*, Temple of the City God
大東門 – *Ta tung-men*, Great East Gate
道署 – *tao shu*, Circuit Intendant's Yamen
火神廟 – *Huo-shen Miao*, Temple of the God of Fire
水仙宮 – *Shui-hsien Kung*, Temple of the Water Sprite
董家渡 – *T'ung-chia-tu*, T'ung Family Ferry
浦東 – *P'u-tung*, Pootung Peninsula (east of the "Poo" river, the Huang-p'u)
龍華寺 – *Lung hwa shih*, the Lungwa Pagoda (south of the city)
徐家匯 – *Hsu-chia-wei*, Siccawei

洋神 *Yang Shen*   *James Lande* 藍德

Yang Shen "Underfoot"

    Following the fashion for interlinears and underbooks in works of fiction, here rests much of the impedimenta that missed the sailing of Yang Shen *and was stowed away out of sight with the other apparatus of glossary and bibliography already encumbering the book. In the "Underfoot," fictional warp is teased apart from factual woof, and readers can themselves decide if the weave of historical fact and informed conjecture yields a tapestry of fictional speculation that will wear. In addition to the contemporary newspapers, journals, letters, accounts and documents that served as firsthand sources for the fiction of* Yang Shen, *here also are noted many fine examples from among the wealth of growing expertise on the later Ch'ing (Qing) dynasty. These include dissertations and studies selected in part to incorporate in the novel the most recent scholarship in the field of Chinese history (regardless of how uncomfortable some such historians might feel in the company of* Yang Shen's *fictional crowd). The "Underfoot" also provides a venue for mulling over issues surrounding incident described in* Yang Shen *as seem to merit further consideration. Sources are referred to here by the author's name unless more than one title is cited for the author in the bibliography, and by the convention of abbreviation for frequently cited titles. For example:*

IWSM   清代籌辦夷務始末 *Ch'ing-tai Chou-p'an I-wu Shih-mo,* "Ch'ing Dynasty Management of Barbarian Affairs from Beginning to End."

NCH   *North China Herald.*

BPP   *British Parliamentary Papers.*

WHTA   吳煦檔案中的太平天國史料選輯 *Wu Hsü Tang-an Chung de T'ai-p'ing Tien-kuo Shih-liao Hsuan-hui,* "Selection of Taiping Historical Materials from the Documents of Wu Hsü."

Abbreviations

    EVA – Ever-victorious Army, *chang-sheng-chün* 常勝軍.
    AEF – Allied Expeditionary Force, of British and French.

Map Sources

    (Maps not cited are freehand drawings based on general sources.)

    U. S. Army Map Service, Corps of Engineers, Series 500: NH 51-1 (Shanghai West), 51-2 (Shanghai East), 51-5 (Hangchou), 51-6 (Tinghai), 51-9 (Tz'u-ch'i), 51-10 (Yin Hsien), 6840s/250/U5, April 1959, from G&M Division, Library of Congress, 3 Nov 1966.

    East China and the Chushan Archipelago – based on British Hydrographic Office chart, China., Sheet IX, 1842, courtesy United Kingdom Hydrographic office, www.ukho.gov.uk. This chart shows the positions of Tsungming and Bush islands upstream from the mouth of the Whangpoo as they were in 1860.

    Shanghai in 1855 – based on H. B. Morse, *The International Relations of the Chinese Empire,* Vol. 1, facing p. 454).

    Maps based on British Hydrographic Office chart, China., Sheets VIII and IX, 1842-3, courtesy United Kingdom Hydrographic office, www.ukho.gov.uk.
        Ningpo and Chushan Island
        Gutzlaff Island to Woosung Bar
        Whangpoo River, Woosung Bar to Shanghai Harbor
        Yangtze River, Woosung to Chen-chiang

    Shanghai Native City and *Shanghai Native City Detail* – from Shanghai County Gazetteer, *Shang-hai hsien-chih* 上海縣志, 同治十一年 1873.

    Volcano Group to Gutzlaff Island – based on British Hydrographic Office chart,

洋神 *Yang Shen*   *James Lande* 藍德

China., Sheet VIII, 1843, courtesy United Kingdom Hydrographic office, *www.ukho.gov.uk.*

Nanking Southern Approaches – adapted from maps in Kuo T'ing-yi 郭廷以, *The Taiping Kingdom Day by Day* 太平天國史事日誌, 1976.

Assault on the Chiang-nan Ta-ying – based on C. A. Curwen, *Taiping Rebel: The Deposition of Li Hsiu-ch'eng*, Map 3, Nanking…, and Kuo, *The Taiping Kingdom Day by Day*, 1976.

Directions for the Langshan crossing – based on S. Wells Williams, *The Chinese Commercial Guide*, 1863. Sailing Directions, p. 146-8.

Nanking in 1860 – see below, Chapter 15: The Rebel Capital.

Yangtze River, Nanking to Wuhoo – based on British Hydrographic Office chart, Yang-tse Kyang, Nanking to Tu-ngliu, 1858, courtesy United Kingdom Hydrographic office, *www.ukho.gov.uk.*

Kiangyin in 1860 – from Kiangyin City Map 江陰市區圖, and Oliphant, …*Earl of Elgin's Mission to China*…p. 293 (1859).

Kiangnan Canal, Yangtze to Hangchow – adapted from Kuo T'ing-yi 郭廷以, *The Taiping Kingdom Day by Day* 太平天國史事日誌, 1976.

Soochow in 1860 – from Soochow Gazetteer and present-day maps.

Country West of Shanghai – see below, Chapter 23: Hiring Foreign Rifles.

Walled City of Sungkiang – Sungkiang Prefecture "Extended" Gazetteer, *Sung-chiang fu hsü-chih* 松江府續志, 光緒九年, 1884.

Water Route, Kuangfulin to Sungkiang, 1860 – same sources as for "Country West of Shanghai." See below, Chapter 23: Hiring Foreign Rifles.

Shanghai City, Sungkiang District, Travel and Tourist Map 上海市松江区交通旅游图, Shanghai Map Society, 2002. See below, Chapter 26: 1st Sungkiang.

In Medias Res…

Incidence of piracy. The incidence of piracy on the China coast in the mid 19th century defies credibility. However, the frequency of reports about piracy in contemporary newspapers and diplomatic correspondence certainly suggests that many ordinary fishermen often did turn pirate, at least long enough to loot any helpless vessel a fisherman happened upon. In her 1940 *British Admirals and Chinese Pirates*, Grace Fox examined the British effort to suppress piracy between 1848 and 1860 and concluded "…the occasional annihilation of pirate junks or fleets had little effect on the evil as a whole. The British made no effort to get at the cause of the piracy or to root it out at its start. The government at Hong Kong did little…in the nature of ship's supply for convoy licenses, and made no attempt to control the traffic. …Furthermore, the economic cause for piracy, the poverty of the Chinese fisherman, though recognized by the current press (China Mail, December 16, 1858: 'The lack of piracies this week is a fact attributable probably to the great cheapness of provisions on the mainland') was beyond the power of the English or Chinese governments of the day to remedy."

Chinese junks. The descriptions of mid-19th century junks and other Chinese vessels that merit first billing in *Yang Shen* are based primarily on more recent works by Worcester, Donnely, and Needham. Worcester's 1971 *The Junks and Sampans of the Yangtze* is the authority the others go to. Donnelly's 1924 *Chinese Junks and Other Native Craft* discusses burning joss money, "paying chin-chin-joss," and Ningpo traders. Needham's 1971 *Science & Civilization in China*, Vol. 4, Part 3, compliments Worcester with what little information there is about old junks in the Chinese language. The extensive and detailed studies of the design and construction of junks in these

洋神 *Yang Shen* James Lande 藍德

sources may be taken as an expression of an abiding Western fascination with the unique character of the Chinese junk. Such interest may have begun with the astonishment of naval officers of the British expeditionary force in 1842, mentioned on p. 402-a of Needham, at Shanghai junks having 141-foot mainmasts 11½ feet in circumference, supporting 111-foot yards, with no shrouds or stays at all for support. Junks had watertight compartments centuries before the Titanic, and were further distinguished by their flat bottoms, high stern, and forward-raked masts. Their battened "balanced lugsails" of bamboo matting attached to a single yard hung obliquely on each mast and were raised and lowered by a halyard run through a block at the top of the mast. An altar was set aside for offerings to any of several manifestations of the goddess of the sea, and an eye, or "oculus," was placed on each side under the bow. Worcester says on p. 39 "In fishing junks the eyeball is often set low in the white so as to be on the alert to observe the fish, unlike the trading junk, wherein the eye looks straight ahead so as to perceive and avoid distant perils invisible to mortal sight." Their watertight compartments rendered junks difficult to sink. With a wind on their beam their flat bottoms caused them to make unwanted leeway, they sailed well before the wind but had to be towed, tracked or sculled against the wind, and their sails were difficult to raise but came down like lead shot. Their variety approached infinity because they were built to varying specifications for specific work everywhere along the China coast. Worcester is also noteworthy for comprehensive descriptions of the reaches of the Yangtze River, from its mouth to well past Chungking. Many fascinating details of the life and beliefs of junkmen and their families, and the Shanghai and Woosung anchorages, the Huangp'u (Whangpoo) River, Soochow Creek, and the lower reaches of the Yangtze west to Wuhoo, found later in *Yang Shen*, come from Worcester.

lodaai 老大**, the old-great**. When Chinese language appears in *Yang Shen*, the English rendering usually precedes or follows the Chinese characters. Occasionally, a line of dialogue in Chinese appears without English attached because someone on the story is translating in the next line. Romanization for Chinese characters and phrases appears only if the Romanized word(s) occur again later in the text, and generally uses the Wade-Giles system of Mandarin Romanization (*lodaai* is Cantonese).

"Have a small heart tonight – be careful." This phrase is the first instance in *Yang Shen* where Chinese idiom, or way of saying something, is rendered in American English for readers. Chinese in the story rarely speak English, of course, unless they are using pidgin English, which is distinct and makes *everyone* speaking in pidgin sound illiterate. When Chinese in the story speak in their own language, the rendering of their speech in English is not distorted, as it is in pidgin, and their grammar and syntax is like any American native speaker of the same class and education – except for idiom selected to characterize them as Chinese. Thus, a common phrase for "be careful" *hsiao-hsin* 小心, "small-heart," is rendered as "have a small heart" and, where the idiom may be ambiguous, followed the American idiom. Lay Wah-duk also says "the sky will soon be black," an instance of non-idiomatic English for "it will soon be dark" *t'ien k'uai hei-le* 天快黑了. In *Yang Shen*, phrases that are not colloquial English generally "reflect" the Chinese language beneath the American English. More on this, and the previous topic, is discussed below in Endnotes: "Why have so much Chinese language in this book?"

Fokie Tom. Fokie Tom actually was a blond-headed English renegade, but accounts of the end of Tom's career as leader of a band of pirates in the Chushan Archipelago differ. D. F. Rennie was a surgeon of the British 31st Regiment who accompanied the allied advance on Peking in 1860, and who later was reported in Shanghai, by the *North China Herald* (NCH) on July 7, 1862, to have introduced a new method of treating smallpox. Rennie tells us in his 1864 *The British Arms in North*

洋神 *Yang Shen*   *James Lande* 藍德

China and Japan, p. 23, that Tom was killed by British and French gunboats, including *Bustard*, *Woodcock*, *Imperieuse* and *Alarme* on June 4, 1860, off the west coast of Chushan Island. Jack Beeching's sources for his 1975 *The Chinese Opium Wars*, p. 283, convinced him that Fokie Tom was captured instead of killed. An NCH article dated June 2, 1860, and included in *Yang Shen*, reported the above incident as having occurred on May 22, 1860, and does not say Tom was either killed or captured. Tom's pedigree and family history were conjured up for *Yang Shen*. H. M. S. Wellesley was on station at the blockade of Canton; that and other details of the 1st opium war are in Beeching, p. 112 and passim.

First China War. Popular contemporary name for the First Anglo-Chinese War, later known as the First Opium War, fought between the British and Chinese in 1839-42, resulting in the Treaty of Nanking. The reprise straggled along between 1856 and 1860, beginning with the Arrow Incident, and ending with the British and French capture of Peking in 1860 and the Treaty of Tientsin. At the time called the Second China War, this war is known variously as the Arrow War, the Second Anglo-Chinese War, and the Second Opium War.

Worship of Ma Tzu. The Reverend Charles Gutzlaff was a pioneering missionary who traveled the South China coast in the early 1830s. He described in some detail in his 1834 *Three Voyages Along the Coast of China*, p. 57 and passim, the elaborate worship of the goddess Ma Tzu he witnessed (and frequently remonstrated against) among coast Chinese, noting especially shrines to Ma Tzu Po 媽祖婆, goddess of the sea, set aboard junks. She is still very popular among the coastal communities of southeast China and Formosa. In 1978 *Chinese Creeds and Customs*, V. R. Burkhardt describes her attendants Thousand Mile Eyes 千里眼, and Fair Wind Ears 順風耳, under the entry for T'ien Hou 天后. The Huan Hua 還華 Chinese Encyclopedia entry for Ma Tzu, [2] 220, has her biography, promotions, history on Taiwan, face colors (the picture caption cites special names for the black faces of Ma Tzu), and attendants. It states there are 380 temples dedicated to her on Formosa.

Romanization of place names. On to the tyranny of style sheets. Even for a novel (maybe especially for a novel). Chinese place names are encumbered with unique spellings from the Postal Atlas of China that are inconsistent with standard systems of romanized Chinese words, but which have seen use for well over 100 years in the popular press. The recent press to use Pinyin has seen these old spellings abandoned, however the older spellings were in use at the time of the story and are consistent with sources, so non-Chinese characters in the story use them. *Yang Shen* follows John King Fairbank's 1970 *Ch'ing Documents: An Introductory Syllabus* and uses unhyphenated postal atlas place names like Nanking, Hangchow, Soochow, and Wuhoo (instead of Nanjing, Hangzhou, Suzhou, and Wuhu). A table of some of these names follows.

Hyphenated Wade-Giles representation is used for other place names by Chinese participants in the story. As Dr Fairbank pointed out, hyphenation of words romanized from Chinese characters avoids ambiguity: Shanan could be Sha-nan or Shan-an. In rare cases, the tyranny of the author prevails, and Wuhoo is used for Wuhu whether it's in the atlas or not (well, it might have been Woohoo). So also with "Taiping."

The cursory reader may be annoyed by more than one spelling for place names, and some other things, and accuse the author of taking the urge for accuracy to a cumbersome extreme. The author agrees. The author himself was hard put to keep it all straight and spent long hours editing romanization to remove Western spellings like "Soochow" from the mouths and minds of Chinese characters, and remove Pinyin that slipped in where Wade-Giles belonged. The fact that much of this was just as confusing for the characters in their day, and that any other approach would have resulted in

洋神 *Yang Shen*   James Lande 藍德

blatant inconsistencies, were justifications that shored the author's choice. Characters appear in text and on maps to clarify Wade-Giles place names for readers of Chinese accustomed to Pinyin. Chinese pronunciation is Mandarin.

Place Names

Postal Atlas Place Name	Wade-Giles Romanization	Pinyin
Peking	Pei-ching	Beijing
Canton	Kuang-chou	Guangzhou
Shanghai	Shang-hai	Shanghai
Nanking	Nan-ching	Nanjing
Szechwan	Ssŭ-ch'uan	Sichuan
Tientsin	T'ien-chin	Tianjin
Ningpo	Ning-po	Ningbo
Kiangyin	Chiang-yin	Jiangyin
Chenkiang	Chen-chiang	Zhenjiang

More Place Names

Chinese (WG)	Western	Chinese (WG)	Western
Ch'ing-p'u 青浦	Tsingpoo, Singpoo	Pai-ho 白河	Peiho
Che-chiang 浙江	Chekiang	Pei-ching 北京	Peking
Chen-chiang 鎮江	Chenkiang, Chinkiang	Pei-t'ang 北塘	Peitang
Chiang-su 江蘇	Kiangsu	Shang-hai 上海	Shanghai
Chiang-nan 江南	Kiangnan	Shan-tung 山東	Shangtung
Chiang-yin 江陰	Kiangyin	Ssŭ-ch'uan 四川	Szechwan
Chia-ting 嘉定	Kahding[1], Kading	Su-chou 蘇州	Soochow
Chih-li 直隸	Chihli	Sung-chiang 松江	Sungkiang
Hang-chou 杭州	Hangchow	T'ai-ts'ang 太倉	Taitsan[1]
Hsiang-kang 香港	Hong Kong	T'ang-ku 塘沽	Tangku
Hsin-ho 新河	Sinho	T'ien-chin 天津	Tientsin
Kuang-chou 廣州	Canton	T'ien-ching 天京 (Nanking)	T'ien-ching
Kun-shan 崑山	Quinshan[1] Kunshan	T'ung-chou 通州	Tungchow
Nan-ch'iao 南橋	Najow[1], Nanchiao	Ta-ku 大沽	Taku
Nan-ching 南京	Nanking	Huang-p'u 黃浦江	Whangpoo, Wampoa
Ning-po 寧波	Ningpo		

[1] Names used by Gordon, *Gordon's Campaign in China*

Romanization of Chinese characters. Several incompatible systems for representing the sound of Chinese characters in Roman alphabets have contended over the decades. English-Chinese dictionaries – Giles, Mathews, etc. – are prefaced by lengthy and complicated discussions of romanization. Put simply, because different language groups use the Roman alphabet in different ways to represent the sounds of their own languages, any romanization devised is likely to reflect those differences. So we have had Wade-Giles (the author's first), Yale, Pinyin (lately acquired), and a host of native Chinese phonetic systems. If memory serves, Romanians developed Pinyin for the Chinese.

    Yale was invented by Americans and most closely supports pronunciation natural to Americans. For Americans – accustomed to pronouncing words as they see them – perplexities like t and t' in Wade-Giles are especially aggravating and inevitably result in Wu-te bring read as "woo-tea" instead of "woo-duh," and *Tung Wang* being read as "toong wang" instead of "doong wong." (Mr. Wade and Mr. Giles have a lot to answer for in the view of average Americans, and perhaps Englishmen as well.) And instead of pondering over the Pinyin "cun" and "xiao," users of Yale romanization are given "tswun" and "hsiao."

    Dr Fairbank, in his introductory syllabus to 1970 *Ch'ing Documents*, p. 12-13, sums

Yang Shen *Underfoot*

洋神 *Yang Shen*　　　　　　　　　　　　　　　　　　　*James Lande* 藍德

it up: "Every form of transliteration (romanization) can be endlessly debated, if one so desires, and the particular devil who lies in wait for sinologists has inspired many of them to waste their energy in argumentation. …It is hopeless to seek a romanization that will convey Chinese sounds correctly to the uninitiated Westerner – the respective sound systems are too dissimilar. Romanization must therefore be an agreed-upon convention." Each approach has peculiarities, so a convention *was* agreed upon.

Pinyin is the current standard, having won the battle on political merit if no other, but Pinyin is as much an obstacle for American speakers as is Wade-Giles. Wade-Giles has its own skewed pronunciation, but was in use at the time of the story and is consistent with sources, so it is used in the novel.

Chapter 1: Fletcher Thorson Wood

Historical persons. Names of many historical persons herein were changed where fictional rendering exceeds the discretion assumed of historians and biographers. Those disciplines require substantial evidence of the facts of history, and very carefully limit conjecture where the historical record does not support speculation. Fictional names chosen usually have the same initials.

Historical characters, entities, and incident are often presented differently in fiction in order to combine some variety of kindred characteristics or compress incident and detail so they fit within the time and space allowed for telling a story. Done well, such storytelling preserves the integrity of known history without distortion or bias. Characters, of course, are often renamed to avoid giving offense to their memory, especially when there is too little reliable information available and their rendering must be filled in with conjecture. Renaming characters may also be appropriate when there is ample information but the story presents less favorable aspects of character or incident.

Fletcher Thorson Wood, of course, is a rendering of Frederick Townsend Ward, drawn from his biographers (Carr, Rantoul, Abend, and Cahill), the academic studies of Richard J. Smith, and the accounts and correspondence of numerous contemporaries.

On the use of secondary sources. *Yang Shen* draws upon a large number of secondary sources for historical fact to inform its narrative. Generally speaking, it is expected that writers of historical fiction will go to historical and biographical sources much as a reader would go to a dictionary or an encyclopedia. When source material merely informs the narrative and is not otherwise misused, historical fiction usually is not held to quite so rigid a standard as academic writing. Thus, historical fiction relies upon the insight of secondary sources as to what is significant, and as a guide to original sources, and sometimes recasts the perceptions of secondary sources in original language. Rarely does historical fiction quote sources in fictional narrative or cite sources in footnotes, although quite often a reading list may be appended which, in effect, acknowledges sources.

A noteworthy exception is William Safire's 1987 *Freedom: A Novel of Abraham Lincoln and the Civil War*, which includes an "Underbook" of sources and commentary that acknowledges writers upon whom the author has depended for information and inspiration and sets out detail of what is fact and what is fiction. This approach removes from fictional narrative formal apparatus not wanted by readers of fiction, yet provides a way for fiction writers to acknowledge sources, distinguish fact from fiction, and consider issues. *Yang Shen*, obviously, takes this approach and appends a receptacle for notes and citations, as well as a glossary and reading list. One objective of *Yang Shen* is to acquire wider exposure for early and recent scholarship in books, studies and dissertations on China and the later Ch'ing (Qing) dynasty, to expand awareness and interest in these sources that might help keep them in print for a new audience.

洋神 *Yang Shen*   *James Lande* 藍德

See Endnotes, below, for more on the use of secondary sources in *Yang Shen*.

Sailing conditions. Southwest soldier's wind: the 1966 edition of Bowditch, *American Practical Navigator*, informs those of us who have never experienced a monsoon that the northeast monsoon of the China Sea ends in about April and the southwest monsoon begins in about May. Aeolus was importuned to declare the winds be from the quarter affording the easiest piloting through the Chushans, to the Volcanoes, on to Gutzlaff, into the Yangtze and up the Woosung river to Shanghai. The wind remained more or less constant from the southwest over the entire course of sailing. This simplified somewhat the task of sailing *Essex* into the Yangtze River (and keeping the author's head above water).

New Jerusalem. In his 1977 *Early Sino-American Relations*, 1841-1912, Swisher relates that Olyphant & Company was the one firm that refused to trade in opium, which earned them the name "Zion's Corner."

Pirate tactics. The tactics employed by the pirates attacking *Essex* evidently were common in the archipelago at this time. Basil Lubbock suggested the notion that a Chinese pilot could be a *pirate* as well, on p. 113 of 1914 *The China Clippers*, and that there were pilots who kept secret the location of uncharted rocks onto which they would drive their hapless charge. This was suspected to be the case when *Norman Court*, an 834-ton, 197-foot tea clipper built the same year as *Cutty Sark*, 1869, struck a rock in the Min River in 1878. Another favored tactic was the "passenger surprise dodge," in which the pirates went aboard as passengers, and took the vessel and drove the crew overboard after the vessel was underway. References to the loss of the lorchas *Silvery Cross* and *Cleopatra* come from March and April 1860 editions of the *North China Herald*.

Another incidence of pirate tactics, related by Robert Fortune in his 1857 book *A Residence Among the Chinese, Inland, on the Coast, and at Sea...*, occurred when Fortune took passage north out of Ningpo on the Jardine Matheson and Co. opium clipper *Erin*. Just beyond Chin-hai, at the entrance to the Yung River, *Erin* came upon the plundering of a Shantung junk by pirate lorchas and junks that had blockaded the passage between Silver Island and the mainland. The pirates had lain in wait behind the islands until a victim approached, then rushed out from hiding and attacked before the victim could flee. Being a fast, heavily armed fighting vessel, *Erin* did not shy from advancing through the pirate line, but as she silently passed the hapless junk, the pirates "seemed to be watching us very narrowly, and in one vessel the crew were getting their guns to bear on our boat." The pirates finally broke the tense standoff and signaled "let us alone and we'll let you" by hoisting a Chinaman's jacket to the rigging, and *Erin* departed the terrible scene without injury.

Secessionist tactics. The view of Elizabeth Fitch's aunt about the tactics of secessionists at the Democratic convention is mentioned in James McPherson's 1988 *The Battle Cry of Freedom* (Oxford History of the U. S.).

Chapter 2: Borrowing American Troops

The house-cricket. The story of "The Fighting Cricket," *Tzu-chih* 促織, is told in Pu Song-ling's *Liao-chai chih-yi* 聊齋誌異, translated by H. A. Giles as *Strange Stories from a Chinese Studio*.

***Taotai* and Superintendent of Customs Wu[2] Hsü[4]** 吳煦. Biographical information on this mandarin is in the *Shanghai County Gazetteer*, 1873, p. 888. 上海縣志: 松江府海防同知(道光二十三年以蘇州督糧水利同知改為松江府海防同知移駐上海縣)咸豐四年任:吳煦. 蘇松太道, 咸豐九年任: 吳煦, 字曉颿(帆)仁和縣人監生兼署江蘇布政使.

Shanghai County Gazetteer: Sub-prefect for Coastal Defense at the Prefecture of Yang Shen Underfoot

洋神 *Yang Shen*   *James Lande* 藍德

Sungkiang (changed from Water-communications Sub-prefect for Grain Supervision at Soochow in 1843 and moved to Shanghai) 4th year of Hsien Feng [1854]: *Wu Hsü. Su-Sung-T'ai Taotai, 9th year of Hsien Feng* [1859]: *Wu Hsü, personal name Hsiao-fan, born in Jen-ho county,* chien-sheng *degree, simultaneously appointed to office of acting Kiangsu provincial treasurer.*

    (See also Sungkiang Prefecture "Extended" Gazetteer 松江府續志, p. 2098-2100, for more on Wu Hsü.)

    These brief entries are from the standard *Shanghai County Gazetteer* of 1873. Each county (*aka* "district") in China came with a "user's manual." A gazetteer was an instruction manual for county magistrates, necessary due to the Manchu policy that no county magistrate was to serve in his home county, or serve in any county for more than a few years. The rapid turnover of these, the lowest level of officials in the empire, necessitated a handy way of becoming familiar with a new locale. The gazetteers were kept up to date by each new magistrate. They were both historical gazetteers and biographical encyclopedias, showing maps of all the land of the county, the roads bridges and canals the magistrate was responsible for maintaining with labor conscripted from the local populace, and describing towns and villages, local organizations, local customs, and other detail. This included defenses, waterways, grain warehouses, collection of duties and taxes, local products, schools, temples, and military facilities. All officers who ever served in the county or superior offices were listed, along with important officials and gentry, important local families and individuals, arts and amusements, exemplary women, local landmarks, local history, and more.

    The entries for Wu Hsü say that in 1854, the 4th year of the reign of the Hsien Feng emperor, Wu Hsü served as a sub-prefect for coastal defense for the prefecture of Sungkiang, at the same time as, or following, Liu Hsün-kao (see below). Wu probably was located in the city of Shanghai. Most likely, he purchased the office. In 1859, the 9th year of the Hsien Feng reign, he was appointed to the office of Su-Sung-T'ai *Tao-t'ai*, which we may speculate he also purchased. A brief biographical note was added to the Shanghai gazetteer giving Wu's personal name, place of birth, official rank, and another office, acting provincial treasurer, over which he had temporary charge in addition to his principal office of *taotai*.

    Wu was his family name, and Hsu was his "given" name; a "personal" name was usually selected at the age of twenty for use by brothers and friends, and Wu Hsü selected *Hsiao-fan* 曉驄, meaning "horse running at dawn," very likely a literary allusion. Wu Hsü was often addressed in correspondence by his personal name, or some elegant variation, by such luminaries as Governor-general Tseng Kuo-fan, and often the character *fan* 帆, sail, was substituted for the character 驄.

    Wu Hsü born in Jen-ho county, which Chinese place-name dictionaries locate in Chekiang Province. He was said to have held the *chien-sheng* degree (see following), which was the lowest level of literary degree. It was easily purchased, especially in the later years of the dynasty after the 1830s when the central government was desperate for cash to defend the empire against the incursions of Westerners, and to suppress the Taiping rebellion. His simultaneous appointment to the office of provincial treasurer made him third in rank in the province, after the governor-general, and the governor, and head of the provincial civil service.

    Evidently, Wu Hsü was too minor an official in the eyes of compilers of Chinese biographical dictionaries to be included with larger lights. To date only some of his Taiping-related documents have been published, in *WHTA* (Selections from Taiping Historical Materials in the Documents of Wu Hsü 吳煦檔案中的太平天國史料選輯),

洋神 *Yang Shen*   *James Lande* 藍德

1958. References to Wu Hsü in *IWSM* (the *I-wu Shih-mo* 夷務始末, 1979), the above fragment from the *Shanghai County Gazetteer*, and gleanings from excerpts in his Taiping-related documents must suffice to fill in a biographical background for this pivotal figure in the life of *Yang Shen*'s Fletcher Thorson Wood.

Historians tell us more about the significance of Wu Hsü's service as the Superintendent of Customs at Shanghai, and the impact of his accomplishment as a "barbarian expert" upon the administration of Shanghai and its custom house. Wu Hsü also was a principle confidant of provincial judge and Kiangsu governor Hsüeh Huan. Hsüeh Huan's expertise in barbarian affairs was so highly valued by the emperor that he was called to Peking to join in the treaty negotiations of 1859.

Details for *Yang Shen*'s fictional representation of Wu Hsü are based on contemporary observations and academic studies, in particular the *North China Herald* (7/21/1860 and *passim*), and Banno, 1964 *China and the West*, p. 274n, citing Rennie, 1864 *The British Arms in North China and Japan*, p. 144. As most contemporary opinions about Wu Hsü are hearesay, *Yang Shen* attempts an evenhanded portrayal with controversial aspects of the fictional character presented as the opinion of Western characters, and Wu Hsü's own language from documents and memorials grafted into the fictional Wu Hsü's thought and dialogue (from *IWSM*, HF 1858 19-20, HF 1859 41-44 and *WHTA*).

The *Chien-sheng* degree. The *chien-sheng* 監生 was an honorary degree appointing the holder to the Imperial Academy which, in contrast to the revered Han-lin Academy, was an institution in title only with neither bureaucratic nor academic functions, but this degree did exempt the holder from torture during judicial inquiry, labor service and official examinations. The *chien-sheng* degree had declined substantially in meaning since the Ming Dynasty, such that by mid-Ch'ing anyone with 100 taels could purchase the degree and wear the robes of a scholar. Degrees higher than the *chien-sheng* could also be purchased for substantially greater payments into the imperial coffers, but more properly were won by passing literary examinations, or were awarded for meritorious service, and serious students seeking public office rigorously studied for advanced examinations. As the system broke down in the latter half of the 19th century, officials who purchased rank, and office, began to outnumber those who followed the proper path of advancement. This phenomenon is said to have contributed to the overall degradation of the Confucian-based philosophy of administration and, consequently, hastened the gradual replacement of reaction by more liberal views of government. Officials with high-rank and a low-level degree might be suspected as having advanced through the purchase-system because, once the *chien-sheng* degree was purchased, further outlays would have been for higher office rather than literary honors. High-level officials who advanced along the proper path might have been expected to have also a high-level literary degree.

Intendant of Circuit. The office of *taotai* usually was translated as Intendant of Circuit. The circuit, or *tao* 道, was an administrative area immediately subordinate to the province, which could contain any number of subordinate areas within it, including prefectures, departments and counties in any combination, and the *taotai* had power over both civil and military offices in his circuit. At the time of *Yang Shen*, there were 84 circuits in China's 18 provinces. In the circuit assigned to Wu Hsü, there were two prefectures and one department, and these comprised most if not all of the strategically critical eastern corner of Kiangsu Province, from Soochow north through Taitsang to the Yangtze River, and from Soochow west through Sungkiang to the coast. In the northern part of this circuit, the department of Taitsang 太倉州, containing three counties, reported directly to the provincial government. In the southwestern part of the circuit was the prefecture of Soochow 蘇州府, with three subordinate counties, and the city of Soochow as its prefectural seat. In the western section of the circuit was the prefecture of Sungkiang 松江府, with two counties, one of which was Shanghai county 上海縣, and the city of Sungkiang as prefectural seat. The romanization is *taotai* when the term is appears in English dialogue or thought, and *tao-t'ai* in Wade-Giles when appears in Chinese dialogue or thought.

Legend of White Snake. One version of this story tells of a white snake that studied the mystical arts for 1000 years and learned to take human form, becoming Miss White. With her sister Hsiao-ch'ing, she came to West Lake at Hangchow, made the acquaintance of an apothecary named Hsu-hsien, and married him. They moved to Suchow and opened a successful apothecary shop, living happily until the jealous monk Fa-hai, fom Gold Mountain Temple, made trouble for them, on one occasion causing her to revert to snake form before her husband's eyes. After several harrowing confrontations, the monk captured Miss White and imprisoned her under the Lei-feng tower – the Tower of Thundering Peak pagoda – next to West Lake. After years of preparation, Hsiao-ch'ing took Hsu-hsien and went to fight Fa-hai and rescue White Snake. In the fierce battle, the pagoda collapsed and White Snake was released to join the fight. They chased the monk into West Lake and made the waters recede, causing Fa-hai to take refuge inside a crab, where he remained a prisoner forever. Thereafter, Chinese visited the collapsed pagoda at West Lake to honor White Snake, and complained about the inedible belly of the crab they ate, made hard by evil monk Fa-hai.

Sedan chairs 轎子. A sedan chair, or palanquin, in China was borne on the shoulders. The emperor had sixteen bearers; a prince of the blood eight; the high provincial authorities eight (though except on religious or ceremonial occasions, or when traveling, they never used more than four). All other officials down to a prefect had four bearers, including a county magistrate if actually in office. The chairs of all officials down to and including provincial treasurers, judges, and salt comptrollers, were green in color. Chairs for the lower ranks were blue, with slight variations of detail; Giles remarks that a *taotai* might change the color of his chair to green because he usually also held the brevet rank of commissioner of justice. Foreign consuls were entitled by treaty to use green chairs with four bearers. Herbert Giles left us all the detail about sedan chairs we might ask for, not just in his 1912 *Chinese Dictionary*, from which most of the below is taken, but also in his 1878 *Glossary of the Far East*.

Chairs were of several designs, with the most elaborate official chairs having lining and curtains, screens, storage space inside, and a knob on top. Military officials rode in open chairs when permitted (usually such officials rode horses or walked). Chinese etiquette made it necessary to get out of a chair to speak with a passing acquaintance. When two or more officials travel together, the highest in rank took the foremost chair. There were light chairs for use in the mountains, and ornamented bridal chairs painted red, the color of happiness. Ordinary mortals were allowed to use simple chairs with only two bearers, and these were advertised for rent to Westerners at hourly or daily rates by the better hotels in Shanghai.

Chinese official ranks. Mandarins took examinations to become eligible for appointment to the bureaucracy. The examinations progressed through several levels, local, provincial, and the highest, held in Peking, and conferred *academic* rank and status. Academic ranks included (1) Student *t'ung sheng* 童生, (2) Licentiate *hsiu ts'ai* 秀才, (3) Senior Licentiate *kung sheng* 貢生, (4) Provincial Graduate *chu-jen* 舉人, and (5) Metropolitan Graduate *chin shih* 進士. Once possessed of academic rank, a

洋神 *Yang Shen*   *James Lande* 藍德

candidate was eligible for appointment as a local magistrate, a provincial officer, or in the imperial bureaucracy. A mandarin also held a grade, from the 9th or lowest, to the 1st grade, which generally advanced with level of academic office, and determined level of pay. The following table shows offices and associated grades for mandarins in the provinces.

Admin Rank	Chinese Name	Grade[1]	Military Rank[2]	Chinese Name	Unit	Chinese Name
Governor-General (Viceroy)	總督	2-1	General-in-chief *Chiang-chün* (Manchu)	將軍	Manchu banner *Pa-ch'i*	八旗
Governor	巡撫 (*fu-tai* 撫台)	2-1	General *T'i-tu*	提督	Provincial Army *Fu-biao*	撫標
Lt Governor (Treasurer)	布政使司	3-2	Lieutenant General *Tu-t'ung* (Manchu)	都統	Banner division *Pa-ch'i kusai*	八旗固山
		3-2	Brigadier General *Tsung-ping*	總兵	Brigade *Chen-piao*[3]	鎮標
Provincial Judge	按察使司	4-3	Colonel *Fu-chiang*	副將, 協台	Brigade *Chen-piao*	鎮標
Salt Comptroller	鹽運使司	4-3				
Grain Intendant	糧道	4-3				
		5-4	Commandant *Ying-tsung*	營總	Brigade *Chuang-yung*	狀勇
Circuit Intendant	分巡道 (*Taotai* 道台)	6-4	Light Colonel *Tsan-chiang*[4]	參將	Regiment *Hsieh*	協
Prefect	知付	7	Major *Yu-chi*	遊擊	Batallion *Ying*	營
Sub-prefect	同知	8	1st Captain *Tu-ssu*	都司	Company *Lien*	連
Department Magistrate	知州	9-8	2nd Captain *Shou-pei*	守備	Company *Lien*	連
District (County) Magistrate	知縣	9	Lieutanant *Ch'ien-tsung*	千總	Platoon *Shao*	哨

(from W. F. Mayer, *The Chinese Government*, 1897)
1. The grade associated with these ranks is an estimate.
2. The equality of military and administrative ranks here is an estimate.
3. The unit commanded by a brigadier general is an extrapolation (Mayers is not specific).
4. Light colonel down through lieutenant have been lowered in this column, so that a light colonel shows as the rough equivalent of a *taotai*, because salt comptroller and grain intendant are the same rank as a provincial judge.

There were a great many more graduates than offices, so a successful academic candidate might languish for years waiting for an appointment. In such cases, employment in the retinue (*mufu* 幕府) of mandarins holding office was an alternative, as was purchase of an appointment. Those scheduled to take up an office when there was a vacancy, the "next in line," were called *expectant*, 候選 or 待詔. In *Yang Shen*, Yang Fang is referred to as expectant *taotai*, next after Wu Hsü in Shanghai "county."

Shanghai County Magistrate Liu[2] Hsün[2]-kao[1] 劉郇膏. Biographical information on this mandarin is based partly on the *Shanghai County Gazetteer*, p. 888, and the *Chinese Biographical Dictionary*, p. 1457. 上海縣志: 松江府海防同知(道光二十三年以蘇州督糧水利同知改為松江府海防同知移駐上海縣) 咸豐 四 年任: 劉郇膏. 上海縣知縣曆官至江蘇布政使署江蘇巡撫有傳.

Shanghai County Gazetteer: Sub-prefect for Coastal Defense at the Prefecture of Sungkiang (changed from Water-communications Sub-prefect for Grain Supervision at Soochow in 1843 and moved to Shanghai) 4th year of Hsien Feng [1854]: Liu Hsün-kao. Shanghai county magistrate, successive appointments as Kiangsu provincial treasurer, appointed acting Governor of Kiangsu Province (see biography).

Yang Shen *Underfoot*

洋神 *Yang Shen* James Lande 藍德

中國人名大辭典,: 劉郇膏. 清太康人. 字松巖. 道光進士. 咸豐間知上海縣. 多善政. 有劉青天 之稱. 李秀成犯上海. 練民兵守禦有功. 官至江蘇布政使卒.

Chinese Biographical Dictionary: Liu Hsün-kao. Ch'ing Dynasty, born in T'ai-k'ang, personal name Sung-yen. Received chin-shih degree during the reign of Tao Kuang [1821-1850], served as Shanghai county magistrate during the reign of Hsien Feng [1850-1862], governed very well, attested by Liu Ch'ing-t'ien, successfully trained militia for defense when Li Hsiu-ch'eng attacked Shanghai, and was last appointed Kiangsu provincial treasurer.

Combining these two sources, we see that Liu Hsün-kao was born in T'ai-k'ang county, which is located in Honan Province, department of Chen-chou, and that his personal name was Sung-yen, "pine cliff." He received his advanced *chin-shih* degree during the reign of the Tao Kuang emperor, and served in 1854 as a sub-prefect for coastal defense at Sungkiang, at the same time as, or immediately prior to, Wu Hsü [see above]. Liu was Shanghai county magistrate in 1860, and later served several times as Kiangsu provincial treasurer, and as acting Kiangsu governor. Liu's incumbency as county magistrate was exemplary, as attested by Liu Ch'ing-t'ien, and during the investment of Shanghai in 1860 by the Taiping general Li Hsiu-ch'eng, Liu was successful at training and leading local militia in the defense of the city.

In 1860, Liu Hsün-kao accompanied Wu Hsü on visits to foreign consulates when, in May and June, the *taotai* was making the rounds of the consulates to enlist the cooperation of Western troops in the defense of Shanghai against the rebels. *Yang Shen* has commandeered him for April perambulations as well.

Taotai and Magistrate. Sources for the conversation between Taotai Wu and Magistrate Liu primarily are Immanual C. Y. Hsu, 1960 *China's Entry into the Family of Nations*, Earl Swisher, 1977 *Early Sino-American Relations, 1841-1912*, and Swisher, 1951 *China's Management of the American Barbarians*. The memorials adapted include Ch'i Ying's 1844 description of the United States, and several memorials of Ho Kuei-ch'ing from the years 1858 and 1859, reproduced in Swisher's *China's Management…* and re-translated for *Yang Shen*. Even though taken out of the context of correspondence with the emperor, the sentiments expressed are assumed to be representative of several treaty port mandarins in Shanghai who were, to one degree or another, protégés of Ho Kuei-ch'ing when he was governor in Kiangnan and, later, Hsüeh Huan, when he became governor. Contemporary Westerners and recent historians have regarded both governors as comparatively progressive in their thought about how to deal with the Western barbarians and save their country from the crisis of the early 1860s.

Poisoned bread. In January of 1857, some four hundred people in British community of Hong Kong were made ill by bread containing arsenic, "sixty grains of white arsenic per pound." The dose was so strong that the poison was vomited up with emetics and no one died, but some became very sick. Ah Lum, the baker responsible, whose own wife and children were poisoned, was arrested and banished from Hong Kong. The community speculated that Ah Lum was enlisted by Cantonese officials and that, at risk for punishment if he disobeyed the mandarins, he may have intentionally overdosed the bread to prevent deaths. S. Couling, 1917 *Encyclopedia Sinica*, p. 8.

Borrowing American troops *(chieh-ping chu-chiao* 借兵助勦*)*. About this time in the story, Chinese authorities in Shanghai approached foreign officials on the subject of using foreign troops to defend the city, and the *taotai* certainly called upon the British and French to ask for help. It may be thin historically to think that Wu Hsü made the same request of the Americans, who had no troops at Shanghai. But he was nothing if not resourceful and could conceivably have suggested that the Americans might bring warships from Hong Kong or Japan (*Hartford, Saginaw* and *Powhatan* were all in the

Far East). If the British and French could be convinced to send troops to save Soochow and defend Shanghai, the Americans could lend support.

Letters to Wu Hsü, from the governors of Kiangsu and Chekiang, which instructed the *taotai* to approach the foreigners and urge them to dispatch troops and steamers to Soochow, appear in the collection of Wu Hsü's documents. It is a minor matter that the letters are dated early in April of the tenth year of Hsien Feng, 1860, which would have been the Chinese lunar month. The solar month of the Western calendar generally occurred then about three to four weeks after the lunar month, so the dates of the letters would actually have been in early to mid-May. This coincides with the dates given by Wang Erh-min in "China's Use of Foreign Military Assistance..." of April 27 to May 5, 1860, for the rebel attack against the *Chiangnan Ta-ying* and the fall of the Imperial camp on May 6, 1860.

Many of the concerns expressed in these letters must, of course, have been anticipated in late April by the Chinese, especially considering the fall of Hangchow, activity already evident around Nanking, and the direction of the rebel march. So it is seems not unreasonable for fictional purposes to have the *taotai* inquire also of the Americans about what help they might be willing to provide. Even if not effective for the expressed purpose, the request could at least been employed as a negotiating tactic to gain advantage in wrangling over other issues with the American consul.

The dispersal three weeks later of the Great Southern Imperial Barracks, *Chiangnan Ta-ying* 江南大營, aka Imperial Battalion or Imperial Encampment, besieging Nanking in mid-1860 caused the military situation in Kiangnan, "south of the Yangtze," to deteriorate dramatically for the Chinese empire. The rebel threat to Soochow and Shanghai became immediate and appalling. As the Westerners had the only viable forces in the area, and some interest vested in defense of their trading entrepôt at Shanghai, a few Chinese officials thought the British and French might be enlisted to defend Soochow and Shanghai against the Taiping rebels. Considering that the same western forces were poised to pounce on Peking, some other Chinese officials were more impressed by the obvious contradiction, *mao-dun* 矛盾. A policy debate ensued in the Ch'ing court and the provinces over the idea of influencing foreigners to commit to the defense of Shanghai.

China has employed barbarians…for thousands of years. Wu Hsü is thinking of Yu Yü 由餘, and Chin Mi-ti 金日磾, two of the earliest examples of employing barbarians. Richard Smith discusses these precedents and many others in 1975 "Employment of Foreign Military Talent," in JHKBRAS. Yu Yü was a Jung 西戎 barbarian in the Ch'in 秦 dynasty who defended the empire against other barbarians. Chin Mi-ti was a Hsiung-nu prince who was loyal to the Western Han 西漢 dynasty. Uighur allies of the T'ang 唐 dynasty helped to put down the rebellion of An-lu-shan 安祿山. Kuo Yao-shih 郭藥師 was a Liao 遼 barbarian who led his Yuan Army 怨军 in defense of the Sung 宋 dynasty (Kuo's 12th century army was renamed Ever-victorious Army 常勝軍 and is a likely precedent for the name given Ward's 19th century EVA). The Mongols of the Yuan 元 dynasty enlisted thousands of Russians in their palace guard, and the Ming 明 dynasty employed Mongol soldiers. In the Ch'ing 清 dynasty, Russian troops served in Manchu banners, Russian and Dutch troops were summoned as allies, and Western warriors and expert soldiers were used on several occasions. Jesuits made guns and cannon during the K'ang-hsi 康熙 period to help put down the *San-fan* 三藩 rebellion of Wu San-kuei 吳三桂. In the 3rd year of the emperor Hsien Feng 咸豐, Shang-hai *Taotai* Wu Chien-chang 吳健彰 hired several foreign steamers and sent them

洋神 *Yang Shen*　　　　　　　　　　　　　　　　　　　James Lande 藍德

to Chen-chiang 鎮江 to help fight the rebels. In the 5th year of Hsien Feng, French forces under Admiral Laguerre joined imperial forces to drive the Small Swords – Triads – out of the walled city of Shanghai. And a year later, the English declared they would defend Shanghai against the Taiping.

Barbarian Experts. Biographies of the several Chinese noted for treating with foreigners in the early days, including Lin Tse-hsiu, Ch'i-shan, Yeh Ming-ch'en, and Ch'i-ying, are in Hummel, 1943 *Emminent Chinese of the Ch'ing Period*.

Calendars and Clocks. This calendar table correlates the two Chinese calendars of the story with the Western calendar. Chinese dates in old China were based on the dynasty and reigning emperor and expressed as, for example, the *"4th year of Hsien Feng,"* meaning the fourth year of the reign of emperor Hsien Feng of the Ch'ing dynasty, or 1854 in the Western calendar. The reigns of three Ch'ing emperors are directly related to the story: Tao Kuang (1821-1851), Hsien Feng (1851-1862), and T'ung Chih (1862-1875). The Taiping used a similar approach, citing years since the start of the Taiping "dynasty."

Calendars		
Western	Ch'ing	Taiping
	Hsien Feng	
1851	1	1
1852	2	2
1853	3	3
1854	4	4
1855	5	5
1856	6	6
1857	7	7
1858	8	8
1859	9	9
1860	10	10
1861	11	11
	T'ung-chih	
1862	1	12

Time of day was kept in two-hour increments correlated with cycles of the watch. The time beat out on a huge drum sounded throughout walled towns from drum towers atop the wall or standing alone at the center of towns.

Time	*Hour of the ...*	*Time*	*Hour of the ...*
1 am – 3 am	Ox, 4th watch	1 pm – 3 pm	Sheep, afternoon
3 am – 5 am	Tiger, 5th watch	3 pm – 5 pm	Monkey
5 am – 7 am	Hare	5 pm – 7 pm	Cock
7 am – 9 am	Dragon	7 pm – 9 pm	Dog, 1st Drum, 1st watch
9 am – 11 am	Snake, forenoon	9 pm – 11 pm	Boar, 2nd Drum, 2nd Watch
11 am – 1 pm	Horse, noon	11 pm – 1 am	Rat, 3rd watch, 三更

Chapter 3: Laws Are Silent

***Ti-pao* 地保, or Local Constable.** The *ti-pao* represented law and order in the countryside and are described on p. 387-88 of John R. Watt's article "The Yamen and Urban Administration" in Skinner, 1977 *The City in Late Imperial China*, as personal agents of magistrates used to represent government authority in villages. They "…began appearing in the late seventeenth and early eighteenth centuries…assigned to natural villages, city blocks, and suburban quarters. …They did not represent any popular organization. Therefore, administrators could exploit them to spread government authority throughout the villages without directly oppressing the rural populace." Note 63 on p. 731-32 of Skinner says "Their [the *tipao*] job was to seek out evildoers contravening the law." A companion country official, the *ti-fang*, is described as "running a certain number of villages and sharing responsibility for management of tax collection, disputes over property, litigation, and investigation of robbery and homicide cases. These country constables were subject to beatings when they did not perform.

Runners were yamen employees with police powers stationed in towns, so perhaps it follows that the *ti-pao* stationed in villages made the collar but afterwards turned the suspects over to the yamen runners for further processing.

Giles dictionary describes the *ti-pao* as an official "beadle" who, in English usage at the time, was a parish officer akin to a bailiff who kept order at church services and

洋神 *Yang Shen*   *James Lande* 藍德

some civil functions and turns up often in the stories of Mr. Dickens.

Monkey 孫悟空. The story of the brash monkey who challenged Heaven is one of a small canon of Chinese popular novels that have seen many editions since being published in the 16th and 17th centuries. It comes down to us as *Hsi Yu Chi* 西遊記, *Journey to the West*, and was translated into English by Arthur Waley with the title *Monkey* (1944). At the heart of the tale is the account of the actual pilgrimage of a T'ang Dynasty priest named Hsüan-tsang 玄奘, also called T'ang San-tsang 唐三藏, or Tripitaka, to India to fetch back to China the Buddhist scriptures. The novel, however, is populated with gods, heroes, magicians, monsters and ogres, and richly embroidered with fantasy, humor, allegory, folklore, religion, history and picaresque satire somewhat like *Don Quixote*. The real hero is the monkey Sun Wu-k'ung 孫悟空, born a stone monkey, from a stone egg birthed by a magic rock, that came to life and immediately got into great mischief, as monkeys will do. He makes himself king of the monkeys, and sets out into the world to learn magic and wisdom and discover the secret of immortality. Inevitably, Monkey's vaulting ambition leads him to steal the Jade Emperor's Peaches of Immortality and he threatens to seize the very throne of Heaven, for which crimes he would have been put to death but for the intervention of Buddha, and the Goddess of Mercy Kuan Yin 觀音. As punishment, Monkey is imprisoned under a mountain for 500 years, until the priest Hsüan-tsang leaves for India and Monkey is offered clemency if he will accompany and protect the priest on his journey to the west, and help return the Buddhist scriptures to China. All manner of fantastic adventures befall the travelers, but this is an honorable Monkey now, and he employs all his many magic powers to protect Hsüan-tsang and see the sutras safely brought home, and in the end is himself made a Bodhisattva as his reward. These days, however, Monkey is commonly banished to the realm of children's literature and is regarded lightly, sometimes with embarrassment, by educated adults. However, much of the original story when stripped out of animated cartoons is well beyond the comprehension of children. *Hsi Yu Chi* was intended to ridicule many aspects of the society in which lived the reputed author, Wu Ch'eng-en 吳承恩, not the least of which was the consequence of unbridled ambition like that of the Monkey King.

Sailing Directions. At the Volcanoes, the flood tide bore WNW at 3 knots, which is why *Essex* was at risk of being pushed further into the mud by the tide flowing against her starboard, and the kedge anchor was put out to keep her off the shoal. Also, as the *Essex* sailors noted with glee, the conflicting wind and tide was the cause of the difficulty the pirates had maneuvering their junks: the current close to the island carried the junks WNW at 3 knots while the wind pushed them ENE at 3 knots.

This location experiences diurnal tides, one low and one high each day. In his 1863 *Commercial Guide Sailing Directions* on p. 131, Williams says that high water full and change (full moon and new moon) is at 11h 30m at the Volcanos, so at 10:00am on this day the tide is still rising, and at springs rises 15 feet.

Laws are silent when drums beat. The original latin, from Cicero, is *Silent enim leges inter arma*, "the law falls silent in the midst of arms" (Safire, *Freedom*, p. 980).

Chapter 4: The Englishman's War

Blaine and Masters. Principal sources for this discussion of issues of British policy are Gregory, John., 1959 "*British Intervention against the Taiping Rebellion*," and Immanual Hsu, 1960 *China's Entry into the Family of Nations*. The depiction of the consul, Masters, was suggested by the description of T. T. Meadows on p. 399 in Lanning and Couling, 1921 *The History of Shanghai*. On p. 395, Lanning and Couling

Yang Shen Underfoot

tell of the career of Chaloner Alabaster, who served as the basis for *Yang Shen*'s Chalmers Alexander. The characterization of Wells, the British interpreter, was informed by James Cooley's 1981 T'oung Pao monograph, "T. F. Wade in China…."

Spelling variations. The spelling of the name Shanghai, like a great many other words of that day, varied considerably. Herein it is spelled differently from Shanghai only when the context suggests it, and usually then as Shanghae, a British rendering. Among the other variants: Shanghay, Changhay, and Xanghay. The Chinese variously called Shanghai 上海 by its ancient name Hu 滬, sometimes in the same paragraph.

Seng-ko-lin-ch'in 僧格林沁**, Prince Seng.** The characterization of Prince Seng and the Manchu rulers of China in 1860 relied predominantly on Hummel, 1943 *Eminent Chinese*…, and the writing of Pamela Kyle Crossley in her 1990 *The Orphan Warriors*. Conflicts between Manchu and Han are delineated by Mark Elliott in a *Late Imperial China* article (Vol. 11, June 1, 1990): "Bannerman and Townsman: Ethnic Tension in 19th-Cen Jiangnan." Detail of the preparations made in 1860 by imperial forces at Taku was suggested by British narratives of the campaign in north China: Wolseley's 1862 *Narrative Of The War With China in 1860*, and Swinhoe's 1861 *Narrative Of The North China Campaign*. Dr. D. F. Rennie was stationed in Peking after the treaties were signed in 1860 and recorded many personal details about Seng-ko-lin-ch'in in 1865 *Peking and the Pekinese, 1st British Embassy, 1860-61*. Seng-ko-lin-ch'in's own language was excerpted from memorials, cited in *IWSM* and Swisher's 1951 *China's Management of the American Barbarians*.

Chapter 5 Fighting Fokie Tom

Field guns and clipper ships. No historical example of firing a field gun from the deck of a clipper ship volunteered to come forward and act as an example for Fletcher and his doughty crew. The action is no more than the result of asking how such a thing might be done. The main difficulties were how to control the recoil in the confined space of the poop deck and forecastle of a clipper ship, how to avoid blowing away the ship's own rigging when firing a 6-pounder from places like a forecastle, where guns ought not to be fired. The rest seemed not difficult: an experienced ship's gun crew should be able to adapt quickly enough to a moveable gun. The loading and firing should not be so different; with the ship aground and not rolling on the swell, any breech-sight would have done just as well as a pendulum sight. The inspiration for "hobbling" the gun to dampen its recoil came from Lieutenant John Gibbon's 1860 *The Artillerist's Manual*, p. 182. A near contemporary to the more terse U. S. Army 1862 *Ordnance Manual*, Gibbon is an excellent adjunct and comprehensive source of practically everything one needs to know to fire a fictional cannon. Including how to tell the age of draft horses pulling gun-carriages and caissons by examining the depth of the infundibulum in their incisors, the little "cups" in their "nippers."

Warping off a shoal. U. S. S. *Powhatan*, in Chinese waters as late as 1859, taking Minister John Ward north to the Peiho for ratification of the Treaty of Tientsin. *Powhatan* went aground in the mud at some point and used a novel method employing two kedges to get off. In Johnston, 1861 *China and Japan…*, p. 221, the *Powhatan* needed two kedges because the flowing tide was pushing her into the mud, one to hold her stern against the tide, and the other to pull her bow around free of the mud.

Chapter 6: Sowing Foreign Discord

Banker, merchant and expectant *Taotai* **Yang² Fang²** 楊坊**.** Biographical information on this mandarin is based partly on the *Shanghai County Gazetteer*, p. 1775. 上海

洋神 *Yang Shen*　　　　　　　　　　　　　　　　　　*James Lande* 藍德

縣志: 楊坊字啟堂浙之鄞縣人多術智賣上海西人通市交易不數年明習各國事咸豐三年劉麗川據滬城[江]蘇[巡]撫吉爾杭阿督勸檄坊使說西人於城東北築土城斷賊接濟城遂復敘勞由同知得道員十年奧賊犯滬坊又奉檄募西勇助勦[剿]名曰常勝軍屢有功同治元年簡放常鎮通海道尋丁憂未赴論者謂聯絡西人借兵助嘩順坊有勞焉性好施輔元育嬰兩堂皆有資助又於虹口創四明公所及義園周[賙]恤甬人之避兵來滬者.

  Shanghai County Gazetteer: Yang Fang, personal name Ch'i-t'ang, born in the Yin district of Chekiang, multi-talented, knowledge of business, familiar with the markets and trade of Shanghai's Westerners. After only a few years understood the practices of all nations. In the 3rd year of Hsien Feng [1853] *Liu Li-ch'uan* [leader of the Hsiao-tao Hui 小刀會 rebels] *occupied the city of Shanghai. Kiangsu Governor Chi-erh-hang-a supervised the defense against the rebels and ordered Yang Fang to call upon the Westerners to build a rammed-earth wall northeast of the city in order to cut off the rebels and relieve the city. Yang Fang then continually arranged for the labor. Yang Fang was promoted from sub-prefect to the post of* [expectant] *taotai. In the 10th year of Hsien Feng* [1860], *when the Cantonese rebels attacked Shanghai, Yang Fang again received orders, and raised an army of Western soldiers to suppress the rebels, called the Ever-Victorious Army, which repeatedly achieved merit. In the 1st year of Tung Chih* [1862], *he was appointed intendant of sea transport at Changchow, but subsequently did not take up the post due to being in mourning for his parents. Memorialists said Yang Fang was energetic in frequently borrowing Western troops to help keep order, and that he was of exemplary character. He established and supported two foundling homes, established the Ningpo Guild at Hongkew, and a charitable group of Ningpo men to provide relief for Shanghai refugees from the rebels.*

  Like the *Taotai* Wu Hsü, Yang Fang was from the province of Chekiang, south of Shanghai on the southern margin of the Chushan Archipelago. In the 1850s, he joined the drift of Ningpo men into Shanghai and eventually established himself as a silk merchant and banker in the network of Ningpo businessmen, and worked for a while as a comprador for Jardine, Matheson & Company. His association with Westerners gave him knowledge of business and unusual familiarity with Western trading practices.

  After the Triads captured the native city of Shanghai and had remained within its walls for some time, the Tartar governor of Kiangsu, Ch'i-erh-hang-a, ordered Yang Fang to negotiate with the Westerners to build a wall of rammed-earth. Placed at the northwestern corner of the city, the wall would cut off the rebels from their source of supplies in the International Settlement. Yang Fang was successful in convincing the Americans and British to cooperate, arranged for labor to assist in construction of the wall, and was allowed to purchase rank and official office, eventually being promoted to expectant *taotai* as was customary then among Chinese compradors for foreign firms.

  During the years when the negotiations of the treaties of Tientsin were in dispute, Governor Hsüeh Huan frequently called upon Yang Fang as an intermediary with foreign merchants. When the Taiping rebels attacked Shanghai in 1860, Yang Fang raised a mercenary army of Western soldiers under the command of Frederick Townsend Ward. When this force later recruited Chinese as soldiers and was repeatedly successful in the field under Ward's leadership, it was recognized by the throne and awarded the name "Ever-Victorious Army." The EVA served as the model for other forces of Chinese soldiers led by Western officers and financed by local Chinese and Western sources. In all this, Yang Fang was lauded as an exemplary promoter of the method of "borrowing foreign troops," and also for his support of a variety of charities.

  Captain Ghent and ***Confucius***. See Chapter 12 notes below.

  "Public life is open." For any half-baked student of old China this little homily is

Yang Shen *Underfoot*

洋神 *Yang Shen* | James Lande 藍德

particularly endearing because it is so easily located and comprehended; it is readily *accessible*, where so much of allusive Chinese is not so abundantly available to the non-native. And it is universal for any culture that has invented its own equivalent of "loose lips sink ships." The common Chinese dictionary Tz'u Hai 辭海, 1967 *A Sea of Terms*, on p. 332 says that in front of the Great Hall of an old yamen in Fuchou county there was erected a stone tablet carved with the characters *kung sheng ming* 公生明. Its purpose was to warn officials and clerks that what they discussed in the yamen belonged there, and should not go beyond the walls. Such a stone tablet appears in the drawing of the layout of the Shanghai county yamen, immediately inside the Ceremonial Gate, *Yi-men* 儀門, and before the Great Hall, *Ta-t'ang* 大堂, shown in the Shanghai county gazetteer of 1873. This leads to the expectation that a *kung sheng ming* stone tablet was not an uncommon accessory in Ch'ing yamens. It would have served as a cold, hard manifestation of the problem of maintaining discretion, if not secrecy, in a large organization staffed by sometimes hundreds of unpaid lackeys who subsisted upon squeeze alone.

The Hunan Army. On pages 145-151 of 1980 *Rebellion and Its Enemies in Late Imperial China*, Philip Kuhn details the formation and structure of Tseng Kuo-fan's Hunan Army in 1853, which drew on local militia to form units based on personal loyalty to leaders. By 1860, Wu Hsü and Yang Fang should have known many of these details and possibly would have been able to discuss specific battles that demonstrated the success of the regional model. The summary in this chapter of Chinese armies of that time is adapted from Richard Smith's 1974 *Journal of Asian History* article "Chinese Military Institutions in the Mid-19th Century, 1850-60," passim.

Shanghai and its yamens. Descriptions of streets and buildings are taken from the *Shanghai County Gazetteer* 上海縣志. The edition is dated 1873, which seemed never to be a problem as far as textual material was concerned, as gazetteers like this are cumulative from previous magistrates forward to the date of the edition. Each edition incorporates the information from the past and adds news of events since the previous edition. However, diagrams and maps represented the city as it was *at the time of the edition*, in this case 1873 rather than 1860. Textual description accompanying the diagrams and maps assigns a date to most of the changes and renovations to the city and its buildings, telling not only of the changes since 1860, but also of many earlier renovations since removed. This could have been used to derive descriptions precise for 1860, and so could have a contemporary edition of the gazetteer, but lacking that *Yang Shen* chose instead to select a mix of characteristics old and new, and to make some descriptions, such as of yamens, rather more representative than precise.

Kiangsu Governor Hsüeh[1] Huan[4] 薛煥. Biographical information on this mandarin is based partly on the *Shanghai County Gazetteer*, p. 887, the *Chinese Biographical Dictionary*, p. 1670, and on Swisher, 1951 *China's Management of the American Barbarians*, p. 721. Also Banno, 1964 *China and The West, 1858-1861*.

上海縣志: 蘇松太道, 咸豐七年任: 薛煥.

Shanghai County Gazetteer: Su-Sung Tao-t'ai, 7th year of Hsien Feng [1857]: *Hsüeh Huan.*

中國人名大辭典: 薛煥.清興文人. 字覲堂. 道光舉人. 選金山知縣. 咸豐時洪楊事起,率川勇力 保上海. 累擢江蘇巡撫. 權兩江總督. 皆以留辦洋務居上海. 後入為工部右侍郎. 總理各國事務大臣. 坐與言事者互劾. 兩罷. 仍留總理衙門.光緒間以病歸.

Chinese Biographical Dictionary: Hsüeh Huan, personal name Chin-t'ang, born in Hsing-wen county, awarded the chü-jen *degree during the reign of Tao Kuang* [1821-1850], *appointed magistrate of Chin-shan county. During the reign of Hsien Feng* [1850-1862], *he became prominent as a result of the Taiping rebellion, leading*

洋神 *Yang Shen*   *James Lande* 藍德

Szechuanese braves in the defense of Shanghai. Appointed governor of Kiangsu, and acting governor-general of the Liang Kiang. In each position, he was retained to handle foreign affairs, residing at Shanghai. Afterwards he joined the Board of Works as a junior vice president, and was a high official of the Tsung-li Yamen. He was dismissed after being implicated in a scandal but kept his position with the Tsung-li Yamen. He retired due to illness in the reign of Kuang Hsü [1875-1908].

    Combining additional information gleaned by Swisher from Hsüeh Huan's memorials, we can say that Hsüeh was born in Hsing-wen county in the province of Szechuan, that his personal name was Chin-t'ang, and that he passed his examinations for the advanced *chü-jen* degree during the reign of Tao Kuang. His first appointment was as magistrate of Gold Mountain county. By 1857 had advanced to the office of Su-Sung-T'ai *taotai* and resided in Shanghai. There he led *yung* forces against the Taiping rebels in engagements around Shanghai, and acquired experience dealing with foreign officials and merchants. For all practical purposes Hsüeh Huan was in charge of China's foreign affairs between 1857 and 1863. By 1858, his reputation for handling foreigners was such that he was appointed judicial commissioner and called to Peking by the emperor to assist with treaty negotiations, and that autumn he assigned to help represent China in the tariff conference at Shanghai. Swisher, in 1951 *China's Management of the American Barbarians*, summarizes the remarkable events that followed. "[Hsüeh] opposed the 'Secret Plan' of the emperor and court to repudiate the treaties of Tientsin and offer the foreigners 'free trade' in exchange and, when the commissioners arrived from Peking [for the tariff conference], persuaded them not to present it to the foreign envoys. Despite the emperor's exasperation with the commissioners for listening to his advice, he recognized Hsüeh Huan's grasp of foreign affairs and made the personal comment that if the foreigners insisted on residence at Peking [for official representatives] 'Hsüeh Huan must be kept in the capital as permanent director'."

    In 1860, Hsüeh was appointed imperial commissioner for trade at the five treaty ports, as well as brevet governor 巡撫銜[1] during the term of Kiangsu Governor Hsü Yu-jen, and governor of Kiangsu province after Hsü's death at Soochow in June of 1860. Hsüeh Huan also held temporary authority as governor-general of the Liang Kiang, the three provinces south of the Yangtze in east China: Kiangsu, Kiangsi, and Anhwei. On p. 722 of *China's Management...*, Swisher says that Hsüeh Huan's memorials from Shanghai revealed a "solid business sense, statesmanship, and diplomacy such as few Chinese officials possessed in this period." In 1862, he was promoted to junior vice-president of the Board of Works in Peking, and was appointed a minister in the Tsung-li Yamen (China's first "foreign office"). Later, he was dismissed from office after being implicated in a scandal, but nevertheless was retained in his position as minister in the Tsung-li Yamen, and retired in 1877 due to illness.

    Reviewing Legal cases. The source for cases at law is Derk Bodde and Clarence

---

[1] Most sources state only that Hsüeh Huan was governor of Kiangsu in 1860, or that he became governor after Hsü Yu-jen. In 1951 *China's Management of the American Barbarians*, p. 650, Swisher cites an edict of March 10, 1860, appointing Hsüeh Huan governor of Kiangsu, at the same time Hsü Yu-jen held that office. *Yang Shen*'s author has not been able to consult the original Chinese of that edict, but it may have specified brevet governor, *hsun-fu hsien* 巡撫銜, which *would* be consistent. Hsüeh Huan is noted as brevet governor in 1860 in a summary of information about him at the National Palace Museum (Taiwan) site *http://npmhost.npm.gov.tw/ttscgi/ttsquery?0:0:npmauac:TM%3D%C1%A7%B7%D8*, and as Kiangsu governor in the same year. *Yang Shen* has therefore assumed that Hsüeh Huan held brevet governor rank when he arrived in Shanghai from Soochow, performed that office while in Shanghai in April, May and into June, and was so regarded by his subordinates, and by the foreign community. NCH makes reference to the arrival of Sieh, newly appointed provincial governor, in issues during that time, such as April 7, 1860.

洋神 *Yang Shen*   James Lande 藍德

Morris, 1973 *Law in Imperial China* [LIC], a seminal work in the study of Chinese law which presents 190 cases documented in original Chinese sources. This extraordinary book describes at length the administration and conduct of Chinese courts, the context of the Ch'ing legal code, and presents a comparison of the interpretation of statutes in China and the West. The three cases adapted for review by Wu Hsü and Liu Hsün-kao in *Yang Shen* are based on the following cases in Bodde and Morris:

    151.8 (1813) – First case: The Tomb Violator, p. 310

      11.1 (1826) – Second case: Criminal Excused to Care for Aged Parents, p. 223 (case cited is on p. 225)

    161.3 (1832) – Third case: The Murdered Businessmen, p. 325

The Ch'ing legal code incorporated degrees of mourning into its statues by determining severity of punishment for crimes according to mourning relationship. Thus, crimes committed against parents were punished more harshly than crimes against cousins, or people more distantly related. The five degrees of mourning, *wu-fu* 五服, are discussed at length on p. 35-38 of Bodde and Morris. The first degree of mourning, *chan-ts'ui* 斬衰, required a son mourning his father to wear garb of unhemmed sackcloth and mourn for three years. The other degrees of mourning are set forth in the following table.

Degree	Designation	Clothing	Term	Example relations
1	斬衰 chan ts'ui	garb of hemmed sackcloth	3 years	Son to father, wife to husband
2	齊衰 tzu (ch'i) ts'ui	garb of hemmed sackcloth		
	a		1 year	Husband to wife
	b		1 year	Father to son, brothers
	c		5 months	Grandparents[1]
	d		3 months	Great grandparents[1]
3	大功 ta kung	garb worked with greater coarseness	9 months	First cousin
4	小功 hsiao kung	garb worked with lesser coarseness	5 months	First cousin once removed
5	緦麻 ssu ma	garb of plain hempen cloth	3 months	First younger cousin

The full detail of the degrees of mourning, *wu-fu* 五服, is found at the front of the book of Ch'ing legal statues, the Ta Ch'ing Hui Tien 大清會典. Note 1. zh.wikipedia.org (the LIC authors do not cite these relations).

The Confucian concept called *li* 理 refers to principles intended to direct proper behavior in society. Five relationships were the basis of proper behavior: father and son, ruler and subject, husband and wife, elder and younger, and friend and friend. Laws derived from Confucian belief recognized these five relationships in the legal code. Rules for mourning, derived from the five relationships, prescribed the manner and length of time for mourning according to degree of relationship.

Chapter 7: Crossing the Bar

Mariner Reef. Mariner Reef is yet another of the flotilla of treacherous submerged rocks named for ships they killed or disabled; in this case, for the brig *Mariner's Hope*, which had struck the reef just three years before the date of *Essex*' passage.

"Like estimating distances with one eye closed." This line is quoted from John King Fairbank's 1970 *Ch'ing Documents: An Introductory Syllabus*, in appreciation of Dr. Fairbank's kindly consideration for a untried writer and inadequate student of Chinese history who approached him during the early development of *Yang Shen* with too many tedious queries. Moreover, Dr Fairbank's syllabus on documentary Chinese was an invaluable portal to learning how to read many of the Chinese source documents for *Yang Shen*.

洋神 *Yang Shen*   *James Lande* 藍德

Sailing directions. The course of *Essex* from the Volcanoes to Gutzlaff Island is based on the British Admiralty Hydrographic Office chart for China, Sheet VIII, Eastern Coast...including Chushan Islands, 1843. Also consulted were the closely corresponding sailing directions for the Chushan Archipelago in the appendix to S. Wells Williams 1863 *The Chinese Commercial Guide*, p. 121-134.

Upon the arrival of *Essex* at Gutzlaff Island, the wind was still steady from the southwest at 3 knots. High water was between 11:00am and 12:00 noon in the vicinity of the island and flowed WNW to NW at 1 to 5 knots, with a spring rise of 15 feet; the ebb tide flowed SE by S with a neap rise of 10 feet.

China Sea Pilots. Basil Lubbock notes in 1914 *The China Clippers* the poor reputation of Western pilots on the China coast, notorious as drunks, and gives anecdotes about a pilot named Hughie Sutherland, who was once so drunk in court his case could not be heard. One more ill-famed example of a disreputable China coast pilot was Richard Savage, another historical footnote resuscitated for *Yang Shen*. Savage was mentioned in British correspondence as having left piloting on the coast to join the Taiping rebels and fought against the Foreign Rifles at Ch'ing-p'u in late 1860. Delevan Slaughter is based loosely on Savage (see Chapter 15, The Rebel Capital).

Clipper *Game Cock*. *Game Cock* actually departed from Woosung on January 8, 1860. No large clippers came downriver on April 20, 1860, as *Essex* approached the Yangtze, thus for fictional purposes it was necessary to shanghai a noteworthy example of a clipper ship from as close a date as possible. *Surprise* departed Shanghai on December 30, 1860. *Indiaman* departed on April 21, 1860. *Game Cock* won out over both *Surprise* and *Indiaman*, one of the few instances where *Game Cock* actually beat another ship. The choice was because *Game Cock* is described by Howe and Matthews as having spread nearly as much sail as *Flying Cloud* (the author's choice until it was verified that *Flying Cloud* was approaching Hong Kong from London in April, 1860). Also, *Game Cock* was leaving Shanghai in ballast bound for Nagasaki, Japan (*North China Herald*, 01/14/1860), under charter to the British government to transport livestock for the Peiho expedition, which indirectly involved her in the events of that moment. *Indiaman* was closer in time, but she was smaller and is not so well known.

Chapter 8: *Essex* at Shanghai

Lord Byron. The lines from Byron's *Don Juan* that Elizabeth recites introduce Smith's book 1978 *Mercenaries and Mandarins*.

The stone-faced wall of the Chinese city. A Chinese wall, like the one encircling Shanghai in 1860, can inspire interest, even awe, for those who never have lived inside a walled city, with its massive size, guarded gates, drum towers, and old brick facings. This wall made a nearly perfect circle around the native city – "Fletcher called that wall the *omphalos* of Shanghai, the middle of all things, the navel of the settlements...." Jen-min (Renmin) Lu 人民路 and Chung-hua (Zhonghua) Lu 中華路 are today where the wall used to be.

Cities surrounded by a wall were called *ch'eng* 城. In his 1928 *A Short History of Shanghai*, F. L. Hawks Pott tells us that in Ming times, the wall around the Shanghai native city kept out Japanese pirates. The original wall's outer face was bricked, and the inner was backed with earth. It was from twenty to twenty-four feet high, three to three and one-quarter miles long, and had twenty *chien-ta* 箭塔, arrow towers (*tsien-t'ai* in Shanghai dialect). Water gates served as the entrances for natural streams flowing through the city. Over time, the eastern wall was made fifteen feet thick, and the moat around the wall was still an effective defense in the 1860s. George Smith wrote, in 1847 *Consular Cities of China*, that a wall three miles in circuit, through which six gates

Yang Shen *Underfoot*   515

opened into the surrounding suburbs, surrounded the city. Four gates opened into the vicinity of the river, where most of the mercantile houses were situated. A canal about twenty feet across surrounded the city outside the wall. Three canals lead through the heart of the city and under the east wall, with several lesser branching dikes. The river opposite was about a quarter of a mile wide,

Making a wall was a large undertaking requiring extensive public participation; official coffers and gentry donations provided the funds and local laborers the work force. Fei Hsiao-t'ung pointed out on p. 558 of "China's Gentry," in Hsiao, 1960 *Rural China: Imperial Control 19th Century*, that the length of a wall, and its size, thickness and height, reflected the affluence and political power of the *ch'eng* it enclosed. Surprisingly, walled cities were not always thought the safest place to be: "Live in the city during minor disturbances; live in the country during a major uprising," was a popular aphorism. In a large-scale revolt or rebellion, the cities were likely to be besieged, and the roads between cities crowded with troops, while the countryside would be comparatively safe from ravaging armies (Hsiao, p. 692).

The wall surrounding Nanking was *thirty* miles in circumference!

Chapter 9: Rebels and Imps

Chung Wang **Li Hsiu-ch'eng** 忠王李秀成, the Loyal King. The description of Li Hsiu-ch'eng is taken liberally from Augustus Lindley's 1866 *Ti-ping Tien-kwoh, The Taiping Heavenly Kingdom*, in spite of reservations about his objectivity. Lindley joined the rebels in late 1860 as an arms buyer and smuggler, and an officer of artillery, served with them for several years. Thus, he can be expected to have been a witness to much detail of life among the rebels, but some historians prefer to leaven his rosy tone of an invariably sweet, just and wholesome Taiping Christian society with corroboration from other contemporary sources. Another crucial source of detail about Li Hsiu-ch'eng, especially about what he may have actually thought, is the confession Li was forced to write just before his execution. This document, which is the subject of C. A. Curwen's 1977 *Taiping Rebel: The Deposition of Li Hsiu-ch'eng*, was liberally edited by Tseng Kuo-fan before the confession was presented to the Emperor. Scholars have pieced it back together from various sources. Together with accounts from Ch'ing generals and other contemporaries, which fill out Curwen's extensive notes with abundant particulars, there is much reasonably consistent detail on events from the siege of Hangchow forward, and on the personalities of the rebel officers.

The retreat from Hangchow. As this chapter occurs at the same time as those preceding, April 19-20, 1860, *Yang Shen* places the Loyal King's forces about midway between Hangchow and Nanking (T'ien-ching) as they return from the feint at Hangchow, intended to draw imperial troops away from Nanking. In 1976 *The Taiping Kingdom Day by Day* 太平天國史事日誌, Kuo T'ing-yi cites Li Hsiu-ch'eng at Chien-p'ing 建平 in Anhui on April 11th, and at Chü-rung 句容 in Kiangsu on April 23rd, after coming from Li-yang 溧陽 and passing Yi-shan 亦山, a length of twelve days. April 17th is six days later, or about one-half the way between, at Li-yang. On the 19th, Li Hsiu-ch'eng may have left Chin-t'an and have been approaching Yi-shan, perhaps within sight of Yi-shan-hu, Yi-shan lake. The day in this chapter was changed to the 20th as the previous chapter takes place on the 20th, expecting Li's location would not change much.

Sources for the retelling of the Loyal King's march toward Hangchow two months earlier, beginning in Section 4, are primarily Kuo Ting-yi, and Jen Yu-wen, 1973 *The Taiping Revolutionary Movement* – these books are fine examples of scholarship that provide ample information for a detailed fictional account. Curwen's 1977 *Taiping*

洋神 *Yang Shen*　　　　　　　　　　　　　　　　　　*James Lande* 藍德

Rebel... was frequently consulted to glean the Loyal's King's personal view of these events from his final "confession." The extraordinary account of the defense of Hangchow by bannermen was made possible by the research of Pamela Kyle Crossley for her book 1990 *Orphan Warriors: Three Manchu Generations and the End of the Qing World*. Archives from the Hangchow garrison, local histories, and journals presented in *Orphan Warriors* give stirring accounts of the battle for the city, and also provide a wealth of detail about how very different the Manchu conquerors of China were from native Han Chinese.

Mongols, Tartars and Manchus. These terms are used interchangeably for the northern tribes that established the Ch'ing Dynasty in 17th-century China and ruled there until 1912. Strictly speaking, Tartar and Mongol are not the same as Manchu, but such *follows 19th century usage*, when the distinctions were no more clear than now. Tartars dwelt in Tatary, dictionaries tell us, a broad sweep geographically and historically of Asia between Europe and Japan home to several ethnic and national groups.

Mongols were the nomadic tribesmen of east Asia whose language is part of the Altaic family; they united under Genghis Khan and overran eastern Europe in the 13th century, eight centuries after Atilla the Hun.

Tartars were peoples of Turkic origin from east-central Asia who spoke a Turkic dialect of Altaic. They joined with Mongols and became part of the Golden Horde led by the grandson of Genghis Khan that invaded Russia later in the 13th century.

Manchus originated in extreme eastern Asia, east of present Mongolia and north of China, along the Great Wall. They were nomads of the Jurchen tribe who federated in the 16th century and developed under the influence of Mongols and Chinese, later taking the name "Manchu" to distinguish themselves from Mongols. The decline of the Ming Dynasty in China gave the rising Manchu empire the opportunity to conquer China and establish their own dynasty, the *Ta Ch'ing* 大清 or "Great Pure" dynasty in 1644.

Chapter 10: Shanghai's U. S. Marshal

Shanghai U. S. Marshal. According to the *North China Herald* of 15 March 1858, p. 317, a Mr. Stanton held the office of U. S. Marshal of the Consular Court in 1858. According to the newspaper, he went aboard the real Chinese war-steamer *Confucius* in pursuit of a Manilaman murder fugitive, pretty much as described in *Yang Shen*. This incident, and another later on involving a ship called the *Wandering Jew*, are the basis for the fictional character Marshal Stanford Hull.

The sketch of his background Fletcher gives the marshal is factual, as is his account of his service aboard Captain Lynch's *Antelope*, and with William Walker in the Republic of Sonora, Mexico.

Description of the Shanghai Bund and its buildings in *Yang Shen* was enhanced considerably by referral to a remarkable collection at the website *Virtual Shanghai* of digital reproductions of old paintings made in Shanghai over the course of the 1850s and 1860s. Of itself, the site says *"Virtual Shanghai is a research and resource platform on the history of Shanghai from the mid-nineteenth century to nowadays. It incorporates four sets of documents: essays, original documents, photographs, and maps. The objective of the project is to write a history of the city through the combined mobilization of these various sets of documents."* http://virtualshanghai.net.

Other sources with detail regarding the Shanghai Bund: Morse, 1918 *The International Relations of the Chinese Empire*; Pott, 1928 *A Short History of Shanghai*; Lanning and Couling, 1921 *The History of Shanghai*; and NCH.

American consul. The concerns of Walter L. G. Shanks draw loosely upon contemporary correspondence between the American consul at Shanghai in 1860, and *Yang Shen Underfoot* his superiors in Washington, available on microfilm from the National Archives, as well as Griffin's description of consular posts in China 1938 *Clippers and Consuls*. The circumstances to which the consul refers in his correspondence reflect the compromising situation of an American consul forced into a position made inferior to that of other consuls at Shanghai by the want of vigorous support for American interests in the Far East from the Buchanan administration. Congress also was increasingly distracted by the threat of approaching civil war. The matters dealt with by the consul on this morning – reporting to the State Department, receiving complaints about acts of piracy against American citizens, enforcing American laws and laws under the treaties with the host nation – were actual and routine duties documented in correspondence to Washington.

Commission Agencies. "No doubt, our firm and many others will have to start investing a great deal more of our own money, instead of just other people's money, into enterprises in China." Augustus Fitch refers here to the changing circumstances of trading in China. American commission houses in China like the fictional Augustus Fitch & Company, which during the 1850s and 1860s conducted business as agents by trading in commodities on the behalf of "constituents" in America, are described by S. C. Lockwood in his 1971 *Augustine Heard and Company, 1858 – 1862: American Merchants in China*. The commission house charged a percentage of each transaction performed using a principal's funds, and did not itself invest in the transactions.

By 1860, this model for business began to decline as recession, changing economic conditions, rebellion and war influenced the rise of competition that lessened the profitability of commission houses and reduced the number of principals willing to continue the relationship. Increasingly, commission houses found they could continue in China only by initiating business on their own behalf, investing their own money in commerce and trade, accepting themselves the risks of success, and themselves managing the business to conclusion. Eventually, greater opportunities for investment in development back home in America lured many Yankee traders out of China.

Chapter 11: American Consular Inquiry

The North China Herald. Samuel Couling, in his 1917 *Encyclopedia Sinica*, tells us on p. 400 that the NCH was a British weekly newspaper established at Shanghai in 1850, which became in 1859 the official publication for announcements of the local British authorities. NCH printed a variety of information besides local news and reports of rebel activity of potential threat to the city [you can believe *Yang Shen* has read a lot of it]. All marine traffic in to, out of, and present in the harbor was reported in detail sufficient to track the movements of specific vessels. The North China Branch of the Royal Asiatic Society saw its papers on life in China printed in NCH, and the "Peking Gazette" – a compendium of imperial Chinese correspondence, edicts, and rescripts – was translated for publication. The editor in 1860, Charles Spencer Compton, did not shy from harsh editorial comment on anything not to his liking or inconsistent with official British policy, in particular the "foreigners in the employ of the *taotai*," the Foreign Rifles. Caleb Carr reports much interesting detail about NCH in his 1992 *The Devil Soldier*, noting the persistent attacks of editor Compton on the Foreign Rifles during 1860 and 1861. Excerpts from NCH articles often open a chapter in *Yang Shen*.

In the consul's office. The correspondence read by Consul Shanks was taken from actual letters to Washington from the Shanghai American consul and reflect accurately issues pressing at the time: ambiguous or insufficient authority to enforce laws, no jails for holding prisoners, American lawbreakers. Ironically, the consuls found that the treaty clause called "extra-territoriality," which was intended to protect Americans from harsh Chinese judicial treatment by making Americans subject only to American authority in

洋神 *Yang Shen*　　　　　　　　　　　　　　　　　　　　　　　*James Lande* 藍德

China, now served to prevent American criminals from being prosecuted. Under treaty, the Chinese had no authority to detain Americans, but the Americans consul was not certain of his authority to act without liability. The sources are files of diplomatic correspondence in the Library of Congress and 1971 *British Parliamentary Papers*.

Fletcher's account of service with Walker accords with the facts. His claim that he was tarred by Walker's notorious activity in Nicaragua, when he served only in Mexico, agrees with the record of his wanderings after he left the Republic of Sonora. The yarn Fletcher tells about Delevan Slaughter is fiction but, then, so is Delevan Slaughter.

The animosity between the China trader Augustus Fitch and the consul is imagined, as are the characters, but is consistent with the conflicts that arose between merchant and consul when their interests clashed. American merchants wanted protection for American trade over that of competing treaty powers, and relief from the caprice of Chinese officials, but they did not wish to be held accountable for their own infractions of business practice or treaty law. Insofar as a consul had to answer to politically sensitive superiors back in Washington, and live together with merchants in the same small community of foreigners, China traders were able to employ more or less subtle pressures to frustrate the best intentions of consular authority. Often, the consul himself was a merchant, which caused complaint early on when the Chinese perceived a consul's self-interest placed Chinese interests at a disadvantage. The British and the French, as well as the Americans in Shanghai, experienced this "Mexican standoff."

The Astor House. The meeting between Fletcher and Hannibal is, of course, fictional, however the detail underlying the characterization of Hannibal begins with Wellman's paper on the "Tarheel" from North Carolina. Further ambiance was skimmed from Hauser, 1940 *Shanghai: City for Sale*, and Lanning and Couling, 1921-3 *The History of Shanghai*. The Astor House is a Shanghai icon still receiving guests after 150 years or so, an inexpensive and colorful place from which to view many of the landmarks of this story. Much of the history of the place – Soochow Creek, the British consulate, harbor and the Bund – has been preserved in photographs on display there. The description presented here is based in an early photo of the hotel at Virtual Shanghai (*http://virtualshanghai.ish-lyon.cnrs.fr/GetFile.php?Table=Image&ID=Image.ID.20804.No.0&Op=T*), taken before the hotel was first remodeled.

The Shanghai custom house. For some time there was a maritime custom house, *Chiang-hai Ta Kuan* 江海大關, at Shanghai, shown in the Shanghai Gazetteer (1873) as located just outside the East Gate, opposite the *Chao-chia-pang* 肇嘉浜 water gate, on the bank of the Huang-p'u (Whangpoo). The accompanying *text*, however, describes it as further north, above the Little East Gate: 江海關向在小東門北今移之老白渡救生局而洋涇浜北復增北新關. The location was convenient to the Huang-p'u junk anchorage, and the *taotai*'s yamen just inside the (greater) East Gate, and presumably served native commerce. When Shanghai became a treaty port in 1843, a fledgling maritime customs station, a *p'an-yen-suo* 盤驗所, was established outside the city wall, beside the Huang-p'u river, north of the *Yang-ching-pang* 洋涇浜. This, in lieu of a full-grown maritime custom house, which could not yet be nurtured by the stripling foreign trade at the port.

As Shanghai changed from a sleepy river town to a bustling entrepôt of foreign commerce in the mid-19th century, the ever-vigilant tax authorities of an empire, strapped for cash to put down rebellion and war with foreigners, decided after some consideration to build a new maritime custom house. The site was downriver where it would be more convenient to the foreign anchorage and the foreign trading houses along the Bund. The new edifice was christened the North Custom House (*Pei Kuan* 北關), or Yang Shen *Underfoot*　　　　　　　　　　　　　　　　　　　　　　　　　　519

洋神 Yang Shen   James Lande 藍德

New Custom House (*Hsin Kuan* 新關), to distinguish it from the older native maritime customs at the East Gate, thereafter called the South Custom House (*Nan Kuan* 南關), or Old Maritime Custom House (*Lao Kiang-hai Kuan* 老江海關).

The New Custom House was ransacked and gutted by fire during the occupation of the city by the Small Swords, *Hsiao Tao Hui* 小刀會, in 1853, and for several years the maritime customs had no permanent home. Briefly, there was a floating custom house, when the *taotai* moored two Chinese gunboats off Pootung Point in 1853. When that proved ineffective, the *taotai* set up shop in a house on the north side of Soochow Creek in 1854, on Chinese soil where foreign consuls fussing about the neutrality of their nations amidst the Small Sword uprising were appeased to see it established.

Finally in 1857, Chinese maritime customs relocated to an old temple on the Bund near Hankow Road, next door to Dent & Co., about one-half mile south of the British Consulate. It took the names of its predecessor (North Custom House, or New Custom House), except that now the names were combined as North New Custom House (*Pei Hsin Kuan* 北新關). There is a photograph of the *Pei Hsin Kuan* compound in Lanning and Couling, 1923 *History of Shanghai*, Vol. I (the caption says it was "in the fifties," but the dress of bystanders seems later, as do the glass windows and an iron fence that Chinese sources say were added in later years). The description in *Yang Shen* of the interior of the place had to be imagined, based on a general familiarity with the interiors of temples. In the many paintings of the Bund of the era, the custom house stands out as the one Chinese-style building in a long façade of Western-style square brick buildings, having the appearance of an old temple with a three-story building flanked by a large wing on each side, a tall monumental arch over the entrance, and two flagpoles out front. In later years, the building was rebuilt several times in Western design.

Kuan Lao-yeh 關老爺. The Chinese God of War, also called Kuan Kung 關公, Kuan Ti 關帝, and Wu Ti 武帝. Originally, he was Kuan Yü 關羽, the bean-curd peddler who became a military hero of the *Romance of the Three Kingdoms* 三國演義 (see below, Chapter 19). He was first ennobled in the 12th century; later, the emperors of the Yuan and Ming deified him as Kuan Ti and, over time, he came to be worshiped in thousands of state and private temples through China, one of the most widely honored deities in the Chinese pantheon. According to Werner's 1961 *Dictionary of Chinese Mythology*, Kuan Ti appeared among the clouds in 1856 and championed an imperialist defeat of the Christian rebels. In gratitude, the Hsien Feng emperor promoted Kuan Ti the same rank as Confucius. Kuan Ti was venerated by warriors, who carried his talisman into battle, and also as the god of literature, because his phenomenal skill at recitation, and, of course, as the patron of bean-curd peddlers.

Chapter 12: Fletcher Meets *Confucius*

Confucius. This gunboat was quite like her appearance in the story, and her description is available entirely through the courtesy of reference librarian William T. La Moy, formerly of the Phillips Library of the Peabody Essex Museum in Salem, Massachusetts, and the library staff. The description of her exterior is based on an oil painting of *Confucius* at the Phillips Library of the Peabody Museum in Salem, found in the library's collection after a diligent search by curator Marla Gearhart, which followed months of fruitless correspondence with East Coast sources. The significance of having a vertical ("walking") beam engine became clear when a careful examination of the painting detail revealed that the Chinese artist in Hong Kong had included the A-frame above deck. The "rope-cutter" reinforcement in her bow is a fictional addition, as is the number and location of her boilers, and the arrangement of her house and hold.

520   Yang Shen *Underfoot*

洋神 *Yang Shen*   *James Lande* 藍德

Other detail came from the New York Marine Register: A Standard Classification of American Vessels, and Other Such Vessels as Visit American Parts, R. C. Root, Anthony & Co., No. 16 Nassau St., New York, 1858, 1859 ("Steamers").

Registry information for Confucius (New York Marine Register):

Description: Side-wheel, 468 tons, 8-foot draft (unloaded), one deck. Built & metalled in 1853 by Thomas Collyer, New York

Measurements: 161, $26^{8/12}$, $11^{6/12}$ (length, beam, depth of hold)

Material: W. O. & C (white-oak and chestnut)

Fastening: IC (iron and copper)

Engine: vertical beam, con'g

Diameter of cylinder: 1 cyl, of 59 inches

Stroke of piston: 9 feet

Steam, fire & bilge pump: 1. Indifferent security & provision against fire (depends on character and condition of lining of the chimney rooms, coating of boilers, and being provided with independent steam fire pumps). Hails from New York. Managed by R. Sturgis and others.

Model: M (tow-boat, open standing pipe)

Class 5 – constructed wholly for navigation of sounds, lakes, and rivers. [*Note: classes 1-4 are all sea-going vessels with 2 or more decks, one or two engines, and s sufficient or "insufficient" spread of sail. Also req'd (possibly only for steamers of 1st class) were two watertight bulkheads, one forward and one abaft of the engines and boilers, reaching at least 2 feet above the deep load line.*]

Rate: A1. [*Note: the rate pertains to the conditions "added" to those of ordinary construction, including security of propeller bearings and rudder post, and of openings in the bottom of the hull; whether the hull is coppered; condition, construction and location of boilers; and if fitted with bilge injection and independent steam pumps.*]

The design of her vertical beam may be of particular interest to readers familiar mostly with Mississippi steamboats of later vintage. Today, only two such engines still exist – one is the ferryboat *Eureka*, at the San Francisco Maritime National Historical Park http://www.nps.gov/safr/historyculture/eureka.htm; the other is the *Ticonderoga*, at the Shelburne Museum in Vermont http://shelburnemuseum.org/collections/steamboat-ticonderoga/. A video showing how a walking beam engine works can be viewed via the link at http://www.steamboatexplorer.org/gunboattypes.html#anchor720294. At the *Mariners' Museum* website, there is a model of a walking beam steam engine. Thomas Main's description of war steamer operation in his 1864 *The Marine Steam Engine* informed much of the operation of Confucius in *Yang Shen*. And R. Sheret's 2005 *Smoke Ash and Steam* is a detailed source on the operation of old steamer engines.

Most the activities attributed to *Confucius* in the story are based on mention of her in the *North China Herald*. Her sale to the Chinese was reported NCH on June 27, 1857. She was lauded in NCH, Jan 26, 1856, "Further Destruction of Pirate Junks," for joining in the destruction of pirate junks at the Volcanoes. In the congressional record [45th Congress], a Capt. Joseph Rouse was deposed and stated he was master of the *Confucius* sometime after 1863. *Confucius* was said to belong to a guild – the "guild" was like a Chinese Chamber of Commerce – and a mandarin was always on board to give the ship received her orders, coal, and payroll [hence the inspiration for the "Littee Mandalin" aboard *Confucius*]. Rouse thought the money for the operation of *Confucius* came from the Shanghai Junk Guild.

The diagrams following were prepared for blocking action aboard the fictional *Confucius*.

Yang Shen *Underfoot*

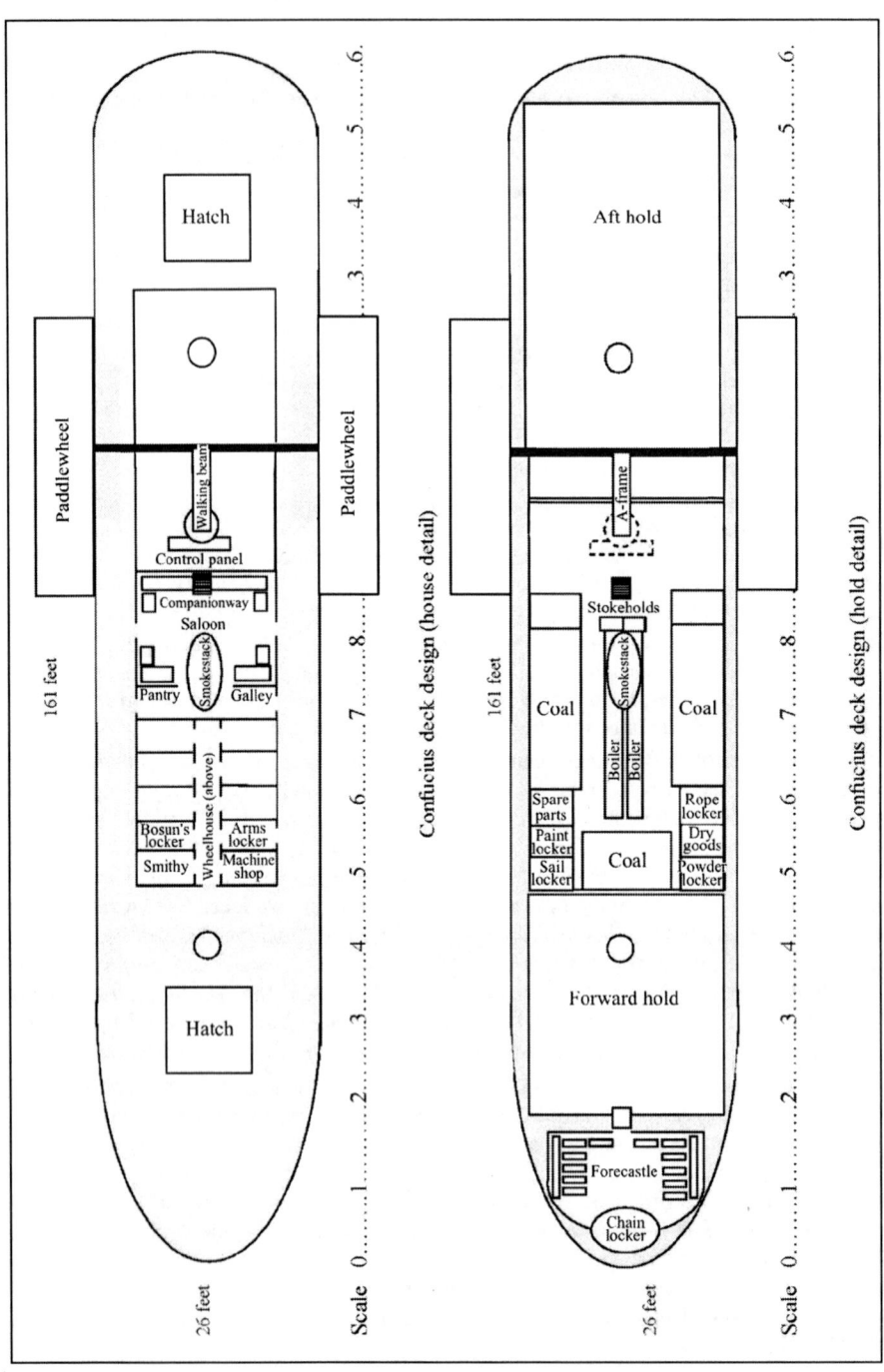

洋神 *Yang Shen*   *James Lande* 藍德

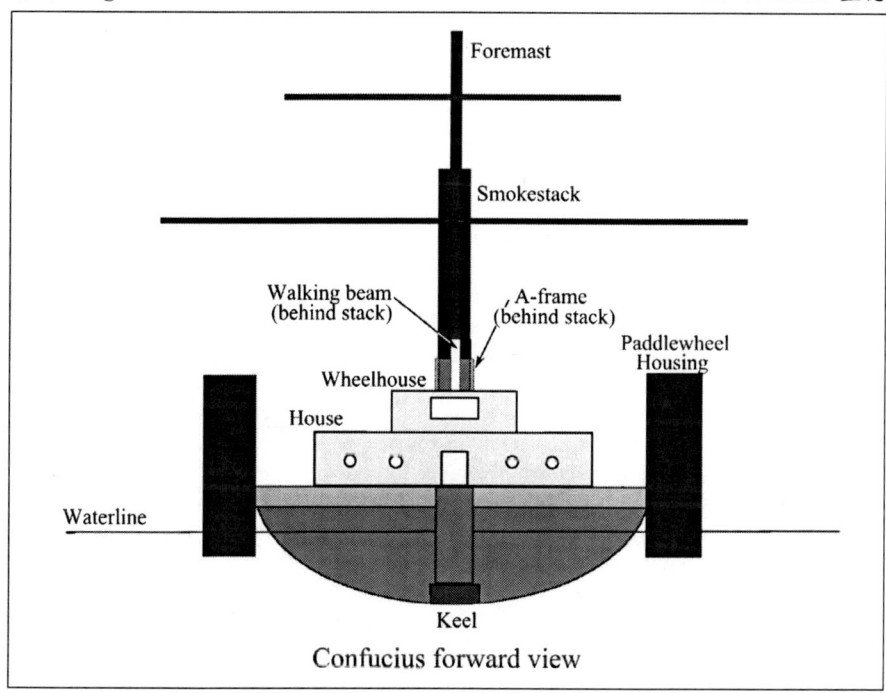

Confucius forward view

Captain Ghent. The captain of *Confucius* is based on historical references to R. S. Gough, the actual captain of the steamer *Confucius*. Captain Gough and *Confucius* appear in NCH at intervals over the years from 1856 to 1862. At least one source has him as an Englishman, but Gough's contemporary Mesny, in his 1899 *The Life and Adventures of a British Pioneer in China*, identified Gough as an American. The online Maritime Heritage Project has archived a letter from a Captain William Ellery that appeared in the *San Francisco Chronicle* on March 4, 1871. The letter stated that Gough "…was a Southerner, and between the years 1830 and 1840 was with the celebrated Captain Wm. Smiley of the schooner *Ohio*, in the sealing business at the Falkland Islands, and on the east coast of South America." Some sources state that Admiral Gough left *Confucius* in 1862 to train Chinese soldiers in Shanghai. It was Mesny's impression that Captain Gough died in 1862 in the explosion of the steamer *Union Star* during trials in the Whangpoo River off Pootung Point, and Captain Ellery's letter confirms Mesny's account of Gough's death. Gough Island in the Whangpoo River may have been named for the Captain R. S. Gough, if not for Sir Hugh Gough, whose force captured Chenkiang in 1842.

Fletcher's letter to his sister. Speculation about the content of correspondence between Frederick Townsend Ward and his sister Elizabeth Ward inspired this fictional correspondence. The original letters have not come down to us. They are reported to have been burnt by Henry Ward's ex-wife, some time after the death of Elizabeth Ward left the ex-wife the sole beneficiary of the settlement of the claims of the Ward estate against the Chinese government. Was there something in the letters to embarrass in-laws tightly laced in their corsets of respectability, or to compromise the pursuit of claims before the courts, or did FTW simply make some injudicious remarks about his sister-in-law? We may never know. Perhaps the hint of opprobrium associated with destruction of the real letters can be circumvented briefly by resurrecting a little of the old 19th century *Yang Shen Underfoot* epistolary style to reveal a more personal side of Fletcher Thorson Wood. Perhaps it may reawaken as well some of the old affection we might like to presume existed between brother and sister.

Chapter 13: The Fitch Soirée

The soirée guests. The vessels and trading firms cited are those actually in Shanghai at the time. The names of diplomats, officers, and traders vary in authenticity; generally those with speaking parts have been changed or invented: Spalding, Barnet, Fitch, Whitfall, Howe, Frazer, Cage, and Wright are all fictional. The soirée itself is also an invention, a set piece devised to round up all the principals and allow them an opportunity to state their positions on pertinent issues, predominant among them being the filibuster Fletcher Wood. Such gatherings, however, appear to have been common in the hermetic little community of foreigners at Shanghai, and one of the few escapes from the grind of a trader's life and the tedium of military duties.

Piratical Attack in Chushans. This *faux* article was created in the style and format of NCH reporting to allow the entire Shanghai foreign community in on the adventures of *Essex* that the reader has been following.

...found a Sebastopol there. Several of the remarks in this conversation were suggested by the lively correspondence between principals of Augustine Heard & Company, an American trading firm with offices in Shanghai in 1860, available in the Augustine Heard Collection, Baker Library Historical Collections, Harvard Business School. Augustus Fitch & Company was contrived using detail of Heard & Company found in the Baker Library collection of letters, and in Stephen Lockwood's 1971 *Augustine Heard and Company: 1858-1862*.

Chalmer's Alexander. This is a fictional rendering of Chaloner Alabaster, who joined the British consular service in 1855 as a Chinese interpreter and held many responsible posts in China over the years, retiring as Consul at Canton in 1892. Lanning and Couling discuss Alabaster's character and accomplishments at length in a section "Some Biographies" in their 1923 *History of Shanghai*, Vol II, listing his service as an assessor with the Shanghai mixed court, and in the Land Office, in addition to his consular duties. In 1858, Alabaster was assigned to accompany Viceroy Yeh of Canton, a prisoner of the British, to Calcutta, and thereby was given an opportunity to observe intimately the workings of a Chinese mind. Alabaster also frequently went into the field with the EVA – his reports to his superiors on Ward's activities have come down to us. He assisted "first Hope, then Stavely, against the rebels. He took part in all the expeditions and was sent on many important missions, for example, to arrange matters with the Ever Victorious Army.... He was probably the only efficient interpreter there was for the British Admiral or General to use, not, of course, [just] by mere knowledge of the spoken language, but by [reason of] his tact and knowledge of the Chinese mind."

Pilloried in the public and the press. The minister is referring to his being blamed for the decision in 1859 that resulted in the allied defeat at the Peiho. When the British returned to China in 1859 for ratification of the treaties won from the Chinese at gunpoint in 1858, the naval force under Admiral Sir James Hope misjudged the response of the Chinese in the Taku forts defending the entrance to the Peiho River. Several emissaries came and went with attempts to negotiate agreement and avoid a confrontation, but the minister insisted that, as he was nine miles off shore aboard a ship, he could not be at hand to conduct diplomacy when the British decided to advance on the booms across the river. The British were soundly thrashed, four gunboats were sunk at the mouth of the river, several more ships damaged, and 89 British died. The defeat was a resounding blow to British prestige, and the minister felt he was made the

洋神 *Yang Shen*   *James Lande* 藍德

scapegoat for the disaster, even after being vindicated by the Foreign Secretary (Morse, 1918 *International Relations of the Chinese Empire*, p. 579-85). Detail underlying the conversations at dinner and after came from NCH, Dennet, Tong. Banno, Morse, and Beeching, and Paske-Smith for Japan.

Chapter 14: The Lower Reaches

Pirate-suppressing Mandarin. The fictional character Yang Hsi-hai, the pirate-suppressing mandarin aboard Confucius, was suggested by the testimony of Mr. Cowie, Master of Confucius, before the 45th Congress, found in Senate Executive Documents, 2nd Session, #48, March 28, 1878, p. 34. Cowie merely mentions the existence of such a person; *Yang Shen* elaborated on that historical footnote to invent the Littee Mandalin.

Malwa opium. One of two varieties of opium, the other being Patna, grown in India in the 1860s and exported to China. The names Malwa and Patna come from the location where the opium was grown.

Piloting the Yangtze River. Several contemporary sources contributed detail for piloting the Lower Reaches. Oliphant describes Lord Elgin's trip up the river in 1858. Blakiston repeated the journey in 1861. S. Wells Williams has distances between towns and landmarks along the way, as well as specific bearings and depths, including the intricate course steered at the Langshan Crossing. British Admiralty charts for the Lower reaches at that time also were consulted and served as the basis for the maps accompanying chapters on the river.

"Isn't Wuhoo in the hands of the rebels?" In February of 1859, the rebel general Li Shih-hsien surrounded imperial forces at Wu-hu and, when imperial reinforcements fail to appear, imperial troops set fire to their own camp and withdrew. The city was still in rebel hands in May of 1860, when the fictional *Confucius* arrived there to purchase tea *(芜湖市地方志 Wuhu City Local Gazetteer www.wuhu.gov.cn:8080/dfz/module/intro/dsjinfo.asp?articleid=68).*

The eve of the break in the siege beginning May 2, 1860. It was only after *Confucius* arrived at Nanking in her fictional journey up the Yangtze that *Yang Shen* realized she had blundered into the middle of one of the most exciting episodes in the rebellion, the breaking of the imperialist siege of Nanking in 1860. There are no records to say if Frederic Townsend Ward was on the river then. We know only that at about this time he served as mate aboard *Confucius*, commanded then by R. S. Gough. Presumably Ward was gathering the experience that would support his proposal to Takee, so he might have been anywhere on the river then. The fictional interlude of the crew of *Confucius* being interviewed in Nanking takes place on May 2nd, when the rebel armies had already converged upon Nanking and that day were signaled to begin the all-out assault on the Southern Imperial Barracks on the following day, May 3rd.

Chapter 15: The Rebel Capital

Nanking in 1860. The particulars of this map are combined from five sources:
(1) Kuo T'ing-yi 郭廷以, 1976 *The Taiping Kingdom Day by Day* 太平天國史事日誌, Map 12.
(2) C. A. Curwen, 1977 *Taiping Rebel: The Deposition of Li Hsiu-ch'eng*, Map 3, p. 73.
(3) F. W. Mote, "The Transformation of Nanking, 1350-1400," in Skinner, 1977 *The City in Late Imperial China*, p. 135, 140.
(4) Spence, 1996 *God's Chinese Son*, p. 187.
(5) "A Concise History of the City of Nanjing...," *nanjingwalls.pomosa.com/history .pdf* (10-6-2009)

Detail is simplified and selected to reflect changes between 1853 and 1860. The

Yang Shen *Underfoot*   525

Eastern King was assassinated in 1856, and Shi Ta-k'ai had long since decamped, so their palaces are marked simply "Taiping Palace," and the Porcelain Tower, torn down after the rebels captured Nanking, has been left off the map, as have been fourteen other gates. Destroyed and rebuilt many times, even Chinese experts sometimes have difficulty locating former features of the old Nanking.

Demons and imps. Both words are used to translate the Chinese *yao* 妖, which was the epithet commonly used in the Taiping Kingdom to refer to soldiers of the Ch'ing emperor. "Imps" is obviously appropriate as it does double-duty as an abbreviation of "imperialist." Demons and imps would correspond roughly to the "rebs" of the American Civil War and, yes, there was an equivalent for "yank," too: the Ch'ing soldiers called the Taiping rebels *tsei* 賊, bandits, or thieves.

Delevan Slaughter. As noted previously, Delevan Slaughter is based on Richard Savage, the china coast pilot and mercenary who served with the Taiping and commanded the repulse of the EVA at Ch'ing-p'u in the autumn of 1860. More detail about Savage is in Lubbock's 1933 *The Opium Clippers*, Carr's 1992 *The Devil Soldier*, p. 100 and passim, and in Abend's biography. According to contemporary British correspondence concerned with reacquiring at Nanking deserters from the British fleet, Savage was formerly a pilot at Shanghai who, during a rebel counter-attack at Sungkiang, led his men against an outer work manned by "Europeans in the service of the Taoutae of Shanghai," the Foreign Rifles, and was knocked down by the first shot. A British acting consul and interpreter named Forrest, with British Admiral James Hope's first expedition up the Yangtze in 1861, reported Savage at Nanking slowly recovering from his Sungkiang wounds (Forrest to Bruce, May 1, 1861 in 1971 *British Parliamentary Papers* 32 1861, No 11, Incl 2). After this, Savage vanishes from the historical record with the same finality as Fokie Tom, walk-on bit players who disappeared when the theater went dark.

Hakka 客家人. A small group of Chinese who migrated as early as the Han Dynasty (206 BC) from the north of China into parts of Fukien, south China, and Taiwan. Called *k'e-chia jen* 客家人 in Mandarin, literally "the guest people," they have their own dialect and a variety of unique traditions that set them apart from the communities in which they settle. Most of the first generation of Taiping leaders came from Hakka villages in southern districts they shared with the local Cantonese majority, referred to generally as *pen-ti jen* 本地人, locals, and Miao tribesman settled more or less in the foothills near *pen-ti* and Hakka villages. When rural leadership failed in south China during the unsettled times of the 1840s, the conflict that grew between villages of these different groups is regarded as one of the reasons for the rise of the God-worshiper Society and the persecution of the Hakka minority that led to the Taiping rebellion.

Conflict between the Loyal King and Hung Jen-k'an. The Loyal King's jealousy of Hung Jen-kan's rapid rise to power depicted here is known from Li's own statements in his confession, documented in Curwen's 1977 *Taiping Rebel*..., and forms the basis for the fictional conflict between Li and Hung over control of the armies, and planning for breaking the siege of Nanking and the thrust eastward toward Shanghai.

Chapter 16: Breaking the Siege

Sailing directions above Nanking. Theodolite point is downstream of the northern limits of the Nanking city wall and the north anchorage (see map *Yangtze River, Nanking to Wuhoo*). Above Nanking, the course is nearly mid-channel to the Pillars, except at "Wells Island" (Wade Island), where USS *Susquehanna* found eight fathoms in the west channel; avoid shallow ground 3½ miles WSW of the Taiping Pagoda,

洋神 *Yang Shen*   *James Lande* 藍德

opposite the village of Tang-tu. Steer a mid-channel course between the East and West Pillars, and through the Wuhoo Reach, and gradually close the right bank on approach to a range of hills 700 feet high, avoiding mud banks that are dry in November. The Wuhoo anchorage is inside a shoal about two cables off shore (S. Wells Williams, 1863 *Commercial Guide*, sailing directions).

Rebel batteries below the Pillars. The incident in which *Confucius* is fired upon by a rebel battery is based on the continuing account of Lord Elgin's journey up the Yangtze in 1858. This was reported in several installments in the *North China Herald*, beginning February 19, 1859, p. 114, col. 5, Extract from a Journal of a Cruise Upon the Yang-tsze Kiang. "In the course of the same afternoon, some flaunting rebels in gay colors had the audacity to wave defiant flags and fire gingals at us… when they brought a gun to bear upon us from a small redoubt, we considered the joke had gone far enough… after two or three shots from the *Retribution* and *Furious*, a well-directed 68-pounder from the former knocked the whole of their gingerbread fort into smithereens, and sent its occupants scampering over the open plain, their long yellow and red robes streaming in the wind in ludicrous dismay and confusion."

Ferrying rebel troops. Sources that describe the crossing of the rebel army across the Yangtze to join the attack on imperial troops at Nanking suggest that by the time *Confucius* arrived at Hsi Liang Shan 西梁山, the West Pillar, on the evening of Tuesday, May 1st, 1860, the army of the rebel Heroic King would have already crossed the river into Kiangnan and joined the battle at Nanking. *Yang Shen* has delayed the rebel crossing in order to put *Confucius* on the scene.

Taiping river pass. The pass issued to Captain Ghent at Nanking is a composite of two examples shown in Michael and Chang, 1971 *The Taiping Rebellion: History and Documents*, Vol. III: (a) a travel pass issued in 1861, on p. 1554, and a customs certificate issued in 1861, on p. 1552. This imaginary pass is intended to resemble actual passes that might have been issued in May of 1860, with an additional countersignature by the fictional officer who interviewed the captain and crew of *Confucius*. The Taiping date was converted to May 1st, 1860, following the Taiping calendar in Kuo T'ing-yi's 1976 *Taiping Kingdom Day-by-Day*. Taiping date conversions are eased by the fact that 1851 was the first year of both the reign of the Chinese emperor then on the throne, and of the Taiping heavenly kingdom. Michael and Chang note that the example of the customs certificate was issued to a merchant traveling to Shanghai from rebel territory and indicates the importance to the rebels of controlling trade and collecting duties.

Tea. Lockwood recounts on p. 46 of 1971 *Augustine Heard…* that in 1860 Heard & Company sent almost a quarter million dollars up-country from Foochow with a comprador, paying five to six dollars per half-chest of tea for almost 50,000 half chests.

The battle for Nanking. The battle witnessed by *Confucius* was pieced together from several sources and is subject to the postulate that the distance from the middle of the river east to the city wall of Nanking was less than five miles, and detailed action could have been viewed through a telescope. Information about the battlefield, and rebel troop movements and disposition in late April and early May, is from Kuo T'ing-yi's 1976 *Taiping Kingdom Day-by-day*, with some reliance on Kuo's maps.

Detail of the general conditions of siege and defense of Chinese walled cities was adapted from Herbert Franke, "Siege and Defense of Towns in Medieval China," in Kierman and Fairbank, ed., 1974 *Chinese Ways in Warfare*, p. 151-201. Changes in the methods of warfare, such as substituting artillery for catapults, were made to reflect the later period of *Yang Shen*.

Particulars of battle were adapted from Augustus F. Lindley, 1866 *Ti-Ping Tien-Kwoh: The History of the Ti-ping Revolution*. Lindley was a Taiping partisan who joined Yang Shen *Underfoot* the rebels after the engagement described, but who by his own heavily-biased account actively participated in later engagements as an artillery and infantry officer under the *Chung Wang* Li Hsiu-ch'eng 忠王李秀成, the Loyal King. Details such as vaulting across moats on bamboo spears, the use of arrow-head rockets, and the rebel infantry tactic for encircling enemy cavalry and shooting them from their horses with musketry and arrows were adapted from Lindley. The wholesale massacre of captured imperial soldiers is speculation based on frequent but unrelated contemporary accounts in the *North China Herald* of executions, or evidence of executions, witnessed by Westerners.

Chapter 17: The River Gauntlet

Rebel lorcha at Silver Island. The captain's brief failure of resolve during the engagement with the rebel lorcha is an adaptation of an occurrence reported in Morse, 1918 *International Relations of the Chinese Empire*. Morse quotes W. S. Wetmore's description, in 1894 *Recollections of Life in the Far East*, p. 33, of an incident that took place in 1857 when Frederick Townsend Ward was mate of a coasting steamer on the China coast, Lynch's *Antelope*. "The steamer ran ashore near Foochow and was threatened by pirates. Our captain quite lost his head. The first officer, fortunately, was cool and collected." Wetmore later recognized the mate as General Ward.

The "Soochow System" of silk purchase. Hicks description of the Takee's method of silk purchase is based on historical detail in Hao Yen-p'ing, 1970 *The Comprador In 19th Century China*, p. 82-3.

Chapter 18: Fletcher Meets Takee

Maskee. "All right," "never mind," "in spite of," "notwithstanding," "but," "however," "anyhow," "it is all good." "Maskee t'at t'ing my no can do. *Without* that thing I can't do it." This pidgin is from Leland's 1876 *Pidgin-English Sing-Song*. Probably the most frustrating term in the entire Chinese pidgin parlance, "maskee" seems to be a universal word that means whatever you like, whenever you'd like it to, according to the situation. Charles Finney, on p. 103 of the 1963 Paperback Library edition of *The Old China Hands*, writing about the period of the 1920s and 1930s when the American 15th Infantry was garrisoned in Tientsin, says that "Maskee is one of the most wonderful words in any language. It means, roughly, 'just do as you please.'"

Fletcher's Resume. The background Fletcher presents to Takee is an amalgam of detail from the several biographies of FTW, none of which agree completely on all facts. For example, the length of FTW's stay at Norwich Academy is given variously as some number of months (Carr, and Wikipedia), over a year (Abend), and nearly two years (Norwich University online archive at *www.archive.org*). The least that can be said is that the fiction writer has quite a lot to choose from even within the confines of accepted biography.

Fletcher's plan to defend Shanghai. Some sources suggest that not all the strategy and tactics set forth by Fletcher to Yang and Wu were actually known to Frederick Townsend Ward at the beginning of his adventure, but were only gradually understood with experience. *Yang Shen* takes the liberty of presenting a plan possibly more detailed than the one the Chinese first heard from Ward. We know little of what passed between the mercenary and his potential backers, or how Ward was so able to impress them that they committed such huge sums, and it seems more likely the Chinese would have been swayed by the specifics offered by Fletcher. In particular, while the need for artillery would have been more apparent to a Westerner, for breaching walls, the tactic of using

洋神 *Yang Shen*   James Lande 藍德

of steamers for swift transport may admittedly have been taken more time to ferment. Still, as it happens shortly in *Yang Shen*, the need for water transport in the labyrinth of streams and creeks west of Shanghai would have been immediately clear upon one's first excursion there from the number of junks alone. The questions remaining then would have been *how* small a steamer was needed and where to get one.

    Ch'ang-mei's lament. Ch'ang Mei is said to cry herself to sleep to the lament of Ts'ui Ying-ying 翠鷹鷹 the cloistered heroine of *Hsi-hsiang Chi*, *The Romance of the West Chamber*. The original version of this poem, from the Yuan Dynasty drama *The Western Chamber* 西廂記 …

        The maiden's boudoir is desolate   金閨極無聊 *Chin-kuei chi wu-liao*
        She cannot greet the new spring   沒能訪春曉 *Mo neng fang ch'ün-hsiao*
        If only some person passing by   料得路過者 *Liao-de lu-kuo che*
        Could feel for the grieving girl   憐憫深嘆人 *Lien-min shen-t'an jen*

…occurs as a song in the old Shaw Brothers' 1960s film *The Western Chamber* 西廂記, produced by Run Run Shaw and starring Ivy Ling Po 凌波 as the student Chang Jün-rei, Fang Ying 方盈 as the rich daughter Ying-ying, and Li Ch'ing 李青 as the slave girl Hung-niang. This charming rendition of the old story is presented in the "light opera" style called *huang-mei-tiao* 黃梅調, "Yellow-plum Melody," similar to American musicals, where songs intermingle with spoken dialogue. The convention of the clever slave girl who comes to the aid of her mistress may have arisen with *The Western Chamber* – Hung-niang has over time become popular in her own right. Fang Ying sings a version of the poem:

        The maiden's boudoir is deeply lonely 蘭閨深寂莫 *Lan-kuei shen chi-mo*
        She cannot enjoy the fragrant spring   無計度芳春 *Wu chi tu fang-ch'ün*
        That fellow who is passing, humming   料得行吟者 *Liao-de hsing-yin che*
        Ought to have pity for her long sighs   應憐長嘆人 *Ying lien ch'ang-t'an jen*

    The first line 蘭閨深寂莫 can be found at many locations on the Internet and seems to be ubiquitous in the collective consciousness of the Chinese-speaking community. The Shaw Brothers video of the film has long been out of print. Copies on VHS of *The Western Chamber*, and many other equally charming old *huang-mei-tiao*, were last available through the licensed representative Ocean Shores Group, #12, Alley 166, Nung-an Street, Taipei, Taiwan.

Chapter 19: Tiger with Wings

    The *Taotai*'s Yamen 道署. The 1873 Shanghai Gazetteer maps the location of this yamen and has a drawing and description of the yamen's layout. The location is recognizable today, a little south from the location old Great East Gate, off of Hsun-tao (Xundao) Street 巡道街.

    The Romance of the Three Kingdoms, *San Kuo Yan-yi* 三國演義. This enduring example of Chinese historical fiction tells of a century-long struggle of ancient heroes to establish a dynasty of Three Kingdoms at the end of the Han. The early Ming author Luo Kuan-chung 羅貫中 combined historical sources with numerous fictional tales to create a complex narrative full of devious political artifice and celebrated proverbs that have become enduring touchstones of Chinese language mastery. The famous passage Yang Fang mentions takes place in the peach garden, *t'ao-yuan* 桃園, and establishes the fundamental loyalties between the heroes Liu Pei 劉備, Chang-fei 張飛, and Kuan-yu 關羽 that form the foundation of the story and persist to the fall of the kingdoms. Over the following centuries, Chinese emperors canonized each of the three heroes. Liu Bei, originally a "seller of straw shoes," was ordained the God of Basket-weavers. Yang Shen *Underfoot*

洋神 *Yang Shen* James Lande 藍德

Chang Fei, who started as a wandering pork-seller, became one of the gods of butchers. And Kuan Yü, a peddler of bean-curd, was promoted to be the God of War, and Literature, and was worshiped throughout the land.

Temple of the Fire God 火神廟. There is no record of this temple being used by the foreign rifles. *Yang Shen* chose to use it because it was near the *taotai*'s yamen. Today the site is occupied, *Yang Shen* believes, by the Universal Complete South Bund Food Market 万有全南外滩菜市场, on He-shun Kai 和顺街. Some locals agree with this identification because in the Shanghai dialect *he-shun* 和顺 is very close to *huo-shen* 火神 in Mandarin, and because the several acres covered by the market are certainly large enough to have once been a temple compound (see below, Chapter 24).

Chinese Maritime Customs. See above, "The Shanghai custom house," in Chapter 11: American Consular Inquiry.

Horatio Nelson Lay. The son of a family with long service in China, H. N. Lay was appointed to the British consular service in 1849 as an interpreter. He left consular service in 1855 to become inspector at Shanghai for the Chinese Maritime Customs Service. In 1859, Lay was appointed Inspector General of customs and remained in that post until dismissed by the Chinese government in 1864 over disagreement about the disposition of a fleet of armed steamers purchased by Lay on behalf of the Chinese, the Lay-Osborn flotilla. Lay was replaced by Robert Hart (Couling, 1917 *Encyclopedia Sinica*, p. 294, 327).

Wu Hsü and Hsüeh Huan. Passages in the conversation between these two mandarins are taken from statements in Hsüeh Huan's memorials from 1860 and 1861 archived in the *IWSM, Ch'ing Dynasty Management of Barbarian Affairs from Beginning to End* 清代籌辦夷務始末, and Wu Hsü's letters in *WHTA, Selection of Taiping Materials in Wu Hsü's Documents* 吳煦檔案中的太平天國史料選輯.

Chapter 20: Sumbitch Tigah Boat

Let him go back into rebel territory…. The passages on the river in this and the next chapter originate in the imagination of *Yang Shen* – there is no record of Ward having ever made scouting trips into rebel territory, and certainly not in the interval immediately following the fall of the *Chiang-nan Ta-ying*. Sources such as Mesny, Lindley, and Blakiston give accounts of Westerners on the Yangtze during the early 60s.

Clearinghouses 錢莊 **and bills of exchange** 憑票 are described by Yoshinobu Shiba in "Ningpo and its Hinterland," in Skinner, 1977 *The City in Late Imperial China*, and appear in Kao Yang's 1986 novel *Hung-ting-shang-jen* 紅頂商人. Kao Yang 高陽 embroiled historical characters including Ward, Yang, Wu, and others in a collection of sophisticated novels set in the Taiping era. The titles are *Hu Hsueh-yen* 胡雪巖 (*Hu Xue-yan* 胡雪岩), *Hung-ting shang-jen* 紅頂商人 (*Hong-ding-shang-ren* 红顶商人), and *Teng-huo lou-t'ai* 燈火樓臺 (*Deng-huo lou-tai* 灯火楼台).

Chapter 21: Tanyang and Changchow

Secret societies, and the *Ko-lao-hui* 哥老會. Sources for this subject include Jean Chesneaux, 1971 *Secret Societies in China*, the entry Hung Men 洪門, by Chang Chi-chieh 長之傑, in the Pan Chinese Encyclopedia 環華百科全書, and Di Wang, "Mysterious Communication: The Secret Language of the Gowned Brotherhood in Nineteenth-Century Sichuan," in *Late Imperial China*, June 2008, 29-1 Supplement.

Chesneaux regards "Hung Men" as another name for Triads (p. 69), but also quotes Sun Yat-sen's use of "Hung Men" as general term for all anti-Manchu societies (p. 145-

46). The encyclopedia entry also treats Hung Men as catch-all term: 洪門又稱洪幫, 或漢留,是所有天地會所派生的幫會的總稱, "Hung Men is also called *hung-pang* 洪幫, or *han-liu* 漢留 [descendants of the Han], and is a general term for all secret societies 幫會 evolved from the original Heaven and Earth Society 天地會." This encyclopedia treats the San Ho Hui 三合會, or Triads, the San Tien Hui 三點會, and the T'ien Ti Hui 天地會 under the entry Hung Men.

Chesneaux points up many similarities between the various manifestations of anti-Manchu secret societies in organization, ritual, and secret signs and language, while Di Wang delves more deeply into arcana of the *Ko-lao-hui*. The date of origin of the *Ko-lao-hui*, Society of Elder Brothers, is a subject of controversy, but is generally regarded as being about 1670, when anti-Manchu brothers dispatched from Taiwan by Cheng Ch'eng-kung established a lodge in Szechuan. From there, the *Ko-lao-hui* spread to provinces across China and is assumed by *Yang Shen* to have been well established in Kiangsu by the 1850s when the junkman Lin Ch'uan joined the society while imprisoned. Secret societies do not figure anywhere in accounts of Frederick Townsend Ward, but the *Ko-lao-hui* was incorporated into *Yang Shen* in order to depict yet another significant dimension of the conflict ongoing in Chinese society of that day.

Entering the Grand Canal. The decision to enter the canal from Tantu instead of from Chenkiang is based on Worcester, 1971 *Junks and Sampans of the Yangtze*, p. 326. The British Hydrographic Office chart (1842), for the reach of the Yangtze below Chenkiang shows the channel from Tantu to the Grand Canal to be less than ½ mile in length. Medhurst's table in p. 86-7 of 1850 *General Description...* shows high tide at 11:00am. The moon will be new in two days, so the tide on the 19th is approaching its highest. Lacking a convenient tide table for all the points at which *Confucius* touches, *Yang Shen* has extrapolated from the British hydrographic charts, and S. Wells Williams sailing directions in 1863 *Commercial Guide*, that the noon flood tide at Chenkiang was perhaps two to four feet. With the river beginning to rise with the "freshets of Spring," the actual flood tide probably would have been higher still.

The Yangtze River. Descriptions of this segment of the river came from Blakiston, 1862 *Five Months On The Yangtse*; Lindley, 1866 *Ti-Ping Tien-Gwoh*; and Worcester, 1971 *Junks and Sampans of the Yangtze*. The streams to Tanyang and Changchow taken by Lin Chuan's junk exist only on the chart of *Yang Shen*'s imagination. However, a persistent reader can with little trouble locate in Google Earth the starting point of streams that exist today along the south bank of the Yangtze and follow one or more of them to these towns. The route of waterways from Shanghai to Kuangfulin was also confirmed using this method.

Cotton farming in the Yangtze delta is described by Medhurst on pages 52-67 of his 1850 *General Description of Shanghai*, and by Mark Elvin in "Market Towns and Waterways," in Skinner, 1977 *The City in Late Imperial China*, p. 444-473 passim.

Wicked clerks 奸胥 and rapacious criminals 蠹犯. The minutia of Lin Chuan's career as a criminal was cadged from Bodde & Morris, 1967 *Law in Imperial China: Exemplified by 190 Ch'ing Dynasty Cases*, cases 230.1, p. 435, and 8.1, p. 218; and from Ch'u T'ung-tsu, 1969 *Local Government in China Under the Ch'ing*, p. 40-54.

Vauban's old book on siegecraft. Vauban's early work 1740 *A Manual for Siegecraft and Fortifications* is discussed in Hinds and Fitzgerald, 1981 *Bulwark and Bastion*, p. 31-4 and passim. By 1860, it is not unlikely that at least some of Vauban had become obsolete with changes in warfare, yet still applied to China, where siegecraft continue to follow centuries old precepts without change.

Li Hsiu-ch'eng saw the small, dark foreigner... Contemporary accounts suggest

洋神 *Yang Shen*   *James Lande* 藍德

that it is highly unlikely Frederick Townsend Ward and the Loyal King ever met, or even laid eyes upon one another. At the risk of slipping from fiction into fantasy, this opportunity is afforded them in *Yang Shen*.

Some detail of Changchow and the actions of the imperial army came from C. A. Curwen, 1977 *Taiping Rebel: The Deposition of Li Hsiu-ch'eng*, p. 116; the *North China Herald*, "Narrative of a journey from Shanghai to Nanking," March 2, 1860, #553, p. 35, col 3; and a recent PRC update of the Changzhou City Gazetteer 常州市志编纂委员会编, Vol 52, p. 1069 passim. The lone figure on the Little New Bridge at Changchow was derived from a contemporary account called *Diary of Living Quietly* 能静居士日记, by Chao Lieh-wen 超烈文, cited in the Ch'ang-chou gazetteer, p. 1072.

Chapter 22: Treachery at Soochow

Expectant *Taotai* Li Wen-ping 李文炳. The facts surrounding this mandarin and his treachery at Soochow come from these principal sources:
Jen Yu-wen, 1973 *The Taiping Revolutionary Movement*
Kuo T'ing-yi, 1976 *The Taiping Kingdom Day by Day* 太平天國史事日誌
C. A. Curwen, 1977 *Taiping Rebel: The Deposition of Li Hsiu-ch'eng*
North China Herald:
    March 2, 1860, "At a meeting of the North-China Branch of the Royal Asiatic Society"
    May 26, 1860
    July 7, 1860, "A Visit to the Insurgent Chief at Soochow"

***Taotai* Wu Chien-chang 吳健彰 (Samqua) escapes from the native city**. Pott's 1928 *Short History of Shanghai* tells how when the Triads took Shanghai, in September of 1853, *Taotai* Wu was put under guard. Two gentlemen from the [American] settlement, a Doctor Hall, and a Caldecott Smith, succeeded in rescuing the *taotai* by going into the native city, locating Wu, disguising him and letting him down by ropes from the city wall. Samqua was first taken to the home of Doctor M. T. Yates, a missionary living close to the wall, then later to the Russell & Company hong.

Arms traffic. The exact circumstances that would allow a British trader at Shanghai to have rifles and muskets for sale were difficult to determine. All but one source make little more than passing reference to arms being available through H. Fogg or Jardine Matheson, as if it were perfectly obvious how Shanghai merchants subject to treaty restrictions on the import and export of arms and ammunition could have or acquire arms. Caleb Carr offers several alternatives on p. 85 and p. 104 of his 1992 *The Devil Soldier* for the acquisition of arms by the first Foreign Rifles, but the issue of how those sources came by arms in 1860 remains (the British military itself enabled the Foreign Rifles to acquire weapons starting in mid-1861). *Yang Shen* relied on two plausible circumstances to make arms available for H. Fogg to sell to Fletcher Wood. Some of the arms could have been acquired prior to the signing of the treaty rules at Shanghai in November of 1858, and treaty contraband could possibly have been imported by non-treaty traders, such as Italy or Spain or, as Artemis Fuller says, leviathans like Schleswig or Piedmont. Just how non-treaty entities conducted business in Shanghai under the Treaty of Tientsin is guesswork on the part of this author because information is lacking in sources consulted for *Yang Shen* or, more likely, *Yang Shen* did not consult the right sources. Non-treaty nationals probably assumed and even claimed treaty right whenever pressed, and disregarded treaty restrictions whenever profitable.

Cost of Equipment for the EVA. From the 45th Congress Record:
    500 muskets, ex *Anglo-Saxon*   4,000 taels, 8 taels each, $12.00
    Howitzers and shells   1,246.30 (no quantity)
    500 haversacks   600 taels, .83 taels each, $1.33

洋神 *Yang Shen*   *James Lande* 藍德

    Canvas, duck, etc. $25.00 [?] (no quantity)
    Serge shirts (Phillips, Moore & Co.)   180 taels (no quantity)
    Hats (Saikee) $197.50 (no quantity)

Bond slave for several *zaibatsu*. Elias Fell is based on Edward Forester, the third officer commanding the early EVA. All sources include Forester with the Foreign Rifles from the start, except Richard Smith's 1978 *Mercenaries and Mandarins*, where documentation showing how Forester could not have been with the Foreign Rifles until much later is cited. *Yang Shen* follows Smith.

Chapter 23: Hiring Foreign Rifles

The first Foreign Rifles. Detail of character, training and action of the first Foreign Rifles is derived from Richard Smith's 1978 *Mercenaries and Mandarins*, Caleb Carr's 1992 *The Devil Soldier*, and the earlier biographers of Frederick Townsend Ward: Rantoul, Cahill, and Abend. Some other sources are:

    Andrew Wilson, 1868 *The Ever-Victorious Army*...
    D. J. Macgowan, 1877 "Memoirs of Generals Ward, Burgevine..."
    Augustus Hayes, 1881 "Another Unwritten Chapter...Late War"
    Augustus Hayes, 1886 "An American Soldier in China"
    Charles Schmidt, 1863 "Memoirs of the Late General Ward, the Hero of Sung-Kiang, and of his Aide-de-camp Vincente Macanaya," *Friend of China*

Carr cites Abend's extract from Mesny's 1896 *The Life and Adventures of a British Pioneer in China*, Chapter 22, about the liberal use of champagne libations as a recruiting tool (p. 84), Hayes' comment that opinion in Shanghai regarded the Foreign Rifles as outlaws (p. 87-9), and the views of Schmidt (p. 84) and Wilson (p. 88) on the character of the first recruits.

Bob Allen's and Fat Jack's (in following chapters) are mentioned by Lanning and Couling on page 387 of Vol. I of their 1921 *History of Shanghai*, and the sailor's home is noted on page 435 of Vol. I, and page 330-1 of Vol. II (1923). The "Crown and Anchor" was also dredged up from this source.

Some of the difficulties encountered with the initial force are suggested by correspondence from Chinese officers with the Foreign Rifles in the field (such as Yang Fang, Hsüeh Huan, Li Heng-sung, and Wu Yün) archived in WHTA and summarized by Smith on p. 37 of 1978 *Mercenaries and Mandarins*.

Discipline among the first recruits is assumed in *Yang Shen* to have been lax at best, based on many of the contemporary recollections of the first force. Correspondence between British officials describing discipline in the force suggest how much more harsh discipline became later (Medhurst to Bruce, 6 May 1861, BPP, China 32, "Correspondence...." 11/3,4, p. 42-3).

Country west of Shanghai. This map, and the description of waterways in this chapter, was cobbled together from several sources old and new, so expect some anomalies. The sources include:

    Medhurst, 1850 *General Description of Shanghai*, description and map following p. 88.
    Kiangsu Complete Province and Maps, 江蘇全省輿圖, in particular maps of Shanghai, Ch'ing-p'u, and Lou counties, 1895.
    Shanghai County Gazetteer maps, 上海縣志、上海縣城圖、上海縣城外街巷圖, 1873.
    Shanghai City, Sungkiang District, Transportation and Tourist Map, 上海市松江区交通旅游图, present day map.
    Worcester, 1971 *The Junks and Sampans of the Yangtze*, map p. 158.

    The P'u-hui T'ang 浦匯塘, "Turbuent Bank Canal," has the same name today it

Yang Shen Underfoot

did in 1860, however some of the other *t'ang* 塘 named were taken from modern maps. Also, several different towns have the same names on the Chinese maps. Southwest a few miles of the New Bridge, Hsin-ch'iao 新橋, on the *Yang Shen* map there is a Hsin-ch'iao Chen 新橋鎮, New Bridge Town, on the Hu-Hang Expressway. The Hundred Flower Slough, Pai-hua Pang 百花浜, has a suspiciously modern ring because the Communist Hundred Flowers movement of the 1950s. The distance from Shanghai to Kuangfulin was roughly estimated at twenty-four miles. The average rate of progress of a junk over these waterways of six knots was a guess, as was the travel time by junk of four hours.

Li Heng-sung (aka Li Ai-tong). Biographies are in Macgowan's *Far East* article of 1877, and the Sungkiang Prefecture "Extended" Gazetteer 松江府續志 of 1883, p. 2103. Sources are uneven on the subject of this officer's rank and command. Macgowan calls him a major-general, but Wu Hsü's letters, and the gazetteer, call him a *ts'an-chiang* 參將. In the Chinese Army chapter of Mayer's 1897 *The Chinese Government*, #443 *ts'an-chiang* is given as a lieutenant colonel, commanding units as large as a provincial brigade. As for the unit Li commanded, Macgowan relates that in the 8th moon of the 10th year (about June of 1860), Li was sent to Shanghai to care for armaments and stores, yet other sources describe Li Heng-sung as commander of an elite force of irregulars known as *chuang-yung* 壯勇. *Chuang-yung* included units "subjected to drill and armed with weapons on the European model" (Mayer, p. 66) and were separate from and superior to ordinary Green Flag troops. Mayer says that *chuang-yung* were led by a *ying-tsung* 營總, a "commandant."

In *Yang Shen,* then, Li Heng-sung is called a lieutenant colonel (*ts'an-chiang* 參將) by Wu Hsü, and a commander (*ying-tsung* 營總) by others. Anticipating that later the EVA would train his soldiers in Western arms and tactics, he commands a force of *chuang-yung* irregulars (and is introduced in this chapter as a brigade commander 鎮標營總, with no certainty that the unit commanded by a *ying-tsung* could ever be called a brigade 鎮標). Also, some writers contest the size of 10,000 given for this force, noting there were not more than a few thousand Green Flag troops in Kiangnan at that time, so the size given for Li's force is left ambiguous.

Chapter 24: Fire God Temple

The Temple of the Fire God 火神廟. In the 1873 Shanghai County gazetteer 上海縣志, the fire god temple was located in the southeast section of a map of the old Shanghai native city, west across one street from the *taotai*'s yamun, just north of the Temple of the Water Sprite 水仙宮. A temple like that of the fire god, Huo Shen 火神, also called the fire king, Huo Wang 火王, was most likely supported by an association of votaries in the neighboring community, who prayed to him to protect them from fire. The temple would have been part of a number of local temples devoted to patron saints venerated by surrounding neighborhood and supported by like associations with overlapping memberships. Each year on the fire god's birthday, his congregation might splurge half their yearly tithings to hire a local restaurant chef for the preparation of a huge banquet in his honor. Perhaps they might even have put his effigy in a sedan chair, taken him out of the temple preceded by incense burners, and paraded him about on the street accompanied by a din of gongs, drums and horns. More detail is in Kristopher M. Schipper, "Neighborhood Cult Associations in Traditional Tainan," in G. William Skinner, 1977 *The City in Late Imperial China*.

Werner's 1961 *Dictionary of Chinese Mythology* lists many fire gods. *Yang Shen*

洋神 *Yang Shen* James Lande 藍德

took its description of the fire god in Chapter 22 from Rita Aero, 1980 *Things Chinese*, p. 92 and 124. Later, the same description was found in Werner's dictionary, where H. C. Du Bose is cited, from p. 389-90 of *The Dragon, Image, and Demon*: "The god of fire, called Huo-li Ta-ti 火力大帝, has three eyes and a red beard, and is worshipped on the third, thirteenth, and twenty-third of each [lunar] month."

Happily, Fletcher and Hannibal arrive at the fire god temple on a day in the Chinese lunar month when festivities were underway. The picture of the Temple of the Fire God compound, heading this chapter, was filched from a picture of the war god temple, Kuan-ti Miao, in the 1873 gazetteer.

Lao Kee Cheong 老旗昌. This dive was a thieves quarter where even the police dared not enter. In 1871, recorded Lanning and Couling on p. 334 of *The History of Shanghai* (1923), Vol. II, it was described as "a sink of iniquity, consisting of one large house split up into a number of small sections, each of which is a gambling, an opium, or a girl hell. It was the focus of every possible abomination, a social, moral, and a sanitary nuisance, and a blot on the fair name of the Settlement. It made night hideous for the neighbors and rest was impossible. …The *Herald* wrote of it in 1875 as a den that ought to be destroyed, full of noise, dirt, and stench."

Bob Allen's. Allen's was a notorious sailor's home and boarding house on the Pootung side of the river nearly opposite the British consulate at Shanghai. Captain Lindsay Anderson said on p. 6 of his 1891 *A Cruise in an Opium Clipper* that it went by the name "Allen's American Boarding-house" and catered to seamen of every country, and deserters from English and American naval and merchant vessels. Bob's crimps "would take men out of one ship to-night and then to-morrow supply the same ship with the men who had been longest on his hands, Bob receiving a good *quid pro quo* on the transaction." Allen's was a refuge from the authorities, and Bob was reputed to have never given up a deserter – the place "was carefully avoided alike by consuls, officers, and captains." Trading in seamen was profitable judging from the returns Allen reported – for a run in a tea-clipper, the crimp received payment of an amount equal to half the sailor's pay, and for other voyages the amount was a month's advance. Crimps were a powerful institution in the early days of sail and a sailor, willingly or not, was subject to their sway every time he left his ship (Alan Villiers, 1953 *The Way of a Ship*, p. 185-6). Lanning and Couling's 1923 *The History of Shanghai*, Vol II, p. 310, has a description of the appalling conditions in sailor's homes at Shanghai.

Chapter 25: Green Flag Immortals

T'ai-ts'ang and Chia-ting. Historical accounts of these early actions of the Foreign Rifles are brief in both Smith (1978 *Mercenaries and Mandarins*, p. 33; Smith's note 47 on p. 207 cites IWSM HF 53:20b-21, 11 July 1860 as a reference of the action) and Carr's 1992 *The Devil Soldier*, p. 90.

Google Earth satellite maps of Chia-ting show a circular canal that *Yang Shen* assumes might have been the moat, and invented action to fit. T'ai-ts'ang is described on p. 39-43 of 1871 *Gordon's Campaign in China* as it was in 1863, and was used as the basis for *Yang Shen*'s fictional engagement there in 1860 (Gordon is also a source for the organization and equipment of the EVA in his day).

Route through the delta. See above, Chapter 23, Country west of Shanghai, for detail of the delta waterways between Shanghai and Kuangfulin, Ch'ing-p'u, T'ai-tsang, and Chia-ting.

Chapter 26: 1st Sungkiang
Yang Shen *Underfoot*

洋神 *Yang Shen* James Lande 藍德

1ˢᵗ Sungkiang. The action for this engagement was invented. What little that is known about "1ˢᵗ Sungkiang" comes from p. 33-4 of Smith's 1978 *Mercenaries and Mandarins*, Carr's description on p. 90 of 1992 *The Devil Soldier*, and Macgowan's article "Memoirs of Generals Ward, Burgevine..." in 1877-78 *The Far East*. Rantoul (p. 81), Cahill (p. 44-5), and Morse's 1927 *In the Days of the Taipings*, p. 192, do not differ significantly. A letter to the editor of the NCH on July 6, 1860, provides information about the presence of vessels near Sungkiang the morning after the attack, flying American, British and French flags, and of Manilamen still nearby.

The brief account of 1ˢᵗ Sungkiang in Abend's biography has four small river steamers taking three hundred men upriver from Shanghai, which seems not to have held much water with later writers. Kuangfulin was northwest only eight miles or so from Sungkiang's east gate (five or so miles from the NW corner of Sungkiang) by boat and it seems more likely the Foreign Rifles would have taken that route, considering also that was the route they are reported to have taken for 2ⁿᵈ Sungkiang. To go to Sungkiang through Shanghai, the Foreign Rifles would have had to travel four hours or more from Kuangfulin back to Shanghai, twenty-seven miles up the Huang-p'u, then march up the creek four miles to Sungkiang.

Yang Shen also proposes a not unlikely rationale to explain the presence of the two steamers and "thirty or more" war junks the next morning noted in the NCH letter. However, Abend's colorful account does consider what the Taiping sentries might have seen as the Foreign Rifles shivaree approached the town wall, and that set *Yang Shen* off on its own little toot of imagining.

Gordon's account, in 1871 *Gordon's Campaign in China*, of his fourteen months leading the EVA was consulted for particulars of many engagements in 1863 that could suggest detail. A major difference is that, while all Gordon's engagements employed artillery, at 1ˢᵗ Sungkiang there was no artillery to breach the town wall and the Foreign Rifles, as Fletcher put it, were left to drubbing the walled town barehanded.

Walled City of Sungkiang. This map of old Sungkiang is based on a present-day map that shows a "Circle Town Street," Huan-ch'eng Lu 環城路, and a village called "East Gate," Tung-men 東門, east of Fang-t'a Park 方塔公園, and another village, Nan-men 南門, south of Fang-t'a Park. In formerly walled cities in China, the old walls often have been replaced by a road, and the former location of the old wall can sometimes be seen on present-day maps as a road running in a circle or square around the early site of a town or city. This is clearly evident in Shanghai, and in Kiangyin (where the old wall is marked on maps today). In several towns, such roads also have names that suggest their ancestry as old walls. In many cities, the walls are gone but the gates are preserved, either physically or in name, such as East Gate, Tung-men 東門, the village on the east side of Sungkiang next to "Circle-town Road," which road circumscribes Sungkiang in an approximate four mile rectangle. Of course, consulting the 1860 gazetteer for Sungkiang would have confirmed this guesswork.

Chapter 27: Fourth of July

The Lahore Gate. ...By 1857, the British East India company had ruled India for 100 years, since the Battle of Plessey in 1757. Their force was made up of about 40,000 British, and a native contingent of 200,000 Muslim and Hindu sepoys. The management of this large native force was thought successful in part because of British accommodation of many native practices, but in the decade before 1857 grievances over perceived abuse mounted.

洋神 *Yang Shen* *James Lande* 蓝德

In March of 1857, indignation over having to bite open new Enfield cartridges greased with lard boiled up out of the regiments and into the streets, and large numbers of disaffected civilian joined the affray. Through April 1857 and into May, unrest spread across Northern India. On May 11, rebels from the 3rd cavalry marched on Delhi and demanded the old king lead their cause; fighting spread through the city, the rebels slaughtering any European they could find.

By July, the British had called in enough Company troops from other stations in India and overseas to begin an effort to retake Delhi, which lasted into September 1857. On September 7, siege guns began battering the Delhi walls. On September 14, the Kashmir Gate was blown and a Company force crossed through town to open the Lahore Gate and admit more Company troops.

The British soldiers and loyal sepoys assaulting the Lahore Gate had to pass up a narrow street under heavy fire from the rooftops, and artillery fire from the far end of the street, to reach the gate. They could not get through this gauntlet – in six hours, the British lost over 1,100 men. Over the next few days, other parts of the town were taken back, and the narrow approach to the Lahore Gate was blasted wide open with artillery. On September 21, 1857, the city fell to the British and the Mogul king fled.

While Delhi was under siege, the rebellion raged on elsewhere across India until June of 1858, and millions died in the fighting and during the retaliations that followed, incited partly by reports of the atrocities at Cawnpore and other places. British East India Company rule in India ceased, the Raj ["reign"] was conveyed to the British crown, and the army was reorganized. India began to look at itself differently.

Many books have been written about the Sepoy Mutiny, often based on the numerous first-hand narratives left by those involved. *Yang Shen* consulted Christopher Hibbert, 1978 *The Great Mutiny: India, 1857*; Eric Stokes, 1986 *The Peasant Armed: The Rebellion of 1857*; and Byron Farwell, 1991 *Armies of the Raj: From Mutiny to Independence, 1858-1947*.

If a British cat could not flog discipline into them.... "If a British cat could not flog discipline into them, why would I expect them to follow my orders?" This thought of Fletcher's was suggested by the observation of FTW's biographer Caleb Carr, who wrote with telling insight on p. 83 of 1992 *The Devil Soldier*, that "These were, after all, men on whom the talents of some of the Western world's most accomplished and brutal disciplinarians had been wasted."

Vulcan. This steamer is described by Morse, on p. 196 of 1927 *In the Days of the Taipings*, as that used by the Foreign Arms Corps for 2nd Sungkiang – a "paddle-wheel [steamer] with high-pressure engines." Caleb Carr wrote on p. 107 of 1992 *The Devil Soldier* that a noisy, shallow-draft river steamer carried the Foreign Arms Corps part of the way to Sungkiang on the occasion of Ward's second attempt on the town. On page 78 of his biography of FTW, Abend mentions that "The *Vulcan* was equipped with notoriously noisy engines...." The only reference to any vessel named *Vulcan* found in research for *Yang Shen* was to one or more large vessels of that name in British service between 1845 and 1862, at least. HMS *Vulcan* was a six-gun second-class iron-hulled paddle steam frigate of 1700 tons built in 1845. An HM[S] *Vulcan* saw service in 1848 as a revenue vessel commanded by C. H. Baker, in 1855 at the assault on Sebastopol, in 1860 transporting the 2nd Queen's regiment to Hong Kong and North China, and in 1862 against the Taiping rebels in the Yangtze delta, commanded by A. C. Strode. Having nothing more specific, the small river-steamer *Vulcan* described in *Yang Shen* was based on the smallest of the steamers known to have seen service with the EVA in later years, the *Kao Jeor* and the *Hyson*. The *Kao Jeor* (41 tons, 70 feet, 3-foot draft) was said by Yang Shen *Underfoot*

W. E. Sherman, in his testimony before the 45th Congress, to be the only one of Ward's steamers small enough to negotiate the water gate at Sungkiang.

Celestial. The *North China Herald* for July 14, 1860, lists a British ship *Celestial* of 494 tons that arrived at Shanghai on July 7, 1860, commanded by a Captain Brail, having sailed from Macao on June 24, 1860, with a cargo of "rattans &c" consigned to Gilman & Company.

MacGregor, in 1952 *The Tea Clippers*, p. 104, cites a British vessel also called the *Celestial*, a wood ship of 438 new tons (452 old tons) built in 1851 by Thomas Bilbe & Co., London. Her dimensions were 134 x 26.8 x 18.2. This vessel was noted as having the Aberdeen bow, essentially greater in length with a slender bow designed to reduce the registered tonnage and, thereby, the tonnage dues. She was a "China trader," and an early British tea clipper, listed as carrying tea to England throughout the 1850s.

About the Aberdeen clipper model, Lubbock says in 1914 *The China Clippers*, p. 71: "It was a very simple improvement, and merely consisted in carrying out the stem to the cutwater and giving the ship a long sharp bow instead of the old-fashioned apple-cheeks."

An American *Celestial* is in Clark's *The Clipper Ship Era*, and Lubbock's *The China Clippers*. She was an extreme clipper ship built in 1850 by William H. Webb, New York, with dimensions of 158 x 34.6 x 19 and capacity of 860 tons. She joined the tea clipper races during the years 1852 through 1857, at least.

Endnotes

More on use of secondary sources. For nonfiction works, common practice and decency require that material from secondary sources be set off by quotes and properly cited in notes and bibliography. Paraphrasing such material generally demands the excerpt be short, and that any restatement be original and add value – that is, expands the selection with additional information, interpretation and/or insight.

For fiction, rules are less precise, largely because of the commercial aspect, and because historical fiction conventionally does not quote source material or cite sources. *Facts* presented in a source apparently are no one's exclusive possession and can be used by others, but the phraseology relating those facts belongs to the original author, in which case the same obligations exist in fiction to avoid infringement, acknowledge substantial sources, and secure permissions if necessary. Paraphrases are not usually placed in quotes but, in the view of *Yang Shen* at least, should still be attributed in notes and/or a critical bibliography. Ideally, the text of the source for the paraphrase is quoted, with permission, in the notes (Underfoot) to simplify comparison.

Another issue particular to historical fiction is the handling of original source material encountered in secondary sources. Use of original source material that is still protected has the same considerations as for use of secondary materials. Secondary source translations of original source material should not be infringed, and confer a responsibility to prepare original translations – here the fiction writer has the same obligation as for any scholar. One's own translations should strive for originality, using different language, and to add value by interpolating new information, implication, or special interpretation and/or insight. Sometimes this can be a challenge with common terms, such as *kuei-chü* 規矩, which in most contexts will always be "rule," "standard," or "manners." One could go to a thesaurus for precept, criterion, or behavior, but the effort can quickly become a pointless exercise in elegant variation. In other cases, a translator might choose a unique way of rendering a phrase and, quite clearly, the

洋神 *Yang Shen*   *James Lande* 藍德

appropriation of such phrasing by another writer would be inappropriate.

As an example, Swisher's 1951 *China's Management of the American Barbarians*, p. 51, gives us "use barbarians to curb barbarians" for *yi-i-chih-yi* 以夷制夷, a unique phrasing. *Yang Shen* renders this as "use barbarians to control barbarians." Fletcher might say that in this example there's not a lot of sea-room for being original – 夷 is "barbarian" and foreigner or Westerner flies in the face of history. 以 can be "employ" or some other pointless variation of "use." But "curb" is unique and belongs to Professor Swisher, forever. So, the conscientious translator (renderer) toddles off to Mr. Giles' dictionary to review 制. In this case, he takes the obvious and easiest choice (anticipating no awards for translation), but one that has a slightly different value because of implications of "control" in English, as well as in Sun Tzu's *The Art of War*. The integrity of the translation of original material in the secondary source has not been infringed, if only barely.

Other examples abound. In his 1977 *Taiping Rebel: The Deposition of Li Hsiu-ch'eng*, Curwen offers on p. 229 n35 a translation of the plan to raise the siege of T'ien-ching (Nanking) taken from the Kan Wang's deposition, on the left below; the *Yang Shen* rendering from Chapter 9 is on the right.

"At this time, when the capital is under siege, it will be difficult to make a direct [counter-]attack. It is necessary to make a determined attack on the weakly-defended towns of Hang-chou and Hu-chou in the [enemy] rear, wait until they draw off forces for a distant campaign, and then turn back and raise the siege. This is certain to succeed."	"Now, it would be difficult for the besieged capital to counterattack," he said. "We must forcefully attack their rear from the direction of Hu-Hang 湖杭, Hu-chou and Hang-chou, compel them to the rescue of Hu-Hang, wait for them to disperse troops far and wide, then return and break the siege. Disguised in imperial hats and uniforms 纓帽號衣, the Loyal King and the Attendant King can together attack both Hu-chou and Hang-chou."

The *Yang Shen* passage is longer [if not bloated] and thus has more "sea-room." Setting aside the *Yang Shen* presentation as dialogue, the *Yang Shen* rendering employs Chinese characters and idiom (Hu-Hang), is closer to the original in some respects ("disperse troops far and wide," and "compel" instead of "wait"), and in the last sentence includes additional content from the original deposition.

In *Yang Shen*, the Underfoot is provided to handle attribution of sources, original and secondary, and discuss how the sources are used. New translations have been prepared and care taken to offer originality and value, to the extent of the translator's scant ability. In the rare event a secondary source is paraphrased, the text of the secondary source was quoted in the Underfoot and permission for use requested. Permissions were requested even when material appeared to be used "fairly," to ensure authors do not *object* to use, especially of academic material in a work of fiction. Liberal acknowledgement, as mentioned before, is one object of *Yang Shen*, to expose sources to as wide a readership as possible and bestir new awareness and interest in their publication and continued availability.

Why have so much Chinese language in this book?

(1) To present meaning, emotion, or sense that has a unique expression in Chinese, but for which there is no direct equivalent in American English. Many words have direct equivalents: door, chair, weather – there is little difference of interest. Other words have no direct equivalent and can only be explained: American *mayonnaise*, and Chinese *temple*, for example. To say *temple* in Chinese one usually has to say what kind of temple – Confucian 廟, Taoist 廟 or 宮, Buddhist 寺 – much as in the classic example from anthropology of Eskimo dialects where to say *snow* one must say what kind of

Yang Shen *Underfoot*   539

snow – wet, dry, slushy, new, old, and so on.

(2) To represent native Chinese idiom – way of saying a thing – when distinctly different from American, as in the example below of "be careful," *hsiao-hsin* 小心, "have a small heart." Other examples: *pu-chang* 補章, a mandarin's large cloth square insignia; *chieh-ping chu-chiao* 借兵助剿, borrow troops to defeat rebels; *fu-mu kuan* 父母官, "father-mother" official, a district or county magistrate; Water can float a craft, but it can also sink a craft *shui neng tsai chou yi neng fu chou* 水能載舟亦能覆舟.

(3) For the visual impact of the Chinese written character. Spanish phrase and idiom in Hemingway's *For Whom the Bell Tolls* has an effect on the American ear that helps create for the reader the Spanish world of the novel[2], and Chinese language in *Yang Shen* does the same, for the eye as well as the ear. The effect occurs usually in one of two ways: (1) Chinese characters occur in phrases and dialogue of the novel; and (2) the rendering in American English of dialogue spoken by Chinese occurs with Chinese syntax and idiom – American phrases that are not colloquial English "reflect" the Chinese language beneath the American English.

In the latter case, the American English language representing dialogue spoken by a Chinese begins as ordinary spoken American, then is rendered into Chinese, and finally is rendered back into American. Chinese idiom is identified in the third step and replaces idiomatic American idiom and syntax where appropriate. The result is a sentence in American that "sounds" spoken by a Chinese.

For example, in the *Yang Shen* preface "In Medias Res" Lay Wah-duc says: "Have a small heart tonight – use care. We are in dangerous water, and the sky will soon be black." This began as: "*Be careful* tonight. We are in dangerous water, and it soon *will be dark.*" The spoken Chinese might be: 晚上小心, 這水危險, 天快黑了 *wan-shang hsiao-hsin, che shui wei-hsien, t'ien k'uai hei-le. Hsiao-hsin* 小心 is "be careful" but literally "have a small heart." And for "it's getting dark" a Chinese commonly might say *t'ien k'uai hei-le* 天快黑了, "the sky will soon be black." This piquant rendering conveys a feel of native Chinese syntax without loss of American English meaning and enhances the characterization.

(4) To identify names of people and places with less ambiguity – there are many confusing methods of romanization for Chinese names, but the characters mostly are always the same (allowing for the difference between short and long forms, and minor differences between dialects).

---

[2] Edward Fenimore, "English and Spanish in *For Whom the Bell Tolls*," in John K. M. McCaffrey ed., *Ernest Hemingway: The Man and His Work*, The World Pub. Co., New York, p. 206.

洋神 *Yang Shen* *James Lande* 藍德

Yang Shen Reading List

One object of writing *Yang Shen* was to resurrect a skeleton of facts about China in the 19th century, diligently unearthed and painstakingly reassembled by accomplished historians and biographers, and fill them out with the flesh, blood, thought and emotion of fictional speculation, to reanimate those old bones, however briefly, with the artifice of the storyteller.

Principal Works Consulted

Among **historical and biographical sources**, the first and finest of the historians consulted about the real-life *Yang Shen*, Frederick Townsend Ward (Fletcher Thorson Wood) was Richard J. Smith, 1978 *Mercenaries and Mandarins,* 1978 *The 'God from the West:' A Chinese Perspective,* and several articles. Nearly all of Smith's English and Chinese sources were gleaned at some point, and they form the best part of a working bibliography of some 700 to 800 titles. Ward's biographers include Caleb Carr, 1992 *The Devil Soldier*; Hallet Abend, 1947 *The God from the West*; Holger Cahill, 1930 *A Yankee Adventurer*; and Robert Rantoul *"Frederick Townsend Ward,"* 1908. The Essex Institute of the Peabody Essex Museum in Salem, Massachusetts, holds a repository established by Ward's estate of the artifacts and correspondence of Frederick Townsend Ward that have come down to us, as well as an oil painting of steamer *Confucius.*

For the **Chinese "handling" of relations with Westerners** in the 19th century, the first source was the *Ch'ing-tai Chou-p'an I-wu Shih-mo* 清代籌辦夷務始末, "Ch'ing Dynasty Management of Barbarian Affairs from Beginning to End," together with Earl Swisher's 1951 *China's Management of the American Barbarians* and 1977 *Early Sino-American Relations, 1841-1982.* Translations of *The Peking Gazette* printed in the *North China Herald* lent insight into the workings of the Ch'ing (Qing) bureaucracy. The diaries and journals of Tseng Kuo-fan, Li Hung-chang and Tso Tsung-t'ang will be gleaned for insight into the character of these famous Chinese generals where they appear in Part II and III of *Yang Shen*.

Contemporary documentary sources in English included National Archive microfilm of Department of State *Diplomatic Despatches, 1843-1861*, *Diplomatic Instructions, 1843-1867* and *Miscellaneous Letters to the Department of State*; British Foreign Office, *Foreign Office General Correspondence, 1862-1865, Papers Related to the Rebellion in China,* and *British Parliamentary Papers (BPP): Taiping Rebellion,1860-64,* and *Treaty of Tientsin, 1860-1864.*

Contemporary correspondence was read in the *Jardine Matheson Archives,* and the *Thomas Wade Collection,* at University Library manuscripts, Cambridge University, Cambridge, England; the *Ward Family Papers* at Phillips Library, Peabody Essex Museum, Salem, MA; the *Jen Yu-wen Collection* in the East Asian Collection of Sterling Library at Yale University, New Haven, CT; and the *Augustine Heard Collection*, Baker Library Historical Collections, Harvard Business School, Harvard University, Cambridge, MA.

Contemporary newspapers consulted were *The North China Herald, The Daily Shipping and Commercial News* (Shanghai)*, The Japan Herald, The Nagasaki Shipping List, The Boston Evening Transcript, Frank Leslie's Illustrated,* and *The London Examiner,* among others.

Of the many **secondary sources** consulted, the following are representative of some general categories.

Yang Shen *Reading List* 541

洋神 *Yang Shen* James Lande 藍德

Clipper ships: Darcey Lever, 1819 *The Young Sea Officer's Sheet Anchor*. Richard Henry Dana, 1863 *The Seaman's Manual*. Alan Villiers, 1953 *The Way of a Ship*. H. A. Gosnell, 1937 *Before the Mast in Clippers*. Basil Lubbock, 1914 *The China Clippers* and 1933 *The Opium Clippers*. David MacGregor, 1952 *The Tea Clippers*. H. Wells Williams, 1863 *The Chinese Commercial Guide* and *Sailing Directions for the Chushan Archipelago*. Howe and Matthews, *American Clipper Ships: 1833-1858*. Edwin H. Daniels, *Eagle Seamanship: A Manual for Square-rigger Sailing*. The first mate, Jim Davis, and crew of the San Diego Maritime Museum Bark *Star of India*. Kenneth D. Reynard, "Restoration of an Iron Star," *Mains'l Haul* (San Diego Maritime Museum), Vol. 33, No. 4, Fall 1997.

Chinese junks: Worchester, C. R. G., 1871 *Junks and Sampans of the Yangtze*. Joseph Needham, 1971 *Science and Civilization in China*. Ivon Donnelly, 1924 *Chinese Junks and Other Native Craft*.

Chinese towns, and walls. G. William Skinner, 1977 *The City in Late Imperial China* (and authors therein: Arthur F. Wright, Chang Sen-dou, John R. Watt, Shiba Yoshinobu, Mark Elvin, Kristopher M. Schipper). Joseph Needham, 1971 *Science and Civilization in China*.

Antebellum America: Carl Bode, 1972 *Midcentury America*. Daniel Howe, *Victorian America*. Daniel Sutherland, 1989 *The Expansion of Everyday Life: 1860-1876*.

American Civil War: Bruce Catton, 1967 *The Coming Fury*, and other Catton books on the Civil War. John Billings 2001 *Hardtack and Coffee* described the minutia daily life in Union camps.

Contemporary language: H. L. Mencken, 1977 *The American Language*. Stewart Flexnor, 1982 *Listening to America*. Joanna Colcord, 1945 *Sea Language Comes Ashore*, was particularly useful (Hannibal's remark that the "oysters in this stew are a day's run apart" is one of Ms Concord's many estimable contributions, from p. 154).

American folklore: Coffin and Cohen, 1970 *Folklore in America*. Duncan Emrich, 1972, *Folklore on the American Land*.

Consular affairs: Tyler Dennet, 1922 *Americans in East Asia*. Department of State, *U. S. Consular System: Manual for Consuls* (1856 and 1868). E. W. A. Tuson, 1856 *The British Consul's Manual*.

Late Ch'ing history and government: John King Fairbank, 1969 *Trade and Diplomacy on the China Coast*. H. B. Morse, 1918 *The International Relations of the Chinese Empire*. Mary Wright, 1957 *The Last Stand of Chinese Conservatism*. T'ung-tsu Ch'u, 1969 *Local Government in China under the Ch'ing*. Derk Bodde and Clarence Morris, 1967 *Law in Imperial China* (containing translations from the Conspectus of Penal Cases, *hsing-an hui-lan* 刑案匯覽 that reference the Ch'ing legal code, *ta-ch'ing lü-li* 大清律例). Kenneth Folsom, 1972 *Friends, Guests and Colleagues*. K'ung-chuan Hsiao, 1960 *Rural China: Imperial Control 19th Century*. William Mayers, 1897 *The Chinese Government*. John Watt, 1972 *The District Magistrate in Late Imperial China*. A comprehensive bibliographic essay pertaining to the Ch'ing [Qing] Dynasty can be found in the 1978 *Cambridge History of China*, Volume 10, p. 591.

British documentation: Great Britain, House of Commons, *British Parliamentary Papers* [BPP], Irish Univ Press, Shannon, Ireland. Numbering – such as 11/3, 4 – refers to Document No. /enclosure.

China 2, "Correspondence, ordinances, orders in council, reports, and other papers respecting consular establishment in China, 1833-81"

China 5, "Correspondence, dispatches, notes and conventions respecting Chinese relations with Great Britain and other countries, 1860-99"

洋神 *Yang Shen* *James Lande* 藍德

    China 6, "Embassy and consular commercial reports, 1854-66"
    China 27, "Correspondence, dispatches, returns and other papers respecting British military affairs in China, 1840-69"
    China 32, "Correspondence, orders in council and other papers respecting the Taiping rebellion in China, 1852-64" and "Further Papers relating to the Rebellion in China"

19th century Chinese society: Sir John Davis, 1836 *The Chinese: a General Description*. Samuel Williams, 1895 *The Middle Kingdom*. Arthur Smith, 1894 *Chinese Characteristics*. Herbert Giles, 1912 *Chinese Dictionary* and 1878 *Glossary on…the Far East*. Headland, Needham, etc. John Hopkins Univ Press journal *Late Imperial China* 清史問題.

Chinese philosophy: Feng Yu-lan, 1934 *A History of Chinese Philosophy*.

Artillery: U. S. Army, 1862 *Ordnance Manual*. John Gibbon, 1860 *The Artillerist's Manual*. Donald Featherstone, 1978 *Weapons and Equipment of the Victorian Soldier*. M. C. Switlik, *The Complete Cannoneer*. Harold Peterson, *Round Shot and Rammers*. Hogg and Batchelor, 1978 *Naval Gun*.

Taiping Rebellion: Kuo T'ing-I 郭廷以, 1976 *Taiping T'ien-kuo Shih-Shih Jih-Chih* 太平天國史事日誌, "The Taiping Kingdom Day by Day" [*Yang Shen*'s rendering of that title]. Jen Yu-wen, 1973 *The Taiping Revolutionary Movement*. Wu Hsü 吳煦, *Wu Hsü Tang-an Chung te T'ai-p'ing T'ien-kuo Shih-liao Hsuan-hui* 吳煦檔案中的太平 天國史料選輯, "Selection of Taiping Historical Materials from the Documents of Wu Hsü," (1958).

Abraham Lincoln: Carl Sandburg, 1981 *Lincoln*. William Safire, 1987 *Freedom*. Gore Vidal, 1984 *Lincoln*.

Contemporary Maps. British Admiralty Office charts created in the 1840s and 1850s, and Chinese gazetteers and related documents, were the basis for freehand drawings of the Yangtze River and Chushan Archipelago. Present-day maps and Google Earth helped to fill in undocumented areas. Compared with maps today, the old charts show how much the profile of the river has changed in just 160 years, altering its shoreline and in effect pushing downstream many islands known in the mid-19th century. The head of Tsungming Island, the "tongue of the river," was much further upstream from the Whangpoo. Bush Island formerly was a large island just above the Woosung bar, but today it is a string of smaller islands down river from Woosung. British Hydrographic Office maps are listed in the Underfoot (permission to adapt the maps was granted by courtesy of the United Kingdom Hydrographic office, *www.ukho.gov.uk*.)

Reading List by Subject

As there are no citations in a novel to be checked against a bibliography, this reading list is ordered by subject, for readers browsing for topics of interest in Yang Shen, *rather than by author or title.*

    Abbreviations
        NCH – North China Herald.
        JAH – Journal of Asian History
        HJAS – Harvard Journal of Asian Studies
        RUSI – Routledge Royal United Service Institute
        USGPO – U. S. Government Printing Office
        JNCBRAS – Journal of the North China Branch of the Royal Asiatic Society.
        JHKBRAS – Journal of the Hong Kong Branch of the Royal Asiatic Society.

洋神 *Yang Shen* │ *James Lande* 藍德

Works in English
American West
Marcy, Randolf, *The Prairie Traveler*, Time-Life Reprint, New York, 1859.
Schlissel, Lillian, *Women's Diaries of the Westward Journey*, Schocken Books, New York, 1982.

Antebellum America
Bode, Carl, *Midcentury America: Life in the 1850s*, So. Illinois Univ Press, Carbondale, 1972.
Coffin and Cohen, *Folklore in America*, Anchor Books, New York, 1970.
Commager, Henry, *The American Mind*, Yale Univ Press, New Haven, 1952.
Dickens, Charles, *American Notes*, Oxford Illustrated, New York, 1842.
Emerson, Ralph, *Essays, Poems, Addresses*, Walter J. Black, New York - 1950, 1844.
Emrich, Duncan, *Folklore on the American Land*, Little Brown & Co., Boston, 1972.
Furness, Clifton, ed., *The Genteel Female*, Knopf, New York, 1931.
Lacour-Gayet, Robert, *Everyday Life in the United States*, Frederick Ungar, New York, 1972.
Stone, John, *Put's Original California Songster*, UCLA Spec. Coll., Los Angeles, 1854.
Stowe, Harriet Beecher, *Old Town Folks*, Houghton Mifflin Co, Boston, 1869.
Sutherland, Daniel, *The Expansion of Everyday Life: 1860-1876*, Harper & Row, New York, 1989.
Thornwell, Emily, *The Lady's Guide to Perfect Gentility*, Huntington Library, San Marino, CA, 1856.
Trollope, Anthony, *North America*, Knopf, New York, 1951.
Wiggington, Eliot ed., *Foxfire, Vols 1-5*, Anchor Books, New York, 1973.

Bibliography
Cheng, J, *Chinese Sources for Taiping Rebellion*, Hong Kong Univ Press, Hong Kong, 1963.
Clarke, Prescott & J. S. Gregory, *Western Reports on the Taiping*, Univ. of Hawaii Press, Honolulu, 1982.
Hucker, Charles, *China: A Critical Bibliography*, Arizona Univ Press, Tucson, 1976.
Macgowan, D. J., "Chinese Bibliography," JNCBRAS, Shanghai, 1859.

Biography
Bancroft, Frederick, *The Life of William Seward*, Peter Smith, Gloucester, Mass, 1967.
Bell, Herbert, *Lord Palmerston*, Archon Books, Hamden CN - 1966, 1936.
Clark, Ronald, *The Survival of Charles Darwin: a Biography...*, Avon Books, New York, 1984.
Crockett, David, *Tour to the North and Down East*, Carey & Hart, Philadelphia, 1835.
Curtis, George, *Life of James Buchanan*, Volume II, Harper & Bros, New York, 1883.
Curwen, C, *Taiping Rebel: The Deposition of Li Hsiu-Ch'eng*, Cambridge Univ Press, New York, 1977.
Detrick, Robert, *Henry Andrea Burgevine in China*, Ph.D Dissertation, Indiana Univ, 1968.
Forester, Edward, "Personal Recollections of the Taiping Rebellion," *Cosmopolitan* 21-22, 1896.
Marshall, Philip, "H. A. Giles and E. H. Parker: Clio's English Servants in Late 19th Century China," *The Historian* XLVI-4, August 1984.
Safire, William, *Freedom: a Novel of Abraham Lincoln and the Civil War*, Doubleday, New York, 1987.
So and Boardman, "Hung Jen-kan, Taiping Prime Minister, 1859-1864," HJAS, June 1957.
Spence, Jonathan, *To Change China: Western Advisors in China 1620-1960*, Penguin, New York, 1980.
Toyama, Gunji, "The Shanghai Gentry-Merchant Yang Fang," Studies in Oriental Hist, Tokyo, 1945.
Wellman, Nancy, "Burgevine: Tar Heel Soldier of Fortune," News and Observer, Raleigh, 1961.
Williams, Frederick, *Life of Samuel Wells Williams...*, G. P. Putnams, New York, 1889.
Wong, J, *Yeh Ming-Ch'en: Viceroy of Liang Kuang*, Cambridge Univ Press, London, 1976.
Wright, S, *Hart and the Chinese Customs*, Wm Mullan & Son, Belfast, 1950.

Chinese Folklore
Bodde, Derk, *Festivals in Classical China*, Princeton Univ Press, New Jersey, 1975.
Burkhardt, V. R., *Chinese Creeds and Customs*, South China Morning Post, Hong Kong, 1954.
Chamberlain, Jonathan, *Chinese Gods*, Huang Chia Pub, Taipei, 1983.
Schipper, Krostofer M., "Neighborhood Cult Associations in Traditional Tainan." in G. William Skinner, *The City in Late Imperial China*, Stanford Univ Press, 1977.
Werner, Edward T. C., *A Dictionary of Chinese Mythology*, Julian Press, New York, 1961.
Werner, Edward T. C., *Ancient Tales and Folklore of China*, Bracken Books, London, 1986.

Chinese Government
Anon, *Peking Gazette*, NCH, Shanghai, 1859-1860.
Bodde, Derk and Clarence Morris, *Law in Imperial China: Exemplified by 190 Ch'ing Dynasty Cases*

洋神 *Yang Shen*   *James Lande* 藍德

(translated from the Hsing-an Hui-lan*)*, *with Historical, Social, and Juridical commentaries by Derk Bodde and Clarence Morris*, Harvard University Press, Cambridge, MA, copyright © 1967 by the Presidents and Fellows of Harvard College.
Chang and Spector, *Guide to Memorials of Seven Officials*, Univ of Washington, Seattle, 1955.
Ch'u, T'ung-tsu, *Local Government in China Under Ch'ing*, Stanford Univ Press, Palo Alto, 1969.
Folsom, Kenneth, *Friends, Guests and Colleagues*, Rainbow Bridge, Taipei, 1972.
Hsiao, Kung-chuan, *Rural China: Imperial Control 19th Century*, Univ of Washington, Seattle, 1960.
Mayers, William, *The Chinese Government*, Ch'eng-wen Reprints, Taipei - 1970, 1897.
Morse, H. B., *The Trade and Administration of China*, Longmans, Green & Co., New York, 1908.
Swisher, Earl, *China's Management of the American Barbarians*, Yale, New Haven, 1951.
Teng, Ssu-yu &, John King Fairbank, *Ch'ing Administration: Three Studies*, Harvard Univ Press, Cambridge, 1960.
Watt, John R., *The District Magistrate in Late Imperial China*, Columbia Univ Press, New York, 1972.
Watt, John R., "The Yamen and Urban Administration," in G. William Skinner, *The City in Late Imperial China*, Stanford Univ Press, 1977.
Wright, Mary, *Last Stand of Chinese Conservatism*, Stanford Univ Press, Palo Alto, 1957.

Chinese Junks

Donnelly, Ivon, *Chinese Junks and other Native Craft*, Kelly and Walsh, Shanghai, 1924.
Needham, Joseph, *Science and Civilization in China IV-3*, Cambridge Univ Press, New York, 1971.
Villiers, Alan, "Chinese Junks" in *The Way of a Ship*, Scribner's, New York, 1953.
Worcester, G. R. G., *The Junks and Sampans of the Yangtze*, Naval Institute Press, Annapolis MD, 1971.

Chinese Literature

Buck, Pearl, tr., *All Men Are Brothers*, John Day and Co, New York, 1933.
de Bary et. al. ed., *Sources of Chinese Tradition*, Columbia Univ Press, New York, 1968.
Hawkes, David, *Ch'u Tz'u, The Songs of the South*, Beacon Press, Boston, 1959.
Hsia, C. T., *The Classic Chinese Novel: a Critical Intro*, Indiana Univ Press, Bloomington, IN, 1980.
Lai Ming, *A History of Chinese Literature*, Capricorn Press, New York, 1964.
Legge, James, *Confucius: Analects, Great Learning, Doctrine of the Mean*, Dover, New York -1971, 1893.
Waley, Arthur, *The Book of Songs*, Grove Press, New York, 1960.
Waley, Arthur, *Monkey*, Grove Press, New York, 1958.
Waley, Arthur, *Translations from the Chinese*, Vintage Books, New York, 1968.

Chinese Philosophy

Ch'u Chai and, Windberg Chai, *The Story of Chinese Philosophy*, Washington Square, New York, 1961.
Feng Yu-lan, *A History of Chinese Philosophy*, Princeton Univ Press, Princeton – 1983, 1934.
Waley, Arthur, *Three Ways of Thought in Ancient China*, Doubleday Anchor, New York, 1983.

Chinese Society

Aero, Rita, *Things Chinese*, Doubleday, New York, 1980.
Chang Chung-li, *The Chinese Gentry*, Univ of Washington, Seattle, 1955.
Chesneaux, Jean, *Secret Societies in China*, Univ of Michigan Press, Ann Arbor, 1971.
Davis, Sir John, *The Chinese: a General Description*, Scholarly Resources, Wilmington, DE - 1972, 1836.
Headland, I, *Home Life in China*, MacMillan, New York, 1914.
Ho Ping-ti, *The Ladder of Success in Imperial China*, John Wiley & Sons, New York, 1964.
Hsu, Francis L. K., *Americans and Chinese*, Doubleday, New York, 1953.
Jones, Susan Mann, "The Ningpo Pang and Financial Power at Shanghai," in Elvin and Skinner, *The Chinese City between Two Worlds*, Stanford Univ Press, Palo Alto, 1974.
Kates, George, *Chinese Household Furniture*, Dover, New York, 1962.
Morse, Hosea, *The Guilds of China*, Ch'eng-wen, Taipei – 1966, 1909.
Needham, Joseph, *Science in Traditional China: a Comparative Perspective*, Harvard Univ Press, Cambridge, 1981.
Smith, Arthur, *Chinese Characteristics*, Fleming H. Revell, New York, 1894.
Wolf, Arthur ed., *Studies in Chinese Society*, Stanford Univ Press, Palo Alto, 1978.

Chinese Cities, Towns, and Villages

Chang Sen-dou, "The Morphology of Walled Capitals," in G. William Skinner, *The City in Late Imperial China*, Stanford Univ Press, Palo Alto, 1977.
Elvin and Skinner, *The Chinese City between Two Worlds*, Stanford Univ Press, Palo Alto, 1974.
Elvin, Mark, "Market Town and Waterways: The County of Shanghai from 1480 to 1910," in G. William

洋神 *Yang Shen*   *James Lande* 藍德

    Skinner, *The City in Late Imperial China*, Stanford Univ Press, 1977.
Shiba, Yoshinobu, "Ningpo and its Hinterland," in G. William Skinner, *The City in Late Imperial China*, Stanford Univ Press, Palo Alto, 1977.
Smith, Arthur, *Village Life in China*, Fleming H. Revell, New York, 1899.
Skinner, G. William, *The City in Late Imperial China*, Stanford Univ Press, Palo Alto, 1977.
Wright, Arthur F., "The Cosmology of the Chinese City," in G. William Skinner, *The City in Late Imperial China*, Stanford Univ Press, Palo Alto, 1977.

Civil War (American)

Billings, John, *Hardtack and Coffee*, Blackstone Audio Inc, 2001.
Catton, Bruce, *The Coming Fury*, Pocket Books, New York, 1967.
Catton, William and Bruce, *Two Roads to Sumter*, McGraw-Hill, New York, 1963.
Catton, Brice, *The Civil War*, Fairfax Press, New York, 1980.
Cole, Arthur, *The Irrepressible Conflict*, MacMillan, New York, 1934.

Clipper Ships

Biddlecombe, George, *Art of Rigging*, Dover Publications, 1990.
Bottomly, Tom, *Practical Celestial Navigation*, Tab Books, Blueridge Summit PA, 1983.
Bowditch, Nathaniel, *American Practical Navigator*, Govt Printing Office, Washington DC, 1966.
Bray, Mary, *A Sea Trip in a Clipper Ship*, Richard G. Badger, Boston, 1920.
Clark, Arthur, *The Clipper Ship Era*, 7 Cs Press, Riverside, Conn., 1911.
Dana, Richard, *The Seaman's Friend*, Dover Publications – 1997, 1879.
Dana, Richard, *Dana's Seaman's Manual*, Edward Moxon, London, 1863.
Dana, Richard, *Two Years Before the Mast*, Walter J Black, New York, 1840.
Daniels, Edwin, *Eagle Seamanship: A Manual for Square-rigger Sailing*, Naval Inst Press, Annapolis, 1990.
Estes, J. Worth, *A Sea of Words: a Lexicon and Companion for Patrick O'Brian's Seafaring Tales*, Henry Holt & Co, 1997.
Gosnell, Harpur, *Before the Mast in Clippers*, Dover, New York, 1937.
Greenhill, Basil, *Travelling by Sea in the 19th Century*, Hastings House, New York, 1974.
Howe & Matthews, *American Clipper Ships, 1833-1858, Vols 1-2*, Dover, New York, 1986.
Lever, Darcy, *The Young Sea Officer's Sheet Anchor*, Edward M. Sweetman, New York - 1963, 1819.
Lubbock, Basil, *The China Clippers*, Hippocrene Books, New York, 1914.
Lubbock, Basil, *The Opium Clippers*, Brown, Son & Ferguson, Glasgow, 1933.
MacGregor, David, *The Tea Clippers*, Percy Marshall, London, 1952.
Maury, M, *Explanations and Sailing Directions...*, U.S. Hydrographic Office, Washington DC, 1860.
Villiers, Alan, *The Way of a Ship*, Scribners, New York, 1953.
Ward, John, "Sailing Directions for the Yang-tsze Kiang, Woosung to Hankow," JNCBRAS, Shanghai, 1859.

Consular Affairs

Cooley, James, "T. F. Wade in China: Pioneer in Global Diplomacy, 1842-1882," E. J. Brill, Leiden, 1981.
Dennet, Tyler, *Americans in East Asia*, MacMillan, New York, 1922.
Dep't of State, *Regs for the Consular Service of the United States*, Gov't Printing Office, Washington, 1870.
Dep't of State, *US Consular System: Manual for Consuls, Merchants, Shipowners...*, Taylor and Maury, Washington, 1856.
Dep't of State, *Despatches from US Consuls in Shanghai, 1860-61*, Nat'l Archives, Washington DC, 1861.
Dep't of State, *Despatches from US Ministers in China, 1859-1860*, Nat'l Archives, Washington DC, 1860.
Dep't of State, *Despatches from US Ministers in China, 1860-1861*, Nat'l Archives, Washington DC, 1861.
Dep't of State, *Miscellaneous Letters of the Dep't of State*, Nat'l Archives, Washington DC.
Dep't of State, *US Consular System: Manual for Consuls*, French & Richardson, Washington DC, 1868.
Great Britain, *Further Papers Related to the Rebellion in China*, Chin Mat Center, San Francisco, 1975.
Great Britain, *Parliamentary Papers: Taiping Rebellion, 1860-64*, Irish Univ Press, Shannon, Ireland, 1971.
Griffin, Eldon, *Clippers and Consuls*, Scholarly Resources, Wilmington, DE - 1972, 1938.
Hinkley, Frank, *American Consular Jurisdiction in Orient*, W. H. Lowdermilk, Washington, 1906.
Porter, Jonathan, "Foreign Affairs...Expertise in Late Ch'ing: Chao Lieh-wen," *Modern Asian Studies*, 13-3, July 1979.
Scarth, John, *British Policy in China...A Supplement*, Edmonston & Douglas, Edinburgh, 1861.
Tong, Te-kong, *United States Diplomacy in China*, Univ of Washington, Seattle, 1964.
Tuson, E. W. A., *The British Consul's Manual*, Longman and Co., London, 1856.

546   Yang Shen *Reading List*

洋神 *Yang Shen*   *James Lande* 藍德

Contemporary Costume

Blum, Stella, *Fashion & Costume from Godey's Lady's Book*, Dover Publications, 1985.
Dalrymple, Priscilla, *American Victorian Costume in Early Photographs*, Dover Publications, 1991.
Foster, Vanda, *A Visual History of Costume: the 19th Century*, B. T. Batsford Ltd, London, 1984.
Garrett, Valery, *Chinese Dress from the Qing Dynasty to the Present*, Tuttle, Vermont, 2007.
Vollmer, John, *In the Presence of the Dragon Throne*, Royal Ontario Museum, Toronto, 1977.

Contemporary Reading

Cooper, James Fenimore, *The Last of the Mohicans*, Airmont Pub, New York - 1962, 1826.
Darwin, Charles, *The Origin of the Species*, 1859.
Dickens, Charles, *Martin Chuzzlewit*, Oxford Univ Press, New York, 1834.
Dickens, Charles, *Great Expectations*, Bantam Classic, New York - 1988, 1860.
Dickens, Charles, *Oliver Twist*, Fawcett Premier, New York - 1966, 1837.
Emerson, Ralph, "Self-Reliance," *The Dial*, Boston, 1841.
Fuller, Margaret, *Women in the 19th Century*, Dover Publications - 1999, 1845.
Gaskell, Elizabeth, *Cranford*, Wordsworth Editions, Hertfordshire - 1993, 1853.
Melville, Herman, *Moby Dick*, Great Books, Chicago - 1956, 1851.
Prescott, William, *History of the Conquest of Mexico...[and] Peru*, Modern Library - 2001, 1843.
Stowe, Harriet Beecher, *Uncle Tom's Cabin*, Penguin, London, 1852.
Trollope, Anthony, *Barchester Towers*, Penguin Books, Baltimore, MD - 1957, 1857.

Filibusters

Scroggs, William, *Filibusterers and Financiers*, Macmillan, New York, 1916.
Wallace, Edward, *Destiny and Glory*, Coward-McCann, New York, 1957.

Frederick Townsend Ward

Abend, Hallet, *The God from the West*, Doubleday, New York, 1947.
Browne, Gerald, "The Last Months of the Taiping War," *Harper's Magazine*, April 1866.
Cahill, Holger, *A Yankee Adventurer: the Story of Ward*, Macaulay, New York, 1930.
Carr, Caleb, *The Devil Soldier*, Random House, New York, 1992.
Carter, Robert, *Barbarians*, Orion Books Ltd, London, 1998.
Hayes, Augustus, "An American Soldier in China," *Atlantic Monthly*, February 1886.
Hayes, Augustus, "Another Unwritten Chapter...Late War," *International Review*, January 1881.
Li, Lillian, "The Ever-Victorious Army...," Harvard Univ Press, Cambridge, 1968.
Macgowan, D, "Memoirs of Generals Ward, Burgevine...," *Far East Magazine* 2-3:1877-1878.
Morse, Hosea, *In the Days of the Taipings*, Essex Institute, Salem, 1927.
Patterson, Richard, "The Mandarin from Salem," *U.S. Naval Inst Proceedings*, February 1953.
Rantoul, Robert, "Frederick Townsend Ward," Essex Institute, Salem, 1908.
Schmidt, Charles, "A Note on Ward's Character," Dept of State, Despatches....
Schmidt, Charles (as "P. C."), "Memoirs of the late General Ward, the hero of Sung-kiang, and of his aid-de-camp, Vincente Macanaya," *Friend of China*, Shanghai, 1863.
Smith, Richard, "The 'God from the West:' A Chinese Perspective," *Essex Institute Historical Collections* 114-3, Salem, 1978.
Smith, Richard, *Mercenaries and Mandarins*, KTO Press, New York, 1978.
U. S. Senate Record, 45th Congress, "US and Chinese Correspondence re 'Ward Claims' against China," Gov't Printing Office, Washington DC.
Ward, Frederick, "Letters from F. T. Ward to Harry Ward, March-April, 1862," Legation Archives, Shanghai Consulate, 1862.
Ward Family Papers, MSS 46, Series III, Box 23, Folder 4, Phillips Library and Peabody Essex Museum, Salem, MA.
Wetmore, W, "Recollections of Life in the Far East," NCH, Shanghai, 1894.
Wilson, Andrew, *The Ever-Victorious Army...*, Wm Blackwood, London, 1868.
Yale University, *Frederick Townsend Ward Collection*, Sterling Library.

General Reference

Brewer & Evans, *Dictionary of Phrase and Fable*, Harper & Row, New York, 1970.
Bryson, Bill, *The Mother Tongue*, Wm Morrow & Co., New York, 1990.
Bulfinch, Thomas, *Mythology*, Thomas Y. Crowell, New York, 1970.
Corbeil, Jean-Claude, *The Visual Dictionary*, Facts On File, New York, 1986.
Giles, Herbert, *A Glossary of Reference on...Far East*, Hong Kong, 1878.

洋神 *Yang Shen*   *James Lande* 藍德

Giles, Herbert, *Chinese Dictionary*, Kelly & Walsh, Shanghai, 1912.
Imperial Maritime Customs, *Names of Places on the China Coast and the Yangtze River*, III, Misc. Series 10, Kelly & Walsh, Shanghai, 1904.

History: America

Appleman, Philip, ed., *1859: Entering an Age of Crisis*, Indiana Univ Press, Bloomington, 1959.
Bassett, John, *A Short History of the United States, 1492-1938*, Macmillan, New York, 1939.
Callcott, George, *History in the United States: 1800-1860*, John Hopkins, Baltimore, 1970.
Griffin, C, *The Ferment of Reform: 1830-1860*, Crowell, New York, 1967.
Langer, William, *Political & Social Upheaval: 1832-1852*, Harper & Row, New York, 1969.
Miller, Douglas, *The Birth of Modern America*, Pegasus, New York, 1970.
Nichols, Thomas, *Forty Years of American Life: 1812-1861*, John Maxwell & Co., New York, 1937.
Riegel, Robert, *Young America: 1830-1840*, Univ of Oklahoma, Norman, OK, 1949.
Tryon, Rolla, *Household Manufactures in the U. S.: 1640-1860*, Chicago, 1917.

History: China

Banno, Masataka, *China and the West, 1858-1861: The Origins of the Tsungli Yamen*, Cambridge, Harvard Univ Press, 1964.
Basu, Philip, *19th Century China: Five Imperialist Perspectives*, Univ of Michigan, Ann Arbor, 1972.
Couling, Samuel, *The Encyclopaedia Sinica*, Kelley & Walsh, Shanghai, 1917.
Crossley, Pamela, *Orphan Warriors: Three Manchu Generations and the End of the Qing World*, Princeton Univ Press, New Jersey, 1990.
Fairbank, John King and Denis Twitchett, eds, *Cambridge History of China*, Volume 10, Part I, Cambridge University Press, Cambridge, 1978.
Fairbank, John King, *China: a New History*, Harvard Univ Press, Cambridge, 1992.
Fairbank, John King, *Chinese-American Interactions...*, Rutgers Univ Press, New Jersey, 1975.
Fairbank, John King, *Ch'ing Documents: An Introductory Syllabus, 3rd Edition*, Vol. I and II, East Asian Research Center, Harvard University, distributed by Harvard University Press, Cambridge, 1970.
Feuerwerker, Albert, *Rebellion in 19th Century China*, Univ of Michigan, Ann Arbor, 1975.
Feuerwerker and Cheng, *Chinese Communist Studies of Modern Chinese History*, Harvard Univ Press, Cambridge, 1961.
Great Britain, *Parliamentary Papers: Treaty of Tientsin, 1860-1864*, Irish Univ Press, Shannon, Ireland, 1971.
Hao Yen-p'ing, *The Commercial Revolution in Nineteenth-Century China: The Rise of Sino-Western Mercantile Capitalism*. Berkeley and Los Angeles: University of California Press, 1986.
Ho and Tsou, eds, *China in Crisis*, Univ of Chicago Press, Chicago, 1968.
Hsu, Immanual C. Y., *China's Entry into the Family of Nations*, Harvard U Press, Cambridge, 1960.
Hsu, Immanual C. Y., *The Rise of Modern China*, 6th Edition, New York, Oxford Univ Press, 2000.
Hummel, Arthur, *Eminent Chinese of the Ch'ing Period*, Ch'eng-wen Reprints, Taipei - 1972, 1943.
King & Clark, *Research Guide to China Coast Newspapers*, Harvard Univ Press, Cambridge, 1965.
Kuhn, Philip, *Rebellion and Its Enemies in...China...*, Harvard Univ Press, Cambridge, 1980.
Levenson, Joseph, *Confucian China and Its Modern Fate*, Univ of California, Berkeley, 1968.
Mayers and Dennys, *The Treaty Ports of China and Japan*, Trübner & Co., London, 1867.
Morse, Hosea, *International Relations of Chinese Empire*, Longmans Green, New York, 1918.
Paske-Smith, *Western Barbarians in Japan and Formosa...: 1603-1868*, Paragon Reprint, New York - 1968, 1930.
Smith, Richard, *Barbarian Officers of Imperial China*, Univ of California, Davis, 1972.
Swisher, Earl, *Early Sino-American Relations: 1841-1912*, Westview Press, Boulder CO, 1977.
Teng Ssu-yu, *Historiography of the Taiping Rebellion*, Harvard Univ Press, Cambridge, 1962.
Teng and Fairbank, *China's Response to the West*, Atheneum, New York, 1966.
Teng and Fairbank, "On Transmission of Ch'ing Documents," *HJAS* 4:1:12-36, 1939.
Teng and Fairbank, "On Types and Uses of Ch'ing Documents," *HJAS* 5:1:1-71, 1940.
Tsiang, T. F., *China, England & Russia in 1860*, Cambridge Hist. Journal, 1929.
Wakeman & Grant, *Conflict and Control in Late Imperial China*, Univ of California, Berkeley, 1975.
Wang Yeh-chien, *Land Taxation in Imperial China 1750-1911*, Harvard U Press, Cambridge, 1973.
Williams, Samuel Wells, *The Chinese Repository, 1832-1851*, Canton, 1832.
Williams, Samuel Wells, *The Middle Kingdom*, Paragon Reprint, New York - 1966, 1895.
Williams, Samuel Wells, *The Chinese Commercial Guide [and Sailing Directions for the China Coast]*, Taipei, Ch'eng Wen Reprint – 1966, 5th edition, 1863.

History: Crimea

洋神 *Yang Shen*   *James Lande* 藍德

Chesney, Kellow, *Crimean War Reader*, Frederick Muller Ltd, London, 1960.
Hamley, Edward, *The War in the Crimea*, Seeley & Co., London, 1891.
James, Lawrence, *Crimea: 1854-1856*, Van Nostrand, New York, 1981.
Wylly, H. C., *The 95th (The Derbyshire) Regiment in the Crimea*, Swan Sonnerschein, London, 1899.

History: England

Cheyney, Edward, *A Short History of England*, Ginn and Co., Boston, 1904.
Knight, Ian, *Queen Victoria's Enemies*, Osprey, London, 1990.
Schultz, Harold, *History of England*, Barnes & Noble, New York, 1971.
Thompson, David, *England in the 19th Century*, Pelican, Middlesex, 1985.
Tull, G. K., and P. Bulwer, *Britain and the World in the 19th Century*, Blanford Press, London, 1966.

History: France

Giquel, Prosper, *A Journal of the Chinese Civil War, 1864*, Univ of Hawaii Press, Honolulu, 1985.
Israeli, Raphael, "Consul de France in Mid-19th-Century China," Modern Asian Studies 23-4, Oct, 1989.
Le Petit Homme Rouge, *The Court of the Tuileries: 1852-1870*, Chatto and Windus, London, 1912.
Maybon and Fredet, *Histoire De La Concession Francaise De Shanghai*, Librairie Plon, Paris, 1929.
Norman, Charles, *Tonkin - or France in the Far East*, London, 1884 (Nabu press reprint).
Williams, Robert, *The World of Napoleon III*, Free Press, New York, 1957.

History: General

Arrian, *Campaigns of Alexander*, Penguin, New York, 1958.
Creasy, Edward, *Fifteen Decisive Battles of the World*, Dorset Press, New York, 1987.
Grun, Bernard, *The Timetables of History*, Simon and Schuster, New York, 1979.

History: Indian Mutiny

Farwell, Byron, *Armies of the Raj: from Mutiny to Independence, 1858-1947*, W. W. Norton, New York.
Fisher, Lt.-Colonel, *Personal Narrative of Three Years Service in China*, Richard Bentley, London, 1863.
Hervey, Albert, *A Soldier of the Company*, Viking Penguin, New York, 1988.
Hibbert, Christopher, *The Great Mutiny: India, 1857*, Penguin, New York, 1978.
Stokes, Eric, *The Peasant Armed: the Rebellion of 1857*, Clarendon Press, Oxford, 1986.

History: Japan

Wallach, Sidney, *Comm. Perry's Naval Expedition to the China Seas...*, Coward-McCann, New York, 1952.
Williams, Harold, *Tales of the Foreign Settlements in Japan*, Charles E. Tuttle, Tokyo, 1958.

History: Opium Wars

Allgood, George, *The China War 1860*, Longmans Green, New York, 1901.
Beeching, Jack, *The Chinese Opium Wars*, Harcourt Brace, New York, 1975.
Knollys, Henry, *Incidents in the China War of 1860*, Wm Lockwood, London, 1875.
O. Bonner-Smith, E. W. R. Lumby, *The Second China War: 1856-60*, Navy Record Society, London, 1954.
Olyphant, Lawrence, *Narrative of the Earl of Elgin's Mission to China and Japan in the Years 1857, 1858 and 1859*, Wm Blackwood and Sons, London, 1859.
Rennie, D, *The British Arms in North China and Japan*, London, John Murray, 1864.
Swinhoe, R, *Narrative of the North China Campaign*, Smith, Elder & Co., London, 1861.
Waley, Arthur, *The Opium War through Chinese Eyes*, Stanford Univ Press, Palo Alto, 1968.
Wolseley, G, *Narrative of the War with China in 1860*, Scholarly Resources, Wilmington, DE - 1972, 1862.

History: Taiping Rebellion

Callery and Yvan, *History of the Insurrection in China*, Paragon Reprints, New York - 1969, 1853.
Editors, *Suppression of Taipings in Departments of Shanghai*, Kelly and Walsh, Shanghai, 1871.
Gordon, Charles, *Gordon's Campaign in China*, Royal Engineers, London, 1871.
Gregory, John, "British Intervention Against Taipings," *Journal of Asian Studies*, 1959.
Gregory, John, *Great Britain and the Taipings*, Praeger, New York, 1969.
Henson, Curtis T., "*The U. S. Navy and Taiping Rebellion*," American Neptune 38, January 1978.
Jen (Chien), Yu-wen, *The Taiping Revolutionary Movement*, Yale Univ Press, New Haven, 1973.
Jen Yu-wen Collection, East Asian Collection, Sterling Library, Yale University, New Haven, CT.
Laai, Yi-faai, "River Strategy: A Phase of Taiping Military Dev," *Oriens* 5-2, Dec 1952.
Lindley, Augustus, *Ti-Ping Tien-Gwoh: History of the Taiping Revolution*, Day & Son, London, 1866.
Meadows, T, *The Chinese and Their Rebellions*, Stanford Univ Press, Palo Alto, 1856.

洋神 *Yang Shen* James Lande 藍德

Michael, Franz and Chang Chung-li, *The Taiping Rebellion, Volumes 1-3*, University of Washington, Seattle, 1966-71.
Mossman, Samuel, *General Gordon's Private Diary...*, Kraus Reprint, New York - 1971, 1885.
Shanghai People's Pub, *The Taiping Revolution*, Foreign Lang Press, Peking, 1976.
Shih, Vincent Y. C., *The Taiping Ideology: Its Source...*, Univ of Washington, Seattle, 1967.
Spence, Jonathan, *God's Chinese Son*, W. W. Norton, New York, 1997.
Teng Ssu-yu, *New Light on History Taiping Rebellion*, Russel & Russel, New York, 1966.
Teng Ssu-yu, *Taiping Rebellion and Western Powers*, Oxford Univ Press, Oxford, 1971.
Wu, James, "Impact of Taiping Rebels on Manchu Fiscal System," *Pacific Historical Review* 19-3, Aug 1950.

Language Reference

Bartlett, Russell, *Dictionary of Americanisms*, Little Brown & Co., Boston, 1859.
Clark, Joseph, "Folk Speech from North Carolina," *Southern Folklore Quarterly* 26, 1962.
Colcord, Joanna, *Sea Language Comes Ashore*, Cornell Maritime/Tidewater, New York, 1945.
Colum, Padraic, "Irish Country Speech" in *The Road Round Ireland*, MacMillan Co., New York, 1927.
Flexnor, Stuart, *I Hear America Talking*, Van Nostrand, New York, 1976.
Flexnor, Stuart, *Listening to America*, Simon and Schuster, New York, 1982.
Fowlie, Wallace, *French Stories* (Bilingual), Bantam Books, New York, 1960.
Herman, Lewis, *Manual of Foreign Dialects for Stage and Screen*, Ziff-Davis Pub Co, Chicago, 1943.
Mayers, William, *The Chinese Reader's Manual*, Ch'eng Wen Reprint, Taipei - 1978, 1874.
McGuffey, William, *Eclectic First Reader*, W B Smith, Cincinnati, 1836.
Mencken, H, *The American Language*, Alfred Knopf, New York, 1977.
Mesny, William, *Mesny's Chinese Miscellany*, Shanghai, 1896.
North China Herald, "Phrases in the Shanghae Dialect," NCH, 1:40, Shanghai, 1851.
Renton and MacDonald, *English-Scottish Gaelic Dictionary*, Hippocrene, New York, 1996.
Smith, Arthur, *Proverbs and Common Sayings...*, Mission Press, Shanghai, 1914.
Smith, Lloyd, *A Book of Useful Phrases*, Haldeman-Julius, Girard, Kansas, 1925.
Smyth, W, *The Sailors' Word Book*, Blackie & Son, London, 1867.
Taylor and Whiting, *Dictionary of American Proverbs and Proverbial Phrases: 1820-1880*, Harvard Univ Press, Cambridge, 1958.
Thurston, Helen, "Sayings & Proverbs from Massachusetts," Amer. Folklore Soc., Columbus, 1906.
Wu Hsiu-liang, Silas, "*Glossary of Ch'ing Administrative Terms*" in Wu Hsiu-liang, Silas, "Memorial Systems of the Ch'ing Dynasty," HJAS, Cambridge, 1967.

***Late Imperial China* Journal** (formerly *Ch'ing-shih Wen-t'i* 清史問題)

Dean, Britten, "Sino-American Relations...View from the Tsungli Yamen Archive," *Ch'ing-shih Wen-t'i* IV-5, John Hopkins Press, Albany, June 1981.
Elliott, Mark, "Bannerman and Townsman: Ethnic Tension in 19th-Cen Jiangnan," *Late Imperial China* 11-1, John Hopkins Press, Albany, June 1990.
Leung Yuen Sang, "Regional Rivalry in Mid-19th Cen. Shanghai: Canton *vs* Ningpo Men," *Ch'ing-shih Wen-t'i* IV-8, John Hopkins Press, Albany, Dec 1982.
Murray, Diane, "Mid-Ch'ing Piracy: An Analysis of Organizational Attributes," *Ch'ing-shih Wen-t'i* IV-8, John Hopkins Press, Albany, Dec 1982.
Wang, Di, "Mysterious Communication: The Secret Language of the Gowned Brotherhood in Nineteenth-Century Sichuan," in *Late Imperial China* 29-1, John Hopkins Press, Albany, June 2008 Supplement.
Watt, John, "Ching Emperors and District Magistrates," *Ch'ing-shih Wen-t'i* I-8, John Hopkins Press, Albany, May 1968.
Yu Li, "Social Change During the Ming-Qing Transition and the Decline of Sichuan Classical Learning in Early Qing," *Late Imperial China* 19-1, John Hopkins Press, Albany, June 1998.

Manchu Language

Crossley and Rawski, "*A Profile of the Manchu Language of Ch'ing History*," HJAS 53-1, 1993.
Editors, "Manchu Grammar," Liaoning Jenmin Chupanshe, Shenyang, 1983.
Norman, Jerry, "*A Manchu-English Dictionary*," privately printed, Taipei, 1967.

Maps and Charts

Tregear, T, *A Geography of China*, Aldine, Chicago, 1965.
Van Slyke, Lyman, *Yangtze: Nature, History, and the River*, Stanford Alumni Assoc., Palo Alto, 1988.

Medicine

Hyatt, Richard, *Chinese Herbal Medicine*, Schocken Books, New York, 1978.

洋神 *Yang Shen* *James Lande* 藍德

Merchants

Barr, Pat, "Jardine's in Japan," in Maggie Keswick, *The Thistle and the Jade*, Octopus Books Ltd, London, 1982.
Dulles, Foster, *The Old China Trade*, Houghton Mifflin, Boston, 1930.
Fairbank, John King, *Trade and Diplomacy on the China Coast: The Opening of the Treaty Ports, 1842-1854*, Harvard University Press, Cambridge, Mass. Copyright 1953 by the President and Fellows of Harvard College. Copyright renewed 1981 by John King Fairbank.Hao Yen-p'ing, *The Comprador in 19th Century China*, Harvard Univ Press, Cambridge, 1970.
Jardine Matheson Archives (private letters, Shanghai, January 1860-1864), University Library manuscripts, Cambridge University, Cambridge, England.
Keswick, Maggie, ed., *The Thistle and the Jade*, Octopus Books Ltd, London, 1982.
Lockwood, Stephen, *Augustine Heard and Company, 1858-1862: American Merchants in China*, Harvard University Asia Center, Cambridge, 1971.
Mason, Mary, *Western Concepts of China and Chinese*, Seeman Printery, New York, 1939.
Personal Records and Correspondence, 1856-1862, Augustine Heard Collection Baker Library Historical Collections, Harvard Business School, Harvard University, Cambridge, MA.
Williams, Samuel, *Chinese Commercial Guide*, A. Shortrede, Hong Kong, 1863.

Military: Chinese

Kierman, and Fairbank, eds, *Chinese Ways in Warfare*, Harvard Univ Press, Cambridge, 1974.
Kuhn, Philip, "The T'uan-lien Local Defense System...," HJAS 27, Cambridge, 1967.
Lamprey, J, "The Economy of the Chinese Army," The RUSI Journal 11-46, London, 1867.
Michael, Franz, "Military Organization...During the Taiping Rebellion," *Pacific Historical Review* 17, Berkeley, 1949.
Scott, James, "The Chinese Brave," *Asiatic Quarterly Review* 1, 1886.
Smith, Richard, "Chinese Military Institutions in the Mid-19th Century," JAH 8.2, 1974.
Smith, Richard, "The Employment of Foreign Military Talent...," JHKBRAS 15, 1975.

Military: Western

Featherstone, Donald, *Weapons and Equipment of the Victorian Soldier*, Blandford Press, Dorset, 1978.
Hinds & Fitzgerald, *Bulwark & Bastion*, privately published, Las Vegas, 1981.
Luvaas, Jay, *The Education of an Army...*, Univ of Chicago, Chicago, 1964.
MacDougall, Sir Patrick, *Modern Warfare as...by Modern Artillery*, John Murray, London, 1864.
Mollo, Borris, *The British Army from Old Photographs*, J M Dent & Sons, London, 1975.
Nickerson, Hoffman, "Nineteenth Century Military Techniques," *Journal of World History* 4, 1958.

New England

Amory, Cleveland, *The Proper Bostonians*, E. P. Dutton, New York, 1947.
Goodman, Paul, "*Ethics and Enterprise: Values of Boston Elite: 1800-60*," *American Quarterly* 18-3, 1966.
Lowell, James, *The Biglow Papers*, Scholarly Press, St Clair Shores, MI, 1848.
Paine, Ralph, *The Old Merchant Marine*, Yale Univ Press, New Haven, 1822.
Paine, Ralph, *Ships and Sailors of Old Salem*, Outing Publishing Co., Boston, 1908.
State Street Trust, *Old Shipping Days in Boston*, State Street Trust, Boston, 1918.
Tharp, Louise, *The Peabody Sisters of Salem*, Little Brown & Co., Boston, 1950.

Newspapers

Boston Evening Transcript, Boston, 1860.
Japan Herald, Nagasaki, 1861.
Leslie's Illustrated Weekly, New York, 1860.
London Examiner (English Literary Examiner), London, 1860.
North China Herald, Shanghai, 1856-1860.
San Francisco Police Gazette, San Francisco, 1860.

Ordnance

Allin, E. S., *Rules for...Cleaning...Rifle Musket Model 1855*, Gov't Printing Office, Washington DC, 1862.
Dawson, Paul, "Artillery Horses: Harness and Draught of the Napoleonic Era, *The Napoleon Series*: Military - Organization, Strategy & Tactics (Other), *www.napoleon-series.org/military/organization /c_artilleryhorses.html*.
Editors, *American Sharps Shooters*, C. Sharps Arms Co., Big Timber, MT, 1985.
Gibbon, John, *The Artillerist's Manual*, Van Nostrand, New York, 1860.
Manucy, Albert, *Artillery through the Ages*, USGPO, Washington, 1949.

Yang Shen *Reading List* 551

洋神 *Yang Shen*   *James Lande* 藍德

Myatt, Major, *Illustrated Encyclopedia of 19th Century Firearms*, Crescent, New York, 1979.
Nonte, George, *The Blackpowder Guide*, Stoeger Pub Co, New Jersey, 1978.
Peterson, Harold, *Notes on Ordinance of American Civil War 1861-1865*, American Ordnance Assoc., Washington DC - 1971, 1959.
Peterson, Harold, *Round Shot and Rammers*, Bonanza Books, New York, 1969.
Richardson, M. T., *Practical Blacksmithing*, Weathervane, New York - 1978, 1889.
Rogers, Pat, "The Navy Colt: One of the Guns That Won the West," *Combat Handguns*, December 1993.
Rywell, Martin, *Sharps Rifle: the Gun...American Destiny*, Pioneer Press, Tennessee, 1979.
Sidney, S., *The Book of the Horse*, Cassell & Co., London, 1893.
Switlik, M. C., *The Complete Cannoneer*, Ray Russell-Books, Rochester, 1971.
Telleen, Maurice, *The Draft Horse Primer*, Rodale Press, Emmaus PA, 1977.
U. S. Army, *Ordinance Manual*, Ordnance Park, Reprint -1970, 1861.
Werner, Edward, *Chinese Weapons*, Royal Asia Soc, Shanghai, 1932.
Worthington, T, *Manual of Arms Sharps Rifle & Colt Revolver*, Applegate & Co, Cincinnati, 1861.

Peking

Rennie, D, *Peking & Pekinese...1st British Embassy, 1860-61*, John Murray, London, 1865.

Philippines

Arcilla, Jose, *An Introduction to Philippine History*, Atenea de Manila Univ Press, Manila, 1971.
Bowring, Sir John, *A Visit to the Philippine Islands*, Filipiniana Book Guild, Manila -1963, 1858.
Foreman, John, *The Philippine Islands*, T. Fisher Unwin, London, 1907.
Phelan, John, *The Hispanization of Philippines*, Univ of Wisconsin Press, Madison, 1959.
Rizal, Jose, *An Eagle Flight [The Social Cancer]*, McClure Phillips & Co., New York, 1900.
Rizal, Jose, *The Reign of Greed*, Philippine Education Co., Manila, 1912.

Photo Studies

Beers, Bertram, *China in Old Photographs: 1860-1910*, Scribners, New York, 1978.
Bergen, Philip, *Old Boston in Photographs*, Dover, New York, 1990.
Gamewell, Mary, *Gateway to China: Pictures of Shanghai*, Ch'eng-wen Reprints, Taipei - 1972, 1916.
Thomson, John, *China and its People in Early Photographs*, Dover, New York - 1982, 1873.
Worswick and Spence, *Imperial China: Photographs: 1850-1912*, Pennwick, New York, 1978.

Pidgin English

Hall, Robert, "Chinese Pidgin-English Grammar & Texts," 1944.
Hayes, A. A., Jr., "Pidgin English," *Scribner's Monthly* 15:3, January 1878, online at
    digital.library.cornell.edu.
Leland, Charles, *Pidgin-English Sing-Song*, Trubner and Co., London, 1876.

Pirates

Fox, Grace, *British Admirals and Chinese Pirates*, Hyperion Press, Westport CT, 1940.
Jeans, T. T., *Ford of H.M.S. Vigilant: A Tale of the Chusan Archipelago*, Blackie & Son, London, 1910.
Laai, Yi-faai, "*The...Pirates of Kwangtung...in the Taiping Insurrection*," Univ of California, Dissertation, 1950.

River Steamers

Coppola, Michael, *Marine Walking Beam Engine* (model), Mariners' Museum, Newport News, 1999.
Harlan & Fisher, *Of Walking Beams and Paddle Wheels*, Bay Books, San Francisco, 1951.
Kubicek, Robert, "The Design of Shallow-draft Steamers for the British...1868-1906," *Technology and Culture* 31-3, July 1990.
Main, Thomas, *The Marine Steam-Engine*, Henry Carey Baird, Philadelphia, 1864.
Milster, Conrad, "Giant American 'Walking' Beam Engines," *Antiquities Magazine*, 1981.
Sykes, Godfrey, *The Colorado Delta*, Carnegie Inst & American Geological Society, New York, 1937.
Taylor, Thomas D. et. al., *New York Marine Register*, R.C. Root, Anthony & Co, New York, 1859.

Shanghai

Black, J. R. ed., *The Far East: a Monthly Journal Illus. With Photographs*, Shanghai, 1876.
Cranston, Earl, "Shanghai in the Taiping Period," *Pacific Historical Review* 5-2, June 1936.
Davidson-Houston, J, *Yellow Creek: the Story of Shanghai*, Putnam, London, 1962.
Hauser, Ernst, *Shanghai: City for Sale*, Chinese-American Publishing, Shanghai, 1940.
Lanning and Couling, *The History of Shanghai*, Kelly and Walsh, Shanghai, 1921.
Medhurst, Walter, *General Description of Shanghai...*, Mission Press, Shanghai, 1850.

洋神 *Yang Shen*   *James Lande* 藍德

Montalto de Jesus, C, *Historic Shanghai*, Shanghai Mercury, Shanghai, 1909.
Pott, F. L. Hawks, *A Short History of Shanghai*, Kelly and Walsh, Shanghai, 1928.

Steamships

Haviland, Kenneth, "American Steamship Navigation in China, 1845-1878," *American Neptune* 16, October 1956.
Hickerson, Mary Greenwalt, "*The Steamboat Builder from Sing-sing*," Westchester Historian, Westchester County, 1965.
Hunter, Louis, *Steamboats on Western Rivers*, Dover, New York, 1994.
Sheret, R, *Smoke Ash and Steam*, Western Isles, Victoria BC, 2005.

Translation

Brower, ed., Reuben, *On Translation*, Harvard Univ Press, Cambridge, 1959.
Cirino, Mark, "*You Don't Know the Italian Language Well Enough: The Bilingual Dialogue of* A Farewell to Arms," *The Hemingway Review* 25-1, Fall 2005.
Fang, Achilles, "Some Reflections on the Difficulty of Translation," in Wright, *Studies in Chinese Thought*, Univ of Chicago Press, Chicago, 1967.
Fenimore, Edward, "English and Spanish in For Whom the Bell Tolls" in John K. M. McCaffrey ed., *Ernest Hemingway: The Man and His Work*, World Publishing, Cleveland, 1950.
Kelly, Louis, *The True Interpreter*, St. Martin's Press, New York, 1979.
Weinberger and Paz, *Nineteen Ways of Looking at Wang-Wei*, Moyer Bell, New York, 1987.
Wright, ed., Arthur F, *Studies in Chinese Thought*, Univ of Chicago Press, Chicago, 1967.

Travel Descriptions

Anderson, Lindsay, *A Cruise in An Opium Clipper*, Chapman Hill, London, 1859.
Augur, Helen, *Tall Ships to Cathay*, Doubleday, New York, 1951.
Bishop, Mrs. J. F., *The Yangtze Valley and Beyond*, G. P. Putnam, New York, 1900.
Blackney, William, "Ascent of the Yang-Tsze-Kiang," Royal Geo. Society Journal, London, 1916.
Blakiston, Thomas, *Five Months on the Yangtze*, John Murray, London, 1862.
Fortune, Robert, *A Residence among the Chinese: 1852-1856*, John Murray, London, 1857.
Gutzlaff, Charles, *Three Voyages along the Coast of China*, Ch'eng Wen Reprint, Taipei - 1968, 1968.
Huc, M, *Recollections of a Journey through...China*, Ch'eng Wen Reprint, Taipei - 1971, 1846.
Johnston, James, *China and Japan: Cruise of Powhatan 1857*, Chas DeSilver, Philadelphia, 1861.
Martin, W. A. P., *A Cycle of Cathay*, Fleming H Revell, New York, 1897.
Medhurst, Walter, *The Foreigner in Far Cathay*, Edward Stanford, London, 1872.
Oliphant, Lawrence, *Narrative of the Earl of Elgin's Mission to China and Japan in the Years 1857, 1858 and 1859*, William Blackwood and Sons, London, 1859.
Oman, Ralph, "*Yankees in China Ports*," Proceedings…U. S. Naval Institute 98, February 1972.
Scarth, John, *Twelve Years in China*, Scholarly Resources, Wilmington, DE - 1972, 1860.
Smith, George, *Consular Cities of China*, Harper Bros, New York, 1847.
Smith, William, *Observations of China and the Chinese*, Carlton Pub, New York, 1863.
Tamarin and Glubok, *Voyaging to Cathay: Americans in the China Trade*, Viking Press, New York, 1976.
Wood, William, *Fankwei: San Jacinto in Seas of China...*, Harcourt & Brace, New York, 1859.

Victorian Society

Best, Geoffrey, *Mid-Victorian Britain: 1851-1875*, Schocken Books, New York, 1972.
Briggs, Asa, *Victorian People: 1851-1867*, Univ of Chicago, Chicago, 1955.
Carlyle, Thomas, *On Heroes, Hero-Worship, and the Heroic...*, John Wiley and Sons, New York, 1876.
Houghton, Walter, *The Victorian Frame of Mind 1830-1870*, Yale Univ Press, New Haven, 1957.
Lasdun, Susan, *Victorians at Home*, Viking, New York, 1981.
Mayhew, Henry, *London Labor and London Poor, Vols II and III*, Penguin USA, New York, 1983.
Seaman, L, *Victorian England: 1837-1901*, Methuen & Co., London, 1973.
Strachey, Lytton, *Emminent Victorians*, Harcourt Brace Jovanovich, New York, 1918.
Young, G, *Early Victorian England: 1830-65*, Oxford Univ Press, London, 1953.

Works in Chinese 中文參考書

Diaries and Biography 日記和人傳

Chao Lieh-wen 趙烈文, *Neng Ching-chu Shih Jih-chi* 能靜居士日記, in Ch'ang-chou city gazetteer 常州市志, 1995, 第52卷專記太平, 天國在常州, p. 1072.

洋神 *Yang Shen*　　　　　　　　　　　　　　　　　　　　　*James Lande* 藍德

Feng Kuei-fen 馮桂芬, *Hsien Chih T'ang Kao* 顯志堂稿, privately published, 1876.
Liang T'ing-nan 梁廷枏, *I Fen Chi Wen* 夷氛記聞, Peiping Yanchiu She, Shanghai, 1937.
Shen Yun-lung 沈雲龍, ed., *Ch'ing-tai Ch'i-pai Ming-jen Chuan* 清代七百名人傳, Wen-hai Pub, Taipei, 1984.
Yao Chi 姚濟, *Hsiao Ts'ang-sang-chi Shang* 小滄桑記上, in Hsiang Ta, *Chung-kuo Chin-tai-shih... Ti-er-chung* 中國近代史…第二种, Shen-chou Kuo-kuang-she, Shanghai, 1952.

Chinese Government 清朝政事

Ch'ing Dynasty (Tao Kuang and Hsien Feng 清道光和咸豐朝), *Ch'ing-tai Ch'ou-pan I-wu Shih-mo* 清代籌辦夷務始末, Chung Hua Shu Chu, Peking, 1979.
Ching Wu 静吾, ed., *Wu Hsu Tang-an Chung-ti T'aip'ing-t'ien-kuo Shih-liao Hsuan-chi* 吳煦檔案中的太平天國史料選輯, Hsin-chih, Peking, 1958.
Feng Kuei-fen 馮桂芬, "On Benevolent Management of Barbarians 善馭夷議," in *Chiao-pin-lu K'ang-i* 校邠廬抗議, 1861.
Feng Kuei-fen 馮桂芬, *Chiao-pin-lu K'ang-i* 校邠廬抗議, privately published, 1861.

Chinese Literature and Fiction 中國文學

Chiang Yun-hsiang 江蔭香, ed., *Ch'ien Chia Shih* 千家詩, Ta Ch'ung Pub, Kaohsiung, 1967.
Kao Yang 高陽, *Hu Hsueh-yen* 胡雪巖, Taipei, Economic Daily, 1994.
Kao Yang 高陽, *Hung-ting Shang-jen* 紅頂商人, Taipei, Economic Daily, 1994.
Kao Yang 高陽, *Teng-huo Lou-t'ai* 燈火樓臺, Taipei, Economic Daily, 1994.
Liu Ta-ch'eng 劉大澄, ed., *T'ang Shih San-pai Shou Hsin-shang* 唐詩三百首欣賞, Wen Hua, Taipei, 1969.
Luo Kuan-chün 羅貫中, *San-kuo Yen-yi* 三国演义, Shih-yi Wen-hua, Tainan, 2003.
Shih Ngai-an 施耐庵, *Shui-hu Chuan* 水滸傳, Ta Chung Pub, Taipei, 1966.
Su T'ung-p'o 蘇東坡, *Su Tung-po Shi-ssu Hsuan-chu* 蘇東坡詞詩選注, Ta Chung Pub, Kaohsiung, 1973.
Tu Fu 杜甫, *Tu-fu Shih Hsuan-chu* 杜甫詩選注, Ta Ch'ung Pub, Kaohsiung, 1969.
Wu Ch'eng-en 吳承恩, *Hsi Yu Chi* 西遊記, Ta Chung-kuo Pub, Taipei, 1963.
Wu, Shao-zhi 吳紹志, ed., *Pai-hua Shi-chi* 白話史記, Xi-bei Chuban She, 1980.

Frederick Townsend Ward 華爾

Feng Kuei-fen, "*Fu-chiang Hua-erh Hsiao-chuan* 副將華爾小傳," in Feng Kuei-fen 馮桂芬, *Hsien Chih T'ang Kao* 顯志堂稿, 1876.

Gazetteers 縣市志

Ch'ang-chou Shih-chih 常州市志, Changzhou City Gazetteer Compilation Committee 常州市志編纂委員会编, 1995.
Kiang-su Ch'uan-sheng Yu T'u 江蘇全省輿圖, Ch'eng-wen Reprints, Taipei – 1967, 1895.
Shang-hai Hsien-chih 上海縣志, Ch'eng-wen Reprints, Taipei – 1966, 1873.
Shang-hai Hsien Hsu-chih 上海縣續志 (Supplement to *Shang-hai Hsien-chih* 1873), Ch'eng-wen Reprints, Taipei – 1969, 1883.
Sung-kiang-fu Hsu-chih 松江府續志, Ch'eng-wen Reprints, Taipei – 1966, 1879.

General Reference 一般參考

Editors 编采组, *Chung-kuo ku-chen-you: Tzu-tung Lü-you Ti-t'u Shou-tse* 中国古镇游:自助旅游地图手册, Shanxi Normal Univ, Xian, 2002.
Chang Chih-chieh 張之傑, ed., *Pan Chinese Encyclopedia* 環華百科全書, Taipei, 1983.
Kao Mo-yeh and Chou Le-shan, ed. 高莫野周樂山合編, *Ch'eng-yu Ku-shih* 成語故事, Cheng-yen, Tainan, 1966.
Lung Hsia-feng 龍乘風, ed., *Chung-kuo Jen-te Pai-pai* 中國人的拜拜, Shih Hsin Pub, San-chung, 1983.
National Palace Museum, *Ch'in-ting Ta-ch'ing Hui-tien-t'u*, 欽定大清會典圖(光绪重修本), Taipei, 1997.

History: China 歷史: 中國

Chou, Gu-ch'eng 周谷城, *Chung-kuo T'ung-shih* 中國通史, Pai-ling Publishers, Hong Kong, 1939.
Editors, *Ch'ing-kung Shih-san Ch'ao* 清宮十三朝, Wen Yuan, Taipei, 1977.
Editors, *Chung-kuo Chin-tai-shih* 中国近代史, Young Lion, Taipei, 1971.

洋神 *Yang Shen*   *James Lande* 藍德

Hsiao I-shan 蕭一山, *Ch'ing-tai T'ung-shih* 清代通史, Shang-wu Yin-shu Guan, Taipei, 1963.
Hsüeh Fu-ch'eng 薛福成, *Chung-kuo Chin-pai-nien-shih Tze-liao Hsüan-chi* 中國近百年史資料選輯, Chung-hua Shu-chü, Taipei, 1958.
Kuo T'ing-i 郭廷以 ed., *Chung-mei Kuan-hsi Shih-liao: Chia-ching, Tao-kuang, Hsien-feng Chau* 中美關係史料:嘉慶道光咸豐朝, Chung-yang Yen-chiu Yuan, Taipei, 1988.
Li, Yun-han 李雲漢, *Chung-kuo Chin-tai-shih* 中國近代史, San Min Book Co., Taipei, 1986.
Li Fang-chen 李方晨, *Chung-kuo T'ung-shih* 中國通史, San Min Pub, Taipei, 1973.

History: Taiping Rebellion 歷史：太平天國

Hsiang Ta 向達, ed., *Chung-kuo Chin-tai-shih Tze-liao Ts'ung-kan Ti-er-chung: T'ai-p'ing T'ien-kuo* 中國近代史資料丛刊第二种:太平天國, Shen-chou Kuo-kuang-she, Shanghai, 1952.
Kuo T'ing-i 郭廷以, *T'ai-p'ing T'ien-kuo Shih-shih Jih-chih* 太平天國史事日誌, Taiwan Shangwu, Taipei, 1976.
Li Jan 李然, *T'ai-p'ing T'ien-kuo* 太平天國, Chung-kuo Jen-shih Chu-pan-she, Peking, 1999.
Mao Ying-chang 毛應章, *T'ai-p'ing T'ien-kuo Shih-wei-chi* 太平天國始末記, Taiwan Shang-wu, Taipei, 1970.
San Jun College 三軍大學, *Chung-kuo Li-tai Chan-cheng Shih 18* 中國歷代戰爭史 18, Li Ming Wen-hua Shi-yeh, 1980.
Shen Yun-lung 沈雲龍, ed., *Chin-tai Chung-kuo Shih-liao Tsung-kan Ti-yi-chi: 0873.1-3 T'ai-p'ing T'ien-kuo Shih-wen* 近代中國史料叢刊第一輯: 0873.1-3 太平天國佚聞, Wen-hai Pub, Taipei 1973.

Reference: Dictionaries 參考書：字辭典

Editors, *Chung-kuo Jen-ming Ta Ts'e-tien* 中国人名大辭典, Taiwan Shang-wu, Taipei, 1982.
Editors, *Chung-kuo Ku-chin Ti-ming Ta Ts'e-tien* 中国古今地名大辭典, Taiwan Shang-wu, Taipei, 1982.
Editors, *Hsin Shih-chieh Han-ying Ts'e-tien* 新世界漢英辭典, Tainan Pei-i Pub, Tainan, 1970.
Editors, *K'ang Hsi Tzu-tien* 康熙字典, Ta Tung Books, Tainan, 1967.
Editors, *T'u-chieh Ying-han Pai-k'e T'se-tien* 圖解英漢百科辭典, 2nd edition, Wen-ho, Taipei, 1996.
Editors, *Ts'e Hai* 辭海, Taipei, Chung-hua, 1967.
Kao Mo-yeh 高莫野, ed., *Chung-kuo Ch'eng-yu Ta Ts'e-tien* 中國成語大辭典, Cheng-yen, Tainan, 1965.

Shanghai 上海

Shen Yun-lung 沈雲龍 ed., *Shang-hai Tzu-chieh Lueh-shih* 上海租界略史, Wen-hai Pub, Taipei, 1971.
Editors, *Shang-hai Ch'un-ch'iu* 上海春秋, Shanghai Jen-min Chu-pan-she, Shanghai, 1997.
Shanghai Tung-she 上海通社, *Shang-hai Yen-chiu Tzu-liao* 上海研究資料, Chung Hua Pub, Shanghai, 1936.
Shao Hui-chao 沙會炤, *Shang-hai-shih Tu-shih She-chi yu T'u-ti Li-yung*, 上海市之都市設計與土地利用, Ch'eng-wen Reprints, Taipei, 1977.
Yeh Meng-chu 葉夢珠 ed., *Shang-hai Ch'ang-Ku Ts'ung-Shu* 上海掌故叢書, Shanghai T'ung-she, Shanghai, 1935.

CPSIA information can be obtained at www.ICGtesting.com
Printed in the USA
LVOW011928031211
257700LV00015B/97/P